The Blight

Shayol Ghul

the Blasted Lands

the Blight

Chachin

KANDOR

Plain of Lances

ravadon

EA

ARAFEL

Shol Arbela

Mountains of Dhoom

Fal Dara

Malkier

Tarwins Gap

Niamh Passes

Ariel Aleste

Fal Moran

SHIENAR

the Black Hills

River Luan

Tar Valon

Dragonmount

WORLD

Kinslayers Dagger

to Rhuidean

the SPINE of the

River Harwin

Caralain Grass

River Gaelin

Cairhien

CAIRHIEN

Tangai Pass

Braem Wood

River Alguenya

ANDOR

Whitebridge   Four Kings   Caemlyn

Aringill

Cary Branch

Steddíng Shangtai

River Manetherendrelle

River Osenn

River Cary

Hills of Kintara

River Erinin

River Manetherendrelle

Lugard

MURANDY

Far Madding

Haddon Mirk

Plains of Maredo

Tear   TEAR

Godan

Dreamed Lands

ILLIAN

Tear

the Fingers of the Dragon

Rivers .... Borders
Roads .... Forests
Towns & Cities   Grasslands & Plains

Illian

Key:

SEA of STORMS

the Sea Folk

Mayene

Cindaking

Praise for Robert Jordan and The Wheel of Time®

"His huge, ambitious Wheel of Time series helped redefine the genre."
—George R. R. Martin, internationally bestselling author of *A Game of Thrones*

"Anyone who's writing epic secondary world fantasy knows Robert Jordan isn't just a part of the landscape, he's a monolith within the landscape."
—Patrick Rothfuss, internationally bestselling author of The Kingkiller Chronicle

"*The Eye of the World* was a turning point in my life. I read, I enjoyed. (Then continued on to write my larger fantasy novels.)"
—Robin Hobb, *New York Times* bestselling author of The Farseer Trilogy

"Robert Jordan's work has been a formative influence and an inspiration for a generation of fantasy writers."   —Brent Weeks, *New York Times* bestselling author of *The Way of Shadow*s

"One of fantasy's most acclaimed series."   —*USA Today*

"Robert Jordan was a giant of fiction whose words helped a whole generation of fantasy writers, including myself, find our true voices. I thanked him then, but I didn't thank him enough."
—Peter V. Brett, internationally bestselling author of The Demon Cycle

"[Robert Jordan's] impact on the place of fantasy in the culture is colossal. . . . He brought innumerable readers to fantasy. He became the *New York Times* Best Seller List's face of fantasy."
—Guy Gavriel Kay, internationally bestselling author of *Tigana*

"Jordan's writing is so amazing! The characterization, the attention to detail!"
—Clint McElroy, cocreator of the #1 podcast *The Adventure Zone*

"The Wheel of Time [is] rapidly becoming the definitive American fantasy saga. It is a fantasy tale seldom equaled and still less often surpassed in English."   —*Chicago Sun-Times*

"Hard to put down for even a moment. A fittingly epic conclusion to a fantasy series that many consider one of the best of all time."
—*San Francisco Book Review* on *A Memory of Light*

The Wheel of Time®

By Robert Jordan

New Spring: The Novel
The Eye of the World
The Great Hunt
The Dragon Reborn
The Shadow Rising
The Fires of Heaven
Lord of Chaos
A Crown of Swords
The Path of Daggers
Winter's Heart
Crossroads of Twilight
Knife of Dreams

By Robert Jordan and Brandon Sanderson

The Gathering Storm
Towers of Midnight
A Memory of Light

By Robert Jordan and Teresa Patterson

The World of Robert Jordan's The Wheel of Time

By Robert Jordan, Harriet McDougal,
Alan Romanczuk, and Maria Simons

The Wheel of Time Companion

LORD
OF
CHAOS

ROBERT JORDAN

TOR

A TOM DOHERTY ASSOCIATES BOOK
NEW YORK

LORD OF CHAOS

Copyright © 1994 by Bandersnatch Group, Inc.

The phrase "The Wheel of Time" and the snake-wheel symbol are trademarks of Bandersnatch Group, Inc.

Excerpt from *A Crown of Swords* copyright © 1996 by Bandersnatch Group, Inc.

Maps by Ellisa Mitchell
Interior illustrations by Matthew C. Nielsen and Ellisa Mitchell

A Tor Book
Published by Tom Doherty Associates
120 Broadway
New York, NY 10271

www.tor-forge.com

Tor® is a registered trademark of Macmillan Publishing Group, LLC.

Jordan, Robert, 1948–2007.
    Lord of chaos / Robert Jordan.—First edition.
        p. cm.—(The wheel of time ; bk. 6)
    ISBN 978-0-312-85428-7 (hardcover)
    ISBN 978-1-4299-6053-3 (ebook)
1. Rand al'Thor (Fictitious character)—Fiction.   I. Title.
    PS3560.O7617 L67 1994
    813'.54—dc20

                                        94030173

ISBN 978-0-7653-3465-7 (trade paperback)

Our books may be purchased in bulk for promotional, educational, or business use. Please contact your local bookseller or the Macmillan Corporate and Premium Sales Department at 1-800-221-7945, extension 5442, or by email at MacmillanSpecialMarkets@macmillan.com.

Printed in the United States of America

0   9   8

For Betsy

CONTENTS

The lions sing and the hills take flight.
The moon by day, and the sun by night.
Blind woman, deaf man, jackdaw fool.
Let the Lord of Chaos rule.

—chant from a children's game
heard in Great Arvalon,
the Fourth Age

the Blight

Shayol Ghul
the Blasted Lands

Mountains of Dhoom

Tarwin's Gap

Chachin   Shol Arbela   Fal Dara

Plain of Lances   Fal   Niamh
KANDOR   ARAFEL   Moran   Passes

SHIENAR

Aiel
Waste

the Black Hills

River Ivo

Tar
Valon   Kinslayer's
Dagger

River Haevin

the
Dragon-
mount

River Gaelin   to
Rhuidean

Caralain Grass   Jangai Pass

Cairhien

Braem Wood   CAIRHIEN

ANDOR

Four Kings Caemlyn
Whitebridge   Aringill

River Storn   River Iralel

River Manetherendrelle

Lugard   Hills of   Kintara   Haddon
MURANDY   Mirk

Far
Madding   Stedding
Shangtai

Plains
of Moredo   TEAR

ALTARA   Tear   Godan   the
Drowned
Lands

ILLIAN

the Fingers of the
Dragon

to the   Illian
Isles of the Sea Folk   Sea of   Cindaking   Mayene
Storms

PROLOGUE

The First Message

Demandred stepped out onto the black slopes of Shayol Ghul, and the gateway, a hole in reality's fabric, winked out of existence. Above, roiling gray clouds hid the sky, an inverted sea of sluggish ashen waves crashing around the mountain's hidden peak. Below, odd lights flashed across the barren valley, washed-out blues and reds, failing to dispel the dusky murk that shrouded their source. Lightning streaked *up* at the clouds, and slow thunder rolled. Across the slope steam and smoke rose from scattered vents, some holes as small as a man's hand and some large enough to swallow ten men.

He released the One Power immediately, and with the vanished sweetness went the heightened senses that made everything sharper, clearer. The absence of *saidin* left him hollow, yet here only a fool would even appear ready to channel. Besides, here only a fool would want to see or smell or feel too clearly.

In what was now called the Age of Legends, this had been an idyllic island in a cool sea, a favorite of those who enjoyed the rustic. Despite the steam it was bitter cold, now; he did not allow himself to feel it, but instinct made him pull his fur-lined velvet cloak closer. Feathery mist marked his breath, barely visible before the air drank it. A few hundred leagues north the world was pure ice, but Thakan'dar was always dry as any desert, though always wrapped in winter.

There was water, of a sort, an inky rivulet oozing down the rocky slope beside a gray-roofed forge. Hammers rang inside, and with every ring, white light flared in the cramped windows. A ragged woman crouched in a hopeless heap against the forge's rough stone wall, clutching a babe in her arms, and a spindly girl buried her face in the woman's skirts. Prisoners from a raid down into the Borderlands, no doubt. But so few; the Myrddraal must be gnashing their teeth. Their blades failed after a time and had to be replaced, no matter that raids into the Borderlands had been curtailed.

One of the forgers emerged, a thick slow-moving man shape that seemed hacked out of the mountain. The forgers were not truly alive; carried any distance from Shayol Ghul, they turned to stone, or dust. Nor were they smiths as such; they made nothing but the swords. This one's two hands held a sword blade in long tongs, a blade already quenched, pale like moonlit snow. Alive or not, the forger took care as it dipped the gleaming metal into the dark stream. Whatever semblance of life it had could be ended by the touch of that water. When the metal came out again, it was dead black. But the making was not done yet. The forger shuffled back inside, and suddenly a man's voice raised a desperate shout.

"No? No! NO!" He shrieked then, the sound dwindling away without losing intensity, as though the screamer had been yanked into unimaginably far distance. Now the blade was done.

Once more a forger appeared—perhaps the same, perhaps another—and hauled the woman to her feet. Woman, babe and child began to wail, but the infant was pulled away and shoved into the girl's arms. At last the woman found a scrap of resistance. Weeping, she kicked wildly, clawed at the forger. It paid no more mind than stone would have. The woman's cries vanished as soon as she was inside. The hammers began ringing again, drowning the sobs of the children.

One blade made, one making, and two to come. Demandred had never before seen fewer than fifty prisoners waiting to give their mite to the Great Lord of the Dark. The Myrddraal must be gnashing their teeth, indeed.

"Do you loiter when you have been summoned by the Great Lord?" The voice sounded like rotted leather crumbling.

Demandred turned slowly—how dare a Halfman address him in that tone—but the quelling words died in his mouth. It was not the eyeless stare of its pasty-pale face; a Myrddraal's gaze struck fear in any man, but he had rooted fear out of himself long ago. Rather, it was the black-clad creature itself. Every Myrddraal was the height of a tall man, a sinuous imitation of a man, as alike as though cast in one mold. This one stood head and shoulders taller.

"I will take you to the Great Lord," the Myrddraal said. "I am Shaidar Haran." It turned away and began climbing the mountain, like a serpent in its fluid motion. Its inky cloak hung unnaturally still, without even a ripple.

Demandred hesitated before following. Halfmen's names were always in the Trollocs' tongue-wrenching language. "Shaidar Haran" came from what people now named the Old Tongue. It meant "Hand of the Dark." Another surprise, and Demandred did not like surprises, especially not at Shayol Ghul.

The entry into the mountain could have been one of the scattered vents, except that it emitted no smoke or steam. It gaped enough for two men abreast, but the Myrddraal kept the lead. The way slanted down almost immediately, the tunnel floor worn smooth as polished tiles. The cold faded as Demandred followed Shaidar Haran's broad back down and down, slowly replaced by increasing heat. Demandred was aware of it, but did not let it touch him. A pale light rose from the stone, filling the tunnel, brighter than the eternal twilight outside. Jagged spikes jutted from the ceiling, stony teeth ready to snap shut, the Great Lord's teeth to rend the unfaithful or the traitor. Not natural, of course, but effective.

Abruptly, he noticed something. Every time he had made this journey, those spikes had all but brushed the top of his head. Now they cleared the Myrddraal's by two hands or more. That surprised him. Not that the height of the tunnel changed—the strange was ordinary here—but the extra space the Halfman was given. The Great Lord gave his reminders to Myrddraal as well as men. That extra space was a fact to be remembered.

The tunnel opened out suddenly onto a wide ledge overlooking a lake of molten stone, red mottled with black, where man-high flames danced, died and rose again. There was no roof, only a great hole rising through the mountain to a sky that was not the sky of Thakan'dar. It made that of Thakan'dar look normal, with its wildly striated clouds streaking by as though driven by the greatest winds the world had ever seen. This, men called the Pit of Doom, and few knew how well they had named it.

Even after all his visits—and the first lay well over three thousand years in the past—Demandred felt awe. Here he could sense the Bore, the hole drilled through so long ago to where the Great Lord had lain imprisoned since the moment of Creation. Here the Great Lord's presence washed over him. Physically, this place was no closer to the Bore than any other in the world, but here there was a thinness in the Pattern that allowed it to be sensed.

Demandred came as close to smiling as he ever did. What fools they were who opposed the Great Lord. Oh, the Bore was still blocked, though more tenuously than when he had wakened from his long sleep and broken free of his own prison in it. Blocked, but larger than when he woke. Still not so large as when he had been cast into it with his fellows at the end of the War of Power, but at each visit since waking, a little wider. Soon the blockage would be gone, and the Great Lord would reach out across the earth again. Soon would come the Day of Return. And he would rule the world for all time. Under the Great Lord, of course. And with those of the other Chosen who survived, also of course.

"You may leave now, Halfman." He did not want the thing here to see the ecstasy overcome him. The ecstasy, and the pain.

Shaidar Haran did not move.

Demandred opened his mouth—and a voice exploded in his head.

DEMANDRED.

To call it a voice was to call a mountain a pebble. It nearly crushed him against the inside of his own skull; it filled him with rapture. He sank to his knees. The Myrddraal stood watching impassively, but only a small part of him could even notice the thing with that voice filling his brain.

DEMANDRED. HOW FARES THIS WORLD?

He was never sure how much the Great Lord knew of the world. He had been as startled by ignorance as by knowledge. But he had no doubt what the Great Lord wanted to hear.

"Rahvin is dead, Great Lord. Yesterday." There was pain. Euphoria too strong became pain quickly. His arms and legs twitched. He was sweating, now. "Lanfear has vanished without a trace, just as Asmodean did. And Graendal says Moghedien failed to meet her as they had agreed. Also yesterday, Great Lord. I do not believe in coincidence."

THE CHOSEN DWINDLE, DEMANDRED. THE WEAK FALL AWAY. WHO BETRAYS ME SHALL DIE THE FINAL DEATH. ASMODEAN, TWISTED BY HIS WEAKNESS. RAHVIN DEAD IN HIS PRIDE. HE SERVED WELL, YET EVEN I CANNOT SAVE HIM FROM BALEFIRE. EVEN I CANNOT STEP OUTSIDE OF TIME. For an instant terrible anger filled that awful voice, and—could it be frustration?

An instant only. DONE BY MY ANCIENT ENEMY, THE ONE CALLED DRAGON. WOULD YOU UNLEASH THE BALEFIRE IN MY SERVICE, DEMANDRED?

Demandred hesitated. A bead of sweat slid half an inch on his cheek; it seemed to take an hour. For a year during the War of Power, both sides had used balefire. Until they learned the consequences. Without agreement, or truce—there had never been a truce any more than there had been quarter— each side simply stopped. Entire cities died in balefire that year, hundreds of thousands of threads burned from the Pattern; reality itself almost un-raveled, world and universe evaporating like mist. If balefire was unleashed once more, there might be no world to rule.

Another point pricked him. The Great Lord already knew how Rahvin had died. And seemed to know more of Asmodean than he. "As you com-mand, Great Lord, so shall I obey." His muscles might be jerking, but his voice was rock steady. His knees began to blister from the hot stone, yet the flesh might as well have been someone else's.

SO YOU SHALL.

"Great Lord, the Dragon can be destroyed." A dead man could not wield balefire again, and perhaps then the Great Lord would see no need for it. "He is ignorant and weak, scattering his attentions in a dozen directions. Rahvin was a vain fool. I—"

WOULD YOU BE NAE'BLIS?

Demandred's tongue froze. Nae'blis. The one who would stand only a step below the Great Lord, commanding all others. "I wish only to serve you, Great Lord, however I may." Nae'blis.

THEN LISTEN, AND SERVE. HEAR WHO WILL DIE AND WHO LIVE.

Demandred screamed as the voice crashed home. Tears of joy rolled down his face.

Unmoving, the Myrddraal watched him.

"Stop fidgeting." Nynaeve testily flipped her long braid over her shoulder. "This won't work if you twitch around like children with an itch."

Neither of the women across the rickety table appeared any older than she, though they were by twenty years or more, and neither was really fidget-ing, but the heat had Nynaeve on edge. The small windowless room seemed airless. She dripped sweat; they appeared cool and dry. Leane, in a Domani dress of too-thin blue silk, merely shrugged; the tall coppery-skinned woman possessed an apparently infinite store of patience. Usually. Siuan, fair and sturdy, seldom had any.

Now Siuan grunted and resettled her skirts irritably; she used to wear fairly plain clothes, but this morning she was in fine yellow linen embroidered with a Tairen maze around a neckline that barely missed being too low. Her blue eyes were cold as deep well water. As cold as deep well water would have been if the weather had not gone mad. Her dresses might have changed, but not her eyes. "It won't work in any case," she snapped. Her manner of speaking was the same, too. "You can't patch a hull when the whole boat's burned. Well, it's a waste of time, but I promised, so get on with it. Leane and I have work to do." The pair of them ran the networks of eyes-and-ears for the Aes Sedai here in Salidar, the agents who sent in reports and rumors of what was going on in the world.

Nynaeve smoothed her own skirts to soothe herself. Her dress was plain white wool, with seven bands of color at the hem, one for each Ajah. An Accepted's dress. It annoyed her more than she could ever have imagined. She would much rather have been in the green silk she had packed away. She was willing to admit her acquired taste for fine clothes, privately at least, but her choice of that particular dress was only for comfort—it was thin, light—not because green seemed one of Lan's favorite colors. Not at all. Idle dreaming of the worst sort. An Accepted who put on anything except the banded white would soon learn she was a *long* step below Aes Sedai. Firmly she put all that out of her head. She was not here to fret over fripperies. He liked blue, too. No!

Delicately she probed with the One Power, first at Siuan, then Leane. In a manner of speaking, she was not channeling at all. She could not channel a scrap unless angry, could not even sense the True Source. Yet it came to the same thing. Fine filaments of *saidar*, the female half of the True Source, sifted through the two women at her weaving. They just did not originate with her.

On her left wrist Nynaeve wore a slender bracelet, a simple segmented silver band. Mainly silver, anyway, and from a special source, though that made no difference. It was the only piece of jewelry she wore aside from the Great Serpent ring; Accepted were firmly discouraged from wearing much jewelry. A matching necklace snugged around the neck of the fourth woman, on a stool against the rough-plastered wall with her hands folded in her lap. Clad in a farmer's rough brown wool, with a farmer's worn sturdy face, she did not sweat a drop. She did not move a muscle either, but her dark eyes watched everything. To Nynaeve, the radiance of *saidar* surrounded

her, but it was Nynaeve who directed the channeling. Bracelet and necklace created a link between them, much in the way Aes Sedai could link to
combine their power. Something about "absolutely identical matrices" was
involved, according to Elayne, after which the explanation truly became
incomprehensible. In truth, Nynaeve did not think Elayne understood half
as much as she pretended. For herself, Nynaeve did not understand at all,
except that she could feel the other woman's every emotion, feel the woman
herself, but tucked away in a corner of her head, and that all the other
woman's grasp of *saidar* was in her control. Sometimes she thought it
would have been better if the woman on the stool were dead. Simpler, certainly. Cleaner.

"There's something torn, or cut," Nynaeve muttered, wiping absently
at the sweat on her face. It was just a vague impression, barely there at all,
but it was also the first time she had sensed more than emptiness. It could
be imagination, and the desperate wanting to find something, anything.

"Severing," the woman on the stool said. "That was what it was called,
what you name stilling for women and gentling for men."

Three heads swiveled toward her; three sets of eyes glared with fury.
Siuan and Leane had been Aes Sedai until they were stilled during the
coup in the White Tower that put Elaida on the Amyrlin Seat. Stilled. A
word to cause shudders. Never to channel again. But always to remember,
and know the loss. Always to sense the True Source and know you could
never touch it again. Stilling could not be Healed any more than death.

That was what everyone believed, anyway, but in Nynaeve's opinion
the One Power should be able to Heal anything short of death. "If you have
something useful to add, Marigan," she said sharply, "then say it. If not,
keep quiet."

Marigan shrank back against the wall, eyes glittering and fixed on
Nynaeve. Fear and hate rolled through the bracelet, but they always did to
one degree or another. Captives seldom loved their captors, even—perhaps
especially—when they knew they deserved captivity and worse. The problem was that Marigan also said severing—stilling—could not be Healed.
Oh, she was full of claims that anything else except death could be Healed
in the Age of Legends, that what the Yellow Ajah called Healing now was
only the crudest hasty battlefield work. But try to pin her down on specif-
ics, on even a hint of how, and you found nothing there. Marigan knew as
much about Healing as Nynaeve did about blacksmithing, which was that
you stuck metal in hot coals and hit it with a hammer. Certainly not
enough to make a horseshoe. Or Heal much beyond a bruise.

Twisting around in her chair, Nynaeve studied Siuan and Leane. Days of this, whenever she could pry them away from their other work, and so far she had learned nothing. Suddenly she realized she was turning the bracelet on her wrist. Whatever the gain, she hated being linked to the woman. The intimacy made her skin crawl. *At least I might learn something*, she thought. *And it couldn't fail any worse than everything else has.*

Carefully she undid the bracelet—the clasp was impossible to find unless you knew how—and handed it to Siuan. "Put this on." Losing the Power was bitter, but this had to be done. And losing the waves of emotion was like taking a bath. Marigan's eyes followed the narrow length of silver as if hypnotized.

"Why?" Siuan demanded. "You tell me this thing only works—"

"Just put it on, Siuan."

Siuan eyed her stubbornly for a moment—Light, but the woman could be obstinate!—before closing the bracelet around her wrist. A look of wonder came onto her face immediately, then her eyes narrowed at Marigan. "She hates us, but I knew that. And there's fear, and . . . Shock. Not a glimmer on her face, but she's shocked to her toes. I don't think she believed I could use this thing, either."

Marigan shifted uneasily. So far only two who knew about her could use the bracelet. Four would give more chances for questions. On the surface she seemed to be cooperating fully, but how much was she hiding? As much as she could, Nynaeve was sure.

With a sigh, Siuan shook her head. "And I cannot. I should be able to touch the Source through her, isn't that right? Well, I can't. A grunter could climb trees first. I've been stilled, and that is that. How do you get this thing off?" She fumbled at the bracelet. "How do you bloody get it off?"

Gently Nynaeve laid a hand over Siuan's on the bracelet. "Don't you see? The bracelet won't work for a woman who can't channel any more than the necklace would work on her. If I put either on one of the cooks, it would be no more than a pretty piece for her."

"Cooks or no cooks," Siuan said flatly, "I cannot channel. I have been stilled."

"But there is something there to be Healed," Nynaeve insisted, "or you'd feel nothing through the bracelet."

Siuan jerked her arm free and stuck her wrist out. "Take it off."

Shaking her head, Nynaeve complied. Sometimes Siuan could be as bullheaded as any man!

When she held the bracelet toward Leane, the Domani woman lifted her wrist eagerly. Leane pretended to be as sanguine over having been stilled as Siuan was—as Siuan pretended to be—but she did not always succeed. Supposedly, the only way to survive stilling for long was to find something else to fill your life, to fill the hole left by the One Power. For Siuan and Leane that something was running their networks of agents, and more importantly, trying to convince the Aes Sedai here in Salidar to support Rand al'Thor as the Dragon Reborn without letting any of the Aes Sedai know what they were doing. The question was whether that was enough. The bitterness on Siuan's face, and the delight on Leane's as the bracelet snapped shut, said that maybe nothing could ever be.

"Oh, yes." Leane had a brisk, clipped way of speaking. Except when talking to men, anyway; she was Domani, after all, and of late making up for time lost in the Tower. "Yes, she really is stunned, isn't she? Beginning to control it now, though." For a few moments she sat silently, considering the woman on the stool. Marigan stared back warily. At last, Leane shrugged. "I cannot touch the Source, either. And I tried to make her feel a fleabite on her ankle. If it had worked, she would have had to show something." That was the other trick of the bracelet; you could make the woman wearing the necklace feel physical sensations. Only the sensations—there was no mark whatever you did, no real damage—but the feel of a sound switching or two had sufficed to convince Marigan that cooperation was her best choice. That and the alternative, a quick trial followed by execution.

Despite her failure, Leane watched closely as Nynaeve undid the bracelet and refastened it on her own wrist. It seemed that she, at least, had not given up completely on channeling again one day.

Regaining the Power was wonderful. Not as wonderful as drawing *saidar* herself, being filled with it, but even touching the Source through the other woman was like redoubling the life in her veins. To hold *saidar* inside was to want to laugh and dance with pure joy. She supposed that one day she would become used to it; full Aes Sedai must. Balanced against that, linking with Marigan was a small price. "Now that we know there's a chance," she said, "I think—"

The door banged open, and Nynaeve was on her feet before she knew it. She never thought of using the Power; she would have screamed if her throat had not closed tight. She was not the only one, but she hardly noticed Siuan and Leane leaping up. The fear cascading through the bracelet seemed an echo of her own.

The young woman who shut the splintery wooden door behind her took no notice of the commotion she had caused. Tall and straight in an

Accepted's banded white dress, with sun-gold curls nestled on her shoulders, she looked spitting mad. Even with her face tight with anger and dripping sweat she somehow managed to look beautiful, though; it was a knack Elayne had. "Do you know what they're doing? They are sending an embassy to . . . to Caemlyn! And they refuse to let me go! Sheriam *forbade* me to mention it again. Forbade me even to *speak* of it!"

"Did you never learn to knock, Elayne?" Straightening her chair, Nynaeve sat down again. Fell, really; relief weakened her knees. "I thought you *were* Sheriam." Just the thought of discovery cored out her middle.

To her credit, Elayne blushed and apologized immediately. Then spoiled it by adding, "But I don't see why you were so goosey. Birgitte is still outside, and you *know* she would warn you if anyone else came close. Nynaeve, they *must* let me go."

"They *must* do nothing of the kind," Siuan said gruffly. She and Leane were seated again, too. Siuan sat up straight, as always, but Leane sagged back, as flimsy as Nynaeve's knees. Marigan was leaning against the wall, breathing hard, eyes closed and hands pressed hard against the plaster. Relief and stark terror surged through the bracelet in alternating jolts.

"But—"

Siuan did not allow Elayne another word. "Do you think Sheriam, or any of the others, will let the Daughter-Heir of Andor fall into the hands of the Dragon Reborn? With your mother dead—"

"I don't believe that!" Elayne snapped.

"You don't believe Rand killed her," Siuan went on relentlessly, "and that's a different thing. I don't, either. But if Morgase were alive, she would come forward and acknowledge him the Dragon Reborn. Or, if she believed him a false Dragon in spite of the proof, she'd be organizing resistance. None of my eyes-and-ears have heard a whisper of either. Not just in Andor, but not here in Altara and not in Murandy."

"They *have*," Elayne forced in. "There's rebellion in the west."

"Against Morgase. Against. If it's not a rumor, too." Siuan's voice was flat as a planed board. "Your mother is dead, girl. Best to admit as much and get your weeping done."

Elayne's chin rose, a very annoying habit she had; she was the picture of icy arrogance, though most men seemed to find it attractive for some reason. "You complain continually over how long it is taking to get in touch with all of your agents," she said coolly, "but I will set aside whether you can have heard all there is to hear. Whether my mother is alive or not, *my* place is in Caemlyn, now. I *am* Daughter-Heir."

Siuan's loud snort made Nynaeve jump. "You've been Accepted long enough to know better." Elayne had as much potential as had been seen in a thousand years. Not as much as Nynaeve, if she ever learned to channel at will, but still enough to make any Aes Sedai's eyes light up. Elayne's nose wrinkled—she knew very well that if she had already been on the Lion Throne, the Aes Sedai still would have gotten her away for training, by asking if possible, by stuffing her into a barrel if necessary—and she opened her mouth, but Siuan did not even slow down. "True, they'd not mind you taking the throne sooner than later; there hasn't been a Queen who was openly Aes Sedai in far too long. But they won't let you go until you're a full sister, and even then, because you *are* Daughter-Heir and will be Queen soon, they won't let you near the Dragon bloody Reborn until they know how far they can trust him. Especially since this . . . *amnesty* of his." Her mouth twisted sourly around the word, and Leane grimaced.

Nynaeve's tongue curdled, too. She had been brought up to fear any man who could channel, fated to go mad and, before the Shadow-tainted male half of the Source killed him horribly, bring terror to everyone around him. But Rand, whom she had watched grow up, was the Dragon Reborn, born both as a sign that the Last Battle was coming and to fight the Dark One in that battle. The Dragon Reborn; humanity's only hope—and a man who could channel. Worse, reports were that he was trying to gather others like him. Of course, there could not be many. Any Aes Sedai would hunt down one of those—the Red Ajah did little else—but they found few, far fewer than once, according to the records.

Elayne was not about to give up, though. That was one admirable thing about her; she would not give up if her head were on the block and the axe descending. She stood there with her chin up, facing Siuan's stare, which Nynaeve often found hard to do. "There are two clear reasons why I should go. First, whatever has happened to my mother, she *is* missing, and as Daughter-Heir, I can calm the people and assure them the succession is intact. Second, I can approach Rand. He trusts me. I would be *far* better than anyone the Hall chooses."

The Aes Sedai here in Salidar had chosen their own Hall of the Tower, a Hall-in-exile, as it were. They were supposed to be mulling over the choice of a new Amyrlin Seat, a rightful Amyrlin to challenge Elaida's claim to the title and the Tower, but Nynaeve had not seen much sign of it.

"So kind of you to sacrifice yourself, child," Leane said dryly. Elayne's expression did not change, yet she colored furiously; few outside this room knew, and no Aes Sedai, but Nynaeve had no doubt that Elayne's first act in Caemlyn would be to get Rand alone and kiss him within an inch of his life. "With your mother . . . missing . . . if Rand al'Thor has you, and Caemlyn, he has Andor, and the Hall won't let him have any more of Andor than they have to, or anywhere else if they can help it. He carries Tear and Cairhien in his pocket, and the Aiel as well, it seems. Add Andor, and Murandy and Altara—with us in it—fall if he sneezes. He is growing too powerful, too fast. He might decide he doesn't need us. With Moiraine dead, there's no one near him we can trust."

That made Nynaeve wince. Moiraine was the Aes Sedai who had brought her and Rand out of the Two Rivers and changed their lives. Her and Rand and Egwene and Mat and Perrin. She had wanted for so long to make Moiraine pay for what she had done to them that losing her was like losing a piece of herself. But Moiraine was dead in Cairhien, taking Lanfear with her; she was fast becoming a legend among the Aes Sedai here, the only Aes Sedai to have killed one of the Forsaken, much less two. The only good thing Nynaeve could find in it, much as it shamed to find any good, was that now Lan was freed from being Moiraine's Warder. If she could ever find him.

Siuan took up immediately where Leane left off. "We can't afford to let the boy go sailing off with no guidance at all. Who knows what he might do? Yes, yes, I know you're ready to argue for him, but I don't care to hear it. I'm trying to balance a live silverpike on my nose, girl. We can't let him grow too strong before he accepts us, and yet we don't dare hold him back too much. And I'm trying to keep Sheriam and the others convinced they *should* support him when half the Hall secretly don't want anything to do with him, and the other half think in their heart of hearts that he should be gentled, Dragon Reborn or not. In any case, whatever your arguments, I suggest you heed Sheriam. You won't change any minds, and Tiana doesn't have enough novices here to keep her busy."

Elayne's face tightened angrily. Tiana Noselle, a Gray sister, was Mistress of Novices here in Salidar. An Accepted had to step considerably further out of line to be sent to Tiana than did a novice, but by the same token, the visit was always that much more shaming and painful. Tiana might show a little kindness to a novice, if only a little; she felt Accepted should know better, and made sure they felt the same long before they left her small cubbyhole of a study.

Nynaeve had been studying Siuan, and now something popped into her head. "You knew all about this . . . embassy, or whatever it is . . . didn't you? You two always have your heads together with Sheriam and her little circle." The Hall might have all the supposed authority until they chose an Amyrlin, but Sheriam and the handful of other Aes Sedai who had first organized the arrivals in Salidar still kept the real control of things. "How many are they sending, Siuan?" Elayne gasped; plainly she had not thought of this. That showed how upset she was. Usually she caught nuances Nynaeve missed.

Siuan denied nothing. Since being stilled she could lie like a wool merchant, but when she decided to be open, she was as open as a slap in the face. "Nine. 'Enough to do honor to the Dragon Reborn'—fish guts! an embassy to a *king* is seldom more than three!—'but not enough to frighten him.' If he's learned enough to be frightened."

"You had better hope he has," Elayne said coldly. "If he hasn't, then nine may be eight too many."

Thirteen was the dangerous number. Rand was strong, perhaps as strong as any man since the Breaking, but thirteen Aes Sedai linked could overwhelm him, shield him from *saidin*, and take him prisoner. Thirteen was the number assigned when a man was gentled, though Nynaeve had begun to think the assignment more custom than requirement. Aes Sedai did a good many things because they always had.

Siuan's smile was far from pleasant. "I wonder why no one else thought of that? Think, girl! Sheriam does, and so does the Hall. Only one will go near him at first, and no more after that than he's comfortable with. But he'll know nine came, and somebody will certainly tell him what an honor that is."

"I see," Elayne said in a small voice. "I should have known one of you would think of it. I'm sorry." That was another good thing about her. She could be stubborn as a cross-eyed mule, but when she decided she was wrong, she admitted it as nicely as any village woman. Most unusual for a noble.

"Min will be going too," Leane said. "Her . . . talents may be useful to Rand. The sisters won't know that part, of course. She can keep her secrets." As if that were the important thing.

"I see," Elayne said again, flatly this time. She made an effort to brighten her tone, a miserable failure. "Well, I see you're busy with . . . with Marigan. I did not mean to disturb you. Please, don't let me interrupt." She was gone before Nynaeve could open her mouth, the door banging shut behind her.

Angrily, Nynaeve rounded on Leane. "I thought Siuan was the mean one of you, but that was vicious!"

It was Siuan who answered. "When two women love the same man, it means trouble, and when the man is Rand al'Thor. . . . The Light knows how sane he still is, or what course they might send him off on. If there's any hair-pulling and clawing to be done, let them do it now, here."

Without thought, Nynaeve's hand found her braid and jerked it back over her shoulder. "I ought to. . . ." Trouble was, there was little she could do, and nothing to make any difference. "We'll go on from where we left off when Elayne came in. But, Siuan. . . . If you ever do something like that to her again," *or to me*, she thought, "I'll make you sorry you— Where do you think you're going?" Siuan had scraped back her chair and risen, and after a glance, Leane did the same.

"We have work," Siuan said curtly, already heading for the door.

"You promised to make yourself available, Siuan. Sheriam told you to." Not that Sheriam thought it any less a waste of time than Siuan, but Nynaeve and Elayne had earned rewards, and a certain amount of indulgence. Like Marigan to be their maid, to give them more time for Accepted's studies.

Siuan gave her an amused look from the door. "Maybe you'll complain to her? And explain how you do your research? I want time with *Marigan* this evening; I have some more questions."

As Siuan left, Leane said sadly, "It would be nice, Nynaeve, but we have to do what we *can* do. You could try Logain." Then she was gone, too.

Nynaeve scowled. Studying Logain had taught her even less than studying the two women. She was no longer certain she could learn anything from him at all. Anyway, the last thing she wanted was to Heal a gentled man. He made her nervous in any case.

"You bite at one another like rats in a sealed box," Marigan said. "On the evidence, your chances are not very good. Perhaps you should consider . . . other options."

"Hold your filthy tongue!" Nynaeve glared at her. "Hold it, the Light burn you!" Fear still oozed through the bracelet, but something else as well, something almost too feeble to exist. A faint spark of hope, perhaps. "The Light burn you," she muttered.

The woman's real name was not Marigan, but Moghedien. One of the Forsaken, trapped with her own overweening pride and held prisoner in the midst of Aes Sedai. Only five women in the world knew, none Aes Sedai, but keeping Moghedien secret was purest necessity. The Forsaken's crimes made her execution as sure as the sun rising. Siuan agreed; for every Aes Sedai who counseled waiting, if any did, ten would demand immediate justice. Into an unmarked grave with her would go all her knowledge from the Age of Legends, when things undreamed of today were done with the Power. Nynaeve was not sure she believed half of what the woman told her of that Age. She certainly understood less than half.

Digging information out of Moghedien was not easy. Sometimes it was like Healing; Moghedien had never been interested in much that could not advance her, preferably by shortcuts. The woman was hardly likely to reveal the truth, but Nynaeve suspected she had been some sort of swindler or the like before swearing her soul over to the Dark One. Sometimes she and Elayne just did not know the questions to ask. Moghedien seldom volunteered anything, that was certain. Even so, they had learned a great deal, and passed most on to the Aes Sedai. As results of their researches and studies as Accepted, of course. They had gained a lot of credit.

She and Elayne would have kept knowledge of her to themselves if they could, but Birgitte had known from the start, and Siuan and Leane had to be told. Siuan had known enough of the circumstances that led to Moghedien's capture to demand a full explanation, and had the leverage to obtain one. Nynaeve and Elayne knew some of Siuan and Leane's secrets; they seemed to know all of her and Elayne's except the truth about Birgitte. It made for a precarious balance, with the advantage to Siuan and Leane. Besides, bits of Moghedien's revelations concerned supposed Darkfriend plots and hints of what the other Forsaken might be up to. The only way to pass those on was to make them seem to have come from Siuan and Leane's agents. Nothing about the Black Ajah—hidden deep and long denied—though that interested Siuan most. Darkfriends disgusted her, but the very idea of Aes Sedai swearing themselves to the Dark One was enough to screw Siuan's anger to an icy rage. Moghedien claimed to have been afraid to go near *any* Aes Sedai, and that was believable enough. Fear was a permanent part of the woman. No wonder she had hidden in the shadows enough to be called the Spider. All in all, she was a treasure trove too valuable to give to the headsman, yet most Aes Sedai would not see it so. Most Aes Sedai might refuse to touch or trust anything learned from her.

Guilt and revulsion stabbed Nynaeve, not for the first time. Could any amount of knowledge justify keeping one of the Forsaken from justice? Turning her in meant punishment, probably dreadful, for everyone involved, not just herself, but Elayne and Siuan and Leane. Turning her in meant Birgitte's secret would come out. And all that knowledge lost. Moghedien might know nothing of Healing, but she had given Nynaeve a dozen hints of what was possible, and there had to be more in her head. With those to guide her, what might she discover eventually?

Nynaeve wanted a bath, and it had nothing to do with the heat. "We will talk about the weather," she said bitterly.

"You know more about controlling weather than I do." Moghedien sounded weary, and an echo slid through the bracelet. There had been enough questions on the subject. "All I know is that what is happening is the Great—the Dark One's work." She had the nerve to smile ingratiatingly at the slip. "No mere human is strong enough to change that."

It took effort for Nynaeve not to grind her teeth. Elayne knew more about working weather than anyone else in Salidar, and she said the same. Including the Dark One part, though any but a fool would know that, with the heat so strong when it should be coming on for snow, with no rain and the streams drying. "Then we'll talk about using different weaves to Heal different illnesses." The woman said that took more time than what was done now, but all the strength for it came from the Power, not from the patient and the woman channeling. Of course, she said *men* had actually been better at some kinds of Healing, and Nynaeve was not about to believe that. "You must have seen it done at least once."

She settled down to bore away for nuggets in the dross. Some knowledge was worth a great deal. She just wished she did not feel that she was digging through slime.

Elayne did not hesitate once she was outside, only waved to Birgitte and went on. Birgitte, her golden hair in an intricate waist-long braid, was playing with two small boys while she kept watch in the narrow alley, her bow propped against a leaning fence beside her. Or trying to play with them. Jaril and Seve stared at the woman in her odd wide yellow trousers and short dark coat, but they showed no more reaction than that. They never did, and they never spoke. They were supposed to be "Marigan's" children. Birgitte was happy playing with them, and a touch sad; she always liked playing with children, especially little boys, and she always felt that way when she did. Elayne knew it as well as she knew her own feelings.

If she had thought Moghedien had anything to do with their condition. . . . But the woman claimed they were as they had been when she picked them up for her disguise in Ghealdan, orphans in the street, and some of the Yellow sisters said they had simply seen too much in the riots in Samara. Elayne could believe it from what she herself had encountered there. The Yellow sisters said time and care would help them; Elayne hoped it was so. She hoped she was not allowing the one responsible to escape justice.

She did not want to think about Moghedien now. Her mother. No, she definitely did not want to think about her. Min. And Rand. There had to be some way to handle this. Barely seeing Birgitte's return nod, she hurried up the alley and out onto the main street of Salidar beneath a cloudless, broiling midday sky.

For years Salidar had stood abandoned, before Aes Sedai fleeing Elaida's coup began to gather there, but now fresh thatch topped the houses, most of which showed considerable new repairs and patches, and the three large stone buildings that had been inns. One, the largest, was called the Little Tower by some; that was where the Hall met. Only what was necessary had been done, of course; cracked glass filled many windows, or none. More important matters were afoot than repointing stonework or painting. The dirt streets were filled to bursting. Not just with Aes Sedai, of course, but Accepted in banded dresses and scurrying novices in pure white, Warders moving with the deadly grace of leopards whether lean or bulky, servants who had followed Aes Sedai from the Tower, even a few children. And soldiers.

The Hall here was preparing to enforce its claims against Elaida by arms if necessary, just as soon as they chose a true Amyrlin Seat. The distant clang of hammers, cutting through the crowds' murmur from forges outside the village, spoke of horses being shod, armor being mended. A square-faced man, his dark hair heavy with gray, went riding slowly down the street in a buff-colored coat and battered breastplate. Picking his way through the crowd, he eyed marching clusters of men with long pikes on their shoulders, or bows. Gareth Bryne had agreed to recruit and lead the Salidar Hall's army, though Elayne wished she knew the full how and why. Something to do with Siuan and Leane, though what, she could not imagine, since he ran both women ragged, especially Siuan, fulfilling some oath Elayne did not have the straight of either. Just that Siuan complained bitterly about having to keep his room and his clothes clean on top of her other duties. She complained, but she did it; it must have been a strong oath.

Bryne's eyes passed across Elayne with barely a hesitation. He had been coolly polite and distant since she arrived in Salidar, though she had known him since her cradle. Until less than a year ago he had been Captain-General of the Queen's Guards, in Andor. Once, Elayne had thought he and her mother would marry. No, she was not going to think of her mother! Min. She had to find Min and talk.

No sooner had she begun to weave through the crowded dusty street, though, than two Aes Sedai found her. There was no choice but to stop and curtsy, while the throng streamed around them. Both women beamed. Neither sweated a drop. Pulling a handkerchief from her sleeve to dab at her face, Elayne wished she had already been taught that particular bit of Aes Sedai lore. "Good day, Anaiya Sedai, Janya Sedai."

"Good day, child. Do you have any more discoveries for us today?" As usual, Janya Frende spoke as though there was no time to get the words out. "Such remarkable strides you've made, you and Nynaeve, especially for Accepted. I still don't see how Nynaeve does it, when she has so many difficulties with the Power, but I must say I'm delighted." Unlike most Brown sisters, often absentminded beyond their books and studies, Janya Sedai was quite neat, every short dark hair tidy around the ageless face that marked Aes Sedai who had worked long with the Power. But the slender woman's appearance did hint at her Ajah. Her dress was plain gray, and stout wool—Browns seldom thought of clothes as more than decent covering— and even when she was talking to you, she wore a little frown, as though squinting in thought about something else entirely. She would have been pretty without that frown. "That way of wrapping yourself in light to become invisible. Remarkable. I'm sure someone will find how to stop the ripples, so you can move about with it. And Carenna is quite excited over that little eavesdropping trick of Nynaeve's. Naughty of her, to think of that, but useful. Carenna thinks she sees how to adapt it to *talk* to someone at a distance. Think of it. To talk with someone a mile away! Or two, or even—" Anaiya touched her arm, and she cut off, blinking at the other Aes Sedai.

"You are making great strides, Elayne," Anaiya said calmly. The bluff-faced woman was always calm. "Motherly" was the word to describe her, and comforting usually, though Aes Sedai features made putting an age to her impossible. She was also one of the small circle around Sheriam who held the real power in Salidar. "Greater than any of us expected, truly, and we expected much. The first to make a *ter'angreal* since the Breaking. That is remarkable, child, and I want you to know that. You should be very proud."

Elayne stared at the ground in front of her toes. Two waist-high boys went dodging by through the crowd, laughing. She wished no one were close enough to hear this. Not that any of the passersby gave them a second glance. With so many Aes Sedai in the village, not even novices curtsied unless an Aes Sedai addressed them, and everyone had errands that needed to be done yesterday.

She did not feel proud at all. Not with all of their "discoveries" coming from Moghedien. There had been a good many, beginning with "inverting," so a weave could not be seen by any but the woman who had woven it, yet they had not passed everything on. How to hide your ability to channel, for one. Without that, Moghedien would have been unmasked in hours—any Aes Sedai within two or three paces of a woman could sense whether she could channel—and if they learned how to do that, they might learn how to penetrate it. And how to disguise yourself; inverted weaves made "Marigan" look nothing at all like Moghedien.

Some of what the woman knew was just too repulsive. Compulsion, for instance, bending people's will, and a way to implant instructions so the recipient would not even remember the orders when he carried them out. Worse things. Too repulsive, and maybe too dangerous to trust anyone with. Nynaeve said they had to learn them in order to learn how to counter them, but Elayne did not want to. They were keeping so many secrets, telling so many lies to friends and people on their side, that she almost wished she could take the Three Oaths on the Oath Rod without waiting to be raised Aes Sedai. One of those bound you to speak no word that was not true, bound you as though a part of your flesh.

"I haven't done as well as I might with the *ter'angreal*, Anaiya Sedai." That, at least, was hers and hers alone. The first had been the bracelet and necklace—a fact kept well hidden, needless to say—but they were an altered copy of a nasty invention, the *a'dam*, that the Seanchan left behind when their invasion was driven into the sea at Falme. The plain green disc that allowed someone not strong enough to work the invisibility trick— not many were—had been her idea from the first. She had no *angreal* or *sa'angreal* to study, so they had been impossible to make so far, and even after her ease in copying the Seanchan device, *ter'angreal* had not proven as easy as she had thought. They used the One Power instead of magnifying it, used it for one specific purpose, to do one thing. Some could even be used by people who could not channel, even men. They should have been simpler. Maybe they were, in function, but not simple to make.

Her modest statement unleashed a torrent from Janya. "Nonsense, child. Absolute nonsense. Why, I've no doubt that as soon as we are back in the Tower and can test you properly and put the Oath Rod in your hand, you'll be raised to the shawl as well as the ring. No doubt. You really are fulfilling all the promise that was seen in you. And more. No one could have expected—" Anaiya touched her arm again; it seemed a set signal, because once more Janya stopped and blinked.

"No need to swell the child's head too far," Anaiya said. "Elayne, I'll have no sulking out of you. You should have outgrown that long since." The mother could be firm as well as kindly. "I won't have you pouting over a few failures, not when your success was so wonderful." Elayne had made five tries at the stone disc. Two did nothing, and two made you appear blurry, as well as sick to your stomach. The one that worked had been the third attempt. More than a few failures in Elayne's book. "Everything you've done is wonderful. You, and Nynaeve, too."

"Thank you," Elayne said. "Thank you both. I'll try not to be sulky." When an Aes Sedai said you were sulky, the one thing you did not do was tell her you were not. "Will you excuse me, please? I understand the embassy to Caemlyn is leaving today, and I want to say goodbye to Min."

They let her go, of course, though Janya might have taken half an hour to do so without Anaiya there. Anaiya eyed Elayne sharply—she surely knew all about the words with Sheriam—but said nothing. Sometimes an Aes Sedai's silences were as loud as words.

Thumbing the ring on the third finger of her left hand, Elayne darted on at a near trot, eyes focused far enough ahead that she could claim not to have seen anyone else who tried to stop her for congratulations. It might work, and it might mean a visit to Tiana; indulgences for good work only went so far. Right that moment, she would much prefer Tiana to praise she did not deserve.

The gold ring was a serpent biting its own tail, the Great Serpent, a symbol of Aes Sedai, but worn by Accepted too. When she donned the shawl, fringed in the color of the Ajah she selected, she would wear it on the finger she chose. It would be the Green Ajah for her, of necessity; only Green sisters had more than one Warder, and she wanted to have Rand. Or as much of him as she could, at least. The difficulty was that she had already bonded Birgitte, the first woman ever to become a Warder. That was why she could sense Birgitte's feelings, how she knew Birgitte had gotten a splinter in her hand that morning. Only Nynaeve knew about the bond. Warders were for full Aes Sedai; for an Accepted who overstepped that bound, no indulgences in the world would save her hide. For them it had been necessity, not whim—Birgitte would have died, else—but Elayne did not think that would make any difference. Breaking a rule with the Power could be fatal for yourself and others; to set that firmly in your mind, Aes Sedai seldom let anyone get away with breaking any rule for any reason.

There was so much subterfuge here in Salidar. Not just Birgitte, and Moghedien. One of the Oaths kept an Aes Sedai from lying, but what was not spoken of did not have to be lied over. Moiraine had known how to weave a cloak of invisibility, maybe the same one they learned from Moghedien; Nynaeve had seen Moiraine do it once, before Nynaeve knew anything of the Power. No one else in Salidar had known, though. Or admitted to it, anyway. Birgitte had confirmed what Elayne had begun to suspect. Most Aes Sedai, maybe all, kept back at least part of what they learned; most had their own secret tricks. Those might become common knowledge taught to novices or Accepted, if enough Aes Sedai learned them—or they might die with the Aes Sedai. Two or three times she thought she had seen a glimmer in someone's eyes when she demonstrated something. Carenna had leaped onto the eavesdropping trick with suspicious quickness. But it was hardly the sort of accusation an Accepted could make against Aes Sedai.

Knowing did not make her own deceptions more palatable, but maybe it helped a little. That and remembering necessity. If only they would stop praising her for what she had not done.

She was sure she knew where to find Min. The River Eldar lay not three miles west of Salidar, and a tiny stream ran through the edge of the village on its way through the forest to the river. Most of the trees that had grown up in the town had been cut down after Aes Sedai began arriving, but a small patch on the stream's bank remained behind some houses, on a scrap of land too narrow to be useful. Min claimed to like cities best, yet she often went to sit among those trees. It was a way to escape the company of Aes Sedai and Warders awhile, and for Min that was almost essential.

Sure enough, when Elayne edged her way around the corner of a stone house onto the slender strip, along a runnel of water no wider, Min was sitting there with her back against a tree, watching the little brook burble over rocks. As much as was left of it; the stream trickled down a bed of dried mud twice as wide as it was. The trees held a few leaves here, though most of the surrounding forest was beginning to go bare. Even the oaks.

A dried branch cracked under Elayne's slipper, and Min jumped to her feet. As usual she wore a boy's gray coat and breeches, but she had had small blue flowers embroidered on the lapels and up the sides of the snug legs. Oddly, since she said the three aunts who raised her had been seamstresses, Min seemed not to know one end of a needle from the other. She stared at Elayne, then grimaced and ran her fingers through dark shoulder-length hair. "You know" was all she said.

"I thought we should talk."

Min scrubbed her hands through her hair again. "Siuan didn't tell me until this morning. I've been trying to work up courage to tell you ever since. She wants me to spy on him, Elayne. For the embassy, and she gave me names in Caemlyn, people who can send messages back to her."

"You won't do it, of course," Elayne said, without a hint of question, and Min gave her a grateful look. "Why were you afraid to come to me? We are friends, Min. And we promised each other not to let a man come between us. Even if we do both love him."

Min's laugh had a huskiness to it; Elayne supposed many men would find that attractive. And she was pretty, in a mischievous sort of way. And a few years older; was that in her favor, or against? "Oh, Elayne, we said that when he was safely away from both of us. Losing you would be like losing a sister, but what if one of us changes her mind?"

Best not to ask which of them that was supposed to be. Elayne tried not to think of the fact that if she bound and gagged Min with the Power and inverted the weave, she might be able to hide the woman in a basement until the embassy was long gone. "We won't," she said simply. No, she could not do that to Min. She wanted Rand all to herself, but she could not hurt Min. Maybe she could just ask the other woman not to go until they both could. Instead, she said, "Is Gareth releasing you from your oath?"

This time Min's laugh was a bark. "Hardly. He says he'll make me work it off sooner or later. Siuan's the one he really wants to hold on to, the Light knows why." A slight tensing of her face made Elayne think there was a viewing involved in it, but she did not ask. Min never talked about those unless they concerned you.

She had an ability known to few in Salidar. Elayne and Nynaeve, Siuan and Leane; that was all. Birgitte did not know, but then Min did not know about Birgitte. Or Moghedien. So many secrets. But Min's was her own. Sometimes she saw images or auras around people, and sometimes she knew what they meant. When she knew, she was always right; for instance, if she said a man and woman would marry, then sooner or later they married, even if they plainly hated one another now. Leane called it "reading the Pattern," but it had nothing to do with the Power. Most people carried the images only occasionally, but Aes Sedai and Warders always. Min's retreats here were to escape that deluge.

"Will you carry a letter to Rand for me?"

"Of course." The other woman's assent was so quick, her face so open, that Elayne blushed and went on hurriedly. She was not sure she would have agreed had the circumstances been reversed. "You mustn't let him know about your viewings, Min. Concerning us, I mean." One thing Min had viewed about Rand was that three women would fall hopelessly in love with him, be tied to him forever, and that one of them would be herself. The second had turned out to be Elayne. "If he learns about the viewing, he might decide it isn't what we want, only the Pattern, or his being *ta'veren*. He could decide to be noble and save us by not letting either of us near him."

"Maybe," Min said doubtfully. "Men are strange. More likely, if he realizes we'll both come running when he crooks a finger, he'll crook it. He won't be able to help himself. I've seen them do it. I think it has something to do with the hair on their chins." She had such a wondering look that Elayne was not sure whether or not that was a joke. Min seemed to know a lot about men; she had worked mainly in stables—she liked horses—but once she had mentioned serving table in a tavern. "Either way, I won't tell. You and I will divide him up like a pie. Maybe we'll let the third have a bit of crust when she shows up."

"What are we going to do, Min?" Elayne had not meant to say that, certainly not in a near wail. Part of her wanted to say unequivocally that *she* would never come for a crooked finger; part wanted him to crook it. Part of her wanted to say she would *not* share Rand, not in any way, not with *anyone*, even a friend, and Min's viewings could go to the Pit of Doom; part wanted to box Rand's ears for doing this to her and Min. It was all so childish she felt like hiding her head, but she could not untangle the snarl in her feelings. Leveling her voice, she answered her own question before Min could. "What we're going to do is sit here awhile and talk." She suited the words, choosing a spot where the dead leaves were particularly thick. A tree made a fine backrest. "Only not about Rand. I am going to miss you, Min. It's so good to have a friend I can trust."

Min sat cross-legged beside her and idly began digging up pebbles and tossing them into the stream. "Nynaeve is your friend. You trust her. And Birgitte certainly seems to be one; you spend more time with her than you do with Nynaeve, even." A slight frown creased her forehead. "Does she really *believe* she's Birgitte out of the legends? I mean, the bow and the braid— every tale mentions those, even if her bow isn't silver—and I can't think she was born with the name."

"She was born with it," Elayne said carefully. It was true, in a way. Best to steer the talk another way. "Nynaeve still can't decide whether I'm a friend or somebody she has to browbeat into doing what she think's right.

And she spends more time remembering I'm her Queen's daughter than I do. I think she holds it against me sometimes. You never do that."

"Maybe I'm not so impressed." Min wore a grin, but on the other she sounded serious. "I was born in the Mountains of Mist, Elayne, at the mines. Your mother's writ runs pretty thin that far west." The smile vanished from her face. "I'm sorry, Elayne."

Stifling a flash of indignation—Min was every bit as much a subject of the Lion Throne as Nynaeve!—Elayne let her head fall back against the tree. "Let's talk of something happy." The sun sat molten overhead through the branches; the sky was a clear sheet of blue, unmarked by even one cloud to the horizon. On impulse, she opened herself to *saidar* and let it fill her, as though all the joy of life in the world had been distilled and every drop in her veins replaced with the essence. If she could make just one cloud form, it would be a sign that everything would come out all right. Her mother would be alive. Rand would love her. And Moghedien . . . would be dealt with. Somehow. She wove a tenuous web through the sky as far as she could see, using Air and Water, searching for the moisture for a cloud. If she only strained hard enough. . . . The sweetness quickly built close to pain, the danger sign; draw much more of the Power, and she could still herself. Just one little cloud.

"Happy?" Min said. "Well, I know you don't want to talk about Rand, but aside from you and me, he's still the most important thing in the world right now. And the happiest. Forsaken fall dead when he appears, and nations line up to bow. The Aes Sedai here are ready to support him. I know they are, Elayne; they have to. Why, next Elaida will hand the Tower over to him. The Last Battle will be a walk for him. He's winning, Elayne. We're winning."

Releasing the Source, Elayne sagged back, staring at a sky as empty as her mood had become. You did not need to be able to channel to see the Dark One's hand at work, and if he could touch the world this much, if he could touch it at all. . . . "Are we?" she said, but too softly for Min to hear.

The manor house was unfinished yet, the greatroom's tall wooden panels pale and unstained, but Faile ni Bashere t'Aybara held court every afternoon, as proper for the lord's wife, in a massive high-backed chair carved with falcons, just in front of a bare stone fireplace that mirrored another at the end of the room. The empty chair by her side, carved with wolves, and a large wolf's head at its peak, should have been occupied by her husband, Perrin t'Bashere Aybara, Perrin Goldeneyes, Lord of the Two Rivers.

Of course, the manor was only an overgrown farmhouse, the greatroom stretched fewer than fifteen paces—how Perrin had stared when she insisted on it being that big; he was still used to thinking of himself as a blacksmith, or even a blacksmith's apprentice—and the name given her at birth had been Zarine, not Faile. These things did not matter. Zarine was a name for a languorous woman who sighed tremulously over poems composed to her smiles. Faile, the name she had chosen as a sworn Hunter for the Horn of Valere, meant falcon in the Old Tongue. No one who got a good look at her face, with its bold nose and high cheekbones and dark tilted eyes that flashed when she was angry, could doubt which suited her best. For the rest, intentions counted a great deal. So did what was right and proper.

Her eyes were flashing at the moment. It had nothing to do with Perrin's stubbornness, and little with the unseasonable heat. Though in truth, futilely working a pheasant feather fan for a breeze against the sweat sliding down her cheeks did not help her temper at all.

This late in the afternoon few remained of the crowd who had come to have her judge their disputes. Actually, they came for Perrin to hear them, but the idea of passing judgment on people he had grown up among horrified him. Unless she managed to corner the man, he vanished like a wolf in fog when it came time for the daily audience. Luckily, the people did not mind it when Lady Faile heard them instead of Lord Perrin. Or few did, anyway, and those wise enough to hide the fact.

"You brought this to me," she said in a flat voice. The two women perspiring before her chair shuffled their feet uneasily and studied the polished floorboards.

Coppery-skinned Sharmad Zeffar's plump curves were covered, if far from obscured, by a high-necked but barely opaque Domani dress, the pale golden silk worn at hem and cuffs, still with a sprinkling of small travel-stains beyond cleaning; silk was silk, after all, and seldom to be had here. Patrols into the Mountains of Mist searching for remnants of the past summer's Trolloc invasion found few of the bestial Trollocs—and no Myrddraal, thank the Light—but they did find refugees nearly every day, ten here, twenty there, five somewhere else. Most came out of Almoth Plain, but a good many from Tarabon and, like Sharmad, from Arad Doman, all fleeing lands ruined by anarchy on top of civil war. Faile did not want to think of how many died in the mountains. Lacking roads or even paths, the mountains were no easy journey in the best of times, and these were far from the best.

Rhea Avin was no refugee, for all she wore a copy of a Taraboner dress in fine-woven wool, soft gray folds that molded and emphasized almost as much as Sharmad's thinner garb. Those who survived the long trek over the mountains brought more than troubling rumors, skills previously unseen in the Two Rivers, and hands to work farms depopulated by the Trollocs. Rhea was a pretty, round-faced woman born not two miles from where the manor now stood, her dark hair in a wrist-thick braid to her waist. In the Two Rivers, girls did not braid their hair until the Women's Circle said they were old enough to marry, whether that was fifteen or thirty, though few went beyond twenty. In fact, Rhea was a good five years older than Faile, her hair four years braided, but at the moment she looked as if she still wore it loose on her shoulders and had just realized that what had seemed a wonderful idea at the time was really the stupidest thing she could have done. For that matter, Sharmad seemed even more abashed, for all she had a year or two on Rhea; for a Domani to find herself in this situation must be humiliating. Faile wanted to slap the pair of them cross-eyed—except that a lady could not do that.

"A man," she said as levelly as she could manage, "is not a horse or a field. Neither of you can own him, and to ask me to say which has the right to him. . . ." She drew a slow breath. "If I thought Wil al'Seen had been leading you both on, I might have something to say on the matter." Wil had an eye for the women, and they for him—he had very well-turned calves— but he never made promises. Sharmad looked ready to sink into the floor; Domani women had a reputation for twining men around their fingers, after all, not the other way around. "As it is, this is my judgment. You will both go to the Wisdom and explain matters to her, leaving nothing out. She will handle this. I expect to hear that she's seen you before nightfall."

The pair flinched. Daise Congar, the Wisdom here in Emond's Field, would not tolerate this sort of nonsense. In fact, she would go well beyond not tolerating it. But they curtsied, muttering "Yes, my Lady" in forlorn unison. If not already, they soon would sorely regret wasting Daise's time.

And mine, Faile thought firmly. Everyone knew Perrin rarely sat in audience, or they would never have brought their fool "problem." Had he been here where he belonged, they would have slipped away rather than air it in front of him. Faile hoped the heat had Daise in a prickle. Too bad there was no way to get Daise to take Perrin in hand.

Cenn Buie replaced the women almost before they could get out of the way on dragging feet. Despite leaning heavily on a walking staff nearly as gnarled as himself, he managed a florid bow, then spoiled it by raking bony fingers through lank thinning hair. As usual, his rough brown coat looked slept in. "The Light shine on you, my Lady Faile, and on your honored husband, the Lord Perrin." The grand words sounded odd in his scratchy voice. "Let me add my wishes for your continued happiness to those of the Council. Your intelligence and beauty make our lives brighter, as does the justice of your pronouncements."

Faile drummed her fingers on the arm of her chair before she could stop herself. Flowery praises instead of the normal sour grumbling. Reminding her that he sat on the Emond's Field Village Council and so was a man of influence, due respect. And playing for sympathy with that staff; the thatcher was as spry as anyone half his age. He wanted something. "What do you bring me today, Master Buie?"

Cenn straightened, forgetting to prop himself up with his stick. And forgetting to keep the acrid note out of his voice. "It's all these outlanders flooding in, bringing all sorts of things we don't want here." He seemed to have forgotten she was an outlander, too; most Two Rivers folks had. "Strange ways, my Lady. Indecent clothes. You'll be hearing from the women about the way those Domani hussies dress, if you haven't already." She had, as it happened, from some of them, though a momentary gleam in Cenn's eye said he would regret it if she gave in to their demands. "Strangers stealing the food from our mouths, taking away our trade. That Taraboner fellow and his fool tile-making, for example. Taking up hands that could be put to useful work. He doesn't care about good Two Rivers people. Why, he. . . ."

Fanning herself, she stopped listening while giving every appearance of paying close attention; it was a skill her father had taught her, necessary at times like this. Of course. Master Hornval's roof tiles would compete with Cenn's thatchwork.

Not everyone felt as Cenn did about the newcomers. Haral Luhhan, the Emond's Field blacksmith, had gone into partnership with a Domani cutler and a whitesmith from Almoth Plain, and Master Aydaer had hired three men and two women who knew furniture making and carving, and gilding as well, though there certainly was no gold lying about for that. Her chair and Perrin's were their work, and as fine as she had seen anywhere. For that matter, Cenn himself had taken on half a dozen helpers, and not all Two Rivers folk; a good many roofs had burned when the Trollocs came, and new houses were going up everywhere. Perrin had no right to make her listen to this nonsense alone.

The people of the Two Rivers might have proclaimed him their lord—as well they might after he led them to victory over the Trollocs— and he might be beginning to realize he could not change that—as he certainly should, when they bowed and called him Lord Perrin to his face right after he told them not to—yet he dug in his heels at the trappings that went with being a lord, all the things that people *expected* from their lords and ladies. Worse, he balked at the duties of a lord. Faile knew those things exactly, as the eldest surviving child of Davram t'Ghaline Bashere, Lord of Bashere, Tyr and Sidona, Guardian of the Blightborder, Defender of the Heartland, Marshal-General to Queen Tenobia of Saldaea. True, she had run away to become a Hunter for the Horn—and then given that up for a husband, which sometimes still stunned her—but she remembered. Perrin listened when she explained, and even nodded his head in the proper places, but trying to make him actually do any of it was like trying to make a horse dance the sa'sara.

Cenn finally ran down in splutters, only just remembering to swallow the invective that bubbled behind his teeth.

"Perrin and I chose to use thatch," Faile said calmly. While Cenn was still nodding in self-satisfaction, she added, "You haven't finished it, yet." He gave a start. "You seem to have taken on more roofs than you can handle, Master Buie. If ours isn't done soon, I fear we will have to ask Master Horn-val about his tiles." Cenn's mouth worked in vigorous silence; if she put a tile roof on the manor, others would follow. "I have enjoyed your discourse, but I am sure you would rather finish my roof than waste time in idle con-versation, however pleasant."

Lips thinning, Cenn glowered for a moment, then made a sketchy bow. Muttering something unintelligible except for a strangled "my Lady" at the end, he stalked out thumping the bare floor with his stick. The things people found to waste her time. Perrin was going to do his share of this if she had to tie him hand and foot.

The rest were not so provoking. A once-stout woman, her patched flower-embroidered dress hanging on her like a sack, who had come all the way from Toman Head, beyond Almoth Plain, wanted to deal in herbs and cures. Hulking Jon Ayellin rubbing his bald head and skinny Thad Torfinn twisting the lapels of his coat, disputing the boundaries of their fields. Two dark Domani men in long leather vests, with close-trimmed beards, min-ers who thought they had seen signs of gold and silver nearby on their way through the mountains. And iron, though they were less interested in that. And finally, a wiry Taraboner, a transparent veil across her narrow face and her pale hair in a multitude of thin braids, who claimed to have been a master carpetweaver and to know the making of rug looms.

The woman with an interest in herbs Faile directed to the local Women's Circle; if Espara Soman knew what she was about, they would find her a place under one of the village Wisdoms. With all the new people coming in, many in a bad way from the journey, not a Wisdom in the Two Rivers but had an apprentice or two, and all were on the lookout for more. Maybe not exactly what Espara wanted, but where she would have to start. A few questions made it plain that neither Thad nor Jon really remembered where the boundary lay—apparently they had been arguing it since before she was born—so she directed them to split the difference. Which seemed to be what each had thought the Village Council would decide, the reason for keeping the argument between themselves so long.

The others she granted the permission they sought. They did not really need permission, but it was best to let them know where authority lay from the start. In return for her consent and enough silver to buy supplies, Faile made the two Domani agree to give Perrin a tenth part of what they found, as well as to locate the iron mentioned in passing. Perrin would not like it, but the Two Rivers had nothing like taxes, and a lord was expected to do things and provide things that required money. And the iron would be as useful as the gold. As for Liale Mosrara, if the Taraboner claimed more skill than she had, her enterprise would not last long, but if she did. . . . Three clothweavers already ensured that the merchants would find more than raw wool when they came down from Baerlon next year, and decent carpets would be another trade item to bring in more coin. Liale promised the first and finest from her looms to the manor, and Faile nodded a gracious acceptance of the gift; she could give more if and when the carpets appeared. The floors did need covering. All in all, everyone seemed reasonably satisfied. Even Jon and Thad.

As the Taraboner woman backed away curtsying, Faile stood, glad to be done, then stopped when four women entered through one of the doorways that flanked the far fireplace, all sweating in dark stout Two Rivers woolens. Daise Congar, as tall as most men and wider, overtopped the other Wisdoms and thrust herself forward to take the lead here on the outskirts of her own village. Edelle Gaelin, from Watch Hill, gray-braided and slender, made it plain with her straight back and stiff face that she thought she should have Daise's place, by virtue of age and her long time in office if no other reason. Elwinn Taron, the Wisdom of Deven Ride, was the shortest, a round woman with a pleasant motherly smile that she wore even when she was making people do what they did not want to. The last, Milla al'Azar, from Taren Ferry, trailed behind; the youngest, almost young enough to be Edelle's daughter, she always appeared uncertain around the others.

Faile remained standing, fanning herself slowly. She truly wished Perrin there, now. Very much. These women had as much authority in their villages as the mayor—sometimes, in some ways, more—and they had to be handled carefully, with due dignity and respect. That made matters difficult. They turned into simpering girls around Perrin, eager to please, but with her. . . . The Two Rivers had had no nobles in centuries; they had not seen so much as a representative of the Queen in Caemlyn for seven generations. Everyone was still working out how to behave toward a lord and a lady, including these four. Sometimes they forgot she was the Lady Faile and saw only a young woman whose marriage Daise had presided over just a few months ago. They could be all curtsies and "yes, of course, my Lady," and right in the middle of it tell her exactly what to do about something without seeing anything at all incongruous. *You are not going to leave this to me anymore, Perrin.*

They curtsied now, with varying degrees of skill, and said, "The Light shine on you, my Lady," on top of one another.

Amenities out of the way, Daise started in before she was completely upright again. "Three more boys have run off, my Lady." Her tone fell halfway between the respect of the words and the now-you-listen-to-me-young-woman she sometimes used. "Dav Ayellin, Ewin Finngar, and Elam Dowtry. Run off to see the world because of Lord Perrin's stories about what's out there."

Faile blinked in surprise. Those three were hardly boys. Dav and Elam were as old as Perrin, and Ewin not really that much younger than she herself. And Perrin's stories, which he told seldom and reluctantly, were hardly the only way Two Rivers youths learned about the outside world now. "I could ask Perrin to speak to you, if you wish."

They stirred, Daise looking for him expectantly, Edelle and Milla automatically smoothing their skirts, Elwinn just as unconsciously drawing her braid over her shoulder and arranging it carefully. Abruptly they realized what they were doing and froze, not looking at one another. Or at her. The one advantage Faile had with them was that they knew the effect her husband had on them. So many times she had seen one or another firm herself up after meeting with Perrin, plainly vowing not to let it happen again; so many times she had seen resolution fly out the window at a sight of him. None was really sure whether she preferred to deal with him or with her.

"That will not be necessary," Edelle said after a moment. "Boys running off are a bother, but only a bother." Her tone had slid a little further from "my Lady" than Daise's, and plump Elwinn added a smile suitable for mother to young daughter.

"As long as we're here, my dear, we really might as well mention something else. Water. You see, some of the people are worried."

"It hasn't rained in months," Edelle added, and Daise nodded.

This time Faile did blink. They were too intelligent to think Perrin could do anything about that. "The springs are all still flowing, and Perrin has ordered more wells dug." Actually he had only suggested it, but it had come to the same thing, fortunately. "And long before planting time, the irrigation canals from the Waterwood will be done." That was her doing; half the fields in Saldaea were irrigated, but no one here had ever heard of the practice. "Anyway, the rains have to come sooner or later. The canals are only in case." Daise nodded again, slowly, and Elwinn and Edelle. But they knew all this as well as she.

"It isn't the rain," Milla muttered. "Not exactly, anyway. It isn't natural. You see, none of us can Listen to the Wind." She hunched her shoulders under the others' sudden frowns. Plainly she was saying too much, and giving away secrets besides. Supposedly all the Wisdoms could predict the weather by Listening to the Wind; at least, they said that they all could. But even so Milla plowed on doggedly. "Well, we can't! We look at clouds instead, and how the birds behave, and the ants and caterpillars and. . . ." Drawing a deep breath, she straightened, but still avoided the other Wisdoms' eyes. Faile wondered how she managed to deal with the Women's Circle in Taren Ferry, much less the Village Council. Of course, they were as new at it as Milla; that village had lost its whole population when the Trollocs came, and everyone there now was new. "It isn't natural, my Lady. The first snows should have been here weeks ago, but it might as well be the middle of summer. We're not worried, my Lady, we're frightened! If nobody else will admit it, I will. I lie awake most nights. I haven't slept properly in a month, and. . . ." She trailed off, color blooming in her face as she realized she might have gone too far. A Wisdom was supposed to be in control in all times; she did not run around saying she was frightened.

The others shifted their gazes from Milla to Faile. They said nothing, faces expressionless enough for Aes Sedai.

Faile understood, now. Milla had spoken simple truth. The weather was *not* natural; it was most *un*natural. Faile often lay awake herself, praying for rain, or better still snow, trying not to think of what lurked behind the heat and drought. Yet a Wisdom was supposed to reassure others. Who could she go to when she needed reassurance herself?

These women might not have known what they were doing, but they had come to the right place. Part of the compact between noble and commoner, ingrained in Faile from her birth, was that nobles provided safety and security. And a part of giving security was to remind people that evil times were not forever. If today was bad, then tomorrow would be better, and if not tomorrow, then the day after. She wished she could be certain of that herself, but she had been taught to give those under her strength even when she had none herself, to soothe their fears, not infect them with her own.

"Perrin told me about his people before I ever came here," she said. He was not a man to brag, but things had a way of coming out. "When hail flattens your crops, when the winter kills half your sheep, you buckle down and keep going. When Trollocs devastated the Two Rivers, you fought back, and when you were done with them, you set about rebuilding without missing a step." She would not have believed that without seeing for herself, not of southerners. These people would have done very well in Saldaea, where Trolloc raids were a matter of course, in the northern parts at least. "I cannot tell you the weather will be what it should tomorrow. I can tell you that Perrin and I will do what needs to be done, whatever can be done. And I don't need to tell you that you will take what each day brings, whatever it is, and be ready to face the next. That is the kind of people the Two Rivers breeds. That is who you are."

They truly were intelligent. If they had not admitted to themselves why they had come, they had to now. Had they been less intelligent, they might have taken umbrage. But even words they had said themselves before had the desired effect coming from someone else. Of course, that carried its own embarrassment. It was a proper muddle, and they were a study in crimson cheeks and unspoken wishes to be somewhere else.

"Well, of course," Daise said. Planting stout fists on ample hips, she stared at the other Wisdoms, daring them to gainsay her. "I've said as much, haven't I? The girl talks sense. I said as much when she first came here. That girl has a head on her, I said."

Edelle sniffed. "Did anyone say she didn't, Daise? I didn't hear it. She does very well." To Faile she added, "You do very well, indeed."

Milla bobbed a curtsy. "Thank you, Lady Faile. I know I've said the same to fifty people, but coming from you, somehow it—" A loud *har-rumph* from Daise cut her short; that was going too far. Milla grew redder in the face.

"This is very nice work, my Lady." Elwinn leaned forward to finger the narrow, divided riding skirt that Faile favored. "There's a Taraboner seamstress down in Deven Ride who could do even better for you, though. If you don't mind my saying. I had a word with her, and she only makes decent dresses now, except for married women." That motherly smile came onto her face again, indulgent and iron at the same time. "Or if they're courting. Beautiful things, she makes. Why, she'd count it a pleasure to work with your coloring and figure."

Daise began smiling complacently before the other woman was done. "Therille Marza, right here in Emond's Field, is already making Lady Faile half a dozen dresses. And the most beautiful gown." Elwinn drew herself up, and Edelle pursed her lips, and even Milla looked thoughtful.

As far as Faile was concerned, the audience was over. The Domani seamstress required a firm hand and constant vigilance to keep her from dressing Faile for the court in Bandar Eban. The gown had been Daise's idea, sprung as a surprise, and even if it was in the Saldaean style rather than Domani, Faile did not know where she was to wear it. It would be a long time before the Two Rivers ran to balls or promenades. Left to themselves, the Wisdoms would soon be competing to see which village would dress her.

She offered them tea, with a casual comment that they could discuss how to hearten the people about the weather. That hit too close to home after the last few minutes, and they nearly tripped over themselves regretting duties that would not allow them to stay.

Thoughtfully, she watched them go, Milla drawing up the rear as usual, a child tagging after older sisters. It might be possible to have a few quiet words with some of the Women's Circle in Taren Ferry. Each village needed a strong mayor and a strong Wisdom to stand up for their interests. Quiet, careful words. When Perrin had discovered she had been talking to the men in Taren Ferry before the election for mayor—if a man had good wits and was strong for her and Perrin, why should the men who were going to vote not know that she and Perrin returned that support?—when he found out. . . . He was a gentle man, slow to anger, but just to be safe she had barricaded herself in their bedroom until he cooled down. Which had not happened until she promised not to "interfere" again in any mayoral

election, in the open or behind his back. That last had been most unfair of
him. It was most inconvenient, too. But it had not occurred to him to
mention Women's Circle voting. Well, what he did not know would do
him a great deal of good. And Taren Ferry, too.

Thinking of him made her remember her promise to herself. The feathered fan picked up speed. Today had not been the worst for nonsense, and
not even the worst with the Wisdoms—there had been no questions about
when Lord Perrin could expect an heir, the Light be blessed!—but maybe
the unrelenting heat had finally screwed her irritation to the sticking place.
Perrin *would* do his duty, or. . . .

Thunder rolled over the manor, and lightning lit the windows. Hope
swelled inside her. If rain had come. . . .

She ran silently on slippered feet, searching out Perrin. She wanted to
share the rain with him. And she still intended a few firm words. More
than a few, if necessary.

Perrin was where she expected, all the way up on the third floor, on the
roofed porch at the front, a curly-haired man in a plain brown coat, with
heavy shoulders and arms. Broad back to her, he was leaning against one of
the porch columns. Staring down at the ground to one side of the manor,
not up at the sky. Faile stopped in the doorway.

Thunder boomed again, and lightning sheeted blue across the sky.
Heat lightning, in a cloudless sky. Not a herald of rain. No rain to break
heat. No snow to follow. Sweat beaded on her face, but she shivered.

"The audience is over?" Perrin said, and she jumped. He had not raised
his head. It was difficult sometimes to remember how sensitive his hearing
was. Or he could have smelled her; she hoped it was the perfume, not the
sweat.

"I half thought I'd find you with Gwil or Hal." That was one of his
worst faults; she tried to train servants, and to him they were men to laugh
with and have a mug of ale. At least he did not have a roving eye, as so
many men did. He never realized Calle Coplin had taken service in the
manor because she hoped to do more for Lord Perrin than make his bed.
He had not even noticed when Faile chased Calle out with a stick of
kindling.

Moving up beside him, she saw what he was watching. Two men,
stripped to the waist, working with wooden practice swords below. Tam
al'Thor was a solid, graying man, Aram slender and young. Aram was learning fast. Very fast. Tam had been a soldier, and a blademaster, but Aram was
pressing him hard.

Automatically her eyes went to the tents clustered in a stone-fenced field half a mile toward the Westwood. The rest of the Tinkers were camped amid half-finished wagons like small houses on wheels. Of course, they no longer acknowledged Aram as one of them, not since he had picked up that sword. The Tuatha'an never did violence, not for any reason. She wondered whether they would go as they planned, when the wagons the Trollocs had burned were replaced. After gathering in all those who had hidden in the thickets, they yet numbered little more than a hundred. Probably they would, leaving Aram behind of his own choice. No Tuatha'an had ever settled in one place that she had ever heard.

But then, people in the Two Rivers used to say nothing there ever changed, yet a great deal had since the Trollocs. Emond's Field, just a hundred paces south of the manor, was larger than she had first seen, all the burned houses rebuilt and new going up. Some in brick, another new thing. And some with tile roofs. At the rate new dwellings were being erected, the manor would be in the village soon. There was talk of a wall, in case the Trollocs returned. Change. A handful of children were following Loial's great height along one of the village streets. Only a few months since the sight of the Ogier, with his tufted ears and broad nose almost as wide as his face, half again as tall as a man, had drawn every child in the village in gaping wonder, and their mothers in a terror to protect them. Now mothers sent their children for Loial to read to them. The outlanders in their strangely cut coats and dresses, dotted among Emond's Fielders, stood out almost as much as Loial, but no one looked at them twice, or at the village's three Aiel, strange, tall folk in browns and grays. Until a few weeks ago there had been two Aes Sedai here, as well, and even they had gotten no more than respectful bows and curtsies. Change. The two flagpoles not far from the Winespring, on the Green, were visible over the rooftops, one bearing the red-bordered red wolf's head that had become Perrin's sigil, the other the crimson eagle in flight that marked Manetheren. Manetheren had vanished in the Trolloc Wars, some two thousand years ago, but this land had been part of it, and the Two Rivers flew that flag almost by acclamation. Change, and they had no notion how large it was, how inexorable it was. But Perrin would see them through it to whatever came beyond. With her help, he would.

"I used to hunt rabbits with Gwil," Perrin said. "He's only a few years older than me, and he used to take me hunting sometimes."

It took her a moment to remember what he was talking about. "Gwil is trying to learn how to be a footman. You don't help him when you invite him to go smoke his pipe with you in the stables and talk horses." She took a deep slow breath. This would not be easy. "You have a duty to these people, Perrin. However hard it is, however much you want not to, you have to do your duty."

"I know," he said softly. "I can feel him tugging at me."

His voice was so strange that she reached up to grip his short beard and make him look down at her. His golden eyes, still as strange and mysterious to her as ever, looked sad. "What do you mean? You might think fondly of Gwil, but he—"

"It's Rand, Faile. He needs me."

The knot inside her that she had been trying to deny clenched even tighter. She had convinced herself this danger had gone with the Aes Sedai. Foolish, that. She was married to a *ta'veren*, a man fated to bend lives around him into the shape the Pattern required, and he had grown up with two more *ta'veren*, one the Dragon Reborn himself. It was a part of him she had to share. She did not like sharing even a hair, but there it was. "What are you going to do?"

"Go to him." His gaze shifted for a moment, and her eyes followed. Against the wall leaned a blacksmith's heavy hammer and an axe with a wicked halfmoon blade and a haft a pace long. "I couldn't. . . ." His voice was almost a whisper. "I couldn't find how to tell you. I'll go tonight, when everyone's asleep. I don't think there's much time, and it could be a long way. Master al'Thor and Master Cauthon will help you with the mayors, if you need it. I spoke to them." He tried to make his voice lighter, a pitiful effort. "You shouldn't have any trouble with the Wisdoms anyway. Funny; when I was a boy the Wisdoms always seemed so fearsome, but they're really easy as long as you're firm."

Faile compressed her lips. So he had spoken to Tam al'Thor and Abell Cauthon, had he, but not to her? And the Wisdoms! She would like to make him wear her skin for a day and see how easy the Wisdoms were. "We can't leave as quickly as that. It will take time to organize a proper entourage."

Perrin's eyes narrowed. "We? You're not going! It will be—!" He coughed, went on in a milder tone. "It will be best if one of us stays here. If the lord goes off, the lady should remain to take care of things. That makes sense. More refugees every day. All those disputes to be settled. If you go, too, it'll be worse than the Trollocs around here."

How could he think she would not notice such a clumsy recovery? He had been going to say it would be dangerous. How could his wanting to keep her out of danger always make her feel so warm inside at the same time it made her so angry? "We will do what you think best," she said mildly, and he blinked suspiciously, scratched his beard, then nodded.

Now it was only necessary to make him see what really was best. At least he had not said right out she *could not* go. Once he dug in his heels, she could as easily shift a grain barn with her hands as shift him, but with care it could be avoided. Usually.

Abruptly she threw her arms around him and buried her face against his broad chest. His strong hands smoothed her hair softly; he probably thought she was worried about him leaving. Well, she was, in a way. Just not about him leaving without her; he had not yet learned what it meant to have a Saldaean wife. They had been getting on so well away from Rand al'Thor. Why did the Dragon Reborn need Perrin now, so strongly that Perrin could feel it across however many hundred leagues lay between them? Why was time so short? Why? Perrin's shirt clung to his sweaty chest, and the unnatural heat sent more sliding down her face, but Faile shivered.

One hand on his sword hilt, Gawyn Trakand bounced a small rock on his palm as he made another circuit of his men, checking their positions around the tree-topped hill. A dry hot wind carrying dust across the rolling brown grasslands fluttered the plain green cloak hanging down his back. Nothing to be seen but dead grass, scattered thickets and a dotting of mostly withered bushes. There was too much front to cover with the men he had if it came to a fight here. He had grouped them in clusters of five swordsmen afoot, with bowmen fifty paces back up the hill. Fifty more waited with lance and horse near the camp on the crest, to be committed where necessary. He hoped it would not be necessary today.

There had been fewer Younglings in the beginning, but their reputation brought recruits. The added numbers would be helpful; no recruit was allowed out of Tar Valon until he was up to standard. It was not that he expected fighting this day more than any other, but he had learned it came most often when unexpected. Only Aes Sedai would wait until the last minute to tell a man about a thing like what was to happen today.

"Is everything well?" he said, stopping beside a group of swordsmen. In spite of the heat, some wore their green cloaks so that Gawyn's white charging boar showed, embroidered on the breast.

Jisao Hamora was the youngest, still with a boy's grin, but he was also the only one of the five with the small silver tower on his collar, marking him a veteran of the fighting in the White Tower. He answered. "All is well, my Lord."

The Younglings deserved their name. Gawyn himself, a few years past twenty, was among the oldest. It was a rule that they accepted none who had served in any army, or borne arms for any lord or lady, or even worked as a merchant's guard. The first Younglings had gone to the Tower as boys and young men to be trained by the Warders, the finest swordsmen, the finest fighters, in the world, and they continued part of that tradition, at least, though Warders no longer trained them. Youth was no detriment. They had held a small ceremony only a week past for the first whiskers Benji Dalfor had ever shaved that were not fuzz, and he bore a scar across his cheek from the Tower fighting. The Aes Sedai had been too busy for Healing in the days right after Siuan Sanche was deposed as Amyrlin. She might still be Amyrlin if the Younglings had not faced many of their former teachers and bested them in the halls of the Tower.

"Is there any point to this, my Lord?" Hal Moir asked. He was two years older than Jisao, and like many who did not wear the silver tower, he regretted not having been there. He would learn. "There isn't a glimmer of Aielmen."

"You think not?" Without any hefting to give warning, Gawyn hurled the rock as hard as he could at the only bush close enough to hit, a scraggly thing. The rustle of dead leaves was the only sound, but the bush shook just a bit more than it should have, as though a man somehow hidden behind it had been struck in a tender place. Exclamations rose from the newer men; Jisao only eased his sword. "An Aiel, Hal, can hide in a fold in the ground you wouldn't even stumble over." Not that Gawyn knew any more of Aiel than he read in books, but he had read every book he could find in the White Tower's library by any man who had actually fought them, every book by any soldier who seemed to know what he was talking about. A man had to ready himself for the future, and it seemed the world's future was war. "But if the Light pleases, there won't be any fighting today."

"My Lord!" came a hail from up the hill as the lookout spotted what he just had: three women emerging from a small thicket a few hundred paces west, coming toward the hill. West; a surprise. But Aiel always liked surprise.

He had read about Aielwomen fighting alongside the men, but these women could never fight in those dark bulky skirts and white blouses. They carried shawls looped over their arms despite the heat. On the other hand, how had they reached that thicket unseen? "Keep your eyes open, and not on them," he said, and then disobeyed himself by watching the three Wise Ones, the emissaries from the Shaido Aiel, with interest. They could be no other, out here.

They came on at a stately pace, not at all as if approaching a large party of armed men. Their hair was long, to the waist—he had read that Aiel kept it cut short—and held back by folded kerchiefs. They wore so many bracelets and long necklaces of gold and silver and ivory that the glitter should have given them away at a mile.

Straight-backed and proud-faced, the three women strode past the swordsmen with hardly a glance and started up the hill. Their leader was a golden-haired woman, her loose blouse unlaced to show considerable tanned cleavage. The other two were gray, with leathery faces; she had to be less than half their age.

"I wouldn't mind asking that one to dance," one of the Younglings said admiringly when the women had gone past. He was a good ten years younger than the golden-haired woman.

"I wouldn't if I were you, Arwin," Gawyn said dryly. "It might be misunderstood." He had read that Aiel called battle "the dance." "Besides, she'd have your liver for dinner." He had caught a glimpse of her pale green eyes, and he had never seen harder.

He watched the Wise Ones until they had climbed the hill to where half a dozen Aes Sedai waited with their Warders. Those who had Warders; two were Red Ajah, and Reds did not. When the women disappeared into one of the tall white tents, and the five Warders had taken up guard around it, he went on with his circuit of the hill.

The Younglings were alert since word of the Aiel's arrival had spread, which did not please him. They should have been this alert before. Even most who did not wear the silver tower had seen fighting around Tar Valon. Eamon Valda, the Whitecloak Lord Captain in command, had pulled nearly all his men out to the west more than a month ago, but the handful he left behind tried to keep together the brigands and bullyboys Valda had gathered. The Younglings had dispersed those, at least. Gawyn wished he could think they had driven Valda off, too—the Tower had certainly kept its own soldiers far from the skirmishing, for all that the Whitecloaks' only reason for being there had been to see what harm they could do the Tower—but he suspected that Valda had his own reasons. Likely orders from Pedron Niall, and Gawyn would have given much to know what they were. Light, but he hated not knowing. It was like fumbling your way in the dark.

The truth was, he admitted, that he was irritated. Not only about the Aiel, about not being told of this meeting until this morning. He had not been told where they were going, either, until he was taken aside by Coiren Sedai, the Gray sister who led the Aes Sedai. Elaida had been closemouthed and imperious when she was his mother's advisor in Caemlyn; since being raised to the Amyrlin Seat she made the old Elaida seem open and warm. No doubt she had pressured him to form this escort as much to get him away from Tar Valon as for any other reason.

The Younglings had sided with her in the fighting—the old Amyrlin was stripped of Staff and Stole by the Hall, the attempt to free her rebellion against the law, clear and simple—but Gawyn had had his doubts about all Aes Sedai long before he heard the charges against Siuan Sanche read. That they pulled strings and made thrones dance was a thing said so often that he had hardly paid it any mind, but then he saw the strings being pulled. The effects at least, and his sister Elayne was the one who danced, danced right out of his sight, out of existence for all he knew. Her, and another. He had fought to keep Siuan imprisoned, then turned around and let her escape. If Elaida ever discovered that, his mother's crown would not keep him alive.

Even with that, Gawyn had chosen to stay, because his mother had always supported the Tower, because his sister wanted to be Aes Sedai. And because another woman wanted to. Egwene al'Vere. He had no right to even think of her, but abandoning the Tower would be abandoning her. For such flimsy reasons did a man choose his fate. Knowing they were flimsy did not change them, though.

He glared at the sere, windswept grasslands as he strode from one position to the next. So here he was, hoping the Aiel did not decide to attack despite—or because of—whatever it was the Shaido Wise Ones were talking over with Coiren and the others. He suspected there might be enough out there to overrun him even with Aes Sedai help. He was on his way to Cairhien, and he did not know how he felt about that. Coiren had made him swear to hold his mission secret, and even then seemed afraid of what she was saying. Well she might be. It was always best to examine carefully what an Aes Sedai said—they could not lie, but they could spin truth like a top—yet even so, he found no hidden meanings. The six Aes Sedai were going to ask the Dragon Reborn to accompany them to the Tower, with the Younglings, commanded by the son of the Queen of Andor, for an escort of honor. There could be only one reason, one that plainly shocked Coiren enough that she only hinted at it. It shocked Gawyn. Elaida intended to announce to the world that the White Tower supported the Dragon Reborn.

It was almost unbelievable. Elaida had been a Red before she became Amyrlin. Reds hated the very idea of men channeling; they did not think much of men in general, for that matter. Yet the fall of the once-invincible Stone of Tear, fulfilling prophecy, said Rand al'Thor was the Dragon Reborn, and even Elaida said the Last Battle was coming. Gawyn could hardly reconcile the frightened farmboy who had literally fallen into the Royal Palace in Caemlyn with the man in the rumors that drifted up the River Erinin to Tar Valon. It was said he had hanged Tairen High Lords and let Aiel loot the Stone. He had certainly brought the Aiel across the Spine of the World, for only the second time since the Breaking, to ravage Cairhien. Perhaps it was the madness. Gawyn had rather liked Rand al'Thor; he regretted that the man had turned out to be what he was.

By the time he came back to Jisao's group, someone else was in sight coming from the west, a peddler in a floppy hat, leading a slab-sided pack mule. Straight toward the hill; he had seen them.

Jisao shifted, then went still again when Gawyn touched his arm. Gawyn knew what the younger man was thinking, but if the Aiel decided to kill this fellow, there was nothing they could do. Coiren would be less than pleased if he started a battle with the people she was talking to.

The peddler shambled along unconcernedly, right by the bush Gawyn had disturbed with his rock. The mule started cropping desultorily at the brown grass as the man pulled off his hat, sketched a bow that took them all in and began mopping his grizzled face with a grimy neckerchief. "The Light shine on you, my Lords. You're well set up for traveling in these parlous times, as any man can see, but if there's any small thing you need, like as not old Mil Tesen's got it in his packs. Ain't no better prices in ten miles, my Lords."

Gawyn doubted there was as much as a farm within ten miles. "Parlous times indeed, Master Tesen. Aren't you afraid of Aiel?"

"Aiel, my Lord? They's all down to Cairhien. Old Mil can smell Aiel, he can. Truth, he wishes there was some here. Fine trading with Aiel. They got lots of gold. From Cairhien. And they don't bother peddlers. Everybody knows that."

Gawyn forbore asking why, if the Aiel in Cairhien made such good trading, the man was not heading south. "What news of the world, Master Tesen? We're from the north, and you may know what hasn't caught up to us yet from the south."

"Oh, big doings southward, my Lord. You'll have heard of Cairhien? Him that calls himself Dragon and all?" Gawyn nodded, and he went on. "Well, now he's taken Andor. Most of it, anyway. Their queen's dead. Some say he'll take the whole world before—" The man cut off with a strangled yelp before Gawyn realized he had seized the fellow's lapels.

"Queen Morgase is dead? Speak, man! Quickly!"

Tesen rolled his eyes looking for help, but he spoke, and quickly. "That's what they say, my Lord. Old Mil don't know, but he thinks it so. Everybody says it, my Lord. Everybody says this Dragon did it. My Lord? Old Mil's neck, my Lord! My Lord!"

Gawyn jerked his hands away as though burned. He felt on fire inside. It had been another neck he wanted in his hands. "The Daughter-Heir." His voice sounded far off. "Is there any word of the Daughter-Heir, Elayne?"

Tesen backed away a long pace as soon as he was free. "Not as old Mil knows, my Lord. Some says she's dead, too. Some says he killed her, but old Mil don't know for sure."

Gawyn nodded slowly. Thought seemed to be drifting up from the bottom of a well. *My blood shed before hers; my life given before hers.* "Thank you, Master Tesen. I. . . ." *My blood shed before hers . . .* That was the oath he had taken when barely tall enough to peer into Elayne's cradle. "You may trade with. . . . Some of my men may need . . ." Gareth Bryne had had to explain to him what it meant, but even then he had known he had to keep that oath if he failed at everything else in his life. Jisao and the others were looking at him worriedly. "Take care of the peddler," he told Jisao roughly, and turned away.

His mother dead, and Elayne. Only a rumor, but rumors on everyone's lips sometimes had a way of turning out true. He climbed half a dozen paces toward the Aes Sedai camp before he knew it. His hands hurt. He had to look to realize they were cramping from the grip he had on his sword hilt, and he had to force them to let go. Coiren and the others meant to take Rand al'Thor to Tar Valon, but if his mother was dead. . . . Elayne. If they were dead, he would see whether the Dragon Reborn could live with a sword through his heart!

Adjusting her red-fringed shawl, Katerine Alruddin rose from the cushions with the other women in the tent. She almost sniffed when Coiren, plump and pompous, intoned, "As it has been agreed, so shall it be." This was a meeting with savages, not the conclusion of a treaty between the Tower and a ruler.

The Aielwomen showed no more reaction, no more expression, than when they first arrived. That was something of a surprise; kings and queens betrayed their innermost feelings when faced by two or three Aes Sedai, much less half a dozen; brutish savages surely should be trembling visibly by now. Perhaps that should have been almost no reaction. Their leader—her name was Sevanna, followed by some nonsense about "septs" and "Shaido Aiel" and "wise"—said, "It is agreed so long as I get to see his face." She had a sulky mouth, and wore her blouse unlaced to attract men's eyes; that the Aiel chose one like her to lead showed how crude they were. "I want to see him, and have him see me, when he is defeated. Only with that will your Tower be allied to the Shaido."

The hint of eagerness in her voice made Katerine suppress a smile. Wise? This Sevanna truly was a fool. The White Tower did not have allies; there were those who served its ends willingly and those who served unwillingly, no others.

A slight thinning at the corners of Coiren's mouth betrayed her irritation. The Gray was a good negotiator, but she did like to have things done just so, every foot placed exactly where it had been planned to go. "Without doubt, your service deserves what you ask."

One of the gray-haired Aiel—Tarva, or some such—narrowed her eyes, but Sevanna nodded, hearing what Coiren had wanted her to hear.

Coiren set out to escort the Aielwomen as far as the foot of the hill, along with Erian, a Green, and Nesune, a Brown, and the five Warders they had between them. Katerine went as far as the edge of the trees to watch. On arrival the Aiel had been allowed to come up alone, like the supplicants they were, but now they were given all honor to make them believe they truly were friends and allies. Katerine wondered whether they were civilized enough to recognize the subtleties.

Gawyn was down there, sitting on a rock, staring off across the grasslands. What would that young man think if he learned he and his children were only here to get them away from Tar Valon? Neither Elaida nor the Hall liked having a pack of young wolves about who refused to accept the leash. Perhaps the Shaido could be prevailed upon to eliminate the problem. Elaida had intimated as much. That way his death would not rebound against the Tower with his mother.

"If you stare so at the young man much longer, Katerine, I will begin to think you should be a Green."

Katerine stamped out a quick spark of anger and inclined her head respectfully. "I was only speculating on his thoughts, Galina Sedai."

That was as much respect as was proper in so public a place, and perhaps even a touch more. Galina Casban looked forty at most but was at least twice Katerine's true age, and for eighteen years the round-faced woman had been the head of the Red Ajah. A fact not known outside the Ajah, of course; such things were for the Ajah alone. She was not even one of the Sitters for the Red in the Hall of the Tower; Katerine suspected that the heads of most other Ajahs were. Elaida would have named her leader of this expedition instead of that self-important Coiren, except that Galina herself had pointed out that a Red might make Rand al'Thor suspicious. The Amyrlin Seat was supposed to be of all Ajahs and none, renouncing her old loyalty, but if Elaida deferred to anyone—which was debatable, true— she deferred to Galina.

"Will he come willingly, as Coiren thinks?" Katerine asked.

"Perhaps," Galina said dryly. "The honor this delegation does him should be enough to make a king carry his throne to Tar Valon on his back."

Katerine did not bother to nod. "The woman Sevanna will kill him, given a chance."

"Then she must not be given a chance." Galina's voice was cold, her plump mouth tight. "The Amyrlin Seat will not be pleased to have her plans disrupted. And you and I will have days to scream in the dark before we die."

Drawing her shawl up over her shoulders reflexively, Katerine shuddered. There was dust in the air; she would get out her light cloak. It would not be Elaida's rage that killed them, though her fury could be terrible. For seventeen years Katerine had been Aes Sedai, but not until the morning before they departed Tar Valon had she learned that she shared more than the Red Ajah with Galina. Twelve years she had been a member of the Black Ajah, never knowing that Galina had too, for far longer. Of necessity Black sisters kept themselves hidden, even from each other. Their rare gatherings were held with faces covered and voices disguised. Before Galina, Katerine had known only three to recognize. Orders were left on her pillow, or in a pocket of her cloak, the ink ready to vanish if any hand but hers touched the paper. She had a secret place to leave messages, and dire orders not to try to see who came to take them. She had never disobeyed.

There might be Black sisters among those following a day behind, but she had no way of knowing.

"Why?" she asked. Orders to preserve the Dragon Reborn made no sense, even if they delivered him into Elaida's hands.

"Questions are dangerous for one sworn to obey without."

Katerine shuddered again, and barely stopped herself from curtsying. "Yes, Galina Sedai." But she could not help wondering. Why?

"They show neither respect nor honor," Therava growled. "They allow us to enter their camp as though we were toothless dogs, then take us out under guard like suspected thieves."

Sevanna did not look around. She would not until safely back among the trees. The Aes Sedai would be watching for signs of nervousness. "They agreed, Therava," she said. "That is enough for now." For now. One day, these lands would be the Shaido's for the looting. Including the White Tower.

"This is all badly thought out," the third woman said in a tight voice. "Wise Ones avoid Aes Sedai; it has always been so. Perhaps it was well enough for you, Sevanna—as Couladin's widow, and Suladric's, you speak as clan chief until we send another man to Rhuidean—but the rest of us should be no part of it."

Sevanna barely forced herself to keep walking. Desaine had spoken against her being chosen as a Wise One, speaking loudly about her having served no apprenticeship and paid no visit to Rhuidean, claiming that her place standing for the clan chief disqualified her. Besides, as the widow of not just one, but two dead chiefs, perhaps she carried bad luck. Fortunately, enough of the Shaido Wise Ones had listened to Sevanna, not Desaine. It was *un*fortunate that Desaine had too many listeners to be safely done away with. Wise Ones were supposed to be inviolate—they even came and went freely among the Shaido from those betrayers and fools down in Cairhien—but Sevanna meant to find a way.

As though Desaine's doubts had infected Therava, she began muttering, only half to herself. "What is ill done is going against Aes Sedai. We served them before the Breaking, and failed them: that is why we were sent to the Three-fold Land. If we fail them again, we will be destroyed."

That was what everyone believed; it was part of the old tales, almost part of custom. Sevanna was not so sure. These Aes Sedai looked weak and foolish to her, traveling with a few hundred men for escort through lands where the true Aiel, the Shaido, could smother them with thousands. "A new day has come," she said sharply, repeating part of one of her speeches to the Wise Ones. "We are no longer bound to the Three-fold Land. Any eye can see that what was, has changed. We must change, or be ended as if we never were." She had never told them how much change she intended, of course. The Shaido Wise Ones would never send a man to Rhuidean, if she had her way.

"New day or old day," Desaine grumbled, "what are we to do with Rand al'Thor if we do manage to take him from the Aes Sedai? Better, and easier, to slip a knife between his ribs while they are escorting him north."

Sevanna did not answer. She did not know what to answer. Not yet. All she knew was that once she had the so-called *Car'a'carn*, the chief of chiefs of all the Aiel, chained before her tent like a vicious dog, then this land would truly belong to the Shaido. And to her. She had known that even before the strange wetlander man somehow found her in the mountains these people called Kinslayer's Dagger. He had given her a small cube of some hard stone, intricately carved in strange patterns, and told her what to do with it, with the aid of a Wise One who could channel, once al'Thor was in her hands. She carried it in her belt pouch at all times; she had not decided what to do about it, but so far she had told no one about man or cube. Head high, she walked on beneath that blistering sun in an autumn sky.

The palace garden might have had a semblance of coolness had there been any trees, but the tallest things were fanciful topiary, tortured into the shapes of running horses or bears performing tumblers' tricks or the like. Shirtsleeved gardeners scurried about with buckets of water beneath the scalding afternoon sun, trying to save their creations. They had given up on the flowers, clearing all the patterned beds and laying them with sod that was dying too.

"A pity the heat is so bad," Ailron said. Sweeping a lace handkerchief from the lace-fringed sleeve of his yellow silk coat, he dabbed delicately at his face, then tossed it aside. A servant in gold-and-red livery quickly snatched it from the graveled walk and faded into the background again: another liveried man laid a fresh replacement in the King's hand to be tucked up his sleeve. Ailron did not acknowledge it, of course, or even appear to notice. "These fellows usually manage to keep everything alive till spring, but I may lose a few this winter. Since it doesn't seem as if we'll have any winter. They take cold better than drought. Don't you think they're very fine, my dear?"

Ailron, Anointed by the Light, King and Defender of Amadicia, Guardian of the Southern Gate, was not as handsome as rumor made him, but then, Morgase had suspected when she first met him, years ago, that he might be the source of those rumors himself. His dark hair was full and wavy—and quite definitely receding in front. His nose was a bit too long, his ears a touch too big. His whole face vaguely suggested softness. One day she would have to ask. The Southern Gate to what?

Working her carved ivory fan, she eyed one of the gardeners' . . . constructs. It seemed to be three huge nude women wrestling desperately with gigantic serpents. "They are quite remarkable," she said. One said what one must when coming as a beggar.

"Yes. Yes, aren't they? Ah, it looks as if affairs of state call me. Pressing matters, I fear." A dozen men, coated as colorfully as the flowers that were no longer there, had appeared on the short marble stair at the far end of the walk and were waiting in front of a dozen fluted columns that supported nothing. "Until this evening, my dear. We will speak further of your dreadful problems, and what I can do."

He bowed over her hand, stopping just short of kissing it, and she curtsied slightly, murmuring appropriate inanities, and then he swept away, followed by all but one of the coterie of servants that had been trailing them everywhere.

With him gone, Morgase worked the fan harder than she could in his presence—the man pretended the heat barely touched him, with sweat streaming down his face—and turned back toward her apartments. Hers by sufferance, just as the pale blue gown she wore was a gift. She had insisted on the high neck despite the weather; she had definite ideas about low necklines.

The lone serving man followed behind her, at a short distance. And Tallanvor, of course, on her heels and still insisting on wearing the rough green coat he had traveled here in, sword on his hip as though he expected an attack in the Seranda Palace, not two miles from Amador. She tried to ignore the tall young man, but as usual, he would not be ignored.

"We should have gone to Ghealdan, Morgase. To Jehannah."

She had let some things go on far too long. Her skirts swished as she whirled to confront him, and her eyes blazed. "On our journey, certain discretions were necessary, but those around us now know who I am. You will remember that too, and show proper respect for your Queen. On your knees!"

To her shock, he did not move. "Are you my Queen, Morgase?" At least he lowered his voice so the servant could not overhear and spread it about, but his eyes. . . . She very nearly backed away from the stark desire there. And the anger. "I will not abandon you this side of death, Morgase, but you abandoned much when you abandoned Andor to Gaebril. When you find it again, I will kneel at your feet, and you can strike off my head if you choose, but until then. . . . We should have gone to Ghealdan."

The young fool would have been willing to die fighting the usurper even after she discovered that no House in Andor would support her, and day by day, week by week since she had decided her only choice was to seek foreign aid, he had grown more insolent and insubordinate. She could ask Ailron for Tallanvor's head, and receive it with no questions asked. But just because they were unasked did not mean they would be unthought. She truly was a beggar here, and could not afford to ask one favor more than absolutely necessary. Besides, without Tallanvor, she would not be here. She would be a prisoner—worse than a prisoner—to Lord Gaebril. Those were the only reasons Tallanvor would keep his head.

Her army guarded the ornately carved doors to her apartments. Basel Gill was a pink-cheeked man with graying hair combed vainly back over a bald spot. His leather jerkin, sewn with steel discs, strained around his girth, and he wore a sword he had not touched in twenty years before belting it on to follow her. Lamgwin was bulky and hard, though heavy-lidded eyes made him look half-asleep. He wore a sword too, but the scars on his face and a nose broken more than once made it plain he was used to employing fists, or a cudgel. An innkeeper and a street tough; aside from Tallanvor, that was the army she had so far to take back Andor and her throne from Gaebril.

The pair were all awkward bows, but she glided past and slammed the door in Tallanvor's face. "The world," she announced in a growl, "would be a far better place without men."

"An emptier place, certainly," Morgase's old nurse said from her chair beside a velvet-draped anteroom window. With her head bent over her embroidery hoop, Lini's gray bun waggled in the air. A reed-thin woman, she was not nearly so frail as she looked. "I assume Ailron was no more forthcoming today? Or is it Tallanvor, child? You must learn not to let men put you in a fret. Fretting makes your face blotchy." Lini still would not admit that she was out of the nursery, despite having been nurse to Morgase's daughter in turn.

"Ailron was charming," Morgase said carefully. The third woman in the room, on her knees taking folded bedsheets from a chest, sniffed loudly, and Morgase avoided glaring at her with an effort. Breane was Lamgwin's . . . companion. The short suntanned woman followed where he went, but she was Cairhienin, and Morgase was no queen of hers, as she made clear. "Another day or two," Morgase continued, "and I think I will get a pledge from him. Today, he finally agreed I need soldiers from outside to retake Caemlyn. Once Gaebril is driven from Caemlyn, the nobles will flock to me once more." She hoped they would; she was in Amadicia because she had let Gaebril blind her, had mistreated even her oldest friends among the Houses at his behest.

"'A slow horse does not always reach the end of the journey,'" Lini quoted, still intent on her embroidery. She was very fond of old sayings, some of which Morgase suspected her of making up on the spot.

"This one will," Morgase insisted. Tallanvor was wrong about Ghealdan; according to Ailron, that country was in near anarchy because of this Prophet all the servants whispered about, the fellow preaching the Rebirth of the Dragon. "I would like some punch, Breane." The woman only looked at her until she added, "If you please." Even then she set about the pouring with a wooden sulkiness.

The mixture of wine and fruit juices was iced, and refreshing in the heat; the silver goblet felt good against Morgase's forehead. Ailron had snow and ice brought down from the Mountains of Mist, though it took nearly a steady stream of wagons to provide enough for the palace.

Lini took a goblet, too. "Concerning Tallanvor," she began after a sip.

"Leave over, Lini!" Morgase snapped.

"So he is younger than you," Breane said. She had poured for herself, as well. The effrontery of the woman! She was supposed to be a servant, whatever she had been in Cairhien. "If you want him, take him. Lamgwin says he is sworn to you, and I have seen him look at you." She laughed huskily. "He will not refuse." Cairhienin were disgusting, but at least most of them kept their dissolute ways decently hidden.

Morgase was about to order her from the room when a knock came at the door. Without waiting permission, a white-haired man who looked all sinew and bone entered. His snowy cloak was emblazoned with a flaring golden sun on the breast. She had hoped to avoid Whitecloaks until she had Ailron's seal on a firm agreement. The chill of the wine abruptly passed straight into her bones. Where were Tallanvor and the others, that he had walked right in?

Dark eyes going straight to her, he made the most minimal of bows. His face was aged, the skin drawn tight, but this man was as feeble as a hammer. "Morgase of Andor?" he said in a firm deep voice. "I am Pedron Niall." Not just any Whitecloak; the Lord Captain Commander of the Children of the Light himself. "Do not fear. I have not come to arrest you."

Morgase held herself straight. "Arrest me? On what charge? I cannot channel." No sooner were the words out of her mouth than she nearly clicked her tongue in exasperation. She should not have mentioned channeling; that she had put herself on the defensive was an indication of how flustered she was. It was true, what she had said, so far as it went. Fifty times trying to sense the True Source to find it once, and when found, twenty times attempting to open herself to *saidar* in order to catch a dribble once. A Brown sister named Verin had told her that there was hardly any need for the Tower to hold her until she learned to handle her tiny ability safely. The Tower did anyway, of course. Still, even that much ability to channel was outlawed in Amadicia, the penalty death. The Great Serpent ring on her hand that so fascinated Ailron now seemed hot enough to glow.

"Tower trained," Niall murmured. "That is forbidden, as well. But as I said, I come not to arrest, but to help. Send your women away, and we will talk." He made himself at home, taking a tall padded armchair and flipping his cloak over the back. "I will have some of that punch before they go." To Morgase's displeasure, Breane brought him a goblet immediately, eyes down and face as expressionless as a board.

Morgase made an effort to take back control. "They stay, Master Niall." She would not give this man the satisfaction of a title. The lack did not appear to faze him. "What has happened to my men outside? I will hold it against you if they've been harmed. And why do you think I need your help?"

"Your men are uninjured," he said dismissively over his punch. "Do you think Ailron will give you what you need? You are a beautiful woman, Morgase, and Ailron prizes women with sun-gold hair. He will come a little closer each day to the agreement you seek, never quite reaching it, until you decide that perhaps, with . . . a certain sacrifice, he will yield also. But he will come no nearer what you want, whatever you give. This so-called Prophet's mobs ravage the north of Amadicia. To the west lies Tarabon, with a ten-sided civil war, brigands sworn to the so-called Dragon Reborn, and rumors of Aes Sedai and the false Dragon himself to frighten Ailron. Give you soldiers? Could he find ten men for every one he has under arms now, or even two, he would mortgage his soul. But I can send five thousand Children of the Light riding to Caemlyn with you at their head if you but ask."

To say she was stunned would have been to minimize Morgase's feeling. She made her way to a chair across from him with a proper stateliness, and sat down before her legs gave way. "Why would you want to help me oust Gaebril?" she demanded. Obviously he knew everything; no doubt he had spies among Ailron's servants. "I've never given the Whitecloaks the free rein they want in Andor."

This time he grimaced. Whitecloaks did not like that name. "Gaebril? Your lover is dead, Morgase. The false Dragon Rand al'Thor has added Caemlyn to his conquests." Lini made a faint noise as if she had pricked herself, but he kept his eyes on Morgase.

For herself, Morgase had to grip the arm of her chair to keep from pressing a hand against her stomach. If her other hand had not been resting the goblet on the other chair arm, she would have slopped punch onto the carpet. Gaebril dead? He had gulled her, turned her into his doxy, usurped her authority, oppressed the land in her name, and finally named himself King of Andor, which had never had a king. How, after all that, could there possibly be this faint regret that she would never feel his hands again? It was madness; if she had not known it was impossible, she would have believed he had used the One Power on her in some way.

But al'Thor had Caemlyn now? That might change everything. She had met him once, a frightened country youth from the west trying his best to show proper respect for his queen. But a youth carrying the heron-mark sword of a blademaster. And Elaida had been wary of him. "Why do you call him a false Dragon, Niall?" If he intended to call her by name, he could do without even a commoner's "master." "The Stone of Tear has fallen, as the Prophecies of the Dragon said. The High Lords of Tear themselves have acclaimed him the Dragon Reborn."

Niall's smile was mocking. "Everywhere he has appeared, there have been Aes Sedai. They do his channeling for him, mark me. He is no more than a puppet of the Tower. I have friends in many places"—he meant spies—"and they tell me there's evidence the Tower set up Logain, the last false Dragon, too. Perhaps he got above himself, so they had to finish him."

"There is no proof of that." She was pleased that her voice was steady. She had heard the rumors about Logain on the way to Amador. But they were only rumors.

The man shrugged. "Believe as you will, but I prefer truth to foolish fancies. Would the true Dragon Reborn do as he has done? The High Lords acclaimed him, you say? How many did he hang before the rest bowed down? He let Aiel loot the Stone, and all of Cairhien. He says Cairhien shall have a new ruler—one he will name—but the only real power in Cairhien is himself. He says there will be a new ruler in Caemlyn, too. You are dead; did you know that? There is mention of the Lady Dyelin, I believe. He has sat on the Lion Throne, used it for audiences, but I suppose it was too small, being made for women. He has put it up as a trophy of his conquest and replaced it with his own throne, in the Grand Hall of your Royal Palace. Of course, all has not gone well for him. Some Andoran Houses think he killed you; there's sympathy for you, now you're dead. He holds what he holds of Andor in an iron fist, though, with a horde of Aiel and an army of Borderland ruffians the Tower recruited for him. But if you think he will welcome you back to Caemlyn and give you back your throne. . . ."

He let the words trail off, but the torrent had hit Morgase like hailstones. Dyelin was next in line for the throne only if Elayne died without issue. Oh, Light, Elayne! Was she still safe in the Tower? Strange to think she had such an antipathy for Aes Sedai, largely because they had lost Elayne for a time, that she had demanded Elayne's return when no one *demanded* anything from the Tower, yet now she hoped they held her daughter tightly. She remembered one letter from Elayne, after she returned to Tar Valon. Had there been others? So much of what had happened while Gaebril held her in thrall was vague. Surely Elayne must be safe. She should be worried about Gawyn too, and Galad—the Light knew where they were—but Elayne was her heir. Peace in Andor depended on a smooth succession.

She had to think carefully. It all hung together, yet well-crafted lies did, and this man would be a master at that craft. She needed facts. That Andor believed her dead was no surprise; she had had to sneak from her own realm to avoid Gaebril and those who might turn her over to him or else avenge Gaebril's wrongs on her. If sympathy came from it, she could make use of it when she rose from the dead. Facts. "I will need time to think," she told him.

"Of course." Niall rose smoothly; she would have risen too, so he did not tower over her, but she was not sure her legs would support her. "I will return in a day or two. In the meantime, I wish to be sure of your safety. Ailron is so wrapped in his own concerns, there is no telling who might slip in, perhaps intent on harm. I have taken the liberty of posting a few of the Children here. With Ailron's consent."

Morgase had always heard that the Whitecloaks were the true power in Amadicia, and she was certain she had just heard proof.

Niall was slightly more formal in his leaving than in coming, making a bow that might have done for an equal. One way and another, he was letting her know that she had no choice.

No sooner had he gone than Morgase pushed to her feet, but Breane was still quicker in darting for the doors. Even so, before either woman had gone three steps, one of them banged open, Tallanvor and the other two men spilling into the room.

"Morgase," Tallanvor breathed, trying to absorb her with his eyes. "I was afraid—"

"Afraid?" she said contemptuously. It was too much; he would not learn. "Is this how you protect me? A boy could have done as much! But then, a boy did."

That smoldering gaze remained on her a moment longer; then he turned and pushed his way past Basel and Lamgwin.

The innkeeper stood wringing his hands. "They were at least thirty, my Queen. Tallanvor would have fought; he tried to cry out, to warn you, but they clubbed him with a hilt. The old one said they didn't mean to hurt you, but they didn't need any but you, and if they had to kill us. . . ." His eyes went to Lini and Breane, who was staring Lamgwin up and down to make sure he had taken no injury. The man appeared as concerned for her. "My Queen, if I'd thought we could do any good. . . . I'm sorry. I failed you."

"'The right medicine always tastes bitter,'" Lini murmured softly. "Most of all for a child who throws a sulky tantrum." At least for once she did not say it for the whole room to hear.

She was right. Morgase knew that. Except about the tantrum, of course. Basel looked miserable enough to welcome beheading. "You did not fail me, Master Gill. I may ask you to die for me one day, but only when there's greater good to come of it. Niall only wanted to talk." Basel perked up right away, but Morgase could feel Lini's eyes on her. Very bitter. "Will you ask Tallanvor to come to me. I—I wish to apologize to him for my hasty words."

"The best way to apologize to a man," Breane said, "is to trap him in a secluded part of the garden."

Something snapped in Morgase. Before she knew it she had hurled her goblet at the woman, spraying punch across the carpet. "Get out!" she shrieked. "All of you, get out! You can deliver my apologies to Tallanvor, Master Gill."

Breane calmly brushed punch from her dress, then took her time walking to Lamgwin and linking her arm through his. Basel was all but bouncing on his toes trying to herd them out.

To Morgase's surprise, Lini went, too. That was not Lini's way; she was much more likely to remain and lecture her old charge as if she were still ten. Morgase did not know why she put up with it. Still, she almost told Lini to stay. But then they were all gone, the door was shut—and she had more important matters to worry about than whether Lini's feelings were bruised.

Pacing across the carpet, she tried to think. Ailron would demand trade concessions—and maybe Niall's "sacrifice"—for help. She was willing to give him the trade concessions, but she feared Niall might be right about how many soldiers Ailron would spare her. Niall's demands would be easier to grant, in a way. Probably free access to Andor for as many Whitecloaks as he chose. And freedom for them to root out the Darkfriends they found in every attic, to rouse mobs against friendless women they accused of being Aes Sedai, to kill real Aes Sedai. Niall might even demand a law against channeling, against women going to the White Tower.

It would be possible—but difficult, and bloody—to oust the White-cloaks once they entrenched themselves, but was it necessary to let them in at all? Rand al'Thor was the Dragon Reborn—she was certain of that no matter what Niall said; she was almost certain—yet ruling nations was no part of the Prophecies of the Dragon that she knew. Dragon Reborn or false Dragon, he could not have Andor. Yet how was she to know?

A timid scratch at the door brought her around. "Come," she said sharply.

The door opened slowly to admit a grinning young man in gold-and-red livery, a tray in his hands bearing a fresh pitcher of iced punch, the silver already beading with cold. She had half-expected Tallanvor. Lamgwin stood guard alone in the corridor, as far as she could see. Or rather lounged against a wall like a tavern bouncer. She waved the young man to put his tray down.

Angrily—Tallanvor should have come; he should have come!—she resumed her pacing. Basel and Lamgwin might hear rumors in the nearest village, but they would be rumors, and maybe planted by Niall. The same held true for the palace servants.

"My Queen. May I speak, my Queen?"

Morgase turned in amazement. Those were the accents of Andor. The young man was on his knees, grin flashing from uncertain to cocky and back. He might have been good-looking except that his nose had been broken and not properly tended. On Lamgwin it looked rugged, if low; this lad looked as if he had tripped and fallen on his face.

"Who are you?" she demanded. "How did you come here?"

"I'm Paitr Conel, my Queen. From Market Sheran. In Andor?" he added, as if she might not realize that. Impatiently she motioned him to go on. "I came to Amador with my uncle Jen. He's a merchant from Four Kings, and he thought he might find some Taraboner dyes. They're dear, with all the troubles in Tarabon, but he thought they might be cheaper—" Her mouth tightened, and he went on in a rush. "We heard about you, my Queen, that you were here in the palace, and given the law in Amadicia, and you being trained in the White Tower and all, we thought we could help you. . . ." He swallowed hard, and finished in a small voice. "Help you escape."

"And are you prepared to help me . . . escape?" Not the best plan, but she could always ride north to Ghealdan. How Tallanvor would gloat. No, he would not, and that would be worse.

But Paitr shook his head wretchedly. "Uncle Jen had a plan, but now there's Whitecloaks all over the palace. I didn't know what else to do but come on to you, the way he told me. He'll think of something, my Queen. He's smart."

"I'm sure he is," she murmured. So Ghealdan went glimmering again. "How long are you gone from Andor? A month? Two?" He nodded. "Then you don't know what is happening in Caemlyn," she sighed.

The young man licked his lips. "I. . . . We're staying with a man in Amador who has pigeons. A merchant. He gets messages from everywhere. Caemlyn, too. But it's all bad news that I hear, my Queen. It may take a day or two, but my uncle will figure out another way. I just wanted to let you know help was nearby."

Well, that was as might be. A race between Pedron Niall and this Paitr's uncle Jen. She wished she were not so sure how to bet. "In the meantime, you can tell me just how bad matters are in Caemlyn."

"My Queen, I was just supposed to let you know about the help. My uncle will be angry if I stay—"

"I *am* your Queen, Paitr," Morgase said firmly, "and your uncle Jen's, too. He will not mind if you answer my questions." Paitr looked as though he might bolt, but she settled herself in a chair and began digging for the truth.

Pedron Niall was feeling quite good as he dismounted in the main court-yard of the Fortress of the Light and tossed his reins to a stableman. Morgase was well in hand, and he had not had to lie once. He did not like lying. It had all been his own interpretation of events, but he was sure of it. Rand al'Thor was a false Dragon and a tool of the Tower. The world was full of fools who could not think. The Last Battle would not be some titanic struggle between the Dark One and a Dragon Reborn, a mere man. The Creator had abandoned mankind to its own devices long ago. No, when Tarmon Gai'don came, it would be as in the Trolloc Wars two thousand years ago and more, when hordes of Trollocs and other Shadowspawn poured out of the Great Blight, tore through the Borderlands and nearly drowned humanity in a sea of blood. He did not mean to let mankind face that divided and unprepared.

A ripple of bows from white-cloaked Children followed him through the stone-walled corridors of the Fortress, all the way to his private audience chamber. In the anteroom, his pinch-faced secretary, Balwer, leaped to his feet with a fussy recitation of papers awaiting the Lord Captain's signature, but Niall's attention was on the tall man who rose easily from one of the chairs against the wall, a crimson shepherd's crook behind the golden sun on his cloak and three golden knots of rank below.

Jaichim Carridin, Inquisitor of the Hand of the Light, looked as hard as he was, but with more gray at his temples than the last time Niall had seen him. His dark, deep-set eyes held a tinge of worry, and it was no wonder. The last two missions he had been given ended in disaster; not auspicious for a man who aspired to be High Inquisitor one day, and perhaps even Lord Captain Commander.

Tossing his cloak to Balwer, Niall motioned Carridin to follow into the audience chamber proper, where captured battle flags and the banners of old enemies made trophies on the dark paneled walls and a huge sunburst set into the floor held enough gold to make most men stare. Aside from that, it was a plain, soldier's room, a reflection of Niall himself. Niall seated himself in a high-backed chair, well made but undecorated. The long twin hearths at either end of the room stood cold and swept at a time of year when they should have held roaring fires. Proof enough that the Last Battle was near. Carridin bowed deeply and knelt on the sunburst, worn smooth by centuries of feet and knees.

"Have you speculated on why I sent for you, Carridin?" After Almoth Plain and Falme, after Tanchico, the man could not be blamed if he believed he was to be arrested. But if he suspected such a possibility, nothing showed in his voice. As usual, he could not help showing that he knew more than anyone else. Definitely more than he was supposed to.

"The Aes Sedai in Altara, my Lord Captain Commander. A chance to wipe out half the Tar Valon witches, right on our doorstep." An exaggeration; a third were in Salidar, perhaps, but no more.

"And have you speculated aloud, among your friends?" Niall doubted that Carridin had any, but there were those he drank with. Of late, got drunk with. The man had certain skills, though; useful skills.

"No, my Lord Captain Commander. I know better than that."

"Good," Niall said. "Because you are not going anywhere near this Salidar, and neither is any other of the Children." He could not be sure whether it was relief that flashed across Carridin's face. If so, it was out of character; the man had never shown any lack of courage. And relief certainly did not suit his reply.

"But they are waiting to be snapped up. This is proof the rumors are true, the Tower is divided. We can destroy this lot without the others raising a hand. The Tower could be weakened enough to fall."

"Think you so?" Niall said dryly. He laced his fingers across his middle and kept his voice mild. Questioners—the Hand despised that name, but even he used it—Questioners never saw anything not shoved under their noses. "Even the Tower can hardly come out openly for this false Dragon al'Thor. What if he turns, as Logain did? But a rebel group? They could support him, and the White Tower's skirts are clean whatever happens." He was sure that was the way of it. If not, there would be ways to use any real split to further weaken the Tower, but he believed he was right. "In any case, what the world sees, matters. I will not let them see merely a struggle between the Children and the Tower." Not until the world saw the Tower for what it was, a sink of Darkfriends meddling with forces mankind was not meant to touch, the force that had caused the Breaking of the World. "This struggle is the world against the false Dragon al'Thor."

"Then if I am not going to Altara, my Lord Captain Commander, what are my orders?"

Niall let his head fall back with a sigh. He felt tired suddenly. He felt all of his years and more. "Oh, you will be going to Altara, Carridin."

Rand al'Thor's name and face had been known to him since shortly after the supposed invasion from across the sea at Falme, an Aes Sedai plot that had cost the Children a thousand men and begun the spread of the Dragonsworn and chaos across Tarabon and Arad Doman. He had known what al'Thor was and believed he could use him as a goad to force the nations to unite. Once bound together, behind his leadership, they could have disposed of al'Thor and been ready for the Trolloc hordes. He had sent emissaries to every ruler of every land to point out the danger. But al'Thor moved faster than he could believe even now. He had meant to let a rabid lion roam the streets long enough to frighten everyone, but the lion had become a giant that moved like lightning.

Yet all was not lost; he had to keep reminding himself. More than a thousand years ago, Guaire Amalasan had named himself the Dragon Reborn, a false Dragon who could channel. Amalasan had conquered more land than al'Thor now held, before a young king named Artur Paendrag Tanreall took the field against him and began his own climb to empire. Niall did not consider himself another Artur Hawkwing, but he was what the world had. He would not give up while he lived.

Already he had begun to counter al'Thor's growing strength. Besides emissaries to rulers, he had sent men to Tarabon and Arad Doman. A few men to find the right ears, to whisper that all their troubles could be laid at the feet of the Dragonsworn, those fools and Darkfriends who had declared for al'Thor. And at the feet of the White Tower. Plenty of rumors already came out of Tarabon of Aes Sedai involved in the fighting, rumors to ready men's ears to hear the truth. Now was time to launch the next part of his new plan, to show the fence-sitters which side to choose. Time. He had so little time. Yet he could not help smiling. There were those, now dead, who had once said, "When Niall smiles, he is going for the throat."

"Altara and Murandy," he told Carridin, "are about to be tormented by a plague of Dragonsworn."

The chamber had the appearance of a palace sitting room—vaulted ceiling of worked plaster, finely woven carpets on the white-tiled floor, elaborately carved paneling for the walls—though it was far from any palace. Indeed, it was far from anywhere, in any way that most humans would understand. Mesaana's russet silk dress rustled as she moved around a lapis-inlaid table, amusing herself with the placement of ivory dominoes in a complex tower, each level larger than the one below. She prided herself on doing this purely with a knowledge of stresses and leverage, not a thread of the Power. She had the tower to nine levels.

In truth, more than amusing herself, she was avoiding conversation with her companion. Semirhage sat doing needlework in a high-backed chair covered in red tapestry, long slender fingers deftly making minuscule stitches to form a labyrinthine pattern of tiny flowers. It was always a surprise that the woman liked an activity so . . . ordinary. Her black dress was a sharp contrast against the chair. Not even Demandred dared suggest to Semirhage's face that she wore black so often because Lanfear wore white.

For the thousandth time Mesaana tried to analyze why she felt uncomfortable around the other woman. Mesaana knew her own strengths and weaknesses, with the One Power and elsewhere. She matched well with Semirhage on most points, and where she did not, she had other strengths to lay against weaknesses in Semirhage. It was not that. Semirhage took delight in cruelty, a pure pleasure in giving anguish, but that surely was not the problem. Mesaana could be cruel where necessary, and she did not care what Semirhage did to others. There had to be a reason, but she could not find it.

Irritably she placed another domino, and the tower collapsed with a clatter, spilling ivory tiles onto the floor. With a click of her tongue, she turned from the table, folding her arms beneath her breasts. "Where is Demandred? Seventeen days since he went to Shayol Ghul, but he waits until now to inform us of a message, then does not appear." She had been to the Pit of Doom twice in that time herself, made that nerve-racking walk with the stone fangs brushing her hair. To find nothing except a strange too-tall Myrddraal that would not speak. The Bore had been there, certainly, but the Great Lord had not answered. She did not remain long either time. She had thought herself beyond fear, at least the sort a Half-man's gaze brought, but twice the Myrddraal's silent eyeless stare had sent her away with quickening steps that only tight self-control kept from becoming a run. Had channeling there not been a sure way to die, she would have destroyed the Halfman, or Traveled from the Pit itself. "Where is he?"

Semirhage raised her eyes from her stitchery, unblinking dark eyes in a smooth dark face, then put aside the needlework and stood gracefully. "He will come when he comes," she said calmly. She was always calm, just as she was always graceful. "If you do not want to wait, then go."

Unconsciously Mesaana raised herself a little on her toes, but she still had to look up. Semirhage stood taller than most men, though so perfectly proportioned that you did not realize it until she stood over you, looking down. "Go? I *will* go. And he can—"

There was no warning, of course. There never was, when a man channeled. A bright vertical line appeared in the air, then widened as the gateway turned sideways to open long enough for Demandred to step through, giving them each a small bow. He was all in dark gray today, with a little pale lace at his neck. He adapted easily to the fashions and fabrics of this Age.

His hawk-nosed profile was handsome enough, though not quite the sort to make every woman's heart beat faster. In a way, "almost" and "not quite" had been the story of Demandred's life. He had had the misfortune to be born one day after Lews Therin Telamon, who would become the Dragon, while Barid Bel Medar, as he was then, spent years almost matching Lews Therin's accomplishments, not quite matching Lews Therin's fame. Without Lews Therin, he would have been the most acclaimed man of the Age. Had he been appointed to lead instead of the man he considered his intellectual inferior, an overcautious fool who too often managed to scrape up luck, would he stand here today? Now, that *was* idle speculation, though she had made it before. No, the important point was that Demandred despised the Dragon, and now that the Dragon had been Reborn, he had transferred that contempt whole.

"Why—?"

Demandred raised a hand. "Let us wait until we are all here, Mesaana, and I will not have to repeat myself."

She felt the first spinning of *saidar* a moment before the glowing line appeared and became a gateway. Graendal stepped out, for once unaccompanied by half-clad servants, and let the opening vanish as quickly as Demandred had. She was a fleshy woman with elaborately curled red-gold hair. Somewhere she had actually managed to find streith for her high-necked gown. High-necked, but mirroring her mood—the fabric was transparent mist. At times Mesaana wondered whether Graendal really took note of anything beyond her sensual pleasures.

"I wondered whether you would be here," the new arrival said lightly. "You three have been so secretive." She gave a gay, slightly foolish laugh. No, it would be a dire mistake to take Graendal at surface value. Most who had taken her for a fool were long since dead, victims of the woman they disregarded.

"Is Sammael coming?" he asked.

Graendal waved a beringed hand dismissively. "Oh, he doesn't trust you. I don't think the man trusts himself anymore." The streith darkened; a concealing fog. "He's marshaling his armies in Illian, moaning over not having shocklances to arm them. When he isn't doing that, he's searching for a usable *angreal* or *sa'angreal*. Something of decent strength, of course."

Their eyes all went to Mesaana, and she drew a deep breath. Any of them would have given—well, almost anything, for a suitable *angreal* or *sa'angreal*. Each was stronger than any of these half-trained children who called themselves Aes Sedai today, but enough half-trained children linked together could crush them all. Except, of course, that they no longer knew how, and no longer had the means in any case. Men were needed to take a link beyond thirteen, more than one to go beyond twenty-seven. In truth, those girls—the oldest seemed girls to her; she had lived over three hundred years, quite aside from her time sealed in the Bore, and had only been considered just into her middle years—those girls were no real danger, but that did not lessen the desire of anyone here for *angreal*, or better yet the more powerful *sa'angreal*. With those remnants from their own time, they could channel amounts of the Power that would have burned them to ash without. Any of them would risk much for one of those prizes. But not everything. Not with no real need. That lack did not still the desire, though.

Automatically Mesaana dropped into a lecturing tone. "The White Tower now has guards *and* wards on their strongrooms, inside and out, plus they count *everything* four times each day. The Great Hold in the Stone of Tear is also warded, with a nasty thing that would have held me fast had I tried to pass through or untie it. I don't think it can be untied except by whoever wove it, and until then it is a trap for any other woman who can channel."

"A dusty jumble of useless rubbish, so I've heard," Demandred said in dismissal. "The Tairens gathered anything with even a rumored connection to the Power."

Mesaana suspected he had more than hearsay to go on. She also suspected there was a trap for men woven around the Great Hold, too, or Demandred would have had his *sa'angreal* and launched himself at Rand al'Thor long since. "No doubt there are some in Cairhien and Rhuidean, but even if you do not walk right into al'Thor, both are full of women who can channel."

"Ignorant girls." Graendal sniffed.

"If a kitchen girl puts a knife in your back," Semirhage said coolly, "are you less dead than if you fall in a sha'je duel at Qal?"

Mesaana nodded. "That leaves whatever might he buried in ancient ruins or forgotten in an attic. If you want to count on finding something by chance, do so. I will not. Unless someone knows the location of a stasis box?" There was a certain dryness to that last. The stasis boxes should have survived the Breaking of the World, but that upheaval had likely as not left them on the bottom of an ocean or buried beneath mountains. Little remained of the world they had known beyond a few names and legends.

Graendal's smile was all sweetness. "I always thought you should be a teacher. Oh. I am sorry. I forgot."

Mesaana's face darkened. Her road to the Great Lord began when she was denied a place in the Collam Daan all those years ago. Unsuited for research, they had told her, but she could still teach. Well, she had taught, until she found how to teach them all!

"I am still waiting to hear what the Great Lord said," Semirhage murmured.

"Yes. Are we to kill al'Thor?" Mesaana realized she was gripping her skirt with both hands and let go. Strange. She never let anyone get under her skin. "If all goes well, in two months, three at most, he will be where I can safely reach him, and helpless."

"Where you can safely reach him?" Graendal arched an eyebrow quizzically. "Where *have* you made your lair? No matter. Bare as it is, it's as good a plan as I've heard lately."

Still Demandred kept silent, stood there studying them. No, not Graendal. Semirhage and her. And when he did speak, half to himself, it was to they two. "When I think where you two have placed yourselves, I wonder. How much has the Great Lord known, for how long? How much of what has happened has been at his design all along?" There was no answer to that. Finally, he said, "You want to know what the Great Lord told me? Very well. But it stays here, held close. Since Sammael chose to stay away, he learns nothing. Nor do the others, whether alive or dead. The first part of the Great Lord's message was simple. 'Let the Lord of Chaos rule.' His words, exact." The corners of his mouth twitched, as close to a smile as Mesaana had ever seen from him. Then he told them the rest.

Mesaana found herself shivering and did not know whether she did so from excitement or fear. It could work; it could hand them everything. But it required luck, and gambling made her uncomfortable. Demandred was the gambler. He was right about one thing; Lews Therin had made his own luck as a mint made coin. In her opinion it seemed that so far Rand al'Thor did the same.

Unless. . . . Unless the Great Lord had a plan beyond the one he had revealed. And that frightened her more than any other possibility.

The gilt-framed mirror reflected the room, the disturbingly patterned mosaics on the walls, the gilded furnishings and fine carpets, the other mirrors and the tapestries. A palace room without a window—or a door. The mirror reflected a woman striding up and down in a dark blood-red gown, her beautiful face a combination of rage and disbelief. Still, disbelief. It reflected his own face, too, and that interested him far more than the woman. He could not resist touching his nose and mouth and cheeks for the hundredth time to make sure they were real. Not young, but younger than the face he had worn on first waking from the long sleep, with all its endless nightmares. An ordinary face, and he had always hated being ordinary. He recognized the sound in his throat as a budding laugh, a giggle, and stifled it. He was not mad. Despite everything, he was not that.

A name had been given to him during this second, far more horrific sleep, before he woke to this face and body. Osan'gar. A name given by a voice he knew and dared not disobey. His old name, given in scorn and adopted in pride, was gone forever. The voice of his master had spoken and made it so. The woman was Aran'gar; who she had been, was no more.

Interesting choices, those names. *Osan'gar* and *aran'gar* were the left- and right-hand daggers in a form of dueling briefly popular early in that long building from the day the Bore had been made to the actual begin- ning of the War of Power. His memories were spotty—too much had been lost in the long sleep, and the short—but he remembered that. The popu- larity had been brief because almost inevitably both duelists died. The daggers' blades were coated with slow poison.

Something blurred in the mirror, and he turned, not too quickly. He had to remember who he was, and make sure others remembered. There still was no door, but a Myrddraal shared the room with them. Neither thing was strange in this place, but the Myrddraal stood taller than any Osan'gar had seen before.

He took his time, letting the Halfman wait to be acknowledged, and before he could open his mouth, Aran'gar spat, "Why has this been done to me? Why have I been put into this body? Why?" The last was almost a shriek.

Osan'gar would have thought the Myrddraal's bloodless lips twitched in a smile, except that was impossible, here or anywhere. Even Trollocs had a sense of humor, if a vile and violent one, but not Myrddraal. "You were both given the best that could be taken in the Borderlands." Its voice was a viper rustling in dry grass. "It is a fine body, strong and healthy. And better than the alternative."

Both things were true. It was a fine body, suitable for a *daien* dancer in the old days, sleekly lush, with a green-eyed ivory oval of a face to match, framed by glossy black hair. And anything bettered the alternative.

Perhaps Aran'gar did not see it that way. Rage mottled that beautiful face. She was going to do something reckless. Osan'gar knew it; there had always been a problem in that regard. Lanfear seemed cautious by contrast. He reached for *saidin*. Channeling here could be dangerous, but less than allowing her to do something truly stupid. He reached for *saidin*—and found nothing. He had not been shielded; he would have felt it, and known how to work around or break it, given time, if it was not too strong. This was as if he had been severed. Shock petrified him where he stood.

Not so for Aran'gar. Perhaps she had made the same discovery, but it affected her differently. With a screech like a cat she launched herself at the Myrddraal, fingernails clawed.

A futile attack, of course. The Myrddraal did not even shift its stance. Casually it caught her by the throat, raised her straight-armed till her feet left the floor. The screech became a gurgle, and she grabbed the Halfman's wrist with both hands. With her dangling in its grasp, it turned that eyeless stare to Osan'gar. "You have not been severed, but you will not channel until you are told you may. And you will never strike at me. I am Shaidar Haran."

Osan'gar tried to swallow, but his mouth was dust. Surely the creature had nothing to do with whatever had been done to him. Myrddraal had powers of a sort, but not that. Yet it knew. He had never liked Halfmen. He had helped make the Trollocs, blending human and animal stock—he was proud of that, of the skill involved, the difficulty—but these occasional throwback offspring made him uneasy at the best of times.

Shaidar Haran turned its attention back to the woman twitching in its fist. Her face was beginning to go purple, and her feet kicked feebly. "You will adapt. The body bends to the soul, but the mind bends to the body. You are adapting already. Soon it will be as if you had never had any other. Or you may refuse. Then another will take your place, and you will be given to . . . my brothers, blocked as you are." Those thin lips twitched again. "They miss their sport in the Borderlands."

"She cannot speak," Osan'gar said. "You're killing her! Don't you know who we are? Put her down, Halfman! Obey me!" The thing had to obey one of the Chosen.

But the Myrddraal impassively studied Aran'gar's darkening face for a long moment more before letting her feet touch the carpet and loosening its grip. "I obey the Great Lord. No other." She hung on, wavering, coughing and gulping air. Had it taken its hand away, she would have fallen. "Will you submit to the will of the Great Lord?" Not a demand, just a perfunctory question in that rasping voice.

"I—I will," she managed hoarsely, and Shaidar Haran let her go.

She swayed, massaging her throat, and Osan'gar moved to help her, but she threatened him with a glare and a fist before he touched her. He backed away with raised hands. That was one enmity he did not need. But it was a fine body, and a fine joke. He had always prided himself on his sense of humor, but this was rich.

"Do you not feel gratitude?" the Myrddraal said. "You were dead, and are alive. Think of Rahvin, whose soul is beyond saving, beyond time. You have a chance to serve the Great Lord again, and absolve yourselves of your errors."

Osan'gar hastened to assure it that he was grateful, that he wanted nothing more than to serve and gain absolution. Rahvin dead? What had happened? No matter; one fewer of the Chosen meant one more chance for true power when the Great Lord was free. It abraded, humbling himself before something that could be said to be as much his creation as the Trollocs, but he remembered death too clearly. He would grovel before a worm to avoid that again. Aran'gar was no less quick, he noted, for all the anger in her eyes. Clearly, she remembered too.

"Then it is time for you to go into the world once more in the service of the Great Lord," Shaidar Haran said. "None but I and the Great Lord know you live. If you succeed, you will live forever and be raised above all others. If you fail. . . . But you will not fail, will you?" The Halfman did smile then. It was like seeing death smile.

CHAPTER
1

Lion on the Hill

T he Wheel of Time turns, and Ages come and pass, leaving memories that become legend. Legend fades to myth, and even myth is long forgotten when the Age that gave it birth comes again. In one Age, called the Third Age by some, an Age yet to come, an Age long past, a wind rose among brown-thicketed hills in Cairhien. The wind was not the beginning. There are neither beginnings nor endings to the turning of the Wheel of Time. But it was *a* beginning.

Westward the wind blew over abandoned villages and farms, many only jumbles of charred timber. War had racked Cairhien, war and civil war, invasion and chaos, and even now that it was done, insofar as it *was* done, only a handful began to trickle back to their homes. The wind held no moisture, and the sun tried to sear away what little remained in the land. Where the small town of Maerone faced larger Aringill across the River Erinin, the wind crossed into Andor. Both towns baked, and if more prayers for rain rose in Aringill, where refugees from Cairhien jammed inside the walls like fish in a cask, even the soldiers packed around Maerone offered up words to the Creator, sometimes drunkenly, sometimes fervently. Winter should have been beginning to send out tendrils, the first snows long past, and those who sweated feared the reason it was not so, though few dared voice those fears.

Westward the wind blew, stirring drought-shriveled leaves on the trees, riffling the surface of shrinking streams bordered in hard-baked mud. There were no burned-out ruins in Andor, but villagers eyed the swollen sun nervously and farmers tried not to look at fields that had produced no fall crops. Westward, until the wind passed across Caemlyn, lifting two banners above the Royal Palace, in the heart of the Ogier-built Inner City. One banner floated red as blood, upon it a disc divided by a sinuous line, half white, half black as deep as the white was brilliant. The other banner slashed snow white across the sky. The figure on it, like some strange golden-maned, four-legged serpent, sun-eyed and scaled scarlet and gold, seemed to ride on the wind. It was a close question which of the two caused more fear. Sometimes, the same breast that held fear, held hope. Hope of salvation and fear of destruction, from the same source.

Many said Caemlyn was the second most beautiful city in the world, and not only Andorans, who often named it first, over-ranking Tar Valon itself. Tall round towers marched along the great outer wall of gray stone streaked silver and white, and within rose even taller towers, and domes of white and gold gleaming in the pitiless sun. The city climbed over hills to its center, the ancient Inner City, encircled by its own shining white wall, containing its own towers and domes, purple and white and gold and glittering tile mosaics, that looked down on the New City, well under two thousand years old.

As the Inner City was the heart of Caemlyn, and more than merely by being its center, the Royal Palace was the heart of the Inner City, a gleeman's tale of snowy spires and golden domes and stonework like lace. A heart that beat in the shadow of those two banners.

Stripped to the waist and balanced easily on the balls of his feet, at the moment Rand was no more aware that he was in a white-tiled courtyard of the Palace than he was of the onlookers among the surrounding colonnades. Sweat slicked his hair to his skull, rolled down his chest. The half-healed round scar on his side ached fiercely, but he refused to acknowledge it. Figures like that on the white banner overhead twined around his forearms, glittering metallically red-and-gold. Dragons, the Aiel called them, and others were taking up the name. He was dimly aware of the heron branded neatly into each of his palms, but only because he could feel them against the long hilt of his wooden practice sword.

He was one with the sword, flowing from stance to stance without thought, boots scraping softly on the pale tiles. Lion on the Hill became Arc of the Moon became Tower of Morning. Without thought. Five sweating, bare-chested men circled him, sidestepping warily from stance to stance, practice swords shifting. They were all he was really aware of. Hard-faced and confident, they were the best he had found so far. The best since Lan went. Without thought, as Lan had taught him. He was one with the sword, one with the five men.

Abruptly he ran forward, the encircling men moving rapidly to keep him centered. Just at the moment when that balance teetered on breaking, when at least two of the five had begun to shift toward breaking it, he suddenly turned in midstep and was running the other way. They tried to react, but it was too late. With a loud clack he caught the downstroke of a practice sword on his own blade of bundled lathes; simultaneously his right foot took the grizzled-haired man next over in the belly. Grunting, the man bent double. Locked blade to blade, Rand forced his broken-nosed opponent to turn, kicking the doubled-over man again as they went around. Grizzle-hair went down gasping for air. Rand's opponent tried to back away to use his blade, but that freed Rand's blade to spiral around his— The Grapevine Twines—and thrust hard against his chest, hard enough to knock him off his feet.

Only heartbeats had passed, few enough that just now were the other three closing in. The first, a quick squat little man, belied his stature by leaping over broken-nose with a yell as broken-nose toppled. Rand's practice blade took him across the shins, half upending him, then again across the back, driving him down to the paving stones.

That left only two, but they were the two best, a limber pole of a man whose sword moved like a serpent's tongue, and a heavy shaven-headed fellow who never made a mistake. They separated immediately, to come at Rand from two sides, but he did not wait. Quickly he closed with the skinny man; he had only moments before the other rounded the fallen.

The skinny man was good as well as fast; Rand offered gold for the best, and they came. He was tall for an Andoran, though Rand overtopped him by a hand, yet height had little bearing with the sword. Sometimes strength did. Rand went at him in all-out attack; the man's long face tightened as he gave ground. The Boar Rushes Down the Mountain crashed through Parting the Silk, broke Lightning of Three Prongs, and the bundled lathes slashed hard against the side of the man's neck. He fell with a strangled grunt.

Immediately Rand threw himself down and to the right, rolling up to his knees on the paving stones, blade streaking into The River Undercuts the Bank. The shaven-headed man was not fast, but somehow he had anticipated. Even as Rand's lathe blade swept across the fellow's wide middle, the man's own blade cracked down on Rand's head.

For a moment Rand wavered, his vision a blur of black flecks. Shaking his head in an effort to clear his eyes, he used the practice sword to push himself to his feet. Panting hard, the shaven-headed man watched him cautiously.

"Pay him," Rand said, and wariness left the shaven-headed man's face. Needless wariness. As if Rand had not promised an extra day's coin to any man who managed to strike him. Triple to any who defeated him one-to-one. It was a way to make sure nobody held back to flatter the Dragon Reborn. He never asked their names, and if they took the omission amiss, so much the better if it made them try harder. He wanted opponents to test him, not become friends. The friends he did have would curse the hour they met him one day, if they did not already. The others were stirring, too; a man "killed" was to stay where he lay until it was all done, an obstruction as a real corpse would be, but the squat man was having to help grizzle-hair up, and having trouble standing unaided himself. The limber fellow worked his head around, wincing. There would be no more practice today. "Pay them all."

A ripple of clapping and praise ran through the watchers among the narrow fluted columns, lords and ladies in colorful silks heavy with elaborate embroidery and braid. Rand grimaced and tossed his sword aside. That lot had all been toadeaters to Lord Gaebril when Queen Morgase—*their* queen—was little more than a prisoner in this palace. Her palace. But Rand needed them. For the moment. *Clutch the bramble, and you will be pricked,* he thought. At least, he hoped it was his thought.

Sulin, the wiry white-haired leader of Rand's escort of Aiel Maidens of the Spear, leader of the Maidens this side of the Spine of the World, pulled a gold Tar Valon mark from her belt pouch, tossed it with a grimace that drew at the nasty scar on the side of her face. The Maidens did not like Rand handling a sword, even a practice blade. They did not approve of any sword. No Aiel did.

The shaven-headed man caught the coin, and answered Sulin's blue-eyed stare with a careful bow. Everyone was careful around the Maidens, in their coats and breeches and soft, laced boots of browns and grays made to fade into the bleak landscape of the Waste. Some had begun adding shades of green, to suit what they called the wetlands despite the drought. Compared to the Aiel Waste, it was still wet; few Aiel had seen water they could not step across before leaving the Waste, and bitter feuds had been fought over pools two or three paces wide.

Like any Aiel warrior, like the twenty other light-eyed Maidens around the courtyard, Sulin kept her hair cut short except for a tail on the nape of her neck. She carried three short spears and a round bull-hide buckler in her left hand, and a pointed heavy-bladed knife at her belt. Like any Aiel warrior, down to those the age of Jalani, all of sixteen and with traces of baby fat still on her cheeks, Sulin knew how to use those weapons well, and would on slight provocation, at least as folk this side of the Dragonwall saw it. Except for her, the Maidens watched everyone, every piercework screened window and pale stone balcony, every shadow. Some had short curved bows of horn with arrows nocked, and more shafts ready in bristling quivers worn at the waist. *Far Dareis Mai*, the Maidens of the Spear, carried the honor of their prophesied *Car'a'carn*, if sometimes in their own peculiar way, and not a one of them but would die to keep Rand alive. The thought made his stomach boil in its own acid.

Sulin continued tossing the gold with a sneer—it pleased Rand to use Tar Valon coins for this debt—another for shaven-head, one for each of the others. Aiel approved of most wetlanders little more than of swords, and that took in anyone not born and bred Aiel. For most Aiel, that would have included Rand despite his Aiel blood, but there were the Dragons on his arms. One marked a clan chief, earned by risking life on strength of will; two marked the *Car'a'carn*, the chief of chiefs, He Who Comes With the Dawn. And the Maidens had other reasons for approval.

Gathering up practice swords, shirts and coats, the men bowed their way from his presence. "Tomorrow," Rand called after them. "Early." Deeper bows acknowledged the order.

Before the bare-chested men were gone from the courtyard, the Andoran nobles swept out of the colonnades, a rainbow of silks crowding around Rand, dabbing at sweaty faces with lace-trimmed handkerchiefs. They made Rand's bile rise. *Use what you must use, or let the Shadow cover the land.* Moiraine had told him that. He almost preferred the honest opposition of the Cairhienin and Tairens to this lot. That nearly made him laugh, calling what those did honest.

"You were wonderful," Arymilla breathed, lightly laying a hand on his arm. "So quick, so strong." Her big brown eyes seemed even more melting than usual. She was apparently fool enough to think him susceptible: her green gown, covered with vines in silver, was cut low by Andoran standards, which meant it showed a hint of cleavage. She was pretty, but easily old enough to be his mother. None of them was any younger, and some older, but all competed at licking Rand's boots.

"That was magnificent, my Lord Dragon." Elenia nearly elbowed Arymilla aside. That smile looked odd on the honey-haired woman's vulpine
face; she had the reputation of a termagant. Not around Rand, of course.
"There has never been a swordsman like you in the history of Andor. Even
Souran Maravaile, who was Artur Hawkwing's greatest general and husband to Ishara, first to sit on the Lion Throne—even he died when confronted by only four swordsmen. Assassins, in the twenty-third year of the
War of the Hundred Years. Though he did kill all four." Elenia seldom
missed a chance to point out her knowledge of Andor's history, especially
in areas where not much was known, like the war that had broken Hawkwing's empire apart after his death. At least today she did not add justifica-
tions of her claims to the Lion Throne.

"Just a bit of bad luck at the end," Elenia's husband, Jarid, put in jovi-
ally. He was a square man, dark for an Andoran. Embroidered scrollwork
and golden boars, the sign of House Sarand, covered the cuffs and long collars of his red coat, and the White Lions of Andor the long sleeves and high
neck of Elenia's matching red gown. Rand wondered whether she thought
he would not recognize the lions for what they were. Jarid was High Seat
of his House, but all the drive and ambition came from her.

"Marvelously well done, my Lord Dragon," Karind said bluntly. Her
shimmery gray dress, cut as severely as her face but heavy with silver braid
on sleeves and hem, almost matched the streaks through her dark hair.
"You surely must be the finest swordsman in the world." Despite her words,
the blocky woman's flat-eyed look was like a hammer. Had she had brains
to match her toughness, she would have been dangerous.

Naean was a slim, palely beautiful woman, with big blue eyes and
waves of gleaming black hair, but the sneer she directed at the five departing men was a fixture. "I suspect they planned it out beforehand so one
would manage to strike you. They will divide the extra coin among them."
Unlike Elenia, the blue-clad woman with the silver Triple Keys of House
Arawn climbing her long sleeves never mentioned her own claims to the
throne, not where Rand could hear. She pretended to be content as High
Seat of an ancient House, a lioness pretending to be content as a housecat.

"Can I always count on my enemies not to work together?" he asked
quietly. Naean's mouth worked in surprise; she was hardly stupid, yet
seemed to think those who opposed her should roll onto their backs as
soon as she confronted them, and seemed to take it as a personal affront
when they did not.

One of the Maidens, Enaila, ignored the nobles to hand Rand a thick length of white toweling to wipe his sweat away. A fiery redhead, she was short for an Aiel, and it grated at her that some of these wetlander women were taller than she. The majority of the Maidens could stare most of the men in the room straight in the eyes. The Andorans did their best to ignore her too, but their pointed looks elsewhere made the attempts glaring failures. Enaila walked away as if they were invisible.

The silence lasted just moments. "My Lord Dragon is wise," Lord Lir said with a small bow and a slight frown. The High Seat of House Baryn was blade-slender and blade-strong in a yellow coat adorned with gold braid, but too smoothly unctuous, too smooth altogether. Nothing but those occasional frowns ever sullied that surface, as if he was unaware of them, yet he was hardly the only one to give Rand strange looks. They all looked at the Dragon Reborn in their midst with wondering disbelief sometimes. "One's enemies usually do work together sooner or later. One must identify them before they have the chance to."

More praise for Rand's wisdom flowed from Lord Henren, blocky, bald and hard-eyed, and from gray-curled Lady Carlys, with her open face and devious mind, from plump giggly Daerilla, and thin-lipped nervous Elegar, and nearly a dozen others who had held their tongues while those more powerful spoke.

The lesser lords and ladies fell silent as soon as Elenia opened her mouth once more. "There is always the difficulty of knowing your enemies before they make themselves known. It is often too late, then." Her husband nodded sagely.

"I always say," Naean announced, "that who does not support me, opposes me. I've found it a good rule. Those who hang back may be waiting until your back is turned to plant a dagger."

This was hardly the first time they had tried to secure their own places by casting suspicion on any lord or lady not standing with them, but Rand wished he could stop them short of telling them to stop. Their attempts to play the Game of Houses were feeble compared to the sly maneuverings of Cairhienin, or even Tairens, and they were irritating besides, but there were thoughts he did not want them to have yet. Surprisingly, aid came from white-haired Lord Nasin, the High Seat of House Caeren.

"Another Jearom," the man said, an obsequious smile awkward on his gaunt, narrow face. He drew exasperated looks, even from some of the minor nobles before they caught themselves. Nasin had been a little addled since the events surrounding Rand's coming to Caemlyn. Instead of the Star and Sword of his House, Nasin's pale blue lapels were incongruously worked with flowers, moondrops and loversknots, and he sometimes wore a flower in his thinning hair like a country youth going courting. House Caeren was too powerful for even Jarid or Naean to push him aside, though. Nasin's head bobbed on a scrawny neck. "Your bladework is spectacular, my Lord Dragon. You are another Jearom."

"Why?" The word cut across the courtyard, souring the Andorans' faces.

Davram Bashere was certainly no Andoran, with his tilted, almost black eyes, a hooked beak of a nose, and thick gray-streaked mustaches curving down like horns around his wide mouth. He was slender, little taller than Enaila, in a short gray coat embroidered with silver on cuffs and lapels, and baggy trousers tucked into boots turned down at the knee. Where the Andorans had stood to watch, the Marshal-General of Saldaea had had a gilded chair dragged to the courtyard, and sprawled in it with a leg over one of its arms, ring-quilloned sword twisted so the hilt sat in easy reach. Sweat glistened on his dark face, but he paid it as little mind as he did the Andorans.

"What do you mean?" Rand demanded.

"All this sword practice," Bashere said easily. "And with five men? No one exercises against five. It's foolish. Sooner or later your brains will be spilled on the ground in a melee like that, even with practice swords, and to no purpose."

Rand's jaw tightened. "Jearom once defeated ten."

Shifting in his chair, Bashere laughed. "Do you think you'll live long enough to equal the greatest swordsman in history?" An angry mutter came from the Andorans—feigned anger, Rand was sure—but Bashere ignored it. "You are who you are, after all." Suddenly he moved like an uncoiling spring; the dagger drawn while shifting flashed toward Rand's heart.

Rand did not move a muscle. Instead he seized *saidin*, the male half of the True Source; it took no more thought than breathing. *Saidin* flooded into him, carrying the Dark One's taint, an avalanche of foul ice, a torrent of reeking molten metal. It tried to crush him, to scour him away, and he rode it like a man balancing atop a collapsing mountain. He channeled, a simple weave of Air that wrapped up the dagger and stopped it an arm's length from his chest. Emptiness surrounded him; he floated in the middle of it, in the Void, thought and emotion distant.

"Die!" Jarid shouted, drawing his sword as he ran toward Bashere. Lir and Henren and Elegar and every Andoran lord had his sword out, even Nasin, though he looked about to drop his. The Maidens had wrapped their *shoufa* around their heads, black veils coming up to cover their faces

to blue or green eyes as they raised long-pointed spears; Aiel always veiled
before killing.

"Stop!" Rand barked, and everyone froze in their tracks, the Andorans
blinking in confusion, the Maidens simply poised on their toes. Bashere had
not moved again beyond settling back into the chair, his leg still hooked
over the arm.

Plucking the horn-hilted dagger from the air with one hand, Rand let
go of the Source. Even with the taint twisting his belly, the taint that eventually destroyed men who channeled, letting go was difficult. With *saidin*
in him, he saw more clearly, heard more sharply. It was a paradox he did
not understand, but when he was floating in that seemingly endless Void,
somehow buffered against bodily feeling and emotions, every sense was
magnified; without it he felt only half-alive. And some of the taint seemed
to remain behind, but not the mitigating glory of *saidin*. The deadly glory
that would kill him if he wavered an inch in the struggle with it.

Turning the dagger in his hands, he walked slowly to Bashere. "Had
I been an eyeblink slower," he said softly, "I'd be dead. I could kill you
where you sit and no law in Andor or anywhere else would say me wrong."
He was ready to do it, he realized. Cold rage had replaced *saidin*. A few
weeks' acquaintance did not cover this.

The Saldaean's tilted eyes were as calm as if he lolled in his own home.
"My wife would not like that. Nor you, for that matter. Deira would probably take command and set out hunting Taim again. She doesn't approve of
my agreement to follow you."

Rand shook his head slightly, the edge of his anger dulled a little by
the man's composure. And his words. It had been a surprise to learn that
among Bashere's nine thousand Saldaean horse all of the nobles had brought
their wives, and most of the other officers as well. Rand did not understand
how a man could take his wife into danger, but it was traditional in Saldaea,
except when campaigning into the Blight.

He avoided looking at the Maidens. They were warriors to their toenails,
but women, too. And he had promised not to keep them from danger, even
death. He had made no promise not to flinch at it, though, and it ripped at
him inside when he had to, but he kept his promises. He did what he had
to do even when he hated himself for it.

With a sigh he tossed the dagger aside. "Your question," he said
politely. "Why?"

"Because you are who you are," Bashere said plainly. "Because you—
and those men you're gathering, I suppose—are what you are." Rand heard

feet shuffling behind him; for all they tried to, the Andorans could never hide their horror at his amnesty. "You can do what you did with the dagger every time," Bashere went on, putting his raised boot down and leaning forward, "but for any assassin to reach you, he has to get past your Aiel. And my horsemen, for that matter. Bah! If anything gets close to you, it won't be human." Throwing his hands wide, he settled back again. "Well, if you want to practice the sword, do it. A man needs exercise, and relaxation. But don't get your skull split open. Too much depends on you, and I don't see any Aes Sedai around to Heal you." His mustache almost hid his sudden grin. "Besides, if you die, I don't think our Andoran friends will maintain their warm welcome for me and my men."

The Andorans had put up their swords, but their eyes remained on Bashere malevolently. Nothing to do with how close he had come to killing Rand. Usually they kept their faces smooth around Bashere, for all he was a foreign general with a foreign army on Andoran soil. The Dragon Reborn wanted Bashere there, and this lot would have smiled at a Myrddraal if the Dragon Reborn wanted it. But if Rand might turn on him. . . . No need to hide anything then. They were vultures who had been ready to feed on Morgase before she died, and they would feed on Bashere given half a chance. And on Rand. He could hardly wait to be rid of them.

The only way to live is to die. The thought came into his head suddenly. He had been told that once, in such a way he had to believe it, but the thought was not his. *I must die. I deserve only death.* He turned away from Bashere clutching at his head.

Bashere was out of his chair in an instant, clutching Rand's shoulder though it was head high to him. "What is the matter? Did that blow really crack your head?"

"I am fine." Rand pulled his hands down; there was never any pain in this, only the shock of having another man's thoughts in his head. Bashere was not the only one watching. Most of the Maidens were eyeing him as closely as they did the courtyard, especially Enaila and yellow-haired Somara, the tallest of them. Those two would probably bring him some sort of herb tea as soon as their duties were done, and stand over him till he drank it. Elenia and Naean and the rest of the Andorans were breathing hard, clutching at coats and skirts, studying Rand with the wide-eyed fear of people afraid they might be seeing the first signs of madness. "I am fine," he told the courtyard. Only the Maidens relaxed, and Enaila and Somara not very far.

Aiel did not care about "the Dragon Reborn"; to them Rand was the *Car'a'carn*, prophesied to unite them, and to break them. They took it in

stride, though they worried about it too, and they seemed to take his channeling in stride as well, and everything that might go with it. The others—
The wetlanders, he thought dryly—called him the Dragon Reborn, and
never speculated on what that meant. They believed he was the rebirth of
Lews Therin Telamon, the Dragon, the man who had sealed the hole into
the Dark One's prison and ended the War of the Shadow three thousand
years ago and more. Ended the Age of Legends as well, when the Dark
One's last counterstroke tainted *saidin*, and every man who could channel
began to go insane, starting with Lews Therin himself and his Hundred
Companions. They called Rand the Dragon Reborn, and never suspected
that some part of Lews Therin Telamon might be inside his head, as mad
as the day he had begun the Time of Madness and the Breaking of the
World, as mad as any of those male Aes Sedai who had changed the face of
the world beyond recognition. It had come on him slowly, but the more
Rand learned of the One Power, the stronger he became with *saidin*, the
stronger Lews Therin's voice became, and the harder Rand had to fight to
keep a dead man's thoughts from taking him over. That was one reason
why he liked sword practice; the absence of thought was a barrier to keep
him himself.

"We need to find an Aes Sedai," Bashere muttered. "If those rumors
are true. . . . The Light burn my eyes, I wish we had never let that one
leave."

A good many people had fled Caemlyn in the days after Rand and the
Aiel seized the city; the Palace itself nearly emptied overnight. There were
people Rand would liked to have found, people who had helped him, but
they had all vanished. Some still slipped away. One fleeing in those first
days had been a young Aes Sedai, young enough that her face still lacked
the distinctive agelessness. Bashere's men sent word when they found her at
an inn, but when she found out who Rand was, she ran screaming. Literally
screaming. He never even learned her name or Ajah. Rumor said another
was somewhere in the city, but a hundred rumors were loose in Caemlyn
now, a thousand, each less likely than the next. Definitely unlikely any
would lead to an Aes Sedai. Aiel patrols had spotted several passing Caemlyn by, each plainly going somewhere in a hurry and none with any intention of entering a city occupied by the Dragon Reborn.

"Could I trust any Aes Sedai?" Rand asked. "It was just a headache.
My head isn't hard enough not to ache a little when it's hit."

Bashere snorted hard enough to stir his thick mustaches. "However
hard your head is, sooner or later you'll have to trust Aes Sedai. Without

them, you'll never bring all the nations behind you short of conquest. People look for such things. However many of the Prophecies they hear you've fulfilled, many will wait for the Aes Sedai to put their stamp on you."

"I won't avoid fighting anyway, and you know it," Rand said. "The Whitecloaks aren't likely to welcome me into Amadicia even if Ailron agrees, and Sammael certainly won't give up Illian without a fight." *Sammael and Rahvin and Moghedien and. . . .* Harshly he forced the thought from his consciousness. It was not easy. They came without warning, and it was never easy.

A thump made him look over his shoulder. Arymilla lay in a heap on the paving stones. Karind was kneeling to pull her skirts down over her ankles and chafe her wrists. Elegar swayed as though he might join Arymilla in a moment, and neither Nasin nor Elenia appeared in much better state. Most of the rest looked ready to sick up. Mention of the Forsaken could do that, especially since Rand had told them that Lord Gaebril really had been Rahvin. He was not sure how much they believed, but just considering the possibility was enough to unhinge the knees of most. Their shock was why they were still alive. Had he believed they had served knowingly. . . . *No,* he thought. *If they'd known, if they were all Darkfriends, you'd still use them.* Sometimes he was so sick of himself that he really was ready to die.

At least he was telling the truth. The Aes Sedai were all dying to keep it secret, the Forsaken being free; they feared that knowing would just bring more chaos and panic. Rand was trying to spread the truth. People might panic, but they would have time to recover. The Aes Sedai way, knowledge and panic might come too late for recovery. Besides, people had a right to know what they faced.

"Illian won't hold out long," Bashere said. Rand's head whipped back around, but Bashere was too old a campaigner to speak of what he should not where others could hear. He was just taking the talk away from the Forsaken. Though if the Forsaken, or anything else, made Davram Bashere nervous, Rand had not seen it yet. "Illian will crack like a nut hit by a hammer."

"You and Mat worked out a good plan." The basic idea had been Rand's, but Mat and Bashere had provided the thousand details that would make it work. Mat more than Bashere.

"An interesting young fellow, Mat Cauthon," Bashere mused. "I look forward to speaking with him again. He never would say who he studied under. Agelmar Jagad? I hear you've both been to Shienar." Rand said nothing. Mat's secrets were his own; Rand was not really sure what they were himself. Bashere tilted his head, scratched at a mustache with one finger. "He's young to have studied under anyone. No older than you. Did he find a library somewhere? I would like to see the books he's read."

"You'll have to ask him," Rand said. "I don't know." He supposed Mat had to have read a book sometime, somewhere, but Mat did not have much interest in books.

Bashere only nodded. When Rand did not want to talk about something, Bashere usually let it alone. Usually. "The next time you jaunt off to Cairhien, why don't you bring back the Green sister who's there? Egwene Sedai? I've heard the Aiel speak of her; they say she's from your home village, too. You could trust her, couldn't you?"

"Egwene has other duties," Rand laughed. A Green sister. If Bashere only knew.

Somara appeared at Rand's side with his linen shirt and his coat, a fine red wool cut in the Andoran style, with dragons on the long collar and laurel leaves thick on the lapels and climbing the sleeves. She was tall even for an Aiel woman, maybe not quite a hand shorter than he. Like the other Maidens, she had lowered her veil, but the gray-brown *shoufa* still hid all but her face. "The *Car'a'carn* will catch a chill," she murmured.

He doubted it. The Aiel might find this heat nothing out of the ordinary, but already sweat streamed down him nearly as hard as while working the sword. Still, he pulled the shirt over his head and tucked it in, though leaving the laces undone, then shrugged into the coat. He did not think Somara would actually try to put the clothes on him, not in front of others, but this way he would avoid lectures from her and Enaila, and very likely some of the others, along with the herb tea.

To most Aiel he was the *Car'a'carn*, and so it was with the Maidens. In public. Alone with these women who had chosen to reject marriage and the hearth in favor of the spear, matters became more complicated. He supposed he could stop it—maybe—but he owed it to them not to. Some had already died for him, and more would—he had promised, the Light burn him for it!—and if he could let them do that, he could let them do the rest. Sweat soaked through the shirt immediately and began making dark patches on the coat.

"You need the Aes Sedai, al'Thor." Rand hoped Bashere was half this dogged when it came to fighting; that was the man's reputation, but he had only reputation and a few weeks to go by. "You can't afford to have them against you, and if they don't at least think they have a few strings tied to you, they might go that way. Aes Sedai are tricksome; no man can know what they'll do or why."

"What if I tell you there are hundreds of Aes Sedai ready to support me?" Rand was aware of the Andorans listening; he had to be careful not to say too much. Not that he knew much. What he did know was probably exaggeration and hope. He certainly doubted the "hundreds," whatever Egwene hinted.

Bashere's eyes narrowed. "If there's been an embassy from the Tower, I would know, so. . . ." His voice dropped to a near whisper. "The split? The Tower has really *split?*" He sounded as if he could not believe the words coming out of his own mouth. Everyone knew Siuan Sanche had been deposed from the Amyrlin Seat and stilled—and executed, so rumor ran— yet to most people a division in the Tower was only conjecture, and few truly believed. The White Tower had remained whole, a monolith towering over thrones, for three thousand years. But the Saldaean was a man who considered all possibilities. He went on in a true whisper, stepping close so the Andorans could not overhear. "It must be the rebels ready to support you. You could strike a better deal with them—they'll need you as much as you need them, maybe more—but rebels, even Aes Sedai rebels, won't carry nearly the weight of the White Tower, certainly not with any crown. Commoners might not know the difference, but kings and queens will."

"They're still Aes Sedai," Rand said just as quietly, "whoever they are." *And wherever they are*, he thought dryly. *Aes Sedai . . . Servants of All . . . the Hall of the Servants is broken . . . broken forever . . . broken . . . Ilyena, my love. . . .* Ruthlessly he quashed Lews Therin's thoughts. Sometimes they had actually been a help, giving him information he needed, but they were growing too strong. If he did have an Aes Sedai there—a Yellow; they knew the most of Healing—perhaps she. . . . There had been one Aes Sedai he trusted, though not until shortly before her death, and Moiraine had left him a piece of advice about Aes Sedai, about every other woman who wore the shawl and the ring. "I'll never trust any Aes Sedai," he rasped softly. "I will use them, because I do need them, but Tower or rebel, I know they'll try to use me, because that is what Aes Sedai do. I'll never trust them, Bashere."

The Saldaean nodded slowly. "Then use them, if you can. But remember this. No one resists for long going the way the Aes Sedai want." Abruptly he barked a short laugh. "Artur Hawkwing was the last, so far as I know. The Light burn my eyes, maybe you'll be the second."

The scrape of boots announced an arrival in the courtyard, one of

Bashere's men, a heavy-shouldered, hatchet-nosed young fellow a head taller than his general, with a luxuriant black beard as well as thick mustaches. He walked like a man more used to a saddle under him than his own feet, but he handled the sword at his hip smoothly as he bowed. To Bashere, more than to Rand. Bashere might follow the Dragon Reborn, but Tumad—Rand thought that was his name; Tumad Ahzkan—followed Bashere. Enaila and three other Maidens fastened their eyes on the new Saldaean; they did not really trust any wetlander around the *Car'a'carn*.

"There is a man has presented himself at the gates," Tumad said uneasily. "He says. . . . It is Mazrim Taim, my Lord Bashere."

CHAPTER
2

A New Arrival

Mazrim Taim. Before Rand, other men through the centuries had claimed to be the Dragon Reborn. The last few years before Rand had seen a plague of false Dragons, some of whom could actually channel. Mazrim Taim was one of those, raising an army and ravaging Saldaea before he was taken. Bashere's face did not change, but he gripped his sword hilt white-knuckle hard, and Tumad was looking at him for orders. Taim's escape, on the way to Tar Valon to be gentled, was the reason Bashere had come to Andor in the first place. That was how much Saldaea feared and hated Mazrim Taim; Queen Tenobia had sent Bashere with an army to pursue the man wherever he went, however long it took, to make sure Taim never troubled Saldaea again.

The Maidens merely stood calmly, but that name burst among the Andorans like a torch tossed in dry grass. Arymilla was just being helped to her feet, yet her eyes rolled up in her head again; she would have gone down in a heap once more if Karind had not eased her to the paving stones. Elegar staggered back among the columns and bent over, retching loudly. The rest were all gasps and panic, pressing handkerchiefs to mouths and clutching at sword hilts. Even stolid Karind licked her lips nervously.

Rand took his hand away from his coat pocket. "The amnesty," he said, and both Saldaeans gave him a long flat look.

"What if he has not come for your amnesty?" Bashere said after a moment. "What if he still claims to be the Dragon Reborn?" Feet shuffled among the Andorans; no one wanted to be within miles of where the One Power might be used in a duel.

"If he thinks that," Rand said firmly, "I will disabuse him." He had the rarest sort of *angreal* in his pocket, one made for men, a carving of a fat little man with a sword. However strong Taim might be, he could not stand up to that. "But if he has come for the amnesty, it is his, the same as any other." Whatever Taim had done in Saldaea, he could not afford to turn away a man who could channel, a man who would not have to be taught from the first steps. He needed such a man. He would turn away no one except one of the Forsaken, not unless he was forced to. *Demandred and Sammael, Semirhage and Mesaana, Asmodean and. . . .* Rand forced Lews Therin down; he could not afford distractions now.

Again Bashere paused before speaking, but finally he nodded and let go of his sword. "Your amnesty holds, of course. But mark me, al'Thor. If Taim ever sets foot in Saldaea again, he will not live to leave. There are too many memories. No command I give—nor Tenobia herself—will stop it."

"I will keep him out of Saldaea." Either Taim had come here to submit to him, or else it was going to be necessary to kill him. Unconsciously Rand touched his pocket, pressing the fat little man through the wool. "Let's have him in here."

Tumad eyed Bashere, but Bashere's short nod came so quickly that it seemed Tumad bowed in response to the spoken command. Irritation flashed in Rand, but he said nothing, and Tumad hurried away in that slightly rolling walk. Bashere folded his arms across his chest and stood with one knee bent, a portrait of a man at his ease. Those dark tilted eyes, fixed on the way Tumad had gone, made it a portrait of a man waiting to kill something.

The scuffling of feet started again among the Andorans, hesitant half-steps away then pulling back. Their breathing sounded as though they had run miles.

"You may leave," Rand told them.

"I for one will stand at your shoulder," Lir began just as Naean said sharply, "I will not run before—"

Rand cut them both off. "Go!"

They wanted to show him they were unafraid, even if they were ready to soil themselves; they wanted to run, abandoning what dignity they had not already tossed at his feet. It was a simple choice. He was the Dragon Reborn, and currying favor meant obedience, and obedience in this case meant doing what they truly wanted. A flurry of extravagant bows and deep skirt-spreading curtsies, hurried murmurs of "By your leave, my Lord Dragon" and "As you command, my Lord Dragon," and they were . . . not exactly scurrying out, but walking as quickly as they could manage without appearing to scurry. In the opposite direction from that in which Tumad had gone; no doubt they did not want to risk a chance encounter with Mazrim Taim on his way in.

The waiting stretched out in the heat—it took time to bring a man through the sprawling corridors from the Palace gates—but once the Andorans were gone no one moved. Bashere kept his gaze steady on the place Taim would appear. The Maidens watched everywhere, but they always did, and if they looked ready to veil themselves again in an instant, they always did that too. Except for their eyes, they could have been statues.

Finally the sound of boots echoed into the courtyard. Rand almost reached out for *saidin*, then held back. The man would be able to tell he held the Power as soon as he entered the court; Rand could not afford to appear afraid of him.

Tumad emerged into the sunlight first, then a black-haired man of well above average height whose dark face and tilted eyes, hooked nose and high cheekbones, marked him another Saldaean, though he was clean-shaven and garbed like a once prosperous Andoran merchant lately fallen on hard times. His dark blue coat had been of fine wool trimmed in darker velvet, but wear had made the cuffs ragged, his breeches bagged at the knee, and dust coated his cracked boots. Still, he walked proudly, no mean feat with four more of Bashere's men behind him, those almost straight, slightly serpentine blades bare and the points inches from his ribs. The heat hardly seemed to touch him. The Maidens' eyes followed his progress.

Rand studied Taim as the man and his escort crossed the courtyard. At least fifteen years older than himself; thirty-five, then, or a few years more at most. Little was known and less written of men who could channel—it was a subject most decent people avoided—but Rand had learned what he could. Relatively few men actually sought it out; that was one of Rand's problems. Since the Breaking, most men who channeled had the ability born in them, ready to spring out as they grew into manhood. Some managed to keep madness at bay for years before Aes Sedai found and gentled them; others were already hopelessly mad when found, at times less than a year after first touching *saidin*. Rand had clung to sanity for close to two years, so far. Yet in front of him he had a man who must have managed it for ten or fifteen. That alone was worth something.

They halted a few paces before him at a gesture from Tumad. Rand opened his mouth, but before he could speak, Lews Therin rose up in a frenzy in his head. *Sammael and Demandred hated me, whatever honors I gave them. The more honors, the worse the hate, until they sold their souls and went over. Demandred especially. I should have killed him! I should have killed them all! Scorched the earth to kill them all! Scorch the earth!*

Face frozen, Rand fought for his own mind. *I am Rand al'Thor. Rand al'Thor! I never knew Sammael or Demandred or any of them! The Light burn me, I am Rand al'Thor!* Like a faint echo, one more thought came from elsewhere. *The Light burn me.* It sounded like a plea. Then Lews Therin was gone, driven back into whatever shadows he lived in.

Bashere took advantage of the silence. "You say you're Mazrim Taim?" He sounded doubtful, and Rand looked at him in confusion. Was this Taim or not? Only a madman would claim that name if it was not his.

The prisoner's mouth quirked in what might have been the beginning of a smile, and he rubbed his chin. "I shaved, Bashere." His voice held more than a hint of mockery. "It is hot this far south, or had you not noticed? Hotter than it should be, even here. Do you want proof of me? Shall I channel for you?" His dark eyes flickered to Rand, then back to Bashere, whose face was growing darker by the minute. "Perhaps not that, not now. I remember you. I had you beat at Irinjavar, until those visions appeared in the sky. But everyone knows that. What does everyone not know, that you and Mazrim Taim will?" Focused on Bashere, he seemed unaware of his guards, or their swords still hovering near his ribs. "I hear you hid what happened to Musar and Hachari and their wives." The mockery was gone; he was just relating what had happened, now. "They shouldn't have tried to kill me under a parley flag. I trust you found them good places as servants? All they'll really want to do now is serve and obey; they won't be happy otherwise. I could have killed them. They all four drew daggers."

"Taim," Bashere growled, hand darting for his hilt, "you . . . !"

Rand stepped in front of him, seizing his wrist with the blade half-drawn. The guards' blades, Tumad's as well, were touching Taim now, very likely touching flesh the way they were shoved against his coat, but he did not flinch. "Did you come to see me," Rand demanded, "or to taunt Lord Bashere? If you do it again, I'll let him kill you. My amnesty pardons what you've done, but it doesn't let you flaunt your crimes."

Taim studied Rand a moment before speaking. Despite the heat, the fellow barely sweated. "To see you. You were the one in the vision in the sky. They say it was the Dark One himself you fought."

"Not the Dark One," Rand said. Bashere was not fighting him exactly, but he could feel the tension in the man's arm. If he let go, that blade would be out and through Taim in a heartbeat. Unless he used the Power. Or Taim did. That had to be avoided, if it could be. He kept his grip on Bashere's wrist. "He called himself Ba'alzamon, but I think he was Ishamael. I killed him later, in the Stone of Tear."

"I hear you've killed a number of the Forsaken. Should I call you my Lord Dragon? I have heard this lot use the title. Do you mean to kill all the Forsaken?"

"Do you know any other way to deal with them?" Rand asked. "They die, or the world does. Unless you think they can be talked into abandoning the Shadow the way they abandoned the Light." This was becoming ridiculous. Here he was, carrying on a conversation with a man who certainly had five sword points drawing blood beneath his coat while he himself held on to another man who wanted to add a sixth and draw more than a trickle. At least Bashere's men were too disciplined to do more without their general's word. At least Bashere was keeping his mouth shut. Admiring Taim's coolness, Rand went on as quickly as he could without seeming to be hurried.

"Whatever your crimes are, Taim, they pale beside the Forsaken's. Have you ever tortured an entire city, made thousands of people assist in breaking each other slowly, in breaking their own loved ones? Semirhage did that, for no more reason than that she could, to prove she could, for the pleasure of it. Have you murdered children? Graendal did. She called it kindness, so they would not suffer after she enslaved their parents and carried them away." He just hoped the other Saldaeans were listening half as closely as Taim; the man had actually leaned forward slightly in interest. He hoped they did not ask too many questions about where all this came from. "Have you given people to Trollocs to eat? All the Forsaken did— prisoners who would not turn always went to the Trollocs, if they weren't murdered out of hand—but Demandred captured two cities just because he thought the people there had slighted him before he went over to the Shadow, and every man, woman and child went into Trolloc bellies. Mesaana set up schools in the territory she controlled, schools where children and young people were taught the *glories* of the Dark One, taught to kill their friends who didn't learn well enough or fast enough. I could go on. I could start from the beginning of the list and go through all thirteen names, adding a hundred crimes as bad to every name. Whatever you've done, it doesn't rank with that. And now you've come to accept my pardon, to walk in the Light and submit to me, to battle the Dark One as hard as you ever battled anyone. The Forsaken are reeling; I mean to hunt them all down, eradicate them. And you will help me. For that, you've earned your pardon. I tell you true, you'll probably earn it a hundred times over again before the Last Battle is done."

At last he felt Bashere's arm relax, felt the man's sword sliding back into its scabbard. Rand barely stopped himself from exhaling in relief. "I don't see any reason to guard him so closely now. Put up your swords."

Slowly, Tumad and the others began sheathing their blades. Slowly, but they were doing it. Then Taim spoke.

"Submit? I had thought more of a compact between us." The other Saldaeans tensed; Bashere was still behind Rand, but Rand could *feel* him stiffening. The Maidens did not move a muscle, except that Jalani's hand twitched toward her veil. Taim tilted his head, unaware. "I would be the lesser partner, of course, yet I have had years more than you to study the Power. There is much I could teach you."

Rage rose up in Rand till his vision filmed red. He had spoken of things he should have no knowledge of, had probably birthed a dozen rumors about himself and the Forsaken, all to make this fellow's deeds seem less dark, and the man had the audacity to speak of *compacts*? Lews Therin raved in his head. *Kill him! Kill him now! Kill him!* For once Rand did not bother to quell the voice. "No compact!" he growled. "No partners! I am the Dragon Reborn, Taim! Me! If you have knowledge I can make use of, I will, but you will go where I say, do as I say, when I say."

Without a pause Taim slipped to one knee. "I submit to the Dragon Reborn. I will serve and obey." The corners of his mouth quivered again in that almost smile as he rose. Tumad gaped at him.

"That fast?" Rand said softly. The rage was not gone; it was white hot. If he gave way, he was not sure what he would do. Lews Therin still babbled in the shadows of his head. *Kill him! Must kill him!* Rand pushed Lews Therin away, to a barely audible murmur. Perhaps he should not be surprised at this; strange things happened around *ta'veren*, especially one as strong as himself. That a man might change his mind in a moment, even if his course had been carved in stone, should be no great surprise. But the anger had him, and a strong streak of suspicion. "You named yourself the Dragon Reborn, fought battles all over Saldaea, were only captured because you were knocked unconscious, and you give up this quickly? Why?"

Taim shrugged. "What are my choices? To wander the world alone, friendless, hunted, while you rise to glory? That's supposing Bashere doesn't manage to kill me before I can leave the city, or your Aielwomen don't. Even if they don't, the Aes Sedai will corner me sooner or later; I doubt the Tower means to forget Mazrim Taim. Or I can follow you, and part of that glory will be mine." For the first time he looked around, at his guards, at the Maidens, and shook his head as if he could not believe it. "I might have been the one. How could I be sure otherwise? I can channel; I'm strong. What said I was not the Dragon Reborn? All I had to do was fulfill just one of the Prophecies."

"Like managing to be born on the slopes of Dragonmount?" Rand said coldly. "That was the first Prophecy to be met."

Taim's mouth quirked again. It really was not a smile; it never touched his eyes. "Victors write history. Had I taken the Stone of Tear, history would have shown I was born on Dragonmount, of a woman never touched by a man, and the heavens opened up in radiance to herald my coming. The sort of thing they say about you, now. But you took the Stone with your Aiel, and the world hails you as the Dragon Reborn. I know better than to stand against that; you are the one. Well, since the whole loaf won't be mine, I will settle for whatever slices fall my way."

"You may find honors, Taim, and you may not. If you begin to fret over them, think what happened to the others who've done what you did. Logain, captured and gentled; rumor says he died in the Tower. A nameless fellow beheaded in Haddon Mirk by the Tairens. Another burned by the Murandians. Burned alive, Taim! That's what the Illianers did to Gorin Rogad four years ago, as well."

"Not a fate I would embrace," Taim said levelly.

"Then forget honors and remember the Last Battle. Everything I do is aimed at Tarmon Gai'don. Everything I tell you to do will be aimed at it. *You* will aim at it!"

"Of course." Taim spread his hands. "You are the Dragon Reborn. I don't doubt that; I acknowledge it publicly. We march toward Tarmon Gai'don. Which the Prophecies say you will win. And the histories will say that Mazrim Taim stood at your right hand."

"Perhaps," Rand told him curtly. He had lived too many prophecies to believe any of them meant exactly what they said. Or even that they ensured anything. In his opinion, prophecy set the conditions that had to be met for a thing to happen; only, meeting them did not mean the thing *would* happen, just that it *could*. Some of the conditions set in the Prophecies of the Dragon more than implied that he had to die for any chance at victory. Thinking of that did nothing for his temper. "The Light send your chance doesn't come too soon. Now. What knowledge do you have that I need? Can you teach men to channel? Can you test a man to know whether he can be taught?" Unlike women, one man who could channel could not simply sense the ability in another. There was as much different between men and women with the One Power as there was between men and women; sometimes it was a matter of hair-fine degree, sometimes stone versus silk.

"Your amnesty? Some fools have actually shown up to learn how to be like you and me?"

Bashere only stared at Taim contemptuously, arms folded and boots spread apart, but Tumad and the guards shifted uneasily. The Maidens did not. Rand had no idea how the Maidens felt about the score of men who had answered his call; they never gave any sign. With the memory of Taim as a false Dragon strong in their heads, few of the Saldaeans could hide their ill ease.

"Just answer me, Taim. If you can do what I want, say so. If not. . . ." That was the anger talking. He could not send the man away, not if every day was a struggle with him. Taim seemed to think he would, though.

"I can do both," he said quickly. "I have found five over the years—not that I was really looking—but only one had the courage to go beyond the testing." He hesitated, then added, "He went mad after two years. I had to kill him before he killed me."

Two years. "You've held it off a deal longer than that. How?"

"Worried?" Taim asked softly, then shrugged. "I can't help you. I don't know how; I just did. I'm sane as . . ." His eyes flickered toward Bashere, ignoring the other man's flat stare. ". . . as Lord Bashere."

But Rand wondered, suddenly. Half the Maidens had returned to watching the rest of the courtyard; they were not likely to focus so deeply on one possible threat that they ignored others. The possible threat was Taim, and the second half of the Maidens still had their eyes fixed on him and Rand for any sign the threat was real. Any man would have to be aware of them, sudden death in their eyes, their hands. Rand was, and they wanted to protect him. And Tumad and the other guards still gripped their sword hilts, ready to draw again. If Bashere's men and the Aiel decided to kill Taim, the man would have a hard time escaping that courtyard however he channeled, unless Rand helped him. Yet Taim paid the soldiers and the Maidens no more outward attention than he did the colonnades' columns or the paving stones beneath his boots. Bravery, real or feigned, or something else? A kind of madness?

After a moment of silence, Taim spoke again. "You don't trust me yet. No reason you should. Yet. In time you will. In token of that future trust, I brought you a present." From under his worn coat he pulled a rag-wrapped bundle a little larger than a man's two fists together.

Frowning, Rand took it, and his breath caught when he felt the hard shape inside. Hastily he pulled away multicolored rags, revealing a disc the size of his palm, a disc like that on the scarlet banner above the palace, half white and half black, the ancient symbol of Aes Sedai, before the Breaking of the World. He ran his fingers across the mated teardrops.

Only seven like this had been made, of *cuendillar*. Seals on the Dark One's prison, seals that held the Dark One away from the world. He had two more, hidden away very carefully. Protected very carefully. Nothing could break *cuendillar*, not even the One Power—the lip of a delicate cup made of heartstone could scratch steel, or diamond—but three of the seven *had* been broken. He had seen them, shattered. And he had watched Moiraine carve a thin sliver from the edge of one. The seals were weakening, the Light alone knew why or how. The disc in his hands had the hard slickness of *cuendillar*, like a blend of the finest porcelain and polished steel—but he was sure it would break if he let it fall to the stones under his feet.

Three broken. Three in his possession. Where was the seventh? Only four seals stood between humankind and the Dark One. Four, if the last was still whole. Only four, standing between humankind and the Last Battle. How well did they still hold, weakened as they were?

Lews Therin's voice came up like thunder. *Break it break them all must break them must must must break them all break them and strike must strike quickly must strike now break it break it break it. . . .*

Rand shook with the effort of fighting that voice down, forcing away a mist that clung like spiderwebs. His muscles ached as if he wrestled with a man of flesh, a giant. Handful by handful he stuffed the fog that was Lews Therin into the deepest crannies, the deepest shadows, he could find in his mind.

Abruptly he heard the words he was muttering hoarsely. "Must break it now break them all break it break it break it." Abruptly he realized he had his hands over his head, holding the seal, ready to smash it to the white pavement. The only thing stopping him was Bashere, up on his toes, hands raised to grip Rand's arms.

"I don't know what that is," Bashere said quietly, "but I think maybe you should wait before deciding to break it. Eh?" Tumad and the others were no longer watching Taim; they gaped wide-eyed at Rand. Even the Maidens had shifted their eyes to him, eyes full of concern. Sulin took a half step toward the men, and Jalani's hand was outstretched toward Rand as if she did not realize it.

"No." Rand swallowed; his throat hurt. "I don't think I should." Bashere stepped back slowly, and Rand brought the seal down just as slowly. If Rand had thought Taim unflappable, he had proof to the contrary now. Shock painted the man's face. "Do you know what this is, Taim?" Rand demanded. "You must, or you wouldn't have brought it to me. Where did you find it? Do you have another? Do you know where another is?"

"No," Taim said, voice unsteady. Not with fear, precisely; more like a man who had felt a cliff unexpectedly crumbling under him and had somehow found himself back on solid ground. "That is the only one I. . . . I've heard all sorts of rumors since I escaped the Aes Sedai. Monsters leaping out of thin air. Strange beasts. Men talking to animals, and the animals talking back. Aes Sedai going mad like we're supposed to. Whole villages going mad, killing each other. Some could be true. Half what I know to be true is no less insane. I heard some of the seals have been broken. A hammer could break that one."

Bashere frowned, stared at the seal in Rand's hands, then gasped. He understood.

"Where did you find it?" Rand repeated. If he could find the last. . . . Then what? Lews Therin stirred, but he refused to listen.

"In the last place you would expect," Taim replied, "which I suppose is the first place to look for the others. A decaying little farm in Saldaea. I stopped for water, and the farmer gave it to me. He was old, with no children or grandchildren to pass it on to, and he thought I was the Dragon Reborn. He claimed his family had guarded it more than two thousand years. Claimed they were kings and queens during the Trolloc Wars, and nobles under Artur Hawkwing. His tale could have been true. No more unlikely than finding that in a hut only a few days ride from the Blightborder."

Rand nodded, then stooped to gather up the rags. He was used to the unlikely happening around him; it had to happen elsewhere, sometimes. Hurriedly rewrapping the seal, he handed it to Bashere. "Guard this carefully." *Break it!* He squashed the voice hard. "Nothing must happen to it."

Bashere took the bundle reverently in both hands. Rand was unsure whether the man's bow was for him or the seal. "For ten hours or ten years, it will be safe until you require it."

For a moment Rand studied him. "Everybody's waiting for me to go mad, afraid of it, but not you. You must have thought I finally was, just now, but you weren't afraid of me even then."

Bashere shrugged, grinning behind his gray-streaked mustaches. "When I first slept in a saddle, Muad Cheade was Marshal-General. The man was as mad as a hare in spring thaw. Twice every day he searched his bodyservant for poison, and he drank nothing but vinegar and water, which he claimed was sovereign against the poison the fellow fed him, but he ate everything the man prepared for as long as I knew him. Once he had a grove of oaks chopped down because they were looking at him. And then insisted they be given decent funerals; he gave the oration. Do you have any idea how long it takes to dig graves for twenty-three oak trees?"

"Why didn't somebody do something? His family?"

"Those not mad as he was, or madder, were afraid to look at him side-ways. Tenobia's father wouldn't have let anyone touch Cheade anyway. He might have been insane, but he could outgeneral anyone I ever saw. He never lost a battle. He never even came close to losing."

Rand laughed. "So you follow me because you think I can out-general the Dark One?"

"I follow you because you are who you are," Bashere said quietly. "The world must follow you, or those who survive will wish themselves dead."

Slowly Rand nodded. The Prophecies said he would break nations and bind them together. Not that he wanted to, but the Prophecies were his only guide to how to fight the Last Battle, how to win it. Even without them, he thought the binding together was necessary. The Last Battle would not be just him against the Dark One. He could not believe that; if he was going mad, he was not yet mad enough to believe he was more than a man. It would be mankind against Trollocs and Myrddraal, too, and every sort of Shadowspawn the Blight could vomit out, and Darkfriends rising out of their hiding places. There would be other dangers on that road to Tarmon Gai'don, and if the world was not united. . . . *You do what must be done.* He was not sure whether that was himself or Lews Therin, but it was the truth, as far as he could see.

Walking quickly to the nearest colonnade, he spoke over his shoulder to Bashere. "I am taking Taim to the farm. Do you want to come along?"

"The farm?" Taim said.

Bashere shook his head. "Thank you, no," he said dryly. He might not allow any nerves to show, but Rand and Taim together were probably as much as he could take; he certainly avoided the farm. "My men are growing soft policing the streets for you. I mean to put some of them back into their saddles properly for a few hours. You were going to inspect them this afternoon. Has that changed?"

"What farm?" Taim said.

Rand sighed, suddenly weary. "No, that hasn't changed. I will be there if I can." It was too important to change, though none but Bashere and Mat knew; he could not let anyone else think it more than a casual matter, a useless ceremony for a man growing taken with the pomp of his position, the Dragon Reborn going out to be cheered by his soldiers. He had another visit to make today, too, one that everyone would think he was trying to keep secret. It might even stay secret, from most, but he had no doubt that those he wanted to learn of it, would.

Taking up his sword from where it stood against one of the narrow columns, he buckled it on over his undone coat. The belt was unadorned dark boarhide, just like the scabbard and the long hilt; the buckle was ornate, a finely worked dragon of etched steel inlaid with gold. He should get rid of that buckle, find something plain. He could not bring himself to do it, though. It had been a gift from Aviendha. Which was the reason he should rid himself of it. He could never think his way out of that circle.

Something else waited there for him, too, a two-foot length of spear with a green-and-white tassel below the sharp head. He hefted it as he turned back to the courtyard. One of the Maidens had carved the short shaft with Dragons. Some people were already calling it the Dragon Scepter, especially Elenia and that lot. Rand kept the thing close to remind himself that he might have more enemies than those he could see.

"What farm are you talking about?" Taim's voice grew harder. "Where is it you mean to take me?"

For a long moment Rand studied the man. He did not like Taim. Something in the fellow's manner would not allow it. Or maybe something in himself. For so long he had been the only man who could even think of channeling without looking over his shoulder in a sweat for Aes Sedai. Well, it seemed a long time, and at least the Aes Sedai would not try to gentle him, not now that they knew who he was. Could it be as simple as that? Jealousy that he was no longer unique? He did not think so. Apart from everything else, he would welcome more men who could channel walking the earth unmolested. Finally he would stop being a freak. No, it would not go that far, not this side of Tarmon Gai'don. He was unique; he was the Dragon Reborn. Whatever his reasons, he just did not like the man.

Kill him! Lews Therin shrieked. *Kill them all!* Rand pushed the voice back down. He did not have to like Taim, only to use him. And trust him. That was the hard part.

"I'm taking you where you can serve me," he said coldly. Taim did not flinch or frown; he merely watched and waited, the corners of his mouth twitching for one moment in that almost smile.

CHAPTER
3

A Woman's Eyes

Stilling his irritation—and Lews Therin's mutters—Rand reached out for *saidin*, launched himself into the now familiar battle for control and survival in the midst of emptiness. The taint oozed through him as he channeled; even within the void he could feel it seeming to filter into his bones, perhaps into his soul. He had no way to describe what he did except as making a fold in the Pattern, a hole through it. This he had learned on his own, and his teacher had not been very good at explaining even what lay behind the things he taught. A bright vertical line appeared in the air, widening quickly into an opening the size of a large doorway. In truth, it seemed to turn, the view through it, a sunlit clearing among drought-draggled trees, rotating to a halt.

Enaila and two more Maidens lifted their veils and leaped through almost before it settled; half a dozen others followed, some with horn bows ready. Rand did not expect there to be anything for them to guard against. He had put the other end—if there *was* another end; he did not understand, but it seemed to him there was only one—in the clearing because a gateway opening up could be dangerous around people, but telling the Maidens, or any Aiel, that there was no need to be on guard was like telling a fish there was no need to swim.

"This is a gateway," he told Taim. "I'll show you how to make one if you didn't catch it." The man was staring at him. If he had been watching carefully, he should have seen Rand's weaving of *saidin*; any man able to channel could do that.

Taim joined him as he stepped through into the clearing, Sulin and the rest of the Maidens following. Some gave the sword at Rand's hip a disdainful glance as they streamed past him, and Maiden handtalk flashed silently among them. Disgustedly, no doubt. Enaila and the foreguard had already spread out warily among the bedraggled trees; their coats and breeches, the *cadin'sor*, made them seem part of the shadows whether or not they had added green to the gray and brown. With the Power in him, Rand could see each dead needle distinctly on each of the pines; more were dead than were alive. He could smell the sour sap of the leatherleafs. The air itself smelled hot, dry and dusty. There was no danger for him here.

"Wait, Rand al'Thor," came a woman's urgent voice from the other side of the gateway. Aviendha's voice.

Rand let go of the weave and *saidin* immediately, and the gateway winked out just as it had come. There were dangers and dangers. Taim looked at him curiously. Some of the Maidens, veiled and unveiled, spared him a moment for looks of their own. Disapproving ones. Fingers flashed in Maiden handtalk. They had the sense to keep their tongues still, though; he had made himself clear on that.

Ignoring curiosity and disapproval alike, Rand started off through the trees with Taim at his side, dead leaves and twigs crackling as they went. The Maidens, in a wide circle around them, made no sound in their soft boots, laced to the knee. Vigilance buried their moment of rebuke. Some had made this journey with Rand before, always without incident, but nothing would ever convince them these woods were not a good site for an ambush. Before Rand, life in the Waste had been nearly three thousand years of raids, skirmishes, feuds and wars, unbroken for any length of time.

There were surely things he could learn from Taim—if not nearly so much as Taim thought—but the teaching would go both ways, and it was time for him to start educating the older man. "Sooner or later you will come up against the Forsaken, following me. Maybe before the Last Battle. Probably before. You don't seem surprised."

"I have heard rumors. They had to break free eventually."

So the word was spreading. Rand grinned in spite of himself. The Aes Sedai would not be pleased. Aside from anything else, there was a certain pleasure in tweaking their noses. "You can expect anything at any time. Trollocs, Myrddraal, Draghkar, Gray Men, *gholam*. . . ."

He hesitated, heron-branded palm stroking his long sword hilt. He had no idea what a *gholam* was. Lews Therin had not stirred, but he knew that was the source of the name. Bits and pieces sometimes drifted across whatever thin barrier lay between him and that voice, and became part of Rand's memories, usually without anything to explain them. It happened more often, lately. The fragments were not something he could fight, like the voice. The hesitation lasted only a moment.

"Not just in the north, near the Blight. Here, or anywhere. They are using the Ways." That was something else he had to deal with. But how? First made with *saidin*, the Ways were dark now, as tainted as *saidin*. The Shadowspawn could not avoid all of the dangers in the Ways that killed men or worse, yet they still managed to use them, and if the Ways were not as quick as gateways and Traveling, or even Skimming, they still allowed hundreds of miles to be covered in a day. A problem for later. He had too many problems for later. He had too many problems for now. Irritably, he slashed at leatherleaf with the Dragon Scepter; pieces of wide, tough leaves fell, most brown. "If you've ever heard a legend about it, expect it. Even Darkhounds, though if they're really the Wild Hunt, at least the Dark One isn't free to ride behind them. They're bad enough anyway. Some you can kill, the way the legends say, but some won't die for anything short of balefire, that I'm sure of. Do you know balefire? If you don't, that is one thing I'll not teach you. If you do, don't use it on anything but Shadowspawn. And do not teach it to anyone.

"The source of some of those rumors you heard might be . . . I don't know what to call them except 'bubbles of evil.' Think of them like the bubbles that sometimes rise up in a bog, only these are rising from the Dark One as the seals weaken, and instead of rotten smells, they are full of . . . well, evil. They drift along the Pattern until they burst, and when they do, anything can happen. Anything. Your own reflection can leap out of the mirror and try to kill you. Believe me."

If the litany dismayed Taim, he did not show it. All he said was "I have been in the Blight; I've killed Trollocs before, and Myrddraal." He pushed a low branch out of the way and held it for Rand. "I have never heard of this balefire, but if a Darkhound comes after me, I will find some way to kill it."

"Good." That was for Taim's ignorance as much as his confidence. Balefire was one bit of knowledge Rand would not mind seeing vanish from the world completely. "With luck you won't find anything like that out here, but you can never be sure."

The woods gave way abruptly to a farmyard, with a sprawling thatch-roofed house of two weathered stories, smoke rising from one of its chimneys, and a large barn that had a distinct lean. The day was no cooler here than in the city a few miles away, the sun no less blistering. Chickens scratched the dust, two dun cows chewed their cud in a rail-fenced enclosure, a flock of tethered black goats busily stripped leaves from bushes within their reach, and a high-wheeled cart stood in the barn's shadow, but the place did not look like a farm. There were no fields in sight; forest stretched all around the yard, broken only by the dirt track meandering northward, used for rare excursions to the city. And there were too many people.

Four women, all but one in her middle years, were hanging wash on a pair of lines, and nearly a dozen children, none older than nine or ten, played among the chickens. There were men about, too, most doing chores. Twenty-seven of them, though in some cases it was a stretch to call them men. Eben Hopwil, the skinny fellow pulling up a bucket of water from the well, claimed to be twenty and was certainly four or five years younger. His nose and ears seemed the biggest parts of him. Fedwin Morr, one of three men sweating on the roof replacing old thatch, was a good deal huskier, with a good deal fewer blotches, but certainly no older. More than half of the men had only three or four years on those two. Rand had almost sent some of them home, Eben and Fedwin at least, save that the White Tower took novices as young and sometimes younger. Gray showed among darker hair on a few heads, and crease-faced Damer Flinn, in front of the barn using peeled branches to show two of the younger men how to handle a sword, had a limp and retained only a thin fringe of white hair. Damer had been in the Queen's Guards until he took a Murandian lance in his thigh. He was no swordsman, but he seemed competent to show the others how not to stab themselves in the foot. Most of the men were Andoran, a few Cairhienin. None had come from Tear yet, though the amnesty had been proclaimed there, too; it would take time for men to come that far.

Damer was the first to notice the Maidens, tossing down his branch and directing his pupils' attention toward Rand. Then Eben dropped his bucket with a yell, splashing water all over himself, and everyone was scrambling, shouting at the house, to cluster anxiously behind Damer. Two more women appeared from inside, aproned and red-faced from cookfires, and helped the others gather the children behind the men.

"There they are," Rand told Taim. "You have nearly half a day left. How many can you test? I want to know who can be taught as soon as possible."

"This lot was dredged from the bottom of . . ." Taim began contemptuously, then stopped in the middle of the farmyard, staring at Rand.

Chickens scratched in the dust around his feet. "You haven't tested any of them? Why, in the name of . . . ? You cannot, can you? You can Travel, but you do not know how to test for the talent."

"Some don't really want to channel." Rand eased his grip on his sword hilt. He disliked admitting gaps in his knowledge to this man. "Some haven't thought beyond a chance at glory or wealth or power. But I want to keep any man who can learn, whatever his reasons."

The students—the men who would be students—were watching him and Taim from in front of the barn with a fair approximation of calm. They had all come to Caemlyn hoping to learn from the Dragon Reborn, after all, or thinking they did. It was the Maidens, making a ring about the farmyard and prowling into the house and barn, that caught their eyes with a wary fascination, even apprehension. The women clutched the children to their skirts, gazes fixed on Rand and Taim, expressions ranging from flat-eyed stares to anxious lip-chewing.

"Come on," Rand said. "It's time to meet your students."

Taim hung back. "Is this truly all you want me for? To try to teach these pathetic dregs? If any of them can be taught. How many do you really think to find in a handful that just straggled to you?"

"This is important, Taim; I'd do it myself, if I could, if I had time." Time was always key, always lacking. And he had made the admission, as much as it curdled his tongue. He realized he did not much like Taim, but he did not have to like him. Rand did not wait, and after a moment the other man caught up with long strides. "You mentioned trust. I'm trusting you with this." *Don't trust!* Lews Therin panted in the dim recesses. *Never trust! Trust is death!* "Test them and start teaching as soon you know who can learn."

"As the Lord Dragon wishes," Taim murmured wryly as they reached the waiting group. Bows and curtsies, none very polished, greeted them.

"This is Mazrim Taim," Rand announced. Jaws dropped and eyes widened, of course. Some of the younger men stared as though they thought he and Taim had come there to fight; a few seemed to be looking forward to watching. "Introduce yourselves to him. From today, he will be teaching you." Taim gave Rand a tight-mouthed look as the students slowly gathered before him and began giving their names.

In truth, the men's reactions varied. Fedwin pushed eagerly to the front, right alongside Damer, while Eben hung to the rear, face white. The others were somewhere in between, hesitant, uncertain, but speaking up finally. Rand's declaration meant an end to weeks of waiting for some of them, to years of dreaming, perhaps. Reality began today, and reality might mean channeling, with all that entailed for a man.

A stocky dark-eyed man, six or seven years older than Rand, ignored Taim and slipped away from the others. In a farmer's rough coat, Jur Grady shifted from foot to foot in front of Rand and twisted a cloth cap in blunt hands. He peered at the cap or the ground under his worn boots, only occasionally glancing up at Rand. "Uh . . . my Lord Dragon, I've been think-ing . . . uh . . . my pa is looking after my croft, a good piece of land if the stream don't dry up there might be a crop yet, if it rains, and . . . and. . . ." He crushed the cap, then straightened it again carefully. "I've been thinking about going home."

The women were not gathering around Taim. In a silent line of wor-ried eyes, they held hard to the children and watched. The youngest, a plump pale-haired woman, a boy of four playing with her fingers, was Sora Grady. Those women had followed their husbands here, but Rand sus-pected that half the talk between husband and wife eventually turned to leaving. Five men had left already, and if none gave marriage as a reason, all had been married. What woman could be comfortable watching her husband wait to learn to channel? It must be like watching him wait to commit suicide.

Some would say this was no place for families, yet most likely those same people would also say the men should not be here, either. In Rand's opinion, the Aes Sedai had made a mistake sealing themselves off from the world. Few entered the White Tower beyond Aes Sedai, women who wanted to be Aes Sedai, and those who served them; only a relative handful seeking help, and then under what they saw as great pressure. When Aes Sedai left the Tower, most held themselves aloof, and some never did leave. To Aes Sedai, people were pieces in a game and the world was the board, not a place to live in. To them, only the White Tower was real. No man could forget the world and ordinary people when he had his family in front of him.

This only had to last until Tarmon Gai'don—how long? A year? Two?—but the question was whether it could even do that. Somehow, it would. He would make it last. Families reminded men what they were go-ing to fight for.

Sora's eyes were fastened on Rand.

"Go, if you want to," he told Jur. "You can leave any time before you actually start learning to channel. Once you take that step, you're the same as a soldier. You know we'll need every soldier we can find before the Last Battle, Jur. The Shadow will have new Dreadlords ready to channel; you can count on it. But it's your choice. Maybe you'll be able to sit it out on your farm. There must be a few places in the world that will escape what's coming. I hope so. Anyway, the rest of us will do our best to make sure as much escapes as possible. At least you can give your name to Taim, though. It would be a shame to leave before you even know whether you could learn." Turning away from Jur's confused face, Rand avoided Sora's eyes. *And you condemn Aes Sedai for manipulating people,* he thought bitterly. He did what he had to do.

Taim was still collecting names out of the shifting pack, and still tossing barely subdued glares at Rand. Abruptly Taim's patience seemed to give out. "Enough of this; names can come later, for those of you who will still be here tomorrow. Who is the first to be tested?" Just that quickly their tongues froze. Some did not even blink as they stared at him. Taim pointed a finger at Damer. "I might as well get you out of the way. Come here." Damer did not move until Taim grabbed his arm and hauled him a few paces apart from the rest.

Watching, Rand moved nearer, too.

"The more Power that's used," Taim told Damer, "the easier it is to detect the resonance. On the other hand, too big a resonance could do un pleasant things to your mind, maybe kill you, so I'll start small." Damer blinked; plainly he barely understood a word, except maybe the part about unpleasant things and dying. Rand knew the explanation was meant for him, though; Taim was covering his ignorance.

Abruptly a tiny flame appeared, an inch tall, dancing in midair equidistant between the three men. Rand could feel the Power in Taim, though only a small amount, and see the thin flow of Fire the man wove. The flame brought a startling relief to Rand, startling because it was proof Taim really could channel. Bashere's first doubts must have stuck in the back of his mind.

"Concentrate on the flame," Taim said. "You are the flame; the world is the flame; there is nothing but the flame."

"Don't feel nothing but an ache starting in my eyes," Damer muttered, wiping sweat from his forehead with the back of a rough, callused hand.

"Concentrate!" Taim snapped. "Do not talk, do not think, do not move. Concentrate." Damer nodded, then blinked at Taim's frown and froze, staring silently at the small flame.

Taim seemed intent, but on what Rand was not sure; he seemed to be listening. A resonance, he had said. Rand focused, listening, feeling for—something.

Minutes stretched out with none of them moving a muscle. Five, six, seven slow minutes, with Damer hardly even blinking. The old man breathed hard, and he sweated so much he looked as though someone had upended a bucket over his head. Ten minutes.

Suddenly Rand felt it. The resonance. A small thing, a tiny echo of the minuscule flow of Power pulsing in Taim, but this seemed to come from Damer. It had to be what Taim meant, but Taim did not move. Perhaps there was more, or maybe this was not what Rand thought.

Another minute or two went by, and finally Taim nodded and let the flame and *saidin* go. "You can learn . . . Damer, was it?" He seemed surprised; no doubt he had not believed the very first man tested would pass, and a nearly bald old man at that. Damer grinned weakly; he looked like he might vomit. "I suppose I shouldn't be surprised if every one of these simpletons passes," the hawk-nosed man muttered with a glance at Rand. "You seem to have luck enough for ten men."

Boots shuffled uneasily among the rest of the "simpletons." Undoubtedly some were already hoping they would fail. They could not back out now, but if they failed, they could go home knowing they had tried without having to face what came with passing.

Rand felt a little surprise himself. There had not been anything more than that echo after all, and he had felt it before Taim, the man who knew what he was looking for.

"In time we'll find out how strong you can be," Taim said as Damer slipped back among the others. They opened a little distance around him and did not meet his eyes. "Perhaps you will turn out strong enough to match me, or even the Lord Dragon here." The space around Damer widened a fraction. "Only time will tell. Pay attention while I test the others. If you are sharp, you should catch on to it by the time I find four or five more." A quick look at Rand said that was meant for him. "Now, who tests next?" No one moved. The Saldaean stroked his chin. "You." He pointed to a lumpy fellow somewhere well beyond thirty, a dark-haired weaver named Kely Huldin. In the line of women, Kely's wife moaned.

Twenty-six more tests were going to take the rest of the daylight, maybe more. Heat or no heat, the days still grew shorter as if winter really was coming on, and a failed test would take a few minutes longer than one passed, just to make certain. Bashere was waiting, and there was Weiramon to visit yet, and . . .

"Carry on with this," Rand told Taim. "I will come back tomorrow to see how you've done. Remember the trust I'm putting in you." *Don't trust him*, Lews Therin groaned. The voice seemed to come from some capering figure in the shadows of Rand's head. *Don't trust. Trust is death. Kill him. Kill them all. Oh, to die and be done, done with it all, sleep without dreams, dreams of Ilyena, forgive me, Ilyena, no forgiveness, only death, deserve to die. . . .* Rand turned away before the struggle inside could show on his face. "Tomorrow. If I can."

Taim caught up to him before he and the Maidens were halfway back to the trees. "If you stay a little longer, you can learn the test." Exasperation touched his voice. "If I really do find four or five more, anyway, which truly won't surprise me. You do seem to have the Dark One's own luck. I assume you want to learn. Unless you mean to dump it all on my shoulders. I warn you, it will be slow. However hard I press, this Damer has days yet, weeks, before he can even sense *saidin*, much less seize it. Just seize it, not channel even a spark."

"I already picked up the test," Rand replied. "It wasn't difficult. And I do mean to put it all on your shoulders, until you can find more and teach them enough so they can help you look. Remember what I said, Taim. Teach them fast." There were dangers in that. Learning to channel the female half of the True Source was learning an embrace, so Rand had been told, learning to submit to something that would obey once you surrendered to it. It was guiding a huge force that would not harm you unless you misused it. Elayne and Egwene thought that natural; to Rand it was almost beyond belief. Channeling the male half was a constant war for control and survival. Leap into it too far, too fast, and you were a boy tossed naked into a pitched battle against armored foes. Even once you learned, *saidin* could destroy you, kill you or obliterate your mind, if it did not simply burn the ability to channel from you. The same price that Aes Sedai exacted from the men they caught who could channel, you could exact from yourself in one careless moment, one instant of letting your guard down. Not that some of the men in front of the barn would not be willing to pay that price right that minute. Kely Huldin's round-faced wife had him by the front of his shirt, talking urgently. Kely was swinging his head uncertainly, and the other married men were looking uneasily toward their wives. But this was a war, and wars had casualties, even among married men. Light, but he was growing calloused enough to sicken a goat. He turned a little, so he did not have to see Sora Grady's eyes. "Walk the edge with them," he told Taim. "Teach them as much as they can learn as fast as they can learn it."

Taim's mouth tightened slightly at Rand's first words. "As much as they can learn," he said flatly. "But what? Things that can be used as weapons, I suppose."

"Weapons," Rand agreed. They had to be weapons, all of them, himself included. Could weapons allow themselves families? Could a weapon allow itself to love? Now, where had *that* come from? "Anything they can learn, but that most of all." They were so few. Twenty-seven, and if there was even one more than Damer who could learn, Rand would thank his being *ta'veren* for drawing the man to him. Aes Sedai only caught and gentled men who actually channeled, but they had become very good at it over the last three thousand years. Some Aes Sedai apparently believed they were succeeding in something they had never intended, culling the ability to channel out of humanity. The White Tower had been built to house three thousand Aes Sedai all the time, and far more if all their numbers had to be called in, with rooms for hundreds of girls in training, but before the split there had only been forty or so novices in the Tower and fewer than fifty Accepted. "I need more numbers, Taim. One way or another, find more. Teach them the test before anything else."

"You mean to try matching the Aes Sedai, then?" Taim seemed unperturbed even if that was Rand's plan. His dark tilted eyes were steady.

"How many Aes Sedai are there altogether? A thousand?"

"Not so many, I think," Taim said cautiously.

Culling the human race. Burn them for it, even if they had cause. "Well, there will be enemies enough anyway." One thing he did not lack was enemies. The Dark One and the Forsaken, Shadowspawn and Darkfriends. The Whitecloaks certainly and very likely Aes Sedai, or some of them, those who were Black Ajah and those who wanted to control him. Those last he counted enemies even if they did not think themselves so. There surely would be Dreadlords, just as he had said. And more beyond that. Enemies enough to crush all his plans, crush everything. His grip tightened on the carved haft of the Dragon Scepter. Time was the greatest enemy of all, the one he had the least chance of defeating. "I am going to defeat them, Taim. All of them. They think they can tear everything down. It's always tearing down, never building up! I'm going to build something, leave something behind. Whatever happens, I will do that! I'll defeat the Dark One. And cleanse *saidin*, so men don't have to fear going mad, and the world doesn't have to fear men channeling. I'll . . ."

The green-and-white tassel swung as he angrily jerked the length of spear. It was impossible. The heat and dust mocked him. Some of it had to be done, but it was all impossible. The best any of them could hope for was to win and die before they went mad, and he did not see how to manage even that much. All he could do was keep trying. There should be a way, though. If there was such a thing as justice, there should be a way.

"Cleanse *saidin*," Taim said softly. "I think that would take more power than you can imagine." His eyes lidded thoughtfully. "I have heard of things called *sa'angreal*. Do you have one you think could actually—"

"Never mind what I have or don't have," Rand snapped. "You teach whoever can learn, Taim. Then find more and teach them. The Dark One won't wait on us. Light! We don't have enough time, Taim, but we have to make do. We have to!"

"I will do what I can. Just do not expect Damer to topple a city's walls tomorrow."

Rand hesitated. "Taim? Keep a watch out for any student who learns too fast. Let me know immediately. One of the Forsaken might try to slip in among the students."

"One of the Forsaken!" It was almost a whisper. For the second time, Taim looked shaken, this time well and truly taken aback. "Why would—?"

"How strong are you?" Rand broke in. "Seize *saidin*. Do it. As much as you can hold."

For a moment Taim only looked at him, expressionless; then the Power flooded into him. There was no glow such as women could see around one another, only a sense of force and menace, but Rand could feel it clearly, and judge it. Taim held enough of *saidin* to devastate the farm and everyone there in seconds, enough to lay waste as far as he could see. It was not much short of what Rand himself could manage, unaided. But then, the man could be holding back. There was no sense of strain and he might not want to show his full strength to Rand; how could he know how Rand might react?

Saidin, the sense of it, faded from Taim, and for the first time Rand realized that he himself was filled with the male half of the Source, a raging flood, every thread he could pull through the *angreal* in his pocket. *Kill him*, Lews Therin muttered. *Kill him now!* For a moment shock gripped Rand; the emptiness surrounding him wavered, *saidin* raged and swelled, and he barely released the Power before it could crush the Void and him both. Had he seized the Source or had Lews Therin? *Kill him! Kill him!*

In a fury, Rand screamed inside his head, *Shut up!* To his surprise, the other voice vanished.

Sweat rolled down his face, and he wiped it away with a hand that wanted to shake. He had grasped the Source himself; it had to have been so. A dead man's voice could not have done it. Unconsciously, he had not been willing to trust Taim holding so much of *saidin* while he stood help-less. That was it.

"Just you keep an eye out for anyone who learns too fast," he muttered. Maybe he was telling Taim too much, but people had a right to know what they might face. As much as they needed to know. He dared not allow Taim or anyone else to find out where he had learned much of what he knew. If they discovered that he had held one of the Forsaken prisoner and allowed him to escape. . . . Rumor would strip away mention of prisoners if that leaked out. The Whitecloaks claimed he was a false Dragon, and very likely a Darkfriend besides; they said as much of anyone who touched the One Power. If the world learned about Asmodean, many more might be-lieve. Never mind that Rand had needed a man to teach him of *saidin*. No woman could have, any more than they could see his weavings, or he theirs. *Men believe the worst easily, and women believe it hides something still darker*; that was an old Two Rivers saying. He would deal with Asmodean himself if the man ever turned up again. "Just you keep an eye out. Quietly."

"As my Lord Dragon commands." The man actually bowed slightly before starting back across the farmyard.

Rand realized the Maidens were looking at him. Enaila and Somara, Sulin and Jalani and all the rest, concern filling their eyes. They accepted almost everything he did, all the things that made him flinch when he did them, all the things everyone but the Aiel flinched at; what put their hack-les up were usually matters he did not understand at all. They accepted, and *worried* about him.

"You must not tire yourself," Somara said quietly. Rand looked at her, and the flaxen-haired woman's cheeks reddened. This might not count as a public place—Taim was already too distant to overhear—but the remark was still going too far.

Enaila, though, pulled a spare *shoufa* from her belt and handed it to him. "Too much sun is not good for you," she murmured.

One of the others muttered, "He needs a wife to look after him." He could not tell which; even Somara and Enaila confined that sort of talk behind his back. He knew who was meant, though. Aviendha. Who better to marry the son of a Maiden than a Maiden who had given up the spear to become a Wise One?

Suppressing a flash of anger, he wound the *shoufa* around his head, and was grateful for it. The sun truly was hot, and the gray-brown cloth deflected a surprising amount of the heat. His sweat dampened it immediately. Did Taim know something like the Aes Sedai trick of not letting heat or cold touch them? Saldaea was in the far north, yet the man hardly seemed to perspire as much as the Aiel. Despite his gratitude, what Rand said was "What I must not do is stand around here wasting time."

"Wasting time?" young Jalani said in a too innocent voice, rewinding her *shoufa* and momentarily exposing short hair nearly as red as Enaila's. "How can the *Car'a'carn* be wasting time? The last time I sweated as much as he is, I had run from sunup to sundown."

Grins and outright laughter spread through the other Maidens, red-haired Maira, at least ten years older than Rand, slapping her thigh, golden-haired Desora hiding her smiles behind a hand as she always did. Scar-faced Liah bounced up and down on her toes, while Sulin almost doubled over. Aiel humor was strange at best. Heroes in stories never had jokes made at their expense, not even odd ones, and he doubted kings did either. Part of the problem was that an Aiel chief, even the *Car'a'carn*, was not a king; he might have the authority of one in many ways, but any Aiel could and would walk up to a chief and say exactly what he thought. The bigger part, however, was something else.

Despite his having been raised in the Two Rivers by Tam al'Thor and, until her death when he was five, Tam's wife, Kari, Rand's true mother had been a Maiden of Spear who died giving birth to him on the slopes of Dragonmount. Not an Aiel, though his father had been, but still a Maiden. Now Aiel customs stronger than law had touched him. No, not touched; enveloped. No Maiden could marry and still carry the spear, and unless she gave up the spear any child she bore was given to another woman by the Wise Ones, in such a way that the Maiden never knew who that woman was. Any child born of a Maiden was believed to be lucky, both in itself and to raise, though none but the woman who raised the child and her husband ever knew it was not her own. Yet beyond that, the Aiel Prophecy of Rhuidean said that the *Car'a'earn* would be such a one, raised by wetlanders. To the Maidens, Rand was all those children come back, the first child of a Maiden ever to be known to everyone.

Most, whether older than Sulin or as young as Jalani, welcomed him like a long-lost brother. In public they gave him as much respect as they did any chief, marginal as that might be sometimes, but alone with them he might as well have been that brother, though whether he was a younger brother or an older did not seem to have anything to do with the woman's own age. He was just glad that only a handful took Enaila and Somara's path; alone or not, it was plain irritating to have a woman no older than himself behaving as though he were her son.

"Then we ought to go somewhere I won't sweat," he said, managing a grin. He owed it to them. Some had already died for him, and more would before it was done. The Maidens quickly subdued their mirth, ready to go where the *Car'a'carn* said, ready to defend him.

The question was, where to go? Bashere was waiting for his carefully casual visit, but if Aviendha had heard about that, she might well be with Bashere. Rand had been avoiding her as much as possible, especially being alone with her. Because he wanted to be alone with her. He had managed to keep that from the Maidens so far, if they ever so much as suspected, they would make his life miserable. The fact was, he *had* to stay away from her. He carried death with him like a contagious disease; he was a target, and people died near him. He had to harden his heart and let Maidens die—the Light burn him forever for that promise!—but Aviendha had given up the spear to study with the Wise Ones. He was not sure what he felt for her, only that if she died because of him, something in him would die, too. It was lucky that she had no emotional tangles where he was concerned. She tried to stay close to him only because the Wise Ones wanted her to watch him for them, and because she wanted to watch him for Elayne. Neither reason made the situation any easier for Rand; exactly the opposite.

The decision was easy, really. Bashere would have to wait, so he could avoid Aviendha; and the visit to Weiramon, intended to begin in the Palace with attempts at stealth meant to be pierced, would come now. A foolish reason to make a decision, but what was a man to do when a woman refused to see sense? It might work out for the best this way. Those who were supposed to learn of that visit still would, and perhaps believe what they were supposed to all the more because it was made in true concealment. Perhaps the call on Bashere and the Saldaeans would even seem more casual because he left it until late in the day. Yes. Twists within twists worthy of a Cairhienin playing the Game of Houses.

Seizing *saidin*, he opened a gateway, the slash of light widening to show the interior of a large green-striped tent, empty save for a carpeting of colorful rugs woven in Tairen maze patterns. There was no chance of an ambush in that tent, less even than around the farm, but Enaila and Maira and others still veiled themselves and darted through. Rand paused to look back.

Kely Huldin was making his way toward the farmhouse, head down and his wife herding their two children at his side. She kept reaching over to pat him consolingly, but even across the farmyard Rand could make out her beaming face. Plainly Kely had failed. Taim was facing Jur Grady, both staring at a tiny flame wavering between them. Sora Grady, her son clasped to her breast, was not watching her husband. Her eyes were still locked on Rand. *A woman's eyes cut deeper than a knife;* another Two Rivers saying.

Stepping through the gateway, he waited for the rest of the Maidens to follow, then released the Source. He did what he had to do.

CHAPTER
4

A Sense of Humor

The tent's dim interior was hot enough to make Caemlyn, some eight hundred miles or so north, seem pleasantly cool, and when Rand pushed the flap open, he blinked. The sun was a hammer that made him glad of the *shoufa*.

A copy of the Dragon banner hung above the green-striped tent, alongside one of the crimson banners bearing the ancient Aes Sedai symbol. More tents stretched across a rolling plain where all but a few tufts of tough grass had long since been beaten to dust by hooves and boots—peak-roofed tents and flat, most white by far if often dirty white, but many in colors or stripes, tents and the colorful banners of lords. An army had gathered here on the border of Tear, on the edge of the Plains of Maredo, thousands upon thousands of soldiers from Tear and Cairhien. The Aiel had made their own camps well away from the wetlanders, five Aiel for every Tairen and Cairhienin and more arriving by the day. It was an army to make Illian shake in its boots, a host already mighty enough to smash anything in its path.

Enaila and the rest of the foreguard were already outside, veils down, with a dozen or so Aielmen. The Aiel kept a constant guard on this tent. Clothed and armed like the Maidens, they were as tall as Rand or taller, lions to the Maidens' leopards, hard-faced sun-dark men with cold eyes of blue or green or gray. Today they were *Sha'mad Conde*, Thunder Walkers, led by

Roidan himself, who headed the society this side of the Dragonwall. The Maidens carried the honor of the *Car'a'carn*, but every warrior society demanded some share of the guard duty.

One thing about some of the men's garb differed from the Maidens'. Half wore a crimson cloth knotted around their temples, with the ancient Aes Sedai symbol a black-and-white disc above their brows. It was a new thing, first seen only a few months earlier. Wearers of the headband considered themselves *siswai'aman*; in the Old Tongue, the Spears of the Dragon. The Spears Owned by the Dragon might be closer. The headbands, and their meaning, made Rand uncomfortable, but there was little he could do when the men refused even to admit they were wearing them. Why no Maidens had donned the things—none he had seen at least—he had no idea. They were almost as reluctant to talk about it as the men.

"I see you, Rand al'Thor," Roidan said gravely. There was considerably more gray than yellow in Roidan's hair, but a blacksmith could have used the heavy-shouldered man's face for hammer or anvil, and by the scars across his cheeks and nose it seemed possible that more than one had. Icy blue eyes made his face soft by comparison. He avoided looking at Rand's sword. "May you find shade this day." That had nothing to do with the molten sun or the cloudless sky—Roidan did not seem to sweat at all—it was simply a greeting among people from a land where the sun was always baking hot and a tree rare.

Equally formal, Rand replied, "I see you, Roidan. May you find shade this day. Is the High Lord Weiramon about?"

Roidan nodded toward a large pavilion with red-striped sides and a crimson roof, ringed by men with tall spears slanted precisely, shoulder-to-shoulder in the burnished breastplates and gold-and-black coats of Tairen Defenders of the Stone. Above it, the Three Crescents of Tear, white on red and gold, and the many-rayed Rising Sun of Cairhien, gold on blue, flanked Rand's own scarlet flag, all three twitching in a breeze that might have come from an oven.

"The wetlanders are all there." Looking Rand straight in the eyes, Roidan added, "Bruan has not been asked to that tent in three days, Rand al'Thor." Bruan was clan chief of the Nakai Aiel, Roidan's clan; they were both Salt Flat sept. "Nor has Han of the Tomanelle, or Dhearic of the Reyn, or any clan chief."

"I will speak with them," Rand said. "Will you tell Bruan and the others I am here?" Roidan nodded gravely.

Eyeing the men sideways, Enaila leaned close to Jalani, then spoke in a whisper that could have been heard clearly at ten paces. "Do you know why they are called Thunder Walkers? Because even when they are standing still, you keep looking to the sky expecting to see lightning." The Maidens hooted with laughter.

A young Thunder Walker leaped in the air, kicking a soft knee-high boot higher than Rand's head. He was handsome except for the puckered white scar that ran up under the strip of black cloth covering a missing eye. He wore the headband, too. "Do you know why Maidens use handtalk?" he shouted at the top of his leap, and, landing, he put on a befuddled grimace. Not directed at the Maidens, though; he spoke to his companions, ignoring the women. "Because even when they are not talking, they cannot stop talking." The *Sha'mad Conde* laughed as hard as the Maidens had.

"Only Thunder Walkers would see honor in guarding an empty tent," Enaila told Jalani sadly, shaking her head. "The next time they call for wine, if the *gai'shain* bring them empty cups, they will no doubt get drunker than we can on *oosquai*."

Apparently the Thunder Walkers thought Enaila had gained the best of the exchange. The one-eyed man and several others raised their bullhide bucklers toward her and rattled spears against them. For her part, she simply listened a moment, then nodded to herself and fell in with the others as they followed Rand.

Musing to himself about Aiel humor, Rand studied the sprawling camp. The aromas of food drifted from hundreds of scattered cookfires, bread baking in coals, meat roasting on spits, soup bubbling in kettles hung on tripods. Soldiers always ate well and often when they could; campaigning usually brought scant meals. The fires added their own sweetish smells; there was more dried ox dung to burn on the Plains of Maredo than wood.

Here and there archers or crossbowmen or pikemen moved about in leather jerkins sewn with steel discs or simply padded coats, but Tairen and Cairhienin nobles alike despised foot and lauded horse, so mounted men were most in evidence. Tairens in helmets rimmed and ridged, and breastplates over fat-sleeved coats striped in the colors of their various lords. Cairhienin in dark coats and battered breastplates and helmets like bells cut away to expose their faces. Small banners called *con*, on short staffs fastened to some men's backs, marked minor Cairhienin nobility and younger sons, and sometimes merely officers, though few Cairhienin commoners rose to rank. Or Tairen, for that matter. The two nationalities did not mingle, and while the Tairens often slouched in their saddles and always directed a sneer at any Cairhienin who came near, the shorter Cairhien sat their horses stiffly, as though straining for the last inch of height, and ignored the Tairens completely. They had fought more than one war against each other before Rand made them ride together.

Roughly dressed, grizzled old men and some little more than boys went poking around the tents with stout sticks, one or another now and again scaring up a rat that he chased down and clubbed before adding it to the others dangling from his belt. A big-nosed fellow in a stained leather vest and no shirt, bow in hand and quiver at his waist, laid a long string of crows and ravens tied together by the feet on a table in front of one tent and received a purse in exchange from the bored-looking helmetless Tairen behind it. Few this far south really believed Myrddraal used rats and ravens and such for spies—Light, except for those who had actually seen them, almost no one this far south truly believed in Myrddraal, or Trollocs!—but if the Lord Dragon wanted the camp kept clear of the creatures, they were happy to oblige, especially since the Lord Dragon paid in silver for every corpse.

Cheers rose, of course; no one else would be walking about with an escort of Maidens of the Spear, and there was the Dragon Scepter. "The Light illumine the Lord Dragon!" and "Grace favor the Lord Dragon!" and the like showered from every side. Many even sounded sincere, though it was difficult to tell with men bellowing at the top of their lungs. Others only stared woodenly, or turned their horses and rode away, not too fast. After all, there was no telling when he might decide to call down lightning or make the ground split open; men who channeled did go mad, and who knew what a madman might do or when? Whether cheering or not, they eyed the Maidens warily. Few had really grown accustomed to seeing women carrying weapons like men; besides, everyone knew Aiel were every bit as unpredictable as madmen.

The noise was not enough to keep Rand from hearing what the Maidens were saying behind him.

"He has a fine sense of humor. Who is he?" That was Enaila.

"His name is Leiran," Somara replied. "A Cosaida Chareen. You think he has humor because he thought your joke better than his. He does look to have strong hands." Several of the Maidens chortled.

"Did you not think Enaila funny, Rand al'Thor?" Sulin was striding at his side. "You did not laugh. You never laugh. Sometimes I do not think you have a sense of humor."

Stopping dead, Rand rounded on them so suddenly that several reached for their veils and looked about for what had startled him. He cleared his throat. "An irascible old farmer named Hu discovered one morning that his best rooster had flown into a tall tree beside his farm pond and wouldn't come down, so he went to his neighbor, Wil, and asked for help. The men had never gotten along, but Wil finally agreed, so the two men went to the pond and began climbing the tree, Hu first. They meant to frighten the rooster out, you see, but the bird only kept flying higher, branch by branch. Then, just as Hu and the rooster reached almost the very top of the tree, with Wil right behind, there was a loud crack, the branch under Hu's feet broke away, and down he went into the pond, splashing water and mud everywhere. Wil scrambled down as fast as he could and reached out to Hu from the bank, but Hu just lay there on his back, sinking deeper into the mud until only his nose stuck out of the water. Another farmer had seen what happened, and he came running and pulled Hu out of the pond. 'Why didn't you take Wil's hand?' he asked Hu. 'You could have drowned.' 'Why should I take his hand now?' Hu grumped. 'I passed him just a moment ago in broad daylight, and he never spoke a word to me.'" He waited expectantly.

The Maidens exchanged blank looks. Finally Somara said, "What happened with the pond? Surely the water is the point of this story."

Throwing up his hands, Rand started for the red-striped pavilion again. Behind him he heard Liah say, "I think it was supposed to be a joke."

"How can we laugh when he doesn't know what happened to the water?" Maira said.

"It was the rooster," Enaila put in. "Wetlander humor is strange. I think it was something about the rooster."

He tried to stop listening.

The Defenders stiffened even more rigidly at his approach, if that was possible, and the two standing before the gold-fringed entry flaps stepped aside smoothly, pulling them open. Their eyes stared past the Aiel women.

Rand had led the Defenders of the Stone once, in a desperate fight against Myrddraal and Trollocs in the halls of the Stone of Tear itself. They would have followed anyone who stepped forward to lead that night, but it had been him.

"The Stone still stands," he said quietly. That had been their battlecry. Quick smiles flashed across some of those faces before they snapped back to wooden stillness. In Tear commoners did not smile at what a lord said unless absolutely sure the lord wanted them to smile.

Most of the Maidens squatted easily outside, spears across their knees, a posture they could hold for hours without moving a muscle, but Sulin followed Rand inside with Liah, Enaila and Jalani. If those Defenders had all been childhood friends of Rand, the Maidens would have been as cautious, but the men inside were not friends at all.

Colorful, fringed carpets floored the pavilion, Tairen mazes and elaborate scrollwork patterns, and in the middle sat a massive table, heavily carved and gilded and garishly inlaid with ivory and turquoise, that very likely needed a wagon all to itself for transport. The map-covered table separated a dozen sweaty-faced Tairens from half as many Cairhienin, who suffered even more from the heat, each man holding a golden goblet that self-effacing servants in black-and-gold livery kept filled with punch. All the nobles were in silk, but the clean-shaven Cairhienin, short, slight and pale compared to the men on the other side of the table, wore coats dark and sober except for bright horizontal slashes of their House colors across the chest, the number indicating the rank of the House, while the Tairens, most with beards oiled and trimmed to neat points, wore padded coats that were a garden of red and yellow and green and blue, satin and brocade, silver thread and thread-of-gold. The Cairhienin were solemn, even dour, most gaunt-cheeked and each with the front of his head shaved and powdered in what had once been the fashion only among soldiers in Cairhien, not lords. The Tairens smiled and sniffed scented handkerchiefs and pomanders that filled the pavilion with their heavy aromas. Beside the punch, the one thing they seemed to have in common was flat-eyed stares for the Maidens, followed hard by the pretense that the Aiel were invisible.

The High Lord Weiramon, oiled beard and hair streaked gray, bowed deeply. He was one of four High Lords there, in elaborately silver-worked boots, the others being unctuous, overly plump Sunamon; Tolmeran, whose iron-gray beard seemed a spear point on the shaft of his leanness; and potato-nosed Torean, looking more a farmer than most farmers—but Rand had given Weiramon the command. For the time being. The other eight were lesser lords, some clean-shaven though with no less gray in their hair; they were here through their oaths of fealty to one or another of the High Lords, yet they all had some experience of fighting.

Weiramon was not short for a Tairen, though Rand stood a head taller, but he always reminded Rand of a banty rooster, all puffed out chest and strutting. "All hail the Lord Dragon," he intoned, bowing, "soon to be Conqueror of Illian. All hail the Lord of the Morning." The rest were no more than a breath behind, Tairens spreading arms wide, Cairhienin touching hand to heart.

Rand grimaced. Lord of the Morning had been one of Lews Therin's titles, or so the fragmentary histories said. A great deal of knowledge had been lost in the Breaking of the World, and more went up in smoke during the Trolloc Wars and later during the War of the Hundred Years, yet surprising shards sometimes survived. He was surprised that Weiramon's use of the title had not brought Lews Therin's mad yammering. Come to think of it, Rand had not heard that voice since shouting at it. As far as he could recall that was the first time he had ever actually addressed the voice sharing his head. The possibilities behind that sent a chill down his back.

"My Lord Dragon?" Sunamon dry-washed fleshy hands. He seemed to be trying not to see the *shoufa* wrapped around Rand's head. "Are you—?" Swallowing his words, he put on an ingratiating smile; asking a potential madman—potential at the very least—whether he was well was perhaps not what he wanted to say. "Would the Lord Dragon like some punch? A Lodanaille vintage mixed with honeymelon." A lanky Lord of the Land sworn to Sunamon, a man named Estevan with a hard jaw and harder eyes, motioned sharply, and a servant darted for a golden goblet from a side table against the canvas wall; another hurried to fill it.

"No," Rand said, then more strongly, "No." He waved the servant away without really seeing him. Had Lews Therin actually *heard*? Somehow that made the whole thing worse. He did not want to think about the possibility now; he did not want to think of it at all. "As soon as Hearne and Simaan get here, almost everything will be in place." Those two High Lords should be arriving soon; they led the last large parties of Tairen soldiers to have left Cairhien, over a month ago. Of course, there were smaller groups on the way south, and more Cairhienin. More Aiel, too; the stream of Aiel would draw things out. "I want to see—"

Abruptly he realized the pavilion had gone very quiet, very still, except for Torean suddenly tipping back his head to gulp down the rest of his punch. He scrubbed a hand across his mouth and held out the goblet for more, but the servants seemed to be trying to fade into the red-striped walls. Sulin and the other three Maidens were suddenly up on their toes, ready to veil.

"What is it?" he asked quietly.

Weiramon hesitated. "Simaan and Hearne have . . . gone to Haddon Mirk. They are not coming." Torean snatched a worked-gold pitcher from one of the servants and filled his own goblet, slopping punch onto the carpets.

"And why have they gone there instead of coming here?" Rand did not raise his voice. He was sure he knew the answer. Those two—and five more High Lords besides—had been sent to Cairhien mainly to occupy minds set to plot against him.

Malicious smiles flickered among the Cairhienin, most half-hidden in quickly raised goblets. Semaradrid, the highest-ranking, slashes of color on his coat to below the waist, wore his sneer openly. A long-faced man with white streaks at his temples and dark eyes that could chip stone, he moved stiffly from wounds suffered in his land's civil war, but his limp came from fighting Tear. His main reason for cooperating with the Tairens was that they were not Aiel. But then, the Tairens' main reason for cooperating was that the Cairhienin were not.

It was one of Semaradrid's countrymen who answered, a young lord named Meneril who had half Semaradrid's stripes on his coat, and on his face a scar from the civil war that pulled up the left corner of his mouth in a permanent sardonic smile. "Treason, my Lord Dragon. Treason and rebellion."

Weiramon might have been hesitant about saying those words to Rand's face, yet he was not about to let an outlander speak for him. "Yes, rebellion," he said hurriedly, glaring at Meneril, but his usual pomposity quickly returned. "And not only them, my Lord Dragon. The High Lords Darlin and Tedosian and the High Lady Estanda are in it, too. Burn my soul, but they all put their names to a letter of defiance! It seems some twenty or thirty minor nobles are involved as well, some little more than jumped-up farmers. Light-blasted fools!"

Rand almost admired Darlin. The man had opposed him openly from the start, fleeing the Stone when it fell and trying to rouse resistance among the country nobles. Tedosian and Estanda were different. Like Hearne and Simaan they had bowed and smiled, called him Lord Dragon and plotted behind his back. Now his forbearance was repaid. No wonder Torean was spilling punch over his white-streaked beard as he drank; he had been involved deeply with Tedosian, and with Hearne and Simaan for that matter.

"They wrote more than defiance," Tolmeran said in a cold voice. "They wrote that you are a false Dragon, that the fall of the Stone and your drawing of The Sword That Is Not a Sword were some Aes Sedai trick." There was a hint of question in his tone; he had not been in the Stone of Tear the night it fell to Rand.

"What do you believe, Tolmeran?" It was a seductive claim in a land where channeling had been outlawed before Rand changed the law, and Aes Sedai were at best tolerated, where the Stone of Tear had stood invincible for close to three thousand years before Rand took it. And a familiar claim. Rand wondered whether he would find Whitecloaks when these rebels were laid by the heels. He thought Pedron Niall might be too smart to allow that.

"I think you drew *Callandor*," the lean man said after a moment. "I think you are the Dragon Reborn." Both times there was a slight emphasis on "think." Tolmeran had courage. Estevan nodded; slowly, but he did it. Another brave man.

Even they did not ask the obvious question, though, whether Rand wanted the rebels rooted out. Rand was not surprised. For one thing, Haddon Mirk was no easy place to root anyone out of, a huge tangled forest lacking villages, roads or even paths. In the choppy mountainous terrain along its northernmost edge a man would be lucky to cover a handful of miles in a long day, and armies could maneuver until their food ran out without finding one another. Perhaps more importantly, whoever asked that question could be suspected of volunteering to lead the expedition, and a volunteer could be suspected of wanting to join Darlin, not lay him by the heels. Tairens might not play *Daes Dae'mar*, the Game of Houses, the way Cairhienin did—that lot read volumes in a glance and heard more in a sentence than you ever meant to put there—but they still schemed and watched one another, suspicious of schemes, and they believed everyone else did the same.

Still, it suited Rand to leave the rebels where they were for now. All of his attention had to be on Illian; it had to be *seen* to be there. But he could not be seen as soft, either. These men would not turn on him, but Last Battle or no Last Battle, only two things kept the Tairens and Cairhienin from each other's throats. They preferred each other to Aielmen, if barely, and they feared the wrath of the Dragon Reborn. If they lost that fear, they would be trying to kill one another, and the Aiel, before you could say Jak o' the Mists.

"Does anyone speak in their defense?" he asked. "Does anyone know any mitigation?" If any did, they held their tongues; counting the servants, nearly two dozen pairs of eyes watched him, waiting. Perhaps the servants most intently of all. Sulin and the Maidens watched everything *except* him. "Their titles are forfeited, their lands and estates confiscated. Arrest warrants are to be signed for every man whose name is known. And every

woman." That could present a problem; the penalty in Tear for rebellion
was death. He had changed some laws, but not that one, and it was too late
now. "Publish it that whoever kills one of them will be absolved of murder,
and whoever aids them will be charged with treason. Any who surrender
will be spared their lives," which might solve the difficulty of Estanda—he
would not order a woman executed—if he could work how to manage it,
"but those who persist will hang."

The nobles shifted uneasily and exchanged glances, whether Tairen or
Cairhienin. Blood drained from more than one face. They had certainly expected the death sentences—there could be no less for rebellion, and with
war in the offing—but the stripping of titles plainly shocked them. Despite all the laws Rand had changed in both lands, despite lords hauled
before magistrates and hanged for murder or fined for assault, they still
thought there was some difference bred in the bone, some natural order
that made them lions by right and commoners sheep. A High Lord who
went to the gibbet died a High Lord, but Darlin and the others would die
peasants in these men's eyes, a much worse fate than the dying itself. The
servants remained poised with their pitchers, waiting to refill any goblet
that had to be tilted very far in drinking. Features as expressionless as ever,
there seemed to be a cheerfulness in some of those eyes not there before.

"Now that that's settled," Rand said, dragging off the *shoufa* as he went
to the table, "let's see the maps. Sammael is more important than a handful of fools rotting in Haddon Mirk." He hoped they did rot. Burn them!

Weiramon's mouth tightened, and Tolmeran quickly smoothed out a
frown. Sunamon's face was so smooth it might have been a mask. The other
Tairens looked as doubtful, and the Cairhienin as well, though Semaradrid
hid it well. Some had seen Myrddraal and Trollocs during that attack on
the Stone, and some had seen his duel with Sammael at Cairhien, yet they
thought his claim the Forsaken were loose a symptom of insanity. He had
heard whispers that he had wrought all the destruction at Cairhien himself, striking out maniacally at friend and foe alike. Going by Liah's stony
face, one of them was going to get a Maiden's spear through him if they
did not guard those looks.

They gathered around the table, though, as he tossed down the *shoufa*
and rummaged through the maps scattered in layers. Bashere was right;
men would follow madmen who won. So long as they won. Just as he
found the map he wanted, a detailed drawing of the eastern end of Illian,
the Aiel chiefs arrived.

Bruan of the Nakai Aiel was first to enter, followed closely by Jheran of the Shaarad, Dhearic of the Reyn, Han of the Tomanelle, and Erim of the Chareen, each acknowledging the nods of Sulin and the three Maidens. Bruan, a massive man with sad gray eyes, really was the leader of the five clans Rand had sent south so far. None of the others objected; Bruan's oddly placid manner belied his battle skills. Clothed in the *cadin'sor, shoufa* hanging loose about their necks, they were unarmed except for their heavy belt knives, but then, an Aiel was hardly unarmed even when he had only his hands and feet.

The Cairhienin simply pretended they were not there, but the Tairens made a point of sneering and sniffing ostentatiously at their pomanders and scented handkerchiefs. Tear had lost only the Stone to the Aiel, and that with the aid of the Dragon Reborn, as they believed—or of Aes Sedai—but Cairhien had twice been ravaged by them, twice defeated and humiliated.

Except for Han, the Aiel ignored them all. Han, white-haired and with a face like creased leather, glared murderously. He was a prickly man at best, and it might not have helped that some of the Tairens were as tall as he. Han was short for an Aiel—which meant well above average for a wetlander—and as touchy about it as Enaila. And of course, Aiel despised "treekillers," one of their names for Cairhienin, beyond any other wetlanders. Their other name for them was "oathbreakers."

"The Illianers," Rand said firmly, smoothing the map out. He used the Dragon Scepter to hold down one end and a gold-mounted inkpot and matching sand-bowl for the other. He did not need these men to start killing each other. He did not think they would—while he was there, at least. In stories allies eventually came to trust and like one another; he doubted these men ever would.

The rolling Plains of Maredo extended a little distance into Illian, giving way to forested hills well short of the Manetherendrelle, and the River Shal branching off from it. Five inked crosses about ten miles apart marked the eastern edge of those hills. The Doirlon Hills.

Rand put his finger on the middle cross. "Are you sure Sammael has not added any new camps?" A slight grimace on Weiramon's face made him snap irritably, "Lord Brend, if you prefer, then, or the Council of Nine, or Mattin Stepaneos den Balgar, if you want the king himself. Are they still like this?"

"Our scouts say so," Jheran said calmly. Slender as a blade is slender, his light brown hair heavily streaked with gray, he was always calm now that the Shaarad's four-hundred-year blood feud with the Goshien Aiel had ended with Rand's coming. "*Sovin Nai* and *Duadhe Mahdi'in* keep a close watch." He nodded slightly in satisfaction, and so did Dhearic. Jheran had been *Sovin Nai*, a Knife Hand, before becoming chief, and Dhearic *Duadhe Mahdi'in*, a Water Seeker. "We know any changes in five days by runners."

"My scouts believe they are," Weiramon said as if Jheran had not spoken. "I send a new troop every week. It takes a full month for them to come and go, but I assure you, I am as up-to-date as the distance allows."

The Aiel's faces might have been carved from stone.

Rand ignored the interplay. He had tried before to hammer shut the gaps between Tairen, Cairhienin and Aiel, and they always sprang apart as soon as his back turned. It was useless effort.

As for the camps. . . . He knew there were still only five; he had visited them, in a manner of speaking. There was a . . . place . . . that he knew how to enter, a strange, unpeopled reflection of the real world, and he had walked the wooden walls of those massive hillforts there. He knew the answers to almost every question he intended to ask, but he was juggling plans within plans like a gleeman juggling fire. "And Sammael is still bringing more men up?" This time he emphasized the name. The Aiel's expressions did not change—if the Forsaken were loose, the Forsaken were loose; the world had to be faced as it was, not as you wished it to be—but the others darted those quick, worried glances at him. They had to get used to it sooner or later. They had to believe sooner or later.

"Every man in Illian who can hold a spear without tripping over it, or so it seems," Tolmeran said with a glum expression. He was as eager to fight the Illianers as any Tairen—the two nations had hated each other since they were wrested from the wreckage of Artur Hawkwing's empire; their history was one of wars fought on the slightest excuse—but he seemed a little less likely than the other High Lords to think every battle could be won by one good charge. "Every scout that makes it back reports the camps larger, with more formidable defenses."

"We should move now, my Lord Dragon," Weiramon said forcefully. "The Light burn my soul, I can catch the Illianers with their breeches around their ankles. They've tied themselves down. Why, they hardly have any horse at all! I'll crush them in detail, and the way will be open to the city." In Illian, as in Tear and Cairhien, "the city" was the city that had given the nation its name. "Burn my eyes, I will put your banner over Illian in a month, my Lord Dragon. Two at most." Glancing at the Cairhienin, he added as if the words were being pulled from him, "Semaradrid and I will." Semaradrid bowed slightly. Very slightly.

"No," Rand said curtly. Weiramon's was a plan for disaster. A good two hundred and fifty miles lay between the camp and Sammael's great hillforts across a plain of grass where a fifty-foot rise was considered a tall hill and a thicket of two hides a forest. Sammael had scouts, too; any rat or raven could be one of Sammael's scouts. Two hundred and fifty miles. Twelve or thirteen days for the Tairens and Cairhienin, with luck. The Aiel could make it in perhaps five, if they pushed—a lone scout or two moved faster than an army, even among Aiel—but they were no part of Weiramon's design. Long before Weiramon reached the Doirlon Hills, Sammael would be ready to crush the Tairen, not the other way around. A fool plan. Even more foolish than the one Rand had given them. "I've given your orders. You hold here until Mat arrives to take command, and even then, no one moves a foot until I think I have enough numbers here. There are more men on their way, Tairens, Cairhienin, Aiel. I mean to smash Sammael, Weiramon. Smash him forever, and bring Illian under the Dragon Banner." That much was true. "I only wish I could be with you, but Andor requires my attention yet."

Weiramon's face became sour stone, Semaradrid's grimace should have turned the wine in his punch to vinegar, and Tolmeran wore such a lack of expression that his disapproval was plain as a fist in the nose. In Semaradrid's case, it was the delay that worried. He had pointed out more than once that if every day brought more men to the camp here, it also brought more to the forts in Illian. No doubt Weiramon's plan was the result of his urgings, though he would have made a better. Tolmeran's doubts centered on Mat. Despite what he had heard from Cairhienin of Mat's skill in battle, Tolmeran thought it flattery from fools for a country man who happened to be a friend of the Dragon Reborn. They were honest objections, and Semaradrid's even had validity—if the plan they had been given had been more than another screen. It was unlikely Sammael depended entirely on rats and ravens for his spying. Rand expected there were human spies in the camp for other Forsaken as well, and probably for the Aes Sedai.

"It shall be as you say, my Lord Dragon," Weiramon said heavily. The man was brave enough when it came to battle, but a pure blind idiot unable to think beyond the glory of the charge, his hatred of Illianers, his contempt for Cairhienin and Aiel "savages." Rand was sure Weiramon was exactly the man he needed. Tolmeran and Semaradrid would not move too soon so long as Weiramon held the command.

For a long while further they talked and Rand listened, asking occasional questions. There was no more opposition, no more suggestions that the attack be made now, no discussion of the attack at all. What Rand questioned Weiramon and the others about was wagons, wagons and what was in them. The Plains of Maredo had few villages and far between, no city except Far Madding in the north, and barely enough farmland to feed the people already there. A huge army would need a constant stream of wagons out of Tear bringing everything from flour for bread to nails for horseshoes. Except for Tolmeran, the High Lords were of the opinion that the army could carry what it needed to cross the plain and then could live off Illian; there seemed to be a certain relish in the thought of stripping their ancient enemy's lands to the ground like a swarm of locusts. The Cairhienin had a different opinion, especially Semaradrid and Meneril. Not only commoners had gone hungry during Cairhien's civil war and the Shaido's siege of their capital; their hollow cheeks spoke eloquently of that. Illian was a fat land, and even the Doirlon Hills held farms and vineyards, but Semaradrid and Meneril did not want to trust their soldiers' bellies to uncertain forage if there was another way. As for Rand, he did not want Illian ravaged any more than could not be avoided.

He did not really press anyone. Sunamon assured him the wagons were being assembled, and he had long since learned his lesson about telling Rand one thing and doing another. Supplies were being gathered all across Tear, despite Weiramon's grimaces of impatience with the whole notion and Torean's sweaty mutters about the expense. The important thing, though, was that the plan he had given them was going forward—and would be seen to be going forward.

Leavetaking involved more grandiose prattle and elaborate bows while he rewound the *shoufa* around his head and took up the Dragon Scepter again, with halfhearted invitations to stay for a banquet and equally insincere offers to attend him to his departure if he could not remain to eat the feast they would have prepared. Tairen or Cairhienin, they avoided the company of the Dragon Reborn as much as they safely could without losing his favor, while pretending that they did no such thing. Most especially they wanted to be elsewhere when he channeled. They did escort him to the entrance and a few steps outside, of course, but Sunamon sighed audibly when he left them, and Rand heard Torean actually giggling in relief.

The Aiel chiefs went with Rand silently, and the Maidens outside joined Sulin and the other three in making a ring around the six men as they started toward the green-striped tent. This time there were only a few cheers, and the chiefs said nothing. They had said almost as little back in the pavilion. When Rand commented on it, Dhearic said, "These wetlanders do not want to hear us." He was a husky man, within a finger width of Rand's height, with a big nose and paler streaks prominent in his golden hair. His blue eyes were filled with contempt. "They hear only the wind."

"Did they tell you of those who rebel against you?" Erim asked. Taller than Dhearic, he had a pugnacious jaw and almost as much white as red in his hair.

"They did," Rand said, and Han frowned at him.

"If you are sending these Tairens after their own kind, it is a mistake. Even if they could be trusted, I do not think they could do it. Send the spears. One clan would be enough and more."

Rand shook his head. "Darlin and his rebels can wait. Sammael is what's important."

"Then let us go to Illian now," Jheran said. "Forget these wetlanders, Rand al'Thor. Already there are nearly two hundred thousand spears gathered here. We can destroy the Illianers before Weiramon Saniago and Semaradrid Maravin can be halfway there."

For a moment Rand squeezed his eyes shut. Was everyone going to argue with him? These were not men who would give way at a frown from the Dragon Reborn. The Dragon Reborn was only a wetlander prophecy; they followed He Who Comes With the Dawn, the *Car'a'carn*, and as he had long since grown tired of hearing, even the *Car'a'carn* was not a king. "I want your word to stay here until Mat tells you to move. A promise from each of you."

"We will stay, Rand al'Thor." Bruan's deceptively mild voice had a tight edge. The others' agreements came in harder voices, but they came.

"But it is wasting time," Han added, twisting his mouth. "May I never know shade if it is not." Jheran and Erim nodded.

Rand had not expected them to give in so quickly. "Now and then you have to waste time to save it," he said, and Han snorted.

Back at the green-striped tent the Thunder Walkers had lifted up the sides on poles, letting the breeze blow through the shaded interior. Hot and dry as it was, the Aiel seemed to find it refreshing. Rand did not think he sweated a drop less than he had in the sun. He pulled off the *shoufa* as he settled to the layered rugs with Bruan and the other chiefs facing him. The Maidens added their number to the Thunder Walkers around the tent; every so often banter between them drifted in, and laughter at it. This time Leiran seemed to be getting the better of it; at least, the Maidens rattled spears against bucklers at him twice. Rand understood almost none of it.

Thumbing his short-stemmed pipe full of tabac, he passed the goatskin pouch around for the chiefs to fill their pipes—he had found a small cask of good Two Rivers leaf in Caemlyn—then channeled his alight while they sent a Thunder Walker for a burning twig from one of the cookfires. When all the pipes were lit they settled down to talk, puffing contentedly.

The conversation lasted fully as long as his discussion with the lords, not because there was that much to talk about but because Rand had talked alone with the wetlanders. Aiel were touchy about honor; their lives were governed by *ji'e'toh*, honor and obligation, with rules as complex and odd as their humor. They talked of the Aiel still on their way down from Cairhien, of when Mat would arrive and of what if anything should be done about the Shaido. They talked about hunting and women and whether brandy was as good as *oosquai*, and about humor. Even patient Bruan finally spread his hands in surrender and gave up trying to explain Aiel jokes. What under the Light was funny about a woman stabbing her husband by accident, whatever the circumstances, or a man ending up married to the sister of the woman he wanted to marry? Han grumped and snorted and refused to believe Rand did not understand; *he* laughed so hard at the one about the stabbing that he nearly fell over. The one thing they did not talk about was the coming war against Illian.

When they left, Rand stood squinting at the sun, halfway down toward the horizon. Han was repeating the story about the stabbing, and the departing chiefs chuckled over it again. Tapping his pipe out on the heel of his palm, Rand ground the dottle underfoot in the dust. There was still time to return to Caemlyn and meet Bashere, but he went back inside the tent and sat watching the sun sink. As it touched the horizon, turning red as blood, Enaila and Somara brought him a plate of mutton stew heaped high enough for two men, a round loaf of bread and a pitcher of mint tea that had been set in a bucket of water to cool.

"You do not eat enough," Somara said, trying to smooth his hair before he moved his head away.

Enaila eyed him. "If you did not avoid Aviendha so, she would see that you ate."

"He attracts her interest, then runs from her," Somara muttered. "You must attract her again. Why do you not offer to wash her hair?"

"He should not be *that* forward," Enaila said firmly. "Asking to brush her hair will be more than enough. He does not want her to think him forward."

Somara sniffed. "She will not think he is forward when he runs from her. You can be too modest, Rand al'Thor."

"You do realize that neither of you is my mother, don't you?"

The two *cadin'sor*-clad women looked at each other in confusion. "Do you think this is another wetlander joke?" Enaila asked, and Somara shrugged.

"I do not know. He does not look amused." She patted Rand on the back. "I am sure it was a good joke, but you must explain it to us."

Rand suffered in silence, grinding his teeth, while they watched him eat. They literally watched every spoonful. Matters became no better when they left with his plate and Sulin joined him. Sulin had some blunt, and most improper, advice on how he could reattract Aviendha's notice; among the Aiel, it was the sort of thing a first-sister might do for a first-brother.

"You must be decently modest in her eyes," the white-haired Maiden told him, "but not so modest she thinks you boring. Ask her to scrape your back in the sweat tent, but shyly, with your eyes downcast. When you undress for bed, let yourself dance as if life pleases you, then apologize when you suddenly realize she is there and put yourself straight into your blankets. Can you blush?"

A great deal of suffering in silence. The Maidens knew too much, and not enough.

When they returned to Caemlyn, well after the sun had gone down, Rand crept into his apartment with his boots in his hands, fumbling his way through the anteroom into his bedchamber in the dark. Even if he had not known Aviendha would be there, already on her pallet on the floor by the wall, he would have felt her presence. In the stillness of the night, he could hear her breathing. For once it seemed he had managed to wait long enough for her to fall asleep. He had tried to stop this, but Aviendha paid him no mind and the Maidens laughed at his "shyness" and "modesty." Good things in a man when alone, they agreed, so long as not carried too far.

He climbed into his bed with a sense of relief that Aviendha was already asleep—and some disgruntlement that he dared not light a lamp to wash—and she turned over on her pallet. Very likely she had been awake all along.

"Sleep well and wake," was all she said.

Thinking what idiocy it was to feel this sudden contentment because a woman he wanted to avoid told him good night, he stuffed a goose-down pillow beneath his head. Aviendha probably thought this the most marvelous joke; taunting was almost an art among Aiel, and the nearer it came to bringing blood, the better. Sleep began to come, and his last conscious thought was that he had a huge joke of his own, though only he and Mat and Bashere knew it yet. Sammael had no sense of humor at all, but that great hammer of an army waiting in Tear was the biggest joke the world had ever seen. With any luck, Sammael would be dead before he knew he should laugh.

CHAPTER
5

A Different Dance

The Golden Stag lived up to its name in most ways. Polished tables and benches with rose-carved legs dotted the large common room. One white-aproned serving girl did nothing but sweep the white stone floor. Blue-and-gold scroll-work made a broad painted band on the plaster walls just below the high beamed ceiling. The fireplaces were well-dressed stone, their hearths decorated with a few evergreen branches, and a stag chiseled above each lintel supporting a winecup in branching antlers. A tall clock with a little gilding stood on one mantel. A knot of musicians played on a small dais at the back, two perspiring men in their shirtsleeves with keening flutes, a pair plucking nine-string bitterns, and a red-faced woman in a blue-striped dress working tiny wooden hammers across a dulcimer on thin legs. More than a dozen serving maids scurried in and out, stepping quickly in their aprons and pale blue dresses. Most were pretty, though some carried nearly as many years as Mistress Daelvin, the round little innkeeper with her wispy gray bun at the nape of her neck. Just the sort of place Mat liked; it fairly oozed comfort and an air of money. He had chosen it because it sat nearly dead center in the town, but the other had not hurt.

Not everything fitted the second-best inn in Maerone, of course. The smells from the kitchen were mutton and turnips again, and the inevitable spicy barley soup, and they mingled with the smell of dust and horses from outside. Well, food was a problem in a town jammed with refugees and soldiers, and more in camps all around it. Men's voices singing raucous marching songs came and went in the street, the sounds of boots and horses' hooves and men cursing the heat. The common room was hot, too, without a breath of air stirring; had the windows been swung out, dust would soon have coated everything inside, and it still would not have done much for the heat inside. Maerone was a griddle.

As far as Mat could see, the whole bloody world was drying up, and he did not want to think about why. He wished he could forget the heat, forget why he was in Maerone, forget everything. His good green coat, gold-embroidered on collar and cuffs, was undone, his fine linen shirt unlaced, yet he still sweated like a horse. It might have helped to remove the black silk scarf looped around his neck, but he seldom did where anyone could see. Draining the last of his wine, he set the burnished pewter cup on the table at his elbow and picked up his broad-brimmed hat to fan himself. Whatever he drank no sooner went in than he sweated it out.

When he chose to stay at the Golden Stag, the lords and officers of the Band of the Red Hand followed his lead, which meant all others stayed clear. That usually did not displease Mistress Daelvin. She could have rented out every bed five times over just among the lords and lordlings of the Band, and that sort paid well, had few fights and usually took them outside before spilling blood. This midday, however, only nine or ten men occupied the tables, and she occasionally blinked at the empty benches, patted at her bun and sighed; she would not sell much wine before evening. A large part of her profits came from wine. The musicians played vigorously, though. A handful of lords pleased with the music—anyone with gold deserved a "my Lord" so far as they were concerned—could be more generous than a room full of common soldiers.

Unfortunately for the musicians' purses, Mat was the only man listening, and he winced at every third note. It really was not their fault; the music sounded fine if you did not know what you were listening to. Mat did—he had taught it to them, clapping the beat and humming—but no one else had heard that tune in more than two thousand years. The best to be said was that they had the rhythms right.

A bit of conversation caught his ear. Tossing his hat down, he waved his cup to signal for more wine and leaned across his table toward the three men drinking around the next. "What was that?"

"We are trying to figure out how to win some of our money back from you," Talmanes said, unsmiling over his winecup. He was not upset. Only

a few years older than Mat's twenty, and a head shorter, Talmanes seldom
smiled. The man always made Mat think of a compressed spring. "No one
can beat you at cards." The commander of half the Band's cavalry, he was a
lord here in Cairhien, but the front of his head was shaved and powdered,
though sweat had washed some of it away. A good many younger Cairhienin
lords had taken up soldiers' styles. Talmanes' coat was plain, too, without a
noble's slashes of color, although he was entitled to quite a few.

"Not so," Mat protested. True, when his luck was in, it was perfect, but
it ran in cycles, especially with things that had as much order as a deck of
cards. "Blood and ashes! You won fifty crowns from me last week." Fifty
crowns; a year or so ago, he would have turned backflips at winning one
crown, and wept at the thought of losing one. A year or so ago, he had not
had one to lose.

"How many hundred behind does that leave me?" Talmanes asked
dryly. "I want a chance to win some back." If he ever did start winning
against Mat with any consistency, he would start worrying too. Like most
of the Band, he took Mat's luck as a talisman.

"Dice are no bloody good," Daerid said. Commander of the Band's
foot, he drank thirstily and ignored a grimace only half-hidden behind
Nalesean's oiled beard. Most nobles Mat had met thought dice common, fit
only for peasants. "I have never seen you end the day behind at dice. It has
to be something you have no control over, no hand in, if you understand."

Just a little taller than his fellow Cairhienin Talmanes, Daerid was a
good fifteen years older, his nose broken more than once and three white
scars crisscrossing his face. The only one of the three not nobly born, he
wore the front of his head shaved and powdered, too; Daerid had been a
soldier all his life.

"We thought horses," Nalesean put in, gesturing with his pewter cup.
A blocky man, taller than either of the Cairhienin, he led the other half of
the cavalry in the Band. Given the heat, Mat often wondered why he kept
his luxuriant black beard, but he trimmed it every morning to keep the
point sharp. And where Daerid and Talmanes wore their plain gray coats
hanging open, Nalesean had his—green silk with those padded Tairen
sleeves striped and cuffed in gold satin—buttoned to the neck. His face
glistened with sweat that he ignored. "Burn my soul, but your luck holds
hard with battle and cards. And dice," he added with another grimace at
Daerid. "But in horse racing, it's all the horse."

Mat smiled and propped his elbows on the table. "Find yourself a good
horse, and we'll see." His luck might not affect a horse race—aside from

dice and cards and the like, he could never be sure what it would touch or when—but he had grown up watching his father trade horseflesh, and his own eye for a horse was fairly sharp.

"Do you want this wine, or not? I cannot pour it if I cannot reach your cup."

Mat glanced over his shoulder. The serving maid behind him with a polished pewter pitcher was short and slim, a dark-eyed, pale-cheeked beauty with black curls nestling on her shoulders. And that precise, musical Cairhienin accent made her voice into chimes. He had had his eye on Betse Silvin since the first day he walked into the Golden Stag, but this was his first chance to speak to her; there were always five things that needed doing immediately and ten that should have been done yesterday. The other men had already buried their faces in their wine, leaving him as alone with the woman as they could without walking out. They had manners, even the two nobles.

Grinning, Mat swung his legs over the bench and held out his cup for her to fill. "Thank you, Betse," he said, and she bobbed a curtsy. When he asked her to pour one for herself and join him, however, she set the pitcher on the table, folded her arms and tilted her head to one side, eyeing him up and down.

"I hardly think Mistress Daelvin would like that. Oh, no, I do not think she would. Are you a lord? They all seem to jump for you, but no one calls you 'my Lord.' They barely even bow; just the commoners."

Mat's eyebrows shot up. "No," he said, more curtly than he wished, "I am *not* a lord." Rand could let people run around calling him Lord Dragon and the like, but that was not for Matrim Cauthon. No, indeed. Taking a deep breath, he put his grin back on. Some women tried to nudge a man off balance, but it was a dance he was good at. "Just call me Mat, Betse. I'm sure Mistress Daelvin won't mind if you just sit with me."

"Oh, yes, she would. But I suppose I can talk a bit; you must be almost a lord. Why are you wearing that in this heat?" Leaning forward, she pushed his scarf down with a finger. He had not been paying attention, and had let it slip a little. "What is this?" She ran her finger along the pale thickened ridge that circled his neck. "Did someone try to hang you? Why? You are too young to be a hardened scofflaw." He pulled his head back and hastily retied the black silk to hide his scar, but Betse was not put off. Her hand dipped into the unlaced front of his shirt to pull up the silver foxhead medallion he wore on a leather thong. "Was it for stealing this? It looks valuable; is it valuable?" Mat snatched the medallion away, stuffed it back where it belonged. The woman hardly drew breath, certainly not enough for him to get a word in. He heard Nalesean and Daerid chuckling behind him, and his face darkened. Sometimes his luck with gambling was stood on its head with women, and they always found it funny. "No, they would not have let you keep it if you stole it, would they?" Betse chattered on. "And if you are almost a lord, I suppose you can own things like that. Perhaps it was because you knew too much. You look a young man who knows a great deal. Or thinks he does." She smiled one of those shrewd little smiles that women wore when they wanted to fuddle a man. It seldom meant they knew anything, but they could make you think they did. "Did they try to hang you for thinking you knew too much? Or was it for pretending to be a lord? Are you sure you are not a lord?"

Daerid and Nalesean were laughing right out, now, and even Talmanes was chuckling, though they tried to pretend it was about something else. Daerid wheezingly interjected some tale about a man falling off a horse whenever he had breath enough, but there was nothing funny in the bits Mat heard.

He kept his grin on, though. He was not going to be routed even if she *could* talk faster than he could run. She was very pretty, and he had spent the last few weeks talking to the likes of Daerid and worse, sweaty men who sometimes forgot to shave and too often had no chance to bathe. Perspiration beaded Betse's cheeks, but she gave off a faint smell of lavender-scented soap. "Actually, I got that scratch for knowing too little," he said lightly. Women always liked it when you played down your scars; the Light knew he was growing enough of them. "I know too much now, but too little then. You could say I was hanged for knowledge."

Shaking her head, Betse pursed her lips. "That sounds like it is supposed to be witty, Mat. Lordlings say witty things all the time, but you say you are not a lord. Besides, I am a simple woman; wit goes right over my head. I think simple words are best. Since you are not a lord, you should speak simply, or else some might think you were playing at being a lord. No woman likes a man pretending to be what he is not. Maybe you could explain what you were trying to say?"

Maintaining his smile was an effort. Bandying words with her was not going at all the way he wanted. He could not tell whether she was a complete nit or just managing to make him trip over his ears trying to keep up. Either way, she was still pretty, and she still smelled of lavender, not sweat. Daerid and Nalesean seemed to be choking to death. Talmanes was humming "A Frog on the Ice." So he was skidding about with his feet in the air, was he?

Mat put down his winecup and rose, bowing over Betse's hand. "I am who I am and no more, but your face drives words right out my head." That made her blink; whatever they said, women always like flowery talk. "Will you dance?"

Not waiting for an answer, he led her toward where a clear floor stretched the length of the common room through the tables. With luck, dancing would slow her tongue a little, and he was lucky, after all. Besides, he had never heard of a woman whose heart was not softened by dancing. *Dance with her, and she will forgive much; dance well, and she will forgive anything.* That was a very old saying. Very old.

Betse hung back, biting her lip and looking for Mistress Daelvin, but the plump little innkeeper only smiled and waved Betse on, then patted ineffectually at the tendrils escaping her bun and went back to chivvying the other serving maids as though the tables were full. Mistress Daelvin would have been all over any man she thought was behaving improperly— despite her placid appearance, she kept a short cudgel in her skirts and sometimes used it; Nalesean still eyed her carefully when she came close— but if a free-spending man wanted a dance, what was the harm in that? He held Betse's hands outstretched to either side. There should be just enough room between the tables. The musicians began to play louder, if no better.

"Follow me," he told her. "The steps are simple to start." In time to the music he began, dip and a gliding sidestep to the right, left foot sliding after. Dip and a gliding step and slide, with arms outstretched.

Betse caught on quickly, and she was light on her feet. When they reached the musicians, he smoothly lifted her hands overhead and spun himself and her back to back. Then it was dip and sidestep, twirl face-to-face, dip, sidestep and twirl, again and again, all the way back to where they began. She fell into that just as swiftly, smiling up at him in delight whenever the turns allowed. She truly was pretty.

"A little more complicated now," he murmured, turning so they faced the musicians side by side, wrists crossed and hands linked in front of them. Right knee up, slight kick left, then glide forward and right. Left knee up, slight kick right, then glide forward and left. Betse laughed as they wove their way to the performers once more. The steps became more intricate with each passage, but she needed only one demonstration to match him, light as a feather in his hands with each twist and turn and spin. Best of all, she did not say a word.

The music caught him up, missed notes and all, and the pattern dance, and memories floated in his head as they floated back and forth across the floor. In memory he was a head taller, with long golden mustaches and blue eyes. He wore a red-sashed coat of amber silk with a ruff of finest Barsine lace and yellow sapphire studs from Aramaelle on his chest, and he danced with a darkly beautiful emissary of the Atha'an Miere, the Sea Folk. The fine gold chain linking her nose ring to one of her multitude of earrings held tiny medallions that identified her as Wavemistress of Clan Shodin. He did not care how powerful she was; that was for the king to worry over, not a middling lord. She was beautiful and light in his arms, and they danced beneath the great crystal dome at the court of Shaemal, when all the world envied Coremanda's splendor and might. Other memories flitted around the edges, sparking off bits of that remembered dance. The morrow would bring news of increasingly heavy Trolloc raids out of the Great Blight, and another month word that Barsine of the golden spires had been ravaged and burned and the Trolloc hordes were sweeping south. So would begin what later would be called the Trolloc Wars, though none gave it that name to begin, three hundred years and more of all but unbroken battle, blood, fire and ruin before the Trollocs were driven back, the Dreadlords hunted down. So would begin the fall of Coremanda, with all its wealth and power, and Essenia, with its philosophers and famed seats of learning, of Manetheren and Eharon and all of the Ten Nations, smashed even in victory to rubble from which other lands would rise, lands that barely remembered the Ten Nations as more than myths of a happier time. But that lay ahead, and he banished those memories in the pleasure of this one. Tonight he danced the pattern dance with. . . .

He blinked, for an instant startled by sunlight streaming through the windows and the fair face beaming up at him through a sheen of perspiration. Very nearly he fumbled the complex interweaving of his feet with Betse's as they whirled down the floor, but he caught himself before tripping her, the steps coming instinctively. This dance was his as surely as those memories were, borrowed or stolen, but so seamlessly woven into those he really had lived that he could no longer tell the difference without thinking. All his, now, filling holes in his own memories; he might as well have lived them all.

It had been true, what he told her about the scar on his neck. Hanged for knowledge, and for lack of it. Twice he had stepped through a *ter'angreal* like a bull-goose fool, a country idiot thinking it simple as a walk across the meadow. Well, almost as simple. The results only hardened his mistrust of anything to do with the One Power. The first time he had been told he was fated to die and live again, among other things he did not want to hear. Some of those other things had set him on the path to his second journey through a *ter'angreal*, and that had led to him having a rope tied around his neck.

A series of steps, each taken for good cause or pure necessity, each seeming so reasonable at the time, and each leading to things he had never imagined. He always seemed to find himself caught in that sort of dance. He had been dead for sure until Rand cut him down and revived him. For the hundredth time he remade a promise to himself. From now on he was going to watch where he put his feet. No more jumping into things without thinking what might come of it.

In truth, he had gained more than the scar that day. The silver foxhead for one, its single eye shaded to look like the ancient symbol of Aes Sedai. Sometimes he laughed so hard over that medallion that his ribs hurt. He did not trust any Aes Sedai, so he even bathed and slept with the thing around his neck. The world was a funny place—funny peculiar, usually.

Another gain really had been knowledge, if unwanted knowledge. Slices of other men's lives packed his head now, thousands of them, sometimes only a few hours, sometimes years altogether though in patches, memories of courts and combats stretching for well over a thousand years, from long before the Trolloc Wars to the final battle of Artur Hawkwing's rise. All his now, or they might as well be.

Nalesean and Daerid and Talmanes were clapping to the music, and the other men scattered around the tables too. Men of the Band of the Red Hand, urging their commander on in his dance. Light but that name made Mat cringe inside. It had belonged to a legendary band of heroes who died trying to save Manetheren. Not a man who rode or marched behind the Band's banner but thought they would end up in the legends too. Mistress Daelvin was clapping as well, and the rest of the maids had stopped to watch.

Those other men's memories were why the Band followed Mat, though they did not know. Because his head held memories of more battles and campaigns than a hundred men could have faced. Whether he had been on the winning side or the losing, he remembered how those battles were won or lost, and it took only a little wit to translate that into winning for the Band. So far it had, at least. When he could find no way to avoid the fighting.

More than once he had wished those bits of other men were out of his head. Without them, he would not be where he was, commanding nearly six thousand soldiers and more wanting to join every day, about to lead them south and take command of the bloody invasion of a land controlled by one of the bloody Forsaken. He was no hero, and did not want to be one. Heroes had a bad habit of getting killed. When you were a hero, it was toss the dog a bone and shove him into a corner out of the way, unless it was promise the dog a bone and send him out to hunt again. The same for soldiers, for that matter.

On the other hand, without those memories he would not have six thousand soldiers around him. He would stand alone, *ta'veren* and tied to the Dragon Reborn, a naked target and known to the Forsaken. Some of them apparently knew entirely too much about Mat Cauthon. Moiraine had claimed he was important, that maybe Rand needed him and Perrin both to win the Last Battle. If she had been right, he would do what he had to—he would; he just had to get used to the idea—but he was not about to be a bloody hero. If he could just figure out what to do about the bloody Horn of Valere. . . . Offering up a small prayer for Moiraine's soul, he hoped she had been wrong.

He and Betse reached the end of the clear space for the final time, and she collapsed against his chest laughing when he stopped. "Oh, that was wonderful. I felt like I was in a royal palace somewhere. Can we do it again? Oh, can we? Can we?" Mistress Daelvin applauded for a moment, then realized the other serving maids were standing about and rounded on them, sending them scurrying like chickens with vigorous waves of her arms.

"Does 'Daughter of the Nine Moons' mean anything to you?" The words just popped out. It was thinking about those *ter'angreal* that did it. Wherever he found the Daughter of the Nine Moons—*Please, Light, let it be a long time yet!* It was a fervent thought—wherever he found her, it would not be serving table at a small-town inn crammed full of soldiers and refugees. Then again, who could say when it came to prophecy? It had been prophecy, in a way. To die and live again. To marry the Daughter of the Nine Moons. To give up half the light of the world to save the world, whatever that meant. He *had* died, after all, swinging on that rope. If that was true, the rest had to be. No way out of that.

"Daughter of the Nine Moons?" Betse said breathlessly. Lack of breath did not slow her down. "Is it an inn? A tavern? Not here in Maerone, I know that. Maybe across the river in Aringill? I have never been to—"

Mat laid a finger across her lips. "It doesn't matter. Let's dance another dance." A country dance this time; something from the here and now, with no memories but his attached to it. Only, he really did have to think to tell them apart now.

A throat clearing made him glance over his shoulder, and he sighed at the sight of Edorion standing in the doorway, steel-backed gauntlets tucked behind his sword belt and helmet beneath his arm. The young Tairen lord had been a plump, pink-cheeked man when Mat gambled with him in the Stone of Tear, but he had grown harder and sun-dark since coming north. The rimmed helmet bore no plumes now, and chips and dents marred the once ornate gilding on his breastplate. His puffy-sleeved coat was blue striped with black, but showing wear.

"You told me to remind you of your rounds at this hour." Edorion coughed into his fist; he ostentatiously did not glance at Betse. "But I could come back later if you wish."

"I'll come now," Mat told him. It was important to make rounds every day, inspect something different every day; those other men's memories told him that, and he had come to trust them about things like this. If he was stuck in this job, he might as well try to do it right. Doing it right might keep him alive. Besides, Betse had drawn away from him and was trying to pat sweat from her face with her apron and straighten her hair at the same time. The euphoria was fading from her face. It did not matter. She would remember. *Dance well with a woman*, he thought smugly, *and she's halfway yours.*

"Give these to the musicians," he told her, folding three gold marks into her hand. However badly they had played, for a time the tune had taken him away from Maerone and the immediate future. Anyway, women liked generosity. This was going very well. With a bow, just short of kissing her hand, he added, "Until later, Betse. We'll dance again when I come back."

To his surprise, she waggled a finger under his nose and gave an admonitory shake of her head as if she had read his mind. Well, he had never claimed to understand women.

Settling his hat on his head, he took up his black-hafted spear from beside the door. That was another gift from the other side of that *ter'angreal*, with its inscription of the shaft in the Old Tongue and its odd head like a short sword blade marked with two ravens.

"We'll do the drinking rooms today," he told Edorion, and they strode out into the full heat of midday, into the bedlam of Maerone.

It was a small, unwalled town, though fifty times larger than anything he had seen before leaving the Two Rivers. An overgrown village, really, few of the brick and stone buildings more than a single story high and only the inns rising as much as three, with as many roofs of wooden shingles or thatch as slate or tile. Now the streets, most hard-packed dirt, were thronged with people. The townsfolk were of every sort, mainly Cairhienin and Andorans. Although it lay on the Cairhienin side of the Erinin, Maerone was in no nation now, but balanced between, with folk from half a dozen lands living there or passing through. There had even been three or four Aes Sedai since Mat arrived. Even wearing the medallion he walked wide of them—no need to seek out trouble—but they all moved on as quickly as they came. His luck did run good when it was important. So far it had.

The townspeople hurried about their business, for the most part ignoring the many ragged men, women and children who wandered about blankly. All Cairhienin, those last usually found their way down to the river before returning to the refugee camps ringing the town. Few left to go home, though. The civil war might be over up in Cairhien, but there were still brigands, and they feared the Aiel. For all Mat knew, they feared running into the Dragon Reborn. The simple truth of it was, they had run as far as they could; none had energy remaining for much beyond those trips to the river to stare at Andor.

The Band's soldiers added to the crowds, ones or threes meandering about the shops and taverns, troops in formation, crossbowmen and archers in jerkins covered with steel discs, pikemen in battered breastplates cast off by their betters or looted from the dead. Everywhere rode breastplated horsemen, Tairen lancers in rimmed helmets and Cairhienin in bell-shaped helmets, even some Andorans in conical helmets with barred face-guards. Rahvin had tossed a good many men out of the Queen's Guards, men too loyal to Morgase, and some had joined the Band. Hawkers wove through the mass with their trays, crying needles and thread, ointments claimed to be good for any wound and remedies for everything from blisters to watery bowels to camp fever, soap, tin pots and cups guaranteed not to rust out, woolen stockings, knives and daggers of the finest Andoran steel—the seller's word on it—every sort of thing that a soldier might need or the vendors thought he might be convinced he did. The din was such that any hawkers' bellows were swallowed up three paces away.

The soldiers recognized Mat right away, of course, and many raised cheers, even men too far away to see more than his broad-brimmed hat and odd spear. Those picked him out as clearly as any noble's sigil. He had heard all the rumors about why he disdained armor and helmet; there were

all sorts, from mad bravery to the claim that only a weapon forged by the
Dark One himself could kill him. Some said the hat had been given him
by Aes Sedai, and as long as he wore it *nothing* could kill him. The fact was
it was an ordinary hat, and he wore it because it gave good shade. And
because it was a good reminder to stay clear of anywhere he might need
helmet and armor. The tales circulating about his spear, with that inscription that few even among the nobles could read, were more extravagant
still. None could match the truth, though. That raven-marked blade
had been made by Aes Sedai during the War of the Shadow, before the
Breaking; it never needed sharpening, and he doubted he could break it if
he tried.

Waving to acknowledge shouts of "The Light illumine Lord Matrim!"
and "Lord Matrim and victory!" and such drivel, he made his way through
the crowds with Edorion. At least he did not have to push; they gave way
as soon as they saw him. He wished so many of the refugees did not stare
as though he had the key to their hopes hidden in his pocket. Aside from
making sure they got food from the wagon trains coming up from Tear, he
did not know what he could do. A good many were dirty as well as ragged.

"Did the soap get out to the camps?" he muttered.

Edorion heard despite the uproar. "It did. Most trade it back to the
peddlers for cheap wine. They don't want soap; they want to cross the river,
or else drown their miseries."

Mat grunted sourly. Passage to Aringill was one thing he could not
give them.

Until civil war and worse tore Cairhien apart, Maerone had been a
transit point for trade between Cairhien and Tear, which meant it had almost as many inns and taverns as it did houses. The first five he poked his
nose into varied little, from The Fox and Goose to The Wagoner's Whip,
stone buildings with packed tables and the occasional budding fistfight,
which Mat ignored. No one was drunk, though.

The River Gate, all the way across town, had been Maerone's best inn,
but heavy planks nailed across its sun-carved doors served as a reminder to
the innkeepers and tapsters not to get the Band's soldiers drunk. Still, even
sober soldiers fought, Tairen against Cairhienin against Andoran, foot
against horse, one lord's men against another's, veterans against new recruits, soldiers against civilians. Fights were quelled before they got out of
hand, though, by soldiers carrying cudgels and wearing red armbands that
stretched from wrist to elbow. Each unit had to take its turn providing
Redarms, different men every day, and the Redarms had to pay for any

damage the day they were on duty. It made them industrious in keeping the peace.

At The Fox and Goose a gleeman was juggling flaming batons, a stout man in his middle years, while another, a skinny balding fellow at The Erinin Inn, had his harp in hand and declaimed part of *The Great Hunt of the Horn*. Despite the heat each wore his distinctive cloak, all covered with patches in a hundred colors that fluttered when he moved; a gleeman would give up a hand before that cloak. They had fairly attentive audiences— many of the onlookers came from villages that eagerly greeted a gleeman's visit—more so than the girl singing on a table in a tavern called The Three Towers. She was pretty enough, with her long dark curls, but a song about true love was not likely to interest the raucously laughing men drinking there. The remaining places had no entertainment beyond a musician or two, yet the crowds were louder still, and dice games at half the tables made Mat's fingers twitch. But he really did almost always win, at least with dice, and it would not be right to take coin from his own soldiers. That was what most of the men at the tables were; few refugees had coin to spend in common rooms.

A handful of others dotted the members of the Band. Here a lean, fork-bearded Kandori with a moonstone the size of his thumbnail in one ear-lobe and silver chains across the chest of his red coat, there a copper-skinned Domani woman, though wearing a modest blue dress, with quick eyes and gemmed rings on all her fingers, elsewhere a Taraboner in a conical flat-topped blue cap, thick mustache hidden behind a transparent veil. Plump men in Tairen coats tight to the waist or bony fellows in Murandian coats hanging to the knee; sharp-eyed women in dresses high-necked or ankle-length, but always in well-cut wool of sober color. Merchants all, ready to leap in when trade reopened between Andor and Cairhien. And in every common room two or three men sat apart from the others, usually alone, for the most part hard-eyed fellows, some well dressed, others little better garbed than the refugees, but every one looking as if he knew how to use the sword at his hip or on his back. Mat identified two women with that lot, though neither showed a weapon; one had a long walking staff propped against her table, and he supposed the other had knives hidden in her riding dress. He carried a few throwing knives tucked about his person, too. He was sure he knew what she and the others were about, and she was a fool if she went at it unarmed.

As he and Edorion stepped out of The Wagoner's Whip, Mat stopped to watch a blocky woman in divided brown skirts wend her way through

the crowds. Unblinking eyes that caught everything in the street belied
the apparent placidity of her round face, and so did the studded cudgel at
her belt, and a dagger heavy-bladed enough to do for an Aielman. So, a
third woman in the lot. Hunters for the Horn was what they were, the
legendary Horn of Valere that would call dead heroes back from the grave
to fight in the Last Battle. Whoever found it would earn a place in the
histories. *If there's anyone left to write a bloody history*, Mat thought wryly.

Some believed the Horn would turn up where there was turmoil and
strife. Four hundred years since the Hunt of the Horn was last called, and
this time people had all but dropped out of the trees to take the oaths. He
had seen flocks of Hunters in the streets of Cairhien, and he expected to see
more flocks when he reached Tear. Without doubt they would be streaming toward Caemlyn now as well. He wished one of them had found the
thing. To the best of his knowledge the Horn of bloody Valere lay somewhere deep in the White Tower, and if he knew anything about Aes Sedai
he would be surprised if a dozen of them were aware of it.

A troop of foot behind a mounted officer in a dented breastplate and a
Cairhienin helmet marched between him and the blocky woman, close to
two hundred pikemen, weapons a tall forest of spikes, followed by fifty or
more archers with quivers on hips and bows slung on shoulders. Not the
Two Rivers longbow Mat had grown up with, but a fair enough weapon.
He had to find enough crossbows to go around, though the archers would
not willingly make the change. They sang as they marched, the massed
voices enough to punch through the rest of the noise.

> You'll feed on beans and on rotten hay,
> and a horse's hoof come your naming day.
> You'll sweat and bleed till you grow old,
> and your only gold will be dreams of gold,
> if you go to be a soldier.
> If you go to be a soldier.

A fat knot of civilians trailed along behind, townsmen and refugees
mingled, young men all, watching curiously and listening. It never ceased
to amaze Mat. The worse the song made soldiering seem—this was far
from the worst—the larger the crowd. Sure as water was wet, some of those
men would be talking to a bannerman before the day was out, and most
who did would sign their names or make their mark. They must think the
song was an attempt to scare them off and keep the glory and loot. At least

the pikes were not singing "Dance with Jak o' the Shadows." Mat hated
that song. Once the lads realized Jak o' the Shadows was death, they
started panting to find a bannerman.

> Your girl will marry another man.
> A muddy grave will be all your land.
> Food for the worms and none to mourn.
> You'll curse the day you were ever born,
> if you go to be a soldier.
> If you go to be a soldier.

"There's a good deal of wondering," Edorion said casually as the formation swung on down the street with its trail of idiots, "about when we'll be
heading south. There are rumors." He peered at Mat from the corner of his
eye, measuring his mood. "I noticed the farriers checking the teams for the
supply wagons."

"We'll move when we move," Mat told him. "No need to let Sammael
know we're coming."

Edorion gave him a level look. This Tairen was no dunce. Not that
Nalesean was—he was just overeager sometimes—but Edorion had a sharp
mind. Nalesean would never have noticed the farriers. Too bad that House
Aldiaya outranked House Selorna, or Mat would have had Edorion in Nalesean's place. Fool nobles and their fool fixation on rank. No, Edorion was
no blockhead; he knew that as soon as the Band moved south word would
speed ahead with the river traffic, and maybe by pigeon as well. Mat would
not have placed a bet against spies in Maerone if he had felt his luck strong
enough to pound his skull apart.

"There's also a rumor the Lord Dragon was in the town yesterday,"
Edorion said, as softly as the street noise would allow.

"The biggest thing that happened yesterday," Mat said wryly, "was I
had my first bath in a week. Now come on. It's going to take half what
daylight is left to finish this as it is."

He would have given a pretty to find out how that rumor began. Only
off by a half day, and there certainly had been no one to see. It had been the
small hours of morning when a slash of light suddenly appeared in his
room at The Golden Stag. He had thrown himself desperately across the
four-posted bed, one boot on and one half off, pulling the knife he wore
hanging between his shoulder blades before he realized it was Rand, stepping out of one of those bloody holes in nothing, apparently from the palace

in Caemlyn by the columns visible before the opening winked out. It was startling, him coming in the middle of the night, without any Aiel, and popping right into Mat's room, which last still made the hair on Mat's neck stand up. That thing could have sliced him in two had he been standing in the wrong place. He did *not* like the One Power. The whole thing had been very strange.

"Make haste slowly, Mat," Rand said, striding up and down. He never looked in Mat's direction. Sweat slicked his face, and his jaw was tight. "He has to see it coming. Everything depends on it."

Seated on his bed, Mat jerked his boot the rest of the way off and dropped it on the scrap of rug Mistress Daelvin had given him. "I know," he said sourly, pausing to rub an ankle he had cracked on a bedpost. "I helped make the bloody plan, remember?"

"How do you know you're in love with a woman, Mat?" Rand did not stop his striding, and he dropped it in as if it fit what he had been saying.

Mat blinked. "How in the Pit of Doom should I know? That's one snare I've never put a foot in. What brought that on?"

But Rand only moved his shoulders as though shrugging something off. "I'll finish Sammael, Mat. I promised that; I owe it to the dead. But where are the others? I need to finish them all."

"One at a time, though." He barely managed to keep the question out of that; there was no telling what Rand might take into his head these days.

"There are Dragonsworn in Murandy, Mat. In Altara, too. Men sworn to me. Once Illian is mine, Altara and Murandy will drop like ripe plums. I'll make contact with the Dragonsworn in Tarabon—and in Arad Doman—and if the Whitecloaks try to keep me out of Amadicia, I'll crush them. The Prophet has Ghealdan primed, and Amadicia almost, so I hear. Can you imagine Masema as the Prophet? Saldaea will come to me; Bashere is sure of it. All the Borderlands will come. They have to! I am going to do it, Mat. Every land united before the Last Battle. I'm going to do it!" Rand's voice had taken on a feverish tone.

"Sure, Rand," Mat said slowly, depositing his other boot beside the first. "But one thing at a time, right?"

"No man should have another man's voice in his head," Rand muttered, and Mat's hands froze in the act of tugging off a woolen stocking. Oddly, he found himself wondering whether the pair had another day's wear in them. Rand knew something of what had happened inside that ter'angreal in Rhuidean—knew he had somehow gained knowledge of soldiering, anyway—but not the whole of it. Mat thought not the whole of it. Not about other men's memories. Rand did not seem to notice anything out of the ordinary. He just scrubbed fingers through his hair *and went on. "He can be gulled, Mat—Sammael always thinks in straight lines—but is there any opening he can slip through? If there's any mistake, thousands will die. Tens of thousands. Hundreds will anyway, but I don't want it to be thousands."*

Mat grimaced so fiercely that a sweaty-faced hawker trying to sell him a dagger, the hilt half-covered in colorful glass "gems," nearly dropped the thing burying himself in the crowd. It had all been like that with Rand, bouncing from the invasion of Illian to the Forsaken to women—Light, Rand was the one who always had the way with women, him and Perrin—from the Last Battle to the Maidens of the Spear to things Mat hardly understood, seldom listening to Mat's replies and sometimes not even waiting for them. Hearing Rand talk about Sammael as if he knew the man was more than just disconcerting. He knew Rand would go mad eventually, but if madness was creeping in already. . . .

And what of the others, those fools Rand was gathering who *wanted* to channel, and this fellow Taim, who already could? Rand had just dropped that in casually; Mazrim Taim, false bloody Dragon, teaching Rand's bloody students or whatever they were. When they all started going insane, Mat did not want to be within a thousand miles.

Only he had as much choice as a leaf in a whirlpool. He was *ta'veren*, but Rand was more so. Nothing in the Prophecies of the Dragon about Mat Cauthon, but he was caught, a shoat under a fence. Light, but he wished he had never seen the Horn of Valere.

It was with a grim face that he stalked through the next dozen taverns and common rooms, circling out from The Golden Stag. They were really no different from the first, packed tables full of men drinking and dicing and arm-wrestling, musicians often as not drowned out by the uproar, Red-arms quashing fights as soon as they began, a gleeman reciting *The Great Hunt* in one—that was popular even without Hunters about—in another a short, pale-haired woman singing a slightly bawdy song somehow made bawdier by her round face of wide-eyed innocence.

His bleak mood held when he left The Silver Horn—idiotic name!—and its innocent-faced singer. Maybe that was why he went running toward the shouting that erupted down the street in front of another inn. The Red-arms would take care of it if it involved soldiers, but Mat shoved his way through the crowd anyway. Rand going mad, leaving him hanging out in the storm. Taim and those other idiots ready to follow him into insanity. Sammael waiting in Illian, and the rest of the Forsaken the Light knew where, all probably looking for a chance to take Mat Cauthon's head in passing. That did not even count what the Aes Sedai would do to him if they laid hands on him again: the ones who knew too much, anyway. And everybody thinking he was going to go out and be a bloody hero! He usually tried to talk his way out of a fight if he could not walk wide of it, but right then he wanted an excuse to punch somebody in the nose. What he found was not anything he expected.

A crowd of townspeople, short, drably clothed Cairhienin and a sprinkling of taller Andorans in brighter colors, made an expressionless ring around two tall lean men with curled mustaches, long Murandian coats in bright silk, and swords with ornate, gilded pommels and quillons. The fellow in a red coat stood grinning in amusement while he watched the one in yellow shake a boy little taller than Mat's waist by the collar like a dog shaking a rat.

Mat held on to his temper; he reminded himself that he did not know what had started all this. "Easy with the boy," he said, laying a hand on yellow-coat's arm. "What did he do to deserve—?"

"He touched me horse!" the man snapped in a Mindean accent, shaking off Mat's hand. Mindeans boasted—boasted!—that they had the worst tempers of anyone in Murandy. "I'll break his skinny peasant neck for him! I'll wring his scrawny—!"

Without another word Mat brought the butt of his spear up hard, straight between the fellow's legs. The Murandian's mouth opened, but no sound came out. His eyes rolled up till almost nothing showed but white. The boy darted off as the man's legs folded, depositing him on knees and face in the street. "No, you won't," Mat said.

That was not the end of it, of course; the man in the red coat snatched at his sword. He managed to bare an inch of blade before Mat cracked his wrist with the spear-butt. Grunting, he let go the sword hilt, but grabbed for the long-bladed dagger on his belt with his other hand. Hastily Mat clipped him over the ear; not hard, but the fellow went down atop the other man. Bloody fool! Mat was not sure whether he was describing red-coat or himself.

Half a dozen Redarms had finally pushed through the onlookers, Tairen cavalrymen awkward afoot in knee boots, their swollen black-and-gold sleeves crushed under the armbands. Edorion had the boy in hand, a gaunt sullen-looking lad of six or so, wriggling bare toes in the dust and now and again giving an experimental tug at Edorion's grip. He was perhaps the ugliest child Mat had ever seen, with a squashed nose, a mouth too wide for his face and ears too big that stuck out besides. By the holes in his coat and breeches, he was one of the refugees. He looked more dirt than anything else.

"Settle this out, Harnan," Mat said. That was a lantern-jawed Redarm, a file leader with a long-suffering expression and a crude tattoo of a hawk on his left cheek. The fashion seemed to be spreading through the Band, but most limited themselves to parts of the body normally covered. "Find out what caused all this, then run these two louts out of town." They deserved that much, whatever the provocation.

A skinny man in a Murandian coat of dark wool wiggled through the onlookers and dropped to his knees beside the pair on the ground. Yellow-coat had begun emitting strangled groans, and red-coat was beginning to clutch his head in his hands and mumble what sounded like imprecations. The newcomer made more noise than both together. "Oh, me Lords! Me Lord Paers! Me Lord Culen! Are you killed?" He stretched trembling hands toward Mat. "Oh, don't kill them, me Lord! Not helpless like this. They're Hunters for the Horn, me Lord. I'm their man, Padry. Heroes, they are, me Lord."

"I'm not going to kill anybody," Mat cut in, disgusted. "But you get these heroes on their horses and out of Maerone by sunset. I don't like grown men who threaten to break a child's neck. Sunset!"

"But, me Lord, they're injured. He's only a peasant boy, and he was molesting Lord Paers' horse."

"I was only sitting on it," the boy burst out. "I was not—what you said."

Mat nodded grimly. "Boys don't get their necks broken for sitting on a horse, Padry. Not even *peasant* boys. You get these two gone, or I'll see about breaking *their* necks." He motioned to Harnan, who nodded sharply to the other Redarms—file leaders never did anything themselves, any more than bannermen did—who snatched Paers and Culen up roughly and hustled them away groaning with Padry trailing behind, wringing his hands and protesting that his masters were in no condition to ride, that they were Hunters for the Horn and heroes.

Edorion still held the source of all this bother by an arm, Mat realized. The Redarms were gone, and the townsfolk drifting away. No one glanced twice at the boy; they had their own children to look after, and a hard enough time doing that. Mat exhaled heavily. "Don't you realize you could be hurt 'just sitting' on a strange horse, boy? A man like that probably rides a stallion that could trample a little boy into the bottom of his stall so no one could ever tell you were there."

"A gelding." The boy gave another jerk at Edorion's grip, and finding it had not loosened, put on a sulky face. "It was a gelding, and it would not have hurt me. Horses like me. I am not a *little boy*: I am nine. And my name is Olver, not *boy*."

"Olver, is it?" Nine? He might be. Mat had trouble telling, especially with Cairhienin children. "Well, Olver, where are your mother and father?" He looked around, but the refugees he saw passed by as quickly as the townsfolk. "Where are they, Olver? I have to get you back to them."

Instead of answering, Olver bit his lip. A tear trickled from one eye, and he scrubbed it away angrily. "The Aiel killed my papa. One of those . . . Shado. Mama said we were going to Andor. She said we were going to live on a farm. With horses."

"Where is she now?" Mat asked softly.

"She got sick. I—I buried her where there were some flowers." Suddenly Olver kicked Edorion and began thrashing in his grip. Tears rolled down his face. "You let me go. I can take care of myself. You let me go."

"Take care of him until we can find somebody," Mat told Edorion, who gaped at him in the middle of trying to fend the boy off and hold on to him at the same time.

"Me? What am I to do with this leopard of a carpet mouse?"

"Get him a meal, for one thing." Mat's nose wrinkled; by the smell, Olver had spent at least a little time on the floor of that gelding's stall. "And a bath. He stinks."

"You talk to me," Olver shouted, rubbing at his face. The tears helped him rearrange the dirt. "You talk to me, not over my head!"

Mat blinked, then bent down. "I'm sorry, Olver. I always hated people doing that to me, too. Now, this is how it is. You smell bad, so Edorion here is going to take you to The Golden Stag, where Mistress Daelvin is going to let you have a bath." The sulkiness on Olver's face grew. "If she says anything, you tell her I said you could have one. She can't stop you." Mat held in a grin at the boy's sudden stare; that would have spoiled it. Olver might not like the idea of a bath, but if someone might try to stop him from having one. . . . "Now, you do what Edorion says. He's a real Tairen lord, and he's going to find you a good hot meal, and some clothes without holes in them. And some shoes." Best not to add "somebody to look after you." Mistress Daelvin could take care of that; a little gold would overcome any reluctance.

"I do not like Tairens," Olver mumbled, frowning first at Edorion then Mat. Edorion had his eyes shut and was muttering to himself. "He is a real lord? Are you a lord, too?"

Before Mat could say anything, Estean came running through the crowd, lumpy face red and sweat-soaked. His dented breast-plate retained few shreds of its former gilded glory, and the red satin stripes on his yellow coatsleeves were worn. He did not at all look the son of the richest lord in Tear. But then, he never had. "Mat," he puffed, shoving fingers through lank hair that kept falling over his forehead. "Mat. . . . Down at the river. . . ."

"What?" Mat cut in irritably. He was going to start having "I am not a bloody lord" embroidered on his coats. "Sammael? The Shaido? The Queen's Guards? The bloody White Lions? What?"

"A ship, Mat," Estean panted, raking at his hair. "A big ship. I think it's the Sea Folk."

That was unlikely; the Atha'an Miere never took their ships farther from open sea than the nearest port. Still. . . . There were not very many villages along the Erinin to the south, and the supplies the wagons could carry were going to run thin before the Band reached Tear. He had already hired riverboats to trail along with the march, but a larger vessel would be more than useful.

"Look after Olver, Edorion," he said, ignoring the man's grimace. "Estean, show me this ship." Estean nodded eagerly and would have set out at a run again if Mat had not grabbed his sleeve to slow him to a walk. Estean was always eager, and he learned slowly; the combination was the reason he bore five bruises from Mistress Daelvin's cudgel.

The numbers of refugees grew as Mat neared the river, both going down and coming back lethargically. Half-a-dozen broad-beamed ferries sat tied to the long tarred-timber docks, but the oars had been carried away and there was not a crewman in sight on any of them. The only boats showing any activity were half-a-dozen rivercraft, stout one- and two-masted vessels that had put in briefly on their way upriver or down. The barefoot crewmen barely stirred on the boats Mat had hired; their holds were full, and their captains assured him they could sail as soon as he gave the word. Ships moved on the Erinin, wallowing bluff-bowed craft with square sails and quick narrow vessels with triangular sails, but nothing crossing between Maerone and walled Aringill, where the White Lion of Andor flew.

That banner had flown above Maerone, too, and the Andoran soldiers who held the town had not been willing to let the Band of the Red Hand enter. Rand might hold Caemlyn, but his command did not extend to the Queen's Guards here, or the units that Gaebril had raised, like the White

Lions. The White Lions were somewhere to the east now—they had fled in that direction, anyway, and any of a dozen rumors of brigands could have been their work—but the rest had crossed the river after sharp skirmishing with the Band. Nothing had crossed the Erinin since.

The only thing Mat really saw, though, was a ship anchored in the middle of the broad river. It really was a Sea Folk vessel, taller and longer than any of the river craft but still sleek, with two raked masts. Dark figures climbed about in the rigging, some bare-chested in baggy breeches that looked black at the distance, some in bright-colored blouses marking the women. Half the crew would be women, near enough. The big square sails had been pulled up to the crossyards, yet they hung in slack folds, ready to be loosed in an instant.

"Find me a boat," he told Estean. "And some rowers." Estean would need to be reminded of that. The Tairen blinked at him, raking at his hair. "Hurry, man!" Estean nodded jerkily and lurched into a run.

Walking down to the end of the nearest dock, Mat propped his spear on his shoulder and dug his looking glass from his coat pocket. When he put the brass-bound tube to his eye, the ship leaped closer. The Sea Folk appeared to be waiting for something, but what? Some glanced toward Maerone, but most were staring the opposite way, including everyone on the tall quarterdeck; that would be where the Sailmistress was, and the other ship's officers. He swung the looking glass to the far side of the river, crossing a long narrow rowboat with dark men at the oars, racing toward the ship.

There was something of a commotion on one of Aringill's long docks, nearly the twins of Maerone's. White-collared red coats and burnished breastplates denoted Queen's Guardsmen, plainly meeting a knot of arrivals from the ship. What made Mat whistle softly was the pair of fringed red parasols among the newcomers, one of two tiers. Sometimes those old memories came in handy; that two-tiered parasol marked a clan Wavemistress, the other her Swordmaster.

"I have a boat, Mat," Estean announced breathlessly at his shoulder. "And some rowers."

Mat turned the looking glass back to the ship. By the activity on deck, they were hauling the small boat up on the other side, but already men at the capstan were hauling the anchor up and the sails were being shaken out. "Looks like I won't need it," he muttered.

On the other side of the river the Atha'an Miere delegation vanished up the dock with an escort of guardsmen. The whole thing made no sense. Sea

Folk nine hundred miles from the sea. Only the Mistress of the Ships outranked a Wavemistress; only the Master of the Blades outranked a Swordmaster. No sense at all, not by any of those other men's memories. But they
were old; he "remembered" that less was known of the Atha'an Miere than
of any people except the Aiel. He knew more of Aiel from his own experience than from those memories, and that little enough. Maybe somebody
who knew the Sea Folk today could make top from bottom in it.

Already sails billowed above the Sea Folk ship, with the anchor still
being hauled dripping onto the foredeck. Whatever had them in such a
hurry, it apparently would not take them back to the sea. With slowly increasing speed the vessel glided upriver, curving toward the marsh-lined
mouth of the Alguenya a few miles north of Maerone.

Well, it was nothing to do with him. With one last regretful look at
the ship—the thing would have carried as much as all the smaller craft he
had hired put together—Mat shoved the looking glass back in his pocket
and turned his back on the river. Estean was still hovering, staring at him.

"Tell the rowers they can go, Estean," Mat sighed, and the Tairen
stumped away muttering to himself and scrubbing his hands through
his hair.

More mud was visible than the last time he had come down to the river
a few days ago. Just a sticky strip less than a hand wide between the water
and the pace-deep band of cracked mud above, but proof even a river like
the Erinin was slowly drying up. Nothing to do with him. Nothing he
could do about it, anyway. He turned and headed back to his rounds of
the taverns and common rooms; it was important that nothing seem out
of the ordinary about today.

When the sun went down, Mat was back in The Golden Stag, dancing
with Betse, minus her apron, while the musicians played as loudly as they
could. Country dances this time, and tables pushed back to make room for
six or eight couples. Dark brought a little coolness, but only by comparison
with daylight. Everyone still sweated. Men laughing and drinking filled
the benches, and the serving girls scurried to put mutton, turnips and
barley soup on the tables and keep ale mugs and winecups full.

Surprisingly, the women seemed to consider dancing a break from lug-
ging trays about. At least, every one of them smiled eagerly when it was
her turn to dab perspiration from her face and doff her apron for a dance,
though she sweated just as hard once it began. Maybe Mistress Daelvin
had worked out some sort of schedule. If she had, Betse was an exception.
That slender young woman fetched wine for no one but Mat, danced with

no one but Mat, and the innkeeper beamed at them so much like a mother at her daughter's wedding that it made Mat uncomfortable. In fact, Betse danced with him till his feet hurt and his calves ached, yet she never ceased smiling, her eyes shining with pure pleasure. Except when they stopped to catch breath, of course. For him to catch breath; she certainly showed no need. As soon as their feet halted, her tongue took off at a gallop. For that matter, it did the same whenever he tried to kiss her, and she always turned her head, exclaiming over something or other, so he kissed an ear or hair instead of lips. She always seemed startled by it, too. He still could not figure out whether she was an utter featherhead or very clever.

It was closer to two hours past midnight than one by the clock when he finally told her he had had enough for one night. Disappointment crossed her face, and a small pout appeared. She looked ready to dance until dawn. She was not alone; one of the older serving women was leaning on one hand against a wall to massage a foot, but most of the others appeared bright-eyed and bushy-tailed as Betse. The greater part of the men appeared to be wearing out, fixed smiles on those letting themselves be dragged away from their benches and a good many just waving the women away. Mat did not understand. It must be because the man did most of the work in dancing, he decided, all the lifting and turning. And women were light; leaping about simply took less energy for them. Blinking at a stout serving maid who was whirling Estean around the floor rather than the other way—the man could dance; he had that talent—Mat pressed a gold coin into Betse's hand, a fat Andoran crown, for her to buy herself something pretty.

She studied the coin for a moment, then lifted up on her toes to kiss him lightly on the mouth, like the brush of a feather. "I would never hang you whatever you did. You will dance with me tomorrow?" Before he could answer she giggled and darted away, eyeing him over her shoulder even when she started trying to pull Edorion out to the dance area. Mistress Daelvin intercepted the pair and, shoving an apron into Betse's hands, jerked a thumb toward the kitchens.

Mat limped slightly as he made his way to the table against the back wall where Talmanes, Daerid and Nalesean had ensconced themselves. Talmanes was staring into his winecup as if to find deep answers. A grinning Daerid was watching Nalesean try to fend off a plump serving maid with gray eyes and light brown hair while not admitting that his feet were sore. Mat leaned his fists on the table. "The Band moves south at first light. You best start making preparations." The three men gaped at him.

"That is only a few hours," Talmanes protested at the same time that Nalesean said, "It will take that long just to root them out of the drinking rooms."

Wincing, Daerid shook his head. "None of us will get any sleep tonight."

"I will," Mat said. "One of you wake me in two hours. First light, and we're marching."

Which was how he found himself astride Pips, his sturdy brown gelding, in the gray predawn, with his spear across his saddle and his unstrung longbow shoved beneath his saddle girth, with not enough sleep and an ache behind his eyes, watching the Band of the Red Hand leave Maerone. All six thousand of them. Half horse, half foot, and all making enough noise to rouse the dead. Despite the hour, people lined the streets and hung gawking from every upper window.

The Band's square red-fringed banner led the way, a red hand on white, the Band's motto crimson-embroidered below. *Dovie'andi se tovya sagain.* "It's time to toss the dice." Nalesean, Daerid and Talmanes rode with the flag, ten mounted men pounding away at brass kettledrums hung with scarlet skirting, and as many trumpeters adding flourishes. Behind came Nalesean's horsemen, a mixture of Tairen armsmen and Defenders of the Stone, Cairhienin lordlings with *con* on their backs and retainers at their heels, and a sprinkling of Andorans, each squadron and troop with its own long banner bearing the Red Hand, a sword and a number. Mat had had them draw lots for who got which number.

The mixing had caused some grumbling; more than a little, truth to tell. In the beginning, Cairhienin horse all followed Talmanes, and Tairens Nalesean. The foot had been a mongrel lot from the start. There had been mutters about making each unit the same size, too, and the numbers on the pennants. Lords and captains had always gathered as many men as would follow, who were known as Edorion's men, or Meresin's, or Alhandrin's. They still did some of that—for example, Edorion's five hundred called themselves Edorion's Hammers, not the First Squadron—but Mat had driven it into their heads that every man belonged to the Band, not whatever land he had happened to be born in, and any who did not like doing things his way were free to leave. The remarkable thing was, none had.

Why they stayed was hard to understand. Certainly, they won when he led them, but some still died. He had a difficult time keeping them fed and seeing they got their pay more or less on time, and they might as well forget the wealth they boasted they were going to loot. Nobody had seen a coin of it so far, and he did not see much chance they ever would. It was madness.

The First Squadron raised a cheer quickly taken up by the Fourth and Fifth. Carlomin's Leopards and Reimon's Eagles, they called themselves. "Lord Matrim and victory! Lord Matrim and victory!"

If Mat had had a rock handy, he would have thrown it at them.

The infantry came next in a flowing snake, each company behind a drum beating cadence as well as one of the long pennants, theirs with a pike instead of a sword across the hand, twenty ranks bristling with pikes followed by five of archers or cross-bowmen. Each company had a flute or two as well, and they sang to the music.

> We drink all night and dance all day,
> and on the girls we spend our pay,
> and when we're done, then we'll away,
> to dance with Jak o' the Shadows.

Mat waited out the song until the first of Talmanes' cavalry appeared, then dug his heels into Pips' flanks. No need to attend the supply wagons at the tail end, or the strings of remounts. Horses would go lame between here and Tear, or die from things the farriers could not remedy, and a cavalryman without a horse was not worth much. On the river seven small ships crept downstream under triangular sails, little faster than the current. Each carried a small white flag with the Red Hand. Other craft were setting forth, too, some sprinting south under every scrap of canvas they could hold.

As he caught up to the head of the column the sun finally peeked above the horizon, sending the first rays across the rolling hills and scattered thickets. He pulled his hat low against the glare of the brilliant sliver. Nalesean had a gauntleted fist to his mouth, stifling an impressive yawn, and Daerid sat slumped in his saddle, heavy-lidded, as if he might drift off to sleep right there. Only Talmanes was straight-backed, wide-eyed and alert. Mat felt more in sympathy with Daerid.

Even so, he raised his voice to be heard over the drums and trumpets. "Put the scouts out as soon as we're beyond sight of the town." Both forest and open country lay farther south, but a fairly well established road cut across both; most traffic went by water, but enough had gone on foot or wagon over the years to mark out a track. "And shut that bloody noise up."

"The scouts?" Nalesean said wonderingly. "Burn my soul, there's no one with so much as a spear inside ten miles of us, unless you think the White Lions have stopped running, and if they have, they won't come closer than fifty miles if they have any notion we're about."

Mat ignored him. "I want to make thirty-five miles today. When we can do thirty-five every day, we'll see how far we can push it." They gaped at him, of course. Horses could not maintain that pace very long, and anybody but Aiel considered twenty-five miles an excellent day's march for foot. But he had to play this out the way it had been dealt. "Comadrin wrote, 'Attack on ground where your enemy believes you will not, from an unexpected direction at an unexpected time. Defend where your enemy believes you are not, and when he believes you will run. Surprise is the key to victory, and speed is the key to surprise. For the soldier, speed is life.'"

"Who is Comadrin?" Talmanes asked after a moment, and Mat had to gather himself to answer.

"A general. Dead a long time. I read his book once." He remembered reading it, anyway, more than once; he doubted a copy existed anywhere now. For that matter, he remembered meeting Comadrin, after losing a battle to him some six hundred years before Artur Hawkwing. Those memories did creep up on him. At least he had not delivered that little speech in the Old Tongue; he usually managed to avoid that sort of thing now.

Watching the mounted scouts fan out ahead across the rolling river plain, Mat relaxed. His part of it was begun, according to plan. A hasty departure on short notice as if he were trying to sneak away south, but showy enough to make sure it was noticed. The combination would make him seem a fool, and that was to the good, too. Teaching the Band to move fast was a good idea—moving fast could keep you away from the fighting—but their progress was sure to be noted from the river if nowhere else. He scanned the sky; no ravens or crows, but that did not mean much. No pigeons, either, yet if none had left Maerone this morning he would eat his saddle.

In a few days at most Sammael would learn the Band was coming, hurrying, and the word Rand had put about down in Tear would have made it clear that Mat's arrival would signal the imminent invasion of Illian. At the best speed the Band could do, it was still more than a month to Tear. With any luck, Sammael would be cracked like a louse between two rocks before Mat ever had to come within a hundred miles of the man. Sammael could see everything coming—almost everything—but it was going to be a different dance than he expected. Different than anyone but Rand, Mat and Bashere expected. That was the real plan. Mat actually found himself whistling. For once everything was going to work out the way he expected.

CHAPTER
6

Threads Woven of Shadow

Cautiously Sammael stepped onto flowery silk carpets, leaving the gateway open in case he needed to retreat and holding hard to *saidin*. Usually he refused meetings except on neutral ground, or his own, but this was the second time he had come here. A matter of necessity. He had never been a trusting man, and was less so since hearing bits of what had passed between Demandred and the three women, and Graendal certainly had told him only enough to support some gain she saw for herself. He quite understood; he had plans of his own the other Chosen knew nothing about. There would only be one Nae'blis, and that was a prize worth as much as immortality itself.

He stood on a deep dais, marble-railed at one end, where tables and chairs of gilded work and carved ivory, some quite disgusting in their details, were arranged to command the rest of the long, columned hall, ten feet below. No stairs led down there; it was a huge, extravagant pit in which to present entertainment. Sunlight sparkled through tall windows where colored glass made elaborate patterns. None of the sun's blistering heat penetrated; the air was cool, though he felt it only remotely. Graendal had no more need than he to make such an effort, but of course she would. The wonder was that she had not extended the net to the entire palace.

There was something different in the lower part of the chamber since his last visit, but he could not see what. Three long wading pools ran down the center of the hall, each with a fountain—sleek forms, motion frozen in stone—that sent water almost to the carved marble ribs of the arched ceiling overhead. Men and women sported in the pools wearing scraps of silk or less, while others garbed in little more performed along the sides, acrobats and jugglers, dancers in varied styles and musicians playing flutes and horns, drums and all sorts of stringed instruments. Of every size, every shade of skin and hair and eyes, each was more physically perfect than the last. It was all meant to amuse whoever stood on the dais. It was idiocy. A waste of time and energy. Typical of Graendal.

The dais had been empty except for himself when he stepped onto it, but with *saidin* filling him, he smelled Graendal's sweet perfume, like an air from a garden of flowers, and heard her slippers whispering on the carpets well before she spoke behind him. "Are my pets not beautiful?"

She joined him at the railing, smiling at the display below. Her thin blue Domani gown clung and more than hinted. As usual she had a ring with different stones on every finger, four or five gem-encrusted bracelets on each wrist, and a wide collar of huge sapphires snugged around the gown's high neck. He did not know about such things, but he suspected hours had gone into arranging those sun-gold curls touching her shoulders, and the moondrops seemingly scattered through them; there was something about their casualness that hinted at precision.

Sammael sometimes wondered about her. He had never met her until he chose to abandon a losing cause and follow the Great Lord, but everyone knew of her, famous and honored, a dedicated ascetic, treating those with disturbed minds Healing could not touch. At that first meeting, when she accepted his initial pledges to the Great Lord, every trace of the abstemious benefactor was gone, as if she had deliberately become the opposite of everything she had been before. On the surface her total fixation was her own pleasure, nearly obscuring a desire to pull down everyone who had a particle of power. And that in turn almost hid her own thirst for power, very seldom exercised openly. Graendal had always been very good at hiding things in plain sight. He thought he knew her better than any of the other Chosen did—she had accompanied him to Shayol Ghul to make his obeisance—but even he did not know all the layers of her. She had as many shades as a *jegal* had scales, slipping from one to another as quickly as lightning. She had been the mistress then, he the acolyte, for all his accomplishments as a general. That situation had changed.

None of the waders or performers looked up, but with her appearance they became more energetic, more graceful if that was possible, attempting to display themselves to best advantage; they existed to please her. Graendal made sure of that.

She gestured to four acrobats, a dark-haired man supporting three slim women, coppery skins oiled and gleaming. "They are my favorites, I think. Ramsid is the Domani king's brother. The woman standing on his shoulders is Ramsid's wife; the other two are the king's youngest sister and eldest daughter. Don't you find it remarkable what can be learned with the proper encouragement? Consider all the talents going to waste." That was one of her favorite concepts. A place for everyone and everyone in their place, chosen for them according to their talents and the needs of society. Which needs always seemed to center on her own desires. The whole thing bored Sammael; had her precepts been applied to him, he would still stand where he was.

The male acrobat turned slowly to give them a good view; he held a woman straight-armed to either side while they hung by one hand from the grip of the one on his shoulders. Graendal had already moved on, to a very dark-skinned man and woman with curly hair, both of great beauty. The slender pair played oddly elongated harps, with chimes that resonated to the plucked strings in crystalline echoes. "My newest acquisitions, from the lands beyond the Aiel Waste. They should thank me for rescuing them. Chiape was Sh'boan, a sort of empress, newly widowed, and Shaofan was to marry her and become Sh'botay. For seven years she would have ruled absolutely, then died. Whereupon he would have chosen a new Sh'boan and ruled absolutely until his death in seven years. They have followed that cycle for nearly three thousand years without a break." She gave a small laugh and shook her head wonderingly. "Shaofan and Chiape insist the deaths are natural. The Will of the Pattern, they call it. To them everything is the Will of the Pattern."

Sammael kept his eyes on the people below. Graendal prattled like a fool, but only a true fool took her for one. What she seemed to let slip among her babbling was often planted as carefully as a *conje* needle. The key was picking out why, and what she meant to gain. Why would she suddenly have snatched pets from so far away? She seldom went out of her way. Was she trying to divert him toward the lands beyond the Waste by making him think she had an interest there? The battlefield was here. The Great Lord's first touch when he broke free would land here. The rest of the world would be whipped by the fringes of storms, even racked by storms, but those storms would generate here.

"Since so much of the Domani king's family met with your approval," he said dryly, "I am surprised no more did." If she wanted to divert him, she would find a way to slide it in again. She never thought anyone knew her tricks well enough to see through them.

A lithe dark-haired woman, not young but with the sort of pale beauty and elegance that would last all her life, appeared at his elbow cradling a crystal goblet of dark wine punch in both hands. He took it, though he had no intention of drinking; beginners watched for a major assault till their eyes burned, and let a lone assassin walk up behind them. Alliances, however temporary, were all very well, but the fewer of the Chosen who remained on the Day of Return, the greater the chance among the survivors to be named Nae'blis. The Great Lord had always encouraged such . . . competition; only the fittest were worthy to serve. At times Sammael believed that the one chosen to rule the world forever would be the last of the Chosen left standing.

The woman turned back to a muscular young man who held a golden tray with another goblet and a tall matching pitcher. Both wore diaphanous white robes, and neither gave so much as the flicker of an eye to the gateway, opening into his apartments in Illian. When she served Graendal, the woman's face was a portrait of worship. There was never any trouble about speaking in front of her servants and pets, though they would not number a single Friend of the Dark among them. She distrusted Friends of the Dark, claiming they were too easily swayed, but the level of Compulsion used on those who served her personally left little room for anything beyond adoration.

"I almost expect to see the king himself here serving wine," he continued.

"You know I choose only the most exquisite. Alsalam is not up to my standard." Graendal took the wine from the woman with barely a glance, and not for the first time Sammael wondered whether the pets were another screen, like the chattering. A little prodding might shake something loose.

"Sooner or later you will slip, Graendal. One of your visitors will recognize one who serves him wine or turns down his bed, and he will have sense enough to hold his tongue until he leaves. What will you do if someone descends on this palace with an army to rescue a husband or a sister? An arrow may not be a shocklance, yet it can still kill you."

She threw back her head and laughed, a trill of gay amusement, plainly too silly to see the implied insult. Plainly, as long as you did not know her. "Oh, Sammael, why would I let them see anything but what I want them to? I certainly do not send my pets to serve them. Alsalam's supporters and his opponents, even the Dragonsworn, leave here thinking I support them and only them. And they do not want to disturb an invalid." His skin tingled slightly as she channeled, and for an instant her image changed. Her skin became coppery but dull, her hair and eyes dark but flat; she appeared gaunt and frail, a once-beautiful Domani woman slowly losing a battle against illness. He barely stopped his lip from curling. One touch would prove the angular contours of that face were not hers—only the most subtle use of Illusion could pass that test—but Graendal seemed wedded to flamboyance. The next moment she was herself again, wearing a wry smile. "You would not believe how they all trust and listen to me."

It never ceased to amaze him that she chose to remain here in a palace well known across Arad Doman, with civil war and anarchy all around her. Of course, he did not think she had let any others of the Chosen know where she had established herself. That she trusted him with the knowledge made him wary. She liked her comforts, and never wanted to expend much effort to keep them, yet this palace was in sight of the Mountains of Mist, and considerable work was necessary to keep the turmoil away from her, to keep anyone from asking where the former owner had gone, along with his family and servants. Sammael would not be surprised if every Domani who visited here left believing that this land had been handed down in her family since the Breaking. She used Compulsion so often like a hammer that one might forget that she could wield the weaker forms of it with great delicacy, twisting a mind's path so subtly that even the closest examination might miss every trace of her. In fact, she might have been the best at that who ever lived.

He let the gateway vanish but held on to *saidin*; her tricks would not work on a man wrapped in the Source. And in truth, he enjoyed the struggle for survival, though it was unconscious now; only the strongest deserved to survive, and he proved his own fitness to himself every day in that battle. There was no way she could know he still grasped *saidin*, but she smiled briefly into her goblet as if she did. He liked people pretending to know things almost as little as he liked them knowing things he did not. "What do you have to tell me?" he said, more roughly than he intended.

"About Lews Therin? You never seem interested in anything else. Now, he would be a pet. I would make him the centerpiece of every display. Not that he is handsome enough, normally, but who he is makes up for that."

Smiling into her goblet again, she added in a murmur that would have been inaudible without *saidin* in him, "And I do like them tall."

It was an effort not to stand up as straight as he could. He was not short, but it rankled that his height did not match his ability. Lews Therin had been a head taller than he; so was al'Thor. There was always an assumption that the taller man was the better. It took another effort not to touch the scar that slanted across his face from hairline to square-cut beard. Lews Therin had given him that; he kept it for a reminder. He suspected she had misunderstood his question on purpose, to bait him. "Lews Therin is long dead," he said harshly. "Rand al'Thor is a jumped-up farmboy, a *choss*-hauler who has been lucky."

Graendal blinked at him as if surprised. "Do you really think so? There has to be more than luck behind him. Luck could not have carried him so far, so fast."

Sammael had not come to talk about al'Thor, yet ice formed at the base of his spine. Thoughts he had forced himself to dismiss came oozing back. Al'Thor was not Lews Therin, but al'Thor was Lews Therin's soul reborn, as Lews Therin himself had been the rebirth of that soul. Sammael was neither philosopher nor theologian, yet Ishamael had been both, and he claimed to have divined secrets hidden in that fact. Ishamael had died mad, true, but even when he was still sane, back when it seemed they surely would drive Lews Therin Telamon to defeat, he claimed this struggle had gone on since the Creation, an endless war between the Great Lord and the Creator using human surrogates. More, he avowed that the Great Lord would almost as soon have turned Lews Therin to the Shadow as have broken free. Maybe Ishamael had been a little mad then, too, but there had been efforts to turn Lews Therin. And Ishamael said that it had happened in the past, the Creator's champion made a creature of the Shadow and raised up as the Shadow's champion.

There were unsettling implications in those claims, ramifications Sammael did not want to consider, but the thing that shoved itself to the front of his mind was the possibility that the Great Lord might really want to make al'Thor Nae'blis. It could not happen in a vacuum. Al'Thor would need help. Help—that could explain his supposed luck so far. "Have you learned where al'Thor is hiding Asmodean? Or anything of Lanfear's whereabouts? Or Moghedien's?" Of course, Moghedien always hid herself; the Spider was forever popping up just when you were sure she was finally dead.

"You know as much as I do," Graendal said blithely, pausing for a sip from her goblet. "Myself, I think Lews Therin killed them. Oh, don't grimace at me. Al'Thor, since you insist." The thought did not seem to disturb her, but then, she would never find herself in open conflict with al'Thor. That had never been her way. If al'Thor ever discovered her, she simply would abandon everything and re-establish herself elsewhere—or else surrender before he could strike a blow, then begin convincing him that she was indispensable. "There are rumors out of Cairhien about Lanfear dying at Lews Therin's hands the same day he killed Rahvin."

"Rumors! Lanfear has been aiding al'Thor since the beginning, if you ask me. I would have had his head in the Stone of Tear except that someone sent Myrddraal and Trollocs to save him! That was Lanfear; I am certain. I'm done with her. The next time I see her, I'll kill her! And why would he kill Asmodean? I would if I could find him, but he has gone over to al'Thor. He's teaching him!"

"Always some excuse for your failures," she whispered into her punch, again too softly for him to have heard without *saidin*. In a louder voice, she said, "Choose your own explanations, if you wish. You may even be right. All I know is that Lews Therin seems to be removing us from the game one by one."

Sammael's hand trembled with anger, nearly slopping punch from his goblet before he could still it. Rand al'Thor was *not* Lews Therin. He himself had outlived the great Lews Therin Telamon, handing out praise for victories he could not have won himself and expecting others to lap it up. His only regret was that the man had not left a grave for him to spit on.

Waving ringed fingers in time to a snatch of music from below, Graendal spoke absently, as though her real attention was on the tune. "So many of us have died confronting him. Aginor and Balthamel. Ishamael, Be'lal and Rahvin. And Lanfear and Asmodean, whatever you believe. Possibly Moghedien; she might be creeping about in the shadows waiting until the rest of us have fallen—she's foolish enough. I do hope you have somewhere prepared to run. There doesn't seem to be any doubt that he is going after you next. Soon, I would say. I'll face no armies here, but Lews Therin is gathering quite a large one to hurl against you. The price you pay if you must be *seen* to wield power as well as wield it."

He did have lines of retreat prepared, as it happened—that was only prudent—but hearing in her voice the certainty of his need infuriated him. "And if I destroy *al'Thor* then, it will violate none of the Great Lord's command." He did not understand, but there was no requirement to understand the Great Lord, only to obey. "As far as you've told it to me. If you have held back. . . ."

Graendal's eyes hardened to blue ice. She might avoid confrontation, but she did not like threats. The next instant she was all inane smiles again. As changeable as the weather in M'jinn. "What Demandred told me that the Great Lord told him, I have passed on to you, Sammael. Every word. I doubt even he would dare lie in the Great Lord's name."

"But you've told me little enough of what he plans to do," Sammael said softly, "him or Semirhage or Mesaana. Practically nothing."

"I have told you what I know." She sighed irritably. Perhaps she was telling the truth. She seemed to regret not knowing herself. Perhaps. With her, anything and everything could be show. "For the rest. . . . Think back, Sammael. We used to plot against one another almost as hard as we fought Lews Therin, yet we were winning before he caught us all gathered at Shayol Ghul." She shuddered, and for a moment her face looked haggard. Sammael did not want to remember that day either, or what came after, a dreamless sleep while the world changed past recognition and all he had wrought vanished. "Now we have awakened in a world where we should stand so far above ordinary mortals as to be another species—and we are dying. For a moment forget who will be Nae'blis. Al'Thor—if you must call him by that name—al'Thor was as helpless as a babe when we woke."

"Ishamael did not find him so," he said—of course, Ishamael *had* been mad then—but she continued as if he had not spoken.

"We behave as if this is the world we knew, when nothing is what we knew. We die one by one, and al'Thor grows stronger. Lands and people gather behind him. And we die. Immortality is mine. I do not want to die."

"If he frightens you, then kill him." Before the words were well out of his mouth he would have swallowed them if he could.

Disbelief and scorn twisted Graendal's face. "I serve the Great Lord and obey, Sammael."

"As do I. As well as any."

"So good of you to deign to kneel to our Master." Her voice was as wintry as her smile, and his face darkened. "All I say is that Lews Therin is as dangerous now as he ever was in our own time. Frightened? Yes, I am frightened. I intend to live forever, not meet Rahvin's fate!"

"Tsag!" The obscenity at least made her blink and truly look at him. "Al'Thor—al'Thor, Graendal! An ignorant boy, whatever Asmodean manages to teach him! A primitive lout who probably still believes that

nine-tenths of what you and I take for granted is impossible! Al'Thor makes a few lords bow and thinks he has conquered a nation. He hasn't the will to close his fist and truly conquer them. Only the Aiel—*Bajad drovja!* Who would have thought they could change so?"—he had to get a grip on himself; he never cursed like this; it was a weakness—"only they truly follow him, and not all of them. He hangs by a thread, and he will fall, one way or another."

"Will he? What if he is . . . ?" She stopped, raising her goblet so rapidly that punch spilled onto her wrist, and gulped until the goblet was almost empty. The elegant serving woman came scurrying with the crystal pitcher. Graendal thrust out the goblet to be refilled and went on breathlessly. "How many of us will die before it is done? We must stand together as we never have before."

That was not what she had started to say. He ignored the ice that gripped his spine once more. Al'Thor would not be chosen Nae'blis. He would not! So she wanted them to stand together, did she? "Then link with me. The pair of us linked would be more than a match for al'Thor. Let that be the beginning of our new standing together." His scar tightened as he smiled at the sudden blankness on her face. The link had to come from her, but with only the two of them, she would have to give him control and trust him to choose when to end it. "So. It seems we will go on as before." There had never been any question of it, really; trust was no part of any of them. "What more do you have to tell me?" That was the reason he had come here, not to listen to her rattle on about Rand al'Thor. Al'Thor would be dealt with. Directly or indirectly.

She stared at him, gathering herself, eyes glittering with enmity. Finally she said, "Little enough." She would not forget that he had seen her lose control. None of her anger came out in her voice; her tone was smooth, even offhand. "Semirhage missed the last gathering; I don't know why, and I do not think Mesaana or Demandred does either. Mesaana in particular was annoyed, though she tried to hide it. She thinks Lews Therin soon will be in our hands, but then she has said the same every time. She was sure Be'lal would kill or capture him in Tear; she was very proud of that trap. Demandred warns you to be careful."

"So Demandred knows you and I meet," he said flatly. Why had he ever expected to receive more than driblets from her?

"Of course he does. Not how much I tell you, but that I tell you something. I am trying to bring us together, Sammael, before it is too—"

He cut in sharply. "You deliver a message to Demandred from me. Tell him I know what he is up to." Events to the south had Demandred's mark all over them. Demandred had always liked using proxies. "Tell *him* to be careful. I won't have him or his *friends* interfering in my plans." Perhaps he could direct al'Thor's attention there; that would likely put an end to him. If other means did not work. "So long as they steer clear of me, his lackeys can carve out what he wants, but they will steer clear or he will answer for it." There had been a long struggle after the Bore was opened into the Great Lord's prison, many years before enough strength was gathered to move openly. This time, when the final seal was shattered, he would present the Great Lord with nations ready to follow. If they did not know who they followed, what did that matter? He would not fail, as Be'lal and Rahvin had. The Great Lord would see who served him best. "You tell him!"

"If you wish it," she said, grimacing reluctantly. An instant later that lazy smile came onto her face again. Changeable. "All these threats weary me. Come. Listen to the music and calm yourself." He started to tell her he had no interest in music, as she knew very well, but she turned to the marble railing. "There they are. Listen."

The very dark man and woman had come to the foot of the dais with their peculiar harps. Sammael supposed the chimes added something to their playing; what, he could not say. They beamed reverently up at Graendal when they saw her watching.

Despite her own advice to listen, Graendal went on talking. "A peculiar place they come from. Women who can channel are required to marry the sons of women who can channel, and everyone of those bloodlines is marked with tattoos on their faces at birth. No one with the markings is allowed to marry anyone without; any child of such a union is killed. Tattooed males are killed in their twenty-first year in any case, and cloistered before, ignorant even of how to read."

So she had come back to it after all. She truly must think he was simple. He decided to plant a small barb of his own. "Do they bind themselves like criminals?"

A look of puzzlement flashed across her face and was hastily suppressed. Plainly she had not reasoned it out; there was no reason she should. Few people in their time had ever committed one violent crime, let alone more. Before the Bore, at least. She did not admit her ignorance, of course. There were times when it was best to hide lack of knowledge, but Graendal often carried the practice to a fault. That was why he had mentioned it; he knew it would dig at her, and serve her right for the useless shreds she doled out.

"No," she said as if she had understood. "The Ayyad, as they call themselves, live in their own small towns, avoiding everyone else, and supposedly never channel without permission or orders from the Sh'botay or Sh'boan. In fact, they are the real power, and the reason the Sh'botay and Sh'boan only rule seven years." Rich laughter bubbled up in her for a moment. She herself had always believed in being the power behind the power. "Yes, a fascinating land. Too far from the center to be of any use for many years, of course." She made a slight, dismissive gesture, fluttering beringed fingers. "There will be plenty of time to see what can be made of it after the Day of Return."

Yes, she definitely wanted him to think she had some interest there. If she really had, she never would have mentioned the place. He set his untouched goblet on the tray the muscular fellow had ready before his hand finished moving. Graendal did train her servants well. "I am sure their music is fascinating," if you cared for that sort of thing, "but I have preparations to see to."

Graendal laid a hand on his arm. "Careful preparations, I trust? The Great Lord will not be pleased if you disturb his plans."

Sammael's mouth tightened. "I have done everything short of surrendering to convince al'Thor I am no threat to him, but the man seems obsessed with me."

"You could abandon Illian, start again elsewhere."

"No!" He had never run from Lews Therin, and he would not run from this provincial buffoon. The Great Lord could not mean to put one like that above the Chosen. Above him! "You have told me all of the Great Lord's command?"

"I dislike repeating myself, Sammael." Her voice held a touch of exasperation, her eyes a hint of anger. "If you did not believe me the first time, you will not now."

He stared at her a moment longer, then nodded brusquely. Very probably she had told the truth there; a lie touching the Great Lord could rebound with deadly force. "I see no reason to meet again until you have something to tell me besides whether Semirhage was there or not." His brief frown at the harpists should be enough to convince her she had succeeded in her misdirection; he turned his gaze into a disapproving sweep across the people splashing in the pools, the acrobats and the rest, so it would not seem obvious. All this wasted effort, all this display of flesh, really did disgust him. "Next time you can come to Illian."

She shrugged as though it did not matter, but her lips moved slightly, and his *saidin*-enhanced hearing plucked "If you are still there" from the air.

Icily Sammael opened a gateway back to Illian. The muscular young man failed to move quickly enough; he did not have time to scream before he was sliced in two down the middle, him and the tray and the crystal pitcher. The edge of a gateway made a razor seem blunt. Graendal pursed her lips peevishly at the loss of one of her pets.

"If you want to help us stay alive," Sammael told her, "find out how Demandred and the others mean to carry out the Great Lord's instructions." He stepped through the gateway, never taking his eyes from her face.

Graendal maintained her vexed expression until the gateway closed behind Sammael, then allowed herself to tap her fingernails on the marble railing. With his golden hair Sammael might have been handsome enough to stand among her pets, if he would let Semirhage remove the burned furrow that slanted across his face; she was the only one remaining with the skill to do what would once have been a simple matter. It was an idle thought. The real question was whether her effort had paid off.

Shaofan and Chiape played their strange atonal music, full of complex harmonies and odd dissonances, quite beautifully; their faces shone with joy that they might be pleasing her. She nodded, and could almost feel their delight. They were much happier now than they would have been left to themselves. So much effort to procure them, and solely for this few minutes with Sammael. Of course, she could have taken less trouble—anyone at all from their lands would have done as well—but she had her standards even when preparing a momentary subterfuge. Long ago she had chosen to seek every pleasure, to deny herself none that did not threaten her standing with the Great Lord.

Her eyes fell on the offal staining her carpet, and her nose twitched irritably. The weaving might be salvaged, but it annoyed her that she would have to remove the blood herself. She gave quick orders, and Osana ran to oversee having the carpet removed. And Rashan's remains disposed of.

Sammael was a transparent fool. No, not a fool. He was deadly enough when he had something to fight directly, something he could see clearly, but he might as well be blind when it came to subtleties. Very likely he believed her ruse was intended to mask what she and the others were up to. One thing he would never consider was that she knew every twitch of his mind, every twist of his thoughts. After all, she had spent

nearly four hundred years studying the workings of minds far more convoluted than his. Transparent, he was. However much he tried to hide it,
he was frantic. He was trapped in a box of his own devising, a box he
would defend to the death rather than abandon, a box in which he very
probably would die.

She sipped her wine, and her forehead furrowed slightly. Possibly she
had already achieved her end with him, though she had expected it to take
four or five visits. She would have to find reason to call on him in Illian; it
was best to observe the patient even after it appeared the desired path had
been taken.

Whether the boy was a simple farm lad or Lews Therin himself truly
come back—she could not make up her mind on that—he had proven
himself far too dangerous. She served the Great Lord of the Dark, but she
did not mean to die, not even for the Great Lord. She would live forever. Of
course, one did not go against even the slightest of the Great Lord's wishes
unless one wished to spend an eternity dying and another eternity wishing
for the lesser agony of that long death. Still, Rand al'Thor had to be removed, but it would be Sammael who earned the blame. If he realized that
he had been aimed at Rand al'Thor like a *dornat* set to hunt, she would be
very much surprised. No, not a man to recognize subtleties.

Far from stupid, though. It would be interesting to discover how he
had found out about the binding. She herself would never have learned
had Mesaana not made a rare slip while venting her anger on an absent
Semirhage; her fury had been strong enough that she did not realize how
much she had revealed. How long had Mesaana been tucked away inside
the White Tower? The mere fact that she was opened interesting avenues.
If there were some way to discover where Demandred and Semirhage had
placed themselves, it might be possible to work out what they intended to
do. They had not trusted her with that. Oh, no. Those three had worked
together since before the War of Power. On the surface, at least. She was
sure they had plotted against one another as assiduously as any of the Chosen, but whether Mesaana undercut Semirhage or Semirhage Demandred,
she had never yet found a crack between them into which a wedge could be
driven.

A scuff of boots announced an arrival, but not men to replace the carpet and remove Rashan. Ebram was a tall, well-made young Domani in
tight red breeches and a flowing white shirt; he could have fit into her collection of pets if he had been more than a merchant's son. His eyes were

intent on her as he knelt, dark and shining. "The Lord Ituralde has come, Great Mistress."

Graendal set the goblet atop a table that at first glance seemed to be inlaid with ivory dancers. "Then he shall speak with the Lady Basene."

Ebram rose smoothly and offered an arm for the frail Domani woman he now saw. He knew who lay behind the weaving of Illusion, but even so the reverence on his face faded slightly; she knew it was Graendal, not Basene, whom he worshiped. At the moment she did not care. Sammael was at the very least pointed at Rand al'Thor, and perhaps launched. As for Demandred and Semirhage and Mesaana. . . . Only she herself knew that she had made her own journey to Shayol Ghul and down to the lake of fire. Only she knew that the Great Lord had all but promised to name her Nae'blis, a promise sure to be fulfilled with al'Thor out of the way. She would be the most obedient of the Great Lord's servants. She would sow chaos till the harvest made Demandred's lungs explode.

Semirhage let the iron-bound door close behind her. One of the glow-bulbs, salvaged from the Great Lord alone knew where, flickered fitfully, but they still gave better light than the candles and oil lamps she had to accept in this time. Aside from the light, the place had the intimidating look of a prison, rough stone walls and a bare floor with a small crude wooden table in one corner. Not her notion; she would have had it all spotless white and gleaming *cueran*, sleek and sterile. This place had been prepared before she knew the need. A pale-haired silk-clad woman hung spread-eagled from nothing in the middle of the room, glaring at her defiantly. An Aes Sedai. Semirhage hated Aes Sedai.

"Who are you?" the patient demanded. "A Darkfriend? A Black sister?"

Ignoring the noise, Semirhage quickly checked the buffer between the woman and *saidar*. If it failed, she could mask the wretch again with no trouble—it was a measure of the woman's weakness that she could afford to leave the knotted buffer unwatched—but taking care was second nature to her, taking each step in its exact turn. Now for the woman's clothing. Someone in garments felt safer than someone without. Delicately she wielded Fire and Wind, slicing away dress and shift and every scrap right down to the patient's shoes. Drawing everything out in front of the woman in one compressed bundle, she channeled again, Fire and Earth, and fine dust rained down onto the stone floor.

The woman's blue eyes bulged. Semirhage doubted she could duplicate those simple feats even if she had been able to follow them.

"Who are you?" This time there was an edge to the demand. Fear perhaps. It was always good if that began early.

Precisely Semirhage located the centers in the woman's brain that received messages of pain from the body, and just as meticulously began to stimulate them with Spirit and Fire. Only a little at first, building slowly. Too much at once could kill in moments, yet it was remarkable how far the system could be taken if fed in finely increasing increments. Working on something you could not see was a difficult task, even this close, but she was as knowledgeable about the human body as anyone had ever been.

The spread-eagled patient shook her head as if she could shake off the pain, then realized she could not and fixed Semirhage with a stare. Semirhage merely watched, and maintained the net. Even in something as hurried as this must be, she could afford a little patience.

How she did hate any who called themselves Aes Sedai. She had been one herself, a true Aes Sedai, not an ignorant fool like the simpleton hanging before her. She had been known, famed, whisked to every corner of the world for her ability to mend any injury, to bring people back from the brink when everyone else said there was nothing more to be done. And a delegation from the Hall of the Servants had offered her a choice that was no choice: to be bound never to know her pleasures again, and with that binding be able to see the end of life approach; or else to be severed, and cast out as Aes Sedai. They had expected her to accept binding; that was the rational, proper thing to do, and they were rational, proper men and women. They never expected her to flee. She had been one of the first to go to Shayol Ghul.

Fat beads of sweat popped out on the patient's pale face. Her jaw knotted, and her nostrils flared as she sucked in air. Now and then she gave a small grunt. Patience. Soon, now.

It had been jealousy, the jealousy of those who could not do what she could. Had anyone she pulled back from death's grasp ever said they would rather have died than suffer the little extra she exacted? And the others? There were always those who deserved to suffer. What matter that she enjoyed giving them their deserts? The Hall and its hypocritical whining about legalities and rights. She had deserved the right to do as she did; she had earned the right. She had been more valuable to the world than all those together who entertained her with their screams. And in jealousy and spite the Hall had tried to pull *her* down!

Well, some of them had fallen into her hands during the war. Given time she could break the strongest man, the proudest woman, mold them exactly as she wanted them to be. The process might be slower than Compulsion, but it was infinitely more enjoyable, and she did not think even Graendal could undo what she did. Compulsion could be unraveled. But her patients. . . . On their knees they had begged to give their souls to the Shadow, and had served obediently until they died. Each time Demandred had been full of what a coup it was, another Counselor of the Hall publicly proclaiming allegiance to the Great Lord, but for her the best part had been the way their faces went pale, even years later, when they saw her, the way they hurried to assure her that they remained faithful to what she had made of them.

The first sob ripped out of the woman hanging in the air and was stifled. Semirhage waited impassively. Haste might be necessary here, but too much haste could spoil everything. More sobbing erupted, overwhelming the patient's efforts to subdue it, growing louder, louder, until it swelled to a howl. Semirhage waited. The woman shone with a greasy slick of sweat; her head flung from side to side, flailing her hair, and she jerked helplessly in her unseen tethers, convulsive flutters. Full-throated, ear-shattering shrieks lasted until breath was exhausted and began again as soon as lungs could be filled. Those wide bulging blue eyes saw nothing; they seemed to be glazing. Now it began.

Semirhage cut off her streams of *saidar* abruptly, but minutes passed before the screams subsided into panting. "What is your name?" she asked gently. The question did not matter as long as it was one the woman would answer. It could have been "Do you still defy me?"—it was often pleasant to keep on with that one until they pleaded to prove they no longer did—but she needed to make every question count this time.

Involuntary shudders ran through the hanging woman. Giving Semirhage a wary, slitted gaze, she licked her lips, coughed, and finally muttered hoarsely, "Cabriana Mecandes."

Semirhage smiled. "It is good to tell me the truth." There were pain centers in the brain, and pleasure centers. She stimulated one of the latter, just for a few moments but hard, as she moved closer. The jolt widened Cabriana's eyes as far as they would go; she gasped and shook. Plucking a handkerchief from her sleeve, Semirhage lifted the woman's wondering face and tenderly dabbed away sweat. "I know this is very hard on you, Cabriana," she said warmly. "You must try not to make it more difficult." With a soft touch she smoothed damp hair away from the woman's face.

"Would you like something to drink?" Not waiting for an answer, she channeled; a battered metal flask floated from the small table in the corner to her hand. The Aes Sedai never took her eyes from Semirhage, but she drank thirstily. After a few swallows, Semirhage took the flask away and returned it to the table. "Yes, that's better, isn't it? Remember, try not to make it difficult for yourself." As she turned away, the woman spoke again, in a rasping voice.

"I spit in the milk of your mother, Darkfriend! Do you hear me? I. . . ."

Semirhage stopped listening. Any other time there would have been a spreading glow of pleasure that the patient's defiance had not been crushed yet. The purest exhilaration came from shaving away defiance and dignity in minute slices, watching the patient finally realize that they were going and struggle vainly to cling to what remained. No time for that now. Carefully she once more set the web on the pain centers of Cabriana's brain and knotted it. Normally she liked to be in personal control, but some haste was necessary. Triggering the net, she channeled to extinguish the lights and left, closing the door behind her. Darkness would work its part, too. Alone, in the dark, with the pain.

Despite herself Semirhage made a vexed sound. There was no finesse in this. She did not like having to hurry. And to be called away from her charge; the girl was willful and obdurate, the circumstances difficult.

The corridor came close to matching the chamber for bleakness, a broad shadowy shaft through stone, with crossing passageways that she had no desire to explore nearly lost in the murk. Only two other doors were in sight, one leading to her present quarters. They were comfortable enough rooms if she had to be here, but she made no move toward them. Shaidar Haran stood in front of that door, black-clad and wreathed in dimness like smoke, so still that it was almost a shock when it spoke, a sound of bone dust being ground.

"What have you learned?"

The summons to Shayol Ghul had resulted in a warning from the Great Lord. *WHEN YOU OBEY SHAIDAR HARAN, YOU OBEY ME. WHEN YOU DISOBEY SHAIDAR HARAN. . . .* However much the warning nettled, there had been no need for more. "Her name. Cabriana Mecandes. I could hardly learn more so quickly."

It flowed across the hallway in that eye-wrenching way, ebon cloak hanging in denial of motion. One moment it was a statue ten paces away, the next it loomed over her so she had the choice of backing away or craning her neck to look up at that dead-white, eyeless face. Backing away was out of the question. "You will drain her completely, Semirhage. You will squeeze her dry, without delay, and tell me every scrap that you learn."

"I promised the Great Lord that I would," she told it coldly.

Bloodless lips twisted in a smile. That was its only reply. Turning sharply, it strode away through patches of shadow—and abruptly was gone.

Semirhage wished she knew how Myrddraal did that. It had nothing to do with the Power, but on the edges of shadow, where light was becoming dark, a Myrddraal could suddenly be elsewhere, in another shadow far away. Long ago Aginor had tested over a hundred of them to destruction in a vain effort to learn how it was done. The Myrddraal themselves did not know; she herself had proved that.

Abruptly she realized that her hands were pressed hard against her stomach, which seemed a ball of ice. It had been many years since she had felt fear anywhere except facing the Great Lord in the Pit of Doom. The frozen lump began to melt as she moved to the other prison door. Later she would analyze the emotion dispassionately; Shaidar Haran might be different from any other Myrddraal she had ever seen, but it was still a Myrddraal.

Her second patient, hanging like the first in midair, was a blocky, square-faced man in a green coat and breeches suitable for fading into a forest. A full half of the glowbulbs here shimmered on the edge of failure—that any had survived so long was a miracle—but Cabriana's Warder was unimportant, really. What was needed, for whatever purpose, rested in the Aes Sedai's mind, yet the Myrddraal apparently had been told to capture an Aes Sedai, and in their minds for some reason Aes Sedai and Warders seemed inseparable. As well they had, though. She had not before had an opportunity to break one of these storied fighters.

His dark eyes tried to bore holes through her head as she removed his clothing and boots and destroyed them as she had Cabriana's. He was hairy, a mass of large hard muscles and scars. He never flinched. He said nothing. His defiance was different from the woman's. Hers was bold, flung in your face, his a quiet refusal to bend. He might be harder to crack than his mistress. Normally he would have been much the more interesting.

Pausing, Semirhage studied him. There was something. . . . A tightness around the mouth and eyes. As if he already fought pain. Of course. That peculiar bond between Aes Sedai and Warder. Strange that these primitives should have come up with something that none of the Chosen understood, yet it was so. From the little she knew, this fellow quite possibly felt at least some of what the other patient was undergoing. Another time that would present interesting possibilities. Now, it only meant that he thought he knew what he was facing.

"Your owner does not take very good care of you," she said. "If she was more than a savage, there would be no need for you to be marred with all those scars." His expression changed only slightly. To a tinge of contempt. "So."

This time she set the net on the pleasure centers and began the slowly increasing stimulation. He was intelligent. He frowned, shook his head, then his eyes narrowed, fixed on her like chips of dark ice. He knew he should not be feeling that rising bliss, and though he could not see her net, he knew it had to be her work, so he set himself to fight it. Semirhage almost smiled. No doubt he thought pleasure easier to fight than pain. On rare occasions she had broken patients with no more than this. It gave her little enjoyment, and afterward they could not think coherently, simply wanting more of the ecstasy that bloomed in their heads, but it was quick, and they would do absolutely anything for more. That lack of coherence was why she had not used it on the other patient; she needed answers there. This fellow would learn the difference soon enough.

Difference. She put a finger to her lips in thought. Why was Shaidar Haran different from every other Myrddraal? She did not like discovering an oddity just when everything seemed to be going in their favor, and a Myrddraal set above the Chosen, even occasionally, was more than a mere oddity. Al'Thor was blinded, his attention all on Sammael, and Graendal was letting Sammael know enough to keep him from ruining everything with his pride. Of course, Graendal and Sammael were certainly scheming for advantage, together or separately. Sammael was a hot *so-far* with warped steering planes, and Graendal not much easier to predict. They had never learned that power came only from the Great Lord, handed out as he chose, for his own reasons. At his whims; she could think that in the safety of her head.

More troubling were the Chosen who had vanished. Demandred insisted they must be dead, but she and Mesaana were not so sure. Lanfear. If there was any justice, time would give her Lanfear. The woman was always there when least expected, always behaving as if she had the right to dabble her fingers in others' plans, always flitting to safety if her dabbling brought ruin. Moghedien. She skulked out of sight, but she had never gone so long before without making herself known, just to remind the rest of them that she, too, was Chosen. Asmodean. A traitor, and so doomed, but he really had vanished, and Shaidar Haran's existence and her own orders here combined to remind her that the Great Lord worked in his own ways toward his own goals.

The Chosen were no more than pieces on the board; they might be Counselors and Spires, but they were still pieces. If the Great Lord moved her here secretly, might he not be moving Moghedien or Lanfear, or even Asmodean? Might Shaidar Haran not be sent to deliver covert commands to Graendal or Sammael? Or for that matter, to Demandred or Mesaana? Their uneasy alliance—if it could be called by so strong a name—had lasted a long time, but neither would tell her if they received secret orders from the Great Lord, any more than she would ever let them learn of the orders that had brought her here, or those that had had her send Myrddraal and Trollocs to the Stone of Tear to battle those sent by Sammael.

If the Great Lord meant to make al'Thor Nae'blis, she herself would kneel to him—and wait for a slip to deliver him into her hands. Immortality meant infinite time to wait. There would always be other patients to amuse her in the meantime. What troubled her was Shaidar Haran. She had never been more than an indifferent *tcheran* player, but Shaidar Haran was a new piece on the board, one of unknown strength and purpose. And one daring way to capture your opponent's High Counselor and turn it to your side was to sacrifice your Spires in a false attack. She would kneel if need be, for as long as need be, but she would not be sacrificed.

An odd feel to the net pulled her out of her thoughts. She took one look at the patient and clicked her tongue in exasperation. His head hung to one side, chin dark with blood where he had chewed his tongue, eyes staring and already filmed over. Inattention, and she had let the stimulation grow too fast, too far. With an irritation that never touched her face, she stopped channeling. There was no point trying to stimulate the brain of a corpse.

A sudden thought occurred to her. If the Warder could feel what the Aes Sedai felt, was the reverse true? Eyeing the scars that decorated the man's body, she was sure it was impossible; even these simple fools would have altered the bond if it meant sharing the feel of *that*. Still, she abandoned the cadaver and stepped across the corridor with some haste.

Screams heard before she opened the iron-bound door onto darkness brought a deep breath of relief. Killing the woman before draining her of everything she knew would probably have meant remaining here until another Aes Sedai was captured. At the least.

There were barely intelligible words among the throat-shredding howls, words that seemed to have all the force of the patient's soul behind them. "Pleeeeaaaase! Oh, Light, PLEEEEAAAASE!"

Semirhage smiled faintly. There was a little fun in this after all.

CHAPTER
7

A Matter of Thought

Seated on her mattress, Elayne finished the one hundred strokes with her left hand, then put the hairbrush away in her small leather traveling case and pushed it back under the narrow bed. A dull ache rested behind her eyes from a day spent channeling, making *ter'angreal*. Too often *trying* to make *ter'angreal* Nynaeve, balanced atop their loose-jointed stool, had long since completed brushing her waist-length hair and was nearly done replaiting her braid loosely for sleep. Sweat made her face glisten.

Even with the one window open, the small room was stifling. The moon hung fat in a star-filled black sky. Their stub of candle provided a fitful glow. Candles and lamp oil were in short supply in Salidar; no one got more than a scrap of light at night unless they had to work with pen and ink. The room truly was cramped, with little space to move around the two short beds. Most of what they owned was packed away in a pair of battered brass-bound chests. Accepted's dresses and cloaks they certainly had no need of now hung from pegs in the walls, where ragged holes in the crazed yellowing plaster showed the lathing beneath. A tiny table with a tilt was shoved between the beds, and a rickety washstand in the corner held a white pitcher and basin with an amazing number of chips between them. Even Accepted who had their heads patted at every turn were not indulged.

A handful of bedraggled blue and white wildflowers—fooled by the

weather into blooming late, and not very well—stuck out of a yellow vase
with a broken neck between a pair of brown pottery cups on the table. The
only other spot of color was a green-striped song sparrow in a wicker cage.
Elayne was nursing it for a broken wing. She had tried her small skill with
Healing on another bird, but songbirds at least were too small to survive
the shock.

No complaining, she told herself firmly. Aes Sedai lived a little better,
novices and servants a little worse, and Gareth Bryne's soldiers slept on the
ground most often. What can't be changed must be endured. Lini used to say
that all the time. Well, Salidar held small enough comfort, and no luxury.
And no coolness, either.

Pulling her shift away from her body, she blew down her front. "We
want to be there ahead of them, Nynaeve. You know how they go on if they
have to wait."

Not a breath of breeze stirred, and the parched air seemed to pull perspiration from every pore. There must be something that could be done
about the weather. Of course, if there was, Sea Folk Windfinders would
probably already have done it, but she still might think of something, if
only the Aes Sedai would give her time enough away from ter'angreal. As
Accepted, she supposedly could take her studies where she wanted, but. . . .
If they thought I could eat and show them how to make ter'angreal at the same
time, I wouldn't have a minute to myself. At least there would be a break in
that tomorrow.

Shifting to her bed, Nynaeve frowned and fiddled with the a'dam bracelet on her wrist. She always insisted one of them wear it even when they
slept, though it produced decidedly odd and unpleasant dreams. There was
hardly need; the a'dam would hold Moghedien just as well hanging on a
peg, and on top of that, she shared a truly tiny cubbyhole with Birgitte.
Birgitte was as good a guard as could be, and besides, Moghedien almost
wept any time Birgitte so much as frowned. She had the least reason to
want Moghedien alive, the most to want her dead, which the woman knew
very well. Tonight the bracelet would be less use than usual.

"Nynaeve, they'll be waiting."

Nynaeve sniffed loudly—she did not do well being at anyone's beck
and call—but she took one of two flattened stone rings from the table between the beds. Both too large for a finger, one was striped and flecked
blue and brown, the other blue and red, and each was twisted so it had
only one edge. Unfastening the leather thong hanging around her neck,
Nynaeve threaded the blue-and-brown ring alongside another, heavy and

gold. Lan's signet. She touched the thick gold band tenderly before tucking both inside her shift.

Elayne picked up the blue-and-red ring, frowning at it.

The rings were *ter'angreal* she had made in imitation of one now in Siuan's possession, and despite their simple appearance, they were complex beyond belief. Sleeping with one next to your skin would take you into *Tel'aran'rhiod*, the World of Dreams, a reflection of the real world. Perhaps of all worlds; some Aes Sedai claimed that there were many worlds, as if all variations of the Pattern had to exist, and that all those worlds together made up a still larger Pattern. The important thing was that *Tel'aran'rhiod* reflected this world, and had properties that were extremely useful. Especially since the Tower knew nothing of entering it, so far as they could discover.

Neither of these rings worked quite as well as the original, though they did work. Elayne was getting a little better at that; of four attempts to produce a copy, only one had been a failure. A *much* better average than with the things she made from scratch. But what if one of her failures did worse than simply not work, or not work very well? Aes Sedai had been stilled studying *ter'angreal*. Burned out, it was called when it happened by accident, yet it was just as final. Nynaeve did not think so, of course but Nynaeve would not be satisfied till she Healed somebody three days dead.

Elayne turned the ring in her fingers. What it did was simple enough to understand, but the "how" still escaped her. "How" and "why" were the keys. With the rings she thought the pattern of colors had as much to do with it as the shape—anything other than the twisted ring did nothing, and the one that had turned out solid blue just gave you horrific nightmares—but she was not sure how to reproduce the original's red, blue and brown. Yet the fine structure of her copies was the same, the way the tiniest bits of them, too small to see or even detect without the One Power, were arranged. Why should the *colors* matter? There seemed to be one common thread in those tiny structures for *ter'angreal* that required channeling to work, and another for those that simply made use of the Power—stumbling on that was what allowed her to even attempt to make original *ter'angreal*—but there was so much she did not know, so much she was guessing at.

"Are you going to sit there all night?" Nynaeve asked dryly, and Elayne gave a start. Setting one of the pottery cups back on the table, Nynaeve arranged herself on her bed, hands folded across her middle. "You *were* the one who mentioned not keeping them waiting. For myself, I don't mean to give those biddies an excuse to chew my tailfeathers."

Hastily Elayne slipped the speckled ring—it was not really stone anymore, though it had started out that way—onto a cord that she tied around her own neck. The second pottery cup also held a tincture of herbs that Nynaeve had prepared, slightly sweetened with honey to negate a bitter taste. Elayne drank about half, from past experience enough to help her sleep even with a headache. Tonight was one of those nights she could not afford to dally.

Stretching out on the cramped bed, she channeled briefly to extinguish the candle, then flapped her shift to produce a little cool. Well, a stir in the air, anyway. "I wish Egwene would get better. I am tired of the scraps Sheriam and the rest of them toss us. I want to know what is happening!"

She had touched on a hazardous topic, she realized. Egwene had been injured a month and a half ago in Cairhien, on the day Moiraine and Lanfear died. The day Lan vanished.

"The Wise Ones say she *is* getting better," Nynaeve murmured sleepily in the dark. For once she did not sound as if she had followed the path to Lan. "That's what Sheriam and her little circle say, and they have no reason to lie even if they could."

"Well, I wish I could look over Sheriam's shoulder tomorrow night."

"As well wish—" Nynaeve stopped for a yawn. "As well wish the Hall will choose you Amyrlin while you're about it. You might have that one, granted. By the time they choose anyone, we'll both be gray-haired enough for the job."

Elayne opened her mouth to reply, but with the other woman's example, it turned into a yawn too. Nynaeve began to snore, not loudly, but with dogged persistence. Elayne let her eyes drift shut, but her thoughts tried to remain focused in spite of herself.

The Hall certainly was being dilatory, the Sitters meeting for less than an hour some days and often not at all. To talk to one, you would think she saw no urgency, though of course the Sitters for the six Ajahs—there were no Reds in Salidar, of course—did not tell other Aes Sedai what they discussed in session, much less an Accepted. They certainly had cause for dispatch. If their intentions remained secret, their gathering surely no longer did. Elaida and the Tower would not ignore them forever. Beyond that, the Whitecloaks were still only a few miles away in Amadicia, and rumors had begun of Dragonsworn right here in Altara. The Light alone knew what Dragonsworn might get up to if Rand had no control over them. The

Prophet was a good example—or rather a horrid one. Riots, homes and farms burned, people murdered for not showing enough fervor in support of the Dragon Reborn.

Nynaeve's snoring sounded like cloth ripping, but in the distance. Another yawn cracked Elayne's jaws; she turned on her side and snuggled into the thin pillow. Reasons for dispatch. Sammael sat in Illian, and it was only a few hundred miles to the Illianer border, far too close with one of the Forsaken. The Light alone knew where the other Forsaken were, or what they were scheming. And Rand; they had to be concerned about Rand. He was not a danger, of course. He could never be that. But he *was* the key to everything; the world truly did bend itself around him now. She *would* bond him, somehow. Min. She and the embassy had to be more than halfway to Caemlyn by now. No snows to slow them. Another month yet for them to arrive. Not that she was concerned about Min going to Rand. What was the girl thinking of? Min. Sleep slid over her, and she slid into *Tel'aran'rhiod* . . .

. . . and found herself standing in the main street of silent night-shrouded Salidar, with the moon gibbous overhead. She could see quite clearly, more so than moonlight alone would have allowed. There was always a sense of light in the World of Dreams, from everywhere and nowhere, as if the darkness itself had some dark glow. But then, dreams were like that, and this was a dream, if not any ordinary dream.

The village here reflected the real Salidar, but in strange facsimile, more still than even night would make it. Every window was dark, and an air of emptiness hung heavily, as if no one occupied any of the buildings. Of course, no one did, here. A nightbird's reedy cry was answered by another, then a third, and something made a faint rustling noise as it skittered away in the odd half-light, but the stables would be empty, and the picket lines outside the village, and the clearings where sheep and cattle had been gathered. Wild creatures there would be in plenty, but none domesticated. Details changed between one glance and the next; the thatch-roofed buildings remained the same, yet a water barrel would be in a slightly different place, or gone, a door that had stood open was closed. The more ephemeral a thing was in the real world, the more its position or condition might change, the less firm its reflection.

Occasionally motion flickered in the dark street, someone appearing and vanishing after a few steps, or even floating across the ground as if flying. Many people's dreams could touch *Tel'aran'rhiod*, but only briefly. Which was lucky for them. Another property of the World of Dreams was that what happened to you here was still real when you woke. If you died here, you did not wake. A strange reflection. Only the heat was the same.

Nynaeve stood there in an Accepted's white dress with the banded hem, impatient beside Siuan and Leane. She had the silver bracelet, too, though it would not work from here to the waking world; it still held Moghedien, but Nynaeve, out of her body, would not be feeling anything through it. Leane was regally slim, though in Elayne's opinion her barely opaque Domani gown of thin silk detracted from her elegance. The color kept shifting, too; that sort of thing happened until you learned what you were doing here. Siuan was better. She wore a simple dress of blue silk, with a scooped neck just low enough to show the twisted ring on a necklace. On the other hand, lace trim sometimes appeared on the dress and the necklace changed from a plain silver chain to elaborate pieces with rubies or firedrops or emeralds set in gold, with earrings to match, then back to the plain chain.

That was the original ring hanging around Siuan's neck; she appeared as solid as any of the buildings. To herself, Elayne looked just as solid, but she knew that to the others she seemed slightly misty, like Nynaeve and Leane. You almost thought you might see the moonlight through them. That was what using a copy did. She could sense the True Source, but as she was, *saidar* felt tenuous; if she tried to channel, that would be meager too. With the ring Siuan wore, it would not be so, but that was the price of having secrets someone else knew and you did not dare have exposed. Siuan trusted the original more than Elayne's copies, so she wore it—or sometimes Leane did—while Elayne and Nynaeve, who could use *saidar*, made do.

"Where are they?" Siuan demanded. Her neckline swooped up and down. The dress was green, now, the necklace a strand of fat moonstones. "It's bad enough they want to stick an oar into my work and row as they please; now they make me wait."

"I do not know why it upsets you for them to come along," Leane told her. "You like watching them make mistakes. They do not know half of what they think they do." For a moment her gown slid dangerously close to transparency; a close torque of fat pearls appeared around her neck and vanished. She did not notice. She had even less experience here than Siuan.

"I need some real sleep," Siuan muttered. "Bryne tries to run me breathless. But I have to wait on the pleasure of women who'll spend half the night remembering how to walk. Not to mention being lumbered with these two." She frowned at Elayne and Nynaeve, then rolled her eyes skyward.

Nynaeve gripped her braid firmly, a sure indication of temper working.

For once, Elayne agreed with her wholeheartedly. It was more than difficult being a teacher with pupils who thought they knew more than they did and were far more likely to call down the teacher than the teacher was to get away with calling them down. Of course, the others were far worse than Siuan or Leane. Where *were* the others?

Movement appeared up the street. Six women, surrounded by the glow of *saidar*, who did not vanish. As usual, Sheriam and the rest of her council had dreamed themselves into their own bedchambers and walked out. Elayne was not sure how far they understood the attributes of *Tel'aran'rhiod* yet. In any case, they often insisted on doing things their own way even when there was a better. Who could know better than an Aes Sedai?

The six Aes Sedai truly were beginners in *Tel'aran'rhiod*, and their dresses changed every time Elayne looked at them. First one was wearing the embroidered Aes Sedai shawl, fringed in the color of her Ajah and with the white Flame of Tar Valon a bold teardrop on the back, then four were, then none. Sometimes it was a light traveling cloak, as to keep dust off, with the Flame on back and left breast. Their ageless faces showed no signs of the heat, of course—Aes Sedai never did—and no sign they were aware of how their clothes were changing, either.

They were as misty as Nynaeve or Leane. Sheriam and the others put more faith in dream *ter'angreal* that required channeling than in the rings. They just did not seem willing to believe that *Tel'aran'rhiod* had nothing to do with the One Power. At least Elayne could not tell which were using her copies. Somewhere about them three would have a small disc of what had once been iron, scribed on both sides with a tight spiral and powered by a flow of Spirit, the only one of the Five Powers that could be channeled in your sleep. Except here, anyway. The other three would be carrying small plaques once amber, with a sleeping woman worked inside each. Even if she had all six *ter'angreal* in front of her, Elayne would not have been able to pick out the two originals; those copies had gone very well. Just the same, it was still copying.

As the Aes Sedai came down the dirt street together, she heard the tail end of their conversation, though she could not make head nor foot of it.

". . . will scorn our choice, Carlinya," fiery-haired Sheriam was saying, "but they will scorn any choice we make. We might as well stay by our decision. You do not need me to list reasons again."

Morvrin, a stout Brown sister with gray-streaked hair, snorted. "After all our work with the Hall, we would have a hard time changing their minds now."

"As long as no ruler scoffs, why should we care?" Myrelle said heatedly. The youngest of the six, not many years Aes Sedai, she sounded decidedly irritated.

"What ruler would dare?" Anaiya asked, much like a woman asking what child would dare track mud on her carpets. "In any case, no king or queen knows enough of what passes among Aes Sedai to understand. Only the sisters' opinions need concern us, not theirs."

"What worries me," Carlinya replied coolly, "is that if she is easily guided by us, she may be as easily guided by others." The pale, almost black-eyed White was always cool, some would say icy.

Whatever they were talking about, it was nothing they wanted to discuss in front of Elayne or the others; they fell silent just before reaching them.

Siuan and Leane's reaction to the newcomers had been to turn their backs on each other sharply, as if they had been having words interrupted by the Aes Sedai's arrival. For Elayne's part, she quickly checked her dress. It was the proper banded white. She did not know how she felt about that, appearing in the right dress without thought; she would have wagered that Nynaeve had had to change her garb after appearing. But then, Nynaeve was far more intrepid than she, struggling against limits that she herself acquiesced to. How could she ever manage to rule Andor? If her mother was dead. If.

Sheriam, slightly plump and with high cheekbones, turned tilted green eyes on Siuan and Leane. For a moment she wore a blue-fringed shawl. "If you two cannot learn to get along, I vow I'll send both of you to Tiana." It had the sound of something said often and no longer really meant.

"You worked together long enough," Beonin said in her heavy Taraboner accent. A pretty Gray with honey-colored hair in a multitude of braids, she had blue-gray eyes that constantly looked startled. Nothing surprised Beonin, though. She would not believe the sun came up in the morning until she saw for herself, yet if one morning it did not, Elayne doubted that Beonin would turn a hair. It would just confirm that she had been right to demand proof. "You can and must work together again."

Beonin sounded as if she had said that so often that she hardly thought of it. All the Aes Sedai were long since used to Siuan and Leane. They had begun handling them as they might have managed two girls who could not stop squabbling. Aes Sedai did have a tendency to see anyone who was not as a child. Even these two who once had been sisters.

"Send them to Tiana or don't," Myrelle snapped, "but don't talk about it." Elayne did not think the darkly beautiful woman was angry at Siuan or Leane. Perhaps not at anyone or anything in particular. She had a volatile temper remarkable even among Greens. Her golden yellow silk dress became high-necked, but with an oval cutout that exposed the tops of her breasts; she wore a peculiar necklace, too, like a wide silver collar supporting three small daggers, hilts nestling in her cleavage. A fourth dagger appeared and was gone so quickly it might have been imagination. She eyed Nynaeve up and down as if searching for fault. "Are we going to the Tower, or aren't we? If we are going to do this, we might as well accomplish something useful while we are about it."

Elayne knew why Myrelle was angry, now. When she and Nynaeve first came to Salidar, they had been meeting Egwene in *Tel'aran'rhiod* every seven days to share what they had learned. Which had not always been easy, since Egwene was always accompanied by at least one of the Aiel dreamwalkers she was studying with. Meeting without a Wise One or two had taken some pains. In any case, all that ended when they reached Salidar. These six Aes Sedai of Sheriam's council had taken over the meetings, when they had had only the three original *ter'angreal* and little more knowledge of *Tel'aran'rhiod* than how to reach it. That had been just when Egwene was injured, which left Aes Sedai facing Wise Ones, two sets of proud resolute women, each suspicious of what the other wanted, neither willing to yield an inch or bow her neck a hair.

Of course, Elayne did not know what went on at those meetings, but she had her own experiences to go by, and fragments dropped here and there by Sheriam and the others.

Aes Sedai were sure they could learn anything once they knew there was something to be learned, usually required the respect due a queen, and always expected to be told what they wanted to know without delays or quibbles. They had apparently demanded answers about everything, from what Rand was planning to when Egwene would be well enough to return to the World of Dreams, to whether it was possible to spy on people's dreams in *Tel'aran'rhiod* or to enter the World of Dreams physically, or bring someone into the dream against their will. They had even asked more than once whether it was possible to affect the real world by what you did in the dream, a pure impossibility they apparently doubted. Morvrin had read a little about *Tel'aran'rhiod*, enough to come up with plenty of questions, though Elayne suspected Siuan supplied her share. She thought Siuan was angling to attend the meetings herself, but the Aes Sedai seemed to think it concession enough to allow her to use the ring as an aid in her work with the eyes-and-ears. Aes Sedai interference in that work was what upset her.

As for the Aiel. . . . Wise Ones—the dreamwalkers, at least, Elayne was aware from her own encounters, not only knew just about everything there was to know about the World of Dreams, but looked on it almost as a private preserve. They did not like anyone coming there in ignorance, and had a rough way of dealing with what they saw as foolishness. Besides which, they were a closemouthed lot, apparently fiercely loyal to Rand, unwilling to say much more than that he was alive, or that Egwene would return to *Tel'aran'rhiod* when she was well enough, and more than unwilling to answer questions they considered improper. Which last could mean that they did not believe the questioner knew enough yet to hear the answer, or that question or answer or both somehow violated their strange philosophy of honor and obligation. Elayne knew little more of *ji'e'toh* than that it existed, and that it made for very peculiar, very touchy behavior.

All in all, it was a recipe for disaster, and Elayne thought it very probably was served up fresh every seven days, at least from the Aes Sedai point of view.

Sheriam and the other five had required lessons every night in the beginning, but now there were only two times they did so. The night before meeting the Wise Ones, as if to hone their skills one last time before a contest. And the night after, usually tight-mouthed, as if to work out what had gone wrong and how to counter it. Myrelle was probably already seething over tomorrow night's disaster. There surely would be one of some kind.

Morvrin turned to Myrelle and opened her mouth, but suddenly there was another woman among them. It took Elayne a moment to recognize Gera, one of the cooks, in those ageless features. Wearing a green-fringed shawl with the Flame of Tar Valon on her back and weighing no more than half what she really did, Gera raised an admonitory finger to the Aes Sedai—and was gone.

"So those are her dreams, are they?" Carlinya said coolly. Her snow-white silk dress grew sleeves that hung in points over her hands, and a high tight neck under her chin. "Someone should speak to her."

"Leave over, Carlinya," Anaiya chuckled. "Gera's a good cook. Let her have her dreams. I can see the attraction myself." Abruptly she became slimmer and taller. Her features did not really alter; she wore the same plain, motherly face as always. With a laugh she changed back. "Can't you see the fun in something for once, Carlinya?" Even Carlinya's sniff was cool.

"Clearly," Morvrin said, "Gera saw us, but will she remember?" Her dark, steely eyes were thoughtful. Her dress, plain dark wool, held the steadiest among the six. Details shifted, but so subtly that Elayne could not really say what was different.

"Of course she will," Nynaeve said acerbically. She had explained this before. Six Aes Sedai looked at her, eyebrows rising, and she moderated her voice. A little. She hated scrubbing pots, too. "If she remembers the dream, she will. But only as a dream."

Morvrin frowned. She ran Beonin a close second in wanting proof. Nynaeve's long-suffering expression was going to get her in trouble, whatever her tone. Before Elayne could say anything to take the Aes Sedai's attention from Nynaeve, though, Leane spoke up with an expression close to a simper.

"Don't you think we should go, now?"

Siuan snorted contemptuously at the timidity, and Leane cut her eyes at her sharply. "Yes, you'll want to have as much time in the Tower as possible," Siuan said, diffident in turn, and Leane sniffed.

They really did it very well. Sheriam and the others never suspected that Siuan and Leane were not simply two stilled women clinging to a purpose that might keep them alive, clinging to the edge of what they had been. Two women childishly at one another's throats all the time. The Aes Sedai should have remembered that Siuan had had the reputation of a strong-willed and devious manipulator, and to a lesser extent so had Leane. Had they presented a unified front, or shown their true faces, the six would have remembered, and looked hard at everything the pair said. But divided, spitting rancor in each other's face, all but groveling to the Aes Sedai and plainly not even aware of it. . . . When one was reluctantly forced to agree with what the other said, it lent extra weight. When one objected on obviously frivolous grounds, so did that. Elayne knew they used the pretense to guide Sheriam and the others toward supporting Rand. She just wished she knew what else they used it for.

"They're right," Nynaeve said firmly, giving Siuan and Leane a disgusted look. Their pretense irked Nynaeve no end: Nynaeve would not have groveled for her life. "You should know by now that the longer you spend here, the less real rest you get. Sleep while you are in *Tel'aran'rhiod* doesn't do as much good as ordinary sleep. Now, remember that if you see anything out of the ordinary, you need to be careful." She truly did hate repeating herself—the fact showed clearly in her voice—but with these women, Elayne had to admit it was too often necessary. If only

Nynaeve did not sound as if she were talking to dim-witted children. "When somebody dreams themselves into *Tel'aran'rhiod* like Gera, but they're having a nightmare, sometimes the nightmare survives, and those are very dangerous. Avoid anything that looks unusual. And try to control your thoughts this time. What you think of here can become real. That Myrddraal that popped out of nowhere last time might have been a leftover nightmare, but I think one of you let her mind wander. You were talking about the Black Ajah, if you'll remember, and discussing whether they were letting Shadowspawn into the Tower." As if that were not bad enough, she had to add, "You won't impress the Wise Ones tomorrow night if you drop a Myrddraal into the middle of everything." Elayne winced.

"Child," Anaiya said gently, adjusting the blue-fringed shawl that was suddenly looped over her arms, "you have been doing very good work, but that doesn't excuse a peevish mouth."

"You have been given a number of privileges," Myrelle said, not at all gently, "but you seem to forget that they *are* privileges." Her frown should have been enough to make Nynaeve quake. Myrelle had been increasingly hard on Nynaeve the past weeks. She had her shawl on, too. They all did, a bad sign.

Morvrin snorted bluntly. "When I was Accepted, any girl who spoke to an Aes Sedai that way would have spent the next month scrubbing floors, if she was due to be raised Aes Sedai the next day."

Elayne spoke up hurriedly, hoping she could forestall their own disaster. Nynaeve had put on what she probably thought was a conciliatory face, but she looked sulky and stubborn. "I am sure she didn't mean anything, Aes Sedai. We have been working very hard. Please forgive us." Adding herself might help, since she had done nothing. It might also have them both scrubbing floors. At least it made Nynaeve look at her. And think, apparently, since her features smoothed into something that did seem appeasing and she made a curtsy and stared at the ground as though abashed. Maybe she really was. Maybe. Elayne rushed on as if Nynaeve had made a formal apology and had it accepted. "I know you all do want to spend as much time as possible at the Tower, so perhaps we shouldn't wait any longer? If you will all visualize Elaida's study, just as you saw it last time?" Elaida was never called the Amyrlin in Salidar, and in the same way the Amyrlin's study in the White Tower had its name shifted. "Everyone fix it in your minds, so we all arrive together."

Anaiya was the first to nod, but even Carlinya and Beonin let themselves be diverted.

It was unclear whether the ten of them moved or *Tel'aran'rhiod* moved around them. It could have been either from the little Elayne really understood; the World of Dreams was almost infinitely malleable. One moment they were standing in the street in Salidar, the next in a large and ornate room. The Aes Sedai gave satisfied nods, still inexperienced enough to be pleased at anything that worked as they thought it should.

As surely as *Tel'aran'rhiod* reflected the waking world, this room reflected the power of the women who had occupied it over the last three thousand years. The gilded stand-lamps were unlit, but there was light, in the odd way of *Tel'aran'rhiod* and dreams. The tall fireplace was golden marble from Kandor, the floor polished redstone from the Mountains of Mist. The walls had been paneled a relatively short time ago—a mere thousand years—in pale wood, oddly striped and carved with marvelous beasts and birds that Elayne was sure had come straight out of the carver's imagination. Gleaming pearly stone framed tall arched windows that let onto the balcony overlooking the Amyrlin's private garden; that stone had been salvaged from a nameless city submerged in the Sea of Storms during the Breaking of the World, and no one had ever found its like elsewhere.

Each woman who used that room put her own mark on it, if only for the time of her possession, and Elaida was no different. A heavy thronelike chair, an ivory Flame of Tar Valon cresting the high back, stood behind a massive writing table ornately carved in triple-linked rings. The tabletop was bare except for three boxes of Altaran lacquerwork, each precisely the same distance from the next. A plain white vase stood atop a severe white plinth against one wall. The vase held roses, the number and color changing at every look, but always arranged with a harsh rigidity. Roses, at this time of year, in this weather! The One Power had been *wasted* to make them grow. Elaida had done the same when she was advisor to Elayne's mother.

Above the fireplace hung a painting in the new style, on stretched canvas, of two men fighting among clouds, hurling lightning. One man had a face of fire, and the other was Rand. Elayne had been at Falme; the painting was not too far from the truth. A tear in the canvas across Rand's face, as though something heavy had been thrown at it, had been mended almost invisibly. Plainly Elaida wanted a constant reminder of the Dragon Reborn, and just as plainly she was not happy having to look at it.

"If you will excuse me," Leane said before all the satisfied nodding was done, "I must see if my people have received my messages." Every Ajah except the White had a network of eyes-and-ears scattered across the nations, and so did a good many individual Aes Sedai, but Leane was rare, perhaps unique, in that as Keeper she had created a net in Tar Valon itself. No sooner had she spoken than she vanished.

"She should not be wandering about alone here," Sheriam said in an exasperated voice. "Nynaeve, go after her. Stay with her."

Nynaeve gave her braid a tug. "I don't think—"

"Very often you do not," Myrelle cut her off. "For once do as you are told, when you are told, Accepted."

Exchanging wry glances with Elayne, Nynaeve nodded, visibly suppressing a sigh, and disappeared. Elayne had little sympathy. Had Nynaeve not indulged her irritation back in Salidar it might have been possible to explain that Leane could be anywhere in the city, that it would be almost impossible to find her, and that she had been venturing into *Tel'aran'rhiod* alone for weeks.

"Now to see what we can learn," Morvrin said, but before anyone could move, Elaida was behind the writing table, glaring.

An unyielding stern-faced woman, handsome rather than beautiful, and dark of hair and eye, Elaida wore a blood-red dress, with the striped stole of the Amyrlin Seat about her shoulders. "As I have Foretold," she intoned. "The White Tower will be reunited under me. Under *me!*" She pointed harshly to the floor. "Kneel, and ask forgiveness of your sins!" With that, she was gone.

Elayne let out a long breath, and was gratified to realize she was not the only one.

"A Foretelling?" Beonin's forehead creased thoughtfully. She did not sound worried, but she might well have. Elaida did have the Foretelling, if fitfully. When the Foretelling laid hold of a woman and she knew a thing would happen, it did.

"A dream," Elayne said, and was surprised at how steady her voice was. "She's asleep and dreaming. No wonder if she dreams everything to her liking." *Please, Light, let it only be that.*

"Did you notice the stole?" Anaiya asked no one in particular. "It had no blue stripe." The Amyrlin's stole was supposed to have one stripe for each of the seven Ajahs.

"A dream," Sheriam said flatly. She sounded unafraid, but she had her blue-fringed shawl on again and was clutching it around her. So was Anaiya.

"Whether it is or not," Morvrin said placidly, "we may as well do what we came for." Not much could frighten Morvrin.

The abrupt stir of activity at the Brown sister's words made it suddenly clear how still everyone had gone. She, Carlinya and Anaiya glided swiftly out to the anteroom, where the Keeper's worktable would be. That was Alviarin Freidhen, under Elaida; a White, strangely, though the Keeper *always* came from the Amyrlin's own Ajah.

Siuan stared after them testily. She claimed there was often more to be learned from Alviarin's papers than from Elaida's, for Alviarin sometimes seemed to know more than the woman she supposedly served, and twice Siuan had found evidence that Alviarin had countermanded Elaida's orders, apparently without repercussions. Not that she had told Elayne or Nynaeve what orders. There were definite limits to Siuan's sharing.

Sheriam, Beonin and Myrelle gathered at Elaida's desk, opened one of the lacquered boxes, and began rifling through the papers inside. Elaida kept her recent correspondence and reports there. The box, worked in golden hawks fighting among white clouds in a blue sky, would suddenly shut again every time one of them let go of the lid, until they remembered to hold it open, and the papers themselves changed even as they were being read. Paper truly was ephemeral. Amid vexed *tsks* and annoyed sighs, the Aes Sedai persevered.

"Here's a report from Danelle," Myrelle said, hastily scanning a page. Siuan tried to join them—Danelle, a young Brown, had been part of the cabal that deposed her—but Beonin gave her a sharp frown that sent her back to a corner grumbling to herself. Beonin had returned her attention to the box and its documents before Siuan had taken three steps; the other two women never noticed. Myrelle went right on talking. "She says that Mattin Stepaneos accepts wholeheartedly, Roedran is still trying to take every side, while Alliandre and Tylin want more time to consider their answers. There's a note here in Elaida's hand. 'Press them!'" She clicked her tongue as the report melted into air in her hand. "It did not say about what, but there can be only two possibilities to take in those four." Mattin Stepaneos was King of Illian and Roedran of Murandy, while Alliandre was Queen of Ghealdan and Tylin of Altara. The subject had to be Rand or the Aes Sedai opposing Elaida.

"At least we know our emissaries still have as good a chance as Elaida's," Sheriam said. Of course, Salidar had sent none to Mattin Stepaneos; Lord Brend of the Council of Nine, Sammael, was the true power in Illian. Elayne would have given a pretty to know what Elaida proposed that Sammael was willing to support, or at least let Mattin Stepaneos say that he would support. She was sure the three Aes Sedai would have given as much, but they just went on snatching documents out of the lacquerwork box.

"The arrest warrant for Moiraine, it is still in force," Beonin said, shaking her head as the sheet in her hand suddenly turned to a fat sheaf. "She does not yet know Moiraine is dead." Grimacing at the pages, she let them fall; they scattered like leaves, and melted into air before settling. "Elaida still means to build herself a palace, too."

"She would," Sheriam said dryly. Her hand jerked as she took in what appeared to be a short note. "Shemerin has run away. The *Accepted* Shemerin."

All three glanced at Elayne before turning back to the box, which they had to open again. None made any comment on what Sheriam had said.

Elayne very nearly ground her teeth. She and Nynaeve had told them Elaida was reducing Shemerin, a Yellow sister, to the Accepted, but of course they had not believed. An Aes Sedai could be made to do penance, she might be cast out, but she could not be demoted short of stilling. Only, it seemed that Elaida was doing exactly as that, whatever Tower law said. Maybe she was rewriting Tower law.

A number of things they had told these women had not really been believed. Such young women, Accepted, could not know enough of the world to know what could be and what not. Young women were credulous, gullible; they might well see and believe what was not there at all. It was an effort not to stamp her foot. An Accepted took what Aes Sedai wished to hand out and did not ask for what Aes Sedai did not choose to give. Such as apologies. She kept her face smooth and her smoldering inside.

Siuan felt under no such restraints. Most of the time she did not. When the Aes Sedai were not looking at her, she bathed them all in a glower. Of course, if one of the three glanced in her direction, her face became meek acceptance in a twinkling. She was very practiced at that. A lion survives by being a lion, she had once told Elayne, and a mouse by being a mouse. Even so, Siuan made a poor and reluctant mouse.

Elayne thought she detected worry in Siuan's eyes. This task had been Siuan's since she proved to the Aes Sedai that she could use the ring safely—after secret lessons for her and Leane from Nynaeve and Elayne, true—and a prime source of information. It took time to reestablish contact with eyes-and-ears scattered across the nations, and redirect their reports from the Tower to Salidar. If Sheriam and the others meant to take this over, Siuan might be less useful. In the history of the Tower no network of agents had ever been run by any but a full sister until Siuan came to Salidar with her knowledge of the Amyrlin's eyes-and-ears, and the Blue Ajah's that she had run before becoming Amyrlin. Beonin and Carlinya were openly reluctant to depend on a woman who was no longer one of them, and the others were not far behind. Truth to tell, they were none of them comfortable around a woman who had been stilled.

There really was nothing for Elayne to do, either. The Aes Sedai might call this a lesson, they might even think of it so, but she knew from past experience that if she tried to do any teaching without being asked, she would have her nose snapped off in short order. She was there to answer any questions they might have and nothing more. She thought of a stool—it appeared, the legs carved in vines—and sat down to wait. A chair would have been more comfortable, but it might occasion comment. An Accepted sitting too comfortably was often considered an Accepted with not enough to do. After a moment Siuan made herself an almost identical stool. She gave Elayne a tight smile—and the Aes Sedai backs a scowl.

The first time Elayne had visited this room in *Tel'aran'rhiod*, there had been a semicircle of such stools, a dozen or more, in front of the heavily carved table. Each visit since had seen fewer, and now none. She was sure that indicated something, though she could not imagine what. She was sure Siuan thought so, too, and very likely had puzzled out a reason, but if she had, she had not shared it with Elayne or Nynaeve.

"The fighting in Shienar and Arafel is dying down," Sheriam murmured half to herself, "but still nothing here to say why it began. Skirmishes only, yet Bordermen do not fight one another. They have the Blight." She was Saldaean, and Saldaea was one of the Borderlands.

"At least the Blight is still quiet," Myrelle said. "Almost too quiet. It cannot last. A good thing that Elaida has plenty of eyes-and-ears through the Borderlands." Siuan managed to combine a wince with a glare at the Aes Sedai. Elayne did not think she had managed yet to make contact with any of her agents in the Borderlands; they lay a long way from Salidar.

"I would feel better if the same could be said of Tarabon." The page in Beonin's hand grew longer and wider; she glanced at it, sniffed, and tossed it aside. "The eyes-and-ears in Tarabon, they are still silent. All of them. The only word she has of Tarabon is rumors from Amadicia that Aes Sedai are involved in the war." She shook her head at the absurdity of committing such rumors to paper. Aes Sedai did not involve themselves in civil wars. Not openly enough to be detected, at any rate. "And there are no more than a handful of confused reports from Arad Doman, it seems."

"We will know about Tarabon soon enough ourselves," Sheriam said soothingly. "A few more weeks."

The search went on for hours. There was never any shortage of documents; the lacquered box never emptied. In fact, the stack inside sometimes increased with the removal of a paper. Of course, only the shortest held steady long enough to be read in full, but occasionally a letter or report that had already been scanned would come out of the box again. Long stretches passed in silence, yet some documents elicited comment; a few the Aes Sedai discussed. Siuan began stringing a cat's-cradle between her hands, apparently paying no attention at all. Elayne wished she could do the same, or better yet read—a book appeared on the floor at her feet, *The Travels of Jain Farstrider*, before she made it go away—but women who were not Aes Sedai were granted more leeway than those training to be. Still, she learned a few things by listening.

Aes Sedai involvement in Tarabon was not the only rumor that had found its way to Elaida's writing table. Pedron Niall's ingathering of the Whitecloaks was rumored to have as its goal everything from seizing the throne of Amadicia—which he certainly had no need of—to crushing the wars and anarchy in Tarabon and Arad Doman, to *supporting* Rand. Elayne would believe that when the sun rose in the west. There were reports of strange occurrences in Illian and Cairhien—there might have been others, but those were the ones they saw—villages taken by madness, nightmares walking in daylight, two-headed calves that talked, Shadowspawn appearing out of thin air. Sheriam and the other two passed over those lightly; the same sort of stories drifted to Salidar from parts of Altara and Murandy and across the river from Amadicia. The Aes Sedai dismissed them as hysteria among people learning of the Dragon Reborn. Elayne was not so sure. She had seen things they had not, for all their years and experience. Her mother was rumored to be raising an army in the west of Andor— under the ancient flag of Manetheren, of all things!—as well as being held prisoner by Rand and fleeing to every nation imaginable, including the Borderlands and Amadicia, which last was purely *un*imaginable. Apparently the Tower believed none of it. Elayne wished she knew what to believe.

She stopped fretting over where her mother really was when she heard Sheriam mention her name. Not speaking to her; reading hurriedly from a square sheet of paper that became a long parchment with three seals at the bottom. Elayne Trakand was to be located and returned to the White Tower at all costs. If there was any more bungling, those who failed would "envy the Macura woman." That made Elayne shiver; on their way to Salidar a woman named Ronde Macura had come within an eyelash of sending her and Nynaeve back to the Tower like bundles of wash to the laundry.

The ruling house of Andor, Sheriam read, was "the key," which made as little sense. The key to what?

None of the three Aes Sedai so much as glanced in her direction. They just exchanged glances and went on with what they were doing. Perhaps they had forgotten her, but then again, perhaps not. Aes Sedai did what they did. If she was to be shielded from Elaida, that was an Aes Sedai decision, and if they decided for some reason to hand her to Elaida bound hand and foot, that was their choice too. *"The pike does not ask the frog's permission before dining,"* as she remembered Lini saying.

Elaida's response to Rand's amnesty was evident in the condition of the report. Elayne could almost see her crumpling the sheet of paper in her fist, starting to rip it apart, then coldly smoothing it out and adding it to the box. Elaida's rages were almost always cold. She had not written anything on that document, but scrawled biting words on another, enumerating the Aes Sedai in the Tower, made clear she was almost ready to declare publicly that any who did not obey her order to return were traitors. Sheriam and the other two discussed the possibility calmly. However many sisters intended to obey, some would have far to travel; some might not even have received the summons yet. In any case, such a decree would confirm to the world all the rumors of a divided Tower. Elaida must be near panic to consider such a thing, or else maddened beyond reason.

A sliver of cold slid down Elayne's backbone, and nothing to do with whether Elaida was fearful or engaged. Two hundred ninety four Aes Sedai in the Tower, supporting Elaida. Nearly one-third of all Aes Sedai, almost as many as had gathered in Salidar. It might be that the best that could be expected was for the rest to split down the middle as well. After a great rush in the beginning, the numbers coming into Salidar had slowed to a trickle. Perhaps the flow to the Tower had dwindled as well. It could be hoped.

For a time they did their searching in silence, then Beonin exclaimed, "Elaida, she has sent emissaries to Rand al'Thor." Elayne leaped to her feet, and barely held her tongue at a clutching gesture from Siuan, spoiled a little by her failure to make the cat's-cradle disappear first.

Sheriam reached for the single sheet, but it became three before her hand touched it. "Where is she sending them?" she asked at the same time Myrelle asked, "When did they leave Tar Valon?" Serenity hung on by its fingernails.

"To Cairhien," Beonin said. "And I did not see when, if it was mentioned. But they certainly will go on to Caemlyn as soon as they discover where he is."

Even so, that was good; it might take a month or more to travel from Cairhien to Caemlyn. The Salidar embassy would reach him first, surely. Elayne had a ragged map tucked away beneath her mattress back in Salidar, and every day she marked off how far she thought they might have traveled toward Caemlyn.

The Gray sister was not finished. "It seems that Elaida, she means to offer him support. And an escort to the Tower." Sheriam's eyebrows rose.

"That is preposterous." Myrelle's olive cheeks darkened. "Elaida was Red." An Amyrlin was of all Ajahs and none, yet no one could simply abandon where they came from.

"That woman will do anything," Sheriam said. "He might find the White Tower's support attractive."

"Perhaps we can send a message to Egwene through the Aiel women?" Myrelle suggested in a doubtful tone.

Siuan gave a loud, and very phony, cough, but Elayne had had all she could stand. Warning Egwene was vital, of course—Elaida's people would surely drag her back to the Tower if they discovered her in Cairhien, and not to a pleasant reception—but the rest . . . ! "How can you think Rand would listen to anything Elaida says? Do you think he does not know she was Red Ajah, and what that means? They aren't going to offer him support, and you know it. We have to warn him!" There was a contradiction in that, and she knew it, but worry had hold of her tongue. If anything happened to Rand, she would die.

"And how do you suggest that *we* do that, Accepted?" Sheriam asked coolly.

Elayne was afraid she must look like a fish, with her mouth hanging open. She had not a clue what answer to give. She was saved suddenly by distant screaming, followed by wordless shouts from the anteroom. She was closest to the door, but she ran through with the others on her heels.

The room was empty except for the Keeper's writing table, with its piles of papers and stacks of scrolls and documents, and a row of chairs against one wall where Aes Sedai would sit while waiting to speak to Elaida. Anaiya, Morvrin and Carlinya were gone, but one of the tall outer doors was still swinging shut. A woman's frantic screams rolled through the narrowing opening. Sheriam, Myrelle and Beonin almost knocked Elayne down in their haste to reach the hall. They might have appeared misty, but they felt solid enough.

"Be careful," Elayne shouted, yet there was really nothing to do but

gather her skirts and follow as quickly as possible with Siuan. They stepped
into a scene from nightmare. Literally.

Some thirty paces to their right, the tapestry-hung corridor suddenly
widened into a stony cavern that seemed to stretch forever, lit in dim
patches by the red glow of scattered fires and braziers. There were Trollocs
everywhere, great manlike shapes, their all-too-human faces distorted by
bestial muzzles and snouts and beaks, sporting horns or tusks or feathered
crests. Those in the distance appeared more indistinct than the nearest,
only half-formed, while the nearest were giants twice as tall as a man, even
larger than any real Trolloc, all clad in leather and black spiked mail,
howling and capering around cookfires and cauldrons, racks and strange
spiked frames and metal shapes.

It really was a nightmare, though larger than any Elayne had heard of
from Egwene or the Wise Ones. Once freed of the mind that created them,
such things sometimes drifted through the World of Dreams and sometimes latched on to a particular spot. Aiel dreamwalkers destroyed each as
a matter of course whenever they found one, but they—and Egwene—had
told her the best thing to do was avoid any she saw altogether. Unfortunately, Carlinya apparently had not listened when she and Nynaeve passed
that on

The White sister was bound and hanging by her ankles from a chain
that disappeared into darkness overhead. To Elayne's eyes the glow of *saidar* still surrounded her, but Carlinya writhed frantically and screamed as
she was slowly lowered headfirst toward a great bubbling black kettle of
boiling oil.

Even as Elayne ran into the corridor, Anaiya and Morvrin halted at the
border where hallway abruptly became cavern. For all of a heartbeat, they
halted, then suddenly their hazy forms seemed to elongate toward the
boundary, like smoke drawn into a chimney. No sooner had they touched
it than they were inside, Morvrin shouting as two Trollocs turned great
iron wheels that stretched her out tighter and tighter, Anaiya dangling by
her wrists as Trollocs danced about her, flogging her with metal-tipped
whips that tore long rents in her dress.

"We must link," Sheriam said, and the glow surrounding her merged
with that around Myrelle and Beonin. Even so, it did not come near the
brightness of that around a single woman in the waking world, a woman
who was not a misty dream.

"No!" Elayne shouted urgently. "You mustn't accept it as real. You must treat it as—" She seized Sheriam's arm, but the flow of Fire the three had woven, tenuous even with them linked, touched the dividing line between dream and nightmare. The weave vanished there as if the nightmare had absorbed it, and in the same instant the three Aes Sedai became drawn out, mist caught in a wind. They had time only for startled yells before they touched the boundary and vanished. Sheriam reappeared inside, her head sticking up from a dark metal bell shape. Trollocs turned handles and jerked levers on the outside, and Sheriam's red hair flailed wildly as she shrieked in rising crescendos. Of the other two there was no sign, but Elayne thought she could hear more screaming in the distance, someone wailing "No!" over and over, another shrieking for help.

"Do you remember what we told you about dispelling nightmares?" Elayne asked.

Eyes fixed on the scene in front of her, Siuan nodded. "Deny its reality. Try to fix things in your mind as they would be without it."

That had been Sheriam's mistake, all the Aes Sedai's mistake probably. By trying to channel against the nightmare they had accepted it as real, and that acceptance had pulled them into it as surely as walking in, leaving them helpless unless they remembered what they had forgotten. Which they showed no sign of doing. The climbing shrieks augered into Elayne's ears.

"The corridor," she muttered, trying to form in her head how it had been when she saw it last. "Think of the corridor the way you remember it."

"I'm trying, girl," Siuan growled. "It isn't working."

Elayne sighed. Siuan was right. Not a line of the scene before them so much as wavered. Sheriam's head was almost vibrating above the metal shroud that enclosed the rest of her. Morvrin's howls came in strained pants; Elayne almost thought she could hear the woman's joints being pulled apart. Carlinya's hair, hanging below her, was almost touching the roiling surface of the hot oil. Two women were not enough. The nightmare was too big.

"We need the others," she said.

"Leane and Nynaeve? Girl, if we knew where to find them, Sheriam and the rest would be dead before. . . ." She trailed off, staring at Elayne. "You don't mean Leane and Nynaeve, do you? You mean Sheriam and. . . ." Elayne only nodded; she was too frightened to speak. "I don't think they can hear us from here, or see us. Those Trollocs haven't even glanced our way. That means we have to try from inside." Elayne nodded again. "Girl," Siuan said in a toneless voice, "you have a lion's courage, and maybe a fisherbird's sense." With a heavy sigh, she added, "But I don't see any other way myself."

Elayne agreed with her about everything except the courage. If she had not had her knees locked, she would have been in a heap on the floor tiles, patterned in all the colors of the Ajahs. She realized she had a sword in her hand, a great gleaming length of steel, absolutely useless even had she known how to wield it. She let it fall, and it vanished before reaching the floor. "Waiting isn't helping anything," she muttered. Much longer, and the little courage she had managed to scrape together would surely evaporate.

Together she and Siuan stepped toward the boundary. Elayne's foot touched that dividing line, and suddenly she felt herself being pulled in, sucked like water through a tube.

One instant she was standing in the hallway, staring at the horrors, the next she was lying on her belly on rough gray stone, wrists and ankles tightly tied in the small of her back, and the horrors were all around her. The cavern stretched endless in every direction; the Tower corridor no longer seemed to exist. Screams filled the air, echoing from rocky walls and a ceiling dripping stalactites. A few paces from her a huge black cauldron stood steaming over a roaring fire. A boar-snouted Trolloc, complete with tusks, was tossing in lumps that seemed to be unidentifiable roots. A cookpot. Trollocs ate anything. Including people. She thought of her hands and feet free, but the coarse rope still dug into her flesh. Even the pale shadow of *saidar* had vanished; the True Source no longer existed for her, not here. A nightmare in truth, and she was well and truly caught.

Siuan's voice cut through the screams in a pained moan. "Sheriam, listen to me!" The Light alone knew what was being done to her; Elayne could not see any of the others. Only hear them. "This is a dream! *Aah . . . aaaaaaah!* Th-think how it should be!"

Elayne took it up. "Sheriam, Anaiya, everybody, listen to me! You must think of the corridor as it was! As it really is! This is only real as long as you believe it!" She set the image of the corridor in her head firmly, colored tiles in ordered rows and gilded stand-lamps and brilliant woven tapestries. Nothing changed. The screams still echoed. "You must think of the corridor! Hold it in your minds, and it will be real! You can defeat this if you try!" The Trolloc looked at her; it had a thick sharp-pointed knife in its hand now. "Sheriam, Anaiya, you have to concentrate! Myrelle, Beonin, concentrate on the corridor!" The Trolloc heaved her onto her side. She tried to wriggle away, but a massive knee held her in place effortlessly while the thing began slicing at her clothes like a hunter skinning a deer carcass. Desperately she held on to the image of the hallway. "Carlinya, Morvrin, for the love of the Light, concentrate! Think of the corridor! The corridor! All of you! Think of it hard!" Grunting something in a harsh language never meant for a human tongue, the Trolloc flipped her face-down again and knelt on her, thick knees crushing her arms against her back. "The corridor!" she screamed. It tangled heavy fingers in her hair, yanked her head back. "The corridor! Think of the corridor!" The Trolloc's blade touched her tight-stretched neck beneath her left ear. "The corridor! The corridor!" The blade began to slide.

Suddenly she was staring at colored floor tiles under her nose. Clapping hands to her throat, marveling that they were free to move, she felt wetness and brought her fingers up to stare at them. Blood, but only a tiny smear. A shudder rippled through her. If that Trolloc had succeeded in cutting her throat. . . . No Healing could have cured that. Shuddering again, she pushed slowly to her feet. It was the Tower hallway outside the Amyrlin's study, with no sign of Trollocs or caverns.

Siuan was there, looking a mass of bruises in a torn dress, and the Aes Sedai, misty forms of near ruin. Carlinya was in the best shape, and she stood wide-eyed and shaking, fingering dark hair that now ended frizzily a hand from her scalp. Sheriam and Anaiya seemed to be weeping heaps of bloody rags. Myrelle huddled in on herself, white-faced, naked and covered with long red scratches and welts. Morvrin moaned every time she moved, and she moved unnaturally, as though her joints did not work properly anymore. Beonin's dress appeared to have been clawed to shreds, and she was panting on her knees, more wide-eyed than ever, holding on to the wall to keep from falling over.

Abruptly Elayne realized that her own dress and shift were hanging from her shoulders, neatly sliced open down the front. A hunter skinning a deer carcass. She shivered so hard she almost fell. Repairing the garments was a simple matter of thought, but she was not sure how long it would take to repair her memories.

"We must go back," Morvrin said, kneeling awkwardly between Sheriam and Anaiya. Despite her stiffness and groans, she sounded as stolid as ever. "There is Healing to be done, and none here can manage it as we are."

"Yes." Carlinya touched her short hair again. "Yes, it might be best if we returned to Salidar." Her voice was a decidedly unsteady version of its normal iciness.

"I will stay a little while, if no one objects," Siuan told them. Or rather suggested, in that ill-fitting humble voice. Her dress was whole again, but the bruises remained. "I might learn a little more that's useful. All that's wrong with me are a few lumps, and I've had worse falling in a boat."

"You look more as if someone had dropped a boat on you," Morvrin told her, "but the choice is yours."

"I will stay, too," Elayne said. "I can help Siuan, and I wasn't hurt at all." She was aware of the nick on her throat every time she swallowed.

"I don't need any help," Siuan said, at the same time that Morvrin said in an even firmer voice, "You kept your head very well tonight, child. Don't spoil it now. You are coming with us."

Elayne nodded grumpily. Arguing would get her nowhere except into hot water. You would have thought the Brown sister was the teacher here, and Elayne the pupil. They probably thought she had stumbled into the nightmare the same way they did. "Remember, you can step out of the dream straight into your own body. You do not have to go back to Salidar first." There was no way of telling whether they heard her. Morvrin had turned away as soon as she nodded.

"Be easy, Sheriam," the stout woman said soothingly. "We will be back in Salidar in a few moments. Be easy, Anaiya." Sheriam at least had stopped crying, though she still moaned in pain. "Carlinya, will you help Myrelle? Are you ready, Beonin? Beonin?" The Gray raised her head and stared at Morvrin a moment before nodding.

The six Aes Sedai vanished.

With a last glance at Siuan, Elayne was only a moment behind, but she did not go to Salidar. Someone would very likely be coming to Heal the scrape on her neck, if they had noticed it, but for a little while they would be concerned with six Aes Sedai who would wake looking as if they had been pushed through some monstrous clockworks. Elayne had those few minutes, and another destination in mind.

The Grand Hall in her mother's palace in Caemlyn did not appear around her with any ease. There was a feel of resistance before she stood on a red-and-white tiled floor beneath the great arched roof, between rows of massive white columns. Once more light seemed to come from everywhere and nowhere. The huge windows overhead, depicting the White Lion of Andor alternating with the earliest queens of the realm and scenes of great Andoran victories, were indistinct with the night outside.

Immediately she saw the difference from what she knew that had made coming here difficult. On the dais at the end of the hall where the Lion Throne should have stood was instead a grandiose monstrosity made of Dragons sparkling gold and red in gilt and enamel, with sunstones for their eyes. Her mother's throne had not been removed from the chamber. It stood on a kind of pedestal, behind and above the monstrous thing.

Elayne walked slowly down the hall and climbed the white marble stairs to stare up at the gilded throne of Andoran Queens. The White Lion of Andor, picked out in moonstones against a field of rubies on the back, would have stood above her mother's head.

"What are you doing, Rand al'Thor?" she whispered harshly. "What do you think you are doing?"

She was terribly afraid that he was bungling matters without her there to guide him between the pitfalls. True, he had handled the Tairens well enough, and apparently the Cairhienin, but her people were different, bluff and straightforward, with a dislike of being maneuvered or bullied. What had worked in Tear or Cairhien could blow up in his face like an Illuminator's display of fireworks.

If only she could be with him. If only she could warn him about the Tower's embassy. Elaida had to have some trick hidden, to spring when he least expected it. Would he be sensible enough to see it? For that matter, she had no idea what the Salidar embassy's orders were. Despite Siuan's efforts, most Aes Sedai in Salidar still seemed of two minds about Rand al'Thor; he was the Dragon Reborn, prophesied savior of humanity, but then again, he was a man who could channel, doomed to madness, death and destruction.

Take care of him, Min, she thought. *Reach him quickly and take care of him.*

A stab of jealousy hit her that Min would be there to do what she wanted to. She might have to share him, but she *would* have part of him all to herself. She *would* bond him as her Warder, whatever it took.

"It will be done." She stretched a hand up toward the Lion Throne, to swear as queens had sworn since there was an Andor. The pedestal was too high for her to reach, but the intent should count. "It *will* be done."

Time was running out. An Aes Sedai would be coming, back in Salidar, to wake her and Heal the pitiful scratch on her neck. With a sigh, she stepped out of the dream.

Demandred moved out from behind the columns of the Grand Hall and looked from the two thrones to where the girl had vanished. Elayne Trakand, unless he missed his guess wildly, and using a minor *ter'angreal* by the faint look of her, one made for training beginning students. He would have given much to know what was in her head, but her words and expression had been plain enough. She did not like what al'Thor was doing here, not in the least, and meant to do something about it. A determined young woman, he suspected. In any case, another thread in the tangle yanked, however feeble the pull turned out to be.

"Let the Lord of Chaos rule," he told the thrones—though he still wished he knew why it had to be so—and opened a gateway to leave *Tel'aran'rhiod*.

CHAPTER
8

The Storm Gathers

Nynaeve woke the next morning at first light feeling grumpy. She had a sense of bad weather coming, yet a glance out of the window revealed not a single cloud marring the still gray sky. Already the day promised to be another oven. Her shift was sweat-damp and twisted from tossing and turning. Once she had been able to rely on her ability to Listen to the Wind, but it seemed to have gone all askew since leaving the Two Rivers, when it did not desert her completely.

Waiting her turn to use the washstand did not help, either, nor listening to Elayne's recital of what had happened after she left them in Elaida's study. Her own night had been one long futile search through the streets of Tar Valon, empty save for herself, pigeons, rats and heaps of garbage. That had been a shock. Tar Valon was always kept spotless; Elaida must be neglecting the city terribly for garbage to show in *Tel'aran'rhiod*. Once she had glimpsed Leane through the window of a tavern near South-harbor, of all places, but when she hurried inside, the common room was empty except for the freshly painted blue tables and benches. She should just have given up, but Myrelle had been badgering her lately, and she wanted a clear conscience when she told the woman that she had tried. Myrelle could pounce on an evasion as quickly as anyone Nynaeve had ever seen or heard of. To finish it off, she had stepped out of *Tel'aran'rhiod* last night to find Elayne's ring already back on the table and Elayne fast asleep. If there had been a prize for useless effort, she would have won it walking away. And now to learn that Sheriam and the rest had nearly gotten themselves killed . . . Even the song sparrow's chirping in its wicker cage earned a sour look.

"They think they know everything," Nynaeve muttered disparagingly. "I told them about nightmares. I warned them, and last night was not the first time." It made no difference that all six sisters had been Healed before she so much as got back from *Tel'aran'rhiod*. Much too easily it could have ended much worse—because they thought they knew it all. The irritated tugs she gave her braid delayed redoing it for the day. The *a'dam* bracelet sometimes caught on her hair, too, but she was not about to take it off. It was Elayne's turn to wear it today, but she was just as likely to leave it on a peg on the wall. Worry tickled through the bracelet, and the inevitable fear, but more than anything else, frustration. Doubtless "Marigan" was already helping with breakfast; having to do chores seemed to grate at her more than being a prisoner did. "That was good thinking on your part, Elayne. You didn't say how you ended up in it yourself after trying to warn everybody else."

Still scrubbing with her facecloth, Elayne shuddered, "It wasn't so hard to think of it. A nightmare that size needed all of us to handle. Maybe they learned a little humility. Maybe their meeting with the Wise Ones tonight won't be so bad."

Nynaeve nodded to herself. As she had thought. Not about Sheriam and the others; Aes Sedai would find humility when goats flew on wings, and a day before the Wise Ones at that. About Elayne. She had probably let herself be caught in the nightmare, though the girl would never admit it. Nynaeve was not sure whether Elayne thought taking credit for bravery was boasting or whether she simply did not realize how brave she was. Either way, Nynaeve was torn between admiration for the other woman's courage and a wish that just once Elayne would acknowledge it. "I thought I saw Rand." That brought the facecloth down.

"Was he there in the flesh?" That was dangerous, according to the Wise Ones; it risked losing some part of what made you human. "You warned him about that."

"When did he start listening to sense? I only glimpsed him. Maybe he just touched *Tel'aran'rhiod* in a dream." Unlikely, that. He apparently hedged his dreams with wards so strong she did not think he could reach the World of Dreams any other way than in the flesh, not even if he had been a Dreamwalker *and* had one of the rings. "Maybe it was somebody who looked a little like him. As I said, I only saw him for a moment, in the square in front of the Tower."

"I should be there with him," Elayne muttered. Emptying the basin into the night jar, she moved aside to let Nynaeve reach the washstand. "He *needs* me."

"What he needs is what he has always needed." Nynaeve glowered as she refilled the basin from the pitcher. She did hate washing in water that had stood all night. At least it was not cold; there was no such thing as cold water anymore. "Somebody to box his ears once a week on general principles and keep him on the straight and narrow."

"It isn't fair." A clean shift going over Elayne's head muffled the words. "I worry about him all the time." Her face popped out the top, looking more worried than indignant whatever her tone, and she pulled a banded white dress from one of the pegs. "I even worry about him in my *dreams*! Do you think he spends all his time fretting about *me*? *I* don't."

Nynaeve nodded, though a part of her considered that it was not exactly the same. Rand had been told Elayne was safe with Aes Sedai, if not where. How could Rand ever be safe? She bent over the basin, and Lan's ring fell out of her shift, dangling on its leather cord. No, Elayne was right. Whatever Lan was doing, wherever he was, she doubted he thought of her half as often as she did of him. *Light, let him be alive even if he doesn't think of me at all.* That possibility made her angry enough to pull her braid out by the roots, if she had not had her hands full of soap and facecloth. "You can't concern yourself over a man all the time," she said sourly, "even if you do want to be a Green. What did they find out last night?"

It was a long tale, though with little meat to it, and after a bit Nynaeve sat down on Elayne's bed to listen and ask questions. Not that the answers told her much either. It was just not the same when you did not see the documents yourself. All very well to learn Elaida finally knew about Rand's amnesty, but what did she mean to do about it? Proof the Tower was approaching rulers might actually be good news; it might light a fire under the Hall. Something had to. Elaida sending an embassy to Rand was certainly a worry, but he could not be fool enough to listen to anyone who came from Elaida. Could he? There just was not enough in what Elayne had overheard. And what was Rand doing putting the Lion Throne on a pedestal? What was he doing with a throne at all? He might be the Dragon Reborn and this Aiel *car*-whatever, but she could not get past the fact that she had tended him when he was a child and paddled his bottom when he needed it.

Elayne went right ahead dressing, and was done before her story was. "I'll tell you the rest later," she said hastily, and flew out the door.

Nynaeve grunted and went back to clothing herself unhurriedly. Elayne was teaching her first class of novices today, something Nynaeve had not been allowed to do yet. But if she was not trusted to teach novices, there was still Moghedien. She would be done with her breakfast chores shortly.

The only trouble was, when Nynaeve found the woman, Moghedien was up to her elbows in soapy water, the silver necklace of the *a'dam* looking especially out of place. She was not alone; a dozen other women were industriously scrubbing clothes on washboards in a wooden-fenced yard, amid steaming kettles of boiling water. More were hanging the first wash on long lines strung between poles, but heaps of bed linens and smallclothes and every sort of thing waited their turn on the washboards. The look Moghedien gave Nynaeve should have been enough to fry her hide. Hatred, shame and outrage rolled through the *a'dam*, nearly enough to swamp the ever-present fear.

The woman in charge, a sticklike gray-haired woman named Nildra, came bustling up, a stirring paddle held like a scepter and her dark woolen skirts tied up to the knee to keep them off ground muddy from spilled water. "Good morning, Accepted. I suppose you want Marigan, eh?" Her tone was a dry blend of respect with knowledge that tomorrow she might find any one of the Accepted added to her laundresses for a day or a month, to be worked and chivvied as hard as the rest if not harder. "Well, I can't let her go, yet. I'm shorthanded as it is. One of my girls is getting married today, another ran off, and two are on light work because they're pregnant. Myrelle Sedai told me I could have her. Maybe I can do without her in a few hours. I'll see."

Moghedien straightened, opening her mouth, but Nynaeve silenced her with a firm look—and a conspicuous touch to the *a'dam* bracelet on her wrist—and she resumed work. All it would take would be a few wrong words from Moghedien, a complaint that would never come from the farm woman she appeared to be, to start her on a path to stilling and the headsman, and Nynaeve and Elayne on one not much better. Nynaeve could not help swallowing in relief when Moghedien bent back to her washboard, mouth working as she muttered under her breath. Immense shame and outright fury surged through the *a'dam*.

Nynaeve managed a smile for Nildra and murmured something, she was not sure what, then stalked off to one of the communal kitchens to find breakfast. Myrelle, again. She wondered if the Green had taken against her personally for some reason. She wondered if she was going to harvest a permanently sour stomach from keeping Moghedien. She was practically eating goosemint like candy since putting the *a'dam* on the woman.

It was easy enough to get a clay mug full of tea with honey and a bun hot from the oven, but once she had them, she walked while she ate. Sweat beaded on her face. Even at that early hour heat was building and the air dry. The rising sun formed a dome of molten gold above the forest.

The dirt streets were full, as usual when there was light to see. Aes Sedai glided past serenely, ignoring dust and heat, mysterious-faced on mysterious errands, often with Warders heeling them, cold-eyed wolves vainly pretending to be tame. There were soldiers everywhere, usually marching or riding in blocks, though Nynaeve did not understand why they were allowed to crowd the streets so when they had camps in the woods. Children darted about, often aping the soldiers with sticks for swords and pikes. White-clad novices trotted through the throng about their chores. Servants moved somewhat more slowly, women with armloads of sheets for Aes Sedais' beds or baskets of bread from the kitchens, men leading ox-carts piled with firewood, hauling chests or shouldering whole sheep carcasses for the kitchens. Salidar had not been made to hold so many people; the village was ready to pop at the seams.

Nynaeve kept moving. An Accepted's day was supposedly her own for the most part, unless she was teaching novices, to be used studying what she chose to, alone or with an Aes Sedai, but an Accepted who appeared to be doing nothing could be snapped up by any Aes Sedai. She did not intend to spend the day helping a Brown sister catalog books or copying out notes for a Gray. She *hated* copying, with all that tongue clicking if she made a blot and all those sighs because her script was not as neat as a clerk's. So she wove through the dust and the crowd, and kept an eye out for Siuan and Leane. She was angry enough to channel without using Moghedien.

Every time she became aware of the heavy gold ring nestling between her breasts she thought, *He has to be alive. Even if he's forgotten me, Light, just let him be alive.* Which last, of course, only made her angrier. If al'Lan Mandragoran so much as let forgetting her cross his mind, she would set him straight. He had to be alive. Warders often died avenging their Aes Sedai— it was as sure as the sun coming up that no Warder would let anything stand in the way of that retribution—but there was no way for Lan to avenge Moiraine any more than if she had fallen off a horse and broken her neck. She and Lanfear had killed one another. He *had* to be alive. And why should she feel guilty over Moiraine's death? True, it had freed Lan for her, but she had had nothing to do with it. Yet her first thought on learning Moiraine was dead, however momentary, had been joy that Lan was free, not sorrow for Moiraine. She could not rid herself of shame over that, and it made her angrier than ever.

Suddenly she saw Myrelle stalking down the street in her direction with yellow-haired Croi Makin, one of her three Warders, striding at her side, a young splinter of a man but hard as rock. A determined look on her face, the Aes Sedai certainly showed no effects from the night before. There was nothing to say Myrelle was looking for her, but Nynaeve quickly ducked into a large stone building that had once been one of Salidar's three inns.

The broad common room had been cleared and furnished like a reception room; its plaster walls and high ceiling had been patched, a few bright tapestries had been hung, and a few colorful rugs lay scattered on a floor that no longer looked precisely splintered but still did not want to hold a polish. The shaded interior actually seemed cool after the street. Cooler, at least. It was also in use.

Logain stood insolently in front of one of the wide unlit fireplaces, the tails of his gold-embroidered red coat shoved behind his back, under the watchful gaze of Lelaine Akashi, her blue-fringed shawl marking the occasion as formal. A slender woman with a dignified air that could sometimes break in a warm smile, she was one of the three Sitters for the Blue Ajah in the Hall of the Tower in Salidar. Today it was her penetrating eye most in evidence as she studied Logain's audience.

Two men and a woman resplendent in embroidered silks and gold jewelry, all three graying, and one of the men nearly bald and wearing a square-cut beard and long mustache to make up for it. Powerful Altaran nobles, they had arrived the day before with strong escorts and as much suspicion for one another as for the Aes Sedai gathering an army inside Altara. Altarans gave allegiance to a lord or a lady or a town, with little if any left for a nation called Altara, and few nobles paid taxes, or heed to what the queen in Ebou Dar said, but they gave heed to an army in their midst. The Light alone knew what effect the rumors of Dragonsworn had on them. For the moment, though, they forgot to stare haughtily at one another or defiantly at Lelaine. Their eyes were fixed on Logain as they might have been on a huge, brightly colored viper.

To complete the cycle, copper-skinned Burin Shaeren, looking carved from an uprooted stump, watched both Logain and the visitors, a man ready to move suddenly and violently in the blink of an eye. Lelaine's Warder was there only partly to guard Logain—supposedly Logain was in Salidar of his own free will, after all—and mainly to protect the man from his visitors and a knife in his heart.

For his part, Logain appeared to flourish under all those stares. A tall man with curling hair that touched his broad shoulders, dark and handsome if hard of face, he looked as proud and confident as an eagle. It was a promise of vengeance that put the light in his eyes, though. If he could not repay everyone he wanted to, he could at least repay some. "Six Red sisters found me in Cosamelle about a year before I proclaimed myself," he said as Nynaeve came in. "Javindhra, the leader was called, though one named Barasine talked a good deal. And I heard Elaida mentioned, as if she knew what these were about. They found me asleep, and I thought I was done when they shielded me."

"Aes Sedai," the listening woman broke in harshly. Stocky and hard-eyed, she had a thin scar across her cheek that Nynaeve found incongruous on a woman. Altaran women did have a reputation for fierceness, of course, though very likely overblown. "Aes Sedai, how can what he claims be true?"

"I do not know how, Lady Sarena," Lelaine said calmly, "but it was confirmed to me by one who cannot lie. He speaks true."

Sarena's face did not change, but her hands clenched into fists behind her back. One of her companions, the tall gaunt-faced man with more gray hair than black, had his thumbs tucked behind his sword belt, trying to appear at ease, but his grip was white-knuckle tight.

"As I was saying," Logain went on with a smooth smile, "they found me, and gave me a choice of death on the spot or taking what they offered. A strange choice, not at all what I expected, but not one I had to think long on. They did not come out and say they had done this before, but there was a practiced feel to it. They gave no reasons, but it seems clear, looking back. Bringing in a man who could channel carried little glory; pulling down a false Dragon, though. . . ."

Nynaeve frowned. He was so casual about it, a man discussing the day's hunting, yet it was his own downfall he spoke of, and every word another nail in Elaida's coffin. Maybe in a coffin for the whole Red Ajah. If the Reds had pushed Logain to name himself the Dragon Reborn, could they have done the same for Gorin Rogad or Mazrim Taim? Perhaps for *all* the false Dragons throughout history? She could all but see the thoughts turning in the Altarans' minds like gears in a mill, reluctantly at first, then spinning faster and faster.

"For a whole year they helped me avoid other Aes Sedai," Logain said, "sent messages when one was near, though there weren't many then. After I proclaimed myself, and began to gather a following, they sent news of where the king's armies were, and in what numbers. How else do you think I always knew where to strike and when?" His listeners shifted their feet, as much for his feral grin as for his words.

He hated Aes Sedai. Nynaeve was sure of that from the few times she had been able to bring herself to study him. Not that she had done so since before Min left, or learned anything when she had. Once she had thought studying him would be looking at the problem from a different angle—never was just how different men were as clear as in using the Power—but it was worse than staring into a dark hole; there was nothing there, not even the hole. All in all, being around Logain was unsettling. He had watched her every move with a burning intensity that made her shiver even knowing she could wrap him up in the Power if he so much as lifted a finger wrong. Not the sort of fervor that men's eyes often directed at women, but a pure contempt that never touched his face at all, which made it all the more horrifying. Aes Sedai had shut him away from the One Power forever; Nynaeve could imagine her own feelings if anyone did that to her. He could not revenge himself on all Aes Sedai, however. What he could do was destroy the Red Ajah, and he was making a fair beginning to it.

This was the first time three had come at once, but every week or so brought another lord or lady to hear his tale, from across Altara and sometimes as far as Murandy, and every one left looking squeezed flat by what Logain had to say. Small wonder; the only news more shocking would have been for the Aes Sedai to admit the Black Ajah really did exist. Well, they were not about to do that, not publicly, and for much the same reason they held news of Logain as close as possible. It might have been the Red Ajah who did this, but they were still Aes Sedai, and too many people could not tell one Ajah from another. All in all, only a few were brought to hear Logain, yet every one of that handful was chosen for the power of the House they led. Houses that now would lend their support to the Aes Sedai in Salidar, if not always openly, or at worst, withhold support from Elaida.

"Javindhra sent me word when more Aes Sedai came," Logain said, "the ones hunting me, and where they would be, so I could come on them before they knew." Lelaine's serene, ageless features hardened for a moment, and Burin's hand drifted toward his sword hilt. Sisters had died before Logain was captured. Logain did not seem to notice their reactions. "The Red Ajah never played me false until they betrayed me in the end."

The bearded man was staring at Logain so hard it was plain he was making himself do it. "Aes Sedai, what of his followers? Perhaps he was safe in the Tower, but he was captured a good many leagues closer to where we stand."

"They were not all killed or captured," the gaunt-faced lord put in right behind him. "Most escaped, melted away. I know my history, Aes Sedai. Raolin Darksbane's followers dared attack the White Tower itself after he was taken, and Guaire Amalasan's as well. We remember too well Logain's army marching across our lands to want it to come again, to rescue him."

"You need have no fear of that." Lelaine eyed Logain with a brief smile, as a woman might a fierce dog she knew tamed to her leash. "He has no more desire for glory, only to make some small restitution for the harm he did. Besides which, I doubt many of his former followers would come if he did call, not after he was carried to Tar Valon in a cage and gentled." Her light laugh was echoed by the Altarans, but only after a moment, and weakly. Logain's face was an iron mask.

Abruptly Lelaine noticed Nynaeve just inside the doorway, and her eyebrows rose. She had exchanged pleasant words with Nynaeve more than once, and praised her and Elayne's supposed discoveries, but she could be as quick as any other Aes Sedai to call down an Accepted who put a foot wrong.

Nynaeve dropped a curtsy, gesturing with the clay mug, now empty of tea. "Pardon me, Lelaine Sedai. I must take this back to the kitchen." She darted out into the baking street before the Aes Sedai could say a word.

Luckily, Myrelle was nowhere in sight now. Nynaeve was in no mood for yet another lecture on showing responsibility or holding her temper or any one of a dozen fool things. An even better piece of luck, Siuan was standing not thirty paces away, facing Gareth Bryne in the middle of the street with the passing throng parting around them. Like Myrelle, Siuan showed no sign of the battering Elayne had reported; perhaps they would have more respect for *Tel'aran'rhiod* if they could not simply step out and have their blunders Healed. Nynaeve moved closer.

"What is the matter with you, woman?" Bryne growled at Siuan. His gray head lowered over her youthful-seeming one; booted feet planted wide and fists on hips made him seem as wide as a boulder. The sweat rolling down his face might have been on someone else's for all the mind he paid it. "I compliment you on how soft my shirts are, and you snap my head off. And I said you looked cheerful, hardly the opening of a battle, I thought. It was a compliment, woman, if not one with roses in it."

"Compliments?" Siuan growled right back, blue eyes blazing up at him. "I don't want your compliments! It just pleases you that I have to iron your shirts. You are a smaller man than I ever thought, Gareth Bryne. Do you expect me to trail after you like a camp follower when the army marches, hoping for more of your *compliments*? And you will *not* address me so, as *woman*! It sounds like 'Here, dog!'"

A vein started throbbing on Bryne's temple. "It pleases me that you keep your word, *Siuan*. And if the army ever does march, I expect you to continue keeping it. I never asked that oath of you; it was your own choice, to try wiggling out of responsibility for what you did. You never thought you'd be called to keep it, did you? Speaking of the army marching, what have you heard while groveling for the Aes Sedai and kissing their feet?"

In one heartbeat Siuan went from fiery rage to icy calm. "That is no part of my oath." You might have thought her a young Aes Sedai, standing there straight-backed with that coolly arrogant defiance, one who had not worked with the Power long enough to take on agelessness. "I will not spy for you. You serve the Hall of the Tower, Gareth Bryne, on *your* oath. Your army will march when the Hall decides. Listen for their words, and obey when you hear."

The change in Bryne was as lightning quick. "You would be an enemy worth crossing swords with," he chuckled admiringly. "You would be a better. . . ." That fast the chuckle faded back into a glower. "The Hall, is it? Bah! You tell Sheriam she might as well stop avoiding me. What can be done here has been done. Tell her a wolfhound kept in a cage might as well be a pig when the wolves come. I didn't gather these men to be sold at market." With a short nod, he went striding off through the crowd. Siuan stared after him, frowning.

"What was that all about?" Nynaeve asked, and Siuan gave a start.

"None of your business is what it was," she snapped, smoothing her dress. You would have thought Nynaeve had sneaked up on her purposely. The woman always took everything personally.

"Let it pass," Nynaeve said levelly. She was not going to let herself be led off down a side trail. "What I won't let pass is studying you." She was going to do something useful today if it killed her. Siuan opened her mouth, looking around. "No, I don't have Marigan, and right now, I don't need her. You've let me near you twice—twice!—since I found a clue that something in you might be Healed. I mean to study you today, and if I don't, I *will* tell Sheriam you're disobeying her orders to make yourself available. I swear I will!"

For a moment she thought the other woman was going to dare her to do her worst, but at last Siuan said grudgingly, "This afternoon. I am busy this morning. Unless you think what you want is more important than helping your Two Rivers friend?"

Nynaeve stepped closer. No one in the street was paying them any mind beyond a glance in passing, but she lowered her voice anyway. "What are they planning about him? You keep saying they haven't made up their minds what to do, but they must have come to *some* conclusion by now." If they had, Siuan would know of it, whether she was supposed to or not.

Abruptly Leane was there, and Nynaeve might as well not have spoken. Siuan and Leane glared at one another, stiff-backed as two strange cats in a small room.

"Well?" Siuan muttered with a tight jaw.

Leane sniffed, and her curls swung as she tossed her head. A sneer twisted her lips, yet her words did not match expression or tone. "I tried to talk them out of it," she spat, but softly. "Only they had not listened to you enough to even consider it. You won't be meeting the Wise Ones tonight."

"Fishguts!" Siuan growled, and turning on her heel, she stalked away, but no more quickly than Leane in the opposite direction.

Nynaeve almost threw up her hands in frustration. Talking as if she were not there, as if she did not know exactly what they were talking about. Ignoring her. Siuan had better appear this afternoon as promised, or she would find a way to wring her out and hang her up to dry! She jumped as a woman spoke behind her.

"Those two should be sent to Tiana for a sound switching." Lelaine stepped up beside Nynaeve, looking first after Siuan then Leane. Going around sneaking up on people! There was no sign of Logain or Burin or the Altaran nobles. The Blue sister shifted her shawl. "They are not what they were, of course, but one would think they could retain a little decorum. It will not do if they actually come to hair-pulling in the street."

"Sometimes people just rub one another the wrong way," Nynaeve said. Siuan and Leane worked so hard to maintain their fiction, the least she could do was support it. How she hated people sneaking up on her.

Lelaine eyed Nynaeve's hand on her braid, and she snatched it away.

Too many knew about that habit; a habit she had tried hard to break. But what the Aes Sedai said was "Not when it impinges on the dignity of Aes Sedai, child. Women who serve Aes Sedai should show some reserve in public however silly they are in private." There was certainly nothing to be said to that; nothing safe, anyway. "Why did you come in where I was showing Logain just now?"

"I thought the room was empty, Aes Sedai," Nynaeve said hastily. "I'm sorry. I hope I did not disturb you." That was no answer—she could hardly say she had been hiding from Myrelle—but the slender Blue only met her eyes for a moment.

"What do you think Rand al'Thor will do, child?"

Nynaeve blinked in confusion. "Aes Sedai, I haven't seen him in half a year. All I know is what I've heard here. Is the Hall . . . ? Aes Sedai, what has the Hall decided about him?"

Scrutinizing Nynaeve's face, Lelaine pursed her lips. Those dark eyes, seeming to see inside your head, were quite unsettling. "A remarkable co-incidence. You come from the same village as the Dragon Reborn, and so does that other girl, Egwene al'Vere. Great things were expected when she became a novice. Do you have any idea where she is?" She did not wait for an answer. "And the other two young men, Perrin Aybara and Mat Cauthon. Both *ta'veren* as well, so I understand. Remarkable, indeed. Then there is you, with your extraordinary discoveries despite your limitations. Wherever Egwene is, does she also venture where none of us have gone? All of you have occasioned a good deal of discussion among the sisters, as you may imagine."

"I hope they say good things," Nynaeve said slowly. There had been many questions about Rand since coming to Salidar, especially since the embassy left for Caemlyn—some Aes Sedai seemed able to speak of little else to her—but this seemed something different. That was the trouble with talking to Aes Sedai. Half the time you could not be sure what they meant or what they were after.

"Do you still have hopes of Healing Siuan and Leane, child?" Nodding as if Nynaeve had answered, Lelaine sighed. "Sometimes I think Myrelle is right. We indulge you too much. Whatever your discoveries, perhaps we should put you in Theodrin's charge until your block against channeling at will is broken. Considering what you have done in the last two months, think what you could do then." Gripping her braid unconsciously, Nynaeve tried to get a word in edgewise, a carefully framed protest, but Lelaine ignored the attempt. Which was probably for the best. "You do Siuan and

Leane no favors, child. Let them forget who and what they were and be content with who and what they are. From the way they behave, the only thing that keeps them from forgetting completely is you, and your foolish attempts to Heal what cannot be Healed. They are no longer Aes Sedai. Why hold out false hope?"

There was a hint of compassion in her voice, and a tinge of contempt too. Those not Aes Sedai were less, after all, and Siuan and Leane's ruse had definitely painted them among the least. Plus, of course, no few here in Salidar blamed the Tower's troubles on Siuan, on her plotting while Amyrlin. Very likely they believed she deserved everything that had happened to her and more.

What *had* been done complicated the whole thing, though. Stilling was rare. Before Siuan and Leane, no woman had been tried and stilled in one hundred and forty years, and none burned out in at least a dozen. A stilled woman usually tried to get as far from Aes Sedai as she could. No doubt if Lelaine had been stilled, she would want to forget being Aes Sedai if she could. No doubt she would like to forget that Siuan and Leane had been, too, that all that had been taken away from them. If they could be seen as two women never able to channel, never Aes Sedai, a good many Aes Sedai would be more comfortable.

"Sheriam Sedai has given me permission to try," Nynaeve said as firmly as she dared to a full sister. Lelaine held her eyes until she let her gaze drop. Her knuckles whitened around her braid before she could let go, but she kept her face smooth. Trying to trade stares with an Aes Sedai was a woolhead's trick for an Accepted.

"We are all fools sometimes, child, yet a wise woman learns to limit how often. Since you seem to have finished breakfast, I suggest you rid yourself of that mug and find something to do before you find yourself in hot water instead. Have you ever considered cutting your hair short? No matter. Off with you."

Nynaeve dropped a curtsy, but it was being made to the Aes Sedai's back before she reached the bottom of it. Safe from Lelaine's eyes, she glowered at the woman. Cut her *hair*? She lifted her braid and shook it at the retreating Aes Sedai. That she had waited until it was safe made her furious, though if she had not waited she would almost certainly be on her way to join Moghedien at the laundry, with a stop to see Tiana on the way. Months sitting here in Salidar doing nothing—for all practical purposes it seemed she was, no matter what she and Elayne managed to pull out of Moghedien—amid Aes Sedai who did nothing except talk and wait while the world went on its way to ruin without them, and Lelaine thought she should cut her hair! She had pursued the Black Ajah, been captured and escaped, captured one of the Forsaken in turn—well, none of them knew that—helped the Panarch of Tarabon regain her throne however briefly, and now all she did was sit and take credit for what she could shake loose from Moghedien. Cut her hair? She might as well shave herself bald for all the good it would do!

She caught sight of Dagdara Finchey striding through the throng, as wide as any man in the street and taller than most, and the round-faced Yellow made her angry, too. One reason she had chosen to remain in Salidar was to study with the Yellows, for they knew more of Healing than anyone else; everyone said so. But if any of them knew more than she already did, they were not sharing it with a mere Accepted. The Yellows should have been the most welcoming to her desire to Heal anything and everything, even stilling, but they were the least. Dagdara would have had her scrubbing floors from sunup to sundown until she gave up "foolish notions and wasting time" if Sheriam had not intervened, while Nisao Dachen, a diminutive Yellow with eyes that could drive nails, refused to even speak to Nynaeve as long as she persisted in trying to "alter how the Pattern has been woven."

To top it all off, her weather sense still told her a storm was on its way, closer now, while the cloudless sky and burning sun taunted her.

Muttering to herself, she tucked the clay mug into the back of a passing woodcart and set off weaving through the crowded street. There was nothing to do except keep moving until Moghedien was free, and the Light knew how long that would be. A whole morning wasted, added to a string of wasted days.

Many of the Aes Sedai nodded and smiled at her, but by the simple expedient of smiling back apologetically and quickening her step for a few paces as if hurrying somewhere, she avoided stopping for the inevitable questions about what new things they might expect out of her. In her present mood she might just tell them exactly what she thought, which would be foolish in the extreme. Doing nothing. Asking *her* what Rand was going to do. Telling her to cut her hair. Bah!

Of course, they were not all smiles. Not only did Nisao look right through Nynaeve; Nynaeve had to step nimbly out of the way before the tiny woman walked right over her. And a haughty, pale-haired Aes Sedai with a prominent chin, guiding a tall roan gelding through the crowd, cast a sharp blue-eyed frown at her as she rode by. Nynaeve did not recognize her. The woman was perfectly neat in a riding dress of pale gray silk, but the light linen dustcloak folded in front of her saddle spoke of travel and named her a new arrival. Adding to the likelihood that she was new come, the lanky green-coated Warder at her heels on a tall gray warhorse looked uneasy. Warders *never* looked uneasy, but Nynaeve supposed joining a rebellion against the Tower might make for an exception. Light! Even new arrivals came ready to put her back up!

And then there was scar-faced Uno, his head shaven except for a topknot and his missing eye covered by a patch painted with a hideous glaring red replacement. Pausing in the leather-lunged flaying of an abashed young man in plate-and-mail armor who stood holding the reins of a horse with a lance lashed to the saddle, Uno directed a warm grin in Nynaeve's direction. Well, it would have been warm without the eyepatch. Nynaeve's grimace made him blink and hurry back to dressing down the soldier.

It was not Uno or his eyepatch that soured her stomach. Not exactly. He had accompanied her and Elayne to Salidar, and once promised to steal horses—"borrow," he called it—if they wanted to leave. No chance of that now. Uno wore a band of golden braid on the cuffs of his worn dark coat now; he was an officer, training heavy cavalry for Gareth Bryne, and much too caught up in it to bother himself with Nynaeve. No, that was not true. If she said she wanted to go, he would procure horses in a matter of hours, and she would ride with an escort of top-knotted Shienarans who had given their allegiance to Rand and were only in Salidar because she and Elayne brought them there. Only, she would have to admit she had been wrong in deciding to stay, admit she had been lying all those times she had told him she was happy right where she was. Making those admissions was just beyond her. Uno's main reason for staying was that he thought he should *look after* her and Elayne. He would hear no admissions from her!

The whole thought of leaving Salidar was a new one, sparked by Uno, and it set her thinking fiercely. If only Thom and Juilin had not gone jaunting off to Amadicia. Not that they had made the trip for the fun of it, really. Back in the days when it seemed the Aes Sedai here might really do something, they had volunteered to scout out what was going on across the river. Meaning to penetrate as far as Amador itself, they had been gone well over a month, and would not return for days more at best. They were not the only scouts, of course; even Aes Sedai and Warders had been sent, though most of those were aimed farther west, at Tarabon. A show of doing something, and the delay before any could return with word, was a good excuse to wait. Nynaeve wished she had not let the two men go. Neither would have, had she said no.

Thom was an old gleeman, though he had once been considerably more, and Juilin a thief-taker from Tear, both competent men who knew how to handle themselves in strange places, and handy in a number of ways. They had accompanied her and Elayne to Salidar, too, and neither would have asked questions if told she wanted to leave. Undoubtedly they would have said a good deal behind her back, but not to her face, the way Uno would.

It was galling to admit that she really needed them, but she was not sure she knew how to go about stealing a horse. In any case, an Accepted would be noticed fooling around the horses, in the stables as much as out on the soldiers' picket lines, and if she changed out of the banded white dress, she would certainly be seen and reported before she got anywhere near a horse. Even if she managed it, she would be pursued. Runaway Accepted, like runaway novices, were almost always brought back to face punishment that erased any thought of a second attempt. When you began training to be Aes Sedai, Aes Sedai were not finished with you until *they* said they were.

It was not fear of punishment that held her, of course. What was a switching or two against the chance of being killed by the Black Ajah, or facing one of the Forsaken? It was just a matter of whether she really wanted to go. Where would she go, for instance? To Rand, in Caemlyn? Egwene in Cairhien? Would Elayne come? Certainly, if they went to Caemlyn. Was it a desire to *do* something, or fear that Moghedien was going to be discovered? The punishment for running away would not be a patch on that! She had reached no conclusion when she rounded a corner and found herself looking at Elayne's novice class, gathered in an open space between two thatch-roofed stone houses where the fallen-in ruins of a third had been cleared away.

More than twenty white-clad women sat on low stools in a semicircle, watching Elayne guide two of their number through an exercise. The glow of *saidar* surrounded all three women. Tabiya, a green-eyed freckle-faced girl of sixteen or so, and Nicola, a slender black-haired woman Nynaeve's age, were unsteadily passing a small flame back and forth. It wavered and sometimes vanished for an instant when one was too slow to catch it up from the other and maintain it. In her present mood, Nynaeve could clearly see the flows they wove.

Eighteen novices had been whisked away when Sheriam and the rest fled—Tabiya was one of those—but most in this group were like Nicola, newly recruited since the Aes Sedai established themselves in Salidar. Nicola was not the only woman there older than usual for a novice; a good half were. When Nynaeve and Elayne went to the Tower, Aes Sedai rarely tested women much older than Tabiya—Nynaeve had been remarked for her age as much as for being a wilder—but perhaps in desperation, the Aes Sedai here had expanded their testing to women even a year or two beyond Nynaeve. The result was that Salidar now held more novices than the White Tower had for years. That success had made the Aes Sedai send sisters out across Altara in a village-by-village search.

"Do you wish you were teaching that class?"

The voice at her shoulder made Nynaeve's stomach turn over. Twice in one morning. She wished she had some goosemint in her belt pouch. If she kept letting herself be taken by surprise, she was going to end up sorting papers for a Brown yet.

Of course, the apple-cheeked Domani woman was not Aes Sedai. Back in the Tower, Theodrin would have been raised to the shawl already, but here she had been raised to something more than Accepted, less than a full sister. She wore her Great Serpent ring on her right hand not her left, and a green dress that went well with her bronze coloring, but she could not choose an Ajah or wear the shawl.

"I have better things to be about than teaching a bunch of thickheaded novices."

Theodrin only smiled at the tartness in Nynaeve's voice. She was quite nice, really. "A thickheaded Accepted to teach thickheaded novices?" Usually, she was nice. "Well, once we have you where you can channel without being ready to thump their heads, you will be teaching novices too. And I would not be surprised if you were raised soon after, the things you've been discovering. You know, you have never told me what your trick was." Wilders almost always had some trick they had learned, the first unveiling of the ability to channel. The other thing most wilders had in common was a block, something they had built up in their minds to hide their channeling even from themselves.

Nynaeve kept her face smooth with an effort. To be able to channel whenever she wanted. To be raised Aes Sedai. Neither would remedy the problem of Moghedien, but she would be able to go where she wanted then, study as she wanted without anyone telling her this or that simply could not be Healed. "People got well when they shouldn't. I would get so mad that somebody was going to die, that everything I knew about herbs wasn't enough . . ." she shrugged. "And they got well."

"Much better than mine." The slender woman sighed. "I could make a boy want to kiss me, or not want to. My block was men, not anger." Nynaeve looked at her incredulously, and Theodrin laughed. "Well, it was emotion, too. If there was a man present, and I liked or disliked him a great deal, I could channel. If I felt neither one way nor the other, or there wasn't a man at all, I might as well have been a tree so far as *saidar* was concerned."

"How did you ever break through that?" Nynaeve asked curiously. Elayne had the novices all paired off now, fumbling their way through passing small flames back and forth.

Theodrin's smile deepened, but a blush stained her cheeks, too. "A young man named Charel, a groom in the Tower stables, began making eyes at me. I was fifteen, and he had the most gorgeous smile. The Aes Sedai let him sit in on my lessons, quietly in a corner, so I could channel at all. What I didn't know was that Sheriam had arranged for him to meet me in the first place." Her cheeks darkened more. "I also didn't know he had a twin sister, or that after a few days, the Charel sitting in the corner was really Marel. When she took off her coat and shirt one day in the middle of my lesson, I was so shocked I fainted. But after that, I could channel whenever I wanted."

Nynaeve burst out laughing—she could not help it—and despite her blushes Theodrin joined in without restraint. "I wish it could be that easy for me, Theodrin."

"Whether it is or not," Theodrin said, her laughter fading, "we will break down your block. This afternoon—"

"I'm studying Siuan this afternoon," Nynaeve cut in hastily, and Theodrin's mouth tightened.

"You have been avoiding me, Nynaeve. In the past month you've managed to wriggle out of all but three appointments. I can accept your trying and failing, but I will not accept you being afraid to try."

"I am not," Nynaeve began indignantly, as a small voice asked whether she was trying to hide the truth from herself. It was so disheartening to try and try and try—and fail.

Theodrin let her have no more than those few words. "Allowing that you have commitments today," she said calmly, "I will see you tomorrow, and every day thereafter, or I will be forced to take other steps. I don't want to do that, and you do not want me to, but I mean to break your block down. Myrelle has asked me to make special efforts, and I vow that I will."

The near echo of what she had told Siuan made Nynaeve's jaw drop. This was the first time the other woman had used the increased authority of her position. It would be just the way Nynaeve's luck was running today for her and Siuan to end up waiting to see Tiana side by side.

Theodrin did not wait for a reply. She merely nodded as if she had received agreement, then glided off up the street. Nynaeve could almost see a fringed shawl around her shoulders. This morning was not going well at all. And Myrelle again! She wanted to scream.

Over among the novices, Elayne gave her a proud smile, but Nynaeve only shook her head and turned away. She was going back to her room. It was a measure of how the day was progressing that before she was halfway there Dagdara Finchey crashed into her running and knocked her flat on her back. Running! An Aes Sedai! The big woman did not stop, either, or as much as shout an apology over her shoulder as she plowed through the crowd.

Nynaeve picked herself up, dusted herself off, stumped the rest of the way to her room and slammed the door behind her. It was hot and close, the beds were unmade until Moghedien could get around to them, and worst of all, Nynaeve's weather sense told her there should have been a hailstorm breaking over Salidar right that minute. But she would not be surprised there, or trampled.

Flinging herself down atop her rumpled sheets, she lay fingering the silver bracelet, thoughts skittering from what she might manage to dig out of Moghedien today to whether Siuan would appear that afternoon, from Lan to her block to whether she was going to stay in Salidar. It would not be running away, really. She would probably go to Caemlyn, to Rand; he did need somebody to keep his head from swelling too big, and Elayne would like that. She just wished leaving—*not* running away!—had not begun to seem even more attractive after Theodrin announced her intentions.

She expected to have some sign in the emotions oozing through the *a'dam* that Moghedien was finished with her work, and to have to go find her—she often hid when she was sulking—but the shame and outrage never decreased, and the door banging open came as a complete surprise.

"So there you are," Moghedien grated. "Look!" She held up her hands. "Ruined!" To Nynaeve they looked no different from any hands that been doing laundry; white and wrinkled, true, but that would fade. "It is not enough that I must live in squalor, fetching and carrying like a servant, now I'm expected to labor like some primitive—!"

Nynaeve cut her off by a simple expedient. She thought of one quick stroke of a switch, what it felt like, then shifted the thought into the part of her mind that held Moghedien's received emotions. The other woman's dark eyes widened, and her mouth clamped shut, lips compressing. Not a hard blow, but a reminder.

"Close the door and sit down," Nynaeve said. "You can make the beds later. We are going to have a lesson."

"I am used to better than this," Moghedien grumbled as she complied. "A night laborer in Tojar was used to better!"

"Unless I miss my guess," Nynaeve told her sharply, "a night laborer in wherever didn't have a death sentence hanging over his head. Any time you want it, we can tell Sheriam exactly who you are." It was pure bluff— Nynaeve's stomach clenched up in a burning ball at the mere thought— but a sickening flood of fear roared out of Moghedien. Nynaeve almost admired how steady the woman's face remained; had she felt like that, she would have been shrieking and gnashing her teeth on the floor.

"What do you want me to show you?" Moghedien said in a level tone. They always had to tell her what they wanted out of her. She practically never volunteered anything unless they pressed her to a point Nynaeve considered the brink of torture.

"We'll try something you haven't been very successful with teaching. Detecting a man's channeling." So far, that was the only thing she and Elayne had not been able to pick up quickly. It could be useful if she did decide to go to Caemlyn.

"Not easy, especially with no man to practice on. A pity you haven't been able to Heal Logain." There was no mockery in Moghedien's voice or on her face, but she glanced at Nynaeve and hurried on. "Still, we can try the forms again."

The lesson truly was not easy. It never was, even with something Nynaeve could learn right away once the weaves became clear. Moghedien could not channel without Nynaeve allowing her to, without Nynaeve guiding her, in fact, but in a new lesson Moghedien had to give the lead for how the flows were to go. It made a pretty tangle, the main reason they were not able to learn a dozen new things from her every day. In this case Nynaeve already had *some* idea of how the flows were woven, but it was an intricate lacework of all of the Five Powers that made Healing seem simple, and the pattern shifted at blinding speed. Its difficulty was the reason it had never been used very often, Moghedien claimed. It also gave you a grinding headache if kept up very long.

Nynaeve lay back on her bed and worked at it as hard as she could, though. If she did go to Rand, she might need this, and there was no telling how soon. She channeled the flows all by herself, too; an occasional thought of Lan or Theodrin kept her anger twisted up tight enough. Sooner or later Moghedien was going to be called to account for her crimes, and where would Nynaeve be then, used to drawing on the other woman's power whenever she wanted? She had to live and work with her own limits. *Could* Theodrin find a way to break her block? Lan had to be alive, so she could find him. The ache became a pain that bored at her temples. A tightness appeared around Moghedien's eyes, and she rubbed at her head sometimes, but underneath the fear the bracelet carried a current of what almost seemed contentment. Nynaeve supposed that even when you did not want to teach, it must bring a certain satisfaction. She was not sure she liked Moghedien displaying such a normal human response.

She was not sure how long the lesson went on, with Moghedien murmuring, "Almost" and "Not quite," but when the door banged open again, she nearly lifted straight up off the mattress. The sudden bolt of fear from Moghedien would have accompanied howling in another woman.

"Have you heard, Nynaeve?" Elayne asked, pushing the door to. "There's an emissary from the Tower, from Elaida."

Nynaeve forgot the words she would have shouted if her heart had not been clogging her throat. She even forgot her headache. "An emissary? You're sure?"

"Of course I'm sure, Nynaeve. Do you think I'd come running for *gossip?* The whole village is aflutter."

"I don't know why," Nynaeve said sourly. The grating inside her skull was back. And all the goosemint in her scrip of herbs under the bed would not have quieted the burning in her stomach. Would the girl never learn to knock? Moghedien had both hands pressed to her belly as though she could use some goosemint as well. "We did tell them Elaida knew about Salidar."

"Maybe they believed us," Elayne said, dropping onto the foot of Nynaeve's bed, "and maybe they didn't, but this drove it home. Elaida knows where we are, and likely what we are up to. Any of the servants could be her eyes-and-ears. Maybe even some of the sisters. I caught a glimpse of the emissary, Nynaeve. Pale yellow hair and blue eyes that could freeze the sun. A Red named Tarna Feir, Faolain said. One of the Warders who was keeping guard escorted her in. When she looks at you, she could be looking at a stone."

Nynaeve looked at Moghedien. "We're done with the lesson for now. Come back in an hour and you can make the beds." She waited until Moghedien had gone, tight-lipped and gripping her skirts in fists, then turned to Elayne. "What . . . message did she bring?"

"They certainly didn't tell me, Nynaeve. Every Aes Sedai I passed was wondering the same thing. I heard when Tarna was told she'd be received by the Hall of the Tower, she laughed. And not as if she was amused. You do not think. . . ." Elayne chewed at her underlip for a moment. "You don't think they could really decide to. . . ."

"Go back?" Nynaeve said incredulously. "Elaida will want them to come the last ten miles on their knees, and the final mile on their bellies! Even if she didn't, even if this Red says, 'Come home. All is forgiven and dinner's waiting,' do you think they could brush aside Logain so easily?"

"Nynaeve, Aes Sedai could brush aside anything to make the White Tower whole again. Anything. You don't understand them the way I do; there were Aes Sedai in the palace from the day I was born. The question now is, what is Tarna saying to the Hall? And what are they saying to her?"

Nynaeve rubbed her arms irritably. She had no answers, only hopes, and her weather sense told her that that hailstorm that was not there was beating the roofs of Salidar like drums. The feeling went on for days.

CHAPTER
9

Plans

"Y ou had these Illuminators brought to Amador?" Many would
have flinched to hear such a cold tone from Pedron Niall, but
not the man standing on the inlaid golden sunburst before
Niall's plain high-backed chair. He exuded confidence and competence.
Niall continued, "There is a reason I have two thousand of the Children
guarding the border with Tarabon, Omerna. Tarabon is quarantined. *No* one
is allowed across the border. Not a sparrow would cross if I had my way."

Omerna was the picture of what an officer of the Children of the Light
was supposed to be, tall and commanding, with a bold, fearless face, a strong
chin and waves of white at his temples. His dark eyes seemed more than
capable of surveying the harshest battlefield undismayed, as indeed they
had. At the moment they seemed to indicate deeply considered thought. The
white-and-gold tabard of a Lord Captain, Anointed of the Light, suited him.
"My Lord Captain Commander, they wish to establish a chapter house here."
Even his voice, deep and mellifluous, fit the image. "Illuminators travel
everywhere. It should be possible to slip agents among them easily. Agents
welcomed into every town, every noble's manor, every ruler's palace." Supposedly Abdel Omerna was a relatively minor member of the Council of
Anointed. In truth, he was the Children of the Light's spymaster. After a
manner of speaking. "Think of it!"

What Niall thought was that the Guild of Illuminators was Taraboner to the last man and woman, and Tarabon was infected with chaos and madness that he would not let loose in Amadicia. If cauterizing that infection had to wait, he could at least isolate it. "They will be treated like anyone else who slips through, Omerna. Kept under guard, allowed to talk to no one, and escorted out of Amadicia without delay."

"If I may insist, my Lord Captain Commander, their usefulness is worth the little gossip they might spread. They keep to themselves. And aside from their use for my agents, the prestige of having an Illuminators' chapter house in Amador would be considerable. The only chapter house, now. The one in Cairhien has been abandoned, and the one in Tanchico surely has been, too."

Prestige! Niall rubbed his left eye to soothe an involuntary flutter. Little point in getting angry with Omerna, but restraint took an effort. The morning heat cooked his temper over a slow fire. "They do indeed keep to themselves, Omerna. They live with their own, travel with their own, and barely speak to anyone else. Do you mean to have these agents marry Illuminators? They rarely marry outside their guild, and there is no way to become an Illuminator except by birth."

"Ah. Well. I am sure a way can be found." Nothing could dent that façade of confidence and competence.

"It shall be done as I say, Omerna." The man actually opened his mouth again, but Niall forestalled him irritably. "As I say, Omerna! I'll hear no more on it! Now what information do you have today? What *useful* information? That is your function. Not providing fireworks for Ailron."

Omerna hesitated, plainly wanting to make another plea for his precious Illuminators, but in the end he said portentously, "The reports of Dragonsworn in Altara are more than rumor, it seems. And perhaps in Murandy as well. The infestation is small, but it will grow. A strong move now could settle for them and the Aes Sedai in Salidar in one—"

"Do you dictate strategy for the Children now? Gather information, and leave its use to me. What else do you have for me?"

The man's response to being cut off was a calm bow of acquiescence. Omerna was very good at remaining calm; it was perhaps what he did best. "I have good news. Mattin Stepaneos is ready to join you. He hesitates to make a public announcement, but my people in Illian report that he soon will. He is reported eager."

"That would be remarkably good," Niall said dryly. Remarkable, certainly. Among the banners and pennants lining the cornices of the chamber, Mattin Stepaneos' Three Leopards, silver on black, hung next to a gold-fringed Illianer Royal Standard, nine bees worked in thread-of-gold on green silk. The Illianer king came out on top in the Troubles finally, at least to the point of forcing a treaty that affirmed the border between Amadicia and Altara where it was at the beginning, but Niall doubted the man would ever forget that he had had the advantage of terrain and numbers at Soremaine and still been defeated and captured. If the Illianer Companions had not covered the field for the rest of the army to escape Niall's trap, Altara would be a fief of the Children today, and very likely Murandy and even Illian. Worse, Mattin Stepaneos had a Tar Valon witch for an advisor, though he hid the fact, and her. Niall sent emissaries because he dared not leave a path untried, but yes, Mattin Stepaneos joining him willingly would be remarkable indeed. "Continue. And be brief. I have a busy day today, and I can read your written reports later."

Despite those instructions Omerna's rendition was long, delivered in a sonorous voice full of certainty. Al'Thor had barely extended his control in Andor beyond Caemlyn. His lightning onslaught was clearly stalled at last—as Omerna carefully pointed out that he had predicted. There was little chance the Borderlands would join the Children against the false Dragon any time soon; lords in Shienar, Arafel and Kandor were taking advantage of the Blight's quiet to rebel, and the Queen of Saldaea had gone into seclusion in the country, in fear of the same according to Omerna. His agents were at work, however, and the Borderland rulers would be brought to heel as soon as these small rebellions were quashed. On the other hand, the rulers of Murandy, Altara and Ghealdan were ready to fall into line, though making ambivalent noises at present to soothe the Tar Valon witches. Alliandre of Ghealdan knew her throne was shaky, knew she needed the Children to avoid plummeting as abruptly as her predecessors, while both Tylin of Altara and Roedran of Murandy hoped that the Children's weight would make them more than figureheads at last. Plainly the man considered those lands already as good as in Niall's coat pocket.

Within Amadicia, the picture was even better, by Omerna's reckoning. Recruits flocked to the Children's banners in greater numbers than for years. Strictly speaking, that was none of Omerna's concern, but he always larded his reports with any good news he could find. The Prophet would not trouble the land much longer; at present his rabble squabbled over looting villages and manors in the north, and might well scatter back into Ghealdan at the next push by Ailron's soldiers. Little room remained in the jails, because Darkfriends and Tar Valon spies were being arrested faster than they could be hanged. The search for Tar Valon witches had found only two so far, but over a hundred women had been put to the question, an indication of how vigilant the patrols were. And fewer refugees from Tarabon were being apprehended, proof the quarantine was becoming more effective; those caught were being thrown back into Tarabon as fast as they could be taken back to the border. He hurried past that last, unsurprising given his stupidity with the Illuminators.

Niall listened just enough to know where to nod. Omerna had been an adequate commander in the field, so long as someone told him what to do, but in his present position, his credulous stupidity was trying. He had reported Morgase dead, her corpse seen and identified beyond doubt, up to the very day Niall brought him face-to-face with her. He had ridiculed "rumors" that the Stone of Tear had fallen, and still denied that the mightiest fortress in the world could have been taken by any outside force; there had been treason, he insisted, a High Lord who had betrayed the Stone to al'Thor and Tar Valon. He maintained that the disaster at Falme and the troubles in Tarabon and Arad Doman were the work of Artur Hawkwing's armies come back across the Aryth Ocean. He was convinced that Siuan Sanche had not been deposed at all, that al'Thor was insane and dying, that Tar Valon had murdered King Galldrian to deliberately set off the civil war in Cairhien, and that these three "facts" were somehow tied into those ridiculous rumors, always from somewhere conveniently far away, of people bursting into flame or nightmares leaping out of thin air and slaughtering whole villages. He was not sure how exactly, but he was working on a grand theory he promised to deliver any day, a theory that supposedly would unravel all the witches' schemes and deliver Tar Valon into Niall's hands.

That was the way with Omerna; he either invented convoluted reasons for what happened, or else seized on gossip in the streets and swallowed it whole. He spent a good deal of his time listening to gossip, in manor houses *and* in the streets. Not only had he been seen drinking in the taverns with Hunters for the Horn, it was an ill-kept secret that he had laid out huge sums for no fewer than three supposed Horns of Valere. Each time he had carried the thing off to the country and puffed on it for days, till even he had to admit that no dead heroes out of legend were going to come riding back from the grave. Even so, the failures were unlikely to stop him from future purchases in dark alleys or the back rooms of taverns. The simple form of it was this: where a spymaster should doubt his own face in the mirror, Omerna believed anything.

Eventually the man ran down, and Niall said, "I will give your reports due consideration, Omerna. You have done well." How the fellow preened, smoothing his tabard. "Leave me, now. On your way out, send Balwer in. I have some letters to dictate."

"Of course, my Lord Captain Commander. Ah." In the middle of his bow, Omerna frowned and fumbled in the pocket of his white undercoat, pulling out a tiny bone cylinder that he handed to Niall. "This arrived at the pigeoncote this morning." Three thin red stripes ran the length of the cylinder, meaning it was to be brought to Niall with the wax seals intact. And the man had almost forgotten it.

Omerna waited, no doubt hoping for a hint of what the cylinder contained, but Niall waved him toward the door. "Do not forget Balwer. If Mattin Stepaneos might join me, I must write and see if I can add a little weight to his making the right decision." Omerna had no choice but to make his bow anew and go.

Even when the door closed behind the man, Niall only fingered the cylinder. These rare special messages seldom brought good news. Rising slowly—of late he sometimes felt age in his bones—he filled a plain silver goblet with punch, but then left it sitting on the table and flipped open a folder of scroll-worked leather lined with linen. It contained a single sheet of heavy paper, crumpled and partly torn, a street artist's drawing in colored chalks of two men fighting in clouds, one with a face made of fire, the other with dark reddish hair. Al'Thor.

All his plans to hinder the false Dragon had gone awry, all his hopes to slow the man's tide of conquest, to divert him. Had he waited too long, let al'Thor grow too powerful? If so, there was only one way to deal with him quickly, the knife in the dark, the arrow from a rooftop. How long did he dare wait? Did he dare risk not waiting? Too much haste could spell disaster as surely as too long a delay.

"My Lord sent for me?"

Niall eyed the man who had entered so silently. On the face of it, it hardly seemed possible that Balwer could move without a dry rustle announcing his presence. Everything about him was narrow and pinched; his brown coat hung from knobby shoulders, and his legs looked as if they might snap under his desiccated weight. He moved like a bird hopping from limb to limb. "Do you believe the Horn of Valere will call dead heroes back to save us, Balwer?"

"Perhaps, my Lord," Balwer said, folding his hands fussily. "Perhaps not. I would not count on it, myself."

Niall nodded. "And do you think Mattin Stepaneos will join me?"

"Again, perhaps. He will not want to finish dead or a puppet. His first and only concern is to hold on to the Laurel Crown, and the army gathering in Tear must make him sweat for that." Balwer smiled thinly, a bare compression of lips. "He has spoken openly about accepting my Lord's proposal, but on the other hand I've just learned he has been communicating with the White Tower. Apparently he has agreed to something, though I don't yet know what."

The world knew that Abdel Omerna was the Children's spymaster. Such a position should have been secret, of course, but stableboys and beggars pointed him out in the street, warily, lest the most dangerous man in Amadicia see them. The truth was that Omerna was a decoy, a fool who did not know himself that he was only a mask hiding the true master of spies in the Fortress of the Light. Sebban Balwer, Niall's prim dried-up little secretary with his disapproving mouth. A man no one would ever suspect, or credit if he was named to them.

Where Omerna believed everything, Balwer believed nothing, perhaps not even in Darkfriends, or the Dark One. If Balwer did believe in anything, it was looking over men's shoulders, listening to their whispers, rooting out their secrets. Of course, he would have served any master as well as he did Niall, but that was all to the good. What Balwer learned was never tainted by what he knew had to be true, or wanted to be true. Disbelieving everything, he always managed to root out truth.

"No more than I expected out of Illian, Balwer, but even he can be brought round." He would have to be. It could not be too late. "Is there any fresh word from the Borderlands?"

"Not yet, my Lord. But Davram Bashere is in Caemlyn. With thirty thousand light horse, my informants claim, but I think no more than half that. He would not weaken Saldaea too far, however quiet the Blight, even if Tenobia commanded him to."

Niall grunted, the corner of his left eye trembling. He fingered the sketch lying in its folder; supposedly it was a fair likeness of al'Thor. Bashere in Caemlyn; a good reason for Tenobia to be hiding in the country from his envoy.

There was no good news from the Borderlands, whatever Omerna thought. The "minor rebellions" Omerna reported were minor, but not rebellions of the sort the man thought. Along the Blightborder men were arguing over whether al'Thor was another false Dragon or the Dragon Reborn. Borderlanders being as they were, sometimes those arguments flared into small-scale battles. The fighting had begun in Shienar about the time

the Stone of Tear was falling, confirmation of the witches' involvement if
any was needed. How it would all be settled was yet in doubt, according to
Balwer.

That al'Thor remained confined to Caemlyn was one of the few things
Omerna had right. Yet why, with Bashere and Aiel and the witches? Not
even Balwer had been able to answer that. Whatever the reason, the Light
be praised for it! The Prophet's mobs had settled in to loot the north of
Amadicia, true, but they were consolidating their hold, killing or putting
to flight any who refused to declare for the Prophet of the Dragon. Ailron's
soldiers had only stopped retreating because the accursed Prophet had
stopped advancing. Alliandre and the others Omerna was certain would
join him were in fact dithering, putting off his ambassadors with flimsy
excuses and delays. He suspected they no more knew how they would leap
than he did.

On the surface everything seemed to be going al'Thor's way at the
moment, except for whatever held him in Caemlyn, but Niall had always
been at his most dangerous when he was outnumbered and with his back
to the wall.

If the rumors could be believed, Carridin was doing well in Altara and
Murandy, though not as quickly as Niall would have liked. Time was as
much an enemy as al'Thor or the Tower. Yet even if Carridin was only doing well in the rumors, that should be enough. Perhaps it was time to extend the "Dragonsworn" into Andor. Perhaps Illian, as well, though if the
army gathering in Tear was not enough to show Mattin Stepaneos the path,
a few farms and villages raided would hardly make a difference. The size of
that army horrified Niall; if it was half what Balwer reported, a quarter, it
still horrified him. Nothing like it had been seen since Artur Hawkwing's
day. Rather than frighten men into joining Niall, an army like that might
intimidate them into falling in behind the Dragon banner. Could he have
found a year, just half a year, he would have accounted it worth al'Thor's
whole army of fools and villains and Aiel savages.

All was not lost, of course. All was never lost as long as you were alive.
Tarabon and Arad Doman were as useless to al'Thor and the witches as to
him, two pits full of scorpions; only a fool would put a hand in there until
more of the scorpions killed one another off. If Saldaea was lost, which he
would not concede, Shienar and Arafel and Kandor still hung in the balance, and balances could be tipped. If Mattin Stepaneos wanted to ride two
horses at once—he had always liked to try that—he could yet be forced to
choose the right one. Altara and Murandy would be prodded to the proper

side, and Andor would drop into his hand whether or not he decided a touch of Carridin's whip was required. In Tear, Balwer's agents had convinced Tedosian and Estanda to join Darlin, turning a show of defiance into real rebellion, and the man was confident the same could be done in Cairhien, and in Andor. Another month, two at the outside, and Eamon Valda would arrive from Tar Valon; Niall could have done without Valda, but then the great majority of the Children's strength would be in one spot, ready to use where it could do the most good.

Yes, he had a good deal on his side yet. Nothing had solidified, but everything coalesced. Time was all that was needed.

Realizing he still held the bone cylinder, he cracked the wax seal with a thumbnail and carefully drew out the thin paper rolled up inside.

Balwer said nothing, but his mouth compressed again, not in a smile this time. Omerna he put up with, knowing the man a fool, much preferring to remain hidden himself, but he did not like Niall receiving reports that bypassed him, from men he did not know.

A tiny, spidery scrawl covered the slip in a cipher that few besides Niall knew, none of them in Amador. For him, reading it was as easy as reading his own hand. The sign at the bottom made him blink, and so did the contents. Varadin was, or had been, one of the best of his personal agents, a rug seller who did good service during the Troubles while peddling his wares through Altara, Murandy and Illian. What he earned there had set him up as a wealthy merchant in Tanchico, regularly supplying fine carpets and wines to the palaces of King and Panarch, as well as to most of the nobles of their courts, and always leaving with his eyes and ears full. Niall had thought him long since dead in the upheaval there; this was the first word from him in a year. From what Varadin wrote, it would have been better if he truly had been a year dead. In the jerky hand of a man on the brink of madness, it was a wild disjointed ramble about men riding strange beasts and flying creatures, Aes Sedai on leashes and the *Hailene*. That meant Forerunners in the Old Tongue, but there was not even an attempt to explain why Varadin was terrified of them or who they were supposed to be. Plainly the man had taken a brain fever from watching his country disintegrate around him.

Annoyed, Niall crumpled the paper and threw it aside. "First I must sit through Omerna's idiocy and now this. What else do you have for me, Balwer?" Bashere. Matters could become nasty with Bashere to general al'Thor's armies. The man had earned his reputation. A dagger in the shadows for him?

Balwer's eyes never left Niall's face by so much as a flicker, but Niall knew the tiny ball of paper on the floor would end up in the man's hands unless he burned it. "Four things that might be of interest, my Lord. The least first. The rumors about meetings between the Ogier *stedding* are true. For Ogier, they seem to be showing some haste." He did not say what the meetings were about, of course; getting a human into an Ogier Stump was as impossible as getting an Ogier to spy. Easier to have the sun rise at night. "Also, there are an unusual number of Sea Folk ships in the southern ports, not taking cargo, not sailing."

"What are they waiting for?"

For a moment Balwer's mouth tightened as though drawstrings had been pulled shut. "I do not know yet, my Lord." Balwer never liked admitting there were any human secrets he could not ferret out. Trying to learn more than the surface of what went on among the Atha'an Miere was like trying to learn how the Guild of Illuminators made fireworks, an exercise in futility. At least the Ogier might eventually make known the decisions of their meetings.

"Continue."

"The news of middling interest is . . . peculiar, my Lord. Al'Thor has reliably been reported in Caemlyn, in Tear and in Cairhien, sometimes on the same day."

"Reliably? Reliable madness. The witches probably have two or three men who look like al'Thor, enough to fool anyone who doesn't know him. That would explain a good deal."

"Perhaps, my Lord. My informants *are* reliable."

Niall slapped the leather folder closed, hiding al'Thor's face. "And the news of greatest interest?"

"I have it from two sources in Altara—reliable sources, my Lord—that the witches in Salidar claim the Red Ajah encouraged Logain to become a false Dragon. All but created him, in fact. They have Logain in Salidar—or a man they say is Logain—and are showing him to nobles they bring there. I have no proof, but I suspect they are telling the same tale to any ruler they can reach."

Frowning, Niall studied the banners overhead. Those represented enemies from nearly every land; no one had ever defeated him twice, and few once. The banners were all faded with age, now. Like him. Yet he was not too faded to see an end to what he had begun. Every banner taken in bloody battle, where you never really knew what was happening beyond sight of your own eyes, where certain victory and certain defeat could be equally ephemeral. The worst battle he had ever fought, armies blundering into one another in the night near Moisen, during the Troubles, had been clear as a bright summer's day compared to the one he fought now.

Could he have been wrong? Could the Tower really be broken? A struggle of some sort between the Ajahs? Over what? Al'Thor? If the witches were fighting among themselves, there would be many in the Children ready to advocate Carridin's solution, a strike to destroy Salidar and as many of the witches as possible. Men who believed thinking of tomorrow was thinking ahead but never considered next week or next month, let alone next year. Valda, for one; perhaps it was just as well he had not reached Amador yet. For another, Rhadam Asunawa, the High Inquisitor of the Questioners. Valda always wanted to use an axe, even when a poniard was best for the task at hand. Asunawa just wanted every woman who had ever spent a night in the Tower hanged as of yesterday, every book that mentioned Aes Sedai or the One Power burned, and the words themselves banned. Asunawa never had a thought beyond those goals, nor a care for costs. Niall had worked too hard, risked too much, to allow this to become a struggle between the Children and the Tower in the eyes of the world.

In truth, it did not matter whether he was wrong. If he was, it still could be very much to his advantage. Perhaps more than if he was right. With a little luck, he could shatter the White Tower past repairing, splinter the witches into shards easily ground to dust. Al'Thor would surely falter then, while remaining enough of a threat to be used as a goad. And he could hold closely to the truth. Fairly closely.

Without taking his eyes from the banners, he said, "The split in the Tower is real. The Black Ajah rose up, the victors hold the Tower and the losers were driven out to lick their wounds in Salidar." He looked at Balwer, and nearly smiled. One of the Children would have been protesting that there was no Black Ajah, or rather that all the witches were Darkfriends; the newest recruit would have. Balwer merely looked at him, not at all as if he had just blasphemed against all the Children stood for. "The only decision to make is whether the Black Ajah won or lost. I think they won. Most people will think of whoever holds the Tower as the real Aes Sedai. Let them associate *real* Aes Sedai with Black Ajah. Al'Thor is a creature of the Tower, a vassal of the Black Ajah." Lifting his winecup from the table, he took a sip; it did not help the heat. "Perhaps I can fit it in with why I haven't moved against Salidar yet." Through his emissaries, he had been using the failure to move as proof of how dire he saw the threat from al'Thor; he was willing to let the witches congregate on Amadicia's doorstep rather than be diverted from the danger of the false Dragon. "The women there, appalled after all these years at how pervasive the Black Ajah is, repelled at last by the evil they've been immersed in. . . ." His inventiveness ran out—they were all servants of the Dark One; what evil could repel them?—but after a moment Balwer took it up.

"Perhaps they've decided to throw themselves on my Lord's mercy, even ask my Lord's protection. Losers in a rebellion, weaker than their enemies, fearing to be crushed; a man falling off a cliff to certain death will stretch out a hand even to his worst enemy. Perhaps. . . ." Balwer tapped bony fingers against his lips in thought. "Perhaps they are ready to repent their sins and renounce being Aes Sedai?"

Niall stared at him. He suspected the Tar Valon witches' sins were among the things Balwer did not believe in. "That is absurd," he said flatly. "It's the sort of thing I might expect from Omerna."

His secretary's face remained as prim as ever, but he began dry-washing his hands the way he did when he felt insulted. "What my Lord might expect to hear from him, but just the sort of thing that will be repeated where he does most of his listening, in the streets and where nobles gossip over wine. Absurdities are never laughed at there; only listened to. What is too absurd to believe is believed because it is too absurd to be a lie."

"How would you present it? I will start no rumor of the Children dealing with witches."

"It would only be rumor, my Lord." Niall's gaze hardened, and Balwer spread his hands. "As my Lord wishes. Each retelling always adds embellishment, so a simple tale has the best chance of the core surviving. I suggest four rumors, my lord, not one. The first, that the division in the Tower was caused by a Black Ajah uprising. The second, that the Black Ajah won, and control the Tower. Third, the Aes Sedai in Salidar, repelled and horrified, are renouncing being Aes Sedai. And fourth, they have approached you, seeking mercy and protection. For most people, each will be a confirmation of the others." Tugging on his lapels, Balwer gave a narrow self-satisfied smile.

"Very good, Balwer. Let it be so." Niall took a deeper drink of wine. The heat was making him feel his age. His bones seemed brittle. But he would last long enough to see the false Dragon put down and the world united to face Tarmon Gai'don. Even if he did not live to lead in the Last Battle, the Light would surely grant him that much. "And I want Elayne

Trakand and her brother Gawyn found, Balwer, and brought to Amador. See to it. You may leave me now."

Instead of going, Balwer hesitated. "My Lord knows I never suggest any course of action."

"But you mean to suggest one now? What is it?"

"Press Morgase, my Lord. More than a month has passed, and she still *considers* my Lord's proposal. She—"

"Enough, Balwer." Niall sighed. Sometimes he wished Balwer were not an Amadician, but a Cairhienin who had taken in the Game of Houses with his mother's milk. "Morgase is more committed to me every day, whatever she believes. I would like it better had she accepted immediately—I could have Andor raised against al'Thor today, with a thick leavening of Children to stiffen it—but every day that she remains my guest ties her to me more tightly. Eventually she will discover she is allied to me because the world believes she is, tangled so tightly she can never escape. And no one will ever be able to say I coerced her, Balwer. That is important. It is always harder to abandon an alliance the world thinks you entered freely than one you can prove you were forced into. Reckless haste leads to ruin, Balwer."

"As my Lord says."

Niall gestured a dismissal, and the man bowed his way out. Balwer did not understand. Morgase was a rugged opponent. Pressed too hard, she would turn and fight whatever the odds. Yet pressed just hard enough, she would fight the enemy she thought she saw and never see the trap building around her until it was too late. Time pressed down on him, all the years he had lived, all the months he desperately needed, but he would not let haste ruin his plans.

The stooping falcon struck the large duck in an explosion of feathers, and the two birds separated, the duck tumbling toward the ground. Banking sharply in the cloudless sky, the falcon swooped back onto her falling prey, clutched it in her talons. The weight of the duck burdened her, but she struggled back toward the people waiting below.

Morgase wondered whether she was like the falcon, too proud and too determined to realize when she had latched on to a prize too heavy for her wings to support. She tried to make her gloved hands loosen their grip on her reins. Her wide-brimmed white hat, with its long white plumes, provided a little protection from the unrelenting sun, but sweat beaded on her face. In a riding dress of green silk embroidered in gold, she did not look a prisoner.

Figures mounted and afoot filled the long pasture of dried brown grass, though they did not crowd it. A cluster of musicians in white-embroidered blue tabards, with flutes and bitterns and tambours, produced a light tune suitable for an afternoon over chilled wine. A dozen handlers in long, elaborately worked leather vests over billowing white shirts stroked hooded falcons perched on their gauntleted arms, or puffed short pipes and blew streams of blue smoke at their birds. Twice as many brightly liveried servants moved about with fruits and wine in golden goblets on golden trays, and a band of men clad in bright mail encircled the pasture just short of the largely bare-branched trees. All in aid of Morgase and her retinue, to ensure their hawking went safely.

Well, that was the reason given, though the Prophet's people were a good two hundred miles north and brigands seemed unlikely this close to Amador. And despite the women clustered around her on their mares and geldings, in bright silk riding dresses and wide-brimmed hats resplendent with colored plumes, their hair in the long ringlets currently in fashion in the Amadician court, Morgase's retinue in truth consisted of Basel Gill, awkward on his horse off to one side, with his jerkin of metal discs straining around his girth over the red silk coat she had procured him so he would not be outshone by the servants, and Paitr Conel, even more awkward in a page's red-and-white coat and displaying the nervousness he had shown since she added him to her party. The women were nobles from Ailron's court, "volunteers" to be Morgase's ladies-in-waiting. Poor Master Gill fingered his sword and eyed the Whitecloak guards disconsolately. That was what they were, though, as usual when escorting her out of the Fortress of Light, not wearing their white cloaks. And they were guards. If she tried to ride too far or remain out too long, their commander, a hard-eyed young man named Norowhin who hated pretending to be other than a Whitecloak, would "suggest" that she return to Amador because the heat was growing too great, or because of a sudden rumor of bandits in the area. There was no arguing with fifty armored men, not with any dignity. Norowhin had come within a hair of taking her reins from her the first time. That was the reason she never let Tallanvor accompany her on these rides. That young fool might insist on her honor and rights if there were a hundred men against him. He spent his spare hours practicing the sword as though he expected to carve a way to freedom for her.

Startlingly a sudden breeze brushed her face, and she realized that

Laurain had leaned from her saddle to fan her with a white lace fan. A slender young woman with dark eyes set slightly too close together, Laurain wore a permanent simper. "It must be so gratifying for Your Majesty to learn that her son has joined the Children of the Light. And to have attained rank so quickly."

"That should be no surprise," Altalin said, fanning her own plump face. "Her Majesty's son would of course rise quickly, as the sun in splendor does." She basked in the appreciative murmurs from some of the other women for her pitiful pun.

Morgase kept her face smooth with difficulty. Niall's news last evening, during one of his surprise visits, had come as a shock. Galad a Whitecloak! At least he was safe, so Niall said. But unable to visit her; the duties of a Child of the Light kept him away. But assuredly he would be part of her escort when she returned to Andor at the head of an army of the Children.

No, Galad was no more safe than Elayne or Gawyn. Perhaps less. The Light send that Elayne was secure in the White Tower. The Light send that Gawyn was alive; Niall claimed not to know where he was, except that he was not in Tar Valon. Galad was a knife to her throat. Niall would never be so crude as to even suggest it, but one simple order from him could send Galad where he would surely die. The one protection he had was that Niall might think she did not care as much for him as for Elayne and Gawyn.

"I am pleased for him if it is what he seeks," she told them in an indifferent tone. "But he is Taringail's son, not mine, Taringail was a marriage of state, you understand. Strange, but he has been dead so long, I can hardly recall his face. Galad is free to do as he will. It is Gawyn who will be First Prince of the Sword when Elayne follows me on the Lion Throne." She waved away a servant with a goblet on a tray. "Niall could at least have provided us with decent wine." A wave of anxious titters answered her. She had had some success in drawing them closer to her, yet none could be easy about offending Pedron Niall, not where it might get back to him. Morgase took every opportunity to do so in their hearing. It convinced them of her bravery, important if she was to gain even partial allegiance. Perhaps more importantly, for her own mind at least, it helped maintain the illusion that she was not Niall's prisoner.

"I hear that Rand al'Thor displays the Lion Throne like a trophy from the hunt." That was Marande, a pretty woman with a heart-shaped face, somewhat older than the others. The sister of the High Seat of House Algoran, she was powerful in her own right, perhaps powerful enough to have resisted Ailron, but not Niall. The others reined their mounts aside for her to heel her bay gelding closer to Morgase. There was no question of gaining any sort of allegiance or friendship from Marande.

"I have heard as much," Morgase replied blithely. "The lion is a dangerous animal to hunt, and the Lion Throne more so. Especially for a man. It always kills men who seek it."

Marande smiled. "I also hear he gives high places to men who can channel."

That produced uneasy glances among the other women, and a worried buzz. One of the younger women, Marewin, slight and little more than a girl, swayed in her high-cantled saddle as if she might faint. News of al'Thor's amnesty had spawned frightening tales; rumors only, Morgase fervently hoped. The Light send it was all rumor, men who could channel gathering in Caemlyn, carousing in the Royal Palace, terrorizing the city.

"You hear a great deal," Morgase said. "Do you spend all your time listening at cracked doors?"

Marande's smile deepened. She had been unable to resist pressure to become one of Morgase's attendants, but she was powerful enough to show her displeasure without fear. She was like a thorn driven deep into the foot, impossible to dislodge and giving a sharp jab at every step. "I have little time left from the pleasure of serving Your Majesty to listen anywhere, but I do try to catch what news I can of Andor. So I may converse with Your Majesty. I hear the false Dragon consorts daily with Andoran nobles. Lady Arymilla and Lady Naean, Lord Jarid and Lord Lir. Others, friends of theirs."

One of the falconers lifted a hooded, sleek gray bird with black wings up to Morgase. Silver bells on the falcon's jesses tinkled as she shifted on the handler's gauntlet.

"Thank you, but I have had enough of hawking for today," Morgase told him, then raised her voice. "Master Gill, gather the escort. I am returning to the city."

Gill gave a start. He knew very well that all he was there for was to ride at her heels, but he began waving and shouting orders to the Whitecloaks as if he believed they would obey. For her part, Morgase turned her black mare immediately. She did not take the animal faster than a walk, of course. Norowhin would have been on her like a flash if he saw a possibility she was considering escape.

As it was, the cloakless Whitecloaks were galloping to form up their escort before the mare had gone ten steps, and before she reached the edge of the meadow, Norowhin was at her side, a dozen men ahead and the rest close behind. The servants and musicians and falconers were left to gather themselves up and follow as quickly as they could.

Gill and Paitr took their places behind her, and then came the ladies-in-waiting. Marande wore her smile like a badge of triumph now, though some of the others frowned in disapproval. Not too openly—even if she had had to yield to Niall, the woman was a force to be reckoned with in Amadicia—but most of them did try to do their best at a task they did not want. For the greater part they would likely have attended Morgase willingly; it was residing inside the Fortress of the Light they did not like.

Morgase would have smiled herself if she could be sure Marande would not see it. The only reason she had not insisted weeks ago that the woman be sent away was how free she was with her tongue. Marande enjoyed pricking her with how far Andor had fallen from her grasp, but the names she chose were a balm to Morgase. All men and women who had opposed her during the Succession, all sycophants of Gaebril. She expected no less of them, and no more. Had Marande named others, the result would have been different. Lord Pelivar or Abelle or Luan, Lady Arathelle or Ellorien or Aemlyn. Others. They had never been part of Marande's stabs, and they would have been if even a whisper from Andor had made her think of them. So long as Marande did not mention them, there was at least hope that they had not knelt to al'Thor. They had supported Morgase's first claim to the throne, and they might yet again, the Light willing.

Nearly leafless forest gave way to a road of hard-packed dirt, and they took it south toward Amador. Stretches of woods alternated with coppiced trees and fallow stone-fenced fields, with thatch-roofed stone houses and barns standing well back from the road. A good many people crowded the way, raising dust that made Morgase tie a silk kerchief across her face, though they scrambled aside onto the verge at the first glimpse of such a large party of armed and armored men. Some even darted into the trees or leaped fences and scurried across the fields. The Whitecloaks ignored them, and no farmers appeared to shake a fist or shout at the trespassers. Several of the farms had an abandoned look, with no chickens or animals in sight.

Among the people on the road there was an ox-cart here, a man with a few sheep there, somewhere else a young woman herding a flock of geese. Plainly they were all local people. Some had a bundle shouldered or a fat scrip, but most were empty-handed, walking as if with no idea where they were going. The numbers of the latter sort had increased every time Morgase had been allowed to leave Amador, no matter in which direction.

Adjusting the kerchief over her nose, Morgase eyed Norowhin sideways. He was about Tallanvor's age and height, but there the resemblance ended. Red-faced under his burnished conical helmet and peeling from the sun, he had never been handsome. A lanky build and a thrusting nose made her think of a pickaxe. Every time she left the Fortress of the Light, he led her "escort," and every time she tried to engage him in conversation. White-cloak or not, every inch she could shift him from being her jailor was a victory. "Are these people refugees from the Prophet, Norowhin?" They could not all be; as many were heading north as south.

"No," he said curtly, without even glancing at her. His eyes scanned the roadsides as if he expected a rescue to appear for her any moment.

That, unfortunately, was the sort of response she had had so far, but she persevered. "Who are they, then? Not Taraboners, surely. You do a very good job of moving them on." She had seen a party of Taraboners, fifty or so men, women and children, dirty and half falling with weariness, being herded west like cattle by mounted Whitecloaks. Only the bitter knowledge that she could do absolutely nothing had enabled her to hold her tongue. "Amadicia is a rich land. Even this drought cannot have driven so many from their farms in just a few months."

Norowhin's face worked. "No," he said finally. "They are refugees from the false Dragon."

"But how? He is hundreds of leagues from Amadicia."

Again a struggle was plain on the man's sunburned face, either for words or against speaking. "They believe he is the true Dragon Reborn," he said at last, sounding disgusted. "They say he has broken all bonds, according to the Prophecies. Men forsake their lords, apprentices desert their masters. Husbands abandon their families, and wives their husbands. It is a plague carried on the wind, a wind that blows from the false Dragon."

Morgase's eyes fell on a young man and woman huddled in each other's arms, watching her party pass. Sweat streaked the dirt on their faces, and dust coated their plain clothes. They looked hungry, their cheeks sunken, their eyes too big. Could this be happening in Andor? Had Rand al'Thor done this to Andor too? *If he has, he will pay.* The problem was making sure the cure was not worse than the disease. To deliver Andor, even from this, and hand it to the Whitecloaks. . . .

She tried to keep the conversation going, but having delivered himself of more words than he had ever before spoken to her at one time, Norowhin retreated into monosyllables. It did not matter; if she could crack his reserve once, she could again.

Twisting in her saddle, she tried to see the young man and woman, but they were hidden behind the Whitecloak soldiers. That did not matter either. Those faces would reside in her memory, alongside her promise.

CHAPTER
10

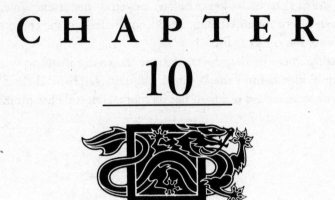

A Saying in the Borderlands

For a moment Rand wished for the days when he could have strolled the Palace corridors alone. This morning he was accompanied by Sulin and twenty Maidens, by Bael, clan chief of the Goshien Aiel, with half a dozen *Sovin Nai*, Knife Hands, from the Jhirad Goshien for Bael's honor, and by Bashere with as many of his hawk-nosed Saldaeans. They crowded the broad, tapestry-hung hallway, the *cadin'sor*-clad *Far Dareis Mai* and *Sovin Nai* staring through servants who bowed or curtsied hastily and got out of the way, and the younger Saldaeans swaggering in their short coats and their baggy breeches tucked into their boots. It was hot even here in the shaded passage, and dust motes danced in the air. Some of the servants wore the red-and-white livery they had worn when Morgase ruled, but most were new, garbed in whatever they had on when they came applying for the job, a motley collection of farmers' and tradesmen's woolens, mainly dark and plain but running the range of colors, with here and there splashes of embroidery or bits of lace.

Rand made a mental note to have Mistress Harfor, the First Maid, find livery enough to go around, so the newcomers would not feel required to work in their best clothes. Palace livery was certainly finer than anything country folk had except perhaps for feastdays. The servants numbered fewer than in Morgase's day, and a good many of the red-and-white attired men and women were gray and stooped, out of the pensioners' quarters.

Instead of fleeing when so many others did, they had quit their retirement rather than see the palace become run down. Another mental note. Have Mistress Harfor—First Maid was an unprepossessing title, but Reene Harfor ran the Royal Palace day-to-day—find enough servants so these old-sters could enjoy their pensions. Were the pensions still being paid with Morgase dead? He should have thought of that before; Halwin Norry, the chief clerk, would know. It was like being beaten to death with feathers. Everything reminded him of something else to be done. The Ways; that was no feather. He had the Waygate here in Caemlyn under guard, and those near Tear and Cairhien, but he could not even be sure how many more there were.

Yes, he would have traded all the bows and curtsies, all the honor guards, all the questions and burdens, all the people whose needs had to be met, for the days when he had to worry about providing a coat for himself. Of course, in those days he would not have been allowed to stroll these cor-ridors at all, certainly not without a different sort of guard, one to make sure he did not slip a silver-and-gold chalice from its niche in the wall, or an ivory carving from a lapis-inlaid table.

At least Lews Therin's voice was not muttering at him this morning. At least he seemed to be getting the way of the mental trick Taim had shown him; sweat trickled down Bashere's face, but the heat hardly touched Rand. He wore his silver-embroidered coat of gray silk buttoned to the neck, and if he felt a little warm, he did not sweat a drop. Taim assured him that in time he would not even feel heat or cold great enough to dis-able another man. It was a matter of distancing from himself, of concen-trating inward, a little like the way he prepared to embrace *saidin*. Strange that it should be so close to the Power yet have nothing to do with it at all. Did Aes Sedai do the same? He had never seen one sweat. Had he?

Abruptly he laughed out loud. Wondering whether Aes Sedai ever sweated! Maybe he was not mad yet, but he could pass fair for a wool-headed fool.

"Did I say something funny?" Bashere asked dryly, knuckling his mus-taches. Some of the Maidens looked at him expectantly; they were making an effort to understand wetlander humor.

How Bashere kept his equanimity, Rand did not know. A rumor had reached the Palace that very morning, of fighting in the Borderlands, be-tween Borderlanders. Travelers' tales sprang up like weeds after rain, but this had come from the north, apparently with merchants who had been at least as far as Tar Valon. Nothing in it said where or who exactly. Saldaea was as likely as anywhere else, and Bashere had had no word from there since he left months ago, yet he might have heard that the price of turnips had risen for all the effect the rumor had had on him.

Of course, Rand knew nothing of what was going on in the Two Rivers either—unless vague mutters of an uprising somewhere in the west touched his home; in these days, that could be anything or nothing—but it was not the same for him. He had abandoned the Two Rivers. Aes Sedai had spies everywhere, and he would not wager a copper that the Forsaken did not as well. The Dragon Reborn had no interest in the flyspeck village where Rand al'Thor had grown up; he was far beyond that. If he was not, then Emond's Field was a hostage to use against him. Still, he would not split hairs with himself. Abandonment was abandonment.

If I could find a way to escape my destiny, do I deserve to? That was his own thought, not Lews Therin's.

Shifting shoulders that suddenly seemed to ache dully, he kept his voice light. "Forgive me, Bashere. Something odd just occurred to me, but I have been listening. You were saying Caemlyn is filling up. For every man who ran away because he was afraid of the false Dragon, two have come because I'm not, and he isn't. You see?"

Bashere grunted, which might have meant anything.

"How many have come for other reasons, Rand al'Thor?" Bael was the tallest man Rand had ever seen, a good hand taller than Rand himself. He made an odd contrast with Bashere, who stood shorter than any of the Maidens except Enaila. Gray streaked thickly through Bael's dark reddish hair, but his face was lean and hard, his blue eyes sharp. "You have enemies enough for a hundred men. Mark me, they will try to strike at you again. There could even be Shadowrunners among them."

"Even if there are no Darkfriends," Bashere put in, "trouble brews in the city like tea left on the boil. A number of people have been severely beaten, evidently for doubting you're the Dragon Reborn, and one poor fellow was hauled from a tavern into a barn and hanged from the rafters for laughing at your miracles."

"My miracles?" Rand said incredulously.

A wrinkled, white-haired serving man in a too-large coat of livery, with a large vase in his hands, trying to bow and step out of the way at the same time, tripped on his heel and fell backward. The pale green vase, paper-thin Sea Folk porcelain, flew over his head and went tumbling end-over-end across the dark red floor tiles, spinning and bouncing until it came to rest, upright, thirty or so paces down the hall. The old man scrambled to his feet with surprising spryness and ran to snatch up the vase, running his hands over it and exclaiming in disbelief as much as relief when he found not a chip or a crack. Other servants stared with just as much incredulity, before abruptly coming to themselves and hurrying on about their tasks. They avoided looking at Rand so hard that several forgot to bow or curtsy.

Bashere and Bael exchanged looks, and Bashere blew out his thick mustaches.

"Strange occurrences, then," he said. "Every day there's another story about a child falling headfirst onto paving stones from a window forty feet up, without so much as a single bruise. Or a grandmother getting in the way of two dozen runaway horses, only somehow they don't even buffet her, much less knock her down and trample her. Some fellow threw five crowns twenty-two times straight at dice the other day, and they lay that at your feet, too. Luckily for him."

"It is said," Bael added, "that yesterday a basket of roof tiles fell from a roof and landed in the street unbroken in the shape of the ancient symbol of the Aes Sedai." He glanced at the openmouthed white-haired servant, clutching the vase to his chest as they passed. "I do not doubt that it did."

Rand exhaled slowly. They did not mention the other sort, of course. The man who stumbled on a step and was hanged when his kerchief caught on the door latch. The loose slate ripped from a roof by a high wind that sailed through an open window and a doorway to kill a woman sitting at table with her family. The sort of thing that did happen, but rarely. Only such things were not rare around him. For good or ill, for ill as often as good, he twisted chance merely by being within a few miles. No, if the Dragons disappeared from his arms and the branded herons from his palms, he was still marked. There was a saying in the Borderlands: *"Duty is heavier than a mountain, death lighter than a feather."* Once you had that mountain firmly on your shoulders, there was no way to put it down. There was no one else to carry it anyway, and no use whining about it.

He made his voice brisk. "Have you found the men who did the hanging?" Bashere shook his head. "Then find them, and arrest them for murder. I want a stop put to this. Doubting me isn't a crime." Rumor said the Prophet had made it one, but there was nothing he could do about that yet. He did not even know where Masema was, beyond somewhere in Ghealdan or Amadicia. If he had not gone elsewhere meantime. Yet another note chalked up in his head; he had to find the man and rein him somehow.

"No matter how far it goes?" Bashere said. "There are whispers you're a false Dragon who killed Morgase with Aes Sedai help. The people are supposed to rise up against you and avenge their queen. There may be more than one someone. It isn't clear."

Rand's face hardened. The first part he could live with—he had to; there were too many variations to stamp out however many times he denied it—but he would not tolerate incitement to rebellion. Andor would be one land he did not split apart in war. He would give Elayne a land as unblemished as it had come to him. If he ever found her, he would. "Find who began it," he said harshly, "and toss them in prison." Light, how to find who started a whisper? "If they seek pardon, they can ask Elayne for it." A young serving woman in a rough brown dress, dusting a blue spunglass bowl, caught sight of his face, and the bowl dropped from her suddenly shaking hands and shattered. He did not always alter chance. "Is there any good news? I could do with some."

The young woman bent unsteadily to gather up the shards of the bowl, but Sulin glanced at her, just glanced, and she sprang back, flattening herself wide-eyed against a tapestry showing a leopard hunt. Rand did not understand it, but some women seemed more frightened of the Maidens than they did of Aiel men. The young woman looked at Bael as if hoping he would protect her. He did not appear to see her at all.

"That depends on how you define good news." Bashere shrugged. "I've learned that Ellorien of House Traemane and Pelivar of House Coelan entered the city three days ago. Sneaked in, you might say, and neither has come near the Inner City that I've heard. Talk in the streets has Dyelin of House Taravin in the country nearby. None of them has responded to your invitations. I've heard nothing to connect any of them to the whispers." He glanced at Bael, who gave a slight shake of his head.

"We hear less than you, Davram Bashere. These people speak more freely around other wetlanders."

It was good news in any case. Those were people Rand needed. If they believed him a false Dragon, he could find a way around that. If they believed he had killed Morgase. . . . Well, so much the better if they remained loyal to her memory, and her blood. "Send them fresh invitations to visit me. Include Dyelin's name; they may know where she is."

"If I send such an invitation," Bashere said doubtfully, "it may do no more than remind them there's a Saldaean army in Andor."

Rand hesitated, then nodded, suddenly grinning. "Ask the Lady Arymilla to carry it. I don't doubt she'll leap at the chance to show them how close she is to me. But you write it out." Moiraine's lessons in playing the Game of Houses were coming in useful once more.

"I do not know whether it is good news or bad," Bael said, "but the Red Shields tell me two Aes Sedai have taken rooms at an inn in the New City." The Red Shields had been helping Bashere's men police Caemlyn and were now taking it over alone. Bael grinned slightly at the chagrin on Bashere's face. "We hear less, Davram Bashere, but perhaps sometimes we see more."

"Is one of them our friend who likes cats?" Rand asked. The stories of an Aes Sedai in the city persisted; sometimes there were two, or three, or a whole party. The closest Bashere or Bael had come to anything at all, though, were a few stories of an Aes Sedai who Healed dogs and cats, but always the next street over, told by someone who had been told by someone who had heard it in a tavern or in the market.

Bael shook his head. "I do not think so. The Red Shields said these two seem to have arrived in the night." Bashere looked interested——he seldom let an opportunity pass to repeat that Rand needed Aes Sedai——but Bael was frowning slightly, so slightly it would not have been noticeable on any-one but an Aiel. Aiel were careful in their dealings with Aes Sedai, even reluctant.

Those few words contained plenty for Rand to think on, and every path came back to himself. Two Aes Sedai had to have a reason to come into Caemlyn, when their sisters were avoiding the city since he appeared there. The most likely reason was something to do with him. In the best of times few people journeyed by night, and these were not the best times. Aes Sedai arriving in the dark might be trying to avoid notice, and the most likely notice for them to avoid was his. On the other hand, they might just be going somewhere urgently. Which could spell a mission for the Tower. The truth of it was, he could not think what might be more important to the Tower right now than himself. Or they might be on their way to join the Aes Sedai that Egwene insisted were going to support him.

Whatever it was, he wanted to know. The Light alone knew what the Aes Sedai were up to——the Tower or Elayne's hidden lot——but he had to find out. There were too many of them, and they could be too dangerous, for him not to. How would the Tower react when Elaida learned of his amnesty? How would any Aes Sedai? Had they heard yet?

As they approached the doors at the end of the corridor, he opened his mouth to tell Bael to ask one of the Aes Sedai to come to the Palace. He could handle two Aes Sedai if it came to that——so long as they did not catch him by surprise—but there was no point taking chances until he knew who they were and what they were about.

Pride fills me. I am sick with the pride that destroyed me!

Rand missed a step. That was the first time today that Lews Therin's voice had spoken inside his head—and too much like a comment on his thoughts of Aes Sedai for comfort—but it was not what made him swallow what he had been going to say and stop dead.

Because of the heat the doors stood open, giving out into one of the Palace gardens. The flowers were gone, and some of the rose and whitestar bushes looked wilted, but the shade trees still stood, if with few leaves, around the white marble fountain that splashed in the garden's heart. A woman in bulky brown wool skirts and a loose white *algode* blouse stood beside the fountain, a gray shawl looped over her arms, staring in wonder as she often did at water with no use except to be looked at. Rand's eyes drank in the lines of Aviendha's face, the waves of reddish hair falling to her shoulders from the folded gray scarf fastened around her temples. Light but she was beautiful. Studying the spray of water, she had not seen him yet.

Did he love her? He did not know. She was all tangled in his head and his dreams with Elayne, and even Min. What he did know was that he was dangerous; he had nothing to offer any woman except pain.

Ilyena, Lews Therin wept. *I killed her! The Light consume me forever!*

"A pair of Aes Sedai showing up like that might be important," Rand said quietly. "I think I should visit this inn and see why they're here." Almost everyone stopped when he did, but Enaila and Jalani exchanged glances and kept on right past him toward the garden. He raised his voice a fraction and hardened it considerably more. "The Maidens here will come with me. Anyone who wants to put on a dress and discuss matchmaking can stay behind."

Enaila and Jalani stiffened and spun to face him, indignation lighting their eyes. A good thing Somara was not in today's guard; she might have gone on anyway. Sulin's fingers flashed in Maiden handtalk, and whatever she had to say, it quenched indignation and set embarrassed flames in the two Maidens' cheeks instead. The Aiel had all sorts of hand signals for when silence was best. Every clan had its private set, and every society as well, besides which there were those all the Aiel knew, but only the Maidens had made a language of them.

Rand did not wait for Sulin to finish before turning away from the garden. These Aes Sedai might leave Caemlyn as quickly as they had come.

He glanced over his shoulder. Aviendha was still staring at the water; she had not seen him. He quickened his step. "Bashere, would you send one of your men to have horses readied? At the South Stable Gate." The main gates of the Palace opened onto the Queen's Plaza, which would be full of people hoping for a glimpse of him. It would have taken half an hour to make a way through, if he was lucky.

Bashere motioned, and one of the younger Saldaeans loped ahead in that rolling stride of a man more used to a saddle. "A man must know when to retreat from a woman," Bashere said to the air, "but a wise man knows that sometimes he must stand and face her."

"Young men," Bael said indulgently. "A young man chases shadows and runs from moonlight, and in the end he stabs himself in the foot with his own spear." Some of the other Aiel chuckled, Maidens and Knife Hands alike. The older ones did.

Irritated, Rand looked over his shoulder again. "Neither of you would look well in a dress." Surprisingly, the Maidens and Knife Hands laughed again, more loudly. Maybe he was getting a grip on Aiel humor.

It was as he expected when he rode out of the South Stable Gate into one of the Inner City's curving streets. Jeade'en's hooves rang on the paving stones as the stallion frisked; the dapple seldom got out of the stable of late. There were plenty of people in the street, but nowhere near the numbers to be expected on the other side of the Palace and all going about their own business. Even so, fingers pointed, and people leaned close to one another, murmuring. Some might have recognized Bashere—unlike Rand, he had been out and about in the city often—but anybody emerging from the Palace, especially with an escort of trotting Aiel, had to be important. The murmurs and pointing fingers followed.

Despite the stares, Rand tried to enjoy the beauties of the Ogier-built Inner City. The few occasions he found to just enjoy anything were precious. Streets curved out from the shining white Royal Palace, flowing along the contours of the hills like a part of the land. Everywhere stood slender towers covered in colored tiles, or domes of gold or purple or white, sparkling in the sunlight. Here a line of sight had been left clear to give a view of tree-filled park, there a rise threw the eyes across the city to the rolling plains and forests beyond the tall silver-streaked white wall that enclosed all of Caemlyn. The Inner City had been laid out to delight and soothe the eye. According to the Ogier, only Tar Valon itself and storied Manetheren had ever surpassed it, and many humans, Andorans foremost among them, believed that Caemlyn matched either.

The pure white walls of the Inner City marked the beginning of the surrounding New City, with its own domes and spires, some trying to match the height of those in the Inner City on its higher hills. Here the narrower streets were packed full of humanity, and even the broad boulevards, split down the middle by tree-lined expanses, were filled with people and ox-carts and horse-drawn wagons, folk on horseback and in carriages and sedan chairs. A buzz hung in the air, as from a huge hive of bees.

Passage was slower here, though the crowds gave way. They did not know who he was any more than did those in the Inner City, but no one wanted to get in the way of striding Aiel. It simply took time with so many people. And there was every sort of person. Farmers in rough woolens and merchants in coats or dresses of finer cut. Craftsmen hurrying about their trades and hawkers crying their wares from trays and pushcarts, everything from pins and ribbons to fruit and fireworks, the last two equally dear now. A gleeman in his patch-covered cloak rubbed shoulders with three Aiel inspecting the blades displayed on tables before a cutler's workshop. Two lean fellows with their dark hair in braids and swords on their backs—Hunters for the Horn, Rand expected—stood chatting with a number of Saldaeans as they listened to a woman playing the flute and a man the tambour on a street corner. Cairhienin, shorter and paler, stood out among the Andorans, and so did the darker Tairens, but Rand saw Murandians in long coats and Altarans in elaborate vests, fork-bearded Kandori, even a pair of Domani with long thin mustaches and earrings.

Another sort of people stood out too, those who wandered about in rumpled coats and wrinkled dresses, often dusty and always blinking and staring, plainly with nowhere to go and no idea of what to do next. That sort had gone as far as they could toward what they sought. Him. The Dragon Reborn. What he was to do with them he had no notion, yet they were his responsibility, one way or another. No matter that he had not asked them to throw over their lives, had not wanted them to abandon everything. They had. Because of him. And if they learned who he was, they might well overwhelm the Aiel and tear him apart in their eagerness just to touch him.

He touched the fat-little-man *angreal* in his coat pocket. A fine thing, if it came to him using the One Power to protect himself against people who had given up everything because of him. That was why he seldom ventured into the city. One reason, anyway. There was just too much to be done to go for an idle ride.

The inn Bael led him to, toward the western end of the city, was called Culain's Hound, three stories of stone with a red tile roof. On the twisting side street, the passing throng backed up both ways, narrowing to crowd around Rand's party when it stopped. Rand touched the *angreal* again—two Aes Sedai; he should be able to handle them without resorting to that—before dismounting and going in. Not before three Maidens and a pair of Knife Hands, of course, all on their toes and a hair from veiling. He could have taught a cat to sing first. Leaving two Saldaeans with the horses, Bashere and the others strode in at his heels along with Bael, the rest of the Aiel following except for those who had taken up guard outside. What they found was not what Rand expected.

The common room could have changed places with any of a hundred or more in Caemlyn, great barrels of ale and wine lining one plain plastered wall, topped with smaller casks of brandy, and a gray-striped cat sprawled on top of all, a pair of stone fireplaces, the hearths swept bare, and three or four aproned serving women moving among tables and benches scattered around a bare wooden floor beneath a beamed ceiling. The innkeeper, a round-faced man with three chins, a white apron straining around his bulk, trotted up washing his hands and eyeing the Aiel only a touch nervously. Caemlyn had learned they were not going to pillage and burn everything in sight—convincing the Aiel that Andor was not a conquered land and they could not take the fifth had been a harder proposition—but that was not to say innkeepers were used to having two dozen appear in their common rooms at once.

The innkeeper concentrated on Rand and Bashere. Mainly on Bashere. Both were clearly men of substance by their clothes, but Bashere was the elder by a good many years and thus likely to be the more important. "Welcome, my Lord, my Lords. What may I offer you? I have wines from Murandy as well as Andoran, brandy from. . . ."

Rand ignored the man. What was not like a hundred other common rooms was the patrons. At this hour he would have expected one or two men perhaps, but there were none. Instead most of the tables were filled with plainly dressed young women, girls really for the most part, who twisted around on their benches, teacups in hand, to gawk at the new arrivals. More than one gasped at Bael's height. Not all of them stared at the Aiel, though, and it was the near dozen who gaped at *him* that made Rand's eyes widen. He knew them. Not all well, but he did know them. One in particular seized his attention.

"Bode?" he said in disbelief. That big-eyed girl staring at him—when had she gotten old enough to put her hair in a braid?—was Bodewhin Cauthon, Mat's sister. And there was plump Hilde Barran sitting next to skinny Jerilin al'Caar, and pretty Marisa Ahan, with her hands clapped to her cheeks the way she always did when surprised, and buxom Emry Lewin and Elise Marwin and Darea Candwin and. . . . They were from Emond's Field, or close by. Darting a look over the rest of the tables, he realized the others must be Two Rivers girls, too. Most of them, anyway—he saw a Domani face, and one or two more that might well be from off—but every dress could have been seen any day on the Green in Emond's Field. "What under the Light are you doing here?"

"We are on our way to Tar Valon," Bode managed despite gaping. The only thing about her that looked at all like Mat was a mischievous something around the eyes. Her astonishment at seeing him vanished quickly in a broad smile of wonder and delight. "To become Aes Sedai, like Egwene and Nynaeve."

"We could ask the same of you," willowy Larine Ayellin put in, arranging her thick braid over her shoulder with studied casualness. The oldest of the Emond's Field girls—a good three years younger than him, but the only one besides Bode to have her hair braided—she had always had a good opinion of herself. She was pretty enough for all the boys to have confirmed it for her. "Lord Perrin hardly said two words about you except to say you were off having adventures. And wearing fine coats, which I see you are."

"Is Mat well?" Bode asked, suddenly anxious. "Is he with you? Mother worries about him so. He wouldn't even remember to put on clean stockings if someone didn't tell him."

"No," Rand said slowly, "he's not here. But he's well."

"We hardly expected to find you in Caemlyn," Jancy Torfinn piped up in her high voice. She could not be more than fourteen; she was the youngest, at least among the Emond's Fielders. "Verin Sedai and Alanna Sedai will be pleased, I'll wager. They're always asking what we know about you."

So those were the two Aes Sedai. He knew Verin, a Brown sister, more than slightly. He did not know what to think about her being here, though. That was hardly most important anyway. These girls were from *home*. "Everything is all right in the Two Rivers, then? In Emond's Field? Perrin got there all right, it seems. Wait! *Lord* Perrin?"

That opened the sluice gate. The rest of the Two Rivers girls were more interested in studying the Aiel with sidelong peeks, especially Bael, and a few spared glances for the Saldaeans, but the Emond's Field girls crowded around Rand, all trying to tell him everything at once, all jumbled up and wrong way round, interspersed with questions about himself and Mat, about Egwene and Nynaeve, most of which he could not have answered in under an hour had they given him a chance.

Trollocs had invaded the Two Rivers, but Lord Perrin drove them off. They went on so about the great battle, everyone talking at the same time, that it was hard to pick out any details except that there had been one. Everybody fought, of course, but it had been Lord Perrin who saved everybody. Always *Lord* Perrin; any time he said just Perrin they corrected him in the perfunctory way they might someone who said horse when he should have said sawhorse.

Even with the news that the Trollocs were beaten, Rand's chest tightened. He had abandoned them to this. If he had gone, there might not have been such a long list of the dead, so many names that he knew. But if he had gone, he would not have the Aiel behind him. Cairhien would not be his, as much as it was, and Rahvin would likely be sending a united Andor against him and the Two Rivers. There was a price to be paid for any decision he made. There was a price for who he was. Other people paid it. He had to keep reminding himself that it was a far smaller price than they would pay without him. The reminder did not help much, though.

Taking his expression for dismay at the listing of Two Rivers' dead, the girls hastened on to happier things. It seemed Perrin had married Faile, too. Rand wished him happiness in that, and wondered how long any happiness they found could last. The girls thought it romantic and wonderful, and only seemed to regret that there had been no time for the usual wedding parties. They were quite approving of Faile, quite admiring, and a touch envious, even Larine.

There had been Whitecloaks, too, and with them Padan Fain, the old peddler who used to come to Emond's Field every spring. The girls seemed unsure whether the Whitecloaks had been friends or enemies, but to Rand, Fain made the difference if there was any real doubt. Fain was a Darkfriend, maybe worse than a Darkfriend, who would do anything to harm Rand and Mat and Perrin. Especially Rand. Maybe the worse news they had to tell him was that no one knew whether Fain was dead. In any case, the Whitecloaks were gone, the Trollocs were gone, and refugees were flooding in across the Mountains of Mist, bringing all sorts of new things, from customs to trades, plants and seeds to clothes. One of the other girls was a Domani, and there were two Taraboners and three from Almoth Plain.

"Larine bought a Domani dress," little Jancy laughed, cutting her eyes, "but her mother made her take it back to the seamstress." Larine raised her hand, then thought better of it and simply rearranged her braid with a sniff. Jancy giggled.

"Who cares about dresses?" Susa al'Seen exclaimed. "Rand doesn't care about dresses." A slight, fluttery girl, Susa had always been excitable, and right now she was bouncing on her toes. "Alanna Sedai and Verin Sedai tested everybody. Well. Almost everybody . . ."

"Cilia Cole wanted to be tested, too," Marce Eldin, a stocky girl, put in. Rand did not much remember her, except that she had always had her nose in a book, even walking in the street. "She insisted! She passed, but they told her she was too old to be a novice."

Susa went right on over Marce. ". . . And we all passed . . ."

"We've been traveling all day and practically all night since White-bridge," Bode put in. "It is so good to stay in one place a little while."

"Have you seen Whitebridge, Rand?" Jancy said on top of Bode. "The White Bridge itself?"

". . . And we're going to Tar Valon to become Aes Sedai!" Susa finished with a glare that took in Bode, Marce and Jancy. "In Tar Valon!"

"We will not be going to Tar Valon just yet."

The voice from the door to the street spun the girls' attention from Rand, but the two Aes Sedai just coming in waved aside their questions offhandedly. The Aes Sedai's regard was all for Rand. They were disparate women, despite the common link of their faces. Either could have been any age at all, but Verin was short and plump, square-faced, with a touch of gray in her hair, while the other, who must be Alanna, was dark and slender, a beautiful vulpine woman with waves of black hair and a light in her eyes that spoke of a temper. And with a slight redness around them, as if she had been crying, though Rand could hardly believe an Aes Sedai weeping. Her riding dress was gray silk slashed with green, and looked as if she had just donned it, while Verin's pale brown appeared slightly rumpled. If Verin paid little heed to her clothes, though, her dark eyes were sharp enough. They latched on to Rand as tightly as mussels on a rock.

Two men in dull green coats followed them into the common room, one stocky and gray-haired, the other a tall dark whip of a man, but each had a sword on his hip, and the fluid way they moved would have named them Warders even without the Aes Sedai. They ignored Rand entirely, instead watching the Aiel and Saldaeans with a stillness that spoke of sudden movement in check. For their part, the Aiel did not move exactly, but there was an air of veils going up about them, Maidens and Knife Hands alike, and the young Saldaeans' fingers suddenly hovered near sword hilts. Only Bael and Bashere appeared truly at ease. The girls noticed nothing except the Aes Sedai, but the fat innkeeper sensed the mood and began wringing his hands, no doubt seeing his common room destroyed, if not his whole inn.

"There will be no trouble," Rand said loudly and levelly, for the innkeeper, for the Aiel. For everyone, he hoped. "No trouble unless you start it, Verin." Several of the girls goggled at him, speaking so to an Aes Sedai, and Larine sniffed loudly.

Verin studied him with birdlike eyes. "Who are we to start trouble near you? You have come far since I saw you last."

For some reason, he did not want to talk about that. "If you've decided not to go to Tar Valon, then you must have heard the Tower is broken." That caused a startled buzz among the girls; they certainly had not heard. The Aes Sedai gave no reaction at all. "Do you know where those who oppose Elaida are?"

"There are things we should discuss in private," Alanna said calmly. "Master Dilham, we will need your private dining room." The innkeeper nearly fell over himself assuring her that it was at her disposal.

Verin started toward a side door. "This way, Rand." Alanna looked at him, raising a questioning eyebrow.

Rand held in a wry grin. They had just walked in and taken charge, but it seemed that Aes Sedai did that as naturally as breathing. The Two Rivers girls stared at him with varying degrees of commiseration. Doubtless they expected the Aes Sedai to skin him if he did not speak right and sit straight. Perhaps Verin and Alanna did, too. With a smooth bow he motioned for Alanna to proceed him. So he had come a long way, had he? They had no idea how far.

Alanna acknowledged his bow with a nod, gathered her skirts and glided after Verin, but trouble followed immediately. The two Warders made as if to trail the Aes Sedai, and before they had taken a full step a pair of cold-eyed *Sovin Nai* moved to block them, while Sulin's fingers flickered in handtalk, sending Enaila and a blocky Maiden named Dagendra toward the door the Aes Sedai were approaching. The Saldaeans looked to Bashere, who gestured for them to stay, but then he himself looked a question at Rand.

Alanna made a vexed sound. "We will speak with him alone, Ihvon." The slender Warder frowned, then nodded slowly.

Verin glanced back, looking slightly startled, as though pulled from deep thought. "What? Oh, yes, of course. Tomas, stay here, please." The gray-haired Warder appeared doubtful, and he gave Rand a hard look before lounging back against the wall beside the door to the street. At least, he was lounging if a tripwire could be said to be lounging. Only then did the Knife Hands relax—as much as Aiel ever relaxed.

"I want to talk to them alone," Rand said, looking straight at Sulin. For a moment he thought she meant to dispute him. Her jaw firmed stubbornly; finally handtalk passed between her, Enaila and Dagendra, and they moved back, looking at him and shaking their heads in disapproval. Sulin's fingers moved again, and all the Maidens laughed. He wished there was some way to learn handtalk; Sulin had been scandalized when he asked.

Confused looks passed among the Two Rivers girls as Rand started after the Aes Sedai, and he closed the door behind them on a rising buzz. It was a small room, but with polished chairs instead of benches and pewter candlesticks on both the polished table and the vine-carved mantel above the fireplace. The two windows were shut, yet no one made a move to open one. He wondered if either Aes Sedai had noticed that the heat touched him no more than it did them.

"Will you be taking them to the rebels?" he asked immediately.

Frowning, Verin smoothed her skirts. "You know considerably more about that than we do."

"We did not hear of events in the Tower until Whitebridge." Alanna's tone was cool, but there was heat in the eyes she kept fixed on him. "What do you know of . . . rebels?" A world of distaste entered her voice with that word.

So they had heard the rumors first in Whitebridge, and made haste here, keeping everything from the girls. And by the reactions of Bode and the others, the decision not to go to Tar Valon was fresh. Seemingly they had found confirmation this morning. "I don't suppose you'll tell me who your spy in Caemlyn is." They merely looked at him, Verin tilting her head to study him. Strange how Aes Sedai gazes had been so unsettling once, so serene whatever was happening, so knowing. Having an Aes Sedai stare at him, or even two, no longer made his stomach turn uneasily. *Pride*, Lews Therin laughed madly, and Rand suppressed a grimace. "I've been told rebels exist. You haven't denied knowing where they are. I mean no harm to them, far from it. I have reason to believe they might support me." He kept back his main reason for wanting to know. Perhaps Bashere was right, perhaps he did need Aes Sedai backing, but mainly he wanted to know because he had been told Elayne was with them. He needed her to gain Andor peacefully. That was his only motive in seeking her. The only one. He was as dangerous to her as to Aviendha. "For the love of the Light, if you know, tell me."

"If we did know," Alanna replied, "we would have no right to tell anyone. Should they decide to support you, you may be certain they will seek you out."

"In their time," Verin said, "not yours."

He smiled grimly. He should have expected as much, or as little. Moiraine's advice was in the front of his head. Trust no woman who wore the shawl on the day she died.

"Is Mat with you?" Alanna asked as if that were the last thing on her mind really.

"If I knew where he was, why should I tell you? Turn and turn about?" They did not seem to think that was funny.

"It is foolish to treat us as enemies," Alanna murmured, moving toward him. "You look tired. Are you getting enough rest?" He stepped back from her raised hand, and she stopped. "Like you, Rand, I mean no harm. Nothing I do here will cause you any injury."

Since she had said it straight out, it must be so. He nodded, and she raised her hand to his head. His skin tingled faintly as she embraced *saidar*, and a familiar warm ripple passed through him, the feel of her checking his health.

Alanna nodded in satisfaction. And suddenly the warmth was heat, one great flash of it, as if he stood for a heartbeat in the middle of a roaring furnace. Even after it passed, he felt odd, aware of himself as he never had been before, aware of Alanna. He swayed, head light, muscles watery. An echo of confusion and unease rang from Lews Therin.

"What did you do?" he demanded. In a fury, he seized *saidin*. The strength of it helped hold him upright. "What did you do?"

Something beat at the flow between him and the True Source. They were trying to shield him! Weaving his own shields, he slammed them into place. He truly had gone far, and learned much, since Verin last saw him. Verin staggered, putting a hand on the table for support, and Alanna grunted as if he had punched her.

"What did you do?" Even deep in the cold emotionless Void as he was, his voice grated. "Tell me! I made no promises not to hurt you. If you don't tell me—"

"She bonded you," Verin said quickly, but if her serenity had been ruffled, it cloaked her again in an instant. "She bonded you as one of her Warders. That is all."

Alanna recovered her composure even faster. Shielded, she faced him calmly, arms folded, a hint of contentment about her eyes. Contentment! "I said I would not injure you, and I have done exactly the opposite of injury."

Drawing deep slow breaths, Rand tried to settle himself. He had walked into it like a puppy. Rage crawled across the outside of the Void. Calm. He must be calm. One of her Warders. She was Green then; not that that made any difference. He knew little of Warders, certainly not how to break the bond, or if it could be broken. All Rand felt from Lews Therin was a sense of stunned shock. Not for the first time Rand wished Lan had not gone galloping away after Moiraine died.

"You said you won't be going to Tar Valon. In that case, since you don't seem to know whether you know where the rebels are, you can remain here in Caemlyn." Alanna opened her mouth, but he rode over her. "Be grateful if I decide not to tie off those shields and leave you like that!" That got their attention. Verin's mouth tightened, and Alanna's eyes could have done for that furnace he had felt. "You will stay away from me, though. Both of you. Unless I send for you, the Inner City is barred to you. Try to break that, and I *will* leave you shielded, and in a cell besides. Do we understand one another?"

"Perfectly." Despite her eyes, Alanna's voice was ice. Verin merely nodded.

Flinging open the door, Rand stopped. He had forgotten the Two Rivers girls. Some were talking to the Maidens, some were just studying them and whispering over their tea. Bode and a handful of the Emond's Fielders were questioning Bashere, who had a pewter mug in his fist and one foot up on a bench. They looked half-entertained, half-aghast. The door banging open whipped their heads around.

"Rand," Bode exclaimed, "this man is saying awful things about you."

"He says you're the Dragon Reborn," Larine spluttered. The girls in the rest of the room apparently had not heard; they gasped.

"I am," Rand said wearily.

Larine sniffed and folded her arms beneath her breasts. "As soon as I saw that coat I knew you had gotten a big head, running off with an Aes Sedai the way you did. I knew it before you talked so disrespectfully to Alanna Sedai and Verin Sedai. But I didn't know you had become a stone blind jack-fool."

Bode's laugh was more appalled than amused. "You shouldn't say such a thing even as a joke, Rand. Tam raised you better than that. You're Rand al'Thor. Now stop this foolishness."

Rand al'Thor. That was his name, but he hardly knew who he was. Tam al'Thor had raised him, but his father had been an Aiel chief, now long dead. His mother had been a Maiden, but not Aiel. That was as much as he really knew of who he was.

Saidin still filled him. Gently he wrapped Bode and Larine in flows of Air and lifted them until their shoes dangled a foot above the floor. "I am the Dragon Reborn. Denying won't change it. Wishing won't change it. I'm not the man you knew back in Emond's Field. Do you understand now? Do you?" He realized he was shouting and clamped his mouth shut. His stomach was lead, and he was trembling. Why had Alanna done what she did? What Aes Sedai scheme was hatching behind that pretty face? Trust none of them, Moiraine had said.

A hand touched his arm, and his head jerked around.

"Please let them down," Alanna said. "Please. They are frightened."

They were more than frightened. Larine's face seemed drained of blood, and her mouth gaped as wide as it would go, as if she wanted to scream and had forgotten how. Bode was sobbing so hard she quivered. They were not the only ones. The rest of the Two Rivers girls had huddled together as far from him as they could get, and most of them were crying too. The serving maids were in that tight cluster as well, weeping as hard as anyone else. The innkeeper had sagged to his knees, goggle-eyed and gurgling wordlessly.

Rand eased the two girls back down and hastily let go of *saidin*. "I'm sorry. I didn't mean to scare you." As soon as they could move, Bode and Larine fled to join the other girls clutching one another. "Bode? Larine? I'm sorry. I won't hurt you, I promise." They did not look at him. None of them did. Sulin was certainly looking at him, and the rest of the Maidens too, blank-faced, flat-eyed disapproving stares.

"What's done is done," Bashere said, setting down his mug. "Who knows? Perhaps it's for the best."

Rand nodded slowly. It probably was. Best that they wanted to stay clear of him. Best for them. He just wished he could have talked a little while longer about home. A little while longer with them seeing only Rand al'Thor. His knees still wobbled from the bonding, but once he began moving, he did not stop until he was back in Jeade'en's saddle. Best that they were afraid of him. Best that he forgot the Two Rivers. He wondered whether that mountain ever got lighter for a time, or only kept on getting heavier.

CHAPTER
11

Lessons and Teachers

A s soon as Rand was out the door Verin let loose the breath she had
been holding. Once she had told Siuan and Moiraine how dangerous he was. Neither had listened, and now the passage of little
more than a year saw Siuan stilled and probably dead, while Moiraine. . . .
The streets crawled with rumors about the Dragon Reborn in the Royal
Palace, most beyond belief, and none that was credible mentioned an Aes
Sedai. Moiraine might have decided to let him think he was going his own
way, but she would never allow him to get far from her, not now when he
was rising to such power. Not now when the hazard he presented had
grown so great. Had Rand turned on her, more violently than he just had
on them? He had aged since she last saw him; his face bore the tightness of
struggle. The Light knew he had reason enough, but could it be the struggle for sanity as well?

So. Moiraine dead, Siuan dead, the White Tower broken, and Rand
possibly on the edge of madness. Verin *tsk*ed irritably. If you took risks,
sometimes the bill came due when you least expected, in the last way you
expected. Almost seventy years of delicate work on her part, and now it
might all go for naught because of one young man. Even so, she had lived
too long, been through too much, to allow herself to be dismayed. *First things
first; take care of what can be done now before worrying too long over what might
never be.* That lesson had been forced on her, but she had taken it to heart.

The first thing was to settle the young women down. They still huddled like a flock of sheep, weeping and holding on to one another and hiding their faces. She quite understood; this was not her first time to confront a man who could channel, much less the Dragon Reborn himself, and her stomach heaved as if on a ship at sea. She began with comforting words, patting a shoulder here, stroking hair there, trying to make her voice motherly. Convincing them that Rand was gone—which in most cases meant convincing them to open their eyes—went a long way toward bringing relative calm. At least the sobbing subsided. But Jancy kept demanding piercingly that someone tell her Rand had been lying, that it had all been a trick, while Bodewhin was just as shrill in wanting her brother found and rescued—Verin would have given a great deal to know where Mat was—and Larine blubbered that they had to leave Caemlyn immediately, on the minute.

Verin drew one of the serving maids aside. A plain-faced woman at least twenty years older than any of the Two Rivers folk, she was wide-eyed, although wiping away tears with her apron and shaking. After requesting her name, Verin said, "Bring them all nice fresh tea, Azril, hot and with plenty of honey, and put a little brandy in it." Considering the younger women for a moment, she added, "Make it more than a little. A generous splash each." That should help soothe their nerves. "And you and the other maids have some, as well." Azril sniffed and blinked and wiped her face, but she curtsied; being sent about her regular duties seemed to lessen her tears, if not her fright.

"Serve them in their rooms," Alanna said, and Verin nodded agreement. A little sleep would do wonders. They were only a few hours out of bed, but brandy atop all their hard travel should do the trick.

The order caused a commotion.

"We can't hide here," Larine managed around sniffles and hiccoughs. "We have to go! Now! He'll kill us!"

Bodewhin's cheeks glistened damply, but her face had taken on a determined cast. That Two Rivers stubbornness was going to cause more than one of these young women trouble. "We have to find Mat. We can't leave him with . . . with a man who can. . . . We can't! Even if it is Rand, we just can't!"

"I want to see Caemlyn," Jancy squeaked, though she was still trembling.

The rest joined in right on top of those three, a handful tremulously supporting Jancy despite their fear, the majority adamantly in favor of departure. One of the young women from Watch Hill, a tall, pretty girl named Elle, fair-haired for the Two Rivers, began to wail again at the top of her lungs.

It was all Verin could do not to smack the lot of them. There was excuse for the youngest, but Larine and Elle and the others with their hair braided were supposed to be women. Most had not been touched, and the danger was gone. On the other hand, they were all tired, Rand's visit had been a shock, and they were likely to face a good many more in the near future, so she held her exasperation in check.

Alanna did not. Even among Greens she was noted for her quicksilver disposition, and it was worse of late. "You will go to your rooms now," she said coolly, but her voice was all that was cool. Verin sighed as the other Aes Sedai wove Air and Fire into Illusion. Gasps filled the room, and already wide eyes bulged. There was no real need for this, but custom frowned on interfering with another sister publicly, and in truth, Verin found the sudden cessation of Elle's howls a relief. Her own nerves were far from their best. The untrained young women could not see the flows, of course; to them it seemed that Alanna was growing taller with every word. Her voice grew with it, tone unchanged, but booming to match her apparent size. "You are to be novices, and the first lesson a novice must learn is to obey Aes Sedai. Immediately. Without complaint or quibble." Alanna stood in the middle of the common room unchanged—to Verin, at least—but the Illusion's head touched the ceiling beams. "Now, run! Whoever is not in her room by the time I count five will regret it to her dying day. One. Two. . . ." Before she reached three there was a mad squealing scramble on the stairs at the back of the room; it was a wonder no one was trampled.

Alanna did not bother to go beyond four. As the last of the Two Rivers girls vanished above, she released *saidar*, the Illusion vanished, and she gave a short satisfied nod. Verin expected the young women would have to be cajoled even to peek out of their rooms now. Perhaps it was just as well. With matters as they were, she did not want anyone sneaking out for a view of Caemlyn and having to be retrieved.

Of course, Alanna had had her effect elsewhere, too. It was necessary to coax the maids out from under the tables where they had hidden, and the one who had collapsed trying to crawl to the kitchen had to be helped back onto her feet. They made no noise; they just trembled like leaves in a high wind. Verin had to give each one a little push to start her moving, and repeated her orders about the brandy and tea three times before Azril stopped gazing at her as if watching her sprout another head. The innkeeper's jaw was on his chest; his eyes seemed ready to fall out of his face. Verin looked at Tomas and motioned to the swaying fellow.

Tomas gave her a wry look—he always did when she asked him to clear up trivial matters, yet he seldom questioned her orders—then clapped an arm around Master Dilham's shoulders and asked in a jovial tone whether the two of them might not share a few mugs of the inn's best wine. A good man, Tomas, skilled in surprising areas. Ihvon had seated himself with his back against the wall and his boots up on a table. He managed to keep an eye on the door to the street and one on Alanna. A very cautious eye on Alanna. He was more than solicitous of her since Owein, her other Warder, had died in the Two Rivers—and wisely more than wary of her temper, though she usually managed to control it better than she had today. Alanna herself showed no interest in helping clean up the mess she had made. She stood in the middle of the common room looking at nothing, arms folded. To anyone not Aes Sedai she probably seemed serenity incarnate. To Verin, Alanna was a woman ready to explode.

Verin touched her arm. "We must talk." Alanna looked at her, eyes unreadable, then without a word glided toward the private dining room.

Behind her Verin heard Master Dilham say in a shaken voice, "Do you suppose I could claim the Dragon Reborn patronized my inn? He did come in, after all." For a brief moment she smiled; he would be all right, at least. Her smile vanished as she closed the door, sealing her and Alanna in.

Alanna was already stalking back and forth in the small room, the silk of her divided skirts whispering like swords sliding from scabbards. There was no face of serenity now. "The gall of the man. The utter gall! Detaining us! *Restricting* us!"

Verin watched her for a few moments before speaking. It had taken her ten years to get over Balinor's death and bond Tomas. Alanna's emotions had been raw since Owein's death, and she had held them in far too long. The occasional bouts of weeping she had allowed herself since departing the Two Rivers were not enough of a release. "I suppose he can keep us out of the Inner City with guards at the gate, but he cannot really hold us in Caemlyn."

That got the withering glance it deserved. They could leave with little difficulty—however much Rand had taught himself, there was little chance he had managed to discover wards—but it would mean relinquishing the Two Rivers girls. No Aes Sedai had found a trove like the Two Rivers in . . . Verin could not imagine how long. Perhaps not since the Trolloc Wars. Even young women of eighteen—the limit they had set for themselves—often found it hard to accept the strictures of the novitiate, yet had they extended the limit only five years, she and Alanna could have brought out twice as many, if not more. Five of these girls—five!—had the spark inborn, including Mat's sister and Wile and young Jancy; they would channel eventually whether anyone taught them or not and be very strong. She and Alanna had left two more behind to be gathered up in a year or so, when they were old enough to leave home. That was safe enough; a girl with the ability born in her very rarely manifested it before fifteen without training. The rest showed exceptional promise; all of them. The Two Rivers was a lode of pure gold.

Now that she had the other woman's attention, Verin changed the subject. She certainly had no intention of abandoning those young women. Or of moving any further from Rand than she had to. "Do you think he is right about rebels?"

Manna's fists tightened for a moment on her skirts. "The possibility repels me! Could we really have come to . . . ?" She trailed off, sounding lost. Her shoulders slumped. Tears bubbled just beneath the surface, barely held in check.

Now that the other woman's anger was dulled, Verin had questions to ask before sharpening it again. "Is there any prospect your butcher can tell you more of what has happened in Tar Valon, if you dig?" The woman was not really Alanna's; she was a Green Ajah agent, discovered because Alanna had noticed an emergency signal of some sort outside her shop. Not that Alanna had told Verin what it was, of course. Verin certainly would not have revealed any Brown signal.

"No. She knows no more than the message she gave me, and that dried her mouth so, she was hardly able to form words. All loyal Aes Sedai to return to the Tower. All is forgiven." That was the essence of it, anyway. A flash of anger lit Alanna's eyes, but only for a moment and not as strong as before. "If not for all those rumors, I'd never have let you know who she is." That, and her emotions being unbalanced. At least she had stopped pacing.

"I know," Verin said, sitting down at the table, "and I will respect the confidence. Now. You must agree that message makes the rumors true. The Tower is broken. In all probability, there *are* rebels somewhere. The question is, what do we do about it?"

Alanna looked at her as if she were mad. Small wonder. Siuan had to have been deposed by the Hall of the Tower, according to Tower law. Even a suggestion of going against Tower law was unthinkable. But then, the Tower broken was unthinkable.

"If you have no answer now, think on it. And think on this. Siuan Sanche was part of finding young al'Thor in the first place." Alanna opened her mouth—doubtless to ask how Verin knew, and whether she had been part of it, too—but Verin gave her no chance. "Only a simpleton would believe that role played no part in bringing her down. Coincidences that large do not exist. So think what Elaida's view of Rand must be. She was Red, remember. While you are thinking, answer me this. What were you at, bonding him like that?"

The question should not have caught Alanna by surprise, yet it did. She hesitated, then drew out a chair and sat, arranging her skirts before she answered. "It was the logical thing to do, with him right there in front of us. It should have been done long ago. You could not—or would not." Like most Greens, she was somewhat amused by other Ajahs' insistence that each sister have only one Warder. What Greens thought of the Reds having none was better left unsaid. "They all should have been bonded at the first chance. They are too important to run loose, him most of all." Color blossomed suddenly in her cheeks; it would be a good while yet before she had full control of her emotions again.

Verin knew what caused the blushes; Alanna had let her tongue run away with her. They had had Perrin under their eyes for long weeks while testing young women in the Two Rivers, but Alanna had quickly gone silent on the subject of bonding him. The reason was as simple as a heated promise from Faile—delivered well out of Perrin's hearing—that if Alanna did any such thing, she would not leave the Two Rivers alive. Had Faile known more of the bond between Aes Sedai and Gaidin, that threat would not have worked, yet her ignorance if nothing else had stayed Alanna's hand. Very likely it had been frustration over that, plus the frayed state of her nerves, that had led to what she did with Rand. Not only bonding him, but doing so without his permission. That had not been done in hundreds of years.

Well, Verin thought dryly, *I have broken a few customs in my time.* "Logical?" she said, smiling to take the sting from her words. "You sound like a White. Well. Now that you have him, what are you going to do with him? Considering the lessons he taught us. I am minded of a fireside tale when I was a girl, about a woman who put saddle and bridle on a lion. She found it a fine and wonderful ride, but then discovered she could never dismount and never sleep."

Shivering, Alanna rubbed her arms. "I still cannot believe he is so strong. If only we had linked sooner. And I tried. . . . I failed. . . . He is so strong!"

Verin barely kept from shivering herself. They could not have linked sooner, not unless Alanna was suggesting they should have linked before she bonded him. Verin was not sure what the result of that would have been. In any case, it had been a series of extremely bad moments, from discovering that they could not cut him off from the True Source to the contemptuous ease with which he had shielded them, snapping their connections to *saidar* like thread. Both of them at once. Remarkable. How many would it take to shield and hold him? The full thirteen? That was only tradition, but it might be necessary with him. At any rate, that was speculation for another day. "And then there is the matter of his amnesty."

Alanna's eyes widened. "Surely you don't believe that! With every false Dragon there have been tales that he was gathering men who could channel, all as false as the men. They wanted power for themselves, not to share it with other men."

"He is not a false Dragon," Verin said quietly, "and that may change everything. If one rumor is true, so can another be, and the amnesty has been on every tongue since Whitebridge."

"Even if it is, perhaps no one has come. No decent man wants to channel. If more than a handful wanted it, we would have had false Dragons every week."

"He is *ta'veren*, Alanna. He draws what he needs to him."

Alanna's mouth worked, her hands now white-knuckled fists on the table. Every shred of Aes Sedai tranquility gone, she trembled visibly. "We can't allow. . . . Men channeling, loosed on the world? If it is true, we must stop it. We must!" She was on the point of springing up again, eyes flashing.

"Before we can decide what to do about them," Verin said calmly, "we need to know where he is keeping them. The Royal Palace seems likely, but finding out may be difficult with the Inner City denied to us. This is what I propose. . . ." Alanna leaned forward intently.

There was a good deal to be worked out, though most would come later. A good many questions to be answered, later. Was Moiraine dead, and if so, how had she died? Were there rebels, and what should her and Alanna's stance be concerning them? Should they try to deliver Rand to Elaida, or to these rebels? Where were they? That knowledge would be valuable whichever way the other questions were answered. How were they to make use of the so very fragile leash Alanna had placed on Rand? Should one or both try to take Moiraine's place? For the first time since Alanna had begun to let her emotions over Owein creep to the surface, Verin was glad she had held them in long enough to become so volatile. In her raveled condition, Alanna was bound to be more amenable to guidance, and Verin knew exactly how some of those questions had to be answered. She did not think Alanna would like some of those answers. Best not to let her learn them until it was too late to change them.

Rand raced back to the Palace at a gallop, slowly outdistancing even the running Aiel, ignoring their shouts as he ignored the shaken fists of people forced to leap out of Jeade'en's way, and the jumble of overturned sedan chairs and coaches locked wheel-to-wheel with market carts in his wake. Bashere and the Saldaeans barely kept up on their smaller horses. He was not sure why he was in such a hurry—the news he carried was not that urgent—but as the shakiness faded from his arms and legs, he realized more and more that he was aware of Alanna still. He could *feel* her. It was as if she had crawled inside his head and taken up residence. If he could feel her, could she feel him the same way? What else could she do? What else? He had to get away from her.

Pride, Lews Therin cackled, and for once Rand did not try to silence the voice.

He had a different destination than the palace in mind, but Traveling required you to know the place you left from even better than the place you were going. At the South Stable he tossed the stallion's reins to a leather-vested groom and ran, his long legs carrying him ahead of the Saldaeans down corridors where servants gaped at him, arresting bows and curtsies as he sped past. In the Great Hall he grasped *saidin*, opened the hole in air and darted through into the clearing near the farm, letting the Source go.

Releasing a long breath, he sank to his knees in the dead leaves. The heat beneath the bare branches hammered him; he had lost the necessary concentration a long while back. He could still feel her, but it was fainter here—if a certainty that she was in *that* direction could be said to be faint. He could have pointed it out with his eyes closed.

For a moment he took hold of *saidin* again, that rage of fire and ice and sour slime. He held a sword in his hands, a sword made of fire, of Fire, a heron dark on the slightly curved red blade, though he did not recall thinking of it. Fire, but the long hilt felt cool and firm against his palms. The Void made no difference, the Power made no difference. Alanna was still there, curled up in a corner of his brain, watching him.

With a bitter laugh he released the Power again and knelt there. He had been so sure. Only two Aes Sedai. Of course he could handle them; he had handled Egwene and Elayne together. What could they possibly do to him? He realized he was still laughing. He did not seem able to stop. Well, it was funny. His fool pride. Overconfidence. It had gotten him in trouble before, and more than him. He had been so sure that he and the Hundred Companions could seal the Bore safely. . . .

Leaves crackled as he forced himself to his feet. "That was not me!" he said hoarsely. "That was not me! Get out of my head! All of you get out of my head!" Lews Therin's voice murmured indistinctly, distantly. Alanna waited silently, patiently, in the back of his head. The voice seemed afraid of her.

Deliberately Rand brushed off the knees of his breeches. He would not surrender to this. Trust no Aes Sedai; he would remember that from now on. *A man without trust might as well be dead*, Lews Therin giggled. He would not surrender.

Nothing had changed about the farm. Nothing and everything. The farmhouse and the barn were the same, the chickens and goats and cows. Sora Grady watched his arrival from a window, blank-faced and cold. She was the only woman now; all the other wives and sweethearts had gone with the men who failed Taim's testing. Taim had the students in a clear area of hard red clay and fitful weeds beyond the barn. All seven of them. Aside from Sora's husband, Jur, only Damer Flinn, Eben Hopwil and Fedwin Morr remained from that first testing. The others were new, all looking almost as young as Fedwin and Eben.

Except for white-haired Damer, the students sat in a line facing away from Rand. Damer stood in front of them, frowning as he stared at a head-sized stone thirty paces away.

"Now," Taim said, and Rand felt Damer seize *saidin*, saw him inexpertly weave Fire and Earth.

The stone exploded, and Damer and the other students threw themselves flat to escape flying shards. Not Taim; stone splinters bounced off the shield of Air that he had thrown up at the last instant. Lifting his head warily, Damer wiped blood from a shallow gouge below his left eye. Rand's mouth tightened; it was only luck that none of those flying pieces had struck him. He glanced back at the farmhouse; Sora was still there, unhurt apparently. And still staring at him. The chickens had hardly paused in their scratching; they seemed to be used to this.

"Perhaps you will remember what I say next time," Taim said calmly, letting his weave vanish. "Shield as you strike, or you may kill yourself."

He glanced at Rand as if he had been aware he was there all the time. "Continue," he told the students, and walked toward Rand. His hawk-nosed face seemed to have a cruel cast today.

As Damer sat down in the line, blotchy-faced Eben stood up, nervously tugging a big ear as he used Air to lift another stone from a pile off to one side. His flows wobbled, and he dropped it once before setting it in place.

"Is it safe to leave them alone like that?" Rand asked as Taim reached him.

The second stone exploded like the first, but this time all of the students had woven shields. So had Taim, surrounding himself and Rand. Without a word Rand took hold of *saidin* again and made his own shield, forcing Taim's away from him. Taim's mouth quirked in that near smile.

"You said to push them, my Lord Dragon, so I push. I make them do everything with the Power, the chores, everything. The newest got his first hot meal last night. If they can't heat it themselves, they eat cold. For most things it still takes twice as long as doing it by hand, but they're learning the Power as fast as they can, believe me. Of course, there still aren't very many."

Ignoring the implied question, Rand looked around. "Where's Haslin? Not drunk again? I told you, he's only to have wine at night." Henre Haslin had been Master of the Sword for the Queen's Guards, in charge of training recruits, until Rahvin began remaking the Guards, discarding everyone faithful to Morgase or sending them off to fight in Cairhien. Too old for campaigning, Haslin had been handed his pension and shown the gate, and when news of Morgase's death spread through Caemlyn, he crawled into a winejar. But he thought Rahvin—Gaebril, to him—had killed Morgase, not Rand, and he could teach. When he was sober.

"I sent him away," Taim said. "What good are swords?" Another rock exploded. "I can barely avoid stabbing myself, and I've never felt the lack. They have the Power, now."

Kill him! Kill him now! Lews Therin's voice echoed hollowly through the Void. Rand stamped the echo out, but he could not stamp out the anger that suddenly seemed a shell around the emptiness containing him. The Void kept his voice drained of emotion, though. "Find him, Taim, and bring him back. Tell him you have changed your mind. Tell the students that. Tell them whatever you choose, but I want him here, giving lessons every day. They need to be part of the world, not apart from it. What are they supposed to do if they can't channel? When you were shielded by the

Aes Sedai, you might still have escaped if you knew how to use a sword, how to fight with your hands."

"I did escape. Here I am."

"Some of your followers broke you free, so I heard, else you'd have ended up in Tar Valon like Logain, gentled. These men won't have followers. Find Haslin."

The other man bowed smoothly. "As my Lord Dragon commands. Was that what brought my Lord Dragon here? Haslin and swords?" The merest hint of contempt tinged his voice, but Rand ignored it.

"There are Aes Sedai in Caemlyn. Trips to the city have to stop, yours and the students' too. The Light only knows what will happen if one of them runs into an Aes Sedai and she recognizes what he is." Or for that matter, when he recognized her, as he assuredly would. He would probably run or strike out in a panic, and either would mark him. Either would doom him. From what Rand saw, Verin or Alanna could wrap up any of the students like a child.

Taim shrugged. "Doing an Aes Sedai's head like one of those rocks isn't beyond them even now. The weave is only a little different." Glancing over his shoulder, he raised his voice. "Concentrate, Adley. Concentrate." The lanky fellow standing in front of the other students, all arms and legs, gave a start and lost *saidin*, then fumbled it back again. Another rock exploded as Taim turned back to Rand. "For that matter, I can . . . remove . . . them myself, if you are not up to it."

"If I wanted them dead, I'd have killed them." He thought he could do it, if they tried to kill him, or gentle him. He hoped he could. But would they try either after bonding him? That was one thing he did not intend to let Taim know; even without Lews Therin's mutters he did not trust the man enough to expose any weakness he could hide. *Light, what sort of hold did I let Alanna get on me?* "If the time comes to kill Aes Sedai, I'll let you know. Until then, no one is to so much as shout at one unless she's trying to take his head off. In fact, you're all to stay as far from Aes Sedai as you can. I want no incidents, nothing to put them against me."

"You think they are not already?" Taim murmured. Again Rand ignored him. This time because he was not sure of the answer.

"And I don't want anybody dead or gentled because his head is too big for his cap. Make sure they know it. I hold you responsible for them."

"As you wish," Taim said with another shrug. "Some will die sooner or later, unless you mean to keep them cooped here forever. Even if you do, some will probably die. It's almost unavoidable, unless I slow the lessons. You would not have to husband them so, if you let me go out looking."

There it was again. Rand looked at the students. A sweating, pale-haired youth with blue eyes was having a hard time moving a stone into place. He kept losing *saidin*, and the rock moved by small leaps across the ground. In a few hours the wagon would be coming out from the Palace with the applicants who had arrived since midday yesterday. Four this time. Some days it was only three, or two, though the numbers had been increasing generally. Eighteen since he brought Taim out here seven days ago, and only three of them could learn to channel. Taim insisted that was a remarkable number considering that they simply walked into Caemlyn looking for the opportunity. He had also pointed out more than once that at this rate, they could match the Tower in six years or so. Rand needed no reminders that he did not have six years. And he did not have time to let them train more slowly.

"How would you do it?"

"Using gateways," Taim had picked that up right away; he was very quick with everything Rand showed him. "I can visit two or even three villages a day. Villages will be easier in the beginning than even small towns. I'll leave Flinn to watch the lessons—he's the furthest along, despite what you saw—and take Grady or Hopwil or Morr. You'll have to supply some decent horses. The nag that pulls our cart won't do."

"What do you intend, though? Just ride in and announce that you're looking for men who want to channel? You'll be lucky if the villagers don't try to hang you."

"I can be a little more circumspect than that," Taim said dryly. "I will say I'm recruiting men to follow the Dragon Reborn." A little more circumspect? Not much. "That should frighten the people just enough to keep them from my throat long enough to gather in whoever is willing. And it culls out anybody who isn't ready to support you. I don't suppose you mean to train up men who'll turn on you the first chance they find." He raised a questioning eyebrow, but did not wait for the unnecessary answer. "Once I have them safely away from the village, I can bring them here through a gateway. Some might panic, but they should not be too hard to handle. Once they've agreed to follow a man who can channel, they can hardly balk at letting me test them. Those who fail, I'll send on to Caemlyn. It's time you started rasing an army of your own instead of depending on others. Bashere could change his mind; he will, if Queen Tenobia tells him to. And who can know what these so-called Aiel will do."

This time he paused, but Rand held his tongue. He had thought along the same lines himself, if certainly not about the Aiel, but Taim had no need to know that. After a moment the man went on as if he had never brought up the subject. "I'll make you a wager. You name the price. The first day I recruit, I will find as many men who can learn as walk into Caemlyn in a month on their own. Once Flinn and some of the others are ready to go out without me. . . ." He spread his hands. "I will match the White Tower for you in less than a year. And every man a weapon."

Rand hesitated. Letting Taim go off was a risk. The man was too aggressive. What would he do if he came across an Aes Sedai on one of his recruiting trips? Maybe he would keep his word and spare her life, but what if she discovered what he was? What if she shielded and captured him? That was a loss Rand could not afford. He could not train students and do everything else he had to do as well. Six years to match the Tower. If Aes Sedai did not find this place first and destroy it and the students before they knew enough to defend themselves. Or less than a year. Finally he nodded. Lews Therin's voice was a mad buzz in the distance. "You will have your horses."

CHAPTER
12

Questions and Answers

"**W**ell?" Nynaeve said as patiently as she could. Keeping her hands in her lap was an effort, as was sitting still on her bed. She stifled a yawn. The hour was early, and she had not slept well for three nights now. The wicker cage was empty, the song sparrow set free. She wished she was free. "Well?"

Elayne was kneeling on her own bed, head and shoulders out the window into the tiny alley behind the house. From there she had just the slimmest line of sight to the rear of the Little Tower, where most of the Sitters were already receiving the Tower envoy this morning. A slight view, but enough to see a bit of the ward against eavesdropping that enclosed the inn. It was the sort that stopped anyone who was trying to listen with the Power. The price of sharing knowledge.

After a moment Elayne sat back on her heels, frustration painting her face. "Nothing. You said those flows could slip through undetected. I don't think I was noticed, but I certainly heard nothing."

That last was directed at Moghedien, on their rickety stool in a corner. The woman's lack of sweat irritated Nynaeve no end. She claimed it took time working with the Power before you could achieve the detachment necessary to ignore heat or cold, not much better than the Aes Sedais' vague promises that it would come "eventually." Nynaeve and Elayne dripped sweat, Moghedien looked cool as an early spring day, and Light, it grated!

"I said they should." Moghedien's dark eyes darted defensively, though mostly she kept her gaze on Elayne; she always concentrated on whoever wore the *a'dam* bracelet. "Should. There are thousands of ways to spin wards. It can take days to spin a hole through one."

Nynaeve held her tongue, but barely. They had been trying for days. This was the third since Tarna Feir's arrival, and the Hall still held the Red sister's message from Elaida closely. Well, Sheriam and Myrelle and that lot knew—Nynaeve would not have been surprised if they had known before the Hall did—but even Siuan and Leane had been shut outside of those daily meetings. At least, they had professed to be.

Nynaeve realized she was plucking at her skirts, and stilled her hands. Somehow, they had to find out what Elaida wanted—and more importantly, the Hall's answer. They had to. Somehow.

"I have to go," Elayne sighed. "I must show some more sisters how I make *ter'angreal*." Very few Aes Sedai in Salidar showed the knack, but they all wanted to learn, and most seemed to think they could, once they made Elayne demonstrate often enough. "You might as well take this," she added, unfastening the bracelet. "I want to try something new in the making after the sisters are done with me, and then I have a novice class." She did not sound happy about that either, not the way she had before the first time. After every class, she came back so full of irritation she bristled like a cat. The youngest girls were overeager, leaping ahead to things they had no idea how to handle, often without asking first, and the oldest, although a little more cautious, were much more likely to argue, or plain balk at an order from a woman six or seven years their junior. Elayne had taken to muttering "fool novices" and "headstrong idiots" like an Accepted of ten years. "You can have time for questions. Maybe you'll have more luck with how to detect a man than I have."

Nynaeve shook her head. "I'm supposed to help Janya and Delana with their notes this morning." She could not help grimacing. Delana was a Sitter for the Gray Ajah as Janya was for the Brown, but Nynaeve would get no glimmer of anything from them. "And then I have another *lesson* from Theodrin." Another waste of time. Everybody in Salidar was wasting time. "Wear it," she said as Elayne started to hang the bracelet on a wall peg with their clothes.

The golden-haired woman gave an affected sigh, but refastened the bracelet. In Nynaeve's opinion, Elayne was entirely too trusting of the *a'dam*. True, so long as the necklace remained on Moghedien's neck, any woman able to channel could find her with the bracelet, and control her. If no one wore the bracelet, she could not move more than a dozen paces from it without falling to her knees retching, and the same if she shifted the bracelet more than a few inches from where it had been left, or tried to unfasten the necklace herself. Maybe it would hold her even on the peg, but maybe one of the Forsaken could reason a way around that, given enough chances. Once, in Tanchico, Nynaeve had left Moghedien shielded and bound with the Power, for just a few moments, and she managed to escape. The how of that had been one of the first things Nynaeve questioned her about once she was captured again, though prying out an answer almost required wringing her neck. A tied-off shield was vulnerable, it seemed, if the woman shielded had a little time and patience. Elayne insisted that would not work against the *a'dam*—there was no knot to attack, and with the necklace around her neck Moghedien could not even *try* to touch *saidar* without permission—but Nynaeve preferred taking no chances.

"Do your copying slowly," Elayne said. "I've copied for Delana before. She *hates* blots or mistakes. She'll make you do it over fifty times to get a clean page if need be."

Nynaeve scowled. Her own hand might not be as clean and delicate as Elayne's, but she was not some lout who had just learned which end of the pen to dip in the ink. The younger woman took no notice, simply slipped out of the room with a final smile. Maybe she had only meant to be helpful. If the Aes Sedai ever learned how much Nynaeve hated copying, they would start assigning it to her for punishment.

"Perhaps you ought to go to al'Thor," Moghedien said abruptly. She was sitting differently, straighter. Her dark eyes held steady on Nynaeve's. Why?

"What do you mean?" Nynaeve demanded.

"You and Elayne should go to Caemlyn, to Rand, She can be queen, and you. . . ." Moghedien's smile was not at all pleasant. "Sooner or later, they will sit you down and dig for how you can make all these marvelous discoveries yet quake like a girl caught with stolen sweets when you try to channel for them."

"I do not—!" She was not going to explain herself, not to this woman. Why was Moghedien so forward all of a sudden? "Just you remember, whatever happens to me if they find out the truth, your head will be on the chopping block before the week is done."

"Whereas you will have much longer to suffer. Semirhage once made a man scream his every waking hour for five years. She even kept him sane, but in the end even she could not keep his heart beating. I doubt any of these children have a tenth of Semirhage's skill, but you may find out firsthand how much they do have."

How could the woman be saying this? Her normal cringing anxiety had been shed like a snake skin. They could have been two equals discussing something of casual interest. No, worse. Moghedien's attitude said it was of casual interest to her, but dire to Nynaeve. Nynaeve wished she had the bracelet. It would have been a comfort. Moghedien's emotions could not possibly be as cool and calm as her face, and her voice.

Nynaeve's breath caught. The bracelet. That was it. The bracelet was not in the room. A ball of ice formed in the pit of her stomach; the sweat suddenly seemed to roll more heavily down her face. Logically, whether the bracelet was there or not made no difference. Elayne had it on—*Please, Light, don't let her have taken it off!*—and the other half of the *a'dam* was firmly around Moghedien's neck. Only, logic had nothing to do with it. Nynaeve had never been alone with the woman without the bracelet there. Or rather, the only times she had had ended in near total disaster. Moghedien had not been wearing the *a'dam* then, but that made no difference either. She was one of the Forsaken, they were alone, and Nynaeve had no way to control her. She gripped her skirts to keep from gripping her belt knife.

Moghedien's smile deepened, as if she had read her thoughts. "In this, you can be sure I have your best interests at heart. This," her hand hovered near the necklace for a moment, carefully not touching it, "will hold me in Caemlyn as well as here. Slavery there is better than death here. But don't take too long to decide. If these so-called Aes Sedai resolve to return to the Tower, what better gift to take the new Amyrlin Seat than you, a woman so close to Rand al'Thor? And Elayne. If he feels for her half what she does for him, holding her will tie a cord to him he'll never be able to cut."

Nynaeve stood, forcing her knees straight. "You can make the beds and clean the room, now. I expect to find it spotless when I return."

"How much time do you have?" Moghedien said before she reached the door. The woman could have been asking whether the water was hot for tea. "A few more days at most before they send their answer back to Tar Valon? A few hours? How will they balance Rand al'Thor, and even Elaida's supposed crimes, against making their precious White Tower whole again?"

"Pay special attention to the chamber pots," Nynaeve said without turning around. "I want them clean this time." She left before Moghedien could say anything else, shutting the door behind her firmly.

She leaned back against the rough wooden planks, breathing deeply in the cramped windowless hallway. Dipping into her belt pouch, she plucked out a small sack and popped two frilly goosemint leaves into her mouth. Goosemint took time to soothe a burning belly, but she chewed and swallowed as though haste could make it work faster. The last few moments had been one blow after another as Moghedien shattered one thing after another that she had *known*. Even with all her distrust, she had believed the woman cowed. False. Oh, Light, false. She had been sure Moghedien knew almost as little about Elayne and Rand as the Aes Sedai did. False. And for her to suggest going to him. . . . They had talked too freely in front of her. What else had they let slip, and what use could Moghedien make of it?

Another Accepted entered the dim hall from the small house's front room, and Nynaeve straightened, tucking the goosemint away and smoothing her dress. Every room but the front one had been made into sleeping quarters, and Accepted and servants filled them, three or four to a room not much larger than the one behind her and sometimes two to a bed. The other Accepted was a slight woman, almost wispy, with gray eyes and a quick grin. An Illianer, Emara did not like Siuan or Leane, which Nynaeve found easy to understand, and thought they should be sent away—decently, as she put it—the way stilled women always had been, but aside from that she was pleasant, not even resenting Elayne and Nynaeve's "extra space" or "Marigan" doing their chores. No few did.

"I hear you do be copying for Janya and Delana," she said in her high-pitched voice, brushing past toward her own room. "Take my advice, and write as fast you can. Janya does care more for getting all her words down than for a few smudges."

Nynaeve glared at Emara's back. Write slow for Delana. Write fast for Janya. A fine lot of counsel that added up to. In any case, she could not make herself worry about blotting copy now. Or even about Moghedien, until she had a chance to talk it over with Elayne.

Shaking her head and muttering under her breath, she stalked outside. Maybe she had been taking things for granted, letting things slip, but it was time to give herself a good shake and stop it. She knew who she had to find.

In the last few days a quiet had settled over Salidar, although the streets were just as crowded. For one thing, the forges outside the village were silent. Everyone had been told to guard their tongues while Tarna was there, about the embassy on its way to Caemlyn, about Logain, who was safely tucked away in one of the soldiers' camps, even about the soldiers themselves, and why they had been gathered. It left most fearful of saying anything at all above a whisper. The low buzz of talk had an anxious note.

Everyone was affected. Servants who normally hurried now moved hesitantly, casting fearful glances over their shoulders. Even Aes Sedai seemed wary beneath their calm, eyeing each other in a calculating manner. There were few soldiers in the streets now, as though Tarna had not seen her fill the first day and come to her own conclusions. The wrong answer to the Hall would put nooses around all their necks; even rulers and nobles who wanted to stand aside from the Tower troubles would likely hang any soldiers they laid hands on, just to keep the notion of rebellion from spreading. Feeling the uncertainty, those few wore carefully blank faces or anxious frowns. Except for Gareth Bryne, waiting patiently in front of the Little Tower. He had been there every day, from before the Sitters arrived until they left. She thought he wanted to make sure they remembered him, and what he was doing for them. The one time she had seen the Sitters coming out, they had not appeared pleased to see him.

Only the Warders seemed no different for the Red sister's arrival. The Warders and the children. Nynaeve gave a start when three small girls burst up in front of her like quail, ribbons in their hair, sweaty, dusty and laughing as they ran. The children did not know what Salidar waited for, and likely would not understand if they did know. Each Warder would follow his Aes Sedai, whatever she decided and wherever she went, and never turn a hair.

Most of the muted talk seemed to be about the weather. That and tales from elsewhere about strange happenings, two-headed calves talking and men smothered by swarms of flies, all the children in a village disappearing in the middle of the night and people struck dead by something unseen in broad daylight. Anyone who could think clearly knew that the drought and unseasonable heat were the Dark One's hand touching the world, but even most Aes Sedai doubted Elayne and Nynaeve's claims that the other happenings were as real, that bubbles of evil were rising from the Dark One's prison as the seals weakened, rising and drifting along the Pattern till they burst. Most people could not think clearly. Some blamed it all on Rand. Some said the Creator was displeased that the world had not gathered behind the Dragon Reborn, or displeased that the Aes Sedai had not captured and gentled him, or displeased that Aes Sedai were opposing a seated Amyrlin. Nynaeve had heard people say the weather would come right as soon as the Tower was whole again. She pushed through the crowd.

". . . swear it's true!" murmured a cook all flour to her elbows. "There's a Whitecloak army massed the other side of the Eldar, just waiting word from Elaida to attack." Aside from the weather and two-headed calves, tales of Whitecloaks outnumbered every other sort, but *Whitecloaks* waiting orders from *Elaida*? The heat had melted the woman's brains!

"The Light stand witness, it's true," a grizzled carter muttered to a frowning woman whose well-cut wool dress marked her an Aes Sedai's maid. "Elaida's dead. The Red's come to summon Sheriam to be the new Amyrlin." The woman nodded, accepting every word of it.

"I say Elaida's a fine Amyrlin," one rough-coated man said, shifting a bundle of fagots on his shoulder. "As fine as any." He did not murmur to his companion. He spoke loudly, trying hard not to look around to see who had heard him.

Nynaeve's mouth twisted sourly. He wanted to be overheard. How *had* Elaida discovered Salidar so quickly? Tarna must have left Tar Valon soon after Aes Sedai began gathering in the village. Siuan had pointed out darkly that a goodly number of Blue sisters were still missing—the original message to gather in Salidar had been aimed at Blues—and Alviarin was accomplished at applying the question. A stomach-turning thought, but not as wrenching as the most common explanation: secret supporters of Elaida here in Salidar. Everybody looked sideways at everybody else, and the woodman was not the first Nynaeve had heard say much the same, in the same manner. Aes Sedai might not say it, but Nynaeve suspected some wanted to. It all stirred Salidar into a stew, and not a tasty one. It made what she was doing even more right.

Finding who she sought took time. She needed groups of children playing, and there were not many children in Salidar. Sure enough, Birgitte was watching five boys scramble about the street throwing a small bag of pebbles at each other, all laughing uproariously whenever one of them was hit, including the one hit. It made no more sense than most boys' games. Or men's.

Birgitte was not alone, of course. She seldom was unless she made an effort to be. Areina stood at her shoulder, dabbing at the perspiration streaming down her face and trying not to show boredom with the children. A year or two younger than Nynaeve, Areina wore her dark hair in a braid patterned after Birgitte's golden one, though still little below her shoulders; Birgitte's hung properly to the waist. Her clothes copied Birgitte, too, a waist-length coat of pale gray and voluminous bronze-colored trousers, gathered at the ankle above short boots with raised heels, as did the bow she carried and the quiver at her waist. Nynaeve did not think Areina had ever held a bow before meeting Birgitte. She ignored the woman.

"I need to talk to you," she told Birgitte. "Alone."

Areina glanced at her, blue eyes close to contempt. "I'd think you'd be wearing your shawl this fine day, Nynaeve. Oh, my. You seem to be sweating like a horse. Why is that?"

Nynaeve's face tightened. She had befriended the woman before Birgitte had, but the friendship melted on reaching Salidar. Learning that Nynaeve was not full Aes Sedai brought something more than disappointment. Only a request from Birgitte had held Areina back from informing the Aes Sedai that she had masqueraded as one. Besides, Areina had taken the oaths as a Hunter for the Horn, and Birgitte was certainly a better model for that life than Nynaeve. To think she had once pitied the woman her bruises!

"From your face," Birgitte said with a sweaty grin, "either you're ready to strangle somebody—probably Areina here—or else your dress fell off in the middle of a pack of soldiers and you weren't wearing a shift." Areina snorted a laugh, but she looked shocked. Why she should, Nynaeve did not know; the woman had had plenty of time to become used to Birgitte's so-called sense of humor, more suited as it was to some unshaven man with his nose in a mug and his belly full of ale.

Nynaeve studied the boys' play for a minute to give her irritation a chance to die down. Worse than useless to let herself get angry when she had a favor to ask.

Seve and Jaril were among the boys dodging and tossing the bag. The Yellows had been right about them; time was what they had needed. After close to two months in Salidar with other children and no fear, they laughed and shouted as loudly as the rest.

A sudden thought hit her like a hammer. "Marigan" still looked after them, if grudgingly, saw that they were bathed and fed, but now that they were talking again, at any time they might tell that the woman was not their mother. Perhaps they already had. That might not cause questions, but then again it might, and questions could bring the house of twigs they had built tumbling down on their heads. The ball of ice reappeared in the pit of Nynaeve's belly. Why had she not thought of this before?

She gave a start as Birgitte touched her arm. "What is wrong, Nynaeve? You look as though your best friend died and cursed you with her last breath."

Areina was striding away, stiff-backed, casting, one look over her shoulder at them. The woman could watch Birgitte drink and flirt with men without turning a hair, and even try to emulate her, yet she bristled every time Birgitte wanted to be alone with Elayne or Nynaeve. Men were no threat; only women could be friends in Areina's book, but only she could be Birgitte's friend. The idea of having two friends seemed foreign to her. Well, enough and be done with her.

"Could you get horses for us?" Nynaeve tried to steady her voice. That was not what she had come to ask, but Seve and Jaril made it an excellent question. "How long will it take?"

Birgitte drew her out of the street, to the mouth of a narrow alley between two weathered houses, and looked around carefully before answering. No one was close enough to overhear, or pay them any mind. "A day or two. Uno was just telling me—"

"Not Uno! We will leave him out of this. Just you, me, Elayne and Marigan. Unless Thom and Juilin return in time. And Areina, I suppose, if you insist."

"Areina's a fool some ways," Birgitte said slowly, "but life will wring that out of her, or wring her out. You know I'd never insist on her going along if you and Elayne don't want her."

Nynaeve kept silent. The woman was behaving as if *she* was the jealous one! It was none of her affair if Birgitte wanted to take up with somebody as fickle as Areina.

Rubbing a knuckle across her lips, Birgitte frowned. "Thom and Juilin are good men, but the best way to avoid trouble is to make sure no one wants to trouble you. A dozen or so Shienarans in armor—or out—would go a long way toward that. I don't understand you and Uno. He is tough, and he'd follow you and Elayne into the Pit of Doom." A sudden grin bloomed on her face. "Besides, he's a well-set-up fellow."

"We do not need anyone to hold our hands," Nynaeve told her stiffly. Well set up? That painted eyepatch flashed queasily across her mind, and the scars. The woman had the strangest taste in men. "We can handle anything that comes our way. I'd think we've already proved that, if it needed proof."

"I know we can, Nynaeve, but we'll draw trouble like flies to a midden. Altara's at a slow boil. Every day brings another tale of Dragonsworn, and I'll wager my best silk dress against one of your old shifts that half of them are really just brigands who'll see four women alone as easy meat. We will have to prove we're not every second day. Murandy's worse, I hear, full of Dragonsworn and bandits and refugees from Cairhien, afraid the Dragon

Reborn will fall on them any day. I assume you don't mean to cross over into Amadicia. I assume it's Caemlyn." Her intricate braid swung slightly as she tilted her head and raised a questioning eyebrow. "Does Elayne agree with you about Uno?"

"She will," Nynaeve muttered.

"I see. Well, when she does, I will procure as many horses as we need. But I want her to tell me why we should not take Uno."

The unyielding finality of her tone heated Nynaeve's face angrily. If she did ask Elayne ever so sweetly to tell Birgitte that Uno was to stay here, they might well find him waiting down the road, and Birgitte all amazement over how he knew they were going and which way. The woman might be Elayne's Warder, but sometimes Nynaeve wondered which of them was really in charge. When she found Lan—when, not if!—she intended to make him swear oaths fit to curl his hair that he would abide by her decisions.

She drew deep calming breaths. No point arguing with a stone wall. She might as well get on to the reason she had hunted up Birgitte in the first place.

Casually she took a step deeper into the narrow alley, making the other woman follow. Brown stubble remained underfoot from the brush that had been cleared out of it. Trying to appear offhanded, she studied the press in the street. Still no one giving them more than a glance. She lowered her voice anyway. "We need to know what Tarna is telling the Hall, and what they're telling her. Elayne and I have tried to find out, but they ward the meetings against eavesdropping. Only with the Power, though. They're so caught up that someone can listen in that way, they seem to have forgotten about pressing an ear to a door. If someone were to—"

Birgitte cut her off in a flat voice. "No."

"At least consider it. Elayne or I are ten times as likely to be caught as you." She thought of adding that Elayne was rather clever, but the other woman sniffed.

"I said no! You've been many things since I've known you, Nynaeve, but never silly. Light, they'll announce it to everyone in a day or two."

"We need to know now," Nynaeve hissed, swallowing. "You man-brained idiot." Silly? Of course she had never been silly! She must not be angry. If she could convince Elayne to go, they might not be here in a day or two. Best not to open that bag of snakes again.

Shuddering—a touch ostentatiously, Nynaeve thought—Birgitte leaned on her bow. "I was caught spying on Aes Sedai once. They tossed me out on my ear three days later, and I left Shaemal as fast as I could reach a horse. I will not go through that to gain you a day you don't need."

Nynaeve remained calm. She made an effort to maintain a smooth face, to not grind her teeth, to not yank her braid. She was calm. "I never heard any story about you spying on Aes Sedai." As soon as the words were out of her mouth, she wanted them back. The core of Birgitte's secret was that she was the Birgitte in the stories. Nothing that made that connection was ever to be mentioned.

For a moment Birgitte's face was stone, hiding everything inside. It was enough to make Nynaeve shiver; there was too much pain wrapped in the other woman's secret. Finally stone became flesh once more, and Birgitte sighed. "Time changes things. I hardly recognize half those tales myself, and the other half not at all. We'll not speak of it again." That was very plainly not a suggestion.

Nynaeve opened her mouth with no clear idea of what to say—her own debt to Birgitte meant she did not want to poke at the woman's pain, but to be balked over two simple requests . . . !—and a third woman's voice spoke suddenly from the mouth of the alley.

"Nynaeve, Janya and Delana want you right this minute."

Nynaeve tried to climb straight up into the air; her heart tried to climb through the roof of her mouth.

In the mouth of the alley, novice-clad Nicola looked startled for a moment. So did Birgitte; then she studied her bow, looking amused.

Nynaeve had to swallow twice before she could force a word out. How much had the woman heard? "If you think that's any way to speak to an Accepted, Nicola, you had best learn better quickly, or you will be taught."

It was a properly Aes Sedai thing to say, but the slender woman's dark eyes surveyed Nynaeve, weighing and measuring. "I am sorry, Accepted," she said, curtsying. "I will try to be more careful."

The curtsy was just exactly deep enough for an Accepted, to the inch, and if the tone was cool, it was not cool enough to call her down for. Areina had not been the only traveling companion disappointed by learning the truth about Elayne and Nynaeve, but Nicola had agreed to keep the secret as if surprised they thought they had to ask. Then, after testing revealed she could learn to channel, the weighing and measuring entered her eyes.

Nynaeve understood all too well. Nicola lacked the inborn spark— without teaching, she would never have touched *saidar*—but already her promise was spoken of, the strength she would have one day if she applied herself. Two years earlier, with more potential than any novice in centuries, she would have caused real excitement. That was before Elayne and Egwene, and Nynaeve herself, though. Nicola never said anything, yet Nynaeve was certain she was determined to match Elayne and Nynaeve, if not better them. She never stepped over the line of propriety, but she often walked it.

Nynaeve gave her a sharp nod. Understanding did not stop her wanting to dose the fool woman with triple-strength sheeps-tongue root for pure idiocy. "See that you do. Go tell the Aes Sedai I will be with them in just a few moments." Nicola curtsied again, but as she turned away, Nynaeve said, "Wait." The woman stopped immediately. It was not there now, but for an instant Nynaeve had been sure she saw a flash of—satisfaction? "Did you tell me everything?"

"I was sent to tell you to come, Accepted, and I did." Bland as water a week in the pitcher.

"What did they say? Their exact words."

"Exact words, Accepted? I don't know that I can remember their *exact* words, but I'll try. Remember it was them who said it; I'm only repeating. Janya Sedai said something like, 'If that fool girl doesn't show up soon, I vow she won't be able to sit down comfortably until she's old enough to be a grandmother.' And Delana Sedai said, 'She'll be that old before she decides to appear. If she isn't here inside the quarter hour, I will turn her hide into dust rags.'" Her eyes were innocence itself. "That was about twenty minutes ago, Accepted. Maybe a little longer."

Nynaeve very nearly swallowed again. Just because Aes Sedai could not lie did not mean every threat had to be taken literally, but sometimes a sparrow would starve on the difference. With anybody but Nicola, she would have yelped "Oh, Light!" and scurried. Not under those eyes. Not in front of a woman who seemed to be storing up a list of her weaknesses. "In that case, I suppose there's no need for you to run ahead of me. Go on about your duties." Turning her back on Nicola's curtsy as if she had no care in the world, she spoke to Birgitte. "I'll talk with you later. I suggest you do nothing about the matter until then." With luck that might keep her away from Uno. With a great deal of luck.

"I will consider your suggestion," Birgitte said gravely, but there was nothing grave about the mixture of sympathy and amusement on her face. The woman knew Aes Sedai. In some ways, she knew more about Aes Sedai than any Aes Sedai.

There was nothing for it but to accept and hope. As Nynaeve started up the street, Nicola fell in beside her. "I told you to be about your duties."

"They said to come back when I found you, Accepted. Is that one of

your herbs? Why do you use herbs? Is it because you can't—? Forgive me,
Accepted. I should not have mentioned that."

Nynaeve blinked at the sack of goosemint in her hand—she did not
remember taking it out—and stuffed it back in her pouch. She wanted to
chew the whole sackful of leaves. She ignored the apology and its cause;
one was surely as false as the other was deliberate. "I use herbs because
Healing isn't always necessary." Would the Yellows disapprove if that got
back to them? They were contemptuous of herbs; they only seemed interested in illnesses that did need Healing. Or those where it was not cracking pecans with a sledgehammer, anyway. What was she doing worrying
over what she said to Nicola in case it should be carried to Aes Sedai? The
woman was a novice, no matter how she looked at her and Elayne. It did
not matter how she looked at them. "Keep quiet," she said irritably. "I
want to think."

Nicola did keep quiet as they wended their way through the crowded
streets, but it seemed to Nynaeve that the woman's steps dragged. Perhaps
it was only imagination, but Nynaeve's knees began to ache from the effort
of not outpacing her. Under no circumstances would she let Nicola see her
even appear to hurry.

The situation set a slow burn inside her. Of everybody who could have
been sent to fetch her, it was hard to imagine anyone worse than Nicola
and her eyes. Birgitte was probably running off to find Uno right that minute. The Sitters were probably telling Tarna they were ready to kneel and
kiss Elaida's ring. Seve and Jaril were probably telling Sheriam they did not
know "Marigan" from a wild goose. It had been that kind of day, and the
molten sun stood only a quarter toward its peak in the cloudless sky.

Janya and Delana were waiting in the front room of the small house
they shared with three other Aes Sedai. Each with her own bedroom, of
course. Each Ajah had a house for its meetings, but Aes Sedai were scattered about through the village depending on when they had come in.
Frowning at the floor, lips pursed, Janya appeared unaware of their arrival.
Pale-haired Delana, though—her hair was so fair there was no telling
whether there was white in it or not—Delana focused her equally pale blue
eyes on them as soon as they set foot inside the door. Nicola jumped.
Nynaeve would have felt better about that had she not done the same.
Usually the stout Gray's eyes were no different from any other Aes Sedai's,
but when she really focused on you, it was as if nothing else existed but
you. Some said Delana was successful as a mediator because both sides
would agree just to make her stop staring at them. You started thinking of

what you had done wrong even if you had done nothing. The list that popped into Nynaeve's head made her curtsy as deeply as Nicola before she knew it.

"Ah," Janya said, blinking as if they had sprung out of the floor, "there you are."

"Forgive me for being late," Nynaeve said hastily. Let Nicola hear whatever she wanted. Delana was staring at her, not Nicola. "I lost track of the time, and—"

"No matter." Delana's voice was deep for a woman, her accent a throaty echo of Uno's Shienaran. It was oddly melodious in such a round woman, but then Delana was oddly graceful for one so stout. "Nicola, be off with you. You'll be running errands for Faolain until your next lesson." Nicola wasted no time dropping another curtsy and darting out. Maybe she had wanted to hear what the Aes Sedai said to Nynaeve for being late, but no one walked any lines with Aes Sedai.

Nynaeve would not have cared if Nicola sprouted wings. She had just realized there was no inkpot on the table where the Aes Sedai took their meals, no sand bowl, no pen, no paper. None of what she would need. Had she been supposed to bring it? Delana was *still* staring at her. The woman *never* stared at anyone that long. She never stared at all unless she had a reason.

"Would you like cool mint tea?" Janya said, and it was Nynaeve's turn to blink. "I do think tea is comforting. It smooths conversation, I always find." Not waiting for an answer, the birdlike Brown sister began filling mismatched cups from a blue-striped teapot on the sideboard. A rock stood in place of one of the sideboard's legs. Aes Sedai might have more room, but their furnishings were just as battered. "Delana and I decided our notes could wait for another time. We will just talk, instead. Honey? I prefer it without, myself. All that sweetness ruins the flavor. Young women always want their honey. Such wonderful things, you've been doing. You and Elayne." A loud throat-clearing made her look at Delana questioningly. After a moment Janya said, "Ah. Yes."

Delana had pulled one of the chairs from the table into the middle of the bare floor. One cane-bottomed chair. From the moment Janya mentioned conversation Nynaeve had known that that was not at all what was going to happen. Delana motioned to the chair, and Nynaeve took a seat on the very edge of it, accepted a cup on a chipped saucer from Janya with a murmured "Thank you, Aes Sedai." She did not have long to wait.

"Tell us about Rand al'Thor," Janya said. She appeared ready to say more, but Delana cleared her throat again; Janya blinked and fell silent, sipping her tea. They stood to either side of Nynaeve's chair. Delana glanced at her, then sighed and channeled the third cup to herself. It floated across the room. Delana fixed on her again in that way that seemed to bore holes in your head, Janya apparently lost in thought and maybe not seeing her at all.

"I've told you everything I know," Nynaeve sighed. "Well, told Aes Sedai, anyway." She had, too. Nothing she knew could harm him—not any more than knowing what he was, anyway—and it might help if she could make the sisters see him as a man. Not a man who could channel; just a man. Not an easy task with the Dragon Reborn. "I don't know any more."

"Don't sulk," Delana snapped. "And don't fidget."

Nynaeve set her cup back in the saucer and wiped her wrist on her skirt.

"Child," Janya said, her tone all compassion, "I know you think you've told all you know, but Delana. . . . I cannot think you would hold back on purpose—"

"Why would she not?" Delana barked. "Born in the same village. Watched him grow up. Her loyalties may be more to him than to the White Tower." That razor gaze descended on Nynaeve again. "Tell us something you haven't told before. I've heard all your stories, girl, so I will know."

"Try, child. I'm sure you don't want to make Delana angry with you. Why—" Janya cut off at another throat-clearing.

Nynaeve hoped they thought her teacup rattling meant she was rattled as well. Dragged here terrified—no, not terrified, but worried at least—over how angry they might be, and now this. Being around Aes Sedai taught you to listen carefully. You still might not catch what they really meant, but you had a better chance than if you listened with half an ear, the way most people usually did. Neither one had really said they thought she was keeping anything back. They just intended to frighten her on the chance that they might shake something else loose. She was not afraid of them. Well, not much. She was furious.

"When he was a boy," she said carefully, "he would accept his punishment without any argument if he thought he deserved it, but if he didn't think so, he fought every step of the way."

Delana snorted. "You've told that to everyone who would listen. Something else. Quickly!"

"You can lead him, or convince him, but he won't be pushed. He digs in his heels if he thinks you're—"

"And that." Hands on broad hips, Delana bent down until her head was level with Nynaeve's. Nynaeve almost wished she had Nicola staring at her again. "Something you've not told every cook and laundress in Salidar."

"Do try, child," Janya said, and for a wonder left it at that.

They dug away, Janya prompting sympathetically, Delana boring without mercy, and Nynaeve brought up every scrap she could remember. It earned her no respite; every scrap had been told so many times before she could identify them by taste. As Delana kindly pointed out. Well, not so kindly. By the time Nynaeve managed to take a sip of her tea, it tasted stale, and the sweetness almost curled her tongue. Janya apparently really did believe young women liked lots of honey. The morning passed slowly. Very slowly.

"This is taking us nowhere," Delana said at last, glaring at Nynaeve as if it were all her fault.

"May I go then?" Nynaeve asked wearily. Every drop of sweat that drenched her seemed to have been squeezed out. She felt limp. She also wanted to slap both those cool Aes Sedai faces.

Delana and Janya exchanged glances. The Gray shrugged and walked over to the sideboard for another cup of tea. "Of course you may," Janya said. "I know this must have been difficult for you, but we really do need to know Rand al'Thor better than he knows himself if we are to decide what's best. Otherwise, everything could turn to catastrophe. Oh, my, yes. You've done very well, child. But then, I never expected any less of you. Anyone who can make the discoveries you've made, with your handicap . . . why, I expect nothing less than excellence from you. And to think. . . ."

It took quite a while for her to run down and let Nynaeve stagger outside. Stagger she did, on wobbly knees. Everybody was talking about her. Of course they were. She should have listened to Elayne and begun leaving all the so-called discoveries to her. Moghedien was right. Sooner or later they were going to start probing for how she did it. So they had to decide what was best, to avoid catastrophe. No clue there to what they intended toward Rand.

A glance at the sun, almost overhead, told her she was already late for her appointment with Theodrin. At least she had a good excuse this time.

Theodrin's house—hers and two dozen other women's—lay beyond the Little Tower. Nynaeve slowed as she came abreast of the onetime inn. The gaggle of Warders out front near Gareth Bryne were evidence the meeting still went on. A residue of anger enabled her to see the ward, a close flat dome mostly of Fire and Air with touches of Water, shimmering to her eyes over the entire building, the knot holding it in tantalizing fashion. Touching that knot would be as good as offering her hide to a tannery; there were plenty of Aes Sedai in the crowded street. Now and then some of the Warders moved back and forth through the shimmer, invisible to them, as one group broke up and another formed. The same ward Elayne had failed to penetrate. A shield against eavesdropping. With the Power.

Theodrin's house stood a hundred paces or so farther up the street, but Nynaeve turned into the yard beside a thatch-roofed house just two beyond the former inn. A rickety wooden fence enclosed the tiny plot of withered weeds behind the house, but it had a gate, hanging on one hinge that was nearly all rust. It squealed murderously when she shifted the gate. She looked around hastily—no one at any of the windows; no one in the street could see her—gathered her skirts and darted through into the narrow alleyway that eventually ran by the room she shared with Elayne.

For a moment she hesitated, wiping sweaty palms on her dress, remembering what Birgitte had said. She knew she was a coward at heart, much as she hated the fact. Once she had thought herself brave enough. Not a hero, like Birgitte, but brave enough. The world had taught her better. Just thinking of what the sisters would do if they caught her—made her want to turn around and run to Theodrin. The chance was vanishingly small that she could actually find a window on the very room where the Sitters were. Impossibly small.

Trying to work some moisture back into her mouth—how could her mouth be so dry when the rest of her was so damp?—she crept closer. One day she wanted to know what it was like to be brave, like Birgitte or Elayne, instead of a coward.

The ward did not tingle when she stepped through. It did not feel like anything at all. She had known it would not. Touching it could do no harm, but she flattened herself against the rough stone wall. Bits of creeper clinging to its cracks brushed her face.

Slowly she edged along to the nearest casement window—and nearly turned around and left right then. It was shut tight, all the glass gone, replaced by oiled cloth that might let in light but certainly did not allow her to see anything. Or hear anything; at least, if there was anybody on the other side, no noise escaped. Taking a deep breath, she inched to the next window. One pane had been replaced here too, but the remainder showed a battered once-ornate table covered with papers and inkpots, a few chairs, and an otherwise empty room.

Muttering a curse she had heard from Elayne—the girl had a surprising stock of such tucked away—she felt her way along the rough stone. The third window was swung out. She pressed her nose close. And jerked back. She had not really believed she would find anything, but Tarna was in there. Not with Sitters, but Sheriam and Myrelle and the rest of that lot. If her heart had not been pounding so hard, she would have heard the murmur of their voices before she looked.

Kneeling down, she moved as close to the casement as she could without being seen by those inside. The bottom of the window rubbed against her head.

". . . sure that is the message you wish me to carry back?" That steely voice had to be Tarna's. "You request more time to consider? What is there to consider?"

"The Hall—" Sheriam began.

"The *Hall*," the Tower envoy scoffed. "Do not believe me blind to where power lies. That so-called *Hall* thinks what you six tell them to think."

"The Hall, it has asked for more time," Beonin said firmly. "Who can say what decision they will reach?"

"Elaida will have to wait to hear their decision," Morvrin said in a fair imitation of Tarna's icy tone. "Can she not wait a small time to see the White Tower whole once more?"

Tarna's reply was even colder, though. "I will carry your . . . the *Hall's* . . . message to the Amyrlin. We shall see what she thinks of it." A door opened and closed with a sharp bang.

Nynaeve could have screamed with frustration. Now she knew the answer, but not the question. If only Janya and Delana had released her a little sooner. Well, it was better than nothing. Better than "We will return and obey Elaida." There was no point staying here, waiting for someone to look out and see her.

She started to ease away, and Myrelle said, "Perhaps we should just send a message. Perhaps we should simply summon her." Frowning, Nynaeve held her place. Her who?

"The forms must be met," Morvrin said gruffly. "The proper ceremonies must be followed."

Beonin spoke on her heels in firm tones. "We must meet every letter of the law. The smallest slip, it will be used against us."

"And if we have made a mistake?" Carlinya sounded heated for perhaps the first time in her life. "How long are we to wait? How long dare we wait?"

"As long as need be," Morvrin said.

"As long as we must." That from Beonin. "I have not waited this long for the biddable child just to abandon all our plans now."

For some reason that produced a silence, although Nynaeve did hear someone murmur "biddable" again as if examining the word. What child? A novice or Accepted? It made no sense. Sisters *never* waited on novices or Accepted.

"We have gone too far to turn back, Carlinya," Sheriam said finally. "Either we bring her here and make sure she does as she should, or we leave everything to the Hall and hope they do not lead us all to disaster." From her tone, she considered that last a hope for fools.

"One slip," Carlinya said coldly, even more coldly than usual, "and we will all end with our heads on pikes."

"But who will put them there?" Anaiya asked thoughtfully. "Elaida, the Hall, or Rand al'Thor?"

Silence stretched, the skirts rustled, and the door opened and closed once more.

Nynaeve risked a peek. The room was empty. She made a vexed sound. That they intended to wait was small consolation; the final answer could still be anything. Anaiya's comment showed they were still as wary of Rand as of Elaida. Maybe more. Elaida was not gathering men who could channel. And who was the "biddable child"? No, that was unimportant. They could have fifty schemes weaving she knew nothing about.

The ward winked out, and Nynaeve jumped. It was past time to be gone from here. Scrambling to her feet, she began dusting her knees vigorously as she stepped away from the wall. One step was all she took. She stopped, bent over with her hands frozen over the dirty spots on her dress, staring at Theodrin.

The apple-cheeked Domani woman met her gaze, not saying a word.

Hastily Nynaeve considered and rejected the fool claim that she had been searching for something she dropped. Instead she straightened and walked slowly by the other woman as if there was nothing to explain. Theodrin fell in beside her silently, hands folded at her waist. Nynaeve considered her options. She could hit Theodrin over the head and run. She could get back on her knees and plead. Both notions had a good deal wrong with them to her way of thinking, but she could not pull up anything in between.

"Have you been keeping calm?" Theodrin asked, looking straight ahead.

Nynaeve gave a start. That had been the other woman's instruction to her after yesterday's attempt to break down her block. Keep calm, very calm; think only quiet composed thoughts. "Of course," she laughed weakly. "What could there be to upset me?"

"That is good," Theodrin said serenely. "Today I mean to try something a little more . . . direct."

Nynaeve glanced at her. No questions? No accusations? The way this day had been going she could not believe she was getting off so lightly.

Neither saw the woman watching them from a second-story window.

CHAPTER
13

Under the Dust

ondering whether to undo her braid, Nynaeve glowered out from under a frayed red-striped towel at her dress and shift, hanging over chairbacks and dripping on the clean-swept floorboards. Another raveled towel, striped green and white and considerably larger, served her as a substitute garment. "Now we know shock doesn't work," she growled at Theodrin, and winced. Her jaw hurt, and her cheek still stung. Theodrin had quick reflexes and a strong arm. "I could channel now, but for a moment there, *saidar* was the furthest thing from my mind." In that drenched moment of gasping for breath, when thought had fled and instinct had taken over.

"Well, channel your things dry," Theodrin muttered.

It made Nynaeve's jaw feel better, watching Theodrin peer into a broken triangle of mirror and finger her eye. The flesh looked a little puffy already, and Nynaeve suspected that left alone the bruise would be spectacular. Her own arm was not so weak. A bruise was the least Theodrin deserved!

Perhaps the Domani thought the same, because she sighed, "I won't try that again. But one way or another, I will teach you to surrender to *saidar* without first being angry enough to bite it."

Frowning at the soaked garments, Nynaeve considered a moment. She had never done anything like this before. The prohibition against doing chores with the Power was strong, and with good reason. *Saidar* was seductive. The more you channeled, the more you wanted to channel, and the more you wanted to channel, the greater the risk that eventually you would draw too much and still or kill yourself. The sweetness of the True Source filled her easily now. Theodrin's bucket of water had seen to that, if the rest of the morning had not. A simple weave of Water drew all the moisture from her clothes to fall on the floor in a puddle that quickly spread to join what the bucket had put there.

"I am not very good at surrendering," she said. Unless there was no point in fighting, anyway. Only a fool went on where there was no chance at all. She could not breathe under water, she could not fly by flapping her arms—and she could not channel except when angry.

Theodrin shifted her frown from the puddle to Nynaeve and planted fists on slim hips. "I am well aware of that," she said in a too level tone. "By all I've been taught, you should not be able to channel at all. I was taught you must be calm to channel, cool and serene inside, open and utterly yielding." The glow of *saidar* surrounded her, and flows of Water gathered the puddle into a ball sitting incongruously on the floor. "You must surrender before you can guide. But you, Nynaeve . . . however hard you try to surrender— and I've seen you try—you hang on with your fingernails unless you're furious enough to forget to." Flows of Air lifted the wobbling ball. For a moment, Nynaeve thought the other woman meant to toss it at her, but the watery sphere floated across the room and out one of the open windows. It made a great splash falling, and a cat screamed in startled fury. Perhaps the prohibition did not apply when you reached Theodrin's level.

"Why not leave it at that?" Nynaeve tried to sound bright, but she thought she failed. She *wanted* to channel whenever she pleased. But as the old saying went, "If wishes were wings, pigs would fly." "No use wasting—"

"Leave that," Theodrin said as Nynaeve started to use the weave of water on her hair. "Let go of *saidar* and allow it to dry naturally. And put on your clothes."

Nynaeve's eyes narrowed. "You don't have another surprise waiting, do you?"

"No. Now start preparing your mind. You are a flower bud feeling the warmth of the Source, ready to open to that warmth. *Saidar* is the river, you the bank. The river is more powerful than the bank, yet the bank contains and guides it. Empty your mind except for the bud. There is nothing in your thoughts but the bud. You are the bud. . . ."

Pulling her shift over her head, Nynaeve sighed as Theodrin's voice droned on hypnotically. Novice exercises. If those worked with her, she would have been channeling whenever she wanted long ago. She should stop this and see to what she really could do, such as convincing Elayne to go to Caemlyn. But she wanted Theodrin to be successful, even if it entailed ten buckets of water. Accepted did not walk out; Accepted did not defy. She hated being told what she could not do even worse than being told what she must.

Hours passed, with them now seated facing one another across a table that looked to have come out of a ramshackle farmhouse, hours of repeating drills that the novices were probably doing right that moment. The flower bud, and the riverbank. The summer breeze, and the babbling brook. Nynaeve tried to be a dandelion seed floating on the wind, the earth drinking in spring rain, a root inching its way through the soil. All without result, or at least the result Theodrin wanted. She even suggested Nynaeve imagine herself in a lover's arms, which turned out a disaster, since it made her think of Lan, and how *dare* he vanish like this! But every time frustration sparked anger like a hot coal in dry grass and put *saidar* in her grasp, Theodrin made her release it and start again, soothing, calming. The way the woman remained fixed on what she wanted was maddening. Nynaeve thought she could teach mules how to be stubborn. She never got frustrated; she had serenity down to an art. Nynaeve wanted to upend a bucket of cold water over *her* head and see how *she* liked it. Then again, considering the ache in her jaw, maybe that was not such a good idea.

Theodrin Healed that ache before Nynaeve left, which was about the extent of her abilities in that Talent. After a moment, Nynaeve gave Healing in return. Theodrin's eye had turned a brilliant purple, and she really hated not leaving it to remind the woman to have a little care what she did in the future, but turnabout was fair, and Theodrin's gasping shivers as the flows of Spirit, Air and Water ran through her were some recompense for Nynaeve's own gasps when that bucket had emptied over her. Of course, she shivered too, at her own Healing, but you could not have everything.

Outside, the sun stood halfway down toward the western horizon. Down the street, a ripple of bows and curtsies moved through the crowd, and then the shifting throng opened to reveal Tarna Feir, gliding along like a queen walking through a pigsty, the red-fringed shawl looped over her arms like a blatant banner. Even at fifty paces her attitude was plain in the way she held her head, the way she kept her skirts out of the dust, the way she ignored even those making courtesy as she passed. The first day there had been many fewer courtesies and much more bluster, but an Aes Sedai was an Aes Sedai, to the sisters in Salidar anyway. To drive that home, two Accepted, five novices and near a dozen serving men and women were spending what would have been their free hours hauling kitchen garbage and chamber-pot emptyings out to the woods and burying them.

As Nynaeve slipped away, before Tarna could see her in turn, her stomach growled loudly enough for a fellow with a basket of turnips on his back to give her a startled look. Breakfast time had gone in Elayne's attempt to pierce the ward, the midday meal in Theodrin's exercises. And she was not finished with the woman today. Theodrin's instructions had been not to sleep tonight. Perhaps exhaustion would work where shock had not. *Any block can be broken*, Theodrin had said, her voice all implacable confidence, *and I* will *break yours. It only takes once. One time channeling without anger, and* saidar *will be yours.*

At the moment all Nynaeve wanted to be hers was some food. The scullions were already cleaning up, of course, and almost done, but the smell of mutton stew and roast pig hanging around the kitchens made her nose twitch. She had to settle for two pitiful apples, a bit of goat cheese and a heel of bread. The day was not getting any better.

Back in their room she found Elayne sprawled atop her bed. The younger woman glanced at her without raising her head, then rolled her eyes back up to stare at the cracked ceiling. "I have had the most *miserable* day, Nynaeve," she sighed. "Escaralde *insists* on learning to make *ter'angreal* when she isn't strong enough, and Varilin did *something*—I don't know what—and the stone she was working on turned into a ball of . . . well, it wasn't quite flame . . . right in her hands. Except for Dagdara, I think she'd have died; no one else there could have Healed her, and I don't think there was time to fetch someone who could. Then I was thinking about Marigan—if we can't learn how to detect a man channeling, maybe we can learn to detect what he's done; I seem to remember Moiraine *implying* that was possible. I *think* I do—anyway, I was thinking about her, and somebody touched me on the shoulder, and I screamed like I'd been stuck with a needle. It was just some poor carter wanting to ask me about a fool rumor, but I frightened him so, he nearly ran."

She drew breath finally, and Nynaeve abandoned the notion of throwing her last apple core at her and darted into the momentary quiet. "Where is Marigan?"

"She was finished tidying—and took her time about it, too—so I sent her off to her own room. I *am* still wearing the bracelet. See?" She waved her arm in the air and let it fall back to the mattress, but the flow of words did not slow. "She was going on in that *awful* whining way about how we should run off to Caemlyn, and I just could *not* stand it another minute, not on top of everything else. My novice class was a disaster. That *horrible* Keatlin woman—the one with the nose?—kept muttering about how she'd never let a *girl* order her around back home, and Faolain came *stalking* up demanding to know why I had Nicola in the class—how was *I* supposed to know Nicola was meant to be running errands for her?—then *Ibrella* decided to see how big a flame she could make and nearly set the whole *class* on fire, and Faolain dressed me down right in front of *everybody* for not keeping my class under control, and Nicola said *she*—"

Nynaeve gave up trying to get a word in edgewise—maybe she should have thrown the apple core—and just shouted. "I think Moghedien's right!"

That name shut the other woman's mouth, and sat her up staring, too. Nynaeve could not help looking around to see if anyone had overheard, even if they were in their own room.

"That is foolish, Nynaeve."

Nynaeve did not know whether Elayne meant the suggestion or speaking Moghedien's name aloud, and she did not intend to inquire. Sitting on her own bed opposite Elayne, she adjusted her skirts. "No, it isn't. Any day now Jaril and Seve will tell somebody Marigan isn't their mother, if they haven't already. Are you ready for the questions that will bring? I'm not. Any day some Aes Sedai is going to start digging into how I can discover anything without being in a fury from sunup to sundown. Every second Aes Sedai I speak to mentions it, and Dagdara has been looking at me in a funny way lately. Besides, they aren't going to do anything here but sit. Unless they decide to go back to the Tower. I sneaked up and listened to Tarna talking with Sheriam—"

"You *what?*"

"I sneaked up and listened," Nynaeve said levelly. "The message they're sending to Elaida is that they need more time to consider. That means they're at least considering forgetting about the Red Ajah and Logain. How they can, I don't know, but they must be. If we stay here much longer, we may end up handed to Elaida as a present. At least if we go now we can tell Rand not to count on any Aes Sedai being behind him. We can tell him not to trust any Aes Sedai."

Frowning prettily, Elayne folded her legs beneath her. "If they're still considering, it means they haven't decided. I think we should stay. Maybe we can help them decide the right way. Besides, unless you mean to talk Theodrin into coming along, you'll never break through your block if we go."

Nynaeve ignored that. A fine lot of good Theodrin had done so far. Buckets of water. No sleep tonight. What next? The woman had as good as said she meant to try anything and everything until she found what worked. Anything and everything took in too much to Nynaeve's way of thinking. "Help them decide? They won't listen to us. *Siuan* hardly listens to us, and if she has us by the scruff of the neck, we at least have her by the toe."

"I still think we should stay. At least until the Hall *does* decide. Then, if worse comes to worst, we can at least tell Rand a fact and not a maybe."

"How are we supposed to find out? We can't count on me finding the right window to listen at twice. If we wait until they announce it, we may be under guard. Me, at least. There isn't an Aes Sedai doesn't know Rand and I both come from Emond's Field."

"Siuan will tell us before anything is announced," the fool girl said calmly. "You don't think she and Leane will go meekly back to Elaida, do you?"

There was that. Elaida would have Siuan and Leane's heads before they could curtsy. "That still doesn't consider Jaril and Seve," she persisted.

"We will think of something. In any case, they aren't the first refugee children cared for by somebody not related to them." Elayne probably thought her dimpled smile was reassuring. "All we need do is put our heads to it. At the very least, we should wait for Thom to return from Amadicia. I cannot leave him behind."

Nynaeve threw up her hands. If looks reflected character, Elayne should have looked like a mule carved in stone. The girl had made Thom Merrilin a replacement for the father who died when she was little. She also sometimes seemed to think he could not find his way to the dinner table unless she held his hand.

The only warning Nynaeve had was the feel of *saidar* being embraced close by, then the door swung open on a flow of Air, and Tarna Feir stepped into the room. Nynaeve and Elayne popped to their feet. An Aes Sedai was an Aes Sedai, and some of those burying refuse were there on Tarna's word alone.

The yellow-haired Red sister scrutinized them, her face arrogant winter marble. "So. The Queen of Andor and the crippled wilder."

"Not yet, Aes Sedai," Elayne replied with a cool politeness. "Not until

I am crowned in the Great Hall. And only if my mother is dead," she added.

Tarna's smile could have frozen a snowstorm. "Of course. They tried to keep you a secret, but whispers do get about." Her gaze took in the narrow beds and the rickety stool, the clothes on their wall pegs and the cracked plaster. "I should think you would have better quarters, considering all the miraculous things you've done. Were you in the White Tower where you belong, I would not be surprised to see you both tested for the shawl by now."

"Thank you," Nynaeve said, to show she could be as civil as Elayne. Tarna looked at her. Those blue eyes made the rest of that face seem warm. "Aes Sedai," Nynaeve added hastily.

Tarna turned back to Elayne. "The Amyrlin has a special place in her heart for you, and for Andor. She has such a search being made for you as you would not believe. I know it would please her greatly if you returned with me to Tar Valon."

"My place is here, Aes Sedai." Elayne's voice was still pleasant, but her chin came up in a good match to Tarna's haughtiness. "I will return to the Tower when the rest do."

"I see," the Red said flatly. "Very well. Leave us now. I wish to speak to the wilder alone."

Nynaeve and Elayne exchanged glances, but there was nothing for Elayne to do but curtsy and go.

When the door closed, a startling change came over Tarna. She sat on Elayne's bed and swung her legs up, crossing her ankles, leaning back against the chipped headboard and folding her hands on her stomach. Her face thawed, and she even smiled. "You look uneasy. Do not be. I will not bite you."

Nynaeve could have believed that better if the other woman's eyes had changed too. The smile never touched them; in contrast, they seemed ten times as hard, a hundred times as cold. The combination made her skin crawl. "I am not uneasy," she said stiffly, planting her feet to keep them from shifting.

"Ah. Offended, is it? Why? Because I called you 'wilder'? I'm a wilder too, you know. Galina Casban beat my block out of me herself. She knew my Ajah long before I did, and took a personal interest in me. She always does in those she thinks will choose Red." She shook her head, laughing, eyes like frozen knives. "The hours I spent howling and weeping before I could find *saidar* without my eyes shut tight; you cannot weave if you cannot see the flows. I understand Theodrin is using gentler methods with you."

Nynaeve's feet moved in spite of herself. Surely Theodrin would not try that! Surely not. Stiffening her knees did nothing for the flutter in her stomach. So she was not supposed to be offended, was she? Was she to dismiss "crippled," too? "What did you wish to speak to me about, Aes Sedai?"

"The Amyrlin wants to see Elayne safe, but in many ways you are every bit as important. Perhaps more. What you have in your head of Rand al'Thor could be beyond price. And what Egwene al'Vere has in hers. Do you know where she is?"

Nynaeve wanted to wipe the sweat from her face, but she kept her hands by her sides. "I have not seen her in a long time, Aes Sedai." Months, since their last meeting in *Tel'aran'rhiod*. "May I ask, what does . . ." No one in Salidar called Elaida Amyrlin, but she was supposed to be respectful to this woman. ". . . the Amyrlin intend about Rand?"

"Intend, child? He's the Dragon Reborn. The Amyrlin knows that, and she intends to give him every honor he deserves." A touch of intensity entered Tarna's voice. "Think, child. This lot will return to the fold once it dawns on them fully what they do, but every day could be vital. Three thousand years the White Tower has guided rulers; there would have been more wars and worse without the Tower. The world faces disaster if al'Thor lacks that guidance. But you cannot guide what you do not know, any more than I could channel with my eyes closed. The best thing for him is for you to return with me and give your knowledge of him to the Amyrlin now, instead of in weeks or months. Best for you, as well. You can never be made Aes Sedai here. The Oath Rod is in the Tower. The testing can only be done in the Tower."

Sweat stung Nynaeve's eyes, but she refused to blink. Did the woman think she could be bribed? "The truth of it is, I never spent much time around him. I lived in the village, you see, and he on a farm off in the Westwood. Mainly all I remember is a boy who never listened to reason. He had to be pushed into doing what he should, or dragged into it. Of course, that was when he was a boy. He may have changed, for all I know. Most men are just the boy grown tall, but he could have."

For a long moment Tarna merely looked at her. A very long moment, under that frigid stare. "Well," she said at last, and flowed onto her feet so quickly Nynaeve almost stepped back, though there was nowhere in the tiny room to step back to. That unsettling smile remained in place. "Such

an odd group gathered here. I haven't seen either, but I understand Siuan
Sanche and Leane Sharif grace Salidar. Not the sort a wise woman would
consort with. And perhaps other odd folk, too? You would do much better
to come with me. I leave in the morning. Let me know tonight whether I
should expect to meet you on the road."

"I'm afraid not—"

"Think on it, child. This could be the most important decision you
ever make. Think very hard." The amiable mask vanished, and Tarna
swept out of the room.

Nynaeve's knees gave way, depositing her on the bed. The woman set
such a gamut of emotions running through her, she did not know what to
make of them. Uneasiness and anger roiled about with exhilaration. She
wished the Red had some way to communicate with the Tower Aes Sedai
seeking Rand. Oh, to be a fly on the wall when they tried using her assess-
ment of him. Trying to bribe her. Trying to frighten her. And doing a fair
job of the latter. Tarna was so sure the Aes Sedai here would kneel to
Elaida; it was a foregone conclusion, only the timing in doubt. And had
that been a hint about Logain? Nynaeve suspected Tarna knew more of
Salidar than the Hall or Sheriam suspected. Perhaps Elaida did have
supporters here.

Nynaeve kept expecting Elayne to return, and when a good half hour
passed without her, she went out hunting, first loping up and down dusty
streets, then trotting, pausing here to climb up on a cart tongue, there to
mount an upended barrel or a stone stoop, and peer across the heads of the
crowd. The sun descended to less than its own height above the tree line
before she stalked back to the room, muttering to herself. And found
Elayne, plainly just arrived herself.

"Where have you been? I thought Tarna might have you tied up somewhere!"

"I was getting these from Siuan." Elayne opened her hand. Two of the
twisted stone rings lay on her palm.

"Is one of those the real one? It's a good idea to take them, but you
should have tried to get the real one."

"Nothing has changed my mind, Nynaeve. I still think we should
stay."

"Tarna—"

"Only convinced me. If we go, Sheriam and the Hall *will* choose the
Tower whole over Rand. I just know it." She put her hands on Nynaeve's
shoulders, and Nynaeve let herself be sat down on her bed. Elayne took the

other opposite her and leaned forward intently. "You remember what you told me about using need to find something in *Tel'aran'rhiod*? What we need is a way to convince the Hall not to go to Elaida."

"How? What? If Logain isn't enough. . . ."

"We will know what when we find it," Elayne said firmly.

Nynaeve fingered her wrist-thick braid absently. "Will you agree to go if we don't find anything? I don't much like the thought of sitting here until they decide to put us under guard."

"I'll agree to go provided you agree to stay if we do find something useful. Nynaeve, as much as I want to see him, we can do more good here."

Nynaeve hesitated before finally muttering, "Agreed." It seemed safe enough. Without some idea of what they were looking for, she could not imagine they would find anything at all.

If the day had seemed to pass slowly before, it began to crawl now. They lined up at one of the kitchens for plates of sliced ham, turnips and peas. The sun sat on the treetops for hours, it seemed. Most in Salidar went to bed with the sun, but a few lights appeared in windows, especially the Little Tower. The Hall was feasting Tarna tonight. Bits of harp music occasionally drifted from the former inn; the Aes Sedai had found a harper of sorts among the soldiers and had him shaved and stuffed into something like livery. People passing by in the street darted quick glances at it before hurrying on or ignored it so hard they practically shook with the effort. Once again Gareth Bryne was the exception. He ate his meal seated on a wooden box in the middle of the street; any of the Hall looking out a window would have to see him. Slowly, ever so slowly, the sun slid down behind the trees. Dark came abruptly, with no twilight to speak of, and the streets emptied. The harper's melody began again. Gareth Bryne still sat on his box on the edge of a pool of light from the Hall's banquet. Nynaeve shook her head; she did not know whether he was being admirable or foolish. Some of each, she suspected.

It was not until she was in her bed with the flecked stone *ter'angreal* on the cord around her neck with Lan's heavy gold signet and the candle snuffed that she remembered Theodrin's instructions. Well, too late for that now. Theodrin would never know whether she slept anyway. Where *was* Lan?

The sound of Elayne's breathing slowed, Nynaeve snuggled into her small pillow with a tiny sigh, and . . .

. . . she stood at the foot of her empty bed, looking at a misty Elayne in the not quite light of night in *Tel'aran'rhiod*. No one to see them here.

Sheriam or one of her circle might be about, or Siuan or Leane. True, the pair of them had a right to visit the World of Dreams, but on tonight's quest neither wanted to answer questions. Elayne apparently saw it as a hunt; consciously or not, she had togged herself out like Birgitte, in green coat and white trousers. She blinked at the silver bow in her hand, and it vanished along with the quiver.

Nynaeve checked her own garments and sighed. A blue silk ball gown, embroidered with golden flowers around the low neckline and in twined lines down the full skirt. She could feel velvet dancing slippers on her feet. What you wore in *Tel'aran'rhiod* did not really matter, but whatever had possessed her mind to choose this? "You realize this might not work," she said, changing to good plain Two Rivers woolens and stout shoes. Elayne had no right to smile that way. A silver bow. Ha! "We're supposed to have some idea at least of what we're looking for, something about it."

"It will have to do, Nynaeve. According to you, the Wise Ones said the stronger the need the better, and we surely need something, or the help we promised Rand is going to vanish except for whatever Elaida is willing to give. I won't let that happen, Nynaeve. I will not."

"Put your chin down. Neither will I, if there's anything we can do about it. We might as well get on with this." Linking hands with Elayne, Nynaeve closed her eyes. *Need*. She hoped some part of her had some notion what it was they needed. Maybe nothing would happen. *Need*. Suddenly everything seemed to slide around her; she felt *Tel'aran'rhiod* tilt and swoop.

Her eyes sprang open immediately. Each step using need was taken blind, of necessity, and while each took you closer to what you sought, any one could drop you down in a pit of vipers, or a lion disturbed at its kill could bite your leg off.

There were no lions, yet what there was was disturbing. It was bright midday, but that did not bother her; time flowed differently here. She and Elayne were holding hands in a cobblestone street, surrounded by buildings of brick and stone. Elaborate cornices and friezes decorated houses and shops alike. Ornate cupolas decorated tile rooftops, and bridges of stone or wood arched across the street, sometimes three or four stories up. Heaps of garbage, old clothes and broken furniture stood piled on street corners, and rats scurried about by the score, sometimes pausing to chitter fearless challenges at them. People dreaming themselves to the brink of *Tel'aran'rhiod* flickered in and out of existence. A man fell shrieking from one of the bridges and vanished before he hit the cobblestones. A howling woman in a torn dress ran a dozen paces toward them before she too winked out.

Truncated screams and shouts echoed through the streets, and sometimes coarse laughter with a maniacal edge.

"I don't like this," Elayne said in a worried tone.

In the distance, a great bone-white shaft reared above the city, far over-topping other towers, many of them linked by bridges that made those where they were seem low. They were in Tar Valon, in the part where Nynaeve had caught a glimpse of Leane last time. Leane had not been very forthcoming about what she had been doing; increasing the awe and legend of the mysterious Aes Sedai, she had claimed with a smile.

"It doesn't matter," Nynaeve said stoutly. "Nobody in Tar Valon even knows about the World of Dreams. We won't run into anybody." Her stomach turned over as a bloody-faced man suddenly appeared, staggering toward them. He had no hands, only spurting stumps.

"That was not what I meant," Elayne muttered.

"Let's be on about it." Nynaeve closed her eyes. Need.

Shift.

They were in the Tower, in one of the tapestry-hung curving hallways. A plump novice-clad girl popped into existence not three paces away, her big eyes going wider when she saw them. "Please," she whimpered, "Please?" And was gone.

Suddenly Elayne gasped, "Egwene!"

Nynaeve whirled around, but the passage was empty.

"I saw her," Elayne insisted. "I know I did."

"I suppose she can touch *Tel'aran'rhiod* in an ordinary dream like any-one else," Nynaeve told her. "Let's just get on with what we're here for." She was beginning to feel more than uneasy. They linked hands again. Need.

Shift.

It was not an ordinary storeroom. Shelves lined the walls and made two short rows out in the floor, neatly lined with boxes of various sizes and shapes, some plain wood, some carved or lacquered, with things wrapped in cloth, with statuettes and figurines, and peculiar shapes seemingly of metal or glass, crystal or stone or glazed porcelain. Nynaeve needed no more to know they must be objects of the One Power, *ter'angreal* most likely, per-haps some *angreal* and *sa'angreal*. Such a disparate collection, stored away so tidily, could not be anything else in the Tower.

"I don't think there is any point to going further here," Elayne said dejectedly. "I don't know how we could ever get anything out of here."

Nynaeve gave her braid a short tug. If there really was something here they could use—there had to be, unless the Wise Ones had lied—then there had to be a way to reach it in the waking world. *Angreal* and the like were not heavily guarded; usually, when she had been in the Tower, only by a lock and a novice. The door here was made of heavy planks with a heavy black iron lock set in it. No doubt it was fastened, but she fixed it in her mind as undone and pushed.

The door swung open into a guardroom. Narrow beds stacked one atop another lined one wall, and racked halberds lined another. Beyond a heavy, battered table ringed by stools was another door, iron-strapped, with a small grille set in it.

As she turned back to Elayne she was suddenly aware that the door was shut again. "If we can't get to what we need here, maybe we can somewhere else. I mean, maybe something else will do. At least we have a hint now. I think these are *ter'angreal* nobody has found how to use yet. That's the only reason they would be guarded like this. It could be dangerous even to channel close to them."

Elayne gave her a wry look. "But if we try again, won't it just bring us right back here? Unless. . . . Unless the Wise Ones told you how to exclude a place from the search."

They had not—they had not been eager to tell her anything at all— but in a place where you open a lock by thinking it was open, anything should be possible. "That's exactly what we do. We fix it in our heads that what we want isn't in Tar Valon." Frowning at the shelves, she added, "And I'll wager it is a *ter'angreal* nobody knows how to use." Though how that would convince the Hall to support Rand, she could not imagine.

"We need a *ter'angreal* that isn't in Tar Valon," Elayne said as if convincing herself. "Very well. We go on."

She held out her hands, and after a moment Nynaeve took them. Nynaeve was not sure how she had become the one to insist on continuing. She wanted to leave Salidar, not find a reason to stay. But if it assured that the Salidar Aes Sedai would support Rand. . . .

Need. A *ter'angreal*. Not in Tar Valon. Need.

Shift.

Wherever they were, the dawn-lit city was certainly not Tar Valon. Not twenty paces away the broad paved street became a white stone bridge with statues at either end, arching over a stone-lined canal. Fifty paces the other way stood another. Slender, balcony-ringed towers stood everywhere, like spears driven through round slices of ornate confection. Every building was white, the doorways and windows large pointed arches, sometimes double or triple arches. On the grander buildings, long balconies of white-painted wrought iron, with intricate wrought-iron screens to hide any occupants, looked down on the streets and canals, and white domes banded with scarlet or gold rose to points as sharp as the towers.

Need. *Shift.*

It might as well have been a different city. The street was narrow and unevenly paved, hemmed in on both sides by buildings five and six stories high, their white plaster flaked away in many places to expose the brick beneath. There were no balconies here. Flies buzzed about, and it was hard to say whether it was still dawn because of the shadows down on the ground.

They exchanged looks. It seemed unlikely they would find a *ter'angreal* here, but they had gone too far to stop now. Need.

Shift.

Nynaeve sneezed before she could open her eyes, and again as soon as they were open. Every shift of her feet kicked up swirls of dust. This storeroom was not at all like that in the Tower. Chests, crates and barrels crowded the small room, piled every which way atop one another, with barely an aisle left between, and all under a thick layer of dust. Nynaeve sneezed so hard she thought her shoes would come off—and the dust vanished. All of it. Elayne wore a small smug smile. Nynaeve said nothing, only fixed the room firmly in her mind *without* dust. She should have thought of that.

Looking over the jumble, she sighed. The room was no larger than the one where their bodies lay sleeping in Salidar, but searching through all that. . . . "It will take weeks."

"We could try again. It might at least show which things to look through." Elayne sounded as doubtful as Nynaeve felt.

Still, it was as good a suggestion as any. Nynaeve closed her eyes, and once more came the *shift.*

When she looked again, she was standing at the end of the aisle away from the door, facing a square wooden chest taller than her waist. The iron straps seemed all rust, and the chest itself looked to have spent the last twenty years being beaten with hammers. A less likely repository for anything useful, especially a *ter'angreal*, Nynaeve could not imagine. But Elayne was standing right beside her, staring at the same chest.

Nynaeve put a hand on the lid—the hinges *would* open smoothly—and pushed it up. There was not even the hint of a squeal. Inside, two heavily rusted swords and an equally brown breastplate with a hole eaten through it lay atop a tangle of cloth-wrapped parcels and what seemed to be the refuse from somebody's old clothespress and a couple of kitchens.

Elayne fingered a small kettle with a broken spout. "Not weeks, but the rest of the night, anyway."

"Once more?" Nynaeve suggested. "It could not hurt." Elayne shrugged. Eyes shut. Need.

Nynaeve reached out, and her hand came down on something hard and rounded, covered with crumbling cloth. When she opened her eyes. Elayne's hand was right next to hers. The younger woman's grin nearly split her face in two.

Getting it out was not easy. It was not small, and they had to shift tattered coats and dented pots and parcels that crumbled to reveal figurines and carved animals and all sorts of rubbish. Once they had it out, they had to hold it between them, a wide flattish disc wrapped in rotted cloth. With the cloth stripped away, it turned out to be a shallow bowl of thick crystal, more than two feet across and carved deeply inside with what appeared to be swirling clouds.

"Nynaeve," Elayne said slowly, "I think this is. . . ."

Nynaeve gave a start and nearly dropped her side of the bowl as it suddenly turned a pale watery blue and the carved clouds shifted slowly. A heartbeat later, the crystal was clear again, the carved clouds still. Only she was certain the clouds were not the same as they had been.

"It is," Elayne exclaimed. "It's a *ter'angreal*. And I will bet anything it has something to do with weather. But I'm not quite strong enough to work it by myself."

Gulping a breath, Nynaeve tried to make her heart stop pounding. "Don't do that! Don't you realize you could still yourself, meddling with a *ter'angreal* when you don't know what it does?"

The fool girl had the nerve to give her a surprised stare. "That *is* what we came to look for, Nynaeve. And do you think there is *anyone* who knows more about *ter'angreal* than I do?"

Nynaeve sniffed. Just because the woman was right did not mean she should not have given a little warning. "I'm not saying it isn't wonderful if this can do something about the weather—it is—but I don't see how it can be what we need. This won't shift the Hall one way or the other about Rand."

" 'What you need isn't always what you want,' " Elayne quoted. "Lini used to say that when she wouldn't let me go riding, or climb trees, but maybe it holds here."

Nynaeve sniffed again. Maybe it did, but right now she wanted what she wanted. Was that so much to ask?

The bowl faded out of their hands, and it was Elayne's turn to give a start, muttering about never getting used to that. The chest was closed, too.

"Nynaeve, when I channeled into the bowl, I felt. . . . Nynaeve, it isn't the only *ter'angreal* in this room. I think there are *angreal*, too, maybe even *sa'angreal*."

"Here?" Nynaeve said incredulously, staring around the cluttered little room. But if one, why not two? Or ten, or a hundred? "Light, don't channel again! What if you make one of them do something by accident? You could still—"

"I do know what I am doing, Nynaeve. Really, I do. The next thing *we* have to do is find out exactly where this room is."

That proved to be no easy task. Though the hinges seemed solid masses of rust, the door was no impediment, not in *Tel'aran'rhiod*. The problems began after that. The dim narrow corridor outside had only one small window at its end, and that showed nothing but a peeling white-plastered wall across the street. Climbing down cramped flights of stone-faced stairs did no good. The street outside could have been the first they had seen in this quarter of the city, wherever that was, all the buildings as near alike as made no difference. The tiny shops along the street had no signs, and the only thing marking inns were blue-painted doors. Red seemed to indicate a tavern.

Nynaeve strode off searching for some landmark, something to pin-point their location. Something to say what the city was. Every street she came to seemed like the last, but she quickly found a bridge, plain stone, unlike the others she had seen, and lacking statues. The center of its arch showed her only the canal, meeting others in both directions, more bridges, more buildings with flaking white plaster.

Suddenly she realized she was alone. "Elayne." Silence, except for the echo of her voice. "Elayne? Elayne!"

The golden-haired woman popped around a corner near the foot of the bridge. "There you are," said Elayne. "This place makes a rabbit warren look well planned. I turned my head for an instant, and you were gone. Did you find anything?"

"Nothing." Nynaeve glanced down the canal again before joining Elayne. "Nothing at all useful."

"At least we can be sure where we are. Ebou Dar. It must be." Elayne's

short coat and wide trousers became a green silk gown with spills of lace
dangling over her hands, a high elaborately embroidered collar, and a narrow neckline deep enough to show considerable cleavage. "I can't think of
another city with so many canals except Illian, and this is certainly not
Illian."

"I should hope not," Nynaeve said faintly. It had never even occurred to
her that a blind search might take them into Sammael's lair. Her own dress
had changed, she realized, to a deep blue silk suitable for traveling, complete with a linen dustcloak. She made the cloak vanish, but left the rest.

"You would like Ebou Dar, Nynaeve. Ebou Dari Wise Women know
more about herbs than anybody. They can cure anything. They have to,
because Ebou Dari fight duels over a sneeze, noble or common, men or
women." Elayne giggled. "Thom says there used to be leopards here, but
they left because they found Ebou Dari too touchy to live with."

"That's all very well," Nynaeve told her, "but they can run each other
through as much as they want for all I care. Elayne, we might as well have
put the rings away and just slept. I couldn't walk back to that room from
here if I was to receive the shawl when I got there. If only there was some
way to make a map. . . ." She grimaced. As well ask for wings in the waking world; if they could take a map out of *Tel'aran'rhiod*, they could take
the bowl.

"Then we will just have to come to Ebou Dar and search," Elayne said
firmly. "In the real world. At least we know what *part* of the city to look in."

Nynaeve brightened. Ebou Dar lay only a few hundred miles down the
Eldar from Salidar. "That sounds a very good notion. And it will get us
away before everything falls on our heads."

"Really, Nynaeve. Is that still the most important thing to you?"

"It is one important thing. Can you think of anything else to do here?"
Elayne shook her head. "Then we might as well go back. I'd like a little
real sleep tonight." There was no telling how much time had passed in the
waking world while you were in *Tel'aran'rhiod*; sometimes an hour there
was an hour here, sometimes a day, or more. Luckily, it did not seem to work
the other way, or at least not as much anyway, or you might starve to death
sleeping.

Nynaeve stepped out of the dream . . .

. . . and her eyes popped open, staring into her pillow, which was as
sweat-damp as she. Not a breath of air stirred through the open window.
Silence had fallen over Salidar, the loudest sound the thin cries of night
herons. Sitting up, she untied the cord around her neck and unstrung the

twisted stone ring, pausing for a moment to finger Lan's thick gold ring. Elayne stirred, then sat up yawning and channeled a stub of candle alight.

"Do you think it will do any good?" Nynaeve asked quietly.

"I do not know." Elayne stopped to muffle a yawn behind her hand. How could the woman manage to look pretty yawning, with her hair a mess and a red wrinkle from a pillow marring one cheek? That was a secret Aes Sedai ought to investigate. "What I do know is that bowl may be able to do something about the weather. I know a cache of *ter'angreal* and *angreal* has to be put in the right hands. It's our duty to hand them over to the Hall. To Sheriam, anyway. I know if it doesn't make them support Rand, I'll keep hunting until I find something that does. And I know I want to sleep. Could we talk about this in the morning?" Without waiting for an answer, she doused the candle, curled up again and was breathing the deep, slow breaths of sleep as soon as her head hit the pillow.

Nynaeve stretched out again, staring at the ceiling through the darkness. At least they would be on their way to Ebou Dar soon. Tomorrow, maybe. A day or two, at most, to ready themselves for the journey and stop a passing riverboat. At least. . . .

Suddenly she remembered Theodrin. If it took two days to get ready, Theodrin would want her two sessions, sure as a duck had feathers. And she expected Nynaeve not to sleep tonight. There was no possible way she could know, but. . . .

Sighing heavily, she climbed out of bed. There was not much room to pace, but she used it all, getting angrier by the minute. All she wanted was to get away. She had said she was not very good at surrendering, but maybe she was getting good at running away. It would be so wonderful to channel whenever she wanted. She never even noticed the tears that began leaking down her cheeks.

CHAPTER
14

Dreams and Nightmares

At the sight of Nynaeve and Elayne, Egwene did not step out of the dream; she leaped out. Not back to her sleeping body in Cairhien—the night was too young yet—but to a vast blackness filled with twinkling pinpricks of light, more by far than the number of stars in the clearest sky, each sharp and distinct as far as the eye could see. If she had had eyes here, that was. Formless, she floated in the infinity between *Tel'aran'rhiod* and the waking world, the narrow gap between dream and reality.

Had she possessed a heart here, it would have been pounding like a mad drum. She did not think they had seen her, but what under the Light were they doing *there*, in a part of the Tower that held nothing of interest? On these nightly excursions she carefully avoided the Amyrlin's study, the novices' quarters, even the Accepted's quarters. It always seemed that if Nynaeve or Elayne or both were not in one of those places, someone else was. She could have approached Nynaeve or Elayne, of course—they certainly knew how to keep secrets—but something told her not to; she had dreamed of doing it, and it always seemed a nightmare. Not the sort that woke you in a cold sweat, but the kind that made you twist fretfully. Those other women. Did the Aes Sedai in Salidar know strangers wandered the Tower in the World of Dreams? Strange to her, at least. If they did not, she had no way to warn them. No way she could take. It was all so frustrating!

The great spangled ocean of darkness swirled around her, seeming to move while she stood still. A fish at home in that ocean, she swam confidently, without really needing to think about it any more than the fish did. Those flickering lights were dreams, all the dreams of all the people of the world. Of all worlds, places that were not quite the world she knew, worlds nothing like it at all. Verin Sedai first told her of those, the Wise Ones affirmed it was so, and she herself had glimpsed things, peeking in, that she simply could not credit, not even in a dream. Not nightmares—those always seemed washed in red, or blue, or a murky gray like deep shadows—but filled with impossible things. Better to avoid them; clearly she did not belong in those worlds. Peering into such a dream was like suddenly being surrounded by broken mirrors, everything whirling and no way to tell up from down. It made her want to empty her stomach, and if she did not have one here, she would again on stepping back into her body. Sicking up was no way to wake yourself.

She had learned a few things alone like this, added to what the Wise Ones had taught her, even ventured where they would have barred the way. And yet. . . . She had no doubt she would know more, much more, if she had had a dreamwalker looking over her shoulder. Telling her that this was too dangerous yet and that forbidden altogether, true, yet suggesting what to try as well. Long past the simple things, easily puzzled out—well, not exactly easily; never that—she had reached a point where she could reason the next step on her own, but they were steps the Wise One dreamwalkers had taken long ago. What took her a month to master for herself, they could teach in a night, in an hour. When they decided she was ready. Never until then. It galled so, when all she wanted was to learn. To learn everything. Right now.

Each light looked identical to every other, yet she had learned to recognize a handful. How exactly, she did not know, a thing that irked her no end. Even the Wise Ones did not know that. Still, once she identified which dream belonged to which person, she could find that person's dreams again like an arrow to the target, no matter if they went to the other side of the world. That light was Berelain, the First of Mayene, the woman Rand had put in charge in Cairhien. Looking into Berelain's dreams made Egwene uncomfortable. Usually they were no different from any other woman's—any woman interested equally in power, politics and the latest fashion in dresses—but sometimes Berelain dreamed of men, even men Egwene knew, in a way that made Egwene blush to remember.

And that slightly muted glow over there was Rand, his dreams guarded behind a ward woven of *saidin*. She almost stopped—it piqued her that something she could not see or feel could shut her out like a stone wall—but instead let it pass. Another night of futility held no attraction.

This place skewed distance the way *Tel'aran'rhiod* did time. Rand was sleeping in Caemlyn, unless he had jaunted to Tear, a thing she very much wanted to know how he did, but only a little way from his dream, Egwene picked out another light she recognized. Bair, in Cairhien, hundreds of leagues from Rand; wherever Rand was, she knew for a fact it was not Cairhien this night. *How* did he do it?

The field of lights streaked by as Egwene darted away from the Wise One's dream. Had she seen Amys and Melaine as well, she might not have fled, but if the other two dreamwalkers were not asleep and dreaming, they could be dreamwalking. One of them might be where she was, even ready to swoop down and haul her out of the dream, or into the dreamwalker's own dream. She doubted she could stop them, not yet. She would be at the other's mercy, just a part of *her* dream. Holding on to yourself inside someone else's dream was hard enough when the dreamer was an ordinary person with no idea what was going on, although no harder than getting out before they stopped dreaming of you, which they were unlikely to do before waking with you actually there in the dream. With a dreamwalker, as aware of her dreams as of the walking world, it was impossible. And that would be the *best* part of it.

It dawned on her that she was being foolish. Running was useless. If Amys or Melaine had found her, she would be somewhere else already. For that matter, she could be racing right toward them. The rush of lights by her did not slow, it simply stopped dead. That was the way here.

Vexed, she considered what to do next. Aside from teaching herself what she could of *Tel'aran'rhiod*, her main purpose here was to glean a few scraps of events in the world. At times it seemed the Wise Ones would not tell her whether the sun was up if she could not see for herself. They said she must not become agitated. How could she avoid it, fretting over what she did not know? That was what she had been doing in the White Tower; trying to pick up some hint of Elaida's intentions. And Alviarin's. Hints were the best she had been able to find, and few of those. She hated not knowing; ignorance was like suddenly going blind and deaf.

Well, the whole Tower was off her list now; it had to be when she could no longer be certain which parts were safe. The rest of Tar Valon had been struck off already, after the fourth time she nearly walked into a copper-skinned woman, this time nodding in satisfaction as, of all things, she studied a stable that seemed freshly painted blue. Whoever she was, she had not dreamed herself into *Tel'aran'rhiod* for a moment by accident; she did not vanish, the way a casual dreamer did, and she appeared made of mist. Using a *ter'angreal*, obviously, which meant she was almost certainly Aes Sedai. Egwene knew of only one *ter'angreal* that allowed access to the World of Dreams without channeling, and Nynaeve and Elayne had that. The willowy woman had not been Aes Sedai long, though. Quite beautiful—and wearing a scandalously thin dress—she appeared Nynaeve's age, not ageless.

Egwene might have tried following her—she might be Black Ajah, after all; they had stolen dream *ter'angreal*—but balancing the risk of being found out, even captured, against the fact that she could tell no one anything she learned, not until she could talk to Nynaeve and Elayne again, not unless she discovered something so dire that everything depended on it. . . . After all, the Black Ajah was Aes Sedai business; quite aside from any other reasons for keeping secrets, she could not tell just anyone. It was no choice at all.

Absently, she studied the nearest lights in the blackness. She did not recognize any of them. They held absolutely still around her, shimmering stars frozen in clear black ice.

There were too many strangers in the World of Dreams lately to suit her peace of mind. Two, but that was two too many. The copper-skinned woman and another, a sturdily pretty woman who moved with a purposeful stride, blue-eyed and with a determined face. The determined woman, as Egwene thought of her, must be able to enter *Tel'aran'rhiod* on her own— she seemed solid, not carved from fog—and whoever she was, for whatever reason she was there, she was about the Tower more often than Nynaeve and Elayne and Sheriam and the rest put together. She seemed to appear everywhere. In addition to the Tower, she had nearly surprised Egwene on her last trip to Tear. *Not* on a meeting night, of course; the woman had been stalking about the Heart of the Stone muttering to herself angrily. And she had been in Caemlyn on Egwene's last *two* trips.

The chances the determined woman was Black Ajah were as great as with the other, but then again, either could be from Salidar. Or both, though Egwene had never seen them together, or with anyone from Salidar. For that matter, either could be from the Tower itself. Divisions enough there for one side to be spying on another, and sooner or later the Tower

Aes Sedai would learn of *Tel'aran'rhiod* if they had not already. The two strangers presented nothing but questions without answers. The only thing Egwene could think to do was avoid them.

Of course, she tried to avoid everyone in the World of Dreams of late. She had taken to looking over her shoulder, to thinking somebody was sneaking up behind her, to seeing things. She thought she had caught glimpses of Rand, of Perrin, even Lan, half-seen out of the corner of her eye. Imagination, of course, or maybe the chance touch of their dreams, but on top of everything else, it had her jumpy as a cat in a dogyard.

She frowned—or would have, had she a face. One of those lights looked. . . . Not familiar; she did not know it. But it seemed to . . . attract her. Wherever her gaze shifted, it came back to that same sparkling pinpoint.

Perhaps she could try finding Salidar again. That meant waiting for Nynaeve and Elayne to leave *Tel'aran'rhiod*—she knew their dreams by sight, of course; in her sleep, she thought with a silent giggle—and so far, a dozen attempts to locate Salidar that way had produced as much result as trying to get through the ward around Rand's dreams. Distance and location here really bore no relation to anything in the waking world; Amys said there *was* no distance or location here. On the other hand, it was as good as any—

Startlingly, the pinpoint her gaze kept returning to began to drift toward her, swelling until what had been a distant star quickly became a full white moon. A spark of fear lit inside her. Touching a dream, peeking inside, was easy—a finger to the surface of water, a touch so light that the water rose to the finger but the surface was never broken—yet it was all supposed to be at her volition. A dreamwalker sought the dream; the dream did not seek her. She willed it to go away, willed the starry scape to move. Only that one light moved, expanding to fill her vision with white light.

Frantically she tried to pull away. White light. Nothing but white light, absorbing her. . . .

She blinked, staring in amazement. Around her stretched a forest of great white columns. Most of it seemed fuzzy, indistinct, especially what was far away, but one thing sharp and real was Gawyn, trotting across the white-tiled floor toward her in a plain green coat, anxiety and relief mingled on his face. It was nearly Gawyn's face, anyway. Gawyn might not be as gorgeous as his half-brother Galad, but he was still a handsome man, yet this face seemed . . . ordinary. She tried to move and could not, not to any extent. Her back was to one of the columns, and chains held her wrists above her head.

This must be Gawyn's dream. Out of all of those countless points of light, she had stopped near his. And somehow been drawn in. How was a question for later. Now she wanted to know why he would dream of holding her captive. Firmly she fixed the truth in her mind. This was a dream, someone else's dream. She was herself, not whatever it was he wanted her to be. She did not accept the reality of anything here. Nothing here touched the true her. Those truths repeated like a chant in her head. It made thinking of anything else difficult, but so long as she held them hard she could risk staying. At least, long enough to find out what peculiar oddities the man had rolling around in his head. Holding her captive!

Abruptly a huge gout of flame bloomed on the floor tiles, and acrid yellow smoke billowed. Rand stepped out of that inferno garbed in gold-embroidered red like a king, facing Gawyn, and the fire and smoke vanished. Only it hardly seemed Rand at all. The real Rand was of a height and size with Gawyn, but this image overtopped Gawyn by a head. The face was just vaguely Rand's, coarser and harder than it should be, the cold face of a murderer. This man wore a sneer. "You will not have her," he snarled.

"You will not keep her," Gawyn replied calmly, and suddenly both men held swords.

Egwene gaped. Not Gawyn holding her prisoner. He dreamed of rescuing her! From Rand! Time to leave this madness. She concentrated on being *outside*, back in the darkness, looking at this from the *outside*. Nothing happened.

Swords met with a clash, and the two men danced a deadly dance. Deadly if it had not been a dream, anyway. It was all nonsense. Dreaming a swordfight, of all things. And it was not a nightmare; everything looked normal, if fuzzy, not washed in color. "A man's dreams are a maze even he cannot know," Bair had told her once.

Egwene closed her eyes, focused her entire mind. Outside. She was outside, looking in. No room for anything else in her head. Outside, looking in. Outside, looking in. Outside!

She opened her eyes once more. The fight was reaching its climax. Gawyn's blade drove into Rand's chest, and as Rand sagged, the steel pulled free, swept in a shining arc. Rand's head spun across the floor almost to her feet; it came to rest staring up at her. A scream bubbled in her throat before she could quell it. A dream. Just a dream. But those dead staring eyes seemed very real.

Then Gawyn was in front of her, sword back in its scabbard. Rand's head and body were gone. Gawyn reached for the manacles holding her, and they were gone, too.

"I knew you would come," she breathed, and gave a start. She was herself! She could not give in to this, not for a moment, or she would be well and truly trapped.

Smiling, Gawyn scooped her up into his arms. "I am glad you knew it," he said. "I would have come sooner if I could. I should never have left you in danger so long. Can you forgive me?"

"I can forgive you anything." There were two Egwenes now, one snuggling contentedly in Gawyn's arms as he carried her down a palace corridor lined with colorful tapestries and great mirrors in ornately gilded frames, the other riding in the back of the first's head.

This was becoming serious. Concentrate as hard as she would on being outside, she stayed there, watching through the eyes of a second her. Hurriedly she stifled curiosity as to what Gawyn dreamed about her. That sort of interest was dangerous. She accepted none of this! But none of it changed.

The corridor appeared quite real where she looked, though what was seen from the corner of her eye seemed hazy. Her own image glimpsed in a mirror caught her attention; she would have twisted to stare at it as they passed, but she was only a passenger in the head of the woman of Gawyn's dreams. The woman reflected for that instant had been her—there was no feature she could have pointed to and said it differed in the slightest from her real face—but somehow the whole was. . . . Beautiful was the only word. Stunningly so. Was that how Gawyn saw her?

No! No curiosity! Outside!

Between one stride and the next the corridor became a hillside carpeted in wildflowers, their scent rich on a soft breeze. The real Egwene gave a mental start. Had she done that? The barrier between her and the other thinned. She focused furiously. It was not real; she refused to accept it; she was herself. Outside. She wanted to be outside, looking in.

Gently Gawyn laid her down on a cloak already spread there on the hillside, in the manner of things in dreams. Kneeling beside her, he brushed a strand of hair from her cheek, let his fingers trail back to the corner of her mouth. Focusing on anything was very hard. She might have no control over the body she rode in, but she felt what it did, and his fingers seemed to make sparks jump.

"My heart is yours," he intoned softly, "my soul, my everything." His coat was scarlet now, elaborately worked in gold leaves and silver lions. He made grand gestures, touching head or heart. "When I think of you, there is no room for any other thought. Your perfume fills my brain and sets my blood afire. My heart pounds till I could not hear the world crack apart. You are my sun and my moon and my stars, my heaven and earth, more precious to me than life or breath or—" Abruptly he stopped, grimacing. "You sound a fool," he muttered to himself.

Egwene would have disagreed had she had any control over her vocal cords. It was very nice hearing those things, even if they were a bit over the top. Just a bit.

When he grimaced, she felt a loosening, but

Flick.

Gently Gawyn laid her down on a cloak already spread there on the hillside, in the manner of things in dreams. Kneeling beside her, he brushed a strand of hair from her cheek, let his fingers trail back to the corner of her mouth. She might have no control over the body she rode in, but she could feel what it felt, and his fingers seemed to make sparks jump.

No! She could not let herself accept any part of his dream!

His face was a map of pain, his coat stark gray. His hands rested on his knees in fists. "I have no right to speak to you as I might wish," he said stiffly. "My brother loves you. I know Galad is in agony with fear for you. He is a Whitecloak at least half because he thinks the Aes Sedai have misused you. I know he—" Gawyn's eyes squeezed shut. "Oh, Light, help me!" he moaned.

Flick.

Gently Gawyn laid her down on a cloak already spread there on the hillside, in the manner of things in dreams. Kneeling beside her, he brushed a strand of hair from her cheek, let his fingers trail back to the corner of her mouth.

No! She was losing the little control she had! She had to get out! *What are you afraid of?* She was not sure whether that was her thought or the other Egwene's. The barrier between them was gauze now. *This is Gawyn. Gawyn.*

"I love you," he said hesitantly. In the green coat again, still less handsome than he really was, he plucked at one of his buttons before letting his hand drop. He looked at her as though afraid of what he might see on her face, hiding it, but not well. "I have never said that to another woman, never wanted to say it. You have no idea how hard it is to say to you. Not that I don't want to," he added hastily, flinging a hand toward her, "but to say it, with no encouragement, is like tossing aside my sword and baring my chest for a blade. Not that I think you would—Light! I can't say this properly. Is there any chance that you . . . might come . . . in time . . . to feel some . . . regard . . . for me? Something . . . more than friendship?"

"You sweet idiot," she laughed softly. "I love you." *I love you*, echoed in the part of her that was really her. She felt the barrier vanishing, had a moment to realize she did not care, and then there was only one Egwene again, an Egwene who happily twined her arms around Gawyn's neck.

Sitting on the stool in the dim moonlight, Nynaeve stuffed a yawn back into her mouth with her knuckles and blinked eyes that felt full of sand. This was going to work; oh, yes, it was. She would fall asleep saying hello to Theodrin, if not before! Her chin sank, and she jerked herself to her feet. The stool had begun feeling like stone—her bottom had gone numb—but that discomfort was apparently not enough anymore. Perhaps a walk outside. Arms outstretched, she felt her way to the door.

Abruptly a distant scream shattered the night, and as it did, the stool struck her hard in the back, knocking her against the rough door with a startled scream of her own. Stunned, she stared at the stool, lying on its side on the floor now, one leg shoved awry.

"What is it?" Elayne cried, coming bolt upright in her bed.

More screams and shouts sounded through Salidar, some from inside their own house, and a vague rumble and clatter that seemed to come from everywhere. Nynaeve's empty bed rattled, then slid a foot across the floor. Elayne's heaved, nearly tossing her out.

"A bubble of evil." Nynaeve was startled at how cool she sounded. There was no point leaping about and flapping her arms, but inside she was doing just that. "We have to wake anybody who's still asleep." She did not know how anyone could sleep through this racket, but those who did could die before they knew it.

Not waiting for a reply, she hurried out and pushed open the next door down the hall—and ducked as a white washbasin hurtled through the space where her head had been to smash against the wall behind her. Four women shared this room, in two beds a little larger than her own. Now one bed lay with its legs in the air, two women trying to crawl from beneath it. On the other, Emara and Ronelle, another Accepted, thrashed and made choking sounds, wrapped tight in their own bedsheet.

Nynaeve grabbed the first woman out from under the overturned bed, a gaping skinny serving woman named Mulinda, and shoved her toward the door. "Go! Wake anybody in the house still sleeping, and help anybody you can! Go!" Mulinda went, stumbling, and Nynaeve hauled her trembling sleeping companion to her feet. "Help me, Satina. Help me with Emara and Ronelle."

Trembling she might have been, but the plump woman nodded and set to with a will. It was not just a matter of unwinding the sheet, of course. The thing seemed alive, like a vine that would tighten until it crushed what it held. Nynaeve and Satina together barely peeled it away from the two women's throats; then the pitcher leaped from the washstand to crash against the ceiling, Satina jumped and lost her hold, and the sheet snapped out of Nynaeve's hands, right back where it had been. The two women's struggles were weakening; one made a rattling noise in her throat, the other no sound at all. Even by the little moonlight that came through the window their faces seemed swollen and dark.

Seizing the sheet again with both hands, Nynaeve opened herself to *saidar*, and found nothing. *I'm surrendering, burn you! I am surrendering! I need the Power!* Nothing. The bed shimmied against her knees, and Satina squeaked. "Don't just stand there!" Nynaeve snapped. "Help me!"

Abruptly the sheet jerked out of her grip once more, but instead of winding around Emara and Ronelle again, it pulled the other way so hard they tumbled over one another, nearly blurring as it unwound. Noticing Elayne in the doorway, Nynaeve closed her mouth with a click of teeth. The sheet hung from the ceiling. The Power. Of course.

"Everybody's awake," Elayne said, handing her a robe. She already had one over her own shift. "A few bruises and scrapes, one or two nasty cuts to be seen to when there's time, and I think *everybody* is going to have bad dreams for a few days, but that's the extent of it. Here." Screams and shouts still rang through the night. Satina jumped again as Elayne let the sheet fall, but it just lay there on the floor. The overturned bed shifted, though, creaking. Elayne bent over the groaning women on the bed. "I think they're dizzy, mainly. Satina, help me get them on their feet."

Nynaeve glowered at the robe in her hands. Well they might be dizzy, spun about like tops. Light, but she was useless. Rushing in like a fool to take charge. Without the Power, she was just useless.

"Nynaeve, could you give me a hand?" Elayne held a swaying Emara upright, while Satina was more than half-carrying Ronelle to the door. "I think Emara's going to sick up, and it better be outside. I think the chamber pots are broken." The smell said she was right. Pottery grated against the floor, trying to slither out from under the overturned bed.

Nynaeve thrust her arms angrily into her robe. She could sense the Source now, a warm glow just out of sight, but she deliberately ignored it. She had done without the Power for years. She could do without it now. Lifting Emara's free arm over her shoulder, she helped guide the moaning woman toward the street. They almost made it.

When they got outside after wiping Emara's mouth, everyone else was already huddled together in front of the house in robes or whatever they had slept in. The still full moon, hanging in a clear sky, gave a bright light. People were spilling out of the other houses in a bedlam of bellows and shrieks. One board in a fence rattled, then another. A bucket suddenly went bouncing down the street. A cart loaded with firewood abruptly rolled forward, shafts plowing shallow furrows in the hard ground. Smoke began to rise a house down the way, and voices began shouting for water.

The dark shape of someone lying in the street drew Nynaeve. One of the nightwatchmen, by the flickering lantern near his outstretched hand. She could see his staring eyes glittering in the moonlight, the blood covering his face, the dent in the side of his head where something had struck him like an axe. She felt his throat for a pulse anyway. She wanted to howl with fury. People should die after a long life, in their own beds, surrounded by family and friends. Anything else was waste. Pure miserable waste!

"So you've found *saidar* tonight, Nynaeve. Good."

Nynaeve jumped, and stared up at Anaiya. She did hold *saidar*, she realized. And useless even with it. Rising, she wearily dusted her knees and tried not to look at the dead man. If she had been quicker, could it have made a difference?

The glow of the Power surrounded Anaiya, but not only her; the single light enveloped as well two more fully clothed Aes Sedai, an Accepted in a robe, and three novices, two in their shifts. One of those in her shift was Nicola. Nynaeve could see other glowing groups, dozens and dozens of them, moving in the street. Some seemed all Aes Sedai, but most not.

"Open yourself to linking," Anaiya went on. "And you, Elayne, and. . . . What is wrong with Emara and Ronelle?" On learning they were just dizzy, she muttered something under her breath, then told them to find a circle and link with it as soon as their heads were steady. Hurriedly she chose out four more Accepted from the cluster around Elayne. "Sammael—if it is him instead of one of the others—will learn we are far from helpless. Quickly now. Embrace the Source, but hold yourself at the point of embracing. You are open and yielding."

"This isn't one of the Forsaken," Nynaeve began, but the motherly Aes Sedai cut her off firmly.

"Don't argue, child, just open yourself. We have expected an attack, if not exactly like this, and planned for it. Quickly, child. There is no time to squander on idle chatter."

Snapping her mouth shut, Nynaeve tried to put herself on that brink where you embraced *saidar*, on the moment of surrender. It was not easy. Twice she felt the Power flow not just into her, but through her into Anaiya, and twice it snapped back. Anaiya's mouth tightened; she stared at Nynaeve as though thinking she did it on purpose. The third time was like being seized by the scruff of the neck. *Saidar* swept through Nynaeve to Anaiya, and when she attempted to pull back—it was her, she realized, not the flow itself—her flow was held, melting into a larger.

A sense of awe came over her. She found herself looking at the faces of the others, wondering if they felt the same. She was a part of something more than herself, greater than herself. Not just the One Power. Emotions tumbled in her head, fear and hope and relief—and yes, awe, more than any other—a sense of calm that had to come from the Aes Sedai, and she could not tell which emotions were hers. It should have been chilling, but she felt closer to these women than she could have to any sister, as if they were all one flesh. A lanky Gray named Ashmanaille smiled warmly at her, seemingly recognizing her thoughts.

Nynaeve's breath caught as it occurred to her that she no longer felt angry. Anger had vanished, swallowed in wonder. Yet somehow, now that control had passed to the Blue sister, the flow of *saidar* continued. Her eyes fell on Nicola and found no sisterly smile, only that considering study. Reflexively Nynaeve tried to pull back from the link, and nothing happened. Until Anaiya broke the circle she was part of it, and that was that.

Elayne joined much more easily, first slipping the silver bracelet into her robe's pocket. Cold sweat broke out on Nynaeve's face. What might have happened had Elayne entered the link already linked to Moghedien by the *a'dam*? She had no notion, which only made the question worse. Nicola frowned from Nynaeve to Elayne. Surely she could not separate out which emotions were which, not when Nynaeve could not tell her own. The final two were brought into the circle just as easily, Shimoku, a pretty dark-eyed Kandori who had become Accepted just before the Tower divided, and Calindin, a Taraboner with her black hair in a multitude of thin braids who had been Accepted for a good ten years. A woman little more than a novice and another who struggled for every scrap she learned, but they had no trouble linking.

Suddenly Nicola spoke, sounding half-asleep. "The lion sword, the dedicated spear, she who sees beyond. Three on the boat, and he who is dead yet lives. The great battle done, but the world not done with battle. The land divided by the return, and the guardians balance the servants. The future teeters on the edge of a blade."

Anaiya stared at her. "What was that, child?"

Nicola blinked. "Did I say something, Aes Sedai?" she asked weakly. "I feel . . . peculiar."

"Well, if you're going to be sick," Anaiya said briskly, "get it over with. Linking takes some women funny the first time. We have no time to coddle your stomach." As if to prove it, she gathered her skirts and started down the street. "Stay close, now, all of you. And sing out if you see something that needs dealing with."

That was hardly a problem. People milled about in the streets, crying out to know what was happening or just crying out, and things moved. Doors slammed and windows banged open with no one touching them. Crashes and splinterings came from inside the houses. Pots, tools, stones, anything loose, might leap or dart at any moment. A stout cook in her shift snagged a hurtling bucket out of the air with a nearly hysterical laugh, but when a pale lean fellow in his smallclothes tried to knock away a stick of firewood, the result was the crack of his arm breaking. Ropes writhed their way about legs and arms, and even people's clothes began to crawl. They found a hairy man with his shirt wrapped around his head, flailing about so hard he kept at bay those who were trying to peel it away before it smothered him. A woman who had managed to pull on a dress if not fasten it up clung to the thatch on the edge of a roof, shrieking at the top of her lungs as the dress tried to haul her across the house, or maybe into the sky.

Dealing with these things proved no more problem than finding them. The flows of Power Anaiya wielded through the link—and those from other circles—would have had no trouble stopping a herd of charging bulls, much less a kettle that took it in mind to fly. And once a thing was stopped, whether by the Power or by hand, it seldom stirred again. There were just so many of them. There was not even time to stop for Healing unless a life was in danger; bruises, bleeding and broken bones had to wait while another fenceboard was slapped to the ground, hopefully before it split a head; another barrel halted in its wild rolling, before it broke a leg.

A sense of frustration grew in Nynaeve. So many things to quell; all

small, but a man with his skull cracked by a frying pan or a woman strangled by her own shift was as dead as someone struck down by the Power. It
was not just her frustration; she thought it came from every woman in the
circle, even the Aes Sedai. But all she could do was march along with the
others, watch Anaiya weave the combination of their flows to battle a thousand small dangers. Nynaeve lost herself in being a conduit, in being one
with a dozen other women.

Finally Anaiya halted, frowning. The link dissolving caught Nynaeve
by surprise. For a moment she sagged where she stood, staring uncompre-
hendingly. Moans and weeping had replaced screams and shouts; the palely
lit street was still except for people trying to help the injured. By the
moon, less than an hour had passed, but it seemed to Nynaeve like ten.
Her back ached where the stool had hit her, her knees wobbled, her eyes
felt scrubbed. She yawned so hard she thought her ears would pop.

"Not at all what I expected from one of the Forsaken," Anaiya muttered only half under her breath. She sounded tired too, but she launched
right into the next thing to be done, catching Nicola by the shoulder. "You
can hardly stand. Bed for you. Off you go, child. I want to speak to you
first thing in the morning, before breakfast, Angla, you stay; you can link
again and lend a little strength for the Healing. Lanita, bed."

"It wasn't the Forsaken," Nynaeve said. Mumbled, really. Light, she
was tired. "It was a bubble of evil." The three Aes Sedai stared at her. For
that matter, so did the rest of the Accepted, except for Elayne, and the novices too. Even Nicola, who had not yet gone. For once, Nynaeve did not
care how much the woman weighed her with her eyes; she was too sleepy to
care.

"We saw one in Tear," Elayne said, "in the Stone." Only the aftermath,
really, but that was closer than either of them had ever hoped to be again.
"If Sammael attacked us, he wouldn't toss sticks about." Ashmanaille exchanged unreadable glances with Bharatine, a Green who managed to
make rail-thin look gracefully slender and a long nose look elegant.

Anaiya never flickered an eyelid. "You seem to have plenty of energy
left, Elayne. You can help with the Healing, too. And you, Nynaeve. . . .
You've lost it again, haven't you? Well, you look as if you ought to be carried to bed, but you will have to find your own way. Shimoku, stand up
and go to bed, child. Calindin, you come with me."

"Anaiya Sedai," Nynaeve said carefully, "Elayne and I found something
tonight. If we could speak to you alo—"

"Tomorrow, child. To bed with you. Now, before you fall down."

Anaiya did not even wait to see whether she was obeyed. Drawing Calindin after her, she strode to a groaning man lying with his head in a woman's lap and bent over him. Ashmanaille pulled Elayne another way, and Bharatine took Angla a third. Before she vanished into the crowd, Elayne looked over her shoulder at Nynaeve and shook her head slightly.

Well, perhaps this was not the best time or place to bring up the bowl and Ebou Dar. There had been something odd in Anaiya's reaction, as though she would be disappointed to learn this truly had not been an attack by the Forsaken. Why? She was too tired to think straight. Anaiya might have controlled the flows, but *saidar* had passed through Nynaeve for a good hour, enough to weary someone who had had a good night's sleep.

Swaying, Nynaeve caught sight of Theodrin. The Domani woman limped along with a pair of white-clad novices at her side, pausing where someone seemed to have an injury her skill at Healing could handle. She did not see Nynaeve.

I will go to bed, Nynaeve thought sullenly. *Anaiya Sedai told me to.* Why had Anaiya seemed disappointed? Some thought nuzzled at the corner of her mind, but she was too sleepy to catch it. Her steps dragged, nearly stumbling on level ground. She *would* go to sleep, and Theodrin could make of it what she wanted.

CHAPTER
15

A Pile of Sand

Egwene's eyes opened, stared at nothing. For a moment she lay on her bedding, idly fingering the Great Serpent ring on its thong around her neck. Wearing it on her hand caused too many odd looks. Easier to fit in as a student of the Wise Ones if no one thought of her as Aes Sedai. Which she was not, of course. She was Accepted, yet had pretended to be Aes Sedai so long, she sometimes almost forgot that she was not.

A bit of early sunlight crept in at the door flap, barely lighting the tent's interior. She might as well not have slept at all, and her temples were throbbing. Since the day Lanfear had nearly killed her and Aviendha, the day the Forsaken and Moiraine had killed each other, her head always hurt after a visit to *Tel'aran'rhiod*, though never enough to be a real bother. Anyway, back home Nynaeve had taught her something of herbs, and she had managed to find a few of the right sort here in Cairhien. Sleepwell root would make her drowsy—or maybe, as weary she was, it might put her under for hours—but it would clear any vestige of a headache.

Climbing to her feet, she straightened her twisted sweat-soaked shift and padded across the layered carpets to the washbasin, a carved crystal bowl that had probably once held wine punch for some nobleman. In any case, it held plain water as well as the blue-glazed pitcher did, water that hardly felt cool at all when she splashed it on her face. Her gaze met her own eyes in the small gilt-framed mirror propped against the dark tent wall, and her cheeks crimsoned.

"Well, what did you think would happen?" she whispered. She would not have thought it possible, but her reflection's face grew redder.

It had only been a dream, not like *Tel'aran'rhiod*, where what happened to you was real when you woke. But she remembered everything, just as if it had been real. She thought her cheeks might burn right off. Just a dream, and Gawyn's dream at that. He had no right to dream about her like that.

"It was all his doing," she told her reflection angrily, "not mine! I had no choice in it!" Her mouth snapped shut ruefully. Trying to hold a man at fault for his dreams. And talking to a mirror like a goosehead.

Pausing at the door flap, she stooped to peer out. Her low tent stood on the edge of the Aiel encampment. The gray walls of Cairhien rose some two miles to the west across the bare hills, with nothing between except the charred ground where Foregate had once encircled the city. By the sharp cast to the light, the sun was just peeking over the horizon, yet Aiel already bustled among the tents.

No early rising for her this morning. After a whole night out of her body—her cheeks heated again; Light, was she going to go the rest of her life blushing over a *dream*? She was very much afraid she might—after that she could sleep until afternoon. The smell of cooking porridge was no competition for heavy eyelids.

Wearily she went back to her blankets and collapsed, rubbing her temples. She was too tired to prepare the sleepwell root, but then, she thought she was too tired for it to matter. The dull pain always faded in an hour or so; it would be gone when she woke.

Given everything, it was no surprise that Gawyn filled her dreams. Sometimes she repeated one of his, though not exactly, of course; in her versions, certain embarrassing events just did not occur, or at least were glossed over. Gawyn spent a good deal more time reciting poetry, and holding her while they watched sunrises and sunsets. He did not stumble over saying he loved her, either. And he looked as handsome as he really was. Others were all her own. Tender kisses that lasted forever. Him kneeling while she cupped his head in her hands. Some made no sense. Twice, right atop one another, she dreamed of taking him by the shoulders and trying to turn him to face the other way against his will. Once he brushed her hands away roughly; the other time, she was somehow stronger than he. The two blended together hazily. In another he began swinging a door closed on her, and she knew if that narrowing gap of light vanished, she was dead.

Dreams tumbled through her head, not all of him, and usually nightmarish.

Perrin came and stood before her, a wolf lying at his feet, a hawk and a falcon perched on his shoulders glaring at each other over his head. Seemingly unaware of them, he kept trying to throw away that axe of his, until finally he ran, the axe floating through the air, chasing him. Again Perrin; he turned away from a Tinker and ran, faster and faster though she called for him to come back. Mat spoke strange words she almost understood—the Old Tongue, she thought—and two ravens alighted on his shoulders, claws sinking through his coat into the flesh beneath. He seemed no more aware of them than Perrin had been of the hawk and falcon, yet defiance passed across his face, and then grim acceptance. In another a woman, face shrouded in shadow, beckoned him toward great danger; Egwene did not know what, only that it was monstrous. Several concerned Rand, not all bad, but all odd. Elayne, forcing him to his knees with one hand. Elayne and Min and Aviendha, sitting in a silent circle around him, each in turn reaching out to lay a hand on him. Him walking toward a burning mountain, something crunching beneath his boots. She stirred and whimpered; the crunching things were the seals on the Dark One's prison, shattering with his every step. She knew it. She did not need to see them to know.

Feeding on fear, her dreams became worse. The two strange women she had been seeing in *Tel'aran'rhiod* caught her and dragged her before a table full of hooded women, and when they took off their hoods, every one was Liandrin, the Black sister who had captured her in Tear. A hard-faced Seanchan woman handed her a silvery bracelet and necklace connected by a silvery leash, an *a'dam*. That made her cry out; Seanchan had put an *a'dam* on her once. She would die before letting it happen again. Rand capered through the streets of Cairhien, laughing as he blasted buildings and people with lightning and fire, and other men ran with him, hurling the Power; that awful amnesty of his had been announced in Cairhien, but surely no man would *choose* to channel. The Wise Ones caught her in *Tel'aran'rhiod* and sold her like an animal in the lands beyond the Aiel Waste; that was what they did to Cairhienin they found in the Waste. She stood outside herself, watching her face melt, her skull crack open, and dimly seen shapes poke at her with hard sticks. Poke at her. Poke. . . .

She bolted up, gasping, and Cowinde sat back on her heels beside the bed, head bowed in the cowl of her white woolen robe.

"Forgive me, Aes Sedai. I only meant to wake you to break the night's fast."

"You didn't have to jab a hole in my ribs," Egwene muttered, and was instantly sorry.

Irritation flared in Cowinde's deep blue eyes, and was snuffed out, hidden behind the *gai'shain* mask of compliant acceptance. Sworn to obey meekly and touch no weapon for a year and a day, *gai'shain* accepted whatever happened, whether a rude word, a blow, even a knife in the heart very likely. Though to an Aiel, killing a *gai'shain* was the same as killing a child. There was no excuse; the perpetrator would be struck down by his own brother or sister. Yet, it was a mask, Egwene was certain. *Gai'shain* worked at it doggedly, but they were still Aiel, and a people less meek Egwene could not imagine. Even one like Cowinde, who refused to put off the white when her year and a day was done. Her refusal was an act of stubborn pride and defiance, as much as any man refusing to retreat from ten enemies. Such tangles the Aiel's *ji'e'toh* got them into.

That was one reason Egwene tried to watch how she spoke to *gai'shain*, especially those like Cowinde. They had no way to fight back without violating everything they believed in. On the other hand, Cowinde had been a Maiden of the Spear, and would be again if she could ever be convinced to put off that robe. Forgetting the Power, she could probably tie Egwene into a knot while honing a spear at the same time.

"I do not want any breakfast," Egwene told her. "Just go away and let me sleep."

"No breakfast?" Amys said, necklaces and bracelets of ivory and silver and gold clicking as she ducked into the tent. She wore no rings—Aiel did not—but for the rest she had on enough to do three women with some to spare. "I thought your appetite at least had recovered fully."

Bair and Melaine followed her in, each as bedecked with jewelry. The three were from different clans, but where most other Wise Ones who had crossed the Dragonwall stayed close to their septs, their tents were together nearby. They took places on bright, tasseled cushions at the foot of her bedding, adjusting the dark shawls Aielwomen never seemed to be without. Those not *Far Dareis Mai*, anyway. Amys was as white-haired as Bair, but where Bair's grandmotherly face bore deep creases, Amys looked oddly young, perhaps because of the contrast between hair and face. She said it had been nearly as pale when she was a child.

Usually Bair or Amys took the lead, but today Melaine, sun-haired and green-eyed, spoke first. "If you stop eating, you cannot get well. We had considered letting you come to the next meeting with the other Aes Sedai—they ask every time when you will come—"

"And make wetlander fools of themselves every time," Amys put in acidly. She was not a sour woman, but the Aes Sedai in Salidar seemed to make her so. Maybe it was just meeting Aes Sedai. By custom, Wise Ones avoided them, especially Wise Ones who could channel, like Amys and Melaine. Besides, they were not pleased that the Aes Sedai had replaced Nynaeve and Elayne at the meetings. Neither was Egwene. She suspected the Wise Ones felt they had impressed those two with the seriousness of *Tel'aran'rhiod*. By the fragments she heard of the meetings now, the Aes Sedai were not impressed at all. Very little impressed Aes Sedai.

"But we may have to think again," Melaine went on calmly. She had been prickly as a thornbush before her recent marriage, but little seemed to crack her composure now. "You must not return to the dream until your body has its full strength back."

"Your eyes are pinched," Bair said in a concerned, reedy voice that matched her face. In many ways she was the hardest of the three, though. "Did you sleep poorly?"

"How could she otherwise?" Amys asked grumpily. "I tried to look in on her dreams three times last night, and found nothing. No one can sleep well if they do not dream."

Egwene's mouth went dry in a heartbeat; her tongue clove to the roof of her mouth. They would have to check on the one night she was not back in her body in just a few hours.

Melaine frowned. Not at Egwene; at Cowinde, still kneeling with her head down. "There is a pile of sand near my tent," she said with something near her old sharpness. "You will search it grain by grain until you find one red grain. If it is not the one I seek, you will have to begin again. Go now." Cowinde merely bowed until her face touched the colorful carpets, then scampered out. Looking at Egwene, Melaine smiled pleasantly. "You seem surprised. If she will not do what is proper on her own, I will make her decide to do it. Since she claims to serve me yet, she is still my responsibility."

Bair's long hair swung as she shook her head. "It will not work." She adjusted her shawl on angular shoulders. Egwene sweated in just her shift, with the sun not really up yet, but the Aiel were used to far hotter. "I have beaten Juric and Beira until my arm wearied, but however many times I tell them to take off the white, they are back in the robes before sunset."

"It is an abomination," Amys muttered. "Since we crossed into the wetlands, a full quarter of those whose time is done have refused to return to their septs. They twist *ji'e'toh* beyond its meaning."

That was Rand's doing. He had revealed to all what only clan chiefs and Wise Ones had known before, that once all Aiel had refused to touch weapons or do violence. Now some believed they all properly should be *gai'shain*. Others refused to accept Rand as the *Car'a'carn* because of it, and still a few each day went to join the Shaido in the mountains to the north. Some simply threw down their weapons and vanished; no one knew what came of them. Taken by the bleakness, the Aiel called it. The strangest part of it to Egwene was that none of the Aiel blamed Rand, except the Shaido anyway. The Prophecy of Rhuidean said that the *Car'a'carn* would take them back and destroy them. Back to what, none seemed certain, but that he would destroy them, somehow, they accepted as calmly as Cowinde had begun a task she knew was hopeless.

Right that moment Egwene would not have cared if every Aiel in Cairhien donned a white robe. Let these Wise Ones even suspect what she had been up to. . . . She would have dug through a *hundred* piles of sand, willingly, but she did not think she would be so lucky. Her punishment would be much worse. Once Amys had said if she failed to do exactly as she was told—the World of Dreams being too dangerous, without that promise—Amys would no longer teach her. No doubt the others would agree; that was the punishment she feared. Better a *thousand* piles of sand under a broiling sun.

"Do not look so shaken," Bair chuckled. "Amys is not angry at all wetlanders, certainly not at you, who have become like a daughter of our tents. It is your sister Aes Sedai. The one called Carlinya suggested we may be holding you against your will."

"Suggested?" Amys' pale eyebrows climbed nearly to her hairline. "The woman said as much!"

"And learned to guard her tongue better." Bair laughed, rocking on her scarlet cushion. "I will wager she did. When we left them, she was still yelping and trying to get those scarlet puffers out of her dress. A scarlet puffer," she confided to Egwene, "looks much like a red adder if your eye is dull like a wetlander's, but it is not poisonous. It does wriggle when confined, though."

Amys sniffed. "They would have been gone if she thought of them gone. The woman learns nothing. The Aes Sedai we served in the Age of Legends could not have been such fools." But she sounded mollified.

Melaine was chortling quite openly, and Egwene found herself giggling too. Some Aiel humor was beyond explaining, but not this. She had only met Carlinya three times, but the image of that stiff, icily supercilious woman dancing about trying to haul snakes out of her dress—it was all she could do to keep from laughing out loud.

"At least your humor is in good fettle," Melaine said. "The head pains have not come back?"

"My head feels fine," Egwene lied, and Bair nodded.

"Good. We were worried when they persisted. So long as you refrain from entering the dream for a while longer, they should stay away. Do not fear you suffer any ill effect from them; the body uses pain to tell us to rest."

That nearly made Egwene laugh again, though not in humor. Aiel ignored gaping wounds and broken bones because they could not be bothered right then. "How much longer do I have to stay out?" she asked. She hated lying to them, but she hated doing nothing even worse. The first ten days after Lanfear hit her with whatever that had been were bad enough; then she could not even think without her head splitting. Once she could, what her mother called "the itchy hands of idleness" had driven her into *Tel'aran'rhiod* behind the Wise Ones' backs. You learned nothing resting. "The next meeting, you said?"

"Perhaps," Melaine replied with a shrug. "We will see. But you must eat. If your desire for food is gone, something is wrong that we do not know."

"Oh, I can eat." The porridge cooking outside did smell good. "I was just being lazy, I suppose." Getting up without wincing was a chore; her head did not like being moved yet. "I thought of some more questions last night."

Melaine rolled her eyes in amusement. "Since, you were hurt you ask five questions for every one you asked before."

Because she was trying to puzzle things out for herself. She could not say that, of course, so she just dug a clean shift from one of the small chests lining the tent wall and exchanged it for her sweaty one.

"Questions are good," Bair said. "Ask."

Egwene chose her words carefully. And went on with her dressing, casually, in the same white *algode* blouse and bulky wool skirt the Wise Ones wore. "Is it possible to be pulled into someone's dream against your will?"

"Of course not," Amys said, "not unless your touch is all thumbs."

But right on top of her, Bair said, "Not unless there is strong emotion involved. If you try to watch the dream of someone who loves or hates you, you can be pulled in. Or if you love or hate them. That last is why we do not dare try to watch Sevanna's dreams, or even to speak with the Shaido Wise

Ones in their dreams." It still surprised Egwene that these women, and the other Wise Ones, all visited and talked with the Shaido Wise Ones. Wise Ones were supposed to be above feuds and battles, but she would have thought opposing the *Car'a'carn*, vowing to kill him, took the Shaido well beyond that. "Leaving the dream of someone who hates you, or loves you," Bair finished, "is like trying to climb from a deep pit with sheer sides."

"There is that." Amys seemed to recover her humor suddenly; she gave Melaine a sidelong glance. "That is why no dreamwalker ever makes the mistake of trying to watch her husband's dreams." Melaine stared straight ahead, face darkening. "She does not make it twice anyway," Amys added.

Bair grinned, deepening the creases of her face, and very pointedly did not look at Melaine. "It can be quite a shock, especially if he is angry with you. If, to choose an example from air, *ji'e'toh* takes him away from you, and you, like some silly child, were foolish enough to tell him he would not go if he loved you."

"This is running far afield from her question," a crimson-faced Melaine said stiffly. Bair cackled loudly.

Egwene stifled curiosity, and amusement. She made her voice ever so offhanded. "What if you don't try to look in?" Melaine gave her a grateful look, and she felt a twinge of guilt. Not enough that she would not ask for the whole story later, though. Anything that made *Melaine* blush so had to be hilarious.

"I heard of such a thing," Bair said, "when I was young and just beginning to learn. Mora, the Wise One of Colrada Hold, trained me, and she said that if the emotion was *very* strong, love or hate so great it left room for nothing else, you could be drawn in merely by letting yourself be aware of the other's dream."

"I have never heard anything like that," Melaine said. Amys merely looked doubtful.

"Nor have I from any save Mora," Bair told them, "but she was a remarkable woman. It was said she was approaching her three hundredth year when she died from a bloodsnake's bite, yet she looked as young as either of you. I was only a girl, but I remember her well. She knew many things, and could channel strongly. Other Wise Ones came from every clan to learn from her. I think love so great, or hate so, is very rare, but she said this happened to her twice, once with the first man she married, and once with a rival for her third husband's interest."

"Three hundred?" Egwene exclaimed, a soft knee-high boot half-laced. Surely even Aes Sedai did not live that long.

"I said that it was said," Bair replied, smiling. "Some women age more slowly than others, like Amys here, and when it is a woman like Mora, tales are born. Someday I will tell you the story of how Mora moved a mountain. Supposedly, at least."

"Another day?" Melaine said a touch too politely. Plainly she still smarted over whatever had happened in Bael's dream, and over the fact the others knew. "I heard every tale of Mora when I was a child; I have them all by heart, I think. If Egwene ever finishes dressing, we must see her fed." A gleam in her green eyes said she meant to watch every bite go down; clearly her suspicions about Egwene's health had not been soothed. "And answer the rest of her questions."

Frantically Egwene fumbled for another. Usually she had a slew of questions, but the events of the night had left her with just that one. If she let it remain at that, they might start wondering whether it had come because she had sneaked off to spy on someone's dream. Another question. Not about her own odd dreams. Some of them probably had meaning, if she could ferret it out. Anaiya claimed Egwene was a Dreamer, able to foretell the course of future events, and these three women thought it might be so, but they said she had to learn it from within. Besides, she was not sure she wanted to discuss her dreams with anyone. These women already knew more than she really liked about what went on inside her head. "Ah . . . what about dreamwalkers who aren't Wise Ones? I mean, do you ever see other women in *Tel'aran'rhiod*?"

"Sometimes," Amys said, "but not often. Without a guide to teach her, a woman may not realize she does more than have vivid dreams."

"And of course," Bair added, "unknowing as she is, the dream may well kill her before she can learn. . . ."

Safely away from the dangerous topic, Egwene relaxed. She had received more answer than she could have hoped for. She already knew she loved Gawyn—*Did you, then?* a voice whispered. *Were you willing to admit it?*—and his dreams certainly indicated he loved her. Though of course, if men could say things waking they did not mean, they very probably could dream them. But to have the Wise Ones confirm it, that he loved her strongly enough to overwhelm anything she. . . .

No. That was to be dealt with later. She did not even have an idea where in the world he was. The important thing now was that she knew the danger. She would be able to recognize Gawyn's dreams the next time, and avoid them. *If you really want to*, that small voice whispered. She hoped the Wise Ones took the color rising in her cheeks for a healthy glow. She wished she knew what her own dreams meant. If they meant anything.

Yawning, Elayne climbed onto a stone stoop so she could see over the heads of the crowd. There were no soldiers in Salidar today, but people packed the street and hung out of windows, waiting in hushed anticipation, all staring at the Little Tower. The shuffling of feet and an occasional cough from the rising dust were the only sounds. Despite the early morning heat, people barely moved beyond stirring a fan or hat to make a little breeze.

Leane stood in the gap between two thatch-roofed houses, on the arm of a tall, hard-faced man Elayne had never seen before. Very much on his arm. No doubt one of Leane's agents. Most Aes Sedai eyes-and-ears were women, but Leane's all seemed to be men. She kept them largely out of sight, but Elayne had noticed her once or twice patting an unfamiliar cheek, smiling up at a pair of strange eyes. She had no idea how Leane did it. Elayne was sure if she tried those Domani tricks, the fellow would think she had promised a good more than she intended, but these men took a pat and a smile from Leane and went trotting away as happy as if handed a chest of gold.

Elsewhere in the crowd, Elayne spotted Birgitte, wisely keeping away from her this morning. For a change that horrid Areina was nowhere to be seen. The night had been well beyond hectic, and Elayne had not gone to bed until the sky was already beginning to lighten toward gray. In truth, she would not have gone at all if Birgitte had not told Ashmanaille she thought Elayne looked unsteady. Not a matter of how she looked at all, of course; the bond with a Warder ran both ways. So what if she had been a little tired? There had been plenty of work to do, and she could still channel more strongly than half the Aes Sedai in Salidar. That bond told her that Birgitte had not slept yet, not her! Elayne sent off to bed like a novice, while Birgitte carried the injured and cleared away wreckage all night!

A glance showed Leane alone now, squeezing into the crowd to find a good place to watch. There was no sign of the tall man.

A yawning, bleary-eyed Nynaeve climbed up beside Elayne, glaring down a leather-vested woodcutter who would have gotten there before her. Muttering to himself, the fellow shoved back into the crowd. Elayne wished Nynaeve would not do that. The yawn, not the glare. Her own jaw cracked in mimicry before she could stop it. There was some excuse for Birgitte— some, maybe; a little—but none for Nynaeve. Theodrin could not possibly expect her to have stayed awake after last night, and Elayne had heard Anaiya tell her to go to bed, yet there she was when Elayne came in, balancing herself on the stool despite its now crooked leg, head nodding every two minutes, muttering about showing Theodrin, showing everyone.

The *a'dam* bracelet conveyed fear to Elayne, of course, but something that might have been amusement as well. Moghedien had spent the night hiding under her bed, untouched and, because she was well hidden, without picking up one single stick of rubbish. She had even gotten a good night's sleep once the first commotion died down. It seemed that old saw about the Dark One's luck held sometimes.

Nynaeve began another yawn, and Elayne jerked her eyes away. Even so, she had to shove her fist against her mouth in a not very successful attempt to avoid imitation. The shuffling feet and coughs took on an impatient sound.

The Sitters were still inside the Little Tower with Tarna, but the Red's roan gelding already stood in the street before the former inn, and a dozen Warders were holding their horses' bridles, their color-shifting cloaks making them uneasy to look at, an escort of honor for the first miles of Tarna's journey back to Tar Valon. The crowd waited for more than the Tower envoy's departure, though most looked as worn out as Elayne felt.

"You'd think she was . . . was. . . ." Nynaeve gaped hard behind her hand.

"Oh, blood and ashes," Elayne muttered, or tried to. Everything after "oh" came out a strangled croak around the fist stuffed in her mouth. Lini said remarks like that were the sign of a slow mind and a dull wit—right before washing your mouth out—but sometimes nothing else could sum up your feelings in as few words. She would have said more, but had no chance.

"Why don't they give her a procession?" Nynaeve growled. "I do not see why they have to give the woman all this to-do." And she yawned again. Again!

"Because she is Aes Sedai, sleepyhead," Siuan said, joining them. "Two sleepyheads," she added with a glance at Elayne. "You'll catch minnows if you keep doing that." Elayne snapped her mouth shut and gave the woman her coldest stare. As usual, it slid off like rain from a glazed roof tile. "Tarna is Aes Sedai, my girls," Siuan went on, peering toward the waiting horses. Or maybe it was the clean cart that had been pulled in front of the stone building that had her eye. "An Aes Sedai is Aes Sedai, and nothing changes that." Nynaeve gave her a look she did not see.

Elayne was glad Nynaeve held her tongue; the obvious reply would have been hurtful. "What was the toll last night?"

Siuan answered without looking away from where Tarna would appear. "Seven dead, here in the village. Nearly a hundred in the soldiers' camps. All those swords and axes and the like lying about, and no one to channel them down. There are sisters out there now, Healing."

"Lord Gareth?" Elayne asked, a touch anxiously. The man might be cold toward her now, but once he had had a warm smile for a child and a pocket that always held hard candies.

Siuan snorted so hard that people turned around to look. "That one," she muttered. "A lionfish would break its teeth on the man."

"You seem in a fine temper this morning," Nynaeve said. "Have you finally learned what the Tower's message is? Gareth Bryne asked you to marry him? Somebody died and left you—?"

Elayne tried not to look at Nynaeve; even the sound of a yawn made her jaws creak.

Siuan gave Nynaeve a level look, but for once Nynaeve met it just as flatly, if a bit watery-eyed.

"If you've learned something," Elayne broke in before they could stare one another senseless, "tell us."

"A woman who claims to be Aes Sedai when she isn't," Siuan murmured as though voicing an idle thought, "is neck-deep in a boiling kettle, true enough, but if she's claimed a particular Ajah, that Ajah has first call on her. Has Myrelle ever told you about the woman she caught claiming to be a Green in Chachin? A former novice who failed her test for Accepted. Ask her, some time when she has an hour or two. It will take that long to tell. The fool girl probably wished she had been stilled before Myrelle was done, stilled and her head cut off as well."

For some reason the threat had no more effect than the glare had on Nynaeve, not even a quiver. Perhaps they were both just too tired. "You tell me what you know," Elayne said in a low voice, "or the next time we're alone, I will teach you to sit up straight, and you can run whining to Sheriam if you want." Siuan's eyes narrowed, and suddenly Elayne yelped, clapping a hand to her hip.

Siuan drew back the hand that had delivered the pinch without any try at stealth. "I don't take well to threats, girl. You know as well as I do what Elaida said; you saw it before anyone here."

"Come back; all is forgiven?" Nynaeve said incredulously.

"More or less. With a load of fish guts about the Tower needing to be

whole more now than ever, and a bit of slippery eeling about no one needing to fear except those who 'have placed themselves in true rebellion.' The
Light knows what that means. I don't."

"Why are they keeping it secret?" Elayne demanded. "They can't possibly think anyone will go back to Elaida. All they need do is trot out
Logain." Siuan said nothing, only frowned at the waiting Warders.

"I still don't see why they're asking for more time," Nynaeve muttered.
"They know what they have to do." Siuan kept silent, but Nynaeve's eyebrows rose slowly. "You didn't know their answer."

"I do now," Siuan clipped the words, and said something under her
breath about "weak-kneed fools." Elayne agreed silently.

Suddenly the front door of the onetime inn opened. Half a dozen Sitters
came out in their fringed shawls, one from each Ajah, then Tarna, followed
by the rest. If the waiting folk had expected some sort of ceremony, they
were sorely disappointed. Climbing into her saddle, Tarna ran her eyes
slowly over the Sitters, glanced at the crowd with an unreadable face, then
heeled the gelding to a walk. Her encircling escort of Warders moved with
her. A concerned buzz, like the sound of disturbed bees, rose from the
onlookers as they gave way.

The murmuring lasted until Tarna passed from sight, out of the village, and Romanda climbed up onto the cart, smoothly hitching her
yellow-fringed shawl into place. Dead silence fell. By tradition the eldest
Sitter made pronouncements from the Hall. Romanda did not move like
an old woman, of course, and her face was as ageless as any, yet even streaks
of gray hair marked considerable age on an Aes Sedai, and the bun gathered at the nape of her neck was pale gray without a trace of anything
darker. Elayne wondered how old she was, but asking an Aes Sedai's age
was about the rudest thing possible.

Romanda wove simple flows of Air to make her high soprano voice
carry; it came to Elayne as if she had been face-to-face with the woman.
"Many of you have been worried these last few days, but needlessly. Had
Tarna Sedai not come to us, we would have sent missives to the White
Tower ourselves. After all, we can hardly be said to be hiding here." She
paused as if to give the crowd time to laugh, but they merely stared at her,
and she adjusted her shawl. "Our purpose here has not changed. We seek
truth and justice, to do what is right . . ."

"Right for who?" Nynaeve murmured.

". . . and we shall neither flag nor fail. Go about your tasks as you have,
assured that you remain sheltered beneath our hands, now and after our

assured return to our proper places in the White Tower. The Light shine upon you all. The Light shine upon all of us."

The murmuring rose again, and the crowd began milling slowly, as Romanda climbed down. Siuan's face might have been carved from stone; her lips were pinched bloodless. Elayne wanted to ask questions, but Nynaeve hopped off the stoop and began pushing toward the three-story stone building. Elayne followed quickly. Last night Nynaeve had been ready to toss out what they had learned with never a care; it had to be presented carefully if it was to be any use in swaying the Hall. And it certainly seemed they did need swaying. Romanda's announcement had been a wagonload of nothing. It had certainly upset Siuan.

Wriggling between two hefty fellows who were glaring at Nynaeve's back—*she* had stepped on toes to get by—Elayne glanced over her shoulder and caught Siuan watching her and Nynaeve. For just a moment; as soon as the woman realized she had been seen, she pretended to spot someone in the crowd and jumped down as if going to them. Frowning, Elayne hurried on. Was Siuan upset, or was she not? How much of her irritation and ignorance were really pretense? Nynaeve's notion of running off to Caemlyn—Elayne was not sure she had given it up yet—was worse than silly, but she herself was looking forward to Ebou Dar, to doing something of real use. All these secrets and suspicions were an itch she could not reach. If only Nynaeve did not put her foot in it.

She caught up to Nynaeve just as the other woman caught Sheriam, near the cart Romanda had spoken from. Morvrin was there too, and Carlinya, all three in their shawls. All the Aes Sedai wore shawls this morning. Carlinya's short hair, worked into a cap of dark curls, was the only sign of their near disaster in *Tel'aran'rhiod*.

"We need to speak to you alone," Nynaeve told Sheriam. "In private."

Elayne sighed. Not the best beginning, but not the worst, either.

Sheriam studied the two of them for a moment, then glanced at Morvrin and Carlinya and said, "Very well. Inside."

When they turned, Romanda was between them and the door, a solidly handsome, dark-eyed woman with her yellow-fringed shawl, all flowers and vines except for the Flame of Tar Valon, high between her shoulders. Ignoring Nynaeve, she smiled warmly at Elayne, one of those smiles Elayne had come to expect, and dread, from Aes Sedai. For Sheriam and Carlinya and Morvrin, though, her face was very different. She stared at them, expressionless, head erect, until they dipped slight curtsies and murmured, "By your leave, Sitter." Only then did she move aside, and even then she sniffed loudly.

The common run of folk never noticed, of course, but Elayne had caught snippets among the Aes Sedai about Sheriam and her little council. Some thought they only saw to the day-to-day running of Salidar, freeing the Hall for more important matters. Some knew they had influence with the Hall, but how much varied according to who spoke. Romanda was one who believed they had entirely too much; worse, they had two Blues and no Yellow in their number. Elayne felt her eyes as she followed the others through the doorway.

Sheriam led them to one of the private chambers just off the former common room, with beetle-chewed paneling and a paper-strewn table against one wall. Her eyebrows lifted when Nynaeve asked them to ward against eavesdropping, but she wove the ward around the inside of the room without comment. Remembering Nynaeve's excursion, Elayne checked to be sure both windows were tightly shut.

"I expect no less than news Rand al'Thor is on his way here," Morvrin said dryly. A quick glance passed between the other two Aes Sedai. Elayne stifled indignation; they really did think she and Nynaeve were holding back secrets about Rand. Them and their secrets!

"Not that," Nynaeve said, "but something as important, in a different way." And out tumbled the story of their trip to Ebou Dar and finding the bowl *ter'angreal.* Not in proper order, and not mentioning the Tower, but all the essential points were there.

"Are you certain this bowl is a *ter'angreal?*" Sheriam asked when Nynaeve ran down. "It can affect the weather?"

"Yes, Aes Sedai," Elayne answered simply. Simple was best, to begin. Morvrin grunted; the woman doubted everything.

Sheriam nodded, shifting her shawl. "Then you have done well. We will send a letter to Merilille." Merilille Ceandevin was the Gray sister sent to convince the queen in Ebou Dar to support Salidar. "We will need all the details from you."

"She'll never find it," Nynaeve burst out before Elayne could open her mouth. "Elayne and I can." Aes Sedai eyes chilled.

"It probably would be impossible for her," Elayne put in hastily. "We *saw* where the bowl is, and it will be difficult for *us.* But at least we *know* what we saw. Describing it in a letter just won't be the same."

"Ebou Dar is no place for Accepted," Carlinya said coldly.

Morvrin's tone was a little more kindly, if still gruff. "We must all do what we can do best, child. Do you think Edesina or Afara or Guisin wanted to go to Tarabon? What can they do to bring order to that unquiet land? But we must try, so they went. Kiruna and Bera are probably in the Spine of the World right this minute, on their way to search for Rand al'Thor in the Aiel Waste because we thought—only thought—when we sent them that he might be there. That we were right makes their journey no less futile now, with him out of the Waste. We all do what we can, what we must. You two are Accepted. Accepted do not go running off to Ebou Dar or anywhere else. What you two can and must do is remain here and study. Were you full sisters, I would still say keep you here. No one has made the sort of discoveries you have, the sheer number in so short a time, in a hundred years."

Nynaeve being Nynaeve, she ignored what she did not want to hear and focused on Carlinya. "We have done very well on our own, thank you. I doubt Ebou Dar can be as bad as Tanchico."

Elayne did not think the woman knew she had a death grip on her braid. Would Nynaeve never learn that simple civility sometimes won what honesty would surely lose? "I understand your concerns, Aes Sedai," Elayne said, "but however immodest it might be, the truth is that I am better qualified to locate a *ter'angreal* than anyone else in Salidar. And Nynaeve and I know better where to look than we could ever put on paper. If you send us to Merilille Sedai, under her guidance I am sure we could locate it in short order. A few days to Ebou Dar by riverboat and a few days back, with a few days under Merilille Sedai's eye in Ebou Dar." It was an effort not to draw a deep breath. "In the meantime, you could send a message to one of Siuan's eyes-and-ears in Caemlyn, so it will be there when Merana Sedai and the embassy arrive."

"Why under the Light should we do that?" Morvrin rumbled.

"I thought Nynaeve told you, Aes Sedai. I'm not sure, but I think the bowl needs a man channeling too, to make it work."

That caused a small commotion, of course. Carlinya gasped, and Morvrin muttered to herself, and Sheriam's mouth actually fell open. Nynaeve gaped as well, but just for an instant; Elayne was sure she covered before the others noticed. They were too stunned to see very much. The thing was, it was a lie, pure and simple. Simple was the key. Supposedly the greatest achievements in the Age of Legends had been done by men and women channeling together, probably linked. Very likely there *were ter'angreal* that needed a man to work. In any case, if *she* could not work the bowl alone, certainly no one in Salidar could. Except Nynaeve, maybe. If it required Rand, they could not pass up the chance to do something about the weather, and by the time she "discovered" that a circle of women could manage the bowl, the Aes Sedai in Salidar would have tied themselves to Rand too tightly to break loose.

"That is all very well," Sheriam said at last, "but it does not change the fact that you are Accepted. We will send a letter to Merilille. There has been some talk about the two of you—"

"Talk," Nynaeve snapped. "That is all you do, you *and* the Hall! Talk! Elayne and I can find this *ter'angreal*, but you would rather prattle like laying hens." Words tumbled over each other coming out of her. She kept such a steady strain on her braid, Elayne half-expected to see it come loose in her hand. "You sit here, hoping Thom and Juilin and the others will come back and tell you the Whitecloaks aren't going to fall on us like a house, when they might come back with Whitecloaks on their heels. You sit, poking at the problem of Elaida instead of doing what you said you would, fumbling over Rand. Do you know how you stand toward him yet? Do you, with your embassy on its way to Caemlyn? Do you know why you sit and talk? I do! You're afraid. Afraid of the Tower divided, afraid of Rand, the Forsaken, the Black Ajah. Last night Anaiya let slip that you had a plan ready in case one of the Forsaken attacked. All those circles linking, right on top of the bubble of evil—do you finally believe in that?—but all mismatched and most with more novices than Aes Sedai. Because only a few Aes Sedai knew beforehand. You think the Black Ajah's right here in Salidar. You were afraid your plan might get back to Sammael, or one of the others. You don't trust each other. You don't trust anybody! Is that why you won't send us to Ebou Dar? Do you think *we're* Black Ajah, or we'll run off to Rand, or . . . or . . . !" She trailed off in furious splutters and panting. She had hardly drawn breath through the entire tirade.

Elayne's first wincing instinct was to smooth it over somehow, though how was a question she could not begin to answer. As easy to smooth over a mountain range. It was the Aes Sedai who made her forget to worry whether Nynaeve had managed to shatter everything. Those expressionless faces, those eyes that seemed able to see through stone, should have conveyed nothing at all. To her, they did convey something. There was none of the cold anger that should have flowed toward anyone foolish enough to rant at Aes Sedai. This was a covering up, and the only thing to hide was truth, a truth they did not want to admit themselves. They were afraid.

"Are you quite done?" Carlinya asked in a voice that should have frozen the sun in its flight.

Elayne sneezed, banging her head on the side of the overturned cauldron. The smell of burned soup filled her nose. The midmorning sun had heated the dark interior of the big cookpot until it felt as if it still sat on a fire; sweat dripped off her. No, it poured off. Dropping the coarse pumice stone, she backed out on her knees and glared at the woman next to her. Or rather, at the half of a woman sticking out of a slightly smaller kettle lying on its side. She poked Nynaeve in the hip, and smiled grimly when the poke produced the bang of a head against iron and a yelp. Nynaeve backed out with a baleful stare, not hindered at all by a yawn she stifled behind a grimy hand. Elayne gave her no chance to speak.

"You just had to blow up, didn't you? You couldn't hold on to your temper for five minutes. We had everything in our hands, and you had to kick us in the ankles."

"They wouldn't have let us go to Ebou Dar anyway," Nynaeve muttered. "And I didn't do all the kicking of ankles." She shoved her chin up in a ridiculous fashion, so she had to look down her nose to see Elayne. " 'Aes Sedai rule their fear,' " she said in tones that might have done for berating a drunken layabout who had staggered into your horse, " 'they do not allow it to rule them. Lead, and we will follow gladly, but you must lead, not cower, hoping that something will make your troubles vanish.' "

Elayne's cheeks heated. She had not looked anything like that. And she certainly had not sounded like that. "Well, perhaps we both overstepped good sense, but—" She cut off at the sound of a footstep.

"So the Aes Sedai's golden children have decided to take a rest, have they?" Faolain's smile was as far from friendly as it was possible for a smile to be. "I am not here for the joy of it, you know. I meant to spend today working on something of my own, something not terribly inferior to what you golden children have done, I think. Instead, I must watch Accepted scrub pots for their sins. Watch so you don't sneak off like the wretched novices the pair of you should be. Now back to work. I can't leave until you're done, and I do not intend to spend the whole day here."

The dark, curly-haired woman was like Theodrin, something more than Accepted, but less than Aes Sedai. As Elayne and Nynaeve would have been, if Nynaeve had not behaved liked a stepped-on cat. Nynaeve and herself, Elayne amended reluctantly. Sheriam had told them as much in the middle of telling them just how long they would be working their "free" hours in the kitchens, the dirtiest work the cooks could find. But no Ebou Dar in any case; that had been made clear, too. A letter would be on its way to Merilille by noon if not already.

"I . . . am sorry," Nynaeve said, and Elayne blinked at her. Apologies from Nynaeve were snow in midsummer.

"I'm sorry, too, Nynaeve."

"Yes you are," Faolain told them. "As sorry as I've seen. Now back to work! Before I find reason to send you to Tiana when you're done here."

With a rueful glance at Nynaeve, Elayne crawled back into the cauldron, attacking the charred soup with the pumice stone as though attacking Faolain. Stone dust and bits of black-burned vegetable flew. No, not Faolain. The Aes Sedai, sitting when they should be acting. She *was* going to get to Ebou Dar, she *was* going to find that *ter'angreal*, and she *was* going to use it to tie Sheriam and all the rest of them to Rand. On their knees! Her sneeze very nearly took her shoes off.

Sheriam turned from where she had been watching the young women through a crack in the fence, and began walking up the narrow alley with its fitful crop of withered weeds and stubble. "I regret that." Considering Nynaeve's words, and her tone—and Elayne's, the wretched child!—she added, "Somewhat."

Carlinya sneered. She was very good at that. "Do you want to tell Accepted what fewer than two dozen Aes Sedai know?" Her mouth clicked shut at a sharp look from Sheriam.

"There are ears where we least expect them," Sheriam said softly.

"Those girls are right about one thing," Morvrin said. "Al'Thor turns my bowels to water. What options are left to us with him?"

Sheriam was not sure they had not long since run out of options.

CHAPTER
16

Tellings of the Wheel

With the Dragon Scepter across his knees, Rand lounged on the Dragon Throne. Or made a show of lounging, at least. Thrones were not made for relaxation, this one least of all, it seemed, but that was only part of the difficulty. Sensing Alanna was part too, for all that it nudged at him constantly. If he told the Maidens, they would. . . . No. How could he even think of that? He had frightened her enough to keep her at bay; she had made no effort to enter the Inner City. He would know if she did. No, for the moment Alanna was less of a problem than the inadequate seat cushion.

Despite the silver-worked blue coat buttoned to its collar, the heat did not reach him—he really was getting the way of Taim's trick—but if pure impatience had produced sweat, he would have dripped as if just climbing out of a river. Keeping cool presented no problem at all. Keeping still did. He intended to give Elayne an Andor whole and unharmed, and this morning would be the first real step to that. If they ever came.

". . . and in addition," the tall bony man standing before the Throne said in a near monotone, "one thousand four hundred twenty-three refugees from Murandy, five hundred sixty-seven from Altara, and one hundred nine from Illian. As far as the head count inside the city proper has gone to this date, I hasten to add." The few wisps of gray hair remaining to Halwin Norry stood up like quill pens stuck behind his ears, appropriate since he had been Morgase's chief clerk. "I have hired twenty-three additional clerks for the enumeration, but the number is still clearly insufficient for. . . ."

Rand stopped listening. Grateful as he was that the man had not run away as so many others had, he was not certain anything was real to Norry except the numbers in his ledgers. He recited the number of deaths during the week and the price of turnips carted in from the countryside in the same dusty tone, arranged the daily burials of penniless friendless refugees with no more horror and no more joy than he showed hiring masons to check the repair of the city walls. Illian was just another land to him, not the abode of Sammael, and Rand just another ruler.

Where are they? he wondered furiously. *Why hasn't Alanna at least tried to sidle up to me?* Moiraine would never have been frightened off so easily.

Where are all the dead? Lews Therin whispered. *Why will they not be silent?*

Rand chuckled grimly. Surely that had to be a joke.

Sulin was sitting easily on her haunches to one side of the throne's dais, and red-haired Urien to the other. Today twenty *Aethan Dor*, Red Shields, waited among the Grand Hall's columns with the Maidens, some wearing the red headband. They stood or squatted or sat, some talking quietly, but as usual looked ready to spring into action in a heartbeat, even the Maiden and two Red Shields who were dicing. At least one pair of eyes always seemed to be watching Norry; few Aiel trusted a wetlander this close to Rand.

Abruptly Bashere appeared in the Hall's tall doorway. When he nodded, Rand sat up. At last. At bloody last. The green-and-white tassel swayed as he gestured with the dragon-carved length of Seanchan spear. "You've done well, Master Norry. Your report left nothing out. I will see that the gold you need is provided. But I must attend to other matters now, if you will forgive me."

The man gave no sign of curiosity or hurt at being cut off so abruptly. He merely stopped in midword, bowed with "As the Lord Dragon commands" in that same dry tone, and backed away three steps before turning. He did not even glance at Bashere in passing. Nothing real but the ledgers.

Impatiently, Rand nodded to Bashere and set himself erect and stiff-backed on the throne. The Aiel went silent. It made them seem twice as ready.

When the Saldaean entered, he did not come alone. Two men and two women followed close behind, none young, in rich silks and brocades. They tried to pretend Bashere did not exist, and almost carried it off, but the

watchful Aiel among the columns were another story. Golden-haired Dyelin missed only a step, but Abelle and Luan, both graying yet hard-faced,
frowned at the *cadin'sor*-clad figures and instinctively felt for the swords
they did not wear today, while Ellorien, a plump dark-haired woman who
would have been pretty were her face not so determinedly stony, stopped
dead and glared before she came to herself and caught up to the others
with a quick stride. Their first good view of Rand took them aback as well,
all of them. Quick wondering glances passed between them. Perhaps they
had thought he would be older.

"My Lord Dragon," Bashere intoned loudly, halting before the dais,
"Lord of the Morning, Prince of the Dawn, True Defender of the Light,
before whom the world kneels in awe, I give to you Lady Dyelin of House
Taravin, Lord Abelle of House Pendar, Lady Ellorien of House Traemane,
and Lord Luan of House Norwelyn."

The four Andorans looked at Bashere then, with tight lips and sharp
sidelong glances. There had been something in his tone that made it sound
as if he was giving Rand four horses. To say their spines stiffened would be
to say water became wetter, yet it seemed so as they stared up at Rand.
Mostly at Rand. Their eyes could not help drifting to the Lion Throne
shining and glittering on its pedestal beyond his head.

He wanted to laugh at their outraged faces. Outraged, but also careful,
and perhaps a touch impressed in spite of themselves. He and Bashere had
worked out that list of titles between them, but the bit about the world
kneeling was new, Bashere's own late addition. Moiraine had given him the
advice, though. He almost thought he heard her silvery voice again. *How
people see you first is what they hold hardest in their minds. It is the way of the
world. You can step down from a throne, and even if you behave like a farmer in a
pigsty, some part in each of them will remember that you did descend from a throne.
But if they see only a young man first, a country man, they will resent him stepping
up to his throne later, whatever his right, whatever his power.* Well, if a title or
two could make anything so, everything would be a deal easier.

I was the Lord of the Morning, Lews Therin mumbled. *I am the Prince of
the Dawn.*

Rand kept his face smooth. "I will not welcome you—this is your land,
and the palace of your queen—but I am pleased you accept my invitation."
After five days, and with just a few hours' notice, but he did not mention
that. Rising, he laid the Dragon Scepter on the throne, then trotted down
from the dais. With a reserved smile—*Never be hostile unless you must,* Moiraine
had said, *but above all never be overly friendly. Never be eager*—he gestured to

five comfortably cushioned chairs with padded backs, set in a circle among the columns. "Join me. We will talk and have some chilled wine."

They followed, of course, eyeing the Aiel and him with equal curiosity and perhaps equal animosity, both poorly hidden. When they were all seated, *gai'shain* came, silent in their hooded white robes, bringing wine and golden goblets already damp with condensation. Another stood behind each chair with a plumed fan, gently stirring the air. Every chair but Rand's. They noted that, noted the lack of sweat on his face. But the *gai'shain* did not perspire either, even in their robes, and neither did the other Aiel. He watched the nobles' faces over his own winecup.

Andorans were proud of being more straightforward than many, and they were not slow to boast that the Game of Houses was far more entwined in other lands than in theirs, yet they still believed they could play *Daes Dae'mar* when they had to. After a fashion they could, but the truth was, Cairhienin and even Tairens considered them simple when it came to the subtle move and countermove of the Great Game. These four kept their composure for the most part, but to someone schooled by Moiraine, schooled harder in Tear and Cairhien, they gave away much with every shift of eye, every slight change of expression.

First it dawned on them that there was no chair for Bashere. Quick looks flickered between them, a slight brightening, especially when they realized Bashere was striding from the throne room. All four actually let themselves glance after him with the faintest of satisfied smiles. They must dislike a Saldaean army in Andor as much as Naean and that lot did. Now their thoughts were obvious: Perhaps the foreigner's influence was less than they had feared. Why, Bashere had been treated as no more than a superior servant.

Dyelin's eyes widened slightly at almost the same instant as Luan's, and only a moment ahead of the other two. For a moment they stared at Rand so closely it was plain they avoided looking at one another. Bashere was an outlander, but also the Marshal-General of Saldaea, three times a lord, and uncle to Queen Tenobia. If Rand used him like a servant. . . .

"Excellent wine." Staring into his goblet, Luan hesitated before adding, "My Lord Dragon." It might have been pulled put of him with a rope.

"From the south," Ellorien said after a sip. "A Tunaighan Hills vintage. A wonder you can find ice in Caemlyn this year. I have heard people already calling this 'the year without a winter.'"

"Do you think I would waste time and effort finding ice," Rand said, "when so many troubles inflict the world?"

Abelle's angular face paled, and he seemed to force himself to take another swallow. On the other hand, Luan emptied his winecup deliberately and thrust it out to be filled by a *gai'shain* whose green eyes flashed a fury at strong odds with the obstinate mildness of his sun-dark face. Serving wetlanders was like being a servant, and Aiel despised the very notion of servants. How that disgust squared with the very concept of *gai'shain* Rand had never been able to determine, but it was so.

Dyelin held her wine firmly on her knees and ignored it thereafter. This close, Rand could see touches of gray in her golden hair; she was still lovely, though in nothing except the hair did she look at all like Morgase or Elayne. Next in line for the throne, she must be a cousin at least, and close. Frowning briefly at him, she seemed on the point of shaking her head, but instead said, "We are concerned with the world's troubles, but more with those inflicting Andor. Did you bring us here to find a cure?"

"If you know one," Rand replied simply. "If not, I must look elsewhere. Many think they know the right cure. If I cannot find the one I want, I will have to accept the next best." That tightened mouths. On the way here, Bashere had taken them through a courtyard where Arymilla and Lir and the rest of those had been left cooling their heels. Taking their ease in the Palace, it would seem. "I would think you'd want to help put Andor back together. You've heard my proclamation?" He did not have to say which one; in this context, there could be only one.

"A reward offered for news of Elayne," Ellorien said flatly, her face becoming even stonier, "who is to be made queen now that Morgase is dead."

Dyelin nodded. "That seemed well, to me."

"Not to me!" Ellorien snapped. "Morgase betrayed her friends and spurned her oldest adherents. Let us see an end to House Trakand on the Lion Throne." She seemed to have forgotten Rand. They all did.

"Dyelin," Luan said curtly. She shook her head as if she had heard this before, but he went on. "She has the best claim. I speak for Dyelin."

"Elayne is the Daughter-Heir," the golden-haired woman told them levelly. "*I* speak for Elayne."

"What does it matter who any of us speak for?" Abelle demanded. "If he killed Morgase, he will——" Abelle cut off abruptly with a grimace, then looked at Rand, not exactly in defiance, but definitely daring him to do his worst. And expecting him to.

"Do you really believe that?" Rand glanced sadly at the Lion Throne on its pedestal. "Why under the Light would I kill Morgase only to hand that to Elayne?"

"Few know what to believe," Ellorien said stiffly. Spots of color still stained her cheeks. "People say many things, most foolish."

"Such as?" He directed the question to her, but it was Dyelin who answered, looking him straight in the eye.

"That you will fight the Last Battle and kill the Dark One. That you are a false Dragon, or an Aes Sedai puppet, or both. That you're Morgase's illegitimate son, or a Tairen High Lord, or an Aielman." She frowned again for a moment, but did not stop. "That you are the son of an Aes Sedai by the Dark One. That you *are* the Dark One, or else the Creator clothed in flesh. That you will destroy the world, save it, subjugate it, bring a new Age. As many tales as there are mouths. Most say you killed Morgase. Many add Elayne. They say your proclamation is a mask to hide your crimes."

Rand sighed. Some of those sayings were worse than any he had heard. "I won't ask which you believe." Why did she keep frowning at him? She was not the only one. Luan did too, and Abelle and Ellorien darted the sort of glances at him that he had come to expect from Arymilla's bunch when they thought he was not looking. *Watching. Watching.* That was Lews Therin, a hoarse giggling whisper. *I see you. Who sees me?* "Instead, will you help me make Andor whole again? I don't want Andor to become another Cairhien, or worse, a Tarabon or Arad Doman."

"I know something of the *Karaethon Cycle*," Abelle said. "I believe you are the Dragon Reborn, but nothing there speaks of you ruling, only fighting the Dark One at Tarmon Gai'don."

Rand's hand tightened on his goblet so hard the dark surface of the wine trembled. How much easier if these four were like most of the Tairen High Lords, or the Cairhienin, but not one of them wanted a shaving more power for themselves than they already had. However the wine had been chilled, he doubted the One Power would intimidate this lot. *In all likelihood, they'd tell me to kill them and be burned for it!*

Burn for it, Lews Therin echoed morosely.

"How many times must I say I don't want to rule Andor? When Elayne sits on the Lion Throne, I will leave Andor. And never return, if I have my way."

"If the throne belongs to anyone," Ellorien said tightly, "it belongs to Dyelin. If you mean what you say, see her crowned, and go. Then Andor will be whole, and I don't doubt Andoran soldiers will follow you to the Last Battle, if that's what is called for."

"I refuse still," Dyelin answered in a strong voice, then turned to Rand. "I will wait and consider, my Lord Dragon. When I see Elayne alive and crowned, and you leave Andor, I will send my retainers to follow you whether anyone else in Andor does the same. But if time passes and you still reign here, or if your Aiel savages do here what I've heard they did in Cairhien and Tear"—she scowled at the Maidens and Red Shields, and the *gai'shain* too, as if she saw them looting and burning—"or you loose here those . . . men you gather with your amnesty, then I will come against you, whether anyone else in Andor does the same."

"And I will ride beside you," Luan said firmly.

"And I," Ellorien said, echoed by Abelle.

Rand threw back his head and laughed in spite of himself, half mirth, half frustration. *Light! And I thought honest opposition would be better than sneaking behind my back or licking my boots!*

They eyed him uneasily, doubtless thinking it was madness at work. Maybe it was. He was not sure himself anymore.

"Consider what you must," he told them, standing to end the audience. "I mean what I said. But consider this as well. Tarmon Gai'don is coming closer. I don't know how long we have for you to spend considering."

They made their goodbyes—a careful bow of the head, as between equals, and at that more than when they arrived—but as they turned to go, Rand caught Dyelin's sleeve. "I have a question for you." The others paused, half turning back. "A private question." After a moment she nodded, and her companions moved a little way down the throne room. They watched closely, but they were not near enough to hear. "You looked at me . . . strangely," he said. *You and every other noble I've met in Caemlyn.* Every Andoran noble, at least. "Why?"

Dyelin peered up at him, then finally nodded slightly to herself. "What is your mother's name?"

Rand blinked. "My mother?" Kari al'Thor was his mother. That was how he thought of her; she had raised him from infancy, until she died. But he decided to give her the cold truth he had learned in the Waste. "My mother's name was Shaiel. She was a Maiden of the Spear. My father was Janduin, clan chief of the Taardad Aiel." Her eyebrows rose doubtfully. "I will swear it on any oath you choose. What does that have to do with what I want to know? They're both long dead."

Relief crept across her face. "A chance resemblance, it seems; no more. I do not mean to say you don't know your parents, but you have the west of Andor on your tongue."

"A resemblance? I grew up in the Two Rivers, but my parents were as I said. Who do I look like to make you stare at me?"

She hesitated, then sighed. "I do not suppose it matters. Someday you must tell me how you had Aiel parents yet were raised in Andor. Twenty-five years ago, more now, the Daughter-Heir of Andor vanished in the night. Her name was Tigraine. She left behind a husband, Taringail, and a son, Galad. I know it is only chance, yet I see Tigraine in your face. It was a shock."

Rand felt a shock of his own. He felt cold. Fragments of the tale the Wise Ones had told him spun through his head. . . . *a golden-haired young wetlander, in silks . . . son she loved; a husband she did not . . . Shaiel was the name she took. She never gave another . . . You have something of her in your features.* "How was it that Tigraine vanished? I have an interest in the history of Andor."

"I will thank you not to call it history, my Lord Dragon. I was a girl when it happened, but more than a child, and here in the Palace often. One morning, Tigraine simply was not in the Palace, and she was never seen again. Some claimed to see Taringail's hand in it, but he was half-mad with grief. Taringail Damodred wanted more than anything else in the world to see his daughter Queen of Andor and his son King of Cairhien. He was Cairhienin, Taringail. That marriage was meant to stop the wars with Cairhien, and it did, yet Tigraine vanishing made them think Andor wanted to break the treaty, which led them to scheme the way Cairhienin do, which led to Laman's Pride. And you of course know where that led," she added dryly. "My father said Gitara Sedai was really at fault."

"Gitara?" A wonder he did not sound strangled. He had heard that name more than once. It had been an Aes Sedai named Gitara Moroso, a woman with the Foretelling, who announced that the Dragon had been Reborn on the slopes of Dragonmount, and so set Moiraine and Siuan on their long search. It had been Gitara Moroso who years before that told "Shaiel" that unless she fled to the Waste, telling no one, and became a Maiden of the Spear, disaster would fall on Andor and the world.

Dyelin nodded, a touch impatiently. "Gitara was counselor to Queen Mordrellen," she said briskly, "but she spent more time with Tigraine and Luc, Tigraine's brother, than with the Queen. After Luc rode north, never to return, whispers said Gitara had convinced him that his fame lay in the Blight, or his fate. Others said it was that he would find the Dragon Reborn there, or that the Last Battle depended on him going. That was about a year before Tigraine disappeared. Myself, I doubt Gitara had anything to do with it, or with Luc. She stayed the Queen's counselor until Mordrellen died. From heartbreak over Tigraine on top of Luc, so it was said. Which began the Succession, of course." She glanced toward the others, who were shifting their feet and frowning with suspicion and impatience, but she could not resist adding one more thing. "You would have found a different Andor, without that. Tigraine queen, Morgase only High Seat of House Trakand, Elayne not born at all. Morgase married Taringail once she had the throne, you see. Who can say what else would be changed?"

Watching her join the others and go, he thought of one thing that would have changed. He would not be in Andor, for he would not have been born. Everything folded back into itself, in endless circles. Tigraine went to the Waste in secret, which made Laman Damodred cut down *Avendoraldera*, a gift of the Aiel, to make a throne, an act which brought the Aiel across the Spine of the World to kill him—that had been their only goal, though the nations called it the Aiel War—and with the Aiel came a Maiden named Shaiel, who died giving birth. So many lives changed, lives ended, so she could give birth to him at the proper time and place and die doing it. Kari al'Thor was the mother he remembered, if dimly, yet he wished he could have known Tigraine or Shaiel or whatever she wanted to call herself, even if only for a little while. Just to have seen her.

Useless dreaming. She was long dead. It was over and done. So why did it still nag at him?

The Wheel of Time and the wheel of a man's life turn alike without pity or mercy, Lews Therin murmured.

Are you really there? Rand thought. *If there's more than a voice and a few old memories, answer me! Are you there?* Silence. He could use Moiraine's advice now, or somebody's.

Abruptly he realized he was staring at the white marble wall of the Grand Hall, staring just north of west. Toward Alanna. She was away from Culain's Hound. *No! Burn her!* He would not replace Moiraine with a woman who would ambush him that way. He could not trust any woman touched by the Tower. Except three. Elayne, Nynaeve and Egwene. He hoped he could trust them. If only just a little.

For some reason he looked up at the great vaulted ceiling, with its colored windows depicting battles and queens, alternating with the White Lion. Those more than life-size women seemed to stare at him, in disapproval, wondering what he was doing there. Imagination, of course, but why? Because he had learned about Tigraine? Imagination, or madness?

"Someone has come I think you should see," Bashere said at his elbow, and Rand jerked away from the women overhead. Had he really been glaring back at them? Bashere had one of his horsemen with him, a taller fellow—not hard to be, beside Bashere—with a dark beard and mustaches, his tilted eyes green.

"Not unless it's Elayne," Rand said, more harshly than he meant, "or somebody with proof the Dark One is dead. I am going to Cairhien this morning." He had had no such intention until the words left his mouth. Egwene was there. And the queens overhead were not. "It's been weeks since I was there last. If I don't keep an eye on them, some lord or lady will claim the Sun Throne behind my back." Bashere looked at him strangely. He was explaining too much.

"As you say, but you will want to see this man first. He says he comes from Lord Brend, and I think he speaks truth." The Aiel were on their feet in the instant; they knew who used that name.

For Rand's part, he stared at Bashere in surprise. The last thing he expected was an emissary from Sammael. "Bring him in."

"Hamad," Bashere said with a jerk of his head, and the younger Saldaean trotted away.

A few minutes later Hamad returned with a knot of Saldaeans warily guarding a fellow in their midst. At first glance nothing about the man accounted for their caution. With no weapon visible, he wore a long gray coat with a raised collar, and a curly beard but no mustache, both in the Illianer fashion. He had a stub of a nose and a wide, grinning mouth. As he came closer, though, Rand realized that grin never altered by a hair. The man's whole face seemed frozen in that one mirthful expression. By contrast, his dark eyes stared out of that mask, swimming with fear.

At ten paces, Bashere raised his hand, and the guard halted. The Illianer, staring at Rand, did not seem to notice until Hamad presented a sword point to his chest, making him stop or be run through. He only glanced at the slightly serpentine blade, then returned to staring at Rand with those terrified eyes in that grinning face. His hands hung at his sides, twitching as much as his face was still.

Rand started to close the distance, but abruptly Sulin and Urien were there, not exactly blocking his way, yet positioned so that he would have to push between them.

"I wonder what has been done to him?" Sulin said, studying the fellow. A number of Maidens and Red Shields had come out from the columns, some even veiled. "If he is not Shadowspawn, he is touched by the Shadow."

"One like that might do things we cannot know," Urien said. He was one of those with a scarlet strip of cloth around his temples. "Kill with a touch, perhaps. A pretty message that would be to send an enemy."

Neither looked at Rand, not directly, but he nodded. Perhaps they were right. "How are you called?" he asked. Sulin and Urien moved a step to either side when they saw he would stay where he was.

"I do come from . . . from Sammael," the man said woodenly through that grin. "I do bring a message for . . . for the Dragon Reborn. For you."

Well, that was direct enough. Was he a Darkfriend, or just some poor soul Sammael had trapped in one of the nastier weavings Asmodean had talked about? "What message?" Rand said.

The Illianer's mouth worked, struggled. What came out bore no relation to the voice he had used before. It was deeper, full of confidence, in a different accent. "We will stand on different sides, you and I, come the day of the Great Lord's Return, but why should we kill each other now and leave Demandred and Graendal to contest for the world over our bones?" Rand knew that voice, in one of those scraps from Lews Therin that had settled in his mind. Sammael's voice. Lews Therin snarled wordlessly. "Already you have much to digest," the Illianer went on—or Sammael did. "Why bite off more? And hard chewing, even if you don't find Semirhage or Asmodean taking you from behind while you are busy with it. I propose a truce between us, a truce until the Day of Return. If you do not move against me, I will not against you. I will pledge not to move east beyond the Plains of Maredo, nor further north than Lugard in the east or Jehannah in the west. You see, I leave the greater share by far to you. I do not claim to speak for the rest of the Chosen, but at least you know you have nothing to fear from me, or out of the lands I hold. I will pledge not to aid them in anything they do against you, nor to help them defend against you. You have done well so far in removing the Chosen from the field. I have no doubt you will continue to do well, better than before, knowing your southern flank is safe and the others fight without my aid. I suspect that on the Day of Return, there will be only you and I, as it should be. As it was meant to be." The man's teeth clicked shut, hidden behind that frozen grin. His eyes looked near madness.

Rand stared. A truce with Sammael? Even if he could have trusted the man to keep it, even if it meant one danger set aside until all the others were dealt with, it also meant leaving countless thousands to Sammael's mercy, a quality the man had never had. He felt rage sliding across the surface of the Void, and realized he had seized *saidin*. That torrent of searing sweetness and freezing filth seemed to echo his anger. Lews Therin. Well enough that he should be mad in his madness. The echo resonated with his own fury till he could not tell one from the other.

"Take this message back to Sammael," he said coldly. "Every death he has caused since waking, I lay at his feet and call due. Every murder he has ever done or caused, I lay at his feet and call due. He escaped justice in the Rorn M'doi, and at Nol Caimaine, and Sohadra. . . ." More of Lews Therin's memories, but the pain of what had been done there, the agony of what Lews Therin's eyes had seen, burned across the Void as if Rand's. ". . . But I will see justice done now. Tell him, no truce with the Forsaken. No truce with the Shadow."

The messenger lifted a spasming hand to wipe sweat from his face. No, not sweat. His hand came away red. Crimson droplets oozed from his pores, and he trembled head to foot. Hamad gasped and stepped back, and he was not the only one. Bashere knuckled his mustaches with a grimace, and even the Aiel stared. Painted red, the Illianer collapsed in a convulsing heap, blood spreading around him in a dark, glistening pool smeared by his thrashing.

Rand watched him die, buried deep in the Void, feeling nothing. The Void walled off emotion, and there was nothing he could have done in any case. Had he known Healing, he did not think it would have stopped that.

"I think," Bashere said slowly, "maybe Sammael will have his answer when this fellow does not return. I have heard of killing a messenger who brought bad news, but never killing him to tell you the news was bad."

Rand nodded. The death changed nothing; it changed no more than learning of Tigraine had. "Have someone see to his burial. A prayer will not hurt, even if it doesn't help either." Why did those queens in their colored windows still seem accusing? Surely they had seen as bad in their lifetimes, maybe even in this chamber. He could still point to Alanna, feel her; the Void was no shield. Could he trust Egwene? She kept secrets. "I may spend the night in Cairhien."

"A strange end to a strange man," Aviendha said, stepping around the dais. Small doors behind it led to robing rooms, and from there to corridors beyond.

Rand started to step between her and what lay on the red-and-white tiles, then stopped. After one curious glance, Aviendha ignored the body. When she was a Maiden of the Spear she had surely seen as many men die as he ever had. By the time she gave up the spear, she had probably killed as many as he had then seen die.

It was him she concentrated on, running her eyes over him to make sure he had taken no hurt. Some of the Maidens smiled at her, and they opened a path to Rand, pushing Red Shields aside where necessary, but she stayed where she was, readjusting her shawl and studying him. It was a good thing that whatever the Maidens thought, she only stayed near him because the Wise Ones told her to, to spy on him, because he found himself wanting to put his arms around her right there. Good that she did not want him. He had given her the ivory bracelet she wore, roses among thorns, suiting her nature. It was her only piece of jewelry except for a silver necklace, the intricate patterns the Kandori called snowflakes. He did not know who had given her that.

Light! he thought disgustedly. Wanting Aviendha *and* Elayne, when he knew he could have neither. *You're worse than Mat ever thought of being.* Even Mat had the sense to stay away from a woman if he thought he would harm her.

"I must go to Cairhien too," she said.

Rand grimaced. One attraction of a night in Cairhien was that it would be a night without her in the same room.

"It has nothing to do with . . ." she began sharply, then bit her full underlip, blue-green eyes flashing. "I must speak with the Wise Ones, with Amys."

"Of course," he told her. "No reason you shouldn't." There was always the chance he could manage to leave her behind there.

Bashere touched his arm. "You were going to watch my horsemen go through their paces again this afternoon." The tone was casual, yet his tilted eyes gave the words heavy weight.

It *was* important, but Rand felt a need to be out of Caemlyn, out of Andor. "Tomorrow. Or the day after." He had to be away from the eyes of those queens, wondering whether one of their blood—Light, he was!—would tear their land apart as he had so many others. Away from Alanna. If only for a night, he had to be away.

CHAPTER
17

The Wheel of a Life

Gathering his sword belt from beside the throne with a flow of Air, and the scepter too, Rand opened the gateway right there before the dais, a slash of light that rotated, widening to give a view of an empty dark-paneled chamber more than six hundred miles from Caemlyn, in the Sun Palace, the Royal Palace of Cairhien. Set aside for his use this way, the room held no furnishings, but dark blue floor tiles and wood-paneled walls glistened from polishing. Windowless, the room was bright anyway; eight gilded stand-lamps burned day and night, mirrors magnifying the oil-fed flames. He paused to buckle on his sword while Sulin and Urien opened the door to the corridor and led veiled Maidens and Red Shields through before him.

In this case he thought their caution ridiculous. The broad corridor outside, the only way to reach the room, was already crowded with thirty or so *Far Aldazar Din*, Brothers of the Eagle, and nearly two dozen of Berelain's Mayeners in red-painted breastplates and rimmed potlike helmets that came down to the nape of the neck in back. If there was one place anywhere that Rand knew he needed no Maidens, it was Cairhien, more so even than Tear.

A Brother of the Eagle was already loping down the hallway by the time Rand appeared, and a Mayener awkwardly clutching spear and shortsword as he followed the taller Aielman. In fact, a small army trailed after the *Far Aldazar Din*, servants in various liveries, a Tairen Defender of the Stone in burnished breastplate and black-and-gold coat, a Cairhienin soldier with the front of his head shaved, his breastplate much more battered than the Tairen's, two young Aielwomen in dark heavy skirts and loose white blouses whom Rand thought he recognized as apprentices to Wise Ones. News of his arrival would spread quickly. It always did.

At least Alanna was far away. Verin, too, but most of all Alanna. He still felt her, even at this distance, just a vague impression that she was somewhere to the west. Like the feel of a hand just a hair from touching the back of his neck. Was there any way to get free of her? He seized *saidin* again for a moment, but that still made no difference.

You never escape the traps you spin yourself. Lews Therin's murmur sounded confused. *Only a greater power can break a power, and then you're trapped again. Trapped forever so you cannot die.*

Rand shivered. Sometimes it really did seem that voice was speaking to him. If only it would make sense once in a while, having it in his head would be easier.

"I see you, *Car'a'carn*," one of the Brothers of the Eagle said. His gray eyes were on a level with Rand's, the scar slashing across his nose stark white against his sun-dark face. "I am Corman of the Mosaada Goshien. May you find shade this day."

Rand had no chance to answer properly before the pink-cheeked Mayener officer was shouldering in. Well, not exactly shouldering—he was too slender to shoulder aside a man a head taller and half again as wide, especially an Aiel, though maybe young enough to think he could—yet he did squeeze himself in front of Rand next to Corman, tucking under his arm a crimson helmet with a single slender red plume. "My Lord Dragon, I am Havien Nurelle, Lord Lieutenant in the Winged Guards"—there were wings worked on the sides of his helmet—"in service to Berelain sur Paendrag Paeron, First of Mayene, and at your service also." Corman gave him an amused sideways look.

"I see you, Havien Nurelle," Rand said gravely, and the boy blinked. Boy? Come to think on it, he might be no younger than Rand. That was a shock! "If you and Corman will show me—" Suddenly he realized Aviendha was gone. He nearly broke his back trying to avoid the woman, and the first time in weeks he agreed to let her near him, she slipped away as soon as his head turned! "Take me to Berelain and Rhuarc," he ordered gruffly. "If they're not together, take me to whoever is closer, and find the other." Running to the Wise Ones, no doubt, to report on what he had been up to. He *would* leave the woman behind here.

What you want is what you cannot have. What you cannot have is what you want. Lews Therin laughed maniacally. It did not bother Rand as much as it once had. Not quite as much. What had to be endured, could be.

Discussing who was nearest, Corman and Havien left their men behind, but they still made quite a procession, with all the Maidens and Red Shields following close, crowding the square-vaulted hallway. The corridor had a dark, heavy feel despite lighted stand-lamps. There was very little color anywhere, except in occasional tapestries, and the Cairhienin tried to make up for it by having everything rigidly arranged, whether embroidered flowers or birds, deer or leopards in a hunt, or nobles in battle. For the Cairhienin servants who scurried out of the way, livery usually meant colored stripes on the cuffs and a house badge embroidered on the breast; sometimes a collar or sleeves in House colors, very seldom an entire coat or dress. Only upper servants would show more color. Cairhienin liked order, and disliked flamboyance. An occasional niche held a golden bowl or a Sea Folk vase, but stark and worked with straight lines, trying to disguise their curves if they had any. Whenever the hall gave way to a square-columned colonnade, if there was a garden below, the walks made a precise grid, every flower bed the same size, shrubs and small trees rigidly pruned and spaced. Had the drought and heat allowed any flowers, he was sure they too would have bloomed in straight lines.

Rand wished Dyelin could see those bowls and vases. The Shaido had carried away whatever they could lift, all the way across Cairhien, and burned what they could when they could not carry it, but such behavior violated *ji'e'toh*. The Aiel who followed Rand and had saved the city had taken, but by their rules, when they took a place in battle they were allowed a fifth of what it held and not a spoon more. Bael had agreed, reluctantly, to forgo even that in Andor, but Rand thought no one without a list would believe anything had been taken here at all.

For all their discussion, Corman and Havien failed to find either Rhuarc or Berelain before they were found themselves instead.

The two came to meet Rand alone in one of the colonnades, without entourage, which only made him feel as though he was leading a parade himself. Rhuarc in his *cadin'sor*, gray streaking his dark red hair, towered over Berelain, a pale, beautiful young woman in a blue and white dress cut low enough to make Rand clear his throat when she curtsied. *Shoufa* looped loosely around his neck, Rhuarc carried no weapon but a heavy Aiel knife. She wore the Diadem of the First, a golden hawk in flight, in shining black hair that made waves to bare shoulders.

Perhaps it was just as well Aviendha had gone; sometimes she had a violent way toward women she even thought were putting themselves forward with him.

Suddenly he realized that Lews Therin was humming tunelessly. Something about it seemed troubling, but what . . . ? Humming. Like a man admiring a pretty woman who was not aware of him.

Stop that! Rand shouted inside his head. *Stop looking through my eyes!* No telling whether he heard—was there someone there to hear?—but the humming stopped.

Havien went to one knee, but Berelain gestured him to rise almost absently. "I trust all is well with my Lord Dragon, and with Andor." She had the sort of voice that made a man listen. "And with your friends, Mat Cauthon and Perrin Aybara, as well."

"All is well," he told her. She always asked after Mat and Perrin, however often he told her one was on his way to Tear and the other he had not seen since before going to the Waste. "And with you?"

Berelain glanced at Rhuarc as they fell in on either side of Rand, proceeding into the next stretch of corridor. "As well as can be expected, my Lord Dragon."

"It is well, Rand al'Thor," Rhuarc said. There was not much expression on his face, but then, there seldom was.

Rand knew both understood why he had put Berelain in charge here. Cold reasons. The first ruler to offer him alliance freely, he could trust her because she needed him, now more than ever since that alliance, to keep Tear from Mayene's throat. The High Lords had always tried to treat Mayene like a province. Besides, a foreigner from a small nation hundreds of leagues south, she had no reason to favor one faction over another in Cairhien, she had no hope of seizing power, and she knew the running of a country. Hard reasons. Given how Aiel felt about Cairhienin and Cairhienin about Aiel, putting Rhuarc in charge would have led to bloodshed, and Cairhien had had enough of that.

The arrangement seemed to be working out well. As with Semaradrid and Weiramon in Tear, the Cairhienin accepted a Mayener as governor as much because she was not Aiel as because Rand appointed her. Berelain did know what she was doing, and she at least listened to advice offered by Rhuarc, speaking for the clan chiefs remaining in Cairhien. No doubt she had to deal with the Wise Ones as well—they would give up meddling, which they did not see as such, a day after Aes Sedai did—but she had not mentioned them so far.

"And Egwene?" Rand said. "Is she any better?"

Berelain's lips compressed slightly. She did not like Egwene. But then, Egwene did not like her. No reason for it, that he knew, but there it was.

Rhuarc spread his hands. "So far as Amys tells me." As well as being a Wise One, Amys was his wife. One of his wives; he had two, one of the odder Aiel customs among many Rand found odd. "She says Egwene yet needs rest, light exercise, plenty of food and fresh air. I think she takes walks in the cool of the day." Berelain gave him a wry look; the faint sheen of perspiration on her face did not detract from her beauty, but of course Rhuarc was not sweating at all.

"I would like to see her. If the Wise Ones permit," Rand added. The Wise Ones were as jealous of their prerogatives as any Aes Sedai he had ever met, making sure of them with sept chiefs, clan chiefs and perhaps most of all with the *Car'a'carn*. "But first we. . . ."

A noise had been catching the edge of hearing as they approached another place where one wall of the corridor was replaced by balustraded columns. The clatter of practice swords. He glanced down in passing. At least that was his intention. What he saw in the stone-paved courtyard below stilled his tongue and stopped his feet. Under the eye of a stiff-backed Cairhienin in a plain gray coat, a dozen sweat-drenched women flailed away in pairs, some wearing riding dresses with divided skirts, some men's coats and breeches. Most were awkward in the forms if vigorous, while others flowed from stance to stance smoothly yet swung the bundled-lathe blades hesitantly. All wore grim determination like a cloak, though grimness was likely to break into rueful laughter when one realized she had made a mistake.

The stiff-backed fellow clapped his hands, and the panting women leaned on their practice swords, some working arms clearly unused to this. From beyond Rand's sight servants darted out, bowing and curtsying right and left as they proffered trays with pitchers and cups. But if they were servants, their livery was odd for Cairhien. They wore white. Dresses or coats and breeches, all pure white.

"What is that?" he asked. Rhuarc made a disgusted sound.

"Some of the Cairhienin women are quite impressed with the Maidens," Berelain said, smiling. "They want to be Maidens. Only, of the sword, I suppose, not the spear." Sulin stiffened indignantly, and handtalk flashed among the Maidens; the gestures seemed outraged. "These are daughters of noble Houses," Berelain went on. "I let them stay here because their parents would not allow this. There are nearly a dozen schools in the city now that will teach the sword to women, but many need to sneak away to attend. It is not only women, of course. The younger Cairhienin in general seem very impressed with the Aiel. They are adopting *ji'e'toh*."

"They are mangling it," Rhuarc growled. "Many ask about our ways, and who would not teach one who would learn what is proper? Even a treekiller." He looked ready to spit. "But they take what they are told and change it."

"Not change, really," Berelain protested. "Only adapt, I think." Rhuarc's eyebrows rose a fraction, and she sighed. Havien's face was a picture of affront, seeing his ruler challenged. Neither Rhuarc nor Berelain noticed, they were intent on Rand. He had the feeling this was an argument the pair had had often.

"They change it," Rhuarc repeated deliberately. "Those fools down there in white claim to be *gai'shain*. *Gai'shain!*" The other Aielmen muttered; handtalk flickered among the Maidens again. Havien began to look a trifle uneasy. "What battle or raid were they taken in? What *toh* have they incurred? You confirmed my ban on fighting in the city, Berelain Paeron, yet they fight duels wherever they think they'll not be found, and the loser puts on white. If one strikes another while both are armed, the one struck pleads for a duel, and if it is refused, puts on white. What has that to do with honor or obligation? They change everything, and do things to make a Sharaman blush. It should be stopped, Rand al'Thor."

Berelain's jaw firmed stubbornly, her hands tightening to fists on her skirts. "Young men always fight." Her tone was condescending enough that you might almost have forgotten she was young herself. "But since they began this, not one has died in a duel. Not one. That alone is worth letting them go on. Besides which, I have faced down fathers and mothers, some powerful, who wanted their daughters sent home. I will not deny those young women what I promised them."

"Keep them if you wish," Rhuarc said. "Let them learn the *sword*, if they wish. But let them stop claiming to follow *ji'e'toh*. Let there be an end to them putting on white and claiming to be *gai'shain*. What they do offends." His chill blue eyes were fixed on Berelain, but her large dark eyes remained steady on Rand.

He hesitated only a moment. He thought he understood what drove the younger Cairhienin to *ji'e'toh*. Twice conquered by Aiel in twenty-odd years, they had to wonder whether the secret lay there. Or maybe they thought their defeats just showed that the Aiel way was better. Clearly the Aiel were upset by what they saw as a mockery of their beliefs, but in truth, some of the ways Aiel became *gai'shain* seemed no less peculiar. For instance, speaking to a man of his father-in-law or to a woman of her mother-in-law—second-father and second-mother, in the Aiel way—was considered hostile enough to justify drawing weapons unless they had mentioned them first. If the offended party instead touched you after you spoke, under *ji'e'toh* it was the same as touching an armed enemy without harming him. That gained much *ji* and incurred much *toh*, but the one touched could demand to be made *gai'shain* to lessen the other's honor and their own obligation. By *ji'e'toh*, a proper demand to be made *gai'shain* had to be honored, so a man or woman could end up *gai'shain* for mentioning somebody's mother-in-law. Hardly less foolish than what these Cairhienin were doing. Really it came down to one thing, though. He had put Berelain in charge; he had to support her. It was as simple as that. "Cairhienin offend you by being Cairhienin, Rhuarc. Leave them be. Who knows, maybe they will eventually learn enough that you won't have to hate them anymore."

Rhuarc grunted sourly, and Berelain smiled. To Rand's surprise, for one moment she seemed about to put her tongue out at the Aielman. Only his imagination, of course. She was only a few years older than himself, but she had been ruling Mayene while he was still guarding sheep in the Two Rivers.

Sending Corman and Havien back to their guard, Rand moved on, with Rhuarc and Berelain to either side and the rest following close. A parade. All it needed was drums and trumpets.

The clatter of practice swords started up again behind him. Another change, however small. Even Moiraine, who had long studied the Prophecies of the Dragon, had not known whether his Breaking the World again meant he would bring on a new Age, but he was certainly bringing changes, one way and another. As many by accident, it seemed, as on purpose.

When they reached the door of the study Berelain and Rhuarc shared—rising suns decorated the long panels of dark polished wood, indicating some royal use once—Rand stopped, turning to Sulin and Urien. If he could not dispense with all these guards here, there was nowhere he could. "I mean to return to Caemlyn an hour or so after sunrise tomorrow. Until then, visit the tents, see your friends, and try not to start any blood feuds. If you insist, two of you can hang about to protect me from mice; I don't think anything larger will jump out at me here."

Urien grinned slightly and nodded, though he did gesture about head-high to a Cairhienin and murmur, "The mice can be big here."

For an instant Rand thought Sulin meant to argue. Her flat stare lasted only a moment, though, before she nodded. Still tight-mouthed, however. Doubtless he would hear the argument in full once there were only Maidens to hear.

A large room, the study presented sharp contrasts even at his second sight of it. On the high worked-plaster ceiling, straight lines and sharp angles made elaborately repeating patterns, and around the walls as well as on a wide fireplace faced with deep blue marble. A massive table stood in the middle of the floor, covered with papers and maps, marking a boundary of sorts. The two tall narrow windows to one side of the fireplace held clay pots on deep stools, filled with small plants that showed a few tiny red-and-white blossoms. On that side of the table a long wall hanging showed ships at sea, and men hauling nets filled with oilfish, the source of Mayene's wealth. An embroidery hoop, with needle and red thread dangling from a piece of half-finished work, sat on a high-backed chair wide enough for Berelain to curl up in if she wished. There was a single carpet on the floor, in flowerlike patterns of gold and red and blue, and a small table beside the chair held a silver wine pitcher and goblets on a silver tray, as well as a slim book bound in red with a gold-worked piece of leather marking Berelain's place.

The floor on the other side of the table was layered in brightly colored rugs, with tasseled cushions of red and blue and green scattered about. A tabac pouch, a short-stemmed pipe, and a pair of tongs sat beside a covered brass bowl atop a small brassbound chest, while a slightly larger chest, strapped with iron, held an ivory carving of a gawky animal Rand doubted really existed. Two dozen books of all sizes, from small enough to fit a coat pocket to large enough that even Rhuarc must need both hands to pick them up, made a neat row across the floor along the wall. Aiel made everything in the Waste that they needed except books; peddlers had made fortunes among Aiel hauling nothing but books.

"Now," Rand said when the door was closed, leaving him alone with Rhuarc and Berelain, "how are things really?"

"As I said," Berelain replied. "As well as can be expected. There is more talk of Caraline Damodred and Toram Riatin in the streets, but most people are too tired to want another war for a time."

"It is said ten thousand Andormen soldiers have joined them." Rhuarc began thumbing his pipe full. "Rumor always multiplies by ten when not twenty, yet it is troubling if true. The scouts say their numbers are not large, but left to grow they could be more than an annoyance. The yellow-fly is almost too small to see, but if you leave its egg in your skin, you will lose an arm or leg before it hatches—if it does not kill you."

Rand grunted noncommittally. Darlin's rebellion in Tear was not the only one he had to face. House Riatin and House Damodred, the last two to hold the Sun Throne, had been bitter rivals before Rand appeared, and likely would be again if he disappeared. Now they had put rivalry aside—on the surface at least; what went on below the surface with Cairhienin could be something else entirely—and, like Darlin, meant to gather strength somewhere Toram and Caraline thought safe. In their case, the foothills of the Spine of the World, as far from the city as they could be and remain in the country. They had gathered the same mix as Darlin, nobles mainly of middle rank, displaced country folk, some outright mercenaries and perhaps a few former brigands. Niall's hand might be there, as well, as it was with Darlin.

Those foothills were not nearly so impenetrable as Haddon Mirk, but Rand held his hand: He had too many enemies in too many places. If he paused to swat Rhuarc's yellowfly here, he might find a leopard on his back somewhere else. He had it in mind to take the leopard first. If only he knew where all the other leopards were.

"What of the Shaido?" he asked, setting the Dragon Scepter down on a half-unrolled map. It showed the north of Cairhien, and the mountains called Kinslayer's Dagger. The Shaido might not be as big a leopard as Sammael, but they were a sight bigger than High Lord Darlin or Lady Caraline. Berelain handed him a goblet of wine, and he thanked her. "Have the Wise Ones said anything at all about Sevanna's intentions?"

He would have thought at least one or two could listen and look around just a little when she journeyed up to Kinslayer's Dagger. He would wager the Shaido Wise Ones did when they came below the River Gaelin. He said neither thing, of course. The Shaido might have abandoned *ji'e'toh*, but Rhuarc had a traditional Aiel view of spying. The Wise Ones' views were another thing again, though exactly what could be hard to pin down.

"They say the Shaido are building holds." Rhuarc paused, using a pair of tongs to hold a hot coal from the sand-filled brass bowl over his pipe. When he had it puffed alight, he went on. "They do not think the Shaido ever mean to return to the Three-fold Land. Nor do I."

Rand scrubbed his free hand through his hair. Caraline and Toram festering, and the Shaido settling in this side of the Dragonwall. A far more dangerous brew than Darlin. And Alanna's unseen finger seemed on the point of touching him. "Is there any other good news?"

"There is fighting in Shamara," Rhuarc said around his pipestem.

"Where?" Rand asked.

"Shamara. Or Shara. They give many names for their land. Co'dansin, Tomaka, Kigali, others. Any could be true, or none. They lie without thought, those people. Unwind every bolt of silk you trade for, or find that only the outside is silk. And if the next time in the tradehold you happen to find the man who traded with you, he will deny seeing you before, or coming to trade before. If you press it, the others kill him to appease you, then say only he could do anything concerning the silk, and try to trade you water as wine."

"Why is fighting in Shara good news?" Rand asked softly. He did not really want to hear the answer. Berelain was listening with interest; no one except the Aiel and the Sea Folk knew much more of the closed lands beyond the Waste than that ivory and silk came from there. That, and the tales in *The Travels of Jain Farstrider*, which were probably too fanciful to be true. Though come to think of it, Rand did remember the lying being mentioned, and the different names, except the examples Farstrider had given matched none of Rhuarc's as far as he could recall.

"There is never fighting in Shara, Rand al'Thor. It is said the Trolloc Wars infested them"—Trollocs had entered the Aiel Waste too; since then the Trolloc name for the Aiel Waste was the Dying Ground—"but if there has been one battle since, no word of it has come to the tradeholds. Not much word of anything outside the holdwalls does come inside. They say their land has always been one, not many as here, always at peace. When you came from Rhuidean as the *Car'a'carn*, word of you spread, and of your title among the wetlanders here. The Dragon Reborn. Word traveled to the tradeholds along the Great Rift and the Cliffs of Dawn." Rhuarc's eyes were calm and steady; this did not trouble him. "Now word comes back across the Three-fold Land. There is fighting in Shara, and Sharamen in the tradeholds ask when the Dragon Reborn will Break the World."

Suddenly the wine tasted sour. Another place like Tarabon and Arad Doman, torn just by hearing of him. How far did the ripples spread? Were there wars he would never hear of in lands he would never hear of, because of him?

Death rides on my shoulder, Lews Therin muttered. *Death walks in my footsteps. I am death.*

Shuddering, Rand set his goblet on the table. How much did the Prophecies demand in all those tantalizing hints and grandly roundabout verses? Was he supposed to add Shara, or whatever it was really called, to Cairhien and the rest? The entire world? How, when he could not even hold Tear or Cairhien completely? It would take more than one man's lifetime. Andor. If he was meant to rip every other land apart, rip the whole world, he would hold Andor safe for Elayne. Somehow.

"Shara, or whatever it's called, is a long way from here. One step at a time, and Sammael is the first step."

"Sammael," Rhuarc agreed. Berelain shivered, and emptied her goblet.

For a time they talked of the Aiel who were still moving south. Rand intended the hammer being made in Tear to be clearly big enough to smash anything Sammael could put in its way. Rhuarc seemed content; it was Berelain who complained that more needed to be kept in Cairhien. Until Rhuarc shushed her. She muttered something about him being too stubborn for his own good, but she went on to the efforts to resettle farmers on the land. She thought by next year there would be no need for grain from Tear. If the drought ever broke. If it did not, Tear would not be supplying grain to itself, much less anywhere else. The first tendrils of trade were beginning to reappear. Merchants had begun coming in from Andor and Tear and Murandy, down from the Borderlands. A Sea Folk ship had even dropped anchor in the river that very morning, which she found strange, so far from the sea, but welcome.

Berelain's face took on an intensity, and her voice a brisk tone, as she moved around the table to take up this sheaf of papers or that, discussing what Cairhien needed to buy and what it could afford to buy, what it had to sell now and what it would have in six months, in a year. Depending on the weather, of course. She brushed by that as if it was of no matter, though giving Rand a level look that said he was the Dragon Reborn and if there was any way to stop the heat, he should find it. Rand had seen her meltingly seductive, he had seen her frightened, defiant, wrapped in arrogance, but never like this. She seemed a different woman altogether. Rhuarc, seated on one of his cushions puffing on his pipe, appeared amused as he watched her.

". . . this school of yours might do some good," she said, frowning at a long sheet covered in a precise hand, "if they would stop thinking of new things long enough to make what they have already thought of." She tapped her lips with a finger, peering at nothing thoughtfully. "You say give them what gold they ask, but if you would let me hold back unless they actually—"

Jalani put her plump face in at the door—Aiel seemed not to understand knocking—and said, "Mangin is here to speak with Rhuarc and you, Rand al'Thor."

"Tell him I'll be happy to talk with him later—" Rand got that far before Rhuarc broke in quietly.

"You should speak with him now, Rand al'Thor." The clan chief's face looked grave; Berelain had replaced the long paper on the table and was studying the floor.

"Very, well," Rand said slowly.

Jalani's head vanished, and Mangin came in. Taller than Rand, he had been one of those who crossed the Dragonwall in search of He Who Comes With the Dawn, one of the handful who took the Stone of Tear. "Six days ago I killed a man," he began without preamble, "a treekiller, and I must know if I have *toh* to you, Rand al'Thor."

"To me?" Rand said. "You can defend yourself, Mangin; Light, you know tha—" For a moment he was silent, meeting gray eyes that were sober but certainly not afraid. Curious, maybe. Rhuarc's face told him nothing; Berelain was still not meeting his gaze. "He did attack you, didn't he?"

Mangin shook his head slightly. "I saw that he deserved to die, so I killed him." He said it conversationally; he saw the drains needed cleaning, so he cleaned them. "But you have said we cannot kill the oathbreakers except in battle, or if they attack us. Do I have *toh* toward you now?"

Rand remembered what he had said. . . . *him will I hang.* His chest felt tight. "Why did he deserve to die?"

"He wore what he had no right to," Mangin replied.

"Wore what? What did he wear, Mangin?"

Rhuarc answered, touching his left forearm. "This." He meant the Dragon coiled around his arm. Clan chiefs did not display them often, or even speak of them; almost everything about the markings were shrouded in mystery, and the chiefs were content to leave it so. "It was a thing of needles and inks, of course." A tattoo.

"He was pretending to be a clan chief?" Rand realized he was searching for an excuse. . . . *him will I hang.* Mangin had been one of the first to follow him.

"No," Mangin said. "He was drinking, and showing off what he should not have had. I see your eyes, Rand al'Thor." He grinned suddenly. "It is a puzzle. I was right to kill him, but now I have *toh* to you."

"You were wrong to kill him. You know the penalty for murder."

"A rope around the neck, as these wetlanders use." Mangin nodded thoughtfully. "Tell me where and when; I will be there. May you find water and shade today, Rand al'Thor."

"May you find water and shade, Mangin," Rand told him sadly.

"I suppose," Berelain said when the door closed behind Mangin, "that he really will walk to his own hanging of his own accord. Oh, don't look at me that way, Rhuarc. I don't mean to impugn him, or Aiel honor."

"Six days," Rand growled, rounding on her. "You knew why he was here, both of you. Six days ago, and you left it to me. Murder is murder, Berelain."

She drew herself up regally, but she sounded defensive. "I am not used to men coming to me and saying they have just committed murder. Bloody *ji'e'toh*. Bloody Aielmen and their bloody honor." The curses sounded odd coming from her mouth.

"You have no cause to be angry with her, Rand al'Thor," Rhuarc put in. "Mangin's *toh* is to you, not to her. Or to me."

"His *toh* was to the man he murdered," Rand said coldly. Rhuarc looked shocked. "The next time somebody commits murder, don't wait for me. You follow the law!" That way, perhaps he would not have to pass sentence again on a man he knew and liked. He would if he had to. He knew that, and it saddened him. What had he become?

The wheel of a man's life, Lews Therin murmured. *No mercy. No pity.*

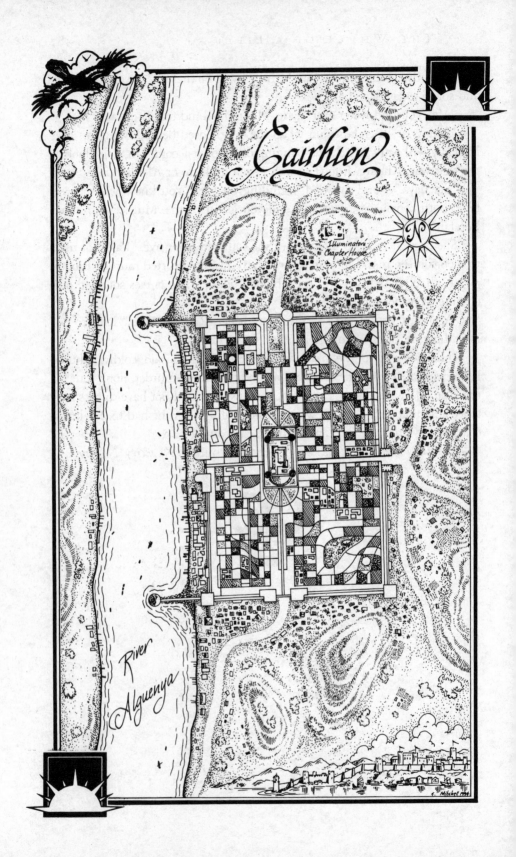

Cairhien

Illuminators
Chapter House

River
Alguenya

S. Mitchell 1994

CHAPTER
18

A Taste of Solitude

"Are there any more problems you want me to deal with?" Rand's tone made it clear he meant problems they should have already solved. Rhuarc shook his head slightly; Berelain's face reddened as well. "Good. Set a date for Mangin's hanging—" *If it hurts too much*, Lews Therin laughed in a hoarse whisper, *make it hurt someone else instead.* His responsibility. His duty. He stiffened his back to keep that mountain from crushing him. "Hang him tomorrow. Tell him I said so." He paused, glaring, then realized he was waiting for Lews Therin's comment, not theirs. Waiting for a dead man's voice, a dead madman. "I'm going to the school."

Rhuarc pointed out that the Wise Ones were probably on their way from the tents, and Berelain that Tairen and Cairhienin nobles alike would be clamoring to know where she was hiding Rand, but he told them to tell the truth. And tell the lot of them not to follow him; he would return when he returned. The pair looked as if they had swallowed sour plums, but he snatched up the Dragon Scepter and left.

In the hallway, Jalani and a yellow-haired Red Shield not much older than she came smoothly to their feet, glancing at one another hastily. Otherwise the corridor was empty except for a few scurrying servants. One of each; it figured, though Rand wondered whether Urien had had to wrestle Sulin to make it so.

Motioning them to follow, he went straight, down to the nearest stable, where the stalls were the same green marble as the columns that held the high ceiling. The head groom, a gnarled fellow with big ears, the Rising Sun of Cairhien worked on his short leather vest, was so shocked by Rand appearing with only two Aiel for escort that he kept staring at the stable doors for more and bowed so often between stares that Rand wondered whether he would ever get a horse. But once the man shouted "A horse for the Lord Dragon!" six stablemen leaped to prepare a tall, fiery-eyed bay gelding with a gold-fringed bridle and a gold-worked saddle atop a sky-blue saddlecloth fringed and embroidered with rising suns in gold.

As quickly as they moved, the big-eared head groom was gone by the time Rand swung into the saddle. To hunt for the coterie of followers the Dragon Reborn must have, possibly. Or to tell someone Rand was leaving the palace practically alone. Cairhien was like that. The sleek bay wanted to frisk, but while still trying to settle his dancing, Rand trotted him out of the palace grounds, past startled Cairhienin guards. He was not worried about assassins laying an ambush from the big-eared man's warning; any-one who ambushed him would find they had come to the shearing without clippers. Any delay, though, and likely he would have nobles crowding around so thickly he could not leave without them. It felt good to be alone for a change.

He glanced at Jalani and the young Aiel man trotting beside the bay. Dedric, he thought; a Jaern Rift Codara. Almost alone. He could feel Alanna still, and Lews Therin moaned in the far distance over his dead Ilyena. He could never be entirely alone. Maybe never again. What he had of solitude felt good, though, after so long.

Cairhien was a large city, its major streets wide enough to dwarf the people crowding them. Each street slashed arrow-straight through hills carved and stone-terraced until they seemed man-made, meeting every other street at a right angle. Throughout the city rose huge towers wrapped in wooden scaffolding that nearly hid elaborate square-arched buttresses, towers that seemed to touch the sky and meant to go higher. Twenty years since the fabled topless towers of Cairhien, a wonder of the world, had burned like torches during the Aiel War, and their rebuilding was still not done.

Making a way was not easy; the trotting did not last. Rand had grown accustomed to crowds opening up before his usual escort, yet with hun-dreds of *cadin'sor*-clad Aiel just within his sight among the slow-flowing throng, it was not quite the same, not for only two. Some of those Aiel recognized him, he thought, but they ignored him, not about to cause embarrassment by calling attention when the *Car'a'carn* wore a sword and, not as bad but hardly to be applauded, rode a horse. To Aiel, shame and embarrassment were far worse than pain, though of course *ji'e'toh* had to complicate things with degrees Rand understood only in part. Aviendha could explain it certainly; she seemed to want him to become Aiel.

Plenty of others jammed the streets too, Cairhienin in their usual drab clothing and also in the shabby bright colors of those who had lived in the Foregate before it burned, Tairens a head taller in the crowd, if not as tall as the Aiel. Ox-carts and horse-drawn wagons threaded through the throng, yielding way to closed lacquer carriages and sedan chairs, sometimes with a House banner. Hawkers cried wares from trays, and peddlers from pushcarts; musicians, tumblers and jugglers performed on street corners. Both were changes. Once Cairhien had been quiet, subdued, except in the Foregate. Some of that sobriety still held. The shops still had small signs, displaying no goods outside. And if the former Foregaters seemed raucous as ever, laughing loudly and shouting at one another, arguing right there in the street, the other Cairhienin still eyed them with prim distaste.

No one but Aiel recognized the bareheaded horseman in a silver-worked blue coat, though occasionally someone glanced twice at his saddlecloth. The Dragon Scepter was not well known here yet. Nobody gave way. Rand felt torn between impatience and the pleasure of not being the focus of every eye.

The school occupied a palace a mile from the Sun Palace, once the property of one Lord Barthanes, now dead and unlamented, a great heap of stone squares with sharply angular towers and severe balconies. The tall gates onto the main courtyard stood open, and when Rand rode in, he found a welcome.

Idrien Tarsin, who headed the school, stood on the broad steps at the far end of the courtyard, a stocky woman in a plain gray dress, straight-backed enough to seem a head taller than she was. She was not alone. Dozens and dozens of others crowded the stone steps, men and women in wool much more often than silk, frequently worn and seldom ornamented. Older folk, mainly. Idrien was not the only one with more gray than black in her hair, or no black at all, or no hair at all, though here and there a younger face peered eagerly at Rand. Younger meaning ten or fifteen years older than he.

They were the teachers, in a way, though this was not exactly a school. Pupils did come to learn—young men and women hung gaping out of every window around the courtyard, now—but for the most part Rand had wanted to gather knowledge in one place. Time and again he had heard how much had been lost in the War of the Hundred Years and the Trolloc Wars. How much more must have vanished in the Breaking of the World? If he was going to Break the World again, he meant to create repositories where knowledge could be preserved. Another school had already started in Tear, though just barely, and he had begun seeking a place in Caemlyn.

Nothing ever goes as you expect, Lews Therin murmured. *Expect nothing, and you will not be surprised. Expect nothing. Hope for nothing. Nothing.*

Suppressing the voice, Rand dismounted.

Idrien came to meet him with a curtsy. As usual, when she rose it was something of a shock to realize yet again that she was barely as tall as his chest. "Welcome to the School of Cairhien, my Lord Dragon." Her voice was surprisingly sweet and youthful, a startling contrast to her blunt face. He had heard it harden, though, with students and teachers; Idrien held a tight rein on the school.

"How many spies do you have in the Sun Palace?" he asked mildly. She looked startled, perhaps that he would suggest such a thing, but more likely because the question was not proper manners in Cairhien.

"We have prepared a small display." Well, he had not really expected an answer. She eyed the two Aiel like a woman eyeing two large and muddy dogs of uncertain temperament, but contented herself with a sniff. "If my Lord Dragon will follow me?"

He followed, frowning. A display of what?

The entry hall of the school was a vast chamber of polished dark gray columns and pale gray floor tiles, with a gray-veined marble balcony all the way around three spans up. Now it was largely filled with . . . contraptions. The teachers crowding in behind him went running to them. Rand stared, suddenly remembering what Berelain had said about the school making things. But what?

Idrien told him—after a fashion—leading him from one to the next, where men and women explained what they had created. He even understood some of it.

An array of screens and scrapers and crocks full of linen scraps produced finer paper than anyone made now, or so its inventor said. A great hulking shape of levers and huge flat plates was a printing press, much better than those already in use, according to its maker. Dedric showed considerable interest in that, until Jalani apparently decided he should be watching for somebody trying to attack the *Car'a'carn*: she trod hard on his foot, and he limped after Rand. There was a plow on wheels meant to turn six furrows at once—Rand could recognize that, at least; he thought it might work—and another thing with shafts for horses that was meant to harvest hay in place of men with scythes, and a new sort of loom that was easier to operate, so the fellow who made it said. There were painted wooden models of viaducts to carry water to places where the wells were going dry, of new drains and sewers for Cairhien, even a tabletop exhibit with tiny figures of men and carts, cranes and rollers, meant to show how roads could be built and paved as well as they had in years long gone.

Rand did not know whether any of it would work, but some looked worth trying. That plow, for instance, could be handy if Cairhien was ever to feed itself again. He would tell Idrien to build it. No, he would tell Berelain to tell her. *Always follow lines of authority in public view*, Moiraine had said, *unless you mean to undercut someone and bring them down.*

Among the teachers he knew was Kin Tovere, a stocky lensmaker who kept wiping his bald head with a striped handkerchief. Aside from looking glasses in various sizes—"Count the hairs in a man's nose at a mile," he said; that was how he talked—he had a lens as big across as his head, a sketch of the looking glass to hold it and more like it, a thing six paces long, and a scheme for looking at the stars, of all things. Well, Kin always wanted to look at things far off.

Idrien wore a look of quiet satisfaction while Rand studied Master To-vere's sketch. She was not much for anything but the practical. During the siege of Cairhien, she herself had built a huge crossbow, all levers and pulleys, that hurled a small spear a full mile hard enough to drive through a man. Had she her way, there would be no time wasted on anything not real and solid.

"Build it," Rand told Kin. Maybe it was of no real use, not like the plow, but he liked Tovere. Idrien sighed and shook her head. Tovere beamed. "And I'm giving you a prize of a hundred gold crowns. This looks interesting." That produced a buzz, and it was close whether Idrien's jaw or Tovere's dropped farther.

Other things in the hall made Tovere seem as levelheaded as the would-be road-builder. The round-faced fellow who did something with cow dung that ended with a bluish flame burning at the end of a brass tube; even he did not seem to know what it was for. The lanky young woman whose display was mainly a shell of paper moored by strings and kept aloft by the heat rising from a small fire in a brazier. She mumbled something about flying—he was sure that was what she said—and birds' wings being curved—she had sketches of birds, and of what seemed to be *wooden* birds—but she was so tongue-tied meeting the Dragon Reborn that he could not understand another word, and Idrien certainly could not explain what it was about.

And then there was the balding man with an assemblage of brass tubes and cylinders, rods and wheels, all covering a heavy wooden table freshly gouged and scraped, some gouges nearly deep enough to pierce the table-top. For some reason half the man's face and one of his hands were swathed in bandages. As soon as Rand appeared in the entry hall, he had begun anxiously building a fire under one of the cylinders. When Rand and Idrien stopped in front of him, he moved a lever and smiled proudly.

The contraption began to quiver, steam hissing out from two or three places. The hiss grew to a shriek, and the thing began trembling. It groaned ominously. The shriek became ear-piercing. It shook so hard the table moved. The balding man threw himself at the table, fumbling a plug loose on the largest cylinder. Steam rushed out in a cloud, and the thing went still. Sucking burned fingers, the man managed a weak grin.

"Very nice brasswork," Rand said before letting Idrien lead him away. "What was that?" he asked quietly when they were out of earshot.

She shrugged. "Mervin will not tell anyone. Sometimes there are bangs in his rooms loud enough to make doors tremble, and he has scalded himself six times so far, but he claims it will bring a new Age when he makes it work." She glanced at Rand uneasily.

"Mervin is welcome to bring it if he can," he told her dryly. Maybe the thing was supposed to make music? All those shrieks? "I don't see Herid. Did he forget to come down?"

Idrien sighed again. Herid Fel was an Andoran who somehow had ended up reading in the Royal Library here—a student of history and philosophy, he called himself—and hardly the sort to endear himself to her. "My Lord Dragon, he never comes out of his study except to go to the Library."

Getting away required a small speech, delivered standing on a stool with the Dragon Scepter in the crook of his arm, telling them that their creations were wonderful. Some might be, for all he knew. Then he was able to slip off with Jalani and Dedric. And Lews Therin, and Alanna. They left behind a pleased babble. He wondered whether any besides Idrien had ever thought of making a weapon.

Herid Fel's study lay on an upper floor, where the view was of nothing much but the dark tile roofs of the school and one square, stepped tower that blocked off anything else. Herid claimed he never looked out of the windows anyway.

"You can wait out here," Rand said on reaching the narrow door—the room inside was narrow, too—and was surprised when Jalani and Dedric agreed right away.

A number of small things suddenly came together. Jalani had not given his sword one disapproving look, something she made a point of, since he came out of the meeting with Rhuarc and Berelain. Neither she nor Dedric had so much as glanced at the horse in the stable, or made a disparaging remark about how his own legs should be good enough for him, another thing she did regularly.

As if for confirmation, as Rand turned to the door, Jalani briefly eyed Dedric up and down. Briefly, but with decidedly open interest and a smile. Dedric ignored her so intently he might as well have stared. That was the Aiel way, pretending not to understand until she made herself clearer. She would have done the same had he begun the looking.

"Enjoy yourselves," Rand said over his shoulder, producing two startled stares, and went inside.

The small room was all books and scrolls and sheafs of paper, or so it appeared. Crowded shelves walled the room to the ceiling except for the doorway and two open windows. Books and papers covered the table that took up most of the floor, lay in a jumble on the extra chair, even here and there on the little remaining of the floor. Herid Fel himself was a stout man who looked as if he had forgotten to brush his thin gray hair this morning. The pipe clenched in his teeth was unlit, and pipe ash sprinkled the front of his rumpled brown coat.

He blinked at Rand for a moment, then said, "Ah. Yes. Of course. I was about to. . . ." He frowned at the book in his hands, then sat down behind the table and fingered through some loose sheets of paper in front of him, muttering quietly. Turning to the title page of the book, he scratched his head. Finally he looked back at Rand, and blinked in surprise again. "Oh, yes. What was it you wanted to talk about?"

Rand cleared the second chair, putting the books and papers on the floor, propped the Dragon Scepter on the pile and sat down. He had tried talking with others here, philosophers and historians, learned women and scholars, and it was like trying to pin down an Aes Sedai. They were very certain of what they were certain of, and about the rest they drowned you in words that could mean anything. They either grew angry when pressed— they seemed to think he was doubting their knowledge, apparently a deep sin—or they increased the torrent of words till he did not know what half of them meant, or they became obsequious, trying to find out what he wanted to hear so they could tell it to him. Herid was different. One of the things that always seemed to slip his mind was that Rand was the Dragon Reborn, which suited Rand very well. "What do you know about Aes Sedai and Warders, Herid? About the bond?"

"Warders? Bond? As much as anybody not Aes Sedai, I suppose. Which isn't saying much, mind." Herid sucked at his pipe, not seeming to realize it had gone out. "What did you want to know?"

"Can it be broken?"

"Broken? Oh, no. I don't think so. Unless you mean when the Warder or the Aes Sedai dies. That breaks it. I think. I remember hearing something about the bond once, but I can't remember. . . ." Catching sight of a sheaf of notes on his table, Herid drew it to him with his fingertips and began reading, frowning and shaking his head. The notes looked to be in his own hand, but he did not seem to agree with them anymore.

Rand sighed; he almost thought if he turned his head quickly enough, he would see Alanna's hand poised over him. "What about the question I posed you last time? Herid? Herid?"

The stout man's head jerked up. "Oh. Yes. Ah, question. Last time. Tarmon Gai'don. Well, I don't know what it will be like. Trollocs, I suppose? Dreadlords? Yes. Dreadlords. But I have been thinking. It can't be the Last Battle. I don't think it can. Maybe every Age has a Last Battle. Or most of them." Suddenly he frowned down his nose at the pipe in his teeth, and began rummaging across the table. "I have a tinderbox here somewhere."

"What do you mean it can't be the Last Battle?" Rand tried to keep his voice smooth. Herid always came to the point; you just had to prod him toward it.

"What? Yes, exactly the point. It can't be the Last Battle. Even if the Dragon Reborn seals the Dark One's prison again as well as the Creator made it. Which I don't think he can do." He leaned forward and lowered his voice conspiratorially. "He isn't the Creator, you know, whatever they say in the streets. Still, it has to be sealed up again by somebody. The Wheel, you see."

"I don't see. . . ." Rand trailed off.

"Yes, you do. You'd make a good student." Snatching his pipe out, Herid drew a circle in the air with the stem. "The Wheel of Time. Ages come and go and come again as the Wheel turns. All the catechism."

Suddenly he stabbed a point on that imaginary wheel. "Here the Dark One's prison is whole. Here, they drilled a hole in it, and sealed it up again." He moved the bit of the pipe along the arc he had drawn. "Here we are. The seal's weakening. But that doesn't matter, of course." The pipestem completed the circle. "When the Wheel turns back to here, back to where they drilled the hole in the first place, the Dark One's prison has to be whole again."

"Why? Maybe the next time they'll drill through the patch. Maybe that's how they could do it the last time—drill into what the Creator made, I mean—maybe they drilled the Bore through a patch and we just don't know."

Herid shook his head. For a moment he stared at his pipe, once more realizing it was unlit, and Rand thought he might have to recall him again, but instead Herid blinked and went on. "Someone had to make it sometime. For the first time, that is. Unless you think the Creator made the Dark One's prison with a hole and patch to begin." His eyebrows waggled at the suggestion. "No, it was whole in the beginning, and I think it will be whole again when the Third Age comes once more. Hmmm. I wonder if *they* called it the Third Age?" He hastily dipped a pen and scribbled a note in the margins of an open book. "Umph. No matter now. I'm not saying the Dragon Reborn will be the one to make it whole, not in this Age necessarily anyway, but it must be so before the Third Age comes again, and enough time passed since it was made whole—an Age, at least—that no one remembers the Dark One or his prison. No one remembers. Um. I wonder. . . ." He peered at his notes and scratched his head, then seemed startled to find he used the hand holding the pen. There was a smudge of ink in his hair. "Any Age where seals weaken must remember the Dark One eventually, because they will have to face him and wall him up again." Sticking his pipe back between his teeth, he tried to make another note without dipping the pen.

"Unless the Dark One breaks free," Rand said quietly. "To break the Wheel of Time, and remake Time and the world in his own image."

"There is that." Herid shrugged, frowning at the pen. Finally he thought of the inkpot. "I don't suppose there's much you or I can do about it. Why don't you come study here with me? I don't suppose Tarmon Gai'don will happen tomorrow, and it would be as good a use of your time as—"

"Is there any reason you can think of to break the seals?"

Herid's eyebrows shot up. "Break the seals? Break the seals? Why would anyone but a madman want to do that? Can they even be broken?

I seem to remember reading somewhere they can't, but I don't recall now that it said why. What made you think of a thing like that?"

"I don't know," Rand sighed. In the back of his head Lews Therin was chanting. *Break the seals. Break the seals, and end it. Let me die forever.*

Fanning herself idly with a corner of her shawl, Egwene peered both ways down the crossing hallway, hoping she had not gotten lost again. She was very much afraid she had, and not pleased if it was so. The Sun Palace had miles of corridor, none much cooler than outside, and she had spent little time in them to learn her way.

There were Maidens everywhere in twos and threes—far more than Rand normally brought with him; certainly far more than usual when he was not there. They simply appeared to be strolling, but to her something about them seemed . . . furtive. A number knew her by sight, and she might have expected a friendly word—the Maidens especially seemed to have decided that being a pupil of the Wise Ones outweighed being Aes Sedai, as they thought she was, to the point that she was not Aes Sedai any longer—but when they saw her, they looked as startled as an Aiel was likely to look. Acknowledging nods came a beat late, and they hurried on without speaking. It was not behavior conducive to asking directions.

Instead she frowned at a sweaty-faced servant with thin blue and gold stripes on his cuffs, wondering whether he knew how to get where she wanted to go from here. The difficulty was, she was not exactly sure where it was she did want to go. Unfortunately, the fellow was plainly on edge with so many Aiel about. Seeing an Aiel woman frowning at him— they never seemed to notice her dark eyes, which certainly no Aiel had— and his head probably full of tales about the Maidens, he turned and ran as hard as he could.

She sniffed irritably. She did not really need directions anyway. Sooner or later she had to come on something she recognized. Certainly no point in going back the way she had come, but which of the other three? Choosing one, she strode off firmly, and even some of the Maidens stepped out of her way.

In truth, she was feeling a bit grumpy. Seeing Aviendha again after all this time would have been wonderful, if the woman had not simply nodded to her coolly and ducked into a private conference in Amys' tent. Private indeed, Egwene learned when she tried to follow.

You were not summoned, Amys had said sharply, while Aviendha sat cross-legged on a cushion, staring dejectedly at the layered carpets in front of her. *Go and take a walk. And eat something. A woman is not meant to look like a reed.*

Bair and Melaine had come hurrying, summoned by *gai'shain*, but Egwene was excluded. It had helped a little seeing a string of Wise Ones turned away too, though only a little. After all, she was Aviendha's friend, and if she was in some sort of trouble, Egwene wanted to help.

"Why are you here?" Sorilea's voice demanded behind her.

Egwene was proud of herself. She turned calmly to face the Wise One of Shende Hold. A Jarra Chareen, Sorilea had thin white hair and a face that was leathery skin pulled tight over her skull. She was all sinew and bone, and though she could channel, she had less strength in the Power than most novices Egwene had met. In fact, in the Tower, she certainly would never have gone beyond novice before being sent away. Of course, channeling did not really count for much among Wise Ones. Whatever the mysterious rules governing Wise Ones, when Sorilea was about, leadership always settled on her. Egwene thought it was pure strength of will.

A good head taller than Egwene, as most Aielwomen were, Sorilea stared at her with a green-eyed gaze that could knock a bull off its feet. That was a relief; it was Sorilea's normal way of looking at everyone. Had she a bone to pick, the walls would have been crumbling wherever she looked and tapestries catching fire. Well, that was how it seemed, anyway.

"I've come to see Rand," Egwene said. "Walking in from the tents seemed as good exercise as any." Certainly better that walking five or six times briskly around the city walls, the usual Aiel notion of light exercise. She hoped Sorilea did not ask why. She truly did not like lying to any of the Wise Ones.

Sorilea stared at her a moment as if she had sniffed something hidden, then hitched her shawl up on narrow shoulders and said, "He is not here. He has gone to his school. Berelain Paeron suggests it would not be wise to follow him, and I agree."

Keeping her face smooth was an effort for Egwene. That the Wise Ones would take to Berelain had been the last thing she expected. They treated her as a woman of sense and respect, which made no sense *at all* to Egwene, and not because Rand had given her authority. They cared not a twig for any wetlander authority. It seemed ridiculous. The Mayener woman flaunted herself in scandalous clothes and flirted outrageously— when she did not do more than flirt, as Egwene darkly believed she did.

Not at all the sort of woman for Amys to smile on like a favorite daughter. Or Sorilea.

Unbidden thoughts of Gawyn floated up in her head. It had only been a dream, and his dream at that. Certainly nothing like what Berelain did.

"When a young woman's cheeks redden for no apparent reason," Sorilea said, "there is usually a man involved. What man has attracted your interest? Can we expect to see you lay a bridal wreath at his feet soon?"

"Aes Sedai seldom marry," Egwene told her coolly.

The leather-faced woman's snort sounded like cloth ripping. The Maidens and the Wise Ones, indeed all the Aiel, might have decided she was not Aes Sedai so long as she studied with Amys and the others, but Sorilea took it further. She seemed to think Egwene had become Aiel. Added to which, there was nowhere Sorilea did not think she had a right to stick a finger. "You will, girl. You are not one to become *Far Dareis Mai* and think men are a sport like hunting, if that. Those hips were made for babies, and you will have them."

"Will you tell me where I can wait for Rand?" Egwene asked, more faintly than she would have liked. Sorilea was not a dreamwalker, able to interpret dreams, and she certainly had none of the Foretelling, but she could be so definite that what she said seemed inevitable. Gawyn's babies. Light, how could she have Gawyn's babies? In truth, Aes Sedai almost never married. Rare was the man who wanted to marry a woman who, with the Power, could handle him like a child if she chose.

"This way," Sorilea said. "Is it Sanduin, that strapping True Blood I saw around Amys' tent yesterday? That scar makes the rest of his face more handsome. . . ."

Sorilea continued to come up with names as she led Egwene through the palace, always watching from the corner of a shrewd eye for any reaction. She also did her best to list each man's charms, and since this included describing what he looked like without clothes—Aiel men and women shared the same sweat tents—she certainly got enough blushes.

By the time they reached the rooms where Rand would be spending the night, Egwene was more than glad to offer hasty thanks and firmly shut the sitting room door on her. Luckily, the Wise One must have had business of her own to see to, or she might well have pushed her way in.

Drawing a deep breath, Egwene began smoothing her skirts and adjusting her shawl. They did not need it, but she felt as if she had been tumbled downhill. The woman more than liked to play matchmaker. She was capable of fashioning the bridal wreath for a woman, dragging her to lay it at the feet of the man Sorilea had chosen, and twisting his arm until he picked it up. Well, not exactly dragging and arm-twisting, but it came to the same thing. Of course, Sorilea would not take it that far with her. The thought made her giggle. After all, Sorilea did not really think she had become Aiel; she knew Egwene was Aes Sedai, or thought she was anyway. No, of course there was no reason to worry over that!

With her hands on the folded gray scarf that held her hair back, she froze at the sound of soft footsteps in the bedchamber. If Rand could leap about from Caemlyn to Cairhien, perhaps he had leaped straight to his bedchamber. And perhaps someone—or something—was waiting for him. She embraced *saidar* and wove several nasty things, ready to use. A *gai'shain* woman came out, arms full of bundled sheets, and gave a start at the sight of her. Egwene released *saidar* and hoped she was not blushing again.

Niella looked enough like Aviendha to startle at first glance in that deep-cowled white robe. Until you realized you had to add six or seven years to a face that was perhaps not quite so tanned, perhaps a little plumper. Aviendha's sister had never been a Maiden of the Spear; a weaver instead, she had completed well over half her year and a day.

Egwene offered no greeting; it would only embarrass Niella. "Do you expect Rand soon?" she asked.

"The *Car'a'carn* will come when he comes," Niella replied, eyes meekly downcast. That truly appeared odd; Aviendha's face, even plumper, did not go well with meekness. "It is for us to be ready when he comes."

"Niella, do you have any idea why Aviendha would need to closet herself with Amys and Bair and Melaine?" It certainly had nothing to do with dreamwalking; Sorilea had as much ability there as Aviendha.

"She is here? No, I know no reason." But Niella's blue-green eyes narrowed slightly as soon as she spoke.

"You do know something," Egwene insisted. She might as well take advantage of *gai'shain* obedience. "Tell me what it is, Niella."

"I know that Aviendha will stripe me till I cannot sit if the *Car'a'carn* finds me standing here with dirty bedding," Niella said ruefully. Egwene did not know whether *ji'e'toh* was involved somehow, yet when they were together, Aviendha held her sister twice as strictly to account as any other *gai'shain*.

Niella's robe trailed across the patterned carpet as she glided hurriedly toward the door, but Egwene caught her sleeve. "When your time is up, will you put off the white?"

It was not a proper question, and meekness vanished in pride enough for any Maiden. "To do otherwise mocks *ji'e'toh*," Niella said stiffly. Abruptly a slight smile flickered on her lips. "Besides, my husband would come looking for me, and he would not be pleased." The mild mask returned; her eyes turned down. "May I go now? If Aviendha is here, I would not meet her can I avoid it, and she will come to these chambers."

Egwene let her go. She had had no right to ask anyway; speaking of a *gai'shain's* life before the white, or after, was shaming. She felt a little ashamed herself, though of course she did not really try to follow *ji'e'toh*. Only enough to be polite.

Alone, she settled into a severely carved and gilded armchair, finding it strangely uncomfortable after so long sitting cross-legged on cushions or the ground. Tucking her legs beneath her, she wondered what Aviendha was discussing with Amys and the other two. Rand, almost certainly. He always concerned the Wise Ones. They did not care about the wetlander Prophecies of the Dragon, but they knew the Prophecy of Rhuidean back to front. When he destroyed the Aiel, as that prophecy said he would, "a remnant of a remnant" would be saved, and they intended to see that the remnant was as large as possible.

That was why they made Aviendha stay close to him. Too close for decency. If she went into the bedchamber, she was sure she would find a pallet made up on the floor for Aviendha. Still, Aiel saw such things differently. The Wise Ones meant Aviendha to teach him Aiel ways and customs, to remind him that his blood was Aiel if not his upbringing. Apparently the Wise Ones thought that needed *every* waking hour, and considering what they faced, she could not fault them entirely. Not entirely. Just the same, it was not decent, making a woman sleep in the same room with a man.

Still, she could do nothing about Aviendha's problem, especially when Aviendha did not seem to see the problem. Leaning on her elbow, Egwene tried to think of how she was going to approach Rand. Her mind went round and round, but she had not settled on anything by the time he entered, murmuring something to two Aiel in the hallway before shutting the door.

Egwene bounded to her feet. "Rand, you have to help me with the Wise Ones; they'll listen to you," she burst out before she could stop herself. That was *not* what she had intended at all.

"It is good to see you again too," he said, smiling. He was carrying that length of Seanchan spear, carved with Dragons since she saw it last. She wished she knew where he had gotten the thing; anything Seanchan made her skin crawl. "I am well, thank you, Egwene. And you? You look to be yourself again, full of ginger as ever." He looked so tired. And hard, hard enough to make that smile appear odd. He seemed harder every time she saw him.

"You needn't think you're amusing," she glowered. Best to go on as she had begun. Better than backing and filling, giving him more reason to grin. "Will you help me?"

"How?" Making himself at home—well, they were his rooms—he tossed the tasseled spearhead on a small table with leopard-carved legs and shed his sword belt and coat. Somehow he was not sweating any more than the Aiel did. "The Wise Ones listen to me, but they only hear what they want to. I've come to recognize that flat-eyed look they get when they decide I'm talking nonsense, and instead of embarrassing me by saying so, or arguing about it, they'll just ignore it." He pulled one of the gilded chairs around to face her and sprawled in it, booted feet stretched in front of him. He managed to do even that with an air of arrogance. He definitely had too many people bowing to him.

"You do talk nonsense sometimes," she muttered. For some reason, having no more time to think concentrated her thoughts. Adjusting her shawl carefully, she placed herself in front of him. "I know that you would like to hear from Elayne again." Why did his face go all sad like that, and at the same time winter cold? Likely because he had not heard from Elayne in so long. "I doubt Sheriam has been giving the Wise Ones very many messages from her for you." None, so far as she knew, though he had seldom been in Cairhien to receive any. "I'm the one Elayne will trust with that sort of missive. I can bring them to you, if you convince Amys that I'm strong enough to . . . to return to my studies."

She wished she had not faltered, but he already knew too much about dreamwalking, if not *Tel'aran'rhiod*. Almost everything about dreamwalking but the name was a close secret among the Wise Ones, particularly those who could dreamwalk. She had no right to give away their secrets.

"Will you tell me where Elayne is?" He might have been asking for a cup of tea.

She hesitated, but the agreement between her, Nynaeve and Elayne—Light, how long ago had they made it?—that agreement held. He was no longer the boy she had grown up with. He was a man full of himself, and whatever his tone, those steady eyes on her face *demanded* an answer. If Aes Sedai and Wise Ones struck sparks, Aes Sedai and he would strike a conflagration. There had to be a buffer between the two, and the only buffers available were the three of them. It had to be done, but she hoped they did not get burned up doing it. "I can't tell you that, Rand. I have no right. It isn't mine to tell." And that was the truth, too. For that matter, it was not as if she could tell him where this Salidar was, beyond Altara, somewhere along the River Eldar.

He leaned forward intently. "I know she's with Aes Sedai. You told me those Aes Sedai support me, or might. Are they afraid of me? I will take oath to stay away from them, if they are. Egwene, I mean to give Elayne the Lion Throne and the Sun Throne. She has claim to both; Cairhien will accept her as quickly as Andor does. I need her, Egwene."

Egwene opened her mouth—and realized that she was about to tell him all she knew about Salidar. Barely in time she clamped her teeth shut so hard her jaws ached, and opened herself to *saidar*. The sweet feel of life, so strong it overwhelmed everything else, seemed to help; slowly the urge to talk began to ebb.

He sat back with a sigh, and she stared at him wide-eyed. It was one thing to know he was the strongest *ta'veren* since Artur Hawkwing, but quite something else to become caught up in it herself. It was all she could do not to hug herself and shiver.

"You won't tell me," he said. Not a question. Briskly he rubbed his forearms through his shirtsleeves, reminding her that she held *saidar*; close like this, he would be feeling it as a faint tingle. "Do you think I meant to force it out of you?" he snapped, suddenly angry. "Am I such a monster now that you need the Power to protect yourself from me?"

"I don't need anything to protect me from you," she said as calmly as she could. Her stomach was still turning over slowly. He was Rand, and he was a man who could channel. A part of her wanted to gibber and wail. She was ashamed of it, but that did not make it go away. Putting away *saidar*, she regretted a tinge of reluctance. Yet it did not matter; if it came to that sort of struggle, unless she managed to shield him he would handle her as easily as if they arm-wrestled. "Rand, I am sorry I can't help you, but I cannot. Even so, I ask you again to help me. You know it would be helping yourself."

His anger was swallowed by a maddening grin; it was frightening how quickly that could happen with him. " 'A cat for a hat, or a hat for a cat,' " he quoted.

But nothing for nothing, she finished mentally. She had heard Taren Ferry folk say that when she was a girl. "You put your cat in your hat and stuff it down your breeches, Rand al'Thor," she told him coldly. She managed not to slam the door on her way out, but it was a near thing.

Striding away, she wondered what she was going to do. Somehow she had to convince the Wise Ones to let her back into *Tel'aran'rhiod*—legally, so to speak. Sooner or later he was going to encounter the Aes Sedai of Salidar, and it would help so much if she could talk to Elayne or Nynaeve again first. She was a little surprised that Salidar had not approached him already; what was holding Sheriam and the rest back? Nothing she could do about it, and they probably knew better than she.

One thing she was eager to tell Elayne. Rand needed her. He sounded as if he meant that more than anything he had ever said in his life. That should set to rest all her worries about whether he still loved her. No man could say he needed you that way unless he loved you.

For a few moments Rand sat staring at the door after it closed behind Egwene. She had changed so much from the girl he grew up with. In those Aiel clothes she managed a good imitation of a Wise One—except for the height, anyway; a short Wise One, with big dark eyes—but then, Egwene always did everything with her whole heart. She had stayed as cool as any Aes Sedai, seizing *saidar* when she thought he was threatening her. That was what he had to remember. Whatever clothes she wore, she wanted to be Aes Sedai, and she would keep Aes Sedai secrets even after he made it clear that he needed Elayne to insure peace in two nations. He had to think of her as Aes Sedai. It was saddening.

Wearily he got to his feet and donned his coat again. There were still the Cairhienin nobles to see, Colavaere and Maringil, Dobraine and the rest. And the Tairens; Meilan and Aracome and that lot would twitch if he gave the Cairhienin a moment more than they got. And the Wise Ones would want their turn at him, and Timolan and the rest of the clan chiefs here he had not met with yet today. Why had he ever wanted to leave Caemlyn? Well, talking with Herid had been pleasant; the questions he brought up were not, but it was nice to talk to someone who never remembered he was the Dragon Reborn. And he had found a little time without a coterie of Aiel surrounding him; he was going to find more of that.

He caught sight of himself in a gilt-framed mirror. "At least you didn't let her see you were tired," he told his reflection. That had been one of

Moiraine's more succinct bits of advice. *Never let them see you weaken.* He just had to become used to thinking of Egwene as one of them.

Apparently squatting at her ease in the garden below Rand al'Thor's rooms, Sulin tossed a small knife into the dirt, seemingly amusing herself with a game of flip. A rock owl's cry from one of the windows brought her to her feet with an oath, slipping the knife behind her belt. Rand al'Thor had left his rooms again. Keeping watch over him this way was not going to work. If she had Enaila or Somara here, she would set them on him. Normally she tried to protect him from that sort of nonsense as she would a first-brother.

Trotting to the nearest doorway, she joined three more Maidens—none had come with her—and began to search the warren of corridors while trying to appear just to be walking. Whatever the *Car'a'carn* wanted, nothing must happen to the only son of a Maiden ever to come back to them.

CHAPTER
19

Matters of Toh

Rand thought that he would sleep well that night. He was nearly tired enough to forget Alanna's touch, and more important, Aviendha was out in the tents with the Wise Ones, not undressing for bed with no regard for his presence, not disturbing his rest with the sound of her breathing. Something else made him toss, though. Dreams. He always warded his dreams, to keep the Forsaken out—and the Wise Ones—but warding could not keep out what was already inside. Dreams came of huge white things like giant birdwings without the bird, sailing across the sky; of great cities of impossibly tall buildings, shining in the sun, with shapes like beetles and flattened water-drops speeding along the streets. He had seen all that before, inside the huge *ter'angreal* in Rhuidean where he had gained the Dragons on his arms, and knew them for images of the Age of Legends, but this time it was all different. Everything seemed twisted, the colors . . . wrong, as though something had gone askew in his eyes. The sho-wings faltered and fell, each carrying hundreds to death. Buildings shattered like glass, cities burned, the land heaved like storm-tossed seas. And time after time he faced a beautiful golden-haired woman, watched love turn to terror on her face. Part of him knew her. Part of him wanted to save her, from the Dark One, from any harm, from what he himself was about to do. So many parts of him, mind splintered in glittering shards, all screaming.

407

He woke in darkness, sweating, shaking. Lews Therin's dreams. That had never happened before, not dreaming the man's dreams. He lay there the hours remaining until sunrise, staring at nothing, afraid to close his eyes. He held on to *saidin* as if he could use it to fight the dead man, but Lews Therin remained silent.

When pale light finally appeared at the windows, a *gai'shain* slipped silently into the room with a cloth-covered silver tray. Seeing Rand awake, he did not speak, only bowed and left just as quietly. With the Power in him, Rand smelled cool sweetberry tea and warm bread, butter and honey, the hot porridge Aiel ate mornings, all as if his nose were in the tray. Releasing the Source, he dressed and buckled on his sword. He did not touch the cloth covering the food; he did not much feel like eating. Holding the Dragon Scepter in the crook of his elbow, he left his apartments.

The Maidens were back in the wide corridor with Sulin, and Urien and his Red Shields, but not alone. People crowded the hallway shoulder to shoulder beyond the guards. And some inside the ring. Aviendha stood among a delegation of Wise Ones, Amys and Bair and Melaine, Sorilea of course, Chaelin, a Smoke Water Miagoma with touches of gray in her dark red hair, and Edarra, a Neder Shiande who looked not much older than himself, though she already had an apparently unshakable calm in her blue eyes and a straight-backed presence to match the others. Berelain was with them, too, but not Rhuarc or any of the other clan chiefs. What he had had to say to them had been said, and Aiel did not draw things out. But then, why were the Wise Ones there? Or Berelain? The green-and-white dress she wore this morning showed a pleasant expanse of pale bosom.

Then there were the Cairhienin, outside the ring of Aiel. Colavaere, strikingly handsome in her middle years, dark hair an elaborate tower of curls and horizontal slashes coloring her gown from high gold-embroidered collar to below her knees, more slashes than anyone else present. Solid, square-faced Dobraine, the front of his mostly gray hair shaved soldier-fashion and his coat worn from the straps of a breastplate. Maringil, straight as a blade, white hair touching his shoulders; he had not shaved his forehead, and his dark silk coat, striped like Dobraine's nearly to his knees, was fit for a ball. Two dozen or more clustered behind, mostly younger men and women, few wearing horizontal stripes even as low as the waist. "Grace favor the Lord Dragon," they murmured, bowing hand to heart or curtsying, and, "Grace honors us with the Lord Dragon's presence."

The Tairens had their contingent as well, High Lords and Ladies with-

out lesser nobles, in peaked velvet hats and silk coats with puffy, satin-
striped sleeves, in bright gowns with broad lace ruffs and close-fitting caps
of pearls or gems, making their respects with "The Light illumine the
Lord Dragon." Meilan stood foremost, of course, lean and hard and expressionless, with his gray pointed beard. Close beside him, Fionnda's stern
expression and iron eyes somehow did not diminish her beauty, while willowy Anaiyella's simpers lessened hers. There were certainly no smiles of
any sort on the faces of Maraconn, a blue-eyed rarity among Tairens, or
bald Gueyam, or Aracome, who looked twice as slender alongside Gueyam's solid width if just as steely. They—and Meilan—had been thick with
Hearne and Simaan. Rand had not mentioned those two yesterday, or their
treason, but he was sure it was known here, and equally sure his silence was
given meaning according to each man's own mind. They had grown used to
such since coming to Cairhien, and this morning they watched Rand as if
he might suddenly produce orders for their arrest.

In truth, nearly everyone was watching someone. A good many eyed
the Aiel nervously, often hiding anger with varying success. Others watched
Berelain almost as closely; he was surprised to see that even the men, even
the Tairens, had more thought than lechery on their faces. Most watched
him, of course; he was who he was, and what he was. Colavaere's cool gaze
shifted between him and Aviendha, where it heated; there was bad blood
there, though Aviendha seemed to have forgotten. Colavaere would certainly never forget the beating she had received from Aviendha after being
discovered in Rand's rooms, or forgive the fact that it was common knowledge now. Meilan and Maringil each made his awareness of the other plain
by avoiding the other's eyes. Both wanted the throne of Cairhien, and both
thought the other his chief rival. Dobraine watched Meilan and Maringil,
though why was anyone's guess. Melaine studied Rand, while Sorilea studied *her*, and Aviendha frowned at the floor. One big-eyed young woman
among the Cairhienin wore her hair loose and cut off at the shoulder instead of piled in ornate curls, and a sword belted over a dark riding dress
with only six slashes of color. Many of the others did not bother to hide
disparaging smiles when they glanced at her; she hardly seemed to notice,
alternating between staring at the Maidens with stark admiration or at
Rand with stark fear. He remembered her. Selande, one of the stream of
beautiful women Colavaere had thought would tie the Dragon Reborn to
her schemes, until Rand convinced her it would not work. With Aviendha's
unasked help, unfortunately. He hoped Colavaere feared him enough to
forget revenge on Aviendha, but he wished he could make Selande believe

she had nothing to fear. *You cannot please everyone*, Moiraine had said. *You cannot soothe everyone.* A hard woman.

To cap it all, the Aiel watched everyone except the Wise Ones, of course. And except Berelain, for some reason. They always eyed wetlanders suspiciously, yet she might as well have been another Wise One.

"You all honor me." Rand hoped he did not sound too dry. Back to a parade. He wondered where Egwene was. Probably lolling in bed. Briefly he considered finding her and making one last effort to. . . . No, if she would not tell, he did not know how to make her. Too bad being *ta'veren* did not work when he most wanted it to. "Unfortunately, I will not be able to talk with you more this morning. I am returning to Caemlyn." Andor was the problem he had to deal with now. Andor, and Sammael.

"Your orders are to be carried out, my Lord Dragon," Berelain said. "This morning, so you may witness it."

"My orders?"

"Mangin," she said. "He was told this morning." Most of the Wise Ones had donned a flat expression, but Bair and Sorilea both wore open disapproval. Surprisingly, it was directed at Berelain.

"I don't mean to be a witness to every murderer who's hung," Rand said coldly. In truth, he had forgotten, or rather shoved it out of his mind. Hanging a man you liked was not something anyone would want to remember. Rhuarc and the other chiefs had not even mentioned it when he spoke with them. Another truth was that he would not make this execution special. Aiel had to live by the law like anyone else; Cairhienin and Tairens had to see that, and know that if he would not play favorites with the Aiel, he certainly would not with them. *You use everything and everybody*, he thought, sickened; at least, he hoped he had thought it. Besides, he did not want to watch any hanging; much less Mangin's.

Meilan certainly looked thoughtful, and sweat was beading on Aracome's forehead, though that might have been the heat. Colavaere, face going pale, seemed to be seeing him for the first time ever. Berelain divided a rueful glance between Bair and Sorilea, who nodded; could they have told her he would answer as he had? It did not seem possible. The others' reactions varied from surprise to satisfaction, but he noted Selande in particular. Wide-eyed, she forgot the Maidens; if she had looked at Rand fearfully before, now she was terrified. Well, so be it.

"I will be leaving for Caemlyn immediately," Rand told them. A soft sound rippled among the Cairhienin and Tairens, very much like sighs of relief.

It was no surprise that they all accompanied him as far as the chamber set aside for his Traveling. Except for Berelain, the Maidens and Red Shields kept the wetlanders back; they did not particularly like letting Cairhienin near him, and he was as glad as they barred the Tairens today. There were plenty of glares, but no one said anything, not to him. Not even Berelain, who followed right behind with the Wise Ones and Aviendha, talking quietly, occasionally laughing softly. That made the hair on his neck stand, Berelain and Aviendha talking together. And laughing?

At the square-carved door to the Traveling chamber, he looked carefully above Berelain's head as she swept him a deep curtsy. "I will tend Cairhien without fear or favor until you return, my Lord Dragon." Perhaps, despite Mangin, she really had come this morning just to say that, and be heard by the other nobles. It brought an indulgent smile from Sorilea for some reason. He needed to find out what was going on there; he was not going to have the Wise Ones interfering with Berelain. The rest of the Wise Ones had drawn Aviendha aside; they seemed to be taking turns speaking to her, quite firmly though he could not make out words. "When you see Perrin Aybarra next," Berelain added, "please give him my warmest wishes. And Mat Cauthon, also."

"We await the Lord Dragon's return eagerly," Colavaere lied, keeping her face carefully neutral.

Meilan glared at her for having managed to speak first, and made a flowery speech, saying no more really than she had, which Maringil of course had to top, for floweriness at least. Fionnda and Anaiyella outdid both, adding enough compliments that he eyed Aviendha anxiously, but the Wise Ones still had her occupied. Dobraine contented himself with, "Until my Lord Dragon's return," while Maraconn, Gueyam and Aracome murmured something indistinct with wary eyes.

It was a relief to duck inside, away from them. The surprise came when Melaine followed him ahead of Aviendha. He raised a questioning eyebrow.

"I must consult with Bael on business of the Wise Ones," she told him in a no-nonsense voice, then immediately shot a sharp look at Aviendha, who had on such an innocent face that Rand knew she was hiding something. Aviendha looked many things naturally, but never innocent; never that innocent.

"As you wish," he said. He suspected the Wise Ones had been waiting a chance to send her to Caemlyn. Who better to make sure Rand did not influence Bael the wrong way than Bael's wife? Like Rhuarc, the man had two, which Mat always said was either a dream or a nightmare and he could not decide which.

Aviendha watched closely as he opened a gateway back to Caemlyn, into the Grand Hall. She usually did, though she could not see his flows. Once she had made a gateway herself, but in a rare moment of panic, and she had never been able to remember how. Today for some reason the rotating slash of light apparently reminded her of what happened that time; red suffused her tan cheeks, and she suddenly refused to look in his direction. With the Power filling him, he smelled her, the herbal scent of her soap, a hint of sweet perfume he could not remember her wearing before. For once truly eager to be rid of *saidin*, he was the first one through into the empty throne room. Alanna seemed to crash home in his head, her presence as palpable as if she had been right in front of him. She had been weeping, he thought. Because he had gone away? Well, let her weep for that. Somehow he had to break free of her.

His going first did not sit well with the Maidens or Red Shields, of course. Urien merely grunted and shook his head disapprovingly. A white-faced Sulin went up on her toes to put herself nose-to-nose with Rand. "The great and powerful *Car'a'carn* gave his honor to *Far Dareis Mai* to carry," she all but hissed in a low whisper. "If the mighty *Car'a'carn* dies in ambush while the Maidens protect him, *Far Dareis Mai* has no honor left. If the all-conquering *Car'a'carn* does not care, perhaps Enaila is right. Perhaps the omnipotent *Car'a'carn* is a willful boy who should be held by the hand lest he run over a cliff because he will not look."

Rand's jaw tightened. In private he gritted his teeth and put up with this—with less pointed than this, usually—for the debt he owed the Maidens, but not even Enaila or Somara had ever openly berated him in public. Melaine was already halfway down the hall, skirts gathered up and almost trotting; apparently she could not wait to reestablish the Wise Ones' influence with Bael. He could not tell whether Urien had heard, though the man seemed awfully intent on directing his veiled *Aethan Dor* as they searched through the columns with the Maidens, something they had no need of direction to do. Aviendha, on the other hand, arms folded beneath her breasts, wore such a mix of frown and approval that he had no doubts about her.

"Yesterday went very well," he told Sulin firmly. "From now on, I think two guards will be more than sufficient." Her eyes almost bulged; she could not seem to find breath to speak. Now that he had taken away, it was time to give back, before she exploded like an Illuminator's fireworks. "It's different when I go outside the Palace, of course. The guard you have been giving me will do then, but here, or in the Sun Palace or the Stone of Tear, two are enough." He turned away while her mouth still worked silently.

Aviendha fell in beside him as he walked around the dais holding the thrones to the small doors behind. He had come here instead of straight to his own rooms in hope that he could lose her. Even without *saidin* he could smell her, or maybe it was the memory. Either way, he wished his head were clogged with a cold; he liked the smell too much.

Shawl wrapped around her tightly, Aviendha stared straight ahead of her as if troubled, not noticing when he held the door into one of the lion-paneled dressing rooms for her, something that usually aroused at least a little ire, perhaps a tart question as to which of her arms was broken. When he asked what was the matter, she gave a start. "Nothing. Sulin was right. But. . . ." Suddenly she gave a reluctant grin. "Did you see her face? No one has set her down like that since . . . since never, I think. Not even Rhuarc."

"I'm a little surprised to find you on my side."

She stared at him with those big eyes. He could spend all day just trying to decide whether they were blue or green. No. He had no right to think about her eyes. What had happened after she made that doorway—to run from him—made no difference. He especially had no right to think about that.

"You trouble me so, Rand al'Thor," she said without a bit of heat. "Light, sometimes I think the Creator made you just to trouble me."

He wanted to tell her it was her own fault—more than once he had offered to send her back to the Wise Ones, though it would just mean them putting someone else in her place—but before he could open his mouth, Jalani and Liah caught up, followed almost immediately by two Red Shields, one a graying fellow with three times the scars Liah had on her face. Rand directed Jalani and the scarred man back to the throne room, which nearly precipitated an argument. Not from the Red Shield, who merely glanced at his fellow, shrugged and went, but Jalani drew herself up.

Rand pointed to the door leading to the Grand Hall. "The *Car'a'carn* expects *Far Dareis Mai* to go where he commands."

"You may be a king to the wetlanders, Rand al'Thor, but not to Aiel." A tough sullenness marred Jalani's dignity, reminding him how young she was. "The Maidens will never fail you in the dance of spears, but this is not the dance." Still, she went, after a rapid exchange of handtalk with Liah.

With Liah and the lean Red Shield, a yellow-haired man named Cassin who stood a good inch taller than Rand, Rand strode quickly through the palace to his rooms. And with Aviendha, of course. If he had thought those bulky skirts might make her fall behind, he was mistaken. Liah and Cassin remained in the hallway outside his sitting room, a large chamber with a marble frieze of lions below the high ceiling and tapestries of hunting scenes and misty mountains, but Aviendha followed him inside.

"Shouldn't you be with Melaine?" he demanded. "Business of the Wise Ones and all that?"

"No," she said curtly. "Melaine would not be pleased if I interfered right now."

Light, but *he* should not be pleased that she was not going. Tossing the Dragon Scepter atop a table with gilded vine-carved legs, he undid his sword belt and added that. "Did Amys and the others tell you where Elayne is?"

For a long moment Aviendha stood in the middle of the blue-tiled floor looking at him, her expression unreadable. "They do not know," she said finally. "I asked." He had expected she would. She had not done it in months, but before coming to Caemlyn the first time with him, every second word out of her mouth had been a reminder that he belonged to Elayne. In her view he did, and what had happened between them beyond that gateway she had made clearly did not alter the fact, and would not happen again, something else she had made quite clear. Exactly as he wanted it; he was worse than a pig to feel regret. Ignoring all the fine gilded chairs, she settled cross-legged on the floor, arranging her skirts gracefully. "They did speak of you, though."

"Why does that not surprise me?" he said dryly, and to his surprise her cheeks reddened. Aviendha was not a woman for blushes, and this made twice in one day.

"They have shared dreams, some of which concern you." She sounded slightly strangled until she paused to clear her throat, then fixed him with a steady, determined gaze. "Melaine and Bair dreamed of you on a boat," she said, the word still awkward after all these months in the wetlands, "with three women whose faces they could not see, and a scale tilting first one way then the other. Melaine and Amys dreamed of a man standing by your side with a dagger to your throat, but you did not see him. Bair and Amys dreamed of you cutting the wetlands in two with a sword." For an instant her eyes darted contemptuously to the scabbarded blade lying atop the Dragon Scepter. Contemptuously, and a bit guiltily. She had given him that, once the property of King Laman, carefully wrapped in a blanket so she could not be said to have actually touched it. "They cannot interpret the dreams, but they thought you should know."

The first was as opaque to him as to the Wise Ones, but the second seemed obvious. A man he could not see with a dagger had to be a Gray Man; their souls given up to the Shadow—not merely pledged, but given away—they could slip past notice even when you looked right at them, and their only real purpose was assassination. Why had the Wise Ones not understood something so plain? As for the last, he feared that was plain as well. He already was cutting lands apart. Tarabon and Arad Doman were ruins, the rebellions in Tear and Cairhien could become more than skulking talk at any time, and Illian would certainly feel the weight of his sword. And that was aside from the Prophet, and the Dragonsworn down in Altara and Murandy.

"I don't see any mystery in two of those, Aviendha." But when he explained, she gave him a doubtful look. Of course. If Wise One dreamwalkers could not interpret a dream, certainly no one else could. He grunted sourly and flung himself into a chair facing her. "What else did they dream?"

"There is one other I can tell you, though it may not concern you." Which meant there were some she would not tell, which made him wonder why the Wise Ones had discussed them with her, since she was not a dreamwalker. "All three had this dream, which makes it especially significant. Rain," that word still came clumsily too, "coming from a bowl. There are snares and pitfalls around the bowl. If the right hands pick it up, they will find a treasure perhaps as great as the bowl. If the wrong hands, the world is doomed. The key to finding the bowl is to find the one who is no longer."

"No longer what?" This certainly sounded more important than the rest. "Do you mean somebody who's dead?"

Aviendha's dark reddish hair swung below her shoulders as she shook her head. "They know no more than I said." To his surprise, she rose smoothly with those automatic adjustments to her clothes that women always made.

"Do you—" He coughed deliberately. *Do you have to go?* he had been about to say. Light, he wanted her to go. Every minute around her was torture. But then, every minute away from her was torture too. Well, he could do what was right and what was good for him, and best for her. "Do you want to go back to the Wise Ones, Aviendha? To resume your studies? There really isn't any point to your staying longer. You've taught me so much, I might as well have been raised Aiel."

Her sniff said volumes, but of course she did not leave it at that. "You know less than a boy of six. Why does a man listen to his second-mother before his own mother, and a woman to her second-father before her own? When can a woman marry a man without making a bridal wreath? When must a roofmistress obey a blacksmith? If you take a silversmith *gai'shain*, why must you let her work one day for herself for each she works for you? Why is the same not true of a weaver?" He floundered for answers short of admitting he did not know, but she suddenly fiddled with her shawl as if she had forgotten him. "Sometimes *ji'e'toh* makes for very great jokes. I would laugh my sides apart if I were not the butt of this one." Her voice dropped to a whisper. "I will meet my *toh*."

He thought she was talking to herself, but he answered. Carefully. "If you mean about Lanfear, it wasn't me who saved you. Moiraine did. She died saving all of us." Laman's sword had rid her of her only other *toh* to him, though he had never been able to understand what that was. The only obligation she knew. He prayed she never learned of the other; she would see it as one, though he certainly did not.

Aviendha peered at him, head tilted and a slight smile flickering on her lips. She had regained a self-possession that would have done Sorilea proud. "Thank you, Rand al'Thor. Bair says it is well to be reminded now and then that a man does not know everything. Be sure to let me know when you mean to go to sleep. I would not come late and wake you."

Rand sat there staring at the door after she had gone. A Cairhienin playing the Game of Houses was usually easier to understand than any woman making no effort to be enigmatic at all. He suspected that what he felt for Aviendha, whatever that was, tangled things up worse.

What I love, I destroy, Lews Therin laughed. *What I destroy, I love.*

Shut up! Rand thought furiously, and the thin-edged laughter vanished. He did not know who he loved, but he knew who he was going to save. From whatever he could, but from him most of all.

In the hallway, Aviendha sagged against the door, taking deep calming breaths. Meant to be calming, anyway. Her heart still tried to tear through her rib cage. Being near Rand al'Thor stretched her naked over hot coals, stretched her till she thought her bones would pop apart. He brought such shame to her as she had never thought she would know. A great joke, she had told him, and part of her did want to laugh. She had *toh* toward him, but much more toward Elayne. All he had done was save her life. Lanfear would have killed her without him. Lanfear had wanted to kill her in particular, as painfully as possible. Somehow, Lanfear had known. Beside what she had incurred toward Elayne, her *toh* toward Rand was a termite mound beside the Spine of the World.

Cassin—the cut of his coat told her he was Goshien as well as *Aethan Dor*; she did not recognize his sept—merely glanced at her from where he squatted with his spears across his knees; he knew nothing, of course. But Liah smiled at her, entirely too encouragingly for a woman she did not know, entirely too knowingly for anyone. Aviendha was shocked to find herself thinking that Chareen, as Liah's coat marked her, were often sneaking cats; she had never thought of any Maiden as anything but *Far Dareis Mai*. Rand al'Thor had unstrung her brain.

Still, her fingers flashed angrily. *Why do you smile, girl? Have you no better use for your time?*

Liah's eyebrows raised slightly, and if anything her smile became amused. Her fingers moved in answer. *Who do you call girl, girl? You are not yet wise, but no longer Maiden. I think you will put your soul in a wreath to lay at a man's feet.*

Aviendha took a furious step forward—there were few insults worse among *Far Dareis Mai*—then stopped. In *cadin'sor* she did not think Liah could match her, but in skirts, she would be defeated. Worse, Liah would probably refuse to make her *gai'shain*; she could, attacked by a woman who was not a Maiden and not yet a Wise One, or demand the right to beat Aviendha before any of the Taardad who could be gathered. A lesser shame than the refusal, but not small. Worst of all, whether she won or lost, Melaine surely would choose a method to remind her she had left the spear behind that would make her wish Liah had drubbed her ten times before all the clans. In a Wise One's hands, shame was keener than a flaying knife. Liah never moved a muscle; she knew all that as well as Aviendha did.

"Now you stare at one another," Cassin said idly. "One day I must learn this handtalk of yours."

Liah glanced at him, her laugh silvery. "You will look pretty in skirts, Red Shield, the day you come to ask to become a Maiden."

Aviendha drew a relieved breath when Liah's eyes left hers; under the circumstances, she could not have looked away first honorably. Automatically her fingers moved in acknowledgment, the first handtalk a Maiden learned, since the phrase a new Maiden used most often. *I have* toh.

Liah signed back without pause. *Very small, spear-sister.*

Aviendha smiled gratefully for the missing hooked little finger that would have made the term mocking, used to women who gave up the spear and then tried to behave as if they had not.

A wetlander servant was running up the hall. Keeping her face clear of the disgust she felt for someone who spent his life serving others, Aviendha strode off the other way, so she would not have to pass the fellow. Killing Rand al'Thor would meet one *toh*, killing herself the second, but each *toh* blocked that solution to the other. Whatever the Wise Ones said, she had to find some way to meet both.

CHAPTER
20

From the Stedding

Rand had just begun thumbing tabac into his short pipe when Liah
put her head in at the door. Before she could speak, a panting
round-faced man in red-and-white livery pushed past her, and fell
to his knees before Rand while she stared in amazement.

"My Lord Dragon," the fellow burst out in a breathless squeak, "Ogier
have come to the Palace. *Three* of them! They have been given wine, and
offered more, but they insist only on seeing the Lord Dragon."

Rand made his voice easy; he did not want to frighten the man. "How
long have you been in the Palace . . . ?" The fellow's livery coat fit him, and
he was not young. "I'm afraid I don't know your name."

The kneeling man goggled. "My name? Bari, my Lord Dragon. Uh,
twenty-two years, my Lord Dragon, come Winternight. My Lord Dragon,
the Ogier?"

Rand had visited an Ogier *stedding* twice, but he was not sure of the
proper etiquette. Ogier had built most of the great cities, the oldest parts
of them, and still came out of their *stedding* occasionally to make repairs,
yet he doubted Bari would have been this excited for anyone else less than
king or Aes Sedai. Maybe not for them. Rand stuffed pipe and tabac pouch
back into his pocket. "Take me to them."

Bari leaped to his feet, all but bouncing on his toes. Rand suspected he
had made the right choice; the man showed no surprise that the Lord

Dragon was going to the Ogier instead of having them brought to him. He left his sword and the scepter behind; Ogier would not be impressed by either. Liah and Cassin came, of course, and it was plain Bari would have run back as well if not for the necessity of keeping his pace to Rand's.

The Ogier waited in a courtyard with a fountain, its basin filled with lily pads and red and gold fish, a white-haired man in a long coat that flared above high boots with their tops turned down, and two women, one noticeably much younger than the other, their skirts embroidered in vines and leaves, the elder's considerably more elaborate than the younger's. Golden goblets made for humans seemed tiny in their hands. Several trees retained some of their leaves, and the Palace itself gave shade. The Ogier were not alone; when Rand appeared, Sulin and a good three dozen Maidens were crowded around them, and Urien, plus fifty or more Aielmen. The Aiel had the grace to fall silent when they saw Rand.

The Ogier man said, "Your name sings in my ears, Rand al'Thor," in a voice like rumbling thunder and gravely made introductions. He was Haman, son of Dal son of Morel. The older woman was Covril, daughter of Ella daughter of Soong, and the younger was Erith, daughter of Iva daughter of Alar. Rand remembered seeing Erith once, in Stedding Tsofu, a hard two-day ride from the city of Cairhien. He could not imagine what she was doing in Caemlyn.

The Ogier made the Aiel seem small; they made the courtyard seem small. Haman stood over half again as tall as Rand and broad in proportion, Covril less than a head—an Ogier head—shorter than that, and even Erith topped Rand by nearly a foot and a half. Yet that was the smallest difference between Ogier and humans. Haman's eyes were as large and round as teacups, his broad nose nearly covered his face, and his ears stood up through his hair, tipped with white tufts. He wore long drooping white mustaches and a narrow beard beneath his chin, and his eyebrows hung down to his cheeks. Rand could not have said precisely how Covril's and Erith's faces differed—except for lacking beards and mustaches, of course, and their eyebrows were not quite so long or thick—but they seemed somehow more delicate. Though Covril's was quite stern at the moment— she looked familiar, too, for some reason—and Erith appeared worried, her ears sagging.

"If you will forgive me a moment," Rand told them.

Sulin did not let him get another word out. "We came to talk with the Treebrothers, Rand al'Thor," she said firmly. "You must know the Aiel have long been waterfriends to the Treebrothers. We go to trade in their *stedding* often."

"That is quite true," Haman murmured. For an Ogier, it was a murmur. An avalanche somewhere out of sight.

"I am sure the others did come to talk," Rand told Sulin. He could pick out the members of her guard this morning by eye, every last one of them; Jalani blushed a deep red. On the other hand, aside from Urien, no more than three or four of the morning's Red Shields were there. "I would not like to think I need to ask Enaila and Somara to take *you* in charge." Sulin's tanned face darkened with indignation, making the scar she had taken following him stand out more. "I would talk with them alone. Alone," he emphasized, eyeing Liah and Cassin. "Unless you think I need protection from them?" If anything that made her more offended, and she gathered up the Maidens with quick flashes of handtalk in what for anyone but an Aiel would surely have been called a huff. Some of the Aielmen were chuckling as they left; Rand supposed he had made a joke of some kind.

As they went, Haman stroked his long beard. "Humans have not always thought us so safe, you know. Um. Um." His musing sounded like a huge bumblebee. "It is in the old records. Very old. Only fragments, really, but dating from just after—"

"Elder Haman," Covril said politely, "if we may stick to the matter at hand?" This bumblebee rumbled at a higher pitch.

Elder Haman. Where had Rand heard that before? Each *stedding* had its Council of Elders.

Haman sighed deeply. "Very well, Covril, but you are showing unseemly haste. You barely gave us time to wash before coming here. I vow, you've begun to leap about like. . . ." Those big eyes flickered toward Rand, and he covered a cough with a hand the size of a large ham. Ogier considered humans hasty, always trying to do now what could not possibly matter until tomorrow. Or until next year; Ogier took a very long view. They also thought it insulting to remind humans of how they leaped about. "This has been a most exacting journey Outside," Haman went on, explaining to Rand, "not the least of it discovering that the Shaido Aiel had besieged Al'cair'rahienallen—most extraordinary, that—and that you were actually there, but then you left before we could speak with you, and. . . . I cannot help feeling we have been impetuous. No. No, you speak, Covril. It is for you I left my studies, and my teaching, to go running across the world. My classes will be in riot by now." Rand almost grinned; the way Ogier normally did things, Haman's classes would take half a year to decide he really was gone and a year more to discuss what to do about it.

"A mother has some right to be anxious," Covril said, tufted ears quivering. She seemed to be battling between the respect due an Elder and a most un-Ogier-like impatience. When she turned to Rand, she drew herself up, ears standing straight and chin firm. "What have you done with my son?"

Rand gaped. "Your son?"

"Loial!" She stared as if he were mad. Erith was peering at him anxiously, hands clutched to her breast. "You told the Eldest of the Elders of Stedding Tsofu that you would look after him," Covril marched on. "They told me you did. You did not call yourself Dragon then, but it was you. Wasn't it, Erith? Did Alar not say Rand al'Thor?" She did not give the younger woman time for more than a nod. As her voice picked up speed, Haman began to look pained. "My Loial is too young to be Outside, too young to be running across the world, doing the things you no doubt have him doing. Elder Alar told me about you. What has my Loial to do with the Ways and Trollocs and the Horn of Valere? You will hand him over to me now, please, so I can see him properly married to Erith. She will settle his itchy feet."

"He's very handsome," Erith murmured shyly, her ears quivering so hard with embarrassment that the dark tufts blurred. "And I think he's very brave, too."

It took Rand a moment to regain his balance mentally. An Ogier being firm sounded much the same as a mountain falling. An Ogier being firm and speaking rapidly. . . .

By Ogier lights, Loial *was* too young to have left the *stedding* alone, little more than ninety. Ogier were very long-lived. From the first day Rand had met him, all full of eagerness to see the world, Loial had been worried over what would happen when the Elders realized he had run away. Most of all, he worried about his mother coming after him with a bride in tow. He said the man had no say in these things among Ogier, and the woman not much; it was all the two mothers' doing. It was not beyond possibility to find yourself betrothed to a woman you had never met before the day your mother introduced you to your prospective bride and mother-in-law.

Loial seemed to think marriage would be the end of everything for him, certainly to all his wishes to see the world, and whether it would or not, Rand could not hand a friend over to what he feared. He was about to say he did not know where Loial was and suggest they return to the *stedding* until he came back—he had his mouth open to say it—when a question occurred to him. It embarrassed him that he could not remember something so important; to Loial, it was. "How long has he been out of the *stedding*?"

"Too long," Haman grumbled like boulders rolling downhill. "The boy never wanted to apply himself. Always talking about seeing Outside, as if anything has really changed from what's in the books he should have been studying. Um. Um. What real change is it if humans change the lines on a map? The land is still—"

"He has been Outside much too long," Loial's mother put in as firmly as a post driven into dry clay. Haman frowned at her, and she managed to stare back at him just as firmly although her ears vibrated in embarrassment.

"M-more than five years now," Erith said. For a moment her ears wilted, then shot up and stubbornly back. In a very good imitation of Covril, she said, "I want him to be my husband. I knew that when I first saw him. I will not let him die. Not from being foolish."

Rand and Loial had talked of many things, and one of them had been the Longing, although Loial had not liked talking about it. When the Breaking of the World drove humans to flee for whatever safety they could find, it drove Ogier from the *stedding* too. For long years humans had wandered in a world that changed sometimes by the day, hunting that safety, and Ogier had wandered, hunting for the *stedding* lost in the changing land. It was then that the Longing entered them. An Ogier away from the *stedding* wanted to return. An Ogier long from the *stedding* needed to return. An Ogier too long from the *stedding* died.

"He told me of an Ogier who stayed out longer," Rand said quietly. "Ten years, I think he said."

Haman was shaking his massive head before Rand finished. "It will not do. That I know of, five have remained Outside that long and survived to return, and I think I would know if more had. Such madness would be written about and talked about. Three of those died within a year of coming home, the fourth was an invalid for the rest of his life, and the fifth little better, needing a stick to walk. Though she did continue writing. Um. Um. Dalar had some interesting things to say concerning—" This time when Covril opened her mouth, his head whipped around; he stared at her, long eyebrows humping up, and she began smoothing her skirts furiously. But she stared right back. "Five years is a short time, I know,"

Haman told Rand, while watching Covril sharply from the corner of his eye, "but we are tied to the *stedding* now. We heard nothing in the city to indicate that Loial is here—and from the excitement we ourselves caused, I think we would have—but if you will tell us where he is, you will be doing him a very great kindness."

"The Two Rivers," Rand said. Saving a friend's life was not betraying him. "When I last saw him, he was setting out in good company, with friends. It's a quiet place, the Two Rivers. Safe." It was now, again, thanks to Perrin. "And he was well a few months ago." Bode had said as much when the girls were telling what had happened back home.

"The Two Rivers," Haman muttered. "Um. Um. Yes, I know where that is. Another long walk." Ogier seldom rode, there being few horses that could bear them, and they preferred their own feet in any case.

"We must start out immediately," Erith said in a firm if light rumble. Light compared to Haman. Covril and Haman looked at her in surprise, and her ears wilted completely. She was, after all, a very young woman accompanying an Elder and a woman Rand suspected was of some importance in her own right from the way she stood up to Haman. Erith was probably not a day over eighty.

Smiling at the thought—a slip of a girl; maybe only seventy—Rand said, "Please accept the hospitality of the Palace. A few days' rest might even make your journey faster. And you might be able to help me, Elder Haman." Of course; Loial was always talking about his teacher, Elder Haman. Elder Haman knew everything, according to Loial. "I need to locate the Waygates. All of them."

All three Ogier spoke at once.

"Waygates?" Haman said, ears and eyebrows both shooting up. "The Ways are very dangerous. Far too dangerous."

"A few days?" Erith protested. "My Loial could be dying."

"A few days?" Covril said on top of her. "My Loial could be—" She cut off, staring at the younger woman, lips compressed and ears quivering.

Haman frowned at them both, stroking his narrow beard irritably. "I do not know why I let myself be talked into this. I should be teaching my classes, and speaking to the Stump. If you were not such a respected Speaker, Covril. . . ."

"You mean if you were not married to my sister," she said stoutly. "Voniel told you to do your duty, Haman." Haman's brows lowered till the long ends hung on his cheeks, and her ears seemed to lose most of their stiffness. "I meant to say she *asked* you," she went on. Not hurriedly, exactly, not losing aplomb, but definitely not hesitating. "By the Tree and stillness, I meant no offense, Elder Haman."

Haman harrumphed loudly—which for an Ogier meant very loudly— and turned to Rand, tugging his coat as if it had been disarrayed.

"Shadowspawn are using the Ways," Rand said before Haman could speak. "I have set guards on the few I can reach." Including the one outside Stedding Tsofu, plainly after their departure. These three could not have walked all the way from Stedding Tsofu after his last futile visit. "A bare handful. All of them need to be guarded, or else Myrddraal and Trollocs can come boiling out of nowhere, as far as anybody they catch is concerned. But I don't even know where they all are."

That would still leave gateways, of course. Sometimes he wondered why one of the Forsaken did not pour a few thousand Trollocs into the Palace by a gateway. Ten thousand, or twenty. He would be hard pressed to stop that, if he could stop it at all. It would be a slaughter at best. Well, he could do nothing about a gateway unless he was there. He could do something about the Waygates.

Haman exchanged looks with Covril. They drew aside, speaking in a whisper, and for a wonder, it was low enough that all he heard was a buzz like a huge swarm of bees on the roof. He must be right about her having some importance. A Speaker; he had heard the capital. He considered seizing *saidin*—he would be able to hear, then—and rejected it disgustedly. He had not sunk to eavesdropping yet. Erith divided her attention evenly between her elders and Rand, all the while unconsciously smoothing her skirts.

Rand hoped they did not inquire why he had not asked his question of the Council of Elders in Stedding Tsofu. Alar, Eldest of the Elders there, had been very firm; the Stump was meeting, and nothing so odd—so peculiar as to never have been thought of before—as handing control of the Waygates to a human could be done unless the Stump concurred. Who he was hardly seemed to matter to her any more than it did to these three.

Finally Haman came back frowning and gripping the lapels of his coat. Covril was frowning too. "This is all very hasty, very hasty," Haman said in slow tones like gravel sliding. "I wish I could discuss it with. . . . Well, I cannot. Shadowspawn, you say? Um. Um. Very well, if there must be haste, there must be haste. Never let it be said that Ogier cannot move quickly when needs require, and perhaps they do now. You must understand, the Council of Elders in any *stedding* may tell you no, and so may the Stump."

"Maps!" Rand shouted, so loudly that all three Ogier jumped. "I need maps!" He spun around looking for one of the servants who always seemed to be about, for a *gai'shain*, anyone. Sulin put her head into the courtyard through a doorway. She would be nearby, after everything he had told her. "Maps," he barked at her. "I want every map in the Palace. And a pen, and ink. Now! Quickly!" She looked at him almost disparagingly—Aiel did not use maps, indeed claimed not to need them—and turned away. "Run, *Far Dareis Mai*!" he snapped. She looked over her shoulder at him—and ran. He wished he knew how his face looked, so he could recall it for use again.

Haman appeared as though he would be wringing his hands if his dignity had been just a little smaller. "Really, there is very little we can possibly tell you that you don't already know. Every *stedding* has one just Outside." The first Waygates could not have been made inside, with the ability to channel blocked by the *stedding* itself; even when Ogier were given the Talisman of Growing, and could themselves make the Ways grow to a new Waygate, the Power was still involved, if not channeling. "And all your cities that have Ogier groves. Though it does seem the city here has grown *over* the grove. And in Al'cair'rahienallen. . . ." He trailed off, shaking his head.

The trouble could be summed up by that name. Three thousand years ago, near enough, there had been a city called Al'cair'rahienallen, built by Ogier. Today it was Cairhien, and the grove the Ogier builders planted to remind them of their *stedding* was part of an estate that had belonged to the same Barthanes whose palace now housed Rand's school. Nobody but Ogier and maybe some Aes Sedai remembered Al'cair'rahienallen. Not even Cairhienin.

Whatever Haman believed, much could change in three thousand years. Great Ogier-built cities had ceased to exist, some leaving not so much as a name behind. Great cities had risen that the Ogier had had no hand in. Amador, begun after the Trolloc Wars, was one, so Moiraine had told him, and Chachin in Kandor, and Shol Arbela in Arafel, and Fal Moran in Shienar. In Arad Doman, Bandar Eban had been built on the ruins of a city destroyed in the War of the Hundred Years, a city Moiraine knew three names for, each suspect, and itself built on the ruins of a nameless city that had vanished in the Trolloc Wars. Rand knew of a Waygate in Shienar, in the countryside near a moderate town that had kept part of the name of the huge city leveled by Trollocs, and another inside the Blight, in Shadow-murdered Malkier. Other places there had simply been change, or growth, as Haman himself had pointed out. The Waygate here in Caemlyn sat in a basement now. A well-guarded basement. Rand knew there was a Waygate in Tear, out in the great pastureland where the High Lords ran their famous horse herds. There should be one somewhere in the Mountains of Mist, where Manetheren had once stood, wherever that was. As far as *stedding* went, he knew where to find Stedding Tsofu. Moiraine had not considered *stedding* or Ogier a vital part of his education.

"You don't know where the *stedding* are?" Haman said incredulously when Rand finished explaining. "Is this Aiel humor? I have never understood Aiel humor."

"For Ogier," Rand said gently, "it has been a long time since the Ways were made. For humans, it has been a *very* long time."

"But you do not even *remember* Mafal Dadaranell, or Ancohima, or Londaren Cor, or . . . ?"

Covril put a hand on Haman's shoulder, but the pity in her eyes was directed at Rand. "He does not remember," she said softly. "Their memories are gone." She made it sound the greatest loss imaginable. Erith, hands clasped to her mouth, appeared ready to cry.

Sulin returned, quite deliberately not running, followed by a fat cluster of *gai'shain*, their arms filled to overflowing with rolled maps of all sizes, some long enough to drag on the courtyard paving stones. One white-robed man carried an ivory-inlaid writing box. "I have set *gai'shain* looking for more," she said stiffly, "and some of the wetlanders."

"Thank you," he told her. A little of the tautness went from her face.

Squatting down, he began spreading maps right there on the paving stones, sorting them. A number were of the city, and many of parts of Andor. He quickly found one showing the whole stretch of the Borderlands, and the Light knew what that was doing in Caemlyn. Some were old and tattered, showing borders that no longer applied, naming countries that had faded away hundreds of years before.

Borders and names were enough to rank the maps by age. On the oldest, Hardan bordered Cairhien to the north; then Hardan was gone and Cairhien's borders swept halfway to Shienar before creeping back as it became clear the Sun Throne simply could not hold on to that much land. Maredo stood between Tear and Illian, then Maredo was gone, and Tear and Illian's borders met on the Plains of Maredo, slowly falling back for the same reasons as Cairhien's. Caralain vanished, and Almoth, Mosara and Irenvelle, and others, sometimes absorbed by other nations, most often eventually becoming unclaimed land and wilderness. Those maps told a story of fading since Hawkwing's empire crumbled, of humanity in slow retreat. A second Borderland map showed only Saldaea and part of Arafel, but it showed the Blightborder fifty miles farther north too. Humanity retreated, and the Shadow advanced.

A bald, skinny man in ill-fitting Palace livery scurried into the court-yard with another armload, and Rand sighed and went on selecting and discarding.

Haman gravely examined the writing box that was held out to him by the *gai'shain*, then produced one almost as large, though quite plain, from a capacious coat pocket. The pen he took from it was polished wood, rather fatter than Rand's thumb and long enough to look slender. It fit the Ogier's sausage-thick fingers perfectly. He got down on hands and knees, crawling among the maps as Rand sorted, occasionally dipping his pen in the *gai'shain's* inkpot, annotating in a handwriting that seemed too large until you realized that for him it was very small. Covril followed, peering over his shoulder even after he asked the second time whether she really thought he would make a mistake.

It was an education for Rand, beginning with seven *stedding* scattered through the Borderlands. But then, Trollocs feared to enter a *stedding*, and even Myrddraal needed some great purpose to drive them into one. The Spine of the World, the Dragonwall, held thirteen, including one in Kin-slayer's Dagger, from Stedding Shangtai in the south to Stedding Qichen and Stedding Sanshen in the north, only a few miles apart.

"The land truly changed in the Breaking of the World," Haman explained when Rand commented. He continued marking briskly, though; briskly for an Ogier. "Dry land became sea and sea dry land, but the land folded as well. Sometimes what was far apart became close together, and what was close, far. Though of course, no one can say whether Qichen and Sanshen were far apart at all."

"You forgot Cantoine," Covril announced, making another liveried ser-vant drop his fresh armload of maps with a start.

Haman gave her a look and lettered in the name just above the River Iralell, not far north of Haddon Mirk. In the strip west of the Dragonwall from the southern border of Shienar to the Sea of Storms, there were only four, all newfound as the Ogier considered it, meaning the youngest, Tsofu, had had Ogier back for six hundred years and none of the others for more than a thousand. Some of the locations were as big a surprise as the Borderlands, such as the Mountains of Mist, which had six, and the Shadow Coast. The Black Hills were included, and the forests above the

River Ivo, and the mountains above the River Dhagon, just north of Arad
Doman.

Sadder was the list of *stedding* abandoned, given up because the numbers
there had grown too few. The Spine of the World and the Mountains of
Mist and the Shadow Coast were in that list too, and so was a *stedding* deep
on Almoth Plain, near the great forest called the Paerish Swar, and one in
the low mountains along the north of Toman Head, facing the Aryth
Ocean. Perhaps saddest was the one marked on the very edge of the Blight
in Arafel; Myrddraal might be reluctant to enter a *stedding*, but as the
Blight marched south year by year, it swept over everything.

Pausing, Haman said sadly, "Sherandu was swallowed by the Great
Blight one thousand eight hundred forty-three years ago, and Chandar
nine hundred sixty-eight."

"May their memories flourish and flower in the Light," Covril and
Erith murmured together.

"I know of one you didn't mark," Rand said. Perrin had told him of
sheltering in it once. He pulled out a map of Andor east of the River Arinelle and touched a spot well above the road from Caemlyn to Whitebridge. It was close enough.

Haman grimaced, almost a snarl. "Where Hawkwing's city was to be.
That was never reclaimed. Several *stedding* were found and never reclaimed.
We try to stay away from the lands of men as much as possible." All of the
marks were in rugged mountains, in places men found hard to enter, or in
a few cases just far from any human habitation. Stedding Tsofu lay far
closer than any other to where humans dwelled, and even then Rand knew
it was a full day to the nearest village.

"This would be a fine discussion another time," Covril said, directing
her words to Rand yet plainly meaning them for Haman, as her sidelong
looks indicated, "but I want to make as far west as I can before nightfall."
Haman sighed heavily.

"Surely you'll stay here awhile," Rand protested. "You must be exhausted, walking all the way from Cairhien."

"Women do not become exhausted," Haman said, "they only exhaust
others. That is a very old saying among us." Covril and Erith sniffed in
harmony. Muttering to himself, Haman went on with his listing, but now
it was cities that the Ogier had built, cities where the groves had been,
each grove holding its Waygate to carry Ogier back and forth to the *stedding* without passing through the so-often troubled lands of men.

Caemlyn he marked, of course, and Tar Valon, Tear and Illian, Cairhien and Maradon and Ebou Dar. That was the end as far as cities that still existed were concerned, and Ebou Dar he wrote as Barashta. Perhaps Barashta belonged with the others, in a way, with the dots made in places where the maps showed nothing but a village if that. Mafal Dadaranell, Ancohima, and Londaren Cor, of course, and Manetheren. Aren Mador, Aridhol, Shaemal, Braem, Condaris, Hai Ecorimon, Iman. . . . As that list grew, Rand began to see damp spots on each map when Haman was done. It took him a moment to realize that the Ogier Elder was weeping silently, letting the tears fall as he marked cities dead and forgotten. Perhaps he wept for the people, perhaps for the memories. The one thing Rand could be sure of was that it was not for the cities themselves, not for the lost works of Ogier masons. To the Ogier, stonework was only something they had picked up during the Exile, and what work in stone could compare with the majesty of trees?

One of those names more than tugged at Rand's memories, and its location as well, east of Baerlon, several days above Whitebridge on the Arinelle. "There was a grove here?" he said, fingering the mark.

"At Aridhol?" Haman said. "Yes. Yes, there was. A sad business, that."

Rand did not raise his head. "In Shadar Logoth," he corrected. "A very sad business. Could you—would you—show me that Waygate if I took you there?"

CHAPTER
21

To Shadar Logoth

"Take us there?" Covril said, frowning formidably at the map in Rand's hands. "It will carry us well out of our way, if I remember where the Two Rivers is correctly. I will not waste another day finding Loial." Erith nodded firmly.

Haman, cheeks still damp with tears, shook his head for their haste but said, "I cannot allow it. Aridhol—Shadar Logoth, as you rightly name it now—is no place for someone as young as Erith. In good truth, it is no place for anyone."

Letting the map fall, Rand stood up. He knew Shadar Logoth better than he wanted to. "You will lose no time. In fact, you'll gain. I will take you there by Traveling, by a gateway; you will be most of the way to the Two Rivers today. We'll not be long. I know you can lead me right to the Waygate." Ogier could sense Waygates, if they were not too far.

This necessitated another conference beyond the fountain, one Erith demanded to be part of. Rand caught only snatches, yet it was plain that Haman, shaking his great head doggedly, opposed the plan while Covril, ears so stiff it seemed she was trying for every inch of height, insisted on it. At first Covril frowned at Erith as much as at Haman; whatever the relationship between mother-in-law and daughter-in-law among Ogier, she clearly thought the younger woman had no business in this. It did not take her long to change her mind, though. The Ogier women flanked Haman, hammering at him relentlessly.

"... too dangerous. Much too dangerous," came like distant thunder from Haman.

"... almost there today. ..." A slighter thunder from Covril.

"... he has been Outside too long already. ..." An almost silvery peal from Erith.

"... haste makes for waste ..."

"... my Loial. ..."

"... my Loial. ..."

"... Mashadar beneath our feet. ..."

"... my Loial. ..."

"... my Loial. ..."

"... as an Elder. ..."

"... my Loial. ..."

"... my Loial. ..."

Haman came back to Rand tugging at his coat as though it had been ripped half off, followed by the women. Covril maintained a smoother face than Erith, who fought to suppress a smile, but their tufted ears were at the same jaunty angle, somehow conveying satisfaction.

"We have decided," Haman said stiffly, "to accept your offer. Let this ridiculous gallivanting be done with so I can return to my classes. And to the Stump. Um. Um. There is much to be said about you before the Stump."

Rand did not care whether Haman told the Stump he was a bully. Ogier held themselves apart from men except for repairing their old stonework, and it was unlikely they would influence any human one way or another about him. "Good," he said. "I will send someone to fetch your belongings from your inn."

"We have everything right here." Covril went back around to the other side of the fountain, bent, and straightened with two bundles that had been hidden behind the basin. Either would have made a heavy load for a man. She handed one to Erith and slipped a strap tied to the other over her head so it slanted across her chest, holding the bundle against her back.

"If Loial were here," Erith explained, donning her bundle, "we would be ready to start back to Stedding Tsofu without delay. If not, we would be ready to go on. Without delay."

"Actually, it was the beds," Haman confided, holding his hands to indicate a size to fit a human child. "Once every inn Outside had two or three Ogier rooms, but they seem very hard to find now. It is difficult to understand." He glanced at the marked maps and sighed. "It was difficult to understand."

Waiting just long enough for Haman to fetch his own bundle, Rand seized *saidin* and opened a gateway right there beside the fountain, a hole in the air that showed a ruined, weed-filled street and collapsing buildings.

"Rand al'Thor." Sulin almost strolled into the courtyard, just ahead of a cluster of map-laden servants and *gai'shain*. Liah and Cassin were with her, pretending to be just as casual. "You asked for more maps." Sulin's glance at the gateway was barely short of accusing.

"I can protect myself better there than you can," Rand told her coldly. He did not intend it to be cold, but wrapped in the Void, he could not make his voice anything but cold and distant. "There is nothing your spears can fight, and some things they can't."

Sulin still wore a good deal of her earlier stiffness. "All the more reason for us to be there."

That could not possibly make sense to anyone not Aiel, but. . . . "I will not argue it," he said. She would try to follow, if he refused; she would summon Maidens who would try to leap through even if he was closing the gateway. "I expect you have the rest of today's guard just inside. Whistle them up. But everyone is to stay close to me and touch nothing. Be quick about it. I want this done with." His memories of Shadar Logoth were not pleasant.

"I sent them away as you insisted," Sulin said disgustedly. "Give me a slow count of one hundred."

"Ten."

"Fifty."

Rand nodded, and her fingers flashed. Jalani darted away inside, and Sulin's hands flickered again. Three *gai'shain* women dropped their armloads of maps, looking startled—Aiel *never* looked that surprised—gathered long white robes and vanished back into the Palace in different directions, but quickly as they moved, Sulin was ahead of them.

As Rand reached, twenty, Aiel began bounding into the courtyard, hurtling though windows, leaping down from balconies. He almost lost the count. Every one was veiled, and only some Maidens. They stared about in confusion when they found only Rand and three Ogier, who blinked at them curiously. Some lowered their veils. The Palace servants huddled together.

The flow continued even after Sulin returned, unveiled, dead on the count of fifty, the courtyard filling with Aiel. Quickly it became clear that she had spread the word the *Car'a'carn* was in danger, the only way she felt she could gather enough spears in the time allotted. A little sour grumping passed among the men, but most decided it was a fine joke, some chuckling or rattling spears on bucklers. None left, though; they looked at the gateway and settled on their haunches to see what was happening.

Ears sharpened with the Power, Rand heard a Maiden named Nandera, sinewy yet still handsome despite more gray than yellow in her hair, whisper to Sulin. "You spoke to *gai'shain* as *Far Dareis Mai.*"

Sulin's blue eyes met Nandera's green levelly. "I did. We will deal with it when Rand al'Thor is safe today."

"When he is safe," Nandera agreed.

Sulin chose out twenty Maidens quickly, some who had been part of the guard that morning and some not, but when Urien began picking Red Shields, men from other societies insisted they should be included. That city through the gateway looked a place where enemies might be found, and the *Car'a'carn* must be protected. If the truth be told, no Aiel turned away from a possible fight, and the younger they were, the more likely to try to find one. Another argument almost started when Rand said the men could not number more than the Maidens—that would dishonor *Far Dareis Mai*, since he had given them his honor to carry—and the Maidens not more than Sulin had already chosen. He truly was taking them where no battle skills could protect them, and every one who came with him was one more he would have to watch out for. That he did not explain; no telling whose honor he would step on if he did.

"Remember," he said once they were sorted out, "touch nothing. Take nothing, not even a sip of water. And stay in sight always; don't go inside any building for any reason." Haman and Covril nodded vigorously, which seemed to impress the Aiel more than Rand's words. So long as they *were* impressed.

They stepped through the gateway into a city long dead, a city more than dead.

A golden sun more than halfway to its zenith roasted the ruins of greatness. Here and there a huge intact dome topped a pale marble palace, but more were holed than not, and most often only a curved and broken fragment remained. Long columned walks ran to towers as tall as anything Cairhien had ever dreamed of, and to towers ending jaggedly. Everywhere roofs had fallen in, bricks and stone fanned across fractured paving stones from collapsed buildings and walls. Shattered fountains and broken monuments decorated every intersection. Stunted trees, dying in the drought, dotted great hills of rubble. Dead weeds lined cracks in streets and buildings. Nothing moved, not a bird, not a rat, not a breeze. Silence shrouded Shadar Logoth. Shadar Logoth. Where the Shadow Waits.

Rand let the gateway vanish. No Aiel unveiled. The Ogier stared around, faces tight and ears laid stiffly back. Rand held on to *saidin* in that fight that Taim said told a man he was alive. Even if he had not been able to channel, maybe especially then, he would have wanted that reminder here.

Aridhol had been a great capital in the days of the Trolloc Wars, an ally of Manetheren and the rest of the Ten Nations. When those wars had lasted long enough to dwarf the War of the Hundred Years, when it seemed the Shadow was everywhere victorious and every victory of the Light did no more than buy time, a man named Mordeth became a councilor in Aridhol, and counseled the rule that to win, to survive, Aridhol must be harder than the Shadow, more cruel than the Shadow, less trusting. Slowly they made it so, until in the end, Aridhol became, if not blacker than the Shadow, as black. With war still raging against the Trollocs, Aridhol finally turned in on itself, turned on itself, consumed itself.

Something was left behind, something that had kept anyone from ever living here again. Not a pebble of this place but was tainted with the hatred and suspicion that had murdered Aridhol and left Shadar Logoth. Not a pebble but could infect, with time.

And more than the taint remained, though that was enough to keep any sane man away.

Rand turned slowly where he stood, staring up at windows like empty eye sockets, the eyes gouged out. With the sun climbing high he could feel unseen watchers. When he had been here before, that feeling had not come this strongly until the sun began to go down. Much more than the taint remained. A Trolloc army had died camping here, vanished except for messages smeared on walls in blood, begging the Dark One to save them. Night was no time to be in Shadar Logoth.

This place frightens me, Lews Therin murmured beyond the Void. *Does it not frighten you?*

Rand's breath caught. Was the voice actually addressing him? *Yes, it frightens me.*

There is darkness here. Blackness blacker than black. If the Dark One chose to live among men, he would choose here.

Yes. He would.

I must kill Demandred.

Rand blinked. *Does Demandred have some connection to Shadar Logoth? To here?*

I remember at last killing Ishamael. There was a sense of wonder in the voice, at a new discovery. *He deserved to die. Lanfear deserved to die, too, but I am glad I was not the one to kill her.*

Was it just happenstance that the voice seemed to speak to him? Was Lews Therin hearing, answering? *How did I—did you kill Ishamael? Tell me how.*

Death. I want the rest of death. But not here. I do not want to die here.

Rand sighed. Just happenstance. He would not want to die here either. A nearby palace, broken columns along its front, had a distinct lean toward the street. It could fall any time, and bury them where they stood. "Lead on," he told Haman. To the Aiel, he added, "Remember what I said. Touch nothing, take nothing, and stay in sight."

"I did not think it would be so bad," Haman muttered. "It almost washes away the Waygate." Erith moaned, and Covril looked as though she would if she were not too dignified. Ogier were sensitive to the mood of a place. Haman pointed. The sweat on his face had nothing to do with the heat. "That way."

Broken pavement crunched beneath Rand's boots like bones grinding. Haman directed them around corners and down streets, past one set of ruins after another, but his direction was sure. The encircling Aiel moved on their toes. Their eyes above the black veils did not look as if they expected attack, but as if the attack had already begun.

The unseen watchers and broken buildings brought back memories Rand would as soon have avoided. Here Mat had begun a road that took him to the Horn of Valere, that almost killed him on the way, maybe the road that had led him to Rhuidean and the *ter'angreal* he did not want to talk about. Here Perrin had disappeared when they were all forced to flee in the night, and when Rand finally saw him again, far from here, he had golden eyes and a sad look and secrets that Moiraine had never shared with Rand.

He had not escaped unscathed himself, though Shadar Logoth had not touched him directly. Padan Fain had followed them all here, himself and Mat and Perrin, Moiraine and Lan, Nynaeve and Egwene. Padan Fain, peddler and frequent visitor to the Two Rivers. Padan Fain, Darkfriend. More than Darkfriend now, and worse, so Moiraine had said. Fain had followed them all here, but what left was more than Fain, or less. Fain, as much as he was still Fain, wanted Rand dead. He had threatened everyone Rand loved if Rand would not come to him. And Rand had not. Perrin had dealt with that, kept the Two Rivers safe, but Light how it hurt. What *had* Fain been doing with the Whitecloaks? Could Pedron Niall be a Darkfriend? If Aes Sedai could be, then so could the Lord Captain Commander of the Children of the Light.

"There it is," Haman said, and Rand gave a start. Shadar Logoth was the last place on earth to lose yourself in thought.

Where the Elder stood had been a spacious square once, though a weathered mound of rubble filled one end now. In the middle of the square, where a fountain might have been, was instead an ornate filigree fence of some shiny metal, Ogier-high and untouched by rust. That enclosed what appeared to be a tall length of stone carved with vines and leaves so delicately done that you expected to feel the breeze that was riffling them, that you were surprised to realize, they were gray not green. The Waygate, though it certainly looked like no kind of gate.

"They cut down the grove as soon as the Ogier departed for the *stedding*," Haman muttered angrily, long brows drawn down, "no more than twenty or thirty years, and extended the city."

Rand touched the fence with a flow of Air, wondering how to get through, and blinked as the whole thing collapsed into twenty or more pieces, which fell with loud shivering clangs that made the Ogier jump. Rand shook his head. Of course. Metal that had survived so long without a spot of rust *must* be Power-wrought, maybe even remnants from the Age of Legends, but the joins that had held them together had long since corroded, awaiting one good shove.

Covril laid a hand on his shoulder. "I would ask you not to open it. No doubt Loial told you how—he always did show too much interest in that sort of thing—but the Ways are dangerous."

"I can lock it," Haman said, "so it cannot be opened again without the Talisman of Growing. Um. Um. A simple matter; simply done." He did not seem eager, though. He certainly did not move any closer.

"It might have to be used without time for fetching anything," Rand told him. All the Ways might have to be used, whatever the dangers. If he could cleanse them somehow. . . . That was almost as grandiose as his boast to Taim that he would cleanse *saidin*.

He began weaving *saidin* around the Waygate, using all Five Powers, even lifting the segments of fence back into place. From the first flow he channeled, the taint seemed to pulse inside him, a slowly building vibration.

It must have been the evil in Shadar Logoth itself, a resonance of evil to evil.
Even in the Void he felt dizzy from those reverberations, as though the world
swung beneath his feet in time to them; they made him want to vomit up
everything he had ever eaten. Still, he persevered. He could not send men to
stand guard here any more than he could have had them search.

What he wove and then inverted was a vicious sort of trap to suit a vicious
place. A ward of surpassing nastiness. Humans could cross it unharmed, perhaps even the Forsaken—he could ward against humans or Shadowspawn,
not both—and even a male Forsaken could not detect it. Should any sort of
Shadowspawn pass through. . . . That was the viciousness. They would not
die right away; they might even live to make it beyond the city walls. Long
enough for the dead to be far off, not here to frighten the next Myrddraal that
came. Long enough for a Trolloc army to exit perhaps, picking up their own
deaths as they did. Cruel enough for a Trolloc. Making the thing sickened
him as much as the taint on *saidin*.

Tying off the weave and loosing *saidin* brought only some relief. The
residue of filth that always seemed to remain behind still throbbed; it almost felt as though the ground were throbbing beneath his boots. His
teeth and ears ached. He could not wait to get away from here.

Taking a deep breath, he prepared to channel again, to open a
gateway—and stopped, frowning. Quickly he counted everyone, then did
it again, more slowly. "Somebody's missing. Who?"

The Aiel took only a moment to confer.

"Liah," Sulin said through her veil.

"She was right behind me." There was no mistaking Jalani's voice.

"Maybe she saw something." He thought that was Desora.

"I told everybody to stay together!" Rage washed across the Void,
waves breaking to froth on a boulder. One of them missing, here, and they
took it with that Light-blasted Aiel coolness. A Maiden missing. A woman
missing, in Shadar Logoth. "When I find her . . . !" Inch by inch he fought
down the fury that threatened to engulf the emptiness around him. What
he wanted to do to Liah was shout at her till she fainted, send her to Sorilea
for the rest of her life. That rage wanted white-hot murder. "Split up in
pairs. Shout, look everywhere, but don't go inside, not for any reason. And
stay out of shadows. You can die here before you know it. You can all die
before any of you know it. If you see her in a building, even if she looks just
fine, find me unless she comes out to you."

"We can search faster if we each search alone," Urien said, and Sulin
nodded agreement. There were far too many nods.

"Pairs!" Rand fought the fury down again. *The Light burn Aiel stubbornness!* "At least that way you have somebody to watch your back. For once do what I say when I say it. I've been here; I know a little about this place."

A few minutes later, most spent in argument over how many should stay with Rand, twenty pairs of Aiel scattered. The one remaining was Jalani, Rand thought, though it was hard to tell with the veil. For once she did not appear to be happy guarding him; the green eyes held a decided touch of sullenness.

"I suppose we could make another pair," Haman said, looking at Covril.

She nodded. "And Erith can remain here."

"No!" Rand and Erith said at almost the same instant. The older Ogier turned with faces of grave disapproval. Erith's ears sagged until they looked ready to fall off.

Rand grabbed hold of his temper firmly. Once it had seemed that in the Void, any anger was off in the far distance somewhere, attached to him by no more than a thread. More and more it threatened to overwhelm him, to overwhelm the Void. Which might be disastrous. Aside from that, though. . . . "I'm sorry. I had no business shouting at you, Elder Haman, or you, Speaker Covril." Was that the right way to say it? Was it even a title of that sort? Nothing in their expressions said either way. "I would appreciate it if you would all stay with me. Then we can all search together."

"Of course," Haman said. "I really don't see how I can offer you more protection than you can offer yourself, but it is yours." Covril and Erith both nodded approvingly. Rand had no idea what Haman was talking about, but it did not seem the time to ask, with the three of them apparently bucked up to protect him. He had no doubt he could safeguard all three as long as they kept close.

"So long as you follow your own rules, Rand al'Thor." The green-eyed Maiden was indeed Jalani, and sounding heartened that she would not have to stand and wait. Rand hoped he had given the others a better idea of what this place was like.

From the beginning the search was frustrating. They walked up and down the streets watched by invisible eyes, sometimes climbing over strewn rubble, taking turns calling, "Liah! Liah!" Covril's shouts made leaning walls creak; Haman's made them groan ominously. Nothing answered. The only other sounds were the shouts of the search parties and mocking echoes along the streets. Liah! Liah!

The sun had climbed nearly overhead when Jalani said, "I do not think she would have gone this far, Rand al'Thor. Not unless she was trying to get away from us, and she would not do that."

Rand turned from peering through shadowed columns at the head of wide stone steps, trying to see into a great chamber beyond. As far as he could make out, there was nothing in there but dust. No footprints. The unseen watchers had faded; they were not gone even now, but almost. "We have to search as much as we can. Maybe she. . . ." He did not know how to finish. "I won't leave her here, Jalani."

The sun swung higher and began to descend, and he was standing atop what had been a palace once, or maybe a whole block of buildings. It was a hill now, weathered enough over the years that only the number of broken bricks and pieces of worked stone sticking out of the dry soil said it had been anything else. "Liah!" he shouted through cupped hands. "Liah!"

"Rand al'Thor," a Maiden called from the street below, lowering her veil so he could see it was Sulin. She and another Maiden, still veiled, stood with Jalani and the Ogier. "Come down."

He scrambled down in a cloud of dust and a shower of bits of brick and stone, moving so fast that he nearly fell twice. "You've found her?"

Sulin shook her head. "We should have by now if she is alive. She would not have gone far on her own. If anyone carried her far, they carried her dead, I think; she would not go easily. And if she was injured too badly to answer our shouts, I think that also must mean she is dead." Haman sighed sadly. The Ogier women's long eyebrows dropped to their cheekbones; for some reason, their sad, pitying looks were directed at Rand.

"Keep looking," he said.

"May we look inside the buildings? There are many rooms we cannot see from outside."

Rand hesitated. Well short of midafternoon yet, and he could feel the eyes again. As strong as they had been with the sun setting his first time here. Shadows were not safe in Shadar Logoth. "No. But we keep looking."

He was not sure how long he went on shouting his way up one street and down the next, but after a time Urien and Sulin stepped in front of him, both unveiled. The sun sat at the treetops to the west, a blood-red ball in a cloudless sky. Shadows stretched long across the ruins.

"I will search as long as you wish," Urien said, "but calling and looking have done what they can. If we could search the buildings—"

"No." It came out a croak, and Rand cleared his throat. Light, but he wanted a drink of water. The invisible watchers filled every window, every opening, thousands of them, waiting, anticipating. And shadows cloaked the city. Shadows were not safe in Shadar Logoth, but darkness brought out death. Mashadar rose with sunset. "Sulin, I. . . ." He could not make himself say they had to give up, leave Liah behind whether she was dead or alive, maybe lying somewhere unconscious, behind a wall, or under a heap of bricks that might have tumbled down on her. She could be.

"Whatever watches us is waiting for nightfall, I think," Sulin said. "I have looked into windows where something was looking back at me, but there was nothing there. Dancing the spears with something we cannot see will not be easy."

Rand realized he had wanted her to say again that Liah must be dead, that they could go. Liah could be injured somewhere; it was possible. He touched his coat pocket; the fat-little-man *angreal* was back in Caemlyn with his sword and the scepter. He was not sure he could protect everyone once night fell. Moiraine had thought the whole White Tower could not kill Mashadar. If it could be said to be alive.

Haman cleared his throat. "From what I remember of Aridhol," he said, frowning, "of Shadar Logoth, that is—when the sun goes down, we will probably all die."

"Yes." Rand breathed the word reluctantly. Liah, maybe alive. All the others. Covril and Erith had their heads together a little way off. He caught a murmur of "Loial."

Duty is heavier than a mountain, death lighter than a feather.

Lews Therin had to have that from him—memories passed both ways across that barrier, it seemed—but it cut to the heart.

"We have to go now," he told them. "Whether Liah is alive or dead, we—must go." Urien and Sulin only nodded, but Erith moved closer and patted him on the shoulder with surprising gentleness for a hand that could have gripped his head.

"If I might trouble you," Haman said, "we have been rather longer than we expected." He gestured to the sinking sun. "If you would do us the favor of carrying us outside the city in the same way you brought us here, I would appreciate it greatly."

Rand remembered the forest outside Shadar Logoth. No Myrddraal or Trollocs there this time, but a thick wood, and the Light alone knew how far to the nearest village or in what direction. "I will do better than that," he said. "I can take you straight to the Two Rivers as quickly."

The two older Ogier nodded gravely. "The blessing of the Light and stillness be on you for your help," Covril murmured. Erith's ears quivered with anticipation, perhaps equally for seeing Loial and leaving Shadar. Logoth.

Rand hesitated a moment. Loial would probably be in Emond's Field, but he could not take them there. Too much chance news of his visit would slip out of the Two Rivers. Away from the village, then, far enough to avoid the farms that clustered close nearby.

The vertical slash of light appeared and widened; the taint pounded inside him again, worse than before; the ground seemed to beat at the soles of the boots.

Half a dozen Aiel leaped through, and the three Ogier followed with a haste that was not at all unseemly in the circumstances. Rand paused, looking back over the ruined city. He had promised to let the Maidens die for him.

As the last of the Aiel went through, Sulin hissed, and he glanced at her, but she was looking at his hand. At the back of his hand, where his fingernails had sliced a gash that oozed blood. Wrapped in the Void as he was, the pain might have belonged to someone else. The physical mark did not matter; it would heal. He had made deeper inside, where no one could see. One for each Maiden who died, and he never let them heal.

"We are done here," he said, and stepped through the gateway into the Two Rivers. The throbbing vanished with the gateway.

Frowning, Rand tried to orient himself. Placing a gateway precisely was not easy where you had never been before, but he had picked a field he did know, a weedy meadow a good two-hour walk south of Emond's Field that no one ever used for anything. In the lurid twilight he could see sheep, though, a sizable flock, and a boy with a crook in his hands and a bow on his back, staring at them from a hundred paces. Rand did not need the Power in him to tell the boy was goggling, as well he might. Dropping the crook, he set off running for a farmhouse that had not been there when Rand was last here. A tile-roofed farmhouse.

For a moment Rand wondered whether he was really in the Two Rivers at all. No, the feel of the place told him he was. The smell of the air shouted home. All those changes Bode and the rest of the girls had told him about—they had not really sunk in; nothing ever really changed in the Two Rivers. Should he send the girls back here, back home? *What you should do is stay clear of them.* It was an irritable thought.

"Emond's Field is that way," he said. Emond's Field. Perrin. Tam might be there, too, at the Winespring Inn, with Egwene's parents. "That is where Loial should be. I don't know if you can make it before dark. You might ask at the farmhouse. I'm sure they will give you a place to sleep. Don't tell them about me. Tell no one how you came." The boy had seen but a boy's tale might well be taken for exaggeration when Ogier appeared.

Adjusting the bundles on their backs, Haman and Covril exchanged looks, and she said, "We will say nothing of how we came. Let people make the stories they wish."

Haman stroked his beard and cleared his throat. "You must not kill yourself."

Even in the Void, Rand was startled. "What?"

"The road ahead of you," Haman rumbled, "is long, dark, and, I very much fear, bloodstained. I also very much fear that you will take us all down that road. But you must live to reach the end of it."

"I will," Rand replied curtly. "Fare you well." He tried to put some warmth into that, some feeling, but he was not sure he succeeded.

"Fare you well," Haman said, and the women echoed it before all three turned toward the farmhouse. Not even Erith sounded as if she believed he would, though.

A moment longer Rand stood there. People had appeared outside the house, watching the Ogier approach, but Rand stared north and west, not toward Emond's Field, but toward the farm where he had grown up. When he turned away and opened a gateway to Caemlyn, it was like tearing his own arm off. The pain was a much more suitable memorial for Liah than a scratch.

CHAPTER
22

Heading South

The five stones made a smoothly spinning circle above Mat's hands, one red, one blue, one clear green, the others striped in interesting ways. He rode on, guiding Pips with his knees, the black-hafted spear thrust behind the saddle girth on the opposite side from his unstrung bow. The stones made him think of Thom Merrilin, who had taught him to juggle, and he wondered whether the old fellow was still alive. Probably not. Rand had sent the gleeman haring after Elayne and Nynaeve what seemed a very long time ago now, supposedly to look out for them. If any two women needed looking out for less, Mat did not know them, but no two were more likely to get a man killed because they would not listen to reason. Nynaeve, poking into everything a man did or said or thought and tugging her bloody braid at a fellow all the time, and Elayne the bloody Daughter-Heir, thinking she could get her way by sticking her nose in the air and telling you what for as bad as Nynaeve ever did, only Elayne was worse, because if frosty high-handedness failed, Elayne smiled and flashed her dimple and expected everybody to fall down because she was pretty. He hoped Thom had managed to survive their company. He hoped they were all right too, but he would not mind if they had found themselves in the pickling kettle at least once since scurrying off to the Light knew where. Let them see what it was like without him to haul them out, and never an honest word of thanks when he was there to do it.

Not too hot a kettle, mind—just enough to make them wish Mat Cauthon were around to rescue them again like an idiot.

"What about you, Mat?" Nalesean asked, reining closer. "Did you ever think what it would be like to be a Warder?"

Mat nearly dropped the stones. Daerid and Talmanes looked at him, sweaty-faced and waiting an answer. The sun was sliding toward the horizon; not long before they would have to stop. Twilight seemed to last a little longer as the days shortened, but Mat wanted to be settled in with his pipe by dusk. Besides, in terrain like this, horses broke legs once the light failed. So did men.

The Band stretched out northward behind them, horse and foot beneath a rising tail of dust, banners flying but drums silent, across low hills covered with sparse scrub and scattered thickets. Eleven days since leaving Maerone, and they were halfway to Tear or a little better, moving faster than Mat had really hoped for. And only one full day spent resting the horses. He was certainly in no hurry to take Weiramon's place, but he could not help wondering how much distance they *could* cover between sunup and sundown if they had to. So far their best had been forty-five miles, as near as anyone could calculate. Of course, the supply wagons took half the night catching up, but the foot had been making a point lately of showing they could match the horse over the long haul if not the short.

A little farther back and to the east, a band of Aiel crested a tree-fringed rise, running easily and slowly closing the distance. Likely they had been trotting since sunrise, and would until nightfall if not later. If they passed the Band while there was still light to see, it would be encouragement for tomorrow. Whenever Aiel passed them, they seemed ready to try for another mile or two the next day.

A few miles ahead the thickets blended into solid forest again; it would be necessary to drop down closer to the Erinin before they reached that. As they crested a hilltop, Mat could see the river, and the five hired riverboats flying the Red Hand. Four more were on their way back to Maerone to reload, mainly with fodder for the horses. What he could not see yet knew were there were the people, some meandering upriver, some down, some changing direction whenever they met a group led by someone with a convincing tongue. A handful had carts, usually pulled by themselves, and a few wagons, but most nothing beyond what they wore on their backs; even the densest brigands had learned there was no point to bothering those. Mat had no idea where they were going and neither did they, yet they were just enough to clog the sorry excuse for a road along the river. Short of clubbing people out of the way, the Band could make much better time up here.

"A Warder?" Mat said, tucking the stones into his saddlebags. He could find more anywhere, but he liked the colors. He had an eagle feather in there, too, and a piece of weathered snow-white stone that might have been carved with scrolls once. There had been a boulder that looked as if it had been the head of a statue, too, but the thing would have needed a wagon. "Never. They're all fools and dupes, letting Aes Sedai lead them around by the nose. What put a notion like that in your head?"

Nalesean shrugged. He fairly oozed sweat, but he still wore his coat—red striped with blue today—buttoned to the neck. Mat's hung open, and he still thought he was broiling. "I suppose it's all the Aes Sedai," the Tairen said. "Burn my soul, it can't but make you think, can it? I mean, burn my soul, what are they up to?" He meant the Aes Sedai on the other side of the Erinin, reportedly scurrying upriver or down a sight quicker than the wanderers that were over there as well.

"Best not to think about them is what I say." Mat touched the silver foxhead through his shirt; even with that, he was glad the Aes Sedai were across the river. A handful of his soldiers traveled on each of the river craft, and few as villages were, they put a boat ashore on his orders at every one they passed on the far side, to see what they could learn. So far the news had been unrevealing and often unpleasant. Aes Sedai swarming was the least of it.

"And how are we not to think of them?" Talmanes asked. "Do you think the Tower really did pull Logain's strings?" That was one of the newer bits, just two days old.

Mat pulled off his hat long enough to mop his forehead before answering. Nightfall would be a little cooler. But no wine, no ale, no women, and no gambling. Who would be a soldier for choice? "There's not much I'd say was beyond Aes Sedai." Sliding a finger behind the scarf around his neck, he eased it. One thing about Warders, by what he knew from observing Lan anyway, they never seemed to sweat. "But that? Talmanes, I'd believe you were Aes Sedai first. You aren't, are you?"

Daerid doubled over the pommel of his saddle laughing, and Nalesean nearly fell off his horse. Talmanes stiffened at first, but finally he grinned. He almost chuckled. The man did not have much sense of humor, but he did have some.

His seriousness reasserted itself quickly, though. "What about the

Dragonsworn? If it is true, Mat, it means trouble." The others' laughter
might as well have been chopped with an axe.

Mat grimaced. That was the newest news or rumor—call it what you
would—picked up yesterday, a village burned somewhere in Murandy.
Worse, supposedly they had killed everybody who would not swear to the
Dragon Reborn, and their families with them. "Rand will settle for them.
If it's true. Aes Sedai, Dragonsworn, all that is his business, and we're well
out of it. We have our own to tend."

That made nobody's face less grim, of course. They had seen too many
burned villages, and thought they would see more soon after reaching
Tear. Who would be a solider?

A horseman appeared over the next rise ahead, galloping toward them,
leaping his mount over brush rather than swerve around even on the
downslope. Mat signed for a halt, adding, "No trumpets." Word rippled
behind him in a fading murmur, but he kept his eyes on the rider.

Dripping sweat, Chel Vanin reined his dun gelding in before Mat. In a
rough gray coat that fit his balding bulk like a sack, he sat his saddle like
a sack, too. Vanin was fat, and no getting around it. Yet improbable as it
seemed, he could ride anything ever born, and he was very good at what
he did.

Long before they reached Maerone, Mat had surprised Nalesean, Daerid and Talmanes by asking for the names of the best poachers and horse
thieves among their men, the ones they knew were guilty but could not
prove anything against. The two nobles in particular had not wanted to
admit having any such men in their commands, but after a little prodding
they came up with the names of three Cairhienin, two Tairens and, surprisingly, two Andorans. Mat had not thought any of the Andorans had
been with the Band long enough to make themselves known like that, but
apparently word got about.

Those seven men he took aside and told that he needed scouts, and that
a good scout used much the same skills as a poacher or horse thief. Ignoring fervent denials that they had ever committed any crime whatsoever—
more from each than from Talmanes and Nalesean combined, and just as
eloquent if far coarser—he offered pardons for any thefts done before that
day, triple pay and no work details as long as they reported the truth. And
a hanging for the first lie; a lot of men could die from a scout's lie. Even
with the threat they leaped at it, probably more for less work than for the
extra silver.

But seven was not enough, so he asked them to suggest others, and to keep in mind what he said about the needed skills, as well as the fact that whether they lived to collect their triple pay would depend in large part on the abilities of those they named. That caused a lot of chin-scratching and edgy looks, but between them they produced eleven more names, emphasizing all the while that they were not implying anything about those fellows. Eleven men, good enough poachers and horse thieves that neither Daerid nor Talmanes nor Nalesean had suspected them but not good enough to avoid the notice of the first seven. Mat made those the same offer, and asked for names again. By the time he reached a point where no more names were to be found, he had forty-seven scouts. Hard times had put a lot of men to soldiering instead of the craft they would rather have followed.

The last, named by all three just before him, had been Chel Vanin, an Andoran who had lived in Maerone but ranged wide on both sides of the Erinin. Vanin could steal a hen pheasant's eggs without disturbing her on the nest, though it was unlikely he would fail to put her in the sack too. Vanin could steal a horse out from under a nobleman without the nobleman knowing it for two days. Or so his recommenders claimed in tones of awe. With a gap-toothed smile and a look of utter innocence on his round face, Vanin had protested he was a stableman and sometime farrier, when he could find work. But he would take the job for four times the Band's normal pay. So far, he had been more than worth it.

Sitting his dun in front of Mat on that hilltop, Vanin looked disturbed. He approved of Mat not wanting to be called "my Lord," since he did not much like bowing to anyone, but he managed to knuckle his forehead casually in a rough sort of salute. "I think you got to see this. I don't know what to make of it myself. You got to look for yourself."

"Wait here," Mat told the others, and to Vanin, "Show me."

It was not a long ride, just over the next two hills and up a winding stream with wide borders of dried mud. The smell announced what Vanin wanted him to see before the first vultures waddled into the air. The others just flapped a few paces before settling again, darting featherless heads and squawking challenges. Worst were those that never looked up from their dinners, milling piles of stained black feathers.

An overturned wagon like a little house on wheels, virulently painted in green and blue and yellow, identified the scene as a Tinker caravan, but few of the wagons had escaped burning. Bodies lay everywhere in bright clothes torn and darkened with dried blood, men and women and children. A part of Mat analyzed it coldly; the rest of him wanted to vomit, or run, anything but sit there on Pips. The attackers had come from the west first. Most of the men and older boys lay there, mingled with what was left of a number of large dogs, as if they had tried to form a line, to hold back killers with their bodies while the women and children ran. A futile flight. Heaped corpses showed where they had run headlong into the second attack. Only the vultures moved now.

Vanin spat disgustedly through a gap in his teeth. "You chase them off before they steal too much—they'll snap up children if you don't look sharp; raise them as their own—maybe you add a kick to speed them, but you don't do this. Who would?"

"I don't know. Brigands." The horses were all gone. But brigands wanted to steal, not kill, and no Tinker would resist if you stole his last penny and his coat to boot. Mat forced his hands to ease their grip on his reins. There was nowhere to look without seeing a dead woman, a dead child. Whoever did this had not wanted any survivors. He rode a slow circuit around the site, trying to ignore the vultures that hissed and flared their wings when he passed—the ground was too dry to hold tracks well, although he thought horses had gone in several directions—and came back to Vanin. "You could have told me about it. I don't need to see." *Light, but I don't!*

"I could've told you there was no good tracks," Vanin said, turning his horse to wade the shallow stream. "Maybe you need to see this."

Fire had taken most of the wagon lying on its side, but the wagon bed survived, propped on yellow wheels with red spokes. A man in a coat that still showed a little eye-wrenching blue lay hard against it, one sprawled hand black with blood. What he had written in shaky letters stood out darker than the wood of the wagon bottom.

TELL THE DRAGON REBORN

Tell him what? Mat thought. That somebody had killed a whole caravan of Tinkers? Or had the man died before he could write whatever it was? It would not have been the first time Tinkers had come onto important information. In a story he would have lived just long enough to scrawl the vital bit that meant victory. Well, whatever the message, nobody was ever going to know a word more now.

"You were right, Vanin." Mat hesitated. Tell the Dragon Reborn what? No reason to start any more rumors than they already had. "See the rest of this wagon burns before you leave. And if anybody asks, there was nothing here but a lot of dead men." And women, and children.

Vanin nodded. "Filthy savages," he muttered, and spat through his teeth again. "Could have been some of them, I suppose."

That band of Aielmen had caught up, three or four hundred strong. They trotted down the slope and crossed the stream no more than fifty paces from the wagons. A number raised a hand in greeting; Mat did not recognize them, but a good many Aiel had heard of Rand al'Thor's friend, he who wore the hat and whom it was better not to gamble against. Across the stream and up the next slope, and all those bodies might as well not have existed.

Bloody Aiel, Mat thought. He knew that Aiel avoided Tinkers, ignored them, if not why, but this. . . . "I don't think so," he said. "See it burns, Vanin."

Talmanes and the other two were right where he had left them, of course. When Mat told them what lay ahead, and that burial parties had to be told off, they nodded grimly, Daerid muttering a disbelieving, "Tinkers?"

"We will camp here," Mat added.

He expected some comment—there was light left for a few more miles, and these three had gotten caught up in how far the Band could move in a day to the point of laying wagers—but Nalesean just said, "I'll send a man down to signal the ships before they get too far ahead."

Maybe they felt the way he did. Unless they swung all the way over to the river, there would be no avoiding at least the sight of vultures scattering into the sky from the burial parties. Just because a man had seen death did not mean he had to enjoy it. For Mat's part, he thought another look at those birds would empty his stomach. In the morning there would only be graves, safely out of eyeshot.

The memory would not go out of his head, though, even after his tent was raised on that very hilltop where it might catch a breeze off the river if one ever decided to rise. Bodies hacked by killers, ravaged by vultures. Worse than the battle around Cairhien against the Shaido. Maidens had died there, but he had not seen any, and there had been no children. A Tinker would not fight even to defend his life. Nobody killed the Traveling People. He picked at his beef and beans, and retired to his tent as soon as he could. Even Nalesean did not want to talk, and Talmanes looked tighter than ever.

Word of the killing had spread. There was a quiet over the camp Mat had heard before. Usually the darkness would be broken by at least a little raucous laughter and sometimes songs off-key and off-color until the bannermen drove the handful who would not admit they were tired to their blankets. Tonight was like the times they had found a village with the dead unburied or a group of refugees who had tried to keep their little from bandits. Few could laugh or sing after that, and those who could were usually silenced by the rest.

Mat lay smoking his pipe while darkness fell, but the tent was close, and sleep would not come for memories of Tinker dead, older memories of older dead. Too many battles, and too many dead. He fingered his spear, traced the inscription in the Old Tongue along the black shaft.

> *Thus is our treaty written; thus is agreement made.*
> *Thought is the arrow of time; memory never, fades.*
> *What was asked is given; the price is paid.*

He had gotten the worst of that deal.

After a time he gathered a blanket, and after a moment the spear, and padded outside in his smallclothes, the silver foxhead on his bare chest catching the light of the clipped moon. There was a slight breeze, a meager stirring with little coolness that scarcely shifted the Red Hand banner on its staff stuck in the ground before his tent, yet better than inside.

Tossing his blanket down among the scrub, he lay on his back. When he was a boy, he'd sometimes used to put himself to sleep naming the constellations. In that cloudless sky, the moon gave enough light to wash out most stars even if it was waning, but it left enough. There was the Haywain, high overhead, and the Five Sisters, and the Three Geese pointing the way north. The Archer, the Plowman, the Blacksmith, the Snake. Aiel called that one the Dragon. The Shield, that some called Hawkwing's Shield—that made him shift; in some of his memories he did not like Artur Paendrag Tanreall at all—the Stag, and the Ram. The Cup, and the Traveler with her staff standing out sharp.

Something caught his ear, he was not sure what. If the night had not been so still, the faint sound might not have seemed furtive, but it was and it did. Who would be sneaking around up here? Curious, he lifted up on an elbow—and froze.

Like moonshadows, shapes moved around his tent. Moonlight caught one enough for him to make out a veiled face. Aiel? What under the Light? Silently they surrounded the tent, closed in; bright metal flashed in the night, whispers of cloth being sliced, and they vanished inside. A moment only and they were back out. And looking around; there was light enough to see that.

Mat gathered his feet under him. If he kept low, he might be able to slip away without being heard.

"Mat?" Talmanes called up the hillside; he sounded drunk.

Mat went still; maybe the man would go back if he thought he was asleep. The Aiel seemed to melt away, but he was sure they had gone to ground where they were.

Talmanes' boots crunched closer. "I have some brandy here, Mat. I think you should take it. It is very good for dreams, Mat. You do not remember them."

Mat wondered whether the Aiel would hear him over Talmanes if he went now. Ten paces or so to where the nearest men would be sleeping—the First Banner of Horse, Talmanes' Thunderbolts, had the "honor" tonight—less than ten to his tent, and the Aiel. They were fast, but with a step or two, they should not catch him before he had fifty men almost within arm's reach.

"Mat? I do not believe you are asleep, Mat. I saw your face. It is better once you kill the dreams. Believe me, I know."

Mat crouched, clutching his spear and taking a deep breath. Two strides.

"Mat?" Talmanes was nearer. The idiot was going to step on an Aiel any time now. They would cut his throat without making a sound.

Burn you, Mat thought. *All I needed was two strides.* "Out swords!" he shouted, leaping upright. "Aiel in the camp!" He sprinted down the slope. "Rally to the banner! Rally to the Red Hand! Rally, you dog-riding grave-robbers!"

That woke everyone, of course, as well it should with him bellowing like a bull in briars. Shouts spread in every direction; drums began beating assembly, trumpets sounding rally. Men of the First Horse roared out of their blankets, racing toward the banner waving swords.

Still, the fact was, the Aiel had a shorter distance to run than the soldiers. And they knew what they were after. Something—instinct, his luck, being *ta'veren*; Mat certainly did not hear anything over the racket—made him turn just as the first veiled shape appeared behind as if springing out of the air. No time to think. He blocked the thrust of a stabbing spear with the haft of his spear, but the Aiel caught his return slash on a buckler and kicked him in the belly. Desperation gave Mat strength to keep his legs straight with no air in his lungs; he twisted aside frantically from a spearhead that sliced his ribs, clipped the Aiel's legs out from under him with his own spear haft, and stabbed him through the heart. Light, but he hoped it was a him.

He jerked the spear free just in time to face the onslaught. *I should have run when I first had the bloody chance!* He worked the thing like a quarterstaff as fast as he ever had in his life, spinning, blocking away lancing Aiel spearpoints, no time to strike back. Too many. *I should have kept my bloody mouth shut and run!* He found breath again. "Rally, you pigeon-gutted sheep-stealers! Are you all deaf? Clean out your ears and rally!"

Wondering why he was not dead yet—he had been lucky with one Aiel, but nobody had enough luck to face this—he suddenly realized he was no longer alone. A skinny Cairhienin in his smallclothes fell nearly under his feet with a shrill yell, only to be replaced by a Tairen with his shirt flapping and sword swinging. More crowded in, shouting everything from "Lord Matrim and victory!" to "The Red Hand!" to "Kill the black-eyed vermin!"

Mat slipped back and left them to it. *The general who leads in the front of battle is a fool.* That came from one of those old memories, a quote from somebody whose name was not part of the memory. *A man could get killed in there.* That was pure Mat Cauthon.

In the end, it was a sheer matter of numbers. A dozen Aiel and, if not the whole Band, several hundred who managed to reach the hilltop before it was done. Twelve Aiel dead and, because they were Aiel, half again as many of the Band, with twice that or more bleeding if still alive to groan while they were tended. Even with his brief exposure, Mat stung and bled at half a dozen places, at least three of which he suspected would need stitching.

His spear made a good walking staff as he limped around to where Talmanes was stretched out on the ground with Daerid tying a tourniquet around his left leg.

Talmanes' white shirt, hanging loose, glistened darkly in two places. "It seems," he panted, "Nerim will get to try his hand as a seamstress on me again, burn him for a ham-fisted bull." Nerim was his serving man, and mended his master as often as his master's clothes.

"Will he be all right?" Mat asked softly.

Daerid shrugged. He wore only his breeches. "He is bleeding less than you, I think." He glanced up. He would have a new scar to add to the collection on his face. "As well you got out of their way, Mat. It is clear they were after you."

"Good not to give them what they came for." Wincing, Talmanes struggled to his feet with the aid of an arm over Daerid's shoulder. "It would be a shame to lose the Band's luck to a handful of savages in the night."

Mat cleared his throat. "That's the way it seemed to me, too." The image of the Aiel vanishing into his tent welled up in his mind, and he shivered. Why under the Light would Aiel want to kill him?

Nalesean appeared from where the dead Aiel were laid out in a row. Even now he had his coat on, though not buttoned; he kept frowning at a bloodstain on the lapel, maybe his blood, maybe not. "Burn my soul, I knew those savages would turn on us sooner or later. I expect they came from that lot who passed us earlier."

"I doubt it," Mat said. "If they had wanted me, they could have had me spitted and over the fire for dinner before any of you knew it." He made himself hobble over and study the Aiel, taking a lantern someone had brought to aid the moonlight. The relief of finding only men's faces nearly unhinged his knees. He did not know any of them, but then, he did not really know many Aiel. "Shaido, I expect," he said, returning to the others with the lantern. They could be Shaido. They could be Darkfriends; he knew all too well that there were Darkfriends among the Aiel. And Darkfriends, of course, did have reason to want him dead.

"Tomorrow," Daerid said, "I think we should try to find one of those Aes Sedai across the river. Talmanes here will live unless all the brandy leaked out of him, but some of the others might not be so fortunate." Nalesean said nothing, but his grunt spoke volumes; he was Tairen, after all, with less love than Mat for Aes Sedai.

Mat did not hesitate in agreeing. He would not be letting any Aes Sedai channel at him—in a way, every scar marked a small victory, another time he had avoided Aes Sedai—but he could not ask a man to die. Then he told them what else he wanted.

"A ditch?" Talmanes said in tones of disbelief.

"All the way around the camp?" Nalesean's pointed beard quivered. "Every night?"

"And a palisade?" Daerid exclaimed. Glancing around, he lowered his voice. There were still quite a few soldiers about, hauling away the dead. "There will be a mutiny, Mat."

"No there won't," Mat said. "By morning, every last man will know Aiel sneaked through the whole camp to reach my tent. Half won't sleep for thinking they will wake with an Aiel spear in their ribs. You three make sure they understand the fact that a palisade just might keep Aiel from sneaking in again." At the least it would slow them down. "Now go away and let me get a little sleep tonight."

After they had gone, he studied his tent. Long slashes in the walls, where Aiel had gone in, stirred in the fitful breeze. Sighing, he started to return to his blanket in the scrub, then hesitated. That noise that had alerted him. The Aiel had not made another, not a whisper. A shadow made as much noise as an Aiel. So what had it been?

Leaning on his spear, he limped around the tent, studying the ground. He was not sure what he was looking for. Soft Aiel boots had left no marks that he could make out by lantern light. Two of the tent ropes hung where they had been cut, but. . . . He set the lantern down and fingered the ropes. That sound could have been taut rope being sliced, yet there was no reason to cut these to get inside. Something about the angle of the cuts, the way they lined up with one another, caught his attention. Taking up the lantern, he cast around. A wiry bush not far away had been trimmed along one side, thin branches with small leaves lying on the ground. A very neat trimming, perfectly flat, the severed branch ends smooth as though planed by a cabinetmaker.

The hair on the back of Mat's neck stirred. One of those holes in the air that Rand used had been opened here. Bad enough that Aiel had tried to kill him, but they had been sent by somebody who could make one of those . . . gateways, Rand called them. Light, if he was not safe from the Forsaken with the Band around him, where was he safe? He wondered how he was going to sleep from now on with watch fires around his tent. And guards; a guard of honor, he could call it to take some of the sting away, to stand sentry around his tent. Next time it would probably be a hundred Trollocs, or a thousand, instead of a handful of Aiel. Or was he important enough for that? If they decided he was too important, the next time it could be one of the Forsaken. Blood and ashes! He had never asked to be *ta'veren*, never asked to be tied to the Dragon bloody Reborn.

"Blood and bloody—!"

Soil crunching underfoot warned him, and he spun swinging the spear with a snarl. Barely in time he stopped the slashing blade, as Olver screamed and fell flat on his back, staring wide-eyed at the spearpoint.

"What in the bloody Pit of Doom are you doing here?" Mat snapped.

"I . . . I. . . ." The boy stopped to swallow. "They say fifty Aiel tried to kill you in your sleep, Lord Mat, but you killed them first, and I wanted to see if you were all right, and. . . . Lord Edorion bought me some shoes. See?" He raised a shod foot.

Muttering under his breath, Mat hauled Olver to his feet. "That wasn't what I meant. Why aren't you in Maerone? Didn't Edorion find somebody to look after you?"

"She just wanted Lord Edorion's coin, not me. She had six children of her own. Master Burdin gives me lots to eat, and all I have to do is feed and water his horses, and rub them down. I like that, Lord Mat. He will not let me ride them, though."

A throat cleared. "Lord Talmanes sent me, my Lord." Nerim was short even for a Cairhienin, a skinny gray-haired man with a long face that seemed to say nothing was going well at the moment and in the long run, this was a better day than most. "If my Lord will pardon me for saying, those bloodstains will never come out of my Lord's smallclothes, but if my Lord will allow it, I may be able to do something for the tears in my Lord." He had his sewing box under one arm. "You, boy, fetch some water. No back talk. Water for my Lord, and quickly." Nerim combined picking up the lantern with a bow. "If my Lord will step inside? Night air is bad for wounds."

In short order Mat was stretched out beside his bedding—"My Lord will not want to stain his blankets"—letting Nerim wash away dried blood and sew him up. Talmanes was right; as a seamstress, the man was a ham-fisted cook. With Olver there, there was no choice but to grit his teeth and bear it.

To try taking his mind elsewhere than Nerim's needle, Mat pointed to the frayed cloth scrip hanging from Olver's shoulder. "What do you have in there?" he panted.

Olver clutched the tattered bag to his chest. He was certainly cleaner than he had been, if no prettier. The shoes appeared stout, and his woolen shirt and breeches looked new. "It is mine," he said defensively. "I did not steal anything." After a moment, he opened the bag and began laying things out. A spare pair of breeches, two more shirts and some stockings had no interest for him, but he listed the other things. "This is my red-hawk's feather, Lord Mat, and this stone is just the color of the sun. See?" He added a small purse. "I have five coppers and a silver penny." A rolled cloth tied with a string and a small wooden box. "My game of Snakes and Foxes; my father made it for me; he drew the board." For a moment his face crumpled, then he went on. "And see, this stone has a fish head in it. I do not know how it got there. And this is my turtle shell. A blue-back turtle. See the stripes?"

Wincing at a particularly hard thrust of the sewing needle, Mat stretched his hand to finger the rolled cloth. Much better if he breathed through his nose. It was odd how those holes in his real memories worked; he could remember how to play Snakes and Foxes, but not ever playing it.

"That's a fine turtle shell, Olver. I had one, once. A green basker." Stretching his hand the other way, he reached his own purse; he dipped out two gold Cairhienin crowns. "Add these to your purse, Olver. A man needs a little gold in his pocket."

Stiffly Olver began stuffing things back into his scrip. "I do not beg, Lord Mat. I can work for my supper. I am not a beggar."

"Never meant to say you are." Mat cast around hurriedly for some reason to pay the boy two crowns. "I . . . I need someone to carry messages for me. Can't ask any of the Band; they are all busy soldiering. Of course, you'd have to take care of your own horse. I could not ask anybody to do it for you."

Olver sat up straight. "I would have my own horse?" he said incredulously.

"Of course. There is one thing. My name is Mat. You call me *Lord* Mat again, and I'll tie your nose in a knot." Bellowing, he jerked half-upright. "Burn you, Nerim, that's a leg, not a bloody side of beef!"

"As my Lord says," Nerim murmured, "my Lord's leg is not a side of beef. Thank you, my Lord, for instructing me."

Olver was feeling his nose hesitantly, as if considering whether it could be tied in a knot.

Mat settled back with a groan. Now he had saddled himself with a boy, and had done the lad no favor—not if he was nearby the next time the Forsaken tried to reduce the number of *ta'veren* in the world. Well, if Rand's plan worked, there would be one less Forsaken. If Mat Cauthon had his way, he intended to stay out of trouble and out of danger until there were no Forsaken.

CHAPTER
23

To Understand a Message

Graendal managed not to stare as she entered the room, but her streith gown went dead black before she could control herself and return it to a blue mist. Sammael had done enough to make anyone doubt that this chamber was in the Great Hall of the Council in Illian. But then, she would be very surprised if anyone but he ever penetrated this far uninvited into "Lord Brend's" apartments.

The air was pleasantly cool; in one corner rose the hollow cylinder of an exchanger. Glowbulbs, bright and steady, stood oddly in heavy gold candleholders, giving much better illumination than candles or oil lamps ever could. A small music box sat on the marble mantelpiece, producing from its memory the soft strains of a sound-sculpture that very likely had not been heard outside this room in well over three thousand years. And she recognized several of the artworks on the walls.

She paused in front of Ceran Tol's "Tempo of Infinity." Not a copy. "One might think you had looted a museum, Sammael." It was hard to keep the envy from her voice, and when she saw his faint smile, she realized she had failed.

Filling two silver-chased goblets with wine, he handed her one. "Only a stasis box. I suppose people tried to save what they could in the last days." His smile pulled at that awful scar across his face as he beamed around the chamber, with especial fondness for the zara board projecting its field of still-transparent boxes in the air; he had always liked the more violent games. Of course, a zara board meant his stasis box had been filled by someone who followed the Great Lord; possession of a single once-human playing piece had meant imprisonment at the least on the other side. What else had he found?

Sipping her wine—and suppressing a sigh; it was from the here and now; she had hoped for a delicate Satare or one of the exquisite Comolads—she stroked her gown with beringed fingers. "I found one as well, but beyond streith, it contained the most appalling collection of useless rubbish." After all, since he had invited her here and let her see this, it was a time for confidences. Small confidences.

"How sad for you." Again that faint smile. He *had* found something more than playthings and pretties. "On the other hand," he went on, "think how awful it would have been to open a box and rouse a nest of cafar, say, or a jumara, or one of Aginor's other little creations. Did you know there are jumara loose in the Blight? Full-grown, though they'll never transform now. They call them Worms." He laughed so hard at that, he shook.

Graendal smiled a good deal more warmly than she felt inside, though if her gown changed color, it was by a hair. She had had an unpleasant, in fact almost fatal, experience with one of Aginor's creations. The man had been brilliant in his way, but mad. None but a madman would have made the *gholam.* "You seem in very good mood."

"Why should I not be?" he said expansively. "I all but have my hands on a cache of *angreal* and who can say what else. Do not look so surprised. Of course I've known that the rest of you have been trying to look over my shoulder in hopes I will lead you to it. Well, it will do you no good. Oh, I will share, but after it's mine, and after I have first choice." Sprawling in a heavily gilded chair—or perhaps it was solid gold; that would be like him—he balanced one boot atop the toe of the other and stroked his golden beard. "Besides, I sent an emissary to al'Thor. And the answer was favorable."

Graendal almost spilled her wine. "It was? I heard that he killed your messenger." If her knowing that much shook him, he held it in. He even smiled.

"Al'Thor killed no one. Andris went there to die; do you think I wanted to wait on couriers, or *pigeons?* How he died told me al'Thor's answer."

"Which was?" she said carefully.

"A truce between us."

Icy fingers seemed to dig into her scalp. It could not be true. Yet he looked more at ease than she had seen him since waking. "Lews Therin would never—"

"Lews Therin is long dead, Graendal." The interruption was amused, even mocking. No anger at all.

She covered a deep breath by pretending to drink. Could it be true? "His army is still gathering in Tear. I have seen it. That hardly looks like a truce to me."

Sammael laughed outright. "It takes time to redirect an army. Believe me, it will never move against me."

"You think not? One or two of my little friends say he wants you dead because you killed some of his pet Maidens. Were I you, I would be thinking about somewhere less conspicuous, somewhere he might not find me." Not a flicker of an eyelid out of him. It was as if all the strings that usually moved him had been cut.

"What should it matter a few Maidens died?" The look on his face was truly puzzled. "It was battle; soldiers die in battle. Al'Thor may be a farmer, but he has generals to fight his battles and explain matters. I doubt he even noticed."

"You really never have looked at these people. They have changed as much as the land, Sammael. Not just the Aiel. In some ways, the rest have changed much more. Those soldiers were women, and to Rand al'Thor, that makes a difference."

He shrugged dismissively, and she suppressed contempt, kept the streith steady in a calm fog. He had never understood that you must understand people to make them do as you wished. Compulsion was all very well, but you could not use Compulsion on the entire world.

She wondered whether the stasis box had been this cache that he claimed he would put his hands on soon. If he had even one *angreal*. . . . If he did, she would find out, but probably not before he let her. "I suppose we shall see how much wiser the primitive Lews Therin has become, then." She raised a doubting eyebrow, managed a smile of her own. No reaction. Where had he found this leash for his temper? Lews Therin's name alone should have been enough to loose it. "If he fails to chase you out of Illian like a cosa scampering up a tree, perhaps—"

"That might be waiting too long," he cut in smoothly. "Too long for you, that is."

"Is that supposed to be a threat, Sammael?" Her gown shifted to a pale rose, but she let it stay. Let him be aware she was angry. "I thought you learned long ago that threatening me is a mistake."

"No threats, Graendal," he replied calmly. All of his pressure points had gone numb; nothing seemed to shift him out of that amused coolness. "Merely facts. Al'Thor will not attack me, and I will not attack him. And of course, I agreed not to aid any other Chosen should al'Thor find them. All very much in accordance with the Great Lord's commands, wouldn't you say?"

"Of course." She kept her face smooth, but the streith had gone a deeper rose, losing some of its mistiness. In part the color was still anger. There was more to this, but how was she to find out?

"Which means," he continued, "that on the Day of Return, I will very likely be the only one remaining to face al'Thor."

"I doubt he will manage to kill all of us," she said acidly, but acid churned in her stomach, as well. Too many of the Chosen had died. Sammael *had* found a way to stand aside until the last; it was the only explanation.

"You think not? Not even if he learns where you all are?" That smile deepened. "I am sure I know what Demandred is scheming, but where is he hiding? Where is Semirhage? Mesaana? What about Asmodean and Lanfear? Moghedien?"

Those cold fingers returned, imprinting themselves on her skull. He would not lounge there and talk this way—he would not dare suggest what he was suggesting—unless. . . . "Asmodean and Lanfear are dead, and I am sure Moghedien must be, too." She was surprised to hear her own voice, hoarse and unsteady. Wine did not seem to dampen her dry throat.

"And the others?" It was just a question; his voice was not in the slightest insistent. It sent a shiver through her.

"I've told you what I know, Sammael."

"Which is nothing. When I am Nae'blis, I will choose who stands just below me. That one will have to be alive to receive the Great Lord's touch."

"Are you saying you have been to Shayol Ghul? That the Great Lord promised you . . . ?"

"You will know all when it is time, and not before. But a small advice, Graendal. Prepare now. Where are they?"

Her mind worked furiously. He must have had that promise. He must. But why him? No, there was no time for speculation. The Great Lord chose as he wished. And Sammael knew where she was, at least. She could flee Arad Doman, establish herself elsewhere; it would not be difficult. Giving up the little games she played there, and even the larger games that might have to be abandoned, would be a small loss compared with having

al'Thor—or Lews Therin—come after her. She had no intention of ever
confronting him directly; if Ishamael and Rahvin had fallen to him, she
was not about to risk his strength, not head-on. Sammael *must* have had
the promise. If he died now. . . . He was certainly holding *saidin*—he
would be mad to say these things otherwise—and he would feel the instant she embraced *saidar*. She would be the one to die. He must have had
it. "I . . . do not know where Demandred or Semirhage is. Mesaana . . .
Mesaana is in the White Tower. That is all I know. I swear it."

A tightness in her chest loosened when he finally nodded. "You will
find the others for me." It was not a question. "All of them, Graendal. If
you want me to believe anyone dead, show me a corpse."

She very much wished she dared turn him into a corpse. Her gown
rippled through violent shades of red, echoing the anger and fear and
shame that rippled through her uncontrollably. Very well, let him think
her cowed for the moment. If he fed Mesaana to al'Thor, if he fed them all
to al'Thor, so be it, so long as that kept al'Thor from her own throat. "I
will try."

"Do more than try, Graendal. More than try."

When Graendal was gone, the gateway back to her palace in Arad Doman
closed, Sammael let the smile dissolve on his face. His jaws ached from
holding it. Graendal thought too much; she was so used to making others
act for her that she failed to think of acting for herself. He wondered what
she would say if she ever discovered that he had manipulated her as deftly
as she had manipulated so many fools in her time. He would wager everything that she never saw his real purpose. So, Mesaana was inside the
White Tower. Mesaana in the Tower, and Graendal in Arad Doman. Had
Graendal been able to see his face then, she would have known real fear.
Whatever happened, Sammael intended to be the one still standing on the
Day of Return, to be named Nae'blis and defeat the Dragon Reborn.

CHAPTER
24

An Embassy

Turning away from the musicians on the street corner, a perspiring woman puffing at a long flute and a red-faced man plucking a nine-string bittern, Egwene threaded her way through the crowd with a light heart. The sun stood high in the sky, molten gold, and the paving stones were hot enough to burn through the soles of her soft boots. Sweat dripped from her nose, her shawl felt like a heavy blanket even looped loosely over her elbows, and there was enough dust in the air that she already wanted to wash, yet she smiled. Some people eyed her askance, when they thought she was not looking, which almost made her laugh. That was how they looked at Aiel. People saw what they expected to see, and they saw a woman in Aiel garb, never noticing her eyes or her height.

Hawkers and peddlers cried their wares, competing against the shouts of butchers and candlemakers, the rattle and clatter from silversmiths' and potters' shops, the squeal of ungreased axles. Rough-tongued wagon drivers and men walking alongside ox-carts loudly contested the way with dark-lacquered sedan chairs and sober coaches with House sigils on the doors. There were musicians everywhere, along with tumblers and jugglers. A knot of pale women in riding dresses, carrying swords, swaggered by, imitating how they imagined men behaved, laughing too raucously and pushing their way in a manner that would have started a dozen fights in a hundred paces had they been men. A blacksmith's hammer rang on his anvil. In general a

babble and hum of bustle hung in the air, the noise of a city that she had
almost forgotten among the Aiel. Perhaps she had missed it.

She did laugh then, right there in the street. The first time she had heard
the noise of a city, it had nearly stunned her. Sometimes it seemed that wide-
eyed girl had been someone else.

A woman working her bay mare through the crowd turned to look at
her curiously. The horse had small silver bells tied in her long mane and
tail, and the woman had more bells in the dark hair that hung halfway
down her back. Pretty, she could not have been much older than Egwene,
but she had a hardness to her face, and a sharp eye, and no fewer than six
knives at her belt, one nearly as large as an Aiel's. A Hunter for the Horn,
no doubt.

A tall handsome man in a green coat, two swords on his back, watched
the woman ride on. He was probably another. They seemed to be everywhere. As the crowd swallowed the woman on the bay, he turned and saw
Egwene looking at him. Smiling with sudden interest, he squared broad
shoulders and started toward her.

Hastily Egwene put on her coldest face, tried to combine Sorilea at her
sternest with Siuan Sanche, the stole of the Amyrlin Seat around her
shoulders.

He stopped, looking surprised. As he turned away, she distinctly heard
him growl, "Flaming Aiel." She could not help laughing again; he must
have heard despite the noise, because he stiffened, shaking his head. But he
did not look back.

The source of her good mood was twofold. One was the Wise Ones finally agreeing that walking in the city provided as much exercise as walking around it outside the walls. Sorilea in particular did not seem to
understand why she wanted to spend a minute more than she had to among
throngs of wetlanders, especially cramped inside walls. Mostly, though, she
felt good because they had told her that now the headaches that had puzzled them so were completely gone—she had not been able to hide them
altogether—she could return to *Tel'aran'rhiod* soon. Not in time for the next
meeting, three nights off, but before the one after.

That was a relief in more ways than one. An end to having to sneak
into the World of Dreams. An end to laboriously working everything out
for herself. An end to being terrified the Wise Ones would catch her and
refuse to teach her any more. An end to needing to lie. It was necessary—
she could not afford to waste time; there was too much to learn, and she

could not believe she would have time to learn it all—but they would never understand.

Aiel dotted the crowd, both in *cadin'sor* and in *gai'shain* white. The *gai'shain* went where they were sent, yet the others might well be inside the walls for their first time, and quite possibly their last. The Aiel really did not seem to like cities, though a good many had come in six days ago, to see Mangin hang. It was said he put the noose around his own neck, and made some Aiel joke about whether the rope would break his neck or his neck the rope. She had heard several Aiel repeat the joke, but never a comment about the hanging. Rand had liked Mangin; she was sure of it. Berelain had informed the Wise Ones of the sentence as though telling them their wash would be ready the next day, and the Wise Ones had listened the same way. Egwene did not think she would ever understand Aiel. She was very much afraid she did not understand Rand anymore. As for Berelain, Egwene understood her all too well; that one was only interested in men who were alive.

With thoughts like those, it took an effort to regain her good mood. The city was certainly no cooler than outside the walls—in fact, with no breeze and people so close, it might have been hotter—and nearly as dusty, but at least she was not trudging along with nothing to look at but the ashes of Foregate. A few more days and she would be able to learn again, to really learn. That put a smile back on her face.

She stopped near a wiry, damp-faced Illuminator; it was easy to tell what he was, or had been. His thick mustaches were not covered by the diaphanous veil Taraboners often wore, but baggy breeches, embroidered on the legs, and an equally loose shirt embroidered across the chest marked him well enough. He was selling finches and warblers in crudely made cages. With their chapter house burned by the Shaido, a number of Illuminators were trying to find the means to return to Tarabon.

"I have it from the most reliable source," he was telling a handsome graying woman in a plainly cut dark blue dress. A merchant, no doubt, catching a jump on those waiting for better times in Cairhien. "The Aes Sedai," the Illuminator confided, leaning over a caged bird to whisper, "they are divided. The Aes Sedai, they are at war. With one another." The merchant nodded agreement.

Egwene stopped pretending to consider a green-headed finch and moved on, though she had to hop out of the way of a round-faced gleeman, striding along with self-important flourishes of his patch-covered cloak.

Gleemen knew very well that they were among the few wetlanders welcome in the Waste; Aiel did not intimidate them. At least, they pretended so.

That rumor troubled her. Not that the Tower had split apart—that could not have been kept secret much longer—but talk of war between Aes Sedai. Knowing that Aes Sedai were set against Aes Sedai was like knowing one part of her family was set against another, just barely tolerable for knowing the reasons, yet the thought that it might come to more. . . . If only there were some way to Heal the Tower, to make it whole again without bloodshed.

A little farther down the street, a perspiring Foregate woman who might have been pretty if her face were cleaner was dispensing rumor along with ribbons and pins from a tray hung from a neckstrap. She wore a blue silk dress, slashed with red in the skirt, that had been made for a shorter woman; the heavily worn hem was high enough to show her stout shoes, and holes in the sleeves and bodice showed where embroidery had been picked out. "I tell you a fact," she informed the women picking over her tray, "there has been Trollocs seen around the city. Ah, yes, that green will set off your eyes. Hundreds of Trollocs and. . . ."

Egwene barely paused. If there had been even one Trolloc anywhere near the city, the Aiel would have known long before it became street gossip. She wished the Wise Ones gossiped. Well, they did, sometimes, but only about other Aiel. As far as Aiel were concerned, nothing about wetlanders was very absorbing. Being able to pop into Elaida's study in *Tel'aran'rhiod* whenever she wanted and read the woman's letters had accustomed her to knowing what was happening in the world, though.

Abruptly Egwene realized she was looking around differently, looking at people's faces. There were Aes Sedai eyes-and-ears in Cairhien as surely as she was sweating. Elaida must receive a report a day by pigeon from Cairhien, if not more. Tower spies, Ajah spies, spies for individual Aes Sedai. They were everywhere, often where and who you least suspected. Why were those two tumblers just standing there? Were they catching their breath, or watching her? They sprang back into action, one leaping up to a handstand on the other's shoulders.

A spy for the Yellow Ajah had once tried to bundle Elayne and Nynaeve off to Tar Valon, on orders issued by Elaida. Egwene did not actually know that Elaida wanted her as well, but assuming anything else would be very foolish. Egwene could not make herself believe that Elaida would forgive anyone who had worked closely for the woman she deposed.

For that matter, some of the Aes Sedai in Salidar probably had eyes-

and-ears here too. If word ever reached them of "Egwene Sedai of the Green Ajah. . . ." It could be anybody. That skinny woman in the shop door, apparently studying a bolt of dark gray cloth. Or the blowsy woman lolling beside the tavern door, flapping her apron at her face. Or that fat fellow with his pushcart full of pies—Why was he looking at her so strangely? She very nearly headed for the nearest city gate.

It was the fat fellow who stopped her, or rather the way he suddenly tried to cover his pies with his hands. He was staring at her because she had been staring at him. He was probably afraid an Aiel "savage" was going to take some of his wares without paying.

Egwene laughed weakly. Aiel. Even people who looked her in the face assumed she was Aiel. A Tower agent who was looking for her would walk right past. Feeling a good deal better, she went back to meandering through the streets, listening where she could.

The trouble was, she had grown used to knowing things just weeks, or even days, after they happened, and with a certainty that they had happened. Rumor might cross a hundred miles in a day or take a month, and it birthed ten daughters every day. Today she learned that Siuan had been executed because she unearthed the Black Ajah, that Siuan *was* Black Ajah and still alive, that the Black Ajah had driven those Aes Sedai who were not Black from the Tower. They were not new tales, only variations on old. One new story, spreading like fire in a summer meadow, was that the Tower had been behind all the false Dragons; that made her so angry she stalked away stiff-backed every time she heard it. Which meant she did a good bit of stiff-backed stalking. She heard that Andorans in Aringill had declared some noblewoman queen—Dylin, Delin, the name varied—now that Morgase was dead, which might be true, and that Aes Sedai were running around Arad Doman doing very improbable things, which was certainly untrue. The Prophet was Coming to Cairhien; the Prophet had been crowned King of Ghealdan—no, Amadicia; the Dragon Reborn had killed the Prophet for blasphemy. The Aiel were all leaving; no, they meant to settle and stay. Berelain was to be crowned on the Sun Throne. A skinny little man with shifty eyes nearly got himself beaten by his listeners outside a tavern for saying that Rand was one of the Forsaken, but Egwene stepped into that without thought.

"Have you no honor?" she demanded coldly. The four coarse-faced men who had been on the point of grabbing the skinny fellow blinked at her. They were Cairhienin, not all that much taller than she, but much bulkier, with the broken noses and sunken knuckles of brawlers, yet she held them where they stood with her sheer intensity. That and the presence of Aiel in the street; they were not fool enough to become rough with an Aiel woman, as they thought, in those circumstances. "If you must face a man for what he says, face him one at a time, in honor. This is not battle; you shame yourselves to go four at one."

They stared at her as if she were mad, and slowly her face reddened. She hoped they thought it anger. Not how dare you pick on someone weaker, but how dare you not let him fight you one by one? She had just lectured them as if they followed *ji'e'toh*. Of course, if they did, there would have been no need to lecture.

One of the men ducked his head in a sort of half-bow. His nose was not only crooked, the tip was missing. "Uh . . . he is gone now . . . uh. . . . Mistress. Can we go too?"

It was true; the skinny man had used her interference to vanish. She felt a flash of contempt. Running because he feared to face four. How could he bear the shame? Light, she was doing it again.

She opened her mouth to say that of course they could—and nothing came out. They took her silence for assent, or maybe excuse, and hurried away, but she barely noticed them go. She was too busy staring at the back of a mounted party making its way up the street.

She did not recognize the dozen or so green-cloaked soldiers forcing a path through the crowd, but who they escorted was a different matter. She could only see the backs of the women—five or six, she thought, between the soldiers—just parts of their backs, but that was more than enough. Much more. The women wore light dustcloaks, pale linen in shades of brown, and Egwene found herself staring right at what seemed to be a pure white disc embroidered on the back of one of those cloaks. Only the stitching picked out the white Flame of Tar Valon from the border signifying the White Ajah. She caught a glimpse of green, of red. Red! Five or six Aes Sedai, riding toward the Royal Palace, where a copy of the Dragon banner waved fitfully atop a stepped tower alongside one of Rand's crimson flags bearing the ancient Aes Sedai symbol. Some called *that* the Dragon banner, and others al'Thor's banner, or even the Aiel banner, and a dozen other names besides.

Wriggling through the crowd, she followed them maybe twenty paces, then stopped. A Red sister—at least one Red that she had seen—had to mean this was the long-expected embassy from the Tower, the one Elaida had written would escort Rand to Tar Valon. More than two months since that letter arrived by a hard-riding courier; this party must have left not long behind.

They would not find Rand—not unless he had slipped in unannounced; she had decided that he had somehow rediscovered the Talent called Traveling, but that put her no closer to knowing how it was done—yet whether they found Rand or not, they must not find Egwene. The best she could expect was to be hauled up short as an Accepted out of the Tower with no full sister to oversee her, and that could be expected only if Elaida really was not hunting for her. Even then they would haul her back to Tar Valon, and Elaida; she had no illusions that she could resist five or six Aes Sedai.

With a last look after the receding Aes Sedai, she gathered her skirts and began to run, dodging between people, sometimes caroming off them, ducking under the noses of teams pulling wagons or carriages. Angered shouts followed her. When she at last dashed through one of the tall square-arched city gates, the hot wind hit her in the face. Unhindered by buildings, it carried sheets of dust that made her cough, but she kept running, all the way back to the Wise One's low tents.

To her surprise a sleek gray mare, saddle and bridle worked and fringed with gold, stood outside Amys' tent, in the charge of a *gai'shain* who kept his eyes down except when patting the spirited animal. Ducking inside, she found the rider, Berelain, sipping tea with Amys and Bair and Sorilea, all stretched out on bright, tasseled cushions. A white-robed woman, Rodera, knelt to one side, meekly waiting to refill cups.

"There are Aes Sedai in the city," Egwene said as soon as she was inside, "heading toward the Sun Palace. It must be Elaida's embassy to Rand."

Berelain rose gracefully; Egwene had to admit, if grudgingly, that the woman was graceful. And her riding dress was decently cut, for even she was not fool enough to go riding in the sun in her usual garb. The others rose with her. "I must return to the palace, it seems," she sighed. "The Light knows how they will feel about no one there to greet them. Amys, if you know where Rhuarc is, could you send a message for him to meet me?"

Amys nodded, but Sorilea said, "You should not depend on Rhuarc so much, girl. Rand al'Thor gave Cairhien to you to tend. Let most men have a finger, and they will have the whole hand before you know. Let a clan chief have a finger, and he will have the entire arm."

"It is true," Amys murmured. "Rhuarc is the shade of my heart, but it is true."

Pulling slim riding gloves from behind her belt, Berelain began tugging them on. "He reminds me of my father. Too much so, sometimes." For an instant she grimaced ruefully. "But he gives very good advice. And he knows when to loom, and how much. I think even Aes Sedai must be impressed by Rhuarc staring at them."

Amys laughed in her throat. "He is impressive. I will send him to you." She kissed Berelain lightly on the forehead and each cheek.

Egwene stared; that was how a mother kissed her son or daughter. What *was* going on between Berelain and the Wise Ones? She could not ask, of course. Such a question would be shaming to her and to the Wise Ones. To Berelain too, though Berelain would not know it, and Egwene would not mind shaming Berelain until her hair fell out.

As Berelain turned to leave the tent, Egwene put a hand on the woman's arm. "They must be handled carefully. They'll not be friendly toward Rand, but the wrong words, a wrong move, could make them open enemies." That was true enough, but not what she needed to say. She would rather have her tongue torn out than ask a favor of Berelain.

"I have dealt with Aes Sedai before, Egwene Sedai," the other woman said dryly.

Egwene refrained from drawing a deep breath. It had to be done, but she would not let this woman see how hard it was. "Elaida means no good to Rand, no more than a weasel means to a chicken, and these Aes Sedai are Elaida's. If they learn of an Aes Sedai on Rand's side, here where they can reach her, she might just disappear one day soon after." Looking into Berelain's unreadable face, she could not make herself say more.

After a long moment, Berelain smiled. "Egwene Sedai, I will do whatever I can for Rand." Both smile and tone of voice . . . insinuated.

"Girl," Sorilea said sharply, and for a wonder, spots of color bloomed in Berelain's cheeks.

Not looking at Egwene, Berelain said in a carefully neutral voice, "I would appreciate it if you did not tell Rhuarc." In fact, she was not looking at anyone, but she tried to ignore Egwene's presence.

"We will not," Amys put in quickly, leaving Sorilea with her mouth open. "We will not." The repetition was directed at Sorilea with a blend of firmness and asking, and at last the eldest Wise One nodded, if somewhat grudgingly. Berelain actually sighed with relief before ducking out of the tent.

"The child has spirit," Sorilea laughed as soon as Berelain was gone. Reclining on the cushions again, she patted the space next to her for Egwene. "We should find the right husband for her, a man to match her. If such exists among wetlanders."

Wiping her hands and face with the damp cloth Rodera brought,

Egwene wondered whether that was enough opening to ask about Berelain in good honor. She accepted a teacup of green Sea Folk porcelain and took her place in the circle of Wise Ones. If one of the others responded to Sorilea, that might be enough.

"Are you certain these Aes Sedai mean harm to the *Car'a'carn?*" Amys asked instead.

Egwene colored. Thinking about gossip when there were important matters to attend. "Yes," she replied quickly, then more slowly, "At least. . . . I don't know that they mean to harm him, exactly. Not intentionally, anyway." Elaida's letter had mentioned "all the honor and respect" he deserved. How much did a former Red sister think any man who could channel deserved? "But I don't doubt they will want to control him somehow, make him do what Elaida wants. They aren't his friends." How much were the Salidar Aes Sedai his friends? Light, she needed to talk with Nynaeve and Elayne. "And they will not care that he is the *Car'a'carn.*" Sorilea grunted sourly.

"You believe they will try to harm you?" Bair asked, and Egwene nodded.

"If they discover I'm here. . . ." She tried to cover a shiver by sipping her mint tea. Whether as a handle on Rand or as an unsupervised Accepted, they would do their best to haul her back to the Tower. "They'll not leave me free if they can help it. Elaida will not want Rand listening to anyone but her." Bair and Amys exchanged grim looks.

"Then the answer is simple." Sorilea sounded as if it had all been decided. "You will stay among the tents, and they will not find you. Wise Ones avoid Aes Sedai, in any case. If you remain with us a few more years, we will make a fine Wise One of you."

Egwene almost dropped her cup. "You flatter me," she said carefully, "but sooner or later, I will have to go." Sorilea did not look convinced. Egwene had learned to hold her own with Amys and Bair, after a fashion, but Sorilea. . . .

"Not soon, I think," Bair told her, with a smile to take the sting out. "You have much to learn yet."

"Yes, and eager to get back to it," Amys added. Egwene struggled not to blush, and Amys frowned. "You look odd. Did you overuse yourself this morning? I was sure you had recovered enough—"

"I have," Egwene said hastily. "Truly, I have. I haven't had a headache in days. It was the dust, running back here. And the crowd in the city was more than I remembered. And I was so excited, I didn't breakfast very well."

Sorilea motioned to Rodera. "Bring some honeybread, if there is any, and cheese, and any fruit you can find." She poked Egwene in the ribs. "A woman should have some flesh to her." That from a woman who looked as if she had been left in the sun till most of her flesh had dried away.

Egwene did not really mind eating—she had been too excited to eat this morning—but Sorilea watched every bite go down, and her scrutiny made swallowing a little difficult. That and the fact that they wanted to discuss what to do about the Aes Sedai. If the Aes Sedai were hostile to Rand, they would have to be watched, and a way found to safeguard him. Even Sorilea was a bit edgy about the possibility that they might be putting themselves against Aes Sedai directly—not afraid; it was going against custom that made them uneasy—but whatever was necessary to protect the *Car'a'carn* had to be done.

For Egwene's part, she worried that they might turn Sorilea's suggestion that she remain among the tents into a command. There would be no way to evade that one, no way to avoid fifty eyes except by staying inside her own tent. How did Rand Travel? The Wise Ones would do whatever was necessary, so long as it did not touch *ji'e'toh*: Wise Ones might interpret it differently here and there, but they held to their interpretation as tightly as any other Aiel. Light, Rodera was Shaido, one of thousands captured in the battle that drove the Shaido away from the city, but the Wise Ones treated her no differently than any other *gai'shain*, and as far as Egwene could see, Rodera behaved no differently than any other *gai'shain*, not in the slightest. They would not go against *ji'e'toh*, no matter how necessary it might be.

Fortunately the subject did not come up. Unfortunately, the question of her health did. The Wise Ones did not know Healing, or how to check someone's health with the Power. Instead, they tested with their own methods. Some seemed familiar from when she had studied under Nynaeve to become a Wisdom: peering into her eyes, listening to her heart through a hollow wooden tube. Some were distinctly Aiel. She touched her toes until she felt dizzy, jumped up and down in one place until she thought her eyes would bounce out of her head, and ran around the Wise One's tents until spots swam before her, then had water poured over her head by a *gai'shain*, drank as much as she could hold, gathered up her skirts, and ran some more. Aiel were great believers in hardiness. Had she been a step too slow, had she staggered to a halt before Amys said she could, they would have decided her health was not sufficiently recovered after all.

When Sorilea finally nodded and said, "You are as sound as a Maiden, girl," Egwene was swaying and gulping for air. A Maiden would not have been, she was sure. Still, she felt pride. She had never thought of herself as soft, but she knew very well that before she began living with the Aiel she would have fallen on her face halfway through the test. *Another year,* she thought, *and I will run as well as any* Far Dareis Mai.

On the other hand, she was hardly up to returning to the city. She joined the Wise Ones in their sweat tent—for once they did not make her pour water over the hot rocks; Rodera did that—luxuriating in the damp heat as it relaxed her muscles, and only left because Rhuarc and two other clan chiefs, Timolan of the Miagoma and Indirian of the Codarra, joined them, tall massive graying men with hard sober faces. That sent her diving out of the tent to hastily wrap her shawl around her. She always expected to hear laughter when she did that, but the Aiel never seemed to understand why she hurried from the sweat tent whenever men came in. It would have fit right into Aiel humor if they had, but luckily they just did not make the connection, for which she was very glad.

Gathering the rest of her clothes in her arms from the neat piles outside the sweat tent, she hurried back to her own. The sun was sitting low now, and after a light meal, she was ready to fall asleep, too tired to even think of *Tel'aran'rhiod.* Too tired to remember most of her dreams, either—that was something the Wise Ones had been teaching her—but most of those she did remember were about Gawyn.

CHAPTER
25

Like Lightning and Rain

For some reason, when Cowinde came to wake her in the gray before dawn, Egwene felt refreshed despite her dreams. Refreshed and ready to see what she could learn in the city. One long yawn and stretch, and she was on her feet, humming as she washed and dressed hurriedly, hardly taking the time to brush her hair properly. She would have hurried away from the tents without wasting time on breakfast, but Sorilea saw her, and that put an abrupt end to that notion. Which turned out to be just as well.

"You should not have left the sweat tent so soon," Amys told her, taking a bowl of porridge and dried fruit from Rodera. Close to two dozen Wise Ones had crowded into Amys' tent, and Rodera, Cowinde and a white-robed man named Doilan, another Shaido, were scurrying to serve them all. "Rhuarc had much to say about your sisters. Perhaps you can add more."

After months of pretense, Egwene did not need to think to know she meant the Tower embassy. "I will tell you what I can. What did he say?"

For one thing, that there were six Aes Sedai, and two of them Red, not one—Egwene could not believe the arrogance, or perhaps stupidity, of Elaida to have sent any at all—but at least a Gray was in charge. The Wise Ones, most lying in a large circle like the spokes of a wheel, some standing or kneeling in the spaces between, turned their eyes to Egwene as soon as the list of names was done.

"I'm afraid I only know two of them," she said carefully. "There are a good many Aes Sedai, after all, and I haven't been a full sister long enough to know many." Heads nodded; they accepted that. "Nesune Bihara is fair-minded—she listens to all sides before reaching a conclusion—but she can find even the smallest flaw in what you say. She sees everything, remembers everything; she can glance at a page once and repeat it back word for word, or the same for a conversation she heard a year ago. Sometimes she talks to herself, though, speaks her thoughts without realizing it."

"Rhuarc said she was interested in the Royal Library." Bair stirred her porridge, watching Egwene. "He said he heard her mutter something about seals." A quick murmur rippled through the other women, silenced when Sorilea cleared her throat loudly.

Spooning up porridge—there were slices of dried plum and some kind of sweet berries in hers—Egwene considered. If Elaida had put Siuan to the question before she was executed, then she knew of three seals that were broken. Rand had two hidden—Egwene wished she knew where; he did not seem to trust anyone of late—and Nynaeve and Elayne had found one in Tanchico and carried it to Salidar, but Elaida had no way of knowing about those. Unless, perhaps, she had spies in Salidar. No. That was speculation for another time, useless now. Elaida must be searching desperately for the rest. Sending Nesune to the second-greatest library in the world after that in the White Tower made sense, and swallowing some dried plum, she told them so.

"I said as much last night," Sorilea growled. "Aeron, Colinda, Edarra, you three go to the Library. Three Wise Ones should be able to find what can be found before one Aes Sedai." That produced three long faces; the Royal Library was huge. Still, Sorilea was Sorilea, and if the named women sighed and muttered, they put down their porridge bowls and left immediately. "You said you know two," Sorilea went on before they were out of the tent. "Nesune Bihara and who?"

"Sarene Nemdahl," Egwene said. "You must understand, I do not know either well. Sarene is like most Whites—she reasons everything out logically, and sometimes she seems surprised when somebody acts from the heart—yet she has a temper. Most of the time she keeps it tightly bottled, but put a foot wrong at the wrong time and she can . . . snap your nose off before you can blink. She listens to what you say, though, and she will admit she was wrong, even after her temper has snapped. Well, once it mends, anyway."

Putting a spoonful of berries and porridge into her mouth, she tried to study the Wise Ones without seeming to; no one appeared to have noticed her hesitation. She had almost said Sarene would send you to scrub floors before you could blink. The only way she knew either woman was from lessons as a novice. Nesune, a slender Kandori with birdlike eyes, could tell when someone's attention drifted even with her back turned; she had taught several classes Egwene had been in. Egwene had only heard two lectures by Sarene, on the nature of reality, but it was hard to forget a woman who told you with absolute seriousness that beauty and ugliness were equally illusion while wearing a face that would make any man look twice.

"I hope you can remember more," Bair said, leaning toward her on an elbow. "It seems you are our only source of information."

That did take a moment for Egwene to puzzle out. Yes, of course. Bair and Amys must have tried to look into the Aes Sedai's dreams last night, but Aes Sedai warded their dreams. It was a skill she regretted not learning herself before leaving the Tower. "If I can. Where are their rooms in the palace?" If she was going to go near Rand the next time he came, it would help if she did not blunder by their apartments trying to find her way. Especially Nesune's. Sarene might not remember one particular novice, but Nesune most certainly would. For that matter, one of those she did not know might, too; there had been a lot of talk about Egwene al'Vere when she was in the Tower.

"They decline Berelain's offer of shade even for one night." Amys frowned. Among Aiel, an offer of hospitality was always accepted; to refuse, even between blood enemies, was shaming. "They stay with a woman named Arilyn, a noble among the treekillers. Rhuarc believes that Coiren Saeldain knew this Arilyn before yesterday."

"One of Coiren's spies," Egwene said with certainty. "Or one of the Gray Ajah's."

Several Wise Ones muttered angrily under their breath; Sorilea snorted loudly in disgust, and Amys gave a heavy, disappointed sigh. Others had a different view. Corelna, a green-eyed hawk of a woman with gray heavy in her flaxen hair, shook her head doubtfully, while Tialin, a lean redhead with a sharp nose, looked at Egwene in open disbelief.

Spying violated *ji'e'toh*, though how that squared with the dreamwalkers' peeking into people's dreams whenever they liked was something Egwene had not worked out. There was no use pointing out that Aes Sedai did not follow *ji'e'toh*. They knew that; they just found it hard to really believe or understand, about Aes Sedai or anyone.

Whatever they thought, she would have wagered anything on being right. Galldrian, the last King of Cairhien, had had an Aes Sedai advisor before he was assassinated. Niande Moorwyn had been all but invisible even before she disappeared following Galldrian's death, but one thing Egwene had learned was that she had occasionally visited the country estates of Lady Arilyn. Niande was a Gray.

"They have apparently placed a hundred guards under that roof," Bair said after a time. Her voice became very bland. "They say the city is still unsettled, but I think they fear the Aiel." Disturbingly interested looks appeared on a number of faces.

"A hundred!" Egwene exclaimed. "They brought a hundred men?"

Amys shook her head. "More than five hundred. Timolan's scouts found most of them camped less than half a day north of the city. Rhuarc spoke of it, and Coiren Saeldain said the men were a guard of honor, but they left most outside the city so as not to *alarm* us."

"They think they will escort the *Car'a'carn* to Tar Valon." Sorilea's voice could have cracked stone, and her expression made her tone seem soft. Egwene had not kept back the contents of Elaida's letter to Rand. The Wise Ones liked it less every time they heard it.

"Rand is not fool enough to accept that offer," Egwene said, but her mind was not on that. Five hundred men could be a guard of honor. Elaida might well think the Dragon Reborn would expect something like that, even be flattered. A number of suggestions occurred to her, but she had to be careful. The wrong word might make Amys and Bair—or worse, Sorilea, dodging Sorilea was like to trying to climb out of a briar patch—give her commands that she could not obey and still do what only she could. Or would, at least. "I assume the chiefs are keeping an eye on those soldiers outside the city?" Half a day north—more like a full day, since they were not Aiel—was too far to be dangerous, but a little caution never hurt. Amys nodded; Sorilea looked at Egwene as though she had asked whether the sun was in the sky at midday. Egwene cleared her throat. "Yes." The chiefs were not likely to make that sort of mistake. "Well. These are my suggestions. If any of these Aes Sedai goes to the palace, some of you who can channel should go behind them and make sure they do not leave any sort of trap." They nodded. Two-thirds of the women there could wield *saidar*, some not much more than Sorilea, others equaling Amys, who was as strong as most Aes Sedai Egwene had yet met; the proportions were about the same for Wise Ones as a whole. Their skills differed from Aes Sedai's— less in some places, more in a few, but generally just different—yet they should be able to sniff out any unwelcome gifts. "And we must make sure there are only six."

She had to explain. They had read wetlanders' books, but even those who could channel did not really know the rituals that had grown up around Aes Sedai dealing with men who had found *saidin*. Among the Aiel, a man who learned he could channel thought he was chosen, and went north into the Blight to hunt the Dark One; none ever returned. For that matter, Egwene had not known the rituals either, until she went to the Tower; the stories she had heard before seldom bore any resemblance to the truth.

"Rand can handle two women at once," she finished. She knew that for a fact. "He might even be able to handle six, but if they are more than they've put themselves forward to be, then it is proof they have lied at the least, even if just by leaving something out." She almost winced at their frowns; if you lied, you incurred *toh* toward whoever you lied to. But in her case, it was necessary. It *was*.

The rest of breakfast was taken up with the Wise Ones deciding who would go through the palace today and which chiefs could be trusted with choosing men and Maidens to watch for more Aes Sedai. Some might be reluctant to put themselves against Aes Sedai in any way; the Wise Ones did not say that right out, but it was clear enough from what they did say, often sourly. Others might think any threat to the *Car'a'carn*, even from Aes Sedai, could best be handled by the spear. A few of the Wise Ones seemed to have moved toward that opinion too; Sorilea stepped heavily on more than one oblique suggestion that the difficulty would be solved if the Aes Sedai were simply no longer there. In the end, Rhuarc and Mandelain of the Daryne were the only two they could agree on.

"Make sure they don't chose any *siswai'aman*," Egwene said. Those would certainly resort to the spear at the slightest hint of a threat. The remark got her a great many stares, ranging from flat to wry. None of the Wise Ones were fools. One thing troubled her. Not one of them mentioned what she was used to hearing almost any time Aes Sedai were discussed: that the Aiel had once failed the Aes Sedai and would be destroyed if they did again.

Aside from that one comment, Egwene kept out of the discussion, busying herself with a second bowl of porridge, with dried pear as well as plums, which earned an approving nod from Sorilea. It was not Sorilea's approval she was after. She was hungry, but mainly she hoped they would forget she was there. It seemed to work.

Breakfast and discussion done, she strolled to her tent, then crouched just inside the entry flap, watching a small knot of Wise Ones make their way to the city, led by Amys. When they vanished through the nearest gate, she popped back outside again. There were Aiel everywhere, *gai'shain* and others, but the Wise Ones were all inside, and no one glanced at her as she walked toward the city wall, not too quickly. If anyone did take notice of her, they should think she was just off for her morning exercise. The wind picked up, blowing waves of dust and old ash from Foregate, but she maintained her steady pace. Just out for exercise.

In the city, the first person she asked, a lanky woman selling wrinkled apples from a cart for an exorbitant price, did not know directions to the Lady Arilyn's palace, nor did a plump seamstress who went wide-eyed at an apparent Aiel woman entering her shop, nor a balding cutler who thought she would be much more interested in his knives. Finally a narrow-eyed silversmith who watched her closely the whole time she was inside her shop told her what she wanted. Striding away through the crowds, Egwene shook her head. She sometimes forgot how big a city like Cairhien really was, that not everyone knew where everything was.

As it was, she got lost three times and had to ask directions twice more before she found herself pressed against the side of a hire stable, peering around the corner at a squat pile of dark stone across the street, all narrow windows and angular balconies and stepped towers. It was small for a palace, though huge for a house; Arilyn was somewhere just above the middle of Cairhien's nobility, if Egwene remembered rightly. Green-coated soldiers in breastplates and helmets stood guard on the broad front stairs, at every gate she could see, even on the balconies. Oddly, they all appeared to be young. Still, that was not what interested her. Women were channeling inside that building, and for her to feel it from down the street, for her to feel it so solidly, they were not handling small quantities of *saidar.* The amount lessened suddenly, but it was still significant.

She chewed at her lip. She could not tell what they were doing, not without seeing the flows, but by the same token, they had to see the flows to weave them. Even if they were at a window, any flows directed out of the mansion that she could not see would have to be aimed south, away from the Sun Palace, away from everything. What were they doing?

One set of gates swung open long enough to emit a matched team of six bays drawing a closed black carriage with a sigil lacquered on its door, two silver stars on a field of red and green stripes. It worked northward through the crowd, the liveried driver plying a long whip as much to make people move aside as to encourage the horses. The Lady Arilyn going somewhere, or some of the embassy?

Well, she had not come here just to stare. Edging back so only one eye peeked around the corner, just enough to see the great house, she drew a small red stone from her belt pouch, took a deep breath and began to channel. If one of them was looking out on this side, she would be able to see the flows, but not Egwene. It had to be risked.

The smooth stone was just that, a stone polished in a stream, but Egwene had learned this trick from Moiraine, and Moiraine had used a stone for a focus—a gem as it happened, but the kind did not matter—so Egwene did too. It was mostly Air she wove, with a touch of Fire, done just so. It allowed you to eavesdrop. Spy, the Wise Ones would say. Egwene did not care what it was called, so long as she learned something of what the Tower Aes Sedai intended.

Her weave touched a window opening carefully, oh so delicately, then another, and another. Silence. Then. . . .

". . . so I says to him," a woman's voice said in her ear, "if you want them beds made, you better leave off tickling my chin, Alwin Rael."

Another woman giggled. "Oh, you never did."

Egwene grimaced. Maids.

A stout woman passing with a basket of bread on her shoulder peered at Egwene in a puzzled manner. As well she might, hearing two women's voices with only Egwene standing there, and her lips not moving. Egwene solved it the quickest way she knew. She glared so furiously that the woman squeaked and nearly dropped her basket dashing off into the crowd.

Reluctantly Egwene lowered the strength of her weave; she might not be able to hear as well, but better that than attracting gawkers. As it was, enough people glanced at her, an Aiel woman pressing herself against a wall, though no one more than hesitated before moving on; no one wanted trouble with Aiel. She put them out of her mind. Window by window she moved the weave, sweating furiously, and not only because of the already rising heat. Just one Aes Sedai glimpsing her flows, even if she did not recognize what they were, would know someone was channeling at them. They would have to suspect the purpose. Egwene inched back, leaving only half an eye showing.

Silence. Silence. A rustle of some sort. Someone moving? Slippers on a carpet? No words, though. Silence. A man muttering, apparently emptying chamber pots and not at all pleased; ears hot, she hurried on. Silence. Silence. Silence.

". . . really believe this is necessary?" Even in a whisper, as it seemed, the woman's voice sounded rich and full of herself.

"We must be prepared for any eventuality, Coiren," another woman replied in a voice like an iron rod. "I heard an arresting rumor—" A door closed firmly, cutting off the rest.

Egwene slumped against the stable's stone wall. She could have screamed with frustration. The Gray sister who was in charge, and the other had to be one of the Aes Sedai or she would never have spoken so to Coiren. None better to say what she wanted to hear, and they had to walk away. What arresting rumor? What eventualities? How did they mean to prepare? The channeling inside the manor changed again, increasing. What were they up to? Drawing a deep breath, she began again, doggedly.

As the sun climbed higher, she heard a great many usually unidentifiable noises, and a good bit of servants' gossip and chatter. Somebody named Ceri was going to have another baby, and the Aes Sedai were to have wine from Arindrim, wherever that was, with their midday meal. The most interesting news was that Arilyn had indeed been in that carriage, off to meet her husband in the country. For all the good knowing that did. A whole morning wasted.

The front doors of the mansion swung wide, liveried servants bowing. The soldiers did not stiffen, but they did look more attentive. Nesune Bihara walked out, followed by a tall young man who seemed to have been carved from a boulder.

Egwene released her weave hastily, released *saidar*, and took a deep calming breath; this was no time to panic. Nesune and her Warder conferred; then the dark-haired Brown sister peered down the street, first one way then the other. She was definitely looking for something.

Egwene decided that perhaps it was a good time to panic after all. Pulling herself back slowly so as not to draw Nesune's sharp eye, she whipped around as soon as she was out of the woman's sight, gathered her skirts and ran, bulling her way into the crowd. For all of three strides she ran. Then she struck a stone wall, bounced off, and sat down in the street so hard that she bounced again on the hot paving blocks.

Dazed, she stared up, becoming more dazed by the heartbeat. The stone wall was Gawyn, staring down at her, looking as stunned as she. His eyes were the most brilliant blue. And those red-gold curls. She wanted to wrap those around her fingers again. She felt her face going scarlet. *You never did that*, she thought firmly. *It was only a dream!*

"Did I hurt you?" he said anxiously, beginning to kneel beside her.

She scrambled to her feet, dusting herself off hurriedly; if she could have had a wish granted right then, it would be never to blush again. Already they had attracted a ring of onlookers. Wrapping an arm in his, she drew him down the street the way she had been going. A glance over her shoulder revealed only the milling throng. Even if Nesune came to that very corner, she would see nothing more. Still, Egwene did not slow; the crowd gave way for an Aiel woman and a man tall enough to be Aiel even if he did wear a sword. The way he moved said he knew how to use it; he moved like a Warder.

After a dozen paces she reluctantly unwound her arm from his. He caught her hand before it got away, though, and she let him hold it as they walked. "I suppose," he mused after a bit, "that I am to ignore the fact that you are dressed like an Aiel. The last I heard, you were in Illian. And I suppose I should not comment on you running away from a palace where six Aes Sedai are staying. Strange behavior for an Accepted."

"I've never been in Illian," she said, hastily looking around to see if any Aiel were close enough to have heard. Several glanced in her direction, but none were in earshot. Suddenly what he had said hit her. She took in his green coat, the same shade as those on the soldiers. "You're with them. The Tower Aes Sedai." Light, she was a fool not to have realized as soon as she saw him.

His face softened; it had been very hard for an instant. "I command the guard of honor the Aes Sedai have brought to escort the Dragon Reborn to Tar Valon." His voice was a curious blend, wryness and anger and weariness. "If he chooses to go, at least. And if he was here. I understand he . . . appears and disappears. Coiren is vexed."

Egwene's heart was in her throat. "I . . . I must ask you a favor, Gawyn."

"Anything except these," he said simply. "I will not harm Elayne or Andor, and I will not become Dragonsworn. Anything else in my power is yours."

Heads turned toward them. Any mention of Dragonsworn caught ears. Four hard-faced men with wagon drivers' whips coiled over their shoulders glared at Gawyn, cracking their knuckles the way some men did before fighting. Gawyn only looked at them. They were not small men, but their belligerence faded under his gaze. Two actually knuckled their foreheads to him before they all slipped away into the river of people. But there were still too many staring, too many trying to look as if they were not listening. Dressed as she was, she attracted eyes without saying a word. Add in a man with red-gold hair, well over a span tall, who looked a Warder, and the combination could not help but draw attention.

"I need to speak with you privately," she said. *If any woman has bonded Gawyn Warder, I'll.* . . . Curiously, the thought had no real heat.

Without a word he took her to a nearby inn, The Long Man, where a golden crown tossed to the round innkeeper produced an almost reverent curtsy and a small private dining room, dark-paneled, with heavily polished table and chairs and dried flowers in a blue vase on the hearth. Gawyn closed the door, and a sudden awkwardness descended as they faced each other alone. Light, but he was gorgeous, easily as gorgeous as Galad, and the way his hair curled around his ears . . .

Gawyn cleared his throat. "The heat seems to get worse every day." He pulled out a handkerchief and wiped his face, then offered it to her. Abruptly realizing it was used, he cleared his throat again. "I have another, I think."

She produced her own while he was searching his pockets. "Gawyn, how can you serve Elaida after what she did?"

"The Younglings serve the Tower," he replied stiffly, but his head swung uneasily. "We do as long as. . . . Siuan Sanche. . . ." For a moment his eyes went icy cold. Just for an instant. "Egwene, my mother always used to say, 'Even a queen must obey the law she makes, or there is no law.'" He shook his head angrily. "I shouldn't be surprised to find you here. I should have known you would be where al'Thor is."

"Why do you hate him?" That had been hate in his voice or she had never heard it. "Gawyn, he really is the Dragon Reborn. You must have heard what happened in Tear. He—"

"I do not care if he is the Creator made flesh," he grated. "Al'Thor killed my mother!"

Egwene's eyes nearly popped out of her head. "Gawyn, no! No, he did not!"

"Can you swear it? Were you there when she died? It's on every tongue. The Dragon Reborn took Caemlyn, and killed Morgase. He probably killed Elayne, too. I can find no word of her." All the anger drained out of him. He slumped where he stood, head falling forward, fists clenched and eyes closed. "I can find out nothing," he whispered.

"Elayne is unharmed," Egwene said, surprised to find herself right in front of him. She reached up, and surprised herself again by running her fingers into his hair as she raised his head. It felt just as she remembered.

Her hands flashed back as if burned. She was sure she would flush so crimson her face would ignite, except. . . . Color stained Gawyn's cheeks. Of course. He remembered too, though only as his own dream. That truly should have set her face afire, but somehow it did the opposite. Gawyn's blush steadied her nerves, even made her want to smile. "Elayne is safe, Gawyn. I *can* swear to that."

"Where is she?" His voice was anguished. "Where has she been? Her place is in Caemlyn now. Well, not Caemlyn—not so long as al'Thor might be there—but in Andor. Where is she, Egwene?"

"I . . . cannot tell you. I can't, Gawyn."

He studied her, face expressionless, then sighed. "You are more Aes Sedai every time I see you." His laugh sounded forced. "Do you know I used to think about being your Warder? How is that for foolish?"

"You will be my Warder." She had not realized the words were coming out of her mouth until they did, but once they did, she knew they were true. That dream. Gawyn kneeling for her to hold his head. It could have meant a hundred things or nothing, but she knew.

He grinned at her. The idiot thought she was joking! "Not me, surely. Galad, I think. Though you'll have to beat away other Aes Sedai with a stick. Aes Sedai, serving girls, queens, chambermaids, merchants, farmwives. . . . I've seen them all look at him. Don't bother claiming you don't think he's—"

The simplest way to silence that nonsense was to put a hand over his mouth. "I do not love Galad. I love you."

The man still tried to pretend it was a jest, smiling against her fingers. "I cannot be a Warder. I'm to be Elayne's First Prince of the Sword."

"If the Queen of Andor can be Aes Sedai, a Prince can be a Warder. And you will be mine. Push that through your thick skull; I am serious. And I love you." He stared at her. At least he was not smiling anymore. But he said nothing, just stared. She took her hand away. "Well? Aren't you going to say anything?"

"When you wish for so long that you could hear something," he said slowly, "and then suddenly, with no warning, you do, it is like a lightning strike and rain on parched ground at the same time. You're stunned, but you cannot hear enough."

"I love you, I love you, I love you," she told him, smiling. "Well?"

For answer, he picked her up and kissed her. It was every bit as good as the dreams. It was better. It was. . . . When he finally set her down, she clung to his arms; her knees did not seem to be working properly. "My

Lady Aiel Egwene Aes Sedai," he said, "I love you, and I cannot wait for you to bond me." Shedding mock formality, he added in a softer tone, "I love you, Egwene al'Vere. You said you wanted a favor. What? The moon on a necklace? I'll set a goldsmith to work within the hour. Stars to wear in your hair? I will—"

"Don't tell Coiren or the others that I am here. Don't mention me to them at all."

She expected some hesitation, but he simply said, "They'll not learn of you from me. Or from anyone else, can I help it." He paused a moment, then took her by the shoulders. "Egwene, I will not ask why you're here. No, just listen. I know Siuan mired you in her schemes, and I understand that you feel loyalty to a man from your own village. That doesn't matter. You should be in the White Tower, studying; I remember them all saying you were going to be a powerful Aes Sedai one day. Do you have a plan for returning without . . . penalties?" She shook her head wordlessly, and he went on in a rush. "Maybe I can think of something, if you don't first. I know you had no choice but to obey Siuan, but I doubt Elaida will give that much weight; even mentioning the name Siuan Sanche around her is nearly as much as your head is worth. I will find some way, somehow I swear it. But promise me that until I do you will not . . . do anything foolish." His hands tightened for a moment almost to the point of pain. "Just promise me you will be careful."

Light, but this was a fine pickle. She could not tell him she had no intention of returning to the Tower as long as Elaida sat on the Amyrlin Seat. And something foolish almost certainly meant anything to do with Rand. He looked so worried. For her. "I will be careful, Gawyn. I promise." *As careful as I can be*, she amended to herself; it was only a small change, but somehow it made what she had to say next more difficult. "I have a second favor to ask. Rand did not kill your mother." How could she word this to put the least strain on him? Strain or no, she had to. "Promise me you will not raise a hand against Rand until I can prove he didn't."

"I swear." Again no hesitation, but his voice was rough, and his hands squeezed again briefly, harder than before. She did not flinch; the slight pain felt like a repayment for the pain she was causing him.

"It has to be that way, Gawyn. He did not do it, but it will take time to prove." How under the Light could she? Rand's word would not be enough. All such a tangle. She had to concentrate on one thing at a time. What were those Aes Sedai up to?

Gawyn startled her by drawing a ragged breath. "I will give over everything, betray everything, for you. Come away with me, Egwene. We will both leave it all behind. I have a small estate south of Whitebridge, with a vineyard and a village, so far into the country that the sun rises two days late. The world will hardly touch us there. We can be married on the way. I don't know how much time we will have—al'Thor; Tarmon Gai'don—I do not know, but we will have it together."

She stared up at him in amazement. Then she realized she had voiced that last thought aloud, What were those Aes Sedai up to?, and a key word—betray—slid into place. He thought she wanted him to spy on them. And he would. Desperately seeking a way not to, he still would, if she asked. Anything, he had promised, and anything he meant, whatever the cost to him. She made a promise to herself; to him really, but it was not the sort of promise she could speak aloud. If he let slip something she could use, she would—she had to—but she would not dig, not for the smallest scrap. Whatever the cost. Sarene Nemdahl would never understand, but it was the only way she could match what he had laid at her feet.

"I cannot," she said softly. "You can never know how much I want to, but I cannot." She laughed abruptly, feeling tears in her eyes. "And you. Betray? Gawyn Trakand, that word fits you as darkness fits the sun." Unspoken promises were all very well, but she could not leave it at that. She would use what he gave her, use it against what he believed. There had to be an offering. "I sleep in the tents, but every morning I walk in the city. I come through the Dragonwall Gate, not long after sunrise."

He understood, of course. Her offering of faith in his word, her freedom put in his pocket. He took her hands in both of his, turned them so he could kiss her palms gently. "A precious thing, what you've given me to hold. If I go to the Dragonwall Gate every morning, someone is sure to notice, and I may not be able to get away every morning, but do not be too surprised if I appear beside you shortly after you enter the city most days."

When Egwene finally got back outside, the sun had moved a considerable distance into the hottest part of the afternoon, thinning the crowds a little. Saying goodbye had taken longer than she thought it would; kissing Gawyn might not be the sort of exercise the Wise Ones intended her to take, but her heart was still racing as if she had been running.

Putting him firmly out of mind—well, pushing him to the back with some effort; putting him out seemed to be beyond her—she returned to her vantage point beside the stable. Someone was still channeling inside the mansion; more than one probably, unless that one was weaving something large; the feel was less than earlier, but still strong. A woman was going into the house, a dark-haired woman Egwene did not recognize, though the agelessness of that hard face marked her. She did not try to eavesdrop again and did not stay long—if they were going in and out, there was too much chance of being seen and recognized despite her clothes—but as she hurried away, one thought hammered at her. What were they up to?

"We intend to offer him escort to Tar Valon," Katerine Alruddin said, shifting slightly. She could never decide whether Cairhienin chairs were as uncomfortable as they looked or one merely believed they were because they looked so uncomfortable. "Once he leaves Cairhien for Tar Valon, there will be . . . a vacuum here."

Unsmiling in the gilded chair opposite her, the Lady Colavaere leaned forward slightly. "You interest me, Katerine Sedai. Leave us," she snapped to the servants.

Katerine smiled.

"We intend to offer him escort to Tar Valon," Nesune said precisely, but she felt the smallest flash of irritation. Despite a smooth face, the Tairen kept shifting his feet, anxious in the presence of an Aes Sedai, perhaps apprehensive that she might channel. Only an Amadician would have been worse. "Once he departs for Tar Valon, there will be a need for strength in Cairhien."

The High Lord Meilan licked his lips. "Why do you tell me this?"

Nesune's smile might have meant anything.

When Sarene entered the sitting room, only Coiren and Erian were there sipping at tea. And a servant waiting to pour, of course. Sarene motioned him out. "Berelain, she may prove to be difficult," she said once the door closed. "I do not know whether the apple or the whip will work best with her. I am supposed to see Aracome tomorrow, am I not, but I think that more time will be necessary with Berelain."

"Apple or whip," Erian said in a tight voice. "Whichever do be necessary." Her face might have been pale marble framed by raven's wings. Sarene's secret vice was poetry, though she would never have let anyone know she could be interested in something so . . . emotional. She would have died of shame had Vitalien, her Warder, ever discovered that she had written lines comparing him to a leopard, among other graceful, powerful and dangerous animals.

"Pull yourself together, Erian." As usual, Coiren sounded as if she were making a speech. "What troubles her, Sarene, is a rumor that Galina heard, a rumor that a Green sister was in Tear with young Rand al'Thor and is now here in Cairhien." She *always* called him "young Rand al'Thor," as though reminding her listeners that he was young and therefore inexperienced.

"Moiraine *and* a Green," Sarene mused. That could indeed indicate trouble. Elaida insisted that Moiraine and Siuan had acted alone in letting al'Thor run without guidance, but if even one additional Aes Sedai was involved, it might mean others had been as well, and that was a string that might lead all the way to some, perhaps many, of those who had fled the Tower when Siuan was deposed. "Still, it is only the rumor."

"Perhaps not," Galina said as she slipped into the chamber. "Have you not heard? Someone channeled at us this morning. For what purpose I cannot say, but we can imagine very closely I believe."

The beads worked in Sarene's tiny dark braids made clicking noises as she shook her head. "It is not the proof of a Green, Galina. It is not even the proof of an Aes Sedai. It could be some poor wretch who was put out of the Tower for failing the test as Accepted. And you know as well as I do that some of these Aielwomen can channel."

Galina smiled, a sliver of teeth in night-eyed sternness. "I think it is proof of Moiraine. I have heard she had a trick of eavesdropping, and I do not believe this story of her so conveniently dead, with no corpse seen and no one able to tell details."

That bothered Sarene as well. Partly because she had liked Moiraine—they had been friends as novices and Accepted, though Moiraine was a year ahead, and that friendship had continued over their few meetings in the years since—and partly because it *was* too vague and too convenient, Moiraine dying, vanishing really, when an arrest warrant hung over her. Moiraine might well be capable of faking her own death under those circumstances. "So you believe we have both Moiraine and a Green sister whose name we do not know to deal with? It is still only the speculation, Galina."

Galina's smile did not change, but her eyes glittered. She was too hard for logic—she believed what she believed whatever the evidence—yet Sarene had always believed great fires roared somewhere in Galina's depths. "What I believe," Galina said, "is that Moiraine *is* the so-called Green.

What better way to hide from arrests than to die and reappear as someone else of another Ajah? I have even heard that this Green is short; we all know Moiraine is far from a tall woman." Erian had sat up stony straight, her brown eyes large smoldering coals of outrage. "When we lay hands on this *Green* sister," Galina told her, "I propose that we give her into your charge for the journey back to the Tower." Erian nodded sharply, but the heat did not fade from her eyes.

Sarene felt stunned. Moiraine? Claim another Ajah than her own? Surely not. Sarene had never married—it was illogical to believe two people could remain compatible for a lifetime—but the only thing she could compare that to was sleeping with another woman's husband. But it was the charge that stunned her, not the possibility that it might be true. She was about to point out that there were many short women in the world, and that shortness was relative, when Coiren spoke in that billowing voice.

"Sarene, you must take your turn again. We must be prepared, whatever happens."

"I do not like it," Erian said firmly. "It does be like preparing for failure."

"It is only logical," Sarene told her. "Dividing time into the smallest possible increments, it is impossible to say with any true certainty what will happen between one and the next. Since chasing al'Thor to Caemlyn might mean we would arrive to find that he has come here, we remain here with as much certainty as we can have that he will eventually return, yet that could be tomorrow or a month from now. Any single event in any hour of that wait, or any combination of events, could leave us with no alternative. Thus, preparation is logical."

"Very nicely explained," Erian said dryly. She had no head for logic; sometimes Sarene thought that beautiful women did not, though there was no logic in the connection that she could see.

"We have as much time as we need," Coiren pronounced. When she was not making a speech, she made pronouncements. "Beldeine arrived today and took a room near the river, but Mayam is not due for two days. We must take care, and that gives us time."

"I still do not like preparing for failure," Erian murmured into her teacup.

"I will not take it amiss," Galina said, "if we find time to take Moiraine to justice. We have waited this long; there is not that much hurry with al'Thor."

Sarene sighed. They did very well at the things they did, but she could not understand it; there was barely a logical bone in one of them.

Retiring upstairs to her chambers, she seated herself in front of the cold fireplace and began to channel. Could this Rand al'Thor really have rediscovered how to Travel? It surpassed belief, yet it was the only explanation. What sort of man was he? That she would discover when she met him, not before. Filled with *saidar* nearly to the point where sweetness became pain, she began running through novice exercises. They were as good as anything. Preparation was only logical.

CHAPTER
26

Connecting Lines

Thunder rolled across the low, brown grassland hills in a continuous peal, though the sky held not a cloud, only the burning sun, still with a way to climb. On a hilltop, Rand held the reins and the Dragon Scepter on the pommel of his saddle and waited. The thunder swelled. It was hard not to look over his shoulder constantly, south toward Alanna. She had bruised her heel this morning and scraped her hand, and she was in a temper. How and what for, he had no notion; he had no real notion how he could be so sure. The thunder crested.

The Saldaean horsemen appeared over the next rise, three abreast at a dead gallop in a long snake that kept coming, down the slope into the broad sweep between the hills. Nine thousand men made a very long snake. At the foot of the slope they divided, the center column coming on while the others peeled off to right and left, each column dividing again and again until they rode by hundreds, swooping past one another. Riders began standing on their saddles, sometimes on feet, sometimes on hands. Others swung impossibly low to slap the ground on first one side of their galloping mounts, then the other. Men left their saddles entirely to crawl underneath speeding horses, or dropped to the ground to run a pace beside the animal before leaping back into the saddle, then dropping on the other side to repeat the performance.

Rand lifted his reins and heeled Jeade'en. As the dapple moved, so did

491

the Aiel surrounding him. This morning the men were Mountain Dancers, *Hama N'dore*, more than half wearing the headband of *siswai'aman*. Caldin, graying and leathery, had tried to get Rand to let him bring more than twenty, what with so many armed wetlanders about; none of the Aiel wasted any time with disparaging looks for Rand's sword. Nandera spent more time watching the two hundred-odd women who trailed after them on horses; she seemed to find more threat in the Saldaean ladies and officers' wives than in the soldiers, and having met some of the Saldaean women, Rand was not ready to argue. Sulin would probably have agreed. It occurred to him that he had not seen Sulin in. . . . Not since returning from Shadar Logoth. Eight days. He wondered if he had done something to offend her.

This was no time to worry about Sulin or *ji'e'toh*. He circled around the valley until he reached the hilltop over which the Saldaeans had first appeared to him. Bashere himself rode about down there examining first one group as they went through their paces, then another; almost coincidentally, he just happened to do this standing up on his saddle.

For an instant Rand seized *saidin*, and released it a heartbeat later. With his vision enhanced, it had not been difficult to see the two white stones lying near the foot of the slope, right where Bashere had placed them personally last night, four paces apart. With luck, no one had seen him. With luck, no one would ask too many questions about this morning. Below, some men were riding two horses now, a foot on each saddle, still at a dead gallop. Others had a man on their shoulders, sometimes in a handstand.

He looked around at the sound of a horse walking toward him. Deira ni Ghaline t'Bashere rode through the Aiel with seeming unconcern; armed only with a small knife at her silver belt, in a riding dress of gray silk embroidered in silver down the sleeves and on the high neck, she appeared to be daring them to attack her. As tall as many of the Maidens, nearly a hand taller than her husband, she was a big woman. Not stout, nor even plump; simply big. She had wings of white in her black hair, and her dark tilted eyes were fixed on Rand. He suspected she was a beautiful woman when his presence did not turn her face to granite.

"Is my husband . . . *amusing* you?" She never gave Rand a title, never used his name.

He looked at the other Saldaean women. They watched him like a troop of cavalry ready to charge, faces also granite, tilted eyes icy. All they awaited was Deira's command. He could well believe the stories of Saldaean women taking up fallen husbands' swords and leading their men back into battle. Being pleasant had gotten him exactly nowhere with Bashere's wife; Bashere himself only shrugged and said she was a difficult woman at times, all the while grinning with what could only be pride.

"Tell Lord Bashere I am pleased," he said. Turning Jeade'en, he started back toward Caemlyn. The Saldaean woman's eyes seemed to press against his back.

Lews Therin was giggling; that was the only word for it. *Never prod at a woman unless you must. She will kill you faster than a man and for less reason, even if she weeps over it after.*

Are you really there? Rand demanded. *Is there more to you than a voice?* Only that soft, mad laughter answered.

He stewed over Lews Therin all the way back to Caemlyn, and even after they had ridden past one of the long markets of tile roofs lining the approaches to the gates and into the New City. He worried over going mad—not just the fact of it, though that was bad enough; if he went insane, how could he do what he had to do?—but he had seen no sign of it. But then, if his mind did crack, would he know it? He had never seen a madman. All he had to go by was Lews Therin maundering in his head. Did all men go mad alike? Would he end like that, laughing and weeping over things no one else saw or knew? He knew he had a chance to live, if a seemingly impossible one. *If you would live, you must die;* that was one of three things he knew must be true, told to him inside a *ter'angreal* where the answers were always true if apparently never easy to understand. But to live like that. . . . He was not sure he would not rather die.

The crowds in the New City gave way before more than forty Aiel, and a handful recognized the Dragon Reborn as well. Maybe more did, but it was a ragged handful of cheers that went up as he rode by. "The Light shine on the Dragon Reborn!" and "The glory of the Light for the Dragon Reborn!" and "The Dragon Reborn, King of Andor!"

That last one jolted him whenever he heard it, and he heard it more than once. He had to find Elayne. He could feel his teeth grinding. He could not look at the people in the street; he wanted to smash them to their knees, roar at them that Elayne was their queen. Trying not to hear, he studied the sky, the rooftops, anything but the crowd. And that was why he saw the man in a white cloak rise up on a red-tiled rooftop and lift a crossbow.

Everything happened in heartbeats. Rand seized *saidin* and channeled as the bolt flew toward him; it struck Air, a silvery blue mass hanging above the street, with a clang as of metal against metal. A ball of fire leaped from Rand's hand, struck the crossbowman in the chest as the bolt was bouncing away from the shield of Air. Flames engulfed the man, and he fell shrieking from the rooftop. And someone leaped into Rand, carrying him out of the saddle.

He hit the paving stones hard with a weight atop him; breath and *saidin* left him together. Struggling for air, he wrestled with the weight, wrenched it off—and found himself holding Desora by the arms. She smiled at him, a beautiful smile; then her head slumped sideways. Sightless blue eyes stared at him, already glazing. The crossbow bolt standing out from her ribs pressed against his wrist. Why had she ever wanted to hide such a beautiful smile?

Hands seized him, hauled him to his feet; Maidens and Mountain Dancers pushed him to the side of the street, close against the front of a tinsmith's shop, and formed a tight, veiled circle around him, horn bows in hand, eyes searching street and rooftops. Shouts and screams rang everywhere, but the street was already clear for better than fifty paces either way, and then it was a milling mass of people struggling to get away. The street was clear except for bodies. Desora, and six others, three of them Aiel. One more a Maiden, he thought. It was hard to be sure from a distance with someone lying crumpled like a heap of rags.

Rand moved, and the Aiel around him pressed together more tightly, a wall of flesh. "These places are rabbit warrens," Nandera said conversationally, without letting her eyes stop their search above her veil. "If you join the dance in there, you can take a blade in the back before you know there is danger."

Caldin nodded. "This reminds me of a time near Sedar Cut, when— We have a prisoner, at least." Some of his *Hama N'dore* had appeared from a tavern across the street, pushing ahead of them a man with his arms and elbows bound behind him. He continued to struggle until they shoved him to his knees on the paving stone and laid spearpoints against his throat. "Perhaps he will tell us who commanded this." Caldin sounded as though he did not doubt it in the least.

A moment later Maidens came out of another building with a second bound man who was limping, his face covered in blood. In short order four men knelt in the street under Aiel guard. Finally the semicircle hemming Rand loosened.

The four were hard-faced men all, though the blood-smeared fellow swayed and rolled his eyes at the Aiel. Two others wore sullen defiance, the fourth a sneer.

Rand's hands twitched. "Are you sure they were part of it?" He could not believe how soft his voice sounded, how steady. Balefire would solve everything. *Not balefire*, Lews Therin panted at him. *Never again*. "Are you sure?"

"They were," a Maiden said; he could not see who, behind her veil. "Those we killed all wore this." She tugged a cloak free from behind the bloodied man's bound arms. A worn white cloak, grimy and stained, with a golden sunburst embroidered on the chest. The other three had them too.

"These were set to watch," a broad Mountain Dancer added, "and report if the attack went badly for the others." He laughed, a short bark. "Whoever sent them did not know how badly it would go."

"None of these men fired a crossbow?" Rand asked. Balefire. *No*, Lews Therin shrieked in the distance. The Aiel exchanged glances, shook *shoufa*-wrapped heads. "Hang them," Rand said. The bloody-faced man nearly collapsed. Rand seized him in flows of Air, dragged him to his feet. It was the first he realized that he held *saidin*. He welcomed the struggle for survival; he even welcomed the taint, staining his bones like acid slime. It made him less aware of things he would rather not remember, emotions he would rather not have. "What is your name?"

"F-Faral, m-my Lord. D-Dimir Faral." Eyes almost popping out of his head stared at Rand through that mask of blood. "P-Please don't h-hang me, m-my Lord. I'll w-walk in the Light, I s-swear!"

"You are a very lucky man, Dimir Faral." Rand's voice sounded as distant in his own ears as Lews Therin's cries. "You are going to watch your friends hang." Faral began to weep. "Then you'll be given a horse, and you will go tell Pedron Niall that one day I will hang him too for what happened here." When he loosed the flows of Air, Faral collapsed in a heap, moaning that he would ride to Amador without stopping. The three who were to die stared contemptuously at the sobbing man. One of them spat at him.

Rand put them out of his mind. Niall was the only one he had to remember. There was something else he had to do yet. He pushed away *saidin*, went through the struggle to escape it without being obliterated, the struggle to make himself release it. For what he had to do, he wanted no screen between him and his emotions.

A Maiden was straightening Desora's body; she had raised Desora's veil. She reached to stop him when he touched that piece of black *algode*, then hesitated, looking at his face, and settled back on her haunches.

Lifting the veil, he memorized Desora's face. She looked as if she were sleeping now. Desora, of the Musara sept of the Reyn Aiel. So many names. Liah, of the Cosaida Chareen, and Dailin, of the Nine Valleys Taardad, and Lamelle, of the Smoke Water Miagoma, and. . . . So many. Sometimes he ran down that list name by name. There was one name in it he had not added. Ilyena Therin Moerelle. He did not know how Lews Therin had put it there, but he would not have erased it if he knew how.

It was both an effort and a relief to turn away from Desora, a pure relief to find that what he had thought was a second dead Maiden was instead a man, short for an Aiel man. He hurt for the men who died for him, but with them he could remember an old saying. *"Let the dead rest, and care for the living."* Not easily, but he could make himself do it. He could not even make himself summon the words when it was a woman who had died.

Skirts spread on the paving stones caught his eye. Not only Aiel had died.

She had taken a crossbow bolt squarely between the shoulder blades. Almost no blood stained the back of her dress; it had been quick, a small mercy. Kneeling, he turned her over as gently as he could; the other end of the bolt stood out from her chest. It was a square face, a woman in her middle years, a touch of gray in her hair. Her dark eyes were open wide; she looked surprised. He did not know her name, but he memorized her face. She had died for being on the same street with him.

He caught at Nandera's arm, and she shook his hand free, not wanting the use of her bow impaired, but she did look at him. "Find this woman's family and see they have whatever they need. Gold. . . ." It was not enough. What they needed was a wife back, a mother back; he could not give them that. "See to them," he said. "And find out her name."

Nandera stretched a hand toward him, then put it back to her bow. When he stood, the Maidens were watching him. Oh, they were watching everything as usual, but those veiled faces turned toward him a little more often. Sulin knew how he felt, if she did not know about the list, but he had no idea whether she had told the others. If she had, he had no idea how they felt about it.

Walking back to where he had fallen, he picked up the tasseled Dragon Scepter. Bending was an effort, and the short length of spear felt heavy. Jeade'en had not gone far once his saddle was empty; the horse was well trained. Rand climbed onto the dapple's back. "I've done as much as I can here," he said—let them think whatever they wanted—and dug in his heels.

If he could not outdistance memory, he outdistanced the Aiel. For a time at least. He had handed Jeade'en over to a stableman and was inside the Palace before Nandera and Caldin caught up to him, with about two-thirds the number of Maidens and Mountain Dancers they had had. Some had been left to care for the dead. Caldin looked sourly irritated. From the heat in Nandera's eyes, Rand thought he should be glad she was not veiled.

Before she could speak, Mistress Harfor approached Rand and curtsied deeply. "My Lord Dragon," she said in a deep, strong voice, "there is a petition for audience with you from the Wavemistress of Clan Catelar, of the Atha'an Miere."

If the fine cut of Reene's red-and-white dress was not enough to say that "first maid" was a misnomer, her manner certainly was. A slightly plump woman with graying hair and a long chin, she looked Rand right in the eye, tilting her head back to manage it, and somehow combined a proper degree of deference, an utter lack of obsequiousness, and an aloofness most noblewomen could not attain. Like Halwin Norry, she had stayed when most others fled, though Rand half-suspected that her motive had been to defend and preserve the Palace from invaders. He would not have been surprised to learn that she periodically searched his chambers for hidden Palace valuables. He would not have been surprised to learn she tried to search the Aiel.

"Sea Folk?" he said. "What do they want?"

She gave him a patient look, trying to make allowances. Very plainly trying. "The petition does not say, my Lord Dragon."

If Moiraine had known anything about the Sea Folk, she had not made it part of his education, but from Reene's attitude, this woman was important. A Wavemistress certainly sounded important. That would mean the Grand Hall. He had not been there since returning from Cairhien. Not that he had any reason to avoid the throne room; there just had been no need to go there. "This afternoon," he said slowly. "Tell her I will see her in the midafternoon. You've given her good apartments? And her retinue?" He doubted anyone with so grand a title traveled alone.

"She refused them; they have taken rooms at The Ball and Hoop." Her mouth flattened slightly; apparently, however lofty a Wavemistress, that was not proper in Reene Harfor's eyes. "They were very dusty and travel-sore, hardly able to stand. They came by horse, not coach, and I do not believe they are used to horses." She blinked as if surprised to have unbent that much, and regained her reserve like donning a cloak. "Someone else wishes to see you, my Lord Dragon." Her tone picked up the faintest hint of distaste. "The Lady Elenia."

Rand almost grimaced himself. No doubt Elenia had another lecture prepared on her claims to the Lion Throne; so far he had managed not to hear more than one word in three. She would be easy enough to turn down. Still, he really should know something of Andor's history, and no one handy knew more of it than Elenia Sarand. "Send her to me in my rooms, please."

"Do you really mean the Daughter-Heir to have the throne?" Reene's tone was not harsh, but all deference was gone. Her face had not changed, yet Rand was sure that with a wrong answer she would shout "For Elayne and the White Lion!" and try to bash his brains in, Aiel or no Aiel.

"I do," he sighed. "The Lion Throne is Elayne's. By the Light and my hope of rebirth and salvation, it is."

Reene studied him a moment, then spread her skirts in another deep curtsy. "I will send her to you, my Lord Dragon." Her back was stiff as she glided away, but it always was; there were no telling whether she believed a word.

"A crafty enemy," Caldin said heatedly before Reene had gone five paces, "will set a weak ambush you are meant to break through. Confident because you have dealt with the threat, your guard relaxed, you walk into the second, stronger ambush."

Right on top of Caldin, Nandera said in a cold voice, "Young men can be impetuous, young men can be rash, young men can be fools, but the *Car'a'carn* cannot let himself be a young man."

Rand glanced over his shoulder before starting off, just long enough to say, "We're back inside the Palace now. Choose your two." It was little surprise that Nandera and Caldin chose themselves, and none at all that they strode after him wrapped in a hard silence.

At the door to his apartments, he told them to send Elenia in when she came and left them in the corridor. There was plum punch in a silver-chased pitcher waiting, but he did not touch it. Instead he stood staring at it, trying to plan out what he was going to say, until he realized what he was doing and grunted in surprise. What was there to plan?

A tap at the door announced honey-haired Elenia, who swept a curtsy in a dress worked with golden roses. On any other woman, Rand would have thought they were just roses; on Elenia, they had to stand for the Rose Crown. "My Lord Dragon is most gracious to receive me."

"I want to ask you some things about Andor's history," Rand said. "Will you take plum punch?"

Elenia's eyes widened in delight before she could stop them. Undoubtedly she had planned how to work Rand around to this in order to lead into her claims, and here it was handed to her. A smile bloomed on her foxlike face. "May I have the honor of pouring for my Lord Dragon?" she said, not waiting for him to wave his assent. She was so pleased with the turn of events that he almost expected her to press him into a chair and urge him to put his feet up. "Upon what point of history may I shed light?"

"A general sort of . . ." Rand frowned; that would give the excuse to be listing her ancestry in detail inside of two sentences ". . . that is, how Souran Maravaile came to bring his wife here. Was he from Caemlyn?"

"Ishara brought Souran, my Lord Dragon." Elenia's smile turned briefly indulgent. "Ishara's mother was Endara Casalain, who was Artur Hawk-wing's governor here then—the province was called Andor—and also the granddaughter to Joal Ramedar, the last King of Aldeshar. Souran was only . . . only a general"—she had been going to say a commoner; he would have wagered on it—"though Hawkwing's finest, of course. Endara resigned her warrant and knelt to Ishara as Queen." Somehow, Rand did not believe it had happened quite that way, or so smoothly. "They were the worst of times, of course, quite as bad as the Trolloc Wars, I am sure. With Hawkwing dead, every noble thought to become High King. Or High Queen. Ishara knew that no one would be able to take it all, though; there were too many factions, and alliances broke as soon as made. She convinced Souran to raise the siege of Tar Valon, and brought him and as much of his army as he could hold together here."

"Souran Maravaile was the one besieging Tar Valon?" Rand said, startled. Artur Hawkwing had laid a twenty-year siege against Tar Valon, and put a price on the head of every Aes Sedai.

"The final year of it," she said, a touch impatiently, "as nearly as the histories record." It was plain she had little real interest in Souran except as Ishara's husband. "Ishara was wise. She promised the Aes Sedai that her el-dest daughter would be sent to study in the White Tower, thus gaining the Tower's backing and an Aes Sedai advisor named Ballair, the first ruler to do so. Others did follow, of course, but they still wanted Hawkwing's throne." She had the bit in her teeth now, face animated, goblet forgotten, gesturing With her free hand. Words bubbled out. "A full generation passed before that idea died, although Narasim Bhuran did try as late as the last ten years of the War of the Hundred Years—a dismal failure that ended with his head on a pike after a year—and Esmara Getares' effort some thirty years earlier gained considerable ground before she tried to conquer Andor and spent the last twelve years of her life as the *guest* of Queen Telaisien. Esmara was assassinated in the end, though there is no record of why anyone would want her dead once Telaisien broke her power. You see, the Queens who came after Ishara, from Alesinde to Lyndelle, followed what she had begun, and not only in sending a daughter to the Tower. Ishara had Souran secure the land around Caemlyn first, only a few villages in the beginning, then slowly expanded her control. Why, it took five years for her sway to reach the River Erinin. But the land that Andor's Queens held was solidly theirs when most others who called themselves kings or queens were still more interested in gaining hew lands than in solidifying what they already had."

She paused for breath, and Rand leaped in quickly. Elenia spoke of these people as if she knew them personally, but his head was spinning with names he had never heard before. "Why is there no House Maravaile?"

"None of Ishara's sons lived past twenty." Elenia shrugged and sipped her punch; the subject did not interest her. But it did give her a new topic. "Nine queens reigned over the course of the War of the Hundred Years, and none had a son live beyond twenty-three. The battles were constant, and Andor was pressed from every side. Why, in Maragaine's reign, four kings brought armies against her—there is a town named for the battle, on the site. The kings were—"

"But all the queens have been descendants of Souran and Ishara?" Rand put in quickly. The woman would give him a day-by-day account if he let her. Sitting, he motioned her to take a chair.

"Yes," she said reluctantly. Probably reluctant to include Souran. But she brightened immediately. "You see, it is a matter of how much of Ishara's blood one has. How many lines connect you to her, and in what degree. In my case—"

"It isn't easy for me to understand. For example, take Tigraine and Morgase. Morgase had the best claim to succeed Tigraine. I suppose that means Morgase and Tigraine were closely related?"

"They were cousins." Elenia made an effort to hide her irritation over being interrupted so often, especially now that she was so close to the heart of what she wanted to say, but her mouth still narrowed. She looked like a fox that wanted to bite, but the chicken kept slipping just out of reach.

"I see." Cousins. Rand drank deeply, half-emptying his goblet.

"We are all cousins. All the Houses." His silence seemed to invigorate her. Her smile returned. "With marriages over a thousand years, there is not a House without some drop of Ishara's blood. But the degree is what is important, that and the number of connecting lines. In my case—"

Rand blinked. "You're *all* cousins? *All* of you? That doesn't seem poss—" He leaned forward intently. "Elenia, if Morgase and Tigraine had been . . . merchants, or farmers . . . how closely would they have been related?"

"Farmers?" she exclaimed, staring at him. "My Lord Dragon, what a peculiar—" The blood drained slowly from her face; he had been a farmer, after all. She wet her lips, a nervous flicker of the tongue. "I suppose . . . I should have to think. Farmers. I suppose that means imagining all the Houses as farmers." A nervous titter broke from her before she drowned it in her punch. "Had they been farmers, I don't think anyone would consider them related at all. All the connections are too far back. But they were not, my Lord Dragon. . . ."

He stopped listening with more than half an ear and sank back in his chair. Not related.

". . . have thirty-one lines to Ishara, while Dyelin has only thirty, and. . . ."

Why did he feel so relaxed suddenly? Knots had vanished from his muscles that he had not even known were there until they went.

". . . if I may say so, my Lord Dragon."

"What? Forgive me. My mind wandered for a moment—the problems of. . . . I missed the last thing you said." There had been something in it that had tugged at his ear, though.

Elenia wore the obsequious, flattering smile that looked so strange on her face. "Why, I was just saying that you yourself bear some resemblance to Tigraine, my Lord Dragon. You might even have some touch of Ishara's blood your—" She cut off with a squeak, and he realized he was on his feet.

"I . . . feel a little tired." He tried to make his voice normal, but it sounded as distant as if he were deep in the Void. "If you would leave me, please."

He did not know how his face looked, but Elenia bounced out of her chair, hurried to set her goblet on the table. She was trembling, and if her face had been bloodless before, now it looked like snow. Dropping a curtsy deep enough for a scullery maid caught stealing, she hurried toward the door, each step faster than the last, all the while watching him over her shoulder, until she tore the door open and the sound of running slippers receded down the hall. Nandera put her head in, checking on him, before pulling the door shut.

For a long time Rand stood staring at nothing. No wonder those ancient queens had been staring at him; they knew what he was thinking when he did not himself. That sudden worm of worry that had gnawed at him unseen since he discovered his mother's real name. But Tigraine had not been related to Morgase. His mother had not been related to Elayne's mother. He was not related to. . . .

"You're worse than a lecher," he said aloud, bitterly. "You're a fool and a. . . ." He wished Lews Therin would speak, so he could say to himself, *That is a madman; I am sane.* Was it those dead rulers of Andor he felt staring at him, or was it Alanna? Striding to the door, he jerked it open. Nandera and Caldin were sitting on their heels beneath a tapestry of brightly colored birds. "Assemble your people," he told them. "I'm going to Cairhien. Please don't tell Aviendha."

CHAPTER
27

Gifts

W alking back out to the great sprawl of tents, Egwene tried to get a grip on herself, but she was not sure her feet actually touched the ground. Well, she knew they did. They added their small portion to the waves of dust swept along by the hot gusting wind; coughing, she wished Wise Ones wore veils. A shawl wrapped around your head was not the same, and it was like wearing a sweat tent besides. Yet she felt as if her feet trod on air. Her brain seemed to be spinning, and not from the heat.

At first she had thought Gawyn was not going to meet her, but then he was suddenly just there as she walked through the crowds. They had spent the entire morning in the private dining room of The Long Man, holding hands and talking over tea. She was absolutely brazen, kissing him as soon as the door closed, before he so much as made a move to kiss her, even sitting on his knee once, though that had not lasted long. It made her start thinking of his dreams, about maybe slipping back into them again, about things no decent woman should be thinking at all! Not an unmarried woman, anyway. She had bounded up like a startled doe, startling him in turn.

Hastily she looked around. The tents were still half a mile off, and there was not a living soul closer. If there had been, they could not have seen her blushes. Realizing she was grinning idiotically behind the shawl,

503

she wiped it away. Light, she had to keep a rein on herself. Forget the feel of Gawyn's strong arms and remember why they had had so much time at The Long Man.

Threading through the crowd, she peered about, looking for Gawyn and trying with some difficulty to pretend casualness; she did not want him to think her eager, after all. Suddenly a man leaned toward her, whispering fiercely. "Follow me to The Long Man."

She jumped; she could not help herself. It took her a moment to recognize Gawyn. He wore a plain brown coat, and a thin dustcloak hung down his back, the hood up and nearly hiding his face. He was not the only one cloaked—any but Aiel who went beyond the city walls wore one—but not many had their hoods raised in that oven heat.

She caught his sleeve firmly as he tried to slide away ahead of her. "What makes you think I'll just go off to an inn with you, Gawyn Trakand?" she demanded, eyes narrowing. She did keep her voice down, though; no need to attract eyes to an argument. "We were going to walk. You are taking entirely too much for granted if you think for a moment—"

Grimacing, he whispered at her hurriedly. "The women I came with are looking for someone. Someone like you. They say little in front of me, but I've caught a word here and there. Now follow me." Without a backward glance he strode off down the street, leaving her to follow with a lurching stomach.

The memory settled her feet firmly. The burned-over ground was nearly as hot as the city paving stones through the soles of her soft boots. She trudged through the dust, thinking furiously. Gawyn had not known much more than he told in that first exchange. He argued that it could not be her they were looking for, that she just had to be careful of her channeling and stay out of sight as much as possible. Only, he had not looked very convinced himself, not wearing a disguise. She refrained from mentioning his clothes; he was so worried that if these Aes Sedai found her she would be in all sorts of troubles, worried that he would lead them to her, so plainly unwilling to stop seeing her even if he did suggest it himself. And so convinced that what she needed was to sneak somehow back to Tar Valon and into the Tower. That, or to make her peace with Coiren and the others and return with them. Light, but she should have been angry at him, thinking he knew what was best for her better than she did, but for some reason it made her want to smile indulgently even now. For some reason she just could not think straight about him, and he seemed to creep into whatever thought she had.

Chewing her lip, she focused on the real problem. The Tower Aes

Sedai. If only she could bring herself to question Gawyn; it would not be betraying him to ask just a few small questions, their Ajahs, where they went, or. . . . No! She had made that promise to herself, but breaking it would dishonor him. No questions. Only what he volunteered.

Whatever he said, she had no reason to think they were looking for Egwene al'Vere. And, she admitted reluctantly, no real reason to think they were not, only a lot of suppositions and hopes. Just because a Tower agent would not recognize Egwene al'Vere in an Aiel woman did not say that the agent had not heard the name, even heard of Egwene Sedai of the Green Ajah. She winced. From now on, she would have to be very careful in the city. More than careful.

She had reached the edge of the tents. The encampment sprawled over miles, covering the hills east of the city whether treed or not. Aiel moved among the low tents, but only a handful of *gai'shain* nearby. None of the Wise Ones were in sight. She had broken a promise to them. To Amys, really, but to all of them. Necessity seemed an increasingly thin reed to support her deception.

"Join us, Egwene," a woman's voice called. Even with her head covered, Egwene was not hard to pick out unless surrounded by girls not yet full grown. Surandha, Sorilea's apprentice, had poked her dark golden head out of a tent and was waving to her. "The Wise Ones are meeting back among the tents, all of them, and they've given us all the day for ourselves. The entire day." That was a luxury seldom offered, and not one Egwene would pass up.

Inside, women lay sprawled on cushions reading by oil lamps—the tent was closed against dust, and thus against light as well—or sat sewing or knitting or doing embroidery. Two were playing cat's cradle. A low murmur of conversation filled the tent, and several smiled greetings. They were not all apprentices—two mothers and several first-sisters had come to visit—and the older women wore as much jewelry as any Wise One. Everyone had their blouses half-unlaced and shawls wrapped around their waists, though the trapped heat did not seem to bother them.

A *gai'shain* moved about refilling teacups. Something in the way he moved said he was a craftsman, not *algai'd'siswai*; he was still hard of face, yet a trifle softer by comparison, and maintaining a meek manner seemed less of a struggle. He wore one of those headbands naming him *siswai'aman*. None of the women gave it a second glance, though *gai'shain* were not supposed to wear anything but white.

Egwene tied her shawl around her waist and gratefully accepted water to wash her face and hands, then undid a few of her blouse laces and took a tasseled red cushion between Surandha and Estair, Aeron's red-haired apprentice. "What are the Wise Ones meeting about?" Her mind was not on the Wise Ones. She had no intention of avoiding the city entirely—she had agreed to look in at The Long Man every morning to see whether Gawyn was there, though the smirk on the stout innkeeper's face made her cheeks grow warm; the Light only knew what that woman thought!—but there definitely would be no more attempts to listen in at Lady Arilyn's mansion. After leaving Gawyn she had gone near enough to sense the channeling continuing inside, but left after one quick peek around the corner. Just standing that close produced the uneasy feeling that Nesune was going to pop up behind her. "Does anyone know?"

"Your sisters, of course," Surandha laughed. She was a handsome woman, with large blue eyes, and laughter made her beautiful. Some five years older than Egwene, she could channel as strongly as many Aes Sedai and was eagerly awaiting the call to a hold of her own. In the meanwhile, of course, she jumped when Sorilea *thought* jump. "What else would make them leap as if they had sat on *segade* spines?"

"We should send Sorilea to talk with them," Egwene said, taking a green-striped cup of tea from the *gai'shain*. While telling her how his Younglings were crowded into all the bedrooms not taken by the Aes Sedai, and some into the stables, Gawyn had let slip that there was no room for even another scullery maid, and that the Aes Sedai were not preparing any. It was good news. "Sorilea could make any number of Aes Sedai sit up straight." Surandha's head went back in gales of laughter.

Estair's laugh was faint, and more than a touch scandalized. A slender young woman with serious gray eyes, she always behaved as if a Wise One was watching her. It never ceased to amaze Egwene that Sorilea should have an apprentice who was full of fun, while Aeron, pleasant and smiling, with never a cross word, had one who seemed to hunt for rules to obey. "I believe it is the *Car'a'carn*," Estair said in the gravest of tones.

"Why?" Egwene asked absently. She was just going to have to avoid the city. Except for Gawyn, of course; embarrassing as it might be to admit, she would not forgo meeting him for anything less than the certainty of Nesune waiting in The Long Man. That meant back to walking around the city walls for exercise, in all that dust. This morning had been an exception, but she was not going to give the Wise Ones any excuse to put off her return to *Tel'aran'rhiod*. Tonight they would meet the Salidar Aes Sedai alone, but in seven nights, she would be with them. "What now?"

"You have not heard?" Surandha exclaimed.

In two or three days she could approach Nynaeve and Elayne, or speak to them in their dreams again. Try to speak to them, anyway; you could never be absolutely certain the other person knew you were more than a dream, not unless they were used to communicating that way, which Nynaeve and Elayne certainly were not. She had only spoken to them that way once before. In any case, the thought of approaching them at all still made her vaguely uneasy. She had had another hazy almost nightmare about it; every time one of them said a word, they tripped and fell on their faces or dropped a cup or plate or knocked over a vase, always something that shattered on impact. Since interpreting the dream about Gawyn becoming her Warder she had been making an effort at all of them. To no real effect so far, but she was sure that one had meaning. Maybe it was best to wait on the next meeting to speak to them. Besides, there was always the chance of running into Gawyn's dreams again, being drawn in. Just the thought made her cheeks color.

"The *Car'a'carn* has returned," Estair said. "He is to meet your sisters this afternoon."

All thoughts of Gawyn and dreams gone, Egwene frowned into her teacup. Twice inside ten days. It was unusual for him to come back so soon. Why had he? Had he learned of the Tower Aes Sedai somehow? How? And as always, his trips themselves triggered their own question. *How* did he do it?

"How does he do what?" Estair asked, and Egwene blinked, startled that she had spoken aloud.

"How does he upset my stomach so easily?"

Surandha shook her head in commiseration, but she grinned too. "He is a man, Egwene."

"He is the *Car'a'carn*," Estair said with heavy emphasis, and more than a touch of reverence. Egwene would not be entirely surprised to see her wind that fool strip of cloth around her head.

Surandha immediately tackled Estair over how she was ever going to deal with a hold chief, much less a sept or clan chief, if she did not realize that a man did not stop being a man just because he led, while Estair maintained stoutly that the *Car'a'carn* was different. One of the older women, Mera, who had come to see her daughter, leaned toward them and said that the way to handle any chief—hold, sept, clan *or* the *Car'a'carn*— was the same as the way to handle a husband, which brought a laugh from Baerin, also there to visit a daughter, and a comment that that would be a good way to have a roofmistress lay her knife at your feet, a declaration of feud. Baerin had been a Maiden before she married, but anyone could declare a feud with anyone other than a Wise One or a blacksmith. Before the words were well out of Mera's mouth everybody except the *gai'shain* joined in, overwhelming poor Estair—the *Car'a'carn* was a chief among chiefs, no more; that was certain—but arguing whether it was better to approach a chief directly or through his roofmistress.

Egwene paid little attention. Surely Rand would not do anything foolish. He had been properly doubtful concerning Elaida's letter, yet he believed Alviarin's, which was not only more cordial, but downright fawning. He thought he had friends, even followers, in the Tower. She did not. Three Oaths or no Three Oaths, she was convinced Elaida and Alviarin had worked up that second letter between them, with all its ridiculous talk of "kneeling in his radiance." It was all a ploy to get him into the Tower.

Looking at her hands regretfully, she sighed and set down her cup. It was snatched up by the *gai'shain* before her hand was well away.

"I must go," she told the two apprentices. "There's something I realize I have to do." Surandha and Estair made noises about going with her— well, more than noises; if Aiel said something, they meant it—but they were caught up in the discussion and did not argue when she insisted they stay. Wrapping her shawl around her head again and leaving the rising voices behind—Mera was telling Estair in no uncertain tones that she might be a Wise One eventually, but until she was she could listen to a woman who had managed a husband and raised three daughters and two sons without a sister-wife to help—Egwene ducked back into the windblown dust.

In the city, she tried to creep through the crowded streets without appearing to creep, tried to look every way while seeming to watch only where she was going. The chances of walking into Nesune were small, but. . . . Ahead of her two women in sober dresses and prim aprons side-stepped to go around one another, but both moved the same way, and they came nose to nose. Murmured apologies, and each woman stepped aside again. In the same direction. More apologies, and as if dancing, they moved together once more. As Egwene passed them, they were still stepping from side to side in perfect unison, faces beginning to redden, apologies swallowed behind compressed lips. How long it might go on she had no idea, but it was well to remember that Rand was in the city. Light, when he was around, it would not be beyond belief for her to walk right up on all six Aes Sedai just as a gust of wind ripped the shawl from around her head and three people shouted her name and called her Aes Sedai. With him around, it would not be entirely beyond belief to walk into Elaida.

She hurried on, increasingly uneasy about being caught in one of his *ta'veren* swirls, increasingly wild-eyed. Fortunately, the sight of a wild-eyed Aiel with her face hidden—what did they know of the difference between a shawl and a veil?—made people move out of her way, which allowed her to speed along at a near trot, but she did not draw a peaceful breath until she slipped into the Sun Palace by a small servant's door in the rear.

A strong smell of cooking hung in the narrow hallway, and liveried men and women scurried back and forth. Others, taking their ease in their shirtsleeves or flapping aprons to make a little breeze, stared at her in astonishment. Likely no one except other servants came this close to the kitchens from one year to the next. Certainly not an Aiel. They looked as though they expected her to produce a spear from under her skirts.

She pointed a finger at a round little man who was wiping his neck with a kerchief. "Do you know where Rand al'Thor is?"

He gave a start, rolling his eyes toward his companions, who were quickly drifting away. His feet shifted, wanting very much to follow. "The Lord Dragon, uh . . . Mistress? In his chambers? I suppose, anyway." He began to shuffle sideways, bowing. "If Mistress . . . uh . . . if my Lady will forgive, I must get back to my—"

"You will take me there," she said firmly. She was not going to wander about this time.

One last eye-rolling after his vanished friends, a sigh quickly suppressed, a hurried frightened look to see whether he had offended, and he scampered off to fetch his coat. He was very efficient in the warren of palace corridors, hurrying along and bowing her way at every turn, but when at last he pointed with yet another bow to tall doors worked with gilded rising suns and guarded by a Maiden and an Aiel man, she felt a flash of contempt as she dismissed him. She could not understand why; he was simply doing what he was paid to do.

The Aiel man stood as she approached, a *very* tall man in his middle years, with bull-like chest and shoulders and cold gray eyes. Egwene did not know him, and he plainly meant to turn her away. Luckily she did know the Maiden.

"Let her pass, Marie," Somara said, grinning. "This is Amys' apprentice, hers and Bair's and Melaine's, the only apprentice I know to serve three Wise Ones. And from the look of her, they have sent her running with strong words for Rand al'Thor."

"Running?" Marie's chuckle softened neither face nor eyes. "Crawling, it looks." He went back to watching the corridor.

Egwene did not have to ask what he meant. Digging her handkerchief out of her belt pouch, she wiped hurriedly at her face; no one could take you seriously dirty, and Rand had to listen. "Important words anyway, Somara. He is alone, I hope. The Aes Sedai haven't come yet?" The handkerchief came away gray and went back into her pouch with a sigh.

Somara shook her head. "It is some good time before they are due. Will you tell him to be careful? I mean no disrespect to your sisters, but he will not look where he leaps. He is headstrong."

"I will tell him." Egwene could not help a grin. She had heard Somara talk this way before—with the sort of exasperated pride a mother might have for an overadventurous son of about ten—and a few other Maidens as well. It had to be some sort of Aiel joke, and even if she did not understand, she was in favor of anything that kept him from getting too big a head. "I'll tell him to wash his ears, too." Somara actually nodded before catching herself. Egwene drew a deep breath. "Somara, my sisters mustn't find out I am here." Marie glanced at her curiously, between studying every servant who entered the hallway. She had to be careful. "We are not close, Somara. In fact, you might say we are as far apart as sisters can be."

"The worst bad blood is between first-sisters," Somara said with a nod. "Go in. They will not hear your name from me, and if Marie's tongue flaps, I will tie a knot in it." Marie, head and shoulders taller and weighing at least twice as much, smiled slightly without looking at her.

The Maidens' habit of sending her in without announcing her had led to embarrassments in the past, but this time Rand was not sitting in his bath. The apartments had obviously belonged to the king, and the anteroom was more a throne room in miniature. Miniature by comparison with the real throne room, anyway. The wavy rays of a golden sun a full span across, set in the polished stone floor, were the only curves in sight. Tall mirrors in severe gold frames lined the walls beneath broad straight bands of gilding, and the deep cornice was made of golden triangles overlapping like scales. Heavily gilded chairs to either side of the rising sun made two facing lines as stiff as their tall backs. Rand sat in another chair, with twice the gilding and a back twice as high, atop a small dais that was itself encrusted with gilt. In a red silk coat embroidered in gold and holding that piece of carved Seanchan spear in the crook of his arm, he wore a dark scowl. He looked a king, and one about to do murder.

She planted her fists on her hips. "Somara says you should wash your ears right this instant, young man," she said, and his head jerked up.

Surprise, and a touch of outrage, lasted only a moment. With a grin he stepped down and tossed the spearhead onto the chair seat. "What under the Light have you been doing?" Striding the length of the chamber, he took her by the shoulders and turned her to face the nearest mirror.

She winced in spite of herself. She was a sight. The dust that had sifted through her shawl—no; mud, with the sweat added—made streaks across her cheeks and swirls across her forehead where she had tried to scrub it away.

"I'll have Somara send for some water," he said dryly. "Perhaps she'll think it is for my ears." That grin was insufferable!

"There is no need," she told him with as much dignity as she could muster. She was not about to have him stand there watching her wash. Pulling out her already grimy handkerchief, she hurriedly tried to clean off the worst. "You're meeting Coiren and the others soon. I don't have to warn you they're dangerous, do I?"

"I think you just did. They aren't all coming. I said no more than three, so that is what they're sending." In the mirror his head tilted as if he were listening, and he nodded, voice dropping to a murmur. "Yes, I can handle three, if they aren't too strong." Abruptly he noticed her looking. "Of course, if one of them is Moghedien in a wig, or Semirhage, I may be in trouble."

"Rand, you must take this seriously." The handkerchief was not doing much good. With the greatest reluctance, she spat on it; there was simply no dignified way to spit on a handkerchief. "I know how strong you are, but they are Aes Sedai. You can't behave like they're women in from the country. Even if you think Alviarin *will* kneel at your feet, and all her friends with her, these were sent by Elaida. You can't think she means anything but to try putting a leash on you. The short and simple of it is, you should send them away."

"And trust your hidden friends?" he asked softly. Much too softly.

There was nothing to be done with her face; she should have let him send for the water. There was no asking for it now, though, not after refusing. "You know you cannot trust Elaida," she said carefully, turning to him. Mindful of what had happened the last time, she did not even want to mention the Aes Sedai in Salidar. "You know that."

"I don't trust any Aes Sedai. They"—there was a hesitation in his voice, as if he had started to use another word, though she could not imagine what—"will try to use me, and I will try to use them. A pretty circle, don't you think?" If she had ever considered the possibility that he could be allowed near the Salidar Aes Sedai, his eyes disabused her of it, so hard, so cold, that she shivered inside.

Maybe if he got angry enough, if he struck enough sparks with Coiren that the embassy went back to the Tower empty-handed, on their own. . . . "If you think it is pretty, I suppose it is; you *are* the Dragon Reborn. Well, since you intend to go through with this, you might as well do it right. Just remember that they are Aes Sedai. Even a king listens to Aes Sedai with respect, even when he doesn't agree, and he'd set out for Tar Valon on the hour if summoned. Even the Tairen High Lords would, or Pedron Niall." The fool man grinned at her again, or at least showed his teeth; the rest of his face was as blank as river rock. "I hope you're paying attention. I am trying to help you." Just not the way he thought. "If you mean to use them, you can't make them bristle like doused cats. The Dragon Reborn won't impress them any more than he does me, with your fancy coats and your thrones and your fool scepter." She shot a scornful look at the tasseled spearhead; Light, the thing made her skin crawl! "They aren't going to fall on their knees when they see you, and it won't kill you when they don't. It will not kill you to be courteous, either. Bend your stubborn neck. It isn't groveling to show a proper deference, a little humbleness."

"Proper deference," he said thoughtfully. With a sigh, he shook his head ruefully, scrubbed a hand through his hair. "I suppose I can't talk to an Aes Sedai the same way I do to some lord who's been plotting behind my back. It's good advice, Egwene. I'll try. I will be humble as a mouse."

Trying not to look hurried, she rubbed at her face again with the handkerchief to hide her goggling. She was not really sure her eyes were popping, but she thought they must be. Her whole life, any time she pointed out that right was a better way, he stuck out his chin and insisted on left! Why did he have to choose now to listen?

Was there anything to the good as matters stood? At least it could not hurt him to display some respect. Even if they followed Elaida, the idea of anyone showing impertinence to any Aes Sedai really did upset her. Only she *wanted* him to be impertinent, to be as arrogant as he had ever been. There was no point in trying to undo it, not now; he was not slow-witted. Only exasperating.

"Was that all you came for?" he asked.

She could not go yet. There might be a chance to put things right, or at least make sure he was not wool-headed enough to go to Tar Valon. "Do you know there's a Sea Folk Wavemistress on a ship in the river? The *White Spray*." That was as good a change of topic as any. "She came to see you, and I hear she is growing impatient." That was from Gawyn. Erian had had herself rowed out to discover what Sea Folk were doing so far inland, and was refused permission to board. She had come back in a mood that would have been called a tail-lashing fury in any woman not Aes Sedai. Egwene more than suspected why they were here, but she was not about to tell Rand; for once let him meet somebody without expecting them to bow down.

"The Atha'an Miere are everywhere, it seems." Rand took a seat in one of the chairs; he looked amused for some reason, but she would swear it had nothing to do with the Sea Folk. "Berelain says I should meet this Harine din Togara Two Winds, but if her temper is anything like Berelain reports, she can wait. I have enough women angry with me for the moment."

That was almost an opening, but not quite. "I cannot understand why. You always have such a winning way about you." Immediately she wished she had the words back; they only reinforced what she did *not* want him to do.

Frowning, he seemed not to have heard her at all. "Egwene, I know you don't like Berelain, but it hasn't gone beyond that, has it? I mean, you make such a good job of playing at Aiel, I could imagine you offering to dance the spears with her. She was troubled about something, uneasy, but she wouldn't say what."

Probably the woman had found a man who told her no; that would be enough to shake Berelain's world to its foundations. "I've not said a dozen words to her since the Stone of Tear, and not many more then. Rand, you don't think—"

One of the doors opened just barely enough to admit Somara, who shut it again behind her quickly. "The Aes Sedai are here, *Car'a'carn*."

Rand's head swiveled toward the door, his face stone. "They weren't to come for another—! Thinking to catch me off guard, were they? They have to learn who sets the rules here."

Right then Egwene did not care if they were trying to catch him in his smallclothes. All thought of Berelain vanished. Somara made a small gesture that might have been commiseration. She did not care about that either. Rand could keep them from taking her, if she asked. All it meant was staying close to him from now on so they could not shield her and hustle her away the first time she put her nose into the street. All it meant was asking, putting herself under his protection. The choice between that and being hauled back to the Tower in a sack was so thin it made her stomach hurt. For one thing, she would never become Aes Sedai hiding behind him, and for another, the idea of hiding behind anyone set her teeth on edge. Only, they were here, right outside the door, and inside the hour she might be in that sack, or as good as. Deep slow breaths did nothing to steady her twitching nerves.

"Rand, is there another way out of here? If there isn't, I will hide in one of the other rooms. They mustn't know I am here. Rand? Rand! Are you listening to me?"

He spoke, but definitely not to her. "You *are* there," he whispered hoarsely. "Too much coincidence for you to think of that now." He was staring at nothing with a look of fury, and maybe fear. "Burn you, answer me! I know you're there!"

Egwene licked her lips before she could stop herself. Somara might be gazing at him with what could be described as fond motherly concern—and him not even noticing her joke—but Egwene's stomach was turning over slowly. He could not have gone mad as suddenly as that. He could not have. But he had seemed to listen to some hidden voice just a little while ago, and maybe spoken to it then too.

She did not remember crossing the intervening space, but abruptly her hand was pressed against his forehead. Nynaeve always said to check for fever first, though what good that would do now. . . . If only she knew more than a scrap of Healing. But that would do no good, either. Not if he was. . . . "Rand, are you . . . ? Are you feeling all right?"

He came to himself, shying back from her hand, peering at her suspiciously. The next moment he was on his feet, gripping her arm, all but hauling her down the chamber so quickly she nearly tripped over her skirts trying to keep up. "Stand right there," he ordered briskly, planting her beside the dais, and backed away.

Rubbing her arm vigorously enough that he could not miss it, she started to follow. Men never realized how strong they were; even Gawyn did not always, though she did not really mind with him. "What do you think—?"

"Don't move!" In a disgusted tone he added, "Burn him, it seems it ripples if you move. I'll fasten it to the floor, but you still can't jump about. I don't know how big I can make it, and this is no time to find out." Somara's mouth had fallen open, though she snapped it shut quickly.

Fasten what to the floor? What was he talking—? It came to her so suddenly that she forgot to wonder who the "him" was. Rand had woven *saidin* around her. Her eyes widened; she was breathing too quickly, but she could not stop. How close was it? Every shred of reason told her the taint could not seep out of whatever he channeled; he had touched her with *saidin* before, but if anything, that thought only made it worse. Instinctively she narrowed her shoulders and held her skirts close in front of her.

"What—? What did you do?" She was very proud of her voice, a trifle unsteady maybe, but nothing like the wail she wanted to let out.

"Look in that mirror," he laughed. Laughed!

Grumpily she obeyed—and gasped. There in the silvered glass was the gilded chair on its dais. Some of the rest of the room. But not her. "I'm . . . invisible," she breathed. Once Moiraine had hidden them all behind a screen of *saidar*, but how had he learned it?

"Much better than hiding under my bed," he said, speaking to air a good hand to the right of her head. As if *that* had ever entered her mind! "I want you to see how respectful I can be. Besides," his tone became more serious, "maybe you'll see something I miss. Maybe you'll even be willing to tell me." With a bark of a laugh he leaped onto the dais, scooped up the tasseled spearhead and took his seat. "Send them in, Somara. Let the embassy of the White Tower approach the Dragon Reborn." His twisted smile made Egwene almost as uncomfortable as the nearness of woven *saidin*. How close *was* the bloody stuff?

Somara vanished, and in moments the doors opened wide.

A plump, stately woman who could only be Coiren led the way in a dark blue gown, flanked a pace to the rear by Nesune in plain brown wool and a raven-haired Aes Sedai in green silk, a pretty, round-faced woman with a plump, demanding mouth. Egwene wished Aes Sedai always wore the colors of their Ajah—Whites did at every chance—because whatever that woman was, she would not believe her Green, not with the hard stare she gave Rand from her first step into the room. Cold serenity barely masked her contempt, perhaps did mask it for anyone not used to Aes Sedai. Would Rand see? Maybe not; he seemed to be concentrating on Coiren, whose face was completely unreadable. Nesune, of course, took in everything, birdlike eyes darting this way and that.

Right then, Egwene was very glad of the cloak he had woven for her. She started to dab at her face with the handkerchief she still held, then froze. He said he would fix it to the floor. Had he? Light, she might be standing there naked for all she knew. Except that Nesune's gaze swept past without pausing. Sweat rolled down Egwene's face. It poured. Burn the man! She would have been perfectly happy hiding under his bed.

Behind the Aes Sedai came a full dozen more women, plainly dressed, with coarse linen dustcloaks hanging down their backs. Most were stocky, but they labored under the weight of two chests, not small, the polished brass strapping worked with the Flame of Tar Valon. The serving women set the chests down with audible sighs of relief, furtively working arms and knuckling backs as the doors swung shut, and Coiren and the other two sank into curtsies in perfect unison, though not very deeply.

Rand was down out of the chair before they straightened. The glow of *saidar* surrounded the Aes Sedai, all three together; they had linked. Egwene tried to remember what she had seen, how they did it; despite the glow, nothing ruffled their outward calm as Rand strode by them to the serving women and peered into each face in turn.

What was he—? Of course; making sure none had the ageless face of an Aes Sedai. Egwene shook her head, then froze again. He was a fool if he thought that enough. Most wore too much age—not all old by any means, but you could put an age to them—yet two were young enough to be Aes Sedai not long raised. They were not—Egwene could only sense the ability in the three Aes Sedai, and she was close enough—but he certainly could not tell by looking.

Tipping up one solid young woman's chin, he smiled into her eyes. "Do not be afraid," he said softly. She swayed as if she might faint. With a sigh, Rand spun on his heel. He did not look at the Aes Sedai as he passed them. "You will not channel around me," he said firmly. "Let it go." A brief look of speculation crossed Nesune's face, but the other two serenely watched him take his seat. Rubbing his arm—Egwene had been there when he learned that tingle—he spoke in a harder tone. "I said you will not channel around me. Or even embrace *saidar.*"

A stretched-out moment, while Egwene prayed silently. What would he do if they held on to the Source? Try to cut them off? Cutting a woman off from *saidar* once she embraced it was far harder than shielding her beforehand. She was not certain even he could manage it with three women, and linked to boot. Worse, what would they do if he tried anything at all? The glow vanished, and she barely stopped a heavy sigh of relief. Whatever he had done made her invisible, but plainly it did not stop sound.

"Much better." Rand's smile took them all in, but it never reached his eyes. "Let us begin again from the beginning. You are honored guests, you only entered this very moment."

They understood, of course. He had not been guessing. Coiren stiffened slightly, and the raven-haired woman's eyes actually widened. Nesune merely nodded to herself, adding to her mental notes. Egwene hoped desperately that he would be careful. Nesune would not miss anything.

With a visible effort Coiren gathered herself, smoothing her dress and very nearly adjusting the shawl she was not wearing. "I have the honor," she announced in ringing tones, "to be Coiren Saeldain Aes Sedai, Ambassador from the White Tower and emissary of Elaida do Avriny a'Roihan, the Watcher of the Seals, the Flame of Tar Valon, the Amyrlin Seat." Somewhat less florid introductions, though with the full honorific Aes Sedai, named the other two; the hard-eyed woman was Galina Casban.

"I am Rand al'Thor." The simplicity was a marked contrast. They had not mentioned the Dragon Reborn and neither had he, but somehow his leaving it out seemed to make the title whisper faintly in the room.

Coiren drew a deep breath, moved her head as if hearing that whisper. "We bring a gracious invitation to the Dragon Reborn. The Amyrlin Seat is fully cognizant that signs have been given and prophecies fulfilled, that. . . ." Those deep round tones took little time to reach the point, that Rand should accompany them, "in all honor as deserved," to the White Tower, and that if he accepted this invitation, Elaida offered not only the protection of the Tower, but the full weight of its authority and influence behind him. Another goodly bit of flowery speech flowed before she finished with, ". . . and in token of this, the Amyrlin Seat sends this trifling gift."

She turned toward the chests, raising her hand, then hesitated with the faintest grimace. She had to gesture twice before the servants understood and lifted the brass-strapped lids; apparently she had planned to fling them open with *saidar*. Leather sacks filled the chests. At another, sharper, gesture, the serving women began untying them.

Egwene swallowed a gasp. No wonder those women had struggled! The opened sacks spilled gold coins of every size, sparkling rings and glittering necklaces and unset gems. Even if those below held dross, it was a fortune.

Leaning back in that thronelike chair, Rand looked at the chests with a near smile. The Aes Sedai studied him, faces masks of composure, yet Egwene thought she detected a hint of complacency in Coiren's eyes, a faint increase of contempt on Galina's full lips. Nesune. . . . Nesune was the real danger.

Abruptly the lids snapped down without a hand touching them, and

the serving women leaped back, not bothering to muffle their squeals. The
Aes Sedai stiffened, and Egwene prayed as hard as she sweated. She wanted
him arrogant and a touch insolent, but just enough to put their backs up,
not to the point of making them decide to try gentling him on the spot.

Suddenly it occurred to her that so far he had shown nothing of that
"humble as a mouse." He had never intended to. The man had been toying
with her! If she were not too frightened to be sure of her knees, she would
go over and box his ears.

"A great deal of gold," Rand said. He seemed relaxed, his smile taking
in his whole face. "I can always find a use for gold." Egwene blinked. He
sounded almost greedy!

Coiren answered with a smile of her own, a definite picture of poised
self-satisfaction now. "The Amyrlin Seat is, of course, most generous.
When you reach the White Tower—"

"When I reach the Tower," Rand cut in as though thinking aloud.
"Yes, I look forward to the day I stand in the Tower." He leaned forward,
elbow on his knee and Dragon Scepter dangling. "It will take a little
time, you understand. I have commitments to meet first, here, in Andor,
elsewhere."

Coiren's mouth tightened for just an instant. Her voice remained as
smooth and round as ever, though. "We surely have no objections to resting a few days before we begin the return journey to Tar Valon. In the
meanwhile, may I suggest that one of us remain close at hand, to offer advice should you wish it? We have, of course, heard of Moiraine's unfortunate demise. I cannot offer myself, but Nesune or Galina would be most
willing."

Rand studied the named pair with a frown, and Egwene held her breath.
He seemed to be listening to something again, or listening for something.
Nesune examined him in return as openly as he did her. Galina's fingers
stroked her skirts unconsciously.

"No," he said at last, sitting back with his arms on the arms of the
chair. He made it look even more a throne than before. "It might not be
safe. I would not like one of you to take a spear through your ribs by accident." Coiren opened her mouth, but he rode over her. "For your own
safety, none of you should come closer to me than a mile without permission. Best if you stay that far from the Palace without permission, too. You
will know when I'm ready to go with you. I promise that." Abruptly he
was on his feet. Atop the dais he stood tall enough that the Aes Sedai had
to crane their necks, and it was plain none of them liked it any more than

they liked his restrictions. Three faces carved in stone stared up at him. "I will let you go back to your resting now. The quicker I can see to certain things, the quicker I can go to the Tower. I will send word when I can see you again."

They were not pleased at so sudden a dismissal, or likely at any dismissal—Aes Sedai were the ones who said when an audience was done—yet there was little they could do except make their minimal curtsies, disgruntlement nearly breaking through Aes Sedai calm.

As they turned to go, Rand spoke again, casually. "I forgot to ask. How is Alviarin?"

"She is well." Galina's mouth hung open for a moment, her eyes widening. She appeared startled to have spoken.

Coiren hesitated on the brink of using the opening to say more, but Rand stood impatiently, all but tapping his foot. When they were gone, he stepped down, hefting that spearhead and staring at the doors that had closed behind them.

Egwene wasted not a moment striding toward him. "What game are you playing at, Rand al'Thor?" She had taken half a dozen steps before a glimpse of her reflection in the mirrors made her realize she had walked right through his weave of *saidin.* At least she had not known when it touched her. "Well?"

"She's one of Alviarin's," he said thoughtfully. "Galina. She is one of Alviarin's friends. I'd bet on it."

Planting herself in front of him, she sniffed. "You'd lose your coin and stick yourself in the foot with a pitchfork, too. Galina is a Red, or I never saw one."

"Because she doesn't like me?" He was looking at her now, and she almost wished he was not. "Because she's afraid of me?" He was not grimacing or glaring, or even staring particularly hard, yet his eyes seemed to know things she did not. She *hated* that. His smile came so suddenly she blinked. "Egwene, do you expect me to believe you can tell a woman's Ajah by her face?"

"No, but—"

"Anyway, even Reds might end following me. They know the Prophecies as well as anybody else. 'The unstained tower breaks and bends knee to the forgotten sign.' Written before there was a White Tower, but what else could 'the unstained tower' be? And the forgotten sign? My banner, Egwene, with the ancient symbol of Aes Sedai."

"Burn you, Rand al'Thor!" The curse came more awkwardly than she could have wished; she was not accustomed to saying such things. "The Light burn you! You can't really be thinking of going with them. You can't!"

He showed his teeth in amusement. Amusement! "Didn't I do what you wanted? What you told me to do *and* what you wanted."

Her lips compressed indignantly. Bad enough that he knew, but throwing it in her face was just rude. "Rand, please listen to me. Elaida—"

"The question now is how to get you back to the tents without them finding out you were here. I expect they have eyes-and-ears in the Palace."

"Rand, you have to—!"

"How about riding in one of those big laundry baskets? I can have a couple of Maidens carry it."

She very nearly threw up her hands. He was as eager to be rid of her as he had been of the Aes Sedai. "My own feet will do well enough, thank you." A laundry basket, indeed! "I wouldn't have to worry if you told me how you step from Caemlyn to here whenever you want." She did not understand why asking should rasp so, yet it did. "I know you can't teach me, but if you told me how, maybe I could work out how to do it with *saidar*."

Instead of the joke at her expense she more than half-expected, he took the end of her shawl in both hands. "The Pattern," he said. "Caemlyn," one finger on his left hand tented the wool, "and Cairhien." A finger on the other hand made a tent, and he brought the two tents together. "I bend the Pattern and bore a hole from one to the other. I don't know what I bore through, but there's no space between one end of the hole and the other." He let the shawl drop. "Does that help?"

Chewing her lip, she frowned at the shawl sourly. It did not help at all. Just the thought of tearing a hole in the Pattern made her queasy. She had hoped it would be like something she had worked out concerning *Tel'aran'rhiod*. Not that she ever meant to use it, of course, but she had had all that time on her hands, and the Wise Ones kept grumbling about the Aes Sedai asking how to enter in the flesh. She thought the way would be to create—a similarity seemed the only way to describe it—a similarity between the real world and its reflection in the World of Dreams. That should make a place where it was possible to simply step from one to the other. If Rand's method of travel had seemed even slightly the same, she would have been willing to try, but this. . . . *Saidar* did as you wanted as long as you remembered it was infinitely stronger than you and had to be guided gently; try to force the wrong thing, and you were dead or burned out before you could scream.

"Rand, are you sure there isn't any sense of making things the same . . . or. . . ." She did not know how to put it, but in any case, he shook his head before she trailed off.

"That sounds like changing the weave of the Pattern. I think it would tear me apart if I so much as tried. I bore a hole." He poked a finger at her to demonstrate.

Well, there was no point in pursuing that. She shifted her shawl irritably. "Rand, about those Sea Folk. I don't know any more than I've read"—she did, but she still was not going to tell him—"but it must be something important to bring them this far to see you."

"Light," he muttered absently, "you jump around like a drop of water on a hot griddle. I'll see them when I have time." For a moment he rubbed at his forehead, and his eyes seemed to see nothing. With a blink he was seeing her again. "Do you intend to stay until they come back?" He really did want to be rid of her.

At the door she paused, but he was already stalking up the room, hands clasped behind his back, talking to himself. Softly, but she could make out some. "Where are you hiding, burn you? I know you're there!"

Shivering, she let herself out. If he really was going mad already, there was no changing it. The Wheel weaved as the Wheel willed, and its weaving must be accepted.

Realizing that she was eyeing the servants passing up and down the hall, wondering which might be Aes Sedai agents, she made herself stop. The Wheel weaved as the Wheel willed. With a nod for Somara, she squared her shoulders and tried very hard not to scuttle on her way to the nearest servants' entrance.

There was little talk as Arilyn's best coach lurched away from the Sun Palace followed by the wagon that had borne the chests, burdened now only with the serving women and driver. Steepling her fingers in the coach, Nesune tapped them thoughtfully against her lips. A fascinating young man. A fascinating subject for study. Her foot touched one of the specimen boxes under the seat; she never went anywhere without proper specimen boxes. One would think that the world must have been catalogued long since, yet since leaving Tar Valon she had tucked away fifty plants, twice as many insects, and the skins and bones of a fox, three sorts of lark, and no fewer than five species of ground squirrel that she was sure were nowhere in the records.

"I did not realize you were friendly with Alviarin," Coiren said after a time.

Galina sniffed. "It is not necessary to be friends to know she was well when we left." Nesune wondered whether the woman knew that she pouted. Only the shape of her mouth perhaps, but one had to learn to live with one's face. "Do you think he truly knew?" Galina went on. "That we had. . . . It is impossible. He must have been guessing."

Nesune's ears perked, though she continued to tap her lips. That was clearly an effort to change the subject, and a sign that Galina was nervous besides. Silence had held as long as it did because no one wanted to mention al'Thor and there seemed no other topic possible. Why did Galina not want to speak of Alviarin? The two certainly were not friends; it was a rare Red who had a friend outside her Ajah. Nesune filed the question in its own mental cubbyhole.

"If he was guessing, he could make his fortune at the fairs." Coiren was no fool. Bombastic beyond all reason, but never a fool. "However ridiculous it might seem, we must assume he can sense *saidar* in a woman."

"That might be disastrous," Galina muttered. "No. It cannot be. He must have guessed. Any man who can channel would assume we would embrace *saidar*."

The woman's pout irritated Nesune. This entire expedition irritated her. She would have been more than happy to join it if asked, but Jesse Bilal had not asked; Jesse had practically shoved her onto her horse physically. However it might be in other Ajahs, the head of the Browns' council was not expected to behave so. Worst of all, though, Nesune's companions were so focused on young al'Thor that they seemed to have gone blind to all else.

"Do you have any notions," she mused aloud, "as to the sister who shared our interview?"

It might not have been a sister—three Aielwomen seemed to turn up whenever she went into the Royal Library, and two could channel—but she wanted to see their reactions. She was not disappointed; or rather, she was. Coiren only sat up straight, but Galina stared. It was all Nesune could do not to sigh. They truly were blind. Only a few paces from a woman able to channel, and they had not sensed her because they could not see her.

"I don't know how she was hidden," Nesune went on, "but it will be interesting to discover." It had to have been his work; they would have seen any weaving of *saidar*. They did not ask whether she was sure; they knew she always identified a guess.

"Confirmation that Moiraine is alive." Galina settled back with a grim smile. "I suggest we set Beldeine to find her. Then we take her and bundle her into the basement. That takes her away from al'Thor, and we can carry her to Tar Valon along with him. I doubt he'll even notice, so long as we let enough gold glitter under his nose."

Coiren shook her head emphatically. "We have no more confirmation than we already had, not of Moiraine. It may be this mysterious Green. As far as finding whoever it is, I agree, but we must consider the rest carefully. I will not risk everything that has been so carefully planned. We must be aware that al'Thor is connected to this sister—whoever she may be—and that his plea for time may be only a strategy. Fortunately, we have time." Galina nodded, however reluctantly; she would marry and settle on a farm before she risked their plans.

Nesune allowed herself a small sigh. Aside from pomposity, stating the obvious was Coiren's only real fault. She did have a good mind, when she used it. And they did have time. Her foot touched one of the specimen boxes again. However events spun out, the paper she intended to write on al'Thor would be the culmination of her life.

CHAPTER
28

Letters

Lews Therin *was* there—Rand was sure of it—but not a whisper
sounded in his head that was not his own. For the rest of the day he
did try to think of other things, useless as they might be. Berelain
was ready to jump out of her skin for the number of times he popped in
on her to ask about something she was perfectly capable of handling
without him; he was not sure, but he thought she started trying to avoid
him. Even Rhuarc began to look a little hunted after the tenth time
Rand cornered him over the Shaido; the Shaido had not stirred, and the
only choices Rhuarc could see were to leave them in Kinslayer's Dagger or
dig them out. Herid Fel had wandered off, as Idrien quickly pointed out he
often did, and was nowhere to be found; when Fel became lost in thought,
he sometimes lost his way in the city, too. Rand shouted at her. Fel was
not her fault, not her responsibility, but Rand left her white and trembling. His temper rippled like a line of thunderstorms sweeping in from
the horizon. He shouted at Meilan and Maringil till they shook in their
boots and left him with pasty faces, reduced Colavaere to incoherent tears
and actually sent Anaiyella running with her skirts hiked to her knees.
For that matter, when Amys and Sorilea came to ask what he had told
the Aes Sedai, he shouted at them as well; from the look on Sorilea's face
as they stalked away, he suspected that might have been the first time
anyone had ever raised voice to her. It was knowing—*knowing*—that

Lews Therin was really there, more than a voice, a man hiding inside his head.

He was almost afraid to fall asleep when night came, afraid Lews Therin might seize control while he slept, and when he did sleep his troubled dreams made him toss and mutter. The first hint of light though the windows woke him in tangled sweat-soaked sheets, with grainy eyes, a mouth that tasted like a horse six days dead, and legs that ached. The dreams he remembered had all been of running from something he could not see. He levered himself out of the great four-posted bed and made his ablutions at the gilded washstand. With the sky just turning gray outside, the *gai'shain* who would bring fresh water had not appeared yet, but last night's did well enough.

He had nearly finished shaving when he stopped, razor poised against his cheek, staring at himself in the mirror on the wall. Running. He had been sure it was the Forsaken he was running from in those dreams, or the Dark One, or Tarmon Gai'don, or maybe even Lews Therin. So full of himself; surely the Dragon Reborn would dream of being pursued by the Dark One. For all his protests that he was Rand al'Thor, it seemed that he could forget as easily as anyone else. Rand al'Thor had run away from Elayne, from his fear of loving Elayne, just as he had run from fear of loving Aviendha.

The mirror shattered, shards dropping into the porcelain washbasin. The pieces remaining in the frame cast back a fragmented image of his face.

Releasing *saidin*, he carefully scraped away the last bit of lather and folded the razor deliberately. No more running. He would do what he had to do, but no more running.

Two Maidens were waiting in the corridor when he emerged. Harilin, a lanky redhead about his age, went running for the others as soon as he appeared. Chiarid, a merry-eyed blonde old enough to be his mother, accompanied him through hallways where only a few servants stirred, surprised to see him so early. Usually Chiarid liked to make jokes at his expense when they were alone—he understood some; she saw him as a younger brother who needed to be kept from getting too big for his hat— but she felt his mood this morning and said not a word. She did give his sword one disgusted glance, but only one.

Nandera and the rest of the Maidens caught up before he was halfway to the Traveling chamber, and caught his silence as quickly. So did the Mayeners and Black Eyes guarding the square-carved door. Rand thought he might leave Cairhien without anyone speaking until a young woman in the red-and-blue of Berelain's personal servants rushed in and bobbed a deep curtsy just as he opened the gateway.

"The First sends this," she panted, extending a letter with a large green seal. Apparently she had run all the way trying to find him. "It's from the Sea Folk, my Lord Dragon."

Rand stuffed the letter into his coat pocket and stepped through the gateway, ignoring the woman's question as to whether there was any reply. Silence suited him this morning. He ran a thumb along the carving on the Dragon Scepter. He would be strong and hard, and put all this self-pity behind him.

The dark Grand Hall in Caemlyn brought Alanna nestling back into his head. Night still held here, but she was awake; he knew as surely as he knew she was weeping, as surely as he knew her tears stopped moments after he closed the gateway behind the last of the Maidens. A small ball of ragged unreadable emotion still sat in the back of his head, yet he was certain she knew he had returned. No doubt she and her bond had played their part in his flight, but he accepted the bond now even if he did not like it. That nearly made him chuckle wryly; he had better accept it, since he could not change it. She had tied a thread to him—no more than a thread; Light, let it be no more—and it should not cause trouble unless he let her close enough to make it a leash. He wished Thom Merrilin were there; Thom probably knew all about Warders and bonds; he knew surprising things. Well, finding Elayne would find Thom. That was all there was to it.

Saidin made a globe of light, Fire and Air, to illumine the way out of the throne room. The ancient queens, hidden in the darkness far overhead, did not bother him at all. They were only pictures in colored glass.

The same could not be said of Aviendha. Outside his apartments Nandera dismissed the Maidens except for Jalani, and the two went in with him to check the rooms while he used the Power to light the lamps and tossed the Dragon Scepter onto a small ivory-inlaid table that had considerably less gilt than it would have had in the Sun Palace. All the furnishings were that way, with less gilding and more carving, usually lions or roses. One large red carpet covered the floor, with gold thread outlining roses.

Without *saidin* in him, he doubted he could have heard the Maidens' soft footfalls, but before they crossed the anteroom Aviendha came stalking out of the still dark bedchamber with her hair in wild disarray and her belt knife in hand. And wearing only her skin. At the sight of him she went stiff as a post and stalked back the way she had come, little short of running. A small light appeared through the doorway, a lamp lit. Nandera laughed softly and exchanged amused glances with Jalani.

"I will never understand Aiel," Rand muttered, pushing the Source away. It was not so much that the Maidens found the situation funny; he had long since given up on Aiel humor. It was Aviendha. She might think it *very* funny to undress for bed in front of him, but let him catch so much as a glimpse of ankle when she did not choose to show it, and she turned into a scalded cat. Not to mention blaming him.

Nandera chortled. "It is not Aiel you cannot understand, but women. No man has ever understood women."

"Men, on the other hand," Jalani put in, "are very simple." He stared at her, with the baby fat still on her cheeks, and she colored faintly. Nandera looked ready to laugh out loud.

Death, Lews Therin whispered.

Rand forgot everything else. *Death? What do you mean?*

Death comes.

What kind of death? Rand demanded. *What are you talking about? Who are you? Where am I?*

Rand felt as though a fist had clutched his throat. He had been sure, but. . . . This was the first time Lews Therin had said anything to him, something clearly and plainly addressed to him. *I am Rand al'Thor. You are inside my head.*

Inside . . . ? No! I am myself! I am Lews Therin Telamon! I am meeeeeeeeee! The cry faded away into the distance.

Come back, Rand shouted. *What death? Answer me, burn you!* Silence. He shifted uneasily. Knowing was one thing, but a dead man, inside him, talking of death, made him feel unclean, like the faintest brush of the taint on *saidin.*

Something touched his arm, and he nearly seized at the Source again before he realized it was Aviendha. She must have flown into her clothes, yet she looked as if she had taken an hour to arrange every hair to her liking. People said Aiel showed no emotion, but it was just that they were more reserved than most. Their faces told as much as anyone else's if you knew what to look for. Aviendha was torn between concern and wanting to be angry.

"Are you well?" she asked.

"I was just thinking," he told her. True enough. *Answer me, Lews Therin! Come back and answer me!* Why had he ever thought silence suited the morning?

Unfortunately, Aviendha took him at his word, and if there was nothing to be concerned about. . . . She put her fists on her hips. That was one thing he understood about women, Aiel, Two Rivers or whoever; fists on hips meant trouble. He need not have bothered lighting the lamps; her eyes were hot enough to light the room. "You went away without me again. I promised the Wise Ones to stay near you until I must go, but you make my promise nothing. You have *toh* to me for this, Rand al'Thor. Nandera, from now on I must be told where he is going and when. He must not be allowed to go without me if I should accompany him."

Nandera hesitated not a moment before nodding. "It shall be as you wish, Aviendha."

Rand squared around on both women. "Now, just you wait! Nobody is to be told my comings and goings unless I say so."

"I have given my word, Rand al'Thor," Nandera said in a flat voice. She looked him in the eye with no notion of backing up.

"As do I," Jalani said just as levelly.

Rand opened his mouth, then closed it again. Bloody *ji'e'toh.* No use mentioning he was the *Car'a'carn*, of course. Aviendha looked faintly surprised that he had even protested; apparently to her it was a foregone conclusion. He shifted his shoulders uneasily, though not because of Aviendha. That unclean feel was still there, and stronger. Maybe Lews Therin had come back. Silently Rand called to him, but there was still no answer.

A tap on the door barely preceded Mistress Harfor, who made her usual deep curtsy. The First Maid showed no sign of the early hour, of course; whatever the time of day, Reene Harfor always looked as if she had just gotten dressed. "There have been arrivals in the city, my Lord Dragon, which Lord Bashere thought you should be told of as soon as possible. Lady Aemlyn and Lord Culhan entered yesterday at noon, and are staying with Lord Pelivar. Lady Arathelle came an hour later, with a large retinue. Lord Barel and Lord Macharan, Lady Sergase and Lady Negara entered separately in the night, with only a few retainers each. None has presented their respects at the Palace." She delivered the last in the same even tone, with no hint of her own opinion.

"That is good news," he told her, and it was, whether they had left respects or not. Aemlyn and her husband Culhan were nearly as powerful as Pelivar, Arathelle more powerful than any except Dyelin and Luan. The others were of minor Houses, and only Barel among them High Seat of his House, but the nobles who had opposed "Gaebril" were beginning to gather. At least, it was good news provided he found Elayne before they decided to try taking Caemlyn away from him.

Mistress Harfor eyed him a moment, then extended a blue-sealed letter. "This was delivered late last evening, my Lord Dragon. By a stableboy. A dirty stableboy. The Sea Folk Wave-mistress was not well pleased that you were gone when she appeared for her audience." This time her disapproval was clear in her voice, though not whether it was for the Wavemistress or Rand missing the audience or the means of the letter's delivery.

He sighed; he had forgotten all about the Sea Folk here in Caemlyn. That reminded him of the letter he had been given in Cairhien, and he dug it out. Both green wax and blue bore the same impression, though he could not make out what it was supposed to be. Two things like flattened bowls with a thick ornate line running from one through the other. Each was addressed to "The Coramoor," whoever or whatever that was. Himself, he supposed. Maybe that was what the Sea Folk called the Dragon Reborn. He broke the blue seal first. There was no salutation, and it was certainly unlike anything else Rand had ever seen addressed to the Dragon Reborn.

The Light willing, you will perhaps return to Caemlyn eventually. As I have traveled far to see you, perhaps I will find time for it when you do.

Zaida din Parede Blackwing
of Clan Catelar, Wavemistress

It seemed Mistress Harfor was right; the Wavemistress was not best pleased. The green seal hid little better.

If it pleases the Light, I will receive you on the deck of White Spray at your earliest convenience.

Harine din Togara Two Winds
of Clan Shodein, Wavemistress

"Are they bad news?" Aviendha asked.

"I don't know." Frowning at the letters, he was barely aware of Mistress Harfor admitting a woman in the red-and-white and exchanging quiet words with her. Neither of these Sea Folk women sounded like anybody he wanted to spend an hour with. He had read every translation of the Prophecies of the Dragon he could find, and though the clearest was often murky, he remembered nothing that indicated the Atha'an Miere. Perhaps, on their ships at sea and their distant islands, they would be one people untouched by him or Tarmon Gai'don. He owed this Zaida an apology, but maybe he could fob her off with Bashere; Bashere certainly had enough titles to flatter anybody's vanity. "I don't think so."

The servant sank to her knees before him, white head bowed low and hands raised high to proffer yet another letter, this one on thick parchment. The posture itself made him blink; even in Tear he had never seen a servant cringe so, much less in Andor. Mistress Harfor was frowning and shaking her head. The kneeling woman spoke, still with her face down. "This has come for my Lord Dragon."

"Sulin?" he gasped. "What are you doing? What are you doing in that . . . *dress*?"

Sulin turned her face up; she looked perfectly horrible, a wolf trying very hard to pretend she was a doe. "It is what women wear who serve and obey as commanded for coins." She waggled the letter in her still upraised hands. "I was commanded to say that this has just come for my Lord Dragon, by a . . . a horseman who left as soon as it was handed over." The First Maid clicked her tongue irritably.

"I want a straight answer," he said, snatching the sealed parchment. She bounded to her feet as soon as it left her hands. "Come back here, Sulin. Sulin, I want an answer!" But she ran as fleetly as she ever had in *cadin'sor*, straight to the doors and out.

For some reason Mistress Harfor glared at Nandera. "I told you this would not work. And I told you both that as long as she wears the Palace livery, I expect her to do the Palace proud whether she's Aiel or the Queen of Saldaea." Curtsying, she gave Rand a hasty "My Lord Dragon" and stalked out talking to herself about crazy Aiel.

He was ready to agree. He looked from Nandera to Aviendha to Jalani. None of them appeared in the least surprised. Not one looked as if she had seen a thing out of the ordinary. "Will you tell me what under the Light is going on? That was Sulin!"

"First," Nandera said, "Sulin and I went to the kitchens. She thought scrubbing pots and the like would be suitable. But a fellow there said he had all the scullions he needed; he seemed to think Sulin would always be fighting the others. He was not very tall," she marked just under Rand's chin, "but just as wide, and I think he would have offered to dance the spears with us if we had not gone away. Then we went to the woman Reene Harfor, since she seems to be roofmistress here." A slight grimace passed over her face; a woman should be roofmistress or not—Aiel thinking held no place for a First Maid. "She did not understand, but at last she agreed. I almost thought Sulin would change her mind when she realized Reene Harfor meant her to put on a dress, but of course she did not. Sulin has more courage than I. I would rather be made *gai'shain* by a new *Seia Doon*."

"I," Jalani said stoutly, "would rather be beaten by the first-brother of my worst enemy in front of my mother every day for a year."

Nandera's eyes tightened in disapproval and her fingers twitched, but instead of handtalk she said deliberately, "You boast like a Shaido, girl." Had Jalani been older, the three calculated insults might have caused trouble, but instead she squeezed her eyes shut to hide the sight of those who had heard her shamed.

Rand scrubbed fingers through his hair. "Reene didn't understand? I don't understand, Nandera. Why is she doing this? Has she given up the spear? If she's married an Andorman"—stranger things had happened around him—"I'll give her enough gold to buy a farm or whatever they want. She doesn't have to become a servant." Jalani's eyes shot open, and the three women were looking at him as if *he* was the one mad.

"Sulin is meeting her *toh*, Rand al'Thor," Aviendha said firmly; she stood very straight and met his gaze directly, a good imitation of Amys. Only there was less imitation in it every day and more her. "It does not concern you."

Jalani nodded a very definite agreement. Nandera only stood there, idly examining a spearpoint.

"Sulin concerns me," he told them. "If something happened to her—" Suddenly he remembered the exchange he had overheard before going to Shadar Logoth. Nandera had accused Sulin of speaking to *gai'shain* as *Far Dareis Mai*, and Sulin admitted it and said they would deal with it later. He had not seen Sulin since returning from Shadar Logoth, but he had assumed she was angry with him and simply letting others do the work of guarding him. He should have known better. Being around any Aiel for long would teach you some of *ji'e'toh*, and Maidens were touchier than anyone, except maybe Stone Dogs and Black Eyes. Then there was Aviendha and her attempts to turn him into an Aiel.

This situation was simple, or as simple as anything ever was in *ji'e'toh*. If he had not been so caught up in himself, he would have realized from the first. You could remind even a roofmistress who she was every day she wore *gai'shain* white—it was deeply shaming, but permitted, even encouraged sometimes—yet for the members of nine of the thirteen societies, that reminder was a deep dishonor except under a handful of circumstances he could not recall. *Far Dareis Mai* was most definitely one of the nine. It was one of the few ways to incur *toh* toward a *gai'shain*, but that was considered the hardest obligation of all to meet. Seemingly Sulin had chosen to meet it by accepting a greater shame, in Aiel eyes, than she had given. It was her *toh*, so her choice how to meet it, her choice how long she continued to do what she despised. Who knew the worth of her honor or the depth of her obligation better than she herself? Still, she had only done what she did in the first place because he had not allowed her enough time. "It is my fault," he said.

That was the wrong thing to say. Jalani gave him a startled stare. Aviendha flushed with embarrassment; she continually drove home that there were no excuses under *ji'e'toh*. If saving your child brought an obligation to a blood enemy, you paid the price without quibble.

The look Nandera shot at Aviendha could charitably be called disparaging. "If you stopped daydreaming about his eyebrows, you would teach him better."

Aviendha's face went dark with indignation, but Nandera flashed handtalk at Jalani, which made Jalani throw back her head and laugh, and made the crimson in Aviendha's cheeks brighten and return to pure embarrassment. Rand half-expected to hear an offer to dance spears. Well, not that exactly; Aviendha had taught him that neither Wise Ones nor their apprentices did that sort of thing. But it would not surprise him if she boxed Nandera's ears.

He spoke quickly to forestall any such thing. "Since I caused Sulin to do what she did, don't I have *toh* toward her?"

Apparently it was possible to make a bigger fool of himself than he already had. Somehow Aviendha's face grew redder still, and Jalani took a sudden interest in the carpet under her feet. Even Nandera looked a little chagrined at his ignorance. You could be told that you had *toh*, though that was insulting, or you could be reminded of it, but asking meant that you did not know. Well, he knew that he did. He could begin by ordering Sulin out of that ridiculous job as a servant, letting her put on *cadin'sor* again, and. . . . And stop her from meeting her *toh*. Anything he did to lighten her burden would interfere with her honor. Her *toh*, her choice. There was something in that, but he could not see what. Maybe he could ask Aviendha. Later, when she would not die from mortification. All three women's faces made it clear he had embarrassed her more than enough for the time being. Light, what a mess.

Wondering how he could find a way out, he realized he still held the letter Sulin had brought. He thrust it into a pocket and unbuckled his sword belt to lay it atop the Dragon Scepter, then retrieved the parchment. Who would send him a message by a rider who did not even stop for breakfast? There was nothing on the outside, no name; only the now vanished courier could have said who it was directed to. Once more the seal was nothing he recognized, some sort of flower impressed in purple wax, but the parchment itself was heavy, of the most expensive sort. The contents, in a fine lacy hand, brought a thoughtful smile.

Cousin,

The times are delicate, but I felt I must write to assure you of my goodwill, and to express my hopes of yours in return. Never fear; I know you and acknowledge you, but there are those who would not smile on anyone who approached you save through them. I ask nothing save that you hold my confidences in the fires of your heart.

Alliandre Maritha

"What are you grinning at?" Aviendha asked, peering at the letter curiously. There was still a touch of anger around her mouth for what he had put her through.

"It's just pleasant to hear from somebody simple in her ways," he told her. The Game of Houses was simple compared with *ji'e'toh*. There was enough of the name to let him know who sent it, but if the parchment fell into the wrong hands, it would seem a note to a friend, or maybe a warm reply to a petitioner. Alliandre Maritha Kigarin, Blessed of the Light, Queen of Ghealdan, would certainly never sign a letter so intimately to someone she had never met, above all not to the Dragon Reborn. Plainly she was worried about the Whitecloaks in Amadicia, and about the Prophet, Masema. He was going to have to do something about Masema. Alliandre was being cautious, not risking any more on paper than she had to. And she reminded him to burn this. The fires of his heart. Still, it was the first time any ruler had approached him without his sword at that nation's throat. Now if he could just find Elayne and give her Andor before he had another battle here.

The door opened gently and he looked up, but saw nothing and returned to the letter, wondering whether he had dug out everything that was in it. Reading, he rubbed his nose. Lews Therin and his talk of death. Rand could not rid himself of that feel of filth.

"Jalani and I will take our places outside," Nandera said.

He nodded absently over the letter. Thom would probably find six things in the first glance that he had missed.

Aviendha put a hand on his arm, then snatched it away. "Rand al'Thor, I must talk with you seriously."

Suddenly everything came together in his head. The door had opened. He was smelling filth, not just feeling it, but it was not really a smell. Dropping the letter, he pushed Aviendha away from him hard enough that she toppled with a startled yell—clear of him, though; clear of danger; everything seemed to have slowed down—and seized *saidin* as he spun.

Nandera and Jalani were just turning back to see what had made Aviendha shout. Rand had to look carefully to see the tall man in a gray coat that neither Maiden saw at all as he glided right by them, dark lifeless eyes fixed on Rand. Even concentrating, Rand found his own gaze wanting to slide past the Gray Man. That was what he was; one of the Shadow's assassins. As the letter was settling to the floor, the Gray Man realized Rand had seen him. Aviendha's shout still hung in the air and she was in mid-bounce from sitting down hard; a knife appeared in the Gray Man's hand, held low, and he darted forward. Rand wrapped him in coils of Air almost contemptuously. And a wrist-thick bar of fire flashed past his shoulder, burned a hole through the Gray Man's chest large enough for a fist. The assassin died before he could twitch; his head fell over, and those eyes, no more dead than they had been, stared at Rand.

Dead, whatever had been done to the Gray Man to make him hard to see no longer held. Dead, he suddenly was as visible as anyone else. Aviendha, just starting to gather herself on the floor, gave a startled yelp, and Rand felt the goose bumps that told him she had embraced *saidar*. Nandera's hand jerked toward her veil with a bit-off exclamation, and Jalani half-raised hers.

Rand let the corpse fall, but he held on to *saidin* as he turned to confront Taim, standing in the doorway of his bedchamber. "Why did you kill him?" Only part of the cold hardness in his voice came from the Void. "I had him captured; he might have told me something, maybe even who sent him. What are you doing here anyway, sneaking in through my bedroom?"

Taim strolled in completely at ease, wearing a black coat with dragons entwined around the sleeves in blue and gold. Aviendha scrambled to her feet, and despite *saidar*, her eyes said she was as ready to use her drawn belt knife on Taim as she was to sheathe it. Nandera and Jalani had veiled, and stood poised on their toes, spears ready. Taim ignored them; Rand felt the Power leave the man. Taim did not even seem concerned that *saidin* still filled Rand. That peculiar almost-smile quirked his lips as he glanced at the dead Gray Man.

"Nasty things, the Soulless." Anybody else would have shivered; not Taim. "I came to your balcony by gateway because I thought you would want to hear the news right away."

"Somebody who learns too fast?" Rand broke in, and Taim flashed that half-smile again.

"No, not one of the Forsaken in disguise, not unless he's managed to disguise himself as a boy not much past twenty. His name is Jahar Narishma, and he has the spark, though it has not come out yet. Men usually show later than women. You should return to the school; you would be surprised by the changes."

Rand did not doubt it. Jahar Narishma was never an Andoran name; Traveling had no limits that he knew, but it seemed Taim's recruiting had ventured far afield. He said nothing, only glanced at the corpse on the carpet.

Taim grimaced, but he was not out of countenance, only irritated. "Believe me, I wish he was still alive as much as you do. I saw him and acted without thinking; the last thing I want is to see you dead. You seized him the moment I channeled, but it was too late to stop."

I must kill him, Lews Therin muttered, and the Power surged in Rand. Frozen, he struggled to push *saidin* away, and it was a struggle. Lews Therin was trying to hang on, trying to channel. Finally, slowly, the One Power faded like water draining from a hole in a bucket.

Why? he demanded. *Why do you want to kill him?* There was no answer, only mad laughter and weeping in the distance.

Aviendha was looking at him with a face full of concern. She had put up her knife, but the tingle along his skin said she retained *saidar*. The two Maidens had unveiled, now that it seemed clear Taim's appearance was no attack; they managed to keep one eye on Taim, one on the rest of the room, and still give each other abashed glances for some reason.

Rand took a chair beside the table where his sword lay atop the Dragon Scepter. The struggle had lasted only moments, but his knees felt weak. Lews Therin had almost taken over, almost taken over *saidin* at least. Before, at the school, he had been able to fool himself, but not this time.

If Taim noticed anything, he showed no sign of it. Bending to pick up the letter, he glanced at it before handing it to Rand with a minimal bow.

Rand stuffed the parchment into his pocket. Nothing shook Taim; nothing disturbed his balance. Why did Lews Therin want to kill him? "The way you were all for going after the Aes Sedai, I'm surprised you don't suggest striking at Sammael. You and me together, maybe a few of the stronger students, dropping right on top of him in Illian through a gateway. That man had to come from Sammael."

"Perhaps," Taim said shortly, glancing at the Gray Man. "I would give a great deal to be sure." That had the ring of simple truth. "As for Illian, I doubt it would be as simple as disposing of a pair of Aes Sedai. I keep thinking what I would do in Sammael's place. I would have Illian warded in boxes, so if a man even thought of channeling, I'd know right where he was, and I would burn even the ground to ash before he had time to take a breath."

That was how Rand saw it, too; no one knew better than Sammael how to defend a place. Maybe it was just that Lews Therin was insane. Maybe jealous, too. Rand tried to tell himself he had not been avoiding the school because *he* was jealous, but he always felt a prickle of something around Taim. "You've delivered your news. I suggest you go see to training this Jahar Narishma. Train him well. He may have to use his ability soon enough."

For a moment Taim's dark eyes glittered, then he bowed his head slightly. Without a word he seized *saidin* and opened a gateway right there. Rand made himself sit, empty, until the man was gone, the gateway thinning in a blazing line of light; he could not risk another struggle with Lews Therin, not when he might lose and find himself fighting Taim. Why *did* Lews Therin want the man dead? Light, Lews Therin seemed to want everybody dead, himself included.

It had been a most eventful morning, especially considering that the sky was still gray. Good news outweighed bad. He eyed the Gray Man sprawled on the carpet; that wound had probably been cauterized as soon as made, but Mistress Harfor would be sure to let him know, without saying a word, if there was even one bloodstain. As for this Sea Folk Wavemistress, she could stew in her own petulance for all of him; he had enough to handle without adding *another* touchy woman.

Nandera and Jalani were still shifting from foot to foot near the door. They should have gone to their places outside as soon as Taim left.

"If you two are upset over the Gray Man," he said, "forget it now. Only a fool expects to notice one of the Soulless except by chance, and neither one of you is a fool."

"It is not that," Nandera said stiffly. Jalani's jaw was so tight she was plainly fighting to hold her tongue.

Just that quickly, he understood. They did not believe they should have spotted the Gray Man, but they were still ashamed they had not. Ashamed of that, and fearful of the shame of having word of their "failure" spread. "I don't want anyone to know Taim was here, or what he said. People are anxious enough knowing the school is somewhere near the city without being afraid Taim or one of the students will just appear. I think the best way is just to keep quiet about everything that happened this morning. We can't keep a corpse secret, but I want you to promise you'll say nothing except that a man tried to kill me and died for it. That's all I intend to tell anybody, and I'd hate for you to make me out a liar."

The gratitude on their faces was remarkable. "I have *toh*," they murmured almost together.

Rand cleared his throat roughly; that was not what he had been after, but at least he had eased their minds. Suddenly a way to deal with Sulin popped into his head. She would not like it, but it would still be meeting her *toh*, maybe the more so because she would not like it, and it would relieve his conscience somewhat and at least meet some of his *toh* to her.

"Get on to your guarding now, or I'll start thinking *you* want to stare at my eyebrows." That *was* what Nandera had said. Aviendha was fascinated by his *eyebrows?* "Go on. And find somebody to haul this fellow away." They left, all smiles and flickering handtalk, and he stood, taking Aviendha by the arm. "You said we had to talk. Come into the bedroom until this room is cleaned up." If there was a stain, maybe he could channel it out.

Aviendha jerked free. "No! Not there!" Drawing a deep breath, she moderated her tone, but she still looked suspicious, and more than a little angry. "Why can we not talk here?" No reason except a dead man on the floor, but that did not count with her. She pushed him back into his chair almost violently, then studied him and took another breath before speaking.

"*Ji'e'toh* is the core of the Aiel. We *are ji'e'toh*. This morning you shamed me to the bone." Folding her arms beneath her breasts and fixing him eye to eye, she lectured him on his ignorance and the importance of hiding it until she could rectify the matter, then went on to the fact that *toh* had to be met at all costs. She spent some time on that.

He was sure this was not what she had meant when she said she had to talk with him, but he was enjoying looking into her eyes too much to wonder. Enjoying it. Bit by bit he chased down the pleasure her eyes gave him and crushed it until only a dull ache remained.

He thought he had hidden it, but his face must have changed. Aviendha slowly trailed off and stood there staring at him, breathing hard. With a visible effort she pulled her eyes away. "At least you understand now," she muttered. "I must. . . . I need to. . . . So long as you understand."

Gathering her skirts, she swept across the room—the corpse might as well have been a bush she had to step around—and out.

Leaving him in a room dimmer for some reason, alone with a dead man. That fit all too well. When *gai'shain* came to bear away the Gray Man, they found Rand laughing softly.

Padan Fain sat with his feet up on a hassock, studying the beauty of new-breaking sunlight glittering on the curved blade of the dagger that he turned over and over in his hands. Carrying it at his belt was not enough; from time to time he simply had to handle it. The large ruby set in the pommel shone with a deep malevolence. The dagger was part of him, or he of it. The dagger was part of Aridhol, what men called Shadar Logoth, but then, he was part of Aridhol too. Or it was part of him. He was quite mad and knew it very well, but being mad, he did not care. Sunlight gleamed on steel, steel more deadly now than any made at Thakan'dar.

A rustling caught his ear, and he glanced toward where the Myrddraal sat waiting his pleasure on the far side of the room. It did not try to meet his gaze; he had broken it of that long since.

He tried to return to his contemplation of the blade, to the perfect beauty of perfect death, the beauty of what Aridhol had been and would be again, but the Myrddraal had broken his concentration. Spoiled it. He very nearly went over and killed the thing. Halfmen took a long time to die; how long if he used the dagger? As if sensing his thoughts, it stirred again. No, it could be useful still.

It was hard for him to concentrate on one thing for long anyway. Except Rand al'Thor, of course. He could feel al'Thor, could point to him, this close. Al'Thor pulled at him, pulled till it hurt. There was a difference lately, a difference that had come suddenly, almost as if someone else had suddenly taken a partial possession of al'Thor, and in doing so pushed away a part of Fain's own possession. No matter. Al'Thor belonged to him.

He wished he could feel al'Thor's pain; surely he had caused him pain at least. Pinpricks only so far, but enough pinpricks would drain him dry. The Whitecloaks were set hard against the *Dragon Reborn*. Fain's lips peeled back in a sneer. Unlikely Niall would have ever supported al'Thor any more than Elaida would have, but it was best not to take too much for granted with Rand bloody al'Thor. Well, he had brushed them both with what he carried from Aridhol; they might possibly trust their own mothers, but never al'Thor now.

The door burst open, and young Perwyn Belman burst into the room pursued by his mother. Nan Belman was a handsome woman, though Fain seldom noticed whether a woman was or not now, a Darkfriend who had thought her oaths were just dabbling in wickedness until Padan Fain appeared on her doorstep. She believed him a Darkfriend too, one high in the councils. Fain had gone far beyond that, of course; he would be dead the moment one of the Chosen laid hands on him. The thought made him giggle.

Perwyn and his mother both shied at the sight of the Myrddraal, of course, but the boy recovered first and reached Fain while the woman was still trying to find her breath.

"Master Mordeth, Master Mordeth," the boy piped, dancing from foot to foot in his red-and-white coat, "I have news you wanted."

Mordeth. Had he used that name? Sometimes he could not recall what name he had used, what name was his. Sheathing the dagger beneath his coat, he put on a warm smile. "And what news would that be now, lad?"

"Someone tried to kill the Dragon Reborn this morning. A man. He's dead now. He got right past all the Aiel and everything, right into the Lord Dragon's rooms."

Fain felt his smile become a snarl. Trying to kill al'Thor? Al'Thor was his! Al'Thor would die by his hand, no other! Wait. The assassin had gotten past the Aiel, into al'Thor's rooms? "A Gray Man!" He did not recognize that grating sound as his own voice. Gray Men meant the Chosen. Would he never be free of their interference?

All that rage had to go somewhere before he burst. Almost casually he brushed his hand across the boy's face. The boy's eyes bulged; he began trembling so hard his teeth rattled.

Fain did not really understand the tricks he could work. A bit of something from the Dark One, perhaps, a bit from Aridhol. It had been after there, after he stopped being just Padan Fain, that the ability began to manifest, slowly. All he knew was that he could do certain things now, as long as he could touch what he worked with.

Nan flung herself to her knees beside his chair, clutching at his coat. "Mercy, Master Mordeth," she panted. "Please, have mercy. He's only a child. Only a child!"

For a moment he studied her curiously, head tilted. She was quite a pretty woman, really. Planting a foot against her chest, he shoved her aside so he could stand. The Myrddraal, peeking furtively, jerked its eyeless face away when it saw him watching. It remembered his . . . tricks very well.

Fain paced; he had to move. Al'Thor's downfall had to be his doing—his!—not the Chosen's. How could he hurt the man again, hurt to the heart? There were those nattering girls at Culain's Hound, but if al'Thor did not come when the Two Rivers was harrowed, what would he care even if Fain burned the inn down and the chits with it? What did he have to work with? Only a few remained of his onetime Children of the Light. That had only been a test really—he would have made the man who actually managed to kill al'Thor beg to be skinned alive!—yet it had cost him numbers. He had the Myrddraal, a handful of Trollocs hidden outside the city, a few Darkfriends gathered in Caemlyn and on the way from Tar Valon. The pull of al'Thor dragged him on. It was the most remarkable thing about Darkfriends. There should be nothing to single out a Darkfriend from anyone else, but of late he found he could tell one at a glance, even someone who had only thought of swearing to the Shadow, as if they had a sooty mark on their foreheads.

No! He had to concentrate. Concentrate! Clear his mind. His eye fell on the woman, moaning and stroking her gibbering son, talking to him softly as if that would help. Fain had no notion how to stop one of his tricks once it began; the boy should survive, if a trifle the worse for wear, once the thing ground to a conclusion. Fain had not put his whole heart into making it. Clear his mind. Think of something else. A pretty woman. How long since he had had a woman?

Smiling, he took her arm. He had to pull her away from the fool boy. "Come with me." His voice was different, grander, the Lugard accent gone, but he did not notice; he never did. "I am sure you, at least, know how to show true respect. If you please me, no harm will come to you." Why was she struggling? He knew he was being charming. He was going to have to hurt her. It was all al'Thor's fault.

CHAPTER
29

Fire and Spirit

Pausing in the shade in front of the Little Tower, Nynaeve carefully
dabbed at her face, then tucked the handkerchief back up her sleeve.
Not that it did much good—sweat popped out again right away—
but she wanted to look her best inside. She wanted to look cool, serene, dignified. Small chance of that. Her temples were throbbing, and her stomach
felt . . . fragile; she had not been able to look at breakfast this morning.
Just the heat, of course, but she wanted to go back to her bed, curl up and
die. To top it off, her weather sense was nagging at her; the molten sun
should have been hidden by roiling black clouds and threatening bolts of
lightning.

The Warders lounging out front did not look like guards at first
glance, but they were. They reminded her of the Aiel she had seen in the
Stone of Tear; they probably looked like wolves even when asleep. A bald,
square-faced man, no taller than she but nearly as wide as he was tall, trotted out of the Little Tower and down the street, the hilt of the sword on his
back thrusting up over his shoulder. Even he—Jori, bonded to Morvrin—
managed it.

Top-knotted Uno passed, threading his horse through the crowd and
hardly seeming to acknowledge the heat despite the steel plates and mail
that covered him from the shoulders down. He twisted in his saddle to
watch her with his good eye, and her face darkened. Birgitte *had* talked.

Every time the man saw her he was obviously waiting for her to ask him for horses. She was almost ready to. Even Elayne could not say they were doing any good. Well, she could, and did, but she should not.

Uno rode out of sight around a corner, and Nynaeve sighed. She was just trying to put off going inside. Myrelle might be there. Blotting her face again, she frowned at her wrinkled hand—today would be the eleventh scrubbing pots, with twenty-nine more to go; twenty-nine!—and went in.

It was slightly cooler in what had been the common room when the Little Tower was an inn, offering a little relief to her aching head. Everyone called it "the waiting room" now. No time had been wasted for repairs here. The fireplaces had stones missing, and lathing showed through holes in the plaster. Areina and Nicola were working brooms with another novice, but making little impression on the age-roughened floor; Areina wore a scowl, but, then, she was never pleased at having to do chores with the novices. No one went choreless in Salidar. At the far end of the room Romanda was speaking with two slender, aged Aes Sedai—their faces might be ageless, but their hair was white—plainly new arrivals by the thin dustcloaks still hanging down their backs. No sign of Myrelle, which brought a sigh of relief; the woman raked Nynaeve over the coals at every opportunity, then raked her the other way! Aes Sedai sat at tables, mismatched but carefully arranged in rows, working over parchments or issuing orders to Warders and servants, but fewer than the first time she had seen the room. Only the Sitters and their servants lived on the floors above now; everyone else had been removed to make space for Aes Sedai to work in. The Little Tower had taken on attributes of the White Tower, the precise formality above all. When Nynaeve first saw this room it had had a bustle about it, an air of something being done. A false air, then. Now it seemed almost slow, but it was the feel of the White Tower.

Approaching one of the tables, not the nearest, she curtsied carefully. "Pardon, Aes Sedai, but I was told Siuan and Leane are here. Could you tell me where to find them?"

Brendas' pen stopped moving and she looked up with cool dark eyes. Nynaeve had chosen her instead of someone nearer the door because Brendas was one of the few Aes Sedai who had never grilled her about Rand. Besides, once, when Siuan was Amyrlin, Siuan had chosen Brendas as one who could be trusted. That had nothing to do with this, but Nynaeve found small comforts where she could.

"They are with some of the Sitters, child." Brendas' voice was chimes, as emotionless as her pale face. Whites seldom showed emotion, but Brendas never showed any.

Nynaeve stifled an irritated sigh. If Sitters had them reporting on their eyes-and-ears, they might not be free for hours yet. Maybe not for the rest of the day. By then she would be head-down among the pots. "Thank you, Aes Sedai."

Brendas stopped her curtsy with a gesture. "Did Theodrin make any progress with you yesterday?"

"No, Aes Sedai." If her voice was bit tight, a touch curt, she had reason. Theodrin had said she meant to try everything, and apparently she really did mean everything. Yesterday's effort had involved sipping wine to relax her, only somehow Nynaeve had ended up taking more than just a few sips. She did not think she would ever forget being carried back to her room singing—singing!—or remember without going red in the face. Brendas had to know. Everyone had to know. Nynaeve wanted to writhe.

"I only ask because your studies seem to be suffering. I've heard several sisters remark that you appear to have reached the end of your remarkable discoveries. Your extra chores might be the problem—but Elayne reveals something new every day, even with teaching her classes and working at the pots. A number of sisters are wondering whether they might not be able to help you more than Theodrin can. If we took it in turns, working you all day every day might prove more fruitful than these informal sessions with someone who is, after all, little more than Accepted herself." It was all delivered in a level tone without the slightest accusation, yet Nynaeve's face heated as if she had been shouted at.

"I'm sure Theodrin will find the key any day, Aes Sedai," she almost whispered. "I will try harder, Aes Sedai." Bobbing a hurried curtsy, she whirled around before Brendas could stop her again. With the result that she bumped into one of the two white-haired newcomers. They looked enough alike to be sisters in truth, almost mirror images of one another, with fine bones and long patrician faces.

The bump was more of a brush, really, and she did try to apologize, but the Aes Sedai fixed her with a stare to do a hawk proud. "Watch where you are going, Accepted. In my day, an Accepted who tried to trample Aes Sedai would have had hair whiter than mine by the time she finished scrubbing floors."

The other touched her arm. "Oh, do let the child go, Vandene. We have work to do."

Vandene directed a sharp sniff at Nynaeve, but allowed herself to be led outside.

Waiting a moment to let them leave, Nynaeve saw Sheriam come out of one of the meeting rooms with Myrelle, Morvrin and Beonin. Myrelle saw her, too, and started in her direction, but only a step before Sheriam and Morvrin each put a hand on the Green sister's arms and spoke quickly and softly, with many a glance at Nynaeve. Still talking, the four crossed the room and disappeared through another door.

Nynaeve waited until she was back in front of the Little Tower before giving her braid a firm, deliberate tug. They had met the Wise Ones last night. Guessing why the others had stopped Myrelle from speaking was easy enough. If Egwene had finally been there in the Heart of the Stone, she was not to be told. Nynaeve al'Meara was in disgrace. Nynaeve al'Meara was scrubbing pots like a novice when she might have been at least a step higher than Accepted. Nynaeve al'Meara was getting nowhere with Theodrin, and all her marvelous discoveries had dried up. Nynaeve al'Meara would never be Aes Sedai. She had known it was a mistake to start funneling everything from Moghedien through Elayne. She had known it!

Her tongue tried to curl up at the memory of a vile taste. Boiled cat-fern and powdered mavinsleaf. An antidote she had used on many a child who would not stop lying. All right; she *had* been the one to suggest it herself, but it was still a mistake. Aes Sedai were no longer talking about her innovations; they talked about the lack of them. Aes Sedai who had never taken more than a passing interest in her block were now caught up in how to break it down. She could not win. One way or another she was going to end up with Aes Sedai examining her from hair to toenails, sunup to sundown.

She yanked harder on her braid, hard enough to hurt her scalp, and the way her head felt, that did nothing for her temper. A soldier in an archer's flat helmet and padded jerkin slowed to look at her curiously, but she gave him such a stare of refined malevolence that he stumbled over his own feet and quickly lost himself in the throng. *Why* did Elayne have to be so stubborn?

A man's hands closed on her shoulders, and she whirled about with words that would rip his head from his neck. They died on her tongue.

Thom Merrilin grinned down at her through his long white mustaches, sharp blue eyes twinkling in his gnarled face. "By the look of you, Nynaeve, I could almost think you were angry, but I know you have such a sweet disposition people ask you to dabble your fingers in their tea."

Juilin Sandar was there beside him, the lean fellow looking carved from dark wood, leaning on his thumb-thick bamboo staff. Juilin was Tairen, not Taraboner, but he still wore that ridiculous flat-topped conical red cap, even more battered than she had last seen it. He snatched it off when she glanced at him. Both men were dusty and travel-worn, their faces gaunt, though neither had been particularly fleshy to begin with. They looked as if they had spent the weeks since leaving Salidar sleeping in their clothes when they were not in the saddle.

Before Nynaeve could open her mouth, they were hit by a human storm. Elayne flung herself at Thom so hard he staggered. He of course put his hands under her arms and hoisted her, whirling her around in a circle like a child despite his slight limp. He was laughing when he set her down again, and so was she. She reached up and tugged at one of his mustaches, and they fell to laughing even harder. He examined her hands, as wrinkled as Nynaeve's, asking what sort of trouble she had dived into without him to keep her on the straight and narrow, and she replied that she had no need of anyone to tell her what to do, only she spoiled it by blushing, and giggling, and biting her lip.

Nynaeve took a deep breath. Sometimes the pair of them took playing at father and daughter entirely too far. Sometimes Elayne seemed to think she was about ten, and so did Thom. "I thought you had a novice class this morning, Elayne."

The other woman glanced at her sideways, then gathered herself in an attempt at decorum that came too late, and set about straightening her banded dress. "I asked Calindin to take it," she said casually. "I thought I might keep you company. And I'm glad I did," she added with a grin for Thom. "Now we can hear everything you learned in Amadicia."

Nynaeve sniffed. Keep her company indeed. She did not remember everything about yesterday, but she remembered Elayne laughing while getting her undressed and putting her to bed with the sun not yet all the way down. And she was sure she remembered the woman asking whether she wanted a bucket of water to cool her head.

Thom noticed nothing; most men were blind, though he was sharp enough usually. "We will have to be quick," he said. "Now Sheriam's drained us dry, she means to have us report to some of the Sitters in person. Luckily, it boils down well enough. There aren't enough Whitecloaks along the Eldar to keep a mouse from crossing, if he had drums and trumpets to announce him a day ahead. Except for a strong force on the Tarabon border and the men he has trying to hold back the Prophet in the north,

Niall seems to be gathering every last Whitecloak around Amadicia, and Ailron is pulling in his soldiers, too. Talk of Salidar had started in the streets before we left, but if Niall has even thought about the place twice, I could find not a hint of it anywhere."

"Tarabon," Juilin muttered, studying his cap. "All ill country for anyone who doesn't know how to take care of herself, or so we heard."

Nynaeve was not sure which of the two was best at dissembling, but she was sure either could lie to your face to make a wool merchant blue with envy. And right then, she was sure they were hiding something.

Elayne saw more than that. Gripping Thom's lapel, she peered up at him. "You heard something about Mother," she said calmly, and it was not a question.

Thom knuckled his mustaches. "There are a hundred rumors on every street in Amadicia, child, each wilder than the last." His gnarled leathery face was pure innocence and openness, but the man had not been innocent the day he was born. "It's said the whole White Tower is here in Salidar, with ten thousand Warders ready to cross the Eldar. It's said Aes Sedai have captured Tanchico, and Rand has wings he uses to fly around in the night, and—"

"Thom?" Elayne said.

He snorted, glaring at Juilin and Nynaeve as though this were their fault. "Child, it's just a rumor, as crazed as any we heard. I could not confirm anything, and believe me, I tried. I meant not to mention it. It just stirs up your pain. Let it pass, child."

"Thom." Much firmer. Shifting his feet, Juilin looked as if he wished he were somewhere else. Thom just looked grim.

"Well, if you must hear it. Everybody in Amadicia seems to think your mother is in the Fortress of the Light, that she's going to lead an army of Whitecloaks back to Andor."

Elayne shook her head, laughing softly. "Oh, Thom, do you think I would worry over something like that? Mother would never go to the Whitecloaks. I could wish she had. I could wish she was alive to. Even though it violates everything she ever taught me—bringing foreign soldiers into Andor; and Whitecloaks!—I could wish it. But if wishes were wings . . ." Her smile was sad, but it was a muted sadness. "I have done my grieving, Thom. Mother is dead, and I must do my best to be worthy of her. She would never have gone running after ridiculous rumors, or wept over them either."

"Child," he said awkwardly.

Nynaeve wondered what if anything he himself felt about Morgase's death. Hard as it was to believe, he had been Morgase's lover once, when she was young and Elayne little more than a babe. Back then he must not have looked as though he had been left to dry in the sun too long. Nynaeve knew little more of how or why it ended than that he had slipped out of Caemlyn with an arrest warrant at his heels. Not the mark of a love to be told in the stories. At the moment he certainly appeared concerned only with whether Elayne was telling the truth or hiding her hurt, with patting her shoulder and stroking her hair. If Nynaeve had not wished they would just once snap at one another like normal people, she would have thought it a pretty picture.

A throat clearing broke up the vignette. "Master Merrilin?" Tabiya said, spreading her white dress in a quick curtsy. "Master Sandar? Sheriam Sedai says the Sitters are ready to receive you. She says you were not supposed to leave the Little Tower."

"The Little Tower, is it?" Thom said dryly, eyeing the former inn. "Elayne, they can't keep us forever. When we're done, you and I can discuss . . . whatever you wish." Motioning Tabiya to lead, he marched inside, his limp obvious, the way it was when he was tired. Juilin squared his shoulders and followed as though walking to a gallows; he was Tairen, after all.

Nynaeve and Elayne stood there, neither quite looking at the other.

Finally, Nynaeve said, "I was not—" at the same time that Elayne said, "I should not—" They cut off together, and moments passed in fidgeting with skirts and blotting faces.

"It is too hot to just stand here," Nynaeve said at last.

It was unlikely that the Sitters who were hearing Siuan and Leane's reports would stop to hear Thom and Juilin's. They split such things among them. That left Logain, much as she wished it did not. She would not learn anything. But it was better than twiddling her thumbs until a dozen Aes Sedai descended on her with an hourly schedule.

With a sigh she started down the street. Elayne came along as though she had been invited. That helped Nynaeve find the anger she was going to need. Abruptly she realized that Elayne's wrists were bare.

"Where is the bracelet?" she asked softly. No one in the street would understand if they heard, but caution once forgotten could be forgotten once too often. "Where is Marigan?"

"The bracelet is in my pouch, Nynaeve." Elayne stepped aside to let a high-wheeled cart pass, then joined Nynaeve again behind the cart.

"Marigan is doing our laundry, with about twenty other women around her. And groaning every time she moves. She said something she didn't think Birgitte would hear, and Birgitte. . . . I *had* to take the thing off, Nynaeve. Birgitte had the right, and it *hurt*. I told Marigan to say she fell down some stairs."

Nynaeve sniffed, but her heart was not in it. She had not been wearing the bracelet much of late. Not because she could not hand over anything she dug out as her own. She was still sure Moghedien knew *something* about Healing even if she did not realize it herself—nobody could be that blind—and there was the trick of detecting a man's channeling that Moghedien kept saying they almost had right. The truth of it was, she was afraid she might do far worse than Birgitte had if she had any more contact with the woman than was absolutely necessary. Maybe it was the way satisfaction seemed to underlie everything else even when Moghedien was groaning from the fed-back pain of Nynaeve trying to master that detection. Maybe it was remembering how afraid she had been, alone with the woman without the bracelet. Maybe growing disgust at keeping one of the Forsaken from judgment. Maybe some of all of it. What she did know was that she had to make herself put on the bracelet now, and that whenever she saw Moghedien's face, she wanted to pound it with her fists.

"I should not have laughed," Elayne said. "I am sorry I did."

Nynaeve stopped dead so suddenly that a horseman had to jerk his reins to keep from riding over her. He shouted something before the crowd carried him away, but shock muffled his words beyond hearing. Not shock at the apology. At what she had to say. The right thing to say. The truth.

Unable to look at Elayne, she started walking again. "You had every right to laugh. I. . . ." She swallowed hard. "I made a complete fool of myself." She had. A few sips, Theodrin said; a cup. And she emptied the pitcher. If you were going to fail, better to have some other reason than that you just could not do it. "You should have sent for that bucket and dunked my head until I could recite *The Great Hunt of the Horn* without a mistake." She risked a glance from the corner of her eye. Small spots of color rested in Elayne's cheeks. So there had been mention of a bucket.

"It could happen to anyone," the other woman said simply.

Nynaeve felt her own cheeks heating. When it had happened to Elayne, she had dunked the girl to wash away the wine. "You should have done whatever you needed to . . . to sober me."

It was quite the oddest argument Nynaeve could remember, with her insisting she had been a total fool and deserved whatever came of it, while Elayne made excuse after excuse for her. Nynaeve did not understand why it felt so refreshing, taking all the blame on herself that way. She could not recall ever doing that before, not without hedging as far as she was able. She very nearly got angry with Elayne for not agreeing that she had been a childish buffoon. It lasted until they reached the small thatched house on the edge of the village where Logain was kept.

"If you don't stop this," Elayne said finally, "I vow I'll send for a bucket of water right this instant."

Nynaeve opened her mouth, then closed it again. Even in this new-found euphoria of admitting she had been wrong, that was going too far. Feeling this good, she could not face Logain. Feeling this good, it would be useless anyway, without Moghedien and the bracelet she definitely felt too fine to put on. She glanced at the two Warders standing guard beside the stone-linteled door. They were not close enough to hear, but she still pitched her voice low. "Elayne, let's go. Tonight." With Thom and Juilin in Salidar, there was no need to ask Uno to find horses. "Not to Caemlyn, if you don't want. To Ebou Dar. Merilille will never find that bowl, and Sheriam will never let us go find it. What do you say? Tonight?"

"No, Nynaeve. What good can we do Rand if they take us for runaways? Which is what we'd be. You promised, Nynaeve. You promised, if we found something."

"I promised if we found something we could use. All we've found is this!" Nynaeve thrust her shriveled hands under the other woman's nose.

The firmness slid from Elayne's face, and her voice; she pursed her lips and studied the ground. "Nynaeve, you know I told Birgitte we were staying. Well, it seems she told Uno that under no circumstances was he to provide you with a horse unless she said so. She told him you were thinking of running away. I didn't find out until it was too late." Her head tossed irritably. "If this is what having a Warder is like, I don't know why anybody wants one."

Nynaeve thought her eyes might burst from indignation. So *that* was why he had been staring at her. Euphoria vanished in a heat of—well, partly anger, partly humiliation. The man *knew*; he thought she. . . . Wait. For a moment she frowned at Elayne, then decided not to voice the question that had come to mind. Was Nynaeve the only name Birgitte had mentioned to Uno, or was Elayne perhaps included? Elayne had found herself quite an adopted family. In Thom, an indulgent father who wanted to teach her everything he knew, and in Birgitte, an older sister who thought it was her job to keep the younger from breaking her neck riding horses she could not handle yet.

"In that case," she said flatly, "let's see what I can learn from Logain."

It was a small house, only two rooms, but thick stone walls made it relatively cool. Logain was in his shirtsleeves, smoking a pipe and reading by a window. The Aes Sedai were taking good care of him. The chairs and tables were as fine as anything in Salidar—nothing elaborate, but well made, though nothing matched anything else—and a scroll-woven red-and-gold carpet covered much of a floor that was swept so clean Nynaeve doubted he did the sweeping.

He set his book down when they entered, seemingly not at all put out by the lack of a knock. Rising leisurely, he tapped out his pipe, donned his coat and only then made a smooth leg. "It is good to see you again after so long. I thought you had forgotten me. Will you join me in some wine? The Aes Sedai keep me on short supply, but what they do let me have is not bad at all."

The offer of wine would have been enough—Nynaeve barely suppressed a wince—if she had needed more. Thinking of Uno, the fact that he was male was enough. No need to pull up any of her anger from the Little Tower. Thinking of it added its bit, though. The True Source was suddenly there, an unseen warmth just out of sight. She opened herself, and *saidar* flooded her; if what she had felt earlier was euphoria, this was beyond ec-stasy. She *was* surrendering to it, burn Theodrin!

"Sit down," she told him coldly. "I'll have no chatter out of you. An-swer when you're spoken to, and otherwise hold your tongue."

Logain only shrugged and complied, meek as a puppy. No, not meek; that smile was pure insolence. Part came from his feelings toward Aes Sedai, Nynaeve was certain, and part. . . . He watched Elayne take another chair, arranging her skirts with a studied care, and even if Nynaeve had not seen what he was looking at, she would have known it was a woman. There was no smirking about it, no leering, just. . . . Nynaeve did not know what, only that he directed the same at her, and she was suddenly very much aware that she was a woman and he a man. Maybe it was just that he was handsome and had broad shoulders, but she liked to think bet-ter of herself. Of course that was not it.

Clearing her throat, she wove filaments of *saidar* into him, Air and Water, Fire and Earth, Spirit. All the elements of Healing, but used now to probe. It would have helped to lay her hands on him, but she could not bring herself to do that. Bad enough to touch him with the Power. He was healthy as a bull and almost as strong, nothing wrong with him in the slightest—except for the hole.

It was not really a hole, more a feeling that what seemed continuous was not, that what seemed smooth and straight was really skirting around an absence. She knew that sensation well, from the early days, back when she thought she might really learn something. It still made her skin crawl.

He looked up at her intently. She did not remember moving closer. His face was fixed in a mask of brazen contempt; she might not be Aes Sedai, but she was the next thing to it.

"How can you do all of that at once?" Elayne asked. "I could not keep track of half of it."

"Hush," Nynaeve murmured. Hiding the effort required, she took Logain's head in her hands roughly. Yes. It was better with physical contact, the impressions sharper.

She directed the full flow of *saidar* into where the hole should have been—and was almost surprised to find an emptiness. Of course, she still did not expect to learn anything. Men were as different from women in the Power as they were in flesh, maybe more so. She might as well study a rock to find out about fish. It was hard to keep her thoughts on what she was doing, knowing she was only going through motions, killing time as it were.

What is Myrelle going to say? Would she keep back a message from Egwene? That emptiness, so small she could pass right over it, was vast once she slipped the flows inside, immense enough to swallow them all. *If only I could talk to Egwene. I'll wager once she knows the Tower is sending an embassy to Rand, and the Aes Sedai here are just sitting on their hands, she'll help me convince Elayne we've done all we can here.* Vast emptiness; nothingness. What about what she had found in Siuan and Leane, the feel of something cut? She was sure it was real, however faint. Men and women might be different, but maybe. . . . *All I need to do is talk to her somehow. She'll see that Rand would be better off with us there. Elayne will listen to her; Elayne thinks Egwene knows Rand better than anybody else.* There it was. Something cut. Just an impression, but the same as in Siuan and Leane. *So how do I find her? If only she'd pop into our dreams again. I'll bet I can talk her into joining us. The three of us would do much better with Rand. Together, we could tell him what we learn in* Tel'aran'rhiod, *keep him from making some wool-headed mistake with the Aes Sedai. She'll see that.* Something about that cut. . . . If it was bridged with Fire and Spirit, so. . . .

It was the slight widening of Logain's eyes that told her what she had done. Breath froze in her throat. She backed away from him so fast she stumbled over her skirt.

"Nynaeve," Elayne said, sitting up straight, "what is the mat—?"

A heartbeat, and Nynaeve had all of *saidar* she could hold redirected into a shield. "Go find Sheriam," she said hurriedly. "Nobody else but Sheriam. Tell her. . . ." She drew a deep breath that seemed like her first in hours; her heart was speeding to beat galloping horses. "Tell her I've Healed Logain."

CHAPTER

30

To Heal Again

Something pushed against the shield Nynaeve had fastened between Logain and the True Source, building until the shield began to bend and the weave trembled on the brink of ripping apart. She let *saidar* flow through her, sweetness reaching the very edge of pain, channeling every thread into Spirit, into the shield. "Go, Elayne!" She did not care one bit if it came out a squeal.

Elayne, the Light shine on her, wasted no time on questions. She bounded out of her chair and was gone at a dead run.

Logain had not moved a muscle. His eyes held Nynaeve's; they seemed to shine. Light, he was big. She fumbled for her belt knife, realized how ridiculous that was—he could probably take it away from her without sweating a drop more than he already was; his shoulders suddenly seemed as wide as she was tall—and diverted some of her weave to Air, to bonds that fastened him right where he sat, arm and leg. He was still big, yet suddenly he looked more normal, entirely manageable. Only then did it occur to her that she had lessened the strength of the shield. But she could not channel a hair more; already the . . . the pure joy of life that was *saidar* was so strong in her that she nearly wanted to weep. He smiled at her.

One of the Warders put his head in at the door, a dark-haired man with a bold nose and a deep, white scar running along his lean jaw. "Is anything amiss? The other Accepted, she went running like she had sat in the nettle patch."

"Everything is quite under control," she told him coolly. As coolly as she could manage. Nobody must know—nobody!—until she had a chance to speak with Sheriam, to get the woman on her side. "Elayne just remembered something she had forgotten." That sounded inane. "You may leave us. I am busy."

Tervail—that was his name; Tervail Dura, bonded to Beonin; and what under the Light did his name matter?—Tervail gave her a wry grin and a mocking bow before retreating. Warders seldom let Accepted get by with playing at Aes Sedai.

Not licking her lips took considerable effort. She studied Logain. He was outwardly calm, as if nothing had changed.

"There's no need for this, Nynaeve. Do you think I'll decide to attack a village with hundreds of Aes Sedai in it? They'd chop me to pieces before I took two steps."

"Be quiet," she said mechanically. Fumbling behind her, she found a chair and sat down, never taking her eyes off him. Light, what was keeping Sheriam? Sheriam had to understand it was an accident. She had to! Anger at herself was the only thing that kept her able to channel. How could she have been so careless, such a blind idiot?

"Don't be afraid," Logain said. "I won't turn against them now. They're succeeding in what I want, whether they know it or not. The Red Ajah is finished. In a year, there won't be an Aes Sedai will dare admit she's Red."

"I said be quiet!" she snapped. "Do you think I'll believe it's only Reds you hate?"

"You know, I saw a man once who will cause more trouble than I ever did. Maybe it was the Dragon Reborn; I don't know. It was when they took me through Caemlyn after I was captured. He was far away, but I saw a . . . a glow, and I knew he'd shake the world. Caged as I was, I couldn't help laughing."

Shifting a small portion of the Air holding him, she forced it between his jaws for a gag. His brows lowered in dark anger, gone in a flash, but she did not care. She had him secure now. At least. . . . He had not attempted to struggle at all, but that could be because he had known from the first that she would only snare him. It could. But how hard had he tried to break through her shield? That push, not exactly slow in building but certainly not fast. Almost like a man stretching muscles long unused, pushing at something not with the intent of moving it but just from the need to feel those muscles again. The thought turned her belly to ice.

Infuriatingly, Logain's eyes crinkled in amusement, almost as though he knew everything that had passed through her head. He sat there with his mouth gaping foolishly, bound and shielded, and he was the one at his ease. How *could* she have been such a fool? She was not fit to be Aes Sedai, not if her block crumbled this instant. She was not fit to be let out alone. They ought to tell Birgitte to make sure she did not fall on her face in the dust trying to cross the street.

It was not intentional, but berating herself kept her anger on a slow simmer until the door burst open. It was not Elayne.

Sheriam followed Romanda in, with Myrelle and Morvrin and Takima close behind, then Lelaine and Janya, Delana and Bharatine and Beonin, more, crowding in until they filled the room. Nynaeve could see others through the door that had no room to close. Those inside peered at her, and her weaving, so intently that she swallowed hard and all her fine anger collapsed. And of course, so did her shield and the bonds holding Logain.

Before Nynaeve could ask somebody to shield him again, Nisao planted herself in front of her. Short as Nisao was, she managed to loom. "Now what is all this nonsense about you Healing him?"

"Is that what she says she did?" Logain actually managed to sound surprised.

Varilin crowded in beside Nisao. The slender red-haired Gray loomed by virtue of being as tall as Logain. "I feared this as soon as everyone began petting her over her discoveries. Once they ran out, the petting stopped, and she was sure to make some wild claim to get it back."

"It was letting her moon over Siuan and Leane," Romanda said firmly. "And this fellow. She should have been told there are things that cannot be Healed, and there's an end to it!"

"But I did!" Nynaeve protested. "I did! Please shield him. Please, you must!" The Aes Sedai in front of her turned to look at Logain, opening just enough space for her to see him too. He met all the stares with a bland face. He even shrugged!

"I think the least we can do is shield him until we are absolutely certain," Sheriam suggested. Romanda nodded, and a shield sprang into being strong enough to hold a giant as the glow of *saidar* surrounded nearly every woman in the room. Romanda restored a little order by briskly naming six to maintain a lesser but adequate shield.

Myrelle's hand closed around Nynaeve's arm. "If you will forgive us, Romanda, we need to talk to Nynaeve alone."

Sheriam's hand closed on the other arm. "Best if we don't leave it too long."

Romanda nodded absently. She was frowning at Logain. Most of the Aes Sedai were; nobody was leaving.

Sheriam and Myrelle pulled Nynaeve to her feet and propelled her toward the door.

"What are you doing?" she demanded breathlessly. "Where are you taking me?" Outside they jostled through the throng of Aes Sedai, many of whom peered at her sharply, even accusingly. They pushed right by Elayne, who grimaced apologetically. Nynaeve looked over her shoulder as the two Aes Sedai hustled her along so quickly she kept stumbling. Not that she expected Elayne to help her, but it might be the last time she saw her. Beonin was saying something to Elayne, who darted away though the crowd. "What are you going to do to me?" Nynaeve moaned.

"We could keep you scrubbing pots for the rest of your natural life," Sheriam said conversationally.

Myrelle nodded. "You could work in the kitchens all day."

"We could have you switched every day instead."

"Peel your hide off in strips."

"Nail you into a barrel and feed you through the bunghole in the end."

"Only mush, though. Stale mush."

Nynaeve's knees sagged. "It was an accident! I swear! I didn't mean to!"

Sheriam gave her a hard shake without slowing a step. "Don't be a fool, child. You may just have done the impossible."

"You believe me? You believe me! Why didn't you say something when Nisao and Varilin and— Why didn't you say something?"

"I said 'may,' child." Sheriam's voice was depressingly neutral.

"Another possibility," Myrelle said, "is that your brain has swollen from strain." Her lidded eyes regarded Nynaeve. "You would be surprised at the number of Accepted, and even novices, who claim they've rediscovered some lost Talent, or found a new. When I was a novice, an Accepted named Echiko was so convinced she knew how to fly, she leaped from the top of the Tower."

Head spinning, Nynaeve looked from one woman to the other. Did they believe her or not? Did they really think her *mind* had bent? *What under the Light are they going to do to me?* She tried to find words to convince them—she was not lying, not crazy; she *had* Healed Logain—but her mouth was still working soundlessly when they hurried her into the Little Tower.

Not until they entered what had been a private dining room, a long chamber where now a narrow table stood with chairs behind it near one wall, did Nynaeve realize they had gained a train of followers. More than a dozen Aes Sedai entered on their heels, Nisao folding her arms tightly beneath her breasts, and Dagdara with her chin thrust forward as though meaning to walk through a wall, Shanelle and Therva and. . . . All Yellow Ajah, save Sheriam and Myrelle. That table suggested a magistrate's chamber; that line of grim faces spoke of a trial. Nynaeve swallowed hard.

Sheriam and Myrelle left her standing and walked over to the table to confer quietly, their backs to her. When they turned again, their faces were unreadable.

"You claim that you Healed Logain." There was a hint of contempt in Sheriam's voice. "You claim you Healed a gentled man."

"You must believe me," Nynaeve protested. "You said you did." She jumped as something unseen struck her hard across the hips.

"Remember yourself, Accepted," Sheriam said coldly. "Do you make this claim?"

Nynaeve stared at the woman. Sheriam was the one crazed, bouncing back and forth this way. Still, she managed a respectful "Yes, Aes Sedai." Dagdara snorted like canvas ripping.

Sheriam gestured to quiet a murmur among the Yellows. "And you did it by accident, you say. If that's the case, I suppose there is no chance of you showing proof by doing it again."

"How could she?" Myrelle said, looking amused. Amused! "If she fumbled her way into it blindly, how could she possibly repeat it? But that would not matter unless she actually did the thing in the first place."

"Answer me!" Sheriam snapped, and that invisible switch struck again. This time Nynaeve managed not to leap. "Is there any chance you can remember even part of what you did?"

"I remember, Aes Sedai," she said sullenly, tensing for another blow. It did not come, but she could see the glow of *saidar* around Sheriam now. That glow seemed threatening.

A small commotion at the door, and Carlinya and Beonin pushed through the line of Yellow sisters, one shoving Siuan ahead of her, the other Leane. "They did not want to come," Beonin announced in an exasperated tone. "Can you believe that they tried to tell us that they were busy?"

Leane was as blank-faced as any Aes Sedai, but Siuan darted sullen, angry looks at everybody, especially Nynaeve.

Finally Nynaeve understood. Finally everything came together. The Yellow sisters' presence. Sheriam and Myrelle believing, then not believing, threatening her, snapping at her. It was all apurpose, all to make her angry enough to work her Healing on Siuan and Leane, to prove herself to the Yellows. No. By their faces, they were here to see her fail, not succeed. She made no effort to hide the firm tug she gave her braid. In fact, she did it again, in case anyone had missed the first time. She wanted to smack *all* their faces. She wanted to dose them with a concoction of herbs that would make them sit down on the floor and cry like babies just from the smell. She wanted to yank their hair out and strangle them with it, to—

"Do I have to put up with this nonsense?" Siuan growled. "I have important work to do, but if it were only heading fish it would be more im—"

"Oh, shut up," Nynaeve broke in testily. One step, and she seized Siuan's head in both hands as if she intended to break the woman's neck. She had believed that nonsense, even the barrel! They had manipulated her like a puppet!

Saidar filled her, and she channeled as she had with Logain, blending all of the Five Powers. She knew what she was looking for this time, that almost-not-there-at-all sense of something cut. Spirit and Fire to mend the break, and. . . .

For a moment Siuan only stared, expressionless. Then the glow of *saidar* enveloped her. Gasps filled the room. Slowly Siuan leaned forward and kissed Nynaeve on either cheek. A tear leaked down her face, then another, and abruptly Siuan was weeping, hugging herself and shaking; the gleaming aura around her faded away. Sheriam quickly folded her into comforting arms; Sheriam looked as though she might cry too.

The rest of the room was staring at Nynaeve. The shock shining through all that Aes Sedai serenity was quite satisfying, and the disgruntlement too. Shanelle's eyes, pale blue in a dark pretty face, seemed about to fall out of her head. Nisao's mouth hung open, until she saw Nynaeve looking at her and snapped it shut.

"What made you think of using Fire?" Dagdara asked in a strangled voice that sounded entirely too high for such a big woman. "And Earth? You used Earth. Healing is Spirit, Water and Air." That opened the floodgate, questions from every throat, but they were all the same question really, just phrased differently.

"I don't know why," Nynaeve replied when she found an opening. "It just seemed right. I've almost always used everything." Which produced a round of admonitions. Healing was Spirit, Water and Air. It was dangerous to experiment with Healing; a mistake could kill not only you but your patient. She said nothing in reply, but the warnings died off quickly in rueful glances and smoothed skirts; she had not killed anyone, and she had Healed what they said could not be Healed.

Leane wore such a hopeful smile that it was almost painful. Nynaeve approached her with a smile of her own, masking the smoldering irritation inside. The Yellow Ajah and all its vaunted knowledge of Healing that she had been ready to beg on her knees to share. She knew more of Healing than any of them! "Watch carefully, now. You'll not get another chance soon to see it done."

She felt the joining clearly as she channeled, though she still could not have said what it was she had joined. It felt different than with Logain—it had with Siuan as well—but as she kept telling herself, men and women *were* different. *Light, I'm lucky this works on them as well as it did on him!* That brought up an uncomfortable line of speculation. What if some things had to be Healed differently in men than in women? Maybe she did not know so very much more than the Yellows after all.

Leane's reaction differed from Siuan's. No tears. She embraced *saidar* and smiled beatifically, then released it, though the smile remained. Then she flung her arms around Nynaeve and hugged her till her ribs creaked, whispering, "Thank you, thank you, thank you," over and over.

A murmur rose among the Yellows, and Nynaeve prepared to bask in their compliments. She would accept their apologies gracefully. Then she heard what they were saying.

". . . used Fire and Earth as if she were trying to bore a hole through stone." That from Dagdara.

"A smoother touch would be better," Shanelle agreed.

". . . see where Fire might be useful in problems with the heart," Therva said, tapping her long nose. Beldemaine, a plump Arafellin with silver bells in her hair, nodded thoughtfully.

". . . if the Earth were combined with Air just so, you see. . . ."

". . . Fire woven into Water. . . ."

". . . Earth blended with the Water. . . ."

Nynaeve gaped. They had forgotten her completely. They thought they could do what she had just showed them better than she could!

Myrelle patted her arm. "You did very well," she murmured. "Don't worry; they will be all praises later. Right now, they are still a little taken aback."

Nynaeve sniffed loudly, but none of the Yellows seemed to notice. "I hope this at least means I don't have to scrub pots anymore."

Sheriam's head whipped around with a startled expression. "Why, child, whatever gave you that notion?" She still had an arm around Siuan, who was dabbing at her eyes with a lace handkerchief in considerable embarrassment. "If anyone could break any rule they chose, do whatever they chose, and escape punishment merely by doing some good to balance it, the world would be chaos."

Nynaeve sighed heavily. She should have known.

Stepping out from the other Yellows, Nisao cleared her throat, and in passing shot Nynaeve a glare that could only be called accusatory. "I suppose this means we will have to gentle Logain again." She sounded as though she wanted to deny any of it had happened.

Heads began nodding, and then Carlinya spoke, like an icicle stabbed into the room. "Can we?" Every eye turned to her, but she went on calmly, coolly. "Ethically, can we consider supporting a man who can channel, a man trying to gather other men who can, while at the same time we go on as before, gentling those we find? Practically, what effect will it have on him when he learns? Distressing as it may be, as matters stand, he will see us as separate from the Tower, and more importantly, from Elaida and the Red Ajah. If we gentle even one man, we may lose that distinction, and with it our chance to gain a hold on him before Elaida does."

Silence cloaked the room when she stopped. Aes Sedai exchanged troubled looks, and those directed at Nynaeve made Nisao's look laudatory. Sisters had died in capturing Logain, and even if he was safely shielded again, she had given them him to deal with all over again, and a worse pickle besides.

"I think you should go," Sheriam said softly.

Nynaeve was not about to argue. She made her curtsies as quickly and carefully as she could, and did her best not to run in leaving.

Outside, Elayne rose from the stone step. "I'm sorry, Nynaeve," she said, brushing her skirt. "I was so excited, I blurted out everything to Sheriam before I realized Romanda and Delana were there."

"It doesn't matter," Nynaeve said heavily, starting down the crowded street. "It would have gotten out sooner or later." It just was not fair, though. *I did something they said couldn't be done, and I still have to scrub pots!* "Elayne, I don't care what you say; we have to go. Carlinya was talking about getting a 'hold' on Rand. This lot won't be any better than Elaida. Thom or Juilin will get horses for us, and Birgitte can just bite her elbow."

"I'm afraid it's too late," Elayne said miserably. "Word is spreading already."

Larissa Lyndel and Zenare Ghodar swooped down from opposite directions like hawks on either side of Nynaeve. Larissa was a bony woman whose plainness almost overcame Aes Sedai agelessness, Zenare slightly plump and haughty enough for two queens, but both wore faces of eager anticipation. They were Yellow Ajah, though neither had been in the room when she Healed Siuan and Leane.

"I want to see you go through everything step by step, Nynaeve," Larissa said, laying hold of an arm.

"Nynaeve," Zenare said, seizing the other arm, "I wager that I will find a hundred things you never thought of, if you repeat the weave often enough."

Salita Toranes, Tairen and almost as dark as one of the Sea Folk, seemed to pop out of nowhere. "Others ahead of me, I see. Well, burn my soul if I'll wait in line."

"I was here first, Salita," Zenare said firmly. And tightened her grip.

"*I* was first," Larissa said, tightening hers.

Nynaeve shot a look of pure horror at Elayne, and got commiseration in return, and a shrug. This was what Elayne had meant about too late. She would not have a waking moment to herself after this.

". . . angry?" Zenare was saying. "I know fifty ways at the front of my head to make her angry enough to chew rocks."

"I can think of a *hundred*," Larissa said. "*I* intend to break her block if it's the last thing I do."

Magla Daronos shouldered her way into the group, and she had the shoulders for it. She looked as if she worked the sword, or a blacksmith's hammer. "You will break it, Larissa? Hah! I do have several ways in mind already to draw it out of her."

Nynaeve just wanted to scream.

It was all Siuan could do not to embrace *saidar* and hold it, but she thought she might start crying again. That would never do. Besides, it would seem like some fool novice's display to the women crowding around her in the waiting room. Every expression of wonder and delight, every warm welcome as if she had been away for years, came as balm, especially from those who had been friends before she became Amyrlin, before time and duty pulled them apart. Lelaine and Delana wrapped their arms around her as they had not in long years. Moiraine had been the only one closer, the only one beside Leane she had managed to keep after donning the stole, and duty had helped keep them together.

"It is so good to have you back," Lelaine laughed.

"So very good," Delana murmured warmly.

Siuan laughed, and had to scrub tears from her cheeks. Light, what was the matter with her? She had not wept this easily as a child!

Maybe it was just joy, at regaining *saidar*, at all the warmth around her. The Light knew, altogether it was enough to unsettle anybody. She had never dared dream this day might come, and now that it had, she held nothing against any of these women, not their cold distance before, not their insistence that she remember her place. The line between Aes Sedai and not Aes Sedai was clear—she had insisted on it before she was stilled, and it went without saying that she would again—and she knew how stilled women had to be dealt with for their own good and the good of those who could still channel. Had had to be dealt with. How strange it was that that would never be so again.

From the corner of her eye she saw Gareth Bryne trotting up the stairs at the side of the room. "Excuse me a moment," she said, and hurried after him.

Even hurrying meant stopping every two steps to accept another congratulation all the way to the stairs, so she did not catch up until he was striding down a corridor on the second floor. Rushing ahead, she planted herself in front of him. His mostly gray hair was windblown, his square face and worn buff coat dusty. He looked as solid as stone.

Lifting a sheaf of papers, he said, "I have to drop this off, Siuan," and tried to step around her.

She moved to block him. "I've been Healed. I can channel again."

He nodded; just nodded! "I heard some talk. I suppose this means you'll be channeling my shirts clean from now on. Maybe they actually will be clean how. I've regretted letting Min go so easily."

Siuan stared at him. The man was no fool. Why was he pretending not to understand? "I am Aes Sedai again. Do you really expect an Aes Sedai to do your *laundry*?"

Just to drive it home, she embraced *saidar*—that missed sweetness was so wonderful she shivered—wrapped him in flows of Air, and lifted him. Tried to lift him. Gaping, she drew more, tried harder, until the sweetness stabbed like a thousand hooks. His boots never stirred from the floor.

It was impossible. True, the simple act of picking something up was one of the hardest in channeling, but she had been able to lift nearly three times her own weight.

"Is this supposed to impress me," Bryne said calmly, "or frighten me? Sheriam and her friends gave their word, the Hall gave its word, and more importantly, you gave yours, Siuan. I wouldn't let you get away from me if you were the Amyrlin again. Now undo whatever it is you've done, or when I get free of it, I'll turn you upside down and smack you for being childish. You're very seldom childish, so you needn't think I will let you start now."

In a near daze, she released the Source. Not for his threat—he was capable of it; he had done it before; but not for that—and not for shock at being unable to pick him up. Tears seemed to well up in her like a fountain; she hoped that letting go of *saidar* might stop them. A few still slid down her cheeks, though, however hard she blinked.

Gareth was cupping her face in his hands before she knew he had moved. "Light, woman, don't, tell me I frightened you. I didn't think being dropped in a pit with a pack of leopards would frighten you."

"I am not frightened," she said stiffly. Good; she could still lie. Tears, building inside.

"We have to work out some way not to be at one another's throat all the time," he said quietly.

"There is no reason for us to work out anything." They were coming. They were coming. Oh, Light, she could not let him see. "Just leave me alone, please. Please, just go." For a wonder, he hesitated only a moment before doing as she asked.

With the sound of his boots behind her, she managed to make it around the corner into the crossing hallway before the dam burst and she sank to her knees weeping piteously. She knew what it was, now. Alric, her Warder. Her dead Warder, murdered when Elaida deposed her. She could lie—the Three Oaths were still gone—but some part of her bond to Alric, a bond flesh to flesh and mind to mind, had been resurrected. The pain of his death, the pain first masked by the shock of what Elaida intended and then buried by stilling, that pain filled her to the brim. Huddled against the wall, bawling, she was only glad Gareth was not seeing this. *I have no time to fall in love, burn him!*

The thought was a bucket of cold water in her face. The pain remained, but the tears stopped, and she scrambled to her feet. Love? That was as impossible as . . . as. . . . She could not think of anything impossible enough. The *man* was impossible!

Suddenly she realized Leane was standing not two paces away, watching. Siuan made one effort at wiping the tears from her face, then gave it up. There was nothing but sympathy on Leane's face. "How did you deal with Anjen's . . . death, Leane?" That had been fifteen years ago now.

"I cried," Leane said. "For a month I held it in during the day, and spent the night in a quivering ball of tears in the middle of my bed. After I had torn the sheets to shreds. For three more, I could find tears in my eyes without warning. Over a year passed before I stopped hurting. That's why I never bonded another. I did not think I could live through that again. It does pass, Siuan." She found a roguish smile somewhere. "Now I think I could manage two or three Warders, if not four."

Siuan nodded. She could cry at night. As for Gareth bloody Bryne. . . . There was no "as for." There was not! "Do you think they're ready?" They had had only a moment to talk below. This hook had to be set quickly or it would not be set at all.

"Perhaps. I did not have much time. And I had to be careful." Leane paused. "Are you sure you want to go through with this, Siuan? It's changing everything we have worked for, on no notice at all, and. . . . I am not as strong as I was, Siuan, and neither are you. Most of the women here can channel more than either of us, now. Light, I think some of the Accepted can, not even counting Elayne or Nynaeve."

"I know," Siuan said. It had to be risked. The other plan had only been a stop-gap, because she was no longer Aes Sedai. But now she was Aes Sedai again, and she had been deposed with only the barest nod to Tower law. If she was Aes Sedai again, was she not Amyrlin again as well?

Squaring her shoulders, she went below to do battle with the Hall.

Lying on her bed in her shift, Elayne stifled a yawn and went back to rubbing the cream Leane had given her into her hands. It seemed to do some good; at least they *felt* softer. A night breeze stirred through the window, making the lone candle flicker. If anything, the air only made the room hotter.

Nynaeve staggered in, banged the door shut, flung herself across her bed, and lay staring at Elayne. "Magla is the most contemptible, hateful, *low* woman in the entire world," she mumbled. "No, Larissa is. No, it's Romanda."

"I take it they made you angry enough to channel." Nynaeve grunted, with the vilest expression, and Elayne hurried on. "How many did you demonstrate for? I expected you long ago. I looked for you at dinner, but I couldn't find you."

"I had a roll for dinner," Nynaeve muttered. "One roll! I demonstrated for all of them, every last Yellow in Salidar. Only they aren't satisfied. They want me one at a time. They set up a rotating schedule. Larissa has me tomorrow morning—before breakfast!—and Zenare right after, then. . . . They discussed how to make me angry as if I was not there!" She raised her head from the coverlet, looking hunted. "Elayne, they are competing over who is going to break my block. They're like boys trying to catch a greased pig on feastday, and I am the pig!"

Yawning, Elayne handed her the pot of hand cream, and after a moment Nynaeve rolled over and began rubbing it on. Nynaeve still had her time at the pots, too.

"I'm sorry I didn't do as you wanted days ago, Nynaeve. We could have woven disguises like Moghedien's and walked right past everybody." Nynaeve's hands stopped. "What is the matter, Nynaeve?"

"I never thought of that. I never *thought* of it!"

"You didn't? I was sure you had. You learned it first, after all."

"I tried not even to think about what we couldn't tell the sisters." Nynaeve's voice was flat as ice and about as cold and hard. "And now it is too late. I'm too tired to channel if you set my hair on fire, and if they have their way, I will be too tired forever. The only reason they let me go tonight was that I couldn't find *saidar* even when Nisao. . . ." She shuddered, and then her hands began moving again, smoothing in the cream.

Elayne let out a small breath. She had very nearly put her foot in it. She was tired, too. Admitting you had been wrong always made the other person feel better, but she hadn't meant to mention using *saidar* for disguises. From the first she had been afraid Nynaeve would do that. Here, at the very least, they could keep an eye on what the Salidar Aes Sedai intended, and maybe pass word to Rand through Egwene, once she returned to *Tel'aran'rhiod*. At the worst, they might have some small influence, through Siuan and Leane.

As if the thought were a summons, the door opened to admit just those women. Leane carried a wooden tray with bread and a bowl of soup, a red pottery cup and a white-glazed pitcher. There was even a sprig of green leaves in a tiny blue vase. "Siuan and I thought you might be hungry, Nynaeve. I hear the Yellows used you hard."

Elayne was uncertain whether she should rise or not. It was just Siuan and Leane, but they were Aes Sedai again. At least, she thought they were. The two solved the problem by sitting, Siuan on the foot of Elayne's bed, Leane on Nynaeve's. Nynaeve eyed them both suspiciously before sitting up with her back against the wall and taking the tray on her knees.

"I heard a rumor you addressed the Hall, Siuan," Elayne said carefully. "Should we have curtsied?"

"Do you mean are we Aes Sedai again, girl? We are. They wrangled like fishwives on Sunday, but they granted that much at least." Siuan exchanged glances with Leane, and Siuan's cheeks colored faintly. Elayne suspected she would never learn what had not been granted.

"Myrelle was kind enough to find me and let me know," Leane said into the momentary silence. "I think I am going to choose Green."

Nynaeve choked around her spoon. "What do you mean? Can you change Ajahs?"

"No, you cannot," Siuan told her. "But what the Hall decided is that although we are Aes Sedai, for a time we weren't. And since they insist on believing that codswallop was legal, all our ties, binds, associations and titles went overboard." Her voice was wry enough to rasp wood. "Tomorrow I ask the Blues whether they'll have me back. I've never heard of an Ajah turning anybody down—by the time you're raised from Accepted, you've been guided to the right Ajah whether you know it or not—but the way matters are proceeding, I wouldn't be completely surprised if they slammed the door on my foot."

"How *are* matters proceeding?" Elayne asked. There was something here. Siuan bullied, prodded, twisted your arm; she did not bring soup, sit on your bed and chat like a friend. "I thought everything was going as well as could be expected." Nynaeve gave her a stare that managed to be incredulous and haggard at the same time. Well, Nynaeve ought to know what she meant.

Siuan twisted around to face her, but she included Nynaeve as well. "I went by Logain's house. Six sisters are maintaining his shield, the same as when he was captured. He tried to break free when he found out we knew he had been Healed, and they said if only five had been holding the shield, he might have. So he's as strong as he ever was, or close enough to make no difference. I'm not. Neither is Siuan. I want you to try again, Nynaeve."

"I knew it!" Nynaeve flung her spoon down on the tray. "I knew you had some reason for this! Well, I'm too tired to channel, and it wouldn't matter if I wasn't. You can't Heal what has been Healed. You get out of here, and take your vile-tasting soup with you!" Less than half the vile-tasting soup remained, and it was a big bowl.

"I know it won't work!" Siuan snapped back. "This morning I knew stilling couldn't be Healed!"

"A moment, Siuan," Leane said. "Nynaeve, do you realize what we are risking, coming here together? This isn't a room in an alley with your archer friend standing guard; there are women all through this house, with eyes to see and tongues to talk. If it is found out that Siuan and I have been playing a game with everybody—even ten years from now—well, suffice it to say, Aes Sedai can be given penance, and we would very likely still be on a farm hoeing cabbages after our hair turns white. We came because of what you did for us, to make a fresh start."

"Why didn't you go to one of the Yellows?" Elayne asked. "Most of them must know as much about it as Nynaeve by now." Nynaeve glared indignantly around the spoon. Vile-tasting?

Siuan and Leane exchanged looks, and at last Siuan said reluctantly, "If we go to a sister, everybody knows, soon or late. If Nynaeve does it, maybe anybody who managed to weigh us today will think they were mistaken. Supposedly, all sisters are equal, and there have been Amyrlins who barely managed to channel enough to earn the shawl, but Amyrlins and the heads of Ajahs aside, by custom, if another is stronger in the Power than you, you're expected to give way to her."

"I don't understand," Elayne said. She was getting quite a lesson out of this; the hierarchy made sense, but she supposed it was one of those things you did not learn until you actually were Aes Sedai. One way and another, she had picked up enough hints to suspect that in many ways your education only began when you put on the shawl. "If Nynaeve *can* Heal you again, then you're stronger."

Leane shook her head. "No one has ever been Healed from stilling before. Maybe the others will see it, say like being wilders. That puts you a little lower than your strength. Maybe having been weaker will count something. If Nynaeve couldn't Heal us all the way the first time, maybe she'll only take us to two-thirds what we were, or half. Even that would be better than now, but still most here would be as strong, and a good many stronger." Elayne stared, more confused than before. Nynaeve looked as if she had been hit between the eyes.

"Everything goes into it," Siuan explained. "Who learned fastest, who spent the least time as novice and Accepted. There are all sorts of shadings. You can't say precisely how strong anyone is. Two women might seem to be the same strength; maybe they are and maybe not, but the only way to say for certain would be a duel, and the Light be blessed, we're above that. Unless Nynaeve returns us to our full strength, we run the risk of standing fairly low."

Leane took it up again. "The hierarchy isn't supposed to rule anything except everyday life, but it does. Advice from somebody with higher standing is given more weight than from somebody with lower. It did not matter while we were stilled. We had no standing at all; they weighed what we said on merit alone. It will not be that way now."

"I see," Elayne said faintly. No wonder people thought Aes Sedai invented the Game of Houses! They made *Daes Dae'mar* look simple.

"It's nice to see that Healing you gave *somebody* more trouble than it did me," Nynaeve grumbled. Peering into the bottom of the bowl, she sighed, then wiped it out with the last bit of bread.

Siuan's face darkened, but she managed to keep her voice level. "You can see, we lay ourselves bare. And *not* just to convince you to try Healing again. You gave me back . . . my life. As simple as that. I had convinced myself I wasn't dead, but it certainly seems so compared to this. So we make Leane's fresh start. Friends, if you'll have me for one. If not, then crewmates in the same boat."

"Friends," Elayne said. "Friends sounds much better to me." Leane smiled at her, but she and Siuan were still watching Nynaeve.

Nynaeve peered from one to the other. "Elayne had a question, so I should have one. What did Sheriam and the others learn from the Wise Ones last night? Don't say you do not know, Siuan. As far as I'm, concerned, you know what they think an hour after they think it."

Siuan's jaw set stubbornly; those deep blue eyes set themselves to intimidate. Suddenly she yelped, and bent to rub her ankle.

"Tell them," Leane said, drawing back her foot, "or I will. All of it, Siuan."

Glaring at Leane, Siuan puffed up till Elayne thought she might burst, but then her gaze touched Nynaeve, and she deflated. Words came out as though dragged, but they came. "The embassy from Elaida has reached Cairhien. Rand's met them, but he seems to be trying to toy with them. At least let us hope that's what he is doing. Sheriam and the others are set up because for once they managed not to make fools of themselves with the Wise Ones. And Egwene will be at the next meeting." For some reason, that last seemed to come most reluctantly of all.

Nynaeve brightened, sitting up straighter. "Egwene? Oh, that's wonderful! So they didn't come off as fools for once. I half wondered why they were not here to drag us off for another lesson." She squinted at Siuan; but even the squint looked cheerful. "A boat, you say? Who's the captain?"

"I am, you wretched little—" Leane cleared her throat, and Siuan took a deep breath. "A share-crew, then; equal shares. But someone has to steer," she added when Nynaeve began to smile, "and that *will* be me."

"All right," Nynaeve said after a long moment. Another hesitation, fiddling with her spoon, then, in a voice so casual Elayne wanted to throw up her hands, "Is there any chance you might help me—us—get us out of the kitchens?" They had faces no older than Nynaeve's, but they had been Aes Sedai for a long time; their eyes remembered that Aes Sedai stare. Nynaeve met it more steadily than Elayne thought she could have—except for just a bit of shifting—but in the end it was no surprise when she muttered, "I suppose not."

"We have to be going," Siuan said, standing. "If anything, Leane understated the cost of discovery. We could be the first Aes Sedai skinned publicly, and I've already been the only first I want to be."

To Elayne's surprise, Leane bent to hug her, whispering, "Friends." Elayne returned the hug and the word warmly.

Leane also hugged Nynaeve, murmuring something Elayne could not hear, and then Siuan did too, with a "Thank you" that sounded gruff and reluctant.

At least, that was how it sounded to her, but once they were gone, Nynaeve said, "She was about to cry, Elayne. Maybe she really meant all of that. I suppose I should try to be nicer to her." She sighed, which became a yawn, muffling "Especially since she's Aes Sedai again." And with that, she fell asleep with the tray still on her knees.

Muffling a yawn of her own behind her hand, Elayne got up and squared everything away neatly, tucking the tray under Nynaeve's bed. It took a little time to get Nynaeve out of her dress and settled down into the bed more comfortably, but even that did not wake her. For herself, once Elayne had the candle snuffed and was hugging her pillow, she lay awake, staring at the darkness and thinking. Rand trying to deal with Aes Sedai sent by Elaida? They would eat him alive. Almost she wished she could have seen her way to accepting Nynaeve's suggestion when it had a chance of success. She could guide him through any snares they set, she was sure—Thom had added a great deal to what her mother taught her—and he would listen to her. Besides, that way she could bond him. After all, she had not waited until she wore the shawl to bond Birgitte; why wait for Rand?

Shifting, she snuggled deeper into her pillow. He had to wait. He was in Caemlyn, not Salidar. Wait, Siuan said he was in Cairhien. How . . . ? She was too tired; the thought drifted. Siuan. Siuan was still hiding something; she was sure of it.

Sleep slid in, and with it a dream, a boat with Leane sitting in the bow flirting with a man whose face was different every time Elayne looked. In the stern, Siuan and Nynaeve were struggling, each trying to steer in a different direction—until Elayne stood up and took charge. A captain keeping secrets could be reason enough for a mutiny if need be.

In the morning Siuan and Leane returned before Nynaeve even opened her eyes, more than sufficient to make her angry enough to channel. It did no good, though. What was already Healed could not be Healed again.

"I will do what I can, Siuan," Delana said, leaning forward to pat the other woman's arm. They were alone in the sitting room, and the teacups on the small table between their chairs stood untouched.

Siuan sighed, looking dejected, though what she could expect after her outburst in front of the Hall, Delana did not know. Early-morning light spilled through the windows, and she thought of the breakfast she had not had yet, but this was Siuan. The situation was disconcerting, and Delana did not like being disconcerted. She had schooled herself not to see her old friend in this woman's face—not hard, since she looked nothing at all like the Siuan Sanche Delana remembered, not at any age—yet seeing Siuan again, a Siuan young and pretty, was only the first shock. The second was Siuan appearing on her doorstep with the sun not up, asking help; Siuan never asked for help. And then there was the biggest shock of all, the one renewed every time she came face-to-face with Siuan since the al'Meara woman had worked her impossible miracle. She was stronger than Siuan, much stronger. The margin had always gone the other way; Siuan had taken the lead when they were novices, even before they were Accepted. Still, she *was* Siuan, and upset, which Delana never remembered before. Siuan could be upset, but she never let you see it. It distressed her that she could not do more for the woman who had stolen honeycakes with her and more than once had taken the blame for pranks they had both been involved in.

"Siuan, I can do this much at least. Romanda would be more than happy to take those dream *ter'angreal* into the Hall's keeping. She doesn't have enough Sitters with her to bring it off, but if Sheriam thinks she does, if she thinks you've used your influence with Lelaine and me to stop it, then she won't be able to refuse you. I know Lelaine will agree. Though why you want to meet these Aielwomen, I cannot imagine. Romanda smiles like a cat in the buttery, watching Sheriam stalk around in a temper after one of those meetings. With your temper, you will likely burst something." Such a change. Once she would never have thought of mentioning Siuan's temper; now she mentioned it without thinking.

Siuan's downcast face broke into a smile. "I hoped you would do something like that. I will speak to Lelaine. And Janya; I think Janya will help. You have to make sure Romanda doesn't actually do it, though. From the little I know, Sheriam has worked out at least a semblance of how to get along with these Aiel. I'm afraid Romanda would need to start from the beginning. Of course, that might not be important to the Hall, but I would just as soon not have my first look at them when everybody has a hook in their gills."

Delana kept her smile inside as she escorted Siuan to the front step and gave her a hug. Yes, it would be very important to the Hall to keep the Wise Ones pacific, though Siuan had no way of knowing that. She watched Siuan hurry down the street before going back in. It seemed she was going to be the one doing the protecting now. She hoped she made as good a job of it as her friend had.

The tea was still warm, and she decided to send Miesa, her serving woman, for some rolls and fruit, but when a timid tap came at the sitting room door, it was not Miesa but Lucilde, one of the novices they had brought from the Tower.

The lanky girl bobbed a nervous curtsy, but Lucilde was always nervous. "Delana Sedai? A woman arrived this morning, and Anaiya Sedai said I should bring her to you? Her name's Halima Saranov? She says she knows you?"

Delana opened her mouth to say that she had never heard of any Halima Saranov, and a woman appeared in the doorway. Delana stared in spite of herself. The woman managed to be slender and lush at the same time, and wore a dark gray riding dress cut ridiculously low; long lustrous black hair framed a green-eyed face that probably made every man who glimpsed it gape. That was not why Delana stared, of course. The woman held her hands at her sides, but with thumbs thrust hard between the first two fingers. Delana had never expected to see that from any woman who did not wear the shawl, and this Halima Saranov could not even channel. She was close enough to be sure of that.

"Yes," Delana said, "it seems to me I do remember. Leave us, Lucilde. And, child, do try to remember that every sentence isn't a question."

Lucilde bobbed a curtsy so quick and deep that she nearly fell. Under other circumstances, Delana would have sighed; she had never done well with novices, though she could not understand why.

Almost before the novice was out of the room, Halima swayed over to the chair Siuan had used and sat without a word of invitation. Picking up one of the untouched cups, she crossed her legs and sipped, watching Delana over the rim.

Delana fixed her with a hard stare. "Who do you think you are, woman? However high you think you stand, none stand higher than Aes Sedai. And where did you learn that sign?" For perhaps the first time in her life, that stare did no good.

Halima smiled at her mockingly. "Do you really think the secrets of the . . . shall we say, *darker* Ajah, are that secret? As for how high you stand, you know very well that if a beggar gave the proper signs, you would leap to obey. My story is that I was traveling companion for a time to one Cabriana Mecandes, a Blue sister. Unfortunately, Cabriana died in a fall from her horse, and her Warder simply refused to leave his blankets or eat after that. He died, too." Halima smiled as if to ask whether Delana was following. "Cabriana and I talked a great deal before she died, and she told me about Salidar. She also told me a number of things she had learned about the White Tower's plans for you here. And for the Dragon Reborn." Another smile, a quick flash of white teeth, and she went back to her tea and her watching.

Delana had never been a woman to give up easily. She had bludgeoned kings into making peace when they wanted war, dragged queens by the scruff of the neck to sign treaties that had to be signed. True, she would have obeyed that hypothetical beggar if he had the proper signs and said the right things, but Halima's hands had identified her as Black Ajah, which she clearly was not. Perhaps the woman thought that was the only way to make Delana acknowledge her, and perhaps she wanted to show off her forbidden knowledge as well. Delana did not like this Halima. "And I suppose I am supposed to make sure the Hall accepts your information," she said gruffly. "It should be no problem so long as you know enough of Cabriana to support your tale. I can't help you there; I never met her above twice. I suppose there is no chance of her appearing to spoil your story?"

"No chance at all." Again that quick, mocking smile. "And I could recite Cabriana's life. I know things she had forgotten herself."

Delana only nodded to that. Killing a sister was always to be regretted, but what must be, must be. "Then there is no problem at all. The Hall will receive you as a guest, and I can make sure they listen."

"A guest is not exactly what I had in mind. Something rather more permanent, I think. Your secretary, or better yet, your companion. I need to make sure your Hall is guided carefully. Beyond this tale of Cabriana's news, from time to time I'll have instructions for you."

"Now you listen to me! I—!"

Halima cut her off without raising her voice. "I was told to mention a name to you. A name I use, sometimes. Aran'gar."

Delana sat down heavily. That name had been mentioned in her dreams. For the first time in years, Delana Mosalaine was afraid.

CHAPTER 31

Red Wax

The sound of the black gelding's hooves was all but swallowed in the noise of Amador as Eamon Valda rode slowly through the crowded streets. Sweat oozed from his every pore, the more for his perfectly polished mail and breastplate, gleaming despite a layer of dust, and the snowy cloak spread over the gelding's powerful rump, yet it might have been a fine spring day for all the notice he took. He did his best to ignore the dirty men and women, even children, with lost expressions and travelworn clothes. Even here. Even here.

For once in his life, the great stone walls of the Fortress of the Light, towered and bannered and impregnable, bastion of truth and right, did not lift his spirits. Dismounting in the main courtyard, he tossed his reins to a Child with grated instructions for caring for the animal; the man knew what to do, of course, but Valda wanted to snap at something. White-cloaked men scurried everywhere in a great show of energy despite the heat. He hoped there was something more than show behind it.

Young Dain Bornhald came trotting across the courtyard, pressing fist to mailed chest in an eager salute. "The Light illumine you, my Lord Captain. You had a good ride from Tar Valon, yes?" His eyes were bloodshot, and a smell of brandy wafted from him. There was no excuse for drinking during the day.

"Fast, at least," Valda growled, jerking off his gauntlets and stuffing them behind his sword belt.

It was not the brandy, though he would make a mark against the man for it. The journey had been fast, for that distance. He intended to give the legion a night in the city by way of reward, once they finished making camp outside the city. A fast journey, but he disapproved of the orders that called him back just when a strong push might have toppled the crippled Tower and buried the witches under the rubble. A ride to be remarked, yet every day had brought worse news. Al'Thor in Caemlyn. It did not really matter whether the man was a false Dragon or the real one; he could channel, and any man who did that had to be a Darkfriend. Dragonsworn rabble in Altara. This so-called Prophet and his scum in Ghealdan, in Amadicia itself.

He had managed to kill some of that filth, at least, though it was hard fighting foes who melted away more often than they stood, who could blend into the accursed streams of refugees, and worse, of brainless wanderers who seemed to think al'Thor had turned all order on its head. He had found a solution, however, if not a completely satisfactory one. The roads behind his legion were littered now, and the ravens fed to bursting. If it was not possible to tell the Prophet's trash from refugee trash, well then, kill whoever clogged the way. The innocent should have remained in their homes where they belonged; the Creator would shelter them anyway. As far as he was concerned, the wanderers were added plums on the cake.

"I heard in the city that Morgase is here," he said. He did not believe it—every other word in Andor had been speculation over who killed Morgase—so he was startled when Dain nodded.

Surprise turned to disgust as the young man babbled about Morgase's apartments and her hunting, how well she was treated, how she was sure to sign a treaty with the Children any day. Valda scowled openly. He should have expected no better from Niall. The man had been one of the best soldiers in his time, accounted a great captain, but he grew old and soft. Valda had known that as soon as his orders reached Tar Valon. Niall should have moved on Tear in strength with the first word of al'Thor. He would have gathered all the numbers he needed on the march; nations would have rallied to the Children against a false Dragon. They would have, then. Now al'Thor was in Caemlyn, and strong enough to frighten the fainthearted. But Morgase was here. If he had Morgase, she would sign that treaty the first day if somebody had to guide her hand to hold the pen.

By the Light, he would teach her to leap when he said leap. If she balked at returning to Andor with the Children, he would lash her to a staff by her wrists. That would be a banner to lead the advance into Andor.

Dain ran down, waiting. No doubt hoping for an invitation to dinner this evening. As a junior, he could not issue one to an officer senior to him, but doubtless he hoped to talk with his old commander, about Tar Valon, perhaps even about his dead father. Valda had not thought much of Geofram Bornhald; the man had been soft. "I will see you at the camp for dinner at six. I will see you sober, Child Bornhald."

Bornhald surely was in drink; he gaped and stammered before making his salute and going. Valda wondered what had happened. Dain had been a fine young officer. One who worried too much over niceties, such as proof of guilt when there was no way to obtain it, yet still fine for all that. Not as weak as his father. A shame to see him waste himself in brandy.

Muttering under his breath—officers drinking in the very Fortress of the Light was another sign that Niall was rotting at the core—Valda went in search of his rooms. He intended to sleep in the camp, but a hot bath would not be amiss.

A square-shouldered young Child approached in the plain stone corridor, the scarlet shepherd's crook of the Hand of the Light behind the flaring golden sun on his chest. Without stopping or even looking at Valda, the Questioner murmured respectfully, "My Lord Captain might wish to visit the Dome of Truth."

Valda frowned after the man—he did not like Questioners; they did good work in their way, yet he could never escape the feeling that they had donned the crook because that way they would never have to face an armed foe—started to raise his voice and dress the fellow down, then stopped. Questioners were sloppy in their discipline, but a simple Child would never speak idly to a Lord Captain. Perhaps the bath could wait.

The Dome of Truth was a wonder that finally did restore some of his essence. Pure white outside, inside gold leaf cast down the light of a thousand hanging lamps. Thick white columns ringed the chamber, plain and polished to glistening, but the dome itself stretched a hundred paces across unsupported and rose fifty at its peak, above the simple white marble dais, centered on the white marble floor, where the Lord Captain Commander of the Children of the Light stood to address the assembled Children in their most solemn moments, their most serious ceremonies. He would stand there, one day. Niall would not live forever.

Dozens of Children wandered about the vast chamber—it was a sight worth seeing, though none but the Children ever did, of course—yet that message had not come so he could admire the Dome. He was sure of it. Behind the great columns ran rows of smaller ones, just as simple and polished just as highly, and tall alcoves where scenes of the Children's triumphs made frescoes of a thousand years. Valda strolled, looking into each recess. Finally he saw a tall, graying man studying one of the paintings, Serenia Latar being raised on the scaffold, the only Amyrlin the Children had ever managed to hang. She had been dead already, of course, live witches being somewhat hard to hang, but that was beside the point. Six hundred and ninety-three years ago, justice had been done according to the law.

"Are you troubled, my son?" The voice was soft, almost mild.

Valda stiffened slightly. Rhadam Asunawa might be the High Inquisitor, but he was still a Questioner. And Valda was a Lord Captain, Anointed of the Light, not "my son." "Not that I have noticed," he said flatly.

Asunawa sighed. His gaunt face was a picture of martyred suffering, so that his sweat might have been taken for tears, but his deep-set eyes seemed to burn with the heat that had boiled away all his spare flesh. His cloak bore only the crook, no flaring golden sun, as though he stood outside the Children. Or perhaps above. "The times are troubled. The Fortress of the Light harbors a witch."

Valda suppressed a wry look before it formed. Cowards or not, Questioners could be dangerous even to a Lord Captain. The man might never be able to hang an Amyrlin, but he probably dreamed of being the first to hang a queen. Valda did not care whether Morgase died, provided it was not before all the use was wrung out of her. He said nothing, and Asunawa's thick gray eyebrows drew down until he seemed to peer out of caverns.

"The times are troubled," he said again, "and Niall must not be allowed to destroy the Children of the Light."

For long minutes Valda examined the painting. Perhaps the artist had been good, perhaps not; he knew nothing of such things and cared even less. The fellow had gotten the weapons and armor right on the guards, though, and the rope and scaffold looked real. Those were things he knew. "I am prepared to listen," he said finally.

"Then we will talk, my son. Later, where there are fewer eyes to see and ears to hear. The Light illumine you, my son." Asunawa strode away without another word, white cloak billowing slightly and the sound of his boots

echoing as if he was trying to drive every step into the stone. Some of the
Children bowed deeply as he passed.

From a narrow window high above the courtyard Niall watched Valda dismount and speak to young Bornhald, then stalk away in a fury. Valda was
always in a fury. Had there been some means to bring the Children home
from Tar Valon and leave Valda there, Niall would have jumped at it. The
man was a fair enough battle commander, but better suited to rousing
mobs. His notion of tactics was the charge, and of strategy—the charge.

Shaking his head, Niall made his way to his audience chamber. He had
more important things than Valda to concern him. Morgase was still resisting like an army on the heights with water and high morale. She refused to
admit she held a valley floor with no way out, and it was her enemy who had
the heights.

Balwer rose from his table as Niall entered the anteroom. "Omerna was
here, my Lord. He left these for you." Balwer touched a sheaf of papers tied
with a red ribbon on the table. "And this." Thin lips tightened as he drew
a tiny bone tube from his pocket.

Niall took the tube with a mutter and stumped into the inner room.
Omerna was becoming more useless every day, for some reason. Leaving
his reports with Balwer was bad enough, nonsense as they were, but even
Omerna knew better than to hand one of these tubes with three red stripes
to anyone but Niall himself. He held the tube close to a lamp to examine
the wax. Unbroken, before his thumbnail pierced it. He would have to
light a fire under Omerna, put the fear of the Light into him. The fool was
no good as a decoy unless he played the consummate spymaster as far as he
was able.

The message was from Varadin again, Niall's private cipher in that
mad, spidery scrawl on a strip of thin paper. He almost burned it unread;
then something at the end caught his eye. Beginning at the beginning, he
consciously worked the cipher in his mind. He wanted to be absolutely
sure. Just as before, it was gibberish about Aes Sedai on leashes and strange
beasts, but right at the last. . . . Varadin had helped Asidim Faisar find a
hiding place in Tanchico; he would try to smuggle Faisar out, but the Forerunners kept such a guard that a whisper could not pass the walls without
permission.

Niall rubbed his chin in thought. Faisar was one of those he had sent
to Tarabon to see if anything could be salvaged. Faisar knew nothing of

Varadin, and Varadin should know nothing of Faisar. The Forerunners kept a such a guard that not a whisper could pass the walls. A madman's scrawl.

Stuffing the paper into his pocket, he returned to the anteroom. "Balwer, what is the latest from the west?" Between them, "the west" always meant the border with Tarabon.

"No change from before, my Lord. Patrols that penetrate very deeply into Tarabon do not return. The worst trouble near the border is refugees trying to cross."

Patrols that penetrated too deeply. Tarabon was a pit writhing with poisonous vipers and rabid rats, but. . . . "How quickly could you get a courier to Tanchico?"

Balwer did not even blink. The man would not show surprise if one day his horse spoke to him. "The problem will be fresh horses once he crosses the border, my Lord. Normally, I would say twenty days there and back, perhaps a few less with luck. Now, twice that, with luck. Maybe twice that just to reach Tanchico." A pit that could swallow a courier and not even leave bones behind.

There would be no need for a return, but Niall kept that to himself. "Let it be arranged, Balwer. I will have a letter ready in an hour. I will speak to the courier myself." Balwer bowed his head in assent, but drywashed his hands at the same time, insulted. Let him be. There was a small chance this could be done without exposing Varadin. Unnecessary precaution if he was insane, of course, but if not. . . . Revealing him would not make anything happen faster.

Back in the audience chamber, Niall studied Varadin's message once more before holding the slip in a lamp flame, watching it catch. He crumpled the ash between his fingers.

He had four rules concerning action and information. Never make a plan without knowing as much as you can of the enemy. Never be afraid to change your plans when you receive new information. Never believe you know everything. And never wait to know everything. The man who waited to know everything was still sitting in his tent when the enemy burned it over his head. Niall followed those rules. Only once in his life had he abandoned them to follow a hunch. At Jhamara, for no reason but a tickling at the back of his head, he had set a third of his army to watch mountains all said were impassable. While he maneuvered the rest of his forces to crush the Murandians and Altarans, an Illianer army that was supposed to be a hundred miles away came out of those "impassable" passes. The only reason he managed to withdraw without being crushed was a "feeling." And now he felt that tickling again.

"I do not trust him," Tallanvor said firmly. "He reminds me of a young sharp I saw at the fair once, a baby-faced fellow who could look you in the eye and grin while he was palming the pea from under its cup."

For once Morgase had no difficulty holding her temper. Young Paitr had reported that his uncle had finally found a way to smuggle her out of the Fortress of the Light, her and the others. The others had been the rub; Torwyn Barshaw had claimed himself able to get her out alone long since, but she would not leave them behind to the mercies of the Whitecloaks. Not even Tallanvor.

"I will make a note of your feelings," she said indulgently. "Just do not let them hinder you. Do you have a saying that fits, Lini? Something for young Tallanvor and his feelings?" Light, why did she take such a delight in taunting him? He came close to treason, but she was his Queen, not. . . . The rest of the thought would not come.

Lini sat near the windows, rolling a ball of blue yarn from the skein Breane held stretched on her hands. "Paitr minds me of that young undergroom, just before you went to the White Tower. The one who got two maids with child and was caught trying to sneak away from the manor with a sackful of your mother's plate."

Morgase's jaw hardened, but nothing could spoil her pleasure, not even the glance Breane gave her, as if she should be allowed to state her opinion as well. Paitr had been overjoyed at Morgase's impending escape. Of course, part of that was because he apparently expected some sort of reward from his uncle for his part—at least, a few of his comments suggested it; something about making up for a failure back home—but the young man practically danced when she agreed to the plan that would have them all out of the Fortress today and out of Amador by sunrise tomorrow. Away from Amador and on the road to Ghealdan, where soldiers would not come with strings to tie to Andor. Two days ago Barshaw himself came to unfold the scheme, disguised as a shopkeeper delivering knitting needles and yarn, a squat big-nosed man with a choleric eye and a sneering mouth, though the words came out respectfully enough. It was hard to believe him Paitr's uncle, they looked so different, much less a merchant. Still, his plan was a marvel of simplicity, if hardly dignified, needing only enough people outside the Fortress to make it work. Morgase was going to ride out of the Fortress of the Light buried in the bottom of a cartload of kitchen refuse.

"Now, you all know what to do," she told them. So long as she herself was in her rooms, the rest could move about with considerable freedom. Everything depended on that. Well, not everything; but certainly every escape but her own. "Lini, you and Breane must be in the laundry yard when the bell sounds High." Lini nodded complacently, but Breane gave her a purse-lipped look. They had been over this twenty times. Even so, Morgase was not going to allow a mistake to result in anyone being left behind. "Tallanvor, you will leave your sword behind and wait at an inn called The Oak and Thorn." He opened his mouth, but she forestalled him firmly. "I have heard your arguments. You can find another sword. They'll believe you mean to return if you leave it." He grimaced, but finally nodded. "Lamgwin is to wait at The Golden Head, and Basel at—"

A hasty tap at the door, and it opened enough to admit Basel's balding head. "My Queen, there's a man . . . a Child. . . ." He glanced over his shoulder into the hall. "There's a Questioner, my Queen." Tallanvor's hands went to his sword hilt, of course, and he would not take them away until she had gestured twice and grimaced at him beside.

"Admit him." She managed a calm voice, but butterflies the size of foxes fluttered frantically in her belly. A Questioner? Was everything that suddenly had been going so well about to turn just as suddenly to disaster?

A tall hawk-nosed man pushed Basel out of the way and closed the door in his face. The white-and-gold tabard with the crimson crook on his shoulder gave his rank as Inquisitor. She had not met Einor Saren, but he had been pointed out to her. There was a set of unalterable certainty to his face. "You are summoned to the Lord Captain Commander," he said coldly. "You will come now."

Morgase's thoughts raced faster than the butterflies. She was used to being summoned—Niall did not come to her, now he had her in the Fortress—called before the man for another lecture on her duty to Andor or for what was supposed to be a friendly chat to show her that Niall had her best interests, and Andor's, at heart. Used to that, but not to this sort of messenger. If she was being given over to the Questioners, there would be no subterfuge. Asunawa would send enough men to drag her away, and everyone with her. Him, she had met briefly; he made her blood freeze. Why had an Inquisitor been sent? She voiced the question, and Saren replied in the same icy tones.

"I was with the Lord Captain Commander, and I was coming this way.

I have finished my business, and now I will take you back. After all, you are a queen, due respect." That all sounded slightly bored, somewhat impatient, until the last, when a note of wry mockery entered. No warmth, though.

"Very well," she said.

"Shall I accompany my Queen?" Tallanvor bowed formally; at least he made a display of deference when any outsider was around.

"No." She would take Lamgwin instead. No, any of the men would make it seem she thought she needed bodyguards. Saren frightened her nearly as much as Asunawa did, and she would not let him catch even a hint of the fact. She put on a casual, tolerant smile. "Surely I need no protection here."

Saren smiled too, or at least his mouth did. He seemed to be laughing at her.

Outside, with Basel and Lamgwin looking at her uncertainly, she almost changed her mind about attendants; she would have, had she not spoken inside. But two men could not protect her if this really was some elaborate trap, and changing her mind would be a show of weakness. Walking through the stone corridors beside Saren, she certainly felt weak, not like a queen at all. No. Maybe she would scream like anyone else if the Questioners had her in their dungeons—well, there was no maybe about it; she was not fool enough to believe royal flesh different from any other in that regard—but until then, she would be what she was. Deliberately, she set about flogging down those butterflies.

Saren led her into a small flagstone-paved courtyard where bare-chested men were hacking at wooden posts with swords. "Where are we going?" she demanded. "This is not the way I have gone to the Lord Captain Commander's study before. Is he somewhere else?"

"I take the shortest way," he replied curtly. "I have more important matters to see to than. . . ." He did not finish, and he did not slow, either.

She had no choice but to follow, down a corridor lined with long rooms full of narrow cots and men often bare-chested or in less. She kept her eyes fixed on Saren's back, composing the blistering sentences she meant to deliver to Niall. Across a stableyard, the smell of horses and dung heavy in the air and a farrier shoeing horses in one corner, along another barracks hallway and then one with kitchens down one side and the thick smell of stew cooking, into another courtyard. . . . She stopped dead.

A long, high scaffold stood in the middle of the yard. Three women and over a dozen men filled every space, hands and feet bound, nooses

snugged around their necks. Some wept piteously; most only looked terrified. The last two men on the far end were Torwyn Barshaw and Paitr, the
boy in his shirtsleeves instead of the red-and-white coat she had had made
for him. Paitr was not weeping, but his uncle was. Paitr appeared too
horrified to think of tears.

"For the Light!" a Whitecloak officer called out, and another Whitecloak shoved a long lever at the end of the scaffold.

Trapdoors snapped opened with loud cracks, and the victims fell from
sight. Some of the stretched ropes quivered as those at the end choked their
lives away instead of dying quickly from a broken neck. Paitr's was one of
those. And her fine escape died with him. Perhaps she should have had as
much concern for him, but it was the escape she thought of, her way out of
the trap she had walked into. Herself trapped, and Andor with her.

Saren was looking at her, plainly expecting her to faint or sick up.

"So many at once?" she said, proud of the steadiness in her voice. Paitr's
rope had stopped jerking; it only swung slowly from side to side, now. No
escape.

"We hang Darkfriends every day," Saren answered dryly. "Perhaps in
Andor you release them with a lecture. We do not."

Morgase met his gaze. The shortest way? So this was Niall's new tactic.
It did not surprise her that no mention had been made of her planned escape. Niall was too subtle for that. She was an honored guest, and Paitr and
his uncle had been hanged by chance, for some crime that had nothing to
do with her. Who would be the next to mount the gallows? Lamgwin or
Basel? Lini or Tallanvor? Strange, but the image of Tallanvor with a rope
around his neck hurt more than the image of Lini. The mind played peculiar tricks. Over Saren's shoulder she caught sight of Asunawa, at a window
overlooking the scaffold. He was staring down at her. Maybe this was his
doing, not Niall's. It made no difference. She could not let her people die
for nothing. She could not let Tallanvor die. Very peculiar tricks.

Arching an eyebrow mockingly, she said, "If this has unhinged your
knees, I suppose we can wait until you find your strength again." A light
voice, not affected at all by what she saw. Light, let her not vomit.

Saren's face darkened, and he turned on his heel and stalked away. She
followed at a stately pace, not looking up at Asunawa's window, trying not
to think of the scaffold.

Perhaps it really was the shortest way, for in the next corridor Saren led
her up steep flights of stairs, delivering her to Niall's audience chamber
more quickly than she remembered making the journey before. As usual

Niall did not rise, and there was no chair for her to take, so she was forced to stand before him like a petitioner. He seemed distracted, sitting silent and staring at her, but not really seeing her.

He had won, and he did not even see her. That irritated her. Light, he had won. Perhaps she should return to her rooms. If she told Tallanvor and Lamgwin and Basel to carve a path for her, they would try. They would die, and so would she; she had never held a sword, but if she gave that command, she would take one up. She would die, and Elayne would ascend the Lion Throne. She would as soon as al'Thor could be pushed from it. The White Tower would see that Elayne got what was hers. The Tower. If the Tower secured the throne for Elayne. . . . It seemed mad, yet she trusted the Tower even less than she did Niall. No, she had to save Andor herself. But the cost. The cost must be paid.

She had to force the words out. "I am ready to sign your treaty."

Niall hardly appeared to hear at first. Then he blinked, and suddenly laughed wryly and shook his head. That irritated her, too. Pretending surprise. She had not tried to escape. She was a guest. She wished she could see him on a gallows.

He moved into action so quickly that he almost dispelled the memory of his earlier apathy. In moments he had his dried-up little secretary in with a long parchment, everything already written out, and even a copy of the Seal of Andor she could not tell from the original.

Choice or no choice, she made a show of reading the terms. They were no different than she had expected. Niall would lead the Whitecloaks to regain her throne, but there was a price, if not named as such. A thousand Whitecloaks quartered in Caemlyn, with their own courts of law, outside Andoran law, in perpetuity. Whitecloaks to stand equal with the Queen's Guards throughout Andor, in perpetuity. It might take her lifetime to undo signing this, and Elayne's as well, but the alternative was al'Thor with the Lion Throne as a trophy. If any woman ever sat on it again, it would be Elenia or Naean or one of that ilk, and as al'Thor's puppet. That, or Elayne as the Tower's puppet; she *could* not make herself trust the Tower.

She signed her name clearly, pressed the copied Seal into the red wax that Niall's secretary dripped at the foot of the sheet. The Lion of Andor surrounded by the Rose Crown. There, she was the first queen ever to accept foreign soldiers on Andoran soil.

"How soon . . . ?" It was harder to say than she had imagined. "How soon will your legions ride?"

Niall hesitated, glancing down the table. There was nothing there except pen and ink, a sand bowl and a freshly burned down stub of sealing wax, as if he had very recently written a letter. He finished scrawling his signature on the treaty and impressed his own seal, a flaring sun in golden wax, then handed the parchment to his secretary. "Put this in the document room, Balwer. I fear I cannot move as quickly as I had hoped, Morgase. There are developments I must consider. Nothing that need concern you. Simply a matter of how best to move in areas unrelated to Andor. I insist you take this as simply more time for me to enjoy your company."

Balwer bowed smoothly if somewhat prissily, yet she was almost certain his eyes nearly jerked toward Niall in surprise. She herself nearly gaped. He pressed her and pressed her, and now he had other matters to consider? Balwer scurried out as though afraid she might try to snatch back the treaty and tear it up, but that was the furthest thing from her mind. At least there would be no more hangings. The rest would be dealt with when it could be. One step at a time. Her dogged resistance had failed, but now she had time again, an unexpected gift not to be wasted. The pleasure of her company?

She put on a warm smile. "It seems as though a weight has lifted from my shoulders. Tell me, do you play stones?"

"I am accounted a fair player." His answering smile was surprised at first, then amused.

Morgase flushed, but managed to keep her face from showing anger. Perhaps it was best that he thought her broken now. No one watched a broken opponent too closely, or regarded them too highly, and if she was careful, with time she could begin recovering what she had given away before his soldiers left Amadicia. She had had a very good teacher in the Game of Houses.

"I will try not to provide too poor a match, if you would like to play." She was well beyond fair, herself, perhaps even beyond good, but she would have to lose, of course, though not so badly that he grew bored. She hated losing.

Frowning, Asunawa drummed his fingers on the gilded arm of his chair. Above his head, the shepherd's crook was worked in brilliant lacquer on a pure white disc. "The witch was taken aback," he murmured.

Saren answered as though it was an accusation. "Some people are affected that way by hanging. The Darkfriends were rounded up yesterday; I'm told they were chanting some catechism to the Shadow when Trom broke down the door. I checked, but no one thought to ask if they had any connection to her." At least he did not shift his feet; he stood as straight as any Hand of the Light should.

Asunawa dismissed explanations with a slight wave of his hand. Of course there was no connection, aside from the fact that she was a witch and they Darkfriends. The witch was in the Fortress of the Light, after all. Still, he was troubled.

"Niall sent me to fetch her as if I were a dog," Saren grated. "I almost spewed up my stomach, standing so close to a witch. My hands wanted her throat."

Asunawa did not bother to respond; he hardly heard. Of course Niall hated the Hand. Most men hated what they feared. No, his mind was on Morgase. She was not weak, by all accounts. She had certainly fended off Niall well enough; most people would have collapsed as soon as they were inside the Fortress. She would ruin some of his plans if she turned out to be weak after all. He had all the details in his mind, each day of her trial with ambassadors on hand from every land that could still produce one, until finally her dramatic confession, wrung from her so skillfully no one would ever find a mark, and then the ceremonies surrounding her execution. A special gallows just for her, to be preserved afterwards to mark the occasion.

"Let us hope she continues to resist Niall," he said, with a smile that some would call mild and pious. Even Niall's patience could not last forever; eventually he would have to hand her to justice.

CHAPTER

32

Summoned in Haste

To Egwene, Rand's visit to Cairhien seemed like one of those grand Illuminators' fireworks displays she had heard of but never seen, exploding all through the city. The echoes seemed to reverberate without end.

She did not go near the palace again, of course, but Wise Ones that went every day to search for traps laid with *saidar* told her what went on. Nobles stared at one another with slitted eyes, Tairen and Cairhienin alike. Berelain seemed to have gone into hiding, refusing to see anyone she did not have to; Rhuarc apparently took her to task for neglecting her duties, with small effect. He appeared to be the only one unaffected in the whole palace. Even the servants jumped if you looked at them, though that might just have been having the Wise Ones themselves poking into every corner.

In the tents, things were no better, among the Wise Ones anyway. The rest of the Aiel were like Rhuarc, calm and solid. Their attitude made the Wise Ones' moodiness even more tense by comparison, not that it needed any. Amys and Sorilea came back from meeting Rand all but hissing. They did not say why, not where Egwene could hear, but the feeling spread through the Wise Ones as fast as thought, until every one of them stalked about like a bristling cat ready to claw anything that moved. Their apprentices stepped lightly and spoke softly, but still were scolded for what would have passed without notice before, and punished for what would have brought only a scolding.

Shaido Wise Ones appearing in the camp did not help. At least, Therava and Emerys were Wise Ones; the third was Sevanna herself, striding around self-importantly with her blouse unlaced enough to rival Berelain no matter how the dust blew. Therava and Emerys said Sevanna was a Wise One, and though Sorilea grumbled, there was no choice but to accept her as one. Egwene was sure they were spying, but Amys merely looked at her when she suggested it. Protected by custom, they had a free run of the tents, welcomed by all the Wise Ones—even Sorilea—as if close friends or first-sisters. Still, their presence honed the edge of everyone's mood. Especially Egwene's. That smirking cat Sevanna knew who she was, and took no pains to hide her delight in sending "the short apprentice girl" to fetch a cup of water or the like at any opportunity. Sevanna looked at her, too, a studying sort of gaze. It made Egwene think of someone studying a chicken, thinking how to cook it after they stole it. Worse than that, the Wise Ones would not tell her what they talked about; it was Wise Ones' business, and none of apprentices'. For whatever reason the Shaido were there, the mood among the other Wise Ones certainly interested them; more than once Egwene saw Sevanna, when she thought herself unobserved, smile as she watched Amys or Malindhe or Cosain stalk by talking to herself and needlessly adjusting her shawl. No one listened to Egwene, of course. Too many comments about the Shaido women finally earned her most of a day spent digging a hole "deep enough to stand in without being seen," and when she climbed out, all sweat and filth to begin filling it in, Sevanna was watching.

Two days after Rand left, Aeron and some other Wise Ones talked three Maidens into sneaking over the wall of Arilyn's palace in the night to see what they could scout out, and that made everything worse. The three avoided Gawyn's guards, if with more difficulty than they expected, but the Aes Sedai were another matter; while they were still climbing from the roof into an attic, they were wrapped up in the Power and whisked inside. Fortunately Coiren and the others seemed to think they were there to steal, though the Maidens might not have thought it was so fortunate. They were tossed into the street, so bruised they could hardly walk and still struggling not to sniffle when they got back to the tents. The other Wise Ones took turns upbraiding Aeron and her friends, usually in private, though Sorilea appeared to make a point of confronting them before as many people as possible. Sevanna and her two companions sneered quite openly whenever they saw Aeron or one of the others, and speculated among themselves in very audible voices about what the Aes Sedai would do when they found out. Even Sorilea looked at them askance for that, but no one said anything, and Aeron and her friends began walking as small as the apprentices. The apprentices began trying to hide when not actually performing their duties or taking lessons. Sharp tempers became like razors.

Except for her hole, Egwene managed to avoid the worst of it, but only because she stayed away from the tents a good deal, largely to stay clear of Sevanna before she taught the woman a lesson. She had no doubt how that would end; Sevanna was accepted as a Wise One, no matter how many grimaces there might be when she was not around. Amys and Bair would probably let the Shaido woman set her punishment. At least staying away was not too difficult. She might be an apprentice, but only Sorilea made any effort to teach her the thousand things a Wise One had to know. Until Amys and Bair gave her final permission to return to *Tel'aran'rhiod*, her days and nights were largely her own, so long as she managed to escape being snapped up with Surandha and the rest to wash dishes or gather dung for the fires or the like.

She could not understand why the days seemed to pass so slowly; she thought it must be waiting on Amys and Bair. Gawyn was at The Long Man every morning. She became used to the fat innkeeper's suggestive smirks, though once or twice she did think of kicking the woman. Maybe three times; no more than that. Those hours went by in a flash. No sooner did she sit on his knee than it was time to straighten her hair and leave. Sitting on his knee no longer frightened her. Not that it had ever frightened her, exactly, but it had come to be more than pleasant. If she sometimes thought things she should not have, if those thoughts made her blush, well, he always brushed her face with his fingers when she blushed, and said her name in a way she could have spent a lifetime hearing. He let slip less about what was going on with the Aes Sedai than she learned elsewhere, and she could hardly make herself care.

It was the other hours that dragged out as though mired in mud. There was so little to do that she thought she might burst from frustration. Wise Ones keeping watch on Arilyn's mansion reported no more Aes Sedai. Chosen from those who could channel, the watchers said the Aes Sedai were still wielding the Power inside day and night without break, but Egwene did not dare go close, and if she had, she could have not told what they were doing without seeing the flows. Had the Wise Ones been less snappish, she might have tried to spend time reading in her tent, but the one time she touched a book except at night by lamplight, Bair muttered so about girls wasting their days lying about lazily that Egwene murmured that she had forgotten something and scurried out of the tent before she was found something more useful to do. A few moments' conversation with another apprentice could be as dangerous. Stopping to talk with Surandha, who was hiding in the shade cast by a tent belonging to some Stone Dogs, earned her an afternoon doing laundry when Sorilea found them. She might actually have been glad of chores, just for something to do, but Sorilea examined the perfectly clean wash hung inside the tent to keep off the ever-present dust, sniffed and told them to do it again. Twice she told them to do it again! Sevanna watched part of that too.

Being in the city always made Egwene look over her shoulder, yet on the third day, she picked her way down to the docks as cautiously as a mouse stealing from a cat. A wizened fellow with a narrow little boat scratched his thinning hair and demanded a silver mark to row her out to the Sea Folk ship. Everything was dear, but that was ridiculous. She fixed him with a level stare, told him he could have a silver penny—still far too much, really—and hoped the bargaining would not take her whole purse; she did not have much. Everybody jumped and flinched at the Aiel, but when it came to bargaining, they forgot all about *cadin'sor* and spears and fought like lions. He opened his toothless mouth, closed it, peered at her, then muttered under his breath and to her surprise told her she was stealing the bread out of his mouth.

"Get in," he grumbled. "Get in. I cannot waste all day for a pittance. Browbeating a man. Stealing the bread." He went on like that even after he began working the oars, pulling the tiny boat out onto the broad waters of the Alguenya.

Egwene did not know whether Rand had met this Wavemistress, but she hoped he had. According to Elayne, the Dragon Reborn was the Sea Folk Coramoor, the Chosen One, and all he had to do was appear to have them running at his beck and call. She hoped they did not grovel too much, though. Rand got more than enough of that already. Still, it was not Rand that sent her out with the muttering boatman. Elayne had actually met some of the Atha'an Miere, had traveled on one of their ships, and she said Sea Folk Windfinders could channel. Some of them anyway; maybe most. That was a secret the Atha'an Miere held close, but the Windfinder on Elayne's vessel had been more than willing to share her knowledge once her secret was penetrated. Sea Folk Windfinder knew weather. Elayne claimed they knew more of weather than the Aes Sedai. She said the Windfinder on her ship had worked enormous flows to produce favorable winds. Egwene had no idea how much of that was true and how much enthusiasm, but learning a little about weather would certainly be better that twiddling her thumbs and wondering whether being caught by Nesune might be a relief from the Wise Ones and Sevanna. With what she knew now, she could not have made it rain if the skies were black except for lightning. At the moment, of course, the sun burned golden in a cloudless sky and heat shimmers danced over the dark water. At least the dust did not make it far onto the river.

When the boatman finally drew in his oars and let the small craft drift beside the ship, Egwene stood up, ignoring his mutters that she would have them both in the river. "Hello!" she called. "Hello? May I come aboard?"

She had been on several riverboats and was proud that she knew the right terms—shipfolk seemed touchy about the right words—but this vessel was outside her experience. She had seen river craft longer, a few, but none so tall. Some of the crew were in the rigging, or clambering up the slanted masts, dark bare-chested men, barefoot in wide, colorful trousers held up by bright sashes, dark women in bright blouses as well.

She was just at the point of shouting again, louder, when a rope ladder uncoiled down the side of the ship. No answering call came from the deck, yet that seemed invitation enough. Egwene climbed. It was difficult—not the climb, but keeping her skirts decently close; she could see why the Sea Folk women wore trousers—but finally she reached the rail.

Immediately her eyes fell on a woman not a span away on the deck. Her blouse and trousers were blue silk, with a darker sash. She wore three worked gold rings in each ear, and a fine chain that supported tiny glittering medallions ran from one to a ring in her nose. Elayne had described this, and even demonstrated using *Tel'aran'rhiod*, but seeing it in the flesh made Egwene wince. But there was something else. She could sense the ability to channel. She had found the Windfinder.

She opened her mouth, and a dark hand flashed in front of her eyes with a gleaming dagger. Before she could scream, the blade sliced through the ropes of the ladder. Still clinging to the useless thing, she plummeted.

She did scream then—for all of a heartbeat, before she went into the river feet first, plunging deep. Water rushed into her open mouth, drowning her scream; she thought she swallowed half the river. Frantically she struggled to unwrap her skirts from around her head and rid herself of the ladder. She was not in a panic. She was not. How far down had she gone? It was all muddy darkness around her. Which way was up? Iron bands gripped her chest, but she breathed out through her nose, watched the bubbles stream, as it seemed to her, down and to her left. Twisting, she stroked for the surface. How far? Lungs burning.

Her head broke through into daylight, and she sucked in air with a coughing gasp. To her surprise, the boatman reached down and hauled her into his boat by increments, muttering at her to stop thrashing before she upset them, adding that Sea Folk were a touchy lot. He leaned over again to reclaim her shawl before it sank once more. She snatched it from him, and he shied back as if he thought she meant to hit him with it. Her skirts hung heavily, her blouse and shift clung; her head scarf slanted across her forehead. A pool began to form in the bottom of the boat under her feet.

The boat had drifted maybe twenty paces from the ship. The Windfinder was at the railing now, and two more women, one in plain green silk, the other brocaded red worked with gold thread. Their earrings and nose rings and chains caught the sun.

"You are refused the gift of passage," the green-clad woman called, and the one in red shouted, "Tell the other, disguises do not fool us. You do not frighten us. You are all refused the gift of passage!"

The wizened boatman picked up his oars, but Egwene pointed a finger straight at his narrow nose. "Stop right where you are." He stopped. Dunking her. Not a word of common courtesy.

Drawing a deep breath, she embraced *saidar* and channeled four flows before the Windfinder could react. So she knew weather, did she? Could she divide her flows four ways? Not many Aes Sedai could. One flow was Spirit, a shield she shoved onto the Windfinder to keep her from interfering. If she knew how. Each of the other three was Air, woven almost delicately around each woman, binding her arms to her sides. Lifting them was not precisely difficult, but not easy either.

A clamor rose on the ship as the women floated into the air and out over the river. Egwene heard the boatman moaning. She was not interested in him. The three Sea Folk women did not even kick. With an effort she hoisted them higher, some ten or twelve paces above the surface; no matter how hard she strained, that seemed to be the limit. *Well, you don't want to actually hurt them,* she thought, and released the weaves. *They'll scream now.*

The Sea Folk women curled into balls as soon as they began to fall, spun, straightened with their arms thrust out before them. They entered the water with three quite small splashes. Moments later three dark heads broke the surface, and the women began swimming rapidly back toward the ship.

Egwene closed her mouth. *If I haul them up by their ankles and dunk their heads, they'll. . . .* What was she thinking? They had to scream because she had? She was no wetter than they. *I must look like a drowned rat!* She channeled carefully—working about yourself always took care; you could not see the flows clearly—and water rolled off her, oozed out of her garments. It made quite a puddle.

It was the boatman staring at her, mouth hanging open and eyes wide, that made her realize what she had done. Channeled, in the middle of the river, with nothing to hide her from any Aes Sedai who happened to be where she could see. Sun or no sun, she suddenly felt cold to the bone.

"You may take me back to shore now." No telling who was on the docks; at this distance she could not tell a man from a woman. "Not to the city. The riverbank." The fellow flung himself against his oars so hard she almost fell over backward.

He took her to a spot where the shore was all smooth rocks the size of her head. There was no one in sight, but she leaped out as soon as the boat grated onto the rocks, hoisted her skirts and darted up the sloping bank at a dead run she maintained all the way back to her tent where she collapsed in a panting pile of sweat. She did not go near the city again. Except to meet Gawyn, of course.

The days passed, and the now almost ceaseless wind carried waves of dust and grit day and night. On the fifth night, Bair accompanied Egwene into the World of Dreams, just a quick jaunt in the nature of a test, a walk in the part of *Tel'aran'rhiod* that Bair knew best, the Aiel Waste, a parched jagged land that made even drought-torn Cairhien seem lush and fair. A quick trip, and then Bair and Amys came to wake her and see whether it had had any ill effect. It had not. No matter how they made her run and jump, no matter how often they peered into her eyes and listened to her heart, they agreed, but agreement or not, the next night Amys took her for another short trip to the Waste, followed by another examination that made her glad to crawl onto her pallet and fall into a deep sleep.

Those two nights she did not return to the World of Dreams, but it was more exhaustion than anything else. Before that she had told herself every night she should stop—a fine thing if she was caught violating their strictures just when they were ready to lift them—but somehow she always decided that just a short trip would be all right, quick enough to reduce the chance of exposure. One thing she did avoid was the place between *Tel'aran'rhiod* and the waking world, the place where dreams floated. Especially she avoided it after she found herself thinking that if she was very careful she might be able to peek into Gawyn's dreams without being drawn in, and that even if she was pulled in, it would only be a dream. She reminded herself firmly that she was a grown woman, not a silly girl. She was just glad no one else knew what a snarl the man made of her thoughts. Amys and Bair would laugh till they cried.

On the seventh night, she prepared herself for bed carefully, putting on a fresh shift and brushing her hair till it shone. All useless so far as *Tel'aran'rhiod* was concerned, but it kept her from thinking about how her stomach was doing backflips. Tonight it would be Aes Sedai waiting in the Heart of the Stone, not Nynaeve or Elayne. That should make no difference, unless. . . . The ivory-backed hairbrush froze in midstroke. Unless one of the Aes Sedai revealed that she was only Accepted. Why had she not thought of that before? Light, but she wished she could talk with Nynaeve and Elayne. Only, she could not see what good it would do, and she was certain that dream of breaking things meant something would go badly wrong if she did speak to them.

Chewing her lip, she considered going to Amys and telling her she was not feeling well. Nothing serious, just an upset stomach, but she did not think she could visit the dream tonight. They were going to start her lessons again after tonight's meeting, but. . . . Another lie, and a coward's way to boot. She would not be a coward. Not everyone could be as brave as everyone else, but cowardice was despicable. Whatever happened tonight, she had to make herself face it, and that was that.

Firmly she put down the brush, blew out the lamp and crawled onto her pallet. She was tired enough that falling asleep presented no problem, though if necessary she knew how to put herself to sleep at any time now, or enter a light trance where she could be in the World of Dreams and still talk—well, mumble—to someone waiting by her body. The last thing before sleep came, she realized something surprising. Her stomach was not turning over anymore.

She stood in a great vaulted chamber forested with thick columns of polished redstone. The Heart of the Stone, in the Stone of Tear. Gilded lamps hung from chains overhead. Unlit, but there was of course light, coming from everywhere and nowhere. Amys and Bair were already there, looking no different than they had that morning, except that all their necklaces and bracelets sparkled a bit more than even gold really should have. They were talking quietly, and looking irritated. Egwene caught only a word here and there, but two of them were "Rand al'Thor."

Abruptly she realized she was wearing an Accepted's white dress with the banded hem. As soon as she did, it became a copy of the Wise Ones' garb, without jewelry. She did not think the other two women had noticed, or would know what the dress meant if they did. There were times when surrender lost less *ji* and earned less *toh* than the alternatives, but no Aiel would ever consider it without even trying to fight.

"They are late again," Amys said wryly, walking out into the open space beneath the chamber's great dome. Driven into the floorstones there was what appeared to be a sword made of crystal, *Callandor* of prophecy, a male *sa'angreal* and one of the most powerful ever made. Rand had put it there to remind the Tairens of him, as if there was any chance of them forgetting, but Amys barely glanced at it. To others The Sword That Is Not a Sword might be a symbol of the Dragon Reborn; to her, it was a wetlander concern. "At least we can hope they will not try to pretend they know everything and we nothing. They were much better, last time."

Bair's snort would have made Sorilea blink. "They will never be better. The least they can do is be where they said they would be when they said they—" She cut off as seven women appeared suddenly on the other side of *Callandor.*

Egwene recognized them, including the young woman with the determined blue eyes she had seen before in *Tel'aran'rhiod.* Who was she? Amys and Bair had mentioned the others—usually in acid tones—but never another. She wore a blue-fringed shawl; they all wore their shawls. Their dresses changed color and cut from moment to moment, but the shawls never flickered.

The Aes Sedai's eyes focused immediately on Egwene. The Wise Ones might as well not have existed.

"Egwene al'Vere," Sheriam said formally, "you are summoned before the Hall of the Tower." Her tilted green eyes shone with some suppressed emotion. Egwene's stomach sank; they knew she had been masquerading as a full sister.

"Ask not why you are summoned," Carlinya said right behind Sheriam, her icy voice making the formality even harder. "It is yours to answer, not to question." For some reason she had cut her dark hair short; that was the sort of unimportant detail that seemed to loom large in Egwene's mind. She certainly did not want to think about what this all meant. The ceremonious phrases rolled on in a stately rhythm. Amys and Bair adjusted their shawls and frowned, their irritation beginning to turn to concern.

"Delay not in your coming." Egwene had always thought Anaiya kindly, but the bluff-faced woman sounded as firm as Carlinya, and not all that much warmer in her formality. "It is yours to obey in haste."

The three spoke in unison. "It is well to fear the summons of the Hall.

It is well to obey in haste and humility, unasking. You are summoned to kneel before the Hall of the Tower and accept their judgment."

Egwene controlled her breathing, at least enough that she managed not to pant. What was the penalty for what she had done? Not light, she suspected, not if all this ceremony went with it. They were all staring at her. She tried to read something on those Aes Sedai faces. Six showed only ageless serenity, with maybe a hint of intensity in the eyes. The young Blue had the cool calmness of one who had been Aes Sedai for years, but she could not hide a slight, satisfied smile.

They seemed to be waiting for something. "I will come as soon as I can," she said. Maybe her stomach was down in her ankles, but she could match them with her voice. No cowardice. She *would* be Aes Sedai. If they let her, after this. "I don't know how quickly, though. It's a long way, and I do not know exactly where Salidar is. Just somewhere along the River Eldar."

Sheriam exchanged glances with the others. Her dress went from pale blue silk to dark gray, with divided skirts. "We are sure there is a way to make the journey quickly. If the Wise Ones will help. Siuan is sure it will require no more than a day or two if you enter *Tel'aran'rhiod* physically—"

"No," Bair snapped at the same instant Amys said, "We will not teach her such a thing. It was used for evil, it is evil, and whoever does it loses part of themselves."

"You cannot be sure of this," Beonin said patiently, "since it seems none of you have ever done it. But if you know of it, you must have some notion of how it is done. We may be able to work out what you do not know."

Patience was exactly the wrong tone. Amys settled her shawl and stood up even straighter than usual. Bair planted fists on hips with a glare that showed teeth. In a moment there was going to be one of those eruptions the Wise Ones had hinted at. They were going to teach these Aes Sedai a few lessons about what could be done in *Tel'aran'rhiod* by way of showing them how little they knew. The Aes Sedai faced them quite calmly, full of confidence. Their shawls held steady, but their dresses flickered almost as fast as Egwene's heartbeat. Only the young Blue's garb had any semblance of holding, changing just once during that long silence.

She had to stop it. She had to go to Salidar, and it certainly would help nothing if she came as witness to the humiliation of these Aes Sedai. "I know how. I think I do. I'm willing to try." If it did not work, she could always ride. "But I still have to know where. Better than I do now, anyway."

Amys and Bair turned their attention from the Aes Sedai to her. Not even Carlinya could have equaled those cold stares, or Morvrin. Egwene's heart sank after her stomach.

Sheriam immediately began giving directions—so many miles west of this village, so many leagues south of that—but the young Blue cleared her throat and said, "This may be more help." The voice sounded familiar, but Egwene could not connect it to the face.

Perhaps she had little better control of her clothing than the others— soft green silk became deep blue as she spoke, a high, embroidered neck became a lace ruff in the Tairen style, a cap of pearls appeared on her head—but she did know something of *Tel'aran'rhiod*. Suddenly a large map hung in the air to one side, with a glowing red dot at one end labeled "Cairhien" in large letters and another as "Salidar" at the other. The map began to expand and change; suddenly the mountains were not just lines, but raised up, the forests took on shades of green and brown, the rivers glittered like blue water in sunlight. It grew until it made a wall hiding the entire side of the Heart. It was like looking down on the world.

Even the Wise Ones were impressed enough to ignore their disapproval, at least, until the woman's Tairen gown turned to yellow silk with a silver-embroidered neckline. The young woman was not interested in them, though. For some reason she stared challengingly at the other Aes Sedai.

"That is splendid, Siuan," Sheriam said after a moment.

Egwene blinked. Siuan? It must be a woman of the same name. This younger Siuan gave a self-satisfied sniff and a sharp nod very reminiscent of Siuan Sanche, but that was impossible. *You're just trying to put it off*, she told herself firmly. "It's certainly enough for me to find Salidar, whether or not I can. . . ." She glanced at Amys and Bair, so full of silent disapproval they could have been carved of winter stone. "Whether or not I can come here in the flesh. One way or another, I promise I will be in Salidar as soon as I can." The map vanished. *Light, what are they going to do to me?*

Her mouth half-formed the question, and Carlinya cut her off sharply, deep in the ceremony again and even harder than before. "Ask not why you are summoned. It is yours to answer, not to question."

"Delay not in your coming," Anaiya said. "It is yours to obey in haste."

The Aes Sedai exchanged glances and vanished so quickly she half-wondered whether they thought she would ask anyway.

That left her alone with Amys and Bair, but when she turned to them, uncertain whether to begin with an explanation or an apology or just a plea for understanding, they vanished too, leaving her there alone, surrounded by the redstone columns, with *Callandor* glittering beside her. There were no excuses in *ji'e'toh*.

Exhaling sadly, she stepped out of *Tel'aran'rhiod* back to her sleeping body.

She woke immediately; waking when you wished was as much a part of a dreamwalker's training as going to sleep when you wished, and she had promised to go as quickly as she could. Channeling, she lit the lamps, all of them. She would need light. She made an effort to be brisk as she knelt beside one of the small chests that stood against the walls of the tent and began digging out clothes she had not worn since going to the Waste. A part of her life was over, but she would not cry over the loss. She would not.

As soon as Egwene disappeared, Rand stepped out from among the columns. He came here sometimes, to look at *Callandor*. The first visit had been after Asmodean taught him to invert his weaves. Then he had changed the traps laid around the *sa'angreal* so only he could see them. If the Prophecies could be believed, whoever drew it out would "follow after" him. He was not sure how much he did believe any longer, but there was no sense taking chances.

Lews Therin rumbled somewhere in the back of his head—he always did when Rand came close to *Callandor*—but tonight the gleaming crystal sword interested Rand not at all. He stared at where the huge map had hung. Not really a map, there at the end, but something more. What was this place? Was it simple chance that drew him here tonight instead of yesterday, or tomorrow? One of his *ta'veren* tugs on the Pattern? No matter. Egwene had accepted that summons meekly, and that she would never do if it came from the Tower and Elaida. This Salidar was where her mysterious friends were hiding. Where Elayne was. They had handed themselves to him.

Laughing, he opened a gateway to the reflection of the Palace in Caemlyn.

CHAPTER
33

Courage to Strengthen

Kneeling in just her shift, Egwene frowned at the dark green silk riding dress she had worn into the Waste, what seemed a very long time ago. There was so much to do. She had given some time to writing a hasty note and rousing Cowinde from her blankets with instructions to leave it at The Long Man in the morning. It said little beyond the fact that she had to go away—she did not know much more—but she could not just disappear without telling Gawyn. A few of the phrases made her blush to remember—saying she loved him was one thing, but actually *asking* him to wait!—yet she had taken care of him as far as was possible. Now she had to ready herself, and she hardly knew for what.

The tent flap was thrown back, and Amys entered, then Bair and Sorilea. They stood in a line, looking down at her. Three faces stern with disapproval. It was very hard not to clutch the dress to her breast; in her shift, she felt very much at a disadvantage. In armor, she would have been at a disadvantage. A matter of knowing she was in the wrong. She was surprised it had taken them so long to come.

She took a deep breath. "If you've come to punish me, I don't have time for carrying water or digging holes or any of it. I am sorry, but I said I would come as soon as I can, and I think they mean to count minutes."

Amys' pale eyebrows rose in surprise, and a puzzled look passed between Sorilea and Bair. "How should we punish you?" Amys asked. "You stopped being a pupil the moment your sisters summoned you. You must go to them as Aes Sedai."

Egwene covered a wince by examining the riding dress again. It had gathered remarkably few wrinkles for having been rolled up in a chest all these months. She made herself face them again. "I know you're angry with me, and you have cause—"

"Angry?" Sorilea said. "We are not angry. I thought you knew us better." It was true she did not sound angry, yet censure still painted all their faces, including hers.

Egwene stared from one to another, especially Amys and Bair. "But you told me how wrong you think what I'm going to do is; you said I must not even think about it. I said I wouldn't, and then I went ahead and worked out how to do it."

Startlingly, a smile bloomed on Sorilea's leathery face. Her multitude of bracelets clattered as she shifted her shawl in a satisfied manner. "You see? I told you she would understand. She could be Aiel."

Some of the tightness faded from Amys, a little more from Bair, and Egwene understood. They were not angry that she meant to try entering *Tel'aran'rhiod* in the flesh. That was wrong in their eyes, but you had to do what you felt you had to do, and even if this worked it incurred no obligation except to herself. Not angry at all really, not yet. What dug at them was her lie. Her stomach fluttered. The lie she had admitted. Maybe her smallest lie.

Another deep breath was required to prime her throat for the words. "I lied about other things, too. I entered *Tel'aran'rhiod* alone after I promised I would not." Amys' face darkened again. Sorilea, not a dreamwalker, only shook her head ruefully. "I promised to obey as a pupil, but when you said the World of Dreams was too dangerous after I was injured, I went anyway." Bair folded her arms, expressionless. Sorilea muttered something about foolish girls, but it hardly sounded heated. A third long breath; this would be the hardest to say. Her middle was not fluttering anymore; it danced so hard she was surprised she was not shaking. "The worst of all is, I am not Aes Sedai. I'm only Accepted. You might call me an apprentice. I will not be raised to Aes Sedai for years, if I ever am, now."

Sorilea's head came up at that, thin lips compressed in a hard line, but still none of them said anything. It was up to Egwene to make matters right. They could never be exactly as before, but. . . .

You've admitted everything, a small voice whispered. *Now you'd better get on with finding out how fast you can reach Salidar. You can still be raised Aes Sedai one day, but not if you make them madder than they already are.*

Egwene lowered her eyes and stared at the colorful layered carpets, her mouth twisting with scorn. Scorn for that small voice. And shame that it could speak in her head, that she could think it. She was going away, but before she did, she had to put matters right. It was possible, under *ji'e'toh*. You did what you had to do, then paid the cost. Long months ago, in the Waste, Aviendha had showed her how a lie was paid for.

Gathering every scrap of courage she could find, hoping it was enough, Egwene put the silk dress aside and stood. Strangely, beginning seemed to make going on easier. She still had to look up to meet their, eyes, but she did it proudly, head high, and she did not have to force the words at all. "I have *toh*." Her stomach was not fluttering any longer. "I ask the favor, that you will help me meet my *toh*." Salidar was going to have to wait.

Leaning on his elbow, Mat examined the game of Snakes and Foxes laid out on the tent floor. Occasionally a drop of sweat fell from his chin, just missing the board. It was not a board at all, really, just a piece of red cloth with the web of lines drawn in black ink, and arrows showing which lines allowed movement only one way and which both. Ten pale wooden discs each with an inked triangle were the foxes, ten with a wavy line the snakes. Two lamps set to either side gave more than enough light.

"We will win this time, Mat," Olver said excitedly. "I know we will."

"Maybe," Mat said. Their two black-stained discs were nearly back to the circle in the middle of the board, but the next roll of the dice would be for the snakes and foxes. Most of the time you did not make it as far as the outer edge. "Roll the dice." He never touched the dice cup himself, not since the day he had given it to the boy; if they were going to play the game, it might as well be without his luck taking a hand.

With a grin, Olver rattled the leather cup and spilled out the wooden dice his father had made. He groaned as he counted the pips; this time three dice showed faces marked with a triangle, the other three wavy lines. On their turn you had to move the snakes and foxes toward your own pieces by the shortest path, and if one landed on the point you occupied. . . . A snake touched Olver, a fox Mat, and Mat could see if the rest of the pips had been played, two more snakes would have reached him.

Only a child's game, and one you would not win so long as you followed the rules. Soon Olver would be old enough to realize that, and like other children, stop playing. Only a child's game, but Mat did not like the fox getting him, and even less the snakes. It brought back bad memories, even if one had nothing to do with the other.

"Well," Olver muttered, "we almost won. Another game, Mat?" Not waiting for an answer, he made the sign that opened the game, a triangle and then a wavy line through it, then chanted the words. " 'Courage to strengthen, fire to blind, music to dazzle, iron to bind.' Mat, why do we say that? There is no fire, no music and no iron."

"I don't know." The line tickled something in the back of his head, but he could not bring it up. The old memories from the *ter'angreal* might as well have been chosen at random—they probably had been—and there were all those gaps in his own, all those fuzzy places. The boy was always asking questions he did not know the answer to, usually beginning with "why."

Daerid ducked in out of the night and gave a start of surprise. Face shining with sweat, he still had his coat on, if hanging undone. His newest scar made a pink furrow across the white lines crisscrossing his face.

"I think it's past your bedtime, Olver," Mat said, pushing himself up. His wounds gave a few twinges, but only a few; they were healing just fine. "Put the board up." He stepped close to Daerid and lowered his voice to a whisper. "If you ever tell about this, I'll cut your throat."

"Why?" Daerid asked dryly. "You are turning into a wonderful father. He shows a remarkable resemblance to you." He seemed to be struggling with a grin, but a moment later it was gone. "The Lord Dragon is coming into camp," he said, as serious as death.

Thoughts of punching Daerid in the nose vanished. Mat pushed the tent flap aside and ducked into the night in his shirtsleeves. Six of Daerid's men, in a circle around the tent, stiffened when he appeared. Crossbowmen; pikes certainly would not be much good for guards. It was night, but not dark in the camp. The bright glow of a waxing three-quarter moon in a cloudless sky was washed out by the light of fires spaced among the rows of tents and men sleeping on the ground. Sentries stood every twenty paces all the way to the log palisade. Not the way Mat would have preferred it, but if an attack could pop out of the air. . . .

The land lay nearly flat here, so he had a clear view of Rand striding toward him. Not alone. Two veiled Aiel moved on their toes, heads swiveling every time one of the Band rolled over in his sleep or a sentry shifted his feet to watch them. That Aiel woman Aviendha was with him as well, a bundle across her back, stalking along as if she would go for the throat of anyone who got in her way. Mat did not understand why Rand kept her around. *Aielwomen are nothing but trouble,* he thought bleakly, *and I've never seen a woman more set to give trouble than that one.*

"Is that really the Dragon Reborn?" Olver asked breathlessly. Clutching the rolled-up game to his chest, he was almost bouncing.

"It is," Mat told him. "Now get off to bed. This is no place for boys."

Olver went, muttering reproachfully, but only as far as the next tent. Out of the corner of his eye Mat saw the boy dart out of sight; his face reappeared, peering around the corner.

Mat left him alone, though after getting a good look at Rand's face, he wondered whether this was any place for grown men, let alone a boy. That face could have been used to hammer down a wall, but some emotion struggled to break through, excitement or maybe eagerness; Rand's eyes held a fevered light. He had a wide piece of rolled parchment in one hand, while the other stroked his sword hilt unconsciously. The Dragon belt buckle glittered in the firelight; sometimes the head of one of the Dragons peeking out from his coatsleeves did too.

When he reached Mat, he wasted no time with greetings. "I need to talk to you. Alone. I need you to do something." The night was a black oven, and Rand wore a gold-embroidered green coat with a high collar, but he was not sweating a drop.

Daerid, Talmanes and Nalesean stood a few paces away in various states of undress, watching. Mat motioned them to wait, then nodded toward his tent. Following Rand in, he fingered the silver foxhead though his shirt. He had nothing to worry about, at least. He hoped he did not.

Rand had said alone, but apparently Aviendha did not think that applied to her. She stayed a firm two paces from him, no more and no less; mostly she watched Rand with an unreadable face, but now and then she glanced at Mat, frowning and eyeing him up and down. Rand paid her no attention, and for all his seeming haste before, he showed none now. He looked around the tent, though Mat wondered uneasily whether he was seeing it. There was not much to see. Olver had set the lamps back on the small folding table. The chair folded, too, and so did the washstand and the cot. All were black-lacquered, with lines of gilt; if a man had coin, he might as well spend it on something. The slits the Aiel had made in the tent wall had been mended neatly, but they still showed.

The silence dug at Mat. "What is this, Rand? I hope you haven't decided to change the plan at this late date." No answer, only a look as if Rand had just remembered he was there. It made Mat nervous. Whatever Daerid and the rest of the Band thought, he worked hard at keeping clear of battles. Sometimes, though, being *ta'veren* worked against his luck; that was the way he saw it. He believed Rand had something to do with that; he was more strongly *ta'veren*, strong enough that at times Mat almost felt a pulling. When Rand put his finger in, Mat would not be surprised to find himself in the middle of a battle if he was asleep in a barn. "A few more days, and I'll be in Tear. The ferries will take the Band across the river, and a few days beyond that will see us with Weiramon. It's too bloody late to go meddling—"

"I want you to bring Elayne to . . . to Caemlyn," Rand broke in. "I want you to see her safe to Caemlyn, whatever happens. Don't leave her side until she's on the Lion Throne." Aviendha cleared her throat. "Yes," Rand said. For some reason his voice went as cold and hard as his face. But then, did he need reasons if he was going mad? "Aviendha is going with you. I think it's best."

"*You* think it is best?" she said indignantly. "If I had not wakened when I did, I would never have known you had found her. You do not send me anywhere, Rand al'Thor. I must speak with Elayne for my . . . my own reasons."

"I am very glad you've found Elayne," Mat said carefully. If he was Rand, he would leave the woman wherever she was. Light, Aviendha would be better! At least Aielwomen did not walk around with their noses in the air, or think you should jump just because they said so. Of course, some of their games were on the rough side, and they did have the habit of trying to kill you now and again. "I just don't understand why you need me. Jump through one of your gateways, give her a kiss, scoop her up and jump back." Aviendha fastened an outraged stare on him; you would have thought he had advised kissing her.

Rand unrolled the large parchment on the table, using the lamps to hold down the ends. "This is where she is." It was a map, a stretch of the River Eldar and maybe fifty miles or so to either side. An arrow had been drawn in blue ink, pointing into forest. "Salidar" was printed beside the arrow. Rand tapped near the eastern edge of the map. That was wooded, too; most of it was. "There is a large clearing here. You can see the nearest village is nearly twenty miles north. I'll put a gateway through to the clearing for you and the Band."

Mat managed to turn a wince into a grin. "Look, if it has to be me, why not just me? Make your gateway to this Salidar, I'll toss her on a horse, and . . ." And what? Was Rand going to make a gateway from Salidar to Caemlyn as well? It was a long way to ride, from the Eldar to Caemlyn. A very long way, with only a snooty noblewoman and an Aiel for company.

"The Band, Mat," Rand snapped. "You and the whole Band!" He drew a long shuddering breath, and his tone became milder. His face did not lose its rigidity, though, and his eyes were still feverish. Mat could almost believe he was sick, or in pain. "There are Aes Sedai in Salidar, Mat. I don't know how many; hundreds, I've heard, but I won't be surprised if it is closer to fifty. The way they go on about the Tower, whole and pure, I doubt you'll see more. I mean to put you out two or three days away so they can learn you're coming. No point in startling them—they might think you were a Whitecloak attack. They're rebels against Elaida, and probably frightened enough that you won't have to do more than loom a little and say Elayne has to be crowned in Caemlyn to make them let her go. If you think they can be trusted, offer your protection. And mine; they're supposed to be on my side, and they might be glad of even my protection by now. Then you escort Elayne—and as many of the Aes Sedai as want to come—straight across Altara and Murandy to Caemlyn. Show my banners, announce what you're doing, and I don't think the Altarans or Murandians will give much trouble, not as long as you keep moving. If you find any Dragonsworn along the way, gather them in as well. Most will probably turn to bandits if I don't tie a rope to them soon—I've heard a rumor or two already—but you will draw them, flying my banners." His sudden grin showed teeth, but never touched those hot eyes. "How many birds with one stone, Mat? You ride through Altara and Murandy with six thousand men and draw the Dragonsworn out after you, and you may hand me both countries."

There was so much in that to set Mat's teeth on edge that he no longer cared whether Rand had ten sore teeth and both boots full of cockleburrs. Make Aes Sedai think he meant to attack them? Indeed not. And he was supposed to intimidate fifty of them? Aes Sedai did not frighten him, maybe not even five or six together, but fifty? He touched the foxhead through his shirt again before he realized it; he might just find out how lucky he really was. As for riding across Altara and Murandy, he could see it now. Every noble whose lands he crossed would swell up like a strutting rooster and try to peck him the moment his back was turned. If that *ta'veren* madness came into it, he would probably find some lord or lady gathering an army right in front of him.

He made one more try. "Rand, don't you think this might draw Sammael's eyes north? You want him looking east. That is why I'm here, remember? To make him look this way."

Rand shook his head emphatically. "All he'll see is a guard of honor escorting the Queen of Andor to Caemlyn, and that's if he learns of it before you reach Caemlyn. How quickly can you be ready?"

Mat opened his mouth, then gave it up. He was not going to budge the man. "Two hours." The Band could be booted and in their saddles faster, but he was in no hurry, and the last thing he wanted was the Band thinking they were moving on the attack.

"Good. I need an hour or so myself." For what, he did not say. "Stay close to Elayne, Mat. Keep her safe. I mean, there's no point to this if she doesn't reach Caemlyn alive for her coronation." Did Rand think he did not know about him and Elayne canoodling in every corner of the Stone the last time they were together?

"I'll treat her like my own sister." His sisters had done their best to make his life miserable. Well, he expected the same from Elayne, just in a different way. Maybe Aviendha would be a little better. "She won't get out of my sight until I plunk her down in the Royal Palace." *And if she tries Mistress Snoot on with me too often, I'll bloody well kick her!*

Rand nodded. "That reminds me. Bodewhin is in Caemlyn. With Verin and Alanna, and some more Two Rivers girls. They're on their way to train for Aes Sedai. I'm not sure where they will do it; I am certainly not letting them go to the Tower the way things are. Maybe the Aes Sedai you bring back will take care of it."

Mat gaped. His sister, Aes Sedai? Bode, who used to run tell their mother every time he did anything that was fun?

"Another thing," Rand went on. "Egwene may be in Salidar before you. I think somehow they found out she's been calling herself Aes Sedai. Do what you can to get her out of it. Tell her I will get her back to the Wise Ones as soon as I can. She'll probably be more than ready to go with you. Maybe not, though; you know how stubborn she's always been. The main thing is Elayne. Remember, don't leave her side till she reaches Caemlyn."

"I promise," Mat muttered. How under the Light could Egwene be somewhere on the Eldar? He was sure she had been in Cairhien when he left Maerone. Unless she had worked out Rand's trick with the gateways. In which case she could jump back any time she wished. Or jump to Caemlyn, and make a gateway for him and the Band at the same time. "Don't worry about Egwene, either. I'll drag her out of whatever trouble she's in, no matter how muley she behaves." It would not be the first time he had pulled her chestnuts off the hearth before they burned. Very likely he would get no thanks for it this time either. *Bode* was going to be Aes Sedai? *Blood and bloody ashes!*

"Good," Rand said. "Good." But he was staring intently at the map. He jerked his eyes away, and for an instant Mat thought he intended to say something to Aviendha. Instead, he turned away from her roughly. "Thom Merrilin should be with Elayne." Rand produced a letter from his pocket, folded and sealed. "See that he gets this." Shoving the letter into Mat's hands, he hurriedly left the tent.

Aviendha took a step after him, half-raising a hand, lips parted to speak. Just as suddenly her mouth snapped shut, and she buried her hands in her skirts and squeezed her eyes shut. So the wind came that way, did it? *And she wants to talk to Elayne.* How did Rand ever get himself in this pickle? Rand was always the one who knew how to handle women, Rand and Perrin.

Still, it was no concern of his. He turned the letter over in his hands. Thom's name was written in a feminine hand; the seal was one he recognized, a snake biting its own tail, set in blue wax. Why would an Aes Sedai be writing to a leathery old man like Thom? Not his concern either. Tossing the letter on the table, he picked up his pipe and pouch. "Olver," he said, stuffing the bowl with tabac, "ask Talmanes, Nalesean and Daerid to come to me."

There was a squeak just outside the door flap, then, "Yes, Mat," and the sound of scurrying feet.

Aviendha looked at him, folding her arms with a firm expression.

He forestalled her. "So long as you travel with the Band, you are under my command. I want no trouble, and I expect you to see there isn't any." Should she start anything, he would deliver her to Elayne tied to a pack-saddle, if it took ten men to put her there.

"I know how to follow, battle leader." She punctuated that with a sharp sniff. "But you should know that not all women are wetlander soft. If you try putting a woman on a horse when she does not want to go, she may put a knife in your ribs."

Mat nearly dropped the pipe. He knew Aes Sedai could not read minds—if they could, his hide would have been hanging on a wall in the White Tower long since—but maybe Aiel Wise Ones. . . . *Of course not. It's just one of those tricks women pull.* He could figure out how she did it if he put his mind to it. He just did not care to put his mind to it.

Clearing his throat, he stuck the unlit pipe between his teeth and bent to study the map. The Band could probably cover the distance from the clearing to Salidar in a day if he pushed, even in that wooded terrain, but he intended to take two, or even three. Give the Aes Sedai plenty of warning; he did not want them any more frightened than they already were. A frightened Aes Sedai was almost a contradiction. Even wearing the medallion he was not eager to learn what a frightened Aes Sedai might do.

He felt Aviendha's eyes on the back of his neck, heard a rasping sound. Sitting cross-legged against the tent wall, she was drawing her belt knife along a honing stone and watching him.

When Nalesean entered with Daerid and Talmanes, he greeted them with, "We are going to tickle some Aes Sedai under the chin, rescue a mule, and put a snip-nosed girl on the Lion Throne. Oh, yes. That's Aviendha. Don't look at her crosswise, or she'll try to cut your throat and probably slit her own by mistake." The woman laughed as if he had made the funniest joke in the world. She did not stop sharpening her knife, though.

For a moment Egwene could not understand why the pain had stopped increasing. Then she pushed herself up from the carpets of her tent and stood, sobbing so hard she quivered. She wanted very much to blow her nose. She did not know how long she had been crying that hard; she only knew she felt on fire from the top of her hips to the backs of her knees. Standing still was a problem she barely mastered. The shift she had thought of as scant protection had been discarded some time back. Tears rolled down her face, and she stood there and bawled.

Sorilea and Amys and Bair regarded her soberly, and they were not the only ones, though most of the rest were sitting about on cushions or stretched out, talking and enjoying tea served by a slender gai'shain. A woman, thank the Light. They were all women, Wise Ones and apprentices, women Egwene had told she was Aes Sedai. She was grateful that just letting them think she was did not count; she could not have survived that! It was the telling, the spoken lie, but there had been surprises. Cosain, a lean yellow-haired Spine Ridge Miagoma, had said gruffly that Egwene had no toh toward her but she would stay for the tea, and so had Estair. Aeron, on the other hand, seemed to want to cut her in two, and Surandha. . . .

Trying to blink away the haze of tears, Egwene glanced toward Surandha. She was sitting with three Wise Ones, chatting and occasionally looking in Egwene's direction. Surandha had been absolutely merciless. Not that any of them had gone easy. The belt Egwene had found in one of her chests was thin and supple, but twice as wide as her hand, and these women all had strong arms. A half-dozen or so strokes from each added up.

Egwene had never felt so ashamed in her life. Not that she was naked and red-faced and weeping like a baby. Well, the weeping was part. Not even that they had all watched her strapped, when not taking their own turns. What shamed her was that she had taken it so badly. An Aiel child would have been more stoic. Well, a child would never have had to face it, but the principle was the simple truth.

"Is it over?" Was that thick, unsteady voice really hers? How these women would laugh if they knew how carefully she had gathered her courage.

"Only you know the worth of your honor," Amys said flatly. She held the belt dangling at her side, using the wide buckle as a handle. The murmur of conversation had ceased.

Egwene drew a long, shaking breath through her sobs. All she had to do was say it was done, and it was. She could have said enough after one blow from each woman. She could. . . .

Wincing, she knelt and stretched herself out on the carpets. Her hands went beneath Bair's skirts to grasp the woman's bony ankles through her soft boots. This time she *would* hold on to her courage. This time she would not cry out. This time she would not kick, or thrash about, or. . . . The belt had not hit her yet. Raising her head, she blinked her eyes clear to glare at them. "What are you waiting for?" Her voice still shook, but there was more than a note of anger too. Making her *wait* on top of everything else? "I have a journey to make tonight, in case you've forgotten. Get on with it."

Amys tossed the belt down beside Egwene's head. "This woman has no *toh* toward me."

"This woman has no *toh* toward me." That was Bair's thin voice.

"This woman has no *toh* toward me," Sorilea said forcefully. Bending, she smoothed damp hair from Egwene's face. "I knew you were Aiel in your heart. Do not be overproud now, girl. You have met your *toh*. Get up before we think you are boasting."

Then they were helping her to her feet, hugging her and wiping away her tears, holding a handkerchief for her to finally blow her nose. The other women gathered around, each announcing that this woman had no *toh* toward her before adding her own hugs and smiles. It was the smiles that were the biggest shock; Surandha beamed at her as brightly as ever. But of course. *Toh* did not exist once it was met; whatever earned it might as well never have happened. A bit of Egwene that was not wrapped up in *ji'e'toh* thought that maybe what she had said at the end helped, too, as well as getting back down in the first place. Perhaps she had not faced it with the indifference of an Aiel in the beginning, but at the end, Sorilea was right.

She had been Aiel in her heart. She thought a part of her heart always would be Aiel.

The Wise Ones and apprentices left slowly. Apparently they should remain the rest of the night or longer, all laughing and talking with Egwene, but that was just custom, not *ji'e'toh*, and with Sorilea's help she managed to convince them that she just did not have the time. At last it was only her, Sorilea and the two dreamwalkers. All the hugs and smiles had slowed her tears to a trickle, and if her lips still trembled no matter what she did, she could still smile. In truth, she wanted to cry again, if for a different reason. Partly for a different reason; she *was* on fire.

"I am going to miss all of you so much."

"Nonsense." Sorilea snorted for emphasis. "If you have luck, they will tell you you can never be Aes Sedai now. Then you can return to us. You will be my apprentice. In three or four years, you will have your own hold. I even know the husband for you. My greatdaughter Amaryn's youngest greatson, Taric. He will be a clan chief one day, I think, so you must watch for a sister-wife to be his roofmistress."

"Thank you." Egwene laughed. It seemed she had something to fall back on if the Hall in Salidar did send her away.

"And Amys and I will meet you in *Tel'aran'rhiod*," Bair said, "and tell you what we know of events here, and with Rand al'Thor. You will go your own way in the World of Dreams now, but if you wish it, I will still teach you."

"I do wish it." If the Hall let her anywhere near *Tel'aran'rhiod*. But then, they could not keep her out; whatever they did, they could not do that. "Please keep a close eye on Rand and the Aes Sedai. I don't know what he is playing, but I'm sure it is more dangerous than he thinks."

Amys said nothing about more teaching, of course. She had given her word on a course of action, and even meeting *toh* did not erase that. Instead, she said, "I know Rhuarc will regret not being here tonight. He has gone north to look at the Shaido for himself. Do not be afraid your *toh* toward him must go unmet. He will give you the opportunity when you meet once more."

Egwene gaped, and covered by blowing her nose for what seemed the tenth time. She had forgotten all about Rhuarc. Of course, nothing said she *had* to pay her obligation to him in the same way. Maybe her heart was at least partly Aiel, but for a moment her mind sought frantically for another method. There had to be one. And she would have plenty of time to find it before seeing him again. "I will be very grateful," she said faintly.

And there was Melaine, too. And Aviendha. Light! She had thought she was done with it. Her feet kept shifting no matter how hard she tried to hold still. There had to be another way.

Bair opened her mouth, but Sorilea cut her off. "We must let her clothe herself. She has a journey to begin." Bair's thin neck stiffened, and Amys' mouth turned down. Clearly neither liked what Egwene was going to try any more than before.

Maybe they meant to stay and try talking her out of it, but Sorilea began muttering only half under her breath about fools who tried to stop a woman from doing what she thought she had to do. The younger pair straightened their shawls—Bair had to be seventy or eighty, but she certainly still was younger than Sorilea—gave Egwene a farewell hug and left with murmurs of, "May you always find water and shade."

Sorilea waited only a moment longer. "Think on Taric. I should have asked him to the sweat tent so you could see him. Until you can, remember this. We are always more afraid than we wish to be, but we can always be braver than we expect. Hold on to your heart, and the Aes Sedai cannot harm what is really you, your heart. They are not nearly so far above us as we believed. May you always find water and shade, Egwene. And always remember your heart."

Alone, Egwene merely stood for a time, staring at nothing and thinking. Her heart. Perhaps she did have more courage than she thought. She had done what she had to do here; she had been Aiel. In Salidar, she was going to need that. Aes Sedai methods differed from the Wise Ones' in some respects, but they would not go easy if they knew she had called herself Aes Sedai. If they knew. She could not imagine why else they would summon her so coldly, but Aiel did not surrender before battle was joined.

With a start she came to herself. *If I'm not going to surrender before fighting*, she thought wryly, *I might as well get on to the battle.*

CHAPTER
34

Journey to Salidar

E gwene washed her face. Twice. Then she found her saddlebags and filled them. Her ivory comb and brush and mirror went in, and her sewing box—a small, finely gilded casket that likely had held some lady's jewels once—plus a white cake of rose-perfumed soap and clean stockings and shifts and handkerchiefs and a host of things, until the leather sides bulged and she could hardly buckle the flaps down. Several dresses and cloaks, an Aiel shawl, remained to make a bundle, which she tied neatly with a cord. That done, she looked around for anything else she might want to take. It was all hers. Even the tent had been given to her, but that was certainly too bulky, as were the carpets and cushions. Her crystal washbasin was beautiful, and far too heavy. The same for the chests, though several had beautiful work on the strapping and lovely carving.

Only then, thinking about the chests of all things, did she realize she was trying to put off the hardest bit of getting ready. "Courage," she said dryly. "Heart of an Aiel."

It turned out to be quite possible to put on stockings without sitting down, so long as you did not mind hopping around. Stout shoes followed, good if she had to walk far, and a silk shift, white and soft. Then the dark green riding dress, with its narrow divided skirts. Unfortunately that fit quite snugly over the hips, enough to remind her, unnecessarily, that she would not enjoy sitting for a while.

There was no point going outside. Bair and Amys were probably in their own tents, but she had no intention of risking the chance one of them might see her do this. It would be like slapping them. If it worked, that was. If not, she had a very long ride ahead of her.

Nervously rubbing her fingers over her palms, she embraced *saidar*, letting it fill her. And shifted her feet. *Saidar* made you more aware of everything, including your own body, which she would just as soon have missed right then. Trying something new, something no one had ever tried before that she knew, should have been done slowly and carefully, but for once she wanted to be rid of the Source. She channeled briskly, flows of Spirit, woven just so.

The air shimmered in the middle of the tent along her weave, cloaking the other side in mistiness. If she was right, she had just created a place where the interior of her tent was so similar to its reflection in *Tel'aran'rhiod* that there was no difference at all right there. One *was* the other. But there was only one way to be sure.

Tossing the saddlebags over her shoulder, she took the bundle under one arm and stepped through the weave, then let go of *saidar*.

She was in *Tel'aran'rhiod*. All it took to tell her was that the lamps that had been lit were no longer burning, yet there was a sort of light. Things moved slightly between one glance and the next, the washbasin, a chest. She was in *Tel'aran'rhiod* in the flesh. It felt no different than when she came in a dream.

She ducked outside. A three-quarter moon shone down on tents where no fire burned and no one moved, on a Cairhien that seemed oddly distant and clouded in shadow. All that remained was the problem of actually getting to Salidar. She had thought about that. A great deal depended on whether she had as much control in the flesh as when she was part of the World of Dreams.

Fixing in her mind what she would find, she walked around the tent—and smiled. There stood Bela, the short shaggy mare she had ridden out of the Two Rivers a lifetime ago. Only a dream-Bela, but the stout mare tossed her nose and whickered at sight of her.

Egwene dropped her burdens and flung her arms around the horse's head. "I'm glad to see you again, too," she whispered. That dark liquid eye looking at her *was* Bela's, reflection or no.

Bela wore the high-cantled saddle she had imagined, too. Comfortable for long travel normally, but not soft. Egwene eyed the thing askance, wondering how it would look padded; then she had a thought. You could change anything in *Tel'aran'rhiod* if you knew how, even yourself. If she had enough control to make Bela while in the flesh. . . . She concentrated on herself.

With a smile she fastened the saddlebags and bundle behind the saddle and climbed up herself, settling quite comfortably. "It isn't cheating," she told the mare. "They would not expect me to ride all the way to Salidar like that." Well, come to think of it, maybe they would. Even so, Aiel heart or no Aiel heart, there were limits. Turning Bela, she heeled the mare's ribs gently. "I need to be as quick as I can, so you will need to run like the wind."

Before she had time to chuckle at the image that came to mind of plump Bela running like the wind, the mare was doing so. The landscape blurred, streaking by. For a moment Egwene clung to the pommel of the saddle, her mouth hanging open. It was as if Bela's every trotting step carried them miles. With the first she had an instant to realize they were on the riverbank below the city, with ships floating out on the dark waters amid streaks of moonlight, and even as she tried to jerk at the reins, to stop Bela running headlong into the river, another step took them into thicketed hills.

Egwene threw back her head and laughed. This was marvelous! Except for the blurring, there was little real sensation of speed; her hair hardly had time to stream back in the wind of that rush before it was gone, only to come again a moment later. Bela's gait felt the same plodding trot she recalled, but the sudden leap of everything around her was exhilarating, one moment a village street, moon-dark and silent, the next a country road winding through hills, the next a meadow with hay standing almost to Bela's shoulders. Egwene only paused now and again to orient herself—no trouble at all with that marvelous map in her head, the one the woman with Siuan's name had made—and otherwise let Bela trot. Villages and towns appeared and vanished in a blur, great cities—one she thought sure was Caemlyn, walls silvery white in the night—and once, in forested hills, the head and shoulders of a huge statue rearing out of the earth, a remnant of some land lost in history, appearing so suddenly at Bela's side with a weathered grimace that Egwene nearly screamed, only it was gone before she could. The moon did not move at all between leaps, and hardly any as they sped along. A day or two to reach Salidar? That was what Sheriam had said. The Wise Ones were right. Everyone had believed for so long that Aes Sedai knew everything that Aes Sedai believed it, too. She was going to prove them wrong tonight, but it was not likely they would take any real notice of her proof. They *knew*.

After a time, when she was sure she was somewhere well into Altara, she began letting Bela make smaller jumps, reining her in more often, even riding normally for a bit, especially if there was a village nearby. Sometimes a night-shrouded inn had a sign that named the village, the Marella Inn or the Ionin Spring Inn, and moonlight added to the odd sense of light in *Tel'aran'rhiod* made reading them easy. Bit by bit she became absolutely certain where she was in relation to Salidar and began to take still smaller leaps, then none at all, only letting Bela trot normally through forest where tall trees had killed most of the undergrowth and drought most of the rest.

Still, she was surprised when a considerable village appeared suddenly, silent and dark in the moonlight. It had to be the right place, though.

At the edge of the thatch-roofed stone houses, she dismounted and took down her belongings. It was late, but people might still be about in the waking world. No need to startle them by popping out of the air. If an Aes Sedai saw that and mistook what she was, she might have no chance to face the Hall.

"You did run like the wind," she murmured, hugging Bela a last time. "I wish I could take you with me." A useless fancy, of course. What was made in *Tel'aran'rhiod* could exist only there. This was not really Bela, after all. Even so, she felt a twinge of regret as she turned her back—she would not stop imagining Bela; let her exist as long as she could—and wove her shimmering curtain of Spirit. Head high, she stepped through, ready to face whatever came with her Aiel heart.

One step she took, and came up short with a sharp, wide-eyed, "Oh!" The changes she had made in *Tel'aran'rhiod* existed in the real world no more than Bela did. The flames returned with a rush, and with them, it was almost as though Sorilea spoke to her. *If you take what you did to meet your* toh *and make it so it might as well never have happened, how have you met* toh? *Remember your Aiel heart, girl.*

Yes. She would remember. She was here to do battle whether the Aes Sedai knew it or not, ready to fight for the right to be Aes Sedai, ready to face. . . . Light, what?

There were people in the streets, a few moving between houses where lighted windows made golden pools. Walking a little gingerly, Egwene approached a wiry woman with a white apron and a harried expression.

"Excuse me. My name is Egwene al'Vere. I am Accepted"—the woman gave her riding dress a sharp look—"and I've just arrived. Can you direct me to Sheriam Sedai? I need to find her." Very likely Sheriam was asleep already, but if she was, Egwene intended to wake her. She had been told to come as soon as possible, and Sheriam was going to know she was here.

"Everyone comes to me," the woman muttered. "Does anybody do anything for themselves? No, they want Nildra to do it. You Accepted are the worst of the lot. Well, I don't have all night. Follow me, if you're coming. If not, you can find her for yourself." Nildra strode off without so much as a backward glance.

Egwene followed silently. If she opened her mouth, she was afraid she would tell the woman what she thought, and that would hardly be the way to start her stay in Salidar. However short it might be. She wished her Aiel heart and her Two Rivers head could get together.

The distance was not long, up the hard-packed dirt street a little way and around the corner into another, narrower street. Sounds of laughter came from some of the houses. Nildra stopped at one that was silent, though light shone in the windows of the front room.

Pausing just long enough to knock on the door, she went in before there was any answer. Her curtsy was perfectly proper, if quick, and she spoke in a somewhat more respectful tone than before. "Aes Sedai, this girl says her name is Egwene, and she—" She got out no more.

They were all there, the seven from the Heart of the Stone, not a one looking ready for bed, though all but the young woman with Siuan's name wore robes. From the way their chairs were pulled together, it seemed that Egwene had walked in on a discussion. Sheriam was the first to leap from her chair, waving Nildra out. "Light, child! Already?"

No one paid any mind at all to Nildra's curtsy, or her put-upon sniff on going.

"We never expected," Anaiya said, taking Egwene's arms with a warm smile. "Not so soon. Welcome, child. Welcome."

"Were there any ill effects?" Morvrin demanded. She had not risen, and neither had Carlinya or the young Aes Sedai, but Morvrin leaned forward intently. All the others' robes were silk of various hues, sometimes brocaded or embroidered; hers was plain brown wool, though it did look soft and finely woven. "Do you feel any changes from the experience? We had precious little to go on. Frankly, I am surprised it worked."

"We shall have to see it work to know how well it does." Beonin paused for a sip of tea, then set cup and saucer down on a rickety-legged side table. The cup and saucer did not match, but then, none of the furniture matched, and most looked as lopsided as the small table. "If there are ill effects, she can be Healed, and they will be done with."

Egwene stepped away from Anaiya quickly, setting her belongings beside the door. "No, I'm quite well. Really, I am." She could have hesitated; Anaiya might well have Healed her without asking. That would have been cheating, though.

"She appears healthy enough," Carlinya said coolly. Her hair really was short, dark curls barely covering her ears; it had not been just something she did in *Tel'aran'rhiod*. She wore white, of course; even the embroidery was white. "We can have one of the Yellows check her thoroughly later, to be sure, if need be."

"Let her get her feet on the ground," Myrelle said with a laugh. Lush flowers in yellow and red so covered her robe that hardly any green showed. "She's just come a thousand leagues in a night. In hours."

"You've no time to let her find her feet," the young Aes Sedai put in firmly. She truly looked out of place in that gathering, in her yellow dress with the skirts slashed with blue and the deep round neckline blue-embroidered. That, and being the only one it was possible to put an age to. "Come morning, the Hall will swarm around her. If she's not ready, Romanda will gut her like a fat carp."

Egwene gaped. That voice registered more than the words. "You're Siuan Sanche. No, it's impossible!"

"Oh, it is possible, all right," Anaiya said dryly, giving the young woman a long-suffering look.

"Siuan is Aes Sedai again." Myrelle's look was more exasperated than long-suffering.

It had to be true—they *had* said so—but Egwene could hardly credit it even when Sheriam explained. Nynaeve had Healed *stilling*? Being *stilled* was why Siuan looked no older than Nynaeve? Siuan had always been a leather-faced taskmistress, and leather-hearted as well, not this pretty, creamy-cheeked woman with an almost delicate mouth.

Egwene watched Siuan while Sheriam talked. Those blue eyes were the same, though. How could she have seen that gaze, strong enough to drive nails, and not known? Well, the face was answer enough there. But Siuan had always been strong in the Power, too. When a girl first began, it required testing to tell how strong she would be, but not once she had gained that strength. Egwene knew enough now to weigh another woman in moments. Sheriam was clearly the strongest woman in the room aside from Egwene herself, and Myrelle next, though it was hard to be certain; the rest all seemed close, except for Siuan. She was weakest by a fair margin.

"This truly is Nynaeve's most remarkable discovery," Myrelle said. "The Yellows are taking what she has done and making their own marvels, but she began it. Sit down, child. It is too long a story to hear standing."

"I prefer to stand, thank you." Egwene eyed the straight-backed chair with a wooden seat that Myrelle indicated, and barely repressed a shudder. "What about Elayne? Is she all right, too? I want to hear all about her and Nynaeve both." Nynaeve's *most* remarkable discovery? That implied more than one. It seemed she had fallen behind with the Wise Ones; she was going to have to run hard to catch up. At least she thought now that she would be allowed to. They would hardly have greeted her so warmly if she was going to be sent away in disgrace. She had not curtsied or called anyone Aes Sedai once—more because she had had no chance than for any other reason; defiance was no way to face Aes Sedai—yet no one had called her down. Maybe they did not know after all. But then, why?

"Except for a little trouble she and Nynaeve have with pots at the moment," Sheriam began, but Siuan broke in harshly.

"Why are you all jabbering like brainless girls? It's too late to be afraid of going on. It has begun; you began it. Either you finish, or Romanda will hang the lot of you in the sun to dry right alongside this girl, and Delana and Faiselle and the rest of the Hall will be there with her to stretch you out."

Sheriam and Myrelle turned to face her almost together. All the Aes Sedai did, Morvrin and Carlinya twisting in their chairs. Cold Aes Sedai eyes stared from cold Aes Sedai faces.

At first Siuan met those stares with a challenging stare of her own, as Aes Sedai as they if seemingly much younger. Then her head fell a little, and spots of color entered her cheeks. She rose from her chair, eyes down. "I spoke in haste," she muttered softly. Those eyes did not change—maybe the Aes Sedai failed to notice, but Egwene saw—yet that was still not like Siuan.

Egwene also saw that she did not know what was going on here at all. Not just Siuan Sanche meek as milk; if she was pushed to it, anyway. That least of all. What had they begun? Why would *she* be hung out to dry if they stopped?

The Aes Sedai exchanged looks as unreadable as Aes Sedai could make them. Morvrin was the first to nod.

"You have been summoned for a very special reason, Egwene," Sheriam said solemnly.

Egwene's heart began to beat faster. They did not know about her. They did not. But what?

"You," Sheriam said, "are to be the next Amyrlin Seat."

CHAPTER
35

In the Hall of the Sitters

Egwene stared at Sheriam, wondering whether she was supposed to laugh. Maybe in her time with the Aiel she had forgotten what passed for humor among Aes Sedai. Sheriam stared back with that ageless, imperturbable face, tilted green eyes not seeming to blink. Egwene looked at the others. Seven faces with no expression, just an air of waiting. Siuan might have been smiling faintly, but the "smile" could as easily have been the natural curve of her lips. Wavering lamplight made their features suddenly strange and inhuman.

Egwene's head felt light, her knees weak. Without thinking she let herself thump down in the straight-backed chair. She stood right up again, too. That certainly cleared her mind; a little, anyway. "I am not even Aes Sedai," she said breathlessly. That seemed noncommittal enough. It had to be some sort of joke, or . . . or . . . or *something*.

"That can be gotten around," Sheriam said firmly, jerking the bow of her pale blue sash tighter for emphasis.

Beonin's honey-colored braids swayed as she nodded. "The Amyrlin Seat, she *is* Aes Sedai—the law is quite clear; several places it is stated, 'the Amyrlin Seat as Aes Sedai'—but nowhere is it said that it is necessary to be Aes Sedai to become Amyrlin." Any Aes Sedai would be familiar with Tower law, but as mediators, Grays had to know the law of every land, and Beonin took on a lecturing tone, as though explaining something that none knew as well as she. "The law that sets forth how the Amyrlin is to be chosen, it merely says 'the woman who is summoned,' or 'she who stands before the Hall' or the like. From beginning to end, the words 'Aes Sedai' are mentioned not once. Never. Some might say that the intent of the framers, it must be considered, but it is clear, whatever the intent of the women who wrote the law, that—" She frowned as Carlinya cut her off.

"No doubt they thought it was understood to such a degree that there was no need to state it. Logically, however, a law means what it says, whatever the framers thought they meant."

"Laws seldom have much concern with logic," Beonin said acidly. "In this case, however," she conceded after a moment, "you are quite correct." To Egwene, she added, "And the Hall, they see it so also."

They were all serious, even Anaiya, when she said, "You will be Aes Sedai, child, just as soon as you are raised Amyrlin Seat. That is the long and short of it." Even Siuan, despite that tiny smile. It was a smile.

"You can take the Three Oaths as soon as we are back in the Tower," Sheriam told her. "We considered having you speak them anyway, but without the Oath Rod, it might be taken for a sham. Best to wait."

Egwene almost sat down again before catching herself. Maybe the Wise Ones had been right; maybe traveling through *Tel'aran'rhiod* in the flesh had done something to her mind. "This, is madness," she protested. "I can't be Amyrlin. I'm . . . I'm. . . ." Objections piled up on her tongue in a tangle that let nothing out. She was too young; Siuan herself had been the youngest Amyrlin ever, and she was thirty when raised. She had barely begun her training, no matter what she knew about the World of Dreams; Amyrlins were knowledgeable and experienced. And wise; they were certainly supposed to be wise. All she felt was confounded and muddled. Most women spent ten years as a novice and ten as Accepted. True, some moved faster, even much faster. Siuan had. But she herself had been a novice less than a year, and Accepted an even shorter time. "It's impossible!" was the best she could manage finally.

Morvrin's snort reminded her of Sorilea. "Settle yourself down, child, or I'll see to it myself. This is no time for you to grow fluttery, or start fainting on us."

"But I wouldn't know what to do! Not the first thing!" Egwene drew a deep breath. It did not really calm her racing heart, but it helped. A little. Aiel heart. Whatever they did, she would not let them bully her. Eyeing Morvrin's bluff, hard face, she added, *She can skin me, but she can't bully me.* "This is ridiculous is what it is. I won't paint myself for a fool in front of everybody, and that is what I'd be doing. If this is why the Hall summoned me, I'll tell them no."

"I fear that is not an option," Anaiya sighed, smoothing her robe, a surprisingly frilly thing in rose silk, with delicate ivory lace bordering every edge. "You cannot refuse a summons to become Amyrlin any more than you could a summons for trial. The words of the summons are even the same." *That* was heartening; oh, yes, it was.

"The choice is the Hall's now." Myrelle sounded a touch sad, which did nothing for Egwene's spirits.

Suddenly smiling, Sheriam put an arm around Egwene's shoulders. "Do not worry, child. We will help you, and guide you. That is why we are here."

Egwene said nothing. She could think of nothing to say; maybe obeying the law was not being bullied, but it felt much the same. They took silence for assent, and she supposed it was. Without delay, Siuan was sent off, grumbling at being handed the task, to wake the Sitters personally and let them know Egwene had arrived.

The house became a whirlwind before Siuan made it out the door. Egwene's riding dress came in for considerable discussion—none of which she was part of—and a plump serving woman was roused from her nap in a chair in a back room and sent off, with dire warnings if she breathed a word, to fetch every Accepted's dress she could find that might come close to fitting Egwene. She tried on eight, right there in the front room, before finding one that did fit, after a fashion. It was too tight in the bosom, but thankfully loose in the hips. All the time the serving woman was bringing in dresses and Egwene was trying them on, Sheriam and the others took turns running out to dress themselves, and in between lectured her on what was going to happen, what she had to do and say.

They made her repeat everything back. The Wise Ones thought saying something once was sufficient, and woe to the apprentice who failed to listen and hear. Egwene remembered some of what she had to say from a novice lecture in the Tower, and she got it word perfect the first time, but the Aes Sedai went over everything again and again, and then again. Egwene could not understand. With anyone else but Aes Sedai, she would have said they were nervous, calm faces or no. She began to wonder whether she was making some mistake, and started emphasizing different words.

"Say them as you are told," Carlinya snapped like a cracking icicle, and Myrelle, sounding hardly less cold, said, "You cannot afford a mistake, child. Not one!"

They put her through it five more times, and when she protested that she had given back every word correctly, listed who would stand where and who would say what just the way they had told her, she thought Morvrin might box her ears if Beonin or Carlinya did not first. In the event, their frowns were as hard as slaps, and Sheriam looked at her as if she were a novice being sulky. Egwene sighed and began yet again. "I enter with three of you escorting me. . . ."

It was a silent procession that made its way through the nearly empty, moon-shadowed streets. Few of the scattered people still out so much as glanced at them; six Aes Sedai with one lone Accepted in their midst might or might not be a common sight here, but apparently it was not odd enough to occasion comment. Windows that had been lit were dark now; quiet lay on the town so their footsteps sounded distinctly on the hard dirt. Egwene fingered the Great Serpent ring, firmly back in place on her left hand. Her knees were trembling. She had been prepared to face anything, but her list of "anything" had never included this.

In front of a rectangular three-story stone building, they stopped. The windows were all dark, but by moonlight it had the look of an inn. Carlinya, Beonin and Anaiya were to remain here, and the first two at least were not much pleased; they made no complaint, as they had not back at the house, but they adjusted their skirts unnecessarily and held their heads stiffly erect, not looking at Egwene.

Anaiya stroked Egwene's hair soothingly. "It will go well, child." She carried a bundle under her arm, the dress Egwene would put on after everything was over. "You are a quick study."

Inside the stone building a gong sounded deeply, once, twice, a third time. Egwene very nearly jumped. Silence for the space of a heartbeat; then the gong repeated its brazen song. Myrelle smoothed her dress unconsciously. Once more silence, followed by the triple call.

Sheriam opened the door, and Egwene followed her in with Myrelle and Morvrin on her heels. The way they surrounded her, Egwene could not help thinking, was like guards set to make sure she did not run away.

The large, high-ceilinged room inside was not dark, far from it. Lamps lined the mantels of four wide stone fireplaces, and more lined the stairs leading to the next floor and the railed walkway overlooking the room. A tall branched stand-lamp, mirrored to increase the light, stood in each corner of the room. Blankets tacked over the window kept all that light in.

Nine chairs made a row down either side of the room, facing inward in groups of three. The women in them, the Sitters for the six Ajahs represented in Salidar, wore their shawls and dresses in the colors of their Ajahs. Their heads swiveled toward Egwene, faces showing nothing but cool serenity.

At the far end of the room was another chair, standing on a small dais more like a flat box. A tall heavy chair, the legs and uprights carved in spirals, it had been painted in yellow and blue, green and white, gray and brown and red. A stole lay across the arms, striped with seven colors. It seemed miles from where Egwene stood to that stole.

"Who comes before the Hall of the Tower?" Romanda demanded in a high, clear voice. She sat just below the colorful chair, opposite the three Blue sisters. Sheriam stepped smoothly aside, revealing Egwene.

"One who comes obediently, in the Light," Egwene said. Her voice should have been shaking. Surely they were not really going to do this.

"Who comes before the Hall of the Tower?" Romanda demanded again.

"One who comes humbly, in the Light." Any moment this would turn into her trial for pretending to be Aes Sedai. No, not that; they would just have shielded her and locked her away until time if that was the case. But surely. . . .

"Who comes before the Hall of the Tower?"

"One who comes at the summons of the Hall, obedient and humble in the Light, asking only to accept the will of the Hall."

Among the Grays below Romanda a dark, slender woman stood. As the youngest Sitter, Kwamesa spoke the ritual question that dated to the Breaking of the World. "Are there any present save women?"

Romanda flung back her shawl deliberately and left it over the back of her chair as she stood. As eldest, she would answer first. Just as deliberately she unfastened her dress and pushed it down to her waist along with her shift. "I am a woman," she pronounced.

Carefully, Kwamesa laid her own shawl across her chair and stripped to the waist. "I am a woman," she said.

The others rose then and began baring themselves, each announcing, once she was showing proof, that she was a woman. Egwene struggled a little with the snug-bodiced Accepted's dress that had been found for her, and had to have Myrelle's help with the buttons, but quickly they four were as bare as anyone else.

"I am a woman," Egwene said with the others.

Kwamesa walked slowly around the room, pausing before each woman for an almost insultingly direct stare, then halted in front of her own chair

again and announced that there were none present but women. The Aes
Sedai sat and most began pulling up their bodices. Not in haste, exactly, but
few wasting any time either. Egwene almost shook her head. She could not
cover until later in the ceremony. Long ago, Kwamesa's question would have
required more proof; in those days, formal ceremonies were held "clad in
the Light," which was to say in nothing but your own skin. What would
these women make of an Aiel sweat tent or a Shienaran bath?

There was no time for thought.

"Who stands for this woman," Romanda said, "and pledges for her,
heart for heart, soul for soul, life for life?" She sat erect and supremely dignified, her plump bosom remaining bare.

"I so pledge," Sheriam said firmly, followed a moment later by the
strong voices of Morvrin and Myrelle in turn.

"Come forward, Egwene al'Vere," Romanda commanded sharply.
Egwene walked forward three paces and knelt; she felt numb. "Why are
you here, Egwene al'Vere?"

She really was numb; she could not feel anything. She could not remember her responses, either, but somehow they rolled from her tongue. "I
was summoned by the Hall of the Tower."

"What do you seek, Egwene al'Vere?"

"To serve the White Tower, nothing more and nothing less." Light,
they *were* going to do it!

"How would you serve, Egwene al'Vere?"

"With my heart and my soul and my life, in the Light. Without fear or
favor, in the Light."

"Where would you serve, Egwene al'Vere?"

Egwene breathed deeply. She *could* still stop this idiocy. She could not
possibly be up to actually. . . . "In the Amyrlin Seat, if it pleases the Hall
of the Tower." Her breath froze. Too late for turning back now. Maybe it
had been too late in the Heart of the Stone.

Delana was the first to stand, then Kwamesa and Janya, more, until nine
Sitters stood before their chairs, signifying acceptance. Romanda was still
firmly in her seat. Nine of eighteen. The acceptance had to be unanimous—
the Hall always sought consensus; in the end, all votes were unanimous,
though it could take a great deal of talking to make it so—but there would
be no talking aside from the ceremonial phrases tonight, and this was one
short of outright rejection. Sheriam and the others had ridiculed her suggestion that that might happen, and did so so quickly that she might have
worried if the whole thing was not so ridiculous, but they had warned her

almost in passing that this could occur. Not a rejection, but a statement that the Sitters who remained in their chairs did not mean to be lapdogs. Only a gesture, a token, according to Sheriam, but looking at Romanda's stern face, and Lelaine's, scarcely less so above her bare chest, Egwene was not certain of that at all. They had said it might be as many as three or four, too.

Without a word the standing women retook their places. No one spoke, but Egwene knew what to do. Her numbness had vanished.

Rising, she moved toward the nearest Sitter, a sharp-faced Green named Samalin who had stayed in her chair. As Egwene went to her knees again in front of Samalin, Sheriam knelt beside her, a wide basin of water in her hands. Ripples danced on the surface of the water. Sheriam appeared cool and dry, while Egwene was beginning to glisten with sweat, but Sheriam's hands were trembling. Morvrin knelt and handed Egwene a cloth, Myrelle waiting at her side with lengths of toweling over her arm. Myrelle looked angry for some reason.

"Please allow me to serve," Egwene said. Looking straight ahead, Samalin raised her skirts to her knees. Her feet were bare. Egwene washed each foot and patted it dry, then moved to the next Green, a slightly plump woman named Malind. Sheriam and the others had given her all the Sitters' names. "Please allow me to serve." Malind had a pretty face with full lips and dark eyes that looked as if they liked to smile, but she was not smiling now. She was one of those who had stood, but her feet were bare too.

Every Sitters' feet were, all the way around the room. As Egwene washed all those feet, she wondered whether the Sitters had known how many would remain sitting. Plainly they had known some would, that this service would be required. She knew little more of how the Hall of the Tower worked than had been in that novice lecture: For all practical purposes, she knew nothing. All she could do was go on.

She washed and dried the last foot—it belonged to Janya, who was frowning as if thinking of something else entirely; at least she had stood—and dropping the cloth in the washbasin, returned to her place at the foot of the rows and knelt. "Please allow me to serve." One more chance.

Once again Delana was first to rise, but Samalin was right behind her this time. No one sprang to her feet, yet one by one they stood, until only Lelaine and Romanda remained sitting, looking at each other, not Egwene. Finally, Lelaine gave the ghost of a shrug, pulled up her bodice unhurriedly, and rose. Romanda turned her head and looked at Egwene. She stared so long that Egwene became conscious of the sweat running down between her breasts and along her ribs. At last, in stately slowness, Romanda reclothed herself and joined the others. Egwene heard a gasp of relief from behind her, where Sheriam and the others were waiting.

It was not over, of course. Romanda and Lelaine came together to lead her up to the brightly painted chair. She stood before it while they pulled up her bodice and draped the stole of the Amyrlin Seat around her shoulders while they and all the Sitters said, "You are raised to the Amyrlin Seat, in the glory of the Light, that the White Tower may endure forever. Egwene al'Vere, the Watcher of the Seals, the Flame of Tar Valon, the Amyrlin Seat." Lelaine removed Egwene's Great Serpent ring from her left hand and gave it to Romanda, who slipped it onto Egwene's right. "May the Light illumine the Amyrlin Seat and the White Tower."

Egwene laughed. Romanda blinked, Lelaine gave a start, and they were not the only ones. "I just remembered something," she said, then added, "daughters." That was what the Amyrlin called Aes Sedai. What she had remembered was what came next. She could not help thinking it was payment for easing her way through *Tel'aran'rhiod*. Egwene al'Vere, the Watcher of the Seals, the Flame of Tar Valon, the Amyrlin Seat, managed to sit in that hard wooden chair without letting herself down gingerly, and without wincing. She considered both triumphs of will.

Sheriam and Myrelle and Morvrin glided forward—whoever had gasped, there was no telling now by their serene faces—and the Sitters formed a line behind them stretching toward the door. It was done in order of age, with Romanda at the very end.

Sheriam spread her skirts in a deep curtsy. "Please allow me to serve, Mother."

"You may serve the Tower, daughter," Egwene replied as gravely as she could. Sheriam kissed her ring and stepped aside, as Myrelle made her curtsy.

Down the line it went. There were some surprises in the arrangements. None of the Sitters were really young despite their Aes Sedai faces, but pale-haired Delana, whom Egwene had thought must be nearly as old as Romanda, stood less than halfway down the line, while Lelaine and Janya, both quite pretty women without a touch of gray in their dark hair, both came just ahead of the white-haired Yellow. Each made her curtsy and kissed Egwene's ring with absolutely no expression—though some did glance at Egwene's banded hem—and left the room by a rear door without another word. Normally there would have been more, but the rest of the ceremony was to wait on morning.

At last Egwene was alone with the three women who had pledged for her. She was still not sure what that meant. Myrelle went to let in the other three as Egwene stood. "What would have happened if Romanda hadn't stood?" Supposedly there would have been one more chance, one more round of foot-washing and asking to be allowed to serve, but she was sure that if Romanda had voted no the second time, she would have the third.

"Then she very probably would have been raised Amyrlin herself in a few days," Sheriam replied. "Her or Lelaine."

"That wasn't what I meant," Egwene said. "What would have happened to me? Would I just have gone back to being Accepted?" Anaiya and the others came hurrying up, smiling, and Myrelle began helping Egwene out of the banded white dress and into a pale green silk that she would wear only long enough to reach her bed. It was late, but the Amyrlin could not walk about in the dress of an Accepted.

"Very probably," Morvrin answered after a moment. "I can't say whether that would be luck or not, being an Accepted that every Sitter knew had almost had the Amyrlin Seat."

"It has seldom happened," Beonin said, "but a woman refused the Amyrlin Seat is usually exiled. The Hall strives for harmony, and she could not help being a source of disharmony."

Sheriam looked straight into Egwene's eyes as if to impress her words. "We surely would have been exiled. Myrelle and Morvrin and I for certain, since we stood pledge for you, and likely Carlinya and Beonin and Anaiya as well." Her smile was abrupt. "But it did not happen that way. The new Amyrlin is supposed to spend her first night in contemplation and prayer, but once Myrelle finishes with those buttons, it might be best if we gave at least a little of it to telling you how matters stand in Salidar."

They were all looking at her. Myrelle was behind her, doing up the last button, but she could feel the woman's eyes. "Yes. Yes, I think that might be best."

CHAPTER
36

The Amyrlin Is Raised

Egwene raised her head from the pillows and looked around, for a moment surprised to find herself in a canopied bed in a large room. Early-morning light spilled in at the windows, and a plumply pretty woman in a simple gray wool dress was setting a large white pitcher of hot water on the washstand. Chesa had been introduced to her last night as her maid. The Amyrlin's maid. A covered tray already sat beside her comb and brush on a narrow table beneath a mirror with a silver-worked frame. The smell of hot bread and stewed pears drifted in the air.

Anaiya had prepared the room for Egwene's arrival. The furnishings still did not match, but they were the best Salidar had to offer, from the padded armchair upholstered in green silk to the stand-mirror in the corner with all its gilding intact to the ornately carved wardrobe where her belongings now hung. Unfortunately, Anaiya's taste seemed to run heavily to frothy lace and frills. Both thickly bordered the canopy of the bed and the drawn-back bed curtains, and one or the other decked the table and its stool, the arms and legs of the padded chair, the coverlet Egwene had tossed on the floor and the thin silk sheet that had followed. The curtains at the windows were lace, too. Egwene put her head back down. Lace edged the pillows as well. The room made her feel she might drown in lace.

There had been a great deal of talk after Sheriam and the others brought her here to what they called the Little Tower, almost all of it on their side. They were not really interested in what she thought Rand was up to, or what Coiren and the others might want. There was an embassy on its way to Caemlyn under Merana, who knew what to do, though they were rather vague about exactly what that was. For the most part, they did the talking, she the listening, her questions brushed aside. The answers to some were unimportant, she was told, for now anyway; those that were answered got a quick gloss before they went on to what was important. Embassies had been sent off to every ruler, each one named in turn, with an explanation of why he or she was absolutely vital to Salidar's cause, which it seemed every one was. They did not quite say everything would fail if even one ruler went against them, but the emphasis they laid on every one said it for them. Gareth Bryne was building an army that would eventually be strong enough to prosecute their—her—claims against Elaida, if it came to that. They did not seem to think it would, despite Elaida's demand that they return to the Tower; they seemed to believe that once word of Egwene al'Vere's elevation to the Amyrlin Seat was spread, Aes Sedai would come to her, even some of those in the Tower now, enough that Elaida would have no choice but to step down on demand. The Whitecloaks were twiddling their thumbs for some reason, so Salidar was as safe as anywhere for as long as was necessary. That Logain had been Healed as well as Siuan—and Leane; of course she would have been Healed if she was here; it was just a surprise to find out she was—came up almost in passing.

"Nothing to worry you there," Sheriam said soothingly. She stood over Egwene, who sat in the padded armchair, with the others in an arc around her. "The Hall will argue whether to gentle him again until old age relieves us of the problem."

Egwene tried to stifle another yawn—it was getting late—and Anaiya said, "We need to let her sleep. Tomorrow is almost as important as tonight was, child." Abruptly she laughed to herself softly. "Mother. Tomorrow is important too, Mother. We will send Chesa to help you get ready for bed."

Even after they left, going to bed was not easy. While Chesa was still undoing Egwene's dress, Romanda appeared with a number of suggestions for the Amyrlin, delivered in a firm no-nonsense voice, and no sooner did she go than Lelaine came, as if the Blue Sitter had been waiting for the Yellow's departure. Lelaine had her own helpful counsel, given with Egwene sitting up in bed after Chesa was gently but firmly put out of the room. It was not a bit like Romanda's advice—neither was much like Sheriam's—and came with a warm, even affectionate, smile, but with just as much certainty that Egwene would need a little guidance in her first months. Neither woman exactly said that she could guide Egwene to what was best for the Tower better than Sheriam, or that Sheriam and her little circle might try to tug in too many directions, or that they might give bad advice, but the strong implications were there. Romanda and Lelaine also each hinted that the other might have her own agenda, one that undoubtedly would cause untold misery.

By the time Egwene channeled the last lamp out, she expected a sleep full of nightmares. In fact there were only two that she remembered the next morning. In one she was Amyrlin—Aes Sedai, but without taking the oaths—and everything she did led to disaster. That wakened her bolt upright, just to get away, yet she was sure it was not a dream with meaning. It was much the same as one of her experiences inside the *ter'angreal* where she had been tested for Accepted; as far as anyone knew, those had no connection to reality. Not to this reality. The other was the sort of foolishness she expected; she knew enough about her own dreams now to know that, even if she had to wake herself finally to escape that one as well. Sheriam had snatched the stole from her shoulders, and then everyone was laughing at her and pointing at the fool who really believed a girl of barely eighteen years could be Amyrlin. Not just the Aes Sedai, but all the Wise Ones, and Rand and Perrin and Mat, Nynaeve and Elayne, almost everyone she had ever met, while she stood there naked, desperately trying to put on an Accepted's dress that might have fit a ten-year-old child.

"Now, you can't be lying abed all day, Mother."

Egwene opened her eyes.

Chesa had an expression of mock severity on her face and a twinkle in her eye. At least twice Egwene's age, at their first meeting she had fallen straight into the blend of respect and familiarity that could be expected of an old retainer. "The Amyrlin Seat can't be lying slugabed, not today of all days."

"The last thing in my mind." Scrambling stiffly from the bed, Egwene stretched before pulling off her sweaty shift. She could not wait until she had worked long enough with the Power to stop sweating. "I'll wear the blue silk with the white morning-stars along the neckline." She noticed Chesa very carefully not looking as the woman handed her a fresh shift. The effects of meeting her *toh* had faded somewhat, but she still appeared faintly bruised. "I had an accident before I got here," she said, hurriedly thrusting her head through the new shift.

Chesa nodded in sudden understanding. "Horses are wicked, untrustworthy beasts. You'll never get me on one, Mother. A good sturdy cart is ever so much safer. If I fell off a horse like that, I'd never let on to a soul. Nildra would say such things, and Kaylin. . . . Oh, you'd never believe the things some women can say the moment your back is turned. Of course, it's different for the Amyrlin Seat, but that's what I'd do." Holding the wardrobe door open, she glanced sideways at Egwene to see whether she understood.

Egwene smiled at her. "People are people, low or high," she said gravely.

Chesa beamed for an instant before bringing out the blue dress. Anaiya might have chosen her, but she was the Amyrlin Seat's maid, and her loyalty was to the Amyrlin Seat. And she was right about today's importance, too.

Eating quickly—despite Chesa's murmurs to herself about how gulping food always upset the stomach; the warm milk with honey and spices was sovereign for settling a nervous stomach—Egwene scrubbed her teeth and washed hurriedly, let Chesa take a few licks at her hair with the brush and dressed as fast as the woman could get the blue silk over her head. Settling the seven-striped stole on her shoulders, she paused to look in the stand-mirror. Stole or no stole, she did not look very much like the Amyrlin Seat. *But I am. This is no dream.*

In the large room below, the tables stood as empty as they had in the night. Only the Sitters were there, wearing their shawls and clustered according to Ajah, and Sheriam standing alone. They quieted as Egwene descended the stair, curtsied when she reached the bottom. Romanda and Lelaine eyed her sharply, then turned away, very obviously not looking at Sheriam, and resumed their conversations. When Egwene remained silent, the others did the same. Occasionally one of them glanced at her. Even in whispers their voices sounded too loud. There was silence outside; utter stillness. Egwene plucked her handkerchief from her sleeve and patted her face. None of *them* sweated a drop.

Sheriam came to stand beside her. "It will go well," she said softly. "Just remember what you are to say." That was another thing they had gone over in detail last night; Egwene had a speech to deliver this morning.

Egwene nodded. It was strange. Her stomach should have been turning over, her knees shaking. They were not, and she could not understand.

"There is no need to be anxious," Sheriam said. She sounded as if she thought Egwene was, and meant to soothe her, but before she could open her mouth again, Romanda spoke loudly.

"It is time."

In a rustle of skirts the Sitters lined up according to age, with Romanda in the lead this time, and marched outside. Egwene moved to just short of the door. Still no flutters. Maybe Chesa was right about the warm milk.

Silence still, then Romanda's voice, too loud for nature. "We have an Amyrlin Seat."

Egwene stepped outside into a heat she would not have expected until later in the day. As her foot left the stoop, it landed on a platform woven of Air. The lines of Sitters stretched out to either side of her, each Sitter glowing with the light of *saidar*.

"Egwene al'Vere," Romanda intoned, her voice carried by weaves of the Power, "the Watcher of the Seals, the Flame of Tar Valon, the Amyrlin Seat."

They lifted her high as Romanda spoke, raising the Amyrlin in truth, until she stood just below the thatched roof, standing on thin air it would seem to any but a woman who could channel.

There were plenty to see her outlined by the rising sun; a second weave made the light into a shimmering weave around her. Men and women packed the street. The crowd disappeared around corners. Every doorway was filled, every window, every rooftop except that of the Little Tower itself. A roar erupted that very nearly drowned out Romanda, waves of cheering that rolled across the village. Egwene scanned the crowd searching for Nynaeve and Elayne, but she could not find them in that sea of upturned faces. An age seemed to pass before there was quiet enough for her to speak. The weave that had carried Romanda's voice shifted to her.

They had prepared her speech, Sheriam and the others, a weighty exhortation she might have been able to deliver without blushing if she was twice her age, or better yet three times. She had made a few changes on her own. "We are gathered together in a quest for truth and justice that will not end until the false Amyrlin Elaida is removed from the place she usurped." The only change in that was "will not" for "cannot," but she thought it stronger and better. "As Amyrlin, I will lead you in that quest, and I will not falter, as I know you will not." And that was quite enough exhortation; in any case, she had no intention of remaining up here long enough to repeat everything they wanted said. It all amounted to what she already had said anyway. "As my Keeper of the Chronicles, I name Sheriam Bayanar."

That produced a much smaller cheer; a Keeper was not an Amyrlin, after all. Egwene glanced down, waiting until she saw Sheriam hurry outside, still draping her shoulders with the stole of the Keeper, blue to show she had been raised from the Blue Ajah. It had been decided not to make a copy of the Amyrlin's staff, topped with a golden flame, that the Keeper carried; until the true staff was recovered from the White Tower, they would have to do without. Sheriam had been expecting a much longer wait, and she looked at Egwene with open exasperation. In the lines of Sitters, Romanda and Lelaine wore no expression at all; each had had her own very strong suggestion for Keeper, and needless to say, neither had been Sheriam.

Egwene drew breath and turned back to the waiting crowd. "In honor of this day, I hereby decree that all Accepted and novices are absolved of penances and punishments." That was customary, and produced shouts of glee only from white-clad girls and a few Accepted who forgot themselves. "In honor of this day, I hereby decree that Theodrin Dabei, Faolain Orande, Nynaeve al'Meara and Elayne Trakand are from this moment raised to the shawl, full sisters and Aes Sedai." A sort of questioning silence greeted that, with here and there a murmur. It was not according to custom at all; far from it. But it was said, and a good thing Morvrin had happened to mention Theodrin and Faolain. Time to return to what they had written out for her. "I hereby decree this a day of feasting and celebration. Let no work be done but what is necessary for enjoyment. May the Light shine on you all, and the Creator's hand shelter you." That last was swallowed by a tumultuous roar that overwhelmed the weave carrying her words. Some people began dancing in the street right there and then, though there was hardly room for them to move.

The platform of Air descended perhaps a trifle more quickly than it had risen. The Sitters were staring at her when she stepped off, and the glow of *saidar* began winking out among them almost before she touched ground.

Sheriam darted up to take Egwene's arm, smiling at the stone-faced Sitters. "I must show the Amyrlin her study. Forgive me." Egwene would not exactly have said Sheriam hustled her inside, but then again, she would not exactly have said she did not. She did not think Sheriam would actually try to drag her, but it seemed best to gather her skirts with her free hand and take longer strides so as not to find out.

Her study, at the back of the waiting room, turned out to be somewhat smaller than her bedroom, with two windows, a writing table, a straight-backed chair behind it and two more in front. Nothing else. The beetle-riddled wall panels had been waxed to a dull shine, but the tabletop was quite bare. There was a piece of flowered carpet on the floor.

"Forgive me if I was abrupt, Mother," Sheriam said, releasing her arm, "but I thought we should speak privately before you spoke to any of the Sitters. They all had a hand in writing your speech, and——"

"I know I made a few changes," Egwene said with a bright smile, "but I felt such a mudgin standing up there with all that to say." *All* of them had a hand? No wonder it had sounded like a pompous old woman who could not stop talking. She almost laughed. "Anyway, I said what had to be said, the heart of it. Elaida must be removed, and I will lead them to do it."

"Yes," Sheriam said slowly, "but there might be a few questions about some of the other . . . changes. Theodrin and Faolain will certainly be raised Aes Sedai as soon as we have the Tower and the Oath Rod back, and very likely Elayne, but Nynaeve still can't light a candle unless she yanks her braid at people first."

"That was exactly the point I wished to raise," Romanda said, coming in without knocking. "Mother," she added after a distinct pause. Lelaine shut the door behind them, nearly in the faces of several other Sitters.

"It seemed necessary," Egwene said, widening her eyes. "I thought of it last night. I've been raised Aes Sedai without being tested or taking the Three Oaths, and if I was the only one, it would just point me out. With four others, I won't seem quite so odd anymore. Not to people here, at least. Elaida might try to make something of it when she hears, but most folk know so little about Aes Sedai, they won't know what to believe anyway. It is the people here who matter most. They must have confidence in me."

Anyone but Aes Sedai would have gaped at her. As it was, Romanda very nearly spluttered.

"That may be so," Lelaine began sharply, giving her blue-fringed shawl a jerk, then stopped. It was so. More, the Amyrlin Seat had publicly decreed those women Aes Sedai. The Hall might be able to keep them Accepted—or whatever Theodrin and Faolain were, in their cases—but the Hall could not erase memories, and it would not stop everyone knowing they had gone against the Amyrlin on her first day. A great deal that would do for confidence.

"I hope, Mother," Romanda said in a tight voice, "that you will consult the Hall first the next time. Going against custom can have unexpected consequences."

"Going against law can have unfortunate ones," Lelaine said bluntly, tacking on a belated, "Mother." That was nonsense, or close to it. The conditions for being raised Aes Sedai were set in law, true, but the Amyrlin could decree almost anything she wished. Still, a wise Amyrlin did not jump into fights with the Hall when they could be avoided.

"Oh, I will consult in the future," Egwene told them earnestly. "But it did seem the right thing to do. Please, would you excuse me now? I really do need to speak with the Keeper."

They practically quivered. Their curtsies were slight, their parting words perfectly correct so far as the words went, but muttered in Romanda's case, and in Lelaine's, sharp enough to cut.

"You handled that very well," Sheriam said when they were gone. She sounded surprised. "But you must remember the Hall can make problems for any Amyrlin. One reason I am your Keeper is so that I can advise you, and keep you away from that sort of problem. You should ask me about any decrees you want to make. And if I'm not at hand, Myrelle and Morvrin and the others. We are here to help you, Mother."

"I understand, Sheriam. I promise to listen carefully to whatever you say. I'd like to see Nynaeve and Elayne, if that is possible."

"It should be," Sheriam said, smiling, "though I may have to pull Nynaeve away from a Yellow physically. Siuan is coming to teach you about the etiquette of being Amyrlin—there is a great deal of it to learn—but I'll tell her to come a little later."

Egwene stared at the door after Sheriam had gone. Then she turned and stared at the table. Absolutely bare. Not a report to be read, no records to study. Not so much as pen and ink to write a note, much less a decree. And Siuan coming to teach her etiquette.

When a timid tap came at the door, she was still standing there. "Come," she said, wondering whether it was Siuan, or perhaps a servant with a snack of honeycakes, already cut into suitably small pieces.

Nynaeve poked her head in hesitantly, then was pushed into the room by Elayne. Side by side, they made perfect deep curtsies, spreading white, banded skirts wide and murmuring, "Mother."

"Please don't do that," Egwene said. Actually, it was more of a wail. "You're the only two friends I have, and if you start. . . ." Light, she was almost ready to cry!

Elayne reached her first by a hair, throwing her arms around her. Nynaeve was silent, fiddling nervously with a slim silver bracelet, but not Elayne. "We're still your friends, Egwene, but you *are* the Amyrlin Seat. Light, remember I told you one day you'd be the Amyrlin when I was. . . ." Elayne grimaced faintly. "Well, in any case, you *are*. We can't just walk up to the Amyrlin and say, 'Egwene, does this dress make me look fat?' It would not be proper."

"Yes it would," Egwene said stoutly. "Well, in private," she allowed after a moment. "When we're alone, I *want* you to tell me a dress makes me look fat, or . . . or whatever you want." Smiling at Nynaeve, she tugged the woman's thick braid gently. Nynaeve gave a start. "And I want you to pull that at me, if you feel like it. I need somebody who is Egwene's friend and doesn't see this . . . this *bloody* stole all the time, or I will go crazy. Speaking of dresses, why are you still in those? I thought sure you could be changed by now."

Nynaeve did pull at her braid then. "That Nisao told me it must be some sort of mistake and dragged me off. She said she wasn't going to waste her turn just for a celebration." The sounds of it were beginning to rise outside, a general hum just loud enough to penetrate the stone walls, and a faint thread of music.

"Well, it was no mistake," Egwene said. Nisao's turn? Well, she was not going to ask now; Nynaeve was not happy about it, and Egwene wanted this to be as happy an occasion as it could. Dragging the chair from behind the table, she saw two plump patchwork cushions on the seat and smiled. Chesa. "We are going to sit here and talk, and then I will help you find the two best dresses in Salidar. Tell me about these discoveries of yours. Anaiya mentioned them, and Sheriam, but I could not make them hold still long enough to give me any details."

Almost as one, the pair paused in the act of sitting and exchanged glances. Unaccountably, they seemed reluctant to talk of anything but Nynaeve's Healing Siuan and Leane—Nynaeve repeated three times rather anxiously that Healing Logain had been an accident—and Elayne's work with *ter'angreal.* Those were remarkable feats, especially Nynaeve's, but there was only so much they could say, and there were only so many times Egwene could tell them how marvelous what they had done was and how much she envied them. Trying to demonstrate did not last long; Egwene had no real feel for Healing, especially not this complicated tapestry Nynaeve wove without thought, and though she had an affinity for metals and very good strength in both Fire and Earth, Elayne lost her almost immediately. Of course they wanted to know what life was like among the Aiel. From the startled blinks and shocked laughs, abruptly cut off, she was not sure they believed everything she told them, and she certainly did not tell everything. The Aiel led naturally into Rand. Both women stared all through her rendition of his meeting with the Aes Sedai. They agreed that he was wading waters deeper than he knew and needed someone to guide him before he stepped into a hole. Elayne thought Min might help with that, once the embassy reached Caemlyn—this was the first Egwene knew

Min was with him, or had been in Salidar—though in truth, Elayne seemed rather halfhearted. And she muttered something truly peculiar, as if it were a truth she did not like hearing.

"Min is a better woman than I am." For some reason, that got a sympathetic look from Nynaeve. "I wish *I* were there," Elayne went on in a stronger voice. "To guide him, I mean." She looked from Egwene to Nynaeve, red touching her cheeks. "Well, that, too." Nynaeve and Egwene began laughing so hard they nearly fell out of their chairs, and Elayne joined in almost immediately.

"There's one good thing to tell, Elayne," Egwene said breathlessly, still trying to recover. Then she realized exactly what she was going to say, and why. Light, what a mire she had stepped into, and while laughing! "I'm sorry about your mother, Elayne. You don't know how I wished I could offer my condolences before this." Elayne looked confused, as well she might. "The point is, Rand means to give you the Lion Throne *and* the Sun Throne." To her surprise, Elayne sat up very straight.

"He does, does he?" she said in a cool flat voice. "He intends to give them to me." Her chin rose slightly. "I have some claim to the Sun Throne, and if I choose to make it, I will do so in my own right. As for the Lion Throne, Rand al'Thor has no right—none!—to *give* me what is mine already."

"I'm sure he didn't mean it that way," Egwene protested. *Did he?* "He loves you, Elayne. I know he does."

"If only it were that simple," Elayne muttered, whatever that was supposed to mean.

Nynaeve sniffed. "Men always say they didn't mean it that way. You would think they spoke a different language."

"When I put my hands on him again," Elayne said firmly, "I will teach him to speak the right language. *Give* me!"

It was all Egwene could do not to laugh again. The next time Elayne laid hands on Rand she would be too busy hunting a secluded spot to teach him anything. This was very like old times. "Now you're Aes Sedai, you can go to him any time you want. Nobody can stop you." A quick look passed between the pair.

"The Hall isn't letting anyone just pick up and leave," Nynaeve said. "And even if she could, we found something I think is more important."

Elayne nodded vigorously. "I think so, too. I'll admit, the first thought I had when I heard you announced Amyrlin was that now maybe Nynaeve and I could go find it. Well, the second; the first was a sort of stunned joy."

Egwene blinked in confusion. "You found something. But now you need to find it." Leaning forward in their chairs, they answered eagerly and almost on top of one another.

"We found it," Elayne said, "but only in *Tel'aran'rhiod*."

"We used need," Nynaeve added. "We certainly needed *something*."

"It's a bowl," Elayne continued, "a *ter'angreal*, and I think it might be strong enough to change the weather."

"Only, the bowl is somewhere in Ebou Dar, in an awful, tangled warren of streets with no signs or anything to help. The Hall sent a letter to Merilille, but she'll never find it."

"Especially since she is supposed to be busy convincing Queen Tylin that the *real* White Tower is here."

"We told them it needed a man in the channeling." Nynaeve sighed. "Of course, that was before Logain, though I don't think they would trust him."

"It doesn't really need a man," Elayne said. "We just wanted to make them believe they *needed* Rand. I don't know how many women it does need; maybe a full circle of thirteen."

"Elayne says it's very powerful, Egwene. It could make the weather right again. I'd welcome that just to get my weather sense straight again."

"The bowl *can* make it right, Egwene." Elayne exchanged happy looks with Nynaeve. "All you have to do is send us to Ebou Dar."

The flood receded, and Egwene leaned back in her chair. "I will do what I can. Maybe there'll be no objection, now that you're Aes Sedai." She had the feeling there would be, though. Raising them had seemed such a bold stroke, but she was beginning to believe it was not quite so simple.

"What you can?" Elayne said incredulously. "You are the Amyrlin Seat, Egwene. You give a command, and Aes Sedai jump." She flashed a quick grin. "Say 'jump,' and I'll prove it."

Grimacing, Egwene shifted on the cushions. "I'm the Amyrlin, but. . . . Elayne, Sheriam doesn't have to think very hard to recall a novice named Egwene, staring goggle-eyed at everything and being sent to rake the New Garden walks for eating apples after bedtime. She means to lead me by the hand, or maybe push me by the scruff of my neck. Romanda and Lelaine both wanted to be Amyrlin, and they see that novice too. They intend to show me where to put my feet as much as Sheriam does."

Nynaeve frowned worriedly, but Elayne was pure indignation. "You can't let them get away with trying to . . . to *bully* you. You are the *Amyrlin*.

The Amyrlin tells the Hall what to do, not the other way around. You have to stand up and make them *see* the Amyrlin Seat."

Egwene's laugh had a touch of bitterness. Had it only been last night that she was so defiant about being bullied? "That will take a little time, Elayne. You see, I finally understood why they chose me. Part is for Rand, I think. Maybe they believe he'll be more amenable if he sees me wearing the stole. The other part is *because* they remember that novice. A woman—no; a girl!—who's so used to doing as she's told that there will be no trouble making her do as they want." She fingered the striped stole around her neck. "Well, whatever their reasons, they chose me Amyrlin, and since they did, I mean to *be* Amyrlin, but I have to be careful, at first anyway. Maybe Siuan made the Hall jump every time she frowned"—she wondered whether that had ever been true—"but if I try that, I might just be the first Amyrlin ever deposed the day after she was raised."

Elayne looked dumbfounded, but Nynaeve nodded slowly. Perhaps being Wisdom and dealing with the Women's Circle back home had given her more insight into how the Amyrlin Seat and the Hall of the Tower actually worked together than all of Elayne's training to be Queen.

"Elayne, once word spreads and rulers know about me, I can begin making the Hall realize they chose an Amyrlin, not a puppet, but until then, they really could take this stole away as fast as they gave it. I mean, if I'm not really Amyrlin, then it isn't hard to push me aside. There might be a few mutters, but I have no doubt they could smooth those over fast enough. If anyone outside Salidar ever heard somebody named Egwene al'Vere was raised Amyrlin, it would just be one of those peculiar rumors that grow up around Aes Sedai."

"What are you going to do?" Elayne asked quietly. "You are not going to accept it meekly." That made Egwene smile wholeheartedly. It was not a question, but a firm statement of fact.

"No, I am not." She had listened to a number of Moiraine's lectures to Rand about the Game of Houses. Back then, she had thought the Game absurd, and worse than underhanded. Now she hoped she could remember everything she had heard. The Aiel always said, "Use the weapons you have." "It may help that they're trying to fit me for three different leashes. I can pretend to be pulled by one or another, depending on which is closest to what I want to do. Once in a while I can just do what I want, the way I did raising you two, but not very often yet." Squaring her shoulders, she met their gazes levelly. "I would like to say I raised you because you deserved it, but the truth is, I did it because you're my friends, and because I hope as full sisters you can help me. I certainly don't know who else I can trust except you two. I will send you to Ebou Dar as soon as I can, but before and after, you are who I can discuss things with. I know you will tell me the truth. That trip to Ebou Dar may not take as long as you might think. You two have made all sorts of discoveries, so I hear, but if I can puzzle a few things out, I may have one of my own."

"That will be wonderful," Elayne said, but she sounded almost absentminded.

CHAPTER
37

When Battle Begins

The silence was very peculiar, and Egwene did not understand at all. Elayne looked at Nynaeve, then they both looked at Nynaeve's slim silver bracelet. Nynaeve shifted her gaze to Egwene, wide-eyed, and quickly put it on the floor.

"I have a confession," she said in a near whisper. Her voice never rose, but words spilled out in a rush. "I captured Moghedien." Without raising her eyes, she lifted her wrist with the bracelet. "This is an *a'dam*. We're holding her prisoner, and nobody knows. Except Siuan and Leane and Birgitte. And now you."

"We had to," Elayne said, leaning forward urgently. "They'd have executed her, Egwene. I know she deserves it, but her head is full of knowledge, things we hardly dream of. That's where all of our *discoveries* came from. Except Nynaeve's Healing Siuan and Leane and Logain, and my *ter'angreal.* They would have killed her without waiting to learn anything!"

Questions whirled through Egwene's head dizzyingly. They had captured one of the Forsaken? How? Elayne had made an *a'dam*? Egwene shivered, barely able to look at the thing. It looked nothing like the *a'dam* she knew far too well. Even with that, how had they managed to keep one of the Forsaken hidden among so many Aes Sedai? One of the Forsaken, prisoner. Not tried and executed. As suspicious as Rand had become, if he ever discovered that, he would never trust Elayne again.

"Bring her here," she managed to say hollowly. Nynaeve bounced out of her chair and ran. The noises of celebration, laughter and music and song, swelled for a moment before the door banged shut behind her. Egwene rubbed her temples. One of the Forsaken. "That is quite a secret to keep."

Elayne's cheeks colored. Why under the Light . . . ? Of course.

"Elayne, I have no intention of asking about . . . anybody I'm not supposed to know about."

The golden-haired woman actually jumped. "I . . . I may be able to talk. Later. Tomorrow. Maybe. Egwene, you have to promise me you won't say anything—not to anybody!—unless I say so. No matter what you . . . what you see."

"If that's what you want." Egwene did not understand why the other woman was so agitated. Not really. Elayne had a secret that Egwene shared, only Egwene had found out by accident, and ever since they had both been pretending it was still Elayne's secret alone. She had met with Birgitte, the hero out of legend, in *Tel'aran'rhiod*; maybe she still did. Wait, that was what Nynaeve had said. Birgitte knew about Moghedien. Did she mean the woman waiting in *Tel'aran'rhiod* for the Horn of Valere to call her back? *Nynaeve* knew the secret that Elayne had refused to admit to Egwene even when she was caught out? No. This was not going to turn into a round of accusations and denials.

"Elayne, I am the Amyrlin—really the Amyrlin—and I already have plans. The Wise Ones who channel handle a good many of their weaves differently from Aes Sedai." Elayne already knew about the Wise Ones, though come to think of it, Egwene did not know whether the Aes Sedai did; the other Aes Sedai, now. "Sometimes what they do is more complicated or more crude, but at times it's simpler than we were taught in the Tower and works just as well."

"You want Aes Sedai to study with the Aiel?" Elayne's mouth quirked in amusement. "Egwene, they'll *never* agree to that, not if you live a thousand years. I suppose they'll want to test Aiel girls for novices when they find out, though."

Shifting on her cushions, Egwene hesitated. Aes Sedai studying with the Wise Ones. As apprentices? It would never happen, but Romanda and Lelaine especially might benefit from a little *ji'e'toh*. And Sheriam, and Myrelle, and. . . . She found a more comfortable way to sit and gave up her fancies. "I doubt the Wise Ones will agree to Aiel girls becoming novices." They might have once, possibly, but certainly not now. Now it would be as much as Egwene could expect for them to speak civilly to Aes Sedai. "I thought some sort of association. Elayne, there are fewer than a thousand Aes Sedai. If you include those who remain in the Waste, I think there are more Wise Ones who can channel than there are Aes Sedai. Maybe many more. Anyway, they don't miss a one with the spark born in her." How many women had died on this side of the Dragonwall, because they suddenly could channel, maybe without realizing what they were doing at all, and had no one to teach them? "I want to bring in more women, Elayne. What about women who can learn, but no Aes Sedai found them before they were thought too old for novices? I say, if she wants to learn, let her try, even if she's forty or fifty or her grandchildren have grandchildren."

Elayne hugged herself laughing. "Oh, Egwene, the Accepted will just love teaching *those* novice classes."

"They'll have to learn how," Egwene said firmly. She did not see the problem. Aes Sedai had always said you could be too old for a novice, but if you wanted to learn. . . . They had changed their minds partway already; in the crowd she had seen faces older than Nynaeve's above novice white. "The Tower has always been severe about excluding people, Elayne. If you aren't strong enough, you're put out. Refuse to take a test, and you're sent away. Fail a test, and out. They should be allowed to stay if they want."

"But the tests are to make sure you're strong enough," Elayne protested. "Not just in the One Power; in yourself. Surely you don't want Aes Sedai who will break the first time they come under pressure? Or Aes Sedai who can barely channel?"

Egwene sniffed. Sorilea would have been put out of the Tower without ever being tested for Accepted. "Maybe they can't be Aes Sedai, but that doesn't mean they are useless. After all, they're already trusted to use the Power with at least some discretion, or they wouldn't be sent off into the world. My dream is for every woman who can channel to be connected to the Tower somehow. Every last one."

"The Windfinders?" Elayne winced when Egwene nodded.

"You didn't betray them, Elayne. I can't believe they kept their secret as long as they did."

Elayne sighed heavily. "Well, what's done is done. 'You can't put honey back in the comb.' But if your Aiel get special protection, the Sea Folk should too. Let the Windfinders teach their girls. No Sea Folk women bundled off by Aes Sedai whatever they will."

"Done." Egwene spat on her palm and held out her hand, and after a moment Elayne spat on hers and grinned as they clasped to seal the bargain.

Slowly that grin faded. "Is this about Rand and his amnesty, Egwene?"

"In part. Elayne, how could the man be so . . . ?" There was no way to finish that, and no answer anyway. The other woman nodded a touch sadly, in understanding or agreement or both.

The door opened, and a sturdy woman in dark wool appeared, a silver tray in her hands with three silver cups and a long-necked silver wine pitcher. Her face was worn, a farmwife's face, but her dark eyes glittered as she studied Egwene and Elayne with a shifting gaze. Egwene had just a moment to feel surprise that the woman wore a close-fitting silver necklace despite her drab dress, and then Nynaeve entered behind heir, shutting the door. She must have run like the wind, because she had found time to exchange the Accepted's dress for a dark blue silk embroidered with golden scrolls around the neckline and hem. It was not nearly so low-cut as what Berelain wore, but still considerably lower than Egwene expected to see on Nynaeve.

"This is 'Marigan,'" Nynaeve said, drawing her braid over her shoulder in a practiced motion. Her Great Serpent ring shone golden on her right hand.

Egwene started to ask why she emphasized the name so, then abruptly realized that "Marigan's" necklace was a match for the bracelet on Nynaeve's wrist. She could not help staring. The woman certainly did not look anything like she expected one of the Forsaken to look. She said as much, and Nynaeve laughed.

"Watch, Egwene."

She did more than watch; she nearly leaped out of her chair, and she did embrace *saidar*. As soon as Nynaeve spoke, the glow had surrounded "Marigan." Only for an instant, but before it faded, the woman in the plain wool dress changed completely. Actually they were rather small changes, but they added up to a different woman, handsome rather than beautiful but not at all worn, a woman who was proud, even regal. Only the eyes remained the same, glittering, but no matter how they shifted, Egwene could believe this woman was Moghedien.

"How?" was all she said. She listened carefully as Nynaeve and Elayne explained about weaving disguises and inverting weaves, but she watched Moghedien. She *was* proud, and full of herself, full of being herself again.

"Put her back," Egwene said when the explanations were done. Again the glow of *saidar* lasted only moments, and once it faded, there were no weaves that she could see. Moghedien was plain and worn again, a country woman who had led a hard life and looked older than her years. Those black eyes glittered at Egwene, filled with hate, and maybe self-loathing as well.

Realizing she still held *saidar*, Egwene felt foolish for a moment. Neither Nynaeve nor Elayne had embraced the Source. But then, Nynaeve was wearing that bracelet. Egwene stood, never taking her gaze from Moghedien, and held out her hand. If anything, Nynaeve seemed eager to have the thing off her wrist, which Egwene could understand.

Handing the bracelet over, Nynaeve said, "Put the tray on the table, Marigan. And be on your best behavior. Egwene has been living with the Aiel."

Egwene turned the silver band over in her hands and tried not to shiver. Cunning work, segmented so cleverly it almost appeared solid. She had been on the other end of an *a'dam* once. A Seanchan device, with a silver leash connecting necklace and bracelet, but still the same. Her stomach roiled as it had not facing the Hall or the crowd; it stewed as though trying to make up for being still before. Deliberately she closed the length of silver around her wrist. She had some idea of what to expect, but she still almost jumped. The other woman's emotions were laid out before her, her physical state, all gathered in one fenced-off portion of Egwene's mind. Mainly there was pulsing fear, but the self-loathing she had thought she saw swelled nearly as strongly. Moghedien did not like her present appearance. Maybe she especially did not like it after a short return to her own.

Egwene thought of who it was she was looking at; one of the Forsaken, a woman whose name had been used to frighten children for centuries, a woman whose crimes deserved death a hundred times over. She thought of the knowledge in that head. She made herself smile. It was not a pretty smile; she did not mean it to be, but she did not think she could have made it one if she tried. "They're right. I have been living with the Aiel. So if you expect me to be as gentle as Nynaeve and Elayne, put it out of your mind. Set just one foot wrong with me, and I'll make you beg for death. Only, I won't kill you. I will just find some way to make that face permanent. On the other hand, if you do more than put a foot wrong. . . ." She widened her smile, until it was just showing teeth.

The fear leaped so high it drowned everything else and bulged against the fence. Standing in front of the table, Moghedien clutched her skirts white-knuckle tight and trembled visibly. Nynaeve and Elayne were looking at Egwene as if they had never seen her before. Light, did they expect her to be polite to one of the Forsaken? Sorilea would stake the woman out in the sun to bring her to heel, if she did not simply slit her throat out of hand.

Egwene moved closer to Moghedien. The other woman was taller, but she cowered back against the table, knocking over the winecups on their tray and rocking the pitcher. Egwene made her voice cold; it did not have far to go. "The day I detect one lie out of you is the day I execute you myself. Now. I have considered traveling from one place to another by boring a hole, so to speak, from here to there. A hole through the Pattern, so there's no distance between one end and the other. How well will that work?"

"Not at all, for you or any woman," Moghedien said, breathless and quick. The fear that boiled inside was plain on her face now. "That is how men Travel." The capital was plain; she was speaking of one of the lost Talents. "If you try, you will be sucked into. . . . I don't know what it is. The space between the threads of the Pattern, maybe. I don't think you would live very long. I know you would never come back."

"Traveling," Nynaeve muttered disgustedly. "We never thought of Traveling!"

"No, we didn't." Elayne sounded no more pleased with herself. "I wonder what else we never thought of."

Egwene ignored them. "Then how?" she asked softly. A quiet voice was always better than shouting.

Moghedien flinched as though she had shouted anyway. "You make the two places in the Pattern identical. I can show you how. It takes a little effort, because of the . . . the necklace, but I can—"

"Like this?" Egwene said, embracing *saidar*, and wove flows of Spirit. This time she was not trying to touch the World of Dreams, but she expected something much the same if it worked. What she got was quite different.

The thin curtain she wove did not produce the shimmering effect, and it lasted only a moment before snapping together in a vertical line that was suddenly a slash of silvery blue light. The light itself widened quickly—or perhaps turned; it looked that way to her—into . . . something. There in the middle of the floor was a . . . a doorway, not at all the misty view she had had of *Tel'aran'rhiod* from her tent, a doorway opening onto a sun-blasted land that made the worst of the drought here look lush. Stone spires and sharp cliffs loomed over a dusty yellow-clay plain cut by fissures and dotted with a few scrub bushes that had a thorny look even at a distance.

Egwene very nearly stared. That was the Aiel Waste halfway between Cold Rocks Hold and the valley of Rhuidean, a spot where it was very unlikely there would be anyone to see—or be hurt; Rand's precautions with his special room in the Sun Palace had suggested she take some too—but she had only hoped to reach it, and she had been sure it would be seen through a shimmering curtain.

"Light!" Elayne breathed. "Do you know what you've done, Egwene? Do you? I think I can do it. If you repeat the weave again, I know I'll remember."

"Remember what?" Nynaeve practically wailed. "How did she do it? Oh, curse this *cursed* block! Elayne, kick my ankle. Please?"

Moghedien's face had gone very still; uncertainty rolled through the bracelet almost as heavily as fear. Reading emotions was hardly like reading words on a page, but those two were clear. "Who . . . ?" Moghedien licked her lips. "Who taught you that?"

Egwene smiled as she had seen Aes Sedai smile; at least, she hoped it conveyed mystery. "Never be too sure I don't already know the answer," she said coolly. "Remember. Lie to me once." Suddenly it occurred to her how this must sound to Nynaeve and Elayne. They had captured the woman, held her captive in the most impossible circumstances, pried all sorts of information out of her. Turning to them, she gave a small, rueful laugh. "I *am* sorry. I didn't mean to just take over."

"Why should you be sorry?" Elayne wore a broad smile. "You are *supposed* to take over, Egwene."

Nynaeve gave her braid a yank, then glared at it. "Nothing seems to work! Why can't I get angry? Oh, you can keep her forever, for all of me. We couldn't take her to Ebou Dar, anyway. *Why* can't I get angry? Oh, blood and bloody ashes!" Her eyes went wide as she realized what she had said, and she clapped a hand over her mouth.

Egwene glanced at Moghedien. The woman was busily setting the winecups upright again and pouring wine with a smell of sweet spices, but something had come through the bracelet while Nynaeve was talking. Shock, perhaps? Maybe she would prefer the mistresses she knew to one who threatened death in almost her first breath.

A firm knock sounded at the door, and Egwene hastily released *saidar*; the opening to the Waste vanished. "Come."

Siuan took one step into the study and stopped, taking in Moghedien, the bracelet on Egwene's wrist, Nynaeve and Elayne. Shutting the door, she made a curtsy as minimal as anything from Romanda or Lelaine. "Mother, I've come to instruct you in etiquette, but if you would rather I returned later . . . ?" Her eyebrows rose, calmly questioning.

"Go," Egwene told Moghedien. If Nynaeve and Elayne were willing to let her run loose, the *a'dam* must limit her, if not as much as one with a leash. Fingering the bracelet—she hated the thing, but she intended to wear it day and night—she added, "But keep yourself available. I'll treat trying to escape the same as a lie." Fear gushed through the *a'dam* as Moghedien scurried out. That could be a problem. How had Nynaeve and Elayne lived with those torrents of dread? Still, that was for later.

Facing Siuan, she folded her arms beneath her breasts. "This won't do, Siuan. I know everything. Daughter."

Siuan tilted her head. "Sometimes knowing gives no advantage whatsoever. Sometimes it only means sharing the danger."

"Siuan!" Elayne said, half-shocked and half-warning, and to Egwene's surprise Siuan did something she had never expected to see Siuan Sanche do. She blushed.

"You can't expect me to become somebody else overnight," the woman muttered grumpily.

Egwene suspected Nynaeve and Elayne could help with what she had to do, but if she was really going to be Amyrlin, she had to do it alone. "Elayne, I know you want to get out of that Accepted's dress. Why don't you do that? And then see what you find out about lost Talents. Nynaeve, you do the same."

A look passed between them, then they glanced at Siuan and rose to make perfect curtsies, respectfully murmuring, "As you command, Mother." There was no evidence of any impression on Siuan; she stood watching Egwene with a wry expression while they left.

Egwene embraced *saidar* again, briefly, to slide her chair back into place behind the table, then adjusted her stole and sat. For a long moment she regarded Siuan silently. "I need you," she said at last. "You know what it is to be Amyrlin, what the Amyrlin can and cannot do. You know the Sitters, how they think, what they want. I need you, and I mean to have you. Sheriam and Romanda and Lelaine may think I still wear novice white under this stole—maybe they all do—but you are going to help me show them differently. I'm not asking you, Siuan. I—will—have—your—help." All there was to do then was wait.

Siuan regarded her, then gave a slight shake of her head and laughed softly. "They made a very bad mistake, didn't they? Of course, I made it first. The plump little grunter for the table turns out to be a live silverpike as long as your leg." Spreading her skirts wide, she made a deep curtsy, inclining her head. "Mother, please allow me to serve, and advise."

"So long as you know it's only advice, Siuan. I have too many people already who think they can tie strings to my arms and legs. I won't put up with it from you."

"I'd as soon try tying strings to myself," Siuan said dryly. "You know, I never really liked you. Maybe it was because I saw too much of myself in you."

"In that case," Egwene said in just as dry a tone, "you can call me Egwene. When we're alone. Now sit down and tell me why the Hall is still sitting here, and how I can get them moving."

Siuan started to pull one of the chairs over before remembering she could move it with *saidar* now. "They are sitting because once they move, the White Tower really is broken. As for how to get them moving, my advice. . . ." Her advice took a long time. Some of it went along lines Egwene had already thought of, and all of it seemed good.

In her room in the Little Tower, Romanda poured mint tea for three other Sitters, only one a Yellow. The room was in the back, but the sounds of festival penetrated; Romanda ignored them studiously. These three had been ready to support her for the Amyrlin Seat; voting for the girl had been as much a way to keep Lelaine from being raised as anything else. Lelaine would burn if she ever knew that. Now that Sheriam had her child Amyrlin installed, these three were still willing to listen. Especially after the business of raising Accepted to the shawl by decree. That had to be Sheriam's doing; she and her little clique had pampered all four; it had been their notion to lift Theodrin and Faolain above the other Accepted, and they had suggested it for Elayne and Nynaeve as well at one time. Frowning, she wondered what was keeping Delana, but she began talking anyway, after sheathing the room in *saidar* against eavesdropping. Delana would just have to catch up when she came. The important thing was that Sheriam was going to learn she had not gained as much power as she thought by snatching the job of Keeper.

In a house halfway across Salidar, Lelaine was serving chilled wine to four Sitters, only one from her own Blue Ajah. *Saidar* laced the room against listeners. The sounds of celebration made her smile. The four women with her had suggested she try for the Amyrlin Seat herself, and she had not been reluctant, but a failure would have meant Romanda being raised instead, which would have pained Lelaine as much as being exiled. How Romanda would gnash her teeth if she ever learned they had all voted for the child just to keep the stole from Romanda's own shoulders. What they had gathered to discuss, though, was how to lessen Sheriam's influence now she had managed to grab the Keeper's stole. That farce of raising Accepted to Aes Sedai by the girl's decree! Sheriam's head must have swollen to madness. As the talk went on, Lelaine began to wonder where Delana was. She should have been there by now.

Delana sat in her room, staring at Halima perched on the edge of Delana's bed. The name Aran'gar was never to be used; sometimes Delana was afraid Halima would know if she even thought it. The ward against eavesdropping was small, enclosing just the pair of them. "That is madness," she managed at last. "Don't you understand? If I continue to try supporting every faction, they will catch me out sooner or later!"

"Everyone must take some risks." The firmness of the woman's voice belied the smile on that lush mouth. "And you will continue to press for gentling Logain again. That, or killing him." A slight grimace actually made the woman more beautiful somehow. "If they ever brought him out of that house, I would attend to it myself."

Delana could not imagine how, but she would not doubt the woman until she failed. "What I don't understand is why you are so afraid of a man with six sisters shielding him from sunup to sunup."

Halima's green eyes blazed as she leaped to her feet. "I am not afraid, and don't you ever suggest it! I want Logain severed or dead, and that is all you have to know. Do we understand one another?"

Not for the first time Delana considered killing the other woman, but as always she had a sinking certainty that she would be the one to die. Somehow Halima knew when she embraced *saidar*, even if Halima could not channel herself. The worst of it was the possibility that because Halima needed her, she would not kill her; Delana could not imagine what she might do instead, but the very vagueness of the threat made her shudder. She should be able to kill the woman right there, right then. "Yes, Halima," she said meekly, and hated herself for it.

"So good of you," Siuan murmured, holding her cup for Lelaine to add a small splash of brandy in her tea. The sun was sinking toward the horizon, giving the light a reddish cast, but the streets outside were still raucous. "You have no idea how tiring it is trying to teach that girl etiquette. She seemed to think as long as she behaves like a *Wisdom* from back home, everything will be fine. The Hall is supposed to be the Women's Circle or some such thing."

Lelaine made sympathetic noises over her own tea. "You say she was complaining about Romanda?"

Siuan shrugged. "Something about Romanda insisting we stay here instead of marching for Tar Valon, as near as I could make out. Light, the girl has a temper like a fisherbird in mating season. I almost wanted to take her by the shoulders and shake her, but of course, she does wear the stole, now. Well, once I finish my lectures I'm done with her. Do you remember . . . ?"

Smiling inside, Siuan watched Lelaine drinking it all in with the tea. Only the first sentence had really been important. The bit about a temper was her own addition, but it might make some of the Sitters walk a little more carefully around Egwene. Besides, she suspected it might be true. She would never be Amyrlin again herself, and she was fairly certain that trying to manipulate Egwene would be as futile as trying to manipulate herself had been, and as painful, yet teaching an Amyrlin to be Amyrlin. . . . She looked forward to that as much as she had anything in a long time. Egwene al'Vere would be an Amyrlin to make thrones tremble.

"But what about my block?" Nynaeve said, and Romanda frowned at her. They were in Romanda's room in the Little Tower, and this was when Romanda was supposed to have her according to the schedule the Yellows had set up. The music and laughter outside seemed to irritate the Yellow.

"You weren't so eager earlier. I heard that you told Dagdara you were Aes Sedai too and she could find a lake and douse her head."

Heat rose in Nynaeve's face. Trust her temper to get in the way. "Maybe I just realized that being Aes Sedai doesn't mean I can channel any more easily than before."

Romanda sniffed. "Aes Sedai. You have a long way to go for that, whatever. . . . Very well, then. Something we haven't tried before. Jump up and down on one foot. And talk." She sat down in a carved armchair near the bed, still frowning. "Gossip, I think. Talk about light things. For instance, what was it the Amyrlin said Lelaine wanted to talk about?"

For a moment Nynaeve stared back indignantly. Jump on one foot?

That was ridiculous! Still, she was not really here about her block anyway. Lifting her skirts, she began jumping. "Egwene . . . the Amyrlin . . . didn't say much. Something about having to stay put in Salidar. . . ." This had better work, or Egwene was going to hear a few choice words, Amyrlin or no.

"I think this one will work better, Sheriam," Elayne said, handing over a twisted blue-and-red flecked ring of what had been stone this morning. In truth, it was no different from any other she had made. They stood apart from the crowd, at the mouth of a narrow alley lit by the red sun. Behind them fiddles squealed and flutes sang.

"Thank you, Elayne." Sheriam tucked the *ter'angreal* into her belt pouch without even looking at it. Elayne had caught Sheriam in a pause from dancing, her face a little flushed beneath all that cool Aes Sedai serenity, but the clear green gaze that had made Elayne's knees shake as a novice was fixed on her face. "Why do I get the feeling this is not your only reason for coming to see me?"

Elayne grimaced, twisting the Great Serpent ring on her right hand. The right hand; she just had to remember she was Aes Sedai too, now. "It's Egwene. The Amyrlin, I guess I should say. She's worried, Sheriam, and I was hoping you could help her. You are the Keeper, and I did *not* know who else to go to. I don't have the straight of it completely. You know how Egwene is; she wouldn't complain if her *foot* was cut off. It's Romanda, I think, though she did mention Lelaine. One or both have been at her, I think, about staying here in Salidar, about not moving yet because it's too dangerous."

"That is good advice," Sheriam said slowly. "I don't know about dangerous, but that is the advice I would give her myself."

Elayne spread her hands in a helpless shrug. "I know. She told me you did, but. . . . She didn't *say* it right out, but I think she's a little afraid of those two. I *know* she's Amyrlin now, but I think they make her feel a novice. I think she's afraid if she does what they want—even if it *is* good advice—they will expect her to do the same next time. I think. . . . Sheriam, she is afraid she won't be *able* to say no the next time if she says yes now. And . . . and I am afraid of it, too. Sheriam, she's the Amyrlin *Seat*; she shouldn't be under Romanda's thumb, or Lelaine's, or anybody's. You are the *only* one who can help her. I do not know how, but you *are*."

Sheriam was quiet so long that Elayne began to think the other woman

was going to tell her every word was ludicrous. "I will do what I can," Sheriam said at last.

Elayne stifled a relieved sigh before she realized it would not have
mattered.

Leaning forward, Egwene rested her arms along the sides of the copper tub
and let Chesa's chatter flow over her as the woman scrubbed her back. She
had dreamed of a real bath, but actually sitting in the soapy water, scented
with a floral oil, felt strange after Aiel sweat tents. She had taken her first
step as Amyrlin, marshaled her outnumbered army and begun her attack.
She remembered hearing Rhuarc say once that when battle began, a battle
leader no longer had any real control of events. Now all she could do was
wait. "Even so," she said softly, "I think the Wise Ones would be proud."

CHAPTER
38

A Sudden Chill

The blazing sun still climbed behind him, and Mat was glad his broad-brimmed hat gave a little shade on his face. This Altaran forest was winter-bare and more than winter-brown, with pines and leatherleafs and other evergreens looking sere, and oak and ash and sweetgum naked. Noon yet to come, the worst heat beyond that, and already the day was like riding through an oven. His coat was slung atop his saddlebags, but sweat made his fine linen shirt cling. Pips' hooves crunched on dead ferns and fallen leaves thick atop the leaf mold, and the Band moved in a crackle from the forest floor. Few birds appeared, quick flashes between the branches, and not a squirrel. There were flies, though, and bitemes, as if this were the heart of summer instead of less than a month to the Feast of Lights. No different from what he had seen back on the Erinin, really, but finding it here too made him uneasy. Was the whole world really burning up?

Aviendha strode along beside Pips with her bundle on her back, apparently unconcerned by dying trees or biting flies, and making considerably less noise than the horse despite her skirts. Her eyes scanned the surrounding trees as though she did not trust the Band's scouts and flankers to keep them out of an ambush. She had not accepted a ride once, which he had not expected anyway, seeing how Aiel felt about riding, but she had made no trouble either, unless sharpening her knife every time they halted could be considered provocative. There had been the incident with Olver, of course. Riding the high-stepping gray gelding Mat had found him among the remounts, Olver kept a wary eye on her. He had tried to stick his belt knife in her the second night, shouting about Aiel killing his father. Of course, she only took it away from him, but even after Mat cuffed him and tried to explain the difference between Shaido and other Aiel—something Mat was not all that sure he understood himself—Olver glared at her constantly. He did not like Aiel. For Aviendha's part, Olver seemed to make her uneasy, which Mat did not understand at all.

The trees stood tall enough to have allowed a breeze to stir under the sparse canopy overhead, but the Red Hand banner hung limp, and so did the two he had dug out once Rand put them through that gateway into a night-covered meadow, a Dragon banner, the red-and-gold shape hidden in white folds, and one of those the Band called Al'Thor's Banner, the ancient Aes Sedai symbol also thankfully wrapped inside. A grizzled senior bannerman had the Red Hand, a fellow with narrow eyes and more scars than Daerid who insisted on actually carrying the banner a part of each day, which few bannermen did. Talmanes and Daerid had supplied second squadmen for the other two, fresh-faced young men who had shown themselves steady enough for a little responsibility.

Three days they had come across Altara, three days in forest without sight of a single Dragonsworn—or anyone else for that matter—and Mat hoped to stretch their loneliness at least through this fourth before reaching Salidar. Aside from Aes Sedai, there was the problem of how to keep Aviendha from Elayne's throat. He had few doubts why she kept sharpening that knife; the edge glittered like gemstones. He was very much afraid he was going to end taking the Aiel woman to Caemlyn under guard, with the bloody Daughter-Heir demanding he hang her every step of the way. Rand and his bloody women! In Mat's view, anything that slowed the Band and kept him from the stew he expected in Salidar was to the good. Halting early and marching late helped. So did the supply wagons at the rear, slow as they were in the forest. But the Band could ride only so slowly. All too soon Vanin was sure to find something.

As if thinking his name had been a summons, the fat scout appeared through the trees ahead with four riders. He had gone out before dawn with six.

Mat raised a clenched fist, signaling a halt, and murmurs passed down the column. His first order on leaving the gateway had been "no drums, no trumpets, no flutes and no bloody singing," and if there had been a few glum faces in the beginning, after the first day in that wooded terrain, where you could never see clearly more than a hundred paces and seldom so far, no one objected at all.

Resting his spear across his saddle, Mat waited until Vanin pulled up and casually knuckled his forehead. "You found them?"

The balding man leaned to one side in his saddle to spit through a gap in his teeth. He was sweating so much he looked to be melting. "I found them. Eight or ten miles west. There's Warders in those woods. I saw one take Mar; just came out nothing in one of those cloaks and swept him out of the saddle. Roughed him considerably, but didn't kill him, though. I expect Ladwin didn't show up for the same reason."

"So they know we're here." Mat breathed heavily through his nose. He did not expect either man would hold back anything from Warders, much less Aes Sedai. But then, the Aes Sedai had to know sooner or later. He had just wanted it to be later. He slapped at a bluefly, but it buzzed away leaving a spot of blood on his wrist. "How many?"

Vanin spat again. "More than I ever figured to see. I got into the village afoot, and there was Aes Sedai faces all over. Two, three hundred, maybe. Maybe four. I didn't want to be too obvious, counting." Before that shock had time to settle, the man delivered another. "They got an army, too. Camped to the north, mainly. More than you got. Maybe twice as many."

Talmanes and Nalesean and Daerid had ridden up during that, sweating and swatting flies and bitemes. "Did you hear?" Mat asked, and they nodded soberly. His battle luck was all very well, yet being outnumbered two to one, with hundreds of Aes Sedai thrown into the bargain, could strain any luck. "We aren't here to fight," he reminded them, but their long faces remained. For that matter, the remark did not make him feel better either. What counted was whether the Aes Sedai wanted this army of theirs to fight.

"Prepare the Band to be attacked," he ordered. "Clear as much ground as you can, and use the logs to make barricades." Talmanes grimaced nearly as hard as Nalesean; they liked to be in the saddle and moving when they fought. "Think. There may be Warders watching us right now." He was surprised to see Vanin nod and glance off to their right in a significant way. "If they see us readying to defend, then plainly we don't mean to attack. It might make them decide to leave us alone, and if it doesn't, at least we're ready." That got through, to Talmanes faster than Nalesean. Daerid had been nodding from the start.

Giving his oiled beard a twist, Nalesean muttered, "What do you intend to do then? Just sit and wait for them?"

"That's what you're going to do," Mat told him. *Burn Rand and his "maybe fifty Aes Sedai"! Burn him and his "loom a little; intimidate them"!* Waiting right there until somebody came out from the village to ask who they were and what they wanted seemed a very good idea. No *ta'veren* twisting this time. Any battle was going to have to come to him; he was not about to walk into it.

"They are that way?" Aviendha said, pointing. Without waiting for an answer, she settled her bundle on her back and began striding west.

Mat stared after her. *Bloody Aiel.* Some Warder would probably try to take her too, and have his head handed to him. Or maybe not, Warders being Warders; if she tried to put a knife in one of those, he might just hurt her. Besides which, if she got to Elayne and began hair-pulling over Rand, or worse, stuck a knife in *her.* . . . She was moving along quickly, almost trotting, eager to reach Salidar. *Blood and bloody ashes!*

"Talmanes, you have the command until I get back, but you don't stir unless somebody jumps on the Band with both boots. These four will tell you what you might have to face. Vanin, you're with me. Olver, stay close to Daerid, in case he needs messages carried. You can teach him to play Snakes and Foxes," he added with a grin at Daerid. "He tells me he'd like to learn." Daerid's jaw dropped, but Mat had already moved on. A fine thing if he ended up hauled into Salidar by a Warder with a lump on his head. How to reduce the chance of that? The banners caught his eye. "You stay here," he told the grizzled bannerman. "You other two come with me. And keep those things furled."

His strange little party caught up to Aviendha quickly. If anything could convince the Warders to let them through unhindered, one look should. No threat in a woman and four men, and obviously making no effort to avoid notice, not carrying two banners. He checked the second squadmen. There was still no breeze, but they held the banners clutched to the staffs. Their faces were tight. Only a fool would want to ride in among Aes Sedai and have those spread in a sudden breeze.

Aviendha glanced at him sideways, then tried to push his boot out of the stirrup. "Let me up," she ordered curtly.

Why under the Light did she want to ride now? Well, he was not going to have her scrambling up and very likely knocking him out of the saddle in the process; he had seen Aiel get on a horse once or twice.

Slapping another fly, he leaned down and caught her hand. "Hold on,"

he said, and heaved her up behind him with a grunt. She was nearly as tall
as he was, and solid to boot. "Just put your arm around my waist." She only
gave him a look and twisted about awkwardly until she sat astride, legs
bared above the knee and not at all concerned with it. Nice legs, but he
would not have involved himself with another Aiel woman even if she was
not moonstruck over Rand.

After a time, she spoke to his back. "The boy, Olver. The Shaido killed
his father?"

Mat nodded without looking around at her. Would he even see any
Warders before it was too late? Leading the way, Vanin rode slumped like
a sack of suet as always, but he had a sharp eye out.

"His mother died of hunger?" Aviendha asked.

"That, or maybe sickness." Warders wore those cloaks that could blend
into anything. You could walk past one without seeing him. "Olver wasn't
too clear, and I didn't press him. He buried her himself. Why? Do you think
you owe him something since Aiel cost him his family?"

"Owe?" She sounded startled. "I killed neither, and if I had, they were
treekillers. How would I have *toh*?" Without a pause she went on as if continuing in the same line. "You do not care for him properly, Mat Cauthon.
I know men know nothing about raising children, but he is too young to
spend all of his time with grown men."

Mat did look at her then, and blinked. She had her headkerchief off
and was busily running a polished greenstone comb through her dark reddish hair. That seemed to be taking all her concentration. That and not
falling off. She had donned an intricately worked silver necklace, too, and a
wide bracelet of carved ivory.

Shaking his head, he went back to studying the forest. Aiel or not, they
were all alike in some ways. *If the world is ending, a woman will want time to fix
her hair. If the world's ending, a woman will take time to tell a man something he's
done wrong.* It would have been enough to make him chuckle if he was not so
busy wondering whether Warders were watching him right that moment.

The sun climbed to its zenith and tipped over by the time the forest
gave way abruptly. Fewer than a hundred paces of cleared ground separated
trees from village, and the ground looked as if it had not been cleared long.
Salidar itself was a considerable village of gray stone buildings and thatched
roofs, and the streets were full and busy. Mat shrugged into his coat; the
finest green wool, embroidered with gold on cuffs and tall collar, it should
be good enough to meet Aes Sedai in. He left it hanging open, though;
even for Aes Sedai he would not die from heat.

No one tried to stop him as they rode in, but people paused and every eye turned to him and his strange little company. They knew, all right. Everyone knew. He gave up counting Aes Sedai faces after reaching fifty; that number was reached too quickly for any peace of mind. There were no soldiers in the crowd, unless you counted Warders, some in those color-shifting cloaks, some fingering a sword hilt as they watched him pass. No soldiers in the village simply meant they were all in the camps Vanin had mentioned. And all the soldiers being in the camps meant they were ready to do something. Mat hoped Talmanes was holding to his instructions. Talmanes had some sense, but he could be almost as eager to go off and charge somebody as Nalesean. He would have left Daerid in charge—Daerid had seen too many battles to be eager—but the noblemen would never have stood for it. There did not seem to be any flies in Salidar, either. *Maybe they know something I don't.*

A woman caught his eye, a pretty woman in odd clothes, wide yellow trousers and a short white coat, her golden hair in an elaborate braid to her waist. She was carrying a bow, of all things. Not many women took up the bow. She saw him looking and ducked down a narrow alleyway. Something about her tickled his memory, but he could not say what. That was one trouble with all those old memories; he was always seeing people who reminded him of somebody who turned out to be a thousand years dead when he finally figured it out. Maybe he had even really seen somebody who looked like her. Those holes in what he remembered of his own life were fuzzy around the edges. *Probably another Hunter for the Horn*, he thought wryly, and put her out of his head.

There was no point in riding about until somebody spoke, because it seemed nobody was going to. Mat reined in and nodded to a thin, dark-haired woman who looked up at him, coolly questioning. Pretty, but too skinny for his taste even without that ageless face. Who wanted to be poked by bones every time you gave a hug? "My name is Mat Cauthon," he said neutrally. If she wanted bowing and scraping, she could take a leap, but antagonizing her would just be foolish. "I'm looking for Elayne Trakand and Egwene al'Vere. And Nynaeve al'Meara, I suppose." Rand had not mentioned her, but she had gone off with Elayne, he knew.

The Aes Sedai blinked in surprise, yet serenity returned in a flash. She studied him and the others one by one, pausing on Aviendha, then looked at the squadmen so long Mat wondered whether she could see the Dragon and the black-and-white disc through the folded cloth. "Follow me," she said finally. "I will see whether the Amyrlin Seat can see you." Gathering her skirts, she started up the street.

As Mat heeled Pips to follow, Vanin let his dun drop back and muttered, "Asking Aes Sedai for anything is never a good notion. I could have shown you where to go." He jerked his head toward a three-story stone cube ahead. "They call it the Little Tower."

Mat shrugged uneasily. The Little Tower? And they had somebody here they called the Amyrlin Seat? He doubted the woman had meant Elaida. Rand was wrong again. This lot were not frightened. They were too puffed-up crazy to be frightened.

In front of the stone cube, the skinny Aes Sedai said peremptorily, "Wait here," and vanished inside.

Aviendha slipped to the ground, and Mat followed quickly, ready to grab her if she tried to dart away. Even if it cost him a little blood he was not going to let her run off and slit Elayne's throat before he even had a chance to talk to this so-called Amyrlin. But she only stood there, staring straight ahead with hands folded at her waist and shawl looped over her elbows. She looked completely at her ease, but he thought she might well be terrified out of her skull. If she had any sense, she was. They had collected a crowd.

Aes Sedai had begun gathering, closing them in against the front of their Little Tower, silently peering at him, and the arc of women thickened the longer he stood there. Actually, they seemed to peer at Aviendha as much as him, but he felt all of those cool, unreadable gazes. He barely stopped himself from fingering the silver foxhead hanging beneath his shirt.

A plain-faced Aes Sedai pushed to the front of the crowd, leading a slender young woman in white, with big eyes. He vaguely remembered Anaiya, but she hardly seemed interested in him at all. "Are you sure, child?" she asked the novice.

The young woman's mouth tightened slightly, but she certainly let no irritation into her voice. "He still seems to glow, or shine. I really do see it. I just don't know why."

Anaiya gave her a delighted smile. "He's *ta'veren*, Nicola. You've uncovered your first Talent. You can see *ta'veren*. Now back to the class with you. Quickly. You don't want to fall behind." Nicola bobbed a curtsy and, with a last glance at Mat, burrowed away through the encircling Aes Sedai.

Anaiya turned her gaze on him then, one of those Aes Sedai gazes that were meant to unsettle a man. It unsettled him right enough. Of course some Aes Sedai knew about him—some knew a good deal more than he could wish, and come to think it, he seemed to remember that Anaiya was one of those—but having things announced that way, in front of the Light knew how many women with those cool Aes Sedai eyes. . . . His hands stroked the carved haft of his spear. Foxhead or no foxhead, there were enough of them to simply lay hands on him and carry him off. *Bloody Aes Sedai! Bloody Rand!*

He only held Anaiya's interest for a moment, though. Stepping up to Aviendha, she said, "And what is your name, child?" Her tone was pleasant, but it expected an answer and no delay about it.

Aviendha faced her squarely, a head taller and using every hair of it. "I am Aviendha, of the Nine Valleys sept of the Taardad Aiel." Anaiya's mouth quirked toward a smile at the note of defiance.

Mat wondered who was going to win that staring match, but before he could make a bet with himself, another Aes Sedai joined them, a woman whose bony-cheeked face gave an impression of age despite smooth cheeks and glossy brown hair. "Do you be aware you can channel, girl?"

"I am," Aviendha said curtly and snapped her mouth shut as if intending to say no more. She concentrated on adjusting her shawl, but she had said enough. Aes Sedai swarmed in around her, crowding Mat away.

"How old are you, child?"

"You have developed much strength, but you could learn very much as a novice."

"Do many Aiel girls die of a wasting sickness when they are a few years younger than you?"

"How long have you . . . ?"

"You could. . . ."

"You really should. . . ."

"You must. . . ."

Nynaeve appeared in the doorway so suddenly she seemed to pop out of the air. Planting her fists on her hips, she stared at Mat. "What are you doing here, Matrim Cauthon? How did you get here? I suppose it's too much to hope you have anything to do with this army of Dragonsworn that's about to descend on us."

"Actually," he said dryly, "I am in command."

"You . . . !" Nynaeve stood there with her mouth open, then gave herself a shake, tugging at her blue dress as if it had been disarrayed. It was cut lower than anything he remembered seeing her wear before, low enough to show cleavage, with yellow scrollwork around the neckline and hem. Altogether different from what she had worn back home. "Well, come with me," she said sharply. "I'll take you to the Amyrlin."

"Mat Cauthon," Aviendha called, a touch breathily. She was looking over and around Aes Sedai to find him. "Mat Cauthon." Just that, but for an Aiel, she looked frantic.

The Aes Sedai surrounding her kept right on, voices calm, reasonable and relentless.

"For you, the best thing, it is to. . . ."

"You must consider. . . ."

"Much the best. . . ."

"You can hardly think of. . . ."

Mat grinned. She might pull her knife in a moment, but in that crowd he doubted it would do her much good. She would not be hunting up Elayne any time soon, that was for sure. Wondering whether he would return to find her wearing a white dress, he tossed his spear up to Vanin. "Lead on, Nynaeve. Let's see this *Amyrlin* of yours."

She gave him a tight frown and led him inside tugging at her braid and muttering only partly to herself. "This is Rand's doing, isn't it? I know it is. Somehow it is. Frightening everybody half out of their wits. You just watch your step, *Lord General* Cauthon, or I swear you will wish I'd caught you stealing blueberries again. Frightening people! Even a man should have more sense! You stop that grinning, Mat Cauthon. I do not know what she's going to make of this."

There were Aes Sedai at the tables inside—it had the feel of a common room to him, even with those careful Aes Sedai scribbling or handing out orders—but they hardly more than glanced at him and Nynaeve as they crossed the room. It only went to show what a raree-show they were running here. An Accepted stalking through muttering to herself, and not a one of those Aes Sedai said a word. He had stayed in the Tower as short a time as he could manage, but he knew that was not the way Aes Sedai ran things.

At the rear of the room, Nynaeve pushed open a door that had seen better days. Everything in the place seemed to have seen better days. Mat followed her in—and stopped dead. There was Elayne, pretty as anything with that golden hair, but playing at the grand lady with every inch of her, in green silk with a high lace neck, and one of those condescending smiles, and raised eyebrows. And there was Egwene, seated behind a table, a questioning smile on her face. And a seven-striped stole over her pale yellow dress.

Taking a quick peek outside, he shoved the door to before any of the Aes Sedai could see in.

"Maybe you think this is funny," he growled, crossing the bit of carpet as fast as he could step, "but they'll have your hide if they find out. They'll *never* bloody let you go, any of you, if they—" Snatching the stole from Egwene's neck, he hauled her hurriedly out of the chair—and the silver foxhead went dead cold against his chest.

Giving Egwene a small shove away from the table, he glared at them. Egwene only looked puzzled, but Nynaeve's mouth was hanging open again, and Elayne's big blue eyes looked ready to pop out onto the floor. One of them had tried to use the Power on him. The only good thing that had come out of his trip into that *ter'angreal* was the foxhead medallion. He supposed it had to be a *ter'angreal* too, but he was grateful for it just the same. So long as it touched his skin, the One Power could not reach him. Not *saidar*, anyway; he had more proof of that than he cared for. It did go cold when someone tried, though.

Tossing the stole and his hat onto the table, he sat down, then hiked up from the seat to pull out some cushions and throw them on the floor. He rested a boot on the edge of the table and regarded the fool women. "You'll need those cushions if this so-called Amyrlin finds out about this little joke of yours."

"Mat," Egwene began in a firm voice, but he cut her off.

"No! If you wanted to talk, you should have talked instead of lashing out with your bloody Power. Now you can listen."

"How did you . . . ?" Elayne said wonderingly. "The flows just . . . vanished."

At almost the same instant, Nynaeve said in a threatening tone, "Mat Cauthon, you are making the biggest—"

"I said listen!" He poked a finger at Elayne. "You, I'm taking back to Caemlyn, if I can keep Aviendha from killing you. If you don't want that pretty throat slit, you stay close to me and do what I say, no questions!" The finger shifted to Egwene. "Rand says he'll send you back to the Wise Ones whenever you want, and if what I've seen so far is any indication what you get up to, my advice is to take him up on it *now*! It seems you know how to Travel"—Egwene gave a small start—"so you can make a gateway to Caemlyn for the Band. I don't want any argument, Egwene! And you, Nynaeve! I ought to leave you here, but if you want to come, you can. Only, I'm warning you. You yank that braid at me just once, and I swear I'll warm your bottom!"

They were staring at him as if he had sprouted horns like a Trolloc, but at least they were keeping their mouths shut. Maybe he had managed to get a little sense into their heads. Not that they would ever thank him for saving their hides. Oh, no; not them. As usual, they would say they would have worked everything out for themselves in just a little while longer. If a woman told you you were interfering when you pulled her out of a dungeon, what would she not say?

He drew a deep breath. "Now. When the poor blind fool they've chosen out for their Amyrlin gets here, I will do the talking. She can't be very bright, or they'd never have been able to shove her into the job. Amyrlin Seat for a bloody village in the middle of bloody nowhere. You keep your mouths shut and curtsy for all you're worth, and I'll pull your bacon off the coals again." They just stared. Good. "I know all about her army, but I have one too. If she's crazy enough to think she can take the Tower away from Elaida . . . well, she probably won't risk any losses just to hold on to you three. You make that gateway, Egwene, and I will have you in Caemlyn tomorrow, the next day latest, and these madwomen can run off and get themselves killed by Elaida. Maybe you'll have some company. They cannot all be mad. Rand's willing to offer sanctuary. A curtsy, a quick oath of fealty, and he'll keep Elaida from putting their heads on pikes in Tar Valon. They can't ask better than that. Well? Anything to say?" They did not even blink as far as he could see. "A simple 'Thank you, Mat' would do." Not a word. Not a blink.

A timid tap on the door was followed by a novice, a pretty green-eyed girl who dropped a deep curtsy, all wide-eyed awe. "I was sent to see if you wanted anything, Mother. For the . . . the general, I mean. Wine, or . . . or. . . ."

"No, Tabiya." Egwene pulled the striped stole from under his hat and settled it on her shoulders. "I want to talk with *General* Cauthon alone a little longer. Tell Sheriam I will send for her shortly, to advise me."

"Close your mouth before you catch flies, Mat," Nynaeve said in tones of deepest satisfaction.

CHAPTER
39

Possibilities

Adjusting her stole, Egwene studied Mat. She expected him to look like a cornered bear, but he just looked poleaxed and sweaty. There were so many questions she wanted to ask—How did Rand know about Salidar? How could he possibly know she had worked out Traveling? What did Rand think he was doing?—but she was not going to ask them. Mat and his Band of the Red Hand had her head buzzing. Maybe Rand had handed her a gift from the sky.

"My chair?" she said quietly. She hoped he had noticed that she was not sweating, nor Elayne or Nynaeve; Nynaeve not very much anyway. Siuan had revealed the trick, nothing to do with the Power at all, just a matter of concentrating in a certain way. Nynaeve had been rather angry, small surprise, that Siuan had not taught it to them before, but Siuan just replied calmly that it was for Aes Sedai, not Accepted. So far Egwene had managed to hold her thoughts properly when there were sisters about, and a cool face instead of a sweaty did seem to help their attitudes a little. Some of them. It should do wonders for Mat. If he ever stopped staring and saw. "Mat? My chair?"

He gave a start, then rose and moved aside, wordlessly staring from her to Elayne to Nynaeve as though they were some sort of puzzle. Well, Nynaeve and Elayne were looking at him in much the same way, and they surely had better reason.

666

She dusted the cushions before replacing them in the chair with a fond thought for Chesa. After two days, she did not need them any longer, not really, but either she gave up bathing or accepted cushions until not a hint of a bruise showed. Chesa would remove the cushions if Egwene said to. Sweaty face or cool, Egwene was the Amyrlin Seat, before whom kings bowed and queens curtsied, even if none had yet, who would have Elaida tried and executed in short order and all put right with the White Tower, and thus with the world. Chesa would do it, and give Egwene such hurt, reproachful glances for not being allowed to take care of her that leaving the cushions there was much easier to bear.

Settling herself with her hands folded on the table, she said, "Mat—" He broke in immediately.

"This really is madness, you know," he said quietly. Quietly, but quite firmly. "You will end with your head off, Egwene. All of you will. Your heads—cut—off."

"Mat," she said in a stronger tone, but he went right on.

"Listen, you can still get out of this. If they think you're the Amyrlin, you can come out with me to . . . to inspect the Band. You make a gateway, and we'll be gone before this bunch of goat-brained lunatics can blink."

Nynaeve had seen *saidar* fail around him, but she had dealt with recalcitrant men long before she learned to channel. With a muttered growl of "Warm *my* bottom?" that Egwene did not think was intended to be heard, Nynaeve deftly hiked up her skirts and kicked Mat squarely in *his*, so hard that he staggered all the way to the wall before catching himself with a hand. Elayne burst into laughter, and suppressed it just as quickly, but she still quivered, and her eyes shone.

Egwene bit her lip to keep from laughing too. It really was comical. Mat turned his head slowly to stare at Nynaeve, all wide-eyed indignation and outrage. Then his brows lowered, and jerking his undone coat as if to straighten it, he began to stalk slowly toward her. Slowly because he was limping. Egwene covered her mouth. It really would not do to laugh.

Nynaeve drew herself up sternly, and then perhaps a few things occurred to her. She might be angry enough to channel, but *saidar* was apparently useless with him. Mat was tall for a Two Rivers man, considerably taller than she, considerably stronger, and there was a decidedly dangerous glint in his eye. She glanced at Egwene, and smoothed her dress, trying to maintain her stern face. Mat stalked nearer, face like thunder. Another hasty glance, worry beginning to show, was followed by a small step back.

"Mat," Egwene said in a level tone. He did not stop. "Mat, stop cutting
the fool. You are in quite a predicament, but I should be able to get you out
of it, if you listen to reason."

Finally he halted. With a glare and a warning shake of his finger at
Nynaeve, he turned his back on her and planted his fists on the writing
table. "*I* am in a predicament? Egwene, you've jumped out of a tree toward
a bear pit, and you think everything is fine because you haven't landed
yet!"

She smiled at him calmly. "Mat, not many here in Salidar think very
well of Dragonsworn. Lord Bryne certainly doesn't, nor his soldiers. We
have heard some very disturbing stories. And some sickening ones."

"Dragonsworn!" he yelped. "What do they have to do with me? I'm no
bloody Dragonsworn!"

"Of course you are, Mat." She made it sound the most obvious thing in
the world. Which it was, if you only thought. "You go where Rand sends
you. What else are you but Dragonsworn? But if you listen to me, I can
stop them from putting *your* head on a pike. Actually, I don't think Lord
Bryne would use a pike—he always complains he doesn't have enough—
but I am sure he would figure out something."

Mat looked at the other two women, and Egwene compressed her lips
for an instant. She had made herself plain, but he appeared to be hunting
for a clue to what she was talking about. Elayne gave him back a tight
smile and a decisively confirming nod. She might not see where Egwene
was going, yet she knew she was not talking for the sound of her voice.
Nynaeve, still struggling to keep a severe face and tugging at her braid,
only glared at him, but maybe that was even better. Though she was
beginning to sweat; Nynaeve lost concentration when she grew angry.

"Now, listen, Egwene," Mat said. Then again, maybe neither response
was really enough. He managed to combine a reasonable tone with indulgence in the most offensive way possible. "If you want to call yourself
Amyrlin, you can call yourself Amyrlin. Rand would welcome you with
open arms in Caemlyn even if you don't bring all these Aes Sedai to him,
but I know he will be overjoyed if you do. Whatever your problems are
with Elaida, he can work them out. She knows he's the Dragon Reborn.
Light, you remember her letter. Why, you will have your White Tower all
mended before you can say Jak o' the Wisps. No battles. No bloodshed.
You know you don't want bloodshed, Egwene."

That she did not. Once the first blood was shed between Salidar and
Tar Valon, it would be difficult to make the Tower whole again. Once the

first Aes Sedai blood was shed, it might be impossible. Still, Elaida had to be brought down, and Egwene would do what she had to do. She just did not like it. And she did not like Mat telling her what she knew, liked it the less so for being right. Definitely the less so in that tone. It was a real effort to keep her hands still on the table. She wanted to stand and box his ears.

"However I deal with Rand," she said coolly, "you can be sure it will not be by leading Aes Sedai to swear fealty to him or any other man." Cool, and not at all arguing; a calm statement of simple facts. "How I deal with Elaida is my concern, and none of yours. If you have any sense at all, Mat, you will keep your mouth shut as long as you are in Salidar and walk small. You start telling other Aes Sedai what Rand is going to do just as soon they kneel to him, and you might not like the answers you get. Talk about carrying me off, or Nynaeve or Elayne, and you will be *very* lucky not to get a sword through you."

He jerked upright with a glare. "I'll talk to you again when you're ready to listen to reason, Egwene. Is Thom Merrilin around?" She gave a curt nod. What did he want with Thom? Probably to douse himself in wine. Well, good luck to him finding a tavern here. "When you're ready to listen," he repeated grimly, and stalked—limped—to the door.

"Mat," Elayne said, "I would not try to leave were I you. Getting into Salidar is much easier than getting out."

He grinned at her insolently, and the way he eyed her up and down, he was lucky Elayne did not slap him hard enough to loosen all his teeth. "You, my fine Lady, I am taking back to Caemlyn if I have to tie you up in a package to hand to Rand, burn me if I don't. And I will bloody well leave when I choose." His bow was mocking, to Elayne and to Egwene. Nynaeve got only a glower and another shake of his finger.

"How *can* Rand have such a low, insufferable lout for a friend?" Elayne asked no one in particular before the door was well closed behind him.

"His language has certainly slipped downhill," Nynaeve grumbled darkly, tossing her head so her braid swung over her shoulder. Egwene thought she might be afraid she would pull it out by the roots if she did not put it out of reach.

"I should have let him do as he wanted, Nynaeve. You have to remember you're Aes Sedai now. You can't go around kicking people, or boxing their ears, or thumping them with sticks." Nynaeve stared at her, mouth working, face growing redder and redder. Elayne began assiduously studying the carpet.

With a sigh, Egwene folded the striped stole and laid it on the table to one side. That was her way of making sure Elayne and Nynaeve remembered they were alone; sometimes the stole made them start talking to the Amyrlin Seat instead of Egwene al'Vere. As usual, it worked. Nynaeve took a very deep breath.

Before she could speak, though, Elayne said, "Do you mean to join him and this Band of the Red Hand to Gareth Bryne?"

Egwene shook her head. The Warders said there were six or seven thousand in Mat's Band now, more than she remembered from Cairhien, and a considerable number, if not nearly so many as those two captured men claimed, but Bryne's soldiers truly would not take kindly to Dragonsworn. Besides, she had her own scheme, which she explained while they drew the other chairs to the table. It was very like sitting in a kitchen talking. She moved the stole farther over.

"That is brilliant." Elayne's grin said she meant it. But then, Elayne always said what she meant. "I didn't think the other would work either, but this really is *brilliant*."

Nynaeve sniffed irritably. "What makes you think Mat will go along? He'll stick a pole through the spokes just for the fun of it."

"I think he made a promise," Egwene said simply, and Nynaeve nodded. Slowly, reluctantly, but she nodded. Elayne looked lost, of course; she did not know him. "Elayne, Mat does exactly as he pleases; he always has."

"No matter how many turnips he had to peel for it," Nynaeve muttered, "or how often he was switched."

"Yes, that is Mat," Egwene sighed. He had been the most irresponsible boy in Emond's Field, maybe in the Two Rivers. "But if he gives his word, he keeps it. And I think he promised Rand to see you back in Caemlyn, Elayne. You notice he retreated to asking me"—in a way he had—"but you he never changed a hair on. I think he'll try to stay as close to you as your belt pouch. But we won't let him even see you unless he does as we want." She paused. "Elayne, if you want to go with him, you can. To Rand, I mean. As soon as we squeeze all of the good out of Mat and his Band."

Elayne hardly hesitated before shaking her head, and she shook it firmly. "No, Ebou Dar is too important." That had been one victory, surprisingly won with a mere suggestion. Elayne and Nynaeve were to join Merilille at Tylin's court. "At least if he stays close, I'll have a few days to try for a look at the *ter'angreal* he is carrying. It has to be that, Egwene. Nothing else could explain it."

Egwene could only agree. She had simply meant to wrap him up in Air where he stood, just a gentle reminder of who he was trying to manhandle, but the flows touched him, and melted. That was the only way to explain it. They ceased to exist where they touched him. She still felt the shock of that moment, remembering, and she realized she was not the only one suddenly adjusting skirts that needed no adjusting.

"We could have some Warders turn out his pockets." Nynaeve sounded more than satisfied with the image. "We'll see how Master Mat Cauthon likes that."

"If we take things away from him," Egwene said patiently, "don't you think he might balk when we start telling him what to do?" Mat had never taken orders very well, and his usual response to Aes Sedai and the One Power was to take the first chance to slip away. Maybe his promise to Rand would stop that—there *had* to be one; nothing else explained his behavior—but she was not going to risk it. Nynaeve nodded, rather grudgingly.

"Maybe. . . ." Tapping her fingers on the table, Elayne stared at nothing thoughtfully for a moment. "Maybe we could take him to Ebou Dar. That way, I might have a better chance at the *ter'angreal*. Though if it stops *saidar*, I can't see how I'll *ever* manage to study it."

"Take that young ruffian along!" Nynaeve sat up straight. "You can't mean it, Elayne. He would make every day a misery; he's very good at that. He'll never do what he's told. Besides, he will never stand still for it. He's so wrapped up in taking you to Caemlyn, you could not budge him from it with a prybar and a team of horses."

"But if he means to keep an eye on me until I reach Caemlyn," Elayne told her, "he'll have no choice but to go. It is perfect."

"It might not be a bad idea," Egwene put in while Nynaeve was searching for another argument. Sending them after the bowl still seemed right, but the more she thought of where they would have to search, the more she worried. "A few soldiers might be a very good idea, unless you've picked out Warders without letting me know. Thom and Juilin are all very well, and Birgitte, but it is a rough place you're going."

"A *few* soldiers might be well enough," Elayne said, coloring slightly. "So long as they know to follow orders."

Nynaeve did not quite glance at Elayne, but there was a distinct pause before she shook her head irascibly. "We're hardly going to be fighting duels, Egwene, however touchy these Ebou Dari are. Thom and Juilin will do quite well enough. Myself, I think all these stories we've been hearing are just meant to make us decide to give it over." Everybody had heard tales of Ebou Dar since word had spread that they were going; Chesa had heard several, each more pitiful and horrific than the last, strangers killed for a wrong glance before they could blink, women widowed and children orphaned over a word, *women* fighting in the streets with knives. "No, if we could survive Tanchico with just Thom and Juilin, and Liandrin and some of her Black sisters around in the bargain, we will do very well in Ebou Dar without Mat Cauthon or any soldiers either. Mat commanding soldiers! He never even remembered to milk his father's cows unless he was put on the stool and handed the bucket."

Egwene gave a faint sigh. Any mention of Birgitte did that; they started as if goosed, then either stammered around her or else went on as if she had not been mentioned at all. One look had convinced Egwene that the woman following Elayne and Nynaeve about—especially Elayne, for some reason—was the woman she had seen in *Tel'aran'rhiod*. Birgitte of the legends, the archer who never missed, one of the dead heroes awaiting the call of the Horn of Valere. A dead hero, not a live woman walking the streets of Salidar, but the same woman nonetheless. Elayne still had provided no explanation, only a careful, embarrassed mumble about not being able to talk of what they had agreed not to talk of. Birgitte herself, the hero of legends, turned the other way or went down alleys if she saw Egwene coming. Ordering the woman to her study and demanding an explanation was out of the question; she had promised, after all, no matter how much a fool the situation made her feel. Anyway, there hardly seemed any harm. She just wished she knew the why of it. And the how.

Putting Birgitte out of her mind for the moment, she leaned across the table toward Nynaeve. "Perhaps we can't make Mat take orders exactly, but wouldn't it be fine to watch him smolder over having to be your bodyguard?"

"It would certainly be worthwhile," Elayne said thoughtfully, "if Rand really has made him a general. Mother often said the best men were reluctant to take orders, and always worth teaching to. I can't see Mat as one of the best—Lini says 'Fools only listen to themselves'—but if we can teach him enough that he doesn't make a *complete* fool of himself where there is nobody to rescue him, we will be doing Rand a large favor. Besides, I need *time* if I am to study that *ter'angreal.*"

Egwene tried not to smile; Elayne always caught on so quickly. Then again, she probably was going to try teaching Mat to sit up straight. That would be something to see. She liked Elayne, and admired her strength, but she would bet on Mat in that contest. By a whisker.

Nynaeve gave ground stubbornly. Mat was wrongheaded; he would say "down" if they said "up" just to spite them. He could make trouble nailed up inside a barrel. They constantly would have to be dragging him out of taverns and gambling dens. Toward the end she was reduced to claiming that Mat would probably pinch Elayne the first time her back was turned, and Egwene knew they were overcoming her objections. Mat certainly gave a lot of time to chasing after women, which Egwene could hardly approve, but Nynaeve surely knew as well as she that for all of looking when and how he should not, he seemed to have an uncanny knack for picking women who wanted to be chased, even the most unlikely. Unfortunately, just when she was sure that Nynaeve was about to give in, a knock at the door announced Sheriam.

Sheriam did not wait on permission to enter; she never did. Cool-eyed in her blue stole, she paused to gaze at Nynaeve and Elayne. Second to the Amyrlin or not, the Keeper had no real authority over Aes Sedai except what the Amyrlin chose to give her, and most assuredly none to dismiss anyone from the Amyrlin's presence, yet that look was clearly a dismissal.

Elayne rose smoothly, making a deep formal curtsy to Egwene. "If you will excuse me, Mother, I should go find Aviendha."

Nynaeve, on the other hand, locked eyes with Sheriam until Egwene cleared her throat and slipped the striped stole back into place on her shoulders.

Flushing, Nynaeve bobbed to her feet. "I should go, too. Janya said she would talk to me about lost Talents."

The recovery of those Talents was not proving as easy as Egwene had hoped. The sisters were willing enough to talk; the problem was in making Moghedien understand what was meant by a vague description or sometimes only a name, then hoping she really knew something. All very well to know, for example, that Aligning the Matrix made metals stronger, but the woman knew less of metals than of Healing, and what under the Light was Spinning Earthfire, or for that matter, Milking Tears?

Moghedien seemed eager to help, desperate to, especially since Siuan taught the trick of ignoring heat. Apparently she had lied to Nynaeve and Elayne about that. Convinced Egwene would take that for her "one lie," the woman had groveled on her knees, weeping and begging, teeth chattering, kissing the hems of their skirts. Eager to help or not, it had raised her fear to new heights. The constant sickening rain of sniveling terror was just too much. Despite her intentions, the *a'dam* bracelet lay in Egwene's pouch now. She would have given it to Nynaeve now—and glad to be rid of it—but handing the thing back and forth in front of others would occasion comment sooner or later.

Instead, she said, "Nynaeve, it might be best for you to avoid Mat until his temper cools." She was not sure that Mat would really carry out his threat, but if anyone could goad him to it, Nynaeve could, and there would be no convincing her after that. "Or at least make sure you only talk to him with a great many people around. Perhaps a few Warders."

Nynaeve opened her mouth; then after a moment closed it again; her cheeks paled a little and she swallowed. "Yes. Yes, I think that might be best, Mother."

Sheriam watched the door close with a small frown that she still wore when she turned to Egwene. "There were hard words, Mother?"

"Only what you expect when old friends meet after a long time. Nynaeve remembers Mat as a scamp, but he isn't ten anymore, and he resents it." Bound by the Oath against lying, Aes Sedai had carried the half-truth, the quarter-truth and the implication to arts. Useful arts, in Egwene's opinion. Especially with Aes Sedai. The Three Oaths did no one any favors, least of all Aes Sedai.

"It's hard sometimes to remember that people change." Taking a chair without being asked, Sheriam arranged her blue silk skirts carefully. "I assume whoever commands the Dragonsworn sent young Mat with a message from Rand al'Thor? I hope you said nothing he might take as a promise, Mother. An army of Dragonsworn not ten miles distant faces us with a delicate situation. It will not help if their commander believes we are going back on pledges."

Egwene studied the other woman a moment. Nothing fazed Sheriam. Not that she let anyone see, at least. Sheriam knew quite a lot about Mat; so did several other sisters in Salidar. Could that be used to press him in the right direction, or would it make him bolt? *Mat for later*, she thought firmly. *Sheriam now.* "Would you ask someone to bring tea, Sheriam? I feel a trifle thirsty."

Sheriam's face altered only slightly, just a tightening around those tilted eyes so small that it barely disturbed her apparent serenity. Egwene could almost see the question wanting to pop out, though. What had she said to Mat that she did not want to talk about? What promises had she made that Sheriam was going to have to rescue her from without losing ground to Romanda or Lelaine?

All Sheriam did was say a few words to someone outside, and when she regained her seat, Egwene gave her no opportunity to open her mouth. Instead, she hit her right between the eyes. So to speak. "It seems Mat is the commander, Sheriam, and in a way, the army is the message. Apparently, Rand would like us all to come to him in Caemlyn. There was some mention of oaths of fealty."

Sheriam's head came up, eyes widening. Only partly in outrage at such a suggestion, though. There was a definite tinge of . . . well, in anyone but an Aes Sedai, Egwene would have called it fear. Very understandable, if so. If she had promised that—and she *was* from the same village; one of her *uses* as Amyrlin was that she had grown up with Rand—it would be a bottomless mire to get out of. Word would spread no matter what Sheriam did; some of the Hall might well blame it on her, or use it as a pretext, anyway. Romanda and Lelaine were not the only Sitters to have cautioned Egwene about following Sheriam's advice without consulting the Hall. In truth, Delana was the only one who really seemed to support Sheriam fully, but she counseled listening to Romanda and Lelaine as well, as if it were really possible to go in three directions at once. And even could the Hall be managed, once news of the promise reached Rand, and of its withdrawal, he would be ten times harder to handle. A hundred times.

Egwene only waited until Sheriam's lips parted, then spoke first again. "Of course, I told him it was ridiculous."

"Of course." Sheriam's voice was not quite as steady as it had been. Very good.

"But you are quite right. The situation is delicate. It's such a pity. Your advice on how to deal with Romanda and Lelaine was good, but I don't think increasing preparations to move will be enough now."

Romanda had cornered her and grimly lectured her on haste leading to ruin; Gareth Bryne's army must be made larger, large enough for news of its size to intimidate Elaida. And by the way, Romanda could not emphasize strongly enough once again that the embassies to rulers *must* be recalled; none but Aes Sedai should be allowed to learn any more of troubles in the Tower than could be avoided. Lelaine cared about neither Lord Bryne's army nor rulers—both were irrelevant—though she did counsel caution and waiting. The proper approaches to Aes Sedai still in the Tower would surely yield dividends; Elaida could be removed from the Amyrlin Seat and Egwene installed in such a fashion that none but a very few sisters would ever be certain what had actually happened. In time, the fact that the White Tower had ever been broken would be taken for no more than a country tale. It might even have worked, if they had had enough time. If waiting did not give Elaida just as much chance to work on sisters here.

The other difference with Lelaine was she had said everything with a smile that would have done very well for a pet novice or Accepted she was very proud of. Egwene's rediscovery of Traveling caused a lot of Aes Sedai to smile, though only a handful were strong enough to make a gateway larger than they could put an arm through and most not even that. Romanda wanted to use gateways to remove the Oath Rod and certain other items—Egwene was not told exactly what—from the Tower so they could make true Aes Sedai in Salidar while depriving Elaida of the ability; surely Egwene wanted to be truly Aes Sedai. Lelaine agreed about that last, but not about using gateways in the Tower; there was too much chance they might be detected, and if those in the Tower learned to Travel, too much advantage would be lost. Those points had carried considerable weight with the Hall, which did not please Romanda at all.

Sheriam had smiled too, over agreeing with Lelaine about something, but she was not smiling now. "Mother, I am not sure I understand," she said, much too tolerantly. "Preparations are certainly enough to show the Hall you will not be bullied. Moving before everything is in place could be disastrous."

Egwene managed to put on a disingenuous expression. "I understand, Sheriam. I don't know what I would do without your advice." How she looked forward to the day she could stop this. Sheriam would make a very good Keeper—she might even have made a good Amyrlin—but Egwene was going to enjoy the day she could teach the woman that she *was* Keeper, not Amyrlin. Sheriam *and* the Hall. "It's just that now Mat has this army of Dragonsworn on our doorstep. What will Lord Bryne do? Or some of his soldiers, on their own? Everybody talks about how he wanted to send men to hunt these Dragonsworn who are supposed to be burning villages. I know he has been told to keep a tight rein on them, but. . . ."

"Lord Gareth will do exactly as we—as you—command, and no more."

"Perhaps." He was not so happy with that tight rein as Sheriam believed. Siuan spent a great deal of time with Gareth Bryne for all her grumbling about the man, and he told her things. Egwene could not afford to give away Siuan's allegiance, though. "I hope the same can be said for every one of his soldiers. We cannot move west into Amadicia, but I thought perhaps we could go downriver, to Ebou Dar. Maybe by gateway. Surely Aes Sedai are welcome there. Lord Bryne could camp outside the city. Moving would emphasize that we aren't going to accept Rand's . . . offer, if it can be called that. And if we are going to make more preparations, I'm sure we would find everything much easier to accomplish in a large city, with roads and ships in and out of the harbor."

Sheriam's control slipped again, to the extent of a breathiness in her voice. "Ebou Dar is not so welcoming as that, Mother. A few sisters are quite different from a few hundred, with an army at their backs. Mother, even a hint of that might make Tylin think we meant to seize the city. Tylin, and a good many Altaran nobles who would like nothing better than an excuse to topple her and take the Throne of the Winds for themselves. A tangle of that kind would ruin us with every ruler. No, Mother, it is quite out of the question."

"But do we dare remain here now? Mat won't do anything, but all it needs is a handful of Lord Bryne's soldiers deciding to take matters into their own hands." Egwene frowned at her skirts, smoothed them as if thinking worriedly, then sighed. "The longer we sit and do nothing with an army of Dragonsworn staring at us, the worse it will be. I won't be surprised to hear rumors they mean to attack us, and people saying we should do for them first." If this did not work, there would be rumors. Nynaeve and Elayne and Siuan and Leane would see to that. It would be dangerous, but she could find some way to make Mat retreat before sparks flew if it came to that. "Why, the way rumors spread, I wouldn't be surprised if half of Altara thinks *we* are Dragonsworn in under a month." That was one rumor she would have stopped if she knew how. The Hall no longer brought nobles to see Logain since he was Healed, but Bryne's recruiters still went out, and parties of Aes Sedai hunting new novices, and men to make the long trek to the nearest villages with their carts and wagons to buy food. A hundred paths for that rumor to take, and it only needed one. "Sheriam, I can't help feeling we are in a box, and if we don't get out of it, nothing good will come. Nothing at all good."

"The answer is to send the Dragonsworn away," Sheriam said, not so patiently as before. "I regret letting Mat out of our hands again, but I fear there's no answer for it. You've told him the *offer* is refused; tell him to go."

"I wish it were that simple. I don't think he will for asking, Sheriam. He implied he was to wait right where he is until something happens. He could be expecting orders from Rand, or even Rand himself. There was a rumor in Cairhien that he's taken to sometimes Traveling with some of those men he's gathered. The ones he's teaching to channel? I do not know what we will do if that happens."

Sheriam stared at her, breathing quite heavily for someone with such calm features.

A scratching at the door was followed by Tabiya with a beaten silver tray. Not catching the mood, she fussed about setting the green porcelain teapot and cups just so, the silver honeypot and small pitcher of cream and lace-edged linen napkins, until Sheriam finally snapped at her so fiercely to be about her work that Tabiya squeaked and dropped a wide-eyed curtsy that nearly put her head on the floor and ran.

For a moment Sheriam busied herself smoothing her skirts while she regained her composure. "Perhaps," she said finally, reluctantly, "it might be necessary for us to leave Salidar after all. Sooner than I could wish."

"But the only way left is north." Egwene widened her eyes. Light, but she hated this! "It will seem we're moving toward Tar Valon."

"I know that," Sheriam almost snapped. Drawing breath, she moderated her tone. "Forgive me, Mother. I feel a little. . . . I do not like being forced into things, and I fear Rand al'Thor has forced our hand before we are ready."

"I will speak quite severely when I see him," Egwene said. "I can hardly think what I would do without your advice." Perhaps she could find a way to send Sheriam to study with the Wise Ones as an apprentice. The thought of Sheriam after, say, half a year with Sorilea made her smile so that Sheriam actually smiled back. "Honey or bitter?" Egwene said, lifting the teapot.

CHAPTER

40

Unexpected Laughter

"You have to help me talk some sense into them," Mat said around his pipestem. "Thom, are you listening?"

They were seated on upended kegs in the scant shade of a two-story house, smoking their pipes, and the lanky old gleeman seemed more interested in staring at the letter Rand had sent on to him. Now he stuffed it into his coat pocket with the blue-wax seal yet unbroken. The buzz of voices and squeak of axles from the street at the end of the alley seemed distant. Sweat dripped from both their faces. At least one thing was taken care of for the moment. Mat had come out of the Little Tower to find that a group of Aes Sedai had hauled Aviendha away somewhere; she would not be sticking a knife in anybody any time soon.

Thom took his pipe from his mouth. It was a long-stemmed thing, carved all over with oak leaves and acorns. "I once tried to rescue a woman, Mat. Laritha was a rose in bud, and married to a glowering brute of a bootmaker in a village where I broke my journey for a few days. A brute. He shouted at her if dinner wasn't ready when he wanted to sit down, and took a switch to her if he saw her say more than two words to another man."

"Thom, what in the Pit of Doom does this have to do with making those fool women see sense?"

"Just listen, boy. How he treated her was common knowledge in the village, but Laritha told me herself, all the while moaning over how she wished someone would rescue her. I had gold in my purse and a fine coach, a driver and a manservant. I was young and good-looking." Thom knuckled his white mustaches and sighed; it was hard to believe that leathery face had ever been good-looking. Mat blinked. A coach? When had a gleeman ever had a coach? "Mat, the woman's plight wrung my heart. And I won't deny her face tugged at it, too. As I said, I was young; I thought I was in love, a hero out of the stories. So one day, sitting beneath a flowering apple tree—well away from the bootmaker's house—I offered to take her away. I'd give her a maid and a house of her own, and court her with songs and verse. When she finally understood, she kicked me in the knee so hard I limped for a month, and hit me with the bench besides."

"They all seem to like kicking," Mat muttered, shifting his weight on the keg. "I suppose she didn't believe you, and who can blame her?"

"Oh, she believed. And was outraged that I thought she would ever leave her beloved husband. Her word; beloved. She ran back to the man as fast as her feet would go, and I had the choice of killing him or leaping into my coach. I had to leave behind almost every stitch I owned. I expect she's still living with him much as before. Holding the purse strings tight in her fist and cracking his head open with whatever lies to hand every time he stops into the inn for an ale. As she always had, so I learned later from a few discreet inquiries." He stuck the pipe back between his teeth as if he had made a point.

Mat scratched his head. "I don't see what that has to do with this."

"Just that you shouldn't think you know the whole story when you've heard part. For instance, do you know Elayne and Nynaeve will be leaving for Ebou Dar in a day or so? Juilin and I are to go along."

"Ebou . . . !" Mat barely caught his pipe before it fell into the dead weeds that carpeted the alley. Nalesean had told some stories about a visit to Ebou Dar, and even counting in the way he exaggerated when it came to women he had known and fights he had been in, the place sounded rough. So they thought they could slip Elayne away from him, did they? "Thom, you have to help me—"

"What?" Thom broke in. "Steal them away from the bootmaker?" He blew up a streamer of blue smoke. "I won't do that, boy. You still don't know the whole story. How do you feel about Egwene and Nynaeve? On second thought, make that just Egwene."

Mat frowned, wondering whether the man thought he could fuddle everything up by going around in circles long enough. "I like Egwene. I. . . . Burn me, Thom, she's Egwene; that's saying enough right there. That's why I am trying to save her fool neck for her."

"Save her from her bootmaker, you mean," Thom murmured, but Mat went right on.

"Her neck and Elayne's as well; even Nynaeve's, if I can stop from throttling her myself. Light! I only want to help them. Besides, Rand will break *my* neck if I let anything happen to Elayne."

"Have you ever thought of helping them do what they want instead of what you want? If I did what I wanted, I'd have Elayne on a horse and riding to Andor. She needs to do other things—*needs* to, I think—so I trot around after her, sweating day and night that somebody will manage to kill her before I can prevent it. She will go to Caemlyn when she's ready." He sucked at his pipe complacently, but there was a slight edge to his voice at the end, as if he did not like his words even as much as he pretended.

"It seems to me they want to hand their heads to Elaida." So Thom would have that silly wench on a horse, would he? A gleeman hauling the Daughter-Heir off to be crowned! He did have a grand sense of himself, Thom did.

"You aren't a fool, Mat," Thom said quietly. "You know better. Egwene. . . . It's hard to think of that child as Amyrlin . . ." Mat grunted sourly in agreement; Thom paid him no mind. ". . . yet I believe she has the backbone for it. It's too early to say whether a few things are just happenstance, but I'm beginning to believe she may have the brains as well. The question is, is she tough enough? If she lacks that, they will eat her alive—backbone, brains and all."

"Who will? Elaida?"

"Oh, her. If she has the chance; that one lacks nothing for toughness. But the Aes Sedai right here hardly think of Egwene as Aes Sedai; Amyrlin maybe, but not Aes Sedai, hard as that is to believe." Thom shook his head. "I don't understand, but it's true. The same for Elayne and Nynaeve. They try to keep it among themselves, but even Aes Sedai don't hide as much as they think, if you watch close and keep your wits about you." He pulled out that letter again, just turning it over in his hands without looking at it. "Egwene is walking the edge of a precipice, Mat, and three factions right here in Salidar—three that I'm sure of—might push her over if she makes one wrong step. Elayne will follow if that happens, and Nynaeve. Or maybe they'll push them over first to pull her down."

"Right here in Salidar," Mat said, flat as a planed board. Thom nodded calmly, and Mat could not stop his voice from rising. "And you want me to leave them here?"

"I want you to stop thinking you're going to *make* them do anything.

They've decided what they are going to do, and you can't change it. But maybe—just maybe—you can help me keep them alive."

Mat jumped to his feet. In his head was an image of a woman with a knife stuck between her breasts; not one of the borrowed memories. He kicked the keg he had been sitting on, sending it rolling along the alley. Help a *gleeman* keep them alive? A faint memory stirred, something about Basel Gill, an innkeeper in Caemlyn, saying something about Thom, but it was like mist, gone as soon as he tried to hold it. "Who's the letter from, Thom? Another woman you rescued? Or did you leave her where she could get her head cut off?"

"I left her," Thom said softly. Rising, he walked away without another word.

Mat half reached out to stop him, started to speak. Only he could not think of what to say. *Crazy old man!* No, he was not crazy. Egwene was mule stubborn, and Nynaeve made her look biddable. Worse, either would climb a tree to see the lightning better. As for Elayne, noblewomen never had enough sense to come in out of the rain. And then they were indignant when they got wet.

Tapping out his pipe, he crushed the embers under heel before the dry weeds could catch, then caught up his hat from the ground and limped out to the street. He needed information from a better source than a gleeman who had delusions of grandeur from running around with that stuck-up chit of a Daughter-Heir. Down to his left he saw Nynaeve coming out of the Little Tower and started toward her, winding between loaded carts drawn by oxen or horses. She could tell him what he needed to know. If she would. His hip gave him a twinge. *Burn me, she owes me a few answers.*

Just then Nynaeve caught sight of him and stiffened visibly. For a moment she watched him approach, then abruptly hurried off in the other direction, plainly trying to avoid him. She looked over her shoulder twice before people and carts hid her.

He stopped, scowling, and pulled his hat low. First the woman kicked him for no reason; now she would not talk to him. They meant to let him stew, her and Egwene, until he would trot off meekly when they pointed a finger. *Well, they chose the wrong man for their game, burn their hides!*

Vanin and the others were outside a stable beside a stone building that had surely been an inn once. Aes Sedai streamed in and out of it now. Pips and the rest of their horses were tied to a hitching rail, and Vanin and the two scouts who had been captured were squatting against the wall. Mar and Ladwin were as different as men could be, one tall, lanky and rough-faced, the other short, stocky and mild-seeming, but both looked plain embarrassed when Mat walked up. Neither had gotten over the ease of his capture. The two squadmen stood stiffly, still holding the banners tight against their staffs as if there was any point to it now. They looked more than a little apprehensive. A battle was one thing; all these Aes Sedai were quite another. A man had a chance in battle. There were two Warders watching them. Not openly, and from across the stableyard, but they had not just picked that spot, standing in the full sun, to talk.

Mat stroked Pips' nose, then after a moment began to examine the horse's eyes. A fellow in a leather vest came out of the stable, shoving a dung barrow up the street. Vanin walked over to peer into Pips' eye. Not looking at him, Mat said, "Could you reach the Band?"

"Maybe." Vanin frowned and lifted Pips' eyelid. "With a little luck, maybe. Hate to leave my horse, though."

Mat nodded, looking closer at the eye. "Tell Talmanes I said to sit tight. I may be staying here a few days, and I don't want any bloody attempted rescue. Try to make it back here. Without being seen, if you can."

Vanin spat into the dust under Pips. "Man mixes with Aes Sedai, he's bridled himself and put a saddle on his back. I'll be back when I can." Shaking his head, he strolled off into the crowd, a fat rumpled man with a rolling walk who no one could suspect of being able to sneak.

One of the squadmen cleared his throat hesitantly and stepped closer. "My Lord, is everything . . . ? This is what you planned, isn't it, my Lord?"

"Right to the plan, Verdin," Mat said, patting Pips. He was headfirst in a sack, and the strings tied tight. He had promised Rand to see Elayne safe to Caemlyn, and he could not leave without her. And he could not go off and let Egwene stretch her neck on the chopping block, either. It might be—Light, how it rankled!—it might be that he was going to have to take Thom's advice. Try to keep those bloody women's bloody heads on their bloody shoulders by somehow helping them make this whole mad impossible scheme actually work. While trying to keep his own neck in one piece, incidentally. And that left out keeping Aviendha from Elayne's throat. Well, at the least, he could be around to get them away when it all fell apart. Small comfort that was. "Everything is just bloody fine."

Elayne expected to find Aviendha in the waiting room or maybe outside, but she hardly had to listen to discover why she was in neither place. There were two topics of conversation among the other Aes Sedai, and everyone was talking, with papers lying abandoned on the tables. Mat occupied most tongues; even the servants and novices bustling about the waiting room paused in running errands to exchange words about him. He was *ta'veren*. Was it safe to let a *ta'veren* remain in Salidar? Had he really been in the Tower and simply allowed to go? Was it true he commanded the Dragonsworn army? Was he to be arrested for the atrocities they had heard of? Was it true he came from the same village as the Dragon Reborn and the Amyrlin? There were rumors of *two ta'veren* connected to the Dragon Reborn; who was the second, and where could he be found? Maybe Mat Cauthon knew. There seemed to be as many opinions as there were people to give them.

There were two questions Elayne expected to hear and did not. What did Mat want in Salidar, and how had Rand known where to send him? Nobody asked them, but here an Aes Sedai suddenly shifted her shawl as if cold or gave a start when she realized someone had spoken to her, there a serving woman stared at nothing in the middle of the floor before coming to herself with a shake or a novice darted frightened glances at the sisters. Mat was not quite a cat set among the pigeons, but he came close. Just the fact that Rand knew where they were seemed enough to set a chill.

Aviendha occasioned less comment, but the sisters could not help talking about her, and not only to change the subject. It was not every day that a wilder simply appeared on her own two feet, especially with such remarkable strength, and an Aiel besides. That last truly fascinated every sister. No Aiel had ever trained in the Tower, and few Aes Sedai had ever entered the Aiel Waste.

A single question sufficed to learn where she was being held. Not held in name, but Elayne knew how Aes Sedai could be when they wanted a woman to become a novice.

"She will be in white by nightfall," Akarrin said confidently. A slim Brown, she nodded for emphasis with almost every word. The two sisters with her nodded just as surely.

Tsking under her breath, Elayne hurried into the street. Ahead of her she could see Nynaeve practically trotting, and looking over her shoulder so often that she was running into people. Elayne thought about catching up—she would not mind having company—but she was not about to run in this heat, concentration or no, and that seemed the only way. Even so, she did lift her skirts slightly and hurried.

Before she had gone fifty paces, she felt Birgitte coming closer and turned to see her running down the street. Areina was with her, but she stopped a little way off and folded her arms with a scowl. The woman was an impossible little wretch, and she certainly had not changed her opinions because Elayne really was Aes Sedai now.

"I thought you should know," Birgitte said quietly. "I just heard that when we leave for Ebou Dar, Vandene and Adeleas are going too."

"I see," Elayne murmured. It could be that the pair were going to join Merilille for some reason, though there were already three Aes Sedai at Tylin's court, or maybe they had a mission of their own in Ebou Dar. She did not believe either. Areina had her mind set, and so did the Hall. Elayne and Nynaeve were to be accompanied by two *real* Aes Sedai as chaperones. "She *does* understand *she* isn't going."

Birgitte glanced the way Elayne was staring, at Areina, then shrugged. "She understands; she is not happy over it. Myself, I can hardly wait to be gone."

Elayne hesitated only a moment. She had promised to keep secrets, which she did not like, but she had not promised to stop trying to convince the other woman there was no need, and no point. "Birgitte, Egwene—"

"No!"

"Why not?" Elayne had not had Birgitte for a Warder long before she decided that when she bonded Rand, she would somehow make him promise to do as he was told, at least when it was important. Lately she had decided on another provision. He was going to have to answer her questions. Birgitte answered when she chose, evaded when she chose and sometimes just put on a stubborn face, as she did now. "Tell me why not, and if it's a good reason, I'll never ask again."

At first Birgitte just glowered, but then she took Elayne's arm and very nearly hustled her to the mouth of an alley. No one passing by glanced at them twice, and Areina remained where she was, if darker of face than before, but Birgitte still looked around carefully and spoke in a whisper. "Always when the Wheel spun me out, I was born, lived and died without ever knowing I was bound to the Wheel. I only knew that in between, in *Tel'aran'rhiod*. Sometimes I became known, even famous, but I was like everyone else, not somebody out of a legend. This time I was ripped out, not spun out. For the first time wearing flesh, I know who I am. For the first time, other people can know too. Thom and Juilin do; they say nothing, but I am sure. They don't look at me the way they do other people. If I said I was going to climb a glass mountain and kill a giant with my bare hands, they'd just ask if I needed any help on the way, and they would not expect me to."

"I don't understand," Elayne said slowly, and Birgitte sighed and let her head hang.

"I don't know that I can live up to that. In other lives, I did what I had to, what seemed to be right, enough for Maerion or Joana or any woman. Now, I'm *Birgitte* of the stories. Everyone who knows will *expect*. I feel like a feather-dancer walking into a Tovan conclave."

Elayne did not ask; when Birgitte mentioned things from past lives, the explanations were usually more confusing than ignorance. "That is nonsense," she said firmly, taking the other woman by the arms. "*I* know, and *I* certainly don't expect you to kill any giants. Egwene doesn't either. And she *already* knows."

"As long as I don't admit it," Birgitte muttered, "it is as if she didn't. Don't bother saying that's nonsense too; I know it is, but that changes nothing."

"Then what about this? She is the Amyrlin, and you are a Warder. She deserves your trust, Birgitte. She needs it."

"Are you done with her yet?" Areina demanded from a pace away. "If you're going to go away and leave me, the least you can do is help me with my archery the way you said you would."

"I will think on it," Birgitte told Elayne quietly. Turning to Areina, she caught the woman's braid at the base of her neck. "We will speak of archery," she said, pushing her up the street, "but first we will speak of manners."

Shaking her head, Elayne suddenly remembered Aviendha and hurried on. The house was not far.

It took her a moment to recognize Aviendha. Elayne was used to seeing her in *cadin'sor*, with her dark reddish hair cut short, not in skirt and blouse and shawl with hair below her shoulders and held back from her face by a folded kerchief. At first glance, she did not appear to be in any difficulty. Sitting rather awkwardly in a chair—Aiel were unused to chairs—she seemed to be peacefully sipping tea with five sisters in a circle in the sitting room. Houses that sheltered Aes Sedai had such things, though Elayne and Nynaeve were still in their cramped little room. At second glance, Aviendha was casting hunted looks at the Aes Sedai over the rim of her teacup. There was no time for a third glance; on sight of Elayne, Aviendha jerked to her feet and dropped her cup to the clean-swept floor. Elayne had seen few Aiel except in the Stone of Tear, but she did know they hid their emotions, and Aviendha did it very well. Only now, naked pain painted her face.

"I'm sorry," Elayne told the room smoothly, "but I must take her away from you for a little while. Perhaps you can talk to her later."

Several of the sisters hesitated on the brink of protest, though there should have been none. She was clearly the strongest in the room by far, except for Aviendha, and none of the Aes Sedai was a Sitter or part of Sheriam's council. She was very happy that Myrelle was not there, since she lived in this house. Elayne had made her choice of Green and been accepted, only to discover that Myrelle was the head of the Green Ajah in Salidar. Myrelle, who had not even been Aes Sedai fifteen years. From things that had been said, Elayne knew there were Greens in Salidar who had worn the shawl at least fifty, though not a one showed a gray hair. Had Myrelle been there, all Elayne's strength would have counted nothing if the head of her Ajah wanted to retain Aviendha. As it was, only Shana, a popeyed White who reminded Elayne of a fish, went as far as opening her mouth further, and she closed it again, though rather sullenly when Elayne arched an eyebrow at her.

The five were more than a bit tight-lipped, but Elayne ignored the tension. "Thank you," she said with a smile she did not feel.

Aviendha slung a dark bundle on her back, but hesitated until Elayne actually asked her to come. In the street, Elayne said, "I apologize for that. I'll see it does not happen again." She could manage that, she was sure. Or Egwene could, surely. "There are not many places to talk alone, I'm afraid. My room is rather hot this time of day. We could try to find some shade, or have some tea, if they haven't already filled you with it."

"Your room." It was not exactly curt, but plainly Aviendha did not want to talk, not yet. Abruptly she darted to a passing cart filled with firewood and snatched out a branch meant to be broken for kindling, longer than her arm and thicker than her thumb. Rejoining Elayne, she began peeling it with her belt knife; the sharp blade shaved away smaller branches like a razor. The pain was gone from her face. She seemed determined now.

Elayne eyed her sideways as they walked. She would not believe Aviendha meant her any harm, whatever that lout Mat Cauthon said. Then again. . . . She knew a little of *ji'e'toh*; Aviendha had explained some of it when they were in the Stone together. Maybe Rand had said or done something. Maybe that bewildering labyrinth of honor and obligation required Aviendha to. . . . It did not seem possible. But maybe. . . .

When they reached her room, she decided to bring it up first. Facing the other woman—and very deliberately not embracing *saidar*—she said, "Mat claims you have come here to kill me."

Aviendha blinked. "Wetlanders always put everything backwards," she said wonderingly. Laying the stick on the foot of Nynaeve's bed, she put the belt knife beside it carefully. "My near-sister Egwene asked me to watch Rand al'Thor for you, which I promised to do." Bundle and shawl went on the floor beside the door. "I have *toh* toward her, but greater to you." Unlacing her blouse, she pulled it over her head, then pushed her shift to her waist. "I love Rand al'Thor, and once I let myself lie with him. I have *toh*, and I ask that you help me meet it." Turning her back, she knelt in the small space available. "You may use the stick or the knife as you wish; the *toh* is mine, but the choice is yours." She tilted up her chin, stretching her neck. Her eyes were closed. "Whichever you choose, I accept."

Elayne thought her knees were going to buckle. Min had said the third woman would be dangerous, but Aviendha? *Wait! She said she. . . . With Rand!* Her hand twitched toward the knife on the bed, and she folded her arms, trapping her hands. "Get up. And put on your blouse. I am *not* going to hit you . . ." Just a few times? She tightened her arms to hold her hands where they were. ". . . and I am *certainly* not going to touch that knife. Please put it away." She would have handed it to the other woman, but she was not certain she was safe to touch a weapon right then. "You have no *toh* toward me." She believed that was the phrase. "I love Rand, but I don't care that you love him too." The lie burned her tongue. Aviendha had actually *lain* with him?

Twisting around on her knees, Aviendha frowned. "I am not certain I understand. Are you proposing that we share him? Elayne, we are friends, I think, but we must be as first-sisters if we are to be sister-wives. It will take time to know if we can be that."

Realizing her mouth was hanging open, Elayne closed it. "I suppose it will," she said faintly. Min kept saying they would share him, but certainly not that way! Even the thought was indecent! "It is a little more complicated than you know. There's another woman who loves him, too."

Aviendha was on her feet so fast she simply seemed to be one place then the other. "What is her name?" Her green eyes blazed, and she had the knife in her hand.

Elayne almost laughed. *One moment talking about sharing, the next as fierce as . . . as. . . . As fierce as me*, she finished, not at all pleased with the thought. This could have been worse, much worse. It could have been Berelain. Since it had to be somebody, it might as well be Aviendha. *And I might as well deal with it instead of kicking my skirts like a child.* Seating herself on the bed, she folded her hands in her lap. "Do sheathe that and sit down, Aviendha. And please put on your blouse. I have a great deal to tell you. There is a woman—my friend, my near-sister—named Min. . . ."

Aviendha did clothe herself, but a considerable time passed before she sat, and considerably more before Elayne could convince her that they should not combine to do Min in. She agreed to that, at least. Reluctantly, she finally said, "I must get to know her. I will not share him with a woman I cannot love as a first-sister." That with a studying look at Elayne, who sighed.

Aviendha would consider sharing him with her. Min was ready to share him with her. Was she the only one of the three who was normal? By the map under her mattress, Min should be in Caemlyn soon, or maybe already was. She did not know what she wanted to have happen there, only that Min should use her viewings to help him. Which meant Min had to stay close to him. While Elayne went to Ebou Dar.

"Is anything in life ever simple, Aviendha?"

"Not when men are involved."

Elayne was not sure which surprised her more, to find that she was laughing or that Aviendha was.

CHAPTER

41

A Threat

Riding slowly through Caemlyn under a baking midmorning sun, Min really saw little of the city. She hardly noticed the people and sedan chairs, wagons and coaches, that clogged the streets except to guide her bay mare around them. One of her dreams had always been to live in a great city and travel to strange places, but today colorful towers covered in glittering tiles and sweeping vistas as the street rounded a hill passed all but unseen. Clumps of Aiel striding through the crowds with space opening around them got a second glance, and so did patrols of hawk-nosed, often bearded men on horseback, but only because they reminded her of the stories they had begun hearing while still in Murandy. Merana had been angered by those, and by the charred evidence of Dragonsworn they had come on twice, but Min thought some of the other Aes Sedai were worried. The less said about what they thought of Rand's amnesty, the better.

At the edge of the plaza in front of the Royal Palace, she drew Wildrose's rein and blotted her face carefully with a lace-edged handkerchief that she tucked back up her coatsleeve. Only a few people dotted the great oval, perhaps because Aiel guarded the open main gates of the palace. More Aiel stood on marble balconies or glided across high, colonnaded walks like leopards. The White Lion of Andor stirred in a breeze above the tallest of the palace domes. Another crimson flag flew from one of the spires, a little lower than the white dome, lifted just enough by the breeze for her to make out the ancient symbol of Aes Sedai, black-and-white.

Those Aiel made her glad she had refused the offer of a pair of Warders as escort; she suspected Aiel and Warders might strike sparks. Well, it had not been precisely an offer, and she had refused by sneaking away an hour beforetime by the clock on the inn mantelpiece. Merana was from Caemlyn, and when they arrived before dawn she took them straight to what she said was the finest inn in the New City.

It was not the Aiel who kept Min sitting there, however. Not entirely, though she had heard all sorts of terrible stories about black-veiled Aiel. Her coat and breeches were the finest, softest wool that could be found in Salidar, in a pale rose, with tiny blue-and-white flowers embroidered on lapels and cuffs and down the outsides of the legs. Her shirt was cut like a boy's too, but in cream silk. In Baerlon, after her father died, her aunts had tried to make her into what they called a decent proper woman, though maybe her Aunt Miren had understood that after ten years running about the mines in boys' clothes, it might be too late to stuff her into dresses. They had tried, even so, and she had fought them as stubbornly as she refused to learn to wield a needle. Aside from that unfortunate episode serving tables at The Miners' Rest—a rough place, but she had not stayed long; Rana, Jan *and* Miren had seen to that emphatically when they found out, and no matter that she was twenty then—aside from that one time, she had never worn a dress willingly. Now she was thinking that maybe she should have had one made instead of this coat and breeches. A dress in silk, cut snug at the bodice and low, and. . . .

He'll have to take me as I am, she thought, twitching the reins irritably. *I'm not changing for any man.* Only, her clothes would have been as plain as any farmer's not that long ago, her hair had not been in ringlets almost to her shoulders, and a small voice whispered, *You'll be whatever you think he wants you to be.* She kicked it down as hard as she had ever kicked any stableman who tried to cut rough, and heeled Wildrose only a little more gently. She hated the very idea of women being weak when it came to men. There was just one problem; she was fairly certain she was going to find out just what it was like very soon now.

Dismounting in front of the Palace gates, she patted the mare, to tell her she had not meant the kick, while eyeing the Aiel uncertainly. Half were women, all but one considerably taller than she. The men towered like Rand, most of them, and some even more. Every one was watching her—well, they seemed to be watching everything, but definitely her as well—and not one blinked that she could see. With those spears and bucklers, the bows on their backs and quivers at their hips, the heavy knives, they looked ready to kill. Those black strips of cloth hanging down onto their chests must be the veils. She had heard Aiel would not kill you without covering their faces. *I hope that's so.*

She addressed herself to the shortest of the women. Framed by bright red hair as short as Min's used to be, her tanned face might as well have been carved from wood, but she was even a little shorter than Min. "I've come to see Rand al'Thor," Min said, a trifle unsteadily. "The Dragon Reborn." Did none of them ever blink? "My name is Min. He knows me, and I have an important message for him."

The red-haired woman turned to the other Aiel, gesticulating quickly with her free hand. The rest of the women laughed as she turned back. "I will take you to him, Min. But if he does not know you, you will leave much faster than you go in." Some of the Aielwomen laughed at that too. "I am called Enaila."

"He knows me," Min told them, flushing. She had a pair of knives up her coatsleeves that Thom Merrilin had showed her how to use, but she had the feeling this woman could take them away and peel her with them. An image flickered above Enaila's head and was gone. A wreath of some sort; Min had no idea what it meant. "Am I supposed to take my horse in, too? I don't think Rand wants to see her." To her surprise, some of the Aiel chuckled, men and women, and Enaila's lips twitched as if she wanted to.

A man came to take Wildrose—Min thought he was Aiel too, despite the downcast eyes and white robe—and she followed Enaila through the gates, across a broad courtyard and into the Palace proper. It was something of a relief to see servants in red-and-white livery scurrying along the tapestry-lined corridors, warily eyeing the Aiel who also walked the halls, but no more so than they might a strange dog really. She had begun to think she would find the Palace filled with none but Aiel, Rand surrounded by them, maybe dressed in coat and breeches all in shades of brown and gray and green, staring at her without blinking.

Before tall wide doors, carved with lions and standing open, Enaila halted, wiggling her hand quickly at the Aiel on guard. They were all women. One, flaxen-haired and considerably taller than most men, waggled fingers back. "Wait here," Enaila said, and went in.

Min took one step after her, and a spear was casually held in her path by the flaxen-haired woman. Or perhaps not casually, but Min did not care. She could see Rand.

He sat on a great gilded throne that seemed made entirely of Dragons, in a red coat worked heavily with gold, holding some sort of green-and-white tasseled spearhead of all things. Another throne stood on a tall pedestal behind him, gilded also, but with a lion picked out in white gemstones against red. The Lion Throne, so the rumors said. At that moment, he could have been using it for a footstool for all she cared. He looked tired. He was so beautiful, her heart ached. Images danced around him continuously. With Aes Sedai and Warders, that deluge was something she tried to escape; she could not tell what they meant any more often than with anyone else, but they were *always* there. With Rand, she had to make herself see them, because otherwise she would just stare at his face. One of those images she had seen every time she saw him. Countless thousands of sparkling lights, like stars or fireflies, rushed into a great blackness, trying to fill it up, rushed in and were swallowed. There seemed to be more lights than she had ever seen before, but the darkness swallowed them at a greater rate, too. And there was something else, something new, an aura of yellow and brown and purple that made her stomach clench.

She tried viewing the nobles facing him—surely that was what they were, in all those fine embroidered coats and rich silk gowns—but there was nothing to see. That was true of most people most of the time, and when she did see something, most often she had no notion what it foretold. Even so, she narrowed her eyes, straining. If she could make out just one image, one aura, it might be a help to him. From the stories she had heard since entering Andor, he could use all the help he could find.

With a heavy sigh, she gave it up finally. Squinting and straining did no good unless there was something to see in the first place.

Suddenly she realized the nobles were withdrawing, Rand was on his feet, and Enaila was waving, motioning her to enter. Rand was smiling. Min thought her heart might burst out of her chest. So this was what it felt like for all those women she had laughed at, throwing themselves at a man's feet. No. She was not a giddy girl; she was older than he, she had had her first kiss while he still thought getting out of tending sheep was the most fun in the world, she. . . . *Light, please, don't let my knees give way.*

Tossing the Dragon Scepter down carelessly where he had been sitting, Rand bounded from the dais in one leap and rushed down the Grand Hall. As soon as he reached Min, he caught her under the arms and swung her into the air and around and around before Dyelin and the others were gone. Some of the nobles stared, and were welcome to, for all of him. "Light, Min, but it's good to see your face," he laughed. Considerably better than Dyelin's stony features or Ellorien's. But if Aemlyn and Arathelle and Pelivar and Luan and all of them had every one proclaimed their joy that Elayne was on her way to Caemlyn instead of staring at him with doubt or even "liar" in their eyes, he would have been as overjoyed to see Min.

When he put her feet back on the floor, she sagged against his chest, clutching his arms and breathing hard. "I'm sorry," he said. "I didn't mean to make you dizzy. It's just that I really am glad to see you."

"Well, you did make me dizzy, you wool-headed sheepherder," she mumbled against his chest. Pushing herself away, she glared up at him through long lashes. "I had a very long ride, I arrived in the middle of the night, or might as well, and you toss me around like a sack of oats. Did you never learn any manners?"

"Woolhead," he laughed softly. "Min, you can name me liar, but I've actually missed hearing you call me that." She did not call him anything; she merely peered up at him, the glare gone completely. Her eyelashes did seem longer than he remembered.

Realizing where they were, he took her hand. A throne room was no place for meeting old friends. "Come on, Min. We can have some cool punch in my sitting room. Somara, I am going to my apartments; you can send everybody away."

Somara did not look happy about it, but she dismissed all the Maidens except for herself and Enaila. Both looked a bit sullen, which he did not understand. He had allowed Somara to gather so many inside the palace in the first place only because Dyelin and the others were coming. Bashere was out at his horsemen's camp north of the city for the same reason. Maidens for a reminder, Bashere because there could be too many reminders. He hoped the two Maidens were not planning on any mothering. They took turns as his guards more than their share, it seemed to him, but Nandera was as adamant as Sulin had been when it came to him saying who specifically was to do what. He could command *Far Dareis Mai*, but he was not a Maiden, and the other was none of his business.

Min studied the tapestries as he led her along the corridor by the hand. She peered at inlaid chests and tables, at golden bowls and tall vases of Sea Folk porcelain in niches. She examined Enaila and Somara head to toe three times each. But she neither looked at him nor spoke a word. His hand engulfed hers, and he could feel the pulse in her wrist racing to beat horses. He hoped she was not really angry over being whirled about.

To his great relief, Somara and Enaila took places on either side of his door, though they both looked at him when he asked for punch, and he had to repeat himself. In the sitting room, he took off his coat and tossed it over a chair. "Sit, Min. Sit. Rest and relax. The punch will be here shortly. You have to tell me everything. Where you've been, how you got here, why you arrived in the night. It isn't safe traveling at night, Min. Now less than ever. I'll give you the best rooms in the Palace—well, the second-best; these are the best—and an Aiel escort to take you wherever you want. Any bullyboy or strongarm will doff his cap and duck his head, if he doesn't run right up the side of a building to get away."

For a moment he thought she might laugh, standing there by the door, but instead she drew a deep breath and took a letter from her pocket. "I can't tell you where I came from—I promised, Rand—but Elayne is there, and—"

"Salidar," he said, and smiled at the way her eyes widened. "I know a few things, Min. Maybe more than some think I do."

"I . . . see that you do," she said faintly. She pushed the letter into his hands then backed away again. Her voice firmed as she added, "I swore I would give that to you first off. Go ahead and read it."

He recognized the seal, a lily in dark yellow wax, and Elayne's flowing hand in his name, and he hesitated before opening it. Clean breaks were best, and he had made one, but with the letter in his hand, he could not stop himself. He read, then sat down atop his coat and read again. It was certainly short.

> *Rand,*
>
> *I have made my feelings clear to you. Know that they have not changed. I hope that you feel for me what I feel for you. Min can help you, if you will only listen to her. I love her like a sister, and hope you love her as I do.*
>
> *Elayne*

Her ink must have been running out, because the last lines were a hurried scrawl, quite unlike the elegance of the rest. Min had been sidling and twisting her head, trying to read the letter without being too obvious, but when he lifted himself to pull his coat out—the fat-little-man *angreal* was in the pocket—she scurried back again. "Do women all *try* to drive a man crazy?" he muttered.

"What!"

He stared at the letter, talking half to himself. "Elayne is so beautiful I can't help staring, but half the time I don't know whether she wants me to kiss her or kneel at her feet. Truth to tell, sometimes I did want to kneel . . . and worship, the Light help me. She says here I know how she feels. Two letters she's written me before this, one full of love, the other saying she never wanted the sight of me again. The times I've sat wishing the first one was true and the other some sort of joke, or mistake, or. . . . And Aviendha. She's beautiful too, but every day with her was a battle. No kisses from her, not anymore, and no doubts how she feels. She was even happier to get away from me than I was to see her go. Only, I keep expecting to see her when I turn around, and when she isn't there, it's as if something inside me is missing. I actually miss the battle, and there are moments when I find myself thinking, *There are things worth fighting for.*" Something in Min's silence made him look up. She was staring at him with a face as blank as an Aes Sedai.

"Did nobody ever tell you it isn't polite to talk to one woman about another?" Her voice was absolutely flat. "Much less two other women."

"Min, you're a friend," he protested. "I don't think of you as a woman." It was the wrong thing to say; he knew it as soon as the words left his mouth.

"Oh?" Tossing back her coat, she placed her hands on her hips. It was not the all-too-familiar angry pose. Her wrists were twisted so her fingers pointed up, and somehow that made it very different. She stood with one knee bent, and that. . . . For the first time he really saw her; not just Min, but the way she looked. Not the usual plain brown coat and breeches, but pale red, and embroidered. Not the usual rough-cut hair that barely covered her ears, but ringlets brushing her neck. "Do I look like a boy?"

"Min, I—"

"Do I look like a man? A horse?" In one quick stride she reached him and plumped herself down in his lap.

"Min," he said, aghast, "what are you doing?"

"Convincing you I'm a woman, woolhead. Don't I look like a woman? Don't I smell like a woman?" She smelled faintly of flowers, now that he noticed. "Don't I feel—? Well, enough of that. Answer the question, sheepherder."

It was the "sheepherder" and "woolhead" that stilled his alarm. The truth was, she felt remarkably nice sitting there. But she was Min, who thought he was a country boy with hay in his hair and not very much common sense. "Light, Min, I know you're a woman. I didn't mean any insult. You're a friend, too. It's just that I feel comfortable with you. It doesn't matter if I look like a fool with you. I can say things to you I wouldn't say to anybody else, not even Mat or Perrin. When I am around you, all the knots unwind, all the tightness in my shoulders I don't even feel till it goes. Do you see, Min? I like being around you. I've missed you."

Folding her arms, she looked at him sideways, frowning. Her leg twitched; if her foot had reached the floor, she would have been tapping it. "All that about Elayne. And this . . . Aviendha. Who is she, by the way? It sounds to me as if you love them both. Oh, stop jerking about. You owe me some answers. Saying I'm not— Just answer me. Do you love both of them?"

"Maybe I do," he said slowly. "Light help me, I think maybe I do. Does that make me a lecher, Min, or just a greedy fool?" Her mouth opened and closed; she tossed her head angrily and compressed her lips. He hurried on before she could tell him which one she had picked to fit him; he did not really want to hear it from her. "It hardly matters now anyway. It is done with. I sent Aviendha away, and I will not let her come back. I won't let myself within a mile of her or Elayne, ten miles if I can help it."

"For the love of . . . ! Why, Rand? What gives you the right to make a choice like that for them?"

"Min, can't you see? I am a target. Any woman I love becomes a target, too. Even if the arrow is aimed at me, it could hit her. It could be aimed at her." Breathing out heavily, he leaned back with his arms on the rose-carved chair arms. She twisted a little, studying him with the most serious expression he had ever seen on her face. Min was always smiling, always a little amused by everything. Just as well she was not now; he was deadly serious himself. "Lan told me he and I are alike in some ways, and it's true. He said there are men who radiate death. Himself. Me. When a man like that falls in love, the best gift he can give her is to put as much distance as possible between himself and her. You see that, don't you?"

"What I see. . . ." She was silent for a moment. "Very well. I'm your friend, and I am glad you know it, but don't bother thinking I will give up. I will convince you I am not a man or a horse."

"Min, I said I—"

"Oh, no, sheepherder. Not good enough." She wriggled round on his lap in a way that made him clear his throat, and pinned a finger against his chest. "I want tears in your eyes when you say it. I want drool on your chin and a stammer in your voice. You needn't think I won't make you pay."

Rand could not help laughing. "Min, it really is good to have you here. All you see is a mudfoot from the Two Rivers, isn't it?"

Her mood changed lightning quick. "I see you, Rand," she said, strangely quiet. "I see you." Clearing her throat, she arranged herself primly, hands on her knees. If it was possible to be prim sitting as she was, anyway. "I might as well get on with why I came. Apparently, you know about Salidar. That is going to raise a few eyebrows, I tell you. What you probably do not know is that I didn't come alone. There's an embassy from Salidar in Caemlyn, to see you."

Lews Therin muttered, thunder in the distance. Mention of Aes Sedai always roused him since Alanna and the bonding, if not as much as being around Taim.

Even with Lews Therin grumbling, Rand very nearly smiled. He had suspected as soon as Min handed him the letter from Elayne. Confirmation was almost as good as proof that they were frightened, as he thought. What else could they be, rebels driven to hiding right on the edge of Whitecloak power? Very likely wishing they knew how to creep back into the White Tower, too, chewing their fingers over how to wriggle back into Elaida's good graces. From what he knew of Elaida, they had small chance, and they had to know it better than he. If they had sent an embassy to the Dragon Reborn, to a man who could channel, then they must be all but ready to accept his protection. This was not like Elaida, who apparently thought he could be bought, and likely kept in a wicker cage like a song sparrow. Egwene's nebulous promises of Aes Sedai who supported him were about to be fulfilled.

"Who came with you?" he asked. "Maybe I know her." He did not really know any Aes Sedai except Moiraine, who was dead, but he had met a few. If she was one of those, it might make things a little harder. He really had been Min's farmboy back then, ready to flinch if an Aes Sedai looked at him.

"There's more than one, Rand. Actually, there are nine." He gave a start, and she went on quickly. "It is meant for an honor, Rand; three times what they'd send a king or queen. Merana—she's in charge; she's Gray Ajah—Merana will come here alone this afternoon, and no more than one at a time will come anywhere near you unless you feel comfortable. They took rooms at The Crown of Roses, in the New City; they practically took it over, with all the Warders and servants. Merana sent me first because I know you, to smooth the way. They don't mean you any harm, Rand. I am sure of it."

"A viewing, Min, or your opinion?" It seemed odd to be carrying on a serious conversation with a woman perched on his knee, but she was Min, after all. That made it different. He just had to keep reminding himself.

"My opinion," she admitted reluctantly. "Rand, I viewed every one of them every day, all the long way from Salidar. If they intended any harm, I would have to have seen something. I can't believe nothing would show in that time." Shifting, she gave him a worried look that quickly changed to a determined firmness. "I might as well tell you something else while I'm about it. I saw an aura around you in the throne room. Aes Sedai are going to hurt you. Women who can channel, anyway. It was all confused; I'm not sure about the Aes Sedai part. But it might happen more than once. I think that's why it seemed all scrambled." He looked at her silently, and she smiled. "I like that about you, Rand. You accept what I can do and what I cannot. You don't ask me if I'm sure, or when it's going to happen. You never ask for more than I know."

"Well, I am to ask one thing, Min. Can you be sure these Aes Sedai in your viewing aren't the Aes Sedai you came with?"

"No," she said simply. That was one thing *he* liked; she never tried to evade.

I have to be careful, Lews Therin whispered intently. *Even these half-trained girls can be dangerous with nine of them. I must—*

I must, Rand thought firmly. A moment of confusion from Lews Therin, and then he fled back to the shadowed recesses. He always did now, if Rand spoke to him. The only problem was that Lews Therin seemed to be seeing and hearing more, and intending to act on it. There had not been another incident of his trying to seize *saidin*, but Rand was careful now. The man wanted Rand's mind and body for his own, thought they were his own, and if he managed to gain control even once, Rand was not certain it would not be just that way. Lews Therin Telamon walking and speaking, while Rand al'Thor was only a voice in his head.

"Rand," Min said anxiously, "don't look at me like that. I am on your side, if it comes to sides. It might; a little. They think I'll tell them what you say. I won't, Rand. They just want to know how to deal with you, what to expect, but I'll not tell one word you don't want me to, and if you ask me to lie, I will. They do not know about my viewings. Those are yours, Rand. You know I will read anyone you say, including Merana and the rest."

He forced the snarl from his face, made sure his voice was mild. "Calm yourself, Min. I know you are on my side." That was simple truth. Suspecting Min would be like suspecting himself. Lews Therin was dealt with for the moment; it was time to deal with this Merana and her embassy. "Tell them they can come three at a time." That was what Lews Therin had advised in Cairhien; no more than three at once. The man seemed to believe he could handle three Aes Sedai. He seemed more than a little contemptuous of those who called themselves Aes Sedai now. But what had been a limit in Cairhien was different here. Merana wanted him calmed and smoothed down before even one Aes Sedai came near. Let her chew on an invitation for three to begin and think what it might mean. "Aside from that, none are to enter the Inner City without my permission. And they aren't to try channeling around me. Tell them that, Min. I'll know the moment they take hold of the Source, and I will not be pleased. Tell them."

"They aren't going to be very pleased either, sheepherder," she said dryly. "But I will tell them."

A crash whipped Rand's head around.

Sulin stood just inside the door in her red-and-white dress, her face so suffused with blood that the scar on her cheek stood out even paler than usual. Her white hair had grown since she put on the livery, but it was still shorter than any of the servants'. Mistress Harfor had had it made into a close cap of curls. Sulin hated that. At her feet was a silver tray bordered in worked gold, with silver-chased golden goblets lying on their sides. The wine pitcher rocked a last time as he looked, and miraculously stopped upright, though there appeared to be as much wine punch on tray and carpet as there could be remaining in the pitcher.

Min was halfway into scrambling to her feet when he caught her by the waist and pulled her back down. Time enough and more to drive home that he was done with Aviendha, and Min would not mind helping. In fact, after a moment of resistance, she leaned into him and put her head on his chest.

"Sulin," he said, "a good servant does not toss trays about. Now, pick it up and do as you're supposed to." Staring at him darkly, she all but quivered.

Figuring out how to let her meet her *toh* while discharging at least some of his obligation to her had been little short of brilliant. Sulin cared for his rooms now, and fetched and carried only for him. She hated it, of course, especially that he saw her doing it every day, but she no longer broke her back scrubbing floors all over the Palace or hauling endless streams of heavy water buckets for laundry. He suspected she would rather every Aiel this side of the Dragonwall saw her shame than allow him to, but he had eased her labors notably, eased his conscience somewhat, and if having to work for him made her decide her *toh* was met sooner, all to the good. Sulin belonged in *cadin'sor* carrying her spears, not in livery folding bed linens.

Picking up the tray, she stalked across the room and pushed it roughly onto an ivory-inlaid table. As she started to turn away, he said, "This is Min, Sulin. She's my friend. She doesn't know Aiel ways, and I would take it amiss should anything untoward happen to her." It had just occurred to him that the Maidens might have their own view of him sending away Aviendha and holding another woman almost as soon as she was gone. Their own view, and their own way of dealing with it. "In fact, if any harm comes to her, I'll consider it done to me."

"Why should any but Aviendha wish to harm this woman?" Sulin said grimly. "She gave too much time to dreaming over you, and not enough to teaching you what you should know." Giving herself a shake, she growled, "My Lord Dragon." He thought it was supposed to be a murmur. She nearly fell over twice in her curtsy before she was upright again, and she slammed the door on her way out.

Min twisted her head to look up at him. "I don't think I have ever seen a maid like—Rand, I believe she'd have stabbed you if she had a knife."

"Kick me, maybe," he chuckled, "but never stab. She thinks I am her long-lost brother." Confusion clouded Min's eyes; he could see a hundred questions rising. "It is a long story. I will tell you another time." Part of it, he would. Nobody was ever going to know what he had to put up with from Enaila and Somara and a few others. Well, the Maidens all knew already, but no one else.

Melaine entered in the Aiel way, which was to say she put her head in at the door, looked around, then followed with the rest of her. He had never puzzled out what would make an Aiel decide not to come in. Chiefs, Wise Ones and Maidens had walked in on him in his smallclothes, in his bed, his bath. Coming closer, the sun-haired Wise One settled herself cross-legged on the carpet a few paces in front of him in a clatter of bracelets and arranged her skirts around her with care. Green eyes regarded Min neutrally.

This time Min made no effort to get up. In fact, from the way she was lying against him, head pressed against his chest, breathing slowly, he was not sure she might not be falling asleep. After all, she had said she had reached Caemlyn in the night. Suddenly he became conscious of his hand fitted in the hollow of her waist, and moved it firmly to the arm of the chair. She sighed almost regretfully and snuggled against him. Going to sleep without a doubt.

"I have news," Melaine said, "and I am uncertain which is the most important. Egwene has gone from the tents. She goes to a place called Salidar, where there are Aes Sedai. These are the Aes Sedai who may uphold you. At her asking, we did not speak to you of them before, but now I will tell you they are froward, undisciplined, contentious and full of themselves beyond reason." Her tone was heated toward the end, and her head was thrust forward.

So one of the dreamwalkers in Cairhien had spoken to Melaine in her dreams. That was about all he knew of the dreamwalkers' skills, and while it could have been useful, they were seldom willing to put it at his disposal. What was different was all that about froward and so forth. Most Aiel behaved as if they thought Aes Sedai might strike them, believed they would deserve it if so, and intended to take the blow without flinching. Even Wise Ones spoke of Aes Sedai respectfully if at all. Clearly a few things had changed. All he said, though, was "I know." If Melaine had any intention of telling him why, she would without his asking. If she did not, asking would get no answers. "About Egwene, and Salidar too. There are nine from Salidar in Caemlyn right now. Min here came with them." Min stirred on his chest and murmured something. Lews Therin was grumbling again, just too low to make out, and Rand was glad of the distraction. Min felt . . . good. She would be offended to the sky if she knew. Then again, considering her promise to make him pay, she might laugh. Maybe. She could be quicksilver at times.

Melaine showed no surprise at his knowledge, not even shifting her shawl. Since marrying Bael she seemed to have—"calmed" was not quite the right word; it was much too placid for Melaine—grown less excitable. "That was my second news. You must be wary of them, Rand al'Thor, and use a firm hand. They will respect nothing else." Most definitely a change.

"You will have two daughters," Min murmured. "Twins like mirrors."

If Melaine had been unsurprised before, she made up for it now. Her eyes went wide, and she gave a start that nearly lifted her from the floor. "How could you . . . ?" she began incredulously, then stopped to gather herself. Even so, she went on in a breathless voice. "I myself was uncertain I was with child until this morning. How could you know?"

Min did get up then, giving him a look he knew all too well. It was his fault for some reason. She was not entirely without flaws, if small ones. Fussing with her coat, she looked everywhere except at Melaine, and when her gaze fell on him again, it was a variation of the first look. He had gotten her into this; it was up to him to get her out.

"It is all right, Min," he said. "She's a Wise One, and I expect she knows things that would curl your hair." Except that already was curly. How did women do that, anyway? "I am sure she will promise to keep your secret, and you can trust her promise." Melaine almost stumbled over her tongue promising.

Just the same, Rand received another look before Min sat down beside Melaine. Reproachful, maybe. How *did* she expect him to get her out of it? Melaine would not forget because he asked, but she would keep a promise, and a secret. She had kept enough from him.

For all her reluctance, once Min began she gave a much fuller explanation than she had ever given him at one time, perhaps helped by the other woman's constant questions, and Melaine's changing attitude as well. It was as if Melaine began to feel that Min's ability made her an equal of sorts, not at all a wetlander.

"It is remarkable," Melaine said at last. "Like interpreting the dream without dreaming. Two, you say? Both girls? Bael will be so pleased. Dorindha has given him three sons, but we both know he would like a daughter." Min blinked and gave her head a hard shake. Of course; she could not know about sister-wives.

From there the two of them passed quickly on to childbirth itself. Neither had ever borne a child, but each had helped midwives.

Rand cleared his throat loudly. It was not that any of the details bothered him. He had helped ewes lamb, mares foal and cows calve. What was irritating was that they sat there with their heads together as though he had ceased to exist. Neither looked around until he cleared his throat again, loud enough that he wondered whether he had strained something.

Melaine leaned closer to Min and spoke in a whisper that could have been heard in the next room. "Men always faint."

"And always at the worst possible time," Min agreed in the same tone.

What would they think if they could have seen him in Mat's father's barn, blood and birthing fluids to his shoulders and three ribs cracked where he had been kicked because the mare had never foaled before and was frightened? A fine colt that had been, and the mare had not kicked at all the next time.

"Before I faint," he said wryly, joining them on the carpet, "perhaps one of you would like to say some more about the Aes Sedai?" He would have stood up or sat on the floor before this had his lap not been full. Among the Aiel, only chiefs had chairs, and a chief's chair was only used for things like pronouncing judgments or receiving the submission of an enemy.

Both women were suitably chastened. Neither said anything, but there was ample shifting of shawl, adjusting of coat and not quite meeting his eye. All that vanished once they got down to talking. Min held tenaciously to her opinion that the Aes Sedai from Salidar meant no harm to Rand and might give aid, suitably handled, which was with all respect in public and in private her reporting to Rand every whisper she overheard. "I'm not being a traitor, you understand, Melaine. I knew Rand before any Aes Sedai except Moiraine, really, and the truth of it is, he took my loyalty long before she died."

Melaine did not think Min a traitor, quite the contrary, and seemed to think even better of her. Wise Ones did have their own version of the Aiel view of spies. But she argued that with notable exceptions, Aes Sedai could be trusted as far as Shaido, which was to say not until they had been taken captive and made *gai'shain*. She did not exactly suggest captivity for the Aes Sedai at The Crown of Roses, but she did not miss far. "How can you trust them, Rand al'Thor? I think they have no honor, except for Egwene al'Vere, and she—" Melaine twitched her shawl again. "When an Aes Sedai shows me she has as much honor as Egwene, I will trust her, and not before."

For his part, Rand listened more than spoke, and saying no more than a dozen or so words, learned a great deal. Answering Melaine's arguments, Min ran through the embassy name by name, listing what each woman had said about support for Rand, and in truth admitting that all was not exactly rosy. Merana Ambrey and Kairen Stang, a Blue, were both Andoran, and for all that Aes Sedai supposedly forsook all allegiances save the White Tower, perhaps because they were estranged from the Tower, they worried that Rand sat in Caemlyn and might have murdered Morgase. Rafela Cindal, also Blue Ajah, might be pleased with the changes Rand had made in Tear, where once channeling had been outlawed and a girl found able to learn was hurried out of the country, but she said little, and Morgase worried her too. Seonid Traighan, a Green, mulled over every rumor from her native Cairhien and kept her own counsel, and Faeldrin Harella, the second Green sister, sometimes compared Dragonsworn atrocities in Altara and Murandy to what Dragonsworn had done in Tarabon, refusing even to talk about the fact that civil war had ripped her land apart before the first man had sworn to the Dragon there. No matter how Melaine pressed, though, Min insisted that every one of those Aes Sedai acknowledged Rand to be the Dragon Reborn and asked her most carefully, all through the journey from Salidar, what he was like and how he could best be approached without either offending or frightening him.

Rand grunted at that—that they were worried about frightening him—but Melaine began insisting that if most of the women in the embassy had so much reason to be against Rand, then the embassy as a whole surely could not be trusted far enough to fetch dung for the fire. Min spared him an apologetic grimace and rushed on. Arad Doman had seen as much of Dragonsworn as Tarabon, as well as its own civil war, but Demira Eriff, of the Brown Ajah, only talked of two things really: meeting Rand, and the rumor that he had started some sort of school in Cairhien; no man who started a school could be all bad in Demira's eyes. Berenicia Morsad, a Yellow sister from Shienar, had heard from Shienarans in Salidar that Rand had been received in Fal Dara by the great captain Lord Agelmar Jagad, an honor that seemed to carry considerable weight with her; Lord Agelmar would hardly have received a ruffian, a fool or a scoundrel. It weighed almost as heavily with Masuri Sokawa; she was a Brown, from Arafel, which bordered Shienar. Finally there was Valinde Nathenos, who according to Min showed an eagerness very unlike the White Ajah to have Rand drive Sammael out of Illian; a promise of that, a promise even to try, and Min would not be surprised to see Valinde offer him an oath of fealty. Melaine expressed disbelief, even rolling her eyes; she had never seen an Aes Sedai with that much sense, an attitude Rand found more than surprising considering that she would probably laugh in his face if he asked for such an oath. Min maintained that it was true, though, whatever the other woman said.

"I will show them as much respect as I can without kneeling," Rand told Min when she finally ran down. For Melaine, he added, "And until they show proof of goodwill, I'll trust them not one jot." He thought that should please them both, since each got what she wanted, but from the frowns he received, it pleased neither.

After all that arguing, he half-expected the pair to be at one another's throats, but it seemed that Melaine's pregnancy and Min's viewing had created a bond. When they stood, the women were all smiles and hugs, and Melaine said, "I did not think I would like you, Min, but I do, and I will name one of the girls after you, because you knew of her first. I must go to tell Bael so he will not be jealous that Rand al'Thor knew before him. May you always find water and shade, Min." To Rand, she added, "Watch these Aes Sedai closely, Rand al'Thor, and give Min your protection when she needs it. They will harm her if they learn she is sworn to you." Of course, she left with exactly the ceremony with which she had arrived, a nod of the head.

Which left him alone with Min again. Which felt awkward for some reason.

CHAPTER
42

The Black Tower

R and and Min stood looking at one another, not moving, until finally he said, "Would you like to come out to the farm with me?"
She gave a little start at the sound of his voice. "The farm?"

"It's a school, really. For the men who come for the amnesty."

Min's face paled. "No, I don't think. . . . Merana will be waiting to hear from me. And I should let them know your rules as soon as possible. Any one of them could wander into the Inner City without knowing, and you wouldn't want. . . . I really ought to go."

He did not understand. Without meeting even one of the students, she was afraid of them, men who could channel, men who wanted to channel. In anyone else it would be understandable, but he could channel, and she was ready to rough his hair and poke his ribs and call him names to his face. "Do you want an escort back to The Crown of Roses? There really are footpads, even by daylight. Not many, but I would not like anything to happen to you."

Her laugh was a bit unsteady. She truly was upset over the farm. "I took care of myself while you were tending sheep, farmboy." Abruptly she had a knife in either hand; a flourish, and they went back up her sleeves, not quite so smoothly as they had come out. In a much more sober tone, she said, "You must take care of yourself, Rand. Rest. You look tired." Startlingly, she went a-tiptoe and stretched her head up to brush his lips with a kiss. "It

is good to see you too, sheepherder." And with another laugh, this one delighted, she slipped out.

Muttering to himself, Rand put his coat back on and went into his
bedchamber to fetch his sword from the back of the wardrobe, a dark,
rose-carved thing tall enough and wide enough for four men's clothes.
He really was turning into a randy goat. Min was just having her fun. He
wondered how long she intended to keep teasing him for one slip of the
tongue.

A cloth bag of moderate size, clinking when he lifted it from under his
stockings in a drawered chest inlaid with lapis, went into one coat pocket,
and a much smaller, velvet bag went in atop his *angreal*. The silversmith
who had made the contents of the larger had been more than happy to
work for the Dragon Reborn and had tried to refuse payment for the honor
of it. The goldsmith who had made the single piece in the other bag had
required four times what Bashere said the work was worth, and a pair of
Maidens to stand over him until it was done.

This trip to the farm had been in Rand's mind for some time already.
He did not like Taim, and Lews Therin would surge around the man, but
he could not go on avoiding the place. Especially not now. So far as he
knew, Taim had done well at keeping the students out of the city—at
least, Rand had heard of no incidents, and he would have—but news of
Merana and the embassy would reach the farm eventually, by the supply
carts or with new students, and in the way of rumors, nine Aes Sedai
would become nine Red sisters, or ninety, hunting men to gentle. Whether
the result of that would be students running off in the night or students
coming into Caemlyn to strike the first blow, he had to quell it before it
began.

Caemlyn held too many rumors of Aes Sedai already as it was, another
reason he had planned to go out. Alanna and Verin and the Two Rivers
girls had grown into half the Tower, by the word in the streets, and there
were plenty of other tales of Aes Sedai sneaking into the city, sneaking
through the gates in the night. That story of an Aes Sedai Healing stray
cats was so prevalent he could almost believe in her himself, but all Bashere's efforts to track the tale down provided as much substance as the tale
that the women who escorted the Dragon Reborn everywhere were really
Aes Sedai in disguise.

Unconsciously Rand turned, staring at a wall banded with white reliefs
of lions and roses, staring beyond it. Alanna was no longer at Culain's
Hound. She was on edge; had she not been Aes Sedai, he would have said

her nerves were jagged. Once last night he had wakened, sure she was weeping; the feel had been that strong. Sometimes he almost found himself forgetting she was there—until something like her waking him happened. He supposed you really could grow used to anything. This morning Alanna was . . . eager, as well; eager seemed the best word. He would wager all of Caemlyn that the plumb line from his eyes to her ran straight to The Crown of Roses. He would wager Verin was with her. Not nine Aes Sedai. Eleven.

Lews Therin murmured uneasily. It was the sound of a man wondering whether his back was against a wall. Rand wondered, too. Eleven, and thirteen could take him as easily as scoop up a child. If he gave them the chance. Lews Therin began laughing softly, a hoarse weeping sort of laugh; he had drifted again.

For a moment Rand considered Somara and Enaila, then opened a gateway right there above the blue-and-gold-patterned carpet in his bedchamber. Sullen as they were this morning, one of them was sure to blurt something before the visit to the farm was done, and remembering his previous visits, he did not want the students all looking over their shoulders for fear of twenty or so Maidens. That sort of thing did little for a man's confidence, and they needed confidence if they were to survive.

Taim was right on one point; holding on to *saidin*, a man knew he was alive, and it went beyond heightened senses. Despite the Dark One's taint, despite the feel of oily offal staining your bones, when the Power was trying to melt you where you stood, freeze you till you shattered, when one misstep or one moment of weakness meant death—Light, you knew you were alive. Still, he pushed the Source away as soon as he was through the gateway, and not only to rid himself of the taint before his stomach emptied itself; it seemed worse than it had been, more vile, if that was possible. His real reason for abandoning the Power was that he did not think he dared face Taim with *saidin* in him and Lews Therin in his head.

The clearing was browner than he remembered, more leaves crackling under his boots and still fewer on the trees. Some of the pines were completely yellow, and a number of leatherleafs stood dead, gray and bare. But if the clearing had changed, the farm was altered almost beyond recognition.

The farmhouse looked in much better repair with its new thatch, and the barn had certainly been rebuilt entirely; it was much larger than before and did not lean at all. Horses filled a large corral beside the barn, and the pens of cows and sheep had been moved farther away. The goats were penned now as well, and neat rows of coops held the chickens. The forest had been cleared back. Over a dozen long white tents made a row beyond the barn, and nearby stood the frames for two buildings much larger than the farmhouse, where a cluster of women sat outside doing their sewing and watching a score of children roll hoops and toss balls and play with dolls. The biggest change was the students, most in close-fitting high-collared black coats and few sweating. There must have been well over a hundred, of all ages. Rand had had no idea Taim's recruiting trips had gone this well. The feel of *saidin* seemed to fill the air. Some men practiced weaves, setting fire to stumps or shattering stones or snaring each other in coils of Air. Others channeled to haul water, the buckets gripped with Air, or to push dung carts from the barn, or stack firewood. Not everyone was channeling. Henre Haslin had a line of bare-chested men under his eye, working the forms with practice swords. With only a fringe of white hair and a bulbous red nose, Haslin sweated more than his students, and doubtless was wishing for his wine, but he watched and corrected as sharply as when he was Master of the Sword for the Queen's Guards. Saeric, a gray-haired Red Water Goshien with no right hand, had two shirtless rows under his stony eyes. One was kicking as high as their heads, pivot and kick, then pivot and kick with the other foot, over and over; the other punched the air in front of them as fast they could. All in all, it was a far cry from the pitiful handful Rand had seen the last time.

A black-coated man just short of his middle years planted himself in front of Rand. He had a sharp nose and a sneering mouth. "And who are you?" he demanded in a Taraboner accent. "I suppose you have come to the Black Tower to learn, yes? You should have waited in Caemlyn for the wagon to bring you. You could have had another day to enjoy that fine coat."

"I am Rand al'Thor," Rand said quietly. Quietly so as not to let out a sudden surge of anger. Civility cost nothing, and if this fool did not decide it was cheap at the price soon. . . .

If anything, the sneer deepened. "So you are him, are you?" He looked Rand up and down insolently. "You do not look so grand to me. I think that I myself could—" A flow of Air solidified just before it clipped him under the ear, and he collapsed in a heap.

"Sometimes we need a hard discipline," Taim said, coming to stand over the man on the ground. His voice was almost jolly, but his dark tilted eyes stared close to murder at the man he had clubbed. "You cannot tell a man he has the power to make the earth shake, then expect him to walk

small." The Dragons climbing the sleeves of his black coat glittered in
the sunlight; thread-of-gold would do for the one, but what could make the
blue shine so? Abruptly he raised his voice. "Kisman! Rochaid! Drag
Torval away and douse him until he wakes. No Healing, mind you.
Maybe an aching head will teach him to mind his tongue."

Two men in black coats, younger than Rand, came running and bent
over Torval, then hesitated, glancing at Taim. After a moment, Rand felt
saidin fill them; flows of Air lifted a limp Torval, and the pair trotted away
with him floating between them.

I should have killed him long ago, Lews Therin panted. *I should have . . .
should have. . . .* There was a stretching toward the Source.

No, burn you! Rand thought. *No, you don't! You're only a bloody voice!*
With a fading wail Lews Therin fled.

Rand took a slow breath. Taim was looking at him, wearing that
almost-smile. "You teach them Healing?"

"The little I know, first thing. Even before how not to sweat to death in
this weather. A weapon loses its utility if it's going to be laid up with the
first wound. As it is, I have had one kill himself drawing too deeply and
three burn themselves out, but no one has died from a sword yet." He
managed to put a good deal of contempt into the word "sword."

"I see," Rand said simply. One dead and three burned out. Did Aes
Sedai lose that many in the Tower? But then, they went slowly. They could
afford to go slowly. "What is this Black Tower the fellow was talking
about? I don't like the sound of it, Taim." Lews Therin was mumbling and
moaning again, just short of making words.

The hawk-nosed man shrugged, studying the farm and the students
with a proprietory pride. "A name the students use. You could not go on
calling this just 'the farm.' They certainly did not feel right about it; they
wanted something more. The Black Tower to balance the White Tower."
He tilted his head, looking at Rand almost sideways. "I can suppress it, if
you wish. It is easy enough to take a word from men's lips."

Rand hesitated. Easy enough to take a word from their lips perhaps,
but not from their minds. It did have to be called something. He had not
thought of that. Why not the Black Tower? Though looking at the farmhouse and the framing—larger, but only wood—the name did make him
smile. "Let it stand." Maybe the White Tower had begun as humbly. Not
that the Black Tower would ever have time to grow into anything to rival
the White. That erased his smile, and he looked at the children sadly. He
was playing as much as they, pretending there was a chance of building

something that might last. "Assemble the students, Taim. I have a few things to say to them."

He had come expecting to gather them round him, and then seeing their numbers, maybe to speak from the back of the rickety cart that now seemed to have vanished. Taim had a platform for making addresses, though, a plain block of black stone dressed and polished so finely that it shone like a mirror in the sunlight, with two steps cut into the back. It stood in an open area beyond the farmhouse, the ground beaten bare and flat and hard around it. The women and children gathered to one side to watch and listen.

From the block, Rand had a chance to see clues to how far Taim's recruiting had ranged. Jahar Narishma, whom Taim had pointed out, the young man with the spark, had dark eyes as big as a girl's, a pale face filled with confidence, and hair in two long braids with silver bells on the ends. Actually, Taim had said he came from Arafel, but Rand recognized a Shienaran's shaved head and topknot on another man, and two with the transparent veils often worn by men and women alike in Tarabon. There were tilted eyes from Saldaea and pale, short fellows from Cairhien. One old man had a beard oiled and cut to a point in imitation of a Tairen lord, which he assuredly was not with that creased leathery face, and no fewer than three wore beards that left their upper lips bare. He hoped Taim had not roused Sammael's interest by recruiting into Illian. He had expected mainly younger men, but fresh faces like Eben's and Fedwin's were balanced by gray or balding heads, some even more grizzled than Damer. Now that he thought of it, though, there was no mystery, no reason there should not be as many grandfathers who could be taught as boys.

He did not know how to make speeches, but he had thought long and hard over what he wanted to say. Not the first part, but that was quickest done, with luck. "You've all probably heard stories that the Tower . . . the White Tower . . . has divided. Well, it's true. There are some rebel Aes Sedai who might just decide to follow me, and they've sent emissaries. Nine of them, sitting in Caemlyn right now and waiting my pleasure. So when you hear about Aes Sedai in Caemlyn, don't believe any rumors. You know why they are here, and you can laugh in the face of the fellow with the rumor."

There was no reaction. They just stood there staring up at him, hardly seeming to blink. Taim looked wry, very wry. Touching the larger bag in his pocket, Rand went on with the part he had labored over.

"You need a name. In the Old Tongue, Aes Sedai means Servants of

All, or something very close. The Old Tongue doesn't translate easily." For himself, he knew only a few words, some from Asmodean, a handful from Moiraine, some that had seeped through from Lews Therin. Bashere had provided what he needed, though. "Another word in the Old Tongue is *asha'man*. It means guardian, or guardians. Or defender, and maybe a couple of other things; I told you, the Old Tongue is very flexible. Guardian seems to be best, though. Not just any defender or guardian, though. You could not call a man who defended an unjust cause *asha'man*, and never one that was evil. An *asha'man* was a man who defended truth and justice and right for everyone. A guardian who would not yield even when hope was gone." The Light knew, hope would go when Tarmon Gai'don came, if not before. "That is what you are here to become. When you finish your training, you will be Asha'man."

Murmurs rustled like leaves in a breeze, the name being repeated, but they died quickly. Attentive faces peered up at him; he could almost see ears pricking for his next words. At least that was a little better than before. The cloth bag gave off a faint clinking as he took it from his coat pocket.

"Aes Sedai begin as novices, then become Accepted, then finally full Aes Sedai. You will have degrees, too, but not like theirs. There will be no putting out or sending away among us." Send away? Light, he would do everything short of tying them hand and foot to stop anyone who wanted to go if he could channel at all. "When a man first comes to the Black Tower . . ." He did not like that name. ". . . he will be called a soldier, because that is what he becomes when he joins us, what you all became, a soldier to fight the Shadow, and not just the Shadow, but anyone who opposes justice or oppresses the weak. When a soldier reaches a certain stage in his skills, he will be called Dedicated, and wear this." From the bag he took one of the badges the silversmith had made, a small gleaming silver sword, perfect with its long hilt and slanting quillons and slightly curved blade. "Taim."

Taim walked to the block stiffly, and Rand bent to pin the silver sword to the tall collar of his coat. It seemed to shine even more brightly against the pitch-black wool. Taim's face had as much expression as the stone beneath Rand's boots. Rand handed him the bag, whispering, "Give these to whoever you think is ready. Just be sure they are."

Straightening, he hoped there were enough; he really had not expected anywhere near so many men. "Dedicated who advance their skill far enough will be called Asha'man, and they will wear this." Taking out the small velvet bag, he held up what it contained. Sunlight sparkled on finely crafted gold and rich red enamel. A sinuous form exactly like the one on the Dragon banner. That went onto Taim's collar too, on the other side, so sword and Dragon shone at the sides of his throat. "I suppose I was the first Asha'man," Rand told the students, "but Mazrim Taim is the second." Taim's face made stone look soft; what was wrong with the man? "I hope that all of you will become Asha'man eventually, but whether you do or not, remember that all of us are soldiers. There are many battles ahead, maybe not always the ones we expect, and at the end, the Last Battle. The Light send it is the last. If the Light shines on us, we will win. We will win because we must win."

There should have been some sort of cheer when he stopped. He did not take himself for the sort of speaker who could make men jump and shout, but these men knew why they were here. Telling them they would win should have produced something, however feeble. There was only silence.

Rand jumped down from the stone block, and Taim snapped, "Disperse to lessons and chores." The students—the soldiers—went their ways almost as silently as they had stood, with only a murmur of quiet words. Taim motioned toward the farmhouse. He was holding the bag of sword pins so tightly it was a wonder none of them stabbed him through the cloth. "If my Lord Dragon has time for a cup of wine?"

Rand nodded; he wanted to get to the bottom of this before returning to the Palace.

The front room of the farmhouse was just what might be expected, a bare floor swept spotless, mismatched ladder-back chairs arranged in front of a red brick fireplace so clean it seemed impossible it had ever held a fire. A white cloth edged with embroidered flowers covered a small table. Sora Grady entered silently and set a wooden tray atop the cloth, with a bright blue pitcher of wine and two white-glazed mugs. Rand had thought her gaze would not hurt after all this time, but the accusation in her eyes made him glad when she left. She had been sweating, he realized. Taim tossed the bag onto the tray and emptied a mug straight away.

"Don't you teach the women that trick of concentrating?" Rand asked. "It's cruel to make them sweat when their men don't."

"Most want no part of it," Taim said curtly. "Their husbands and sweethearts try to teach them, but most refuse even to listen. It might have to do with *saidin*, you see."

Rand peered into his mug at the dark wine. He had to feel his way here. No blowing up just because irritation prickled. "I'm pleased to see the recruiting going so well. You said you'd match the Tower . . . the White Tower . . ." White Tower; Black Tower. What would the stories make of that? If there were any. ". . . in less than a year, and if you keep on at this rate, you will. I don't see how you find so many."

"Sift enough sand," Taim said stiffly, "and you will find a few grains of gold eventually. I leave that to others now, except for a trip or two. Damer, Grady, there are a dozen men I can trust alone for a day; they have enough years not to do anything stupid, and there are enough younger men with the strength to make a gateway, if not much more, to accompany the older who don't. You will have your thousand before the year. What of those I send on to Caemlyn? Have you made an army of them yet? You have your thousand there, and times over."

"I leave that to Bashere," Rand said quietly. Taim's mouth quirked derisively, and Rand set his mug down before it could break in his grip. Bashere was making what he could of them, he understood, in a camp somewhere west of the city; what he could considering that they were, as the Saldaean put it, a ragtag collection of penniless farmers, runaway apprentices and failed craftsmen who had never held a sword, ridden a horse with a saddle or been more than five miles from where they were born. Rand had too much to concern him to worry about the likes of that; he had told Bashere to do what he wanted with them and not bother him unless they ran riot.

Looking at Taim, who was making no effort to hide his disdain, he stuck his hands behind his back, where they clenched into fists. Lews Therin rumbled in the distance, an echo of his anger. "What has gotten into you? You've had a burr in your breeches ever since I put those badges on you. Is it something to do with them? If so, I don't understand. Those men will think more of theirs for seeing you receive yours from the Dragon Reborn. For that matter, they'll think more of you for it. Maybe you won't have to keep discipline by clubbing men over the head. Well, what have you to say?" That began well enough, in a calm tone if not exactly mild—he had not intended it to be mild—but along the way his voice grew firmer and louder. Not to a shout, yet that final question cracked like a whip.

The most remarkable transformation came over the other man. Taim shook visibly—with rage, Rand would have said, not fear—but when the shaking stopped, he was his old self again. Not friendly certainly, a touch mocking, but very much relaxed and in control of himself. "Since you must know, what worries me are Aes Sedai, and you. Nine Aes Sedai come to

Caemlyn, plus two, make eleven. Then there might just be one or two more. I haven't been able to find them yet, but—"

"I told you to stay out of the city," Rand said flatly.

"I found a few men to ask questions for me." Taim's tone was dry as dust. "I've been no closer than here since I saved you from that Gray Man."

Rand let that pass. Barely. Almost. The voice in his head was too low to be understood, but cold thunder for that. "They'll catch smoke with their fingers before they catch rumors." That came out with all the contempt he felt—Taim had *saved* him?—and the man jerked. Outwardly he still appeared at his ease, yet his eyes could have been dark gemstones.

"And if they join with the Red Aes Sedai?" His voice was cool and amused, but his eyes glittered. "There are Red sisters in the countryside. Several parties of them, arrived in the last few days. Trying to intercept men coming here."

I will kill him, Lews Therin shouted, and Rand felt that fumbling reach toward *saidin.*

Go away, he said firmly. The fumbling continued, and so did the voice.

I will kill him, and then them. They must serve him. It is plain; they must serve him.

Go away, Rand shouted back silently. *You are nothing but a voice!* Stretching toward the Source.

Oh, Light, I killed them all. All that I loved. If I kill him, it will be well, though. I can make it up, if I kill him finally. No, nothing can make up, but I must kill him anyway. Kill them all. I must. I must.

No! Rand screamed inside his head. *You're dead, Lews Therin. I am alive, burn you, and you are dead! You are dead!*

Abruptly he realized he was leaning on the table, holding himself up with sagging knees. And muttering, "You are dead! I am alive, and you are dead!" But he had not seized *saidin.* And neither had Lews Therin. Shivering, he looked at Taim and was surprised to see concern on the man's face.

"You must hold on," Taim said softly. "If sanity can be held, you must. The price is too high, if you fail."

"I won't fail," Rand said, pushing himself upright. Lews Therin was silent. There seemed to be nothing in his head but himself. And the feel of Alanna, of course. "Have these Reds taken anyone?"

"Not that I have heard." Taim was watching him cautiously, as if he expected another outburst. "Most of the students come through gateways now, and with all the people on the roads, it cannot be easy to pick out a man heading here unless he talks too freely." He paused, "They could be disposed of easily enough in any case."

"No." Was Lews Therin really gone? He wished it, and knew he would be a fool to believe. "If they start taking men, I'll have to do something, but as it is, they're no threat out in the country. And believe me, nobody Elaida sends is likely to join those Aes Sedai in the city. Either lot would probably welcome you before they did each other."

"What about those who are not in the countryside? Eleven of them? A few accidents could reduce that to a much safer number. If you don't want to soil your own hands, I am willing to—"

"No! How many times do I have to say, no! If I feel a man channel in Caemlyn, I will come for you, Taim. I swear I will. And don't think you can stay far enough from the Palace that I won't feel it and be safe. If one of those Aes Sedai keels over dead for no reason, I will know who to blame. Mark me!"

"You set wide boundaries," Taim said dryly. "If Sammael or Demandred decides to taunt you with a few dead Aes Sedai on your doorstep, my veins are opened?"

"They haven't so far, and you had better hope they do not start. Mark me, I say."

"I hear my Lord Dragon and obey, of course." The hawk-nosed man bowed slightly. "But I still say eleven is a dangerous number."

Rand laughed in spite of himself. "Taim, I intend to teach them to dance to my flute." Light, how long since he had played the flute? Where *was* his flute? Faintly, he heard Lews Therin chuckling.

CHAPTER
43

The Crown of Roses

Merana's hired coach swayed its slow way through the densely packed streets toward The Crown of Roses. Outwardly she was calm, at least, a dark-haired woman with cool hazel eyes, slim-fingered hands folded peacefully on her pale gray silk skirts. Inside, she was not so serene. Thirty-eight years ago she had been in place by chance to negotiate a treaty between Arad Doman and Tarabon that was supposed to put an end to the squabbling over Almoth Plain, with Domani and Taraboners dodging at every turn and three times nearly starting a war in the middle of the exchanges and all the while maintaining smiling faces of utter good-will. By the time the signatures were dry, she felt as if she had been rolled over rough hills in a barrel full of splinters, and after all that, the treaty turned out to be worth considerably less than the wax and ribbons for its seals. She hoped what she had begun this afternoon at the Royal Palace ended better—it had to—but inside, she felt as though she had just climbed out of another barrel.

Min was sitting back with her eyes closed; the young woman seemed to take catnaps any time an Aes Sedai was not actually speaking to her. The other two sisters in the coach occasionally shot quick glances at the girl. Seonid, cool and reserved in her brocaded green. Masuri, slim and merry-eyed in brown embroidered with flowering vines around the hem. They had all dressed formally, in shawls and Ajah colors.

Merana was sure they had the same thought as herself when they looked at Min. Seonid should certainly understand, though who could be certain? Seonid was very methodical and practical about her Warders, almost like a woman with a pair of prize wolfhounds she felt some affection for. Masuri might understand. She did like to dance and even flirt, though she was liable to forget the poor man when she heard a rumor of an old manuscript hidden away. Merana herself had not been in love since well before that Fifth Treaty of Falme, but she did remember, and all it had taken was one glimpse of Min staring at al'Thor to see a woman who had tossed sense out the window and was riding her heart at a gallop.

Not proof that Min had ignored all their cautions, broken her promise and told al'Thor everything, but he knew about Salidar. He knew Elayne was there, and had been amused—amused!—at their evasions. Aside from whether Min had broken confidence—care would have to be used in what was said around her from now on in any case—it was frightening when taken with everything else. Merana was not used to being frightened. She had been, often, in the year after Basan died—she had never bonded another Warder, at least partly because she did not want to go through that again; and also partly because she was simply too busy to search out the right man—but that was the last time she had known anything more than apprehension, before the Aiel War. Now she felt fear, and she did not like it. Everything could still go well, nothing truly disastrous had happened, but al'Thor himself turned her knees to water.

The hired coach rocked to a stop in the stableyard of The Crown of Roses, stablemen in vests worked with roses rushing out to take bridles and open doors.

The common room suited the three stories of finely dressed white stone, all dark polished panels with tall fireplaces faced in white marble. One mantelpiece held a wide clock, with chimes for the hours and a few lines of gilding. The serving women wore blue dresses and white aprons embroidered with a ring of roses; they were all smiling, polite, efficient, and those not pretty were handsome. The Crown of Roses was a favorite of nobles in from the country who had no mansions of their own in Caemlyn, but now the tables held only Warders. And Alanna and Verin, seated at the rear; had Merana had her wishes, they would have been waiting in the kitchens with the servants. The rest of the sisters were all out. There was no time to waste.

"If you don't mind," Min said, "I would like to walk around. I'd like to see some of Caemlyn before dark."

Merana gave her assent and, as the young woman darted back outside, exchanged looks with Seonid and Masuri, wondering how long it would take Min to return to the Palace.

Mistress Cinchonine appeared at once, as round as any innkeeper Merana had ever seen, bobbing bows and dry-washing her pink hands. "Is there anything I can do for you, Aes Sedai? Anything I can fetch?" She had accommodated Merana often, and well, both before and after learning she was Aes Sedai.

"Berry tea," Merana told her, smiling. "In the private sitting room upstairs." The smile went as the innkeeper scurried away calling for one of the serving women. Merana motioned sharply for Alanna and Verin to join her on the stairs, and the five of them climbed in silence.

The sitting-room windows gave a good view of the street for those who wished it, which Merana did not particularly. She pulled in the windows that were open, to shut out some of the noise, and turned her back on them. Seonid and Masuri had taken chairs. Alanna and Verin remained standing, between the other two. Verin's dark wool dress had an air of being rumpled, though it was not, and she had an inkstain on the tip of her nose, but her eyes were birdlike, sharp and watchful. Alanna's eyes shone too, but very likely with anger, and now and then her hands quivered slightly, gripping the skirts of her yellow-bodiced blue silk dress; it looked as if she had slept in it. There was some excuse for her, of course. Some, but not enough.

"I do not know yet, Alanna," Merana said firmly, "whether your actions have had any adverse effect. He did not bring up your bonding him— against his will—but he was sharp, very sharp, and—"

"Has he set further restrictions?" Verin broke in, tilting her head slightly. "All seems to be going well, to me. He did not fly away at news of you. He has received three; in some courtesy, at least, or you would be at thunderheads. He is a little frightened of us, which is to the good, or he would not have set limits, but unless he has set more, we still have as much freedom as before, so he is not terrified. Above all, we must not frighten him too far."

The difficulty was that Verin and Alanna were not part of Merana's delegation; she had no authority over them. They had heard the news of Logain and the Reds and agreed that Elaida could not be allowed to remain in the Amyrlin Seat, yet that meant nothing. Of course, Alanna was not really a problem, only potentially. She and Merana were so close in strength that the only way to say which had the greater would be an actual contest, the sort of thing novices did until they were caught. Alanna had been six years a novice, Merana only five, but more importantly, Merana had been Aes Sedai above thirty years the day the midwife laid Alanna at her mother's breast. That took care of that. Merana had precedence. No one actually thought in those terms unless something made them, but they both knew and adjusted automatically. Not that Alanna would take orders, yet instinctive deference would surely keep her in hand to some degree. That, and knowing what she had done.

Verin was the problem, the one who had Merana thinking of strengths and precedence. Merana let herself sense the other woman's strength in the Power again, though of course she knew what she would find. No way to tell which of them was stronger. Five years as novice for each, six as Accepted; that was one thing every Aes Sedai knew about every other if she knew nothing else. The difference was that Verin was older, maybe almost as much older than she as she was older than Alanna. The touch of gray in Verin's hair emphasized it. Had Verin been part of the embassy, there would have been no difficulty at all, but she was not, and Merana found herself listening attentively, deferring without thinking. Twice in the morning she had had to remind herself that Verin was not in charge. The only thing that made the situation tolerable was that Verin must feel she shared some of Alanna's guilt. Without that she surely would have been in a chair as soon as anyone else, not standing beside Alanna. If only there were some way to make her remain at Culain's Hound day and night to watch over that wonderful treasure of girls from the Two Rivers.

Seating herself so she, Seonid and Masuri surrounded the pair, Merana adjusted her skirts and shawl carefully. There was some moral ascendancy in being seated while the others remained standing. To her, what Alanna had done was little short of rape. "In fact, he has placed another restriction. It is all very well that you two have located his *school*, but now I strongly suggest you abandon whatever thoughts you may have had in that direction. He has . . . charged us . . . to stay away from his . . . men." She could see him still, leaning forward in that monstrosity of a throne with the Lion Throne on exhibit behind him and a carved piece of spear in his fist; no doubt an Aiel custom, that.

"*Hear me, Merana Sedai,*" *he said, quite pleasantly and quite firmly.* "*I want no trouble between Aes Sedai and Asha'man. I have told the soldiers to stay clear of you, but I do not mean them to be Aes Sedai meat. If you go hunting at the Black Tower, you may be dinner yourself. We both want to avoid that.*"

Merana had been Aes Sedai long enough not to shiver every time a goose walked over her grave, but it was close this time. Asha'man. The Black Tower. Mazrim Taim! How could it have gone so far? Yet Alanna was certain there were over a hundred men, though she gave no details of how she knew, of course; no sister willingly exposed her eyes-and-ears. It did not matter. "If you pursue two hares, both will escape you," the old saying went, and al'Thor was the most important hare in the world. The others had to wait.

"Is he . . . ? Is he still here, or has he gone?" Verin and Alanna seemed to take it very calmly that al'Thor apparently could Travel; it still made Merana a trifle queasy. What else had he taught himself that Aes Sedai had forgotten? "Alanna? Alanna!"

The slender Green sister jerked, pulling herself back from wherever her mind had been. She seemed to drift quite often. "He is in the city. In the Palace, I think." She still sounded a little dreamy. "It was. . . . He has a wound in his side. An old wound, yet only half-healed. Every time I let myself dwell on it, I want to weep. How can he live with it?"

Seonid gave her a sharp look; any woman who had a Warder had felt his injuries. But she knew what Alanna was going through, having lost Owein, and when she spoke, her voice was almost gentle and only a little brisk. "Why, Teryl and Furen have taken wounds that almost made me faint, even feeling them as softly as we do, and they never slowed a step. Not one step."

"I think," Masuri said quietly, "we are going afield." She always spoke quietly, but unlike many Browns, always to the point.

Merana nodded. "Yes. I considered taking Moiraine's place with him. . . ."

A rap at the door announced a white-aproned woman with the tea tray. A silver teapot and porcelain cups; The Crown and Rose was used to the nobility. By the time the tray was settled and the serving woman gone, Alanna was no longer dreamy. Her dark eyes flashed with all the fire Merana had ever seen in them. Greens particularly were jealous of their Warders, and al'Thor belonged to her now, however she had bonded him. Deference went down the well when it came to that. Straight as a blade she stood, just waiting for Merana's next words to see whether to slash and cut. Still, Merana waited until the blueberry tea was poured and everyone back in her chair. She even told Verin and Alanna to sit. The fool woman deserved a little upset, even atop Owein. Maybe it was not short of rape at all.

"I considered it," she went on at last, "and rejected it. I might have done so if you had not done what you did, Alanna, but he is so suspicious of Aes Sedai now that he might well laugh in my face if I suggested it."

"He is as arrogant as any king," Seonid said curtly.

"Everything Elayne and Nynaeve said and more," Masuri added, shaking her head. "Claiming that he knows when a woman channels. I almost embraced *saidar* to show him he was mistaken, but of course, whatever I did to show him might have alarmed him too much."

"All those Aiel." Seonid's voice was tight; she *was* Cairhienin. "Men *and* women. I think they would have tried to spear us if we blinked too quickly. One, a sun-haired woman who was at least wearing skirts, made no effort at all to hide her dislike."

At times, Merana thought, Seonid did not fully realize that al'Thor himself might be a danger.

Alanna unconsciously began chewing her underlip like a girl. It was good she had Verin to take care of her; she was not fit to be out alone in her state. Verin merely sipped her tea and watched; Verin's eyes could be most disconcerting.

Merana found herself relenting. She remembered too well the fragile bundle of nerves she had been after Baran. "Fortunately, it seems there may be a good side to his suspicion. He has received emissaries from Elaida, in Cairhien. He was quite open about it. Suspicion will make him keep them at a long arm's length, I believe."

Seonid rested her cup in its saucer. "He thinks to play us one against the other."

"And he might still," Masuri said dryly, "except that we know more of him than Elaida possibly can. I think she must have sent her envoys to meet a shepherd, if a shepherd in a silk coat. Whatever he is, he is no longer that. Moiraine taught him well, it seems."

"We were forearmed," Merana said. "I think it unlikely they were."

Alanna stared at them, blinking. "Then I have not ruined everything?" They all three nodded, and she took a deep breath, then smoothed at her skirts with a frown as if just noticing the wrinkles. "I may yet be able to make him accept me." The wrinkles were abandoned, and her face and voice became calmer and more confident by the word. "As for his amnesty, we may have to hold any plans in abeyance, but that doesn't mean we should not make them. That sort of danger cannot be ignored."

For a moment Merana regretted her relenting. The woman had done that to a man and all that truly worried her was whether it damaged their chances of success. Reluctantly, though, she admitted that had it made al'Thor biddable, she would have held her nose, and her tongue. "First we must bring al'Thor to heel, so to speak. The abeyance will last as long as it must, Alanna." Alanna's mouth tightened, but after a moment she nodded in acquiescence. Or at least assent.

"And how is he to be brought to heel?" Verin asked. "He must be handled delicately. A wolf on a leash one thread thick."

Merana hesitated. She had not meant to share everything with this pair, who had only the most tenuous allegiance to the Hall in Salidar. She dreaded what would happen if Verin tried to take over here, if in fact she did manage to take over. She herself knew how to handle this; she had been chosen because of a lifetime spent mediating sensitive disputes, nego-tiating treaties where the hatreds seemed implacable. That agreements were broken eventually and treaties violated was the nature of humanity, yet in eighty years, the Fifth Treaty of Falme was her only real failure. She knew all of that, but all of those years had ingrained some instincts deeply. "We are approaching certain nobles, who by good luck are all in Caemlyn now. . . ."

"My worry is Elayne," Dyelin said firmly. The more firmly for being alone in the sitting room with an Aes Sedai; Aes Sedai could press hard if you weakened when you were alone. Especially when no one else knew you were alone with her.

Kairen Sedai smiled, but neither smile nor cool blue eyes gave away anything. "It is quite possible the Daughter-Heir will yet be found to sit on the Lion Throne. What may seem insurmountable to others is seldom so to Aes Sedai."

"The Dragon Reborn says—"

"Men say many things, Lady Dyelin, but you know I do not lie."

Luan patted the Tairen stallion's gray neck, looking both ways in case one of the grooms came into the stables, and barely dodged a bite from wicked teeth. Rafela's Warder would give warning, but Luan was not sure he trusted anyone of late. Especially not with a visit of this sort. "I am not sure I understand," he said curtly.

"Unity is better than division," Rafela said, "peace better than war, patience better than death." Luan's head jerked at the odd end to the platitudes, and the round-faced Aes Sedai smiled. "Will Andor not be better off if Rand al'Thor leaves the land in peace and unity, Lord Luan?"

Holding her robe shut, Ellorien stared at the Aes Sedai who had managed to reach her in her bath without being announced, possibly without being seen. The coppery-skinned woman looked back from the stool on the other side of the marble tub full of water as though this were all natural and ordinary. "Who," Ellorien asked finally, "would have the Lion Throne then, Demira Sedai?"

"The Wheel weaves as the Wheel wills" was the reply, and Ellorien knew she would get no other.

CHAPTER
44

The Color of Trust

O nce Vanin was gone to tell the Band to sit tight, Mat found that not an inn remained in Salidar but was taken over by Aes Sedai, and the five stables were all full to bursting. Yet when he slipped a little silver to a narrow-jawed stableman, the fellow had the sacks of oats and bales of hay shifted from a stone-walled yard that was fine for six horses. He also showed Mat and the remaining four men of the Band places to sleep in the loft, which was little cooler than anywhere else.

"Ask for nothing," Mat told his men as he divided the rest of his coins among them. "Pay for everything, and accept no gifts. The Band isn't going to be beholden to anybody here."

His false air of confidence communicated itself to them, and they did not even hesitate when he ordered them to fix the banners out the loft door so they hung down in front of the stable, crimson and white, the black-and-white disc and the Dragon plain to everybody. On the other hand, the stableman's eyes bulged, and they almost danced as they demanded to know what Mat was doing.

He only grinned and tossed the narrow-jawed fellow a gold mark. "Just letting everybody know for sure who's come to call." He wanted Egwene to realize he was not going to be pushed around, and sometimes making people see that meant you had to act like jack-fool.

The trouble was, the banners had no effect. Oh, everybody who walked by gaped and pointed; a number of Aes Sedai came just to look, cool-eyed and expressionless, but he more than half expected an indignant demand to take them down, and that never materialized. When he returned to the Little Tower, an Aes Sedai who somehow managed to be prune-faced despite smooth ageless cheeks shifted her brown-fringed shawl and told him in no uncertain terms that the Amyrlin Seat was busy; perhaps she could see him in a day or two. Perhaps. Elayne appeared to have vanished, and so did Aviendha, but no one was crying murder yet; he suspected the Aiel might be somewhere having a white dress pulled over her head. All the same to him if it kept the peace; he did not want to be the one to tell Rand one had killed the other. He did catch a sight of Nynaeve, but she ducked around a corner and was gone by the time he reached it.

He spent most of the afternoon looking for Thom and Juilin; either one surely could tell him more of what was going on, and besides, he needed to apologize to Thom for his remarks about that letter. Unfortunately nobody seemed to know where they were either. Long before nightfall he concluded that they were being kept out of his way. Egwene really did mean for him to stew, but he intended to let her know he was not even simmering. In aid of that, he went dancing.

It seemed that celebrations over a new Amyrlin were supposed to go on for a month, and though everyone in Salidar seemed to be working at a run during the day, once darkness fell bonfires were lit at every street crossing, and fiddles and flutes appeared and even a dulcimer or two. Music and laughter filled the air, and festival reigned until bedtime. He saw Aes Sedai dancing in the streets with carters and stablemen still in their rough clothes, and Warders dancing with serving women and cooks who had put aside their aprons. No Egwene, though; the Amyrlin bloody Seat was not going to caper in the streets. No Elayne or Nynaeve, either, and no Thom or Juilin. Thom would not have missed a dance with both legs broken unless he was deliberately kept away. Mat settled down to enjoy himself, to let everybody see he had not a care in the world. It did not work exactly as he wished.

He danced a short time with the most beautiful woman he had ever seen in his life, a slim yet buxom armful who wanted to know all about Mat Cauthon. Very flattering, especially when she had asked him to step out. But after a while he noticed that Halima had a way of brushing against him, a way of leaning to look at something so he could not help seeing down her dress. He might have enjoyed it, if not for the fact that she glanced at his face every time with a sharp eye and an amused smile. She was not a

very good dancer—she kept trying to lead, for one thing—and he finally
begged off.

It should have been nothing, but before he had gone ten paces the foxhead went icy cold on his chest. He spun around, looking furiously for anything at all. What he saw was Halima staring at him in the firelight. Only
for an instant before she seized a tall Warder's arm and whirled back into
the dance, but he was sure he had seen shock on that beautiful face.

The fiddles were wailing a tune he recognized. At least, one of his old
memories did, not very much changed considering the passage of well over a
thousand years. The words must have changed altogether, for the old words
that echoed in his head would never have found favor here.

> Give me your trust, said the Aes Sedai.
> On my shoulders I support the sky.
> Trust me to know and to do what is best,
> And I will take care of the rest.
> But trust is the color of a dark seed growing.
> Trust is the color of a heart's blood flowing.
> Trust is the color of a soul's last breath.
> Trust is the color of death.

"Aes Sedai?" a plump young woman said contemptuously to his question. She was pretty, and he might have tried for a bit of kiss and cuddle in
different circumstances. "Halima's just Delana Sedai's secretary. Always
teasing the men, she is. Like a child with a new toy; teasing just to see if
she can. She'd be in hot water to her neck ten times over if Delana didn't
protect her."

> Give me your trust, said the queen on her throne,
> for I must bear the burden all alone.
> Trust me to lead and to judge and to rule,
> and no man will think you a fool.
> But trust is the sound of the grave-dog's bark.
> Trust is the sound of betrayal in the dark.
> Trust is, the sound of a soul's last breath.
> Trust is the sound of death.

Maybe he had been mistaken. Maybe she had just been shocked that he
walked off. Not many men would walk away from a woman who looked

like that, no matter how she teased or danced. That had to be it. But that left the question of who and why. He looked around, at the dancers, and the people watching from the edge of the shadows and waiting their turns. The golden-haired Hunter for the Horn who had seemed familiar went spinning by with a particularly lumpy-faced fellow, her braid almost standing out behind her. Mat could pick out Aes Sedai by their faces—most of them he could—but there was no way to tell which had tried to . . . whatever it was she had tried.

He strode on down the street to the next bonfire as much to get away from that song as anything, before it went on through "the king on high" and "the lady and lord" to "the love of your life" in his head. In that old memory he remembered writing that song, because of the love of his life. *Trust is the taste of death.* At that next corner a fiddler and a woman with a flute were playing what sounded like "Fluff the Feathers," a good country dance.

How far could he trust Egwene? She was Aes Sedai now; she must be, if she was Amyrlin, even a ragtag Amyrlin in a ragtag village. Well, whatever she was, she was Egwene; he could not believe she would strike at him out of the dark that way. Of course, Nynaeve might, though not to injure him really. His hip still hurt, though; the bruise had made a knot. And the Light only knew what a woman like Elayne might do. They were still trying to chase him away, he decided. He could probably expect more attempts. The best thing was to ignore them; he almost hoped they did try again. They could not touch him with the Power, and the more they tried and failed, why, the more they would have to see he was not to be budged.

Myrelle came to stand beside him, watching the dancers. He remembered her, vaguely. He did not think she knew anything dangerous about him. He did not think so. She was not as beautiful as Halima, of course, but still much more than merely pretty. Flickering shadows washed her face so he could almost forget she was Aes Sedai.

"A warm night," she said, smiling, and went on in such a casual way while he enjoyed looking at her that it took him some time to realize what she was getting at.

"I don't think so," he said politely when she gave an opening. This was what came of forgetting; Aes Sedai were Aes Sedai.

She only smiled. "There would be many advantages, and I would not try to pin you to my skirts. Many advantages. You've chosen a perilous life, or had it chosen for you. A Warder might have a better chance of survival."

"I really don't think so. No, but thank you for the offer."

"Think on it, Mat. Unless. . . . Has the Amyrlin bonded you?"

"No." Egwene would not do that. Would she? She could not so long as he wore the medallion, but would she if he did not have it? "If you will excuse me?" He gave her a shallow bow and walked quickly to where a pretty, blue-eyed young woman was tapping her foot to the music. She had a sweet mouth, just right for kissing, and he bloody well wanted to enjoy himself. "I saw your eyes, and I couldn't help coming over. Will you dance?"

Too late he saw the Great Serpent ring on her right hand, and then that sweet mouth opened and a voice he recognized said dryly, "I asked you once whether you'd be there when the house was burning down, boy, but it seems you make a habit of jumping into fires. Now go away and find somebody who wants to dance with you."

Siuan Sanche! She was stilled and dead! She was glaring at him with some young woman's face she had stolen, was what she was, and wearing an Aes Sedai ring! He had asked *Siuan Sanche* to dance!

While he was still staring, a willowy young Domani woman swirled up in a pale green dress thin enough for the light of the bonfire to silhouette her through it. Giving Siuan a frosty look that was returned with interest, the Domani all but snatched him out among the dancers. She was as tall as an Aiel woman, dark eyes actually a little higher than his. "I am Leane, by the way," she said in a voice like a honeyed caress, "in case you did not recognize me." Her low laugh was almost a caress too.

He jumped and nearly fumbled the first turn. She also wore the ring. He moved by rote. Tall or not, she was a feather in his hands, a gliding swan, but that was certainly not enough to stop the question that kept popping in his head like an Illuminator's fireworks. How? How under the Light? To top it all, when the dance was done, she said, "You are a very good dancer," in that stroking voice, and then kissed him about as thoroughly as he had ever been kissed. He was so shocked he did not even try to get away. Sighing, she patted his cheek. "A very good dancer. Think of it as dancing next time, and you will do better." And off she went laughing, back into the dance with some fellow she snagged from the onlookers.

Mat decided he had had as much as one man could take in a night. He went back to the stable and went to sleep, with his saddle for a pillow. His dreams would have been pleasant, except that they all involved Myrelle and Siuan and Leane and Halima. When it came to dreams, a man just naturally lacked the sense to pour water out of a boot.

The next day had to be better, he thought, especially when dawn found Vanin in the loft, asleep on his saddle. Talmanes understood and would hold where he was; Warders had been seen watching the Band's preparations, no doubt letting themselves be seen, but no one had come near the Band. A less pleasant surprise was finding Olver's gray in the yard behind the stable, and Olver himself curled up in his blankets in a corner.

"You need somebody to watch your back," he told Mat darkly. "She cannot be trusted." There was no need for him to name Aviendha.

Olver had no interest in playing with the children in the village, so Mat had to endure the stares and smiles as the boy trailed him around Salidar, doing his best to imitate a Warder's flowing stride and looking nine ways at once for Aviendha. Who was still nowhere to be seen, any more than Elayne or Nynaeve. And "the Amyrlin" was still busy. Thom and Juilin were also "busy." Vanin managed to hear a few things, but nothing that made Mat happy. If Nynaeve had really Healed Siuan and Leane, she would be worse than ever; she had always had a large opinion of herself, and after doing what could not be done, her head would be bigger than a dewmelon. Yet that was the mildest of it. Logain and the Red Ajah made Mat wince. That sounded the sort of thing no Aes Sedai would forgive. If Gareth Bryne was leading their army, it was no mob of farmers and street sweepings with a few Warders for stiffening. Add in the foodstuffs Vanin saw being wrapped or stuck in barrels for travel, and it sounded like trouble. The worst kind of trouble Mat could imagine, short of finding one of the Forsaken across the table from him and a dozen Trollocs coming in the door. None of it made them any less fools; it made them very dangerous fools. Thom and his "help them make it work." If the gleeman ever came out of hiding, maybe he could pull a "how" out of one of his tales.

In the evening Myrelle spoke to him again about becoming a Warder, and went a little tight around the eyes when he told her hers would be the fifth offer he had refused since sunup. He was not sure she believed him; she flounced off in as much of a huff as he had ever seen from an Aes Sedai. It was true, though. The very first, while he was still trying to eat breakfast, had been the very Delana that Halima worked for, a stout pale-haired woman with watery blue eyes who came close to trying to bully him into it. That night he stayed away from the dancing and went to sleep with music and laughter in his ears; they sounded sour this time.

It was midafternoon of his second full day in Salidar when a girl in a white dress, pretty and freckled and working very hard at an icy dignity that she almost reached, found him with a summons, and it was exactly that. "You will present yourself before the Amyrlin Seat at once." Full stop, and not another word. Mat motioned her to lead; it seemed proper, and she seemed to like doing it.

They were all there in that room in the Little Tower, Egwene and Nynaeve, Elayne and Aviendha, though he had to look twice to recognize the Aiel woman in a blue dress of fine wool with a lace collar and cuffs. At least neither Aviendha nor Elayne was trying to strangle the other, but they were both stony-faced. Which made them no different from Egwene and Nynaeve. Not a flicker of expression in the four, and all eyes on him. He managed to hold his tongue while Egwene laid out his choices as she saw them, sitting behind the table with that striped stole draped on her shoulders.

"Should you think you can do neither," she finished, "remember that I can have you tied to your horse and returned to your Band of the Hand. There is no room in Salidar for slackers and malingerers. I will not allow it. For you, Mat, it's either Ebou Dar with Elayne and Nynaeve, or off to see who you can impress with flags and banners."

Which really left no choice at all, of course. When he said so, nobody's expression changed. If anything, Nynaeve grew more wooden. And Egwene just said, "I'm glad that is done, Mat. Now, I have a thousand things to do. I will try to see you before you go." Dismissed like a stableboy; the Amyrlin was busy. The least she could have done was toss him a copper.

That was why Mat's third morning in Salidar found him just outside it, on the cleared ground between village and forest. "They may stay right here till I get back," he told Talmanes, glancing over his shoulder toward the houses. They would be coming soon, and he did not want any of this getting back to Egwene. She would try to drive a spike through it if she could. "I hope so, anyway. If they move, follow wherever they go, but never close enough to frighten. And if a young woman named Egwene shows up, you ask no questions, just take her and ride to Caemlyn if you have to cut a hole through Gareth Bryne." Of course, they might be intending to go to Caemlyn; there might be a chance. He was afraid it was Tar Valon they were aiming at, though; Tar Valon and the headsman's axe. "And take Nerim with you."

Talmanes shook his head. "If you are taking Nalesean, I will be offended if you do not let me send my man to care for your things." Mat wished Talmanes would smile once in a while; it would help to know when he was serious. He certainly sounded serious.

Nerim stood a little distance off, with Pips, and his own short plump brown mare towering over him, and two packhorses with wicker panniers stuffed to the top. Nalesean's man, a stout fellow named Lopin, only led one pack animal in addition to his hammer-nosed gelding and Nalesean's tall black stallion.

That was not all the party. No one seemed ready to tell him more than where to be and when, but in the middle of yet another talk about becoming a Warder, Myrelle had let him know it was now all right for him to communicate with the Band so long as he did not try to bring them nearer Salidar. That had been the last thing in his mind. Vanin was there this morning because he could probably spy out the lay of the land anywhere, and a dozen cavalrymen chosen from the Band for heavy shoulders and having kept order well as Redarms back in Maerone. From what Nalesean said, quick fists and cudgels should be able to quell any inconvenience Nynaeve and Elayne got into, at least long enough to spirit them away. Last of all was Olver on the gray he had named Wind, which the leggy animal might even deserve. Olver had been no hard choice. The Band might well find trouble if they actually had to follow that lot of madwomen. Maybe not trouble with Bryne, but enough nobles would bristle at two armies crossing their lands to provide nightly attempts at the horses and arrows flying from every second thicket. Any city had to be safer than that for a boy.

Still no sign of any Aes Sedai, and the sun beginning to bake above the treetops.

Mat jerked his hat down irritably. "Nalesean knows Ebou Dar, Talmanes." The Tairen grinned through his sweat and nodded. Talmanes' face did not change. "Oh, all right. Nerim comes." Talmanes inclined his head; maybe he had been serious.

At last there was a stir in the village, a group of women leading horses. Not just Elayne and Nynaeve, though he had not expected anyone else. Aviendha wore a gray riding dress, but she looked at her lean dun mare more than doubtfully. That Hunter with the golden braid showed more confidence with a heavy-haunched mouse-colored gelding and seemed to be trying to convince Aviendha of something about her mare. What was either of them doing there? There were two Aes Sedai, as well—other Aes Sedai besides Nynaeve and Elayne, he supposed he should say—slender women with white hair, which he had not seen on an Aes Sedai before. An old fellow trailed after them with a packhorse in addition to his own mount, a stringy man without much hair and that gray. It took Mat a moment to realize he was a Warder, with one of those color-shifting cloaks hanging down his back. That was what being a Warder meant; Aes Sedai worked you till your hair fell out, then probably worked your bones after you were dead.

Thom and Juilin came not far behind, and they had a packhorse too.

The women stopped some fifty paces to the left with their aged Warder, not so much as looking at Mat and his men. The gleeman glanced at Nynaeve and the others, then spoke to Juilin, and they led their horses toward Mat, stopping short as if uncertain of their welcome. Mat went to them.

"I have to apologize, Mat," Thom said, knuckling his mustaches. "Elayne put it in no uncertain terms that I wasn't to talk with you further. She only relented this morning. In a weak moment some months back I promised to follow her orders, and she flings it in my face at the most awkward times. She wasn't very pleased that I had said as much as I did."

"Nynaeve threatened to punch my eye if I went near you," Juilin said glumly, leaning on his bamboo staff. He was wearing a red Taraboner cap that could not give much protection from the sun, and even that looked glum.

Mat looked toward the women. Nynaeve was peeking at him over her saddle, but when she saw him looking, she ducked behind her horse, a plump brown mare. He would not have thought even Nynaeve could beat Juilin down, but the dark thief-taker was a far cry from the man he had known briefly in Tear. That Juilin had been ready for anything; this Juilin, with a permanently furrowed brow, looked as if he never stopped worrying. "We will teach her some manners this trip, Juilin. Thom, I'm the one who has to apologize. What I said about the letter. It was the heat talking, and worry over fool women. I hope it was good news." Too late he remembered what Thom had said. He had left the woman who wrote that letter to die.

But Thom only shrugged. Mat did not know what to make of him without his gleeman's cloak. "Good news? I haven't puzzled that out yet. Often you don't know whether a woman is friend, enemy or lover until it is too late. Sometimes, she is all three." Mat expected a laugh, but Thom frowned and sighed. "Women always seem to like making themselves mysterious, Mat. I can give you an example. Do you remember Aludra?"

Mat had to think. "The Illuminator we kept from getting her throat slit in Aringill?"

"The very one. Juilin and I met her during our travels, and she didn't know me. Not that she failed to recognize me; you say things to a stranger you travel with, to get to know them. Aludra did not want to know me, and even if I didn't know why, I saw no reason to impose. I met her a stranger and left her a stranger. Now, would you call her a friend or an enemy?"

"Maybe a lover," Mat said dryly. He would not mind meeting Aludra again; she had given him some fireworks that proved very useful. "If you want to know about women, ask Perrin, not me. I don't know anything at all. I used to think Rand knew, but Perrin surely does." Elayne was talking with the two white-haired Aes Sedai under the Hunter's watchful eye. One of the older Aes Sedai gazed in Mat's direction consideringly. They had the same sort of bearing Elayne did, cool as a queen on her bloody throne. "Well, with luck I won't have to put up with them long," he muttered to himself. "With luck, whatever they're doing won't take long, and we can be back here in five or ten days." With luck, he might be back before the Band had to begin shadowing the madwomen. Tracking not one army but two would be easy as stealing a pie, of course, but he did not look forward to any more days in Elayne's company than necessary.

"Ten days?" Thom said. "Mat, even with this 'gateway' it will take five or six just to reach Ebou Dar. Better than twenty or so, but. . . ."

Mat stopped listening. Every shred of irritation that had been building since he first laid eyes on Egwene again came to a head at once. Snatching off his hat, he stalked to where Elayne and the others were. Keeping him in the dark was bad enough—how was he supposed to keep them out of trouble when they told him nothing?—but this was ridiculous. Nynaeve saw him coming and darted behind her mare for some reason.

"It will be interesting traveling with a *ta'veren*," one of the white-haired Aes Sedai said. Up close, he still could not fasten any age to her, yet somehow her face conveyed an impression of long years. It must have been the hair. She could have used the other for a mirror; maybe they really were sisters. "I am Vandene Namelle."

Mat was in no mood to talk about being *ta'veren*. He was never in that mood, but certainly not now. "What's this nonsense I hear about five or six days to reach Ebou Dar?" The old Warder straightened, staring hard, and Mat reevaluated him as well; stringy, but hard as old roots. It made no difference in his tone. "You can open a gateway in sight of Ebou Dar. We aren't any bloody army to scare anyone, and as for popping out of air, you're Aes Sedai. People expect you to pop out of air and walk through walls."

"I fear you are speaking to the wrong one of us," Vandene said. He looked at the other white-haired woman, who shook her head as Vandene said, "Nor Adeleas, I fear. It appears we are not strong enough for some of the new things."

Mat hesitated, then settled his hat low and turned to Elayne.

Her chin came up. "Apparently you know rather less than you believe, Master Cauthon," she said coolly. She was not sweating, he realized, no more than the two . . . the other two . . . Aes Sedai. The Hunter was staring at him challengingly. What had put a bee in her ear? "There are villages and farms around Ebou Dar for a hundred miles," Elayne went on, explaining the obvious to a fool. "A gateway is quite dangerous. I do not intend to kill some poor man's sheep or cows, much less the poor man himself."

He hated more than her tone. She was right, and he hated that too. He was not about to admit she was, though, not to her, and searching for a way to retreat, he saw Egwene coming out of the village with two dozen or more Aes Sedai, most wearing fringed shawls. Or rather, she came, and they followed. Head held high, she looked straight ahead, that striped stole hanging about her neck. The others strolled along behind her in little clumps. Sheriam, wearing the blue Keeper's stole, was talking with Myrelle and a bluff-faced Aes Sedai who managed to look motherly. Except for Delana, he recognized none of the others—one had gray hair in a bun; how old did Aes Sedai have to be for their hair to go completely gray or white?—but they were all talking among themselves, ignoring the woman they had named Amyrlin. Egwene might as well have been alone; she looked alone. Knowing her, she was trying very hard to be what they had named her, and they let her walk alone, with everybody watching.

To the Pit of Doom with them if they think they can treat a Two Rivers woman that way, he thought grimly.

Striding to meet Egwene, he swept off his hat and bowed, making the best leg he knew how, and he could flourish with the best when he had to. "Good morning, Mother, and the Light shine on you," he said, loud enough to be heard in the village. Kneeling, he seized her right hand and kissed her Great Serpent ring. A quick glare and a grimace directed at Talmanes and the others, and hidden by Egwene from those behind her, had them all scrambling to kneel and call out, "The Light illumine you, Mother," or some variation. Even Thom and Juilin.

Egwene looked startled at first, though she hid it quickly. Then she smiled, and said softly, "Thank you, Mat."

For a moment he stared up at her, then cleared his throat and stood, brushing off his knees. Sheriam and all those others behind Egwene were staring at him. "I didn't expect you out here," he said in a low voice, "but then, it seems there are all sorts of things I didn't expect. Does the Amyrlin always see people off on trips? You wouldn't by any chance want to tell me what it's all about now, would you?"

At first he thought she might; then her mouth tightened for an instant and she gave a slight shake of her head. "I will always see friends off, Mat.

I'd have spoken with you before this if I was not so busy. Mat, do try to stay out of trouble in Ebou Dar."

He stared indignantly. Here he went kneeling and kissing rings, and she told *him* to stay out of trouble, when the whole point was for him to keep Elayne and Nynaeve with whole skins. "I will try, Mother," he said wryly, but not too. Sheriam and some of those might be close enough to hear. "If you will excuse me, I must see to my men."

Another bow, and he backed away a few steps before stalking over to where Talmanes and the rest were still on their knees. "Do you mean to stay there till you take root?" he growled. "Mount up." He followed his own order, and everyone but Talmanes scrambled into their saddles.

Egwene passed a few words with Elayne and Nynaeve, while Vandene and Adeleas went to speak to Sheriam, and then it was time, as quick as that after all their dawdling. Mat half-expected some sort of ceremony, with Egwene there in the Amyrlin's stole, but she and the others who were not going merely withdrew a little distance. Elayne stepped out, and suddenly there was a slash of light in front of her, widening into a hole, the view through it, what seemed to be a low hilltop covered in brown grass, rotating to a halt. Just like when Rand did it. Almost.

"Dismount," Mat ordered. Elayne looked quite pleased with herself—you would never suspect the sort of woman she was from that delighted smile, asking Nynaeve and Aviendha to share her pleasure—but pleased or not, the gateway was not as large as the one Rand had made for the Band. Of course, they were not nearly so many as the Band, but the least she could have done was make it tall enough to ride through.

On the other side, low rolling brown-grass hills ran as far as Mat could see even when he climbed back onto Pips, though a darkness to the south suggested forest. Dusty hills.

"We must not press the horses too hard in this," Adeleas said, swinging quite easily onto her round bay mare as soon as the gateway vanished. The animal looked as if it would be more at home in a barn.

"Oh, indeed not," Vandene said. Her mount was a slab-sided black gelding that had a light step. The pair of them started south, motioning everyone to follow. The old Warder rode right at their heels.

Nynaeve and Elayne exchanged irritated looks, then booted their mares to catch the older women, hooves beating up dust until they were level. The yellow-braided Hunter dogged them the way the Warder did the other pair.

Sighing, Mat undid the black kerchief around his neck and retied it over his nose and mouth. Much as he might enjoy seeing the older Aes Sedai teach those two to sit up straight, what he really wanted was an uneventful ride, a short stay in Ebou Dar, and a quick jump back to Salidar before Egwene did anything stupid and irretrievable. Women always gave him trouble; he did not understand it.

When the gateway winked out, Egwene sighed. Maybe Elayne and Nynaeve between them could keep Mat from getting into too much trouble. Keeping him out entirely was probably too much to ask. She felt a pang of regret for using him, but he might be some use where he was, and he had had to be gotten away from the Band. Besides, he deserved it. Maybe Elayne *would* teach him a few manners.

Turning to the others, the Hall and Sheriam and her circle, she said, "Now we must get on with what we're about."

All eyes went to the Cairhienin in the dark coat just now mounting his horse near the trees. Talmanes, Egwene thought Mat had said his name was; she had not dared ask too many questions. He studied them for a moment and shook his head before riding into the forest.

"A man who means trouble if I ever saw one," Romanda said.

Lelaine nodded. "It will be well to put miles between ourselves and that sort."

Egwene did not let herself smile. Mat's Band had served its first purpose, but a great deal depended on exactly what orders Mat had left with this Talmanes. She thought she could depend on Mat in this. Siuan said that man Vanin had rooted out things before she had a chance to put them under his nose. And if she was to "come to her senses" and run to the Band for protection, then the Band would have to be close to her. "Shall we go to our horses?" she said. "If we leave now, we should catch up to Lord Bryne well before sunset."

CHAPTER 45

A Bitter Thought

As Vilnar led his mounted patrol through the streets of the New City, not far from the tall outer city wall, its gray stone streaked with silver and white in the midday sun, he thought about shaving his beard. Some others already had shaved; even if everyone said the heat was unnatural, it must be cooler back in Saldaea.

Letting his thoughts roam was safe enough. He could guide his horse in his sleep, and only the most foolhardy cutpurse would ply his trade anywhere hear ten Saldaeans. They rode about at random so the fellows would not know where they were safe. In truth, more often than having to catch thieves, they merely arrested those who came to them. The toughest bullyboy in Caemlyn would come running for Saldaeans to take him up before the Aiel could. So Vilnar kept half an eye on the street and let his mind drift. He thought about the girl back home in Mehar he would like to marry; Teryane's father was a merchant, and wanted a soldier for a son perhaps more than Teryane wanted one for a husband. He thought about the game those Aielwomen had suggested; Maiden's Kiss sounded innocent enough, but there had been a gleam in their eyes he did not quite trust. Most of all, though, he thought about Aes Sedai.

Vilnar had always wanted to see an Aes Sedai, and certainly there could be no better place than Caemlyn now, unless he went to Tar Valon one day. Apparently there were Aes Sedai all over Caemlyn. He had ridden to Culain's Hound, where rumor had a hundred, but at the last moment he could not make himself go in. He was brave enough with a sword in his hand and a horse between his knees and men or Trollocs in front of him, but the thought of Aes Sedai turned him shy. Besides, the inn would not have accommodated a hundred women, and none of the girls he saw could possibly be Aes Sedai. He had gone to The Crown of Roses, too, and watched from across the street, but he was not sure any of the women he had seen was Aes Sedai, and that made him sure they were not.

He cocked an eye at a thin woman with a wide nose coming out of a tall house that must belong to a merchant; she stood frowning at the street before finally donning a wide-brimmed straw hat and hurrying off. Vilnar shook his head. He could not have said how old she was, but that was not enough. He knew how to recognize an Aes Sedai. Let Jidar claim they were so beautiful they could kill a man by smiling, and let Rissen insist they were all a foot taller than any man. Vilnar knew it was the face you could tell by, the timeless face of an immortal. It must be impossible to mistake that.

As the patrol came opposite the towered, vaulting arch of the White-bridge Gate, Vilnar forgot about Aes Sedai. Outside, one of the farmer's markets stretched alongside the road, long open stone sheds roofed in red or purple tiles, pens full of calves and pigs and sheep, chickens and ducks and geese, stalls selling everything from beans to turnips. Usually those markets were a cacophony of farmers crying their wares, but now except for the clamor of the animals silence marched along the market toward the gate, beside one of the oddest processions Vilnar had ever seen.

A long column of farmers four abreast on horseback made the bulk of it, and there seemed to be wagons behind. Farmers for sure in those rough coats, but every one of them in Vilnar's sight had the longest bow he had ever seen slung across his back, a full quiver at one hip and a long knife or short sword at the other. Leading the procession was a white banner bordered in red with a red wolf's head, and a mix of people as odd as the column. There were three Aiel, afoot of course, two of them Maidens, and a fellow whose bright green-striped coat and virulent yellow breeches said he was a Tinker, except he had a sword on his back. He was leading a horse as big as a Nashun draft horse, with a saddle meant for a giant. The leader seemed to be a heavy-shouldered shaggy-haired fellow with a short beard and a wicked axe on his belt, and at his side rode a Saldaean woman in dark narrow divided skirts who kept looking up at him with the fondest. . . .

Vilnar sat forward in his saddle. He recognized that woman. He thought of Lord Bashere, in the Royal Palace right that moment. More, he thought of Lady Deira, and his heart sank; she was in the Palace too. If some Aes Sedai had waved her hand and turned that column into Trollocs, Vilnar would have been overjoyed. Maybe this was the price for daydreaming. Had he kept his mind on his duty, the patrol would have been long past here by now. Still, he had his orders.

Wondering whether Lady Deira would have his head for a ball, he deployed his men in the gate.

Perrin let his dun stallion walk within ten paces of the city gate before drawing rein. Stepper was as happy to stop; he did not like the heat. The mounted men blocking the gate were Saldaeans, by those bold noses and tilted eyes; some wore glossy black beards, some thick mustaches, and some were clean-shaven. Every man save one had a hand on his sword hilt. The air stirred from them, not quite a breeze; there was no fear smell. Perrin looked at Faile, but she was bent over Swallow's arched neck, intent on fiddling with the black mare's bridle; she smelled faintly of herbal soap and anxiety. They had heard news of Saldaeans in Caemlyn these last two hundred miles and more, led by Faile's father supposedly. That did not seem to worry Faile, but she was certain her mother would be in Caemlyn as well. She said that did not worry her either.

"We don't even need the bowmen," Aram said quietly, stroking the hilt that stuck up over his shoulder. His dark eyes seemed eager; he certainly smelled eager. "There are only ten. You and I could cut through them ourselves." Gaul had veiled himself, and almost certainly, Bain and Chiad had too, on the other side of Faile.

"No archers, and no cutting," Perrin said. "And no spears, Gaul." He did not say anything to Bain or Chiad; they only listened to Faile anyway. Who did not appear ready to look up or say a word any time soon. Gaul merely lowered his veil with a shrug; Aram frowned in disappointment.

Perrin kept his expression mild as he turned back to the Saldaeans. Yellow-gold eyes made some men nervous. "My name is Perrin Aybara. I think Rand al'Thor will want to see me."

The bearded fellow who had not touched his sword gave a small bow from the saddle. "I am Vilnar Barada, Lord Aybara, Underlieutenant sword-sworn to Lord Davram Bashere." He said that very loudly, and come to think of it, he had been avoiding looking at Faile. She sighed at mention of her father and scowled at Barada, the more so when he continued to ignore her. "Lord Bashere's orders," the man went on, adding as an after-thought, "and the Lord Dragon's, are that no noble can enter Caemlyn with more than twenty armed men or fifty servants."

Aram shifted on his horse. He was even more prickly about Perrin's supposed honor than Faile, which was saying something, but thank the Light, he would not unsheathe his sword unless Perrin said to.

Perrin spoke over his shoulder. "Dannil, take everybody back to that meadow we passed about three miles back and make camp. If a farmer shows up to complain, give him some gold and smooth him down. Let him know he'll be paid for any damage. Aram, you go with them."

Dannil Lewin, a beanpole of a man with a thick mustache that almost hid his mouth, knuckled his forehead despite all the times Perrin had told him a simple "all right" would do, and immediately began giving orders to turn everyone around. Aram stiffened, of course—he never liked being far from Perrin—but he said nothing, equally of course. Sometimes Perrin thought he had acquired a wolfhound in the former Tinker. Not good for a man to be that way, but he did not know what to do about it.

He expected Faile to say a good deal about sending everyone back—he expected her to bring up what was due his so-called position and insist on the twenty Barada had mentioned, and as close to the fifty as they could manage as well—but she was leaning out of her saddle to speak in whis-pers with Bain and Chiad. He made a point of not listening, though he could still make out parts of words. Something about men, sounding amused; women always seemed either amused or angry when they talked of men. Faile was the reason he had all these people trailing after him, and the banner to boot, though he had not yet figured out exactly how she had done it. There were *servants* back in the wagons, men and women wearing *livery* with a wolf's head on the shoulder. Even the Two Rivers folk had not com-plained; they seemed as proud of it as any of the refugees.

"Does that satisfy?" he asked Barada. "You can escort the rest of us to Rand, if you don't want us running loose."

"I think. . . ." Barada's dark eyes darted to Faile and away. "I think that would be best."

As Faile straightened, Bain and Chiad trotted to the line of horsemen and pushed through as if they were not there. The Saldaeans did not even look surprised, but then, they must be used to Aiel; all the rumors said Caemlyn was full of Aiel already.

"I must find my spear-brothers," Gaul said abruptly. "May you always find water and shade, Perrin Aybara." And away he darted after the women. Faile hid an amused smile behind a gray-gloved hand.

Perrin shook his head. Gaul wanted Chiad to marry him, but by Aiel custom, she had to ask him, and though according to Faile she was willing to become his lover, she would not give up the spear and marry. He seemed as affronted as a Two Rivers girl would have been in the same circumstance. Bain seemed to be part of it too, somehow; Perrin did not understand how. Faile professed not to know, if a bit too quickly, and Gaul grew sullen when asked. An odd people.

The Saldaeans made a way through the crowds, but Perrin paid little mind to crowds or city. He had seen Caemlyn once, some of it, and he did not much like cities anymore. Wolves seldom came close to a city; he had not sensed one for two days. What he did do was study his wife with sideways looks, trying not to let her notice. He might as well have stared. She always rode erect, but now she was stiff in her saddle, glaring at Barada's back. The man's shoulders were hunched as if he could feel her eyes. A falcon could not glare as well as Faile.

Perrin expected she was thinking of the same thing as he, though maybe not along the same lines. Her father. She might have a few explanations to make—she had run away, after all, to become a Hunter for the Horn—but Perrin was the one who had to face the Lord of Bashere, Tyr and Sidona and tell the man a blacksmith had married his daughter and heir. It was not something Perrin looked forward to. He did not think he was particularly brave—doing what you had to do was not bravery—but he had never really thought he might be a coward until now. The thought of Faile's father dried his mouth. Maybe he should see to setting up the camp. A letter sent to Lord Bashere could explain everything. A carefully composed letter might take two or three days to write. Maybe more. He was no hand with words.

A glimpse of the crimson banner waving lazily above the Royal Palace brought him back with a thump. The rumors had spoken of that. Perrin knew it was not the Dragon banner, whatever the rumors said—some claimed it meant the Aes Sedai served Rand; others that he served them—and he wondered why Rand was not flying the Dragon banner itself. Rand. He could still feel Rand pulling at him, greater *ta'veren* tugging at lesser. It did not tell him where Rand was; it was not that kind of pull. He had left the Two Rivers expecting to ride to Tear or maybe the Light alone knew where, and only a river of rumors and tales flowing west across Andor had brought him here. Some very disturbing tales and rumors. No, what he felt was more a need to be near Rand, or maybe Rand's need for him, like an itch between his shoulders he could not scratch. Now it was close to being scratched, and he almost wished it was not. He had a dream, one that Faile would laugh at, adventurous as she was. He dreamed of living in a small house with her, somewhere in the country, far from cities and strife. There was always strife around Rand. But Rand needed him, and he would do what he had to.

In a great, column-ringed courtyard overlooked by marble balconies and pointed spires, Perrin slung his belt, weighted by his axe, on the saddle—it was a relief to be rid of it for a while—and a white-robed man and woman took Stepper and Swallow. With a few words Barada turned Faile and him over to cold-eyed Aielmen, many wearing scarlet headbands marked with the black-and-white disc, who led them inside and with even fewer words handed them to Maidens who were just as frosty. Perrin did not recognize any of them from the Stone, and his efforts at making conversation were met with blank looks. Their hands flashed Maiden handtalk, and one was chosen out to take him and Faile deeper into the Palace, a lean sandy-haired woman he thought might be about Faile's age. She named herself Lerian, the only words she spoke except to warn them not to wander. He wished Bain or Chiad were there; a familiar face would have been pleasant. Faile glided down the corridors like the grand lady she was, yet at every crossing hallway she looked both ways quickly. Plainly she did not want to be surprised by her father.

Finally they reached a pair of doors, each carved with a lion, where two more Maidens rose from squatting on their heels and still more handtalk flickered before the sandy-haired Maiden went in without knocking.

Perrin was wondering whether it was always like this around Rand now, Aiel guards and nobody speaking, when suddenly the doors were flung open, and there was Rand in his shirtsleeves.

"Perrin! Faile! The Light shine on your wedding day," he laughed, kissing Faile lightly. "I wish I could have been there for it." She looked as confused as Perrin felt.

"How did you know?" he exclaimed, and Rand laughed again, clapping him on the shoulder

"Bode's here, Perrin. Bode and Jancy and all of them. In Caemlyn, anyway. This is as far as Verin and Alanna got them before they heard about the Tower." He looked tired, his eyes drawn, though his laughter did not sound it. "Light, Perrin, the things they told me you've been up to. Lord Perrin of the Two Rivers. What does Mistress Luhhan say to that?".

"She calls me Lord Perrin," Perrin muttered wryly. Alsbet Luhhan had smacked his bottom more often growing up than his mother had. "She curtsies, Rand. She actually curtsies." Faile eyed him askance. She said he embarrassed people when he tried to stop all the bowing and curtsying, as for his embarrassment when they did, she said it was part of the price he had to pay.

The Maiden who had gone in squeezed by Rand coming out, and he gave a start. "Light, I'm keeping you in the door. Come in; come in. Lerian, tell Sulin I need more punch. The melon. And tell her to hop." For some reason the three Maidens laughed as if Rand had said something funny.

One step inside the sitting room, a floral scent of perfume told Perrin there was another woman there before he saw her. When he did, he stared. "Min?" The hair in short curls, the embroidered blue coat and breeches were wrong, but the face was right. "Min, it is you!" Laughing, he caught her up in a hug. "We are gathering everybody, aren't we? Faile, this is Min. I told you about her."

That was when he realized what he was smelling from his wife, and put Min down while she was still grinning at him. Suddenly he was too much aware that those tight breeches showed the shape of Min's legs very well. Faile had very few faults, but she did have a slight tendency toward jealousy. He was not supposed to know she had chased Calle Coplin half a mile with a stick, as if he would ever look twice at another woman when he had her.

"Faile?" Min said, holding out her hands. "Any woman who can put up with this hairy lummox long enough to marry him has my admiration. I suppose he might make a good husband at that, once you housebreak him."

Faile took Min's hands smiling, but oh, that acrid, bristly scent. "I've not succeeded in the housebreaking yet, Min, but I intend to keep him at least until I do."

"Mistress Luhhan curtsies?" Rand shook his head in disbelief. "I will have to see that to believe it. Where's Loial? Did he come? You didn't leave him outside?"

"He came," Perrin said, trying to keep an eye on Faile without being obvious, "but not all the way, not yet. He said he was tired, and needed a *stedding*, so I told him one I know of, an abandoned one north of the road from Whitebridge, and he set off for it afoot. He said he would be able to feel it once he was within ten miles or so."

"I suppose you know Rand and Perrin very well?" Faile asked, and Min glanced at Rand.

"For a while, anyway. I met them right after they first left the Two Rivers. They thought Baerlon was a grand city."

"On foot?" Rand said.

"Yes," Perrin said slowly. Faile's scent was changing, the thorny jealousy dwindling away. Why? "He would rather use his feet, you know. He bet me a gold crown he would be here in Caemlyn no more than ten days after us." The two women were looking at one another, Faile smiling and Min coloring slightly; Min smelled faintly embarrassed, Faile pleased. And surprised, though only a hint showed on her face. "I didn't want to take his coin—he has to go fifty miles or more out of his way—but he insisted. He wanted to make it five days."

"Loial always did say he could outrun a horse," Rand laughed, but there had been a pause. Laughter faded. "I hope he makes it safely," he said more seriously. He *was* tired, and different in other ways, too. The Rand Perrin had last seen in Tear had not been soft, far from it, but this Rand made that one look an innocent farmboy. He did not blink often enough, as if a blink might hide what he needed to see. Perrin recognized something of that look; he had seen it on the faces of Two Rivers men after the Trolloc attacks, after the fifth, the tenth, when it seemed hope was gone but you went on fighting because the cost of giving up was too great.

"My Lord Dragon," Faile said, startling Perrin; she had always called him Rand before, though they had been hearing the title since Whitebridge, "if you will forgive me, I will just have a word with my husband then leave you two to talk."

She hardly waited for Rand's surprised assent to close on Perrin, turning him so her back was to Rand. "I will not go far, my dear heart. Min and I will have our own conversation about things that would very likely bore you." Fussing with his lapels, she began speaking hurriedly under her breath, so softly that anyone except him would have had to strain their ears. She did recall his hearing sometimes. "Remember he is not your boyhood friend any longer, Perrin. At least, not only that. He is the Dragon Reborn, the Lord Dragon. But you are Lord of the Two Rivers. I know you will stand up for yourself, and for the Two Rivers." The smile she gave him was full of love and confidence; he wanted to kiss her right there. "There," she said in a normal tone. "You are all straight again." She no longer gave off the slightest scent of jealousy.

Offering Rand a graceful curtsy and a murmur of "My Lord Dragon," she held out a hand to Min. "Come, Min." Min's curtsy was considerably less practiced, and made Rand start.

Before they reached the doorway, one of the doors banged open and a tall liveried woman entered with a silver tray holding goblets and a pitcher that gave off the smell of wine and honeymelon juice. Perrin almost stared. Despite the red-and-white dress, she could have been Chiad's mother, or maybe grandmother with that short curled white hair. Frowning at the departing women, she stalked to the nearest table and set down the tray, her face a mask of meekness that seemed frozen in place. "I was told four, my Lord Dragon," she said oddly; he thought she might be trying for humble respect but had something caught in her throat, "so I brought for four." Her curtsy made Min's look elegant, and she slammed the door on her way out.

Perrin looked at Rand. "Do you ever think women are . . . strange?"

"Why are you asking me? You are the married man." Rand filled a silver-chased goblet with punch and handed it to him. "If you don't know, you will have to ask Mat. I know less every day."

"So do I," Perrin sighed. The punch was certainly cooling, Rand did not seem to be sweating at all. "Where is Mat, anyway? If I had to guess, I would say in the nearest tavern, and odds or evens whether he has a dice cup in his hands or a girl on his knee."

"He had better have neither," Rand said grimly, setting down his punch untouched. "He is supposed to be bringing Elayne here to be crowned. And Egwene and Nynaeve, I hope. Light, there's so much to do before she gets here." His head swung like a bear's, at bay; then he fixed on Perrin. "Would you go to Tear for me?"

"Tear! Rand, I have been over two months on the road. My bottom's taken on the shape of the saddle."

"I can have you there tonight. Today. You can sleep in a general's tent, and stay away from saddles as long as you like."

Perrin stared at him; the man seemed serious. Suddenly he found himself wondering how Rand's sanity was holding. Light, it had to hold, at least until Tarmon Gai'don. He took a long swallow of the punch to wash the bitter thought out of his mouth. What a way to think about a friend. "Rand, if you could set me down in the Stone of Tear right now, I would still say no. I have to talk to someone here in Caemlyn. And I'd like to see Bode and the others."

Rand did not seem to be listening. He flung himself into one of the gilded chairs and stared at Perrin bleakly. "You remember how Thom used to juggle all those balls and make it look easy? Well, I'm juggling now for all I am worth, and it isn't easy. Sammael in Illian; the rest of the Forsaken the Light only knows where. Sometimes I don't even think they are the worst of it. Rebels who think I'm a false Dragon. Dragonsworn who think they can burn villages in my name. Have you heard of the Prophet, Perrin? No matter; he's no worse than the rest. I have allies who hate each other, and the best general I can name to face Illian wants nothing better than to charge off and be killed. Elayne should be here in maybe a month and a half with luck, but I may just have a rebellion on my hands here before then. Light, I want to give her Andor whole. I thought of going to get her myself, but that is the worst thing I could do." He rubbed his face with both hands, speaking behind them. "The very worst."

"What does Moiraine say?"

Rand's hands came down far enough for him to look over them. "Moiraine is dead, Perrin. She killed Lanfear and died, and that's an end to that."

Perrin sat down. Moiraine? It did not seem possible. "If Alanna and Verin are here. . . ." He rolled the goblet between his palms. He could not really make himself trust either woman. "Have you asked their advice?"

"No!" Rand's hand slashed a sharp cutting gesture. "They stay clear of me, Perrin; I made that plain."

Perrin decided to ask Faile to find out what was going on from Alanna or Verin. The two Aes Sedai often made him vaguely uneasy, but Faile seemed to get on well with them. "Rand, you know as well as I do it's dangerous to anger Aes Sedai. Moiraine came looking for us—for you, anyway—but there were times I thought she was ready to kill Mat, me *and* you." Rand said nothing, but at least he seemed to be listening, with his head tilted. "If a tenth of the stories I've been hearing ever since Baerlon are even half-true, this might be the worst possible time to have Aes Sedai angry with you. I don't pretend to know what's going on in the Tower, but—"

Rand gave himself a shake and leaned forward. "The Tower's split right down the middle, Perrin. Half think I am a pig to buy at market, and the other half. . . . I don't know what they think, exactly. Three days in a row, I've met some of their embassy. I am supposed to meet again this afternoon, and I still cannot pin them down. They ask a sight more questions than they answer, and don't seem much pleased I won't give them any more answers than they give me. At least Elaida—she is the new Amyrlin, if you've not heard—at least her people say something, even if they do seem to think I'll be so impressed by Aes Sedai curtsying that I won't dig too deep."

"Light," Perrin breathed. "Light! You mean to say part of the Aes Sedai really have rebelled, and you've put yourself square between the Tower and the rebels? Two bears ready to fight, and you go picking cloudberries between them! Did you never think you might have enough trouble from Aes Sedai without that? I tell you true, Rand. Siuan Sanche made my toes curl up in my boots, but at least you knew where you stood with her. She made me feel like I was a horse and she was trying to decide whether I'd do for a long hard ride, but at least she made it plain she didn't mean to saddle me herself."

Rand's laugh was too hoarse to hold any mirth. "Do you really think Aes Sedai would leave me alone just because I left them alone? Me? The Tower splitting is the best thing that could have happened for me. They're too busy staring at one another to turn full attention on me. Without that, there'd be twenty Aes Sedai everywhere I turned. Fifty. I have Tear and Cairhien behind me, after a fashion, and a toehold here. Without the split, every time I opened my mouth, there'd be somebody saying, 'Yes, but the Aes Sedai say.' Perrin, Moiraine did her best to tie cords to me until I forced her to stop, and truth to tell, I'm not so sure she stopped then. When an Aes Sedai says she'll advise you and let you decide, she means she knows what you should do and will make you do it if she can." Taking up his goblet, he drank deeply. When he lowered it, he seemed calmer. "If the Tower was whole, I'd have so many strings tied to me by now, I could not move a finger without asking six Aes Sedai for permission."

Perrin very nearly laughed himself, and no more in mirth than Rand. "So you think it's better to—what?—play the rebel Aes Sedai off against the Tower? 'Cheer the bull, or cheer the bear; cheer both, and you will be trampled and eaten.'"

"Not that simple, Perrin, though they don't know it," Rand said smugly, shaking his head. "There's a third side, ready to kneel to me. If they make contact again. Light! This isn't how we should be spending our first hour together again, talking about Aes Sedai. Emond's Field, Perrin." His face softened almost to the Rand Perrin remembered, and he grinned eagerly. "I only had a short time with Bode and the others, but they mentioned all kinds of changes. Tell me what's changed, Perrin. Tell me what's the same."

For a long while they talked about the refugees and all the new things they had brought, new kinds of beans and squash, new varieties of pear and apple, the weaving of fine cloth and maybe carpets, making bricks and tiles, stonework and furniture more ornate than anything the Two Rivers had seen in a long time if ever. Perrin had grown used to the sheer numbers of people who had come across the Mountains of Mist, but it seemed to stun Rand. The advantages and disadvantages of the wall some wanted to put around Emond's Field, and the other villages, were gone into in depth, and stone walls versus log. At times Rand sounded his old self, laughing over how all the women had been so hard against Taraboner or Domani dresses in the beginning, and now were divided into those who would wear nothing but good stout Two Rivers dresses and those who had cut up all theirs for rags. Or over how a number of the younger men were growing mustaches like Taraboners or Domani, occasionally with an Almoth Plain goatee as well, which made the unwise wearer look as though a small animal had latched on under his nose. Perrin did not bother to add to that beards like his own were even more popular.

It came as a shock, though, when Rand made it clear he had no intention of visiting the camp, though there were any number of men there he knew. "I can't protect you or Mat," he said softly, "but I can them."

After that the conversation naturally lagged, until even Rand realized he had draped a blanket over it. Finally he stood with a sigh, scrubbing his hands through his hair and looking around in a disgruntled way. "You must want to wash and rest, Perrin. I should not keep you from it. I'll have rooms set aside for you." Seeing Perrin to the door, he suddenly added, "You will think about Tear, Perrin? I need you there. There is no danger involved. I will tell you the whole plan, if you decide to go. You'll be only the fourth man to know the real plan." Rand's face hardened. "You must keep that to yourself, Perrin. Don't tell even Faile."

"I can hold my tongue," Perrin said stiffly. And a little sadly. The new Rand was back. "And I will think on Tear."

CHAPTER
46

Beyond the Gate

Perrin paid scant attention as Rand instructed a Maiden, "Tell Sulin to prepare rooms for Perrin and Faile, and obey them as she would me." The two Aielwomen took that as some sort of great joke, from the way they laughed and slapped thighs, but Perrin was staring at a slender man standing a little way down the tapestry-hung corridor. He had no doubt at all that the man was Davram Bashere. It was not just that he was Saldaean, and he surely looked nothing like Faile with those thick gray-streaked mustaches curving down to almost hide his mouth. He was no taller than Faile either, maybe a little shorter, but the way he stood, arms folded, face like a hawk staring down into a henyard, made Perrin certain. The man knew; that was certain, too.

Making last goodbyes to Rand, Perrin took a deep breath and walked up the hallway. He found himself wishing he had his axe; Bashere was wearing his sword. "Lord Bashere?" Perrin made a bow that was not returned. The man reeked of cold fury. "I am Perrin Aybara."

"We will talk," Bashere said curtly and turned on his heel. Perrin had no choice but to follow, and to take quick strides despite his longer legs.

Two turnings later, Bashere entered a small sitting room and closed the door behind them. Tall windows let in plenty of light, and even more heat than the high ceiling could handle. Two chairs with padded seats and high, scroll-carved backs had been placed facing each other. A silver pitcher with a tall neck and two silver cups stood on a lapis-inlaid table. Not punch, this time; strong wine, by the smell.

Bashere filled the cups and thrust one at Perrin, gesturing peremptorily to one of the chairs. He wore a smile behind his mustaches, but eyes and smile could have belonged to two different men. The eyes could have driven nails. "I suppose Zarine told you all about my estates before you . . . married her. All about the Broken Crown. She was always talkative as a girl."

The man remained standing, so Perrin did as well. Broken crown? Faile had certainly never mentioned any broken crown. "First she told me you were a fur trader. Or maybe it was a lumber merchant first, and then a fur trader. You sold ice peppers, too." Bashere gave a start, repeating "Fur trader?" incredulously under his breath. "Her story changed," Perrin went on, "but once too often she repeated something you had said about how a general should behave, and I asked her straight out, and . . ." He peered into his wine, then made himself meet the other man's eyes. "When I found out who you were, I almost changed my mind about marrying her, only she had her mind set, and when Faile has her mind set, shifting her is like shifting a hitch of mules that have all decided to sit down at once. Besides, I loved her. I love her."

"Faile?" Bashere barked. "Who in the Pit of Doom is Faile? We are talking about my daughter Zarine, and what you've done to her!"

"Faile is the name she took when she became a Hunter for the Horn," Perrin said patiently. He had to make a good impression on this man; being at odds with your father-in-law was almost as bad as being at odds with your mother-in-law. "That was before she met me."

"A Hunter?" Pride shone in the man's voice, and his sudden grin. The scent of anger almost vanished. "The little minx never said a word to me about that. I must say, Faile suits her better than Zarine. That was her mother's notion, and I—" Suddenly he gave himself a shake, and Perrin a suspicious stare. Anger began scenting the air again. "Don't try changing the subject, boy. What we are about is you and my daughter and this supposed marriage of yours."

"Supposed?" Perrin had always been good at holding his temper; Mistress Luhhan said he never had one. When you were bigger and stronger than the other boys growing up, and might hurt somebody by accident, you learned to hold your temper. Right then he was having a little difficulty, though. "The Wisdom performed the ceremony, the same as everybody's been married in the Two Rivers since time out of mind."

"Boy, it wouldn't matter if you had the words said by an Ogier Elder with six Aes Sedai standing witness. Zarine *still* isn't old enough to marry without her mother's permission, which she never asked, much less received. She is with Deira right now, and if she doesn't convince her mother she's old enough to be married, she goes back to the camp, probably doing duty as her mother's saddle. And you. . . ." Bashere's fingers stroked the hilt of his sword, though he did not seem aware of it. "You," he said in an almost jolly tone, "I get to kill."

"Faile is mine," Perrin growled. Wine slopped over his wrist, and he looked down in surprise at the winecup, crushed in his fist. He set the twisted piece of silver on the table carefully, beside the pitcher, but he could do nothing about his voice. "Nobody can take her from me. Nobody! You take her back to your camp—or anywhere!—and I'll come for her."

"I have nine thousand men with me," the other man said in a surprisingly mild tone.

"Are they any harder to kill than Trollocs? Try taking her—try!—and we'll find out!" He was shaking, Perrin realized, his hands clenched into fists so hard they hurt. It shocked him; he had not been angry, really angry, in so long that he no longer remembered what it was like.

Bashere studied him up and down, then shook his head. "It might be a shame to kill you. We need some new blood. It's getting thin in the House. My grandfather used to say we were all becoming soft, and he was right. I'm half the man he was, and much as it shames me to say it, Zarine is terribly soft. Not weak, mind . . ." He frowned hard for a moment, nodding when he saw Perrin was not going to say Faile was weak. ". . . but soft, just the same."

And that shocked Perrin so, he sat down before he realized he had moved to the chair. He almost forgot to be angry. Was this man mad, changing about like that? And Faile, soft? She could be deliriously soft at times, true, but any man who thought she was soft in the way her father meant would probably have his head handed to him. Himself included.

Bashere picked up the crushed winecup, studied it, then replaced it and took the other chair. "Zarine told me a good bit about you before she went with her mother, all about Lord Perrin of the Two Rivers, Slayer of Trollocs. That's good, that. I like a man who can stand toe to toe with a Trolloc and not back up. Now I want to know what kind of man you are." He waited expectantly, sipping his wine.

Perrin wished he had some more of Rand's melon punch, or even his winecup undented. His throat had gone dry. He wanted to make that good impression, but he had to start with the truth. "The fact of it is, I am not really a lord. I'm a blacksmith. You see, when the Trollocs came. . . ." He trailed off because Bashere was laughing so hard the man had to wipe his eyes.

"Boy, the Creator never made the Houses. Some forget it, but go far enough back in any House, and you'll find a commoner who showed uncommon courage or kept his head and took charge when everybody else was running around like plucked geese. Mind you, another thing some like to forget is the road down can be just as sudden. I've two maids in Tyr who would be ladies if their forebears two hundred years ago hadn't been fools even a fool wouldn't follow, and a woodcutter in Sidona who claims his ancestors were kings and queens before Artur Hawkwing. He might be telling the truth; he's a good woodcutter. As many roads down as up, and the roads down as slippery as the others." Bashere snorted hard enough to make his mustaches stir. "A fool moans when fortune takes him down, and it takes a true fool to moan when fortune takes him up. What I want to know about you isn't what you were, or even so much what you are, as what you are inside. If my wife leaves Zarine with a whole hide, and I don't kill you, do you know how to treat a wife? Well?"

Mindful of that good impression, Perrin decided not to explain that he would much rather be a blacksmith again. "I treat Faile as well as I know how," he said carefully.

Bashere snorted again. "As well as you know how." His flat tone became a growl. "You had better know well enough, boy, or I'll. . . . You hear me. A wife isn't a trooper to go running when you shout. In some ways, a woman is like a dove. You hold her half as hard as you think is necessary, or you might hurt her. You don't want to hurt Zarine. You understand me?" He grinned suddenly, disconcertingly, and his voice grew almost friendly. "You might do very well for a son-in-law, Aybara, but if you make her unhappy. . . ." He was stroking his sword hilt again.

"I try to make her happy," Perrin said seriously. "Hurting her is the last thing I'd want to do."

"Good. Because it would be the last thing you do, boy." That was delivered with a grin too, but Perrin had no doubts Bashere meant every word. "I think it's time to take you to Deira. If she and Zarine haven't finished their discussion by now, best we step in before one of them kills the other. They always did get a little carried away when they argued, and Zarine's too big now for Deira to put an end to it by spanking her." Bashere put his cup on the table, and went on as they started for the door. "One thing you have to be aware of. Just because a woman says she believes something, doesn't mean it is true. Oh, she'll believe it, but a thing is not necessarily true just because a woman believes it is. You keep that in mind."

"I will." Perrin thought he understood what the man meant. Faile sometimes had only a passing acquaintance with the truth. Never about anything important, or at least not what she considered important, but if she promised to do something she did not want to do, she always managed to leave herself a hole to wriggle through and keep the letter of the promise while doing exactly as she wished. What he did not understand was what that could have to do with meeting Faile's mother.

It was a long walk through the Palace, along colonnades and up flights of stairs. There did not seem to be many Saldaeans about, but a good many Aielmen and Maidens, not to mention red-and-white-liveried servants, who bowed or curtsied, and white-robed men and women like those who had taken the horses. Those last scurried along with trays or armloads of toweling, eyes down, and seemed to take no notice of anyone. With a start Perrin realized that a number of them wore the same length of scarlet cloth around their temples that many of the Aielmen did. They must be Aiel, too. He noticed a small thing as well. As many women as men in the white robes wore the headband, and men in the drab coats and breeches, but no Maidens that he saw. Gaul had told him a little about the Aiel, but he had never mentioned the headbands.

As he and Bashere entered a room with ivory-inlaid chairs and small tables set on a patterned carpet of red and gold and green, Perrin's ears picked up the muffled sound of women's voices raised in an inner room. He could not make out words through the thick door, but he could tell that one of them was Faile. Abruptly there was a slap, followed almost immediately by another, and he winced. Only a complete woolhead stepped between his wife and her mother when they were arguing—by what he had seen, usually they both rounded on the poor fool—and he knew very well that Faile could stand up for herself in normal circumstances. But then again, he had seen strong women, themselves mothers and even grandmothers, allow themselves to be treated like children by their own mothers.

Squaring his shoulders, he strode for the inner door, but Bashere was there before, rapping with his knuckles as if they had all the time in the world. Of course, Bashere could not hear what sounded to Perrin like two cats in a sack. Wet cats.

Bashere's rap cut off the snarling as though with a knife. "You may come," a composed voice said loudly.

It was all Perrin could do not to push past Bashere, and once he was inside, his eyes sought out Faile anxiously, where she sat in a wide-armed chair just where the light from the windows became less sharp. The carpet was mostly dark red in here, making him think of blood, and one of the two wall hangings showed a woman on horseback killing a leopard with a spear. The other was a furious battle swirling around a White Lion banner. Her scent was a jumble of emotions he could not separate, and her left cheek bore a red handprint, but she smiled at him, if faintly.

Faile's mother made Perrin blink. With all Bashere's talk of doves, he expected a fragile woman, but Lady Deira stood inches taller than her husband, and she was . . . statuesque. Not big like Mistress Luhhan, who was round, or like Daise Congar, who looked as if she could take over a blacksmith's hammer. She was buxom, which a man certainly should not think of his mother-in-law, and he could see where Faile got her beauty. Faile's face was her mother's face, without the slash of white through her dark hair on her temples. If that was how Faile would look when she reached that age, he was a very fortunate man. On the other hand, that bold nose gave Lady Deira the look of an eagle as those dark tilted eyes fastened on him, a fiery-eyed eagle ready to sink talons deep into a particularly insolent rabbit. She smelled of fury and contempt. The real surprise, though, was the crimson handprint on her cheek.

"Father, we were just talking of you," Faile said with an affectionate smile, gliding to him and taking his hands. She kissed his cheeks, and Perrin felt a sudden stab of disgruntlement; a father did not deserve all that when there was a husband standing right there with only one brief smile to sustain him.

"Should I ride away and hide then, Zarine?" Bashere chuckled. Oh, a very rich chuckle. The man did not even seem to see that his wife and daughter had hit each other!

"She prefers Faile, Davram," Lady Deira said absently. Arms folded beneath that ample bosom, she eyed Perrin up and down without any effort to disguise it.

He heard Faile whisper softly to her father, "It depends on him, now."

Perrin supposed it did, if she and her mother had come to blows. Squaring his shoulders, he prepared to tell Lady Deira that he would be as gentle with Faile as if she were a kitten, that he himself would be meek as a lamb. The last part would be a lie, of course—Faile would spit a meek man and roast him for dinner—but peace had to be maintained. Besides, he *did* try to be gentle with her. Maybe the Lady Deira was why Bashere talked so about gentleness; no man would have the nerve to be anything else with this woman.

Before he could open his mouth, Faile's mother said, "Yellow eyes do not make a wolf. Are you strong enough to handle my daughter, young man? From what she tells me, you're a milksop, indulging her every whim, letting her twine you around her fingers whenever she wants to play cat's cradle."

Perrin stared. Bashere had taken the chair Faile had been sitting in, and now he was complacently studying his boots, one propped atop the toe of the other. Faile, seated on the broad arm of her father's chair, gave her mother one indignant frown, then smiled at Perrin with all the confidence she had showed when telling him to stand up to Rand.

"I don't think she twists me around her finger," he said carefully. She tried, true, but he did not think he had ever let her. Except once in a while, to please her.

Lady Deira's sniff spoke volumes. "Weaklings never think so. A woman wants a strong man, stronger than she, here." Her finger poked his chest hard enough to make him grunt. "I'll never forget the first time Davram took me by the scruff of the neck and showed me he was the stronger of us. It was magnificent!" Perrin blinked; that was an image his mind could not hold. "If a woman is stronger than her husband, she comes to despise him. She has the choice of either tyrannizing him or else making herself less in order not to make him less. If the husband is strong enough, though . . ." She poked him again, even harder. ". . . she can be as strong as she is, as strong as she can grow to be. You will have to prove to Faile that you're strong." Another poke, harder still. "The women of my family are leopards. If you cannot train her to hunt on your command, Faile will rake you as you deserve. Are you strong enough?" This time her finger drove Perrin back a step.

"Will you stop that?" he growled. He refrained from rubbing his chest. Faile was giving no help at all, merely smiling at him encouragingly. Bashere was studying him with pursed lips and a cocked eyebrow. "If I indulge her sometimes, it's because I want to. I like to see her smile. If you expect me to trample on her, you can forget it." Maybe he had lost with that. Faile's mother began staring at him in a most peculiar way, and her scent was a tangle he could not make out, though anger was still in it, and icy disdain. But good impression or no, he was done with trying to say what Bashere and his wife wanted to hear. "I love her, and she loves me, and that's the whole of it as far as I'm concerned."

"He says," Bashere said slowly, "that if you take our daughter away, he will take her back. He seems to think nine thousand Saldaean horse no match for a few hundred Two Rivers bowmen."

His wife gazed at Perrin consideringly, then visibly took herself in hand, her head coming erect. "That is all very well, but any man can swing a sword. What I want to know is whether he can tame a willful, head-strong, disobedient—"

"Enough, Deira," Bashere cut in mildly. "Since you've obviously de-cided Zarine . . . Faile . . . is no longer a child, I think Perrin will do well enough."

To Perrin's surprise, Bashere's wife bowed her head meekly. "As you say, my heart." Then she glared at Perrin, not meekly at all, as if to say that was the way a man should handle a woman.

Bashere murmured something under his breath about grandchildren and making the blood strong again. And Faile? She smiled at Perrin with an expression he had never seen on her face before, an expression that made him decidedly uncomfortable. With her hands folded and her ankles crossed and her head tilted to one side, she somehow managed to look . . . submissive. Faile! Maybe he had married into a family where *every*one was mad.

Closing the door on Perrin, Rand finished his goblet of punch, then sprawled in a chair, thinking. He hoped Perrin got on well with Bashere. But then, if they struck sparks, maybe Perrin would be more amenable to Tear. He needed either Perrin or Mat there to convince Sammael that that was the true attack. The thought brought a soft, bitter laugh. Light, what a way to think about a friend. Lews Therin was giggling and muttering indistinctly about friends and betrayal. Rand wished he could sleep for a year.

Min entered without knocking or being announced, of course. The Maidens sometimes looked at her oddly, but whatever Sulin had said, or maybe Melaine, Min was now on the short list of those sent on in whatever he was doing. She took advantage, too; once already she had insisted on tak-ing a stool beside his bathtub and talking as if nothing were out of the ordi-nary at all. Now she just paused to fill herself a goblet of punch and dropped into his lap with a little bounce. A faint sheen of sweat glistened on her face. She would not even try to learn how to ignore the heat, just laughing and saying she was not Aes Sedai and had no plans to be. He had become her favorite chair for these visits, it seemed, but he was certain if he merely pretended not to notice, she would give up her game sooner or later. That was why he had hid as best he could in his bathwater instead of blindfolding her with Air. Once she knew she was affecting him, she would never stop the joke. Besides, much as it shamed him to admit it about Min, having a girl on his knees did feel nice. He was not made of wood.

"Did you have a good talk with Faile?"

"It didn't last long. Her father came and got her, and she was too busy flinging arms around his neck to notice me. I went for a little walk after."

"You didn't like her?" he said, and Min's eyes widened, her lashes making them look even larger. Women never expected a man to see or understand anything they did not want him to.

"It isn't that I dislike her exactly," she said drawing the words out. "It's just. . . . Well, she wants what she wants when she wants it, and she will not take no for an answer. I pity poor Perrin, married to her. Do you know what she wanted with me? To make sure I had no designs on her precious husband. You may not have noticed—men never see these things—" She cut off, looking up at him suspiciously through those long lashes. He had showed he could see some things, after all. Once she was satisfied he did not mean to laugh, or bring it up, she went on. "I could see at a glance he's besotted with her, the poor fool. And she with him, for all the good it will do him. I don't think he would even look twice at another woman, but she doesn't believe it, not if the other woman looks first anyway. He's found his falcon, and I wouldn't be surprised if she kills him when the hawk appears." Her breath caught, and she glanced up at him again then busied herself drinking from the goblet.

She would tell him what she meant if he asked. He remembered her as saying nothing of her viewings unless they concerned him, but if that was so, she had changed for some reason. She would view anyone he asked now, and tell him everything she saw. Yet doing so made her uncomfortable.

Shut up! he shouted at Lews Therin. *Go away! You're dead!* It had no effect; it often did not, now. That voice went on mumbling, maybe about being betrayed by friends, maybe about betraying them.

"Did you see anything that concerns me?" he asked.

With a grateful grin, Min settled companionably against his chest— well, she probably meant it to be companionable; or then again; very likely not—and began talking between sips of punch. "When you two were together, I saw those fireflies and the darkness stronger than ever. Um. I like melon punch. But with the two of you in the same room, the fireflies were holding their own instead of being eaten faster than they can swarm, the way they do when you're alone. And something else I saw when you were together. Twice he's going to have to be there, or you. . . ." She peered into her goblet so he could not see her face. "If he's not, something bad will happen to you." Her voice sounded small and frightened. "Very bad."

Much as he would have liked to know more—like when and where and what—she would have told him already had she known. "Then I'll just have to keep him around," he said, as cheerfully as he could. He did not like for Min to be frightened.

"I don't know that that will be enough," she mumbled into her punch. "It *will* happen if he is not there, but nothing I saw said it won't because he is. It will be very bad, Rand. Just thinking of that viewing makes me. . . ."

He turned her face up, and was surprised to see tears leaking from her eyes. "Min, I didn't know these viewings could hurt you," he said gently. "I am sorry."

"A fat lot you know, sheepherder," she muttered. Plucking a lace-edged handkerchief from her sleeve, she dabbed at her eyes. "It was just dust. You don't make Sulin dust in here often enough." The handkerchief went back with a flourish. "I should go back to The Crown of Roses. I just had to tell you what I saw about Perrin."

"Min, be careful. Maybe you shouldn't come so often. I can't think Merana would be easy on you if she discovered what you are doing."

Her grin looked very much her old self, and her eyes looked amused even if they did still shine from the tears. "You let me worry about me, sheepherder. They think I am gawking at the sights of Caemlyn like every other country simpleton. If I didn't come every day, would you know they are meeting with the nobles?" She had glimpsed that by chance on her way to the Palace yesterday, Merana appearing for an instant at the window of a palace Min had learned belonged to Lord Pelivar. There was as much chance that Pelivar and his guests were the only ones as there was that Merana had gone to clear Pelivar's drains.

"You be careful," he told her firmly. "I don't want you hurt, Min."

For a moment she studied him silently, then rose up enough to kiss him lightly on the lips. At least. . . . Well, it was light, but this was a daily ritual when she left, and he thought maybe those kisses were getting a little less light every day.

Despite all his promises to himself, he said, "I wish you wouldn't do that." Letting her sit on his knee was one thing, but kisses were carrying the joke too far.

"No tears yet, farmboy," she smiled. "No stammer." Ruffling his hair as if he were ten, she walked to the door, but as she sometimes did, she moved in a gracefully swaying fashion that might not have produced tears and stammer but certainly did make him stare however hard he tried not to. His eyes whipped to her face as she turned around. "Why, sheepherder, your face is flushed. I thought the heat never touched you now. Never mind. I wanted to tell you, I will be careful. I'll see you tomorrow. Be sure to put on clean stockings."

Rand let out a long breath once the door was firmly shut behind her. Clean stockings? He put on clean every day! There were only two choices. He could keep pretending she was having no effect until she quit, or he could resign himself to stammering. Or maybe to begging; she might stop if he begged, but then she would have that to tease him with, and Min did like teasing. The only other option—keeping their time together short, being cold and distant—was out of the question. She was a friend; he could as well have been cold toward. . . . Aviendha and Elayne were the names that came to mind, and they did not fit. Toward Mat or Perrin. The only thing he did not understand was why he still felt so comfortable around her. He should not, with her taunting him in this way, but he did.

Lews Therin's maundering had grown louder from the moment the Aes Sedai were mentioned, and now he said quite clearly, *If they are plotting with the nobles, I have to do something about them.*

Go away, Rand commanded.

Nine are too dangerous, even untrained. Too dangerous. Can't allow them. No. Oh, no.

Go away, Lews Therin!

I am not dead! the voice howled. *I deserve death, but I am alive! Alive! Alive!*

You are dead! Rand shouted back in his head. *You are dead, Lews Therin!*

The voice dwindled, still howling *Alive!* when it faded from hearing.

Shaking, Rand got up and refilled his goblet, draining the punch in one long swallow. Sweat dripped from his face, and his shirt clung to him. Finding the concentration again was an effort. Lews Therin was growing more persistent. One thing was certain. If Merana was plotting with the nobles, especially the nobles ready to declare rebellion if he did not produce Elayne soon enough to satisfy them, then he did have to do something. Unfortunately, he had no idea what.

Kill them, Lews Therin whispered. *Nine are too dangerous, but if I kill*

*some, if I chase them away . . . kill them . . . make them fear me . . . I will not die
again . . .*

I deserve death, but I want to live. . . . He began to weep, but the whispered rambling continued.

Rand filled his goblet again and tried not to listen.

When the Origan Gate into the Inner City came into sight, Demira Eriff slowed. A number of men in the crowded street eyed her admiringly as they squeezed past, and for perhaps the thousandth time she made a note to stop wearing dresses from her native Arad Doman, and for the thousandth time promptly forgot it. Dresses were hardly important—she had been having the same six duplicated for years—and if a man who did not realize she was Aes Sedai became too impudent, it was always a simple matter to let him know who he was being saucy to. That got them out of her hair quickly enough, usually as fast as they could run.

Right then all she was interested in was the Origan Gate, a great white marble arch in the gleaming white wall, the stream of people, carts and wagons passing through it watched by a dozen Aielmen she suspected were not so desultory as they appeared at first glance. They might recognize an Aes Sedai on sight. Surprising people did sometimes. Besides, she had been followed from The Crown of Roses; those coats and breeches made to fade into rock and brush stood out on a city street. So even had she wanted to enter the Inner City, even had she been willing to risk Merana's wrath by entering without first asking al'Thor's permission, she would not have. How that did gall, Aes Sedai being required to ask a man's *permission*. All she wanted was a sight of one Milam Harnder, Second Librarian in the Royal Palace, and her agent for nearly thirty years.

The library in the Palace here could not compare with that in the White Tower, or the Royal Library in Cairhien, or the Terhana Library in Bandar Eban, but she might as well wish to fly as for access to one of those. Still, if her message had reached Milam, he would have begun searching for the books she wanted. The Palace library might well have some information about the Seals on the Dark One's prison, perhaps even cataloged sources, though that might be too much to hope. Most libraries had volumes lying in corners that should have been recorded long ago yet somehow had remained forgotten for a hundred years, or five hundred, sometimes even more. Most libraries held treasures even the librarians did not suspect.

She waited patiently, letting the crowd flow by her, attending only to the people coming out of the gate, but she did not see Milam's bald head and round face. At last she sighed. Plainly he had not received her message; if he had, he would have made whatever excuse was necessary to be there at the appointed time. She was going to have to wait on her turn to accompany Merana to the Palace and hope young al'Thor would give her permission—permission again!—to search in the library.

Turning away from the gate, her eyes chanced to meet those of a tall, lean-faced fellow in a carter's vest who was gazing at her much too admiringly. When their eyes met, he winked!

She was not going to put up with that all the way back to the inn. *I really must remember to have some plain dresses made*, she thought, wondering why she had never done it before. Luckily, she had been in Caemlyn before, some years ago, and Stevan would be waiting at The Crown of Roses, a beacon she could use to guide her if it came to that. She slipped into the narrow shaded gap between a cutler's shop and a tavern.

The narrow alleyways of Caemlyn had been muddy the last time she was in them, but even dry, the deeper she went, the more unfortunate the smell. The walls were blank, with never a window and seldom a cramped door or narrow gate, and those with the look of not having been open in a long time. Scrawny cats peered at her silently from atop barrels and back walls, and stray dogs with knobby ribs laid back their ears, sometimes growling before they skulked off down a crossing run, as alleys were called here. She felt no worry about being scratched or bitten. Cats seemed to sense something about Aes Sedai; she had never heard of an Aes Sedai being scratched by even the most feral cat. Dogs were hostile, true, almost as if they thought Aes Sedai *were* cats, but they almost always slinked away after a little show.

There were far more dogs and cats in the runs than she remembered, and gaunter, but many fewer people. She had not seen anyone at all before she rounded a corner to find five or six Aielmen coming toward her, laughing and talking among themselves. They seemed startled to see her.

"Pardon, Aes Sedai," one of them muttered, and they all pressed against the side of the run, though there was plenty of room.

Wondering if they were the same who had followed her—one of those faces looked familiar, that of a squat fellow with villainous eyes—she nodded and murmured thanks as she started past.

The spear going into her side was such a shock she did not even cry out. Frantically she reached for *saidar*, but something else pierced her side, and she was down in the dust. That remembered face was thrust into hers, black eyes mocking, growling something she ignored as she tried to reach *saidar*, tried to. . . . Darkness closed in.

When Perrin and Faile finally left the interminable interview with her parents, that odd serving woman, Sulin, was waiting for them in the hallway. Sweat drenched Perrin, making dark patches on his coat, and he felt as if he had run ten miles while being pummeled every stride. Faile had a smile on her face and a spring in her step; she looked radiant, beautiful, and as proud of herself as when she brought the Watch Hill men just as the Trollocs were about to overrun Emond's Field. Sulin curtsied every time one of them looked at her, nearly falling over every single time; that leathery face with its scar down her cheek was fixed in an obsequious smile that seemed ready to shatter at a breath. Passing Maidens flashed handtalk at one another, and Sulin curtsied to them as well, though grinding her teeth loud enough for Perrin to hear clearly. Even Faile began to eye her warily.

Once the woman led them to their rooms, a sitting room and a bedchamber with a canopied bed big enough for ten and a long marble balcony overlooking a fountained courtyard, she insisted on explaining or showing them everything, even what they could see. Their horses had been stabled and curried. Their saddlebags were unpacked and hung in the wardrobe with Perrin's axe belt, most of the scant contents laid in the drawers of a chest-on-chest in a precise array. Perrin's axe was propped beside the gray marble fireplace as though to chop kindling. One of the two silver pitchers glistening with condensation held cool tea flavored with mint, the other plum punch. Two gilt-framed mirrors on the wall were pointed out and touched, one over a table where Faile's ivory comb and brush were laid, and a great stand-mirror with carved uprights that a blind man could not have missed.

While Sulin was still explaining about bathwater being brought, and copper tubs, Perrin pressed a gold crown into her calloused palm. "Thank you," he said, "but if you will leave us now. . . ." For a moment he thought she was going to throw the fat coin at him, but instead he got another wavering curtsy and a slammed door as she departed.

"I suppose whoever trains the servants doesn't know her job," Faile said. "That was very good, by the way. Polite but firm. If you would only do that with *our* servants." As she turned her slim back, her voice dropped to a murmur. "Will you unbutton me?"

He always felt very thick-fingered undoing her small buttons, half-afraid he was going to pop them off or tear her dress. On the other hand, he did enjoy undressing his wife. She usually had a maid do it, because of lost buttons he was sure. "Did you mean any of that nonsense you told your mother?"

"Have you not tamed me, my husband," she said without looking at him, "and taught me to perch on your wrist when you call? Do I not run to please you? Am I not obedient to your smallest gesture?" She smelled amused. She certainly sounded amused. The only thing was, she sounded as if she meant it, too, the same as when she told her mother practically the same thing, head high and as proud as she could be. Women were strange, that was all there was to it. And her mother . . . ! For that matter, her father!

Maybe he should change the subject. What was that Bashere had mentioned? "Faile, what is a broken crown?" He was sure that had been it.

She made a vexed noise, and suddenly began to smell upset. "Rand is gone from the Palace, Perrin."

"And if he is?" Bending to peer at a tiny mother-of-pearl button, he frowned at her back. "How do you know?"

"The Maidens. Bain and Chiad taught me some of their handtalk. Don't let on, Perrin. From the way they behaved when they heard there were Aiel here, I think maybe they shouldn't have. Besides, it might be good to understand what the Maidens are saying without them knowing it. They seem thick around Rand." She twisted around to give him a roguish look and stroke his beard. "Those first Maidens we met thought you have nice shoulders, but they did not think much of this. Aielwomen do not know a good beard when they see one."

Shaking his head, he waited until she turned again, then pocketed the button that had come off when she twisted. Maybe she would not notice; he had gone a week with a button missing from his coat, and had not known until she pointed it out. As for beards, from what Gaul said, Aiel always shaved clean; Bain and Chiad had thought his beard a subject for odd jokes. He had thought of shaving himself more than once in this heat. But Faile did like the beard. "What about Rand? Why should it matter if he's left the Palace?"

"Just that you should know what he's doing behind your back. Obviously you didn't know he was going off. Remember, he *is* the Dragon Reborn. That is very like a king, a king of kings, and kings sometimes use up even friends, by accident and on purpose."

"Rand wouldn't do that. What are you suggesting, anyway? That I spy on him?"

He meant it as a joke, but she said, "Not you, my love. Spying is a wife's work."

"Faile!" Straightening so fast he nearly yanked another button loose, he took her shoulders and turned her to face him. "You are not going to spy on Rand, do you hear me?" She put on a dogged look, mouth drawing down, eyes narrowing—she practically reeked of stubbornness—but he could be dogged, too. "Faile, I want to see some of that obedience you were boasting about." As far as he could see, she did what he said when she good and well pleased and otherwise not, and forget whether he was in the right or not. "I mean it, Faile. I want your promise. I'll be no part of anyb—"

"I promise, my heart," she said, placing her fingers over his mouth. "I promise I will not spy on Rand. You see, I am obedient to my lord husband. Do you remember how many grandchildren my mother said she expects?"

The sudden change of direction made him blink. But she had promised; that was the important thing. "Six, I think. I lost count when she started telling us which were to be boys and which girls." Lady Deira had had some startlingly frank advice on how this was to be achieved; thankfully he had missed most of it from wondering whether he should leave the room till she finished. Faile had just nodded away as though it was the most natural thing in the world, with her husband and her father there.

"At least six," she said with a truly wicked grin. "Perrin, she will be looking over our shoulders unless I can tell her she can expect the first soon, and I thought, if you ever managed to undo the rest of my buttons. . . ." After months of marriage she still blushed, but that grin never faded. "The presence of a real bed after so many weeks makes me forward as a farmgirl at harvest."

Sometimes he wondered about these Saldaean farmgirls she was always bringing up. Blushes or no blushes, if they were as forward as Faile when he and she were alone, no crops would ever be harvested in Saldaea. He broke off two more buttons getting her dress undone, and she did not mind a bit. She actually managed to tear his shirt.

Demira was surprised to open her eyes, surprised to find herself lying on the bed in her own room in The Crown of Roses. She expected to be dead, not undressed and tucked under a linen sheet. Stevan was sitting on a stool at the foot of her bed, managing to look relieved, concerned and stern all at the same time. Her slender Cairhienin Warder was a head shorter than she and nearly twenty years younger for all the gray streaking his temples, but sometimes he tried to behave like a father, all but claiming she could not take care of herself without him holding her hand. She very much feared this incident would give him the high ground in that struggle for months to come. Merana was on one side of the bed looking grave, Berenicia on the other. The plump Yellow sister always looked grave, but now she looked absolutely somber.

"How?" Demira managed. Light, but she felt weak. Healing did that, but putting her arms outside the sheet was an effort. She must have been very close to death. Healing left no scars, but memories and weakness were quite enough.

"A man came into the common room," Stevan said, "claiming he wanted some ale. He said he had seen Aiel following an Aes Sedai—he described you exactly—and saying they were going to kill her. As soon as he spoke, I felt. . . ." He grimaced bleakly.

"Stevan asked me to come," Berenicia said, "he all but dragged me—and we ran the whole way. Truth, I was not certain we were in time until you opened your eyes just now."

"Of course," Merana said in a flat voice, "it was all part of the same trap, the same warning. The Aiel and the man. A pity we let him get away, but we were so concerned over you that he managed to slip off before anyone thought to hold him."

Demira had been thinking about Milam and how this was going to affect the search in the library, about how long it was going to take Stevan to calm down, and what Merana was saying did not really penetrate until the last. "Hold him? A warning? What are you talking about, Merana?" Berenicia muttered something about her understanding if they showed it to her in a book; Berenicia had an acid tongue at times.

"Have you seen anyone come into the common room for a drink since we arrived, Demira?" Merana asked patiently.

It was true; she had not. One or even two Aes Sedai made little difference to an inn's custom in Caemlyn, but nine was another matter. Mistress Cinchonine had remarked on it openly of late. "Then it was intended you should know Aiel had killed me. Or maybe that I was to be found before I died." She had just recalled what that villainous-faced fellow had growled at her. "I was told to tell you all to stay away from al'Thor. Exact words. 'Tell the other witches to stay away from the Dragon Reborn.' I could hardly deliver that message dead, could I? How were my wounds placed?"

Stevan shifted on his stool, darting a pained look at her. "Both missed any organ that would have killed you on the spot, but the amount of blood you lost—"

"What are we to do now?" Demira cut in, directing her question to Merana, before he could start in on how foolish she had been to let herself be caught that way.

"I say we should find the Aiel responsible," Berenicia said firmly, "and make an example of them." She came from the Border Marches of Shienar, and Aiel raids had been a feature of her growing up. "Seonid agrees with me."

"Oh, no!" Demira protested. "I will not have my first chance to study the Aiel ruined. They'll hardly say two words as it is. It was my blood, after all. Besides, unless the man who gave you warning was Aiel too, it seems obvious to me that they acted under orders, and I think there is only one man in Caemlyn who orders Aiel."

"The rest of us," Merana said, eyeing Berenicia firmly, "agree with you, Demira. I want to hear no more talk of wasting time and energy finding one pack of hounds among hundreds while the man who set them to hunt walks about grinning." Berenicia bristled a little before bowing her head, but she always did.

"We must at least show al'Thor he cannot treat Aes Sedai in this fashion," Berenicia said sharply. A glance from Merana moderated her tone, though she did not sound happy. "Yet not so sharply that it ruins everything we've planned, of course."

Demira steepled her fingers against her lips and sighed. She did feel weak. "A thought occurs to me. If we charge him openly with what he's done, he will deny it, of course, and we have no proof to fling in his face. Not only that, it might be wise to let it be learned that he feels free to hunt Aes Sedai like rabbits." Merana and Berenicia exchanged glances and nodded quite firmly. Poor Stevan frowned furiously; he had never let anyone walk away from hurting her. "Might it not be better to say nothing? That will certainly make him ponder and sweat. Why haven't we said anything? What are we going to do? I don't know how much we can do, but we can at least make him look over his shoulder."

"A valid point," Verin said from the doorway. "Al'Thor has to respect Aes Sedai, or there will be no working with him." She motioned Stevan to leave—he waited for Demira's nod, of course—then took his stool. "I thought since you were the target—" She frowned at Merana and Berenicia. "Will you sit down? I do not mean to get a crick in my neck staring up at you." Verin went on while they were still placing the room's only chair and a second stool beside the bed. "Since you were the target, Demira, you should help decide how Master al'Thor is to be taught his lesson. And you seem to have made a beginning already."

"What I think," Merana began, but Verin cut her off.

"In a moment, Merana. Demira has the right to first suggestions."

Demira's breath caught as she waited for the explosion. Merana always seemed to want her decisions approved by Verin, which was natural enough under the circumstances, if awkward, but this was the first time Verin had simply taken charge. In front of others, at least. Yet all Merana did was stare at Verin for a moment, lips compressed, and then bow her head. Demira wondered whether this meant Merana was going to resign the embassy to Verin; there did not seem anything else she could do, now. All eyes turned to Demira, waiting. Verin's were particularly penetrating.

"If we want him to worry over what we intend to do, I suggest no one go to the Palace today. Perhaps without any explanation, or if that is too strong, with one he must see through." Merana nodded. More importantly, as things were turning out, Verin did as well. Demira decided to venture a little more. "Maybe we should send no one for several days, to let him stew. I'm sure watching Min will tell us when he is nicely on the boil, and. . . ." Whatever they decided to do, she wanted to be part of it. It *had* been her blood, after all, and the Light only knew how long she would have to put off her researches in the library now. That last was almost as much reason to teach al'Thor a lesson as his forgetting who Aes Sedai were.

CHAPTER
47

The Wandering Woman

Mat wanted a quiet ride to Ebou Dar, and he got one, in a way. But traveling with six women, four of them Aes Sedai, he had plenty of irritations.

They reached the distant forest that first day with the sun still fairly well up in the sky, and rode several hours beneath a high canopy of mostly bare branches, with dead leaves and dry branches crunching under the horses' hooves, until making camp near a dwindling stream just before sunset. Lantern-jawed Harnan, the file leader with the hawk tattooed on his cheek, saw to getting the troopers from the Band settled, the horses curried and hobbled, sentries set and fires lit. Nerim and Lopin bustled about moaning over not having brought tents, and how was a man to know they would be spending nights on the ground when his master said nothing, and if his master caught his death of something, it was not his fault. Skinny and stout, they managed to sound like echoes. Vanin took care of himself, of course, though he did keep an eye on Olver and even curried the parts of Wind that the boy could not reach even using his saddle for a stool. Everybody took care of Olver.

The women shared the camp, but in a way their area was as separate as if it had been fifty paces away. An invisible line seemed to split the campsite in half, with invisible signs telling the troopers not to cross. Nynaeve and Elayne and the two white-haired women gathered around their own fire with Aviendha and the golden-haired Hunter, rarely even glancing toward where Mat and his men were laying out their blankets. The murmured conversation Mat heard, as much as he could make out, had to do with Vandene and Adeleas' concern that Aviendha meant to lead her horse all the way to Ebou Dar instead of riding. Thom tried to get a word in with Elayne and received an absent pat on the cheek, of all things, before he was sent back to sit with Juilin and Jaem, the stringy old Warder, who belonged to Vandene and seemed to spend all of his time sharpening his sword.

Mat had no objection to the women staying apart. A tension he could not understand hung around them. At least, it did around Nynaeve and Elayne, and the Hunter seemed to be infected too. They sometimes stared at the Aes Sedai—the other Aes Sedai; he was not sure he would ever become used to thinking of Nynaeve and Elayne that way—a bit too intently, though Vandene and Adeleas appeared as oblivious as Aviendha. Whatever the reason, Mat wanted no part of it. It smelled like an argument burning to leap out, and whether it burst into flame or smoldered underground, a wise man stepped wide of women's arguments. Medallion or no medallion, a wise man stepped very wide if the women were Aes Sedai.

A small irritant that, and so was the next, which was his own fault. Food. The smell of lamb and some sort of soup quickly wafted from the Aes Sedai's fire. Expecting a quick arrival in Ebou Dar, he had said nothing about food to Vanin and the others, which meant they had a little dried meat and hard cakes of flatbread in their saddlebags. Mat had seen hardly a bird or squirrel, let alone sign of a deer, so hunting was out of the question. When Nerim set up a small folding table and stool for Mat— Lopin was putting up another for Nalesean—Mat told him to share out what he had tucked away in the packhorses' panniers. The result was not as good as he hoped.

Nerim stood by Mat's table, pouring water from a silver pitcher as if it were wine and mournfully watching delicacies vanish down the trooper's gullets. "Pickled quail eggs, my Lord," he would announce in a funereal tone. "They would have gone very well for my Lord's breakfast in Ebou Dar." And, "The best smoked tongue, my Lord. If my Lord only knew what I went through to find honey-smoked tongue in that wretched village, with no time to find anything and all the best taken by the Aes

Sedai." Actually, his biggest grievance seemed to be that Lopin had found potted larks for Nalesean. Every time Nalesean crunched one between his teeth, Lopin's smug smile grew wider and Nerim's face grew longer. For that matter, it was plain from the way some of the men sniffed the air that they would rather have had a slice of lamb and a bowl of soup than any amount of honey-smoked tongue or goose-liver pudding. Olver stared at the women's fire with open wistfulness.

"You want to eat with them?" Mat asked him. "It's all right, if you do."

"I like kippered eel," Olver said stoutly. In a darker tone, he added, "Anyway, she might put something in it." His eyes followed Aviendha every time she shifted, and he seemed to have taken against the Hunter too, perhaps because she spent a good bit of time in obviously friendly chat with the Aiel woman. Aviendha at least must have felt the boy's stare, because she glanced at him and frowned.

Wiping his chin and eyeing the Aes Sedai's fire—come to think of it, he would rather have had lamb and soup himself—Mat noticed that Jaem was missing. Vanin grumped about being sent out again, but Mat sent him for the same reason he had had the man scout ahead during the day despite the fact that Jaem did too. He did not want to rely on what the Aes Sedai chose to tell him. He might have trusted Nynaeve—he did not think she would actually lie to him; as Wisdom, Nynaeve had always been death on anyone lying—but she kept peeping at him past Adeleas' shoulder in a very suspicious way.

To his surprise, Elayne rose as soon as she finished eating and came gliding across that invisible line. Some women just seemed to skim over the ground. "Will you walk aside with me, Master Cauthon?" she asked coolly. Not polite, exactly, but not exactly rude either.

He motioned her to lead the way, and she floated out into the moon-shadowed trees beyond the sentries. That golden hair nestled about her shoulders, framing a face to make any man stare, and the moonlight softened her arrogance. If she had been anything but what she was. . . . And he did not mean just Aes Sedai, nor even that she belonged to Rand. Rand did seem to be tangling himself with the worst sort of woman for a man who had always known how to handle them. Then Elayne began talking, and he forgot everything else.

"You have a *ter'angreal*," she said without preamble, and without looking at him. She just glided along, rustling the leaves on the ground, as if she expected him to heel like a hunting hound. "Some hold that *ter'angreal*

are rightfully the property of Aes Sedai, but I do not require you to surrender it. No one will take it from you. Such things need study, however.
For that reason, I want you to give the *ter'angreal* to me each evening when
we stop. I will return it each morning before we start out."

Mat gave her a sidelong look. She was serious, no doubt about it.
"That's very kind of you, letting me keep what's mine. Only, what makes
you think I have one of these . . . what did you call it? A ter-something?"

Oh, she did stiffen up at that, and looked at him too. He was surprised
not to see fire leap from her eyes to light up the night. Her voice, on the
other hand, was purest crystal ice. "You know very *well* what a *ter'angreal* is,
Master Cauthon. I heard Moiraine speak of them to you in the Stone of
Tear."

"The Stone?" he said blandly. "Yes, I remember the Stone. A fine time
we all had there. Do you remember something in the Stone that gives you
a right to make demands of me? I don't. I am just here to keep you and
Nynaeve from getting holes poked in your hides in Ebou Dar. You can ask
Rand about *ter'angreal* after I deliver you to him."

For a long moment she stared at him as though meaning to beat him
down by force of will, then turned on her heel without another word. He
followed her back to the camp and was surprised to see her walk along
the line of hobbled horses. She examined the fires and how the blankets
were laid out, shook her head over the remains of the troopers' meal. He
had no idea what she was about until she returned to him with her chin
raised.

"Your men have done very well, Master Cauthon," she said, loud
enough for everyone to hear. "In general I am more than satisfied. But if
you had planned ahead properly, they would not have had to gorge themselves on foods that will at the very least keep them awake tonight. Still,
on the whole, you have done well. I'm sure you will think ahead in future."
Cool as you please she strode back to her own fire before he could say
a word, leaving him staring.

Had that been the whole of it, though, the bloody Daughter-Heir
thinking he was one of her subjects, and her and Nynaeve tight-lipped
around Vandene and Adeleas—had that been all, he would have danced a
jig. Right after Elayne's "inspection," before he could even reach his
blankets, the foxhead went cold.

He was so shocked that he stood there staring down at his chest before
he even thought to look toward the Aes Sedai's fire. There they stood in a

row along that unseen dividing line, Aviendha as well. Elayne murmured something he could not make out and the two white-haired Aes Sedai nodded, Adeleas all the while hastily dipping a pen in an inkjar in a sort of scabbard at her belt and jotting notes in a small book. Nynaeve was tugging her braid and muttering to herself.

It only lasted a few moments altogether. Then the chill faded, and they returned to their fire talking softly among themselves. Now and then one of them would glance in his direction until he finally bedded himself down.

The second day they joined a road, and Jaem put his color-shifting cloak away. It was a broad stretch of hard-packed dirt where sometimes an edge of old paving stone still showed, but the highway did not make travel that much faster. For one thing, it curved through increasingly hilly forest. Some of those hills deserved the name of small mountain at least, jagged things with sheer cliffs and stony spires sticking up through the trees. For another, a thin yet steady stream of people drifted in both directions, mostly clumps of grubby blank-faced folk who barely seemed to have sense to step out of the way of a farmer's high-wheeled ox-cart, much less a merchant's train with its canvas-topped wagons clipping along behind teams of six or eight horses. Farmhouses and barns of pale stone appeared clinging to the slopes of the hills, and midway through the third day, they saw the first village of white-plastered buildings with flat roofs of pale reddish tile.

The pinpricks kept up, though. Elayne continued her evening inspections. When he told her sarcastically that he was glad she was pleased, in the second night's camp beside the road, she smiled one of those deliberate regal smiles and said, "You should be, Master Cauthon," sounding as if he had meant every word!

Once they began stopping at inns, she inspected the horses in the stables *and* the troopers' sleeping places in the lofts. Asking her not to brought a coolly arched eyebrow and no answer. Telling her not to brought not even the eyebrow; she just plain ignored him altogether. She told him to do things he had already decided to do—such as having all the horses' shoes checked at the first inn that had a farrier—and, more grating, things he would have seen to had he known of them before her. How she discovered Tad Kandel was trying to hide a boil on his bottom, Mat did not know, or that Lawdrin Mendair had no fewer than five flasks of brandy secreted in his saddlebags. Irritating did not begin to describe doing a thing after she told him to, but Kandel's boil had to be lanced—some of the

Band had adopted Mat's attitude toward being Healed—and Mendair's brandy poured out, and a dozen things more.

Mat almost prayed for her to tell him to do something that did not need doing, just once, so he could tell her no. Emphatically, absolutely, no! Another demand for the *ter'angreal* would have been perfect, but she never mentioned it again. He explained to the troopers that they had no obligation to obey her, and he never actually caught one at it, but they began grinning in a pleased way at her compliments on how well they cared for their horses and puffed out their chests when she told them they looked like good soldiers to her. The day Mat saw Vanin knuckle his forehead to her, heard him murmur, "Thank you, my Lady," without a trace of irony, that day Mat nearly swallowed his tongue.

He tried to be pleasant, but none of the women were having any, not just Elayne. Aviendha told him that he had no honor, of all things, and if he could not show more respect to Elayne, she herself would undertake to teach him respect. Aviendha! The woman he still suspected was waiting her chance to slit Elayne's throat! She called Elayne her near-sister! Vandene and Adeleas peered at him as if he were a strange bug pinned to a board. He offered to shoot with the Hunter for coin or the fun of it—the bow she carried must have fevered her imagination; her name as a Hunter was Birgitte—but she just gave him a very odd look and declined. For that matter, she stayed clear of him after that. She stuck to Elayne's side like a burr except when Elayne came near him. And Nynaeve. . . .

All the way from Salidar she avoided him as if he smelled bad. Their third night on the way, the first at an inn, a little place called The Marriage Knife, Mat saw her in the tile-roofed stable feeding a wizened carrot to her plump mare and decided that whatever else was going on, he could at least talk to her about Bode. It was not every day a man's sister went off to become Aes Sedai, and Nynaeve would know what Bode was facing, "Nynaeve," he said, striding toward her, "I want to talk to you—" He got no further.

She practically leaped straight up in the air, and came down shaking a fist at him, though she immediately hid it in a fold of her skirts. "You leave me alone, Mat Cauthon," she all but shouted. "Do you hear me? You leave me alone!" And she scurried out, sidling past him and bristling so that he expected to see her braid stand up like a cat's tail. After that, he not only smelled bad, he had some sickness that was both loathsome and catching. If he so much as tried to come near her, she hid behind Elayne and glared at him past the other woman's shoulder for all the world as if she was about to stick her tongue out at him. Women were plain mad; that was all.

At least Thom and Juilin were willing to ride alongside him during the day, whenever Elayne did not demand their attention. She did sometimes, just to keep them away from him, he was sure, though he could not fathom the why. Once they found inns, the pair were more than happy to share a mug of ale or punch with him and Nalesean of an evening. They were country common rooms, brick-walled and quiet, where watching a brindle cat was the entertainment and the innkeeper herself served table, inevitably a woman with hips that looked as though a man's fingers might break trying a pinch. The talk was of Ebou Dar mainly, of which Thom knew a good deal despite never having been there. Nalesean was more than willing to recount his one visit there as often as asked, though he wanted to focus on duels he had seen and the gambling on horse races. Juilin had stories from men who knew men who had been there, if not three or four removed, that sounded beyond belief until Thom or Nalesean confirmed them. Men fought duels over women in Ebou Dar, and *women* over *men*, and in both cases the prize—that was the word used—agreed to go with the winner. Men gave women a knife when they married, asking her to use it to kill him if he displeased her—*displeased* her!—and a woman killing a man was considered justified unless it was proven differently. In Ebou Dar, men walked small around women, and forced a smile at what they would kill another man for. Elayne would love it. So would Nynaeve.

Something else came out in those talks. Mat had not imagined Nynaeve and Elayne's displeasure at Vandene and Adeleas, however they tried to hide it. Nynaeve apparently contented herself with glaring and mumbling under her breath. Elayne did not frown or mutter, but she did continually try to take charge; she seemed to think she was already Queen of Andor. However many years those Aes Sedai faces hid, Vandene and Adeleas had to be old enough to be the younger women's mothers if not grandmothers. Mat would not have been surprised to learn they were Aes Sedai when Nynaeve and Elayne were born. Even Thom could not fathom the tension, and he did seem to comprehend a great many things for a simple gleeman. Elayne had snapped Thom's nose off and *told* him he did not understand, and could not, when he tried to remonstrate with her gently. It seemed the two older Aes Sedai were remarkably tolerant. Adeleas often did not appear to register the fact when Elayne gave orders, and both she and Vandene seemed surprised when they did notice.

"Vandene said, 'Well, if you really want to, child, of course we will,' "

Juilin muttered into his ale, recounting one incident. "You would think somebody who was only Accepted just a few days ago would be pleased. Elayne's eyes minded me of a winter storm. Nynaeve ground her teeth so hard, I thought they'd crack."

They were in the common room of The Marriage Knife. Vanin and Harnan and others occupied benches at other tables, together with a number of locals. The men were in long vests, some bright enough for a Tinker and often with no shirt, the women in pale dresses with deep narrow necklines, their skirts gathered up to the knee on one side to expose petticoats colorful enough to make the vests fade. Many of the men and all of the women wore large hoop earrings, and on their hands usually three or four rings sparkling with colored glass. Men and women alike fingered long curved knives stuck through their belts and eyed the strangers darkly. There were two merchant's trains from Amadicia stopped at The Marriage Knife, but the merchants had eaten in their rooms, and their drivers remained with the wagons. Elayne and Nynaeve and the rest of the women were upstairs too.

"Women are . . . different," Nalesean said, laughing, in response to Juilin, though he directed the words at Mat, fingering the point of his beard. He was not usually so stiff with commoners, but Juilin was a Tairen commoner, and that seemed to make a difference, especially since Juilin made a point of staring when he spoke to him. "There's a peasant saying in Tear. 'An Aes Sedai is ten women in one skin.' Peasants have a good bit of wisdom sometimes, burn my soul if they don't."

"At least no one has done anything, shall we say, drastic," Thom said, "though I thought it was close when Elayne let slip that she had made Birgitte her first Warder."

"The Hunter?" Mat exclaimed. Several of the locals looked at him hard, and he lowered his voice. "She's a Warder as well? Elayne's Warder?" That certainly explained a few things.

Thom and Juilin exchanged looks over the rims of their mugs.

"She will be gratified to know you puzzled out that she is a Hunter for the Horn," Thom said, wiping ale from his mustaches. "Yes, she is, and a right set-to it nearly caused, too. Jaem took to her right away like a younger sister, but Vandene and Adeleas. . . ." He sighed heavily. "Neither was very pleased Elayne had already chosen a Warder—apparently most Aes Sedai go years before finding one—and they especially were not pleased she chose a woman. And their not being pleased has Elayne's back up even more."

"They don't seem to like doing things that have not been done before," Juilin added.

"A woman Warder," Nalesean muttered. "I knew everything would change with the Dragon Reborn, but a woman Warder?"

Mat shrugged. "I suppose she'll do well enough as long as she really can shoot that bow. Down the wrong hole?" he asked Juilin, who had begun choking on his ale. "Give me a good bow over a sword any day. Better a quarterstaff, but a bow is just fine. I only hope she doesn't try to get in my way when it's time to take Elayne to Rand."

"I think she can shoot it." Thom leaned across the table to slap Juilin on the back. "I think she can, Mat."

But if Nynaeve and the others had any thoughts of hair-pulling—and Mat would not want to be within ten miles of that, foxhead or no—they showed none of it to him. All he saw was a solid front, and more attempts to channel at him, beginning while he was saddling Pips the morning after the first attempt. Luckily, he was busy fending off Nerim, who thought saddling Mat's horse was his job and implied he could do it better, and the flash of cold lasted only a moment, so Mat gave no outward indication that he had noticed anything at all. That, he determined, would be his response. No stares, no glares, no accusations. He would ignore them and let them cook in their own broth.

He had plenty of opportunity to ignore them. The silver medallion went cold twice more before they found the road, then several times more during the day, that evening, and every day and evening thereafter. Sometimes it came and went in two blinks of an eye, and sometimes he was sure it went on for an hour. He could never tell which one was responsible, of course. Or usually not. Once, when the heat had given him a rash on his back and the scarf around his neck seemed about to saw his head off, he · caught Nynaeve looking at him when the medallion grew cold. She was scowling so hard that a passing farmer, who was poking his ox with a stick, trying to make the animal lumber faster, peered over his shoulder at her as though he feared that gaze might turn on him any moment and maybe kill his ox in the cart shafts. Only when Mat scowled back at her, she gave a jump and almost fell out of her saddle, and the chill vanished. For the rest, he just could not say. At times he might see two or three of them watching him, including Aviendha, who was still walking and leading her horse. Others, by the time he peeked, were talking among themselves or looking at an eagle drifting across the cloudless sky or a great black bear, half again as tall as a man, standing among the trees on a steep hillside in sight of the road. The only truly good thing in it was that he got the impression Elayne was not pleased. He did not know why, and he did not care. Inspecting his men. Patting him on the head with compliments. If he had been the kind of man to do that sort of thing, he would have kicked her.

In truth, though, he began to feel more than a little smug. Whatever they were doing, it had no effect on him that a touch of one of Nerim's ointments rubbed onto his chest could not cure. Nerim assured him it was not frostbite. He felt smug until the fourth afternoon. He was making his way from stabling Pips to The Southern Hoop, a scruffy two stories of white-plastered bricks in a scruffy village of white-plastered bricks and flies called So Tehar, when something soft hit him squarely between the shoulders. With the smell of horse dung in his nostrils he spun around, ready to chew a hole in a stableboy or one of So Tehar's sullen-eyed louts, knife or no knife. There was no stable-boy and no lout. Only Adeleas, busily scribbling away in her little book and nodding to herself. Her hands were quite clean.

Mat went inside and called for punch from the innkeeper, then changed his mind and had her bring brandy instead, a cloudy liquid the lanky woman insisted was made from plums, but which tasted as if it might re-move rust. Juilin contented himself with a sniff, and Thom would not even do that. Even Nalesean only took one sip before asking for punch, and Na-lesean would drink anything. Mat lost count of how many of the tiny pew-ter cups he emptied, but however many it was, it took Nerim and Lopin together to get him to bed. He had never really let himself think whether the foxhead had any limits. He had proof and more than enough that it would stop *saidar*, but if all they had to do was pick something up with the Power and throw it at him. . . . *Better than nothing*, he kept telling himself, lying on his lumpy mattress and watching moonshadows crawl across the ceiling. *A lot better than nothing*. But if he had been able to stand by himself, he would have gone back down for more brandy.

Which was why he was in a vile temper, with a tongue that seemed coated with feathers and a head that had drummers pounding away inside, and sweat pouring down him from the sun overhead, when the road topped a rise on the fifth day to reveal Ebou Dar spread out below, straddling the broad River Eldar with a great bay full of ships beyond.

His first impression of the city was white. White buildings, white palaces, white towers and spires. Domes like sharp white turnips or pears often bore bands of crimson or blue or gold, but mainly the city was white, and reflected sunlight till it almost hurt his eyes. The gate the road led to was a broad tall pointed arch in a white-plastered wall so thick that he rode in shade for twenty paces before emerging into the sun again. It seemed to be a city of squares and canals and bridges, large squares full of people with fountains or statues in the center, canals broad and narrow with men poling barges along them, bridges in every size, some low, some arching high, some big enough that shops lined their sides. Palaces with thick columned porticos stood alongside shops displaying rugs and cloth; houses of four stories with huge arched windows hidden behind louvered shutters stood beside stables and cutlers and fishmongers.

It was in one of those squares that Vandene drew rein to confer with Adeleas while Nynaeve frowned at them and Elayne stared as if icicles should have been hanging from her nose and chin. At Elayne's urging, Aviendha had climbed onto her lanky dun for the entry to the city, but now she scrambled down again as awkwardly as she had climbed on. She looked about almost as curiously as Olver, who had been wide-eyed since the city first came into view. Birgitte seemed to be trying to heel Elayne in imitation of Jaem with Vandene.

Mat took the opportunity to fan himself with his hat and look around.

The largest palace he had seen yet filled one entire side of the square, all domes and spires and colonnades three and four stories above the ground. The other three sides mixed great houses with inns and shops, each as white as the next. A statue of a woman in flowing robes, taller than an Ogier, stood on an even taller pedestal in the middle of the square, one arm raised to point south toward the sea. There were only a handful of people walking across the pale paving stones, and no wonder in that heat. A few were eating their midday meal on the lowest step of the pedestal, and pigeons and seagulls flocked about fighting for scraps. It was a picture of tranquility. Mat did not understand why he suddenly felt the dice rolling in his head.

He knew that sensation well. Sometimes he felt it when his luck was running strong in the gambling. It was always there when a battle was in the offing. And it seemed to come when there was a vital decision to make, the sort where the wrong choice might well get his throat cut.

"We will go in now, by one of the lesser gates," Vandene announced.

Adeleas was nodding. "Merilille will see that we are given rooms to freshen."

That must mean this was the Tarasin Palace, where Tylin Quintara of House Mitsobar sat on the Throne of the Winds and ruled in truth maybe as much as a hundred miles around Ebou Dar. One of the few things he had managed to learn about this trip was that the Aes Sedai were to meet one of their number in the palace, and of course Tylin. Aes Sedai would meet the Queen. Mat looked at that great heap of gleaming marble and white-plastered stone, and he thought what it would be like to stay in there. He liked palaces, usually; at least, he liked anywhere with servants and gold, and feather beds did not hurt. But a Royal Palace meant nobles every time you turned around. Mat preferred nobles a few at a time; even Nalesean could be irritating. A palace that size meant either constant wondering where Nynaeve and Elayne were or else an attempt to mount guard over them. He was not sure whether it would be worse if they let him tag along in there as a bodyguard or refused. He could almost hear Elayne saying in that cool voice, *Pray find some accommodation for Master Cauthon and my men. See they are fed and watered.* She would do it, too. She would pop in for her inspections and tell him to do whatever he was already about to. Yet if she and Nynaeve were safe from trouble anywhere, it would be inside a Queen's Palace. Besides, what he wanted was somewhere he could put his feet up and drink punch with a girl on his knee to soothe his temples. Damp towels would be good. His head hurt. The prim-mouthed lecture Elayne had delivered that morning, about the evils of drink and setting an example, still rang in his ears. That was another reason he had to put his foot down. He had been too weak to reply, just out of bed and wondering whether he could heave himself onto Pips, and she had already gotten away with too much. If he did not put a stop to it now, she would have *him* knuckling his forehead.

All that ran through his mind in the time it took Vandene to turn her slab-sided bay gelding toward the palace. "I'll take rooms at one of these inns for my men," he said loudly. "If you or Elayne mean to go out in the streets, Nynaeve, you can send word, and I'll bring a few men to walk you about." They probably would not—nobody could top a woman for thinking she could take care of herself in a bear pit with her bare hands—but he would wager Vanin could figure out a way to know when they went out. And if not, then Juilin; a thief-catcher should know how. "That one will do." Choosing at random, he pointed to a wide building across the square. A sign he could not make out swung over the arched doorway.

Vandene looked at Adeleas. Elayne looked at Nynaeve. Aviendha frowned at him.

He gave none of them a chance to speak, though. "Thom, Juilin, what do you say to a few mugs of punch?" Maybe water would be better; he had never drunk that much before in his life.

Thom shook his head. "Later perhaps, Mat. I should stay close in case Elayne needs me." The almost fatherly smile he directed at her faded when he saw her staring nonplussed at Mat. Juilin did not smile—he seldom did anymore—but he too said he should stay close, maybe later.

"As you wish," Mat said, replacing his hat. "Vanin. Vanin!" The fat man gave a start and stopped staring worshipfully at Elayne. He actually blushed! Light, the woman was a bad influence.

As Mat turned Pips, Elayne's voice hit him in the back, even more prim than that morning. "You are not to let them drink to excess, Master Cauthon. Some men do not know when to stop. You should certainly not allow a young boy to see men in drink."

He gritted his teeth and rode on across the square without looking back. Olver was looking at him. He was going to have to warn the men about getting drunk in front of the boy, especially Mendair. Light, but he hated her telling him what he should do!

The inn turned out to be called The Wandering Woman, but the sign over the door, and the common room, promised everything that Mat wanted. The high-ceilinged room was certainly cooler than outside, with its wide, arched windows screened behind wooden shutters carved into arabesques. There seemed to be more hole than wood, but they shaded the room. Outlanders sat among the locals, a lanky Murandian with curling mustaches, a stout Kandori with two silver chains across the chest of his coat, others Mat did not recognize offhand. A faint haze of pipe smoke filled the air, and two women playing shrill flutes and a fellow with a drum between his knees provided an odd sort of music. Best of all, the serving women were pretty, and men were tossing dice at four tables. The Kandori merchant was playing at cards.

The stately innkeeper introduced herself as Setalle Anan, though her hazel eyes had never been born in Ebou Dar. "Good my Lords . . ." Large gold hoops in her ears swayed as she bowed her head equally to Mat and Nalesean. ". . . may The Wandering Woman offer you her humble accommodation?"

She was pretty despite a touch of gray in her hair, but Mat watched her eyes. She wore a marriage knife hanging from a close-fitting necklace, the hilt set with red and white stones nestling in her generous cleavage, and she also had one of those curving knives in her belt. Still, he could not help grinning. "Mistress Anan, I feel like I've come home."

The odd thing was, the dice had stopped rolling in his head.

CHAPTER
48

Leaning on the Knife

C limbing out of the big copper tub with a length of white toweling wrapped around her head, Nynaeve dried slowly. The plump gray-haired serving woman tried to dress her, but Nynaeve sent her away, ignoring the startled looks and protests, and did it herself, with great care, examining the dark green dress with its wide collar of pale Merada lace in the tall narrow stand-mirror. Lan's heavy gold ring lay in her pouch—best not to think of that—alongside one of the twisted ring *ter'angreal*, and the Great Serpent gleamed golden around the third finger of her right hand. Her right hand. Best not to think of that either.

The high ceiling was quite pleasantly painted in blue sky and white clouds, and if the furnishings stood on disconcertingly large gilded lion feet and the slim bedposts and chair legs and everything else vertical had too much fluting and gilding for her taste, it was still a more comfortable room than she had stayed in for some considerable time. A pleasant room. Moderately cool. What she was trying to do was calm herself.

It did not work, of course. She had felt *saidar* being woven, and as soon as she stepped from her bedchamber she saw the ward against eavesdropping Elayne had made and tied off around the sitting room. Birgitte and Aviendha were already there as well, all of them freshly scrubbed and dressed.

In what Birgitte claimed was a rather ordinary arrangement here, four bedchambers flanked the one sitting room, which also had a ceiling painted as sky and clouds. Four tall arched windows opened onto a long balcony of white-painted wrought iron, so intricate they could peer down from it unseen at the Mol Hara Square in front of the palace. A faint breeze stirred through the windows, carrying the salt scent of the sea, and for a wonder it actually was a little cool. Anger interfered with her concentration, and Nynaeve had been feeling the heat since shortly after arriving in the Tarasin Palace.

Thom and Juilin had been given a room somewhere deep in the servants' quarters, which in truth seemed to irritate Elayne more than it did either of the men. Thom had actually laughed. But then, he could afford to.

"Have some of this excellent tea, Nynaeve," Elayne said, laying a white napkin across gleaming blue silk skirts. Like everything else in the sitting room, her wide chair had gilded balls for feet, and more standing along the tall back above her head. Aviendha sat by her side, but on the floor, legs folded beneath the skirt of a high-necked dress that almost matched the pale green tile. Her labyrinthine silver necklace went very well with the dress. Nynaeve did not think she had seen the Aiel woman sit in a chair once. People had certainly stared at her in those two inns.

"Mint and cloudberries," Birgitte added to Elayne's offer, filling another delicate golden porcelain cup without waiting. Birgitte wore wide gray trousers and a short blue coat. She did wear dresses occasionally, but her taste made Nynaeve glad it was seldom. All three of them dressed and primped, and no one wanted them.

The silver pitcher glistened damply, and the tea was cool and refreshing. Nynaeve admired Elayne's face, cool and dry. She herself already felt moist again despite the breeze. "I must say," she muttered, "I expected a different reception."

"Did you really?" Elayne asked. "After the way Vandene and Adeleas treated us?"

Nynaeve sighed. "Very well, then, I hoped. I am finally Aes Sedai, really Aes Sedai, and nobody seems to believe it. I truly hoped leaving Salidar would make a difference."

Their meeting with Merilille Ceandevin had not gone well. Their presentation to her, in truth. Vandene's introduction had been almost perfunctory, and then they were dismissed, sent away so the real Aes Sedai could talk. Merilille had said she was sure they wanted to freshen up, but it was a dismissal, with a choice of going like obedient Accepted or refusing like sulky children. Just remembering ruined all Nynaeve's attempts at calm; sweat began to run down her face.

Being sent away was not the worst of it, really. Merilille was a slender, palely elegant Cairhienin with glossy black hair and large liquid eyes, a Gray who looked as if nothing had ever surprised her and nothing ever could. Only those dark eyes had gone wide when told Nynaeve and Elayne were Aes Sedai, and wider still on learning Egwene was the Amyrlin Seat. Birgitte as a Warder clearly astounded her, though by that time she managed to hold her reaction to one stare and a brief tightening of her lips. Aviendha came out of it the easiest; Merilille gave her only a murmur about how much she would enjoy being a novice. Then came the dismissal. And a suggestion, more in the nature of a command, that they spend several days *recuperating* from the *rigors* of their journey.

Nynaeve plucked her handkerchief from her sleeve and fanned her face uselessly with the lacy square. "I still think they're hiding something."

"Really, Nynaeve," Elayne said, shaking her head. "I do *not* like how we're treated any more than you, but you are trying to make a bull out of a mouse. If Vandene and Adeleas want to look for runaways, let them. Would you rather have them trying to take over looking for the bowl?" During the whole journey they had hardly mentioned the *ter'angreal* they sought, for fear the pair would do just that.

Whether they would have or not, Nynaeve still thought they were hiding things. Elayne just did not want to admit it. Adeleas had not realized that Nynaeve had overheard that remark about looking for runaways once they reached Ebou Dar, and when Nynaeve asked whether they really expected to find any, Vandene replied just a bit too quickly that they always kept an eye out for young women who had run from the Tower. It did not make sense. No one had run away from Salidar, but novices did run sometimes—the life was hard, especially with years of obedience to look forward to before you could even think of thinking for yourself—and an occasional Accepted who had begun to despair of ever reaching the shawl tried to slip away, yet even Nynaeve knew that few made it off the island of Tar Valon and almost all were dragged back. You could be put out at any time, for not being strong enough to go on, for refusing or failing your test for Accepted or the test for Aes Sedai that she and Elayne had slipped by, but leaving was never your decision unless you wore the shawl.

So if successful runaways were so rare, why did Vandene and Adeleas think they might find one in Ebou Dar, and why had they shut up like mussels when she asked? She was afraid she knew the answer to the last, anyway. Not tugging her braid required considerable self-control. She thought she was becoming better at that.

"At least Mat finally knows we're Aes Sedai," she growled. At least she could deal with him now. Let him try anything, and he would see what it was like being thumped with everything she could wrap a flow around. "He had better."

"Is that why you've been avoiding him like a Cheltan flinching from the tax collector?" Birgitte asked with a grin, and Nynaeve felt her face coloring. She thought she had hidden her feelings better than that.

"He is very irritating, even for a man," Aviendha murmured. "You must have traveled very far, Birgitte. You often speak of places I have never heard of. One day I would like to travel the wetlands and see all these strange places. Where is this . . . Cheltan? Chelta?"

That wiped Birgitte's grin right off; wherever it was, it might be dead a thousand years, or since an earlier Age altogether. Her and her slipping ancient places and things into the conversation. Nynaeve wished she had been there to see her admit to Egwene what Egwene already knew. Egwene had grown impressively forceful in her time with the Aiel, and put up with little she considered nonsense. Birgitte had actually come back looking chastened.

Even so, Nynaeve liked Birgitte rather better than she did Aviendha, who made her very uneasy at times with her hard stares and bloodthirsty talk. And however irritating Birgitte could be, Nynaeve had promised to help her keep her secret.

"Mat . . . threatened me," she said hurriedly. It was the first way that came to mind to divert Aviendha and the last thing she wanted anyone else to know. Her cheeks heated all over again. Elayne actually smiled, though she had the grace to hide it in her teacup. "Not like that," Nynaeve added when Aviendha began frowning and fingering her belt knife. The Aiel woman seemed to think the proper response to everything was a violent one. "It was just. . . ." Aviendha and Birgitte looked at her, all ears and interest. "He just said. . . ." As she had rescued Birgitte, Elayne rescued her.

"I really think that is enough about Master Cauthon," Elayne said firmly. "He is only here to pull him out of Egwene's hair, and I can puzzle out what to do about the *ter'angreal* later." Her lips compressed for a moment. She had not been happy when Vandene and Adeleas began channeling at Mat without so much as a by-your-leave, and even less when he slipped off to that inn. There had been nothing she could do, of course. She claimed that by only telling him to do what he had to do anyway in the beginning, she could bring him into the habit. Well, good luck to her. "He is the least important part of this trip," she said, even more firmly.

"Yes." Nynaeve just kept the relief out of her voice. "Yes, the bowl is what's important."

"I suggest I scout about first," Birgitte said. "Ebou Dar seems rougher than I remember, and the district you describe could be rougher than . . ." She did not quite glance at Aviendha. ". . . Than the rest of the city," she finished with a sigh.

"If there is scouting to be done," Aviendha put in eagerly, "I wish to be part of it. I have a *cadin'sor.*"

"A scout is supposed to blend in," Elayne said gently. "I think we should find Ebou Dari dress for *all* of us; then we can all search together from the start, and none of us will stand out. Though Nynaeve will have the easiest time of it," she added, smiling at Birgitte and Aviendha. The Ebou Dari they had seen so far all had dark hair, and most seemed to have nearly black eyes.

Aviendha exhaled glumly, and Nynaeve felt like echoing her, thinking of those deep necklines. Very deep, however narrow. Birgitte actually grinned; the woman had no shame at all.

Before the discussion could go any further, a woman with short black hair, in the livery of House Mitsobar, entered without knocking, which Nynaeve thought rude no matter what Elayne said was proper for servants. Her dress was white, the skirt sewn up to the knee on the left side to expose a green petticoat, with a snug bodice embroidered on the left breast with a green Anchor and Sword. Even the livery's narrow neckline plunged as far as Nynaeve recalled. Plump and somewhere in her middle years, the woman hesitated, then curtsied and addressed herself to everyone. "Queen Tylin wishes to see the three Aes Sedai, if it pleases them."

Nynaeve exchanged wondering looks with Elayne and the others.

"There are only two of us Aes Sedai here," Elayne said after a moment. "Perhaps you meant to go to Merilille?"

"I was directed to this apartment . . . Aes Sedai." The pause was barely long enough to notice, and the woman just missed turning the title into a question.

Elayne rose, smoothing her skirts; no stranger would suspect that that smooth face hid anger, but there was a hint of tightness at the corners of eyes and mouth. "Shall we go, then? Nynaeve? Aviendha? Birgitte?"

"I am not Aes Sedai, Elayne," Aviendha said, and the serving woman put in hurriedly, "I was told only the Aes Sedai."

"Aviendha and I could have a look around the city while you see the Queen," Birgitte said before Elayne could open her mouth. Aviendha's face lit up.

Elayne gave the pair of them a sharp look, then sighed. "Well, at least be careful. Nynaeve, are you coming, or do you want to see the city too?" That last was in a dry tone, with another glance at Birgitte.

"Oh, I would not miss it," Nynaeve told her. "It will be good to finally meet someone who thinks. . . ." She could not finish it with the maid there. "We should not keep the Queen waiting."

"Oh, no," the liveried woman said. "It'd be as much as my ears are worth."

However much her ears were worth, it took some time to walk through the palace corridors. As though to make up for all the white outside, the palace was full of color. In one corridor the ceiling was painted green and the walls blue, in another the walls were yellow and the ceiling pale rose. The floor tiles were diamonds of red and black and white, or blue and yellow, or almost any combination in any shade. There were very few tapestries, usually scenes of the sea, but a good many tall vases of golden Sea Folk porcelain stood in arched niches, and also large pieces of carved crystal, statuettes and vases and bowls, that caught Elayne's eye as well as Nynaeve's.

Of course servants scurried about everywhere, the men's version of the livery entailing white breeches and a long green vest over a white shirt with wide, pleated sleeves, but before they had gone very far Nynaeve saw someone striding toward them who made her stop and catch Elayne's arm. It was Jaichim Carridin. She did not take her eyes off the tall graying man as he strode on past them, those cruel deep-set eyes never turning in their direction, white cloak spreading behind him. Sweat covered his face, but he ignored it as he ignored them.

"What is he doing here?" Nynaeve demanded. That man had unleashed slaughter in Tanchico, and the Light only knew where else.

The serving woman looked at her quizzically. "Why, the Children of the Light sent an embassy too, months gone. The Queen . . . Aes Sedai?" Again, that hesitation.

Elayne managed to nod graciously, but Nynaeve could not blank the asperity from her own voice. "Then we should not keep her waiting." One thing Merilille had let slip about this Tylin was that she was a punctilious woman, stiffly formal. But if she too started doubting they were Aes Sedai, Nynaeve was in just the mood to prove it.

The serving woman left them in a large room with a pale blue ceiling and yellow walls, where a row of tall triple-arched windows gave onto a long wrought-iron balcony and let in a quite comfortable salty breeze, and before the Queen Nynaeve and Elayne made their curtsies, proper for Aes Sedai to ruler, a slight dip, a tiny bow of the head.

Tylin was a most impressive woman. No taller than Nynaeve, she stood with a regal bearing that Elayne would have had to strain to match on her best day. She should have replied to their courtesies with the same, but she did not. Instead her large black eyes examined them with imperious intensity.

Nynaeve returned the favor as well as she could. Waves of glossy black hair, gray at the temples, hung well below Tylin's shoulders, framing a face that was handsome if not unlined. Shockingly, there were two scars on the woman's cheeks, fine and so old they had all but vanished. Of course, she did have one of those curved knives stuck through a belt of woven gold, with hilt and scabbard encrusted in gems, Nynaeve was sure it must be for show. Tylin's blue silk dress was certainly nothing anyone could wear fighting a duel, with falls of snowy lace that would nearly hide her fingers if she lowered her hands, and skirts drawn up above her knees in front to expose layers of green and white silk petticoats and trailing behind her a pace or more. The bodice, trimmed in the same lace, was snug enough that Nynaeve was not sure whether sitting in it or standing would be more uncomfortable. A collar of woven gold fastened around the gown's high neck, which put more lace under her chin, supported a white-sheathed marriage knife hanging hilt-down into an oval cut-out that easily equalled any of those deep necklines.

"You two must be Elayne and Nynaeve." Tylin took a chair carved to resemble bamboo, though covered in gilt, and arranged her skirts carefully without taking her eyes from them. Her voice was deep, melodious and commanding. "I understood there was a third. Aviendha?"

Nynaeve exchanged glances with Elayne. There had been no invitation for them to sit, not so much as a flicker of eyes toward a chair. "She is not Aes Sedai," Elayne began calmly.

Tylin spoke before she could say more. "And you are? You've seen eighteen winters at most, Elayne. And you, Nynaeve, staring at me like a cat with its tail caught, how many have you seen? Twenty-two? Twenty-three perhaps? Stab my liver! I visited Tar Valon once, and the White Tower. I doubt any woman your age has ever worn that ring on her right hand."

"Twenty-six!" Nynaeve snapped. With a good part of the Women's

Circle back in Emond's Field thinking she was too young to be Wisdom, it had become habit with her to flourish every naming day she could claim. "I am twenty-six and an Aes Sedai of the Yellow Ajah." She still felt a thrill of pride saying that. "Elayne may be eighteen, but she is Aes Sedai as well, and Green Ajah. Do you think Merilille or Vandene would let us wear these rings as a joke? A good many things have changed, Tylin. The Amyrlin Seat, Egwene al'Vere, is no older than Elayne."

"Is she?" Tylin said in a flat voice. "I was not told that. When the Aes Sedai who counseled me from the day I took the throne, and my father before me, abruptly leaves for the Tower without explanation, and I then learn that rumors of a Tower divided are true; when Dragonsworn seem to spring out of the ground; when an Amyrlin is chosen to oppose Elaida and an army gathered under one of the great captains, inside Altara, before I hear of it—when all of that has happened, you cannot expect me to be enamored of surprises."

Nynaeve hoped her face did not look as sickly as she felt. Why could she not learn to hold her tongue occasionally? Abruptly she realized she could no longer sense the True Source; anger and embarrassment did not go together very well. It was probably to the good. If she could channel, she might make an even bigger fool of herself.

Elayne moved to smooth things over without a pause. "I know you have heard this before," she told Tylin, "but let me add my apologies to those of Merilille and the others. Gathering an army inside your borders without your permission was unconscionable. All I can say in mitigation is that events moved quickly and we in Salidar were caught up, but that is no excuse. I swear to you, no harm is intended to Altara, and no insult was meant to the Throne of the Winds. Even as we speak, Gareth Bryne leads that army north, out of Altara."

Tylin stared at her, unblinking. "I have heard no word of apology or excuse until yours. But any ruler of Altara must learn to swallow insult from greater powers without salt." Taking a deep breath, she gestured, lace waving. "Sit, sit. Both of you sit. Lean back on your knife and let your tongue go free." Her sudden smile was very close to a grin. "I don't know how you say it in Andor. Be at ease, and speak your mind as you wish."

Nynaeve was glad that Elayne's blue eyes widened in surprise, because she herself gasped aloud. This was the woman who Merilille had claimed required ceremony carved in polished marble? Nynaeve was more than glad to take a chair. Thinking of all the hidden currents in Salidar, she wondered whether Tylin was trying to . . . to what? She had come to expect everyone who was not a close friend to try manipulating her. Elayne sat on the very front of her chair, and stiffly.

"I mean what I say," Tylin insisted. "Whatever you say, I will hear no insult." From the way her fingers tapped the jeweled hilt at her waist, though, silence might be heard as one.

"I am not certain where to begin," Nynaeve said carefully. She did wish Elayne had not actually nodded at that; Elayne was supposed to know how to handle kings and queens. Why did she not say something?

"With why," the Queen said impatiently. "Why do four more Aes Sedai come to Ebou Dar from Salidar? It cannot be to outshine Elaida's embassy—Teslyn does not even call it that, and there are only her and Joline. . . . You did not know?" Falling back in her chair laughing, she pressed the fingers of one hand to her lips. "Do you know about the Whitecloaks? Yes?" Her free hand made a slashing gesture, and her mirth began to subside in small ripples. "That for Whitecloaks! But I must listen to all who court me, Lord Inquisitor Carridin as well as the others."

"But why?" Nynaeve demanded. "I am glad you don't like Whitecloaks, but in that case, why must you listen to a word Carridin says? The man's a butcher." She knew she had made another mistake. The way Elayne suddenly seemed to be studying the broad white fireplace, where the deep lintel was carved into towering waves, told her that even before the last vestige of Tylin's laughter snuffed out like a candle.

"You take me at my word," the Queen said quietly. "I said let your tongue go free, and. . . ." Those dark eyes went to the floor tiles, and she seemed to be gathering herself.

Nynaeve looked to Elayne, hoping for some hint of what she had done wrong, or better, how to make it right, but Elayne only gave her one sideways glance and the smallest shake of her head before returning to her study of the marble waves. Maybe she should avoid looking at Tylin, too? Yet the woman staring at the floor drew her eyes. With one hand Tylin stroked the hilt of her curved dagger, with the other fingered the smaller hilt nestled between her breasts.

The marriage dagger told quite a lot about Tylin; Vandene and Adeleas had been more than willing to explain some things concerning Ebou Dar, usually those that made the city seem unsafe for anyone not surrounded by a dozen armored guards. The white sheath meant the Queen was widowed and did not intend to remarry. The four pearls and one firedrop set in the gold-wrapped hilt said she had borne four sons and one daughter; the white-enameled setting of the firedrop and the red-enameled of three of the pearls said only one son survived. All had been at least sixteen when they died, and died in duels, or the settings would have been black. What must it be like to constantly carry a reminder of that sort! According to Vandene, women saw a red or white setting as a source of pride, whether her stones were pearls and firedrops or colored glass. Vandene said many Ebou Dari women removed the stones of their children past sixteen who refused a duel, and never acknowledged them again.

At long last Tylin raised her head. Her face was pleasant, and her hand left the dagger in her belt, but she continued to finger the marriage knife absently. "I want my son to follow me on the Throne of the Winds," she said mildly. "Beslan is your age, Elayne. This would be a matter of course in Andor, though he would have to be a woman"—she actually grinned, in apparently genuine amusement—"or in any other land save Murandy, where matters are much the same as here in Altara. In the thousand years since Artur Hawkwing, only one House has held the throne for five generations, and Anarina's fall was so precipitous that to this day House Todande is a lapdog for anyone who wants them. No other House has ever had more than two rulers in succession.

"When my father took the throne, other Houses had more of the city itself than Mitsobar. Had he stepped outside this palace without guards, he would have been sewn into a sack with rocks and tossed into the river. When he died, he gave me what I have now. Small, compared to other rulers. A man riding fresh horses could reach the end of my writ in one day's hard ride. I have not been idle, though. When news of the Dragon Reborn came, I was certain I could hand on to Beslan twice what I hold, and allies of a sort beyond that. The Stone of Tear and *Callandor* changed everything. Now I thank Pedron Niall when he arranges for Illian to take a hundred-mile swathe of Altara instead of invading. I listen to Jaichim Carridin, and I do not spit in his eye, however many Altarans died in the Whitecloak War. I listen to Carridin, and to Teslyn, and to Merilille, and I pray that I can pass something to my son instead of being found drowned in my bath on the day Beslan meets with an accident hunting."

Tylin drew a long breath. The pleasant face remained, but an edge entered her voice. "Now. I have stood bare-breasted in the fishmarket for you. Answer me mine. Why do I have the honor of four more Aes Sedai?"

"We are here to find a *ter'angreal*," Elayne said, and as Nynaeve stared in amazement, she told everything from *Tel'aran'rhiod* to the dust in the room where the bowl was.

"To make the weather right again would be a miraculous blessing,"

Tylin said slowly, "but the quarter you describe sounds like the Rahad, across the river. Even the Civil Guard steps lightly there. Forgive me—I understand that you are Aes Sedai—but in the Rahad, you could have a knife in your back before you knew it. If the clothes are fine, they use a very narrow blade so there is little blood. Perhaps you should leave this search to Vandene and Adeleas. I think they have had a few more years than you to see such places."

"They told you about the bowl?" Nynaeve said with a frown, but the Queen shook her head.

"Only that they were here to search for something. Aes Sedai never tell a word more than they absolutely must." Once again that sudden grin flashed; it looked quite merry, though it did make her scars show as thin lines across her cheeks. "Until you two, at least. May the years not change you too much. I often wish Cavandra had not returned to the Tower; I could talk with her in this way." Standing, she motioned them to remain seated and glided across the room to tap a silver gong with an ivory mallet; it produced quite a loud chime for such a small cylinder. "I will send for cool mint tea, and we will talk. You will tell me how I can help—if I send soldiers into the Rahad, it will be the Wine Riots all over again—and per-haps you will even be able to explain why the bay is full of Sea Folk ships that neither dock nor trade. . . ."

A goodly time passed over tea and talk, mostly about the dangers of the Rahad and what Tylin could not do, and Beslan was brought in, a soft-spoken youth who bowed respectfully and stared with beautiful black eyes that perhaps held relief when his mother said he could go. He certainly never doubted they were Aes Sedai. Finally, though, the pair of them were finding their way back to their apartment through the brightly painted corridors.

"So they mean to take over the search too," Nynaeve murmured, glancing about to make sure none of the liveried servants was close enough to hear. Tylin had known too much about them too soon. And however she grinned, she had been upset over the Aes Sedai in Salidar. "Elayne, do you think it was wise to tell her everything? She might decide the best way to make sure that boy gets the throne is to let us find the bowl and then tell Teslyn." She re-membered Teslyn slightly; a Red, and an unpleasant woman.

"I know how my mother felt about Aes Sedai traveling about Andor, never letting her know what they were doing. I know how I would feel. Besides, I finally remembered being taught about that phrase—lean back on your knife and the rest. The only way to insult somebody who says that to you is to lie." Elayne's chin rose slightly. "As for Vandene and Adeleas, they only think they've taken over. This Rahad may be dangerous, but I cannot think it is any worse than Tanchico, and we won't have the Black Ajah to worry about. I wager in ten days we will have the bowl, I will know what makes Mat's *ter'angreal* do what it should not be able to do and we will be on our way to join Egwene, with him knuckling his forehead as fast as Master Vanin, and Vandene and Adeleas will be left sitting here with Merilille *and* Teslyn trying to puzzle out what happened."

Nynaeve could not help it; she laughed out loud. A lanky serving man shifting a large vase of golden porcelain stared at her, and she stuck out her tongue at him. He nearly dropped the vase. "I won't take that wager, except about Mat. Ten days it is."

CHAPTER
49

The Mirror of Mists

R and puffed contentedly on his pipe, sitting in his shirtsleeves with his back against one of the slender white columns that surrounded the small oval courtyard, and watched the water spray up in the marble fountain, sparkling like gems in the sunlight. The morning still left this part of the courtyard in pleasant shade. Even Lews Therin was still. "Are you sure you won't reconsider Tear?"

Seated against the next column and also coatless, Perrin blew two smoke rings before replacing his pipe, a rather ornate thing carved with wolfheads. "What about what Min saw?"

Rand's attempt at his own ring ran afoul of a sour grunt and came out just a puff of smoke. Min had had no right to bring that up where Perrin could hear. "Do you really want to be tied to my belt, Perrin?"

"What I want hasn't seemed to count much since the first time we saw Moiraine back in Emond's Field," Perrin said dryly. He sighed. "You are who you are, Rand. If you fail, everything fails." Suddenly he sat forward, frowning toward a wide doorway behind the columns to their left.

A long moment later Rand heard footsteps in that direction, too heavy for any human. The broad shape that ducked through the doorway and strode into the courtyard was more than twice as tall as the serving woman who was almost running to keep up with the Ogier's long legs.

"Loial!" Rand exclaimed, scrambling to his feet. He and Perrin reached the Ogier together. The grin on Loial's wide mouth really did almost split his huge face in two, but his long coat, spreading out above turned-down knee-high boots, still carried travel dust. The big pockets bulged with squarish shapes, too; Loial was never far from books. "Are you all right, Loial?"

"You look tired," Perrin said, urging the Ogier toward the fountain. "Sit on the coping."

Loial let himself be led, but his long dangling eyebrows rose and tufted ears quivered in puzzlement as he stared from one of them to the other. Sitting, he was as tall as Perrin standing. "All right? Tired?" His voice was a rumble like the earth moving. "Of course I am all right. And if I'm tired, I have walked a long way. I must say it felt good to be back on my own feet. You always know where your feet are taking you, but you never can be sure with a horse. Anyway, my feet are faster." Abruptly he let out a thunderous laugh. "You owe me a gold crown, Perrin. You and your ten days. I will wager another crown you've not been here more than five days before me."

"You'll get your crown." Perrin laughed. In an aside to Rand that had Loial's ears vibrating indignantly, he added, "Gaul corrupted him. He dices now, and bets on horse races when he can barely tell one horse from another."

Rand grinned. Loial always had looked at horses rather dubiously, and small wonder since his legs were longer than theirs. "Are you sure you're all right, Loial?"

"Did you find that abandoned *stedding*?" Perrin asked around his pipestem.

"Did you stay long enough?"

"What are you two talking about?" Loial's uncertain frown trailed the ends of his eyebrows down onto his cheeks. "I just wanted to see a *stedding* again, to feel one. I am ready for ten more years."

"That isn't what your mother says," Rand said seriously.

Loial was on his feet before Rand finished, staring wildly in every direction, ears laid back and trembling. "My mother? Here? She is here?"

"No, she isn't," Perrin said, and Loial's ears almost went limp with relief. "It seems she's in the Two Rivers. Or was a month ago. Rand used some way of hopping about he has to take her and Elder Haman— What's the matter?"

Halfway to sitting down again, Loial froze with his knees bent at Elder Haman's name. Eyes closed, he lowered himself slowly the rest of the way. "Elder Haman," he muttered, rubbing his face with a thick-fingered hand. "Elder Haman and my mother." He peered at Perrin. He peered at Rand. In a voice that was low and much too casual, he asked, "Was anyone else with them?" Well, it was low for an Ogier; a giant bumblebee buzzing in a huge waterjar.

"A young Ogier woman named Erith," Rand told him. "You—" That was as far as he got.

With a moan Loial leaped to his feet again. Servants' heads appeared at doorways and windows to see what that vast noise was, and vanished again when they saw Rand. Loial began pacing back and forth, ears and eyebrows both drooping so much that he seemed to be melting. "A wife," he mumbled. "It cannot mean anything else, not with Mother and Elder Haman. A wife. I'm too young to get married!" Rand hid a smile behind his hand; Loial might be young for an Ogier, but in his case that meant more than ninety. "She'll drag me back to Stedding Shangtai. I know she won't let me travel with you, and I still don't have near enough notes for my book. Oh, you can smile, Perrin. Faile does whatever you say." Perrin choked on his pipe, wheezing until Rand slapped his back. "It is different with us," Loial went on. "It is considered very rude not to do as your wife says. Very rude. I know she'll make me settle down to something solid and respectable, like treesinging or. . . ." Abruptly he frowned and stopped pacing. "Did you say Erith?" Rand nodded; Perrin seemed to be getting his breath back, but he was glaring at Loial in a sort of malevolent amusement. "Erith, daughter of Iva daughter of Alar?" Rand nodded again, and Loial sank back to his place on the fountain coping. "But I know her. You remember her, Rand. We met her at Stedding Tsofu."

"That is what I was trying to tell you," Rand said patiently. And with no little amusement himself. "She was the one who said you're handsome. And gave you a flower, as I recall."

"She might have said," Loial muttered defensively. "She might have done; I cannot recall." But one hand strayed toward a coat pocket full of books, where Rand would have wagered anything that flower was carefully pressed. The Ogier cleared his throat, a deep rumble. "Erith is very beautiful. I've never seen anyone so beautiful. And intelligent. She listened very attentively when I explained Serden's theory—that is Serden, son of Kolom son of Radlin; he wrote about six hundred years ago—when I explained his theory of how the Ways. . . ." He trailed off as if he had just noticed their grins. "Well, she did listen. Attentively. She was very interested."

"I'm sure she was," Rand said noncommittally. Mention of the Ways made him think. Most of the Waygates were near *stedding*, and if Loial's mother and Elder Haman were to be believed, the *stedding* were what Loial needed. Of course, he could not take Loial any closer than the edge of one; you could not channel into a *stedding* any more than you could channel inside one. "Listen, Loial. I want to put guards on all the Waygates, and I need somebody who can not only find them, but can talk to the Elders as well and get their permission."

"Light," Perrin growled disgustedly. He tapped out his pipe and ground the dottle into the courtyard paving stone under his boot heel. "Light! You send Mat off to face down Aes Sedai, you want to dump me into the middle of a war with Sammael and a few hundred Two Rivers men with me, some of them you know, and now you want to send Loial off when he's only just arrived. Burn you, Rand, look at him! He needs rest. Is there anybody you won't use? Maybe you want Faile to go hunt Moghedien or Semirhage. Light!"

Anger welled up in Rand, a tempest that made him shake. Those yellow eyes stared at him grimly, but he stared back like thunder. "I will use anybody I must. You said it yourself; I am who I am. And I'm using myself up, Perrin, because I have to. Just like I'll use anybody I have to. We don't have a choice anymore. Not me, not you, not anybody!"

"Rand, Perrin," Loial murmured worriedly. "Be still, be calm. Don't fight. Not you." A hand the size of a ham patted each of them awkwardly on the shoulder. "You should both rest in a *stedding*. The *stedding* are very peaceful, very soothing."

Rand stared at Perrin staring at him. Anger still flashed in him, lightning flashes in a storm that would not quite die. Lews Therin's mutters rumbled fitfully, far off. "I'm sorry," he muttered, meaning it for both.

Perrin made an offhand gesture, maybe meaning there was nothing to apologize for, maybe accepting the apology, but he did not offer one himself. Instead his head swung toward the columns again, toward the door Loial had come through. Once more moments passed before Rand heard running footsteps.

Min dashed into the courtyard at a dead run. Ignoring Loial and Perrin, she seized Rand's arms. "They're coming," she panted. "They are on their way right now."

"Easy, Min," Rand said. "Calm yourself. I was beginning to think they were all taking to their beds like—what did you say her name is? Demira?" In truth, he felt considerable relief, though Lews Therin's grumbling and wheezing laughter grew louder with the mention of Aes Sedai. For three days Merana had appeared with two sisters each afternoon as regular as the finest clockmaker's art, but the visits had suddenly stopped five days ago without a word of explanation. Min had no idea why. He had been worried that they had taken offense enough at his rules to leave.

But Min stared up at him with a face of anguish. She was trembling, he realized. "Listen to me! It is seven of them, not three, and they didn't send me to ask permission or let you know or anything. I slipped out ahead of them, and galloped Wildrose the whole way. They mean to be inside the Palace before you know they're here. I heard Merana talking to Demira when they didn't know I was there. They mean to reach the Grand Hall ahead of you, so you have to come to them."

"Is this your viewing, do you think?" he asked calmly. Women who could channel would hurt him badly, she had said. *Seven!* Lews Therin whispered hoarsely. *No! No! No!* Rand ignored him; there was little else he could do.

"I don't know," Min said in an agonized voice. Rand was startled to realize the shine in her dark eyes came from unshed tears. "Do you think I wouldn't tell you if I knew? All I know is, they are coming, and—"

"And there is nothing to be afraid of," he broke in firmly. The Aes Sedai must really have frightened her for Min to be near crying. *Seven*, Lews Therin groaned. *I cannot handle seven, not at once. Not seven.* Rand thought of the fat-little-man *angreal*, and the voice faded to murmurs; it still sounded uneasy, though. At least Alanna was not one of them; Rand could feel her at some distance, not moving, certainly not toward him. He was not sure he dared come face-to-face with her again. "There's no time to waste, either. Jalani?"

The plump-cheeked young Maiden popped out from behind a column so suddenly that Loial's ears shot straight up. Min seemed to see the Ogier for the first time, and Perrin; she gave a start too.

"Jalani," Rand said, "tell Nandera I am going to the Grand Hall, where I expect Aes Sedai shortly."

She tried to maintain a smooth face, but the beginnings of a self-satisfied grin made her cheeks seem even plumper. "Beralna has already gone to inform Nandera, *Car'a'carn.*" Loial's ears flickered in surprise at the title.

"Then would you tell Sulin to meet me at the dressing rooms behind the Grand Hall with my coat? And the Dragon Scepter?"

Jalani's grin widened openly. "Sulin has already gone running in her wetlander dress as fast as a gray-nosed hare that sat on *segade* spines."

"In that case," Rand said, "you can bring my horse to the Grand Hall." The young Maiden's jaw dropped, especially when Perrin and Loial doubled over laughing.

Min's fist in Rand's shortribs made him grunt. "This is no joking matter, you thick-skulled sheepfarmer! Merana and the rest were wrapping themselves in their shawls as though putting on armor. Now, listen to me. I will stand over to one side, behind the columns, so you can see and they cannot, and if I see anything, I'll make some sort of signal."

"You will stay here with Loial and Perrin," he told her. "I don't know what kind of signal you could make that I'd understand, and if they catch even a glimpse of you, they will know you warned me." She gave him one of those fists-on-hips, glaring-up-through-her-eyelashes, sullen stubborn stares. "Min?"

To his surprise, she sighed and said, "Yes, Rand," just as meek as milk-water. That sort of thing from her made him as suspicious as it would have from Elayne or Aviendha, but he had no time for digging if he was to be in the Grand Hall before Merana. Nodding, he hoped he did not look as uncertain as he felt.

Wondering whether he should have asked Perrin and Loial to keep her there—she would have loved that—he trotted all the way to the dressing rooms behind the Grand Hall with Jalani at his heels muttering about whether the horse had been a joke. Sulin was already there with a gold-embroidered red coat and the Dragon Scepter; the spearhead got an approving grunt, though no doubt she would have found it more acceptable without the green-and-white tassel and with a proper length of shaft and no carvings. Rand felt to be sure the *angreal* was in the pocket. It was, and he breathed more easily, though Lews Therin still seemed to be panting anxiously.

When Rand hurried through one of the lion-paneled dressing rooms into the Grand Hall, he discovered that everyone had been as quick as Sulin. Bael towered at one side of the throne dais with his arms folded, while Melaine stood on the other, calmly adjusting her dark shawl. What must have been a hundred or more Maidens lined the way from the doors on one knee, under Nandera's watchful gaze, complete with spears and bucklers, horn bows cased on their backs and full quivers at their hips. Only their eyes showed above black veils. Jalani ran to join one of those lines. Behind them more Aiel crowded among the thick columns, men and Maidens, though none appeared armed beyond their heavy-bladed knives. There were a number of grim faces, though. They could not be enjoying the thought of a confrontation with Aes Sedai, and not for fear of the Power. However Melaine and the other Wise Ones might speak of them now, most Aiel had that ancient failure of the Aiel firmly fixed in their heads.

Bashere was not there, of course—he and his wife were out at one of

Bashere's training camps—and neither were any of the Andoran nobles who flocked around the Palace. Rand was sure that Naean and Elenia and Lir and that entire lot would have learned of this gathering as soon as it began. They never missed an audience from the throne unless he sent them away. Their absence could only mean that on their way to the Grand Hall, they had learned the reason too, and that meant the Aes Sedai were already in the Palace.

Indeed, Rand had no sooner seated himself on the Dragon Throne with the Dragon Scepter on his knee than Mistress Harfor scurried into the Grand Hall looking flustered, quite unusual for her. Staring at him and all the Aiel with equal amazement, she said, "I sent servants everywhere to find you. There are Aes Sedai—" That was as far as she got before seven Aes Sedai appeared in the wide doorway.

Rand felt Lews Therin reaching for *saidin*, touching the *angreal*, but Rand took hold of it himself, holding that raging torrent of fire and ice, filth and sweetness, as hard as he did the piece of Seanchan spear.

Seven, Lews Therin mumbled darkly. *I told them three, and seven come. I must be cautious. Yes. Cautious.*

I said three, Rand snapped back at the voice. *Me! Rand al'Thor!* Lews Therin fell silent, but then the distant muttering began again.

Glancing from Rand to the seven women in their fringed shawls, Mistress Harfor apparently decided between was no place to be. The Aes Sedai received her first curtsy, Rand the second, and she walked with a good show of calm to one side of the doorway. When the Aes Sedai entered, though, forming a line abreast, she did slip out behind them with just a touch of haste.

On each of her three visits Merana had brought different Aes Sedai, and Rand recognized all but one of these, from Faeldrin Harella on the right, her dark hair in a multitude of thin braids worked with brightly colored beads, to stout Valinde Nathenos on the left in her white-fringed shawl and white dress. They were all clothed in their Ajah colors. He knew who the one he did not recognize must be. That coppery skin made the gracefully beautiful woman in dark bronze silk Demira Eriff, the Brown sister who Min had reported had taken to her bed. But she stood in the center of the line, a pace ahead of the others, while Merana stood between Faeldrin and plump, round-faced Rafela Cindal, who looked even more serious today than she had when he saw her with Merana six days ago. They all looked very serious.

For one moment they paused, looking at him impassively, ignoring the

Aiel; then they glided forward, first Demira, then Seonid and Rafela, then Merana and Masuri, forming an arrowhead pointed straight at Rand. He did not need the faint tingle in his skin to tell him they had embraced *saidar*. With every step each woman appeared noticeably taller than before.

They think to impress me spinning the Mirror of Mists? Lews Therin's incredulous laugh faded into mad giggles. Rand did not need the man's explanation; he had seen Moiraine do something like this once. Asmodean had called it the Mirror of Mists too, and also Illusion.

Melaine shifted her shawl irritably and sniffed loudly, but Bael suddenly looked as if he were facing, all alone, a charge by hundreds. He meant to stand against it, but he did not expect any good outcome. For that matter, some of the Maidens stirred until Nandera glared at them over her veil, and that did not stop the soft sound of shifting feet from the Aiel among the columns.

Demira Eriff began to speak, and plainly channeling was involved there too. She did not shout, but her voice filled the Grand Hall, seeming to come from everywhere. "Under the circumstances, it was decided that I should speak for all. We intend you no harm here today, but the strictures we accepted before, that you would feel safe, we must now reject. Obviously you have never learned the respect due Aes Sedai. You must learn it now. Henceforth we shall come and go as we please, saving only that at our choice, we will still inform you first in the future when we wish to speak with you. Your Aiel watchers around our inn must be removed, and no one is to watch or follow us. Any future insult to our dignity will be punished, though those we must punish are as children, and you will be responsible for their pain. This is how it must be. This is how it shall be. Know that we are Aes Sedai."

As that long arrowhead halted before the throne, Rand noticed Melaine glancing at him, frowning, no doubt wondering whether he was impressed. If he had not some notion of what was happening, he would have been; he was not sure he was not anyway. The seven Aes Sedai stood twice as tall as Loial, maybe more, heads nearly halfway to the vaulted ceiling with its colored-glass windows. Demira gazed down at him, cool and dispassionate, as if she might be contemplating picking him up in one hand, which she appeared big enough to do.

Rand made himself lean back casually, his mouth tightening when he realized that it had taken an effort, if not very great. Lews Therin chittered and screamed, but in the distance, something about not waiting, striking now. She had laid emphasis on certain words, as if he should understand the significance. Under what circumstances? They had accepted the restrictions before; why were they suddenly a breach of respect? Why did they suddenly decide that far from needing to make him feel safe, they could threaten? "The Tower emissaries in Cairhien accept the same constraints as you and do not seem offended." Well, not very offended. "Instead of vague threats, they offer gifts."

"They are not us. They are not here. We will not buy you."

The contempt in Demira's voice stung. Rand's knuckles ached from his grip on the Dragon Scepter. His anger had an echo from Lews Therin, and suddenly he realized the man was struggling again to reach the Source.

Burn you! Rand thought. He meant to shield them, but Lews Therin spoke, panting in near panic.

Not strong enough. Even with the angreal, *maybe not strong enough, not to hold seven. You fool! You waited too long! Too dangerous!*

Shielding anyone did take a fair amount of strength. With the *angreal*, Rand was sure he could make seven shields, even with them embracing *saidar* already; but if even one could break that shield. . . . Or more than one. He wanted to impress them with his strength, not give them a chance to overcome it. But there was another way. Weaving Spirit, Fire and Earth just so, he struck almost as if intending to shield.

Their Mirror of Mists shattered. Suddenly there were only seven normal women standing in front of him with stunned faces. Shock vanished behind Aes Sedai tranquility in an instant, however.

"You have heard our requirements," Demira said in a normal voice, but a commanding one, just as if nothing had happened at all. "We expect them to be met."

Rand stared in spite of himself. What did he have to do to show them he would not be browbeaten? *Saidin* raged in him, a boiling fury. He did not dare release it. Lews Therin was screaming maniacally now, trying to claw the Source out of his grip. It was all he could do to hold on. Slowly he stood. With the extra height of the dais, he towered over them. Seven unruffled Aes Sedai faces looked up at him. "The restrictions stand," he said quietly. "And one more requirement of my own. From now on I expect to see the respect I deserve from you. I am the Dragon Reborn. You may go now. The audience is at an end."

For perhaps ten heartbeats they stood there, not even blinking, as though to show they would not move a single slipper at his command. Then Demira turned without so much as a nod of her head. As she passed Seonid and Rafela, they fell in behind her, and the others in turn, all gliding smoothly, without hurry, across the red and white tiles and out of the Grand Hall.

Rand stepped down from the dais as they vanished into the corridor.

"The *Car'a'carn* handled them well," Melaine said, loudly enough to be heard in every corner. "They must be taken by the scruff of the neck and taught honor though they weep for it." Bael did not quite manage to hide his discomfort, hearing Aes Sedai spoken of so.

"Perhaps it is the way to handle Wise Ones too?" Rand asked, managing a smile.

Melaine lowered her voice, shifting her shawl emphatically. "Do not be a complete fool, Rand al'Thor."

Bael chuckled, though his wife glared at him. At least he had brought a chuckle. Rand did not feel the humor of the small joke, though, and not because of the buffering of the Void. He almost wished he had let Min come. There were too many undercurrents here he could not understand, and he was afraid there were some he did not even see. What were they really after?

Closing the small door of the dressing room, Min leaned back against a dark lion-carved wall panel and drew a very deep breath. Faile had come for Perrin, and however much Loial had protested that Rand wanted her to stay there, he had crumpled before the simple truth that Rand had no right to make her stay anywhere. Of course, if Loial had had any idea what she intended, he might have tucked her under his arm—quite gently, of course—and sat there in the courtyard reading to her.

The thing was, while she had heard everything, she had not seen very much, aside from Aes Sedai towering over throne and dais. They must have been channeling, which did tend to obscure the images and auras, but she had been so astounded she would not have noticed had any been present. By the time she recovered, they were no longer towering, and Demira's voice no longer boomed from every angle.

Chewing her underlip, she thought furiously. There were two problems, as she saw it. First, Rand and his demands for respect, whatever he meant by that. If he expected Merana to curtsy with her head to the floor, he was going to have a long wait, and in the meantime, he had surely put their backs up. There had to be some way she could smooth that over, if she could just see how. The second problem was the Aes Sedai. Rand seemed to think this was some sort of snit that he could end by putting his foot down. Min was not certain Aes Sedai had snits, but if they did, she was sure this was something more serious. The only place to find out, though, was The Crown of Roses.

Reclaiming Wildrose at the forecourt stable, she trotted the bay mare back to the inn and handed her over to a big-eared stableman with a request that the horse be rubbed down well and fed some oats. Her gallop to the Palace had been just that, and Wildrose deserved a reward for helping spike Merana and the others' scheme. From the cold fury in Rand's voice, she was not certain what would have happened had he suddenly learned out of a clear sky that seven Aes Sedai were awaiting him in the Grand Hall.

The common room of The Crown of Roses looked almost the same as when she had scuttled out through the kitchens earlier. Warders sat about at the tables, some playing dominoes or stones, others tossing dice. Almost as one they glanced up as she entered, and, recognizing her, went back to what they were doing. Mistress Cinchonine was standing in front of the wine-room door—no barrels of ale and wine stacked along the common-room wall in The Crown of Roses—with her arms folded and a sour expression on her face. The Warders were the only ones at the tables, and as a rule, Warders drank little and seldom. Any number of pewter mugs and cups stood on tables, but Min did not see one of them touched. She did see a man who might be willing to tell her a little.

Mahiro Shukosa sat at a table by himself working tavern puzzles, the two swords he usually wore on his back propped against the wall in easy reach. With graying temples and a noble nose, Mahiro was handsome in a rugged sort of way, though certainly only a woman in love would have called him beautiful. In Kandor he was a lord. He had visited the courts of almost every land, traveled with a small library, and won or lost gambling with the same easy smile. He could recite poetry and play the harp and dance like a dream. In short, except for being Rafela's Warder, he was exactly the sort of man she had liked before meeting Rand. Still liked, actually, when she could see them for thinking about Rand. Whether fortunately or unfortunately, Mahiro saw her in a way Min suspected might be peculiar to Kandor, as a sort of younger sister who occasionally needed someone to talk to and a little advice so she would not break her neck while sowing her wild oats. He told her she had pretty legs, would never think of touching them, and would break the neck of any man who did think of it without her permission.

Deftly slipping the intricate iron pieces back together, he placed the puzzle on a stack of those already worked and took up one from another stack as she sat down across from him. "So, cabbage," he said with a grin, "back with your neck unbroken, not kidnapped and not married." One day she was going to ask him what that meant; he always said it.

"Has anything happened since I went out, Mahiro?"

"You mean aside from the sisters returning from the Palace looking like a storm in the mountains." As usual, the puzzle came apart in his hands as though channeled.

"What upset them?"

"Al'Thor, I suppose." The puzzle went back together just as easily and joined the pile of discards; immediately one from the other pile did, too. "I worked that one years ago," he confided.

"But how, Mahiro? What happened?"

Dark eyes regarded her; a leopard's eyes would look like Mahiro's if they were nearly black. "Min, a yearling who puts her nose into the wrong den may have her ears bitten off."

Min winced. All too true. The fool things a woman did because she was in love. "That is what I would like to avoid, Mahiro. The only reason I'm here is to carry messages back and forth between Merana and the Palace, but I walk in there with no idea what I'm walking into. I don't know why the sisters stopped meeting him every day, or why they started back, or why a whole fistful went today instead of just three. I could get more than my ears bitten, not knowing. Merana isn't going to tell me. She doesn't tell me anything except go there, do that. Just a hint, Mahiro? Please?"

He began studying the puzzle, yet she knew he was thinking, because the interlocked pieces shifted about in his long fingers but nothing came loose.

A motion at the back of the common room caught her eye and she half-turned her head before her neck froze. Two Aes Sedai were coming back from the baths, by the freshly washed look of them. The last time she had seen that pair was months ago, before they were sent out from Salidar because Sheriam had a hunch Rand was in the Aiel waste somewhere. That was where Bera Harkin and Kiruna Nachiman had been headed; the Waste, not Caemlyn.

Except for her ageless face, Bera would have looked like a farmwife with her brown hair cut close around a square face, but at the moment that face was set in grim determination. Kiruna, elegant and statuesque, seemed every inch exactly what she was, sister to the King of Arafel and a powerful lady in her own right. Her large dark eyes gleamed as if she was about to order an execution and enjoy it. Images and auras flickered about them as always around Aes Sedai and Warders. One caught Min's eye when it flashed around both women at the same instant, brownish yellow and deep purple. The colors themselves meant nothing, but that aura made Min stop breathing.

The table was not far from the foot of the stairs, but the two women did not glance at Min as they turned to climb. Neither had ever given her more than two looks in Salidar, and now they were engrossed in their own conversation.

"Alanna should have brought him to heel long since." Kiruna's voice was low, yet close to open anger. "I would have. When she arrives, I will tell her so, and the Dark One take convention."

"He should be leashed," Bera agreed in a flat tone, "and before he can do more damage to Andor." She was Andoran. "The sooner, the better, I say."

As the pair sailed up the stairs, Min realized Mahiro was looking at her. "How did they get here?" she asked, and was surprised her voice sounded perfectly ordinary. Kiruna and Bera made thirteen. Thirteen Aes Sedai. And there was that aura.

"They followed word of al'Thor. They were halfway to Cairhien when they heard he was here. I would walk wide of them, Min. Their Gaidin tell me neither is in a good temper." Kiruna had four Warders, and Bera three.

Min managed a smile. She wanted to dart out of the inn, but that would raise all sorts of suspicions, even in Mahiro. "That sounds good advice. What about my hint?"

He hesitated another moment, then set the puzzle down. "I will not say what is or is not, but a word in a good ear. . . . Maybe you should expect al'Thor to be upset. Maybe you should even consider asking if someone else can deliver any messages, perhaps one of us." He meant the Warders. "Maybe the sisters have decided to teach al'Thor a small lesson in humility. And that, cabbage, is maybe a word more than I should have said. You will think on it?"

Min did not know whether the "small lesson" was what had happened at the Palace or something to come, but it all fit together. And that aura. "That sounds good advice too. Mahiro, if Merana comes looking for me to carry a message, will you tell her I am looking at the sights in the Inner City for the next few days?"

"A long journey," he chuckled, gently mocking. "You will kidnap a husband yet if you are not careful."

The big-eared ostler stared when Min insisted he root Wildrose out of her stall and saddle her again. She rode out of the stableyard at a walk, but as soon as the first turning hid The Crown of Roses, Min dug her heels and sent people leaping from her path as she galloped toward the Palace as fast as Wildrose could carry her.

"Thirteen," Rand said flatly, and just saying it was enough for Lews Therin to try seizing control of *saidin* from him again. It was a wordless struggle with a snarling beast. When Min first said there actually were thirteen Aes Sedai in Caemlyn, Rand had barely managed to seize the Power before Lews Therin could. Sweat rolled down Rand's face; there were dark patches on his coat. He only had room for concentrating on one thing. Keeping *saidin* away from Lews Therin. A muscle in his cheek jumped from the strain. His right hand trembled.

Min stopped pacing across his sitting-room carpet, and bounced on her toes. "It isn't only that, Rand," she said frantically. "It's the aura. Blood, death, the One Power, those two women and you, all in the same place at the same time." Her eyes were shining again, but this time tears leaked silently down her cheeks. "Kiruna and Bera do not like you, not at all! Remember what I saw around you? Women who can channel, hurting you. It is the auras, and the thirteen, and everything, Rand. It is too much!"

She always said her viewing always came true, though she could never tell whether in a day or a year or ten, and if he remained in Caemlyn, he thought it might be the day. Even with only a snarling in his head to go on, he knew Lews Therin wanted to strike at Merana and the others before they could strike at him. For that matter, the idea appealed uncomfortably to Rand. Maybe it was only happenstance, maybe his *ta'veren* twisting of chance had worked against him, but the fact remained. Merana had decided to challenge him on the very day the number of Aes Sedai reached thirteen.

Rising, he strode into his bedchamber long enough to fetch his sword from the back of the wardrobe and fasten the Dragon-shaped buckle. "You're coming with me, Min," he told her as he snatched up the Dragon Scepter and headed for the door.

"Coming where?" she demanded, wiping her cheeks with a handkerchief, but she did follow, and he was already in the hallway. Jalani bounced to her feet a touch more quickly than Beralna, a bony redhead with blue eyes and a feral grin.

With none but Maidens about, Beralna would stare at him as though considering whether to do him the great favor of doing as he asked, but he gave her a sharp stare of his own. The Void made his voice distant and cold. Lews Therin had subsided to muted whimpers, but Rand dared not relax. Not in Caemlyn; not anywhere near Caemlyn. "Beralna, find Nandera and tell her to meet me in Perrin's rooms with however many Maidens she wants to take." He could not leave Perrin behind, and not because of any viewing; when Merana found Rand gone, one of them might well bond Perrin the way Alanna had him. "I may not be coming back here. If anyone sees Perrin or Faile or Loial, tell them to meet me there too. Jalani, find Mistress Harfor. Tell her I need pen and ink and paper." He had letters to write before he left. His hand trembled again, and he added, "Lots of paper. Well? Go! Go!" They exchanged one look, and went at a run. He headed in the opposite direction, with Min almost trotting to keep up.

"Rand, where are we going?"

"Cairhien." With the Void around him, that came out cold as a slap in the face. "Trust me, Min. I won't hurt you. I will cut off my arm before I hurt you." She was silent, and he finally looked down to find her peering up at him with a strange expression.

"That's very nice to hear, sheepherder." Her voice was as odd as her face. The thought of thirteen Aes Sedai coming for him must have really frightened her, and small wonder.

"Min, if it comes down to facing them, I promise to send you away out of danger somehow." How could any man face thirteen? The thought made Lews Therin surge again, screaming.

To his surprise, she flourished those knives out of her coatsleeves and opened her mouth, but then slid the blades back just as smoothly—she must have been practicing—before she spoke. "You can lead me by the nose to Cairhien or anywhere else, sheepherder, but you better dig deep and try hard if you think to send me anywhere at all." For some reason, he was sure that was not what she had been going to say.

When they reached Perrin's rooms, Rand found quite a gathering. At one side of the sitting room Perrin and Loial were in shirtsleeves, cross-legged on the blue carpet and smoking their pipes with Gaul, a Stone Dog Rand remembered from the fall of the Stone. On the other side of the room sat Faile, also on the floor, with Bain and Chiad, who had also been at the Stone. Through the open door to the other room, Rand could see Sulin changing bed linens, flinging them about as though she would rather rip them to shreds. Everyone looked up when he and Min entered, and Sulin came to the bedchamber door.

There was a good bit of scrambling about once he explained about the thirteen Aes Sedai and what Min had overheard. Not the viewings, though; some in the room knew, some might not, and he was not going to tell anyone unless she did. Which she did not. And not about Lews Therin, of course; not that he was afraid of what might happen to him in a city with thirteen Aes Sedai even if they sat on their hands. Let them think he was panicky if they wished; he was not sure he was not. Lews Therin had gone silent, but Rand could feel him, like heated eyes watching in the night. Anger and fear, and maybe panic too, crawled outside the Void like large spiders.

Perrin and Faile immediately began a hasty packing, and Bain and Chiad flickered fingers at one another before announcing that they meant to accompany Faile, whereupon Gaul announced that he was accompanying Perrin. Rand did not understand what was going on there, but it involved a great deal of Gaul not looking at Bain or Chiad and them not looking at him. Loial went running off, muttering under his breath, as he thought about Cairhien being much farther from the Two Rivers than Caemlyn and his mother being a famous walker. When he returned, he had a half-done bundle under one arm and huge saddlebags over his shoulder, shirts hanging out. Loial was ready to go on the spot. Sulin vanished as well, coming back with a bundle in her arms that seemed made out of red-and-white dresses. With her face fixed in that incongruous mildness, she growled at Rand that she had been commanded to serve him *and* Perrin *and* Faile, and only a sun-crazed lizard would think she could do that in Caemlyn when they were all in Cairhien. She even added a "my Lord Dragon" that sounded a curse, and a curtsy, amazingly without a single wobble. The latter seemed to amaze her too.

Nandera arrived at almost the same instant as Mistress Harfor, who was carrying a writing case with several steel-nibbed pens and enough paper and ink and sealing wax for fifty letters. Which turned out to be fortunate.

Perrin wanted to send word to Dannil Lewin telling him to follow with the rest of the Two Rivers men—he did not intend to leave any of them for the Aes Sedai, either—and he only refrained from telling Dannil to bring Bode and the other girls from Culain's Hound when both Rand and Faile pointed out that in the first place, the Aes Sedai were not going to let them go, and in the second, it was not very likely they would want to. Perrin and she had both been to the inn more than once, and even Perrin had to admit that the girls mainly seemed impatient to get on with becoming Aes Sedai.

Faile herself had two hasty letters to write, to her mother and father, so they would not worry, she said. Rand did not know which was which, but they were very different in tone, the one begun half a dozen times then torn up, and every word frowned over, the other dashed off with smiles and chuckles. He thought that must be to her mother. Min wrote to a friend named Mahiro at The Crown of Roses, and for some reason made a point of telling Rand he was an old man, though she blushed at saying it. Even Loial took pen in hand after some hesitation. His own pen; a human pen would have vanished in his huge hands. Sealing his note, he handed it to Mistress Harfor with a diffident request that she deliver it personally if the chance arose. A thumb the size of a fat sausage covered most of the recipient's name, in both human script and Ogier, but with the One Power sharpening his eyes, Rand noticed the name "Erith." Still, he showed no sign of wanting to wait and give it to her himself.

Rand's own letters were as difficult as Faile's, but for different reasons. Sweat dripping from his face made the ink run, and his hand shook so that he had to start over more than once for inkblots. He knew exactly what he wanted to say, though. To Taim, a warning about thirteen Aes Sedai and a reiteration of his orders to stay away from them. And to Merana, a different sort of warning, and an invitation of a kind; it was no use him trying to hide; Alanna could find him anywhere in the world eventually. It had to be on his terms, though, if he could manage that.

When he finally sealed them—the presence of a greenstone seal carved with a Dragon earned Mistress Harfor a stare, which she returned with the utmost blandness—Rand turned to Nandera. "Do you have your twenty Maidens outside?"

Nandera's eyebrows rose. "Twenty? Your message said however many I wanted, and that you might not return. I have five hundred, and would have more had I not drawn the line."

He only nodded. In his head was silence except for his own thoughts, but he could *feel* Lews Therin, inside the Void with him, waiting like a coiled spring. Not until he had passed everyone through the gateway to the chamber in Cairhien and let the hole close, cutting his sense of Alanna to that vague impression of somewhere west, not until then did Lews Therin seem to go away. It was as if, wearied by grappling with Rand, the man had gone to sleep. At last Rand pushed *saidin* away, and with that he realized how wearied he had been by the struggle. Loial had to carry him to his rooms in the Sun Palace.

Merana sat quietly by the sitting-room window, her back to the view of the street and Rand al'Thor's letter on her lap. She knew its contents by heart.

Merana, it began. Not Merana Aes Sedai, nor even Merana Sedai.

> *Merana,*
>
> *A friend of mine once told me that in most dice games, the number thirteen is considered nearly as unlucky as rolling the Dark One's Eyes. I also think thirteen is an unlucky number. I am going to Cairhien. You may follow me as you can with no more than five other sisters. That way you will be on an equal footing with the emissaries from the White Tower. I will be displeased if you try to bring more. Do not press me again. I have little trust left in me.*
>
>

Rand al'Thor
The Dragon Reborn

At the end, his pen had pressed so hard that it nearly tore the paper; the last two lines almost seemed a different hand from the rest.

Merana sat very quietly. She was not alone. The rest of the embassy, if it could still be called that, sat in chairs around the walls, in various states. Irritatingly, only Berenicia sat as small as Merana, plump hands folded in her lap, head bowed slightly and grave eyes watchful; she did not say a word unless spoken to. Faeldrin sat quite proudly and spoke when she wished, and so did Masuri and Rafela. For that matter, Seonid appeared scarcely less eager, sitting on the edge of her chair and often smiling determinedly. The rest were more like Valinde, almost placid. Everyone was there except Verin and Alanna, and Gaidin had been sent to find them. Kiruna and Bera, standing in the middle of the floor, were most definitely there.

"That anyone could send such a letter to Aes Sedai disgusts me." Kiruna did not thunder; her voice managed to be cool and calm and forceful all at once. But her dark eyes did provide lightning. "Demira, can your informant confirm that al'Thor has gone to Cairhien?"

"Traveling," Bera murmured in disbelief. "To think that he would rediscover that."

The bright beads in Faeldrin's braids clicked as she nodded. "We can think of no other thing it can be. It will be well to remember that he is perhaps more powerful even than Logain, or Mazrim Taim, yes?"

"Can nothing be done about Taim?" Rafela's round face, normally mild and pleasant, was quite stern, and her usually sweet voice flat. "There are at least one hundred men who can channel—one hundred!—not twenty miles from where we sit." Kairen nodded resolutely but did not speak.

"They must wait," Kiruna said firmly. "Light and honor, I do not know how many sisters will be required to handle so many. Al'Thor is the important matter, and one we can handle. Demira?"

Demira had waited for the others to finish, of course. With a slight bow of her head, she said, "I know only that he is gone, apparently with a large number of Aiel, and possibly with Perrin Aybara as well."

Verin had slipped into the room as Demira began, and she added, "There can be no doubt of Perrin. I sent Tomas to look at the Two Rivers men's camp. It seems they have sent two men to the Palace for Perrin's horse, and his wife's. The rest have left the wagons and servants and are already riding east as hard as they can go. Behind Perrin's wolfhead, and the Red Eagle of Manetheren." A faint smile curved her lips as though she found that amusing. Kairen plainly did not; she gasped, then clamped her mouth shut in a hard line.

Merana did not find it amusing either, but it was such a small thing compared to the rest. A faint whiff of something spoiled when you already sat on a midden heap; a dog snarling at you when wolves already had hold of your skirts. To think that she had worried so over Verin, struggled so hard. Verin had hardly touched her own plans really, except for guiding Demira into suggesting today's unfortunate confrontation. It had been done quite skillfully; Merana did not believe anyone but a Gray would have noticed. Yet she herself had agreed even with that. Facing al'Thor down—trying to face him down—was the least they could have done. She had worried about Verin, and then Kiruna and Bera appeared, neither with any tie to her authority, both at least as strong as Masuri or Faeldrin or Rafela.

"Now, that's a rotten turnip tossed in the stew," Bera muttered grimly. Kairen and a number of others nodded agreement.

"A small turnip," Kiruna told her in a dry tone. Nearly everyone nodded, except Merana and Verin. Merana just sighed softly; Verin watched Kiruna with that birdlike gaze, her head tilted. "What is keeping Alanna?" Kiruna demanded of no one in particular. "I do not want to go over everything twice."

Merana supposed she herself had begun it, deferring to Verin. She had still been the head of the delegation, everyone still followed her orders, even Masuri and Rafela and Faeldrin. But they all knew. She was not certain yet whether Kiruna or Bera had taken charge—that one was born on a farm and the other in a palace mattered not at all; that had nothing to do with being Aes Sedai—but the one thing Merana was sure of was that the embassy was crumbling around her. It was the sort of thing that would never have happened when the White Tower was whole, when an ambassador had the full power of the Tower and the Amyrlin Seat behind her, and no matter if she had taken thirty years to reach the shawl and barely had enough strength to keep from being sent away. They were only a collection of Aes Sedai now, slipping into their relative places without thought.

As if speaking her name had been a summons, Alanna appeared just as Bera was opening her mouth. She and Kiruna rounded on Alanna together. "Al'Thor claims to have gone to Cairhien," Bera said baldly. "Can you add anything?"

Alanna faced them proudly, a dangerous gleam in her dark eyes. They were speaking of her Warder, after all. "He is somewhere to the east. That is all I know. It could be Cairhien."

"If you had to bond a man without asking him," Kiruna demanded in that commanding voice, "why, by the Light most holy, have you not used the bond to bend him to your will? Compared to the other, that is only slapping his wrist."

Alanna still had small control of her emotions. Color actually flooded her cheeks, partly in anger by the way her eyes flashed, and assuredly partly in shame. "Has no one told you?" she asked, too brightly. "I suppose no one wants to think of it. I certainly do not." Faeldrin and Seonid looked at the floor, and they were not the only ones. "I tried to compel him moments after I bonded him," Alanna continued as if noticing none of it. "Have you ever attempted to uproot an oak tree with your bare hands, Kiruna? It was much the same."

Kiruna's only reaction was a slow widening of her eyes, a slow deep breath. Bera actually muttered, "That's impossible. Impossible."

Alanna threw back her head and laughed. Her hands on her hips made the laughter seem contemptuous, which tightened Bera's mouth and brought a cold gleam to Kiruna's eyes. Verin peered at them, reminding Merana uncomfortably of a robin peering at worms. Somehow Verin seemed to defer without deferring, though Merana could not understand how.

"No one ever before has bonded a man who can channel," Alanna said when her mirth subsided. "Perhaps that has something to do with it."

"Be that as it may," Bera said firmly. Her gaze was just as firm. "Be that as it may. You can still locate him."

"Yes," Kiruna said. "You will come with us, Alanna." Alanna blinked as though coming to herself. Her head bowed slightly in acquiescence.

It was time, Merana decided. If she was to hold the delegation together, this was her last chance. She stood, folding al'Thor's letter to give her hands something to do. "When I brought this embassy to Caemlyn," she began, to remind them all that she *was* the head; thank the Light that her voice was steady, "I was given great leeway, yet it seemed obvious what should be done, and we," to remind them they were a delegation, "set about it with a fair expectation of success. Al'Thor was to be enticed out of Caemlyn so that we could return Elayne and see her crowned, placing Andor firmly behind us. Slowly al'Thor was to be brought to trust us, that we would not harm him. And he would have been brought to show a proper respect as well. Two or three of us, carefully selected, would have taken Moiraine's place advising and guiding him. Including Alanna, of course."

"How do you know he did not kill Moiraine," Bera interrupted, "as he is said to have killed Morgase?"

"We have heard every sort of rumor concerning her death," Kiruna added. "Some even say she died fighting Lanfear. Most say she was alone with al'Thor when she died."

With an effort, Merana stopped herself from answering. If she allowed those ingrained instincts a word, they would take them all in the end. "All that was in hand," she went on, "when you two arrived. Only by chance, I know, and only following your instructions to find him, yet you brought our number to thirteen. What man of al'Thor's sort would not flee as fast as he could hearing of thirteen Aes Sedai together? The simple fact is, whatever damage has been done to our plans must be laid at your feet, Kiruna, and yours, Bera." She could only wait then. If she had managed to gain any moral ascendancy at all. . . .

"Are you quite finished?" Bera said coolly.

Kiruna was even more blunt. She turned to the others. "Faeldrin, you will come with us to Cairhien, if you will. And you also, Masuri, Rafela."

Merana trembled, the folded letter crumpling in her fist. "Don't you see?" she shouted. "You talk as if we can go on as before, as if nothing has changed. There is an embassy from Elaida in Cairhien, from the White

Tower. That is how al'Thor must see it. We need him more than he needs us, and I fear he knows it!"

For a moment, shock covered every face save Verin's. Verin only nodded thoughtfully, smiling a small, secretive smile. For a moment, every other face was full of wide eyes, stunned. Those words seemed to ring in the air. *We need him more than he needs us.* They did not need the Three Oaths to know it for truth.

Then Bera said quite firmly, "Sit down, Merana, and calm yourself." Merana was sitting before she realized it; still trembling, still wanting to shout, but sitting with her hands clutched together around al'Thor's missive.

Kiruna turned her back deliberately. "Seonid, you will come, of course. Another pair of Gaidin are always useful. And Verin, I think." Verin nodded as if it were a request. "Demira," Kiruna went on, "I know you have grievance against him, but we do not want to panic the man again, and someone must shepherd that extraordinary collection of girls from the Two Rivers to Salidar. You, Valinde, Kairen and Berenicia must assist Merana in that."

The other four named murmured acceptance without the slightest hesitation, but Merana felt cold. The delegation was not crumbling; it was gone to dust.

"I. . . ." She trailed off as Bera's gaze turned to her, and Kiruna's. And Masuri's and Faeldrin's and Rafela's as well. Gone to dust, and all her authority with it. "You may find some need for a Gray," she said faintly. "There will certainly be negotiations, and. . . ." Words failed her again. This would *never* have happened when the Tower was whole.

"Very well," Bera said at last, in such a tone that all Merana's control only just kept her cheeks from going crimson in shame.

"Demira, you will see the girls to Salidar," Kiruna said.

Merana sat very still. She prayed that the Hall had chosen an Amyrlin by now. Someone very strong, in the Power and in her heart. It would take another Deane, another Rashima, to make them once more what they had been. She prayed Alanna led them to al'Thor before he decided to acknowledge Elaida. Even another Rashima would not save them then.

CHAPTER
50

Thorns

R and spent the rest of that day in his apartments in the Sun Palace, a good part lying on his bed, a huge thing with four square blackwood posts thicker than his leg, polished till they shone between the inlaid ivory wedges. As if to contrast with all the gilding in the anteroom and sitting room, the bedchamber furnishings were all blackwood and ivory, if no less angular.

Sulin rushed in and out, fluffing his feather pillows and adjusting the linen sheet over him, grumbling that blankets on the floor were healthier, bringing him mint tea he did not ask for and punch he did not want, until he ordered her to stop. "As my Lord Dragon commands," she growled through a sweet smile. She made her second perfect curtsy, but she still stalked out as though she might not bother to open the door.

Min also stayed with him, sitting on the mattress and holding his hand and frowning until he suspected she thought he was dying. Finally he chased her out too, long enough to put on a dark gray silk robe that he had always left in the wardrobe before. He found something else in there as well, way in the back. A narrow, plain wooden case holding a flute, a gift from Thom Merrilin in what seemed another lifetime. Sitting by one of the tall narrow windows, he tried playing. After so long, he produced more squeaks and silences than anything else at first. It was the odd sounds that drew Min back.

"Play for me," she said, laughing in delight, or perhaps astonishment, and of course settled herself on his knee while he tried with small success to produce something near a recognizable tune. Which was how the Wise Ones walked in on him, Amys and Bair and Sorilea and a dozen or so more. Min scrambled up quickly enough blushing at that, tugging her coat straight to such an extent you would have thought they had been wrestling.

Bair and Sorilea were at his side before he could say a word.

"Look left," Sorilea commanded, thumbing back his eyelid and thrusting her leathery face into his, "Look right."

"Your pulse is too quick," Bair muttered, holding bony fingers against the side of his throat.

It seemed that Nandera had sent a Maiden running as soon as his knees gave way. It seemed that Sorilea had winnowed the small army of Wise Ones who had intended to descend on the palace into this smaller horde. And it seemed that Sorilea or no Sorilea, everyone wanted her turn at the Car'a'carn. When she and Bair were done, her place was taken by Amys, and Bair's by Colinda, a lean woman with penetrating gray eyes who looked short of her middle years yet had almost as strong a presence as Sorilea. But then, so did Amys, of course, and any number of them. He was poked, prodded, stared at, and called stubborn when he refused to jump up and down. They really seemed to think he would.

Min was not ignored while the Wise Ones were taking their turns with him; the others surrounded her, asking a hundred questions, all about her viewings. Which widened her eyes to say the least, and had her staring at them *and* Rand as if wondering whether her mind was being read. Amys and Bair explained—Melaine had not been able to keep the news of her daughters to herself—and instead of growing any wider, which they probably could not at that point, Min's eyes looked ready to fall out of her face. Even Sorilea seemed to accept Melaine's view that Min's ability put her on an equal footing of sorts with them, but Wise Ones being Wise Ones— very much in the manner of Aes Sedai being Aes Sedai—she had to repeat everything nearly as many times as there were Wise Ones, because those fussing over him at any given time wanted to be sure they had not missed anything.

Once Sorilea and the rest reluctantly concluded that all he needed was rest, and departed ordering him to see that he got it, Min made herself comfortable on his lap again. "They talk in *dreams*?" she said, shaking her head. "It doesn't seem possible, like something out of a story." A frown creased her forehead. "How old do you think Sorilea is? And that Colinda. I

saw— No. No, it doesn't have anything to do with you. Maybe the heat is
affecting me. When I know, I *always* know. It must be the heat." A mischievous light appeared in her eyes, and she slowly leaned closer, pursing her
lips as if for a kiss. "If you put them like this," she murmured when they
were almost touching his, "it might help. There were bits in that last piece
that almost sounded like 'Rooster in the Gumtree.'" It took him a moment
to understand, with her eyes filling his vision, and when he did, his face
must have been a sight, because she collapsed on his chest laughing.

A note arrived from Coiren a short time later, inquiring after his
health, wishing he was not ill, and asking whether she might come to see
him with two of her sisters; she offered Healing, should he desire. Lews
Therin stirred as if rousing from sleep while Rand read, but his vague,
discontented mumbling was hardly a patch on his rage in Caemlyn, and he
seemed to go back to sleep when Rand put the short letter down.

It was a sharp contrast to how Merana had behaved. And a reminder
that nothing happened in the Sun Palace at midday that Coiren did not
know in full before sunset, if not sooner. He sent back polite thanks for
her wishes, and a polite refusal. Out of bed or not, he still felt tired, and
he wanted his wits about him when he faced any Aes Sedai. That was part
of it.

In that same return note Rand also asked Gawyn to visit. He had only
met Elayne's brother once, but he liked the man. Gawyn never came,
though, and he never replied. Sadly, Rand concluded that Gawyn believed
the stories about his mother. That was hardly the sort of thing you could
just ask a man to stop believing. It put him in a such a gray humor whenever he thought of it that even Min seemed to despair of cheering him;
neither Perrin nor Loial would stay around him when he was like that.

Three days later another request came from Coiren, just as courteous,
and a third three days after that, but he made excuses for those as well. In
part that was because of Alanna. The feel of her was still distant and
vague, but she was coming nearer by the hour. No surprise in that; he had
been sure Merana would choose Alanna for one of the six. He had no intention of letting Alanna within a mile of him, or not within sight anyway,
but he had said he would put them on an equal footing with Coiren, and
he meant it. So Coiren would have to abide in patience for a little while.
Besides, he was busy, one way and another.

A quick visit to the school in Barthanes' onetime palace turned out not
so quick. Idrien Tarsin was once again waiting at the door to show him all

sorts of inventions and discoveries, often incomprehensible, and also the shops where various new plows and harrows and reapers were now being made for sale, but the difficulty was Herid Fel. Or maybe Min. Fel's thoughts wandered as usual, his tongue wandered after them, and he plainly forgot Min was there. He forgot her a good many times. But no sooner would Rand have the man aimed at a point, than Fel suddenly noticed her for the first time again and gave a great start. He was constantly apologizing to her for the half-smoked pipe he still never seemed to remember to light, constantly brushing ash from his stout belly, constantly smoothing his thin gray hair. Min seemed to enjoy it, though why she enjoyed a man forgetting her presence, Rand could not begin to say. She even kissed Fel on top of his head when she and Rand rose to go, which left the man looking poleaxed. It did not help a great deal with learning what Fel had puzzled out about the Seals on the Dark One's prison or the Last Battle.

The next day brought a note crammed onto a torn-off corner of parchment.

Belief and order give strength. Have to clear rubble before you can build. Will explain when see you next. Do not bring girl. Too pretty.

Fel

It was a hasty scrawl with the signature jammed into the point of the fragment, and to Rand it made no sense. When he tried to reach Fel again, though, it seemed that the man had told Idrien that he felt young again and was going fishing. In the middle of a drought. Rand wondered whether the old man's wits had finally cracked. Min certainly found the note amusing; she asked if she could have it, and several times he caught her grinning over it.

Cracked wits or whole, Rand decided that he would leave Min behind the next time, but in truth, it was difficult to keep her at his side when he wanted her. She seemed to spend more time with the Wise Ones than with him. He could not understand why that should irritate him so, but he noticed a tendency to snap at people when Min was out among the tents. It was a good thing she was not with him too often. People would notice. People would talk, and wonder. In Cairhien, where even the servants played their own version of the Game of Houses, it could be dangerous for her to have people wondering whether she was important. A good thing. He tried not to snap.

What he wanted Min for, of course, was to view the nobles who began coming to him one at a time, asking after his health—those sagging knees must have started rumors—smiling, inquiring how long he intended to remain in Cairhien this time, what his plans were if they might ask, smiling more, always smiling. The only one who did not smile at him so intently was Dobraine, still with the front of his head shaved like a soldier and the stripes across his coat worn by the breastplate he did not wear to the palace, and Dobraine was so glum in asking exactly the same questions that Rand was almost happier to see him go than any of the others.

Min did manage to be at those audiences, squeezing it in between whatever she was doing with the Wise Ones; Rand had no intention of asking. The problem was keeping her hidden.

"I could just pretend to be your lightskirt," Min laughed. "I could drape myself on you and feed you grapes—well, raisins; I haven't seen a grape in some time—and you could call me your little honey-lips. Nobody would wonder why I was there then."

"No," he snapped, and her face grew solemn.

"Do you really think the Forsaken would come after me just for that?"

"They might," he told her just as seriously. "A Darkfriend like Padan Fain would, if he's still alive. I won't risk that, Min. In any case, I won't have these filthy-minded Cairhienin thinking of you that way, or the Tairens either." The Aiel were different; they thought her teasing very funny, very amusing indeed.

Min certainly was changeable. She went straight from solemn to radiant with no in-between, all smiles that hardly faded for a moment. Until the audiences actually began.

A paneled screen of gilded fretwork set up in the corner of the anteroom was a failure. Maringil's dark glittering eyes avoided looking at it to such an extent that Rand knew the man would turn the Sun Palace end over end to find out who or what it hid. The sitting room turned out better, with Min peeping through cracked doors into the anteroom, but not everyone showed image or aura to her eyes during the audience with him, and what she did see, there and simply walking about in the hallways, was bleak. Maringil, white-haired and blade-slim and cool as ice, was going to die by poison. Colavaere, her more than handsome face calm and collected once she learned Aviendha was not with Rand this time, would die by hanging. Meilan, with his pointed beard and oily voice, would die by the knife. The future carried a heavy toll for the High Lords of Tear. Aracome and Maraconn and Gueyam were all going to die too, bloody deaths, in battle, Min thought. She said she had never seen death so often in one group of people.

By the time she saw blood covering Gueyam's broad face, their fifth day in Cairhien, she felt so ill at the thought that Rand made her lie down and had Sulin bring damp cloths to lay on her forehead. This time he was the one to sit on the mattress and hold her hand. She held on very tight.

She did not give up her teasing, though. The two times he could be absolutely sure she would be there were when he practiced the sword, dancing the forms with four or five of the best he could find among the Tairen and Cairhienin soldiers, and when he and Rhuarc or Gaul were tossing each other about and trying to kick each other in the head. Inevitably Min ran a finger across his bare chest and made some joke about sheepfarmers not sweating because they were used to having wool as thick as their sheep or the like. Sometimes she touched the half-healed, never-healing scar on his side, that circle of pale pink flesh, but differently, softly; she never made any jokes about that. She pinched his bottom—startling to say the least when other people were about; Maidens and Wise Ones nearly fell over laughing every single time he jumped; Sulin looked as if she might burst from not laughing—snuggled in his lap and kissed him at every opportunity, she even threatened to come scrub his back in his bath one of these nights. When he pretended to weep and stammer, she laughed and said it was not good enough.

Min did quit quickly enough if a Maiden stuck her head in to announce someone, especially Loial, who never stayed long and talked of the Royal Library the whole time, or Perrin, who stayed even more briefly and for some reason looked increasingly tired. Most especially Min leaped up if Faile happened to be with either one. The two times that happened, Min hastily found a book among those Rand had in the bedchamber and sat pretending to read, opening it somewhere in the middle as if she had been at it for some time. Rand did not understand the cool looks the two women exchanged. It was not precisely animosity, or even unfriendliness exactly, but Rand suspected that if either made a list of those she would just as soon not spend time with, the other's name would be prominent.

The amusing thing of it was, the second time, the book turned out to be the leather-bound first volume of Daria Gahand's *Essays on Reason*, which he had found heavy going and intended to send back to the Library the next time Loial stopped in. Min actually went on reading for a time after Faile left, and for all her frowning and muttering, that night Min took it back to her own rooms in the guest apartments.

If cool disinterest reigned between Min and Faile, between Min and Berelain animosity was not in it. When Somara announced Berelain on the second afternoon, Rand put on his coat, strode into the anteroom and took the tall gilded chair on the dais before telling Somara to admit her. Min was slow in reaching the sitting room, though. Berelain swept in, as beautiful as ever, in a soft blue dress cut as deeply as ever—and her eyes fell on Min, in her pale rose coat and breeches. For several long moments Rand might as well not have existed. Berelain openly eyed Min up and down. Min forgot about the sitting room; she put her hands on her hips and stood there with one knee bent, studying Berelain just as openly. They smiled at each other; Rand thought the hair on his head would stand up when they did that. He was minded of nothing so much as two strange cats who had just discovered they were shut up in the same small room. Apparently deciding there was no point hiding now, Min walked—undulated would have been a better word; she managed to make Berelain's way of walking look like a boy's!—and sat with one knee over the other, still smiling. Light, how those women did smile.

At last Berelain turned to Rand, spreading her skirts wide and bending low. He heard Lews Therin humming in his head, enjoying the sight of a very beautiful woman who was more than generous in displaying her charms. Rand appreciated what he was seeing too, despite wondering whether he should look away at least until she was erect again, but he had put himself on the dais for a reason. He tried to make his voice both reasonable and firm.

"Rhuarc let slip that you were neglecting your duties, Berelain. It seems you hid away in your rooms for days after I was last here. I gather he had to speak to you severely to make you come out." Rhuarc had not actually said so, but that had been the impression. Crimson bloomed in her cheeks, suggesting Rand had the right of it. "You know why you are in charge here and not him. You're supposed to listen to his advice, not leave everything to him. I don't need Cairhienin deciding to rebel because they think I've put an Aiel to rule them."

"I was . . . concerned, my Lord Dragon." Despite the hesitation, and the red cheeks, her voice was composed. "Since the Aes Sedai came, rumors grow like weeds. May I ask, who *do* you mean to rule here?"

"Elayne Trakand. The Daughter-Heir of Andor. The Queen of Andor, now." Soon, at least. "I don't know what rumors you mean, but you worry about putting Cairhien straight, and let me worry about the Aes Sedai.

Elayne will be grateful for what you do here." Min sniffed quite loudly for some reason.

"She is a good choice," Berelain said thoughtfully. "The Cairhienin will accept her, I think, perhaps even the rebels in the hills." That was good to hear; Berelain was astute at judging political currents, maybe as good as any Cairhienin. She took a deep breath, making Lews Therin's hum pause. "As for the Aes Sedai . . . rumor says they have come to escort you to the White Tower."

"And *I* said, leave the Aes Sedai to me." It was not that he mistrusted Berelain. He trusted her to rule Cairhien until Elayne took the Sun Throne, he even trusted her not to have any ambitions for the throne herself. But he also knew that the fewer who were aware he had any plan at all regarding the Aes Sedai, the less chance that Coiren would learn he had a thought beyond her gold and jewels.

As soon as the doors closed behind Berelain, Min sniffed again. Actually, it was more of a snort this time. "I wonder she bothers to wear any clothes at all. Well, she'll be snubbed up sooner or later. I saw nothing of any use to you. Just a man in white who will make her fall head over heels. Some women have no shame at all!"

That very afternoon she asked him for coin to engage a whole roomful of seamstresses, since she had come away from Caemlyn with only what she stood in, and they proceeded to produce a stream of coats and breeches and blouses in silks and brocades of all colors. Some of the blouses seemed quite low-cut, even beneath a coat. Some of the breeches, he was not sure how she could get into. She also practiced throwing her knives every day. Once he saw Nandera and Enaila showing her their way of fighting with hands and feet, which differed significantly from how the men did it; the Maidens did not like him watching, and refused to go on until he left. Maybe Perrin would have understood it all, but Rand decided for the thousandth time that he himself did not understand women and never would.

Every day Rhuarc came to Rand's apartments or Rand went to the study Rhuarc shared with Berelain. Rand was pleased to see her hard at work over reports of grain shipments and resettlement of refugees and repairs to damage from what some Cairhienin were calling the Second Aiel War, in spite of every effort to name it the Shaido War. Rhuarc claimed to have decided to ignore the Cairhienin playing, as he called it, at *ji'e'toh*, though he still grumbled every time he saw a Cairhienin woman with a sword or young men and women garbed all in white. The rebels still seemed to be sitting in the hills waiting, their numbers growing, but they did not concern him either. What did concern him were the Shaido, and how many spears still moved south each day toward Tear. Scouts, those who returned, reported the Shaido stirring in Kinslayer's Dagger. There was no sign of which direction they intended to move or when. Rhuarc actually mentioned the number of Aiel who still gave way to the bleakness and tossed down their spears, the number who refused to put off *gai'shain* white when their time was done, even those few who still headed north to join the Shaido. It was a sign of his unease. Surprisingly, Sevanna had been in the tents, even in the city itself, leaving the day after Rand arrived. Rhuarc only mentioned it in passing.

"Would it not have been better to seize her?" Rand asked. "Rhuarc, I know she is supposed to be a Wise One, but she can't be, the way I understand it. I'd not be surprised if the Shaido turned reasonable without her."

"I doubt that," Rhuarc said dryly. He was seated on one of his cushions against the study wall, smoking his pipe. "Amys and the others pass looks behind Sevanna's back, but they receive her as a Wise One. If the Wise Ones say Sevanna is a Wise One, then she is. I have seen chiefs I would not waste a waterskin on if I stood between ten pools, but they were still chiefs."

Sighing, Rand studied the map spread on the table. Rhuarc truly did not seem to need it; without looking he could name any feature of the terrain the map showed. Berelain sat in her high-backed chair on the other side of the table, her feet curled up beneath her and a sheaf of papers on her lap. She had a pen in her hand, and an ink jar stood on the small table beside her chair. Every so often she glanced at him, but whenever she saw Rhuarc looking she would bend her head over the reports again. For some reason, Rhuarc frowned whenever he looked at her, and she always blushed and firmed her jaw stubbornly. Sometimes Rhuarc looked disapproving, which made no sense. She was taking care of her duties now.

"You will have to stop sending spears south," Rand said at last. He did not like it. It was vital that Sammael see the biggest hammer in the world coming at him, but not at the cost of having to root the Shaido out of Cairhien again. "I don't see any other way."

The days passed, and every one filled somehow. He had smiling lords and ladies so cordial to one another that he was sure they were scheming against each other beneath the surface. Wise Ones counseled him on how to deal with Aes Sedai, whether from the Tower or Salidar; Amys and Bair made Melaine appear mild; Sorilea made his blood run cold. Young

Cairhienin rioted in the streets against Rhuarc's ban on dueling. Rhuarc handled it by giving them a taste of what it was really like to be made *gai'shain*; sitting naked in the sun all day under guard quenched their ardor somewhat, but Rhuarc was not about to go against custom so far as to put wetlanders in white, and those the Red Shields had caught actually began to swagger over the affair. Rand overheard Selande telling another young woman with a sword and her hair cut short, in a very self-important tone, that the other woman would never truly understand *ji'e'toh* until she had been captive to Aiel. It was uplifting, whatever that was supposed to mean.

But despite Shaido and nobles, Wise Ones and riot, despite wondering whether Fel was ever going to come back from fishing, those days seemed . . . pleasant. Refreshing. Maybe it was just because he had been so tired on arrival. And maybe it really was only by comparison with those last hours in Caemlyn, yet it did seem that Lews Therin was quieter. Rand even found himself enjoying Min's teasing enough that once or twice he had to remind himself that it was only teasing. By the time he had been ten days in Cairhien, he thought this would not be such a bad way to spend the rest of his life. Of course, he knew it could not last.

For Perrin those ten days were not pleasant at all. Before very long he sought Loial's company, but Loial had found a paradise in the Royal Library, where he spent the better part of every daylight. Perrin liked to read, and he might have enjoyed those seemingly endless rooms full of books to their high vaulted ceilings, but an Aes Sedai haunted those rooms, a slender dark-haired woman who seldom seemed to blink. She did not appear to notice him, but he had not been particularly trusting of Aes Sedai even before events in Caemlyn. With Loial's company largely denied to him, Perrin went hunting a great deal with Gaul, and a few times with Rhuarc, who he had met in the Stone and liked. Perrin's problem was his wife. Or maybe it was Berelain. Or both. If Rand had not been so busy, Perrin would have asked his advice. In a general sort of way; Rand knew women, but there were things a man simply could not talk about right out.

It began that very first day, when he had been in Cairhien scarcely long enough to be shown to rooms in the Sun Palace. Faile went off with Bain and Chiad to explore, and he was stripped to the waist and washing when he suddenly smelled perfume, not heavy but strong to his nose, and a warm voice behind him said, "I always did think you must have a beautiful back, Perrin."

He spun around so fast he nearly knocked over the washstand.

"I hear that you have come with . . . a wife?" Berelain stood in the door to the sitting room, smiling.

Yes, he had; a wife who would not be pleased at finding him alone and shirtless with any woman wearing that dress. Especially not the First of Mayene. Tugging a shirt over his head, he told Berelain that Faile was out, that he did not know when she would be back for visitors, and put *her* out into the hall as fast as he could without picking her up and tossing her. He thought it was done with; Berelain was gone, and he had managed to call Faile wife six times in as many sentences and say how much he loved her twice. Berelain knew he was married, knew he loved his wife, and that should have been that.

When Faile returned a short time later, she took two steps into the bedchamber and began radiating the smells of jealousy and rage, prickly and knife-sharp, a blend that should have made his nose bleed. Perrin did not understand; he could still smell Berelain's perfume, but his sense of smell was nearly as acute as a wolf's. Surely Faile could not. It was very strange. Faile smiled. Not one untoward word passed her lips. She was as loving as ever, and even more fierce than usual, raking deep furrows into his shoulders with her fingernails, which she had never done before.

Afterwards, examining the bleeding gouges by lamplight, she nipped his ear between her teeth, not at all lightly, and laughed. "In Saldaea," she murmured, "we notch a horse's ears, but I think that will do to mark you." And the whole while she fairly reeked of jealousy and rage.

If that had been all, matters would have settled down. Faile's jealousy might flare up like a forge fire roaring in a high wind, yet it always died just as fast as it caught, once she realized there was no cause. The very next morning, though, he saw her talking to Berelain down the corridor, both smiling to beat anything. His ears caught the last thing Berelain said before she turned away. "I always keep my promises." An odd remark to send that acrid thorny smell leaping from Faile.

He asked Faile what promises Berelain was talking about, and maybe that was a mistake. She blinked—she did forget his hearing sometimes—and said, "I really do not remember. She's the sort of woman who makes all sorts of promises she cannot keep." His shoulders got a *second* set of furrows, and it was not even midmorning!

Berelain began stalking him. He did not think of it that way at first. The woman had flirted with him once, in the Stone of Tear, in a mild sort of way, not really meaning anything he was sure, and she knew he was married now. It was only a series of chance encounters in hallways, it seemed, a few innocuous words almost in passing. But after a while he knew either his being *ta'veren* was twisting chance completely out of shape or Berelain was arranging matters, unlikely as that seemed. He tried telling himself that was ridiculous. He tried telling himself he must think he was handsome as Wil al'Seen. Wil was the only man he had ever seen women chase after; they certainly never had after Perrin Aybara. There were just too many of those "chance" encounters, though.

She always touched him. Not blatantly, just fingers on his hand for a moment, on his arm, his shoulder. Hardly worth noticing. The third day a thought occurred that made the hair on the nape of his neck rise. When you were taming a horse that had never been ridden, you began with light touches, until the animal knew your touch would not hurt, until it stood still for your hand. After that came the saddlecloth, and later the saddle. The bridle was always last.

He began to dread the scent of Berelain's perfume, wafting around a corner. He began to head in the opposite direction at the first whiff, only he could not give every moment to watching for it. For one thing, there seemed to be a great many swaggering young Cairhienin fools going in and out of the palace, most of them women. Women carrying swords! He walked around any number of men and women who planted themselves deliberately in his path. Twice he had to knock a fellow down when the idiot simply would not let him walk around, but kept dancing back in front of him. He felt bad about that—Cairhienin were nearly all considerably smaller than he—but you could not take chances with a man who had his hand on his sword hilt. Once a young woman tried that, and after he took her sword away, she made a nuisance of herself until he gave it back, which seemed to shock her, then shouted after him that he had no honor, until some Maidens led her off, talking to her fiercely.

For another thing, people knew he was Rand's friend. Even had he not arrived as he did, some of the Aiel and Tairens remembered him from the Stone, and word spread. Lords and ladies he had never seen in his life introduced themselves in hallways, and Tairen High Lords who had stared down their noses at him in Tear addressed him like an old friend in Cairhien. Most smelled of fear, and an odor he could not put a name to. They all wanted the same thing, he realized.

"I'm afraid the Lord Dragon doesn't always take me into his confidence, my Lady," he said politely to a cold-eyed woman named Colavaere, "and when he does, you wouldn't expect me to break that confidence." Her smile seemed to come from a great height; she seemed to be wondering how he would skin out for a lap rug. She had a strange smell, hard and smooth and somehow . . . high.

"I don't really know what Rand intends to do," he told Meilan. The man very nearly repeated his nose-staring, for all he smiled nearly as much as Colavaere. He had the smell too, just as potently. "Maybe you should ask him."

"If I did know, I'd hardly talk it all over the city," he told a white-haired weasel with too many teeth, a fellow called Maringil. By then he was growing tired of attempts to milk him. Maringil also gave off the smell, every bit as heavily as Colavaere or Meilan.

They three carried it far more than anyone else, a dangerous smell, he knew in his bones, like a dry mountain top before an avalanche.

Between keeping an eye out for young idiots and having that smell in his nose, he could not recognize Berelain's scent until she had crept close enough to pounce. Well, truth to tell, she glided up along the hallways, a swan on a smooth pond, but it certainly felt like being pounced on.

He mentioned Faile more times than he could count; Berelain did not seem to hear. He asked her to stop; Berelain asked him whatever did he mean? He told her to leave him alone; Berelain laughed and patted his cheek and asked what she was to stop doing. Which of course had to be the exact moment that Faile came out of the next crossing corridor, just the instant *before* he jerked back. It must have seemed to Faile that he moved away because he saw her. Without a moment's hesitation, Faile turned smoothly on her heel, her pace not a whit slower or faster.

He ran after her, caught up and walked alongside in pained silence. A man could hardly say what he had to say where people could hear. Faile smiled quite pleasantly all the way back to their rooms, but oh, that thorny, thorny, thorny scent in his nose.

"That wasn't what it looked like," he said as soon as the door was closed. Not a word out of her; her eyebrows just rose in a silent question. "Well, it was—Berelain patted my cheek—" Still smiling, but eyebrows lowered darkly, and sharp anger among the thorns. "—but she just did it. I didn't encourage her, Faile. She just did it." He wished Faile would say something; she only stared. He thought she was waiting, but for what? Inspiration took him by the throat, and as so often seemed to happen when he was talking to her, put a noose around it. "Faile, I'm sorry." Anger became a razor.

"I see," she said flatly, and glided out of the room.

So, both feet put wrong; straight into his mouth, it seemed, though he could not understand how. He had apologized, and he had not even done anything to apologize for.

That afternoon he overheard Bain and Chiad discussing whether they should help Faile beat him, of all things! No telling whether Faile had suggested it—she was fierce, but was she that fierce?—yet he suspected the pair meant him to hear, which made him angry. Plainly his wife was discussing affairs between him and her with them, matters which should have remained between husband and wife, which made him angrier. What other parts of their life did she chat about over tea? That night, as he watched in amazement, Faile put on a thick wool nightgown despite the heat. When he tried to kiss her cheek, almost timidly, she muttered that she had had a tiring day and rolled over with her back to him. She smelled furious, sharp enough to split a razor edgewise.

He could not sleep with that smell, and the longer he lay there beside her, studying the ceiling in the darkness, the angrier he became. Why was she doing this? Could she not see he loved her and only her? Had he not shown her time and again that what he wanted more than anything in life was to hold her forever? Was he to blame because some fool woman got a bee up her nose and wanted to flirt? What he ought to do was turn her upside down and smack her bottom till she saw sense. Only he had done that once before, when she thought she could hit him with her fist whenever she wanted to make a point. In the long run it had hurt him a lot more than it had her; he did not like even the thought of Faile being hurt. He wanted peace with her. With her and only her.

Which was why he made the decision he made lying there with gray first light of their sixth day in Cairhien showing in the windows. In the Stone, Berelain had flirted with a dozen men that he knew of; whatever had made her choose him as her quarry, she would settle on another if he was out of sight for very long. And once Berelain chose another victim, Faile would come to her senses. It seemed simple.

So as soon as he could throw on some clothes he went off to find Loial and breakfast with him, then accompanied him to the Royal Library. And once he saw that slender Aes Sedai and Loial told him she was there every day—Loial was diffident around Aes Sedai, but he did not mind fifty of them around him—Perrin sniffed out Gaul and asked whether he would like to go hunting. There were not many deer or rabbits in the hills close to the city, of course, and those few suffering as much from the drought as the people, yet Perrin's nose could have led them to any number they

needed if meat had really been what he was after. He never even nocked an
arrow, but he insisted on remaining out until Gaul asked whether he intended hunting bats by the light of the half-moon; sometimes Perrin forgot
that other people could not see as well as he in the night. The next day he
hunted into the darkness as well, and every day thereafter.

The problem of it was, his simple plan seemed to be falling on its nose.
The first night when he returned to the Sun Palace, with his unstrung bow
on his shoulder, pleasantly tired from all that walking, only a chance stir in
the air brought Berelain's scent in time to stop him from walking into the
main entry hall of the palace. Motioning the Aiel guards to silence, Perrin
sneaked all the way around to a servants' door, where he had to pound to
make a bleary-eyed fellow let him in. The next night Berelain was waiting
in the hallway outside his rooms; he had to hide around a corner half the
night before she gave up. Every night she was waiting somewhere, as if she
could pretend a chance encounter when no one else was awake but a few
servants. It was utter madness; why had she not gone on to someone else?
And every night when he at last crept into his bedchamber with his boots
in his hands, Faile was asleep in that bloody thick nightgown. Long before
his sixth sleepless night in a row he was ready to admit he had blundered,
though he still could not see how. It had seemed so bloody simple. All he
wanted was one word from Faile, one hint of what he should say or do. All
he got was the sound of his own teeth grinding in the darkness.

On the tenth day, Rand received another request from Coiren for an audience, just as politely, worded as the first three. For a time he sat rubbing
the thick creamy parchment between thumb and forefinger, thinking.
There was really no way to tell how far Alanna was yet from his sense of
her, but comparing how strong it had been the first day with how strong it
was now, he thought she might be halfway to Cairhien. If that was so,
Merana was not dawdling. That was good; he wanted her eager. Penitent,
at least a little, would help too, but as well wish for the moon; she was Aes
Sedai. Ten more days until they reached Cairhien, if they kept that pace,
and they should be able to. Time enough to meet twice more with Coiren,
so he would have given each group three audiences. Let Merana consider
that when she arrived. No advantage to her at all, the White Tower on the
other side, and no need for her to know he would as soon stick his hand
into a viper pit as go anywhere near the Tower, especially with Elaida as
Amyrlin. Ten more days, and he would eat his boots if ten more passed

beyond that before Merana agreed to throw Salidar's support to him, with no nonsense about guiding or showing the way. Then, at last, he could turn his full attention on Sammael.

As Rand sat to write Coiren that she could bring two of her sisters to the Sun Palace tomorrow afternoon, Lews Therin began muttering audibly. *Yes. Sammael. Kill him this time. Demandred and Sammael and all of them, this time. Yes, I will.*

Rand hardly noticed.

CHAPTER
51

The Taking

R and let Sulin hold his coat for him to put on for the simple reason
that he would have had to rip it out of her hands physically to do
otherwise. As usual, she tried to shove the garment onto him with
no regard to details such as where his arms happened to be. The result was a
small dance in the middle of his bedchamber. Lews Therin cackled with a
sort of mad delight, just loud enough to be heard. *Sammael, oh, yes, but Demandred first. First of all I rid myself of him, then Sammael. Oh, yes.* If the man had
had hands, he would have been rubbing them in glee. Rand ignored him.

"Be respectful," Sulin muttered under her breath. "You did not show
respect to those Aes Sedai in Caemlyn, and you saw what came of it. The
Wise Ones. . . . I have heard the Wise Ones say things. . . . You must be
respectful. My Lord Dragon," she added, as an afterthought.

At last he managed to wrench the coat on the rest of the way. "Has
Min come yet?"

"Do you see her? My Lord Dragon." Picking imaginary lint from the
red silk, Sulin began doing up his buttons. It was faster to put his hands
down and let her. "Min will come when she comes, if she comes. Sorilea
will be done with her in the tents when she is done." Suddenly she peered
up at him sharply. "What do you want with her? You hardly want your
bottom pinched while the Aes Sedai are here." There was no hidden smile
this afternoon. "My Lord Dragon."

834

It was very hard not to scowl. Everything was going so well, and now this. Sorilea knew he wanted Min today more than for any previous audience; a chance for her to view Coiren and two more of Elaida's emissaries was not to be missed. Sorilea had promised to have her back. He moved away again, but Sulin followed, working at the buttons. "Sulin, I want you to go to Sorilea's tent. Find Min and bring her here. No questions, Sulin. Just do it."

She managed to smile and grind her teeth at the same time, a remarkable sight. "As my Lord Dragon commands." A smooth curtsy spread red-and-white skirts wide and lowered her face halfway to the floor.

"How long?" he asked as she turned to go. There was no need to say until what; her hesitation showed that she understood.

At last she spoke, calmly and firmly, not grumbling at all. "Until my shame equals theirs." She looked him straight in the eye for a moment, the Sulin of old, if with longer hair, but just as quickly the mask returned. "If my Lord Dragon will excuse me, I must run if I am to obey his command." Which she did, lifting her skirts to her knees and darting out of the room. Rand shook his head and did up the last buttons himself.

In truth, he felt good. Except about Min, of course. Sorilea had promised. Min had promised. Once he fended off Coiren's inevitable questions as to whether he had decided to return to Tar Valon with her, he was going to sit Min down and. . . . He was not sure what. But Alanna was another day closer. A short time of listening to Coiren, and he would go work the sword for an hour.

Demandred, Lews Therin snarled. *He wanted Ilyena!* As usual, the thought of Ilyena sent him off into distant weeping and moaning. *Ilyena! Oh, Light, Ilyena!*

Rand took the Dragon Scepter into the anteroom. Wondering who Coiren would bring, he sat in the tall chair on the dais to keep from pacing. Not over the Aes Sedai. Over Min. She knew he needed her. She knew that.

At last one of the doors opened just enough to admit a woman, but it was Chiad, not Min. "The Aes Sedai are here, *Car'a'carn*." She said the title stiffly, still not sure about a wetlander as the chief of chiefs, and for that matter, still not certain how to see him as the son of a Maiden.

Rand nodded, shifting himself upright and standing the Dragon Scepter erect on his knee. "Send them in." He was going to speak sharply to Min about this. Giving all her time to the Wise Ones.

Coiren glided in like a plump self-important swan, followed by Galina and another raven-haired, hard-eyed woman with an Aes Sedai face. They were all in shades of gray today, chosen he suspected because it would not show the dust. To his surprise, once more serving women with light dust-cloaks hanging down their backs came behind the Aes Sedai, a full dozen laboring under the weight of two brass-bound chests, neither small. Some of the young women glanced at him, but most had their heads down, in concentration on their burdens or maybe in fear.

Rand's lip very nearly curled before he could stop it. They really did think they could buy him.

"A pity your *Green* sister is not here today," Galina said.

His eyes whipped from the serving women to her. All three Aes Sedai were staring at him intently. How could they possibly know about Al-anna?

There was no time for wondering, though; almost at the same instant, his skin began to tingle.

Fury leaped inside him, and in Lews Therin too. Rand seized *saidin* nearly out of Lews Therin's teeth. White-hot rage roiled along the bound-aries of the Void, and contempt, as he glared at Coiren and Galina and whoever the third was. Coiren's soft round jaw was set with determination; the other two actually smiled, eagerly and not at all pleasantly. They were as much fools as Merana and that lot.

The shield sliding between him and the True Source was like the clos-ing of a sluice gate; the flow of *saidin* vanished, leaving only the filthy resi-due of the taint. Beside that, the air seeming to turn solid around him from his ankles to his head was as nothing. That shield made his eyes bulge; it was impossible. No three women could block him from the Source once he had taken hold of *saidin*, not unless they were as strong as Semirhage or Mesaana or. . . . He reached for the Source, battered at that invisible stone wall, harder, harder. Lews Therin was snarling like a beast, battering, clawing frantically. One of them had to be able to reach *saidin*; one of them had to be able to break a buffer held by only three.

The block had only been in place moments when one of the serving women stepped up beside Galina, and Rand felt the blood drain from his face. Four sets of eyes in four ageless faces examined him.

"It is a great pity that it came to this." In those calm, rolling tones, Coiren might better have been addressing a gathering than one man. "I very much wanted you to come to Tar Valon on your own, but it became obvious you only intended to put us off. I suppose that you have had some contact from those poor fools who fled after the Sanche woman was stilled.

Did you really believe they could offer you anything? As against the White Tower?" She actually sounded disappointed in him.

His eyes were the only part of him that could move; they slid toward the serving women, busy around one of the chests. It stood open, and they were lifting out a shallow tray. Some of those faces looked young, but the others. . . . They were all Aes Sedai, he was sure, the five young women only new enough that they had not yet assumed the agelessness, five to look at him and lull his suspicions while the others hid their faces. Fifteen Aes Sedai. Thirteen to link and weave a shield no man could break, and two to bind him. Thirteen to. . . . Lews Therin fled screaming.

Galina plucked the Dragon Scepter from Rand's hand, shaking her head over it. "I am in charge now, Coiren." She never even looked at him; he might as well have been part of the chair. "It was agreed, if it came to this, the Red Ajah would take charge." Handing the Dragon Scepter to the other black-haired woman in gray, she said, "Put this somewhere, Katerine. It might make an amusing souvenir for the Amyrlin."

Red Ajah. Sweat oozed down Rand's face. If only the Maidens outside would walk in now, Wise Ones, Sulin, anybody who could scream a warning, rouse the palace. Thirteen Aes Sedai, and Red Ajah in charge. Had he been able to open his mouth, he would have howled.

Bain looked up in surprise when the doors opened—Rand al'Thor had received the Aes Sedai a very little while ago—and automatically averted her eyes when she saw the serving women bringing out the chests. One of the black-haired Aes Sedai planted herself in front of her, and Bain hurriedly straightened from her crouch by the door. She hardly knew what to make of the tale the other Maidens had told her in Caemlyn, the things only chiefs and Wise Ones had known once, but this woman's dark eyes seemed to know all about how the Aiel had failed so long ago. Those eyes held Bain's till she was only vaguely aware of the other night-haired Aes Sedai confronting Chiad, and the pompous one leading the women away down the corridor with the chests. Bain wondered whether the Aes Sedai facing her meant to kill her for the Aiel's failure. Surely they would have begun killing before now if they intended to—surely they knew—but this woman's dark eyes glittered with a hardness that surely presaged death. Bain was not afraid to die; she only hoped she would have time to veil first.

"It seems young Master al'Thor is accustomed to coming and going from Cairhien when he chooses," the Aes Sedai told her in a voice like stone. "We are not accustomed to anyone walking away from us rudely. If he returns to the palace in the next few days, we will return also. If not. . . . Our patience is not infinite." She glided away, she and the other, after the women with the chests.

Bain exchanged quick looks with Chiad, and they hurried into Rand al'Thor's chambers.

"What do you mean, he's gone?" Perrin demanded. Loial's ears twitched toward him, but the Ogier kept his eyes on the stones board as firmly as Faile did. She smelled. . . . Perrin could make out nothing in the jumble of scents from her; that jumble made him want to bite his hands.

Nandera only shrugged. "He does this sometimes." She appeared calm enough, with her arms folded and her face impassive, but she smelled irritated, a scent like tiny burrs. "He slips away without even one Maiden to guard his back, sometimes for as long as half a day. He thinks we do not know. I thought you might know where he has gone." Something in her voice made Perrin think that if she found out, she intended to follow.

"No," he sighed. "I have no idea."

"Pay attention to the game, Loial," Faile murmured. "Surely you didn't mean to put a stone there."

Perrin sighed again. Today he had decided to stay every moment at Faile's side. She would have to speak to him sooner or later, and besides, Berelain would surely leave him alone if he was with his wife. Well, at least Berelain had indeed left him alone, but as soon as Faile realized he was not going hunting again, she had collared Loial before he could run off to the Library, and they had been playing endless games of stones ever since. In silence, for all practical purposes. Perrin wished he were wherever Rand was.

Lying on his back on the bed, Rand stared up at the thick basement rafters, not really seeing them. The bed was not large, but it had two feather mattresses and goose-down pillows and good linen sheets. There was a sturdy chair, and a small table, plain yet well made. His muscles still ached from being transported here inside one of the chests. The Power had doubled him up easily, with his head between his knees; simple cords had sufficed to make a package of him.

Metal grating on metal made him turn his head. Galina had used a

large iron key to unlock a flap in the iron cage that surrounded bed and
table and chair. A graying woman with a wrinkled face thrust her arms
inside the cage long enough to set a cloth-covered tray on the table, then
all but leaped back.

"I intend to deliver you to the Tower in reasonable health," Galina said
coldly as she relocked the flap. "Eat, or you will be fed."

Rand turned his eyes back to the rafters. Six Aes Sedai sat in chairs
around the cage, sustaining the shield on him. He maintained the Void, in
case they should slip, but he did not lunge at the barrier. When they first
pushed him stumbling into the cage, he had; some of them had laughed,
those who took any notice. Now he reached gingerly instead toward the
fury of *saidin*, a storm of fire and ice still just out of sight beyond the corner
of his eye. He reached, and felt at the invisible wall cutting him off from
the Source, slid along it as though trying to find an edge. What he found
was a place where the wall seemed to become six points; they stopped him
as effectively, but they were six, not one, and definitely points.

How long had he been here? A gray bleakness had settled over him,
blanketing time, blanketing him in lethargy. He had been here long
enough to be hungry, but the Void made sensation distant, and even the
smell of hot stew and warm bread coming from the covered tray sparked
no interest. Rising seemed too much effort. So far, twelve Aes Sedai had
taken turns around the cage, and not one a face he had seen before they
appeared in the basement. How many were there in the house? That might
be important later. Where was the house? He had no notion how far he
had been carried in that chest, most of the way jolted about in a wagon or
cart. Why had he forgotten Moiraine's advice. Trust no Aes Sedai, not an
inch, not a hair. Six Aes Sedai channeling enough of *saidar* to hold that
shield should be felt outside by any woman who could channel. All he
needed was Amys or Bair or some other to pass by in the street and wonder. They had to be thinking now that he had vanished when Coiren left
the palace. If there was a street outside. All he needed. . . .

He felt at the shield again, softly, so they would not feel. Six points. Six
soft points, somehow. That had to mean something. He wished Lews
Therin would speak again, but the only sound in his head was his own
thoughts sliding along the Void. Six points.

Hurrying along the dusk-covered street by the great stone house where the
Aes Sedai were, Sorilea could barely sense them still channeling inside. She

could only just sense it because she could only just channel at all, but that was not why she ignored it. They had been channeling day and night in there since their arrival; none of the Wise Ones wasted thought on why any longer. Sorilea certainly had more important matters to think of now. Back at the treekiller's palace, the Maidens were beginning to grow itchy over Rand al'Thor, muttering that the *Car'a'carn* would have some explaining to do when he returned this time. Sorilea had lived a great deal longer than any of those Maidens, longer than any other Wise One, weak in the Power or not, and she was uneasy. Like most men, Rand al'Thor went when he wished, where he wished—men were like cats in that—but this time, at the same time he was flitting off, Min had vanished somewhere between the tents and the palace. Sorilea did not like coincidences, no matter how many surrounded the *Car'a'carn*. Wrapping her shawl against a sudden feel of chill in her bones, she hurried on toward the tents.

CHAPTER
52

Weaves of the Power

The men sitting around the table in the common room of The Wandering Woman were mainly local. Those who wore the long vest sported it in bright silk, often brocaded, over pale shirts with wide sleeves. Garnets or pearls adorned finger rings, hoop earrings were gold not gilded, and moonstones and sapphires sparkled on the pommels of curved knives stuck through belts. Several men had silk coats slung about their shoulders, with a chain of silver or gold strung between the narrow lapels embroidered with flowers or animals. The coats looked odd, really—too small to put on; never meant for anything but a cape—but their wearers carried long narrow swords as well as the curved dagger, and seemed equally willing to use either, for a wrong word, a wrong look, or because they happened to feel like it.

It was a varied crowd, altogether. Two Murandian merchants with curled mustaches and those ridiculous little beards on the point of the chin, and a Domani with hair below his shoulders and thin mustaches who wore a gold bracelet, a close-fitting gold necklace, and a large pearl in his left ear. A dark Atha'an Miere in a bright green coat, with tattooed hands and two knives thrust into a red sash, and a Taraboner with a transparent veil covering thick mustaches that almost hid his mouth, and a number of outlanders who might have been from anywhere. But every man had a pile of coins in front of him, though the size did vary. So close to the Tarasin Palace, The Wandering Woman attracted patrons with gold to spare.

Rattling the five dice in the leather cup, Mat spun them out on the table. They stopped with two crowns, two stars and a cup showing. A fair toss; no better. His luck ran in waves, and at the moment the wave seemed low, meaning he won no more than half his tosses at most. So far he had managed to lose ten in a row, an unusual run for him at any time. The dice passed to a blue-eyed outlander, a hard, narrow-faced man who seemed to have plenty of coin to fling about despite his plain brown coat.

Vanin bent to whisper in Mat's ear. "They're out again. Thom says he still doesn't know how." Mat directed a grimace at the fat man that made him straighten more quickly than you would think someone his size could.

Swallowing half the dewmelon punch in his silver cup, Mat frowned down the table. Again! The blue-eyed man's toss rolled across the table, and the dice stopped showing three crowns, a rose and a rod. Murmurs rounded the table at his win.

"Blood and ashes," Mat muttered. "Next, the Daughter of the Nine Moons is going to walk in and claim me." The blue-eyed fellow choked on his celebratory drink. "Do you know the name?" Mat asked.

"My punch went down the wrong way," the man said in a soft, slurring accent Mat did not recognize. "What name was that?"

Mat made a pacifying gesture; he had seen fights start over less. Scraping his gold and silver back into his purse, he stuffed it into his coat pocket as he rose. "I am done. The Light's blessing on all here." Everyone at the table repeated the benison, even the outlanders. People were very polite in Ebou Dar.

Even short of midmorning, the common room was fairly full, and another dice game added its share of laughter and groans. Two of Mistress Anan's younger sons were helping the serving girls hand out late breakfasts. The innkeeper herself was sitting at the back of the room near the railless white stone stairs, keeping an eye on everything, with a young, pretty woman whose big black eyes had a merry twinkle, as though she knew a joke no one else did. Her face was a perfect oval framed by glossy black hair, and the deep neckline of her red-belted gray dress showed a tantalizing view. The amusement in her eyes deepened as she smiled at Mat.

"With your luck, Lord Cauthon," Mistress Anan said, "my husband should ask you where to send his fishing boats." For some reason, her tone was very dry.

Mat accepted the title without a blink. In Ebou Dar, few would challenge a lord except other lords; it was a simple calculation of numbers to him. There were a lot fewer lords than commoners, which meant fewer chances somebody would try to stick a knife in him. Even so, he had had to crack three heads in the last ten days. "I'm afraid my luck doesn't run to things like that, Mistress."

Olver seemed to just pop up at his side. "Can we go horse-racing, Mat?" he demanded eagerly.

Frielle, Mistress Anan's middle daughter, trotted up to catch the boy by the shoulders. "Your pardon, Lord Cauthon," she said anxiously. "He just slipped away from me. Light's truth, he did." Soon to be married—the snug silver necklace for her marriage knife already encircled her slim throat—she had volunteered to look after Olver, laughing about how she wanted six sons of her own. Mat suspected she was beginning to hope for daughters.

It was Nalesean, coming down the stairs, who got Mat's glare, hard enough to stop the Tairen in his tracks. It was Nalesean who had entered Wind in two races, with Olver riding—boys did the riding here—and Mat not knowing a thing till it was done. That Wind had proven as fast as his name did not help matters. Two victories gave Olver a taste for more. "Not your fault, Mistress," Mat told Frielle. "Put him in a barrel if you must, with my blessing."

Olver gave him an accusatory look, but a moment later he whipped around to give Frielle an insolent grin he had picked up somewhere. It looked odd with his big ears and wide mouth; he was never going to be a handsome lad. "I will sit quietly if I can look at your eyes. You have beautiful eyes."

Frielle had a lot of her mother in her, and not just her looks. She laughed sweetly and chucked him under the chin, making him blush. Her mother and the big-eyed young woman smiled at the tabletop.

Shaking his head, Mat started up the stairs. He had to speak to the boy. He could not just grin like that at every woman he saw. And telling a woman she had beautiful eyes! At his age! Mat did not know where Olver got it.

As he came abreast of Nalesean, the man said, "They have sneaked away again, haven't they." It was not a question, and when Mat nodded, he gave his pointed beard a yank and cursed. "I'll assemble the men, Mat."

Nerim was fussing about Mat's room, wiping the table with a cloth as if the maids had not dusted this morning already. He shared a smaller room next door with Olver, and rarely left The Wandering Woman. Ebou Dar was dissolute and uncivilized, he claimed.

"My Lord is going out?" Nerim said lugubriously as Mat picked up his hat. "In that coat? I fear there is a wine stain from last night on the shoulder. I would have removed it if my Lord had not donned the garment in haste this morning, and a gash in the sleeve—from a knife, I believe—that I would have mended."

Mat let him bring out a gray coat with silver scrolls embroidered on the cuffs and high collar and gave him the gold-embroidered green.

"I trust my Lord will at least try not to get blood on it today. Bloodstains are very difficult to remove."

It was a compromise they had worked out. Mat put up with Nerim's dismal face and gloomy observations, and let the man fetch, clean and hand him things he could just as easily pick up himself; in return Nerim agreed, reluctantly, not to try actually dressing him.

Checking the knives snugged up his sleeves, under his coat and in the turned-down tops of his boots, Mat left his spear leaning in the corner with his unstrung bow and went down to the front of the inn. That spear seemed to draw idiots who wanted to fight the way honey drew flies.

In spite of his hat, sweat beaded on Mat's face the moment he stepped from the shade and relative coolness of the inn. The morning sun would have done for high noon in midsummer in ordinary times, but Mol Hara Square was thronged with people. At first he stood frowning at the Tarasin Palace. With Juilin and Thom watching inside and Vanin out, how were they managing to leave without being seen? They went out almost every single day. After it happened three times, Mat had set men watching every way out of that domed heap of white stone and plaster, taking their places before dawn. There were just enough of them, with him and Nalesean. No one had seen hide nor hair, but just before midday Thom came out to say the women had gone somehow. The old gleeman seemed at his wits' end, ready to tear out his mustaches. Mat knew what was going on. They were doing it just to spite him.

Nalesean and the others were waiting in a glum sweating knot. Nalesean was fingering his sword hilt as though he would like an opportunity to use it today.

"We'll look across the river today," Mat said. Several of the Redarms exchanged uneasy glances; they had heard the stories.

Vanin shifted his feet, shook his head. "A waste of time," he said flatly. "Lady Elayne would never go anywhere like that. The Aiel woman maybe, or Birgitte, but not Lady Elayne."

Mat closed his eyes for a moment. How had Elayne managed to ruin a good man in so short a time? He kept hoping that enough time away from her influence would set Vanin right, but he was beginning to lose hope. Light, but he despised noblewomen. "Well, if we don't see them today, we can forget the Rahad—they'll stand out like painted larks in a flock of black-birds over there—but I intend to find them if they're hiding under a bed in the Pit of Doom. Search in pairs, as usual, and watch each other's back. Now to find some boatmen to ferry us across. Burn me, I hope they're not all out selling fruit to the Sea Folk ships."

To Elayne the street looked as it had in *Tel'aran'rhiod*, brick buildings five and six stories high, covered patchily with flaking white plaster, crowded together and looming above uneven pavement. Only at this time of day, with the golden sun burning overhead, did shadows vanish completely from these narrow ways. Flies buzzed everywhere. The only differences from the World of Dreams were the laundry hanging from windows, the people—not many outdoors at the moment, of course—and the smell, a deep pungent miasma of decay that made her try not to breathe too deeply. Unfortunately, every street looked alike in the Rahad.

Halting Birgitte with a hand on her arm, she eyed a scabrous pile of brick with dingy washing dangling from half the windows. The thin wail of a baby crying came from somewhere inside. It had the right number of floors, six. She was certain it had been six. Nynaeve insisted on five.

"I don't think we should stand staring," Birgitte said softly. "People are looking."

That was not quite true, just Birgitte worrying about her. Shirtless men in often ragged vests strutted down the street with sunlight glinting on their brass hoop earrings, and brass finger rings set with colored glass, or slunk along like the sort of cur dog that might snarl and might bite. For that matter, so did the women, in their usually worn dresses and *their* jewelry of brass and glass. Everyone had a curved knife stuck through a belt, and frequently a plain work knife as well.

In truth, no one gave her and Birgitte a second glance, though Birgitte's aged face was often challenging and she herself was tall for an Ebou Dari woman. That was what they saw, by way of not so simple weaves of Air and Fire that Elayne had inverted and tied off herself. When Elayne looked at Birgitte, she saw a woman with fine wrinkles at the corners of black eyes and black hair touched with gray. The disguises were easier the closer you stayed to how a person really was, so the hair flowing down Birgitte's back, tied in four places with tattered green ribbon, was considerably longer than Ebou Dari women wore it, but then Elayne had not cut her hair either, and no one seemed to pay it any mind. It was a perfect disguise; she just wished she did not have to sweat as well. With the addition of the even more complex weave of Spirit that masked a woman's ability to channel, Elayne had walked right by Merilille on her way out of the palace that morning. She wore it still; they had seen Vandene and Adeleas on this side of the river more than once.

Their clothes were not part of the weaves, of course, but threadbare woolen dresses with frayed embroidery on the sleeves and around the deep narrow necklines. Their shifts and stockings were wool too, and Elayne's, at least, itched. Tylin had provided the garments, along with various pieces of advice, and the white-sheathed marriage knives. It seemed that married women were less likely to be challenged than unmarried, and widows who rejected another marriage least of all. Age helped, too. No one challenged a gray-haired grandmother, though she might you.

"I think we should go in," Elayne said, and Birgitte moved ahead of her, one hand on the knife in her coarse brown woolen belt, to push open the unpainted door. Inside was a dim hallway lined with rough doors, and a steep narrow stairway of chipped brick at the back. Elayne did not quite sigh in relief.

White sheaths or no white sheaths, walking into a building where you did not belong was one good way to end up in a knife fight here. So was asking questions, or being curious. Tylin had counseled against that, but on the first day they had visited inns, marked only by blue doors, planning to say they were buying things out of old storerooms to refurbish and sell. She had paired with Birgitte and set Nynaeve with Aviendha so they could cover more ground. The common rooms were dark, grimy places, and twice in as many stops, Birgitte had hustled her out, both of them with daggers in hand, just before serious trouble started. The second time, Elayne had to channel briefly, tripping a pair of women who came after them into the street, and even so Birgitte had been certain that someone *had* followed them the rest of the day. Nynaeve and Aviendha had the same sort of difficulty, except for being followed; Nynaeve had actually hit another woman with a stool. So even innocuous questions were abandoned, and they hoped they did not walk through a doorway into a knife.

Birgitte climbed the steep stairs ahead, though she often glanced behind, too. The smells of cooking blended with the general stench of the Rahad in a quite sickening fashion. The baby stopped crying, but somewhere in the building a woman began shouting. On the third floor a thick-shouldered man without shirt or vest opened a door just as they came up. Birgitte frowned at him, and he raised both hands, palms toward them, and backed out of the hallway again, kicking the door shut as he did. On the top floor, where the storeroom should have been if this was the right building, a gaunt woman in a coarse linen shift was sitting on a stool in the doorway, catching what little breeze was stirring while she sharpened her dagger. Her head swiveled toward them, and the blade stopped moving across the honing stone. She did not look away from them as they backed slowly down the stairway, and the soft rasp of metal on stone did not begin again until they reached the bottom of the flight. Elayne did let out a relieved breath then.

She was more than glad Nynaeve had not taken her wager. Ten days. She had been an optimistic fool. This was the eleventh day since her boast, eleven days when sometimes she thought she was on the same street in the evening as the morning, eleven days without a clue to the bowl. Sometimes they had remained in the palace just to clear their heads. It was all so frustrating. At least Vandene and Adeleas were having no luck either. As far as Elayne could see, no one in the Rahad would speak two willing words to Aes Sedai. People melted away as soon as they realized what they were; she had seen two women try to stab Adeleas, no doubt to rob the fool walking the Rahad in a silk dress, and by the time the Brown sister lifted the pair on flows of Air and stuffed them through a window two floors up, there was not another person in sight. Well, she was not going to allow those two to find her bowl and snatch it from under her nose.

Once back in the street, she had yet another reminder that there were worse things in the Rahad than frustration. Right in front of her, a slender man with blood all over his chest and a knife in his hand came leaping out of a doorway, spinning immediately to face another man who followed; the second was taller and heavier and bleeding down the side of his face. They circled each other, eyes locked, extended blades flickering and probing. A small crowd gathered to watch as though springing from the rough pavement; none came running, but no one passed by.

Elayne and Birgitte moved to the side of the street, but they did not leave. In the Rahad, leaving would attract attention, the last thing they wanted. Blending in meant watching, but Elayne managed to focus beyond the two men, seeing only vague blurs of quick motion until suddenly the motion slowed. She blinked and made herself look. The man with blood on his chest was parading about, grinning and gesturing with a blade that dripped red. The bigger man lay facedown in the street, giving harsh feeble coughs, not twenty paces from her.

Elayne moved instinctively—her minuscule ability in Healing was better than none when a man was bleeding to death, and to the Pit of Doom with what anyone here thought of Aes Sedai—yet before she took a second step, another woman was kneeling at the man's side. A little older than Nynaeve perhaps, she wore a red-belted blue dress in somewhat better repair than most in the Rahad. Elayne took her for the dying man's sweetheart at first, especially when the victor in the duel grew sober. No one moved to go; everyone watched silently as the woman turned the man onto his back.

Elayne gave a start as, far from tenderly wiping the blood from his lips, the woman pulled what seemed to be a handful of herbs from her pouch and hurriedly thrust some of them into the man's mouth. Before her hand left his face, the glow of *saidar* surrounded her, and she began to weave the flows of Healing more deftly than Elayne could have done. The man gasped hard enough to expel most of the leaves, shuddered—and lay still, half-open eyes staring at the sun.

"Too late, it seems." Standing, the woman faced the lean fellow. "You must tell Masic's wife you've killed her husband, Baris."

"Yes, Asra," Baris replied meekly.

Asra turned away without another glance at either man, and the thin crowd opened up before her. As she passed within a few paces of Elayne and Birgitte, Elayne noticed two things about her. One was her strength; Elayne felt for that on purpose. She expected to feel a fair amount, but Asra likely would never have been allowed to take the test for Accepted. Healing must have been her strongest Talent—perhaps her only one, since she must be a wilder—and very well honed from use. Maybe she even believed those herbs were necessary. The second thing Elayne noticed was the woman's face. It was not sun-dark, as she had supposed at first. Asra was most certainly Domani. What under the Light was a Domani wilder doing in the Rahad?

Elayne might have followed the woman, except that Birgitte drew her the other way. "I recognize that look in your eyes, Elayne." Birgitte's eyes scanned the street as if she expected some of the passersby to be eavesdroppers. "I don't know why you want to chase after that woman, but she seems to be respected. Accost her, and you might have more blades drawn than you and I can handle together."

That was simple truth, and so was the fact that Domani wilders were not what she had come to Ebou Dar to find.

Touching Birgitte's arm, she nodded toward two men just rounding the corner ahead. In his satin-striped blue coat, Nalesean looked every inch the Tairen lord; the padded coat was done up to his neck, and his sweaty face glistened almost as much as his oiled beard. He glared at anyone who so much as glanced at him, to such an extent that he surely would have been in a fight by now except that he was caressing his sword hilt as if he would welcome one. Mat, on the other hand, did not grimace at all. He swaggered along, and except for an air of disgruntlement, he could have been enjoying himself. With his coat hanging open and his hat pulled low and that scarf tied around his neck, he looked as if he had spent the night crawling through taverns, which he might very well have. To her surprise, she realized she had not thought of him in days. She itched to lay hands on his *ter'angreal*, but the bowl was infinitely more important.

"It never struck me before," Birgitte murmured, "but I think Mat is the more dangerous of those two. A N'Shar in Mameris. I wonder what they're doing this side of the Eldar."

Elayne stared at her. A what where? "They have probably drunk all the wine on the other side. Really, Birgitte, I do wish you'd keep your mind on what we are about." This time she was *not* going to ask.

As Mat and Nalesean sauntered on past, Elayne put them out of her mind again and began to study the street. It would be wonderful to find the bowl today. Not least because the next time they came, she would be paired with Aviendha. She was beginning to like the woman—despite her extremely peculiar notions about Rand and them; extremely!—but she did have a tendency to encourage women who seemed ready to draw a knife. Aviendha even seemed disappointed that men dropped their eyes if she stared, instead of pulling out a blade the way the women would!

"That one," Elayne said, pointing. Nynaeve could not be right about five stories. Could she? Elayne did hope Egwene had found a solution.

Egwene waited patiently while Logain drank some more water. His tent was not so spacious as his quarters had been in Salidar, but it was still larger than most in the camp. There had to be room for the six sisters sitting on stools, maintaining the shield on him. Egwene's suggestion that it be tied off had been met with close to shock and not far from scorn; no one was willing to countenance it, particularly now, so soon after she had raised four women Aes Sedai without testing or Oath Rod, and perhaps not ever. Siuan had said they would not. Custom said six, though if he was as much reduced as Siuan and Leane, any three sisters in the camp could surely have held him, and custom said the shield on a man must be maintained, not tied. A single lamp gave a fitful illumination. She and Logain sat on blankets laid for rugs.

"Let me understand," Logain said when he lowered the pewter cup. "You want to know what *I* think of al'Thor's amnesty?" Some of the sisters shifted on their stools, maybe because he had omitted calling her "Mother," but more likely because they despised the subject.

"I want your thoughts, yes. Surely you must have some. In Caemlyn with him, you would very likely be given a place of honor. Here, you may be gentled any day. Now. You've held off the madness six years, you say. How much chance is there, do you think, that any men who come to him might do as well?"

"Do they truly mean to gentle me again?" His voice was quiet, his tone injured and angry. "I've thrown my lot in with you I've done all that was asked. I've offered to swear any oath you name."

"The Hall will decide soon. Some would as soon you died conveniently. If Aes Sedai tell your tale, all know Aes Sedai cannot lie. But I don't believe you need fear that. You have served us too well for me to allow you to be harmed. And whatever happens, you can still serve, and see the Red Ajah punished, as you wish."

Logain jerked up onto his knees, snarling, and she embraced *saidar* and had him wrapped securely in flows of Air in the space of a heartbeat. The sisters shielding him had all their strength directed into that—another custom; you must use every bit of your strength to shield a man—but several could split their weaves, and one might have diverted part to him if they thought he might harm her. She did not want to risk him being injured.

The flows held him there kneeling, but he seemed to ignore them. "You want to know what I think of al'Thor's amnesty? I wish I were with him now! Burn you all! I have done everything you asked! The Light, burn you all!"

"Be calm, Master Logain." Egwene was surprised her voice came out so steady. Her heart was racing, though certainly not for fear of him. "I swear this to you. I will never harm you, nor allow you to be harmed by any who follow me if I can help it, unless you turn against us." The rage had gone from his face, replaced by woodenness. Was he listening? "But the Hall will do as it decides. Are you calm, now?" He nodded wearily, and she released the flows. He sank back to the ground, not looking at her. "I will speak with you about the amnesty when you are more composed. Perhaps in a day or two." He nodded again, curtly, still not looking.

As she ducked out into the dusk, the two Warders standing guard outside bowed to her. At least the Gaidin did not care that she was eighteen, an Accepted raised Aes Sedai only because she was raised Amyrlin. To the Warders, an Aes Sedai was an Aes Sedai, and the Amyrlin was the Amyrlin. Still, she did not let herself exhale until she was far enough away for the two not to hear.

The camp was quite large, tents for hundreds of Aes Sedai spreading through the forest, for Accepted and novices and servants, carts and wagons and horses everywhere. The cooking smell of the evening meal hung thick in the air. Around it stretched the cookfires of Gareth Bryne's army; most men there would be sleeping on the ground, not in tents. The so-called Band of the Red Hand lay camped no more than ten miles south; Talmanes never let that distance vary more than a mile or so either way, day or night for over two hundred miles. Already they had served part of her plan for them, as suggested by Siuan and Leane.

Gareth Bryne's force had grown in the sixteen days since leaving Salidar. Two armies marching slowly northward through Altara, plainly not friendly toward each other, drew attention. Nobles flocked in with their levies to ally themselves with the stronger of the two. True, none of those lords and ladies would have sworn the oaths they had if they had known there would be no great battle in their own lands. True, given free choice, every last one would have ridden the moment they realized Egwene's target was Tar Valon, not an army of Dragonsworn. But they *had* made those oaths, to *an* Amyrlin at least, before Aes Sedai who called themselves the Hall of the Tower, with hundreds more watching. Breaking that kind of vow came back to haunt you. Besides, even if Egwene's head ended on a pike in the White Tower, not a one of them believed Elaida would forget they had sworn. Trapped into alliance they might have been, and into fealty of a sort, but they would be among the most fervent of her supporters. Their only way out of that trap with their necks intact was to see Egwene wearing the stole in Tar Valon.

Siuan and Leane were quite set up over it. Egwene was not certain how she felt. If there had been some way to remove Elaida without a drop of blood being shed, she would have leaped at it. She did not think there was, though.

After a small dinner of goat, turnip and something she did not inquire after too closely, Egwene retired to her tent. Not the largest in the camp,

but certainly the largest occupied by one person. Chesa was there, waiting
to help Egwene undress, bubbling over the news that she had acquired
some of the finest linen imaginable from an Altaran lady's maid, filmy material that would make the coolest shifts imaginable. Often Egwene let
Chesa sleep in the tent with her for the company, though a pallet of blankets hardly equaled Chesa's own cot. Tonight she sent the woman away
once she was ready for bed. Being Amyrlin entailed a few privileges. Such
as a tent of her own for your maid. Such as sleeping alone on nights when
it was necessary.

Egwene was not tired enough to go to sleep yet, but that was no trouble.
Putting herself to sleep was a simple matter; she had been trained by Aiel
dreamwalkers. She stepped into *Tel'aran'rhiod* . . .

. . . and was standing in the room that had been her study in the Little
Tower for such a brief time. The table and chairs remained, of course. Furniture was not something you took away when you set out with an army.
Any place felt empty in the World of Dreams, but those that really were
more than most. Already the Little Tower felt . . . hollow.

Abruptly, she realized the Amyrlin's stole was draped around her neck.
She made it vanish just in time. An instant later Nynaeve and Elayne were
there, Nynaeve as solid as she, Elayne misty. Siuan had been reluctant to let
go of the original ring *ter'angreal*; a firm order had been necessary. Elayne
wore a green dress with lace spilling over her hands and outlining a narrow
yet startlingly deep neckline that revealed a small knife dangling from a
snug gold necklace, the hilt nestled between her breasts a mass of pearls
and firedrops. Elayne always did seem to embrace the local fashions immediately wherever she went. Nynaeve, as expected, wore stout Two Rivers
woolens, dark and plain.

"Success?" Egwene said hopefully.

"Not yet, but we will." Elayne sounded so optimistic that Egwene almost stared; she had to really try to sound that way.

"I'm sure it will not be much longer," Nynaeve said, sounding even
more positive. They must be beating their heads against a wall.

Egwene sighed. "Maybe you should join me again. I'm sure you could
find the bowl in a few more days, but I keep thinking about all these stories." They could take care of themselves. She knew that, and it would be a
fine thought to have over their graves. Siuan said that *none* of the stories
they had told were exaggerations.

"Oh, no, Egwene," Nynaeve protested. "The bowl is too important. You
know it is. Everything is going to cook in its own juice if we don't find it."

"Besides," Elayne added, "what kind of trouble can we fall into? We sleep every night in the Tarasin Palace, in case you've forgotten, and if Tylin doesn't tuck us in, she is still there to talk." Her dress was different, the cut unaltered, but the material was coarse and worn. Nynaeve wore a near copy of it, except that her knife had no more than nine or ten glass beads on the hilt. Hardly clothes for any palace. Worse, she was trying to look innocent. Nynaeve had no practice at that.

Egwene let it pass. The bowl *was* important, they *could* take care of themselves, and she knew very well they were not looking in the Tarasin Palace. She almost let it pass, anyway. "You are making use of Mat, aren't you?"

"We—" Abruptly Elayne became aware of her dress and gave a start. For some reason, though, it seemed to be the small knife that truly startled her. Eyes popping, she clutched the hilt, a mass of large red and white glass beads, and her face went absolutely crimson. An instant later she was in a high-necked Andoran gown of green silk.

The funny thing was, Nynaeve realized what she was wearing only a heartbeat behind Elayne, and reacted exactly the same. Exactly. Except maybe that if Elayne blushed like a sunset, Nynaeve blushed for two. She was back into Two Rivers woolens even before Elayne changed.

Clearing her throat, Elayne said breathily, "Mat is quite useful, I'm sure, but we cannot allow him to get in our way, Egwene. You know how he is. You can be sure, though, if we do anything dangerous, we will have him and all his soldiers cheek to cheek around us." Nynaeve was silent, and looking sour. Perhaps remembering Mat's threat.

"Nynaeve, you won't push at Mat too hard, will you?"

Elayne laughed. "Egwene, she is not pushing at him at all."

"That's the simple truth," Nynaeve put in quickly. "I've not said a cross word to him since we arrived in Ebou Dar."

Egwene nodded doubtfully. She could reach the bottom of this, but it would take. . . . She glanced down to make sure the stole had not reappeared, and saw only a flicker that even she could not recognize.

"Egwene," Elayne said, "have you been able to speak with the dreamwalkers yet?"

"Yes," Nynaeve said. "Do they know what the problem is?"

"I have." Egwene sighed. "They don't, not really."

It had been an odd meeting, only a few days ago, begun by finding Bair's dreams. Bair and Melaine had met her in the Stone of Tear; Amys had said she would not teach Egwene more, and she did not come. At first,

Egwene felt awkward. She could not bring herself to tell them she was Aes Sedai, much less Amyrlin, afraid they might believe it another lie. There had certainly been no difficulty with the stole appearing then. And then there was her *toh* to Melaine. She brought it up, thinking all the while about how many miles she had to spend in a saddle the next day, but Melaine was so full of pleasure that she was going to have daughters—she rhapsodized over Min's viewing—that she not only announced straight away that Egwene had no *toh* toward her, but said she was going to name one of the girls Egwene. That had been a small pleasure in a night full of futility and irritation.

"What they said," she went on, "was that they had never heard of anyone trying to find something with need again after they had already found it. Bair thought maybe it was like trying to eat the same . . . apple twice." The same *motai* was what Bair had said; a *motai* was a kind of grub found in the Waste. Quite sweet and crunchy—until Egwene found out what she was eating.

"You mean we just *can't* go back to the storeroom?" Elayne sighed. "I was hoping we were doing something wrong. Oh, well. We'll find it anyway." She hesitated, and her dress changed again, though she did not seem to notice. It was still Andoran, but red, with the White Lions of Andor climbing the sleeves and marching across the bodice. A queen's dress, even without the Rose Crown resting on her red-gold curls. But a queen's dress with a close-fitting bodice that showed perhaps more cleavage than an Andoran queen would. "Egwene, did they say anything about Rand?"

"He's in Cairhien, lolling about in the Sun Palace, it seems." Egwene managed to not wince. Neither Bair nor Melaine had been very forthcoming, but Melaine muttered darkly about Aes Sedai while Bair said that they should all be beaten at regular intervals; whatever Sorilea said, a simple beating should be enough. Egwene was very much afraid that somehow Merana had managed to put a foot very wrong. At least he was putting Elaida's emissaries off; she did not think he knew how to handle them nearly as well as he thought he did. "Perrin is with him. And Perrin's wife! He married Faile!" That brought exclamations; Nynaeve said Faile was much too good for him, but said it smiling broadly; Elayne said she hoped they would be happy, but she sounded doubtful for some reason. "Loial is there, too. And Min. All it needs is Mat and the three of us."

Elayne bit her underlip. "Egwene, would you pass a . . . a message to the Wise Ones for Min? Tell her. . . ." She hesitated, chewing her lip in thought. "Tell her I hope she can come to like Aviendha as much as she likes me. I know that sounds odd," she laughed. "It's a private matter between us." Nynaeve looked at Elayne as oddly as Egwene knew she herself was.

"I will, of course. I don't mean to talk with them again for some time, though." There was not much point when they were as uncommunicative concerning Rand as they were. And as hostile toward Aes Sedai.

"Oh, that is fine," Elayne said quickly. "It really isn't important. Well, if we can't use need, then we must use feet, and in Ebou Dar, mine are aching right now. If you don't mind, I will go back to my body and get some real sleep."

"You go ahead," Nynaeve said. "I will be just a little while." When Elayne vanished, she turned to Egwene. Her dress had changed too, and Egwene thought she knew very well why. It was a soft blue, cut low. There were flowers in her hair, and ribbons through her braid, as there would be for her wedding back home. Egwene's heart went out to her. "Have you heard anything of Lan?" Nynaeve asked quietly.

"No, Nynaeve, I haven't. I am so sorry; I wish I could tell you better. I know he's still alive, Nynaeve. And I know he loves you as much as you love him."

"Of course he is alive," Nynaeve said firmly. "I won't allow anything else. I mean to make him mine. He *is* mine, and I won't let him be dead."

When Egwene woke herself, Siuan was sitting beside her cot, dimly seen in the darkness. "Is it done?" Egwene asked.

The glow surrounded Siuan as she wove a small ward against eavesdropping around the pair of them. "Of the six sisters on duty beginning at midnight, only three have Warders, and those Gaidin will be on guard outside. They will have mint tea brought to them, with a small addition they shouldn't taste."

Egwene closed her eyes for a moment. "Am I doing the right thing?"

"You ask *me?*" Siuan choked out. "I did as I was commanded, Mother. I'd as soon jump into a school of feeding silverpike as help that man escape if it were up to me."

"They will gentle him, Siuan." Egwene had been over this with her, but she needed to go over it again for herself, to convince herself she was not making a mistake. "Even Sheriam doesn't listen to Carlinya anymore, and Lelaine and Romanda are pressing for it. That or someone really will do what Delana has been hinting at. I won't allow murder! If we cannot try a man and execute him, we have no right to *arrange* for him to die. I will not let him be murdered, and I cannot allow him to be gentled. If Merana really has put Rand's back up somehow, that will be tossing fat-wood in the fire. I just wish I could be sure he will go to Rand and join him instead of running off the Light knows where, doing the Light knows what. At least that way there might be some way to control what he does." She heard Siuan shift in the darkness.

"I always thought the stole weighed about as much as three good men," Siuan said quietly. "The Amyrlin has few easy decisions to make, and fewer where she can be sure. Do what you must, and pay the price if you're wrong. Sometimes if you are right, too."

Egwene laughed softly. "It does seem to me I have heard that before." After a while her mirth died. "Make sure he doesn't hurt anyone leaving, Siuan."

"As you command, Mother."

"This is terrible," Nisao muttered. "If it becomes known, the condemnation will be enough to drive you into exile, Myrelle. And me with you. Four hundred years ago, it might have been commonplace, but no one will think it so today. Some will call it crime."

Myrelle was glad the moon was down already. It hid her grimace. She could handle the Healing herself, but Nisao had been studying how to deal with sicknesses of the mind, things the Power could not touch. Myrelle was not sure this counted as a sickness, but she would try whatever tool might work. Nisao could say what she would; Myrelle knew she would cut off her own hand rather than pass up this chance to further her studies.

She could feel him out there in the night, coming closer. They were well away from the tents, well beyond the soldiers, with only scattered trees round them. She had felt him from the moment his bond passed to her, the crime Nisao fretted over. A Warder's bond passed from one Aes Sedai to another without his consent. Nisao was right in one point; they would have to keep this secret as long as they could. Myrelle could feel his wounds, some almost healed, some almost fresh. Some badly infected. He would not have gone aside to seek battle. He had to come to her, as surely as a boulder tipped down a mountain had to roll on to the bottom. He would not have moved one foot to stand aside from battle either. She had felt his journey in distance and blood; his blood. Across Cairhien and Andor, Murandy and now Altara, through lands infested with rebels and rogues, bandits and Dragonsworn, focused on her like an arrow speeding to the target, carving his way through any armed man who stood in his path.

Even he could not do that unharmed. She toted up his injuries in her mind, and wondered that he was still alive.

The sound of a horse's hooves came to her first, a steady walk, and only then did she make out the tall black warhorse in the night. Night seemed to be the rider, too. He would be wearing his cloak. The horse stopped a good fifty paces from her.

"You shouldn't have sent Nuhel and Croi out to find me," the unseen rider called in a rough voice. "I almost killed them before I saw who they were. Avar, you might as well come out from behind that tree." Off to the right, the night seemed to move; Avar wore his cloak too, and he would not have expected to be seen.

"This is madness," Nisao muttered.

"Be quiet," Myrelle hissed. In a louder voice, she called, "Come to me." The horse did not move. A wolfhound mourning his dead mistress did not come to a new mistress willingly. Delicately she wove Spirit and touched the part of him that contained her bond; it had to be delicate, or he would be aware of it, and only the Creator knew what sort of explosion might result. "Come to me."

This time the horse came forward, and the man swung down to stride the last paces, a tall man, moonshadows making his angular face seemed carved of stone. Then he was standing in front of her, standing over her, and as she stared up into Lan Mandragoran's cold blue eyes, she saw death. The Light help her. How was she ever to keep him alive long enough?

CHAPTER

53

The Feast of Lights

T he people dancing in the streets of Cairhien exasperated Perrin;
making a way through was near to impossible. A line-dance snaked
past him behind a big-nosed fellow with a flute and no shirt; last
in line pranced a round little woman who laughed merrily and took a hand
from the waist of the man in front of her to try pulling Perrin in behind.
He shook his head, and either his yellow eyes frightened her or his face
looked as grim as he felt, because she swallowed her mirth and let the line
lead her on, glancing back over her shoulder at him until the crowd hid
her. A graying woman, still handsome, with slashes of color halfway to the
waist of her dark silk dress, flung slender arms around Perrin's neck and
stretched up her mouth hungrily toward his. She looked startled when he
picked her up gently under the arms and set her down out of his way. A
group of men and women his own age, capering to tambours, bumped into
him, laughing gaily and plucking at his coat. They ignored his head-
shaking until finally he pushed one of the men away hard and snarled a
lead-wolf growl at the others. Laughter vanished in gaping astonishment
for a moment, but they were roaring again, and trying to imitate his growl,
before they frolicked away into the throng.

It was the first day of the Feast of Lights, the shortest day of the year,
the last day of the year, and the city celebrated in ways Perrin could never
have imagined. There would be dancing in the Two Rivers, but this . . . !

The Cairhienin seemed determined to make up for a year of staid reserve in the two days of the feast. Propriety had gone down the well and with it every barrier between common and noble, in public at least. Perspiring women in plain rough wool seized sweaty men in color-striped dark silks and pulled them into the dance; men in carters' coats and stablemen's vests whirled women whose dresses bore slashes of color sometimes to the waist. Bare-chested men poured wine over themselves and anyone else close to them. Apparently any man could kiss any woman, any woman kiss any man, and they were doing so with great abandon everywhere Perrin looked. He tried not to look too closely. Some of the noblewomen with their hair in elaborate towers of curls were bare to the waist beneath light cloaks that they made little effort to keep closed. Among the commoners, few women who had abandoned blouses bothered with any sort of covering beyond their hair, and that seldom near long enough; they flung wine over themselves and everyone else as wildly as any man. Boisterous laughter warred with a thousand different tunes from flutes and drums and horns, zithers and bitterns and dulcimers.

The Women's Circle in Emond's Field would have had a screaming fit, and the Village Council swallowed their tongues in apoplexy, but the depraved goings-on were only a small burr added to Perrin's irritation. A few hours, Nandera had said, but Rand had been gone six days now. Min had either gone with him or was staying with the Aiel. And no one seemed to know anything. Except for the one called Sorilea, the Wise Ones were evasive as any Aes Sedai when Perrin managed to corner one; Sorilea told him bluntly to tend to his wife and keep his nose out of affairs that did not concern wetlanders. How Sorilea knew of the trouble between Faile and him, he had no idea, but he did not care. He could feel Rand's need like an itch everywhere under his skin, stronger every day. He was coming from Rand's school now, a last resort, but everyone there was as caught in drink, dance and debauchery as the rest of Cairhien. A woman named Idrien had been named to him as the head of the school, but after he managed, with some difficulty and no small embarrassment, to interrupt her kissing a man young enough to be her son, long enough to ask his question, all she could say was that maybe a man named Fel might know something, and Fel turned out to be dancing with three young women who could have been his granddaughters. With all three at once. Fel hardly seemed able to remember his own name, perhaps not surprising in the circumstances. Burn Rand! He had gone off without a word, when he knew about Min's viewing, knew he was going to need Perrin desperately. Even the Aes Sedai had grown disgusted, apparently. Just that morning Perrin had learned they were three days on their way back to Tar Valon, having said there was no further point in remaining. What was Rand up to? That itch had Perrin wanting to bite something.

When he reached the Sun Palace, every lamp was lit and candles burned everywhere one could be placed; the corridors glittered like gems in the sun. In the Two Rivers, too, every house would be illuminated, with every available lamp and candle, until sunrise the day after tomorrow. Most of the palace servants were out in the streets, and the few who remained seemed to laugh and dance and sing as much as work. Even here some women were bare to the waist, girls barely old enough to have their hair braided in the Two Rivers and gray-haired grandmothers. The Aiel in the corridors looked disgusted when they noticed, which in truth they did not seem to do very often. The Maidens in particular appeared furious, though Perrin suspected that had nothing to do with Cairhienin women exposing themselves; the Maidens had been more and more cats lashing their tails every day since Rand went.

Perrin strode through the hallways openly for a change. He almost wanted Berelain to pounce on him. The image that flashed in his mind was of him seizing the scruff of her neck in his teeth and shaking her until she was ready to run away with her tail curled under. Perhaps fortunately, he reached his rooms without seeing a hair of her.

Faile almost looked up from the stones board when he entered; Perrin was sure she did. The scent of jealousy still wafted from her, but it was not the strongest; anger was sharper, if not at its worst, and most powerful was a flat, dull odor he identified as disappointment. Why was she disappointed in him? Why would she not speak to him? One word even hinting at everything returning to how it had been, and he would be on his knees to accept blame for anything she wanted to pile on his head. But she only placed a black stone and murmured, "It is your turn, Loial. Loial?"

Loial's ears were twitching uneasily, and his long eyebrows drooped. The Ogier might have no sense of smell to speak of—well, no better than Faile's, say—but he could sense mood where no human would see anything. When Perrin and Faile were in the same room, Loial looked as though he wanted to cry. Now he just sighed like wind blowing through a cavern and put a white stone where he would begin trapping a large part of Faile's stones if she did not notice. She probably would; she and Loial were evenly matched, far better players than Perrin.

Sulin came to the bedchamber door with a pillow in her arms, frowning at Faile and at Perrin. Her scent reminded Perrin of a she-wolf who had taken about all of cubs nipping her tail in play that she could stand. She also smelled worried. And afraid, oddly. Though why a white-haired serving woman smelling afraid should be odd—even one with Sulin's scarred leathery face—Perrin did not understand.

Scooping up a book with a leather cover worked in gilt, Perrin sank into a chair and flung the volume open. Yet he did not read, or even see the book well enough to know which one he had picked up. He inhaled deeply, filtering out everything but Faile. Disappointment, anger, jealousy, and underneath that, underneath even the faint fresh herbal smell of her soap, was her. Perrin breathed her in hungrily. One word; that was all she had to say.

When a knock sounded at the door, Sulin stalked out of the bedroom, flouncing her red-and-white skirts and glaring at Perrin and Faile and Loial as if wondering why one of them had not answered it. She sneered quite openly when she saw Dobraine—she seemed to do that quite often since Rand left—but then took a deep breath as if steeling herself and visibly forced an almost cringing mildness. Her deep curtsy might have done to greet a king who enjoyed being his own headsman, and there she remained, her face nearly on the floor. Suddenly she began trembling. The smell of her anger melted, and even the worry was overwhelmed by a scent like thousands of hair-fine, needle-sharp splinters. Perrin had smelled shame from her before, but this time he would have said she might die from it. He smelled the bitter sweetness women gave off when they wept from emotion.

Of course, Dobraine never even glanced at her. Instead his deep-set eyes studied Perrin, his face sober, even somber, below his shaved and powdered forehead. Dobraine did not smell of drink even faintly, and he hardly looked as if he had been dancing. The one time Perrin had met him before, he had thought the man smelled wary; not afraid, but as though he was padding through tangled woods full of poisonous snakes. That smell was ten times stronger today. "Grace favor you, Lord Aybara," Dobraine said, inclining his head. "May I speak with you alone?"

Perrin set the book on the floor beside his chair and motioned to one opposite him. "The Light shine on you, Lord Dobraine." If the man wanted to be formal, Perrin could be formal. But there were limits. "Whatever you have to say, my wife can hear. I keep no secrets from her. And Loial is my friend."

He could feel Faile's gaze on him. The sudden scent of *her* nearly overpowered him. For some reason, he associated that with her loving him;

when she was at her tenderest, or when her kisses were fiercest, that aroma almost overwhelmed him. He thought about telling Dobraine to go—and Loial and Sulin too; if Faile smelled that way, surely he could make it all right somehow—but the Cairhienin was already sitting.

"A man who has a wife he can trust, Lord Aybara, is favored of grace beyond wealth." Still, Dobraine eyed her a moment before going on. "Today Cairhien has suffered two misfortunes. This morning, Lord Maringil was found dead in his bed, of poison it appears. And only a short while later High Lord Meilan apparently fell victim to a footpad's blade in the streets. Most unusual during the Feast of Lights."

"Why are you telling me this?" Perrin said slowly.

Dobraine spread his hands. "You are the Lord Dragon's friend, and he is not here." He hesitated, and when he went on, it seemed he was forcing words. "Last night, Colavaere dined with guests from a number of the smaller Houses. Daganred, Chuliandred, Annallin, Osiellin, others. Small by themselves, but numerous. The subject was alliance with House Saighan and support for Colavaere for the Sun Throne. She made little effort to hide the meeting." Again he paused, weighing Perrin with his eyes. Whatever Dobraine saw, he seemed to think it called for more explanation. "This is most strange, because both Maringil and Meilan wanted the throne, and either would have had her smothered with her own pillows had they learned of it."

At last Perrin understood, though not why the man needed to beat around the bush so. He wished Faile would speak up; she was so much better at this sort of thing than he. From the corner of his eye he could see her, head bent over the stones board, and watching him from the corner of her eye. "If you think Colavaere committed a crime, Lord Dobraine, you should go to . . . to Rhuarc." He had been going to say Berelain, but even so, the thread of jealousy increased slightly in Faile's scent.

"The Aiel savage?" Dobraine snorted. "Better to go to Berelain, and that not much. I admit the Mayener wench knows how to order a city, but she thinks every day is the Feast of Lights. Colavaere will have her sliced and cooked with peppers. You are the Dragon Reborn's friend. Colavaere—" This time he stopped because he finally realized that Berelain had entered the room without knocking, something long and narrow and wrapped in a blanket cradled in her arms.

Perrin had heard the door latch click, and at the sight of her, with half her bosom exposed, fury almost washed everything else out of his head. The woman came *here*, to carry on her flirting in front of his *wife*? Rage drove him to his feet, and his hands slapped together with a thunder crack. "Out! Out, woman! Out, now! Or I will throw you out, and I will throw you so far you bounce twice!"

Berelain gave such a start at his first shout that she dropped her burden and took a wide-eyed step back, although she did not leave. By the last word, Perrin realized that everyone was looking at him. Dobraine's face appeared impassive, but his scent was all astonishment, like one tall stone spike in the middle of a flat plain. Loial's ears were as stiffly erect as that spike, and his jaw on his chest. And Faile, wearing that cool smile. . . . Perrin did not understand at all. He expected the waves of jealousy, with Berelain right there in the room, but why did she smell just as strongly of hurt?

Suddenly Perrin saw what Berelain had dropped. The blanket had fallen away to reveal Rand's sword and the belt with the Dragon buckle. Would Rand have left that behind? Perrin liked to think things through; when you were hasty, you could hurt people without meaning to. But that sword lying there was like a strike of lightning. Fast was foolish, and sloppy, in forge work, but Perrin's hackles rose, and a growl rumbled deep in his throat.

"They have taken him!" Sulin wailed suddenly, shockingly. Head thrown back, eyes squeezed shut, she moaned at the ceiling, and the sound of her voice was enough to make Perrin shiver. "The Aes Sedai have taken my first-brother!" Her cheeks glistened with tears.

"Be calm, good woman," Berelain said firmly. "Go into the next room, and be calm." To Perrin and Dobraine she added, "We cannot allow her to spread word—"

"You do not recognize me," Sulin broke in savagely, "wearing this dress and with my hair grown longer. Speak of me again as though I am not here, and I will give you what I hear Rhuarc gave you in the Stone of Tear, and should have since."

Perrin exchanged confused glances with Dobraine and Loial, even with Faile before her eyes jerked away. Berelain, on the other hand, went pale and crimson by turns; her scent was pure mortification, shriveled and small.

Striding to the door, Sulin had flung it open before anyone could move; Dobraine at least started to, but a yellow-haired young Maiden passing by saw her and grinned in amusement. "Wipe your face, Luaine," Sulin snapped. Her hands seemed to be moving, hidden from the room by her body. Luaine's grin was indeed wiped away. "Tell Nandera she must come here at once. And Rhuarc. And bring me *cadin'sor*, and scissors to cut my

hair properly. Run, woman! Are you *Far Dareis Mai* or *Shae'en M'taal?*"
The yellow-haired Maiden darted away, and Sulin turned back to the room
with a satisfied nod, slamming the door. Faile was gaping.

"Grace favors us," Dobraine growled. "She told the Aiel nothing; the
woman must be mad. We can decide what to tell them after we tie and gag
her." He moved as if to do it, even pulling a dark green scarf from his coat
pocket, but Perrin caught his arm.

"She is Aiel, Dobraine," Berelain said. "A Maiden of the Spear. I do not
understand the livery." Surprisingly, it was Berelain who received a warning glare from Sulin.

Perrin exhaled slowly. And he had wanted to protect the white-haired
old woman from Dobraine. The Cairhienin looked at him questioningly,
raised the hand holding the scarf a little; apparently he still favored binding and gagging. Perrin stepped between the two and picked up Rand's
sword.

"I want to be sure." Suddenly he realized his steps had put him very
close to Berelain. She glanced at Sulin uneasily and moved closer to him, as
though seeking protection, but her scent was determined, not uneasy; she
smelled like a hunter. "I don't like leaping to conclusions," he said, walking
over to stand beside Faile's chair. Not quickly; just a man going to stand by
his wife. "This sword isn't really proof of anything." Faile rose and glided
around the table to peer at the board past Loial's shoulder; well, closer to
his elbow, really. Berelain glided too, toward Perrin; she was still casting
fearful looks at Sulin without the slightest fear scent, and her hand came
up as if to take his arm. He moved after Faile, trying to appear casual.
"Rand said three Aes Sedai could not harm him, if he was watchful." Faile
sailed around the other side of the table back to her chair. "I understand he
never let more than three near him." Berelain followed with piteous looks
for him and plainly fearful ones for Sulin. "I was told only three came here
the day he left." He went after Faile, a little faster. She popped out of her
chair again, returning to Loial's side. Loial had his head in his hands and
was moaning, softly for an Ogier. Berelain stalked after Perrin with her
already big eyes wide, the very picture of a woman seeking protection.
Light, she smelled determined!

Whirling to face her, Perrin shoved stiffened fingers against her chest
hard enough to make her squeak. "Stop right there!" Abruptly he realized
exactly where his fingers were nestled and snatched them away as if
burned. He managed to keep his voice hard, though. "Stay right there!"
He backed away from her, glaring hard enough to crack a stone wall. He

could understand why Faile's jealousy was a cloud filling his nose, but why, why, why did she smell even more hurt than before?

"Few men can make me obey," Berelain laughed softly, "but I think you are one." Her face and tone—and more importantly, her scent—became serious. "I went searching in the Lord Dragon's apartments because I was afraid. Everyone knew the Aes Sedai had come to escort him to Tar Valon, and I could not understand why they had given up. I myself received no fewer than ten visits from various sisters, advising me on what I should do when he returned to the Tower with them. They seemed very certain." She hesitated, and though she did not look at Faile, Perrin got the impression she was considering whether to say something in front of her. In front of Dobraine as well, but more Faile. The hunter smell returned. "I received the strong impression that I should return to Mayene, and that if I did not, I might well be escorted there."

Sulin muttered under her breath, but Perrin's ears heard clearly. "Rhuarc is a fool. If she was truly his daughter, he would have no time to do anything else for having to beat her."

"Ten?" Dobraine said. "I had only one visit. I thought she was disappointed when I made it clear I had sworn fealty to the Lord Dragon. But whether ten or one, Colavaere is the key. She knows as well as any that the Lord Dragon means the Sun Throne for Elayne Trakand." He grimaced. "Elayne Damodred, she should be. Taringail should have insisted Morgase marry into Damodred instead of marrying into Trakand himself; she needed him enough to have done it. Well, Elayne Trakand or Elayne Damodred, she has as strong a claim to the throne as any, stronger than Colavaere's by far, yet I am convinced Colavaere had Maringil and Meilan killed to make her own way to the throne safe. She would never have dared had she thought the Lord Dragon would ever return."

"So that is why." A small, vexed frown creased Berelain's forehead. "I have proof she had a servant put poison in Maringil's wine—she was careless, and I brought two good thief-catchers with me—but I did not know why." She bowed her head slightly, acknowledging Dobraine's admiring look. "She will hang for that. If there is any way to get the Lord Dragon back. If not, I fear we must all look to how we are to stay alive."

Perrin's hand tightened on the boarhide scabbard. "I will get him back," he growled. Dannil and the other Two Rivers men could not be more than halfway to Cairhien yet, burdened with the wagons. But there were the wolves. "If I have to go alone, I'll get him back."

"Not alone," Loial said, as grimly as stone grinding. "Never alone while

I am here, Perrin." Abruptly his ears shifted in embarrassment; he always seemed embarrassed when anyone saw him being brave. "After all, my book will not end very well if Rand is imprisoned in the Tower. And I can hardly write of his rescue if I am not there."

"You will not go alone, Ogier," Dobraine said. "I can have five hundred men I trust by tomorrow. What we can do against six Aes Sedai, I do not know, but I keep my oaths." Looking at Sulin, he fingered the scarf that he still held. "But how far can we trust the savages?"

"How far can we trust treekillers?" Sorilea demanded in a voice leathery and tough as she herself, striding in without knocking. A grim-smelling Rhuarc was with her, and Amys, her too-youthful face cool as any Aes Sedai's in that incongruous frame of white hair, and Nandera, reeking of murderous fury and carrying a bundle of gray and brown and green.

"You know?" Perrin said incredulously.

Nandera tossed the bundle at Sulin. "Past time you saw your *toh* as met. Almost four and a half weeks, an entire month and a half. Even *gai'shain* say your pride is too strong." The two women vanished into the bedchamber.

A smell of irritation had wafted from Faile as soon as Perrin spoke. "Maiden handtalk," she murmured, too softly for any ear but his to hear. He gave her a grateful look, but she appeared to be concentrating on the stones board. Why was she not taking part? She gave good advice, and he would be grateful for any she was willing to offer. She placed a stone and frowned at Loial, who was intent on Perrin and the others.

Trying not to sigh, Perrin said flatly, "I don't care who trusts who. Rhuarc, are you willing to send your Aiel against Aes Sedai? Six of them. A hundred thousand Aiel would give them pause though." The number coming out of his mouth made him blink—ten thousand men was a not inconsiderable army—but those were the numbers Rand had spoken of, and what Perrin had seen of the Aiel camp in the hills made him believe. To his surprise, Rhuarc smelled hesitant.

"So many are not possible," the clan chief said slowly, and paused before going on. "Runners came this morning. The Shaido are moving south from Kinslayer's Dagger in force, into the heart of Cairhien. I may have enough to stop them—they do not all seem to be coming—but if I take so many spears out of this land, all that we have done will have to be redone. At the least, the Shaido will have looted this city long before we return. Who can say how far they will have gone, into other lands even, and how many carried off claiming they are *gai'shain*." A strong odor of contempt came from him at that last, but Perrin understood none of it. What did it matter how much land had to be reconquered—or even how many people died, though that thought came reluctantly, painfully—stacked against Rand, the Dragon Reborn, being taken prisoner to Tar Valon?

Sorilea had been studying Perrin. Wise Ones' eyes often made Perrin feel as Aes Sedai's did, that he had been weighed to the ounce and measured to the inch. Sorilea made him feel he had been disassembled like a broken plow, every pin hefted and examined to see whether it should be mended or replaced. "Tell him everything, Rhuarc," she said sharply.

Amys laid a hand on Rhuarc's arm. "He has the right to know, shade of my heart. He is Rand al'Thor's near-brother." Her voice was gentle, her smell quite firm.

Rhuarc gave the Wise Ones a hard look, and Dobraine a contemptuous one. Finally he straightened to his full height. "I can take only Maidens and *siswai'aman*." By his tone and his smell, he would rather lose an arm than speak those words. "Too many of the others will not dance the spears with Aes Sedai." Dobraine's lip curled in contempt.

"How many Cairhienin will fight Aes Sedai?" Perrin asked quietly. "Six Aes Sedai, and we have nothing but steel." How many of the Maidens and these sis-whatever could Rhuarc gather? No matter; there were always the wolves. How many wolves would die?

The curl went out of Dobraine's lip. "I will, Lord Aybara," he said stiffly. "I and my five hundred, if there were sixty Aes Sedai."

Even Sorilea's cackle was leathery. "Do not fear the Aes Sedai, treekiller." Suddenly, shockingly, a tiny flame danced in the air before her. She could channel!

She let the flame vanish as they began planning, but it remained in Perrin's thoughts. Small, flickering weakly, somehow it had seemed a declaration of war stronger than trumpets, war to the knife.

"If you cooperate," Galina said conversationally, "life will be more pleasant for you."

The girl stared back sullenly and shifted on her stool, a little painfully yet. She was sweating freely, though her coat was off. The tent must be hot; Galina sometimes forgot temperature altogether. Not for the first time, she wondered about this Min, or Elmindreda, or whatever her real name was. The first time Galina had seen her, she had been garbed like a boy, keeping company with Nynaeve al'Meara and Egwene al'Vere. And Elayne

Trakand as well, but the other two were tied to al'Thor. The second time, Elmindreda had been the sort of woman Galina hated, frilly and sighing, and as near under the personal protection of Siuan Sanche as made no difference. How Elaida had ever been fool enough to allow her to leave the Tower, Galina could not imagine. What knowledge was in this girl's head? Perhaps Elaida would not have her right away. Properly used in the Tower, the girl might enable Galina to net Elaida like a swallow. For all of Alviarin, Elaida had become one of those strong, capable Amyrlins who took every rein firmly into their own hands; caging her would surely weaken Alviarin. Properly used right now . . . .

A change in the flows she had been sensing made Galina sit up straight. "I will talk with you again when you have had time for thought, Min. Think carefully on how many tears a man is worth."

Once outside, Galina snapped at the stocky Warder on guard. "Watch her properly, this time." Carilo had not been on guard during the incident last night, but there was too much mollycoddling of the Gaidin. If they had to exist at all, they should be treated as soldiers and no more.

Ignoring his bow, she glided away from the tent, looking for Gawyn. That young man had been withdrawn since al'Thor was captured, and much too quiet. She was not about to have everything ruined by him trying to avenge his mother. But she saw Gawyn sitting his horse on the edge of the camp, talking to a knot of those boys who called themselves the Younglings.

They had stopped early of necessity today, and the afternoon sun made long shadows of the tents and wagons beside the road. Rolling plains and low hills surrounded the camp, with only a few scattered thickets in sight, most sparse and small. Thirty-three Aes Sedai added to the original six, with their servants—and Warders; nine were Green, only thirteen Red, and the rest White, Alviarin's former Ajah—made a considerable encampment even without counting Gawyn and his soldiers. A number of sisters were standing outside or looking out of their tents, having felt what Galina had. The focus of attention was seven Aes Sedai, six seated on stools around a brass-bound chest set where it could catch whatever strength remained in the sun. The seventh was Erian; she had not been far from the chest since al'Thor was put back into it last night. He had been allowed out once they were away from Cairhien, but Galina suspected Erian was going to want him to make the rest of the journey inside that box.

The Green rounded on her as soon as she came close. Erian was quite beautiful usually, her face a pale exquisite oval, but now crimson suffused her cheeks, as it had almost constantly since the night before, and her lovely dark eyes were red-rimmed. "He did try to break through the shield again, Galina." Wrath mingled with contempt for the man's foolishness, making her voice thick and harsh. "He must be punished again. I do want to be the one to punish him."

Galina hesitated. Much better would be to punish Min; that would quell al'Thor. He had certainly raged enough seeing her punished for her outburst last night, which had in turn come from seeing him punished. The entire incident had begun because al'Thor discovered Min was in the camp, after one of the Warders carelessly allowed her to walk in the darkness instead of keeping her closely confined in her tent. Who would have thought that al'Thor, shielded and surrounded, would have gone mad that way? Not just trying to break through the shield, but killing a Warder with his bare hands and severely wounding another with the dead man's sword, to such an extent that the second died in the Healing. All that in the moments required for the sisters to overcome their shock and bind him with the Power.

For herself, Galina would have gathered the other Red sisters and gentled al'Thor days ago. Since that was prohibited, she would just as soon have delivered him to the Tower unmarked, so long as he was reasonably polite. Even now efficiency was what she cared for, and what would be efficient would be to bring Min out here and let him hear her wail and weep again, let him know that he was the cause of her pain. But by chance both the dead Warders belonged to Erian. Most of the sisters would feel she had the right. And Galina herself wanted the doll-like Illianer Green to rid herself of her rage as soon as possible. Much better to travel the rest of the way able to admire that porcelain face unruffled.

Galina nodded.

Rand blinked when light suddenly flooded into the chest. He could not help flinching too; he knew what was coming. Lews Therin fell silent, and still. Rand held the Void by a fingernail, yet he was all too aware of cramped muscles groaning as he was pulled upright. He clamped his teeth shut and tried not to squint against what seemed the brightness of noon. The air seemed wonderfully fresh; his sodden shirt clung to him, dripping with sweat. No cords held him, but he could not have moved a step for his life. If not held up with the Power, he would have fallen over. Until he saw how low the sun sat, he had no idea how long he had been in there with his head between his knees, in a puddle of his own sweat.

The sun got only a notice, though. Involuntarily his eyes went to Erian even before she placed herself squarely in front of him. The short slender woman peered up at him, dark eyes full of fury, and he almost flinched again. Unlike last night, she said nothing, only began.

The first unseen blow struck him across the shoulders, the second the chest, third the backs of his thighs. The Void shattered. Air. Only Air. It sounded softer, that way. Each blow felt a whip, though, wielded by an arm stronger than any man's. Before she began, bruised welts crisscrossed him from shoulders to knees. He had been aware of them, not so dimly as he could have wished; even inside the Void he had wanted to weep. After the Void went, he wanted to howl.

Instead he clenched his jaws. Sometimes a grunt escaped through his teeth, and when one did, Erian's efforts redoubled as if she wanted more. He refused to give it. He could not stop a shudder at each stroke of that invisible lash, but no more than that would he give her. He fixed his eyes on hers, refused to look away, to blink.

I killed my Ilyena, Lews Therin moaned every time a blow landed.

Rand had his own litany. Pain flailing his chest. *This comes of trusting Aes Sedai*. Fire striping his back. *Never again; not an inch; not a hair*. Like a razor's slash. *This comes of trusting Aes Sedai*.

They thought they could break him. They thought they could make him crawl to Elaida! He made himself do the hardest thing he had ever done in his life. He smiled. Certainly it touched nothing but his lips, yet he looked Erian in the eye, and he smiled. Her eyes widened, and she hissed. The scourges began to come from everywhere at once.

The world was pain and fire. He could not see, only feel. Agony and inferno. For some reason he was aware of his hands trembling uncontrollably in their invisible bonds, but he concentrated on holding his teeth shut. *This comes of—Won't cry out! I will not cry ou—! Never again; not an in—! Not an inch; not a hair! Never agai—! I will not! Never a—! Never! Never! NEVER!*

First there was a perception of breathing. Air, gulped hungrily through his nostrils. He throbbed—he was a pulsing flame—but the beating had stopped. It almost came as a shock, realizing that. The end of something that part of him had been convinced would never end. He tasted blood, and realized that his jaws hurt almost as much as the rest of him. Good.

He had not cried out. The muscles of his face were locked in a knotted cramp; it would take effort to open his mouth even if he wanted to.

Sight was the last thing to return, and when it did, he wondered whether pain was making him hallucinate. Among the Aes Sedai stood a group of Wise Ones, shifting their shawls and staring at the Aes Sedai with all the arrogance they could muster. When he decided they were real—unless he was fantasizing Galina talking to one of his fancies—his first thought was rescue. Somehow the Wise Ones had . . . It was impossible, but somehow they would. . . . Then he recognized the woman speaking with Galina.

Sevanna strolled toward him, a smile on that plump greedy mouth. Those pale green eyes peered up at him from that beautiful face framed by hair like spun gold. Rand would as soon have looked into the face of a rabid wolf. There was something odd in the way she stood, leaning forward slightly, shoulders back. She was watching his eyes. Abruptly, as much as he hurt, he wanted to laugh; he would have, if he could have been sure what sound would emerge if he opened his mouth. Here he was, a prisoner, beaten within an inch of his life, welts burning, sweat stinging, and a woman who hated him, he was sure, who probably blamed him for the death of her lover, was trying to see whether he would look down the front of her blouse!

Slowly she ran a fingernail across his throat—in fact, as far around his neck as she could reach—as though imagining cutting off his head. Fitting, considering Couladin's fate. "I have seen him," she said with a satisfied sigh and a small shiver of pleasure. "You have kept your part of the bargain, and I have kept mine."

The Aes Sedai doubled him again then, shoved him back down into the chest with his head between his knees, crouching in that thin puddle of sweat. The lid closed, and darkness enclosed him.

Only then did he work his jaws until his mouth could open and let out a long shuddering breath. He had not been sure whether he might not whimper even now. Light, but he was on fire!

What was Sevanna doing there? What bargain? No. All very well to know there was some bargain between the Tower and the Shaido, but worrying about it was for later. Now was for Min. He had to get free. They had hurt her. That thought was so grim it almost dulled the pain. Almost.

Assuming the Void again was a labor of wading through a swamp of agony, but at last he was surrounded by emptiness, reaching out toward *saidin*. . . . Only to find Lews Therin there as soon as he was, like two sets of hands fumbling to grasp something only one could hold.

Burn you! Rand growled in his head. *Burn you! If you'd only work with me just once instead of against me!*

You work with me! Lews Therin snapped back.

Rand nearly lost the Void in shock. There could be no mistake this time; Lews Therin had heard him and answered. *We could work together, Lews Therin.* He did not want to work with the man; he wanted him out of his head. But there was Min. And how many days yet to Tar Valon. Somehow he was sure if they got him that far, there would be no more chances. Ever.

An uncertain, apprehensive laugh answered him. Then, *Together?* Another laugh, and this mad as a loon. *Together. Whoever you are.* And voice and presence vanished.

Rand shivered. Kneeling there, adding more sweat to the puddle his head rested in, he shivered.

Slowly he reached for *saidin* again. . . . And came against the shield, of course. The thing he had been seeking in any case. Slowly, ever so gently, he felt his way along it, to where a hard plane suddenly turned to six soft points.

Soft, Lews Therin said, panting. *Because they are there. Sustaining the buffer. Hard when they knot. Nothing to be done when they are soft, but I can unravel the web if they knot it. With time.* He paused so long Rand thought he was gone again, then he whispered, *Are you real?* And then he really was gone.

Gingerly Rand felt along the shield to the soft points. To six Aes Sedai. With time? If they tied it, which they had not so far in. . . . What was it? Six days? Seven? Eight? No matter. He could not afford to wait too long. Every day was one closer to Tar Valon. Tomorrow, he would try to break through the barrier again; it had been like beating his hands against stone, but he had beaten with all his strength. Tomorrow when Erian flogged him—he was sure it would be her—he would smile at her again, and when the pain built, he would let the screams come. The next day he would not more than brush the shield, maybe hard enough to let them feel it, but only that, and not again after whether they punished him or not. Maybe he would beg for water. They had given him some at dawn, but he was thirsty again; even if they let him drink more than once a day, begging would fit. If he was still in the box then, he might plead to be let out, too. He thought he would be; small chance of them allowing him out for long until they were sure he had learned his lesson. Cramped muscles twitched at the thought of two or three more days stuffed in here. There was no room to move anything, but his body tried. Two or three days, and they would be sure he was broken. He would look fearful and avoid meeting anyone's gaze. A wretch they could safely let out of the chest. More importantly, a wretch they did not need to guard so closely. And then, perhaps, they would decide they did not need six to hold the shield, or that they could tie it off, or . . . or something. He needed some crack. Something!

It was a desperate thought, but he realized that he was laughing, and he could not stop. He could not stop feeling at the barrier, either, a blind man sliding his fingers desperately across a piece of smooth glass.

Galina frowned after the departing Aielwomen until they topped a rise and vanished down the other side. Every one of those women except Sevanna herself had been able to channel, several quite strongly. No doubt Sevanna had thought herself safer, surrounded by a dozen or so wilders. Amusing thought. These savages were an untrusting lot. In a few days she would make use of them again, in the second part of Sevanna's "bargain." The regrettable death of Gawyn Trakand, and the better part of his Younglings.

Returning to the heart of the camp, she found Erian still standing over the chest containing al'Thor.

"He do be weeping, Galina," she said fiercely. "Can you hear him? He do be—" Suddenly tears were sliding down Erian's face; she simply stood there sobbing quietly, her hands fists clutching her skirts.

"Come to my tent," Galina said soothingly. "I have some nice blueberry tea, and I will put a cool, damp cloth on your brow."

Erian smiled through her tears. "Thank you, Galina, but I cannot. Rashan and Bartol will be waiting for me. They do suffer worse than I, I fear. They do not only feel my suffering, but do suffer because they *know* I do. I must comfort them." One grateful squeeze of Galina's hand, and she glided away.

Galina frowned at the chest. Al'Thor did seem to be weeping; either that or he was laughing, and she very much doubted that. She looked after Erian, just disappearing into her Warders' tent. Al'Thor would weep. They had at least two weeks more to Tar Valon and Elaida's planned triumphal entry; yes, at least twenty days more. From now on, whether Erian wished to do it or not, he was to be punished each day at dawn and at sunset. When she brought him into the White Tower, he would kiss Elaida's ring, speak when spoken to and kneel in the corner when he was not wanted. Eyes tight, she went to drink her blueberry tea by herself.

As they entered the largish stand of trees, Sevanna turned to the others, thinking how remarkable it was that she should think of the trees so casually. Before crossing the Dragonwall, she had never seen so many trees. "Did you all see the means they used to hold him?" she asked, making it sound as if she had said "also" instead of "all."

Therava looked at the others, who nodded. "We can weave all they have done," Therava said.

Nodding, Sevanna fingered the small stone cube, with its intricate carvings, in her pouch. The strange wetlander who had given it to her had said she should use it now, when al'Thor was captive. Until she had actually looked on him, she had intended to; now she decided to throw the cube away. She was the widow of a chief who had been to Rhuidean and of a man who had been called chief without making that visit. Now she was going to be the wife of the *Car'a'carn* himself. Every spear of the Aiel would be grounded to her. Her finger still retained the feel of al'Thor's neck, where she had traced the line of the collar she would put on him.

"It is time, Desaine," she said.

Of course, Desaine blinked in surprise, and then she had time only to scream before the others began their work. Desaine had contented herself with grumbling about Sevanna's position. Sevanna had put her time to better use. Except for Desaine, every woman here was solidly behind her, and more beside.

Sevanna watched very closely what the other Wise Ones did; the One Power fascinated her, all those things done so miraculously, so effortlessly, and it was very important that it would be seen that what was done to Desaine could only have been done with the Power. She thought it quite astounding that a human body could be taken apart with so little blood.

CHAPTER
54

The Sending

With the sun just a thin glowing slice on the horizon, the second day of the Feast of Lights saw the streets of Cairhien already filled with revelers. Indeed, they had never really emptied through the night. There was a frenzied air to the celebration, and few gave more than a glance to the curly-bearded man with the grim face and the axe on his hip, riding a tall bay down the arrow-straight streets toward the river. Some did look at his companions; an Aiel man was a common enough sight now, though they had abandoned the streets when the celebrations began, but it was not every day that you saw an Ogier, taller than the man on horseback, especially one carrying an axe propped across one shoulder, with a haft nearly as long as he was tall. The Ogier made the bearded man look jolly.

The ships on the Alguenya had all their lanterns lit, including the Sea Folk ship that occasioned so much rumor, for being in Cairhien at all, for remaining at anchor so long with barely any contact with the shore. By the rumors Perrin had heard, the Sea Folk disapproved of the carrying on in the city even more than the Aiel did, and he had thought Gaul would die from shock at all the men and women kissing. Whether or not the woman wore a blouse did not appear to bother Gaul nearly as much as the fact that they were kissing where they could be seen. That was indecent.

Long stone piers thrust out into the river between tall flanking walls, and boats of all sizes and types were tied along them, including ferries that could take one horse or fifty, but Perrin did not see more than one man on any of them. He reined in the bay as he came to a broad, mastless craft some six or seven spans long lashed to stone posts. Its ramp to the dock was in place. A stout, gray-haired man with no shirt was sitting on an up-ended cask on the deck, a gray-haired woman with half a dozen bright slashes across the bosom of her dark dress on his knees.

"We want to cross," Perrin said loudly, trying to look only enough to see whether the pair took their arms from around each other. They did not. Perrin tossed an Andoran crown down onto the ferry, and the sound of the fat gold coin bouncing on the deck brought the fellow's head around. "We want to cross," Perrin said, hefting a second gold crown on his palm. After a moment, he added another.

The ferryman licked his lips. "I will have to find oarsmen," he muttered, staring at Perrin's hand.

Sighing, Perrin pulled two more from his purse; he could remember when his eyes would have fallen out at having one of those coins.

The ferryman leaped up, dropping the noblewoman onto her bottom with a thump, and scrambled up the ramp panting that he would be only moments, my Lord, only moments. The woman gave Perrin a very reproachful look, and glided away down the dock with a dignity somewhat spoiled by rubbing herself; before she had gone very far, though, she gathered her skirts and ran to join a group of dancers capering along the waterfront. Perrin could hear her laughing.

It took more than moments, but apparently the promise of gold was enough, for in not too long a time the ferryman had enough fellows gathered to man most of the long sweeps. Perrin stood stroking the bay's nose as the vessel swung out into the river. He had not decided on a name, yet; the animal came from the Sun Palace stable. Well-shod, with white forefeet, the horse looked a stayer, though not a patch on Stepper.

His unstrung Two Rivers bow was thrust through the saddle girth on one side, and the full quiver hung in front of the high-cantled saddle, balancing a long, narrow, neatly wrapped bundle. Rand's sword. Faile had tied that package herself and handed it to him without a word. She had said something, after he had turned away realizing he would receive no kiss.

"If you fall," she whispered, "I will take up your sword."

He was still not sure whether she meant him to hear or not. Her scent had been such a jumble he could make nothing out.

He knew he should be thinking of what he was about, but Faile always crept softly back into his mind. At one point he had been sure she was about to announce that she was coming with him, and his heart had clenched. Had she done so, he did not think he could have made himself refuse her—not that or anything, after all the hurt he had given her—but there were six Aes Sedai ahead, and blood and death. If Faile died, Perrin knew he would go mad. That point had come when Berelain said she would be leading her Mayener Winged Guards in this chase. Luckily, the moment had been gotten past quickly, if in an odd way.

"If you leave the city Rand al'Thor has given to you as his hand," Rhuarc said quietly, "how many rumors will grow of it? If you send all of your spears, how many rumors? What will grow from those tales?" It sounded like advice, and then again it did not; something in the clan chief's voice made it much stronger.

Berelain gazed at him, smelling stubborn and head high. Slowly the stubborn smell faded, and she muttered to herself, "Sometimes I think there are too many men who can. . . ." It was just audible to Perrin. Smiling, she spoke aloud, in a remarkably regal tone. "That is sound advice, Rhuarc. I think that I will take it."

The most remarkable thing, however, had been the way their scents combined, Rhuarc's and hers. To Perrin they had seemed he-wolf and near-grown cub; an indulgent father, fond of his daughter and she of him, though sometimes he still had to nip her nose to make her behave properly. But what was important was that Perrin could see the intention fading from Faile's eyes. What was he to do? If he lived to see her again, what was he to do?

In the beginning the coarsely dressed, sometimes bare-chested oarsmen made rough jokes, not too unfriendly, about how any amount of gold was hardly worth what they were missing. They laughed as they strode back and forth along the deck, working the sweeps, and every one claimed he had been dancing with or kissing a noblewoman. One lanky fellow with a big chin even claimed he had a *Tairen* noblewoman on his knee before he came out to Manal's shout, but no one believed that. Perrin certainly did not; the Tairen men had taken one look at what was going on and dived headfirst into the celebrations; the Tairen women had taken one look and shut themselves up in their rooms with guards on the doors.

Jokes and laughter did not last long. Gaul stood as near the center of the boat as he could, slightly wild eyes fixed on the far shore, up on his toes as though ready to leap. It was all that water, of course, but the boatmen could not know that. And Loial, leaning on the long-handled axe he had found in the Sun Palace, with its ornately engraved head like the head of a huge wood-axe, stood still as a statue with his broad face truly looking carved from granite. The ferrymen shut their mouths and worked their oars as hard as they could, hardly daring to look at their passengers. When the ferry finally pulled into a stone dock on the west bank of the Alguenya, Perrin gave the owner—come to think of it, he hoped the man was the owner—the rest of the gold and a handful of silver to pass around besides, to soothe them for being frightened by Loial and Gaul. The fat man flinched back from him in taking it, and bowed so deeply in spite of his bulk that his head nearly touched his knees. Perhaps Gaul and Loial did not have the only frightening faces.

Huge windowless buildings stood surrounded by wooden scaffolding, the stone blackened, and fallen in many places. The granaries had been burned in riots some time ago, and repairs were only now really taking hold, but there was no one in sight at all on the streets lined with granaries and stables, warehouses and wagon yards. Every last man who worked here was in the city. There was no one in sight until two men rode out of a side street.

"We are ready, Lord Aybara," Havien Nurelle said eagerly. The pink-cheeked young man, considerably taller than his companion, appeared gaudy in his red-painted breastplate and helmet, with a single slender red plume. He even smelled eager, and young.

"I began to think you were not coming," Dobraine muttered. Helmet-less, he wore steel-backed gauntlets and a battered breastplate that retained remnants of once ornate gilding. He glanced at Perrin's face and added, "Under the Light, I meant no disrespect, Lord Aybara."

"We have a long way to go," Perrin said, turning the bay. Stayer? What was he to do about Faile? Rand's need seethed beneath his skin. "They've four days on us, now." He dug in his heels lightly and put Stayer to a steady walk. A long chase; it would not do to founder the horses. Neither Loial nor Gaul had any difficulty keeping up.

The widest of the straight streets abruptly became the Tar Valon Road—Cairhien's Tar Valon Road; there were others—a wide band of hard-packed earth winding west and north through forested hills lower than those the city stood on. A mile into the forest, they were joined by two hundred Mayener Winged Guards and five hundred armsmen of House Tabor-win, all mounted on the best animals that could be found.

The Mayeners were all in red breastplates and helmets like rimmed pots that covered the nape of the neck, and their lances bore red streamers. Many of them seemed almost as eager as Nurelle. The shorter Cairhienin wore plain breastplates and helmets like bells cut away to expose hard

faces, helmets and breastplates alike often dented. Their lances were unadorned, though here and there Dobraine's *con*, a small stiff square on a
short staff, blue with two white diamonds, marked officers or minor lords
of House Taborwin. None of them looked eager, only grim. They had seen
fighting. In Cairhien, they called it "seeing the wolf."

That nearly made Perrin laugh. It was not time for the wolves yet.

Near midday, a small cluster of Aiel trotted out of the trees and down
the slope to the road. Two Maidens loped at Rhuarc's shoulder, Nandera
and, Perrin realized after a moment, Sulin. She looked very different in
cadin'sor, with her white hair cut close except for the tail on the back of her
neck. She looked . . . natural . . . which she never had in livery. Amys and
Sorilea came with them, shawls looped over their arms, clattering with
necklaces and bracelets of gold and ivory, holding up their bulky skirts on
the slope, but matching the others stride for stride.

Perrin swung down to walk with them, ahead of everyone else. "How
many?" was all he said.

Rhuarc glanced back to where Gaul and Loial were walking alongside
Dobraine and Nurelle in advance of the column. Too far maybe for even
Perrin to hear anything over the clump of hooves and jingle of bridles and
creak of saddles, but Rhuarc held his voice low anyway. "Five thousand
men from different societies; a few more than five. I could not bring many.
Timolan was suspicious as it is that I did not go with him against the
Shaido. If it becomes common knowledge that Aes Sedai hold the *Car'a'carn*,
I fear the bleakness will swallow us all." Nandera and Sulin coughed loudly
at the same time; the two women glared at one another, and after a moment Sulin looked away, blushing. Rhuarc spared them a glance—he
smelled exasperated—and muttered, "I also have nearly a thousand Maidens. Had I not tightened my fist, I would have every last one of them running after me, carrying a torch to tell the world that Rand al'Thor is in
danger." Abruptly his voice hardened. "Any Maiden I find following us will
learn that I mean what I say."

Sulin and Nandera both went red, the color startling on those hard
sun-dark faces. "I—" both began at the same instant. Again those glares
passed, and again Sulin looked away, her face even more crimson. Perrin
did not remember all this blushing from Bain and Chiad, the only two
Maidens he really knew. "I have promised," Nandera said stiffly, "and *every*
Maiden has promised on pledge. It will be as the chief has commanded."

Perrin forbore asking what the bleakness was, just as he did not ask how
Rhuarc had gotten the Aiel across the Alguenya without ferries when water

they could not step across was the only thing in the world that could give an Aiel pause. He would have liked to know, but the answers were unimportant. Six thousand Aiel, five hundred of Dobraine's armsmen, and two hundred Winged Guards. Against six Aes Sedai, their Warders and some five hundred guards apparently, that should be enough. Except. The Aes Sedai held Rand. If they put a knife to his throat, would anyone dare lift a hand?

"There are also ninety-four Wise Ones," Amys said. "They are the strongest in the One Power of those near the city." That came out reluctantly—he had the idea Aielwomen did not like to admit they could channel—but her voice picked up. "We would not have brought so many, but all wanted to come." Sorilea cleared her throat, and this time Amys blushed. He was going to have to ask Gaul. Aiel were so unlike anyone else he had ever met; maybe they began blushing when they grew older. "Sorilea leads us," Amys finished, and the older woman gave a snort that sounded extremely satisfied. She certainly smelled satisfied.

For Perrin, he only just stopped from shaking his head. What he knew of the One Power could be stuffed into a thimble with room left for a fat thumb, but he had traveled with Moiraine, seen what Verin and Alanna could do, and he had seen that flame Sorilea had made. If she was one of the strongest in the Power among the Wise Ones, he was not sure six Aes Sedai would not wrap all ninety-four of them into a bundle. At this point, though, he would not have turned aside field mice.

"They must be seventy or eighty miles ahead of us," he said. "Maybe as much as a hundred, if they're pushing their wagons. We will have to press as hard as we can." As he climbed back to his saddle, Rhuarc and the other Aiel were already trotting back up the hill. Perrin raised his hand, and Dobraine signaled the horsemen to advance. It never occurred to Perrin to wonder why men old enough to be his father, women old enough to be his mother, men and women used to command, were following him.

What he did wonder about, worry about, was how fast they could move. Aiel in *cadin'sor* could keep up with the horses, he knew, yet at first he had worried about Wise Ones in skirts, some maybe as old as Sorilea. Skirts or no, white hair or no, the Wise Ones walked as quickly as anyone, keeping up with the horses while talking quietly in groups.

The road wound clear ahead; no one set out during the Feast of Lights, and few for days before, unless their business was as urgent as his. The sun climbed higher, and the hills grew lower, and by the time they made camp at twilight, he estimated they might have come as much as thirty-five miles. A good day's travel, excellent for so large a party; half again what the Aes Sedai could manage unless they were willing to kill the teams drawing their wagons. He no longer worried whether he could catch them before they reached Tar Valon, only what he could do once he did.

Lying on his blankets with his head pillowed on his saddle, Perrin smiled up at the waxing quarter-moon. With any clouds at all, the night would not have been nearly so bright. It was a good night for hunting. A good night for wolves.

In his mind he formed an image. A curly-haired young wild bull, proud, with horns that gleamed like polished metal in morning sunlight. His thumb ran across the axe lying beside him, with its wicked curving blade and sharp spike. The steel horns of Young Bull; that was what the wolves called him.

He let his mind quest, sent the image out into the night. There would be wolves, and they would know of Young Bull. News of a human able to speak with wolves would pass across the land like a rushing wind. Perrin had only met two. One a friend, the other a poor wretch who had not been able to hold on to humanity. He had heard tales from the refugees who trickled into the Two Rivers. They had old stories of men turning into wolves, stories few really believed, told to entertain children. Three claimed to have known men who became wolves and ran wild, though, and if the details had seemed wrong to Perrin, the uneasy way two of them had avoided his yellow eyes made confirmation of a sort. Those two, a woman from Tarabon and a man from Almoth Plain, would not go outdoors at night. They also kept giving him gifts of garlic for some reason, which he ate with great pleasure. But he no longer tried to find others like himself.

He felt wolves, and their names began coming to him. Two Moons and Wildfire and Old Deer and dozens more cascading into his head. They were not names as such, really, but images and sensations. Young Bull was a very simple image to name a wolf. Two Moons was really a night-shrouded pool, smooth as ice in the instant before the breeze stirred, with a tang of autumn in the air, and one moon hanging full in the sky and another reflected so perfectly on the water that it was difficult to tell which was real. And that was cutting it to the bone.

For a time there was only the exchanging of names and scents. Then he thought, *I seek people who are ahead of me. Aes Sedai and men, with horses and wagons.* That was not exactly what he thought, of course, any more than Two Moons was just two moons. People were "two-legs" and horses "hard-footed four-legs." Aes Sedai were "two-leg shes who touch the wind that moves the sun and call fire." Wolves did not like fire, and they were even more wary of Aes Sedai than of other humans; they thought it amazing that he could not tell an Aes Sedai; he had only learned they could by chance. They took the ability as much for granted as he took being able to pick out one white horse among a herd of black, certainly nothing to mention, and certainly nothing they could explain clearly.

In his head the night sky seemed to whirl, suddenly capping a camp of wagons and tents and campfires. They did not look quite right—wolves cared little for anything human, so the wagons and tents seemed vague; the campfires appeared to roar dangerously; the horses looked quite tasty—and this was passed from wolf to wolf before reaching him. The camp was larger than Perrin expected, but Wildfire was in no doubt. Her pack was even then skirting wide of where the "two-leg shes who touch the wind that moves the sun and call fire" were. Perrin tried asking how many, but wolves had no grasp of numbers; they told how many things there were by showing how many they had seen, and once Wildfire and her pack sensed Aes Sedai, they had no intention of going any closer.

How far? received a better answer, again passed wolf to wolf, if one that had to be puzzled out. Wildfire said she could walk to the hill where a sour male named Half Tail had his pack feeding on a deer while the moon moved so far across the sky, at that angle. Half Tail could reach Rabbit Nose—apparently a young and very fierce male—while the moon moved that far, at another angle. And so it went until Two Moons was reached. Two Moons maintained a dignified silence, suitable for an old male with a muzzle more white than not; he and his pack were not much beyond a mile from Perrin, and it would have been insulting to think Perrin did not know exactly where they sat.

Reasoning it out as best he could, Perrin came up with a figure of sixty or seventy miles. Tomorrow, he would be able to tell how fast he was closing on them. They surely could not be moving as fast as he with wagons.

Why? That was Half Tail, passed along and scent-marked.

Perrin hesitated before answering. He had dreaded this. He felt about the wolves as he did about Two Rivers people. *They have caged Shadowkiller,* he thought at last. That was what the wolves called Rand, but he had no idea whether they considered Rand important.

The shock filling his mind was answer enough, but howls filled the night, near and far, howls filled with anger and fear. In the camp horses whinnied fearfully, stamping their hooves as they shied against the picket ropes. Men ran to calm them, and others to peer into the darkness as if expecting a huge pack to come after the mounts.

We come, Half Tail replied at last. Only that, and then others answered, packs Perrin had spoken to and packs that had listened silently to the two-legs who could speak as the wolves did. *We come*. No more.

Rolling over, Perrin went to sleep, and dreamed he was a wolf running across endless hills. The next morning there was no sign of wolves—not even the Aiel reported seeing one—but Perrin could feel them, several hundred of them and more on the way.

The land flattened into rolling plains over the next four days, where the tallest rises hardly seemed to warrant the name hill compared to what had been around them back by the Alguenya. The forest thinned and faded into grassland, brown and sere, with thickets increasingly far between. The rivers and streams they crossed barely wet the horses' hooves, and would not have done much more before they had narrowed between banks of sun-hardened mud and stones. Each night the wolves told Perrin what they could of the Aes Sedai ahead, which was not much. Wildfire's pack shadowed, but well back. One thing did become clear. Perrin was covering as much ground each day as he had the first, and each day he sliced as much as ten miles from the Aes Sedai lead. But when he caught up, what then?

Before the wolves each night, Perrin would sit talking quietly with Loial, as they smoked their pipes together. It was the "what then" that Perrin wanted to talk about. Dobraine seemed to think they should charge in and die doing their best. Rhuarc only said that they must wait to see what the sun shone on tomorrow and that all men must wake from the dream, which was not so different from Dobraine. Loial might be a young Ogier, but he was still ninety-odd; Perrin suspected Loial had read more books than he himself had seen, and he often came out with surprising knowledge about Aes Sedai.

"There are several books about Aes Sedai dealing with men who can channel." Loial frowned around his pipe; its leaf-carved bowl was as big as Perrin's two fists. "Elora, daughter of Amar daughter of Coura, wrote *Men of Fire and Women of Air* in the early days of Artur Hawkwing's reign. And Ledar, son of Shandin son of Koimal, wrote *A Study of Men, Women and the One Power Among Humans* only some three hundred years ago. Those are the two best, I think. Elora in particular; she wrote in the style of. . . . No. I will be brief." Perrin doubted that, brevity was seldom numbered among Loial's virtues when he spoke of books. The Ogier cleared his throat. "By Tower law, the man must be taken to the Tower for trial before he can be gentled." For a moment Loial's ears twitched violently, and his long eyebrows drew down grimly, but he patted Perrin's shoulder in an effort at comfort. "I cannot think they mean to do that, Perrin. I hear they spoke of honoring him, and he is the Dragon Reborn. They know that."

"Honor?" Perrin said quietly. "Maybe they're letting him sleep on silk, but a prisoner is still a prisoner."

"I am sure they are treating him well, Perrin. I am sure." The Ogier did not sound sure, and his sigh was a hollow gale. "And he is safe until he does reach Tar Valon. What I do not understand is how they captured him." That huge head swung in open puzzlement. "Perrin, both Elora and Ledar say that when Aes Sedai find a man of great power, they always gather thirteen to take him. Oh, they recount stories of four or five, and both mention Caraighan—she brought a man nearly two thousand miles to the Tower by herself after he killed both of her Warders—but. . . . Perrin, they wrote of Yurian Stonebow and Guaire Amalasan. Of Raolin Darksbane and Davian, as well, but the others are who worry me." Those were four of the most powerful among the men who had called themselves the Dragon Reborn, all long ago, before Artur Hawkwing. "Six Aes Sedai tried to capture Stonebow, and he killed three and captured the others himself. Six tried to take Amalasan; he killed one and stilled two more. Surely Rand is as strong as Stonebow or Amalasan. Are there really only six ahead of us? It would explain much."

Perhaps it did, but no comfort in it. Thirteen Aes Sedai might be able to beat off any attack Perrin could mount by themselves, without their Warders and guards. Thirteen Aes Sedai could threaten to gentle Rand if Perrin attacked. Surely they would not—they did know Rand was the Dragon Reborn; they knew he had to be there at the Last Battle—but could Perrin risk it, Tower law or no Tower law? Who knew why Aes Sedai did anything? He had never been able to make himself trust even Aes Sedai who had tried to show themselves friends. They always held their secrets, and how could a man ever be sure when he could feel them moving behind his back, however much they smiled to his face? Who could say what Aes Sedai would do?

In truth, Loial did not know much that would help when the day came, and besides, he was much more interested in talking about Erith. Perrin knew he had left two letters with Faile, one addressed to his mother and the other to Erith, to be delivered when she could if anything untoward should happen. Which Loial had nearly bent over backward trying to assure her would not happen; he always worried terribly about worrying anyone else. Perrin had left his own letter for Faile; Amys had carried it out to leave with the Wise Ones in the Aiel camp.

"She is so beautiful," Loial murmured, staring at the night as if seeing her. "Her face is so delicate, yet strong at the same time. When I looked at her eyes, it seemed I could see nothing else. And her ears!" Abruptly his own ears were vibrating wildly, and he choked on his pipe. "Please," he gasped, "forget I mentioned. . . . I should not have spoken of. . . . You know I am not coarse, Perrin."

"I've forgotten already," Perrin said weakly. Her *ears?*

Loial wanted to know what it was like being married. Not that he had any intention of marrying yet, he was quick to add; he was too young, and he had his book to finish, and he was not ready to settle down to a life of never leaving the *stedding* except to visit another, which a wife would assuredly insist on. He was just curious. No more than that.

So Perrin spoke of life with Faile, how she had transplanted his roots before he knew it. Once the Two Rivers had been home; now home was wherever Faile was. The thought that she was waiting quickened his step. Her presence brightened a room, and at her smile, every trouble receded. Of course, he could not speak of how thinking of her made his blood leap, or looking at her his heart pound—it would not have been decent—and he certainly had no intention of mentioning the trouble she had planted in his bones. What was he to do? He really was ready to go on his knees to her, but a stubborn iron seed in him required that one word from her first. If only she would just say she wanted things to be as they had been.

"What about her jealousy?" Loial asked, and it was Perrin's turn to choke. "Are wives all like that?"

"Jealousy?" Perrin said stoutly. "Faile is not jealous. Where did you get that idea? She is perfect."

"Of course she is," Loial said faintly, peering into his pipe bowl. "Do you have any more Two Rivers tabac? All I have after this is some sharp Cairhienin leaf."

Had it all been like that, the journey would have been peaceful in a way, as much as such a chase could be. The land rolled by without another soul in sight. If the sun was molten gold, turning the air to an oven, hawks often wheeled in the cloudless blue sky. The wolves, not wanting humans coming out where they were, drove deer toward the road in such numbers that there were more than even such a large group needed, and it was not unusual to see a proud buck with a tall forked rack and his does and a few spike-horns standing in plain sight as the column passed. But there was an old saying. "The only man completely at peace is a man without a navel."

The Cairhienin were not easy with the Aiel, of course, frequently frowning at them, or sneering openly. More than once Dobraine muttered about being outnumbered twelve to one. He respected their fighting abilities, but in the way you respected the dangerous qualities of a pack of rabid leopards. The Aiel did not glare or sneer; they just made it plain the Cairhienin were beneath notice. Perrin would not have been surprised to see one of them try to walk through a Cairhienin for refusing to admit he was there. Rhuarc said there would be no trouble, so long as the treekillers started none. Dobraine said there would be no trouble, so long as the savages kept out of his way. Perrin wished he could be certain they would not start killing one another before they even saw the Aes Sedai holding Rand.

He had some hope the Mayeners might be a bridge between the two, though at times he found himself regretting it. The men in red breastplates got on well with the shorter men in plain armor—there had never been a war between Mayene and Cairhien—and the Mayeners also got on with the Aiel. Except for the Aiel War, Mayeners had never fought Aiel. Dobraine was quite friendly with Nurelle, often sharing the evening meal, and Nurelle took to smoking a pipe with various of the Aiel. Especially Gaul. That was where the regret came from.

"I have been talking with Gaul," Nurelle said diffidently. It was the fourth day on the road, and he had come up from the Mayeners to ride beside Perrin at the head of the column. Perrin was only half-listening; Wildfire had allowed one of the younger males in her pack to creep close soon after the Aes Sedai began moving that morning, and he had not smelled Rand. Every wolf knew the scent of Shadowkiller, it seemed. Still, for all the sketchiness of what Morning Clouds had seen, every wagon but one appeared to have a canvas cover on hoops. Rand was probably inside one of the others, and a good deal more comfortable out of the sun than Perrin was, with sweat rolling down his neck. "He was telling me of the Battle of Emond's Field," Nurelle went on, "and your Two Rivers Campaign. Lord Aybara, it would honor me greatly to hear of your battles from yourself."

Abruptly Perrin sat up stiff in his saddle, staring at the boy. No, not a boy, despite those pink cheeks and that open face. Nurelle was surely as old as he himself. But the man's scent, all bright and quivering slightly. . . . Perrin very nearly groaned. He had smelled that from young boys back home, but to be hero-worshiped by a man his own age was almost more than he could take.

If that had been the worst of it, though, he would hardly have minded. He expected the Aiel and the Cairhienin not to like one another. He should have expected a young man who had never seen a battle to look up

to one who had fought Trollocs. It was the things he could not have fore-
seen that frayed his nerves. The unforeseen could bite you on the ankle
when you least expected it and could least afford to be distracted.

Except for Gaul and Rhuarc, every Aiel man wore a strip of crimson
cloth tied around his temples, with that black-and-white disc above his
brows. Perrin had seen them in Cairhien, and in Caemlyn, but now when he
asked Gaul, and then Rhuarc, if that marked them as this *siswai'aman*
Rhuarc had spoken of, both men tried to pretend they did not know what
he was talking about, as if they could not see red headbands on five thousand men. Perrin even asked the man who seemed to be in charge under
Rhuarc, Urien, a Two Spires Reyn whom Perrin had met long ago, but
Urien seemed not to understand either. Well, Rhuarc had said he could only
bring *siswai'aman*, so that was how Perrin thought of them, even if he did
not know what it meant.

What he did know was there might be trouble between the *siswai'aman*
and the Maidens. When some of those men looked at the Maidens, Perrin
caught a whiff of jealousy. When some of the Maidens looked at the
siswai'aman, their scent made him think of a wolf hunkering over the carcass of a deer, not meaning to let any other of the pack have a bite if she
choked to death swallowing it all. He could not begin to fathom why, but
there it was, and sharp.

That was a "maybe" though, some time to come. Other things were
not. For the first two days after leaving the city, Sulin and Nandera both
put themselves forward whenever Rhuarc said anything concerning the
Maidens; every time Sulin backed away, blushing, but she was right there
the next time, every time. The second evening, when camp was made, they
tried to kill each other with their bare hands.

At least, that was what it looked like to Perrin, kicking each other, hit-
ting with fists, tossing each other to the ground, bending arms so that he
was sure bones must break—until whoever was at a disadvantage managed
to free herself with a twist or a blow. Rhuarc stopped him when he tried to
interfere, and looked surprised that he wanted to. A good many of the
Cairhienin and Mayeners gathered around to watch and place bets, but no
Aiel so much as glanced at the fight, not even the Wise Ones.

Finally Sulin had Nandera facedown with an arm doubled painfully
behind her; seizing Nandera's hair, she slammed the other woman's head
against the ground until she lay limp. For a long time the older woman
stood looking down at the one she had beaten. Then Sulin heaved the unconscious Nandera up onto her shoulders and staggered away with her.

Perrin assumed that Sulin would do the talking from then on, but such was not the case at all. She was still always there, but a bruised Nandera answered Rhuarc's questions and took his commands while an equally bruised Sulin kept silent, and when Nandera asked Sulin to do something, she did it without hesitation. Perrin could only scratch his head and wonder whether he actually had seen the fight end as he thought it had.

The Wise Ones always walked alongside the road in groups that varied in size and seemed to shift members constantly. By the end of the first day Perrin realized that all that shifting really centered around two women, Sorilea and Amys. By the end of the second, he was sure the two were urging very different view-pointers; there were too many glares and frowns. Now and then Perrin heard Aes Sedai mentioned; he caught snatches about "custom" and "battle," but never enough to understand. Amys began backing down more slowly, and blushing considerably less. Sometimes Rhuarc smelled faintly anxious when he looked at his wife, but that was the only sign he saw anything. By the third camp out of the city, Perrin half-expected to see Sulin and Nandera's fight repeated between Wise Ones.

Instead, the two women took a waterskin and went off a little distance, where they sat by themselves on the ground and removed their folded scarves so their long hair hung loose. He watched them into moonlit darkness, keeping far enough back that he would not eavesdrop even by accident, until he went to his own bed, but all they did was drink cups of water and talk. The next morning, the rest of the Wise Ones still shifted from group to group, but before the long column had covered three miles, Perrin realized that all centered on Sorilea now. Now and then she and Amys went off to one side of the road by themselves to talk, but there were no more glares. Had they been wolves, Perrin would have said a challenge to the pack leader had been defeated, but by their scents, Sorilea accepted Amys as almost an equal now, which did not fit wolves at all.

The seventh day out of Cairhien, riding beneath a broiling morning sun, he was worrying about what sort of surprise the Aiel were going to give him next, worrying about whether the Aiel and Cairhienin would stay away from each others' throats another day, about what he was going to do when he caught the Aes Sedai in another three or four days.

All of that vanished at a sending from Half Tail. There was a large party of men—and women maybe; wolves sometimes had difficulty telling male humans from female—only a few miles to the west, and riding hard in the same direction Perrin was heading. It was the sketchy image of the two banners they rode behind that drew Perrin up.

He was surrounded quickly, by Dobraine and Nurelle, Rhuarc and
Urien, Nandera and Sulin, Sorilea and Amys. "Keep on," he told them,
turning Stayer west. "We may have a few friends to join us, but we don't
want to lose any time."

They did keep on as he rode away, but they did not let him go alone.
Before he covered a quarter of a mile he was trailed by a dozen of the
Winged Guards and as many Cairhienin, at least twenty Maidens led by
Sulin and an equal number of *siswai'aman* behind a gray-haired man with
green eyes and a face that appeared to have been used to break stone, Perrin
was only surprised there was not a Wise One or two.

"Friends," Sulin murmured to herself, trotting at his stirrup. "Friends
who appear suddenly, with no warning, and he suddenly just knows they
are there." Looking up at him, she spoke louder. "I would not like to see
you trip over a pillow and fall on your nose again."

Perrin shook his head, wondering what other cudgels he had given her
while she masqueraded as a servant. Aiel were strange.

By the sun he rode for nearly an hour, guided by the wolves, as surely
as arrow to target, and when he topped a low rise, he was not surprised by
what he saw perhaps two miles ahead, mounted men in a long column of
twos, Two Rivers men with his own Red Wolfhead banner at their head
streaming on a light breeze. What did surprise him was that there really
were women with them—nine, he counted—and a number of men he was
sure were not Two Rivers folk. What tightened his jaw was the second
banner. The Red Eagle of Manetheren. He could not say how many times
he had told them not to take one of those out of the Two Rivers; one of the
few things he had not been able to stop back home just by suggesting was
the flying of that flag. Still, the wolves' imperfect sending of the banners
had prepared him.

They saw him and his companions quickly, of course. There were good
eyes in that band. They drew up, waiting, and some unlimbered bows
from their backs, the great Two Rivers bows that could kill a man at three
hundred paces and more.

"No one get in front of me," Perrin said. "They'll not shoot if they recognize me."

"It seems yellow eyes see far," Sulin said flatly. A number of the others
were looking at him oddly.

"Just stay behind me," Perrin sighed.

As he rode closer at the head of his strange party, bows that had been
raised were, lowered and arrows un-nocked. They had Stepper, he saw with

delight, and with less delight, Swallow. Faile would never forgive him if he let her black mare be injured. It would be good to be back on his dun, but maybe he would keep Stayer as well; a lord could have two horses. Even a lord who might not have more than another four days to live.

Dannil rode out from the Two Rivers column, knuckling his thick mustaches, and Aram, and the women rode with them. Perrin recognized ageless Aes Sedai faces even before he picked out Verin and Alanna, both riding to the rear of the women. He did not know any of the others, but he was certain who they were, if not how they had gotten here. Nine. Nine Aes Sedai could be more than useful in three or four days now, yet how far could he trust them? They were nine, and Rand had told them only six could follow him. He wondered which one was Merana, their leader.

A square-faced Aes Sedai who looked like a farmer beneath her ageless-ness spoke before Dannil could. Her mount was a solid brown mare. "So you are Perrin Aybara. Lord Perrin, I should say. We've heard a great deal about you."

"It is a surprise to meet you here," an arrogant if beautiful woman said coolly, "with such odd companions." She rode a dark gelding with a fierce eye; Perrin would have wagered the animal was trained as a warhorse. "We thought sure you would be ahead of us yet."

Ignoring them—one of those two must be Merana, and he was not certain what to say to her yet—Perrin looked at Dannil. "Not that I'm displeased, but how did you come here?"

Dannil glanced at the Aes Sedai and stroked his mustaches furiously. "We started out like you said, Lord Perrin, and as fast as we could. I mean, we left the wagons and all, since it seemed there must be some reason for you to leave so quick. Then Kiruna Sedai and Bera Sedai and the others caught us up, and they said Alanna could find Rand—the Lord Dragon, I mean—and since you went with him, I thought sure you'd be wherever he was, and no way to tell us if you'd gone from Cairhien, and. . . ." He drew a deep breath. "Anyway, it seems they were right, weren't they, Lord Perrin."

Perrin frowned, wondering how Alanna could find Rand. But she must be able to, or Dannil and the rest would not be here. She and Verin were continuing to stay back, with a slim, hazel-eyed woman who seemed to sigh often.

"I am Bera Harkin," the square-faced woman said, "and this is Kiruna Nachiman." She indicated her haughty companion. Apparently the others could do without introductions yet. "Will you tell us why you are here when young al'Thor—the Lord Dragon—is several days north?"

It did not take much consideration. If these nine meant to join the Aes Sedai ahead, there was little he could do to stop it. Nine Aes Sedai on his side, however. . . . "He's being held prisoner. An Aes Sedai named Coiren and at least five others are taking him to Tar Valon. At least, they mean to. I mean to stop them." That caused considerable shock, with Dannil's eyes widening and Aes Sedai all talking at once. Aram was the only one who did not appear affected, but then, he did not seem to care much about anything except Perrin and his sword. The smells from the Aes Sedai were all outrage and fear for all their calm faces.

"We have to stop them, Bera," came from a woman with her hair in beaded Taraboner braids, just as a pale Cairhienin woman on a lanky bay mare said, "We cannot allow Elaida to have him, Bera."

"Six?" the hazel-eyed woman said incredulously. "Six could not take him. I am sure of it."

"I told you he was injured," Alanna half-wept. Perrin knew her scent well enough to pick it out; she smelled of pain. "I told you." Verin kept silent, but she smelled furious—and afraid.

Kiruna ran a dark, contemptuous gaze over Perrin's party. "You mean to stop Aes Sedai with this, young man? Verin did not say you were a fool."

"I have a few more than this back on the Tar Valon Road," he said dryly.

"Then you may join them to us," Kiruna told him, as though making a concession. "That will be all right, Bera, will it not?" Bera nodded.

He could not understand why Kiruna's attitude grated at him so, but this was no time to try puzzling it out. "I also have three hundred Two Rivers archers I intend to take back to the road with me." How could Alanna know whether Rand was hurt? "You Aes Sedai are welcome to come along."

They did not like it, certainly. They rode off a dozen paces to one side to discuss it—even his ears heard nothing; they must have been using the Power somehow—and for a time, Perrin thought they were going to ride on alone.

In the end they did come, but Bera and Kiruna rode on either side of him all the way back to the road, taking turns telling him how dangerous and delicate this situation was, and he must do nothing that might endanger young al'Thor. Bera at least remembered to call Rand the Dragon Reborn sometimes. One thing they made quite clear was that Perrin was not to so much as put one foot in front of the other without asking them first. Bera began to seem a little vexed that he would not repeat her words back to her; Kiruna seemed to take them for said. Perrin began to wonder whether he had made a mistake asking them to come.

If the Aes Sedai were impressed by the collection of Aiel and Mayeners and Cairhienin marching along the road, they gave no sign to either eye or nose. They did add their little bit to the bubbling of the kettle, though. The Mayeners and Cairhienin seemed very heartened at the appearance of nine Aes Sedai and sixteen Warders, and they nearly bowed and scraped whenever one of the women came close. Maidens and *siswai'aman* looked at the Aes Sedai as though they expected the women to crush them underfoot, but though the Wise Ones kept faces as smooth as the Aes Sedai, Perrin smelled waves of pure fury from them. Except for a Brown named Masuri, the Aes Sedai ignored the Wise Ones entirely at first, but after Masuri had been rebuffed at least two dozen times over the next few days—she was persistent, yet the Wise Ones avoided the Aes Sedai so smoothly that Perrin thought they must do it by instinct—after that, Bera and Kiruna and all the rest were constantly looking at the Wise Ones and talking among themselves behind some invisible barrier that kept Perrin from hearing what they said.

He would have eavesdropped if he could; they were hiding more than talk about the Aielwomen. For one thing, Alanna refused to tell him how she knew where Rand was—"There is knowledge that would burn any mind but Aes Sedai," she had told him, cool and mysterious, but she fairly reeked of anxiety and pain—and she would not even admit to having said he was injured in some way. Verin hardly said a word to him, only watched everything with those dark birdlike eyes and a small secret smile, yet she gave off waves of frustration and anger. By smell he would have said Bera or Kiruna was the leader; Bera, he thought, though it was close and sometimes seemed to shift the other way for a time. It was hard to say otherwise, though one or the other rode beside him a good hour every day, repeating variations of their original "advice" and generally assuming they were in charge. Nurelle seemed to think they were, taking their commands without so much as a glance at Perrin, and Dobraine did no more than glance first. For a full day and a half Perrin assumed Merana had remained in Caemlyn, and it came as a shock to hear the slim hazel-eyed woman addressed by that name. Rand had said she headed the embassy from Salidar, but for all that the Aes Sedai appeared equals on the surface, Perrin marked her as low wolf in the pack; dull resignation and anxiety filled her scent. No surprise that Aes Sedai kept secrets, of course, but he intended to rescue Rand from Coiren and the lot ahead, and he would have liked a hint as to whether he would have to rescue him from Kiruna and her friends.

At least it was good being reunited with Dannil and the others even if they were nearly as bad around the Aes Sedai as the Mayeners and Cairhienin. The Two Rivers men were so glad to see him that few even grumbled when he told them to put away the Red Eagle; it would come out again, Perrin was sure, but Dannil's brother Tell, who looked almost exactly like him except for a pickaxe nose and long thin mustaches in the Domani manner, folded it carefully into his saddlebags. They did not go on without banners, of course. For one thing, there was his own Red Wolf-head. They might have ignored him if he told them to pack that away, and for some reason, Kiruna's cool, disdainful gaze made him want to display it. But beside that, Dobraine and Nurelle produced banners, since one had been shown already. Not the Rising Sun of Cairhien or the Golden Hawk in flight of Mayene. Each had brought a pair of Rand's standards, the Dragon red-and-gold on white, and the black-and-white disc on crimson. The Aiel did not seem to care one way or another, and the Aes Sedai grew very cold, but they seemed fitting ensigns to go on behind.

On the tenth day, with the sun almost halfway to its peak, Perrin was feeling grim despite banners and Two Rivers men and Stepper under him. They should overtake the Aes Sedai wagons not long after noon, but he still did not know what to do after that. It was then that the sending came from the wolves. *Come now. Many two-legs. Many, many, many! Come now!*

CHAPTER

55

Dumai's Wells

Gawyn tried to keep his mind on the landscape as he rode at the head of the column. This sort of rolling terrain with its scattered bunches of trees was just flat enough to make you think you could see a long way, when in truth some of those occasional long ridges and low hills were not quite so low as they seemed. The wind was gusting up waves of dust today, and dust could hide a lot, too. Dumai's Wells lay just off the road to his right, three stone wells in a small copse; the water barrels could stand topping, and it was at least four days to the next sure water, if the Alianelle Spring had not gone dry, but Galina had ordered no stopping. He tried to hold his attention where it should be, but he could not.

From time to time he twisted in his saddle, looking back at the long snake of wagons stretching along the road, with Aes Sedai and Warders riding alongside, and servants who were not in the wagons walking. Most of the Younglings were at the rear, where Galina had ordered them. He could not see the one wagon, in the center of the column with six Aes Sedai always riding beside it, that had no canvas cover. He would have killed al'Thor if he could, but this sickened him. Even Erian had refused to take part any longer after the second day, and the Light knew she had cause. Galina was adamant, though.

Putting his eyes firmly forward, he touched Egwene's letter in his coat pocket, where it lay carefully wrapped in layers of silk. Just a few words to say she loved him, that she must go; no more. He read it five or six times a day. She never mentioned his promise. Well, he had not raised a hand against al'Thor. He had been stunned to learn the man was a prisoner and had been for days when he heard of it. Somehow he must make her understand that. He had promised her not to raise his hand against the man, and he would not if he died for it, but he would not raise a hand to help him either. Egwene had to understand that. Light, she had to.

Sweat trickled down his face, and he wiped his eyes with his sleeve. Egwene he could do nothing about yet except pray. He could about Min. Somehow he had to. She did not deserve to be carried to the Tower a prisoner; he would not believe it. If the Warders would only slacken the guard on her, he could. . . .

Suddenly Gawyn became aware of a horse galloping back down the road toward the wagons through sheets of dust, seemingly with no rider. "Jisao," he ordered, "tell the wagon drivers to halt. Hal, tell Rajar to ready the Younglings." Without a word they wheeled their horses and galloped. Gawyn waited.

That was Benji Dalfor's steel-dust gelding, and as it came closer, Gawyn could see Benji doubled over and clinging to the gelding's mane. The horse almost went past before Gawyn could seize the reins.

Benji turned his head without straightening, peered at Gawyn with glazed eyes. There was blood around his mouth, and he had one arm tight against his middle as if trying to hold himself together. "Aiel," he mumbled. "Thousands. All sides, I think." Suddenly he smiled. "Cold today, isn't—" Blood gushed out of his mouth, and he toppled to the road, staring unblinking at the sun.

Gawyn spun his stallion around, galloping toward the wagons. There would be time for Benji later, if any of them were alive.

Galina rode to meet him, linen dustcloak flaring behind her, dark eyes blazing fury in that serene face. She had been furious constantly since the day after al'Thor tried to escape. "Who do you think you are, ordering the wagons stopped?" she demanded.

"There are thousands of Aiel closing on us, Aes Sedai." He managed to keep his tone polite. The wagons were stopped at least, and the Younglings forming up, but wagon drivers fingered their reins impatiently, servants peered about fanning themselves, Aes Sedai chatted with Warders.

Galina's lips writhed contemptuously. "You fool. No doubt those are the

Shaido. Sevanna said she would give us an escort. But if you doubt, take
your Younglings and see for yourself. These wagons will keep moving toward Tar Valon. It is time you learned that I give the orders here, not—"

"And if they are not your tame Aiel?" This was not the first time in the
last few days that she had suggested he lead a scout himself; he suspected if
he did, he would find Aiel, and not tame. "Whoever they are, they've killed
one of my men." At least one; there were still six scouts out. "Maybe you
should consider the possibility these are al'Thor's Aiel, come to rescue him.
It will be too late when they start spitting us."

It was only then that he realized he was shouting, but Galina's anger
actually faded. She looked up the road to where Benji lay, then nodded
slowly. "Perhaps it would not be unwise to be cautious this once."

Rand labored for breath; the air inside the chest felt thick and hot. Luckily
he could not smell it any longer. They sluiced him off with a bucket of
water each night, but that was hardly a bath, and for a time after they
closed the lid on him each morning and latched it, the stench added by yet
another day exposed to the full blast of the sun assaulted his nose. Holding
the Void was an effort. He was a mass of stripes; not an inch of him from
shoulders to knees but burned even before sweat touched it, and those ten
thousand flames flickered on the borders of emptiness, trying to consume
it. The half-healed wound in his side throbbed in the distance, but the
emptiness around him quivered with every throb. Alanna. He could feel
Alanna. Close. No. He could not waste time thinking about her; even if
she had followed, six Aes Sedai would not be able to free him. If they did
not decide to join Galina. No trust. Never again trust for any Aes Sedai.
Maybe he was imagining it anyway. Sometimes he did imagine things in
here, cool breezes, walking. Sometimes he lost thought of anything else
and hallucinated about walking free. Just walking. Hours lost in what was
important. He labored for breath, and he felt his way across the ice-slick
barrier that divided him from the Source. Again and again, fumbling to
those six soft points. Soft. He could not stop. The fumbling was important.

Dark, Lews Therin moaned in the depths of his head. *No more dark. No
more.* Over and over again. Not too badly, though. Rand just ignored him
this time.

Suddenly he gasped; the chest was moving, grating loudly along the
wagon bed. Was it night already? Welted flesh flinched involuntarily.
There would be another beating before he was fed and doused with water

and trussed like a goose to sleep however he could. But he would be out of the box. The darkness around him was incomplete, a deep dark gray. The tiny crack around the lid let in the smallest amount of light, though he could not see with his head jammed between his knees, and his eyes took as long each day to see anything but blackness as his nose did to grow deadened. Even so, it must be night.

He could not help groaning as the chest tilted; there was no room for him to slide, but he shifted, putting new strains on muscles sore beyond sore. His tiny prison thumped to the ground hard. The lid would open soon. How many days in the broiling sun? How many nights? He had lost count. Which one would it be this time? Faces spun through his head. He had marked down every woman when she took her turn at him. They were a jumble now; remembering which came where or when seemed beyond him. But he knew that Galina and Erian and Katerine had beaten him most often, the only ones to do so more than once. Those faces glowed in his mind with a feral light. How often did they want to hear him scream?

Abruptly it came to him that the chest should have been opened by now. They intended to leave him in here all night, and then there would be tomorrow's sun, and— Muscles too bruised and sore to move managed a frantic heave. "Let me out!" he shouted hoarsely. Fingers scrabbled pain-fully behind his back, futilely. "Let me out!" he screamed. He thought he heard a woman laugh.

For a time he wept, but then tears dried up in rage like a furnace. *Help me*, he snarled at Lews Therin.

Help me, the man groaned. *The Light help me.*

Muttering darkly, Rand returned to feeling blindly across that smooth plain to the six soft points. Sooner or later, they would let him out. Sooner or later, they would slacken their guard. And when they did. . . . He did not even know it when he began a rasping laugh.

Crawling up the gentle slope on his belly, Perrin peered over the crest into a scene from the Dark One's dreams. The wolves had given him some no-tion of what to expect, but notions paled beside reality. Perhaps a mile from where he lay beneath the midday sun, a huge milling mass of Shaido completely surrounded what seemed to be a ring of wagons and men cen-tered on a small clump of trees not far from the road. A number of the wagons were bonfires, flames dancing. Balls of fire, small as a fist and large as boulders, hurtled into the Aiel, gouts of fire flared, turning a dozen at a

time to torches; lightning fell from a cloudless sky, hurling earth and
cadin'sor-clad figures into the air. But silver flashes of lightning struck at
the wagons, too, and fire leaped from the Aiel. Much of that fire suddenly
died or exploded short of any target, many of the lightning bolts stopped
abruptly, but if the battle seemed slightly in favor of the Aes Sedai, the
sheer number of Shaido had to prove overwhelming eventually.

"There must be two or three hundred women channeling down there,
if not more." Kiruna, lying beside him, sounded impressed. Sorilea, beyond the Green sister, certainly looked impressed. The Wise One smelled
concerned; not afraid, but troubled. "I have never seen so many weaves at
once," the Aes Sedai went on. "I think there are at least thirty sisters in the
camp. You have brought us to a boiling cauldron, young Aybara."

"Forty thousand Shaido," Rhuarc muttered grimly on Perrin's other
side. He even smelled grim. "Forty thousand at the least, and small satisfaction to know why they did not send more south."

"The Lord Dragon is down there?" Dobraine asked, looking across
Rhuarc. Perrin nodded. "And you mean to go in there and bring him out?"
Perrin nodded again, and Dobraine sighed. He smelled resigned, not afraid.
"We will go in, Lord Aybara, but I do not believe we will come out." This
time Rhuarc nodded.

Kiruna looked at the men. "You do realize there are not enough of us.
Nine. Even if your Wise Ones can actually channel to any effect, we are
not enough to match that." Sorilea snorted loudly, but Kiruna kept her
eyes where they were.

"Then turn around and ride south," Perrin told her. "I'll not let Elaida
have Rand."

"Good," Kiruna replied, smiling. "Because I will not either." He
wished her smile did not make his skin crawl. Of course, had she seen the
malevolent look Sorilea directed at the back of her head, her skin might
have crawled too.

Perrin signaled to those at the bottom of the ridge, and Sorilea and the
Green slid down until they could straighten, then hurried in opposite
directions.

It was not much of a plan that they had. It boiled down to reaching
Rand somehow, freeing him somehow, then hoping he was not injured too
badly to make a gateway for as many as could to escape with him before
either the Shaido or the camp's Aes Sedai managed to kill them. Minor
problems, no doubt, for a hero in a story or a gleeman's tale, but Perrin
wished there had been time for some sort of real planning, not just what he

and Dobraine and Rhuarc had hammered out with the clan chief running as fast as he could between their horses. Time was one of many things they did not have, though. No telling if the Tower Aes Sedai would be able to hold off the Shaido for even another hour.

First to move were the Two Rivers men and the Winged Guards, divided into two companies, one surrounding Wise Ones afoot and the other mounted Aes Sedai and Warders. To left and right they crossed the ridge. Dannil had let them bring out the Red Eagle again, in addition to the Red Wolfhead. Rhuarc did not even glance toward where Amys walked not far from Kiruna's dark gelding, but Perrin heard him murmur, "May we see the sun rise together, shade of my heart."

At the end, the Mayeners and Two Rivers men were to cover the Wise Ones and Aes Sedai in retreat, or maybe it would be the other way around. In either case, Bera and Kiruna did not seem to like the plan; they very much wanted to be where Rand was.

"Are you sure you will not ride, Lord Aybara?" Dobraine asked from his saddle; to him, the notion of fighting on foot was anathema.

Perrin patted the axe hanging at his hip. "This is not much use from horseback." It was, in truth, but he did not want to ride Stepper or Stayer into what lay ahead. Men could choose whether they threw themselves into the midst of steel and death; he chose for his horses, and today he chose no. "Maybe you'll lend me a stirrup when the time comes." Dobraine blinked—Cairhienin made little use of foot soldiers—but he seemed to understand, and nodded.

"It is time for the pipers to play the dance," Rhuarc said, lifting his black veil, though today there would be no pipers playing, which some of the Aiel did not like. Many of the Maidens did not like the required strips of red cloth tied around their arms, to distinguish them from Shaido Maidens for the wetlanders; they seemed to think anyone should know at a glance.

Black-veiled Maidens and *siswai'aman* began trotting up the slope in a thick column, and Perrin walked with Dobraine to where Loial already stood at the head of the Cairhienin, gripping his axe in both hands and ears laid back. Aram was there, too, afoot and his sword bare; the former Tinker wore a dark smile of anticipation. Dobraine waved his arm for the advance, behind Rand's twin banners, and saddles creaked as a small forest of five hundred lances climbed beside the Aiel.

Nothing had changed in the battle, which surprised Perrin until he realized only moments had passed since he last saw it. The time had seemed much longer. The great mass of Shaido still pressed inward; wagons still burned, perhaps more than before; lightning still struck from the sky, and fire leaped in balls and billows.

The Two Rivers Men were almost to their position, with the Mayeners and Aes Sedai and Wise Ones, moving almost unhurriedly across the rolling plain. Perrin would have held them farther back, to give them a better chance at escape when the time came for that, but Dannil kept insisting they had to close to at least three hundred paces for their bows to be effective, and Nurelle had been just as anxious not to hang back. Even the Aes Sedai, who Perrin was sure only had to be near enough to see clearly, had insisted. None of the Shaido had looked around yet. At least, none were pointing at the threat moving slowly toward their backs; none were wheeling about to face it. All seemed fixed on rushing at the circle of wagons, falling back before fire and lightning, then rushing in again. All it would take would be one looking behind, but the inferno ahead held them.

Eight hundred paces. Seven hundred. The Two Rivers men dismounted, taking bows in hand. Six hundred. Five. Four.

Dobraine drew his sword, raised it high. "The Lord Dragon, Taborwin and victory!" he shouted, and the shout came from five hundred throats as lances snapped down.

Perrin had just time to seize hold of Dobraine's stirrup before the Cairhienin were thundering forward. Loial's long legs matched the horses pace for pace. Loping along, letting the horse pull him in long leaping strides, Perrin sent his mind out. *Come.*

Ground covered with brown grass, seemingly empty, suddenly gave birth to a thousand wolves, lean brown plains wolves, and some of their darker, heavier forest cousins, running low to hurl themselves into the backs of the Shaido with snapping jaws just as the first long Two Rivers shafts rained out of the sky beyond them. A second flight already arched high. New lightnings fell with the arrows, new fires bloomed. Veiled Shaido turning to fight wolves had only moments to realize they were not the only threat before a solid spear of Aiel stabbed into them alongside a hammer of Cairhienin lancers.

Snatching his axe free, Perrin hacked down a Shaido in his way and leaped over the man as he fell. They had to reach Rand; everything rested on that. Beside him Loial's great axe rose and fell and swung, carving a path. Aram seemed to dance with his sword, laughing as he cut down everyone in his way. There was no time to think of anyone else. Perrin worked his axe methodically; he was hewing wood, not flesh; he tried not to see the blood that spurted, even when crimson sprayed his face. He had to reach Rand. He was slashing a path through brambles.

All he focused on was the man, in front of him—he thought of them as men even when height said it might be a Maiden; he was not sure he could swing that red-dripping half-moon blade if he let himself think it was a woman he swung at—he focused, but other things drifted across his vision as he cut his way forward. A silvery lightning strike hurled *cadin'sor*-clad figures into the air, some wearing the scarlet headband, some not. Another bolt threw Dobraine from his horse; the Cairhienin labored to his feet, laying about him with his sword. Fire enveloped a knot of Cairhienin and Aiel, men and horses turned to screaming torches, those who could still scream.

These things passed before his eyes, but he did not let himself see them. There were only the men before him, the brambles, to be cleared by his axe and Loial's, and Aram's sword. Then he saw something that pierced his concentration. A rearing horse, a toppling rider being pulled from his saddle as Aiel spears stabbed him. A rider in a red breastplate. And there was another of the Winged Guards, and a clump of them, thrusting their lances, with Nurelle's plume waving above his helmet. A moment later he saw Kiruna, face serenely unconcerned, striding like a queen of battles along a path carved for her by three Warders and the fires that leaped from her own hands. And there was Bera, and farther over, Faeldrin and Masuri and. . . . What under the Light were they all doing here? What were any of them doing? They were supposed to be back with the Wise Ones!

From somewhere ahead came a hollow boom, like a thunderclap cutting through the din of screams and shouts. A moment later, a slash of light appeared not twenty paces from him, slicing through several men and a horse like a huge razor as it widened into a gateway. A black-coated man with a sword jumped out of it, and went down with a Shaido spear through his middle, but a moment later eight or nine more sprang through as the gateway vanished, forming a circle around the fallen man with their swords. With more than swords. Some of the Shaido who rushed at them fell to a blade, but more simply burst into flame. Heads exploded like melons dropped onto stone from a height. Maybe a hundred paces beyond them, Perrin thought he saw another circle of men in black coats, surrounded by fire and death, but he had no time to wonder. Shaido were closing around him, too.

Setting himself back-to-back with Loial and Aram, he slashed and hacked desperately. There was no going forward now. It was all he could do to remain standing where he was. Blood pounded in his ears, and he could hear himself gasping for breath. He could hear Loial, too, panting like a huge bellows. Perrin knocked aside a stabbing spear with his axe, slashed at another Aiel with the spike on the backswing, caught a spearhead with his hand, unmindful of the bloody gash it made, split a black-veiled face. He did not think they were going to last much longer. Every part of him centered on staying alive for one heartbeat more. Almost every part. One corner of his mind held an image of Faile, and the sad thought that he would not be able to apologize for not coming back to her.

Doubled painfully inside the chest, panting, Rand fumbled at the shield between him and the Source. Moaning floated across the Void, grim fury and burning fear slid along the edge of it; he was no longer altogether certain which was his and which Lews Therin's. Suddenly his breath froze. Six points, but one was hard now. Not soft; hard. And then a second. A third. Rasping laughter filled his ears; that was his, he realized after a moment. A fourth knot became hard. He waited, trying to stifle what sounded uncomfortably like deranged giggling. The last two points remained soft. Those muffled cackles died.

They will feel it, Lews Therin groaned desperately. *They will feel it and call the others back.*

Rand licked cracked lips with a tongue nearly as dry; all the moisture in him seemed to have gone into the sweat that slicked him and bit his welts. If he tried and failed, there would never be another chance. He could not wait. There might never be another chance anyway.

Cautiously, blindly, he felt at the four hard points. There was nothing there, any more than the shield itself was anything he could feel or see, but somehow he could feel *around* this nothingness, feel a shape to it. Like knots. There was always space between the cords in a knot, however tightly pulled, gaps finer than a hair, where only air could go. Slowly, ever so slowly, he fumbled into one of those gaps, squeezing through infinitesimal spaces between what seemed not to be there at all. Slowly. How long before the others returned? If they took it up again before he found a way through this tortuous labyrinth. . . . Slowly. And suddenly he could feel the Source, like brushing it with a fingernail; the bare edge of a fingernail. *Saidin* was still beyond him—the shield was still there—but he could feel hope welling in Lews Therin. Hope and trepidation. Two Aes Sedai were still holding their part of the barrier, still aware of what they held.

Rand could not have explained what he did next, though Lews Therin had explained how; explained between drifting off into his own mad fancies, between towering rages and wailing over his lost. Ilyena, between gibbering that he deserved to die and shouting that he would not let them sever him. It was as if he flexed what he had extended through the knot, flexed it as hard as he could. The knot resisted. It trembled. And then it burst. There were only five. The barrier thinned. He could feel it grow less. An invisible wall only five bricks thick now instead of six. The two Aes Sedai would have felt it, too, though they might not understand exactly what had happened, or how. Please, Light, not now. Not yet.

Quickly, almost frantically, he attacked the remaining knots in turn. A second went; the shield thinned. It was quicker now, quicker with each, as if he were learning the path through, though it was different each time. The third knot gone. And a third soft point appeared; maybe the Aes Sedai did not know what he was doing, but they would not simply sit while the shield grew less and less. Truly frantic, Rand hurled himself at the fourth knot. He had to unravel it before a fourth sister came into the shield; four might be able to hold it whatever he did. Almost weeping, he struggled through the complex windings, slipping between nothingness. Frenziedly, he flexed, bursting the knot. The shield remained, but held by only three now. If he could only move fast enough.

When he reached for *saidin*, the invisible barrier was still there, but it no longer seemed stone or brick. It gave as he pressed, bending under his pressure, bending, bending. Suddenly it tore apart before him like rotted cloth. The Power filled him, and as it did, he seized at those three soft points, crushing them ruthlessly in fists of Spirit. Aside from that, he still could only channel where he could see, and all he could see, dimly, was the inside of the chest, what he could glimpse of it with his head forced between his knees. Before he even finished with the fists of Spirit, he channeled Air. The chest exploded away from him with a loud boom.

Free, Lews Therin breathed, and it was an echo of Rand's thought. *Free*. Or maybe the other way around.

They will pay, Lews Therin growled. *I am the Lord of the Morning*.

Rand knew he had to move even more quickly now, move quickly and violently, but at first he struggled to move at all. Muscles beaten twice a day for he did not know how long, crammed into a chest every day, those muscles screamed as he gritted his teeth and slowly pushed up to hands and knees. It was a distant screaming, someone else's body in pain, but he could not make that body move faster however strong *saidin* made him feel. Emptiness buffered emotion, but something close to panic tried to wriggle creepers into the Void.

He was in a large clump of scattered trees, with broad shafts of sunlight filtering through nearly leafless branches; he was shocked to realize it was still daylight, maybe even midday. He had to move; more Aes Sedai would be coming. Two lay on the ground near him, apparently unconscious, one with a nasty gash bleeding across her forehead. The third, an angular woman, was on her knees staring at nothing, clutching her head in both hands and screaming. She seemed untouched by all the splinters and pieces of the chest. He did not recognize any of them. An instant of regret that it was not Galina or Erian he had stilled—he was not sure he had intended to do that; Lews Therin had gone on at length about how he intended to sever every one of them who had imprisoned him; Rand hoped it had been his own idea, however hasty—an instant, and he saw another shape stretched out on the ground beneath bits of the chest. In rose-colored coat and breeches.

The angular woman did not look at him or stop shrieking even when he knocked her over against the low stone coping of a well as he crawled past. Desperately he wondered why no one came to her screams. Halfway to Min he became aware of lightning bolts lancing out of the sky and fireballs exploding overhead. He could smell wood burning, hear men shouting and screaming, the clash of metal, the cacophony of battle. He did not care if it was Tarmon Gai'don. If he had killed Min. . . . Gently he turned her over.

Big dark eyes stared up at him. "Rand," she breathed. "You're alive. I was afraid to look. There was an awful roar, and pieces of wood everywhere, and I recognized part of the chest, and . . ." Tears began spilling down her cheeks. "I thought they had. . . . I was afraid you were. . . ." Scrubbing at her face with bound hands, she drew a deep breath. Her ankles were bound too. "Will you untie me, sheepherder, and make one of your gateways away from here? Or don't bother with untying. Just toss me over your shoulder and go."

Deftly he wielded Fire, parting the cords that held her. "It isn't that simple, Min." He did not know this place at all; a gateway opened from here might go anywhere, if it opened at all. If he could open one at all. Pain and weariness shaved at the borders of the Void. He was not sure how much of the Power he could draw. Suddenly he realized he could feel *saidin* being channeled in every direction. Through the trees, beyond burning wagons, he could see Aiel fighting Warders and Gawyn's green-coated soldiers, being driven back by Aes Sedai fire and lightning, yet coming on again. Somehow Taim had found him and brought Asha'man soldiers and Aiel. "I cannot go just yet. I think some friends have come for me. Don't worry; I will protect you."

A jagged silver blaze split a tree on the edge of the copse, close enough to make Rand's hair stir. Min gave a start. "Friends," she muttered, rubbing her wrists.

He motioned her to stay where she was—except for that one errant bolt, the thicket appeared untouched—but when he shoved himself to his feet, she was right there, holding him up on one side. Staggering to the sparse tree line, he was grateful for her support, but he made himself straighten and stop leaning on her. How could she believe he would protect her if he needed her not to fall on his face? A hand on the shattered trunk of the lightning-struck tree helped. Tendrils of smoke rose from it, but it had not caught fire.

The wagons made a great ring around the trees. Some of the servants seemed to be trying to keep the horses together—the teams were all still harnessed—but most huddled wherever they could in hope of avoiding the fury falling from above. In truth, except for that one bolt, it all seemed aimed at the wagons and men fighting. Maybe at the Aes Sedai too. Each sat her horse a little way back from the whirl of spears and swords and flame, but not too far, sometimes standing in her stirrups for a better view.

Rand spotted Erian quickly, slender and dark-haired on a pale gray mare. Lews Therin snarled, and Rand struck almost without thinking. He felt the other man's disappointment as he did. Spirit to shield her, with the slight resistance that told of slicing through her connection of *saidar*, and even as that was tied, a club of Air to knock her unconscious from the saddle. If he decided to still her, he wanted her to know who was doing it and why. One of the Aes Sedai shouted for someone to tend Erian, but no one looked toward the trees. No one out there could feel *saidin*; they thought she had been felled by something from outside the wagons.

His eyes searched among the other mounted women, stopped on Katerine, wheeling her long-legged bay gelding back and forth, fire blazing wherever she looked among the Aiel. Spirit and Air, and she fell limply, one foot tangled in a stirrup.

Yes, Lews Therin laughed. *And now Galina. Her I want especially.*

Rand squeezed his eyes shut. What was he doing? It was Lews Therin who wanted those three so badly he could think of nothing else. Rand wanted to repay them for what they had done to him, but there was battle going on, men dying while he hunted for particular Aes Sedai. Maidens dying too, no doubt.

He took the next Aes Sedai, twenty paces to Katerine's left, with Spirit and Air, then moved to another tree and put Sarene Nemdahl on the ground, unconscious and shielded. Slowly he staggered along the edge of the thicket, striking like a cutpurse time and again. Min stopped trying to hold him up, though her hands hovered, ready to catch him.

"They're going to see us," she muttered. "One of them is going to look around and see us."

Galina, Lews Therin growled. *Where is she?*

Rand ignored him, and Min. Coiren fell, and two more whose names he did not know. He had to do what he could.

The Aes Sedai had no way of telling what was happening. Steadily along the ringwall of wagons, sisters toppled from their horses. Those still conscious spread themselves out more, trying to cover the whole perimeter, an air of anxiety suddenly in the way they handled their horses, the re-doubled fury with which fire blazed into the Aiel and lightning struck from the sky. It had to be something from outside, but Aes Sedai fell, and they did not know how or why.

Their numbers dwindled, and the effects began to tell. Fewer lightning bolts fizzled abruptly in midair, and more struck among the Warders and soldiers. Fewer balls of fire suddenly vanished or exploded before reaching the wagons. Aiel began pressing through the gaps between wagons; wag-ons were heaved over. In moments there were black-veiled Aiel everywhere, and chaos. Rand stared in amazement.

Warders and green-coated soldiers fought in clumps against Aiel, and Aes Sedai surrounded themselves with rains of fire. But there were Aiel fighting Aiel as well; men with the scarlet *siswai'aman* headband and Maid-ens with red strips tied to their arms fighting Aiel without. And Cairhienin lancers in their bell-shaped helmets and Mayeners in red breastplates were suddenly among the wagons too, striking at Aiel as well as Warders. Had he finally gone mad? He was conscious of Min, pressed against his back and trembling. She was real. What he was seeing must be real.

A dozen or so Aielmen, each as tall as he or taller, started trotting to-ward him. They wore no red. He watched them curiously until, within a pace of him, one raised a reversed spear like a cudgel. Rand channeled, and fire seemed to shoot out of the dozen everywhere. Charred and twisted bodies tumbled at his feet.

Suddenly Gawyn was reining a bay stallion up not ten steps in front of him, sword in hand and twenty or more green-coated men riding at his heels. For a moment they stared at one another, and Rand prayed he would not have to harm Elayne's brother.

"Min," Gawyn grated, "I can take you out of here."

She peeked past Rand's shoulder to shake her head; she was holding on to him so tightly, he did not think he could have pried her loose had he wanted to. "I'm staying with him, Gawyn. Gawyn, Elayne loves him."

With the Power in him, Rand could see the man's knuckles go white on his sword hilt. "Jisao," he said in a flat voice. "Rally the Younglings. We are cutting a way out of here." If his voice had been flat before, now it went dead. "Al'Thor, one day I will see you die." Digging his heels in, he galloped away, he and all the others shouting "Younglings!" at the top of their lungs, and more men in green coats cutting a way to join them with every stride.

A man in a black coat darted in front of Rand, staring after Gawyn, and the ground erupted in a gout of fire and earth that toppled half a dozen horses as they reached the wagons. Rand saw Gawyn sway in the saddle in the instant before he beat the black-coated man to the ground with a mace of Air. He did not know the hard-faced young man who snarled at him, but the fellow wore both the sword and Dragon on his high collar, and *saidin* filled him.

In an instant, it seemed, Taim was there, blue-and-gold Dragons twined around the sleeves of his black coat, staring down at the fellow. His collar bore neither pin. "You would not strike at the Dragon Reborn, Gedwyn," Taim said, at once soft and steely, and the hard-faced man scrambled to his feet, saluting with fist to heart.

Rand looked toward where Gawyn had been, but all he could see was a large group of men with a White Boar banner slashing their way deeper into the surrounding Aiel, with more green-coated men fighting to join them.

Taim turned to Rand, that almost-smile on his lips. "Under the circumstances, I trust you will not hold it against me, violating your command about confronting Aes Sedai. I had reason to visit you in Cairhien, and. . . ." He shrugged. "You look the worse for wear. You will allow me to—" The slight twist of his lips flattened as Rand stepped back from his outstretched hand, pulling Min with him. She hung on tighter than ever.

Lews Therin had begun ranting about killing as he always did when Taim appeared, rambling madly about the Forsaken and killing everybody, but Rand stopped listening, walled the man off to the buzzing of a fly. It was a trick he had learned inside the chest, when there was nothing to do but feel at the shield and listen to a voice in his head that was insane more often than not. Yet even without Lews Therin, he did not want to be Healed by the man. He thought if Taim ever touched him with the Power, however innocently, he would kill him.

"As you wish," the hawk-nosed man said wryly. "I have the campsite secured, I believe."

That seemed true enough. Bodies littered the ground, but in only a few places did men still fight inside the ring of wagons. A dome of Air suddenly covered the entire camp, smoke from the fires sliding up to a hole left in the top. It was not one solid weave of *saidin*; Rand could see where individual weaves butted one against another to make it. He thought there might have been as many as two hundred black-coated men beneath the dome. A hail of lightning and fire struck that barrier and exploded harmlessly. The sky itself seemed to crackle and burn; the constant roar of it filled the air. Maidens with strips of red dangling from their arms and *siswai'aman* stood along the wall they could not see, mingled with Mayeners and Cairhienin, many of them afoot as well. On the other side, a solid mass of Shaido stared at the invisible barricade keeping them from their enemies, sometimes stabbing at it with spears or hurling themselves against it bodily. Spears stopped short, and bodies bounced back.

Inside the dome, the last fighting died even as Rand looked. Under the eyes of a scant handful of red-marked men and Maidens, disarmed Shaido were removing their garments with stolid faces; taken in battle, they would wear *gai'shain* white for a year and a day even if the Shaido somehow succeeded in overrunning the camp. Cairhienin and Mayeners provided guards for a large knot of angry Warders and Younglings mixed with fearful servants, almost as many guards as prisoners. Nearly a dozen Aes Sedai were being shielded by an equal number of Asha'man wearing sword and Dragon. The Aes Sedai looked sick and frightened. Rand recognized three, though Nesune was the only one he could name. He did not recognize any of their Asha'man jailers. A number of the women Rand had shielded and rendered unconscious were laid out with those prisoners, some of them beginning to stir, while black-coated soldiers and Dedicated with the silver sword on their collars were using *saidin* to drag others across the ground and lay them in that row. Some of them brought the two unconscious Aes Sedai and the angular woman out of the copse; she was still screaming. When they were added to the cluster, some of the Aes Sedai abruptly turned away and vomited.

There were other Aes Sedai present, surrounded by Warders and watched by black-coated men though not shielded, watching the Asha'man as uneasily as did the women under guard. They stared at Rand, too, and plainly would have come to him if not for the Asha'man. Rand glared back. Alanna was there; he had not been hallucinating. He did not recognize all of her companions, but enough. They were nine altogether. Nine. Sudden rage stormed outside the Void, and Lews Therin's fly-buzz grew louder.

At that point it seemed no surprise at all to see Perrin stagger up, face and beard bloody, followed by a limping Loial with a huge axe, and a bright-eyed fellow who looked a Tinker in a red-striped coat, except for the sword he carried, blade crimson from end to end. Rand almost looked around to see whether Mat was also there somehow. He did see Dobraine, on foot with a sword in one hand and the staff of Rand's crimson banner in the other. Nandera joined Perrin, letting her veil drop, and another Maiden Rand almost did not recognize at first. It was good to see Sulin in *cadin'sor* once more.

"Rand," Perrin gasped, "thank the Light you're still alive. We meant for you to make a gateway for us to escape, but it's all fallen to pieces. Rhuarc and most of the Aiel are still out among the Shaido, most of the Mayeners and Cairhienin too, and I don't know what has happened to the Two Rivers folk, or the Wise Ones. The Aes Sedai were supposed to stay with them, but. . . ." Putting the head of his axe on the ground, he leaned on the shaft panting; he looked as if he might fall without the support.

Along the barrier, mounted men were appearing, as well as Aielmen in red headbands and Maidens with strips of red dangling from their arms. The barrier held them out as well. Wherever they appeared, Shaido swarmed over them, swallowed them up.

"Let the dome go," Rand ordered. Perrin sighed in relief, of all things. Had he thought Rand would let his own people be slaughtered? But Loial sighed too. Light, what did they think of him? Min began rubbing his back, murmuring under her breath in a soothing tone. For some reason, Perrin gave her a very surprised look.

Taim might have been surprised, but he was certainly not relieved. "My Lord Dragon," he said in a tight voice, "I would say there are still several hundred Shaido women out there, some not insignificant it seems. And that is not to mention some thousands of Shaido with spears. Unless you truly want to find out whether you are immortal, I suggest waiting a few hours until we know this place well enough to make gateways with some certainty where they will come out, then leaving. There are casualties in battle. I lost several soldiers today, nine men who will be harder to re-place than any number of renegade Aiel. Whoever dies out there, dies for the Dragon Reborn." If he had been paying any attention to Nandera or

Sulin, he might have moderated his tone and chosen his words more carefully. Handtalk flashed between them; they looked ready to strike him down on the spot.

Perrin pushed himself upright, yellow eyes fixed on Rand, firm and anxious at the same time. "Rand, even if Dannil and the Wise Ones held back the way they were supposed to, they'll not leave as long as they see this." He gestured to the dome overhead, where fire and lightning made a continuous sheet of light. "If we sit here for hours, the Shaido will turn on them sooner or later, if they haven't already. Light, Rand! Dannil and Ban and Wil and Tell . . . Amys is out there, and Sorilea, and . . . ! Burn you, Rand, more have died for you already than you know!" Perrin drew a deep breath. "At least let me out. If I can make it that far, I can let them know that you're alive and they can retreat before they get killed."

"Two of us can slip out," Loial said quietly, hefting that huge axe. "Two will stand a better chance." The Tinker only smiled, but almost eagerly.

"I will have a place opened in the barrier," Taim began, but Rand broke in on him sharply.

"No!" Not for the Two Rivers folk. He could not appear to worry over them any more than over the Wise Ones. Truth to tell, he had to seem to worry less. Amys was out there? The Wise Ones never took part in battle; they walked untouched through battles and blood feuds. They had ripped apart custom if not law to come for him. He would as soon let Perrin go back into that maelstrom as abandon them. But it could not be for the Wise Ones or the Two Rivers folk. "Sevanna wants my head, Taim. Apparently she thought she could take it today." The emotionless quality the Void gave to his voice, was appropriate. It did seem to worry Min, though; she was stroking his back as though to calm him. "I mean to let her know her mistake. I told you to make weapons, Taim. Show me just how deadly they are. Disperse the Shaido. Break them."

"As you command." If Taim had been stiff before, he was stone now.

"Put my standard up where they can see it," Rand commanded. At least that would tell everyone outside who held the camp. Maybe the Wise Ones and Two Rivers folk would pull back when they saw that.

Loial's ears wriggled uneasily, and Perrin grabbed Rand's arm as Taim walked away. "I saw what they do, Rand. It's. . . ." With his bloody face and bloody axe, he still sounded disgusted.

"What would you have me do?" Rand demanded. "What else can I do?"

Perrins's hand fell away, and he sighed. "I do not know. I do not have to like it, though."

"Grady, raise the Banner of Light!" Taim called, and the Power made his voice boom. On flows of Air, Jur Grady lifted the crimson banner out of a surprised Dobraine's hand and raised it all the way through the hole in the top of the dome. Fire burst around it and lightning flashed as brilliant red lifted amid the smoke billowing up from the burning wagons. Rand recognized a number of the men in black coats, but he knew only a few names aside from Jur's. Damer and Fedwin and Eben, Jahar and Torval; of those, only Torval wore the Dragon on his collar.

"Asha'man, form line of battle!" Taim boomed.

Black-coated men rushed to place themselves between the barrier and everyone else, all of them except Jur and those watching Aes Sedai. Except for Nesune, who peered intently at everything, the Tower lot had sunk listlessly to their knees, not even looking at the men who had them shielded, and even Nesune still looked on the point of sicking up. The Salidar group stared coldly at the Asha'man guarding them for the most part, though now and then they turned those icy eyes on Rand. Alanna stared only at Rand. His skin was tingled faintly, he realized; for him to feel it at that distance, all nine must be embracing *saidar*. He hoped they had enough sense not to channel; the stony men facing them held *saidin* to bursting, and they looked as tense as the Warders fingering their swords.

"Asha'man, raise the barricade two spans!" At Taim's command, the edges of the dome rose all around. Surprised Shaido who had been pushing at what they could not see stumbled forward. They recovered instantly, a black-veiled mass surging forward, but they had time for only a stride before Taim's next shout. "Asha'man, kill!"

The front rank of the Shaido exploded. There was no other way to put it. *Cadin'sor*-clad shapes burst apart in sprays of blood and flesh. Flows of *saidin* reached through that thick mist, darting from figure to figure in the blink of an eye, and the next row of Shaido died, then the next, and the next, as though they were running into an enormous meat grinder. Staring at the slaughter, Rand swallowed. Perrin bent over to empty his stomach, and Rand understood fully. Another rank died. Nandera put a hand over her eyes, and Sulin turned her back. The bloody ruins of human beings began to make a wall.

No one could stand up to that. Between one blast of death and the next, the Shaido in front were suddenly struggling the other way, forcing themselves back into the mass fighting to get forward. The milling tangle itself began to explode, and then all of them were falling back. No, running. The rain of fire and lightning against the dome faltered.

"Asha'man," Taim's voice rang out, "rolling ring of Earth and Fire!"

Beneath the feet of the Shaido nearest the wagons the ground suddenly erupted in fountains of flame and dirt, hurling men in every direction. While bodies still hung in the air, more gouts of flame roared from the ground, and more, in an expanding ring all the way around the wagons, pursuing the Shaido for fifty paces, a hundred, two hundred. There was nothing but panic and death out there now. Spears and bucklers were cast aside. The dome above stood clear except for the smoke rising from the burning wagons.

"Stop!" The roar of explosions swallowed Rand's shout as well as it did men's screams. He wove the flows Taim had used. "Stop it, Taim!" His voice crashed like thunder over everything.

One more ring of eruptions, and Taim called, "Asha'man, rest!"

For a moment a deafening silence seemed to fill the air. Rand's ears rang. Then he could hear screams and moans. Wounded heaved among the piles of dead. And beyond them the Shaido ran, leaving behind scattered clusters of *siswai'aman* and Maidens with red armcloths, Cairhienin and Mayeners, some still on their horses. Almost hesitantly those began to move toward the wagons, some of the Aiel lowering their veils. With Power enhancing his eyes, he could make out Rhuarc, limping, one arm dangling, but on his feet. And well beyond him, a large group of women in dark bulky skirts and pale blouses, with an escort of men in Two Rivers coats carrying longbows. They were too far for him to make out faces, but from the way the Two Rivers men at least were staring at the fleeing Shaido, they were as stunned as anyone else.

A great sense of relief welled up inside Rand, though not enough to still the distant churning in his stomach. Min had her face pressed against his shirt; she was weeping. He smoothed her hair. "Asha'man"—he had never been more glad of the Void draining emotion from his voice—"you have done well. I congratulate you, Taim." He turned away so he would not have to see the carnage anymore, hardly hearing the cheers of "Lord Dragon!" and "Asha'man!" that thundered from the black-coated men.

When he turned, he found Aes Sedai. Merana was all the way at the back, but Alanna stood almost face-to-face with him beside two Aes Sedai he did not recognize.

"You have done well," the square-faced one of the pair said. A farmer, with an ageless face and eyes just holding on to serenity, ignoring the Asha'man around her. Obviously ignoring them. "I am Bera Harkin, and this is Kiruna Nachiman. We came to rescue you—with Alanna's aid"—that was an obvious addition, at Alanna's sudden frown—"though it seems you had small need of us. Still, intentions do count, and—"

"Your place is with them," Rand said, pointing to the Aes Sedai shielded and under guard. Twenty-three, he saw, and Galina not among them. The buzzing of Lews Therin swelled, but he refused to listen. Now was no time for insane rages.

Kiruna drew herself up proudly. Whatever she was, she was certainly no farmer. "You forget who we are. They may have mistreated you, but we—"

"I forget nothing, Aes Sedai," Rand said coldly. "I said six could come, but I count nine. I said you would be on an equal footing with the Tower emissaries, and for bringing nine, you will be. They are on their knees, Aes Sedai. Kneel!"

Coldly serene faces stared back at him. He felt Asha'man readying shields of Spirit. Defiance grew on Kiruna's face, on Bera's, on others. Two dozen black-coated men made a ring around Rand and the Aes Sedai.

Taim appeared as close to a smile as Rand had ever seen him. "Kneel and swear to the Lord Dragon," he said softly, "or you will be knelt."

As stories do, the tale spread, across Cairhien and north and south, by merchant train and peddler and simple traveler gossiping at an inn. As stories do, the tale changed with every telling. The Aiel had turned on the Dragon Reborn and killed him, at Dumai's Wells or elsewhere. No, the Aes Sedai had saved Rand al'Thor. It was Aes Sedai who had killed him—no, gentled him—no, carried him to Tar Valon where he languished in a dungeon beneath the White Tower. Or else where the Amyrlin Seat herself knelt to him. Unusually for stories, it was something very close to truth that was most often believed.

On a day of fire and blood, a tattered banner waved above Dumai's Wells, bearing the ancient symbol of Aes Sedai.

On a day of fire and blood and the One Power, as prophecy had suggested, the unstained tower, broken, bent knee to the forgotten sign.

The first nine Aes Sedai swore fealty to the Dragon Reborn, and the world was changed forever.

EPILOGUE

The Answer

The man only paused long enough to rest his hand on the door of the sedan chair, and was away as soon as Falion took the note from his fingers. Her rap had the two bearers moving almost before the fellow in Tarasin Palace livery stepped back into the crowd of the square.

There was only one word on the small square of paper. *Gone.* She crumpled it in her fist. Somehow they had slipped out again without her people inside seeing. Months of futile search had convinced her there was no cache of *angreal*, whatever Moghedien believed. She had even considered putting a Wise Woman or two to the question; one of them might know its whereabouts, if it existed. And horses might fly. All that kept her here in this wretched city was the simple fact that when one of the Chosen gave a command, you obeyed until it was changed. Anything else was a short road to a painful death. Yet if Elayne and Nynaeve were here. . . . They had ruined everything in Tanchico. Whether or not they really were full sisters—impossible as that seemed—Falion would not take their presence as coincidence. Maybe there was a cache. For the first time she was glad that Moghedien had ignored her since giving her her orders so many months ago in Amadicia. What had felt like abandonment might yet be a chance for advancement in the Chosen's eyes. That pair might yet lead her to the cache, and if not, if there was no cache. . . . Moghedien had seemed to have interest in Elayne and Nynaeve themselves. Delivering them would certainly be better than nonexistent *angreal*.

Leaning back, she let the sway of the chair soothe her. She did hate this city—she had come here as a runaway, when she was a novice—but perhaps this visit would end pleasantly after all.

Sitting in his study, Herid was peering into his pipe and wondering whether he had the means of lighting it at hand when the *gholam* squeezed under the door. Of course, even if Fel had been paying attention, he would not have believed, and once the *gholam* was inside the room, few men would have stood any chance.

When Idrien came to Fel's study later, she stared at what was piled none too neatly on the floor beside the table. It took her a moment to realize what it was, and when she did, she fainted before she could get a scream out. However many times she heard of someone torn limb from limb, she had never seen it before.

The rider turned his horse at the top of the hill for a last look back at Ebou Dar, gleaming white in the sun. A good city for looting, and from what he had learned of the local people, they would resist, so the Blood would allow looting. They would resist, but he hoped the other eyes were bringing back reports of disunity such as he had seen. Resistance would not last long, where a so-called queen ruled a tiny patch of ground, and that combined the best possibilities. Wheeling his mount, he rode west. Who knew? Perhaps that fellow's comment had been an omen. Perhaps the Return would come soon, and the Daughter of the Nine Moons with it. Surely that would be the greatest omen of victory.

Lying on her back in the night, Moghedien stared at the roof of the tiny tent she was allowed to herself as one of the Amyrlin's servants. From time to time her teeth ground, but as soon as she realized it, she stilled them again, very conscious of the *a'dam* necklace tight around her neck. This Egwene al'Vere was harder than Elayne or Nynaeve had been; she tolerated less and demanded more. And when she passed the bracelet to Siuan or

Leane, especially Siuan. . . . Moghedien shivered. That must be what it would be like if Birgitte could wear the bracelet.

The tent flap moved aside, admitting just enough moonlight for her to make out a woman ducking in.

"Who are you?" Moghedien demanded roughly. When they sent for her in the night, whoever came always brought a lantern.

"Call me Aran'gar, Moghedien," an amused voice said, and a small light bloomed inside the tent.

Her own name clove Moghedien's tongue to the roof of her mouth; that name meant death here. She was struggling to speak, to say her name was Marigan, when suddenly she became truly aware of the light. A small glowing white ball, pale, hanging in the air near her head. With the *a'dam* on her, she could not do more than think of *saidar* without permission, but she could still feel it channeled, see the webs woven. This time she felt nothing, saw nothing. Just a tiny ball of pure light.

She stared at the woman who had called herself Aran'gar, recognizing her now. Halima, she thought; secretary to one of the Sitters, she believed. But a woman certainly, if one who looked as though she had been designed by a man. A woman. But that ball of light had to be *saidin*! "Who are you?" Her voice shook slightly, and she was surprised it was so steady.

The woman smiled at her—a very amused smile—as she settled beside the pallet. "I told you, Moghedien. My name is Aran'gar. You will learn that name in the future, if you are lucky. Now, listen to me carefully, ask no more questions. I will tell you what you need to know. In a moment I will remove your pretty necklace. When I do, you will vanish as quickly and silently as Logain did. If you do not, you will die here. And that will be a shame, because you are summoned to Shayol Ghul this very night."

Moghedien licked her lips. Summoned to Shayol Ghul. That could mean eternity in the Pit of Doom, or immortality ruling the world, or anything in between. Little chance it meant being named Nae'blis, not if the Great Lord knew enough of how she had spent the past months to send someone to free her. Yet it was a summons she could not refuse. And it meant an end to the *a'dam* at last. "Yes. Remove it. I will go immediately." There was no point to delaying anyway; she was stronger than any woman in the camp, but she did not intend to give a circle of thirteen a chance at her.

"I thought you would see it so," Halima—or Aran'gar—chuckled richly. She touched the necklace, flinching slightly, and Moghedien wondered again about a woman who apparently channeled *saidin* and was hurt, however faintly, by touching what should only hurt a man who could channel. Then the necklace was off, being slipped hastily into the woman's pouch. "Go, Moghedien. Go, now."

When Egwene reached the tent and put her head and lantern in, she found only disturbed blankets. She withdrew slowly.

"Mother," Chesa fussed behind her, "you should not be out in the night air. Night air is bad air. If you wanted Marigan, I could have fetched her."

Egwene looked around. She had felt the necklace come off, and felt the flash of pain that meant a man who could channel had brushed the link. Most people were already asleep, but a few still sat outside their tents around low fires, and some not far. It might be possible to find out which man had come to "Marigan's" tent.

"I think she has run away, Chesa," she said. Chesa's angry mutterings about women who deserted their mistresses followed her back to her own tent. It could not have been Logain, could it? He would not have come back, could not have known. Could he?

Demandred knelt in the Pit of Doom, and for once he did not care that Shaidar Haran watched his trembling with that eyeless, impassive gaze. "Have I not done well, Great Lord?"

The Great Lord's laughter filled Demandred's head.

The unstained tower breaks and bends knee to the forgotten sign.
The seas rage, and stormclouds gather unseen.
Beyond the horizon, hidden fires swell, and serpents nestle in the
    bosom.
What was exalted is cast down; what was cast down is raised up.
Order burns to clear his path.

—*The Prophecies of the Dragon*
translation by Jeorad Manyard
Governor of the Province of Andor for
the High King, Artur Paendrag Tanreall

The End
of the Sixth Book of
The Wheel of Time

GLOSSARY

A Note on Dates in This Glossary. The Toman Calendar (devised by Toma dur Ahmid) was adopted approximately two centuries after the death of the last male Aes Sedai, recording years After the Breaking of the World (AB). So many records were destroyed in the Trolloc Wars that at their end there was argument about the exact year under the old system. A new calendar, proposed by Tiam of Gazar, celebrated freedom from the Trolloc threat and recorded each year as a Free Year (FY). The Gazaran Calendar gained wide acceptance within twenty years after the Wars' end. Artur Hawkwing attempted to establish a new calendar based on the founding of his empire (FF, From the Founding), but only historians now refer to it. After the death and destruction of the War of the Hundred Years, a third calendar was devised by Uren din Jubai Soaring Gull, a scholar of the Sea Folk, and promulgated by the Panarch Farede of Tarabon. The Farede Calendar, dating from the arbitrarily decided end of the War of the Hundred Years and recording years of the New Era (NE), is currently in use.

Accepted: Young women in training to be Aes Sedai who have reached a certain level of power and passed certain tests. It normally takes five to ten years to be raised from novice to Accepted. Somewhat less confined by rules than novices, they are allowed to choose their own areas of study, within limits. Accepted wear a Great Serpent ring on the third finger of the left hand. When an Accepted is raised Aes Sedai, she chooses her Ajah, gains the right to wear the shawl, and may wear the ring on any finger or not at all if circumstances warrant. *See also* Aes Sedai.

a'dam (AYE-dam): A device for controlling a woman who can channel, usable only by either a woman who can channel or a woman who can be taught to channel, and having no effect on any woman who cannot channel. It creates a link between the two women. The Seanchan version consists of a collar and bracelet linked by a leash, all of silvery metal. If a man who can channel is linked to a woman by an *a'dam*, the likely result is death for both. Simply touching an *a'dam* can result in pain for a man who can channel when the *a'dam* is being worn by a woman who can channel. *See also* linking; Seanchan.

Aes Sedai (EYEZ seh-DEYE): Wielders of the One Power. Since the Breaking of the World ended, all are women. Respected and honored by many, yet widely distrusted and feared, even hated. Also widely blamed for the Breaking of the World, and thought to meddle in the affairs of nations. At the same time, few rulers are without an Aes Sedai advisor, even where such a connection must be secret. Apparently after some years of channeling the One Power, Aes Sedai take on an ageless quality, so that one old enough to be a grandmother may show no signs of age except perhaps a few gray hairs. *See also* Ajah; Amyrlin Seat; Breaking of the World.

Age of Legends: Age ended by the War of the Shadow and the Breaking of the World. A time when Aes Sedai performed wonders now only dreamed of. *See also* Breaking of the World; War of the Shadow.

Aiel (eye-EEL): The people of the Aiel Waste. Fierce and hardy. They veil their faces before they kill. Deadly warriors with weapons or bare hands, they will not touch a sword even on the point of death, nor ride a horse unless pressed. Aiel call battle "the dance," and "the dance of spears." They are divided into twelve clans: the Chareen, the Codarra, the Daryne, the Goshien, the Miagoma, the Nakai, the Reyn, the Shaarad, the Shaido, the Shiande, the Taardad, and the Tomanelle. Each clan is divided into septs. Sometimes they speak of a thirteenth clan, the Clan That Is Not, the Jenn, who were the builders of Rhuidean. All know that Aiel supposedly once failed the Aes Sedai and were banished to the Aiel Waste for that sin, and that they will be destroyed if they ever fail the Aes Sedai again. *See also* Aiel warrior societies; Aiel Waste; *gai'shain*; bleakness; Rhuidean.

Aiel War (976–78 NE): When King Laman (LAY-mahn) of Cairhien cut down *Avendoraldera*, four clans of the Aiel crossed the Spine of the World. They looted and burned the capital city of Cairhien as well as many other cities and towns, and the conflict extended into Andor and Tear. By the conventional view, the Aiel were finally defeated at the Battle of the Shining Walls, before Tar Valon; in fact, Laman was killed in that battle, and having done what they came for, the Aiel recrossed the Spine. *See also Avendoraldera*; Cairhien; Spine of the World.

Aiel warrior societies: Aiel warriors are all members of one of twelve societies. These are Black Eyes (*Seia Doon*), Brothers of the Eagle (*Far Aldazar Din*), Dawn Runners (*Rahien Sorei*), Knife Hands (*Sovin Nai*), Maidens of the Spear (*Far Dareis Mai*), Mountain Dancers (*Hama N'dore*), Night Spears (*Cor Darei*), Red Shields (*Aethan Dor*), Stone Dogs (*Shae'en M'taal*), Thunder Walkers (*Sha'mad Conde*), True Bloods (*Tain Shari*), and Water Seekers (*Duadhe Mahdi'in*). Each has its own customs, and sometimes specific duties. For example, Red Shields act as police, and Stone Dogs are often used as rear guards during retreats, while Maidens are often scouts. Aiel clans frequently raid and battle one another, but members of the same society will not fight each other even if their clans do so. Thus there are always lines of contact between the clans, even during open warfare. *See also* Aiel; Aiel Waste; *Far Dareis Mai*.

Aiel Waste: Harsh, rugged and all-but-waterless land east of the Spine of the World. Called the Three-fold Land by the Aiel. Few outsiders enter; the Aiel consider themselves at war with all other peoples and do not welcome strangers. Only peddlers, gleemen, and the Tuatha'an are allowed safe entry, although Aiel avoid all contact with the Tuatha'an, whom they call "the Lost Ones." No maps of the Waste itself are known to exist.

Ajah (AH-jah): Societies among the Aes Sedai, seven in number and designated by colors: Blue, Red, White, Green, Brown, Yellow and Gray. All Aes Sedai except the Amyrlin Seat belong to one. Each follows a specific philosophy of the use of the One Power and the purposes of the Aes Sedai. The Red Ajah bends its energies to finding men who can channel, and to gentling them. The Brown forsakes the mundane world and dedicates itself to seeking knowledge, while the White, largely eschewing both the world and the value of worldly knowledge, devotes itself to questions of philosophy and truth. The Green Ajah (called the Battle Ajah during the Trolloc Wars) holds itself ready for

Tarmon Gai'don, the Yellow concentrates on the study of Healing, and Blue sisters involve themselves with causes and justice. The Gray are mediators, seeking harmony and consensus. A Black Ajah, dedicated to serving the Dark One, is officially and vehemently denied.

Altara (al-TAH-rah): A nation on the Sea of Storms, though in truth little unifies it except a name. The people of Altara think of themselves as inhabitants of a town or village, or as this lord's or that lady's people, first, and only second if at all as Altaran. Few nobles pay taxes to the crown or offer more than lip service, and that often slight. The ruler of Altara (currently Queen Tylin Quintara of House Mitsobar; TIE-lihn quin-TAHR-ah; MIHT-soh-bahr) is seldom more than the most powerful noble in the land, and at times has not even really been that. The Throne of the Winds holds so little power that many powerful nobles have scorned to take it when they could have.

Amyrlin Seat (AHM-ehr-lihn SEAT): (1) Leader of the Aes Sedai. Elected for life by the Hall of the Tower, which consists of three representatives (called Sitters, as in "a Sitter for the Green") from each Ajah. The Amyrlin Seat has, theoretically, supreme authority among the Aes Sedai, and ranks as the equal of a king or queen. A slightly less formal usage is "the Amyrlin." (2) The throne on which the leader of the Aes Sedai sits.

Amys (ah-MEESE): Wise One of Cold Rocks Hold, and a dreamwalker. An Aiel of the Nine Valleys sept of the Taardad Aiel. Wife of Rhuarc, sister-wife to Lian (lee-AHN), who is roofmistress of Cold Rocks Hold. Amys is sister-mother to Aviendha.

angreal (ahn-gree-AHL): Remnants of the Age of Legends that allow anyone capable of channeling to handle a greater amount of the Power than is safe or even possible unaided. Some were made for use by women, others by men. Rumors of *angreal* usable by both men and women have never been confirmed. Their making is no longer known, and few remain in existence. *See also* channel; *sa'angreal*; *ter'angreal*.

Arad Doman (AH-rad do-MAHN): Nation on the Aryth Ocean. Presently racked by civil war and simultaneously by wars against those who have declared for the Dragon Reborn and against Tarabon. Domani women are famous—or infamous—for their beauty, seductiveness and scandalous clothes.

Artur Hawkwing: Legendary king, Artur Paendrag Tanreall (AHR-tuhr PAY-ehn-DRAG tahn-REE-ahl). Ruled FY 943–94. United all lands west of the Spine of the World. Sent armies across the Aryth Ocean

(FY 992), but contact with these was lost at his death, which set off the War of the Hundred Years. His sign was a golden hawk in flight. *See also* War of the Hundred Years.

Atha'an Miere (ah-thah-AHN mee-EHR): *See* Sea Folk.

Avendoraldera (AH-ven-doh-ral-DEH-rah): Tree grown in the city of Cairhien from a sapling of *Avendesora*, a gift from the Aiel in 566 NE, although no record shows any connection between the Aiel and the legendary Tree of Life.

Bair (BAYR): A Wise One of the Haido sept of the Shaarad Aiel. A dreamwalker. She cannot channel. *See also* dreamwalker.

Berelain sur Paendrag (BEH-reh-lain suhr PAY-ehn-DRAG): First of Mayene, Blessed of the Light, Defender of the Waves, High Seat of House Paeron (pay-eh-ROHN). A beautiful and willful young woman, and a skillful ruler. *See also* Mayene.

Birgitte (ber-GEET-teh): Hero of legend and story, renowned for her beauty almost as much as for her bravery and skill at archery. Supposedly carried a silver bow and silver arrows with which she never missed. One of the heroes to be called back when the Horn of Valere is sounded. Always linked with the hero-swordsman Gaidal Cain. Except for her beauty and skill with a bow, she is little like the stories of her. *See also* Horn of Valere.

Bleakness, the: Term given by the Aiel to the effects on many of learning that rather than having always been fierce warriors, their ancestors were strict pacifists forced into defending themselves during the Breaking of the World and the years following. Many feel that this was their failure of the Aes Sedai. Some throw down their spears and run away. Others refuse to put off *gai'shain* white when their time is up. Still others deny the truth of this, and with it deny necessarily that Rand al'Thor is truly the *Car'a'carn*; these either return to the Aiel Waste or go to join the Shaido opposing him. *See also* Aiel; Aiel Waste; *Car'a'carn*; *gai'shain*.

Blight, the: *See* Great Blight.

Borderlands: The nations bordering the Great Blight: Saldaea, Arafel, Kandor, and Shienar. Their history is one of unending raids and war against Trollocs and Myrddraal. *See also* Great Blight.

Breaking of the World: During the Time of Madness, male Aes Sedai who had gone insane changed the face of the earth. They leveled mountain ranges and raised new mountains, lifted dry land where seas had been and made oceans cover once dry land. Much of the world was completely depopulated, the survivors scattered like dust on the wind. This destruction is remembered in stories, legends, and history as the Breaking of the World.

Bryne, Gareth (BRIHN, GAH-rehth): Once Captain-General of the Queen's Guards in Andor. Exiled by Queen Morgase. Considered one of the greatest generals living. The sigil of House Bryne is a wild bull, the rose crown of Andor around its neck. Gareth Bryne's personal sigil is three golden stars, each of five rays.

cadin'sor (KAH-dihn-sohr): Garb of Aiel warriors; coat and breeches in browns and grays that fade into rock or shadow, along with soft, laced knee-high boots. In the Old Tongue, "working clothes," though this is of course an imprecise translation.

Cairhien (KEYE-ree-EHN): Both a nation along the Spine of the World and the capital city of that nation. The city was burned and looted during the Aiel War, as were many other towns and villages. The abandonment of farmland near the Spine of the World after the war made necessary the importation of grain. The assassination of King Galldrian (998 NE) resulted in war for succession to the Sun Throne, disrupting grain shipments and bringing famine. The city was besieged by the Shaido in what some now call the Second Aiel War; this siege was lifted by other Aiel under the command of Rand al'Thor. The banner of Cairhien is a many-rayed golden sun rising on a field of sky blue. *See also* Aiel War.

calendar: There are 10 days to the week, 28 days to the month and 13 months to the year. Several feast days are not part of any month; these include Sunday (the longest day of the year), the Feast of Thanksgiving (once every four years at the spring equinox), and the Feast of All Souls Salvation, also called All Souls Day (once every ten years at the autumn equinox).

Callandor (CAH-lahn-DOOR): The Sword That Is Not a Sword, the Sword That Cannot Be Touched. Crystal sword once held in the Stone of Tear. A powerful male *sa'angreal*. Its removal from the chamber called the Heart of the Stone was, along with the fall of the Stone, a major sign of the Dragon's Rebirth and the approach of Tarmon Gai'don. Replaced in the Heart, driven into the stone, by Rand al'Thor. *See also* Dragon Reborn; *sa'angreal*; Stone of Tear.

Car'a'carn: In the Old Tongue, "chief of chiefs." According to Aiel prophecy, a man who would come from Rhuidean at dawn, marked with two

Dragons, and lead them across the Dragonwall. The Prophecy of Rhuidean says that he will unite the Aiel and destroy them, all but a remnant of a remnant. *See also* Aiel; Rhuidean.

Caraighan Maconar (kah-RYE-gihn mah-CON-ahr): Legendary Green sister (212 AB–373 AB), the heroine of a hundred adventures credited with exploits that even some Aes Sedai consider improbable despite their inclusion in the records of the White Tower, such as single-handedly putting down a rebellion in Mosadorin and quelling the Co-maidin Riots at a time when she had no Warders. Considered by the Green Ajah to be the archetype of a Green sister. *See also* Aes Sedai; Ajah.

Carridin, Jaichim (CAHR-ih-dihn, JAY-kim): An Inquisitor of the Hand of the Light, a high officer of the Children of the Light and a Dark-friend.

Cauthon, Abell (CAW-thon, AY-bell): A farmer in the Two Rivers. Father of Mat Cauthon. Wife: Natti (NAT-tee). Daughters: Eldrin (EHL-drihn), and Bodewhin (BOHD-wihn), called Bode.

channel (verb): To control the flow of the One Power. *See also* One Power.

Children of the Light: Society of strict ascetic beliefs, owing allegiance to no nation and dedicated to the defeat of the Dark One and the destruction of all Darkfriends. Founded during the War of the Hundred Years to proselytize against an increase in Darkfriends, they evolved during the war into a completely military society. Extremely rigid in beliefs, and certain that only they know the truth and the right. Consider Aes Sedai and any who support them to be Darkfriends. Known disparagingly as Whitecloaks. Their sign is a golden sunburst on a field of white. *See also* Questioners.

Darkfriends: Adherents of the Dark One. They believe they will gain great power and rewards, even immortality, when he is freed. Among themselves, they sometimes use the ancient name Friends of the Dark.

Dark One: Most common name, used in every land, for Shai'tan (SHAY-ih-TAN). The source of evil, antithesis of the Creator. Imprisoned by the Creator in Shayol Ghul at the moment of Creation. An attempt to free him brought about the War of the Shadow, the tainting of *saidin*, the Breaking of the World and the end of the Age of Legends. *See also* Dragon, Prophecies of the.

Daughter-Heir: Title of the heir to the Lion Throne of Andor. Without a surviving daughter, the throne goes to the nearest female blood relation of the Queen. Dissension over exactly who was nearest by blood has several times led to power struggles, the latest being "the Succession"—so called in Andor and "the Third War of Andoran Succession" elsewhere—which brought Morgase of House Trakand to the throne.

Deane Aryman (dee-AHN-eh AH-rih-mahn): Amyrlin Seat who saved the White Tower from the damage done by Bonwhin in attempting to control Artur Hawkwing. Born circa FY 920 in the village of Salidar, in Shiota, she was raised Amyrlin from the Blue Ajah in FY 992. Credited with convincing Souran Maravaile to raise the siege of Tar Valon (which had begun in FY 975) at Hawkwing's death. Deane restored the Tower's prestige, and it is believed that at the time of her death in FY 1084, in a fall from a horse, she was on the point of convincing the nobles warring over the remains of Hawkwing's empire to accept the leadership of the White Tower as a means of restoring unity to the land. *See also* Amyrlin Seat; Artur Hawkwing.

Dragon, false: Name given to various men who have claimed to be the Dragon Reborn. Some began wars that involved many nations. Over the centuries most were unable to channel, but a few could. All, however, either disappeared or were captured or killed without fulfilling any of the Prophecies of the Dragon. Among those who could channel, the most powerful were Raolin Darksbane (335–36 AB), Yurian Stonebow (circa 1300–1308 AB), Davian (FY 351), Guaire Amalasan (FY 939–43), Logain (997 NE) and Mazrim Taim (998 NE). *See also* Dragon Reborn.

Dragon, Prophecies of the: Little known except among the well-educated and seldom spoken of, the Prophecies, given in *The Karaethon Cycle* (ka-REE-ah-thon), foretell that the Dark One will be freed again, and that Lews Therin Telamon, the Dragon, will be Reborn to fight Tarmon Gai'don, the Last Battle against the Shadow. He will, say the Prophecies, save the world—and Break it again. *See also* Dragon, the.

Dragon, the: Name by which Lews Therin Telamon was known during the War of the Shadow, some three thousand or more years ago. In the madness that overtook all male Aes Sedai, Lews Therin killed everyone who carried any of his blood, as well as everyone he loved, thus earning the name Kinslayer. *See also* Dragon, Prophecies of the; Dragon Reborn.

Dragon Reborn: According to the Prophecies of the Dragon, the man who is the Rebirth of Lews Therin Kinslayer. Most people, but not all, acknowledge Rand al'Thor as the Dragon Reborn. *See also* Dragon, false; Dragon, Prophecies of the; Dragon, the.

Dreadlords: Men and women able to channel, who went over to the Shadow during the Trolloc Wars, acting as generals over armies of Trollocs and Darkfriends. Occasionally confused with the Forsaken by the less well educated.

Dreamer: *See* Talents.

dreamwalker: Aiel name for a woman able to enter *Tel'aran'rhiod*, interpret dreams and speak to others in their dreams. Aes Sedai also use the term, referring to Dreamers, but rarely, and they capitalize it—Dreamwalker. *See also* Talents; *Tel'aran'rhiod*.

Elaida do Avriny a'Roihan (eh-LY-da dob. AHV-rih-nee ah-ROY-han): An Aes Sedai, formerly of the Red Ajah, now raised to the Amyrlin Seat. Once advisor to Queen Morgase of Andor. She sometimes has the Foretelling.

Far Dareis Mai (FAHR DAH-rize MY): In the Old Tongue, literally, "Of the Spear Maidens." Aiel warrior society which, unlike any other, admits women and only women. A Maiden may not marry and remain in the society, nor may she fight while carrying a child. Any child born to a Maiden is given to another woman to raise, in such a way that no one knows the child's mother. ("You may belong to no man, nor may any man belong to you, nor any child. The spear is your lover, your child and your life.") *See also* Aiel; Aiel warrior societies.

first-sister; first-brother: Aiel kinship term meaning having the same mother. Among the Aiel, having the same mother means a closer relationship than having the same father.

Five Powers: There are threads to the One Power, named according to the sorts of things that can be done using them—Earth, Air (sometimes called Wind), Fire, Water and Spirit, which are called the Five Powers. A wielder of the Power will have a greater strength with one, possibly two but rarely more, and lesser with the others. In the Age of Legends, Spirit was found equally in men and in women, but great ability with Earth and/or Fire occurred much more often among men, ability with Water and/or Air among women. Despite exceptions, it was so often so that Earth and Fire came to be regarded as male Powers, Air and Water as female.

Flame of Tar Valon: Symbol of Tar Valon, the Amyrlin Seat, and the Aes Sedai. A stylized representation of a flame; a white teardrop, point upward.

Forsaken, the: Name given to thirteen of the most powerful Aes Sedai of the Age of Legends, thus among the most powerful ever known, who went over to the Dark One during the War of the Shadow in return for the promise of immortality. Their own name for themselves was "the Chosen." According to both legend and fragmentary records, they were imprisoned along with the Dark One when his prison was reseated. The names given to them are still used to frighten children. They were: Aginor (AGH-ih-nohr), Asmodean (ahs-MOH-dee-an), Balthamel (BAAL-thah-mell), Be'lal (BEH-lahl), Demandred (DEE-man-drehd), Graendal (GREHN-dahl), Ishamael (ih-SHAH-may-EHL), Lanfear (LAN-feer), Mesaana (meh-SAH-nah), Moghedien (moh-GHEH-dee-ehn), Rahvin (RAAV-ihn), Sammael (SAHM-may-EHL) and Semirhage (SEH-mih-RHAHG).

Gaidin (GYE-deen): In the Old Tongue, "Brother to Battles." A title used by Aes Sedai for the Warders. *See also* Warder.

gai'shain (GYE-shain): In the Old Tongue, "Pledged to Peace in Battle" is as close a translation as is possible. An Aiel taken prisoner by other Aiel during raid or battle is required by *ji'e'toh* to serve his or her captor humbly and obediently for one year and a day, touching no weapon and doing no violence. A Wise One, a blacksmith, a child or a woman with a child under the age of ten may not be made *gai'shain*. *See also* Bleakness, the.

Galad (gah-LAHD): Lord Galadedrid Damodred (gah-LAHD-eh-drihd DAHM-oh-drehd). Half-brother to Elayne and Gawyn, sharing the same father, Taringail (TAH-rihn-gail) Damodred. His sign is a winged silver sword, point down.

Game of Houses: Name given the scheming, plots and manipulations for advantage by noble Houses. Great value is given to subtlety, to aiming at one thing while seeming to aim at another, and to achieving ends with the least visible effort. Also known as the Great Game, and sometimes by its name in the Old Tongue: *Does Daemar* (DAH-ess day-MAR).

Gawyn (GAH-wihn) of House Trakand (trah-KAND): Queen Morgase's son, and Elayne's brother, who will be First Prince of the Sword when Elayne ascends to the throne. Half-brother to Galad. His sign is a white boar.

gentling: The act, performed by Aes Sedai, of shutting off a male who can channel from the One Power. Necessary because any man who channels will go insane from the taint on *saidin* and almost certainly do horrible things with the Power in his madness before the taint kills him. One who has been gentled can still sense the True Source, but cannot touch it. Whatever madness has come before gentling is arrested but not cured, and if it is done soon enough death can be averted. A man who is gentled, however, inevitably gives up wanting to live; those who do not succeed in committing suicide usually die anyway within a year or two. *See also* One Power; stilling.

gleeman: A traveling storyteller, musician, juggler, tumbler and all-around entertainer. Known by trademark cloaks of many-colored patches, gleemen perform mainly in the villages and smaller towns.

Gray Man: One who has voluntarily surrendered his or her soul in order to become an assassin serving the Shadow. Gray Men are so ordinary in appearance that the eye can slide right past without noticing them. The vast majority of Gray Men are indeed men, but a small number are women. Also called the Soulless.

Great Blight, the: A region in the far north, entirely corrupted by the Dark One. A haunt of Trollocs, Myrddraal and other creatures of the Shadow.

Great Lord of the Dark: Name by which Darkfriends refer to the Dark One, claiming that to speak his true name would be blasphemous.

Great Serpent: A symbol for time and eternity, ancient before the Age of Legends began, consisting of a serpent eating its own tail. A ring in the shape of the Great Serpent is awarded to women who have been raised to the Accepted among the Aes Sedai.

High Lords of Tear: Acting as a council, the High Lords are historically the rulers of the nation of Tear, which has neither king nor queen. Their numbers are not fixed, and have varied from as many as twenty to as few as six. Not to be confused with the Lords of the Land, who are lesser Tairen lords.

Horn of Valere (vah-LEER): The legendary object of the Great Hunt of the Horn, it can call back dead heroes from the grave to fight against the Shadow. A new Hunt of the Horn has been called, and sworn Hunters for the Horn can now be found in many nations.

Illian (IHL-lee-an): A great port on the Sea of Storms, capital city of the nation of the same name.

Juilin Sandar (JUY-lihn sahn-DAHR): A thief-catcher from Tear.

Lan (LAN); **al'Lan Mandragoran** (AHL-LAN man-DRAG-or-an): Uncrowned King of Malkier, a land swallowed by the Blight in the year he was born (953 NE), Dai Shan (Battle Lord), and the last surviving Malkieri lord. At the age of sixteen he began a one-man war against the Blight and the Shadow, which continued until he was bonded as a Warder by Moiraine in 979 NE. *See also* Warder; Moiraine.

length, units of: 10 inches = 1 foot; 3 feet = 1 pace; 2 paces = 1 span; 1,000 spans = 1 mile; 4 miles = 1 league.

Lews Therin Telamon; Lews Therin Kinslayer: *See* Dragon, the.

Lini (LIHN-nee): Childhood nurse to the Lady Elayne, and before her to Elayne's mother, Morgase, as well as to Morgase's mother. A woman of vast inner strength, considerable perception, and a great many sayings.

linking: The ability of women who can channel to combine their flows of the One Power. While the combined flow is not as great as the sum total of the individual flows, it is directed by the person who leads the link and that can be used much more precisely and to far greater effect than the individual flows could be. Men cannot link their abilities without the presence of a woman or women in the circle. Up to thirteen women can link without the presence of a man. With the addition of one man, the circle can increase to twenty-six women. Two men can take the circle to include thirty-four women, and so on until the limit of six men and sixty-six women is reached. There are links that include more men and fewer women, but except in the linking of one man and one woman, one woman and two men, or of course, two men and two women, there must always be at least one more woman in the circle than there are men. In most circles, either a man or a woman can control the link, but a man must control in the circle of seventy-two as well as in mixed circles of fewer than thirteen. Although men are in general stronger in the Power than women, the strongest circles are those which contain as near as possible to equal numbers of men and women. *See also* Aes Sedai.

Logain (loh-GAIN): A man who once claimed to be the Dragon Reborn. Captured after carrying war across Ghealdan, Altara and Murandy, he was carried to the White Tower and gentled, later escaping in the confusion after Siuan Sanche was deposed. A man who yet has greatness ahead of him.

Manetheren (mahn-EHTH-ehr-ehn): One of the Ten Nations that made the Second Covenant. Also the capital city of that nation. Both city and nation were utterly destroyed in the Trolloc Wars. The sign of Manetheren was a Red Eagle in flight. *See also* Trolloc Wars.

Mayene (may-EHN): City-state on the Sea of Storms, hemmed in and historically oppressed by Tear. The ruler of Mayene is styled the First, which was once the First Lord or Lady; Firsts claim to be descendants of Artur Hawkwing. The title of Second, once held by a single lord or lady, has in the last four hundred years or so been held by as many as nine at once. The banner of Mayene is a golden hawk in flight on a field of blue.

Mazrim Taim (MAHZ-rihm tah-EEM): A false Dragon who raised havoc in Saldaea until he was defeated and captured. Not only able to channel, but of great strength. *See also* Dragon, false.

Melaine (meh-LAYN): A Wise One of the Jhirad sept of Goshien Aiel. A dreamwalker. Moderately strong in the One Power. Married to Bael, clan chief of the Goshien. Sister-wife to Dorindha, roof mistress of Smoke Springs Hold. *See also* dreamwalker.

Moiraine Damodred (mwah-RAIN DAHM-oh-drehd): Aes Sedai of the Blue Ajah. Born 956 NE in the Royal Palace of Cairhien. After coming to the White Tower as a novice in 972 NE, her rise was meteoric, being raised Accepted in just three years and Aes Sedai only three more after that, at the end of the Aiel War. From that time she began a search for the young man who had (according to Gitara Morose, an Aes Sedai with the Foretelling) been born on the slopes of Dragonmount during the Battle of the Shining Walls and who would be the Dragon Reborn. It was she who took Rand al'Thor, Mat Cauthon, Perrin Aybara and Egwene al'Vere out of the Two Rivers. She vanished into a *ter'angreal* in Cairhien while battling Lanfear, apparently killing both herself and the Forsaken.

Morgase (moor-GAYZ): By the Grace of the Light, Queen of Andor, Defender of the Realm, Protector of the People, High Seat of House Trakand. Now in exile and believed dead, murdered by the Dragon Reborn, so many think. Her sign is three golden keys. The sign of House Trakand is a silver keystone.

Myrddraal (MUHRD-draal): Creatures of the Dark One, commanders of the Trollocs. Twisted offspring of Trollocs in which the human stock used to create the Trollocs has resurfaced, but tainted by the evil that made the Trollocs. They have no eyes, but can see like eagles in light or dark. They have certain powers stemming from the Dark One, including the ability to cause paralyzing fear with a look, and to vanish wherever there are shadows. Among Myrddraal's known weaknesses is that they are reluctant to cross running water. Mirrors reflect them only mistily. In different lands they are known by many names, among them Halfman, the Eyeless, Shadowman, Lurk, Fetch and Fade.

near-sister; near-brother: Aiel kinship terms meaning friend as close as first-sisters or first-brothers. Near-sisters often adopt one another formally as first-sisters. Near-brothers almost never do.

Oaths, Three: The oaths taken by an Accepted on being raised to Aes Sedai. Spoken while holding the Oath Rod, a *ter'angreal* that makes oaths binding. They are: (1) To speak no word that is not true. (2) To make no weapon with which one man may kill another. (3) Never to use the One Power as a weapon except against Darkfriends or Shadowspawn, or in the last extreme of defense of her own life, or that of her Warder or another Aes Sedai. The second oath was the first adopted after the War of the Shadow. The first oath, while held to the letter, is often circumvented by careful speaking. It is believed that the last two are inviolable.

Ogier (OH-gehr): (1) A nonhuman race, characterized by great height (ten feet is average for adult males), broad, almost snoutlike noses and long, tufted ears. They live in areas called *stedding*, which they rarely leave, and they typically have little contact with humankind. Knowledge of them among humans is sparse, and many believe Ogier to be only legends, though they are wondrous stonemasons and built most of the great cities constructed after the Breaking. Although they are thought to be a pacific people and extremely slow to anger, some old stories say they fought alongside humans in the Trolloc Wars, and call them implacable enemies. By and large, they are extremely fond of knowledge, and their books and stories often contain information lost to humans. A typical Ogier life span is at least three to four times that of a human. (2) Any individual of that nonhuman race. *See also* Breaking of the World; *stedding*.

Old Tongue: The language spoken during the Age of Legends. It is generally expected that nobles and the educated can speak it, but most know only a few words. Translation is often difficult, as it is a language capable of many subtly different meanings. *See also* Age of Legends.

One Power: The power drawn from the True Source. The vast majority of people are completely unable to learn to channel the One Power. A very small number can be taught to channel, and an even tinier number have the ability inborn. These few have no need to be taught; eventually they will channel whether they want to or not, often without even realizing what they are doing. This inborn ability usually manifests itself in late adolescence or early adulthood. If control is not taught, or self-learned (extremely difficult, with a success rate of only one in four), death is certain. Since the Time of Madness, no man has been able to channel the Power without eventually going completely, horribly mad, and then, even if he has learned some control, dying from a wasting sickness that causes the sufferer to rot alive, a sickness caused, as is the madness, by the Dark One's taint on *saidin*. *See also* Aes Sedai; Breaking of the World; channel; Five Powers; True Source.

Padan Fain (PAD-an FAIN): Once a peddler trading into the Two Rivers, and a Darkfriend, he was transformed at Shayol Ghul not only to enable him to find the young man who would become the Dragon Reborn as a hound finds prey for the hunter, but to ingrain the need to find him. The pain of this induced in Fain a hatred both of the Dark One and of Rand al'Thor. While following al'Thor, he encountered the trapped soul of Mordeth in Shadar Logoth, and this soul tried to take Fain's body. Because of what had been made of Fain, though, the result was an amalgamation which was mostly Fain and which has abilities beyond what either man had originally, though Fain does not understand them fully yet. Most men feel fear at a Myrddraal's eyeless gaze; Myrddraal feel fear at Fain's gaze.

Pattern of an Age: The Wheel of Time weaves the threads of human lives into the Pattern of an Age, often called simply the Pattern, which forms the substance of reality for that Age. *See also ta'veren.*

Questioners, the: An order within the Children of the Light. Avowed purposes are to discover the truth in disputations and uncover Darkfriends. In the search for truth and the Light, their normal method of inquiry is torture, their normal manner that they know the truth already and must only make their victim confess to it. Refer to themselves as the Hand of the Light, the Hand that digs out truth, and at times act as if they were entirely separate from the Children and the Council of the Anointed, which commands the Children. The head of the Questioners is the High Inquisitor, who sits on the Council of the Anointed. Their sign is a blood-red shepherd's crook. *See also* Children of the Light.

Rashima Kerenmosa (rah-SHE-mah keh-rehn-MOH-sah): Called the Soldier Amyrlin. Born circa 1150 AB. Raised Amyrlin from the Green Ajah in 1251 AB. Personally leading the Tower armies, she won innumerable victories, most notably Kaisin Pass, the Soralle Step, Larapelle, Tel Norwin and Maighande, where she died in 1301 AB. Her body was discovered after the battle surrounded by her five Warders and a vast wall of Trollocs and Myrddraal which contained the corpses of no fewer than nine Dreadlords. *See also* Aes Sedai; Ajah; Amyrlin Seat; Dreadlords; Warders.

Rhuidean (RHUY-dee-ahn): A great city, the only one in the Aiel Waste and totally unknown to the outside world. Abandoned for nearly three thousand years. Once men among the Aiel were allowed to enter Rhuidean only once, in order to be tested inside a great *ter'angreal* for fitness to become clan chief (only one in three survived), and women only twice, for testing to become Wise Ones, the second time in the same *ter'angreal*, though with a considerably higher survival rate than the men. Now the city is inhabited again, by Aiel, and a great lake occupies one end of the valley of Rhuidean, fed by an underground ocean of fresh water and in turn feeding the only river in the Waste. *See also* Aiel.

sa'angreal (SAH-ahn-GREE-ahl): Remnants of the Age of Legends that allow channeling much more of the One Power than is otherwise possible or safe. A *sa'angreal* is similar to, but more powerful than, an *angreal*. The amount of the Power that can be wielded with a *sa'angreal* compares to the amount that can be handled with an *angreal* as the Power wielded with the aid of an *angreal* does to the amount that can be handled unaided. The making of them is no longer known. As with *angreal*, there are male and female *sa'angreal*. Only a handful remain, far fewer even than *angreal*.

saidar (sah-ih-DAHR); *saidin* (sah-ih-DEEN): *See* True Source.

Sea Folk: More properly, the Atha'an Miere, the People of the Sea. A secretive people. Inhabitants of islands in the Aryth (AH-rihth) Ocean and the Sea of Storms, they spend little time ashore, living most of their lives on their ships. Most seaborne trade is carried by Sea Folk ships.

Seanchan (SHAWN-CHAN): (1) Descendants of the armies Artur Hawkwing sent across the Aryth Ocean, who conquered the lands there. They believe that any woman who can channel must be controlled for the safety of everyone else, and any man who can channel must be killed for the same reason. (2) The land from which the Seanchan come.

Shayol Ghul (SHAY-ol GHOOL): A mountain in the Blasted Lands, beyond the Great Blight. Site of the Dark One's prison.

sister-wife: Aiel kinship term. Aielwomen who are near-sisters or first-sisters who discover they love the same man, or who simply do not want a man to come between them, will both marry him, thus becoming sister-wives. Women who love the same man will sometimes try to find out whether they can become near-sisters and adopted first-sisters, a first step to becoming sister-wives.

Sorilea (soh-rih-LEE-ah): The Wise One of Shende Hold, a Jarra Chareen. Barely able to channel, she is the oldest living Wise One, though not by as much as many think.

Spine of the World: A towering mountain range, with few passes, which separates the Aiel Waste from the lands to the west. Also called the Dragonwall.

stedding (STEHD-ding): An Ogier (OH-gehr) homeland. Many *stedding* have been abandoned since the Breaking of the World. They are shielded in some way, no longer understood, so that within them no Aes Sedai can channel the One Power, nor even sense the True Source. Attempts to wield the One Power from outside a *stedding* have no effect inside the *stedding* boundary. No Trolloc will enter a *stedding* unless driven, and even Myrddraal will do so only at the greatest need and with the greatest reluctance. Even Darkfriends, if truly dedicated, feel uncomfortable within a *stedding*.

stilling: The removal of a woman's ability to channel. A woman who has been stilled can sense but not touch the True Source. Officially, stilling is the result of trial and sentence for a crime. Novices in the White Tower are required to learn the name and crimes of all women who have suffered stilling. When the ability to channel is lost accidentally, it is called being burned out, though "stilling" is often used for that also. Women who are stilled, however it occurs, seldom survive long; they seem to simply give up and die unless they find something to replace the emptiness left by the One Power.

Stone of Tear: A great fortress in the city of Tear, said to have been made with the One Power soon after the Breaking of the World. Attacked and besieged unsuccessfully countless times, it fell in a single night to the Dragon Reborn and a few hundred Aiel, thus fulfilling two parts of the Prophecies of the Dragon. *See also* Dragon, Prophecies of the.

Talents: Abilities in the use of the One Power in specific areas. Aptitude in various Talents varies widely from individual to individual and is seldom related to the strength of the individual's ability to channel. There are major Talents, the best known and most widespread of which is Healing. Other examples are Cloud Dancing, the control of weather, and Earth Singing, which involves controlling movements of the earth—for example, preventing, or causing, earthquakes or avalanches. There are also minor Talents, seldom given a name, such as the ability to see *ta'veren* or to duplicate the chance-twisting effect of *ta'veren*, though in a very small and localized area rarely covering more than a few square feet. Many Talents are now known only by their names and sometimes vague descriptions. Some, such as Traveling (the ability to shift from one place to another without crossing the intervening space) are only now being rediscovered. Others, such as Foretelling (the ability to foretell future events, but in a general way) and Delving (the location of ores and possibly their removal from the ground), are found rarely. Another Talent long thought lost is Dreaming, interpreting the Dreamer's dreams to foretell future events in more specific fashion than Foretelling. Some Dreamers had the ability to enter *Tel'aran'rhiod*, the World of Dreams, and (it is said) even other people's dreams. The last acknowledged Dreamer previously was Corianin Nedeal (coh-ree-AHN-ihn neh-dee-AHL), who died in 526 NE, but there is now another. *See also Tel'aran'rhiod.*

Tallanvor, Martyn (TAL-lahn-vohr, mahr-TEEN): Guardsman-Lieutenant of the Queen's Guards who loves his queen more than life or honor.

Tam al'Thor (TAM al-THOR): A farmer and shepherd in the Two Rivers. As a young man, he left to become a soldier, returning with a wife (Kari, now deceased) and a child (Rand).

Tarabon (TAH-rah-BON): Nation on the Aryth Ocean. Once a great trading nation, a source of rugs, dyes and fireworks produced by the Guild of Illuminators, among other things. Little news has come out of Tarabon since the land became racked by anarchy and civil war compounded by simultaneous wars against Arad Doman and the Dragonsworn, people who have sworn to follow the Dragon Reborn.

Tarmon Gai'don (TAHR-mohn GAY-dohn): The Last Battle. *See also* Dragon, Prophecies of the; Horn of Valere.

ta'veren (tah-VEER-ehn): A person around whom the Wheel of Time weaves all surrounding life-threads, perhaps ALL life-threads. *See also* Pattern of an Age.

Tear (TEER): A nation on the Sea of Storms. Also the capital city of that nation, a great seaport. The banner of Tear is three white crescent moons slanting across a field half-red, half-gold. *See also* Stone of Tear.

Telamon, Lews Therin (TEHL-ah-mon, LOOZ THEH-rihn): *See* Dragon, the.

Tel'aran'rhiod (tel-AYE-rahn-rhee-ODD): In the Old Tongue, "the Unseen World," or "the World of Dreams." A world or place, glimpsed in dreams, which was believed by the ancients to permeate and surround all other possible worlds. Many can touch *Tel'aran'rhiod* for a few moments in their dreams, but few have ever had the ability to enter it at will, though some *ter'angreal* confer that ability. Unlike other dreams, what happens to living things in the World of Dreams is real; a wound taken there will still exist on awakening, and one who dies there does not wake at all. Otherwise, though, nothing done there affects the waking world in any way. *See also ter'angreal.*

ter'angreal (TEER-ahn-GREE-ahl): Remnants of the Age of Legends that use the One Power. Unlike *angreal* and *sa'angreal*, each *ter'angreal* was made to do a particular thing. Some *ter'angreal* are used by Aes Sedai, but the original purposes of many are unknown. Some require channeling, while others may be used by anyone. Some will kill or destroy the ability to channel of any woman who uses them. Like *angreal* and *sa'angreal*, the making of them has been lost since the Breaking of the World. *See also angreal; sa'angreal.*

Thom Merrilin (TOM MER-rih-lihn): A not-so-simple gleeman and traveler. *See also* Game of Houses; gleeman.

Tinkers: Properly, the Tuatha'an (too-AH-thah-AHN), also called the Traveling People. A wandering folk who live in brightly painted wagons and follow a totally pacifist philosophy called the Way of the Leaf. They are among the few who can cross the Aiel Waste unmolested, for the Aiel strictly avoid all contact with them. Very few people even suspect that the Tuatha'an are descended from Aiel who broke away during the Breaking of the World in an attempt to find a way back to the time of peace. *See also* Aiel.

Trollocs (TRAHL-lohks): Creatures of the Dark One, created during the War of the Shadow. Huge of stature, they are a twisted blend of animal and human stock. Vicious by nature, they kill for the pure pleasure of killing. Deceitful in the extreme, they cannot be trusted unless coerced by fear. They will eat anything—or anyone. *See also* Trolloc Wars.

Trolloc Wars: A series of wars, beginning about 1000 AB and lasting more than three hundred years, during which Trolloc armies ravaged the world under the command of Myrddraal and Dreadlords. Eventually the Trollocs were driven back into the Great Blight, but some nations ceased to exist, and others that survived were almost depopulated. All records of the time are fragmentary. *See also* Dreadlords; Myrddraal; Trollocs.

True Source: The driving force of the universe, which turns the Wheel of Time. Divided into a male half (*saidin*) and a female half (*saidar*), which work at the same time with and against each other. Only a man can draw on *saidin*, only a woman on *saidar*. For more than three thousand years, *saidin* has been tainted by the Dark One's touch. *See also* One Power.

Warder: A warrior bonded to an Aes Sedai. The bonding is a thing of the One Power: by it he gains such gifts as quick healing, the ability to go long periods without food, water, or rest and the ability to sense the taint of the Dark One at a distance. So long as a Warder lives, the Aes Sedai to whom he is bonded knows he is alive however far away he is, and when he dies she will know the moment and manner of his death. While most Ajahs believe an Aes Sedai may have one Warder bonded to her at a time, the Red Ajah refuses to bond any Warders at all, and the Green Ajah believes an Aes Sedai may bond as many as she wishes. Ethically the Warder must accede to the bonding voluntarily, but it has been known to be done against the Warder's will. What the Aes Sedai gain from the bonding is a closely held secret. *See also* Aes Sedai.

War of Power: *See* War of the Shadow.

War of the Hundred Years (FY 994–FY 1117): A series of overlapping wars among constantly shifting alliances, precipitated by the death of Artur Hawkwing and the resulting struggle for his empire. The War of the Hundred Years depopulated large parts of the lands between the Aryth Ocean and the Aiel Waste, from the Sea of Storms to the Great Blight. So great was the destruction that only fragmentary records of the time remain. The empire of Artur Hawkwing was pulled apart, and the nations of the present day were formed. *See also* Hawkwing, Artur.

War of the Shadow: Also known as the War of Power. Began shortly after the attempt to free the Dark One, and soon involved the whole world. In a world where even the memory of war had been forgotten, every facet of war was rediscovered, often twisted by the Dark One's touch on the world, and the One Power was used as a weapon. The war was ended by the resealing of the Dark One into his prison in a strike led by Lews Therin Telamon, the Dragon, and one hundred male Aes Sedai called the Hundred Companions. The Dark One's counterstroke tainted *saidin* and drove Lews Therin and the Hundred Companions insane, thus beginning the Time of Madness and the Breaking of the World. *See also* Dragon, the; One Power, the.

weight, units of: 10 ounces = 1 pound; 10 pounds = 1 stone; 10 stone = 1 hundredweight; 10 hundredweight = 1 ton.

Wheel of Time, the: Time is a wheel with seven spokes, each spoke an Age. As the Wheel turns, Ages come and go, each leaving memories that fade to legend, then to myth, and are forgotten by the time that Age comes again. The Pattern of an Age is slightly different each time an Age comes, and each time it is subject to greater change.

Whitecloaks: *See* Children of the Light.

White Tower: The center and heart of Aes Sedai power, located in the heart of the great island city of Tar Valon.

wilder: A woman who has learned to channel the One Power on her own; only one in four survive this. Such women usually build barriers against knowing what it is they are doing, but if these can be broken down, wilders are among the most powerful of channelers. The term is often used in derogatory fashion.

Wisdom: In villages, a woman chosen by the Women's Circle for her knowledge of such things as healing and foretelling the weather, as well as common good sense. Generally considered the equal of the Mayor, and in some villages his superior. She is chosen for life, and it is very rare for a Wisdom to be removed from office before her death. Depending on the land, she may instead have another title, such as Guide, Healer, Wise Woman or Seeker, among others.

Wise One: Among the Aiel, Wise Ones are women chosen by other Wise Ones and trained in healing, herbs and other things, much like Wisdoms. They have great authority and responsibility, as well as great influence with sept and clan chiefs, though these men often accuse them of meddling. A good many Wise Ones can channel to one degree or another; they find every Aiel woman born with the spark in her and most of those who can learn. The fact that Wise Ones can channel is not spoken of among Aiel, by custom. Also by custom, Wise Ones avoid all contact with Aes Sedai, even more so than other Aiel. Wise Ones stand outside all feuds and battle, and according to *ji'e'toh* may not be harmed or impeded in any way. For a Wise One to take part in a battle would be a great violation of custom and tradition. Three Wise Ones now living are dreamwalkers, with the ability to enter *Tel'aran'rhiod* and to speak to other people in their dreams among other things. *See also* dreamwalker; *Tel'aran'rhiod*.

PROLOGUE

A preview of
A Crown of Swords

Book Seven of
The Wheel of Time

Lightnings

From the tall arched window, close onto eighty spans above the ground, not far below the top of the White Tower, Elaida could see for miles beyond Tar Valon, to the rolling plains and forests that bordered the broad River Erinin, running down from north and west before it divided around the white walls of the great island city. On the ground, long morning shadows must have been dappling the city, but from this prominence all seemed clear and bright. Not even the fabled "topless towers" of Cairhien had truly rivaled the White Tower: Certainly none of Tar Valon's lesser towers did, for all that men spoke far and wide of them and their vaulting sky-bridges.

This high, an almost constant breeze lessened the unnatural heat gripping the world. The Feast of Lights past, snow should have covered the ground deep, yet the weather belonged in the depths of a hard summer. Another sign that the Last Battle approached and the Dark One touched the world, if more were needed. Elaida did not let the heat touch her even when she descended, of course. The breeze was not why she had had her quarters moved up here, despite the inconvenience of so many stairs, to these simple rooms.

Plain russet floor tiles and white marble walls decorated by a few tapestries could not compare with the grandeur of the Amyrlin's study and the rooms that went with it far below. She still used those rooms occasionally—they held associations with the power of the Amyrlin Seat in some minds—but she resided here, and worked here more often than not. For the view. Not of city or river or forests, though. Of what was beginning in the Tower grounds.

Great diggings and foundations spread across what had been the Warders' practice yard, tall wooden cranes and stacks of cut marble and granite. Masons and laborers swarmed over the workings like ants, and endless streams of wagons trailed through the gates onto the Tower grounds, bringing more stone. To one side stood a wooden "working model," as the masons called it, big enough for men to enter crouching on their heels and see every detail, where every stone should go. Most of the workmen could not read, after all—neither words nor mason's drawn plans. The "working model" was as large as some manor houses.

When any king or queen had a palace, why should the Amyrlin Seat be relegated to apartments little better than those of many ordinary sisters? Her palace would match the White Tower for splendor, and have a great spire ten spans higher than the Tower itself. The blood had drained from the chief mason's face when he heard that. The Tower had been Ogier-built, with assistance from sisters using the Power. One look at Elaida's face, however, set Master Lerman bowing and stammering that of course all would be done as she wished. As if there had been any question.

Her mouth tightened with exasperation. She had wanted Ogier masons again, but the Ogier were confining themselves to their *stedding* for some reason. Her summons to the nearest, Stedding Jentoine, in the Black Hills, had been met with refusal. Polite, yet still refusal, without explanation, even to the Amyrlin Seat. Ogier were reclusive at best. Or they might be withdrawing from a world full of turmoil; Ogier stayed clear of human strife.

Firmly Elaida dismissed the Ogier from her mind. She prided herself on separating what could be from what could not. Ogier were a triviality. They had no part in the world beyond the cities they had built so long ago and seldom visited now except to make repairs.

The men below, crawling beetle-like over the building site, made her frown slightly. Construction went forward by inches. Ogier might be out of the question, yet perhaps the One Power could be used again. Few sisters possessed real strength in weaving Earth, but not that much was required to reinforce stone, or bind stone to stone. Yes. In her mind, the palace stood finished, colonnaded walks and great domes shining with gilt and that one spire reaching to the heavens. . . . Her eyes rose to the cloudless sky, to where the spire would peak, and she let out a long sigh. Yes. The orders would be issued today.

The towering case clock in the room behind her chimed Third Rise, and in the city gongs and bells pealed the hour, the sound faint here, so high above. With a smile, Elaida left the window, smoothing her red-slashed dress of cream silk and adjusting the broad, striped stole of the Amyrlin Seat on her shoulders.

On the ornately gilded clock, small figures of gold and silver and enamel moved with the chimes. Horned and snouted Trollocs fled from a cloaked Aes Sedai on one level; on another a man representing a false Dragon tried to fend off silver lightning bolts that had obviously been hurled by a second sister. And above the clockface, itself above her head, a crowned king and queen knelt before an Amyrlin Seat in her enameled stole, with the Flame of Tar Valon, carved from a large moonstone, atop a golden arch over her head.

She did not laugh often, but she could not help a quietly pleased chuckle at the clock. Cemaile Sorenthaine, raised from the Gray, had commissioned it dreaming of a return to the days before the Trolloc Wars, when no ruler held a throne without the Tower's approval. Cemaile's grand plans came to naught, however, as did Cemaile, and for three centuries the clock sat in a dusty storage room, an embarrassment no one dared display. Until Elaida. The Wheel of Time turned. What was once, could be again. Would be again.

The case clock balanced the door to her sitting room, and her bedchamber and dressing room beyond. Fine tapestries, colorful work from Tear and Kandor and Arad Doman, with thread-of-gold and thread-of-silver glittering among the merely dyed, hung each exactly opposite its mate. She had always liked order. The carpet covering most of the tiles came from Tarabon, patterned in red and green and gold; silk carpets were the most precious. In each corner of the room a marble plinth carved in unpretentious verticals held a white vase of fragile Sea Folk porcelain with two dozen carefully arranged red roses. To make roses bloom now required the One Power, especially with the drought and heat; a worthwhile use, in her opinion. Gilded carving covered both the only chair—*no* one sat in her presence now—and the writing table, but in the stark style of Cairhien. A simple room, really, with a ceiling barely two spans high, yet it would do until her palace was ready. With the view, it would.

The tall chairback held the Flame of Tar Valon picked out in moonstones above her dark head as she sat. Nothing marred the polished surface of the table except for three boxes of Altaran lacquerwork, arranged just so. Opening the box covered with golden hawks among white clouds, she removed a slim strip of thin paper from atop the pile of reports and correspondence inside.

For what must have been the hundredth time, she read the message come from Cairhien by pigeon twelve days ago. Few in the Tower knew of its existence. None but she knew its contents, or would have a glimmer of what it meant if they did. The thought almost made her laugh again.

The ring has been placed in the bull's nose. I expect a pleasant journey to market.

No signature, yet she needed none. Only Galina Casban had known to send that glorious message. Galina, whom Elaida trusted to do what she would have trusted to no one else save herself. Not that she trusted anyone fully, but the head of the Red Ajah more than any other. She herself had been raised from the Red, after all, and in many ways still thought of herself as Red.

The ring has been placed in the bull's nose.

Rand al'Thor—the Dragon Reborn, the man who had seemed on the point of swallowing the world, the man who had swallowed entirely too much of it—Rand al'Thor was shielded and in Galina's control. And none who might support him knew. Even a chance of that, and the wording would have been different. By various earlier messages, it seemed he had rediscovered how to Travel, a Talent lost to Aes Sedai since the Breaking, yet that had not saved him. It had even played into Galina's hands. Apparently he had a habit of coming and going without warning. Who would suspect that this time he had not gone, but been taken? Something very like a giggle rose in her.

Inside another week, two at most, al'Thor would be in the Tower, closely supervised and guided safely until Tarmon Gai'don, his ravaging of the world stopped. It was madness to allow any man who could channel to run free, but most of all the man prophecy said must face the Dark One in the Last Battle, the Light send that it lay years off yet in spite of the weather. Years would be needed to arrange the world properly, beginning with undoing what al'Thor had done.

Of course, the damage he had wrought was nothing beside what he could have caused, free. Not to mention the possibility that he might have gotten himself killed before he was needed. Well, that troublesome young man would be wrapped in swaddling and kept safe as an infant in his mother's arms until time to take him to Shayol Ghul. After that, if he survived. . . .

Elaida's lips pursed. The Prophecies of the Dragon seemed to say he would not, which undeniably would be for the best.

"Mother?" Elaida almost gave a start as Alviarin spoke. Entering without so much as a knock! "I have word from the Ajahs, Mother." Slim and cool-faced, Alviarin wore the Keeper's narrow stole in white, matching her dress, to show she had been raised from the White, but in her mouth "Mother" became less a title of respect and more an address to an equal.

Alviarin's presence was enough to dent Elaida's good mood. That the Keeper of Chronicles came from the White, not the Red, always served as a biting reminder of her weakness when she was first raised. Some of that had been dispelled, true, but not all. Not yet. She was tired of regretting that she had so few personal eyes-and-ears outside Andor. And that her predecessor and Alviarin's had escaped—been helped to escape; they must have had help!—escaped before the keys to the Amyrlin's great network could be wrested out of them.

She more than wanted the network that was hers by right. By strong tradition the Ajahs sent to the Keeper whatever dribbles from their own eyes-and-ears they were willing to share with the Amyrlin, but Elaida was convinced the woman kept back some of even that trickle. Yet she could not ask the Ajahs for information directly. Bad enough to be weak without going begging to the world. The Tower, anyway, which was as much of the world as really counted.

Elaida kept her own face every bit as cool as the other woman's, acknowledging her only with a nod while she pretended to examine papers from the lacquered box. Slowly she turned them over one by one, returned them to the box slowly. Without really seeing a word. Making Alviarin wait was bitter, because it was petty, and petty ways were all she had to strike at one who should have been her servant.

An Amyrlin could issue any decree she wished, her word law and absolute. Yet as a practical matter, without support from the Hall of the Tower, many of those decrees were wasted ink and paper. No sister would disobey an Amyrlin, not directly at least, yet many decrees required a hundred other things ordered to implement them. In the best of times that could come slowly on occasion so slowly it never happened, and these were far from the best.

Alviarin stood there, calm as a frozen pond. Closing the Altaran box, Elaida kept out the strip of paper that announced her sure victory. Unconsciously she fingered it, a talisman. "Has Teslyn or Joline finally deigned to send more than word of their safe arrival?"

That was meant to remind Alviarin that no one could consider herself immune. Nobody cared what happened in Ebou Dar, Elaida least of all; the capital of Altara could fall into the sea, and except for the merchants, not even the rest of Altara would notice. But Teslyn had sat in the Hall nearly fifteen years before Elaida had commanded her to resign her chair. If Elaida could send a Sitter—a *Red* Sitter—who had supported her rise off as ambassador to a flyspeck throne with no one sure why but a hundred rumors flowering, then she could come down on anyone. Joline was a different matter. She had held her chair for the Green only a matter of weeks, and everyone was sure the Greens had selected her to show they would not be cowed by the new Amyrlin, who had handed her a fearsome penance. That bit of insolence could not be allowed to pass, of course, and had not been. Everyone knew that, too.

It was meant to remind Alviarin that she was vulnerable, but the slim woman merely smiled her cool smile. So long as the Hall remained as it was, she *was* immune. She riffled through the papers in her hand, plucking one out. "No word from Teslyn or Joline, Mother, no, though with the news you have received so far from the thrones. . . ." That smile deepened into something dangerously close to amusement. "They all mean to try their wings, to see if you are as strong as . . . as your predecessor." Even Alviarin had enough sense not to speak the Sanche woman's name in her presence. It was true, though; every king and queen, even mere nobles, seemed to be testing the limits of her power. She must make examples.

Glancing at the paper, Alviarin went on. "There is word from Ebou Dar, however. Through the Gray." Had she emphasized that, to drive the splinter deeper? "It appears Elayne Trakand and Nynaeve al'Meara are there. Posing as full sisters, with the blessings of the rebel . . . *embassy* . . . to Queen Tylin. There are two others, not identified, who may be doing the same. The lists of who is with the rebels are incomplete. Or they may just be companions. The Grays are uncertain."

"Why under the Light would they be in Ebou Dar?" Elaida said dismissively. Certainly Teslyn would have sent news of *that*. "The Gray must be passing along rumors, now. Tarna's message said they are with the rebels in Salidar." Tarna Feir had reported Siuan Sanche there, too. And Logain Ablar, spreading those vicious lies no Red sister could lower herself to acknowledge, much less deny. The Sanche woman had a hand in that obscenity, or the sun would rise in the west tomorrow. Why could she not simply have crawled away and died, decently out of sight, like other stilled women?

It required effort not to draw a deep breath. Logain could be hanged quietly as soon as the rebels were dealt with; most of the world thought him dead long since. The filthy slander that the Red Ajah had set him up as a false Dragon would die with him. When the rebels were dealt with, the Sanche woman could be made to hand over the keys to the Amyrlin's eyes-and-ears. And name the traitors who had helped her escape. A foolish hope to wish that Alviarin would be named among them. "I can hardly see the al'Meara girl running to Ebou Dar claiming to be Aes Sedai, much less Elayne, can you?"

"You did order Elayne found, Mother. As important as putting a leash on al'Thor, you said. When she was among three hundred rebels in Salidar, it was impossible to do anything, but she will not be so well protected in the Tarasin Palace."

"I have no time for gossip and rumors." Elaida bit off each word with contempt. Did Alviarin know more than she should, mentioning al'Thor, and leashing? "I suggest you read Tarna's report again, then ask yourself whether even *rebels* would allow Accepted to pretend to the shawl."

Alviarin waited with visible patience for her to finish, then examined her sheaf again and pulled out four more sheets. "The Gray agent sent sketches," she said blandly, proffering the pages. "He is no artist, but Elayne and Nynaeve are recognizable." After a moment, when Elaida did not take the drawings, she slipped them under the rest.

Elaida felt the color of anger and embarrassment rising in her cheeks. Alviarin had led her down this path deliberately by not bringing out those sketches at the first. She ignored that—anything else would only be more embarrassing still—but her voice became cold. "I want them taken, and brought to me."

The lack of curiosity on Alviarin's face made Elaida wonder again how much the woman knew that she was not supposed to. The al'Meara girl might well provide a handle on al'Thor, coming from the same village. All the sisters knew that, just as they knew that Elayne was Daughter-Heir of Andor, and that her mother was dead. Vague rumors linking Morgase to the Whitecloaks were so much nonsense, for she would never have gone to the Children of the Light for help. She was dead, leaving not even a corpse behind, and Elayne would be Queen. If she could be wrested away from the rebels before the Andoran Houses put Dyelin on the Lion Throne instead. It was not widely known what made Elayne more important than any other noble with a strong claim to a throne. Aside from the fact that she would be Aes Sedai one day, of course.

Elaida had the Foretelling sometimes, a Talent many thought lost before her, and long ago she had Foretold that the Royal House of Andor held the key to winning the Last Battle. Twenty-five years gone and more, as soon as it became clear that Morgase Trakand would gain the throne in the Succession, Elaida had fastened herself to the girl, as she was then. How Elayne was crucial, Elaida did not know, but Foretelling never lied. Sometimes she almost hated the Talent. She hated things she could not control.

"I want all four of them, Alviarin." The other two were unimportant, certainly, but she would take no chances. "Send my command to Teslyn immediately. Tell her—*and* Joline—that if they fail to send regular reports from now on, they will wish they had never been born. Include the information from the Macura woman." Her mouth twisted around that last.

The name made Alviarin shift uneasily, too, and no wonder. Ronde Macura's nasty little infusion was something to make any sister uncomfortable. Forkroot was not lethal—at least you woke, if you drank enough to sleep—but a tea that deadened a woman's ability to channel seemed aimed too directly at Aes Sedai. A pity the information had not been received before Galina went; if fork-root worked on men as well as it seemed to on women, it would have made her task considerably easier.

Alviarin's ill ease lasted only a moment; a mere instant and she was all self-possession again, unyielding as a wall of ice. "As you wish, Mother. I am sure they will leap to obey, as of course they should."

A sudden flash of irritation swept Elaida like fire in dry pasture. The fate of the world in her hands, and petty stumbling blocks kept rising beneath her feet. Bad enough that she had rebels and recalcitrant rulers to handle, but too many Sitters still brooded and grumbled behind her back, fertile ground for the other woman to plow. Only six were firmly under her own thumb, and she suspected as many at least listened closely to Alviarin before they voted. Certainly nothing of importance passed through the Hall unless Alviarin agreed to it. Not open agreement, not with any acknowledgment that Alviarin bore a shred more influence or power than a Keeper should, but if Alviarin opposed. . . . At least they had not gone so far as to reject anything Elaida sent them. They simply dragged their feet and too often let what she wanted starve on the floor. A pitifully small thing for which to be happy. Some Amyrlins had become little more than puppets once the Hall acquired a taste for rejecting what they put forward.

Her hands clenched, and a tiny crackle came from the strip of paper.

The ring has been placed in the bull's nose.

Alviarin looked as composed as a marble statue, but Elaida no longer cared. The shepherd was on his way to her. The rebels would be crushed and the Hall cowed, Alviarin forced to her knees and every fractious ruler brought to heel, from Tenobia of Saldaea, who had gone into hiding to avoid her emissary, to Mattin Stepaneos of Illian, who was trying to play all sides at once again, trying to agree with her *and* the Whitecloaks, and with al'Thor for all she knew. Elayne would be placed on the throne in Caemlyn, without her brother to get in the way and with a full knowledge of who had set her there. A little time back in the Tower would make the girl damp clay in Elaida's hands.

"I want *those men* rooted out, Alviarin." There was no need to say who she meant; half the Tower could talk of nothing but *those men* in their *Black* Tower, and the other half whispered about them in corners.

"There are disturbing reports, Mother." Alviarin looked through her papers once more, but Elaida thought it was only for something to do. She did not pluck out any more pages, and if nothing else disturbed the woman for long, this unholy midden outside Caemlyn must.

"*More* rumors? Do you believe the tales of thousands flocking to Caemlyn in answer to that obscene *amnesty*?" Not the least of what al'Thor had done, but hardly cause for worry. Just a pile of filth that must be safely cleared before Elayne was crowned in Caemlyn.

"Of course not, Mother, but—"

"Toveine is to lead; this task belongs properly to the Red." Toveine Gazal had been fifteen years away from the Tower, until Elaida summoned her back. The other two Red Sitters who had resigned and gone into a "voluntary" retreat at the same time were nervous-eyed women now, but unlike Lirene and Tsutama, Toveine had only hardened in her solitary exile. "She is to have fifty sisters." There could not be more than two or three men at this *Black* Tower actually able to channel, Elaida was certain. Fifty sisters could overwhelm them easily. Yet there might be others to deal with. Hangers-on, camp followers, fools full of futile hopes and insane ambitions. "And she is to take a hundred—no, two hundred—of the Guard."

"Are you certain that is wise? The rumors of thousands are certainly madness, but a Green agent in Caemlyn claims there are over four hundred in this Black Tower. A clever fellow. It seems he counted the supply carts that go out from the city. And you are aware of the rumors Mazrim Taim is with them."

Elaida fought to keep her features smooth, and barely succeeded. She had forbidden mention of Taim's name, and it was bitter that she did not dare—did not dare!—impose the penalty on Alviarin. The woman looked her straight in the eyes; the absence of so much as a perfunctory "Mother" this time was marked. And the *temerity* of asking whether her actions were *wise*! She was the Amyrlin Seat! Not first among equals; the Amyrlin Seat!

Opening the largest of the lacquered boxes revealed carved ivory miniatures laid out on gray velvet. Often just handling her collection soothed her, but more, like the knitting she enjoyed, it let whoever was attending her know their place, if she seemed to give more attention to the miniatures than to what they had to say. Fingering first an exquisite cat, sleek and flowing, then an elaborately robed woman with a peculiar little animal, some fantasy of the carver, almost like a man covered in hair, crouched on her shoulder, at length Elaida chose out a curving fish, so delicately carved that it seemed nearly real despite the aged yellow of the ivory.

"Four hundred rabble, Alviarin." She felt calmer already, for Alviarin's mouth had thinned. Just a fraction, but she savored any crack in the woman's façade. "If there are that many. Only a fool could believe that more than one or two can channel. At most! In ten years, we have found only six men with the ability. Just twenty-four in the last twenty years. And you know how the land has been scoured. As for Taim. . . ." The name burned her mouth; the only false Dragon ever to escape being gentled once in the hands of Aes Sedai. Not a thing she wanted in the Chronicles under her reign, certainly not until she decided how it should be recorded. At present the Chronicles told nothing after his capture.

She stroked her thumb along the fish's scales. "He is dead, Alviarin, else we would have heard from him long since. And not serving al'Thor. Can you think he went from claiming to be the Dragon Reborn to *serving* the Dragon Reborn? Can you think he could be in Caemlyn without Davram Bashere at least trying to kill him?" Her thumb moved faster on the ivory fish as she reminded herself that the Marshal-General of Saldaea was in Caemlyn taking orders from al'Thor. What *was* Tenobia playing at? Elaida held it all inside, though, presenting a face as calm as one of her carvings.

"Twenty-four is a dangerous number to speak aloud," Alviarin said with an ominous quiet, "as dangerous as two thousand. The Chronicles record only sixteen. The last thing needed now is for those years to rear up again. Or for sisters who know only what they were told to learn the truth. Even those you brought back hold their silence."

Elaida put on a bemused look. So far as she knew, Alviarin had learned the truth of those years only on being raised Keeper, but her own knowledge was more personal. Not that Alviarin could be aware of that. Not for certain, anyway. "Daughter, whatever comes out, I have no fear. Who is going to impose a penance on *me*, and on what charge?" That skirted truth nicely, but apparently it impressed the other woman not at all.

"The Chronicles record a number of Amyrlins who took on public penance for some usually obscure reason, but it has always seemed to me that is how an Amyrlin might have it written if she found herself with no choice except—"

Elaida's hand slapped down on the table. "Enough, daughter! I *am* Tower law! What has been hidden will remain hidden, for the same reason it has for twenty years—the good of the White Tower." Only then did she feel the bruise beginning on her palm; she lifted her hand to reveal the fish, broken in two. How old had it been? Five hundred years? A thousand? It was all she could do not to quiver with rage. Her voice certainly thickened with it. "Toveine is to lead fifty sisters and two hundred of the Tower Guards to Caemlyn, to this Black Tower, where they will gentle any man they find able to channel and hang him, along with as many others as they can take alive." Alviarin did not even blink at the violation of Tower law.

Elaida had spoken the truth as she meant it to be; with this, with everything, she *was* Tower law. "For that matter, hang up the dead as well. Let them be a warning to any man who thinks of touching the True Source. Have Toveine attend me. I will want to hear her plan."

"It will be as you command, Mother." The woman's reply was as cool and smooth as her face. "Though if I may suggest, you might wish to reconsider sending so many sisters away from the Tower. Apparently the rebels found your offer wanting. They are no longer in Salidar. They are on the march. The reports come from Altara, but they must be into Murandy by now. And they have chosen themselves an Amyrlin." She scanned the top sheet of her sheaf of papers as if searching for the name. "Egwene al'Vere, it seems."

That Alviarin had left this, the most important piece of news, until now, should have made Elaida explode in fury. Instead, she threw back her head and laughed. Only a firm hold on dignity kept her from drumming her heels on the floor. The surprise on Alviarin's face made her laugh harder, till she had to wipe her eyes with her fingers.

"You do not see it," she said when she could speak between ripples of mirth. "As well you are Keeper, Alviarin, not a Sitter. In the Hall, blind as you are, within a month the others would be holding you in a cabinet and taking you out when they needed your vote."

"I see enough, Mother." Alviarin's voice held no heat; if anything, it should have coated the walls with frost. "I see three hundred rebel Aes Sedai, perhaps more, marching on Tar Valon with an army led by Gareth Bryne, acknowledged a great captain. Discounting the more ridiculous reports, that army may number over twenty thousand, and with Bryne to lead they will gain more at every village and town they pass. I do not say they have hope of taking the city, of course, but it is hardly a matter for laughter. High Captain Chubain should be ordered to increase recruiting for the Tower Guard."

Elaida's gaze fell sourly on the broken fish, and she stood and stalked to the nearest window, her back to Alviarin. The palace under construction took away the bitter taste, that and the slip of paper she still clutched.

She smiled down on her palace-to-be. "Three hundred rebels, yes, but you should read Tarna's account again. At least a hundred are on the point of breaking already." She trusted Tarna to some extent, a Red with no room in her head for nonsense, and she said the rebels were ready to jump at shadows. Quietly desperate sheep looking for a shepherd, she said. A wilder, of course, yet still sensible. Tarna should be back soon, and able to give a fuller report. Not that it was needed. Elaida's plans were already working among the rebels. But that was her secret.

"Tarna has always been sure she could make people do what it was clear they would not." Had there been an emphasis in that, a significance of tone? Elaida decided to ignore it. She had to ignore too much from Alviarin, but the day would come. Soon.

"As for their army, daughter, she says two or three thousand men at most. If they had more, they would have made sure she saw them, to overawe us." In Elaida's opinion, eyes-and-ears always exaggerated, to make their information seem more valuable. Only sisters could be truly trusted. Red sisters, anyway. Some of them. "But I would not care if they did have twenty thousand, or fifty, or a hundred. Can you even begin to guess why?" When she turned, Alviarin's face was all smooth composure, a mask over blind ignorance. "You seem to be conversant with all the aspects of Tower law. What penalty do rebels face?"

"For the leaders," Alviarin said slowly, "stilling." She frowned slightly, skirts swaying just barely as her feet shifted. Good. Even Accepted knew this, and she could not understand why Elaida asked. Very good. "For many of the rest, too."

"Perhaps." The leaders might themselves escape that, most of them, if they submitted properly. The minimum penalty in law was to be birched in the Grand Hall before the assembled sisters, followed by at least a year and a day in public penance. Yet nothing said the penance must be served all at once; a month here, a month there, and they would still be atoning their crimes ten years from now, constant reminders of what came of resisting her. Some would be stilled, of course—Sheriam, a few of the more prominent so-called Sitters—but only sufficient to make the rest fear putting a foot wrong again, not enough to weaken the Tower. The White Tower had to be whole, and it had to be strong. Strong, and firmly in her grasp.

"Only one crime among those they have committed *demands* stilling." Alviarin opened her mouth. There had been ancient rebellions, buried so deep that few among the sisters knew; the Chronicles stood mute, the lists of stilled and executed confined to records open only to Amyrlin, Keeper and Sitters, aside from the few librarians who kept them. Elaida allowed Alviarin no opportunity to speak. "Any woman who falsely claims the title of Amyrlin Seat *must* be stilled. If they believed they had any chance of success, Sheriam would be their *Amyrlin*, or Lelaine, or Carlinya, or one of the others." Tarna reported that Romanda Cassin had come out of her retirement; Romanda surely would have seized the stole with both hands if she saw the tenth part of a chance. "Instead, they have plucked out an *Accepted*!"

Elaida shook her head in wry amusement. She could quote every word of the law setting out how a woman was chosen Amyrlin—she had made good use of it herself, after all—and never once did it require that the woman be a full sister. Obviously she *must* be, so those who framed the law never stated it, and the rebels had squirmed through that crack. "They know their cause is hopeless, Alviarin. They plan to strut and bluster, try to dig out some protection against penalty for themselves, then yield the girl as a sacrifice." Which was a pity. The al'Vere girl was another possible handle on al'Thor, and when she reached her full strength in the One Power, she would have been one of the strongest in a thousand years or more. A true pity.

"Gareth Bryne and an army hardly sound like strutting to me. It will take their army five or six months to reach Tar Valon. In that time, High Captain Chubain could increase the Guard—"

"Their *army*," Elaida sneered. Alviarin was such a fool; for all her cool exterior, she was a rabbit. Next she would be spouting the Sanche woman's nonsense about the Forsaken being loose. Of course, she did not know the secret, but just the same. . . . "Farmers carrying pikes, butchers with bows and tailors on horseback! And every step of the way, thinking of the Shining Walls, that held Artur Hawkwing at bay." No, not a rabbit. A weasel. Yet soon or late, she would be weasel-fur trim on Elaida's cloak. The Light send it soon. "Every step of the way, they will lose a man, if not ten. I would not be surprised if our rebels appear with nothing more than their Warders." Too many people knew of the division in the Tower. Once the rebellion was broken, of course, it could be made to seem all a ploy, a part of gaining control of young al'Thor perhaps. An effort of years, that, and generations before memories faded. Every last rebel would pay for that on her knees.

Elaida clenched her fist as though she held all the rebels by the throat. Or Alviarin. "I mean to break them, daughter. They will split open like a rotten melon." Her secret assured that, however many farmers and tailors Lord Bryne hung on to, but let the other woman think as she would. Suddenly the Foretelling took hold of her, a certainty about things she could not see stronger than if they had been laid out before her. She would have been willing to step blindly over a cliff on that certainty. "The White Tower will be whole again, except for remnants cast out and scorned, whole and stronger than ever. Rand al'Thor will face the Amyrlin Seat and know her anger. The Black Tower will be rent in blood and fire, and sisters will walk its grounds. This I Foretell."

As usual, the Foretelling left her trembling, gasping for breath. She forced herself to stand still and straight, to breathe slowly; she never let anyone see weakness. But Alviarin. . . . Her eyes were wide as they could open, lips parted as if she had forgotten the words she meant to speak. A paper slid from the sheaf in her hands and almost fell before she could catch it. That recalled her to herself. In a flash she regained her serene mask, a perfect picture of Aes Sedai calm, but she definitely had been jolted to her heels. Oh, very good. Let her chew on the certain surety of Elaida's victory. Chew and break her teeth.

Elaida drew a deep breath and seated herself behind her writing table again, putting the broken ivory fish to one side where she did not have to look at it. It was time to exploit her victory. "There is work to be done today, daughter. The first message is to go to the Lady Caraline Damodred. . . ."

Elaida spun out her plans, enlarging on what Alviarin knew, revealing some that she did not, because at the last an Amyrlin did have to work through her Keeper, however much she hated the woman. There was a pleasure in watching Alviarin's eyes, watching her wonder what else she still did not know. But while Elaida ordered, divided and assigned the world between the Aryth Ocean and the Spine of the World, in her mind frolicked the image of young al'Thor on his way to her like a caged bear, to be taught to dance for his dinner.

The Chronicles could hardly record the years of the Last Battle without mentioning the Dragon Reborn, but she knew that one name would be written larger than all others. Elaida do Avriny a'Roihan, youngest daughter of a minor House in the north of Murandy, would go down in history as the greatest and most powerful Amyrlin Seat of all time. The most powerful woman in the history of the world. The woman who saved humankind.

The Aiel standing in a deep fold in the low, brown-grass hills seemed carved figures, ignoring sheets of dust sweeping ahead of a gusting wind. That snow should have been deep on the ground this time of year did not bother them; none had ever seen snow, and this oven heat, with the sun still well short of its peak, was less than where they came from. Their attention remained fixed on the southern rise, waiting for the signal that would announce the arrival of the destiny of the Shaido Aiel.

Outwardly, Sevanna looked like the others, though a ring of Maidens marked her out, resting easily on their heels, dark veils already hiding their faces to the eyes. She also waited, and more impatiently than she let on, but not to the exclusion of everything else. That was one reason why she commanded and the rest followed. The second was that she saw what could be if you refused to let outworn custom and stale tradition tie your hands.

A slight flicker of her green eyes to the left showed twelve men and one woman, each with round bull-hide buckler and three or four short spears, garbed in gray-and-brown *cadin'sor* that blended as well with the terrain here as in the Three-fold Land. Efalin, short graying hair hidden by the *shoufa* wrapped around her head, sometimes glanced Sevanna's way; if a Maiden of the Spear could be said to be uneasy, Efalin was. Some Shaido Maidens had gone south, joining the fools capering around Rand al'Thor, and Sevanna did not doubt others talked of it. Efalin must be wondering whether providing Sevanna with an escort of Maidens, as if she had been *Far Dareis Mai* once herself, was enough to balance that. At least Efalin had no doubts where true power lay.

Like Efalin, the men led Shaido warrior societies, and they eyed one another between watching the rise. Especially blocky Maeric, who was *Seia Doon*, and scar-faced Bendhuin, of *Far Aldazar Din*. After today, no longer would anything hold back the Shaido from sending a man to Rhuidean, to be marked as the clan chief if he survived. Until that happened, Sevanna spoke as the clan chief since she was the widow of the last chief. Of the last two chiefs. And let those who muttered that she carried bad luck choke on it.

Gold and ivory bracelets clattered softly as she straightened the dark shawl over her arms and adjusted her necklaces. Most of those were gold and ivory too, but one was a mass of pearls and rubies that had belonged to a wetlander noblewoman—the woman now wore white and hauled and fetched alongside the other *gai'shain* back in the mountains called Kinslayer's Dagger—with a ruby the size of a small hen's egg nestled between her breasts. The wetlands held rich prizes. A large emerald on her finger caught sunlight in green fire; finger rings were one wetlander custom worth adopting, no matter the stares often aimed at hers. She would have more, if they matched this one for magnificence.

Most of the men thought Maeric or Bendhuin would be first to receive the Wise Ones' permission to try Rhuidean. Only Efalin in that group suspected that none would, and she only suspected; she also was astute enough to voice her suspicions circumspectly to Sevanna and not at all to anyone else. Their minds could not encompass the possibility of shedding the old, and in truth, if Sevanna was impatient to don the new, she was also aware that she must bring them to it slowly. Much had changed already in the old ways since the Shaido crossed the Dragonwall into the wetlands—still wet, compared to the Three-fold Land—yet more would change. Once Rand al'Thor was in her hands, once she had wed the *Car'a'carn*, the chief of chiefs of all the Aiel—this nonsense of the Dragon Reborn was wetlander foolishness—there would be a new way of naming clan chiefs, and sept chiefs as well. Perhaps even the heads of the warrior societies. Rand al'Thor would name them. Pointing where she told him, of course. And that would be only the beginning. The wetlander notion of handing down rank to your children, and their children, for instance.

The wind swept higher for a moment, blowing south. It would cover the sound of the wetlanders' horses and wagons.

She shifted her shawl again, then suppressed a grimace. At all costs she must not appear nervous. A glance to the right stilled worry as soon as begun. Over two hundred Shaido Wise Ones clustered there, and normally at least some would be watching her like vultures, but their eyes were all on the rise. More than one adjusted her shawl uneasily or smoothed bulky skirts. Sevanna's lip curled. Sweat beaded on some of those faces. Sweat! Where was their honor that they showed nerves before every gaze?

Everyone stiffened slightly as a young *Sovin Nai* appeared above them, lowering his veil as he scrambled down. He came straight to her, as was proper, but to her irritation he raised his voice enough for all to hear. "One of their forward scouts escaped. He was wounded, but still on his horse."

The society leaders began to move before he finished speaking. That would never do. They would lead in the actual fighting—Sevanna had never more than held a spear in her life—but she would not let them forget for a moment who she was. "Throw every last spear against them," she ordered loudly, "before they can ready themselves." They rounded on her as one.

"Every spear?" Bendhuin demanded incredulously. "You mean except for the screens—"

Glowering, Maeric spoke right on top of him. "If we keep no reserve, we can be—"

Sevanna cut them both off. "Every spear! These are Aes Sedai we dance with. We must overwhelm them immediately!" Efalin and most of the others schooled their faces to stillness, but Bendhuin and Maeric frowned, ready to argue. Fools. They faced a few dozen Aes Sedai, a few hundred wetlander soldiers, yet with the more than forty thousand *algai'd'siswai* they had insisted on, they still wanted their screens of scouts and their spears in reserve as if they faced other Aiel or a wetlander army. "I speak as the clan chief of the Shaido." She should not have to say that, but a reminder could do no harm. "They are a handful." She weighted every word with contempt now. "They can be run down if the spears move quickly. You were ready to avenge Desaine this sunrise. Do I smell fear now? Fear of a few wetlanders? Has honor gone from the Shaido?"

About the Author

Robert Jordan was born in 1948 in Charleston, South Carolina. He taught himself to read when he was four with the incidental aid of a twelve-years-older brother, and was tackling Mark Twain and Jules Verne by five. He was a graduate of the Citadel, the Military College of South Carolina, with a degree in physics. He served two tours in Vietnam with the U.S. Army; among his decorations are the Distinguished Flying Cross with bronze oak leaf cluster, the Bronze Star with "V" and bronze oak leaf cluster, and two Vietnamese Gallantry Crosses with Palm. A history buff, he also wrote dance and theater criticism. He enjoyed the outdoor sports of hunting, fishing, and sailing, and the indoor sports of poker, chess, pool, and pipe collecting. He began writing in 1977 and continued until his death on September 16, 2007.